BLOOD OF ELVES

By Andrzej Sapkowski

The Last Wish
Sword of Destiny
Blood of Elves
The Time of Contempt
Baptism of Fire
The Tower of Swallows
The Lady of the Lake

The Malady and Other Stories:
An Andrzej Sapkowski Sampler (e-only)

BLOOD OF ELVES

ANDRZEJ SAPKOWSKI

Translated by Danusia Stok

www.orbitbooks.net

Original text copyright © 1994 by Andrzej Sapkowski
English translation copyright © 2008 by Danusia Stok
Excerpt from *The Time of Contempt* copyright © 1995 by Andrzej Sapkowski
Excerpt from *Kings of the Wyld* copyright © 2017 by Nicholas Eames

Cover design by Lauren Panepinto
Cover illustration by Bartłomiej Gaweł, Paweł Mielniczuk, Marcin Błaszczak, Arkadiusz Matyszewski, Marian Chomiak
Cover copyright © 2012 by Hachette Book Group, Inc.

Originally published in Polish as *Krew Elfów*

Orbit
Hachette Book Group
1290 Avenue of the Americas
New York, NY 10104
orbitbooks.net

Published by arrangement with Literary Agency 'Agence de l'Est'

Originally published in mass market paperback and ebook by Orbit in May 2009
Originally published in hardcover by Gollancz in Great Britain in 2008

First Trade Paperback Edition: October 2017

Orbit is an imprint of Hachette Book Group.
The Orbit name and logo are trademarks of Little, Brown Book Group Limited.

The publisher is not responsible for websites (or their content) that are not owned by the publisher.

The Hachette Speakers Bureau provides a wide range of authors for speaking events. To find out more, go to www.hachettespeakersbureau.com or call (866) 376-6591.

ISBNs: 978-0-316-43898-8 (trade paperback), 978-0-316-02919-3 (mass market paperback), 978-0-316-07371-4 (ebook)

Printed in the United States of America

LSC-C

10 9 8

BLOOD OF ELVES

Verily I say unto you, the era of the sword and axe is nigh, the era of the wolf's blizzard. The Time of the White Chill *and the White Light is nigh, the Time of Madness and the Time of Contempt: Tedd Deireádh, the Time of End. The world will die amidst frost and be reborn with the new sun. It will be reborn of the Elder Blood, of Hen Ichaer, of the seed that has been sown. A seed which will not sprout but will burst into flame. Ess'tuath esse! Thus it shall be! Watch for the signs! What signs these shall be, I say unto you: first the earth will flow with the blood of Aen Seidhe, the Blood of Elves . . .*

Aen Ithlinnespeath,
Ithlinne Aegli aep Aevenien's prophecy

CHAPTER ONE

The town was in flames.

The narrow streets leading to the moat and the first terrace belched smoke and embers, flames devouring the densely clustered thatched houses and licking at the castle walls. From the west, from the harbour gate, the screams and clamour of vicious battle and the dull blows of a battering ram smashing against the walls grew ever louder.

Their attackers had surrounded them unexpectedly, shattering the barricades which had been held by no more than a few soldiers, a handful of townsmen carrying halberds and some crossbowmen from the guild. Their horses, decked out in flowing black caparisons, flew over the barricades like spectres, their riders' bright, glistening blades sowing death amongst the fleeing defenders.

Ciri felt the knight who carried her before him on his saddle abruptly spur his horse. She heard his cry. "Hold on," he shouted. "Hold on!"

Other knights wearing the colours of Cintra overtook them, sparring, even in full flight, with the Nilfgaardians.

3

Ciri caught a glimpse of the skirmish from the corner of her eye – the crazed swirl of blue-gold and black cloaks amidst the clash of steel, the clatter of blades against shields, the neighing of horses—

Shouts. No, not shouts. Screams.

"Hold on!"

Fear. With every jolt, every jerk, every leap of the horse pain shot through her hands as she clutched at the reins. Her legs contracted painfully, unable to find support, her eyes watered from the smoke. The arm around her suffocated her, choking her, the force compressing her ribs. All around her screaming such as she had never before heard grew louder. What must one do to a man to make him scream so?

Fear. Overpowering, paralysing, choking fear.

Again the clash of iron, the grunts and snorts of the horses. The houses whirled around her and suddenly she could see windows belching fire where a moment before there'd been nothing but a muddy little street strewn with corpses and cluttered with the abandoned possessions of the fleeing population. All at once the knight at her back was racked by a strange wheezing cough. Blood spurted over the hands grasping the reins. More screams. Arrows whistled past.

A fall, a shock, painful bruising against armour. Hooves pounded past her, a horse's belly and a frayed girth flashing by above her head, then another horse's belly and a flowing black caparison. Grunts of exertion, like a lumberjack's when chopping wood. But this isn't wood; it's iron against iron. A shout, muffled and dull, and something huge and black collapsed into the mud next to her with a splash, spurting blood. An armoured foot quivered, thrashed, goring the earth with an enormous spur.

A jerk. Some force plucked her up, pulled her onto another saddle. *Hold on!* Again the bone-shaking speed, the mad gallop. Arms and legs desperately searching for support. The horse rears. *Hold on!* . . . There is no support. There is no . . . There is no . . . There is blood. The horse falls. It's impossible to jump aside, no way to break free, to escape the tight embrace of these chainmail-clad arms. There is no way to avoid the blood pouring onto her head and over her shoulders.

A jolt, the squelch of mud, a violent collision with the ground, horrifically still after the furious ride. The horse's harrowing wheezes and squeals as it tries to regain its feet. The pounding of horseshoes, fetlocks and hooves flashing past. Black caparisons and cloaks. Shouting.

The street is on fire, a roaring red wall of flame. Silhouetted before it, a rider towers over the flaming roofs, enormous. His black-caparisoned horse prances, tosses its head, neighs.

The rider stares down at her. Ciri sees his eyes gleaming through the slit in his huge helmet, framed by a bird of prey's wings. She sees the fire reflected in the broad blade of the sword held in his lowered hand.

The rider looks at her. Ciri is unable to move. The dead man's motionless arms wrapped around her waist hold her down. She is locked in place by something heavy and wet with blood, something which is lying across her thigh, pinning her to the ground.

And she is frozen in fear: a terrible fear which turns her entrails inside out, which deafens Ciri to the screams of the wounded horse, the roar of the blaze, the cries of dying people and the pounding drums. The only thing which exists, which counts, which still has any meaning, is fear. Fear embodied in the figure of a black knight wearing a helmet decorated with feathers frozen against the wall of raging, red flames.

The rider spurs his horse, the wings on his helmet fluttering as the bird of prey takes to flight, launching itself to attack its helpless victim, paralysed with fear. The bird – or maybe the knight – screeches terrifyingly, cruelly, triumphantly. A black horse, black armour, a black flowing cloak, and behind this – flames. A sea of flames.

Fear.

The bird shrieks. The wings beat, feathers slap against her face. *Fear!*

Help! Why doesn't anyone help me? Alone, weak, helpless – I can't move, can't force a sound from my constricted throat. Why does no one come to help me?

I'm terrified!

Eyes blaze through the slit in the huge winged helmet. The black cloak veils everything—

"Ciri!"

She woke, numb and drenched in sweat, with her scream – the scream which had woken her – still hanging in the air, still vibrating somewhere within her, beneath her breastbone and burning against her parched throat. Her hands ached, clenched around the blanket; her back ached . . .

"Ciri. Calm down."

The night was dark and windy, the crowns of the surrounding pine trees rustling steadily and melodiously, their limbs and trunks creaking in the wind. There was no malevolent fire, no screams, only this gentle lullaby.

6

Beside her the campfire flickered with light and warmth, its reflected flames glowing from harness buckles, gleaming red in the leather-wrapped and iron-banded hilt of a sword leaning against a saddle on the ground. There was no other fire and no other iron. The hand against her cheek smelled of leather and ashes. Not of blood.

"Geralt—"

"It was just a dream. A bad dream."

Ciri shuddered violently, curling her arms and legs up tight.

A dream. Just a dream.

The campfire had already died down; the birch logs were red and luminous, occasionally crackling, giving off tiny spurts of blue flame which illuminated the white hair and sharp profile of the man wrapping a blanket and sheepskin around her.

"Geralt, I—"

"I'm right here. Sleep, Ciri. You have to rest. We've still a long way ahead of us."

I can hear music, she thought suddenly. *Amidst the rustling of the trees ... there's music. Lute music. And voices. The Princess of Cintra ... A child of destiny ... A child of Elder Blood, the blood of elves. Geralt of Rivia, the White Wolf, and his destiny. No, no, that's a legend. A poet's invention. The princess is dead. She was killed in the town streets while trying to escape ...*

Hold on ...! Hold ...

"Geralt?"

"What, Ciri?"

"What did he do to me? What happened? What did he ... do to me?"

"Who?"

7

"The knight . . . The black knight with feathers on his helmet . . . I can't remember anything. He shouted . . . and looked at me. I can't remember what happened. Only that I was frightened . . . I was so frightened . . ."

The man leaned over her, the flame of the campfire sparkling in his eyes. They were strange eyes. Very strange. Ciri had been frightened of them; she hadn't liked meeting his gaze. But that had been a long time ago. A very long time ago.

"I can't remember anything," she whispered, searching for his hand, as tough and coarse as raw wood. "The black knight—"

"It was a dream. Sleep peacefully. It won't come back."

Ciri had heard such reassurances in the past. They had been repeated to her endlessly; many, many times she had been offered comforting words when her screams had woken her during the night. But this time it was different. Now she believed it. Because it was Geralt of Rivia, the White Wolf, the Witcher, who said it. The man who was her destiny. The one for whom she was destined. Geralt the Witcher, who had found her surrounded by war, death and despair, who had taken her with him and promised they would never part.

She fell asleep holding tight to his hand.

The bard finished the song. Tilting his head a little he repeated the ballad's refrain on his lute, delicately, softly, a single tone higher than the apprentice accompanying him.

No one said a word. Nothing but the subsiding music and the whispering leaves and squeaking boughs of the enormous oak could be heard. Then, all of a sudden, a goat tethered to one of the carts which circled the ancient tree bleated lengthily. At that moment, as if given a signal, one of the men seated in the large semi-circular audience stood up. Throwing his cobalt blue cloak with gold braid trim back over his shoulder, he gave a stiff, dignified bow.

"Thank you, Master Dandelion," he said, his voice resonant without being loud. "Allow me, Radcliffe of Oxenfurt, Master of the Arcana, to express what I am sure is the opinion of everyone here present and utter words of gratitude and appreciation for your fine art and skill."

The wizard ran his gaze over those assembled – an audience of well over a hundred people – seated on the ground, on carts, or standing in a tight semi-circle facing the foot of the oak. They nodded and whispered amongst themselves. Several people began to applaud while others greeted the singer with upraised hands. Women, touched by the music, sniffed and wiped their eyes on whatever came to hand, which differed according to their standing, profession and wealth: peasant women used their forearms or the backs of their hands, merchants' wives dabbed their eyes with linen handkerchiefs while elves and noblewomen used kerchiefs of the finest tight-woven cotton, and Baron Vilibert's three daughters, who had, along with the rest of his retinue, halted their falcon hunt to attend the famous troubadour's performance, blew their noses loudly and sonorously into elegant mouldgreen cashmere scarves.

"It would not be an exaggeration to say," continued the wizard, "that you have moved us deeply, Master Dandelion. You have prompted us to reflection and thought; you have stirred our hearts. Allow me to express our gratitude, and our respect."

The troubadour stood and took a bow, sweeping the heron feather pinned to his fashionable hat across his knees. His apprentice broke off his playing, grinned and bowed too, until Dandelion glared at him sternly and snapped something under his breath. The boy lowered his head and returned to softly strumming his lute strings.

The assembly stirred to life. The merchants travelling in the caravan whispered amongst themselves and then rolled a sizable cask of beer out to the foot of the oak tree. Wizard Radcliffe lost himself in quiet conversation with Baron Vilibert. Having blown their noses, the baron's daughters gazed at Dandelion in adoration – which went entirely unnoticed by the bard, engrossed as he was in smiling, winking and flashing his teeth at a haughty, silent group of roving elves, and at one of them in particular: a dark-haired, large-eyed beauty sporting a tiny ermine cap. Dandelion had rivals for her attention – the elf, with her huge eyes and beautiful toque hat, had caught his audience's interest as well, and a number of knights, students and goliards were paying court to her with their eyes. The elf clearly enjoyed the attention, picking at the lace cuffs of her chemise and fluttering her eyelashes, but the group of elves with her surrounded her on all sides, not bothering to hide their antipathy towards her admirers.

The glade beneath Bleobheris, the great oak, was a place of frequent rallies, a well-known travellers' resting place and meeting ground for wanderers, and was famous for its tolerance and openness. The druids protecting the ancient tree called it the Seat of Friendship and willingly welcomed all comers. But even during an event as exceptional as the world-famous troubadour's just-concluded performance the travellers kept to themselves, remaining in clearly delineated groups. Elves stayed with elves. Dwarfish craftsmen gathered with their kin, who were often hired to protect the merchant caravans and were armed to the teeth. Their groups tolerated at best the gnome miners and halfling farmers who camped beside them. All non-humans were uniformly distant towards humans. The humans repaid in kind, but were not seen to mix amongst themselves either. Nobility looked down on the merchants and travelling salesmen with open scorn, while soldiers and mercenaries distanced themselves from shepherds and their reeking sheepskins. The few wizards and their disciples kept themselves entirely apart from the others, and bestowed their arrogance on everyone in equal parts. A tight-knit, dark and silent group of peasants lurked in the background. Resembling a forest with their rakes, pitchforks and flails poking above their heads, they were ignored by all and sundry.

The exception, as ever, was the children. Freed from the constraints of silence which had been enforced during the bard's performance, the children dashed into the woods with wild cries, and enthusiastically immersed themselves in a game whose rules were incomprehensible to all those who had bidden farewell to the happy years of childhood. Children of elves, dwarves, halflings, gnomes, half-elves, quarter-elves and toddlers of mysterious provenance neither knew nor recognised racial or social divisions. At least, not yet.

"Indeed!" shouted one of the knights present in the glade, who was as thin as a beanpole and wearing a red and black tunic emblazoned with three lions passant. "The

wizard speaks the truth! The ballads were beautiful. Upon
my word, honourable Dandelion, if you ever pass near
Baldhorn, my lord's castle, stop by without a moment's
hesitation. You will be welcomed like a prince— What am
I saying? Welcomed like King Vizimir himself! I swear
on my sword, I have heard many a minstrel, but none
even came close to being your equal, master. Accept the
respect and tributes those of us born to knighthood, and
those of us appointed to the position, pay to your skills!"

Flawlessly sensing the opportune moment, the troubadour winked at his apprentice. The boy set his lute aside
and picked up a little casket which served as a collection
box for the audience's more measurable expressions of
appreciation. He hesitated, ran his eyes over the crowd,
then replaced the little casket and grabbed a large bucket
standing nearby. Master Dandelion bestowed an approv-
ing smile on the young man for his prudence.

"Master!" shouted a sizeable woman sitting on a cart,
the sides of which were painted with a sign for "Vera
Loewenhaupt and Sons," and which was full of wicker-
work. Her sons, nowhere to be seen, were no doubt busy
wasting away their mother's hard-earned fortune. "Master
Dandelion, what is this? Are you going to leave us in suspense? That can't be the end of your ballad? Sing to us of
what happened next!"

"Songs and ballads" – the musician bowed – "never
end, dear lady, because poetry is eternal and immortal, it
knows no beginning, it knows no end—"

"But what happened next?" The tradeswoman didn't
give up, generously rattling coins into the bucket Dandelion's apprentice held out to her. "At least tell us about it,
even if you have no wish to sing of it. Your songs men-

12

tion no names, but we know the witcher you sing of is no other than the famous Geralt of Rivia, and the enchantress for whom he burns with love is the equally famous Yennefer. And the Child Surprise, destined for the witcher and sworn to him from birth, is Cirilla, the unfortunate Princess of Cintra, the town destroyed by the Invaders. Am I right?"

Dandelion smiled, remaining enigmatic and aloof. "I sing of universal matters, my dear, generous lady," he stated. "Of emotions which anyone can experience. Not about specific people."

"Oh, come on!" yelled a voice from the crowd. "Everyone knows those songs are about Geralt the Witcher!"

"Yes, yes!" squealed Baron Vilibert's daughters in chorus, drying their sodden scarves. "Sing on, Master Dandelion! What happened next? Did the witcher and Yennefer the Enchantress find each other in the end? And did they love each other? Were they happy? We want to know!"

"Enough!" roared the dwarf leader with a growl in his throat, shaking his mighty waist-length red beard. "It's crap — all these princesses, sorceresses, destiny, love and women's fanciful tales. If you'll pardon the expression, great poet, it's all lies, just a poetic invention to make the story prettier and more touching. But of the deeds of war — the massacre and plunder of Cintra, the battles of Marnadal and Sodden — you did sing that mightily, Dandelion! There's no regrets in parting with silver for such a song, a joy to a warrior's heart! And I, Sheldon Skaggs, declare there's not an ounce of lies in what you say — and I can tell the lies from the truth because I was there at Sodden.

I stood against the Nilfgaard invaders with an axe in my hand . . ."

"I, Donimir of Troy," shouted the thin knight with three lions passant blazoned across his tunic, "was at both battles of Sodden! But I did not see you there, sir dwarf!"

"No doubt because you were looking after the supply train!" Sheldon Skaggs retorted. "While I was in the front line where things got hot!"

"Mind your tongue, beardy!" said Donimir of Troy flushing, hitching up his sword belt. "And who you're speaking to!"

"Have a care yourself!" The dwarf whacked his palm against the axe wedged in his belt, turned to his companions and grinned. "Did you see him there? Frigging knight! See his coat of arms? Ha! Three lions on a shield? Two shitting and the third snarling!"

"Peace, peace!" A grey-haired druid in a white cloak averted trouble with a sharp, authoritative voice. "This is not fitting, gentlemen! Not here, under Bleobheris' crown, an oak older than all the disputes and quarrels of the world! And not in Poet Dandelion's presence, from whose ballads we ought to learn of love, not contention."

"Quite so!" a short, fat priest with a face glistening with sweat seconded the druid. "You look but have no eyes, you listen but have deaf ears. Because divine love is not in you, you are like empty barrels—"

"Speaking of barrels," squeaked a long-nosed gnome from his cart, painted with a sign for "Iron hardware, manufacture and sale", "roll another out, guildsmen! Poet Dandelion's throat is surely dry – and ours too, from all these emotions!"

"—Verily, like empty barrels, I tell ye!" The priest, determined not to be put off, drowned out the ironware gnome. "You have understood nothing of Master Dandelion's ballad, you have learned nothing! You did not see that these ballads speak of man's fate, that we are no more than toys in the hands of the gods, our lands no more than their playground. The ballads about destiny portrayed the destinies of us all, and the legend of Geralt the Witcher and Princess Cirilla – although it is set against the true background of that war – is, after all, a mere metaphor, the creation of a poet's imagination designed to help us—"

"You're talking rubbish, holy man!" hollered Vera Loewenhaupt from the heights of her cart. "What legend? What imaginative creation? You may not know him, but I know Geralt of Rivia. I saw him with my own eyes in Wyzima, when he broke the spell on King Foltest's daughter. And I met him again later on the Merchants' Trail, where, at Gildia's request, he slew a ferocious griffin which was preying on the caravans and thus saved the lives of many good people. No. This is no legend or fairy-tale. It is the truth, the sincere truth, which Master Dandelion sang for us."

"I second that," said a slender female warrior with her black hair smoothly brushed back and plaited into a thick braid. "I, Rayla of Lyria, also know Geralt the White Wolf, the famous slayer of monsters. And I've met the enchantress, Lady Yennefer, on several occasions – I used to visit Aedirn and her home town of Vengerberg. I don't know anything about their being in love, though."

"But it has to be true," the attractive elf in the ermine toque suddenly said in a melodious voice. "Such a beautiful ballad of love could not but be true."

"It could not!" Baron Vilibert's daughters supported the elf and, as if on command, wiped their eyes on their scarves. "Not by any measure!"

"Honourable wizard!" Vera Loewenhaupt turned to Radcliffe. "Were they in love or not? Surely you know what truly happened to them, Yennefer and the witcher. Disclose the secret!"

"If the song says they were in love," replied the wizard, "then that's what happened, and their love will endure down the ages. Such is the power of poetry."

"It is said," interrupted Baron Vilibert all of a sudden, "that Yennefer of Vengerberg was killed on Sodden Hill. Several enchantresses were killed there—"

"That's not true," said Donimir of Troy. "Her name is not on the monument. I am from those parts and have often climbed Sodden Hill and read the names engraved on the monument. Three enchantresses died there: Triss Merigold, Lytta Neyd, known as Coral . . . hmm . . . and the name of the third has slipped my mind . . ."

The knight glanced at Wizard Radcliffe, who smiled wordlessly.

"And this witcher," Sheldon Skaggs suddenly called out, "this Geralt who loved Yennefer, has also bitten the dust, apparently. I heard he was killed somewhere in Transriver. He slew and slew monsters until he met his match. That's how it goes: he who fights with the sword dies by the sword. Everyone comes across someone who will better them eventually, and is made to taste cold hard iron."

"I don't believe it." The slender warrior contorted her pale lips, spat vehemently on the ground and crossed her chainmail-clad arms with a crunch. "I don't believe there is anyone to best Geralt of Rivia. I have seen this witcher handle a sword. His speed is simply inhuman—"

"Well said," threw in Wizard Radcliffe. "Inhuman. Witchers are mutated, so their reactions—"

"I don't understand you, magician." The warrior twisted her lips even more nastily. "Your words are too learned. I know one thing: no swordsman I have ever seen can match Geralt of Rivia, the White Wolf. And so I will not accept that he was defeated in battle as the dwarf claims."

"Every swordsman's an arse when the enemy's not sparse," remarked Sheldon Skaggs sententiously. "As the elves say."

"Elves," stated a tall, fair-haired representative of the Elder Race coldly, from his place beside the elf with the beautiful toque, "are not in the habit of using such vulgar language."

"No! No!" squealed Baron Vilibert's daughters from behind their green scarves. "Geralt the Witcher can't have been killed! The witcher found Ciri, the child destined for him, and then the Enchantress Yennefer, and all three lived happily ever after! Isn't that true, Master Dandelion?"

"'Twas a ballad, my noble young ladies," said the beer-parched gnome, manufacturer of ironwares, with a yawn. "Why look for truth in a ballad? Truth is one thing, poetry another. Let's take this – what was her name? – Ciri? The famous Child Surprise. Master Dandelion trumped that up for sure. I've been to Cintra many a time and the king and queen lived in a childless home, with no daughter, no son—"

"Liar!" shouted a red-haired man in a sealskin jacket,

a checked kerchief bound around his forehead. "Queen Calanthe, the Lioness of Cintra, had a daughter called Pavetta. She died, together with her husband, in a tempest which struck out at sea, and the depths swallowed them both."

"So you see for yourselves I'm not making this up!" The ironware gnome called everyone to be his witnesses. "The Princess of Cintra was called Pavetta, not Ciri."

"Cirilla, known as Ciri, was the daughter of this drowned Pavetta," explained the red-haired man. "Calanthe's granddaughter. She was not the princess herself, but the daughter of the Princess of Cintra. She was the Child Surprise destined for the witcher, the man to whom – even before she was born – the queen had sworn to hand her granddaughter over, just as Master Dandelion has sung. But the witcher could neither find her nor collect her. And here our poet has missed the truth."

"Oh yes, he's missed the truth indeed," butted in a sinewy young man who, judging by his clothes, was a journeyman on his travels prior to crafting his masterpiece and passing his master's exams. "The witcher's destiny bypassed him: Cirilla was killed during the siege of Cintra. Before throwing herself from the tower, Queen Calanthe killed the princess's daughter with her own hand, to prevent her from falling into the Nilfgaardians' claws alive."

"It wasn't like that. Not like that at all!" objected the red-haired man. "The princess's daughter was killed during the massacre while trying to escape from the town."

"One way or another," shouted Ironware, "the witcher didn't find Cirilla! The poet lied!"

"But lied beautifully," said the elf in the toque, snuggling up to the tall, fair-haired elf.

"It's not a question of poetry but of facts!" shouted the journeyman. "I tell you, the princess's daughter died by her grandmother's hand. Anyone who's been to Cintra can confirm that!"

"And I say she was killed in the streets trying to escape," declared the red-haired man. "I know because although I'm not from Cintra I served in the Earl of Skellige's troop supporting Cintra during the war. As everyone knows, Eist Tuirseach, the King of Cintra, comes from the Skellige Isles. He was the earl's uncle. I fought in the earl's troop at Marnadal and Cintra and later, after the defeat, at Sodden—"

"Yet another veteran," Sheldon Skaggs snarled to the dwarves crowded around him. "All heroes and warriors. Hey, folks! Is there at least one of you out there who didn't fight at Marnadal or Sodden?"

"That dig is out of place, Skaggs," the tall elf reproached him, putting his arm around the beauty wearing the toque in a way intended to dispel any lingering doubts amongst her admirers. "Don't imagine you were the only one to fight at Sodden. I took part in the battle as well."

"On whose side, I wonder," Baron Vilibert said to Radcliffe in a highly audible whisper which the elf ignored entirely.

"As everyone knows," he continued, sparing neither the baron nor the wizard so much as a glance, "over a hundred thousand warriors stood on the field during the second battle of Sodden Hill, and of those at least thirty thousand were maimed or killed. Master Dandelion should be thanked for immortalising this famous, terrible battle in one of his ballads. In both the lyrics and melody of his work I heard not an exaltation but a warning. So I repeat: offer praise and everlasting renown to this poet for his ballad, which may, perhaps, prevent a tragedy as horrific as this cruel and unnecessary war from occurring in the future."

"Indeed," said Baron Vilibert, looking defiantly at the elf. "You have read some very interesting things into this ballad, honoured sir. An unnecessary war, you say? You'd like to avoid such a tragedy in the future, would you? Are we to understand that if the Nilfgaardians were to attack us again you would advise that we capitulate? Humbly accept the Nilfgaardian yoke?"

"Life is a priceless gift and should be protected," the elf replied coldly. "Nothing justifies wide-scale slaughter and sacrifice of life, which is what the battles at Sodden were – both the battle lost and the battle won. Both of them cost the humans thousands of lives. And with them, you lost unimaginable potential—"

"Elven prattle!" snarled Sheldon Skaggs. "Dim-witted rubbish! It was the price that had to be paid to allow others to live decently, in peace, instead of being chained, blinded, whipped and forced to work in salt and sulphur mines. Those who died a heroic death, those who will now, thanks to Dandelion, live on forever in our memories, taught us to defend our own homes. Sing your ballads, Dandelion, sing them to everyone. Your lesson won't go to waste, and it'll come in handy, you'll see! Because, mark my words, Nilfgaard will attack us again. If not today, then tomorrow! They're licking their wounds now, recovering, but the day when we'll see their black cloaks and feathered helmets again is growing ever nearer!"

"What do they want from us?" yelled Vera Loewen-haupt. "Why are they bent on persecuting us? Why don't they leave us in peace, leave us to our lives and work? What do the Nilfgaardians want?"

"They want our blood!" howled Baron Vilibert.

"And our land!" someone cried from the crowd of peasants.

"And our women!" chimed in Sheldon Skaggs, with a ferocious glower.

Several people started to laugh – as quietly and fur-tively as they could. Even though the idea that anyone other than another dwarf would desire one of the excep-tionally unattractive dwarf-women was highly amusing, it was not a safe subject for teasing or jests – especially not in the presence of the short, stocky, bearded individ-uals whose axes and short-swords had an ugly habit of leaping from their belts and into their hands at incredible speed. And the dwarves, for some unknown reason, were entirely convinced that the rest of the world was lech-erously lying in wait for their wives and daughters, and were extremely touchy about it.

"This had to happen at some point," the grey-haired druid declared suddenly. "This had to happen. We forgot that we are not the only ones in this world, that the whole of creation does not revolve around us. Like stupid, fat, lazy minnows in a slimy pond we chose not to accept the existence of pike. We allowed our world, like the pond, to become slimy, boggy and sluggish. Look around you – there is crime and sin everywhere, greed, the pursuit of profit, quarrels and disagreements are rife. Our traditions are disappearing, respect for our values is fading. Instead of living according to Nature we have begun to destroy

21

it. And what have we got for it? The air is poisoned by the stink of smelting furnaces, the rivers and brooks are tainted by slaughter houses and tanneries, forests are being cut down without a thought . . . Ha – just look! – even on the living bark of sacred Bleobheris, there just above the poet's head, there's a foul phrase carved out with a knife – and it's misspelled at that – by a stupid, illiterate vandal. Why are you surprised? It had to end badly—"

"Yes, yes!" the fat priest joined in. "Come to your senses, you sinners, while there is still time, because the anger and vengeance of the gods hangs over you! Remember Ithlin's oracle, the prophetic words describing the punishment of the gods reserved for a tribe poisoned by crime! 'The Time of Contempt will come, when the tree will lose its leaves, the bud will wither, the fruit will rot, the seed turn bitter and the river valleys will run with ice instead of water. The White Chill will come, and after it the White Light, and the world will perish beneath blizzards.' Thus spoke Seeress Ithlin! And before this comes to pass there will be visible signs, plagues will ravish the earth – Remember! – the Nilfgaard are our punishment from the gods! They are the whip with which the Immortals will lash you sinners, so that you may—"

"Shut up, you sanctimonious old man!" roared Sheldon Skaggs, stamping his heavy boots. "Your superstitious rot makes me sick! My guts are churning—"

"Careful, Sheldon." The tall elf cut him short with a smile. "Don't mock another's religion. It is not pleasant, polite or . . . safe."

"I'm not mocking anything," protested the dwarf. "I don't doubt the existence of the gods, but it annoys me when someone drags them into earthly matters and tries to pull the wool over my eyes using the prophecies of some crazy elf. The Nilfgaardians are the instrument of the gods? Rubbish! Search back through your memories to the past, to the days of Dezmod, Radowid and Sambuk, to the days of Abrad, the Old Oak! You may not remember them, because your lives are so very short – you're like mayflies – but I remember, and I'll tell you what it was like in these lands just after you climbed from your boats on the Yaruga Estuary and the Pontar Delta onto the beach. Three kingdoms sprang from the four ships which beached on those shores; the stronger groups absorbed the weaker and so grew, strengthening their positions. They invaded others' territories, conquered them, and their kingdoms expanded, becoming ever larger and more powerful. And now the Nilfgaardians are doing the same, because theirs is a strong and united, disciplined and tightly knit country. And unless you close ranks in the same way, Nilfgaard will swallow you as a pike does a minnow – just as this wise druid said!"

"Let them just try!" Donimir of Troy puffed out his lion-emblazoned chest and shook his sword in its scabbard. "We beat them hollow on Sodden Hill, and we can do it again!"

"You're very cocksure," snarled Sheldon Skaggs. "You've evidently forgotten, sir knight, that before the battle of Sodden Hill, the Nilfgaard had advanced across your lands like an iron roller, strewing the land between Marnadal and Transriver with the corpses of many a gallant fellow like yourself. And it wasn't loud-mouthed smart-arses like you who stopped the Nilfgaardians, but the united strengths of Temeria, Redania, Aedirn and Kaedwen. Concord and unity, that's what stopped them!"

"Not just that," remarked Radcliffe in a cold, resonant voice. "Not just that, Master Skaggs."

The dwarf hawked loudly, blew his nose, shuffled his feet then bowed a little to the wizard.

"No one is denying the contribution of your fellowship," he said. "Shame on he who does not acknowledge the heroism of the brotherhood of wizards on Sodden Hill. They stood their ground bravely, shed blood for the common cause, and contributed most eminently to our victory. Dandelion did not forget them in his ballad, and nor shall we. But note that these wizards stood united and loyal on the Hill, and accepted the leadership of Vilgefortz of Roggeveen just as we, the warriors of the Four Kingdoms, acknowledged the command of Vizimir of Redania. It's just a pity this solidarity and concord only lasted for the duration of the war, because, with peace, here we are divided again. Vizimir and Foltest are choking each other with customs taxes and trading laws, Demavend of Aedirn is bickering with Henselt over the Northern Marches while the League of Hengfors and the Thyssenids of Kovir don't give a toss. And I hear that looking for the old concord amongst the wizards is useless, too. We are not closely knit, we have no discipline and no unity. But Nilfgaard does!"

"Nilfgaard is ruled by Emperor Emhyr var Emreis, a tyrant and autocrat who enforces obedience with whip, noose and axe!" thundered Baron Vilibert. "What are you proposing, sir dwarf? How are we supposed to close ranks? With similar tyranny? And which king, which kingdom, in your opinion, should subordinate the others? In whose hands would you like to see the sceptre and knout?"

"What do I care?" replied Skaggs with a shrug. "That's a human affair. Whoever you chose to be king wouldn't be a dwarf anyway."

"Or an elf, or even half-elf," added the tall representative of the Elder Race, his arm still wrapped around the toque-wearing beauty. "You even consider quarter-elves inferior—"

"That's where it stings," laughed Vilibert. "You're blowing the same horn as Nilfgaard because Nilfgaard is also shouting about equality, promising you a return to the old order as soon as we've been conquered and they've scythed us off these lands. That's the sort of unity, the sort of equality you're dreaming of, the sort you're talking about and trumpeting! Nilfgaard pays you gold to do it! And it's hardly surprising you love each other so much, the Nilfgaardians being an elven race—"

"Nonsense," the elf said coldly. "You talk rubbish, sir knight. You're clearly blinded by racism. The Nilfgaardians are human, just like you."

"That's an outright lie! They're descended from the Black Seidhe and everyone knows it! Elven blood flows through their veins! The blood of elves!"

"And what flows through yours?" The elf smiled derisively. "We've been combining our blood for generations, for centuries, your race and mine, and doing so quite successfully – fortunately or unfortunately, I don't know. You started persecuting mixed relationships less than a quarter of a century ago and, incidentally, not very successfully. So show me a human now who hasn't a dash of Seidhe Ichaer, the blood of the Elder Race."

Vilibert visibly turned red. Vera Loewenhaupt also flushed. Wizard Radcliffe bowed his head and coughed. And, most interestingly, the beautiful elf in the ermine toque blushed too.

"We are all children of Mother Earth." The grey-haired druid's voice resounded in the silence. "We are children of Mother Nature. And though we do not respect our mother, though we often worry her and cause her pain, though we break her heart, she loves us. Loves us all. Let us remember that, we who are assembled here in this Seat of Friendship. And let us not bicker over which of us was here first: Acorn was the first to be thrown up by the waves and from Acorn sprouted the Great Bleobheris, the oldest of oaks. Standing beneath its crown, amongst its primordial roots, let us not forget our own brotherly roots, the earth from which these roots grow. Let us remember the words of Poet Dandelion's song—"

"Exactly!" exclaimed Vera Loewenhaupt. "And where is he?"

"He's fled," ascertained Sheldon Skaggs, gazing at the empty place under the oak. "Taken the money and fled without saying goodbye. Very elf-like!"

"Dwarf-like!" squealed Ironware.

"Human-like," corrected the tall elf, and the beauty in the toque rested her head against his shoulder.

"Hey, minstrel," said Mama Lantieri, striding into the room without knocking, the scents of hyacinths, sweat, beer and smoked bacon wafting before her. "You've got a guest. Enter, noble gentleman."

Dandelion smoothed his hair and sat up in the enormous carved armchair. The two girls sitting on his lap quickly jumped up, covering their charms and pulling down their disordered clothes. The modesty of harlots, thought the poet, was not at all a bad title for a ballad. He got to his feet, fastened his belt and pulled on his doublet, all the while looking at the nobleman standing at the threshold.

"Indeed," he remarked, "you know how to find me anywhere, though you rarely pick an opportune moment. You're lucky I'd not yet decided which of these two beauties I prefer. And at your prices, Lantieri, I cannot afford them both."

Mama Lantieri smiled in sympathy and clapped her hands. Both girls – a fair-skinned, freckled islander and a dark-haired half-elf – swiftly left the room. The man at the door removed his cloak and handed it to Mama along with a small but well-filled money-bag.

"Forgive me, master," he said, approaching the table and making himself comfortable. "I know this is not a good time to disturb you. But you disappeared out from beneath the oak so quickly . . . I did not catch you on the High Road as I had intended and did not immediately come across your tracks in this little town. I'll not take much of your time, believe me—"

"They always say that, and it's always a lie," the bard interrupted. "Leave us alone, Lantieri, and see to it that we're not disturbed. I'm listening, sir."

The man scrutinised him. He had dark, damp, almost tearful eyes, a pointed nose and ugly, narrow lips.

"I'll come to the point without wasting your time," he declared, waiting for the door to close behind Mama. "Your ballads interest me, master. To be more specific, certain characters of which you sang interest me. I am concerned with the true fate of your ballad's heroes. If I am not mistaken, the true destinies of real people inspired the beautiful work I heard beneath the oak tree? I have in mind . . . Little Cirilla of Cintra. Queen Calanthe's granddaughter."

Dandelion gazed at the ceiling, drumming his fingers on the table.

"Honoured sir," he said dryly, "you are interested in strange matters. You ask strange questions. Something tells me you are not the person I took you to be."

"And who did you take me to be, if I may ask?"

"I'm not sure you may. It depends if you are about to convey greetings to me from any mutual friends. You should have done so initially, but somehow you have forgotten."

"I did not forget at all." The man reached into the breast pocket of his sepia-coloured velvet tunic and pulled out a money-bag somewhat larger than the one he had handed the procuress but just as well-filled, which clinked as it touched the table. "We simply have no mutual friends, Dandelion. But might this purse not suffice to mitigate the lack?"

"And what do you intend to buy with this meagre purse?" The troubadour pouted. "Mama Lantieri's entire brothel and all the land surrounding it?"

"Let us say that I intend to support the arts. And an artist. In order to chat with the artist about his work."

"You love art so much, do you, dear sir? Is it so vital for you to talk to an artist that you press money on him before you've even introduced yourself and, in doing so, break the most elementary rules of courtesy?"

"At the beginning of our conversation" – the stranger's

dark eyes narrowed imperceptibly – "my anonymity did not bother you."

"And now it is starting to."

"I am not ashamed of my name," said the man, a faint smile appearing on his narrow lips. "I am called Rience. You do not know me, Master Dandelion, and that is no surprise. You are too famous and well known to know all of your admirers. Yet everyone who admires your talents feels he knows you, knows you so well that a certain degree of familiarity is permissible. This applies to me, too. I know it is a misconception, so please graciously forgive me."

"I graciously forgive you."

"Then I can count on you agreeing to answer a few questions—"

"No! No you cannot," interrupted the poet, putting on airs. "Now, if you will graciously forgive *me*, I am not willing to discuss the subjects of my work, its inspiration or its characters, fictitious or otherwise. To do so would deprive poetry of its poetic veneer and lead to triteness."

"Is that so?"

"It certainly is. For example, if, having sung the ballad about the miller's merry wife, I were to announce it's really about Zvirka, Miller Loach's wife, and I included an announcement that Zvirka can most easily be bedded every Thursday because on Thursdays the miller goes to market, it would no longer be poetry. It would be either rhyming couplets, or foul slander."

"I understand, I understand," Rience said quickly. "But perhaps that is a bad example. I am not, after all, interested in anyone's peccadilloes or sins. You will not slander anyone by answering my questions. All I need is one small piece of information: what really happened to Cirilla, the Queen of Cintra's granddaughter? Many people claim she was killed during the siege of the town; there are even eye-witnesses to support the claim. From your ballad, however, it would appear that the child survived. I am truly interested to know if this is your imagination at work, or the truth? True or false?"

"I'm extremely pleased you're so interested." Dandelion smiled broadly. "You may laugh, Master whatever-your-name-is, but that was precisely what I intended when I composed the ballad. I wished to excite my listeners and arouse their curiosity."

"True or false?" repeated Rience coldly.

"If I were to give that away I would destroy the impact of my work. Goodbye, my friend. You have used up all the time I can spare you. And two of my many inspirations are waiting out there, wondering which of them I will choose."

Rience remained silent for a long while, making no move to leave. He stared at the poet with his unfriendly, moist eyes, and the poet felt a growing unease. A merry din came from the bawdy-house's main room, punctuated from time to time by high-pitched feminine giggles. Dandelion turned his head away, pretending to show derisive haughtiness but, in fact, he was judging the distance to the corner of the room and the tapestry showing a nymph sprinkling her breasts with water poured from a jug.

"Dandelion," Rience finally spoke, slipping his hand back into the pocket of his sepia-coloured tunic, "answer my questions. Please. I have to know the answer. It's incredibly important to me. To you, too, believe me, because if you answer of your own free will then—"

"Then what?"

A hideous grimace crept over Rience's narrow lips. "Then I won't have to force you to speak."

"Now listen, you scoundrel." Dandelion stood up and pretended to pull a threatening face. "I loathe violence and force, but I'm going to call Mama Lantieri in a minute and she will call a certain Gruzila who fulfils the honourable and responsible role of bouncer in this establishment. He is a true artist in his field. He'll kick your arse so hard you'll soar over the town roofs with such magnificence that the few people passing by at this hour will take you for a Pegasus."

Rience made an abrupt gesture and something glistened in his hand.

"Are you sure," he asked, "you'll have time to call her?"

Dandelion had no intention of checking if he would have time. Nor did he intend to wait. Before the stiletto had locked in Rience's hand Dandelion had taken a long leap to the corner of the room, dived under the nymph tapestry, kicked open a secret door and rushed headlong down the winding stairs, nimbly steering himself with the aid of the well-worn banisters. Rience darted after him, but the poet was sure of himself – he knew the secret passage like the back of his hand, having used it numerous times to flee creditors, jealous husbands and furious rivals from whom he had, from time to time, stolen rhymes and tunes. He knew that after the third turning he would be able to grope for a revolving door, behind which there was a ladder leading down to the cellar. He was sure that his persecutor would be unable to stop in time, would run on and step on a trapdoor through which he would fall and land in the pigsty. He was equally sure that – bruised, covered in shit and mauled by the pigs – his persecutor would give up the chase.

Dandelion was mistaken, as was usually the case whenever he was too confident. Something flashed a sudden blue behind his back and the poet felt his limbs grow numb, lifeless and stiff. He couldn't slow down for the revolving door, his legs wouldn't obey him. He yelled and rolled down the stairs, bumping against the walls of the little corridor. The trapdoor opened beneath him with a dry crack and the troubadour tumbled down into the darkness and stench. Before thumping his head on the dirt floor and losing consciousness, he remembered Mama Lantieri saying something about the pigsty being repaired.

The pain in his constricted wrists and shoulders, cruelly twisted in their joints, brought him back to his senses. He wanted to scream but couldn't; it felt as though his mouth had been stuck up with clay. He was kneeling on the dirt floor with a creaking rope hauling him up by his wrists. He tried to stand, wanting to ease the pressure on his shoulders, but his legs, too, were tied together. Choking and suffocating he somehow struggled to his feet, helped considerably by the rope which tugged mercilessly at him.

Rience was standing in front of him and his evil eyes glinted in the light of a lantern held aloft by an unshaven ruffian who stood over six feet tall. Another ruffian, probably no shorter, stood behind him. Dandelion could hear his breathing and caught a whiff of stale sweat. It was the reeking man who tugged on the rope looped over a roof beam and fastened to the poet's wrists.

Dandelion's feet tore off the dirt floor. The poet whistled through his nose, unable to do anything more.

"Enough," Rience snapped at last – he spoke almost immediately, yet it had seemed an age to Dandelion. The bard's feet touched the ground but, despite his most heartfelt desire, he could not kneel again – the tight drawn rope was still holding him as taut as a string.

Rience came closer. There was not even a trace of emotion on his face; the damp eyes had not changed their expression in the least. His tone of voice, too, remained calm, quiet, even a little bored.

"You nasty rhymester. You runt. You scum. You arrogant nobody. You tried to run from me? No one has escaped me yet. We haven't finished our conversation, you clown, you sheep's head. I asked you a question under much pleasanter circumstances than these. Now you are going to answer all my questions, and in far less pleasant circumstances. Am I right?"

Dandelion nodded eagerly. Only now did Rience smile and make a sign. The bard squealed helplessly, feeling the rope tighten and his arms, twisted backwards, cracking in their joints.

"You can't talk," Rience confirmed, still smiling loathsomely, "and it hurts, doesn't it? For the moment, you should know I'm having you strung up like this for my own pleasure – just because I love watching people suffer. Go on, just a little higher."

Dandelion was wheezing so hard he almost choked.

"Enough," Rience finally ordered, then approached the poet and grabbed him by his shirt ruffles. "Listen to me, you little cock. I'm going to lift the spell so you can talk. But if you try to raise your charming voice any louder than necessary, you'll be sorry."

He made a gesture with his hand, touched the poet's cheek with his ring and Dandelion felt sensation return to his jaw, tongue and palate.

"Now," Rience continued quietly, "I am going to ask you a few questions and you are going to answer them quickly, fluently and comprehensively. And if you stammer or hesitate even for a moment, if you give me the slightest reason to doubt the truth of your words, then . . . Look down."

Dandelion obeyed. He discovered to his horror that a short rope had been tied to the knots around his ankles, with a bucket full of lime attached to the other end.

"If I have you pulled any higher," Rience smiled cruelly, "and this bucket lifts with you, then you will probably never regain the feeling in your hands. After that, I doubt you will be capable of playing anything on a lute. I really doubt it. So I think you'll talk to me. Am I right?"

Dandelion didn't agree because he couldn't move his head or find his voice out of sheer fright. But Rience did not seem to require confirmation.

"It is to be understood," he stated, "that I will know immediately if you are telling the truth, if you try to trick me I will realise straight away, and I won't be fooled by any poetic ploys or vague erudition. This is a trifle for me – just as paralysing you on the stairs was a trifle. So I advise you to weigh each word with care, you piece of scum. So, let's get on with it and stop wasting time. As you know, I'm interested in the heroine of one of your beautiful ballads, Queen Calanthe of Cintra's granddaughter, Princess

Cirilla, endearingly known as Ciri. According to eye-witnesses this little person died during the siege of the town, two years ago. Whereas in your ballad you so vividly and touchingly described her meeting a strange, almost legendary individual, the . . . witcher . . . Geralt, or Gerald. Leaving the poetic drivel about destiny and the decrees of fate aside, from the rest of the ballad it seems the child survived the Battle of Cintra in one piece. Is that true?"

"I don't know . . ." moaned Dandelion. "By all the gods, I'm only a poet! I've heard this and that, and the rest . . ."

"Well?"

"The rest I invented. Made it up! I don't know anything!" The bard howled on seeing Rience give a sign to the reeking man and feeling the rope tighten. "I'm not lying!"

"True." Rience nodded. "You're not lying outright, I would have sensed it. But you are beating about the bush. You wouldn't have thought the ballad up just like that, not without reason. And you do know the witcher, after all. You have often been seen in his company. So talk, Dandelion, if you treasure your joints. Everything you know."

"This Ciri," panted the poet, "was destined for the witcher. She's a so-called Child Surprise . . . You must have heard it, the story's well known. Her parents swore to hand her over to the witcher—"

"Her parents are supposed to have handed the child over to that crazed mutant? That murderous mercenary? You're lying, rhymester. Keep such tales for women."

"That's what happened, I swear on my mother's soul,"

35

sobbed Dandelion. "I have it from a reliable source . . . The witcher—"

"Talk about the girl. For the moment I'm not interested in the witcher."

"I don't know anything about the girl! I only know that the witcher was going to fetch her from Cintra when the war broke out. I met him at the time. He heard about the massacre, about Calanthe's death, from me . . . He asked me about the child, the queen's granddaughter . . . But I knew everyone in Cintra was killed, not a single soul in the last bastion survived—"

"Go on. Fewer metaphors, more hard facts!"

"When the witcher learned of the massacre and fall of Cintra he forsook his journey. We both escaped north. We parted ways in Hengfors and I haven't seen him since . . . But because he talked, on the way, a bit about this . . . Ciri, or whatever-her-name-is . . . and about destiny . . . Well, I made up this ballad. I don't know any more, I swear!"

Rience scowled at him.

"And where is this witcher now?" he asked. "This hired monster murderer, this poetic butcher who likes to discuss destiny?"

"I told you, the last time I saw him—"

"I know what you said," Rience interrupted. "I listened carefully to what you said. And now you're going to listen carefully to me. Answer my questions precisely. The question is: if no one has seen Geralt, or Gerald, the Witcher for over a year, where is he hiding? Where does he usually hide?"

"I don't know where it is," the troubadour said quickly. "I'm not lying. I really don't know—"

"Too quick, Dandelion, too quick." Rience smiled ominously. "Too eager. You are cunning but not careful enough. You don't know where it is, you say. But I warrant you know what it is."

Dandelion clenched his teeth with anger and despair.

"Well?" Rience made a sign to the reeking man. "Where is the witcher hiding? What is the place called?"

The poet remained silent. The rope tightened, twisting his hands painfully, and his feet left the ground. Dandelion let out a howl, brief and broken because Rience's wizardly ring immediately gagged him.

"Higher, higher." Rience rested his hands on his hips. "You know, Dandelion, I could use magic to sound out your mind, but it's exhausting. Besides, I like seeing people's eyes pop out of their sockets from pain. And you're going to tell me anyway."

Dandelion knew he would. The rope secured to his ankles grew taut, the bucket of lime scraped along the ground.

"Sir," said the first ruffian suddenly, covering the lantern with his cloak and peering through the gap in the pigsty door, "someone's coming. A lass, I think."

"You know what to do," Rience hissed. "Put the lantern out."

The reeking man released the rope and Dandelion tumbled inertly to the ground, falling in such a way that he could see the man with the lantern standing at the door and the reeking man, a long knife in his hand, lying in wait on the other side. Light broke in from the bawdyhouse through gaps in the planks, and the poet heard the singing and hubbub.

The door to the pigsty creaked open, revealing a short

figure wrapped in a cloak and wearing a round, tightly fitting cap. After a moment's hesitation, the woman crossed the threshold. The reeking man threw himself at her, slashing forcefully with his knife, and tumbled to his knees as the knife met with no resistance, passing through the figure's throat as though through a cloud of smoke. Because the figure really was a cloud of smoke – one which was already starting to disperse. But before it completely vanished another figure burst into the pigsty, indistinct, dark and nimble as a weasel. Dandelion saw it throw a cloak at the lantern man, jump over the reeking one, saw something glisten in its hand, and heard the reeking man wheeze and choke savagely. The lantern man disentangled himself from the cloak, jumped, took a swing with his knife. A fiery lightning bolt shot from the dark figure with a hiss, slapped over the tough's face and chest with a crack and spread over him like flaming oil. The ruffian screamed piercingly and the grim reek of burning meat filled the pigsty.

Then Rience attacked. The spell he cast illuminated the darkness with a bluish flash in which Dandelion saw a slender woman wearing man's clothes gesticulating strangely with both hands. He only glimpsed her for a second before the blue glow disappeared with a bang and a blinding flash. Rience fell back with a roar of fury and collapsed onto the wooden pigsty walls, breaking them with a crash. The woman dressed in man's clothing leapt after him, a stiletto flashing in her hand. The pigsty filled with brightness again – this time golden – beaming from a bright oval which suddenly appeared in the air. Dandelion saw Rience spring up from the dusty floor, leap into the oval and immediately disappear. The oval dimmed but, before it went out entirely, the woman ran up to it shouting incomprehensibly, stretching out her hand. Something crackled and rustled and the dying oval boiled with roaring flames for a moment. A muffled sound, as if coming from a great distance, reached Dandelion's ears – a sound very much like a scream of pain. The oval went out completely and darkness engulfed the pigsty again. The poet felt the power which gagged him disappear.

"Help!" he howled. "Help!"

"Stop yelling, Dandelion," said the woman, kneeling next to him and slicing through the knots with Rience's stiletto.

"Yennefer? Is that you?"

"Surely you're not going to say you don't remember how I look. And I'm sure my voice is not unfamiliar to your musical ear. Can you get up? They didn't break any bones, did they?"

Dandelion stood with difficulty, groaned and stretched his aching shoulders.

"What's with them?" He indicated the bodies lying on the ground.

"We'll check." The enchantress snicked the stiletto shut. "One of them should still be alive. I've a few questions for him."

"This one," the troubadour stood over the reeking man, "probably still lives."

"I doubt it," said Yennefer indifferently. "I severed his windpipe and carotid artery. There might still be a little murmur in him but not for long."

Dandelion shuddered.

"You slashed his throat?"

"If, out of inborn caution, I hadn't sent an illusion in

first, I would be the one lying there now. Let's look at the other one . . . Bloody hell. Such a sturdy fellow and he still couldn't take it. Pity, pity—"

"He's dead, too?"

"He couldn't take the shock. Hmm . . . I fried him a little too hard . . . See, even his teeth are charred— What's the matter with you, Dandelion? Are you going to be sick?"

"I am," the poet replied indistinctly, bending over and leaning his forehead against the pigsty wall.

"That's everything?" The enchantress put her tumbler down and reached for the skewer of roast chickens. "You haven't lied about anything? Haven't forgotten anything?"

"Nothing. Apart from 'thank you'. Thank you, Yennefer."

She looked him in the eyes and nodded her head lightly, making her glistening, black curls writhe and cascade down to her shoulders. She slipped the roast chicken onto a trencher and began dividing it skilfully. She used a knife and fork. Dandelion had only known one person, up until then, who could eat a chicken with a knife and fork as skilfully. Now he knew how, and from whom, Geralt had learnt the knack. *Well*, he thought, *no wonder. After all, he did live with her for a year in Vengerberg and before he left her, she had instilled a number of strange things into him.* He pulled the other chicken from the skewer and, without a second thought, ripped off a thigh and began eating it, pointedly holding it with both hands.

"How did you know?" he asked. "How did you arrive with help on time?"

"I was beneath Bleobheris during your performance."

"I didn't see you."

"I didn't want to be seen. Then I followed you into town. I waited here, in the tavern – it wasn't fitting, after all, for me to follow you in to that haven of dubious delight and certain gonorrhoea. But I eventually became impatient and was wandering around the yard when I thought I heard voices coming from the pigsty. I sharpened my hearing and it turned out it wasn't, as I'd first thought, some sodomite but you. Hey, innkeeper! More wine, if you please!"

"At your command, honoured lady! Quick as a flash!"

"The same as before, please, but this time without the water. I can only tolerate water in a bath, in wine I find it quite loathsome."

"At your service, at your service!"

Yennefer pushed her plate aside. There was still enough meat on the chicken, Dandelion noticed, to feed the innkeeper and his family for breakfast. A knife and fork were certainly elegant and refined, but they weren't very effective.

"Thank you," he repeated, "for rescuing me. That cursed Rience wouldn't have spared my life. He'd have squeezed everything from me and then butchered me like a sheep."

"Yes, I think he would." She poured herself and the bard some wine then raised her tumbler. "So let's drink to your rescue and health, Dandelion."

"And to yours, Yennefer," he toasted her in return. "To health for which – as of today – I shall pray whenever the occasion arises. I'm indebted to you, beautiful lady, and I shall repay the debt in my songs. I shall explode the myth which claims wizards are insensitive to the pain of others, that they are rarely eager to help poor, unfortunate, unfamiliar mortals."

"What to do." She smiled, half-shutting her beautiful violet eyes. "The myth has some justification; it did not spring from nowhere. But you're not a stranger, Dandelion. I know you and like you."

"Really?" The poet smiled too. "You have been good at concealing it up until now. I've even heard the rumour that you can't stand me, I quote, any more than the plague."

"It was the case once." The enchantress suddenly grew serious. "Later my opinion changed. Later, I was grateful to you."

"What for, if I may ask?"

"Never mind," she said, toying with the empty tumbler. "Let us get back to more important questions. Those you were asked in the pigsty while your arms were being twisted out of their sockets. What really happened, Dandelion? Have you really not seen Geralt since you fled the banks of the Yaruga? Did you really not know he returned south after the war? That he was seriously wounded – so seriously there were even rumours of his death? Didn't you know anything?"

"No. I didn't. I stayed in Pont Vanis for a long time, in Esterad Thyssen's court. And then at Niedamir's in Hengfors—"

"You didn't know." The enchantress nodded and unfastened her tunic. A black velvet ribbon wound around her neck, an obsidian star set with diamonds hanging from it. "You didn't know that when his wounds healed

Geralt went to Transriver? You can't guess who he was looking for?"

"That I can. But I don't know if he found her."

"You don't know," she repeated. "You, who usually know everything, and then sing about everything. Even such intimate matters as someone else's feelings. I listened to your ballads beneath Bleobheris, Dandelion. You dedicated a good few verses to me."

"Poetry," he muttered, staring at the chicken, "has its rights. No one should be offended—"

"'Hair like a raven's wing, as a storm in the night . . .'" quoted Yennefer with exaggerated emphasis, "'. . . and in the violet eyes sleep lightning bolts . . .' Isn't that how it went?"

"That's how I remembered you." The poet smiled faintly. "May the first who wishes to claim the description is untrue throw the first stone."

"Only I don't know," the Enchantress pinched her lips together, "who gave you permission to describe my internal organs. How did it go? 'Her heart, as though a jewel, adorned her neck. Hard as if of diamond made, and as a diamond so unfeeling, sharper than obsidian, cutting—' Did you make that up yourself? Or perhaps . . . ?"

Her lips quivered, twisted.

". . . or perhaps you listened to someone's confidences and grievances?"

"Hmm . . ." Dandelion cleared his throat and veered away from the dangerous subject. "Tell me, Yennefer, when did you last see Geralt?"

"A long time ago."

"After the war?"

"After the war . . ." Yennefer's voice changed a little.

"No, I never saw him after the war. For a long time . . . I didn't see anybody. Well, back to the point, Poet. I am a little surprised to discover that you do not know anything, you have not heard anything and that, in spite of this, someone searching for information picked you out to stretch over a beam. Doesn't that worry you?"

"It does."

"Listen to me," she said sharply, banging her tumbler against the table. "Listen carefully. Strike that ballad from your repertoire. Do not sing it again."

"Are you talking about—"

"You know perfectly well what I'm talking about. Sing about the war against Nilfgaard. Sing about Geralt and me, you'll neither harm nor help anyone in the process, you'll make nothing any better or worse. But do not sing about the Lion Cub of Cintra."

She glanced around to check if any of the few customers at this hour were eavesdropping, and waited until the lass clearing up had returned to the kitchen.

"And do try to avoid one-to-one meetings with people you don't know," she said quietly. "People who 'forget' to introduce themselves by conveying greetings from a mutual acquaintance. Understand?"

He looked at her surprised. Yennefer smiled.

"Greetings from Dijkstra, Dandelion."

Now the bard glanced around timidly. His astonishment must have been evident and his expression amusing because the sorceress allowed herself a quite derisive grimace.

"While we are on the subject," she whispered, leaning across the table, "Dijkstra is asking for a report. You're on your way back from Verden and he's interested in hearing what's being said at King Ervyll's court. He asked me to convey that this time your report should be to the point, detailed and under no circumstances in verse. Prose, Dandelion. Prose."

The poet swallowed and nodded. He remained silent, pondering the question.

But the enchantress anticipated him. "Difficult times are approaching," she said quietly. "Difficult and dangerous. A time of change is coming. It would be a shame to grow old with the uncomfortable conviction that one had done nothing to ensure that these changes are for the better. Don't you agree?"

He agreed with a nod and cleared his throat. "Yennefer?"

"I'm listening, Poet."

"Those men in the pigsty . . . I would like to know who they were, what they wanted, who sent them. You killed them both, but rumour has it that you can draw information even from the dead."

"And doesn't rumour also have it that necromancy is forbidden, by edict of the Chapter? Let it go, Dandelion. Those thugs probably didn't know much anyway. The one who escaped . . . Hmm . . . He's another matter."

"Rience. He was a wizard, wasn't he?"

"Yes. But not a very proficient one."

"Yet he managed to escape from you. I saw how he did it – he teleported, didn't he? Doesn't that prove anything?"

"Indeed it does. That someone helped him. Rience had neither the time nor the strength to open an oval portal suspended in the air. A portal like that is no joke. It's clear that someone else opened it. Someone far more powerful.

That's why I was afraid to chase him, not knowing where I would land. But I sent some pretty hot stuff after him. He's going to need a lot of spells and some effective burn elixirs, and will remain marked for some time."

"Maybe you will be interested to hear that he was a Nilfgaardian."

"You think so?" Yennefer sat up and with a swift movement pulled the stiletto from her pocket and turned it in her palm. "A lot of people carry Nilfgaardian knives now. They're comfortable and handy – they can even be hidden in a cleavage—"

"It's not the knife. When he was questioning me he used the term 'battle for Cintra', 'conquest of the town' or something along those lines. I've never heard anyone describe those events like that. For us, it has always been a massacre. The Massacre of Cintra. No one refers to it by any other name."

The magician raised her hand, scrutinised her nails. "Clever, Dandelion. You have a sensitive ear."

"It's a professional hazard."

"I wonder which profession you have in mind?" She smiled coquettishly. "But thank you for the information. It was valuable."

"Let it be," he replied with a smile, "my contribution to making changes for the better. Tell me, Yennefer, why is Nilfgaard so interested in Geralt and the girl from Cintra?"

"Don't stick your nose into that business." She suddenly turned serious. "I said you were to forget you ever heard of Calanthe's granddaughter."

"Indeed, you did. But I'm not searching for a subject for a ballad."

"What the hell are you searching for then? Trouble?"

"Let's take it," he said quietly, resting his chin on his clasped hands and looking the enchantress in the eye. "Let's take it that Geralt did, in fact, find and rescue the child. Let's take it that he finally came to believe in the power of destiny, and took the child with him. Where to? Rience tried to force it out of me with torture. But you know, Yennefer. You know where the witcher is hiding."

"I do."

"And you know how to get there."

"I know that too."

"Don't you think he should be warned? Warned that the likes of Rience are looking for him and the little girl? I would go, but I honestly don't know where it is . . . That place whose name I prefer not to say . . ."

"Get to the point, Dandelion."

"If you know where Geralt is, you ought to go and warn him. You owe him that, Yennefer. There was, after all, something between you."

"Yes," she acknowledged coldly. "There was something between us. That's why I know him a bit. He does not like having help imposed on him. And if he was in need of it he would seek it from those he could trust. A year has gone by since those events and I . . . I've not had any news from him. And as for our debt, I owe him exactly as much as he owes me. No more and no less."

"So I'll go then." He raised his head high. "Tell me—"

"I won't," she interrupted. "Your cover's blown, Dandelion. They might come after you again; the less you know the better. Vanish from here. Go to Redania, to

Dijkstra and Philippa Eilhart, stick to Vizimir's court. And I warn you once more: forget the Lion Cub of Cintra. Forget about Ciri. Pretend you have never heard the name. Do as I ask. I wouldn't like anything bad to happen to you. I like you too much, owe you too much—"

"You've said that already. What do you owe me, Yennefer?"

The sorceress turned her head away, did not say anything for a while.

"You travelled with him," she said finally. "Thanks to you he was not alone. You were a friend to him. You were with him."

The bard lowered his eyes.

"He didn't get much from it," he muttered. "He didn't get much from our friendship. He had little but trouble because of me. He constantly had to get me out of some scrape . . . help me . . ."

She leaned across the table, put her hand on his and squeezed it hard without saying anything. Her eyes held regret.

"Go to Redania," she repeated after a moment. "To Tretogor. Stay in Dijkstra's and Philippa's care. Don't play at being a hero. You have got yourself mixed up in a dangerous affair, Dandelion."

"I've noticed." He grimaced and rubbed his aching shoulder. "And that is precisely why I believe Geralt should be warned. You are the only one who knows where to look for him. You know the way. I guess you used to be . . . a guest there . . . ?"

Yennefer turned away. Dandelion saw her lips pinch, the muscles in her cheek quiver.

"Yes, in the past," she said and there was something

elusive and strange in her voice. "I used to be a guest there, sometimes. But never uninvited."

The wind howled savagely, rippling through the grasses growing over the ruins, rustling in the hawthorn bushes and tall nettles. Clouds sped across the sphere of the moon, momentarily illuminating the great castle, drenching the moat and few remaining walls in a pale glow undulating with shadows, and revealing mounds of skulls baring their broken teeth and staring into nothingness through the black holes of their eye sockets. Ciri squealed sharply and hid her face in the witcher's cloak.

The mare, prodded on by the witcher's heels, carefully stepped over a pile of bricks and passed through the broken arcade. Her horseshoes, ringing against the flagstones, awoke weird echoes between the walls, muffled by the howling gale. Ciri trembled, digging her hands into the horse's mane.

"I'm frightened," she whispered.

"There's nothing to be frightened of," replied the witcher, laying his hand on her shoulder. "It's hard to find a safer place in the whole world. This is Kaer Morhen, the Witchers' Keep. There used to be a beautiful castle here. A long time ago."

She did not reply, bowing her head low. The witcher's mare, called Roach, snorted quietly, as if she too wanted to reassure the girl.

They immersed themselves in a dark abyss, in a long, unending black tunnel dotted with columns and arcades. Roach stepped confidently and willingly, ignoring the impenetrable darkness, and her horseshoes rang brightly against the floor.

In front of them, at the end of the tunnel, a straight, vertical line suddenly flared with a red light. Growing taller and wider it became a door beyond which was a faint glow, the flickering brightness of torches stuck in iron mounts on the walls. A black figure stood framed in the door, blurred by the brightness.

"Who comes?" Ciri heard a menacing, metallic voice which sounded like a dog's bark. "Geralt?"

"Yes, Eskel. It's me."

"Come in."

The witcher dismounted, took Ciri from the saddle, stood her on the ground and pressed a bundle into her little hands which she grabbed tightly, only regretting that it was too small for her to hide behind completely.

"Wait here with Eskel," he said. "I'll take Roach to the stables."

"Come into the light, laddie," growled the man called Eskel. "Don't lurk in the dark."

Ciri looked up into his face and barely restrained her frightened scream. He wasn't human. Although he stood on two legs, although he smelled of sweat and smoke, although he wore ordinary human clothes, he was not human. *No human can have a face like that*, she thought.

"Well, what are you waiting for?" repeated Eskel.

She didn't move. In the darkness she heard the clatter of Roach's horseshoes grow fainter. Something soft and squeaking ran over her foot. She jumped.

"Don't loiter in the dark, or the rats will eat your boots."

Still clinging to her bundle Ciri moved briskly towards

the light. The rats bolted out from beneath her feet with a squeak. Eskel leaned over, took the package from her and pulled back her hood.

"A plague on it," he muttered. "A girl. That's all we need."

She glanced at him, frightened. Eskel was smiling. She saw that he was human after all, that he had an entirely human face, deformed by a long, ugly, semi-circular scar running from the corner of his mouth across the length of his cheek up to the ear.

"Since you're here, welcome to Kaer Morhen," he said. "What do they call you?"

"Ciri," Geralt replied for her, silently emerging from the darkness. Eskel turned around. Suddenly, quickly, wordlessly, the witchers fell into each other's arms and wound their shoulders around each other tight and hard. For one brief moment.

"Wolf, you're alive."

"I am."

"All right." Eskel took a torch from its bracket. "Come on. I'm closing the inner gates to stop the heat escaping."

They walked along the corridor. There were rats here, too; they flitted under the walls, squeaked from the dark abyss, from the branching passages, and skittered before the swaying circle of light thrown by the torch. Ciri walked quickly, trying to keep up with the men.

"Who's wintering here, Eskel? Apart from Vesemir?"

"Lambert and Coën."

They descended a steep and slippery flight of stairs. A gleam was visible below them. Ciri heard voices, detected the smell of smoke.

The hall was enormous, and flooded with light from a huge hearth roaring with flames which were being sucked up into the heart of the chimney. The centre of the hall was taken up by an enormous, heavy table. At least ten people could sit around that table. There were three. Three humans. Three witchers, Ciri corrected herself. She saw nothing but their silhouettes against the fire in the hearth.

"Greetings, Wolf. We've been waiting for you."

"Greetings, Vesemir. Greetings, lads. It's good to be home again."

"Who have you brought us?"

Geralt was silent for a moment, then put his hand on Ciri's shoulder and lightly pushed her forward. She walked awkwardly, hesitantly, huddled up and hunched, her head lowered. *I'm frightened*, she thought. *I'm very frightened. When Geralt found me, when he took me with him, I thought the fear wouldn't come back. I thought it had passed . . . And now, instead of being at home, I'm in this terrible, dark, ruined old castle full of rats and dreadful echoes . . . I'm standing in front of a red wall of fire again. I see sinister black figures, I see dreadful, menacing, glistening eyes staring at me—*

"Who is this child, Wolf? Who is this girl?"

"She's my . . ." Geralt suddenly stammered. She felt his strong, hard hands on her shoulders. And suddenly the fear disappeared, vanished without a trace. The roaring red fire gave out warmth. Only warmth. The black silhouettes were the silhouettes of friends. Carers. Their glistening eyes expressed curiosity. Concern. And unease . . .

Geralt's hands clenched over her shoulders.

"She's our destiny."

Verily, there is nothing so hideous as the monsters, so contrary to nature, known as witchers for they are the offspring of foul sorcery and devilry. They are rogues without virtue, conscience or scruple, true diabolic creations, fit only for killing. There is no place amidst honest men for such as they.

And Kaer Morhen, where these infamous beings nestle, where they perform their foul practices, must be wiped from the surface of this earth, and all trace of it strewn with salt and saltpetre.

Anonymous, *Monstrum,* or *Description of the Witcher*

Intolerance and superstition has always been the domain of the more stupid amongst the common folk and, I conjecture, will never be uprooted, for they are as eternal as stupidity itself. There, where mountains tower today, one day there will be seas; there where today seas surge, will one day be deserts. But stupidity will remain stupidity.

Nicodemus de Boot, *Meditations on Life, Happiness and Prosperity*

CHAPTER TWO

Triss Merigold blew into her frozen hands, wriggled her fingers and murmured a magic formula. Her horse, a gelding, immediately reacted to the spell, snorting and turning its head, looking at the enchantress with eyes made watery by the cold and wind.

"You've got two options, old thing," said Triss, pulling on her gloves. "Either you get used to magic or I sell you to some peasants to pull a plough."

The gelding pricked up its ears, snorted vapour through its nostrils and obediently started down the wooded mountainside. The magician leaned over in the saddle, avoiding being lashed by the frosty branches.

The magic worked quickly; she stopped feeling the sting of cold in her elbows and on her neck, and the unpleasant sensation of cold which had made her hunch her shoulders and draw her head in disappeared. The spell, warming her, also muffled the hunger which had been eating at her for several hours. Triss cheered up, made herself comfortable in the saddle and, with greater attention than before, started to take stock of her surroundings.

Ever since she had left the beaten track, she had been guided by the greyish-white wall of mountains and their snow-capped summits which glistened gold in those rare moments when the sun pierced the clouds – usually in the morning or just before sunset. Now that she was closer to the mountain chain she had to take greater care. The land around Kaer Morhen was famous for its wildness and inaccessibility, and the gap in the granite wall that was a vital landmark was not easy for an inexperienced eye to find. It was enough to turn down one of the numerous gullies and gorges to lose sight of it. And even she who knew the land, knew the way and knew where to look for the pass, could not allow herself to lose her concentration for an instant.

The forest came to an end. A wide valley opened before the enchantress, strewn with boulders which ran across the valley to the sheer mountain-slope on the other side. The Gwenllech, the River of White Stones, flowed down the heart of the valley, foam seething between the boulders and logs washed along by the current. Here, in its upper reaches, the Gwenllech was no more than a wide but shallow stream. Up here it could be crossed without any difficulty. Lower down, in Kaedwen, in its middle reaches, the river was an insurmountable obstacle, rushing and breaking against the beds of its deep chasms.

The gelding, driven into the water, hastened its step, clearly wanting to reach the opposite bank as quickly as possible. Triss held it back lightly – the stream was shallow, reaching just above the horse's fetlocks, but the pebbles covering the bed were slippery and the current was sharp and quick. The water churned and foamed around her mount's legs.

The magician looked up at the sky. The growing cold and increasing wind here, in the mountains, could herald a blizzard and she did not find the prospect of spending yet another night in a grotto or rocky nook too attractive. She could, if she had to, continue her journey even through a blizzard; she could locate the path using telepathy, she could – using magic – make herself insensitive to the cold. She could, if she had to. But she preferred not to have to.

Luckily, Kaer Morhen was already close. Triss urged the gelding on to flat scree, over an enormous heap of stones washed down by glaciers and streams, and rode into a narrow pass between rocky outcrops. The gorge walls rose vertically and seemed to meet high above her, only divided by a narrow line of sky. It grew warmer, the wind howling above the rocks could no longer reach to lash and sting at her.

The pass broadened, leading through a ravine and then into the valley, opening onto a huge depression, covered by forest, which stretched out amidst jagged boulders. The magician ignored the gentle, accessible depression rim and rode down towards the forest, into the thick backwoods. Dry branches cracked under the gelding's hooves. Forced to step over fallen tree trunks, the horse snorted, danced and stamped. Triss pulled at the reins, tugged at her mount's shaggy ear and scolded it harshly with spiteful allusions to its lameness. The steed, looking for all the world as though it were ashamed of itself, walked with a more even and sprightly gait and picked its way through the thicket.

Before long they emerged onto clearer land, riding along the trough of a stream which barely trickled along the ravine bed. The magician looked around carefully, finally finding what she was looking for. Over the gully, supported horizontally by enormous boulders, lay a mighty tree trunk, dark, bare and turning green with moss. Triss rode closer, wanting to make sure this was, indeed, the Trail and not a tree accidentally felled in a gale. But she spied a narrow, indistinct pathway disappearing into the woods. She could not be mistaken – this was definitely the Trail, a path encircling the old castle of Kaer Morhen and beset with obstacles, where witchers trained to improve their running speeds and controlled breathing. The path was known as the Trail, but Triss knew young witchers had given it their own name: The Killer.

She clung to the horse's neck and slowly rode under the trunk. At that moment, she heard stones grating. And the fast, light footsteps of someone running.

She turned in her saddle, pulled on the reins and waited for the witcher to run out onto the log.

A witcher did run out onto the log, flitted along it like an arrow without slowing down, without even using his arms to aid his balance – running nimbly, fluently, with incredible grace. He flashed by, approaching and disappearing amongst the trees without disturbing a single branch. Triss sighed loudly, shaking her head in disbelief.

Because the witcher, judging by his height and build, was only about twelve.

The magician eased the reins, nudged the horse with her heels and trotted upstream. She knew the Trail cut across the ravine once more, at a spot known as the Gullet. She wanted to catch a glimpse of the little witcher once again – children had not been trained in Kaer Morhen for near to a quarter of a century.

She was not in a great hurry. The narrow Killer path meandered and looped its way through the forest and, in order to master it, the little witcher would take far longer than she would, following the shortcut. However, she could not loiter either. Beyond the Gullet, the Trail turned into the woods and led straight to the fortress. If she did not catch the boy at the precipice, she might not see him at all. She had already visited Kaer Morhen a few times, and knew she saw only what the witchers wanted her to see. Triss was not so naïve as to be unaware that they wanted to show her only a tiny fraction of the things to be seen in Kaer Morhen.

After a few minutes riding along the stony trough of the stream she caught sight of the Gullet – a leap over the gully created by two huge mossy rocks, overgrown with gnarled, stunted trees. She released the reins. The horse snorted and lowered its head towards the water trickling between pebbles.

She did not have to wait long. The witcher's silhouette appeared on the rock and the boy jumped, not slowing his pace. The magician heard the soft smack of his landing and a moment later a rattle of stones, the dull thud of a fall and a quiet cry. Or rather, a squeal.

Triss instantly leaped from her saddle, threw the fur off her shoulders and dashed across the mountainside, pulling herself up using tree branches and roots. Momentum aided her climb until she slipped on the conifer needles and fell to her knees next to a figure huddled on the stones. The youngster, on seeing her, jumped up like a spring, backed away in a flash and nimbly grabbed the sword slung across his back – then tripped and collapsed between the junipers and pines. The magician did not rise from her knees; she stared at the boy and opened her mouth in surprise.

Because it was not a boy.

From beneath an ash-blonde fringe, poorly and unevenly cut, enormous emerald eyes – the predominant features in a small face with a narrow chin and upturned nose – stared out at her. There was fear in the eyes.

"Don't be afraid," Triss said tentatively.

The girl opened her eyes even wider. She was hardly out of breath and did not appear to be sweating. It was clear she had already run the Killer more than once.

"Nothing's happened to you?"

The girl did not reply; instead she sprang up, hissed with pain, shifted her weight to her left leg, bent over and rubbed her knee. She was dressed in a sort of leather suit sewn together – or rather stuck together – in a way which would make any tailor who took pride in his craft howl in horror and despair. The only pieces of her equipment which seemed to be relatively new, and fitted her, were her knee-high boots, her belts and her sword. More precisely, her little sword.

"Don't be afraid," repeated Triss, still not rising from her knees. "I heard your fall and was scared, that's why I rushed here—"

"I slipped," murmured the girl.

"Have you hurt yourself?"

"No. You?"

The enchantress laughed, tried to get up, winced and swore at the pain in her ankle. She sat down and carefully straightened her foot, swearing once more.

"Come here, little one, help me get up."

"I'm not little."

"If you say so. In that case, what are you?"

"A witcher!"

"Ha! So, come here and help me get up, witcher."

The girl did not move from the spot. She shifted her weight from foot to foot, and her hands, in their finger-less, woollen gloves, toyed with her sword belt as she glanced suspiciously at Triss.

"Have no fear," said the enchantress with a smile. "I'm not a bandit or outsider. I'm called Triss Merigold and I'm going to Kaer Morhen. The witchers know me. Don't gape at me. I respect your suspicion, but be reasonable. Would I have got this far if I hadn't known the way? Have you ever met a human on the Trail?"

The girl overcame her hesitation, approached and stretched out her hand. Triss stood with only a little assis-tance. Because she was not concerned with having help. She wanted a closer look at the girl. And to touch her.

The green eyes of the little witcher-girl betrayed no signs of mutation, and the touch of her little hand did not produce the slight, pleasant tingling sensation so charac-teristic of witchers. Although she ran the Killer path with a sword slung across her back, the ashen-haired girl had not been subjected to the Trial of Grasses or to Changes. Of that, Triss was certain.

"Show me your knee, little one."

"I'm not little."

"Sorry. But surely you have a name?"

"I do. I'm . . . Ciri."

"It's a pleasure. A bit closer if you please, Ciri."

"It's nothing."

"I want to see what 'nothing' looks like. Ah, that's what I thought. 'Nothing' looks remarkably like torn trousers and skin grazed down to raw flesh. Stand still and don't be scared."

"I'm not scared . . . Awww!"

The magician laughed and rubbed her palm, itching from casting the spell, against her hip. The girl bent over and gazed at her knee.

"Oooh," she said. "It doesn't hurt anymore! And there's no hole . . . Was that magic?"

"You've guessed it."

"Are you a witch?"

"Guessed again. Although I prefer to be called an enchantress. To avoid getting it wrong you can call me by my name, Triss. Just Triss. Come on, Ciri. My horse is waiting at the bottom. We'll go to Kaer Morhen together."

"I ought to run." Ciri shook her head. "It's not good to stop running because you get milk in your muscles. Geralt says—"

"Geralt is at the keep?"

Ciri frowned, pinched her lips together and shot a glance at the enchantress from beneath her ashen fringe. Triss chuckled again.

"All right," she said. "I won't ask. A secret's a secret, and you're right not to disclose it to someone you hardly know. Come on. When we get there we'll see who's at the castle and who isn't. And don't worry about your muscles – I know what to do about lactic acid. Ah, here's my mount. I'll help you . . ."

She stretched out her hand, but Ciri didn't need any help. She jumped agilely into the saddle, lightly, almost without taking off. The gelding started, surprised, and stamped, but the girl quickly took up the reins and reassured it.

"You know how to handle a horse, I see."

"I can handle anything."

"Move up towards the pommel." Triss slipped her foot into the stirrup and caught hold of the mane. "Make a bit of room for me. And don't poke my eye out with that sword."

The gelding, spurred on by her heels, moved off along the stream bed at a walking pace. They rode across another gully and climbed the rounded mountainside. From there they could see the ruins of Kaer Morhen huddled against the stone precipices – the partially demolished trapezium of the defensive wall, the remains of the barbican and gate, the thick, blunt column of the donjon.

The gelding snorted and jerked its head, crossing what remained of the bridge over the moat. Triss tugged at the reins. The decaying skulls and skeletons strewn across the river bed made no impression on her. She had seen them before.

"I don't like this," the girl suddenly remarked. "It's not as it should be. The dead should be buried in the ground. Under a barrow. Shouldn't they?"

"They should," the magician agreed calmly. "I think so, too. But the witchers treat this graveyard as a . . . reminder."

"Reminder of what?"

"Kaer Morhen," Triss said as she guided the horse towards the shattered arcades, "was assaulted. There was a bloody battle here in which almost all the witchers died. Only those who weren't in the keep at the time survived."

"Who attacked them? And why?"

"I don't know," she lied. "It was a terribly long time ago, Ciri. Ask the witchers about it."

"I have," grunted the girl. "But they didn't want to tell me."

I can understand that, thought the magician. *A child trained to be a witcher, a girl, at that, who has not undergone the mutations, should not be told such things. A child like that should not hear about the massacre. A child like that should not be terrified by the prospect that they too may one day hear words describing it like those which were screamed by the fanatics who marched on Kaer Morhen long ago. Mutant. Monster. Freak. Damned by the gods, a creature contrary to nature. No, I do not blame the witchers for not telling you about it, little Ciri. And I shan't tell you either. I have even more reason to be silent. Because I am a wizard, and without the aid of wizards those fanatics would never have conquered the castle. And that hideous lampoon, that widely distributed* Monstrum *which stirred the fanatics up and drove them to such wickedness was also, apparently, some wizard's anonymous work. But I, little Ciri, do not recognise collective responsibility, I do not feel the need to expiate the events which took place half a century before my birth. And the skeletons which are meant to serve as an eternal reminder will ultimately rot away completely, disintegrate into dust and be forgotten, will disappear with the wind which constantly whips the mountainside . . .*

"They don't want to lie like that," said Ciri suddenly. "They don't want to be a symbol, a bad conscience or a warning. But neither do they want their dust to be swept away by the wind."

Triss raised her head, hearing a change in the girl's voice. Immediately she sensed a magical aura, a pulsating and a rush of blood in her temples. She grew tense but did not utter a word, afraid of breaking into or disrupting what was happening.

"An ordinary barrow." Ciri's voice was becoming more and more unnatural, metallic, cold and menacing. "A mound of earth which will be overgrown with nettles. Death has cold blue eyes, and the height of the obelisk does not matter, nor does the writing engraved on it matter. Who can know that better than you, Triss Merigold, the Fourteenth One of the Hill?"

The enchantress froze. She saw the girl's hands clench the horse's mane.

"You died on the Hill, Triss Merigold." The strange, evil voice spoke again. "Why have you come here? Go back, go back at once and take this child, the Child of Elder Blood, with you. Return her to those to whom she belongs. Do this, Fourteenth One. Because if you do not you will die once more. The day will come when the Hill will claim you. The mass grave, and the obelisk on which your name is engraved, will claim you."

The gelding neighed loudly, tossing its head. Ciri jerked suddenly, shuddered.

"What happened?" asked Triss, trying to control her voice.

Ciri coughed, passed both hands through her hair and rubbed her face.

"Nn . . . nothing . . ." she muttered hesitantly. "I'm tired, that's why . . . That's why I fell asleep. I ought to run . . ."

The magical aura disappeared. Triss experienced a

sudden cold wave sweeping through her entire body. She tried to convince herself it was the effect of the defensive spell dying away, but she knew that wasn't true. She glanced up at the stone blocks of the castle, the black, empty eye sockets of its ruined loop holes gaping at her. A shudder ran through her.

The horse's shoes rang against the slabs in the courtyard. The magician quickly leaped from the saddle and held out her hand to Ciri. Taking advantage of the touch of their hands she carefully emitted a magical impulse. And was astounded. Because she didn't feel anything. No reaction, no reply. And no resistance. In the girl who had, just a moment ago, manifested an exceptionally strong aura there was not a trace of magic. She was now an ordinary, badly dressed child whose hair had been incompetently cut.

But a moment ago, this child had been no ordinary child.

Triss did not have time to ponder the strange event. The grate of an iron-clad door reached her, coming from the dark void of the corridor which gaped behind the battered portal. She slipped the fur cape from her shoulders, removed her fox-fur hat and, with a swift movement of the head, tousled her hair – long, full locks the colour of fresh chestnuts, with a sheen of gold, her pride and identifying characteristic.

Ciri sighed with admiration. Triss smiled, pleased by the effect she'd had. Beautiful, long, loose hair was a rarity, an indication of a woman's position, her status, the sign of a free woman, a woman who belonged to herself. The sign of an unusual woman – because "normal" maidens wore their hair in plaits, "normal" married women hid theirs beneath a caul or a coif. Women of high birth, including queens, curled their hair and styled it. Warriors cut it short. Only druids and magicians – and whores – wore their hair naturally so as to emphasise their independence and freedom.

The witchers appeared unexpectedly and silently, as usual, and, also as usual, from nowhere. They stood before her, tall, slim, their arms crossed, the weight of their bodies on their left legs – a position from which, she knew, they could attack in a split second. Ciri stood next to them, in an identical position. In her ludicrous clothes, she looked very funny.

"Welcome to Kaer Morhern, Triss."

"Greetings, Geralt."

He had changed. He gave the impression of having aged. Triss knew that, biologically, this was impossible – witchers aged, certainly, but too slowly for an ordinary mortal, or a magician as young as her, to notice the changes. But one glance was enough for her to realise that although mutation could hold back the physical process of ageing, it did not alter the mental. Geralt's face, slashed by wrinkles, was the best evidence of this. With a sense of deep sorrow Triss tore her gaze away from the white-haired witcher's eyes. Eyes which had evidently seen too much. What's more, she saw nothing of what she had expected in those eyes.

"Welcome," he repeated. "We are glad you've come."

Eskel stood next to Geralt, resembling the Wolf like a brother apart from the colour of his hair and the long scar which disfigured his cheek. And the youngest of the Kaer Morhen witchers, Lambert, was there with his usual ugly, mocking expression. Vesemir was not there.

"Welcome and come in," said Eskel. "It is as cold and blustery as if someone has hung themselves. Ciri, where are you off to? The invitation does not apply to you. The sun is still high, even if it is obscured. You can still train."

"Hey." The Enchantress tossed her hair. "Politeness comes cheap in Witchers' Keep now, I see. Ciri was the first to greet me, and brought me to the castle. She ought to keep me company—"

"She is undergoing training here, Merigold." Lambert grimaced in a parody of a smile. He always called her that: "Merigold," without giving her a title or a name. Triss hated it. "She is a student, not a major domo. Welcoming guests, even such pleasant ones as yourself, is not one of her duties. We're off, Ciri."

Triss gave a little shrug, pretending not to see Geralt and Eskel's embarrassed expressions. She did not say anything, not wanting to embarrass them further. And, above all, she did not want them to see how very intrigued and fascinated she was by the girl.

"I'll take your horse," offered Geralt, reaching for the reins. Triss surreptitiously shifted her hand and their palms joined. So did their eyes.

"I'll come with you," she said naturally. "There are a few little things in the saddlebags which I'll need."

"You gave me a very disagreeable experience not so long ago," he muttered as soon as they had entered the stable. "I studied your impressive tombstone with my own eyes. The obelisk in memory of your heroic death at the battle of Sodden. The news that it was a mistake only reached me recently. I can't understand how anyone could mistake anyone else for you, Triss."

"It's a long story," she answered. "I'll tell you some time. And please forgive me for the disagreeable moment."

"There's nothing to forgive. I've not had many reasons to be happy of late and the feelings I experienced on hearing that you lived cannot compare to any other. Except perhaps what I feel now when I look at you."

Triss felt something explode inside her. Her fear of meeting the white-haired witcher, which had accompanied her throughout her journey, had struggled within her with her hope of having such a meeting. Followed by the sight of that tired, jaded face, those sick eyes which saw everything, cold and calculating, which were unnaturally calm but yet so infused with emotion . . .

She threw her arms around his neck, instantly, without thinking. She caught hold of his hand, abruptly placed it on the nape of her neck, under her hair. A tingling ran down her back, penetrated her with such rapture she almost cried out. In order to muffle and restrain the cry her lips found his lips and stuck to them. She trembled, pressing hard against him, her excitement building and increasing, forgetting herself more and more.

Geralt did not forget himself.

"Triss . . . Please."

"Oh, Geralt . . . So much . . ."

"Triss." He moved her away delicately. "We're not alone . . . They're coming."

She glanced at the entrance and saw the shadows of the approaching witchers only after some time, heard their steps even later. Oh well, her hearing, which she considered very sensitive, could not compete with that of a witcher.

"Triss, my child!"

"Vesemir!"

Vesemir was really very old. Who knows, he could be even older than Kaer Morhen. But he walked towards her with a brisk, energetic and sprightly step; his grip was vigorous and his hands strong.

"I am happy to see you again, Grandfather."

"Give me a kiss. No, not on the hand, little sorceress. You can kiss my hand when I'm resting on my bier. Which will, no doubt, be soon. Oh, Triss, it is a good thing you have come . . . Who can cure me if not you?"

"Cure, you? Of what? Of behaving like a child, surely! Take your hand from my backside, old man, or I'll set fire to that grey beard of yours!"

"Forgive me. I keep forgetting you are grown up, and I can no longer put you on my knee and pat you. As to my health . . . Oh, Triss, old age is no joke. My bones ache so I want to howl. Will you help an old man, child?"

"I will." The enchantress freed herself from his bear-like embrace and cast her eye over the witcher accompanying Vesemir. He was young, apparently the same age as Lambert, and wore a short, black beard which did not hide the severe disfigurement left behind by smallpox. This was unusual; witchers were generally highly immune to infectious diseases.

"Triss Merigold, Coën." Geralt introduced them to each other. "This is Coën's first winter with us. He comes from the north, from Poviss."

The young witcher bowed. He had unusually pale, yellow-green irises, and the whites of his eyes, riddled with red threads, indicated difficult and troublesome processes during his mutation.

"Let us go, child," uttered Vesemir, taking her by the arm. "A stable is no place to welcome a guest, but I couldn't wait to see you."

In the courtyard, in a recess in the wall sheltered from the wind, Ciri was training under Lambert's instructions. Deftly balancing on a beam hanging on chains, she was attacking – with her sword – a leather sack bound with straps to make it resemble a human torso. Triss stopped to watch.

"Wrong!" yelled Lambert. "You're getting too close! Don't hack blindly at it! I told you, the very tip of the sword, at the carotid artery! Where does a humanoid have its carotid artery? On top of its head? What's happening? Concentrate, Princess!"

Ha, thought Triss. *So it is truth, not a legend. She is the one. I guessed correctly.*

She decided to attack without delay, not allowing the witchers to try any ruses.

"The famous Child Surprise?" she said indicating Ciri. "I see you have applied yourselves to fulfilling the demands of fate and destiny? But it seems you have muddled the stories, boys. In the fairy-tales I was told, shepherdesses and orphans become princesses. But here, I see, a princess is becoming a witcher. Does that not appear somewhat daring to you?"

Vesemir glanced at Geralt. The white-haired witcher remained silent, his face perfectly still; he did not react with even the slightest quiver of his eyelids to Vesemir's unspoken request for support.

"It's not what you think." The old man cleared his throat. "Geralt brought her here last autumn. She has no one apart from— Triss, how can one not believe in destiny when—"

"What has destiny to do with waving a sword around?"

"We are teaching her to fence," Geralt said quietly, turning towards her and looking her straight in the eyes. "What else are we to teach her? We know nothing else. Destiny or no, Kaer Morhen is now her home. At least for a while. Training and swordsmanship amuse her, keep her healthy and fit. They allow her to forget the tragedy she has lived through. This is her home now, Triss. She has no other."

"Masses of Cintrians," the enchantress said, holding his gaze, "fled to Verden after the defeat, to Brugge, Temeria and the Islands of Skellige. Amongst them are magnates, barons, knights. Friends, relations . . . as well as this girl's subjects."

"Friends and relations did not look for her after the war. They did not find her."

"Because she was not destined for them?" She smiled at him, not very sincerely but very prettily. As prettily as she could. She did not want him to use that tone of voice.

The witcher shrugged. Triss, knowing him a little, immediately changed tactics and gave up the argument.

She looked at Ciri again. The girl, agilely stepping along the balance beam, executed a half-turn, cut lightly, and immediately leaped away. The dummy, struck, swayed on its rope.

"Well, at last!" shouted Lambert. "You've finally got it! Go back and do it again. I want to make sure it wasn't a fluke!"

"The sword," Triss turned to the witchers, "looks sharp. The beam looks slippery and unstable. And Lambert looks like an idiot, demoralising the girl with all his shouting. Aren't you afraid of an unfortunate accident? Or maybe you're relying on destiny to protect the child against it?"

"Ciri practised for nearly six months without a sword," said Coën. "She knows how to move. And we are keeping an eye on her because—"

"Because this is her home," finished Geralt quietly but firmly. Very firmly. Using a tone which put an end to the discussion.

"Exactly. It is." Vesemir took a deep breath. "Triss, you must be tired. And hungry?"

"I cannot deny it," she sighed, giving up on trying to catch Geralt's eye. "To be honest, I'm on my last legs. I spent last night on the Trail in a shepherd's hut which was practically falling apart, buried in straw and sawdust. I used spells to insulate the shack; if it weren't for that I would probably be dead. I long for clean linen."

"You will have supper with us now. And then you will sleep as long as you wish, and rest. We have prepared the best room for you, the one in the tower. And we have put the best bed we could find in Kaer Morhen there."

"Thank you." Triss smiled faintly. *In the tower*, she thought. *All right, Vesemir. Let it be the tower for today, if appearances matter so much to you. I can sleep in the tower in the best of all the beds in Kaer Morhen. Although I would prefer to sleep with Geralt in the worst.*

"Let's go, Triss."

"Let's go."

* * *

The wind hammered against the shutters and ruffled the remains of the moth-eaten tapestries which had been used to insulate the window. Triss lay in perfect darkness in the best bed in the whole of Kaer Morhen. She couldn't sleep – and not because the best bed in Kaer Morhen was a dilapidated antique. Triss was thinking hard. And all the thoughts chasing sleep away revolved around one fundamental question.

What had she been summoned to the fortress for? Who had summoned her? Why? For what purpose?

Vesemir's illness was just a pretext. Vesemir was a witcher. The fact that he was also an old man did not change the fact that many a youngster could envy him his health. If the old man had been stung by a manticore or bitten by a werewolf Triss would have accepted that she had been summoned to aid him. But "aching bones" was a joke. For an ache in his bones, not a very original complaint within the horrendously cold walls of Kaer Morhen, Vesemir could have treated with a witchers' elixir or – an even simpler solution – with strong rye vodka, applied internally and externally in equal proportions. He didn't need a magician, with her spells, philtres and amulets.

So who had summoned her? Geralt?

Triss thrashed about in the bedclothes, feeling a wave of heat come over her. And a wave of arousal, made all the stronger by anger. She swore quietly, kicked her quilt away and rolled on to her side. The ancient bedstead squeaked and creaked. *I've no control over myself*, she thought. *I'm behaving like a stupid adolescent. Or even worse – like an old maid deprived of affection. I can't even think logically.*

She swore again.

Of course it wasn't Geralt. Don't get excited, little one. Don't get excited, just think of his expression in the stable. You've seen expressions like that before. You've seen them, so don't kid yourself. The foolish, contrite, embarrassed expressions of men who want to forget, who regret, who don't want to remember what happened, don't want to go back to what has been. By all the gods, little one, don't fool yourself it's different this time. It's never different. And you know it. Because, after all, you've had a fair amount of experience.

As far as her erotic life was concerned, Triss Merigold had the right to consider herself a typical enchantress. It had began with the sour taste of forbidden fruit, made all the more exciting by the strict rules of the academy and the prohibitions of the mistress under whom she practised. Then came her independence, freedom and a crazy promiscuity which ended, as it usually does, in bitterness, disillusionment and resignation. Then followed a long period of loneliness and the discovery that if she wanted to release her tension and stress then someone who wanted to consider himself her lord and master – as soon as he had turned on his back and wiped the sweat from his brow – was entirely superfluous. There were far less troublesome ways of calming her nerves – ones with the additional advantages of not staining her towels with blood, not passing wind under the quilt and not demanding breakfast. That was followed by a short-lived and entertaining fascination with the same sex, which ended in the conclusion that soiling towels, passing wind and greediness were by no means exclusively male attributes. Finally, like all but a few magicians, Triss moved to affairs with other wizards, which proved sporadic and frustrating in their cold, technical and almost ritual course.

Then Geralt of Rivia appeared. A witcher leading a stormy life, and tied to her good friend Yennefer in a strange, turbulent and almost violent relationship.

Triss had watched them both and was jealous even though it seemed there was little to be jealous of. Their relationship quite obviously made them both unhappy, had led straight to destruction, pain and yet, against all logic . . . it had lasted. Triss couldn't understand it. And it had fascinated her. It had fascinated her to such an extent that . . .

. . . she had seduced the witcher – with the help of a little magic. She had hit on a propitious moment, a moment when he and Yennefer had scratched at each other's eyes yet again and had abruptly parted. Geralt had needed warmth, and had wanted to forget.

No, Triss had not desired to take him away from Yennefer. As a matter of fact, her friend was more important to her than he was. But her brief relationship with the witcher had not disappointed. She had found what she was looking for – emotions in the form of guilt, anxiety and pain. His pain. She had experienced his emotions, it had excited her and, when they parted, she had been unable to forget it. And she had only recently understood what pain is. The moment when she had overwhelmingly wanted to be with him again. For a short while – just for a moment – to be with him.

And now she was so close . . .

Triss clenched her fist and punched the pillow. *No*, she thought, *no. Don't be silly. Don't think about it. Think about . . .*

About Ciri. Is she . . .

Yes. She was the real reason behind her visit to Kaer Morhen. *The ash-blonde girl who, here in Kaer Morhen, they want to turn into a witcher. A real witcher. A mutant. A killing machine, like themselves.*

It's clear, she suddenly thought, feeling a passionate arousal of an entirely different nature. *It's obvious. They want to mutate the child, subject her to the Trial of Grasses and Changes, but they don't know how to do it.* Vesemir was the only witcher left from the previous generation, and he was only a fencing instructor. The Laboratorium, hidden in the vaults of Kaer Morhen, with its dusty demijohns of elixirs, the alembics, ovens and retorts . . . None of the witchers knew how to use them. The mutagenic elixirs had been concocted by some renegade wizard in the distant past and then perfected over the years by the wizard's successors, who had, over the years, magically controlled the process of Changes to which children were subjected. And at a vital moment the chain had snapped. There was no more magical knowledge or power. The witchers had the herbs and Grasses, they had the Laboratorium. They knew the recipe. But they had no wizard.

Who knows, she thought, *perhaps they have tried? Have they given children concoctions prepared without the use of magic?*

She shuddered at the thought of what might have happened to those children.

And now they want to mutate the girl but can't. And that might mean . . . They may ask me to help. And then I'll see something no living wizard has seen, I'll learn something no living wizard has learned. Their famous Grasses and herbs, the secret virus cultures, the renowned, mysterious recipes . . .

And I will be the one to give the child a number of elixirs, who will watch the Changes of mutation, who will watch, with my own eyes . . .

Watch the ashen-haired child die.

Oh, no. Triss shuddered again. *Never. Not at such a price.*

Besides, she thought, *I've probably got excited too soon again. That's probably not what this is about. We talked over supper, gossiped about this and that. I tried to guide the conversation to the Child Surprise several times to no avail. They changed the subject at once.*

She had watched them. Vesemir had been tense and troubled; Geralt uneasy, Lambert and Eskel falsely merry and talkative, Coën so natural as to be unnatural. The only one who had been sincere and open was Ciri, rosy-cheeked from the cold, dishevelled, happy and devilishly voracious. They had eaten beer potage, thick with croutons and cheese, and Ciri had been surprised they had not served mushrooms as well. They had drunk cider, but the girl had been given water and was clearly both astonished and revolted by it. "Where's the salad?" she had yelled, and Lambert had rebuked her sharply and ordered her to take her elbows off the table.

Mushrooms and salad. In December?

Of course, thought Triss. *They're feeding her those legendary cave saprophytes – a mountain plant unknown to science – giving her the famous infusions of their mysterious herbs to drink. The girl is developing quickly, is acquiring a witcher's infernal fitness. Naturally, without the mutation, without the risk, without the hormonal up-*

heaval. But the magician must not know this. It is to be kept a secret from the magician. They aren't going to tell me anything; they aren't going to show me anything.

I saw how that girl ran. I saw how she danced on the beam with her sword, agile and swift, full of a dancer's near-feline grace, moving like an acrobat. I must, she thought, *I absolutely must see her body, see how she's developing under the influence of whatever it is they're feeding her. And what if I managed to steal samples of these "mushrooms" and "salads" and take them away? Well, well . . .*

And trust? I don't give a fig for your trust, witchers. There's cancer out there in the world, smallpox, tetanus and leukaemia, there are allergies, there's cot death. And you're keeping your "mushrooms", which could perhaps be distilled and turned into life-saving medicines, hidden away from the world. You're keeping them a secret even from me, and others to whom you declare your friendship, respect and trust. Even I'm forbidden to see not just the Laboratorium, but even the bloody mushrooms!

So why did you bring me here? Me, a magician?
Magic!

Triss giggled. *Ha*, she thought, *witchers, I've got you! Ciri scared you just as she did me. She "withdrew" into a daydream, started to prophesy, gave out an aura which, after all, you can sense almost as well as I can. She automatically reached for something psychokinetically, or bent a pewter spoon with her will as she stared at it during lunch. She answered questions you only thought, and maybe even some which you were afraid to ask yourselves. And you felt fear. You realised that your Surprise is more surprising than you had imagined.*

You realised that you have the Source in Kaer Morhen.

And that, you can't manage without a magician.

And you don't have a single friendly magician, not a single one you could trust. Apart from me and . . .

And Yennefer.

The wind howled, banged the shutter and swelled the tapestry. Triss rolled on to her back and, lost in thought, started to bite her thumbnail.

Geralt had not invited Yennefer. He had invited her. *Does that mean . . . ?*

Who knows. Maybe. But if it's as I think then why . . . ? Why . . . ?

"Why hasn't he come to me?" she shouted quietly into the darkness, angry and aroused.

She was answered by the wind howling amidst the ruins.

The morning was sunny but devilishly cold. Triss woke chilled through and through, without having had enough sleep, but finally assured and decided.

She was the last to go down to the hall. She accepted the tribute of gazes which rewarded her efforts – she had changed her travel clothes for an attractive but simple dress and had skilfully applied magical scents and non-magical but incredibly expensive cosmetics. She ate her porridge, chatting with the witchers about unimportant and trivial matters.

"Water again?" muttered Ciri suddenly, peering into her tumbler. "My teeth go numb when I drink water! I want some juice! That blue one!"

"Don't slouch," said Lambert, stealing a glance at Triss

from the corner of his eye. "And don't wipe your mouth with your sleeve! Finish your food; it's time for training. The days are getting shorter."

"Geralt." Triss finished her porridge. "Ciri fell on the Trail yesterday. Nothing serious, but it was because of that jester's outfit she wears. It all fits so badly, and it hinders her movements."

Vesemir cleared his throat and turned his eyes away. *Aha*, thought the enchantress, *so it's your work, master of the sword. Predictable enough, Ciri's short tunic does look as if it has been cut out with a knife and sewn together with an arrowhead.*

"The days are, indeed, getting shorter," she continued, not waiting for a comment. "But we're going to make today shorter still. Ciri, have you finished? Come with me, if you please. We shall make some vital adjustments to your uniform."

"She's been running around in this for a year, Merigold," said Lambert angrily. "And everything was fine until . . ."

". . . until a woman arrived who can't bear to look at clothes in poor taste which don't fit? You're right, Lambert. But a woman has arrived, and the old order's collapsed; a time of great change has arrived. Come on, Ciri."

The girl hesitated, looked at Geralt. Geralt nodded his agreement and smiled. Pleasantly. Just as he had smiled in the past when, when . . .

Triss turned her eyes away. His smile was not for her.

Ciri's little room was a faithful replica of the witchers' quarters. It was, like theirs, devoid of almost all fittings and furniture. There was practically nothing there beside a few planks nailed together to form a bed, a stool and a trunk. Witchers decorated the walls and doors of their quarters with the skins of animals they killed when hunting – stags, lynx, wolves and even wolverines. On the door of Ciri's little room, however, hung the skin of an enormous rat with a hideous scaly tail. Triss fought back her desire to tear the stinking abomination down and throw it out of the window.

The girl, standing by the bed, stared at her expectantly.

"We'll try," said the enchantress, "to make this . . . sheath fit a little better. I've always had a knack for cutting and sewing so I ought to be able to manage this goatskin, too. And you, little witcher-girl, have you ever had a needle in your hand? Have you been taught anything other than making holes with a sword in sacks of straw?"

"When I was in Transriver, in Kagen, I had to spin," muttered Ciri unwillingly. "They didn't give me any sewing because I only spoilt the linen and wasted thread; they had to undo everything. The spinning was terribly boring – yuk!"

"True," giggled Triss. "It's hard to find anything more boring. I hated spinning, too."

"And did you have to? I did because . . . But you're a wi— magician. You can conjure anything up! That amazing dress . . . did you conjure it up?"

"No." Triss smiled. "Nor did I sew it myself. I'm not that talented."

"And my clothes, how are you going to make them? Conjure them up?"

"There's no need. A magic needle is enough, one

which we shall charm into working more vigorously. And if there's a need . . ."

Triss slowly ran her hand across the torn hole in the sleeve of Ciri's jacket, murmuring a spell while stimulating an amulet to work. Not a trace remained of the hole. Ciri squealed with joy.

"That's magic! I'm going to have a magical jacket! Wow!"

"Only until I make you an ordinary – but good – one. Right, now take all that off, young lady, and change into something else. These aren't your only clothes, surely?"

Ciri shook her head, lifted the lid of the trunk and showed her a faded loose dress, a dark grey tunic, a linen shirt and a woollen blouse resembling a penitent's sack.

"This is mine," she said. "This is what I came in. But I don't wear it now. It's woman's stuff."

"I understand." Triss grimaced mockingly. "Woman's or not, for the time being you'll have to change into it. Well, get on with it, get undressed. Let me help you . . . Damn it! What's this? Ciri?"

The girl's shoulders were covered in massive bruises, suffused with blood. Most of them had already turned yellow; some were fresh.

"What the hell is this?" the magician repeated angrily. "Who beat you like this?"

"This?" Ciri looked at her shoulders as if surprised by the number of bruises. "Oh, this . . . That was the windmill. I was too slow."

"What windmill? Bloody hell!"

"The windmill," repeated Ciri, raising her huge eyes to look up at the magician. "It's a sort of . . . Well . . . I'm using it to learn to dodge while attacking. It's got these paws made of sticks and it turns and waves the paws. You have to jump very quickly and dodge. You have to learn a lefrex. If you haven't got the lefrex the windmill wallops you with a stick. At the beginning, the windmill gave me a really terribly horrible thrashing. But now—"

"Take the leggings and shirt off. Oh, sweet gods! Dear girl! Can you really walk? Run?"

Both hips and her left thigh were black and blue with haematomas and swellings. Ciri shuddered and hissed, pulling away from the magician's hand. Triss swore viciously in Dwarvish, using inexpressibly foul language.

"Was that the windmill, too?" she asked, trying to remain calm.

"This? No. This, this was the windmill." Ciri pointed indifferently to an impressive bruise below her left knee, covering her shin. "And these other ones . . . They were the pendulum. I practise my fencing steps on the pendulum. Geralt says I'm already good at the pendulum. He says I've got . . . Flair. I've got flair."

"And if you run out of flair" – Triss ground her teeth together – "I take it the pendulum thumps you?"

"But of course," the girl confirmed, looking at her, clearly surprised at this lack of knowledge. "It thumps you, and how."

"And here? On your side? What was that? A smith's hammer?"

Ciri hissed with pain and blushed.

"I fell off the comb . . ."

". . . and the comb thumped you," finished Triss, controlling herself with increasing difficulty. Ciri snorted.

"How can a comb thump you when it's buried in the ground? It can't! I just fell. I was practising a jumping pirouette and it didn't work. That's where the bruise came from. Because I hit a post."

"And you lay there for two days? In pain? Finding it hard to breathe?"

"Not at all. Coën rubbed it and put me straight back on the comb. You have to, you know? Otherwise you catch fear."

"What?"

"You catch fear," Ciri repeated proudly, brushing her ashen fringe from her forehead. "Didn't you know? Even when something bad happens to you, you have to go straight back to that piece of equipment or you get frightened. And if you're frightened you'll be hopeless at the exercise. You mustn't give up. Geralt said so."

"I have to remember that maxim," the enchantress murmured through her teeth. "And that it came from Geralt. Not a bad prescription for life although I'm not sure it applies in every situation. But it is easy to put into practise at someone else's expense. So you mustn't give up? Even though you are being thumped and beaten in a thousand ways, you're to get up and carry on practising?"

"Of course. A witcher's not afraid of anything."

"Is that so? And you, Ciri? You aren't afraid of anything? Answer truthfully."

The girl turned away and bit her lip.

"You won't tell anybody?"

"I won't."

"I'm frightened of two pendulums. Two at the same time. And the windmill, but only when it's set to go fast. And there's also a long balance, I still have to go on that . . . with a safety de— A safety device. Lambert says I'm a sissy and a wimp but that's not true. Geralt told me my weight is distributed a little differently because I'm a girl. I've simply got to practise more unless . . . I wanted to ask you something. May I?"

"You may."

"If you know magic and spells . . . If you can cast them . . . Can you turn me into a boy?"

"No," Triss replied in an icy tone. "I can't."

"Hmm . . ." The little witcher-girl was clearly troubled. "But could you at least . . ."

"At least what?"

"Could you do something so I don't have to . . ." Ciri blushed. "I'll whisper it in your ear."

"Go on." Triss leaned over. "I'm listening."

Ciri, growing even redder, brought her head closer to the enchantress's chestnut hair.

Triss sat up abruptly, her eyes flaming.

"Today? Now?"

"Mhm."

"Hell and bloody damnation!" the enchantress yelled, and kicked the stool so hard that it hit the door and brought down the rat skin. "Pox, plague, shit and leprosy! I'm going to kill those cursed idiots!"

"Calm down, Merigold," said Lambert. "It's unhealthy to get so worked up, especially with no reason."

"Don't preach at me! And stop calling me 'Merigold'! But best of all, stop talking altogether. I'm not speaking to you. Vesemir, Geralt, have any of you seen how terribly battered this child is? She hasn't got a single healthy spot on her body!"

"Dear child," said Vesemir gravely, "don't let yourself get carried away by your emotions. You were brought up differently, you've seen children being brought up in another way. Ciri comes from the south where girls and boys are brought up in the same way, like the elves. She was put on a pony when she was five and when she was eight she was already riding out hunting. She was taught to use a bow, javelin and sword. A bruise is nothing new to Ciri—"

"Don't give me that nonsense," Triss flared. "Don't pretend you're stupid. This is not some pony or horse or sleigh ride. This is Kaer Morhen! On these windmills and pendulums of yours, on this Killer path of yours, dozens of boys have broken their bones and twisted their necks, boys who were hard, seasoned vagabonds like you, found on roads and pulled out of gutters. Sinewy scamps and good-for-nothings, pretty experienced despite their short lives. What chance has Ciri got? Even though she's been brought up in the south with elven methods, even growing up under the hand of a battle-axe like Lioness Calanthe, that little one was and still is a princess. Delicate skin, slight build, light bones . . . She's a girl! What do you want to turn her into? A witcher?"

"That girl," said Geralt quietly and calmly, "that petite, delicate princess lived through the Massacre of Cintra. Left entirely to her own devices, she stole past Nilfgaard's cohorts. She successfully fled the marauders who prowled the villages, plundering and murdering anything that still lived. She survived on her own for two weeks in the forests of Transriver, entirely alone. She spent a month roaming with a pack of fugitives, slogging as hard as all the others and starving like all the others. For almost half a year, having been taken in by a peasant family, she worked on the land and with the livestock. Believe me,

Triss, life has tried, seasoned and hardened her no less than good-for-nothings like us, who were brought to Kaer Morhen from the highways. Ciri is no weaker than un-wanted bastards, like us, who were left with witchers in taverns like kittens in a wicker basket. And her gender? What difference does that make?"

"You still ask? You still dare ask that?" yelled the ma-gician. "What difference does it make? Only that the girl, not being like you, has her days! And bears them excep-tionally badly! And you want her to tear her lungs out on the Killer and some bloody windmills!"

Despite her outrage, Triss felt an exquisite satisfac-tion at the sight of the sheepish expressions of the young witchers, and Vesemir's jaw suddenly dropping open.

"You didn't even know." She nodded in what was now a calm, concerned and gentle reproach. "You're pathetic guardians. She's ashamed to tell you because she was taught not to mention such complaints to men. And she's ashamed of the weakness, the pain and the fact that she is less fit. Has any one of you thought about that? Taken any interest in it? Or tried to guess what might be the matter with her? Maybe her very first bleed happened here, in Kaer Morhen? And she cried to herself at night, unable to find any sympathy, consolation or even understanding from anyone? Has any one of you given it any thought whatsoever?"

"Stop it, Triss," moaned Geralt quietly. "That's enough. You've achieved what you wanted. And maybe even more."

"The devil take it," cursed Coën. "We've turned out to be right idiots, there's no two ways about it, eh, Vesemir, and you—"

"Silence," growled the old witcher. "Not a word."

It was Eskel's behaviour which was most unlikely; he got up, approached the enchantress, bent down low, took her hand and kissed it respectfully. She swiftly withdrew her hand. Not so as to demonstrate her anger and annoyance but to break the pleasant, piercing vibration triggered by the witcher's touch. Eskel emanated powerfully. More powerfully than Geralt.

"Triss," he said, rubbing the hideous scar on his cheek with embarrassment, "help us. We ask you. Help us, Triss."

The enchantress looked him in the eye and pursed her lips. "With what? What am I to help you with, Eskel?"

Eskel rubbed his cheek again, looked at Geralt. The white-haired witcher bowed his head, hiding his eyes behind his hand. Vesemir cleared his throat loudly.

At that moment, the door creaked open and Ciri entered the hall. Vesemir's hawking changed into something like a wheeze, a loud indrawn breath. Lambert opened his mouth. Triss suppressed a laugh.

Ciri, her hair cut and styled, was walking towards them with tiny steps, carefully holding up a dark-blue dress – shortened and adjusted, and still showing the signs of having been carried in a saddlebag. Another present from the enchantress gleamed around the girl's neck – a little black viper made of lacquered leather with a ruby eye and gold clasp.

Ciri stopped in front of Vesemir. Not quite knowing what to do with her hands, she planted her thumbs behind her belt.

"I cannot train today," she recited in the utter silence, slowly and emphatically, "for I am . . . I am . . ."

She looked at the enchantress. Triss winked at her, smirking like a rascal well pleased with his mischief, and moved her lips to prompt the memorised lines.

"Indisposed!" ended Ciri loudly and proudly, turning her nose up almost to the ceiling.

Vesemir hawked again. But Eskel, dear Eskel, kept his head and once more behaved as was fitting.

"Of course," he said casually, smiling. "We understand and clearly we will postpone your exercises until your indisposition has passed. We will also cut the theory short and, if you feel unwell, we will put it aside for the time being, too. If you need any medication or—"

"I'll take care of that," Triss cut in just as casually.

"Aha . . ." Only now did Ciri blush a little – she looked at the old witcher. "Uncle Vesemir, I've asked Triss . . . that is, Miss Merigold, to . . . that is . . . Well, to stay here with us. For longer. For a long time. But Triss said you have to agree forsooth. Uncle Vesemir! Say yes!"

"I agree . . ." Vesemir wheezed out. "Of course, I agree . . ."

"We are very happy." Only now did Geralt take his hand from his forehead. "We are extremely pleased, Triss."

The enchantress nodded slightly towards him and innocently fluttered her eyelashes, winding a chestnut lock around her finger. Geralt's face seemed almost graven from stone.

"You behaved very properly and politely, Ciri," he said, "offering Miss Merigold our ongoing hospitality in Kaer Morhen. I am proud of you."

Ciri reddened and smiled broadly. The enchantress gave her the next pre-arranged sign.

"And now," said the girl, turning her nose up even higher, "I will leave you alone because you no doubt wish to talk over various important matters with Triss. Miss Merigold. Uncle Vesemir, gentlemen . . . I bid you goodbye. For the time being."

She curtseyed gracefully then left the hall, walking up the stairs slowly and with dignity.

"Bloody hell." Lambert broke the silence. "To think I didn't believe that she really is a princess."

"Have you understood, you idiots?" Vesemir cast his eye around. "If she puts a dress on in the morning I don't want to see any exercises . . . Understood?"

Eskel and Coën bestowed a look which was entirely devoid of respect on the old man. Lambert snorted loudly. Geralt stared at the enchantress and the enchantress smiled back.

"Thank you," he said. "Thank you, Triss."

"Conditions?" Eskel was clearly worried. "But we've already promised to ease Ciri's training, Triss. What other conditions do you want to impose?"

"Well, maybe 'conditions' isn't a very nice phrase. So let us call it advice. I will give you three pieces of advice, and you are going to abide by each of them. If, of course, you really want me to stay and help you bring up the little one."

"We're listening," said Geralt. "Go on, Triss."

"Above all," she began, smiling maliciously, "Ciri's menu is to be more varied. And the secret mushrooms and mysterious greens in particular have to be limited."

Geralt and Coën controlled their expressions wonderfully, Lambert and Eskel a little less so, Vesemir not at all. *But then*, she thought, looking at his comically embarrassed expression, *in his day the world was a better place. Duplicity was a character flaw to be ashamed of. Sincerity did not bring shame.*

"Fewer infusions of your mystery-shrouded herbs," she continued, trying not to giggle, "and more milk. You have goats here. Milking is no great art. You'll see, Lambert, you'll learn how to do it in no time."

"Triss," started Geralt, "listen—"

"No, you listen. You haven't subjected Ciri to violent mutations, haven't touched her hormones, haven't tried any elixirs or Grasses on her. And that's to be praised. That was sensible, responsible and humane. You haven't harmed her with any of your poisons – all the more so you must not cripple her now."

"What are you talking about?"

"The mushrooms whose secrets you guard so carefully," she explained, "do, indeed, keep the girl wonderfully fit and strengthen her muscles. The herbs guarantee an ideal metabolic rate and hasten her development. All this taken together and helped along by gruelling training causes certain changes in her build, in her adipose tissue. She's a woman, and as you haven't crippled her hormonal system, do not cripple her physically now. She might hold it against you later if you so ruthlessly deprive her of her womanly . . . attributes. Do you understand what I'm saying?"

"And how," muttered Lambert, brazenly eyeing Triss's breasts which strained against the fabric of her dress.

Eskel cleared his throat and looked daggers at the young witcher.

"At the moment," Geralt asked slowly, also gliding his eyes over this and that, "you haven't noticed anything irreversible in her, I hope?"

"No." She smiled. "Fortunately, not. She is developing healthily and normally and is built like a young dryad – it's a pleasure to look at her. But I ask you to be moderate in using your accelerants."

"We will," promised Vesemir. "Thank you for the warning, child. What else? You said three . . . pieces of advice."

"Indeed. This is the second: Ciri must not be allowed to grow wild. She has to have contact with the world. With her peers. She has to be decently educated and prepared for a normal life. Let her wave her sword about for the time being. You won't turn her into a witcher without mutation anyway, but having a witcher's training won't harm her. Times are hard and dangerous; she'll be able to defend herself when necessary. Like an elf. But you must not bury her alive here, in the middle of nowhere. She has to enter normal life."

"Her normal life went up in flames along with Cintra," murmured Geralt, "but regarding this, Triss, as usual you're right. We've already thought about it. In spring I'm going to take her to the Temple school. To Nenneke. To Ellander."

"That's a very good idea and a wise decision. Nenneke is an exceptional woman and Goddess Melitele's sanctuary an exceptional place. Safe, sure, and it guarantees an appropriate education for the girl. Does Ciri know yet?"

"She does. She kicked up a fuss for a few days but finally accepted the idea. Now she is even looking forward to spring with impatience, excited by the prospect of an expedition to Temeria. She's interested in the world."

"So was I at her age." Triss smiled. "And that comparison brings us dangerously close to the third piece of advice. The most important piece. And you already know what it is. Don't pull silly faces. I'm a magician, have you forgotten? I don't know how long it took you to recognise Ciri's magical abilities. It took me less than half an hour. After that I knew who, or rather what, the girl is."

"And what is she?"

"A Source."

"That's impossible!"

"It's possible. Certain even. Ciri is a Source and has mediumistic powers. What is more, these powers are very, very worrying. And you, my dear witchers, are perfectly well aware of this. You've noticed these powers and they have worried you too. That is the one and only reason you brought me here to Kaer Morhen. Am I right? The one and only reason?"

"Yes," Vesemir confirmed after a moment's silence.

Triss breathed an imperceptible sigh of relief. For a moment, she was afraid that Geralt would be the one to confirm it.

The first snow fell the following day, fine snowflakes initially, but soon turning into a blizzard. It fell throughout the night and, in the early morning, the walls of Kaer Morhen were drowned beneath a snowdrift. There could be no question of running the Killer, especially since Ciri was still not feeling very well. Triss suspected that the witchers' accelerants might be the cause of the girl's menstrual problems. She could not be sure, however, knowing practically nothing about the drugs, and Ciri was, beyond doubt, the only girl in the world to whom they had been administered. She did not share her suspicions with the witchers. She did not want to worry or annoy them and preferred to apply her own methods. She gave Ciri elixirs to drink, tied a string of active jaspers around her waist, under her dress, and forbade her to exert herself in any way, especially by chasing around, wildly hunting rats with a sword.

Ciri was bored. She roamed the castle sleepily and finally, for lack of any other amusement, joined Coën, who was cleaning the stable, grooming the horses and repairing a harness.

Geralt – to the enchantress's rage – disappeared somewhere and appeared only towards evening, bearing a dead goat. Triss helped him skin his prey. Although she sincerely detested the smell of meat and blood, she wanted to be near the witcher. Near him. As near as possible. A cold, determined resolution was growing in her. She did not want to sleep alone any longer.

"Triss!" yelled Ciri suddenly, running down the stairs, stamping. "Can I sleep with you tonight? Triss, please, please say yes! Please, Triss!"

The snow fell and fell. It brightened up only with the arrival of Midinváerne, the Day of the Winter Equinox.

On the third day all the children died save one, a male barely ten. Hitherto agitated by a sudden madness, he fell all at once into deep stupor. His eyes took on a glassy gaze; incessantly with his hands did he clutch at clothing, or brandish them in the air as if desirous of catching a quill. His breathing grew loud and hoarse; sweat cold, clammy and malodorous appeared on his skin. Then was he once more given elixir through the vein and the seizure it did return. This time a nose-bleed did ensue, coughing turned to vomiting, after which the male weakened entirely and became inert.

For two days more did symptoms not subside. The child's skin, hitherto drenched in sweat, grew dry and hot, the pulse ceased to be full and firm – albeit remaining of average strength, slow rather than fast. No more did he wake, nor did he scream.

Finally, came the seventh day. The male awoke and opened his eyes, and his eyes were as those of a viper . . .

Carla Demetia Crest, *The Trial of Grasses and other secret Witcher practices, seen with my own eyes*, manuscript exclusively accessible to the Chapter of Wizards

CHAPTER THREE

"Your fears were unfounded, entirely ungrounded." Triss grimaced, resting her elbows on the table. "The time when wizards used to hunt Sources and magically gifted children, tearing them from their parents or guardians by force or deceit, is long gone. Did you really think I might want to take Ciri away from you?"

Lambert snorted and turned his face away. Eskel and Vesemir looked at Geralt, and Geralt said nothing. He continued to gaze off to the side, playing incessantly with his silver witcher medallion, depicting the head of a snarling wolf. Triss knew the medallion reacted to magic. On such a night as Midinváerne, when the air itself was vibrating with magic, the witchers' medallions must be practically humming. It must be both irritating and bothersome.

"No, child," Vesemir finally said. "We know you would not do such a thing. But we also know that you do, ultimately, have to tell the Chapter about her. We've known for a long time that every wizard, male or female, is burdened with this duty. You don't take talented children from their parents and guardians any more. You observe such children so that later – at the right moment – you can fascinate them in magic, influence them—"

"Have no fear," she interrupted coldly. "I will not tell anyone about Ciri. Not even the Chapter. Why are you looking at me like that?"

"We're amazed by the ease with which you pledge to keep this secret," said Eskel calmly. "Forgive me, Triss, I do not mean to offend you, but what has happened to your legendary loyalty to the Council and Chapter?"

"A lot has happened. The war changed many things, and the battle for Sodden Hill changed even more. I won't bore you with the politics, especially as certain issues and affairs are bound by secrets I am not allowed to divulge. But as for loyalty . . . I am loyal. And believe me, in this matter I can be loyal to both you and to the Chapter."

"Such double loyalty" – Geralt looked her in the eyes for the first time that evening – "is devilishly difficult to manage. Rarely does it succeed, Triss."

The enchantress turned her gaze on Ciri. The girl was sitting on a bearskin with Coën, tucked away in the far corner of the hall, and both were busy playing a hand-slapping game. The game was growing monotonous as both were incredibly quick – neither could manage to slap the other's hand in any way. This, however, clearly neither mattered to them nor spoiled their game.

"Geralt," she said, "when you found Ciri, on the Yaruga, you took her with you. You brought her to Kaer Morhen, hid her from the world and do not let even those closest to the child know she is alive. You did this because something – about which I know nothing – convinced you that destiny exists, holds sway over us, and guides us in everything we do. I think the same, and have always done so. If destiny wants Ciri to become a magician, she will become one. Neither the Chapter nor the Council have to know about her; they don't have to observe or encourage her. So in keeping your secret I won't betray the Chapter in any way. But as you know, there is something of a hitch here."

"Were it only one," sighed Vesemir. "Go on, child."

"The girl has magical abilities, and that can't be neglected. It's too dangerous."

"In what way?"

"Uncontrolled powers are an ominous thing. For both the Source and those in their vicinity. The Source can threaten those around them in many ways. But they threaten themselves in only one. Mental illness. Usually catatonia."

"Devil take it," said Lambert after a long silence. "I am listening to you half-convinced that someone here has already lost their marbles and will, any moment now, present a threat to the rest of us. Destiny, sources, spells, hocus-pocus . . . Aren't you exaggerating, Merigold? Is this the first child to be brought to the Keep? Geralt didn't find destiny; he found another homeless, orphaned child. We'll teach the girl the sword and let her out into the world like the others. True, I admit we've never trained a girl in Kaer Morhen before. We've had some problems with Ciri, made mistakes, and it's a good thing you've pointed them out to us. But don't let us exaggerate. She is not so remarkable as to make us fall on our knees and raise our eyes to the heavens. Is there a lack of female warriors roaming the world? I assure you, Merigold, Ciri will leave here skilful and healthy, strong and able to face life. And, I warrant, without catatonia or any other epilepsy. Unless you delude her into believing she has some such disease."

"Vesemir," Triss turned in her chair, "tell him to keep quiet, he's getting in the way."

"You think you know it all," said Lambert calmly, "but you don't. Not yet. Look."

He stretched his hand towards the hearth, arranging his fingers together in a strange way. The chimney roared and howled, the flames burst out violently, the glowing embers grew brighter and rained sparks. Geralt, Vesemir and Eskel glanced at Ciri anxiously but the girl paid no attention to the spectacular fireworks.

Triss folded her arms and looked at Lambert defiantly.

"The Sign of Aard," she stated calmly. "Did you think to impress me? With the use of the same sign, strengthened through concentration, willpower and a spell, I can blow the logs from the chimney in a moment and blast them so high you will think they are stars."

"You can," he agreed. "But Ciri can't. She can't form the Sign of Aard. Or any other sign. She has tried hundreds of times, to no effect. And you know our Signs require minimal power. Ciri does not even have that. She is an absolutely normal child. She has not the least magical power – she has, in fact, a comprehensive lack of ability. And here you are telling us she's a Source, trying to threaten us—"

"A Source," she explained coldly, "has no control over their skills, no command over them. They are a medium, something like a transmitter. Unknowingly they get in touch with energy, unknowingly they convert it. And when they try to control it, when they strain trying to form the Signs perhaps, nothing comes of it. And nothing will come of it, not just after hundreds of attempts but after thousands. It is one characteristic of a Source. Then, one day, a moment comes when the Source does not exert itself, does not strain, is daydreaming or thinking about cabbage and sausages, playing dice, enjoying themselves in bed with a partner, picking their nose . . . and suddenly something happens. A house might go up in flames. Or sometimes, half a town goes up."

"You're exaggerating, Merigold."

"Lambert." Geralt released his medallion and rested his hands on the table. "First, stop calling Triss 'Merigold'. She has asked you a number of times not to. Second, Triss is not exaggerating. I saw Ciri's mother, Princess Pavetta, in action with my own eyes. I tell you, it was really something. I don't know if she was a Source or not, but no one suspected she had any power at all until, save by a hair's breadth, she almost reduced the royal castle of Cintra to ashes."

"We should assume, therefore," said Eskel, lighting the candles in yet another candlestick, "that Ciri could, indeed, be genetically burdened."

"Not only could," said Vesemir, "she *is* so burdened. On the one hand Lambert is right. Ciri is not capable of forming Signs. On the other . . . We have all seen . . ."

He fell silent and looked at Ciri who, with a joyful squeal, acknowledged that she had the upper hand in the game. Triss spied a small smile on Coën's face and was sure he had allowed her to win.

"Precisely," she sneered. "You have all seen. What have you seen? Under what circumstances did you see it?

Don't you think, boys, that the time has come for more truthful confessions? Hell, I repeat, I will keep your secret. You have my word."

Lambert glanced at Geralt; Geralt nodded in assent. The younger witcher stood and took a large rectangular crystal carafe and a smaller phial from a high shelf. He poured the contents of the phial into the carafe, shook it several times and poured the transparent liquid into the chalices on the table.

"Have a drink with us, Triss."

"Is the truth so terrible," she mocked, "that we can't talk about it soberly? Do I have to get drunk in order to hear it?"

"Don't be such a know-all. Take a sip. You will find it easier to understand."

"What is it?"

"White Seagull."

"What?"

"A mild remedy," Eskel smiled, "for pleasant dreams."

"Damn it! A witcher hallucinogenic? That's why your eyes shine like that in the evenings!"

"White Seagull is very gentle. It's Black Seagull that is hallucinogenic."

"If there's magic in this liquid I'm not allowed to take it!"

"Exclusively natural ingredients," Geralt reassured her but he looked, she noticed, disconcerted. He was clearly afraid she would question them about the elixir's ingredients. "And diluted with a great deal of water. We would not offer you anything that could harm you."

The sparkling liquid, with its strange taste, struck her throat with its chill and then dispersed warmth throughout her body. The magician ran her tongue over her gums and palate. She was unable to recognise any of the ingredients.

"You gave Ciri some of this . . . Seagull to drink," she surmised. "And then—"

"It was an accident," Geralt interrupted quickly. "That first evening, just after we arrived . . . she was thirsty, and the Seagull stood on the table. Before we had time to react, she had drunk it all in one go. And fallen into a trance."

"We had such a fright," Vesemir admitted, and sighed. "Oh, that we did, child. More than we could take."

"She started speaking with another voice," the magician stated calmly, looking at the witchers' eyes gleaming in the candlelight. "She started talking about events and matters of which she could have no knowledge. She started . . . to prophesy. Right? What did she say?"

"Rubbish," said Lambert dryly. "Senseless drivel."

"Then I have no doubt" – she looked straight at him – "that you understood each other perfectly well. Drivel is your speciality – and I am further convinced of it every time you open your mouth. Do me a great favour and don't open it for a while, all right?"

"This once," said Eskel gravely, rubbing the scar across his cheek, "Lambert is right, Triss. After drinking Seagull Ciri really was incomprehensible. That first time it was gibberish. Only after—"

He broke off. Triss shook her head.

"It was only the second time that she started talking sense," she guessed. "So there was a second time, too. Also after she drank a drug because of your carelessness?"

"Triss." Geralt raised his head. "This is not the time for your childish spitefulness. It doesn't amuse us. It worries and upsets us. Yes, there was a second time, too, and a third. Ciri fell, quite by accident, during an exercise. She lost consciousness. When she regained it, she had fallen into another trance. And once again she spoke nonsense. Again it was not her voice. And again it was incomprehensible. But I have heard similar voices before, heard a similar way of speaking. It's how those poor, sick, demented women known as oracles speak. You see what I'm thinking?"

"Clearly. That was the second time, get to the third."

Geralt wiped his brow, suddenly beaded with sweat, on his forearm. "Ciri often wakes up at night," he continued. "Shouting. She has been through a lot. She does not want to talk about it but it is clear that she saw things no child should see in Cintra and Angren. I even fear that . . . that someone harmed her. It comes back to her in dreams. Usually she is easy to reassure and she falls asleep without any problem . . . But once, after waking . . . she was in a trance again. She again spoke with someone else's, unpleasant, menacing voice. She spoke clearly and made sense. She prophesied. Foresaw the future. And what she foretold . . ."

"What? What, Geralt?"

"Death," Vesemir said gently. "Death, child."

Triss glanced at Ciri, who was shrilly accusing Coën of cheating. Coën put his arms around her and burst out laughing. The magician suddenly realised that she had never, up until now, heard any of the witchers laugh.

"For whom?" she asked briefly, still gazing at Coën.

"Him," said Vesemir.

"And me," Geralt added. And smiled.

"When she woke up—"

"She remembered nothing. And we didn't ask her any questions."

"Quite so. As to the prophecy . . . Was it specific? Detailed?"

"No." Geralt looked her straight in the eyes. "Confused. Don't ask about it, Triss. We are not worried by the contents of Ciri's prophecies and ravings but about what happens to her. We're not afraid for ourselves but—"

"Careful," warned Vesemir. "Don't talk about it in front of her."

Coën approached the table carrying the girl piggy-back.

"Wish everybody goodnight, Ciri," he said. "Say goodnight to those night owls. We're going to sleep. It's nearly midnight. In a minute it'll be the end of Midinváerne. As of tomorrow, every day brings spring closer!"

"I'm thirsty." Ciri slipped off his back and reached for Eskel's chalice. Eskel deftly moved the vessel beyond her reach and grabbed a jug of water. Triss stood quickly.

"Here you are." She gave her half-full chalice to the girl while meaningfully squeezing Geralt's arm and looking Vesemir in the eye. "Drink."

"Triss," whispered Eskel, watching Ciri drink greedily, "what are you doing? It's—"

"Not a word, please."

They did not have to wait long for it to take effect. Ciri suddenly grew rigid, cried out, and smiled a broad, happy smile. She squeezed her eyelids shut and stretched out her arms. She laughed, spun a pirouette and danced on tiptoes. Lambert moved the stool away in a flash, leaving Coën standing between the dancing girl and the hearth.

Triss jumped up and tore an amulet from her pouch – a sapphire set in silver on a thin chain. She squeezed it tightly in her hand.

"Child . . ." groaned Vesemir. "What are you doing?"

"I know what I'm doing," she said sharply. "Ciri has fallen into a trance and I am going to contact her psychically. I am going to enter her. I told you, she is something like a magical transmitter – I've got to know what she is transmitting, how, and from where she is drawing the aura, how she is transforming it. It's Midinváerne, a favourable night for such an undertaking . . ."

"I don't like it." Geralt frowned. "I don't like it at all."

"Should either of us suffer an epileptic fit," the magician said, ignoring his words, "you know what to do. A stick between our teeth, hold us down, wait for it to pass. Chin up, boys. I've done this before."

Ciri ceased dancing, sank to her knees, extended her arms and rested her head on her lap. Triss pressed the now-warm amulet to her temple and murmured the formula of a spell. She closed her eyes, concentrated her willpower and gave out a burst of magic.

The sea roared, waves thundered against the rocky shore and exploded in high geysers amidst the boulders. She flapped her wings, chasing the salty wind. Indescribably happy, she dived, caught up with a flock of her companions, brushed the crests of the waves with her claws, soared into the sky again, shedding water droplets, and glided, tossed by the gale whistling through her pinfeathers. *Force of suggestion*, she thought soberly. *It is only force of suggestion. Seagull!*

Triiiss! Triiss!

Ciri? Where are you?

Triiiss!

The cry of the seagulls ceased. The magician still felt the wet splash of the breakers but the sea was no longer below her. Or it was – but it was a sea of grass, an endless plateau stretching as far as the horizon. Triss, with horror, realised she was looking at the view from the top of Sodden Hill. But it was not the Hill. It could not be the Hill.

The sky suddenly grew dark, shadows swirled around her. She saw a long column of indistinct figures slowly climbing down the mountainside. She heard murmurs superimposed over each other, mingling into an uncanny, incomprehensible chorus.

Ciri was standing nearby with her back turned to her. The wind was blowing her ashen hair about.

The indistinct, hazy figures continued past in a long, unending column. Passing her, they turned their heads. Triss suppressed a cry, watching the listless, peaceful faces and their dead, unseeing eyes. She did not know all of the faces, did not recognise them. But some of them she did know.

Coral. Vanielle. Yoël. Pox-marked Axel . . .

"Why have you brought me here?" she whispered. "Why?"

Ciri turned. She raised her arm and the magician saw a trickle of blood run down her life-line, across her palm and onto her wrist.

"It is the rose," the girl said calmly. "The rose of Shaerrawedd. I pricked myself. It is nothing. It is only blood. The blood of elves . . ."

The sky grew even darker, then, a moment later, flared with the sharp, blinding glare of lightning. Everything froze in the silence and stillness. Triss took a step, wanting to make sure she could. She stopped next to Ciri and saw that both of them stood on the edge of a bottomless chasm where reddish smoke, glowing as though it was lit from behind, was swirling. The flash of another soundless bolt of lightning suddenly revealed a long, marble staircase leading into the depths of the abyss.

"It has to be this way," Ciri said in a shaky voice. "There is no other. Only this. Down the stairs. It has to be this way because . . . Va'esse deireádh aep eigean . . ."

"Speak," whispered the magician. "Speak, child."

"The Child of Elder Blood . . . Feainnewedd . . . Luned aepHenIchaer . . . Deithwen . . . TheWhiteFlame . . . No, no . . . No!"

"Ciri!"

"The black knight . . . with feathers in his helmet . . . What did he do to me? What happened? I was frightened . . . I'm still frightened. It's not ended, it will never end. The lion cub must die . . . Reasons of state . . . No . . . No . . ."

"Ciri!"

"No!" The girl turned rigid and squeezed her eyelids shut. "No, no, I don't want to! Don't touch me!"

Ciri's face suddenly changed, hardened; her voice became metallic, cold and hostile, resounding with threatening, cruel mockery.

"You have come all this way with her, Triss Merigold? All the way here? You have come too far, Fourteenth One. I warned you."

"Who are you?" Triss shuddered but she kept her voice under control.

"You will know when the time comes."

"I will know now!"

The magician raised her arms, extended them abruptly, putting all her strength into a Spell of Identification. The magic curtain burst but behind it was a second . . . A third . . . A fourth . . .

Triss sank to her knees with a groan. But reality continued to burst, more doors opened, a long, endless row leading to nowhere. To emptiness.

"You are wrong, Fourteenth One," the metallic, inhuman voice sneered. "You've mistaken the stars reflected on the surface of the lake at night for the heavens."

"Do not touch— Do not touch that child!"

"She is not a child."

Ciri's lips moved but Triss saw that the girl's eyes were dead, glazed and vacant.

"She is not a child," the voice repeated. "She is the Flame, the White Flame which will set light to the world. She is the Elder Blood, Hen Ichaer. The blood of elves. The seed which will not sprout but burst into flame. The blood which will be defiled . . . When Tedd Deireádh arrives, the Time of End. Va'esse deireádh aep eigean!"

"Are you foretelling death?" shouted Triss. "Is that all you can do, foretell death? For everyone? Them, her . . . Me?"

"You? You are already dead, Fourteenth One. Everything in you has already died."

"By the power of the spheres," moaned the magician, activating what little remained of her strength and drawing her hand through the air, "I throw a spell on you by water, fire, earth and air. I conjure you in thought, in dream and in death, by all that was, by what is and by what will be. I cast my spell on you. Who are you? Speak!"

Ciri turned her head away. The vision of the staircase leading down into the depths of the abyss disappeared, dissolved, and in its place appeared a grey, leaden sea, foaming, crests of waves breaking. And the seagull's cries burst through the silence once more.

"Fly," said the voice, through the girl's lips. "It is time. Go back to where you came from, Fourteenth of the Hill. Fly on the wings of a gull and listen to the cry of other seagulls. Listen carefully!"

"I conjure you—"

"You cannot. Fly, seagull!"

And suddenly the wet salty air was there again, roaring with the gale, and there was the flight, a flight with no beginning and no end. Seagulls cried wildly, cried and commanded.

Triss?

Ciri?

Forget about him! Don't torture him! Forget! Forget, Triss!

Forget!

Triss! Triss! Trisss!

"Triss!"

She opened her eyes, tossed her head on the pillow and moved her numb hands.

"Geralt?"

"I'm here. How are you feeling?"

She cast her eyes around. She was in her chamber, lying on the bed. On the best bed in the whole of Kaer Morhen.

"What is happening to Ciri?"

"She is asleep."

"How long—"

"Too long," he interrupted. He covered her with the duvet and put his arms around her. As he leaned over, the wolf's head medallion swayed just above her face. "What you did was not the best of ideas, Triss."

"Everything is all right." She trembled in his embrace. *That's not true*, she thought. *Nothing's all right.* She turned her face so that the medallion didn't touch her. There were many theories about the properties of witcher amulets and none advised magicians to touch them during the Equinox.

"Did . . . Did we say anything during the trance?"

"You, nothing. You were unconscious throughout. Ciri . . . just before she woke up . . . said: 'Va'esse deireádh aep eigean'."

"She knows the Elder Speech?"

"Not enough to say a whole sentence."

"A sentence which means, 'Something is ending.'" The magician wiped her face with her hand. "Geralt, this is a serious matter. The girl is an exceptionally powerful medium. I don't know what or who she is contacting, but I think there are no limits to her connection. Something wants to take possession of her. Something which is too powerful for me. I am afraid for her. Another trance could end in mental illness. I have no control over it, don't know how to, can't . . . If it proved necessary, I would not be able to block or suppress her powers; I would not even be capable, if there were no other option, of permanently extinguishing them. You have to get help from another magician. A more gifted one. More experienced. You know who I'm talking about."

"I do." He turned his head away, clenched his lips.

"Don't resist. Don't defend yourself. I can guess why

you turned to me rather than her. Overcome your pride, crush your rancour and obstinacy. There is no point to it, you'll torture yourself to death. And you are risking Ciri's health and life in the process. Another trance is liable to be more dangerous to her than the Trial of Grasses. Ask Yennefer for help, Geralt."

"And you, Triss?"

"What about me?" She swallowed with difficulty. "I'm not important. I let you down. I let you down . . . in everything. I was . . . I was your mistake. Nothing more."

"Mistakes," he said with effort, "are also important to me. I don't cross them out of my life, or memory. And I never blame others for them. You are important to me, Triss, and always will be. You never let me down. Never. Believe me."

She remained silent a long while.

"I will stay until spring," she said finally, struggling against her shaking voice. "I will stay with Ciri . . . I will watch over her. Day and night. I will be with her day and night. And when spring is here . . . when spring is here we will take her to Melitele's Temple in Ellander. The thing that wants to possess her might not be able to reach her in the temple. And then you will ask Yennefer for help."

"All right, Triss. Thank you."

"Geralt?"

"Yes."

"Ciri said something else, didn't she? Something only you heard. Tell me what it was."

"No," he protested and his voice quivered. "No, Triss."

"Please."

"She wasn't speaking to me."

"I know. She was speaking to me. Tell me, please."

"After coming to . . . When I picked her up . . . She whispered: 'Forget about him. Don't torture him.'"

"I won't," she said quietly. "But I can't forget. Forgive me."

"I am the one who ought to be asking for forgiveness. And not only asking you."

"You love her that much," she stated, not asking.

"That much," he admitted in a whisper after a long moment of silence.

"Geralt."

"Yes, Triss?"

"Stay with me tonight."

"Triss . . ."

"Only stay."

"All right."

Not long after Midinváerne the snow stopped falling. The frost came.

Triss stayed with Ciri day and night. She watched over her. She surrounded her with care, visible and invisible.

The girl woke up shouting almost every night. She was delirious, holding her cheek and crying with pain. The magician calmed her with spells and elixirs, put her to sleep, cuddling and rocking her in her arms. And then she herself would be unable to sleep for a long time, thinking about what Ciri had said in her sleep and after she came to. And she felt a mounting fear. Va'esse deireádh aep eigean . . . Something is ending . . .

That is how it was for ten days and nights. And finally it passed. It ended, disappeared without a trace. Ciri calmed, she slept peacefully with no nightmares, and no dreams.

But Triss kept a constant watch. She did not leave the girl for a moment. She surrounded her with care. Visible and invisible.

"Faster, Ciri! Lunge, attack, dodge! Half-pirouette, thrust, dodge! Balance! Balance with your left arm or you'll fall from the comb! And you'll hurt your . . . womanly attributes!"

"What?"

"Nothing. Aren't you tired? We'll take a break, if you like."

"No, Lambert! I can go on. I'm not that weak, you know. Shall I try jumping over every other post?"

"Don't you dare! You might fall and then Merigold will tear my—my head off."

"I won't fall!"

"I've told you once and I'm not going to say it again. Don't show off! Steady on your legs! And breathe, Ciri, breathe! You're panting like a dying mammoth!"

"That's not true!"

"Don't squeal. Practise! Attack, dodge! Parry! Half-pirouette! Parry, full pirouette! Steadier on the posts, damn it! Don't wobble! Lunge, thrust! Faster! Half-pirouette! Jump and cut! That's it! Very good!"

"Really? Was that really very good, Lambert?"

"Who said so?"

"You did! A moment ago!"

"Slip of the tongue. Attack! Half-pirouette! Dodge! And again! Ciri, where was the parry? How many times do I have to tell you? After you dodge you always parry, deliver a blow with the blade to protect your head and shoulders! Always!"

"Even when I'm only fighting one opponent?"

"You never know what you're fighting. You never know what's happening behind you. You always have to cover yourself. Foot and sword work! It's got to be a reflex. Reflex, understand? You mustn't forget that. You forget it in a real fight and you're finished. Again! At last! That's it! See how such a parry lands? You can take any strike from it. You can cut backwards from it, if you have to. Right, show me a pirouette and a thrust backwards."

"Haaa!"

"Very good. You see the point now? Has it got through to you?"

"I'm not stupid!"

"You're a girl. Girls don't have brains."

"Lambert! If Triss heard that!"

"If ifs and ands were pots and pans. All right, that's enough. Come down. We'll take a break."

"I'm not tired!"

"But I am. I said, a break. Come down from the comb."

"Turning a somersault?"

"What do you think? Like a hen off its roost? Go on, jump. Don't be afraid, I'm here for you."

"Haaaa!"

"Nice. Very good – for a girl. You can take off the blindfold now."

"Triss, maybe that's enough for today? What do you think? Maybe we could take the sleigh and ride down the hill? The sun's shining, the snow's sparkling so much it hurts the eyes! The weather's beautiful!"

"Don't lean out or you'll fall from the window."

"Let's go sleighing, Triss!"

"Suggest that again in Elder Speech and we'll end the lesson there. Move away from the window, come back to the table . . . Ciri, how many times do I have to ask you? Stop waving that sword about and put it away."

"It's my new sword! It's real, a witcher's sword! Made of steel which fell from heaven! Really! Geralt said so and he never lies, you know that!"

"Oh, yes. I know that."

"I've got to get used to this sword. Uncle Vesemir had it adjusted just right for my weight, height and arm-length. I've got to get my hand and wrist accustomed to it!"

"Accustom yourself to your heart's content, but outside. Not here! Well, I'm listening. You wanted to suggest we get the sleigh out. In Elder Speech. So – suggest it."

"Hmmm . . . What's 'sleigh'?"

"Sledd as a noun. Aesledde as a verb."

"Aha . . . Vaien aesledde, ell'ea?"

"Don't end a question that way, it's impolite. You form questions using intonation."

"But the children from the Islands—"

"You're not learning the local Skellige jargon but classical Elder Speech."

"And why am I learning the Speech, tell me?"

"So that you know it. It's fitting to learn things you don't know. Anyone who doesn't know other languages is handicapped."

"But people only speak the common tongue anyway!"

"True. But some speak more than just it. I warrant, Ciri, that it is better to count yourself amongst those few than amongst everyone. So, I'm listening. A full sentence: 'The weather today is beautiful, so let's get the sleigh.'"

"Elaine . . . Hmmm . . . Elaine tedd a'taeghane, a va'en aesledde?"

"Very good."

"Ha! So let's get the sleigh."

"We will. But let me finish applying my make-up."

"And who are you putting make-up on for, exactly?"

"Myself. A woman accentuates her beauty for her own self-esteem."

"Hmmm . . . Do you know what? I feel pretty poorly too. Don't laugh, Triss!"

"Come here. Sit on my knee. Put the sword away, I've already asked you! Thank you. Now take that large brush and powder your face. Not so much, girl, not so much! Look in the mirror. See how pretty you are?"

"I can't see any difference. I'll do my eyes, all right? What are you laughing at? You always paint your eyes. I want to too."

"Fine. Here you are, put some shadow on your eyelids with this. Ciri, don't close both your eyes or you won't see anything – you're smudging your whole face. Take a tiny bit and only skim over the eyelids. Skim, I said! Let me, I'll just spread it a little. Close your eyes. Now open them."

"Oooo!"

"See the difference? A tiny bit of shadow won't do any harm, even to such beautiful eyes as yours. The elves knew what they were doing when they invented eye shadow."

"Elves?"

"You didn't know? Make-up is an elvish invention. We've learned a lot of useful things from the Elder People. And we've given bloody little back in return. Now take the pencil and draw a thin line across your upper lids, just above the lashes. Ciri, what are you doing?"

"Don't laugh! My eyelid's trembling! That's why!"

"Part your lips a little and it'll stop trembling. See?"

"Ooooh!"

"Come on, now we'll go and stun the witchers with our beauty. It's hard to find a prettier sight. And then we'll take the sleigh and smudge our make-up in the deep snowdrifts."

"And we'll make ourselves up again!"

"No. We'll tell Lambert to warm the bathroom and we'll take a bath."

"Again? Lambert says we're using up too much fuel with our baths."

"Lambert cáen me a'báeth aep arse."

"What? I didn't understand . . ."

"With time you'll master the idioms, too. We've still got a lot of time for studying before spring. But now . . . Va'en aesledde, me elaine luned!"

"Here, on this engraving . . . No, damn it, not on that one . . . On this one. This is, as you already know, a ghoul. Tell us, Ciri, what you've learned about ghouls . . . Hey, look at me! What the devil have you got on your eyelids?"

"Greater self-esteem!"

"What? Never mind, I'm listening."

"Hmm . . . The ghoul, Uncle Vesemir, is a corpse-devouring monster. It can be seen in cemeteries, in the vicinity of barrows, anywhere the dead are buried. At nec— necropolia. On battlegrounds, on fields of battle . . ."

"So it's only a danger to the dead, is that right?"

"No, not only. A ghoul may also attack the living if it's hungry or falls into a fury. If, for example, there's a battle . . . A lot of people killed . . ."

"What's the matter, Ciri?"

"Nothing . . ."

"Ciri, listen. Forget about that. That will never return."

"I saw . . . In Sodden and in Transriver . . . Entire fields . . . They were lying there, being eaten by wolves and wild dogs. Birds were picking at them . . . I guess there were ghouls there too . . ."

"That's why you're learning about ghouls now, Ciri. When you know about something it stops being a nightmare. When you know how to fight something, it stops being so threatening. So how do you fight a ghoul, Ciri?"

"With a silver sword. The ghoul is sensitive to silver."

"And to what else?"

"Bright light. And fire."

"So you can fight it with light and fire?"

"You can, but it's dangerous. A witcher doesn't use light or fire because it makes it harder to see. Every light creates a shadow and shadows make it harder to get your bearings. One must always fight in darkness, by moon or starlight."

"Quite right. You've remembered it well, clever girl. And now look here, at this engraving."

"Eeeueeeuuueee—"

121

"Oh well, true enough, it is not a beautiful cu— creature. It's a graveir. A graveir is a type of ghoul. It looks very much like a ghoul but is considerably larger. He can also be told apart, as you can see, by these three bony combs on his skull. The rest is the same as any other corpse-eater. Take note of the short, blunt claws, adapted for digging up graves, and churning the earth. Strong teeth for shattering bones and a long, narrow tongue used to lick the decaying marrow from them. Such stinking marrow is a delicacy for the graveir . . . What's the matter?"

"Nnnnothing."

"You're completely pale. And green. You don't eat enough. Did you eat breakfast?"

"Yeeees. I diiiidddddd."

"What was I . . . Aha. I almost forgot. Remember, because this is important. Graveirs, like ghouls and other monsters in this category, do not have their own ecological niche. They are relics from the age of the interpenetration of spheres. Killing them does not upset the order and interconnections of nature which prevail in our present sphere. In this sphere these monsters are foreign and there is no place for them. Do you understand, Ciri?"

"I do, Uncle Vesemir. Geralt explained it to me. I know all that. An ecological niche is—"

"All right, that's fine. I know what it is. If Geralt has explained it to you, you don't have to recite it to me. Let us return to the graveir. Graveirs appear quite rarely, fortunately, because they're bloody dangerous sons-of-bitches. The smallest wound inflicted by a graveir will infect you with corpse venom. Which elixir is used to treat corpse venom poisoning, Ciri?"

" 'Golden Oriole'."

"Correct. But it is better to avoid infection to begin with. That is why, when fighting a graveir, you must never get close to the bastard. You always fight from a distance and strike from a leap."

"Hmm . . . And where's it best to strike one?"

"We're just getting to that. Look . . ."

"Once more, Ciri. We'll go through it slowly so that you can master each move. Now, I'm attacking you with tierce, taking the position as if to thrust . . . Why are you retreating?"

"Because I know it's a feint! You can move into a wide sinistra or strike with upper quarte. And I'll retreat and parry with a counterfeint!"

"Is that so? And if I do this?"

"Auuu! It was supposed to be slow! What did I do wrong, Coën?"

"Nothing. I'm just taller and stronger than you are."

"That's not fair!"

"There's no such thing as a fair fight. You have to make use of every advantage and every opportunity that you get. By retreating you gave me the opportunity to put more force into the strike. Instead of retreating you should have executed a half-pirouette to the left and tried to cut at me from below, with quarte dextra, under the chin, in the cheek or throat."

"As if you'd let me! You'll do a reverse pirouette and get my neck from the left before I can parry! How am I meant to know what you're doing?"

"You have to know. And you do know."

"Oh, sure!"

"Ciri, what we're doing is fighting. I'm your opponent.

123

I want to and have to defeat you because my life is at stake. I'm taller and stronger than you so I'm going to watch for opportunities to strike in order to avoid or break your parry – as you've just seen. What do I need a pirouette for? I'm already in sinistra, see? What could be simpler than to strike with a seconde, under the arm, on the inside? If I slash your artery, you'll be dead in a couple of minutes. Defend yourself!"

"Haaaa!"

"Very good. A beautiful, quick parry. See how exercising your wrist has come in useful? And now pay attention – a lot of fencers make the mistake of executing a standing parry and freeze for a second, and that's just when you can catch them out, strike – like so!"

"Haa!"

"Beautiful! Now jump away, jump away immediately, pirouette! I could have a dagger in my left hand! Good! Very good! And now, Ciri? What am I going to do now?"

"How am I to know?"

"Watch my feet! How is my body weight distributed? What can I do from this position?"

"Anything!"

"So spin, spin, force me to open up! Defend yourself! Good! And again! Good! And again!"

"Owwww!"

"Not so good."

"Uff . . . What did I do wrong?"

"Nothing. I'm just faster. Take your guards off. We'll sit for a moment, take a break. You must be tired, you've been running the Trail all morning."

"I'm not tired. I'm hungry."

"Bloody hell, so am I. And today's Lambert's turn and he can't cook anything other than noodles . . . If he could only cook those properly . . ."

"Coën?"

"Aha?"

"I'm still not fast enough—"

"You're very fast."

"Will I ever be as fast as you?"

"I doubt it."

"Hmm . . . And are you—? Who's the best fencer in the world?"

"I've no idea."

"You've never known one?"

"I've known many who believed themselves to be the best."

"Oh! What were they? What were their names? What could they do?"

"Hold on, hold on, girl. I haven't got an answer to those questions. Is it all that important?"

"Of course it's important! I'd like to know who these fencers are. And where they are."

"Where they are? I know that."

"Ah! So where?"

"In cemeteries."

"Pay attention, Ciri. We're going to attach a third pendulum now – you can manage two already. You use the same steps as for two only there's one more dodge. Ready?"

"Yes."

"Focus yourself. Relax. Breathe in, breathe out. Attack!"

"Ouch! Owwww . . . Damn it!"

"Don't swear. Did it hit you hard?"

"No, it only brushed me . . . What did I do wrong?"

"You ran in at too even a pace, you sped the second half-pirouette up a bit too much, and your feint was too wide. And as a result you were carried straight under the pendulum."

"But Geralt, there's no room for a dodge and turn there! They're too close to each other!"

"There's plenty of room, I assure you. But the gaps are worked out to force you to make arrhythmic moves. This is a fight, Ciri, not ballet. You can't move rhythmically in a fight. You have to distract the opponent with your moves, confuse his reactions. Ready for another try?"

"Ready. Start those damn logs swinging."

"Don't swear. Relax. Attack!"

"Ha! Ha! Well, how about that? How was that, Geralt? It didn't even brush me!"

"And you didn't even brush the second sack with your sword. So I repeat, this is a fight. Not ballet, not acrobat-ics— What are you muttering now?"

"Nothing."

"Relax. Adjust the bandage on your wrist. Don't grip the hilt so tightly, it distracts you and upsets your equilib-rium. Breathe calmly. Ready?"

"Yes."

"Go!"

"Ouch! May you— Geralt, it's impossible! There's not enough room for a feint and a change of foot. And when I strike from both legs, without a feint . . ."

"I saw what happens when you strike without a feint. Does it hurt?"

"No. Not much . . ."

"Sit down next to me. Take a break."

"I'm not tired. Geralt, I'm not going to be able to jump over that third pendulum even if I rest for ten years. I can't be any faster—"

"And you don't have to be. You're fast enough."

"Tell me how to do it then. Half-pirouette, dodge and hit at the same time?"

"It's very simple; you just weren't paying attention. I told you before you started – an additional dodge is necessary. Displacement. An additional half-pirouette is superfluous. The second time round, you did everything well and passed all the pendulums."

"But I didn't hit the sack because . . . Geralt, without a half-pirouette I can't strike because I lose speed, I don't have the . . . the, what do you call it . . ."

"Impetus. That's true. So gain some impetus and energy. But not through a pirouette and change of foot because there's not enough time for it. Hit the pendulum with your sword."

"The pendulum? I've got to hit the sacks!"

"This is a fight, Ciri. The sacks represent your opponent's sensitive areas, you've got to hit them. The pendulums – which simulate your opponent's weapon – you have to avoid, dodge past. When the pendulum hits you, you're wounded. In a real fight, you might not get up again. The pendulum mustn't touch you. But you can hit the pendulum . . . Why are you screwing your nose up?"

"I'm . . . not going to be able to parry the pendulum with my sword. I'm too weak . . . I'll always be too weak! Because I'm a girl!"

"Come here, girl. Wipe your nose, and listen carefully.

No strongman, mountain-toppling giant or muscle-man is going to be able to parry a blow aimed at him by a dracolizard's tail, gigascorpion's pincers or a griffin's claws. And that's precisely the sort of weapons the pendulum simulates. So don't even try to parry. You're not deflecting the pendulum, you're deflecting yourself from it. You're intercepting its energy, which you need in order to deal a blow. A light but very swift deflection and instantaneous, equally swift blow from a reverse half-turn is enough. You're picking impetus up by rebounding. Do you see?"

"Mhm."

"Speed, Ciri, not strength. Strength is necessary for a lumberjack axing trees in a forest. That's why, admittedly, girls are rarely lumberjacks. Have you got that?"

"Mhm. Start the pendulums swinging."

"Take a rest first."

"I'm not tired."

"You know how to now? The same steps, feint—"

"I know."

"Attack!"

"Haaa! Ha! Haaaaa! Got you! I got you, you griffin! Geraaaalt! Did you see that?"

"Don't yell. Control your breathing."

"I did it! I really did it!! I managed it! Praise me, Geralt!"

"Well done, Ciri. Well done, girl."

In the middle of February, the snow disappeared, whisked away by a warm wind blowing from the south, from the pass.

*   *   *

Whatever was happening in the world, the witchers did not want to know.

In the evenings, consistently and determinedly, Triss guided the long conversations held in the dark hall, lit only by the bursts of flames in the great hearth, towards politics. The witchers' reactions were always the same. Geralt, a hand on his forehead, did not say a word. Vesemir nodded, from time to time throwing in comments which amounted to little more than that "in his day" everything had been better, more logical, more honest and healthier. Eskel pretended to be polite, and neither smiled nor made eye contact, and even managed, very occasionally, to be interested in some issue or question of little importance. Coën yawned openly and looked at the ceiling, and Lambert did nothing to hide his disdain.

They did not want to know anything, they cared nothing for dilemmas which drove sleep from kings, wizards, rulers and leaders, or for the problems which made councils, circles and gatherings tremble and buzz. For them, nothing existed beyond the passes drowning in snow or beyond the Gwenllech river carrying ice floes in its leaden current. For them, only Kaer Morhen existed, lost and lonely amongst the savage mountains.

That evening Triss was irritable and restless – perhaps it was the wind howling along the great castle's walls. And that evening they were all oddly excited – the witchers, apart from Geralt, were unusually talkative. Quite obviously, they only spoke of one thing – spring. About their approaching departure for the Trail. About what the Trail would have in store for them – about vampires, wyverns, leshys, lycanthropes and basilisks.

This time it was Triss who began to yawn and stare at

the ceiling. This time she was the one who remained silent – until Eskel turned to her with a question. A question which she had anticipated.

"And what is it really like in the south, on the Yaruga? Is it worth going there? We wouldn't like to find ourselves in the middle of any trouble."

"What do you mean by trouble?"

"Well, you know . . ." he stammered, "you keep telling us about the possibility of a new war . . . About constant fighting on the borders, about rebellions in the lands invaded by Nilfgaard. You said they're saying the Nilfgaardians might cross the Yaruga again—"

"So what?" said Lambert. "They've been hitting, killing and striking against each other constantly for hundreds of years. It's nothing to worry about. I've already decided – I'm going to the far South, to Sodden, Mahakam and Angren. It's well known that monsters abound wherever armies have passed. The most money is always made in places like that."

"True," Coën acknowledged. "The neighbourhood grows deserted, only women who can't fend for themselves remain in the villages . . . scores of children with no home or care, roaming around . . . Easy prey attracts monsters."

"And the lord barons and village elders," added Eskel, "have their heads full of the war and don't have the time to defend their subjects. They have to hire us. It's true. But from what Triss has been telling us all these evenings, it seems the conflict with Nilfgaard is more serious than that, not just some local little war. Is that right, Triss?"

"Even if it were the case," said the magician spitefully, "surely that suits you? A serious, bloody war will lead to more deserted villages, more widowed women, simply hordes of orphaned children—"

"I can't understand your sarcasm." Geralt took his hand away from his forehead. "I really can't, Triss."

"Nor I, my child." Vesemir raised his head. "What do you mean? Are you thinking about the widows and children? Lambert and Coën speak frivolously, as youngsters do, but it is not the words that are important. After all, they—"

". . . they defend these children," she interrupted crossly. "Yes, I know. From the werewolf who might kill two or three a year, while a Nilfgaardian foray can kill and burn an entire settlement in an hour. Yes, you defend orphans. While I fight that there should be as few of those orphans as possible. I'm fighting the cause, not the effect. That's why I'm on Foltest of Temeria's council and sit with Fercart and Keira Metz. We deliberate on how to stop war from breaking out and, should it come to it, how to defend ourselves. Because war is constantly hovering over us like a vulture. For you it's an adventure. For me, it's a game in which the stakes are survival. I'm involved in this game, and that's why your indifference and frivolity hurt and insult me."

Geralt sat up and looked at her.

"We're witchers, Triss. Can't you understand that?"

"What's there to understand?" The enchantress tossed her chestnut mane back. "Everything's crystal-clear. You've chosen a certain attitude to the world around you. The fact that this world might at any moment fall to pieces has a place in this choice. In mine, it doesn't. That's where we differ."

"I'm not sure it's only there we differ."

"The world is falling to ruins," she repeated. "We can watch it happen and do nothing. Or we can counteract it."

"How?" He smiled derisively. "With our emotions?"

She did not answer, turning her face to the fire roaring in the hearth.

"The world is falling to ruins," repeated Coën, nodding his head in feigned thoughtfulness. "How many times I've heard that."

"Me, too," Lambert grimaced. "And it's not surprising – it's a popular saying of late. It's what kings say when it turns out that a modicum of brains is necessary to rule after all. It's what merchants say when greed and stupidity have led them to bankruptcy. It's what wizards say when they start to lose their influence on politics or income. And the person they're speaking to should expect some sort of proposal straight away. So cut the introduction short, Triss, and present us with your proposition."

"Verbal squabbling has never amused me," the enchantress declared, gauging him with cold eyes, "or displays of eloquence which mock whoever you're talking to. I don't intend to take part in anything like that. You know only too well what I mean. You want to hide your heads in the sand, that's your business. But coming from you, Geralt, it's a great surprise."

"Triss." The white-haired witcher looked her straight in the eyes again. "What do you expect from me? To take an active part in the fight to save a world which is falling to pieces? Am I to enlist in the army and stop Nilfgaard? Should I, if it comes to another battle for Sodden, stand with you on the Hill, shoulder to shoulder, and fight for freedom?"

"I'd be proud," she said quietly, lowering her head. "I'd be proud and happy to fight at your side."

"I believe that. But I'm not gallant enough. Nor valiant enough. I'm not suited to be a soldier or a hero. And having an acute fear of pain, mutilation and death is not the only reason. You can't stop a soldier from being frightened but you can give him motivation to help him overcome that fear. I have no such motivation. I can't have. I'm a witcher: an artificially created mutant. I kill monsters for money. I defend children when their parents pay me to. If Nilfgaardian parents pay me, I'll defend Nilfgaardian children. And even if the world lies in ruin – which does not seem likely to me – I'll carry on killing monsters in the ruins of this world until some monster kills me. That is my fate, my reason, my life and my attitude to the world. And it is not what I chose. It was chosen for me."

"You're embittered," she stated, tugging nervously at a strand of hair. "Or pretending to be. You forget that I know you, so don't play the unfeeling mutant, devoid of a heart, of scruples and of his own free will, in front of me. And the reasons for your bitterness, I can guess and understand. Ciri's prophecy, correct?"

"No, not correct," he answered icily. "I see that you don't know me at all. I'm afraid of death, just like everyone else, but I grew used to the idea of it a very long time ago – I'm not under any illusions. I'm not complaining about fate, Triss – this is plain, cold calculation. Statistics. No witcher has yet died of old age, lying in bed dictating his will. Not a single one. Ciri didn't surprise or frighten me. I know I'm going to die in some cave which stinks of carcases, torn apart by a griffin, lamia or manticore.

But I don't want to die in a war, because they're not my wars."

"I'm surprised at you," she replied sharply. "I'm surprised that you're saying this, surprised by your lack of motivation, as you learnedly chose to describe your supercilious distance and indifference. You were at Sodden, Angren and Transriver. You know what happened to Cintra, know what befell Queen Calanthe and many thousands of people there. You know the hell Ciri went through, know why she cries out at night. And I know, too, because I was also there. I'm afraid of pain and death too, even more so now than I was then – I have good reason. As for motivation, it seems to me that back then I had just as little as you. Why should I, a magician, care about the fates of Sodden, Brugge, Cintra or other kingdoms? The problems of having more or less competent rulers? The interests of merchants and barons? I was a magician. I, too, could have said it wasn't my war, that I could mix elixirs for the Nilfgaardians on the ruins of the world. But I stood on that Hill next to Vilgefortz, next to Artaud Terranova, next to Fercart, next to Enid Findabair and Philippa Eilhart, next to your Yennefer. Next to those who no longer exist – Coral, Yoël, Vanielle . . . There was a moment when out of sheer terror I forgot all my spells except for one – and thanks to that spell I could have teleported myself from that horrific place back home, to my tiny little tower in Maribor. There was a moment, when I threw up from fear, when Yennefer and Coral held me up by the shoulders and hair—"

"Stop. Please, stop."

"No, Geralt. I won't. After all, you want to know what happened there, on the Hill. So listen – there was a din and flames, there were flaming arrows and exploding balls of fire, there were screams and crashes, and I suddenly found myself on the ground on a pile of charred, smoking rags, and I realised that the pile of rags was Yoël and that thing next to her, that awful thing, that trunk with no arms and no legs which was screaming so horrifically was Coral. And I thought the blood in which I was lying was Coral's blood. But it was my own. And then I saw what they had done to me, and I started to howl, howl like a beaten dog, like a battered child— Leave me alone! Don't worry, I'm not going to cry. I'm not a little girl from a tiny tower in Maribor any more. Damn it, I'm Triss Merigold, the Fourteenth One Killed at Sodden. There are fourteen graves at the foot of the obelisk on the Hill, but only thirteen bodies. You're amazed such a mistake could have been made? Most of the corpses were in hard-to-recognise pieces – no one identified them. The living were hard to account for, too. Of those who had known me well, Yennefer was the only one to survive, and Yennefer was blind. Others knew me fleetingly and always recognised me by my beautiful hair. And I, damn it, didn't have it any more!"

Geralt held her closer. She no longer tried to push him away.

"They used the highest magics on us," she continued in a muted voice, "spells, elixirs, amulets and artefacts. Nothing was left wanting for the wounded heroes of the Hill. We were cured, patched up, our former appearances returned to us, our hair and sight restored. You can hardly see the marks. But I will never wear a plunging neckline again, Geralt. Never."

The witchers said nothing. Neither did Ciri, who had

slipped into the hall without a sound and stopped at the threshold, hunching her shoulders and folding her arms.

"So," the magician said after a while, "don't talk to me about motivation. Before we stood on that Hill the Chapter simply told us: 'That is what you have to do.' Whose war was it? What were we defending there? The land? The borders? The people and their cottages? The interests of kings? The wizards' influence and income? Order against Chaos? I don't know! But we defended it because that's what had to be done. And if the need arises, I'll stand on the Hill again. Because if I don't, it will make the sacrifices made the first time futile and unnecessary."

"I'll stand beside you!" shouted Ciri shrilly. "Just wait and see, I'll stand with you! Those Nilfgaardians are going to pay for my grandmother, pay for everything . . . I haven't forgotten!"

"Be quiet," growled Lambert. "Don't butt into grown-ups' conversations—"

"Oh sure!" The girl stamped her foot and in her eyes a green fire kindled. "Why do you think I'm learning to fight with a sword? I want to kill him, that black knight from Cintra with wings on his helmet, for what he did to me, for making me afraid! And I'm going to kill him! That's why I'm learning it!"

"And therefore you'll stop learning," said Geralt in a voice colder than the walls of Kaer Morhen. "Until you understand what a sword is, and what purpose it serves in a witcher's hand, you will not pick one up. You are not learning in order to kill and be killed. You are not learning to kill out of fear and hatred, but in order to save lives. Your own and those of others."

The girl bit her lip, shaking from agitation and anger.

"Understood?"

Ciri raised her head abruptly. "No."

"Then you'll never understand. Get out."

"Geralt, I—"

"Get out."

Ciri spun on her heel and stood still for a moment, undecided, as if waiting – waiting for something that could not happen. Then she ran swiftly up the stairs. They heard the door slam.

"Too severe, Wolf," said Vesemir. "Much too severe. And you shouldn't have done it in Triss's presence. The emotional ties—"

"Don't talk to me about emotions. I've had enough of all this talk about emotions!"

"And why is that?" The magician smiled derisively and coldly. "Why, Geralt? Ciri is normal. She has normal feelings, she accepts emotions naturally, takes them for what they really are. You, obviously, don't understand and are therefore surprised by them. It surprises and irritates you. The fact that someone can experience normal love, normal hatred, normal fear, pain and regret, normal joy and normal sadness. That it is coolness, distance and indifference which are considered abnormal. Oh yes, Geralt, it annoys you, it annoys you so much that you are starting to think about Kaer Morhen's vaults, about the Laboratorium, the dusty demi-johns full of mutagenic poisons—"

"Triss!" called Vesemir, gazing at Geralt's face, suddenly grown pale. But the enchantress refused to be interrupted and spoke faster and faster, louder and louder.

"Who do you want to deceive, Geralt? Me? Her? Or maybe yourself? Maybe you don't want to admit the truth, a truth everyone knows except you? Maybe you don't want to accept the fact that human emotions and feelings weren't killed in you by the elixirs and Grasses! You killed them! You killed them yourself! But don't you dare kill them in the child!"

"Silence!" he shouted, leaping from the chair. "Silence, Merigold!"

He turned away and lowered his arms defencelessly. "Sorry," he said quietly. "Forgive me, Triss." He made for the stairs quickly, but the enchantress was up in a flash and threw herself at him, embracing him.

"You are not leaving here alone," she whispered. "I won't let you be alone. Not right now."

They knew immediately where she had run to. Fine, wet snow had fallen that evening and had covered the forecourt with a thin, impeccably white carpet. In it they saw her footsteps.

Ciri was standing on the very summit of the ruined wall, as motionless as a statue. She was holding the sword above her right shoulder, the cross-guard at eye level. The fingers of her left hand were lightly touching the pommel.

On seeing them, the girl jumped, spun in a pirouette and landed softly in an identical but reverse mirror position.

"Ciri," said the witcher, "come down, please."

It seemed she hadn't heard him. She did not move, not even a muscle. Triss, however, saw the reflection of the moon, thrown across her face by the blade, glisten silver over a stream of tears.

"No one's going to take the sword away from me!" she shouted. "No one! Not even you!"

"Come down," repeated Geralt.

She tossed her head defiantly and the next second leaped once more. A loose brick slipped beneath her foot with a grating sound. Ciri staggered, trying to find her balance. And failed.

The witcher jumped.

Triss raised her hand, opening her mouth to utter a formula for levitation. She knew she couldn't do it in time. She knew that Geralt would not make it. It was impossible.

Geralt did make it.

He was forced down to the ground, thrown on his knees and back. He fell. But he did not let go of Ciri.

The magician approached them slowly. She heard the girl whisper and sniff. Geralt too was whispering. She could not make out the words. But she understood their meaning.

A warm wind howled in the crevices of the wall. The witcher raised his head.

"Spring," he said quietly.

"Yes," she acknowledged, swallowing. "There is still snow in the passes but in the valleys . . . In the valleys, it is already spring. Shall we leave, Geralt? You, Ciri and I?"

"Yes. It is high time."

Upriver we saw their towns, as delicate as if they were woven from the morning mist out of which they loomed. It seemed as if they would disappear a moment later, blown away on the wind which rippled the surface of the water. There were little palaces, white as nenuphar flowers; there were little towers looking as though they were plaited out of ivy; there were bridges as airy as weeping willows. And there were other things for which we could find no word or name. Yet we already had names for everything which our eyes beheld in this new, reborn world. Suddenly, in the far recesses of our memories, we found the words for dragons and griffins, mermaids and nymphs, sylphs and dryads once more. For the white unicorns which drank from the river at dusk, inclining their slender necks towards the water. We named everything. And everything seemed to be close to our hearts, familiar to us, ours.

Apart from them. They, although so resembling us, were alien. So very alien that, for a long time, we could find no word for their strangeness.

Hen Gedymdeith, *Elves and Humans*

A good elf is a dead elf.

Marshal Milan Raupenneck

CHAPTER FOUR

The misfortune behaved in the eternal manner of misfortunes and hawks – it hung over them for some while waiting for an appropriate moment before it attacked. It chose its moment, when they had passed the few settlements on the Gwenllech and Upper Buina, passed Ard Carraigh and plunged into the forest below, deserted and intersected by gorges. Like a hawk striking, this misfortune's aim was true. It fell accurately upon its victim, and its victim was Triss.

Initially it seemed nasty but not too serious, resembling an ordinary stomach upset. Geralt and Ciri discreetly tried to take no notice of the stops the enchantress's ailment necessitated. Triss, as pale as death, beaded with sweat and painfully contorted, tried to continue riding for several hours longer, but at about midday, and having spent an abnormally long time in the bushes by the road, she was no longer in any condition to sit on a saddle. Ciri tried to help her but to no avail – the enchantress, unable to hold on to the horse's mane, slid down her mount's flank and collapsed to the ground.

They picked her up and laid her on a cloak. Geralt unstrapped the saddlebags without a word, found a casket containing some magic elixirs, opened it and cursed. All the phials were identical and the mysterious signs on the seals meant nothing to him.

"Which one, Triss?"

"None of them," she moaned, with both hands on her belly. "I can't . . . I can't take them."

"What? Why?"

"I'm sensitised—"

"You? A magician?"

"I'm allergic!" she sobbed with helpless exasperation and despairing anger. "I always have been! I can't tolerate elixirs! I can treat others with them but can only treat myself with amulets."

"Where is the amulet?"

"I don't know." She ground her teeth. "I must have left it in Kaer Morhen. Or lost it—"

"Damn it. What are we going to do? Maybe you should cast a spell on yourself?"

"I've tried. And this is the result. I can't concentrate because of this cramp . . ."

"Don't cry."

"Easy for you to say!"

The witcher got up, pulled his saddlebags from Roach's back and began rummaging through them. Triss curled up, her face contracted and her lips twisted in a spasm of pain.

"Ciri . . ."

"Yes, Triss?"

"Do you feel all right? No . . . unusual sensations?"

The girl shook her head.

"Maybe it's food poisoning? What did I eat? But we all ate the same thing . . . Geralt! Wash your hands. Make sure Ciri washes her hands . . ."

"Calm down. Drink this."

"What is it?"

"Ordinary soothing herbs. There's next to no magic in them so they shouldn't do you any harm. And they'll relieve the cramps."

"Geralt, the cramps . . . they're nothing. But if I run a fever . . . It could be . . . dysentery. Or paratyphoid."

"Aren't you immune?"

Triss turned her head away without replying, bit her lip and curled up even tighter. The witcher did not pursue the question.

Having allowed her to rest for a while they hauled the enchantress onto Roach's saddle. Geralt sat behind her, supporting her with both hands, while Ciri rode beside them, holding the reins and leading Triss's gelding. They did not even manage a mile. The enchantress kept falling from Geralt's hands; she could not stay in the saddle. Suddenly she started trembling convulsively, and instantly burned with a fever. The gastritis had grown worse. Geralt told himself that it was an allergic reaction to the traces of magic in his witcher's elixir. He told himself that. But he did not believe it.

"Oh, sir," said the sergeant, "you have not come at a good time. Indeed, you could not have arrived at a worse moment."

The sergeant was right. Geralt could neither contest it nor argue.

The fort guarding the bridge, where there would usually be three soldiers, a stable-boy, a toll-collector and – at most – a few passers-by, was swarming with people. The witcher counted over thirty lightly armed soldiers wearing the colours of Kaedwen and a good fifty shield bearers, camping around the low palisade. Most of them were lying by campfires, in keeping with the old soldier's rule which dictates that you sleep when you can and get up when you're woken. Considerable activity could be seen through the thrown-open gates – there were a lot of people and horses inside the fort, too. At the top of the little leaning lookout tower two soldiers were on duty, with their crossbows permanently at the ready. On the worn bridge trampled by horses' hooves, six peasant carts and two merchant wagons were parked. In the enclosure, their heads lowered sadly over the mud and manure, stood umpteen unyoked oxen.

"There was an assault on the fort – last night." The sergeant anticipated his question. "We just got here in time with the relief troops – otherwise we'd have found nothing here but charred earth."

"Who were your attackers? Bandits? Marauders?"

The soldier shook his head, spat and looked at Ciri and Triss, huddled in the saddle.

"Come inside," he said, "your Enchantress is going to fall out of her saddle any minute now. We already have some wounded men there; one more won't make much difference."

In the yard, in an open, roofed shelter, lay several people with their wounds dressed with bloodied bandages. A little further, between the palisade fence and a wooden well with a sweep, Geralt made out six still bodies wrapped in sacking from which only pairs of feet in worn, dirty boots protruded.

"Lay her there, by the wounded men." The soldier indicated the shelter. "Oh sir, it truly is bad luck she's sick. A few of our men were hurt during the battle and we wouldn't turn down a bit of magical assistance. When we pulled the arrow out of one of them its head stuck in his guts. The lad will peter out by the morning, he'll peter out like anything . . . And the enchantress who could have saved him is tossing and turning with a fever and seeking help from us. A bad time, I say, a bad time—"

He broke off, seeing that the witcher could not tear his eyes from the sacking-wrapped bodies.

"Two guards from here, two of our relief troops and two . . . two of the others," he said, pulling up a corner of the stiff material. "Take a look, if you wish."

"Ciri, step away."

"I want to see, too!" The girl leaned out around him, staring at the corpses with her mouth open.

"Step away, please. Take care of Triss."

Ciri huffed, unwilling, but obeyed. Geralt came closer.

"Elves," he noted, not hiding his surprise.

"Elves," the soldier confirmed. "Scoia'tael."

"Who?"

"Scoia'tael," repeated the soldier. "Forest bands."

"Strange name. It means 'Squirrels', if I'm not mistaken?"

"Yes, sir. Squirrels. That's what they call themselves in elvish. Some say it's because sometimes they wear squirrel tails on their fur caps and hats. Others say it's because they live in the woods and eat nuts. They're getting more and more troublesome, I tell you."

Geralt shook his head. The soldier covered the bodies again and wiped his hands on his tunic.

"Come," he said. "There's no point standing here. I'll take you to the commandant. Our corporal will take care of your patient if he can. He knows how to sear and stitch wounds and set bones so maybe he knows how to mix up medicines and what not too. He's a brainy chap, a mountain-man. Come, witcher."

In the dim, smoky toll-collector's hut a lively and noisy discussion was underway. A knight with closely cropped hair wearing a habergeon and yellow surcoat was shouting at two merchants and a greeve, watched by the toll-collector, who had an indifferent, rather gloomy expression, and whose head was wrapped in bandages.

"I said, no!" The knight thumped his fist on the rickety table and stood up straight, adjusting the gorget across his chest. "Until the patrols return, you're not going anywhere! You are not going to roam the highways!"

"I's to be in Daevon in two days!" the greeve yelled, shoving a short notched stick with a symbol branded into it under the knight's nose. "I have a transport to lead! The bailiff's going to have me head if it be late! I'll complain to the voivode!"

"Go ahead and complain," sneered the knight. "But I advise you to line your breeches with straw before you do because the voivode can do a mean bit of arse-kicking. But for the time being I give the orders here – the voivode is far away and your bailiff means no more to me than a heap of dung. Hey, Unist! Who are you bringing here, sergeant? Another merchant?"

"No," answered the sergeant reluctantly. "A witcher, sir. He goes by the name Geralt of Rivia."

To Geralt's astonishment, the knight gave a broad smile, approached and held a hand out in greeting.

"Geralt of Rivia," he repeated, still smiling. "I have heard about you, and not just from gossip and hearsay. What brings you here?"

Geralt explained what brought him there. The knight's smile faded.

"You have not come at a good time. Or to a good place. We are at war here, witcher. A band of Scoia'tael is doing the rounds and there was a skirmish yesterday. I am waiting here for relief forces and then we'll start a counterattack."

"You're fighting elves?"

"Not just elves! Is it possible? Have you, a witcher, not heard of the Squirrels?"

"No. I haven't."

"Where have you been these past two years? Beyond the seas? Here, in Kaedwen, the Scoia'tael have made sure everybody's talking about them, they've seen to it only too well. The first bands appeared just after the war with Nilfgaard broke out. The cursed non-humans took advantage of our difficulties. We were fighting in the south and they began a guerrilla campaign at our rear. They counted on the Nilfgaardians defeating us, started declaring it was the end of human rule and there would be a return to the old order. 'Humans to the sea!' That's their battle cry, as they murder, burn and plunder!"

"It's your own fault and your own problem," the greeve

commented glumly, tapping his thigh with the notched stick, a mark of his position. "Yours, and all the other noblemen and knights. You're the ones who oppressed the non-humans, would not allow them their way of life, so now you pay for it. While we've always moved goods this way and no one stopped us. We didn't need an army."

"What's true is true," said one of the merchants who had been sitting silently on a bench. "The Squirrels are no fiercer than the bandits who used to roam these ways. And who did the elves take in hand first? The bandits!"

"What do I care if it's a bandit or an elf who runs me through with an arrow from behind some bushes?" the toll-collector with the bandaged head said suddenly. "The thatch, if it's set on fire above my head in the night, burns just the same. What difference does it make who lit the fire-brand? You say, sir, that the Scoia'tael are no worse than the bandits? You lie. The bandits wanted loot, but the elves are after human blood. Not everyone has ducats, but we all have blood running through our veins. You say it's the nobility's problem, greeve? That's an even greater folly. What about the lumberjacks shot in the clearing, the tar-makers hacked to pieces at the Beeches, the refugee peasants from the burned down hamlets, did they hurt the non-humans? They lived and worked together, as neighbours, and suddenly they got an arrow in the back . . . And me? Never in my life have I harmed a non-human and look, my head is broken open by a dwarf's cutlass. And if it were not for the soldiers you're snapping at, I would be lying beneath an ell of turf—"

"Exactly!" The knight in the yellow surcoat thumped his fist against the table once again. "We are protecting your mangy skin, greeve, from those, as you call them, oppressed elves, who, according to you, we did not let live. But I will say something different – we have emboldened them too much. We tolerated them, treated them as humans, as equals, and now they are stabbing us in the back. Nilfgaard is paying them for it, I'd stake my life, and the savage elves from the mountains are furnishing them with arms. But their real support comes from those who always lived amongst us – from the elves, half-elves, dwarves, gnomes and halflings. They are the ones who are hiding them, feeding them, supplying them with volunteers—"

"Not all of them," said another merchant, slim, with a delicate and noble face – in no way a typical merchant's features. "The majority of non-humans condemn the Squirrels, sir, and want nothing to do with them. The majority of them are loyal, and sometimes pay a high price for that loyalty. Remember the burgomaster from Ban Ard. He was a half-elf who urged peace and co-operation. He was killed by an assassin's arrow."

"Aimed, no doubt, by a neighbour, some halfling or dwarf who also feigned loyalty," scoffed the knight. "If you ask me, none of them are loyal! Every one of them— Hey there! Who are you?"

Geralt looked around. Ciri stood right behind him casting her huge emerald eyes over everyone. As far as the ability to move noiselessly was concerned, she had clearly made enormous progress.

"She's with me," he explained.

"Hmmm . . ." The knight measured Ciri with his eyes then turned back to the merchant with the noble face, evidently considering him the most serious partner in the discussion. "Yes, sir, do not talk to me about loyal non-humans. They are all our enemies, it's just that some are better than others at pretending otherwise. Halflings, dwarves and gnomes have lived amongst us for centuries – in some sort of harmony, it would seem. But it sufficed for the elves to lift their heads, and all the others grabbed their weapons and took to the woods too. I tell you, it was a mistake to tolerate the free elves and dryads, with their forests and their mountain enclaves. It wasn't enough for them, and now they're yelling: 'It's our world! Begone, strangers!' By the gods, we'll show them who will be gone, and of which race even the slightest traces will be wiped away. We beat the hides off the Nilfgaardians and now we will do something about these rogue bands."

"It's not easy to catch an elf in the woods," said the witcher. "Nor would I go after a gnome or dwarf in the mountains. How large are these units?"

"Bands," corrected the knight. "They're bands, witcher. They can count up to a hundred heads, sometimes more. They call each pack a 'commando'. It's a word borrowed from the gnomes. And in saying they are hard to catch you speak truly. Evidently you are a professional. Chasing them through the woods and thickets is senseless. The only way is to cut them off from their supplies, isolate them, starve them out. Seize the non-humans who are helping them firmly by the scruff of their necks. Those from the towns and settlements, villages and farms—"

"The problem is," said the merchant with noble features, "that we still don't know which of the non-humans are helping them and which aren't."

"Then we have to seize them all!"

"Ah." The merchant smiled. "I understand. I've heard that somewhere before. Take everyone by the scruff of their neck and throw them down the mines, into enclosed camps, into quarries. Everyone. The innocent, too. Women and children. Is that right?"

The knight raised his head and slammed his hand down on his sword hilt.

"Just so, and no other way!" he said sharply. "You pity the children, yet you're like a child yourself in this world, dear sir. A truce with Nilfgaard is a very fragile thing, like an egg-shell. If not today then the war might start anew tomorrow, and anything can happen in war. If they defeated us, what do you think would happen? I'll tell you what – elven commandos would emerge from the forests, they'd emerge strong and numerous and these 'loyal elements' would instantly join them. Those loyal dwarves of yours, your friendly halflings, do you think they are going to talk of peace, of reconciliation then? No, sir. They'll be tearing our guts out. Nilfgaard is going to deal with us through their hands. And they'll drown us in the sea, just as they promise. No, sir, we must not pussyfoot around them. It's either them or us. There's no third way!"

The door of the hut squeaked and a soldier in a bloodied apron stood in the doorway.

"Forgive me for disturbing you," he hawked. "Which of you, noble sirs, be the one who brought this sick woman here?"

"I did," said the witcher. "What's happened?"

"Come with me, please."

They went out into the courtyard.

"It bodes not well with her, sir," said the soldier, indicating Triss. "Firewater with pepper and saltpetre I gave her – but it be no good. I don't really . . ."

Geralt made no comment because there was nothing to

say. The magician, doubled over, was clear evidence of the fact that firewater with pepper and saltpetre was not something her stomach could tolerate.

"It could be some plague." The soldier frowned. "Or that, what's it called . . . Zintery. If it were to spread to our men—"

"She is a wizard," protested the witcher. "Wizards don't fall sick . . ."

"Just so," the knight who had followed them out threw in cynically. "Yours, as I see, is just emanating good health. Geralt, listen to me. The woman needs help and we cannot offer such. Nor can I risk an epidemic amongst my troops. You understand."

"I understand. I will leave immediately. I have no choice – I have to turn back towards Daevon or Ard Carraigh."

"You won't get far. The patrols have orders to stop everyone. Besides, it is dangerous. The Scoia'tael have gone in exactly that direction."

"I'll manage."

"From what I've heard about you" – the knight's lips twisted – "I have no doubt you would. But bear in mind you are not alone. You have a gravely sick woman on your shoulders and this brat . . ."

Ciri, who was trying to clean her dung-smeared boot on a ladder rung, raised her head. The knight cleared his throat and looked down. Geralt smiled faintly. Over the last two years Ciri had almost forgotten her origins and had almost entirely lost her royal manners and airs, but her glare, when she wanted, was very much like that of her grandmother. So much so that Queen Calanthe would no doubt have been very proud of her granddaughter.

"Yeeessss, what was I . . ." the knight stammered, tugging at his belt with embarrassment. "Geralt, sir, I know what you need to do. Cross beyond the river, south. You will catch up with a caravan which is following the trail. Night is just around the corner and the caravan is certain to stop for a rest. You will reach it by dawn."

"What kind of caravan?"

"I don't know." The knight shrugged. "But it is not a merchant or an ordinary convoy. It's too orderly, the wagons are all the same, all covered . . . A royal bailiff's, no doubt. I allowed them to cross the bridge because they are following the Trail south, probably towards the fords on the Lixela."

"Hmmm . . ." The witcher considered this, looking at Triss. "That would be on my way. But will I find help there?"

"Maybe yes," the knight said coldly. "Maybe no. But you won't find it here, that's for sure."

They did not hear or see him as he approached, engrossed as they were in conversation, sitting around a campfire which, with its yellow light, cadaverously illuminated the canvas of the wagons arranged in a circle. Geralt gently pulled up his mare and forced her to neigh loudly. He wanted to warn the caravan, which had set up camp for the night, wanted to temper the surprise of having visitors and avoid a nervous reaction. He knew from experience that the release mechanisms on crossbows did not like nervous moves.

The campers leaped up and, despite his warning, performed numerous agitated movements. Most of them, he saw at once, were dwarves. This reassured him somewhat

– dwarves, although extremely irascible, usually asked questions first in situations such as these and only then aimed their crossbows.

"Who's that?" shouted one of the dwarves hoarsely and with a swift, energetic move, prised an axe from a stump by the campfire. "Who goes there?"

"A friend." The witcher dismounted.

"I wonder whose," growled the dwarf. "Come closer. Hold your hands out so we can see them."

Geralt approached, holding his hands out so they could be seen even by someone afflicted with conjunctivitis or night blindness.

"Closer."

He obeyed. The dwarf lowered his axe and tilted his head a little.

"Either my eyes deceive me," he said, "or it's the witcher Geralt of Rivia. Or someone who looks damn like him."

The fire suddenly shot up into flames, bursting into a golden brightness which drew faces and figures from the dark.

"Yarpen Zigrin," declared Geralt, astonished. "None other than Yarpen Zigrin in person, complete with beard!"

"Ha!" The dwarf waved his axe as if it were an osier twig. The blade whirred in the air and cut into a stump with a dull thud. "Call the alarm off! This truly is a friend!"

The rest of the gathering visibly relaxed and Geralt thought he heard deep sighs of relief. The dwarf walked up to him, holding out his hand. His grip could easily rival a pair of iron pincers.

"Welcome, you warlock," he said. "Wherever you've

come from and wherever you're going, welcome. Boys! Over here! You remember my boys, witcher? This is Yannick Brass, this one's Xavier Moran and here's Paulie Dahlberg and his brother Regan."

Geralt didn't remember any of them, and besides they all looked alike, bearded, stocky, practically square in their thick quilted jerkins.

"There were six of you," one by one he squeezed the hard, gnarled hands offered him, "if I remember correctly."

"You've a good memory," laughed Yarpen Zigrin. "There were six of us, indeed. But Lucas Corto got married, settled down in Mahakam and dropped out of the company, the stupid oaf. Somehow we haven't managed to find anybody worthy of his place yet. Pity, six is just right, not too many, not too few. To eat a calf, knock back a barrel, there's nothing like six—"

"As I see," with a nod Geralt indicated the rest of the group standing undecided by the wagons, "there are enough of you here to manage three calves, not to mention a quantity of poultry. What's this gang of fellows you're commanding, Yarpen?"

"I'm not the one in command. Allow me to introduce you. Forgive me, Wenck, for not doing so straight away but me and my boys have known Geralt of Rivia for a long time – we've a fair number of shared memories behind us. Geralt, this is Commissar Vilfrid Wenck, in the service of King Henselt of Ard Carraigh, the merciful ruler of Kaedwen."

Vilfrid Wenck was tall, taller than Geralt and near twice the dwarf's height. He wore an ordinary, simple outfit like that worn by greeves, bailiffs or mounted messengers, but there was a sharpness in his movements, a stiffness and sureness which the witcher knew and could faultlessly recognise, even at night, even in the meagre light of the campfire. That was how men accustomed to wearing hauberks and belts weighed down with weapons moved. Wenck was a professional soldier. Geralt was prepared to wager any sum on it. He shook the proffered hand and gave a little bow.

"Let's sit down." Yarpen indicated the stump where his mighty axe was still embedded. "Tell us what you're doing in this neighbourhood, Geralt."

"Looking for help. I'm journeying in a threesome with a woman and youngster. The woman is sick. Seriously sick. I caught up with you to ask for help."

"Damn it, we don't have a medic here." The dwarf spat at the flaming logs. "Where have you left them?"

"Half a furlong from here, by the roadside."

"You lead the way. Hey, you there! Three to the horses, saddle the spare mounts! Geralt, will your sick woman hold up in the saddle?"

"Not really. That's why I had to leave her there."

"Get the sheepskin, canvas sheet and two poles from the wagon! Quick!"

Vilfrid Wenck, crossing his arms, hawked loudly.

"We're on the trail," Yarpen Zigrin said sharply, without looking at him. "You don't refuse help on the Trail."

"Damn it." Yarpen removed his palm from Triss's forehead. "She's as hot as a furnace. I don't like it. What if it's typhoid or dysentery?"

"It can't be typhoid or dysentery," Geralt lied with conviction, wrapping the horse blankets around the sick woman. "Wizards are immune to those diseases. It's food poisoning, nothing contagious."

"Hmm . . . Well, all right. I'll rummage through the bags. I used to have some good medicine for the runs, maybe there's still a little left."

"Ciri," muttered the witcher, passing her a sheepskin unstrapped from the horse, "go to sleep, you're barely on your feet. No, not in the wagon. We'll put Triss in the wagon. You lie down next to the fire."

"No," she protested quietly, watching the dwarf walk away. "I'm going to lie down next to her. When they see you keeping me away from her, they won't believe you. They'll think it's contagious and chase us away, like the soldiers in the fort."

"Geralt?" the enchantress moaned suddenly. "Where . . . are we?"

"Amongst friends."

"I'm here," said Ciri, stroking her chestnut hair. "I'm at your side. Don't be afraid. You feel how warm it is here? A campfire's burning and a dwarf is just going to bring some medicine for . . . For your stomach."

"Geralt," sobbed Triss, trying to disentangle herself from the blankets. "No . . . no magic elixirs, remember . . ."

"I remember. Lie peacefully."

"I've got to . . . Oooh . . ."

The witcher leaned over without a word, picked up the enchantress together with her cocoon of caparisons and blankets, and marched to the woods, into the darkness. Ciri sighed.

She turned, hearing heavy panting. Behind the wagon appeared the dwarf, hefting a considerable bundle under his arm. The campfire flame gleamed on the blade of the axe behind his belt; the rivets on his heavy leather jerkin also glistened.

"Where's the sick one?" he snarled. "Flown away on a broomstick?"

Ciri pointed to the darkness.

"Right." The dwarf nodded. "I know the pain and I've known the same nasty complaint. When I was younger I used to eat everything I managed to find or catch or cut down, so I got food poisoning many a time. Who is she, this Enchantress?"

"Triss Merigold."

"I don't know her, never heard of her. I rarely have anything to do with the Brotherhood anyway. Well, but it's polite to introduce oneself. I'm called Yarpen Zigrin. And what are you called, little goose?"

"Something other than Little Goose," snarled Ciri with a gleam in her eyes.

The dwarf chuckled and bared his teeth.

"Ah." He bowed with exaggeration. "I beg your forgiveness. I didn't recognise you in the darkness. This isn't a goose but a noble young lady. I fall at your feet. What is the young lady's name, if it's no secret?"

"It's no secret. I'm Ciri."

"Ciri. Aha. And who is the young lady?"

"That," Ciri turned her nose up proudly, "is a secret."

Yarpen snorted again.

"The young lady's little tongue is as sharp as a wasp. If the young lady will deign to forgive me, I've brought the medicine and a little food. Will the young lady accept it or will she send the old boor, Yarpen Zigrin, away?"

"I'm sorry . . ." Ciri had second thoughts and lowered

her head. "Triss really does need help, Master . . . Zigrin. She's very sick. Thank you for the medicine."

"It's nothing." The dwarf bared his teeth again and patted her shoulder amicably. "Come on, Ciri, you help me. The medicine has to be prepared. We'll roll some pellets according to my grandmother's recipe. No disease sitting in the guts will resist these kernels."

He unwrapped the bundle, extracted something shaped like a piece of turf and a small clay vessel. Ciri approached, curious.

"You should know, Ciri," said Yarpen, "that my grandmother knew her medicine like nobody's business. Unfortunately, she believed that the source of most disease is idleness, and idleness is best cured through the application of a stick. As far as my siblings and I were concerned, she chiefly used this cure preventively. She beat us for anything and for nothing. She was a rare old hag. And once when, out of the blue, she gave me a chunk of bread with dripping and sugar, it was such a surprise that I dropped it in astonishment, dripping down. So my gran gave me a thrashing, the nasty old bitch. And then she gave me another chunk of bread, only without the sugar."

"My grandmother," Ciri nodded in understanding, "thrashed me once, too. With a switch."

"A switch?" The dwarf laughed. "Mine whacked me once with a pickaxe handle. But that's enough reminiscing, we have to roll the pellets. Here, tear this up and mould it into little balls."

"What is it? It's sticky and messy . . . Eeeuuggh . . . What a stink!"

"It's mouldy oil-meal bread. Excellent medicine. Roll

it into little balls. Smaller, smaller, they're for a magician, not a cow. Give me one. Good. Now we're going to roll the ball in medicine."

"Eeeeuuuugggghh!"

"Stinks?" The dwarf brought his upturned nose closer to the clay pot. "Impossible. Crushed garlic and bitter salt has no right to stink, even if it's a hundred years old."

"It's foul, uugghh. Triss won't eat that!"

"We'll use my grandmother's method. You squeeze her nose and I'll shove the pellets in."

"Yarpen," Geralt hissed, emerging abruptly from the darkness with the magician in his arms. "Watch out or I'll shove something down you."

"It's medicine!" The dwarf took offence. "It helps! Mould, garlic . . ."

"Yes," moaned Triss weakly from the depths of her cocoon. "It's true . . . Geralt, it really ought to help . . ."

"See?" Yarpen nudged Geralt with his elbow, turning his beard up proudly and pointing to Triss, who swallowed the pellets with a martyred expression. "A wise magician. Knows what's good for her."

"What are you saying, Triss?" The witcher leaned over. "Ah, I see. Yarpen, do you have any angelica? Or saffron?"

"I'll have a look, and ask around. I've brought you some water and a little food—"

"Thank you. But they both need rest above all. Ciri, lie down."

"I'll just make up a compress for Triss—"

"I'll do it myself. Yarpen, I'd like to talk to you."

"Come to the fire. We'll broach a barrel—"

"I want to talk to *you*. I don't need an audience. Quite the contrary."

"Of course. I'm listening."

"What sort of convoy is this?"

The dwarf raised his small, piercing eyes at him.

"The king's service," he said slowly and emphatically.

"That's what I thought." The witcher held the gaze. "Yarpen, I'm not asking out of any inappropriate curiosity."

"I know. And I also know what you mean. But this convoy is . . . hmm . . . special."

"So what are you transporting?"

"Salt fish," said Yarpen casually, and proceeded to embellish his lie without batting an eyelid. "Fodder, tools, harnesses, various odds and ends for the army. Wenck is a quartermaster to the king's army."

"If he's quartermaster then I'm a druid," smiled Geralt. "But that's your affair – I'm not in the habit of poking my nose into other people's secrets. But you can see the state Triss is in. Let us join you, Yarpen, let us put her in one of the wagons. Just for a few days. I'm not asking where you're going because this trail goes straight to the south without forking until past the Lixela and it's a ten-day journey to the Lixela. By that time the fever will have subsided and Triss will be able to ride a horse. And even if she isn't then I'll stop in a town beyond the river. Ten days in a wagon, well covered, hot food . . . Please."

"I don't give the orders here. Wenck does."

"I don't believe you lack influence over him. Not in a convoy primarily made up of dwarves. Of course he has to bear you in mind."

"Who is this Triss to you?"

"What difference does it make in this situation?"

"In this situation – none. I asked out of an inappropriate curiosity born of the desire to start new rumours going around the inns. But be that as it may, you're mighty attracted to this enchantress, Geralt."

The witcher smiled sadly.

"And the girl?" Yarpen indicated Ciri with his head as she wriggled under the sheepskin. "Yours?"

"Mine," he replied without thinking. "Mine, Zigrin."

The dawn was grey, wet, and smelled of night rain and morning mist. Ciri felt she had slept no more than a few minutes, as though she had been woken up the very minute she laid her head down on the sacks heaped on the wagon.

Geralt was just settling Triss down next to her, having brought her in from another enforced expedition into the woods. The rugs cocooning the enchantress sparkled with dew. Geralt had dark circles under his eyes. Ciri knew he had not closed them for an instant – Triss had run a fever through the night and suffered greatly.

"Did I wake you? Sorry. Sleep, Ciri. It's still early."

"What's happening with Triss? How is she?"

"Better," moaned the magician. "Better, but . . . Listen, Geralt . . . I'd like to—"

"Yes?" The witcher leaned over but Triss was already asleep. He straightened himself, stretched.

"Geralt," whispered Ciri, "are they going to let us travel on the wagon?"

"We'll see." He bit his lip. "Sleep while you can. Rest."

He jumped down off the wagon. Ciri heard the sound

of the camp packing up – horses stamping, harnesses ringing, poles squeaking, swingle-trees grating, and talking and cursing. And then, nearby, Yarpen Zigrin's hoarse voice and the calm voice of the tall man called Wenck. And the cold voice of Geralt. She raised herself and carefully peered out from behind the canvas.

"I have no categorical interdictions on this matter," declared Wenck.

"Excellent." The dwarf brightened. "So the matter's settled?"

The commissar raised his hand a little, indicating that he had not yet finished. He was silent for a while, and Geralt and Yarpin waited patiently.

"Nevertheless," Wenck said finally, "when it comes to the safe arrival of this caravan, it's my head on the line."

Again he said nothing. This time no one interrupted. There was no question about it – one had to get used to long intervals between sentences when speaking to the commissar.

"For its safe arrival," he continued after a moment. "And for its timely arrival. Caring for this sick woman might slow down the march."

"We're ahead of schedule on the route," Yarpen assured him, after a significant pause. "We're ahead of time, Wenck, sir, we won't miss the deadline. And as for safety . . . I don't think the witcher's company will harm that. The Trail leads through the woods right up to the Lixela, and to the right and left there's a wild forest. And rumour has it all sorts of evil creatures roam the forest."

"Indeed," the commissar agreed. Looking the witcher straight in the eye, he seemed to be weighing out every single word. "One can come across certain evil creatures in Kaedwen forests, lately incited by other evil creatures. They could jeopardise our safety. King Henselt, knowing this, empowered me to recruit volunteers to join our armed escort. Geralt? That would solve your problem."

The witcher's silence lasted a long while, longer than Wenck's entire speech, interspersed though it had been with regular pauses.

"No," he said finally. "No, Wenck. Let us put this clearly. I am prepared to repay the help given Lady Merigold, but not in this manner. I can groom the horses, carry water and firewood, even cook. But I will not enter the king's service as a soldier. Please don't count on my sword. I have no intention of killing those, as you call them, evil creatures on the order of other creatures whom I do not consider to be any better."

Ciri heard Yarpen Zigrin hiss loudly and cough into his rolled-up sleeve. Wenck stared at the witcher calmly.

"I see," he stated dryly. "I like clear situations. All right then. Zigrin, see to it that the speed of our progress does not slow. As for you, Geralt . . . I know you will prove to be useful and helpful in a way you deem fit. It would be an affront to both of us if I were to treat your good stead as payment for aid offered to a suffering woman. Is she feeling better today?"

The witcher gave a nod which seemed, to Ciri, to be somewhat deeper and politer than usual. Wenck's expression did not change.

"That pleases me," he said after a normal pause. "In taking Lady Merigold aboard a wagon in my convoy I take on the responsibility for her health, comfort and safety. Zigrin, give the command to march out."

"Wenck."

"Yes, Geralt?"

"Thank you."

The commissar bowed his head, a bit more deeply and politely, it seemed to Ciri, than the usual, perfunctory politeness required.

Yarpen Zigrin ran the length of the column, giving orders and instructions loudly, after which he clambered onto the coachman's box, shouted and whipped the horses with the reins. The wagon jolted and rattled along the forest trail. The bump woke Triss up but Ciri reassured her and changed the compress on her forehead. The rattling had a soporific effect and the magician was soon asleep; Ciri, too, fell to dozing.

When she woke the sun was already high. She peered out between the barrels and packages. The wagon she was in was at the vanguard of the convoy. The one following them was being driven by a dwarf with a red kerchief tied around his neck. From conversations between the dwarves, she had gathered that his name was Paulie Dahlberg. Next to him sat his brother Regan. She also saw Wenck riding a horse, in the company of two bailiffs.

Roach, Geralt's mare, tethered to the wagon, greeted her with a quiet neigh. She couldn't see her chestnut anywhere or Triss's dun. No doubt they were at the rear, with the convoy's spare horses.

Geralt was sitting on the coachman's box next to Yarpen. They were talking quietly, drinking beer from a barrel perched between them. Ciri pricked up her ears but soon grew bored – the discussion concerned politics and was mainly about King Henselt's intentions and plans, and some special service or missions to do with secretly aiding his neighbour, King Demavend of Aedirn, who was being threatened by war. Geralt expressed interest about how five wagons of salted fish could help Aedirn's defence. Yarpen, ignoring the gibe in Geralt's voice, explained that some species of fish were so valuable that a few wagon-loads would suffice to pay an armoured company for a year, and each new armoured company was a considerable help. Geralt was surprised that the aid had to be quite so secretive, to which the dwarf replied that was why the secret was a secret.

Triss tossed in her sleep, shook the compress off and talked indistinctly to herself. She demanded that someone called Kevyn kept his hands to himself, and immediately after that declared that destiny cannot be avoided. Finally, having stated that everyone, absolutely everyone, is a mutant to a certain degree, she fell into a peaceful sleep.

Ciri also felt sleepy but was brought to her senses by Yarpen's chuckle, as he reminded Geralt of their past adventures. This one concerned a hunt for a golden dragon who instead of allowing itself to be hunted down had counted the hunters' bones and then eaten a cobbler called Goatmuncher. Ciri began to listen with greater interest.

Geralt asked about what had happened to the Slashers but Yarpen didn't know. Yarpen, in turn, was curious about a woman called Yennefer, at which Geralt grew oddly uncommunicative. The dwarf drank more beer and started to complain that Yennefer still bore him a grudge although a good few years had gone by since those days.

"I came across her at the market in Gors Velen," he recounted. "She barely noticed me – she spat like a she-cat and insulted my deceased mother horribly. I fled for all I was worth, but she shouted after me that she'd catch up with me one day and make grass grow out of my arse."

Ciri giggled, imagining Yarpen with the grass. Geralt grunted something about women and their impulsive natures – which the dwarf considered far too mild a description for maliciousness, obstinacy and vindictiveness. Geralt did not take up the subject and Ciri fell into dozing once more.

This time she was woken by raised voices. Yarpen's voice to be exact – he was yelling.

"Oh yes! So you know! That's what I've decided!"

"Quieter," said the witcher calmly. "There's a sick woman in the wagon. Understand, I'm not criticising your decisions or your resolutions . . ."

"No, of course not," the dwarf interrupted sarcastically. "You're just smiling knowingly about them."

"Yarpen, I'm warning you, as one friend to another: both sides despise those who sit on the fence, or at best they treat them with suspicion."

"I'm not sitting. I'm unambiguously declaring myself to be on one side."

"But you'll always remain a dwarf for that side. Someone who's different. An outsider. While for the other side . . ."

He broke off.

"Well!" growled Yarpen, turning away. "Well, go on, what are you waiting for? Call me a traitor and a dog on a human leash who for a handful of silver and a bowl of lousy food, is prepared to be set against his rebelling kinsmen who are fighting for freedom. Well, go on, spit it out. I don't like insinuations."

"No, Yarpen," said Geralt quietly. "No. I'm not going to spit anything out."

"Ah, you're not?" The dwarf whipped the horses.

"You don't feel like it? You prefer to stare and smile? Not a word to me, eh? But you could say it to Wenck! 'Please don't count on my sword.' Oh, so haughtily, nobly and proudly said! Shove your haughtiness up a dog's arse, and your bloody pride with it!"

"I just wanted to be honest. I don't want to get mixed up in this conflict. I want to remain neutral."

"It's impossible!" yelled Yarpen. "It's impossible to remain neutral, don't you understand that? No, you don't understand anything. Oh, get off my wagon, get on your horse, and get out of my sight, with your arrogant neutrality. You get on my nerves."

Geralt turned away. Ciri held her breath in anticipation. But the witcher didn't say a word. He stood and jumped from the wagon, swiftly, softly and nimbly. Yarpen waited for him to untether his mare from the ladder, then whipped his horses once again, growling something incomprehensible, sounding terrifying under his breath.

She stood up to jump down too, and find her chestnut. The dwarf turned and measured her with a reluctant eye.

"And you're just a nuisance, too, little madam," he snorted angrily. "All we need are ladies and girls, damn it. I can't even take a piss from the box – I have to stop the cart and go into the bushes!"

Ciri put her hands on her hips, shook her ashen fringe and turned up her nose.

"Is that so?" she shrilled, enraged. "Drink less beer, Zigrin, and then you won't have to!"

"My beer's none of your shitin' business, you chit!"

"Don't yell, Triss has just fallen asleep!"

"It's my wagon! I'll yell if I want to!"

"Stumpy!"

"What? You impertinent brat!"

"Stump!"

"I'll show you stump . . . Oh, damn it! Pprrr!"

The dwarf leaned far back, pulling at the reins at the very last moment, just as the two horses were on the point of stepping over a log blocking their way. Yarpen stood up in the box and, swearing in both human and Dwarvish, whistling and roaring, brought the cart to a halt. Dwarves and humans alike, leaping from their wagons, ran up and helped lead the horses to the clear path, tugging them on by their halters and harnesses.

"Dozing off, eh Yarpen?" growled Paulie Dahlberg as he approached. "Bloody hell, if you'd ridden over that the axle would be done for, and the wheels shattered to hell. Damn it, what were you—"

"Piss off, Paulie!" roared Yarpen Zigrin and furiously lashed the horses' hindquarters with the reins.

"You were lucky," said Ciri, ever so sweetly, squeezing onto the box next to the dwarf. "As you can see, it's better to have a witcher-girl on your wagon than to travel alone. I warned you just in time. But if you'd been in the middle of pissing from the box and ridden onto that log, well, well. It's scary to think what might have happened—"

"Are you going to be quiet?"

"I'm not saying any more. Not a word."

She lasted less than a minute.

"Zigrin, sir?"

"I'm not a sir." The dwarf nudged her with his elbow and bared his teeth. "I'm Yarpen. Is that clear? We'll lead the horses together, right?"

"Right. Can I hold the reins?"

"If you must. Wait, not like that. Pass them over your

index finger and hold them down with your thumb, like this. The same with the left. Don't tug them, don't pull too hard."

"Is that right?"

"Right."

"Yarpen?"

"Huh?"

"What does it mean, 'remain neutral'?"

"To be indifferent," he muttered reluctantly. "Don't let the reins hang down. Pull the left one closer to yourself!"

"What's indifferent? Indifferent to what?"

The dwarf leaned far out and spat under the wagon.

"If the Scoia'tael attack us, your Geralt intends to stand by and look calmly on as they cut our throats. You'll probably stand next to him, because it'll be a demonstration class. Today's subject: the witcher's behaviour in the face of conflict between intelligent races."

"I don't understand."

"That doesn't surprise me in the least."

"Is that why you quarrelled with him and were angry? Who are these Scoia'tael anyway? These . . . Squirrels?"

"Ciri," Yarpen tussled his beard violently, "these aren't matters for the minds of little girls."

"Aha, now you're angry at me. I'm not little at all. I heard what the soldiers in the fort said about the Squirrels. I saw . . . I saw two dead elves. And the knight said they also kill. And that it's not just elves amongst them. There are dwarves too."

"I know," said Yarpen sourly.

"And you're a dwarf."

"There's no doubt about that."

"So why are you afraid of the Squirrels? It seems they only fight humans."

"It's not so simple as that." He grew solemn. "Unfortunately."

Ciri stayed silent for a long time, biting her lower lip and wrinkling her nose.

"Now I know," she said suddenly. "The Squirrels are fighting for freedom. And although you're a dwarf, you're King Henselt's special secret servant on a human leash."

Yarpen snorted, wiped his nose on his sleeve and leaned out of the box to check that Wenck had not ridden up too close. But the commissar was far away, engaged in conversation with Geralt.

"You've got pretty good hearing, girl, like a marmot." He grinned broadly. "You're also a bit too bright for someone destined to give birth, cook and spin. You think you know everything, don't you? That's because you're a brat. Don't pull silly faces. Faces like that don't make you look any older, just uglier than usual. You've grasped the nature of the Scoia'taels quickly, you like the slogans. You know why you understand them so well? Because the Scoia'taels are brats too. They're little snotheads who don't understand that they're being egged on, that someone's taking advantage of their childish stupidity by feeding them slogans about freedom."

"But they really are fighting for freedom." Ciri raised her head and gazed at the dwarf with wide-open green eyes. "Like the dryads in the Brokilon woods. They kill people because people . . . some people are harming them. Because this used to be your country, the dwarves' and the elves' and those . . . halflings', gnomes' and other . . . And now there are people here so the elves—"

"Elves!" snorted Yarpen. "They – to be accurate – happen to be strangers just as much as you humans, although they arrived in their white ships a good thousand years before you. Now they're competing with each other to offer us friendship, suddenly we're all brothers, now they're grinning and saying: 'we, kinsmen', 'we, the Elder Races'. But before, shi— Hm, hm . . . Before, their arrows used to whistle past our ears when we—"

"So the first on earth were dwarves?"

"Gnomes, to be honest. As far as this part of the world is concerned – because the world is unimaginably huge, Ciri."

"I know. I saw a map—"

"You couldn't have. No one's drawn a map like that, and I doubt they will in the near future. No one knows what exists beyond the Mountains of Fire and the Great Sea. Even elves, although they claim they know everything. They know shit all, I tell you."

"Hmm . . . But now . . . There are far more people than . . . Than there are you."

"Because you multiply like rabbits." The dwarf ground his teeth. "You'd do nothing but screw day in day out, without discrimination, with just anyone and anywhere. And it's enough for your women to just sit on a man's trousers and it makes their bellies swell . . . Why have you gone so red, crimson as a poppy? You wanted to know, didn't you? So you've got the honest truth and faithful history of a world where he who shatters the skulls of others most efficiently and swells women's bellies fastest reigns. And it's just as hard to compete with you people in murdering as it is in screwing—"

"Yarpen," said Geralt coldly, riding up on Roach. "Restrain yourself a little, if you please, with your choice of words. And Ciri, stop playing at being a coachwoman and have a care for Triss, check if she's awake and needs anything."

"I've been awake for a long time," the magician said weakly from the depths of the wagon. "But I didn't want to . . . interrupt this interesting conversation. Don't disturb them, Geralt. I'd like . . . to learn more about the role of screwing in the evolution of society."

"Can I heat some water? Triss wants to wash."

"Go ahead," agreed Yarpen Zigrin. "Xavier, take the spit off the fire, our hare's had enough. Hand me the cauldron, Ciri. Oh, look at you, it's full to the brim! Did you lug this great weight from the stream by yourself?"

"I'm strong."

The elder of the Dahlberg brothers burst out laughing.

"Don't judge her by appearances, Paulie," said Yarpen seriously as he skilfully divided the roasted grey hare into portions. "There's nothing to laugh at here. She's skinny but I can see she's a robust and resilient lass. She's like a leather belt: thin, but it can't be torn apart in your hands. And if you were to hang yourself on it, it would bear your weight, too."

No one laughed. Ciri squatted next to the dwarves sprawled around the fire. This time Yarpen Zigrin and his four "boys" had lit their own fire at the camp because they did not intend to share the hare which Xavier Moran had shot. For them alone there was just enough for one, at most two, mouthfuls each.

"Add some wood to the fire," said Yarpen, licking his fingers. "The water will heat quicker."

"That water's a stupid idea," stated Regan Dahlberg, spitting out a bone. "Washing can only harm you when you're sick. When you're healthy, too, come to that. You remember old Schrader? His wife once told him to wash, and Schrader went and died soon afterwards."

"Because a rabid dog bit him."

"If he hadn't washed, the dog wouldn't have bitten him."

"I think," said Ciri, checking the temperature of the water in the cauldron with her finger, "it's excessive to wash every day too. But Triss asked for it – she even started crying once . . . So Geralt and I—"

"We know." The elder Dahlberg nodded. "But that a witcher should . . . I'm constantly amazed. Hey, Zigrin, if you had a woman would you wash her and comb her hair? Would you carry her into the bushes if she had to—"

"Shut up, Paulie." Yarpen cut him short. "Don't say anything against that witcher, because he's a good fellow."

"Am I saying anything? I'm only surprised—"

"Triss," Ciri butted in cheekily, "is *not* his woman."

"I'm all the more surprised."

"You're all the more a blockhead, you mean," Yarpen summed up. "Ciri, pour a bit of water in to boil. We'll infuse some more saffron and poppy seeds for the magician. She felt better today, eh?"

"Probably did," murmured Yannick Brass. "We only had to stop the convoy six times for her. I know it wouldn't do to deny aid on the trail, and he's a prick who thinks otherwise. And he who denies it would be an arch-prick and base son-of-a-bitch. But we've been in these woods too long, far too long, I tell you. We're tempting fate, damn it, we're tempting fate too much, boys. It's not safe here. The Scoia'tael—"

"Spit that word out, Yannick."

"Ptoo, ptoo. Yarpen, fighting doesn't frighten me, and a bit of blood's nothing new but . . . If it comes to fighting our own . . . Damn it! Why did this happen to us? This friggin' load ought to be transported by a hundred friggin' cavalrymen, not us! The devil take those know-alls from Ard Carraigh, may they—"

"Shut up, I said. And pass me the pot of kasha. The hare was a snack, damn it, now we have to eat something. Ciri, will you eat with us?"

"Of course."

For a long while all that could be heard was the smacking of lips, munching, and the crunch of wooden spoons hitting the pot.

"Pox on it," said Paulie Dahlberg and gave a long burp. "I could still eat some more."

"Me, too," declared Ciri and burped too, delighted by the dwarves' unpretentious manners.

"As long as it's not kasha," said Xavier Moran. "I can't stomach those milled oats any more. I've gone off salted meat, too."

"So gorge yourself on grass, if you've got such delicate taste-buds."

"Or rip the bark off the birch with your teeth. Beavers do it and survive."

"A beaver – now that's something I could eat."

"As for me, a fish." Paulie lost himself in dreams as he crunched on a husk pulled from his beard. "I've a fancy for a fish, I can tell you."

"So let's catch some fish."

"Where?" growled Yannick Brass. "In the bushes?"

"In the stream."

"Some stream. You can piss to the other side. What sort of fish could be in there?"

"There are fish." Ciri licked her spoon clean and slipped it into the top of her boot. "I saw them when I went to get the water. But they're sick or something, those fish. They've got a rash. Black and red spots—"

"Trout!" roared Paulie, spitting crumbs of husk. "Well, boys, to the stream double-quick! Regan! Get your breeches down! We'll turn them into a fishing-trap."

"Why mine?"

"Pull them off, at the double, or I'll wallop you, snot-head! Didn't mother say you have to listen to me?"

"Hurry up if you want to go fishing because dusk is just round the corner," said Yarpen. "Ciri, is the water hot yet? Leave it, leave it, you'll burn yourself and get dirty from the cauldron. I know you're strong but let me – I'll carry it."

Geralt was already waiting for them; they could see his white hair through the gap in the canvas covering the wagon from afar. The dwarf poured the water into the bucket.

"Need any help, witcher?"

"No, thank you, Yarpen. Ciri will help."

Triss was no longer running a high temperature but she was extremely weak. Geralt and Ciri were, by now, efficient at undressing and washing her. They had also learned to temper her ambitious but, at present, unrealistic attempts to manage on her own. They coped exceptionally well – he supported the enchantress in his arms, Ciri washed and dried her. Only one thing had started to surprise and annoy Ciri – Triss, in her opinion, snuggled up to Geralt too tightly. This time she was even trying to kiss him.

Geralt indicated the magician's saddlebags with his head. Ciri understood immediately because this, too, was part of the ritual – Triss always demanded to have her hair combed. She found the comb and knelt down beside her. Triss, lowering her head towards her, put her arms around the witcher. In Ciri's opinion, definitely a little too tightly.

"Oh, Geralt," she sobbed. "I so regret . . . I so regret that what was between us—"

"Triss, please."

". . . it should have happened . . . now. When I'm better . . . It would be entirely different . . . I could . . . I could even—"

"Triss."

"I envy Yennefer . . . I envy her you—"

"Ciri, step out."

"But—"

"Go, please."

She jumped out of the wagon and straight onto Yarpen who was waiting, leaning against a wheel and pensively chewing a blade of grass. The dwarf put his arm around her. He did not need to lean over in order to do so, as Geralt did. He was no taller than her.

"Never make the same mistake, little witcher-girl," he murmured, indicating the wagon with his eyes. "If someone shows you compassion, sympathy and dedication, if they surprise you with integrity of character, value it but don't mistake it for . . . something else."

"It's not nice to eavesdrop."

"I know. And it's dangerous. I only just managed to jump aside when you threw out the suds from the bucket. Come on, let's go and see how many trout have jumped into Regan's breeches."

"Yarpen?"

"Huh?"

"I like you."

"And I like you, kid."

"But you're a dwarf. And I'm not."

"And what diff— Ah, the Scoia'tael. You're thinking about the Squirrels, aren't you? It's not giving you any peace, is it?"

Ciri freed herself from his heavy arm.

"Nor you," she said. "Nor any of the others. I can plainly see that."

The dwarf said nothing.

"Yarpen?"

"Yes?"

"Who's right? The Squirrels or you? Geralt wants to be . . . neutral. You serve King Henselt even though you're a dwarf. And the knight in the fort shouted that everybody's our enemy and that everyone's got to be . . . Everyone. Even the children. Why, Yarpen? Who's right?"

"I don't know," said the dwarf with some effort. "I'm not omniscient. I'm doing what I think right. The Squirrels have taken up their weapons and gone into the woods. 'Humans to the sea,' they're shouting, not realising that their catchy slogan was fed them by Nilfgaardian emissaries. Not understanding that the slogan is not aimed at them but plainly at humans, that it's meant to ignite human hatred, not fire young elves to battle. I understood – that's why I consider the Scoia'tael's actions criminally stupid. What to do? Maybe in a few years time I'll be called a traitor who sold out and they'll be heroes . . . Our history, the history of our world, has seen events turn out like that."

He fell silent, ruffled his beard. Ciri also remained silent.

"Elirena . . ." he muttered suddenly. "If Elirena was a hero, if what she did is heroism, then that's just too bad. Let them call me a traitor and a coward. Because I, Yarpen Zigrin, coward, traitor and renegade, state that we should not kill each other. I state that we ought to live. Live in such a way that we don't, later, have to ask anyone for forgiveness. The heroic Elirena . . . She had to ask. Forgive me, she begged, forgive me. To hell with that! It's better to die than to live in the knowledge that you've done something that needs forgiveness."

Again he fell quiet. Ciri did not ask the questions pressing to her lips. She instinctively felt she should not.

"We have to live next to each other," Yarpen continued. "We and you, humans. Because we simply don't have any other option. We've known this for two hundred years and we've been working towards it for over a hundred. You want to know why I entered King Henselt's service, why I made such a decision? I can't allow all that work to go to waste. For over a hundred years we've been trying to come to terms with the humans. The halflings, gnomes, us, even the elves – I'm not talking about rusalkas, nymphs and sylphs, they've always been savages, even when you weren't here. Damn it all, it took a hundred years but, somehow or other, we managed to live a common life, next to each other, together. We man-

aged to partially convince humans that we're not so very
different—"

"We're not different at all, Yarpen."

The dwarf turned abruptly.

"We're not different at all," repeated Ciri. "After all,
you think and feel like Geralt. And like . . . like I do. We
eat the same things, from the same pot. You help Triss
and so do I. You had a grandmother and I had a grandmother . . . My grandmother was killed by the Nilfgaardians. In Cintra."

"And mine by the humans," the dwarf said with some
effort. "In Brugge. During the pogrom."

"Riders!" shouted one of Wenck's advance guards.
"Riders ahead!"

The commissar trotted up to Yarpen's wagon and Geralt approached from the other side.

"Get in the back, Ciri," he said brusquely. "Get off the
box and get in the back! Stay with Triss."

"I can't see anything from there!"

"Don't argue!" growled Yarpen. "Scuttle back there
and be quick about it! And hand me the martel. It's under
the sheepskin."

"This?" Ciri held up a heavy, nasty-looking object, like
a hammer with a sharp, slightly curved hook at its head.

"That's it," confirmed the dwarf. He slipped the handle
into the top of his boot and laid the axe on his knees.
Wenck, seeming calm, watched the highway while shel-
tering his eyes with his hand.

"Light cavalry from Ban Gleán," he surmised after
a while. "The so-called Dun Banner – I recognise them
by their cloaks and beaver hats. Remain calm. And stay

sharp. Cloaks and beaver hats can be pretty quick to change owners."

The riders approached swiftly. There were about ten of them. Ciri saw Paulie Dahlberg, in the wagon behind her, place two readied crossbows on his knee and Regan covered them with a cloak. Ciri crept stealthily out from under the canvas, hiding behind Yarpen's broad back. Triss tried to raise herself, swore and collapsed against her bedding.

"Halt!" shouted the first of the riders, no doubt their leader. "Who are you? From whence and to where do you ride?"

"Who asks?" Wenck calmly pulled himself upright in the saddle. "And on whose authority?"

"King Henselt's army, inquisitive sir! Lance-corporal Zyvik asks, and he is unused to asking twice! So answer at the double! Who are you?"

"Quartermaster's service of the King's army."

"Anyone could claim that! I see no one here bearing the King's colours!"

"Come closer, lance-corporal, and examine this ring."

"Why flash a ring at me?" The soldier grimaced. "Am I supposed to know every ring, or something? Anyone could have a ring like that. Some significant sign!"

Yarpen Zigrin stood up in the box, raised his axe and with a swift move pushed it under the soldier's nose.

"And this sign," he snarled. "You know it? Smell it and remember how it smells."

The lance-corporal yanked the reins and turned his horse.

"Threaten me, do you?" he roared. "Me? I'm in the king's service!"

"And so are we," said Wenck quietly. "And have been for longer than you at that, I'm sure. I warn you, trooper, don't overdo it."

"I'm on guard here! How am I to know who you are?"

"You saw the ring," drawled the commissar. "And if you didn't recognise the sign on the jewel then I wonder who *you* are. The colours of your unit bear the same emblem so you ought to know it."

The soldier clearly restrained himself, influenced, no doubt, equally by Wenck's calm words and the serious, determined faces peering from the escort's carts.

"Hmm . . ." he said, shifting his fur hat towards his left ear. "Fine. But if you truly are who you claim to be, you will not, I trust, have anything against my having a look to see what you carry in the wagons."

"We will indeed." Wenck frowned. "And very much, at that. Our load is not your business, lance-corporal. Besides, I do not understand what you think you may find there."

"You do not understand." The soldier nodded, lowering his hand towards the hilt of his sword. "So I shall tell you, sir. Human trafficking is forbidden and there is no lack of scoundrels selling slaves to the Nilfgaardians. If I find humans in stocks in your wagons, you will not convince me that you are in the king's service. Even if you were to show me a dozen rings."

"Fine," said Wenck dryly. "If it is slaves you are looking for, then look. You have my permission."

The soldier cantered to the wagon in the middle, leaned over from the saddle and raised the canvas.

"What's in those barrels?"

"What do you expect? Prisoners?" sneered Yannick Brass, sprawled in the coachman's box.

"I am asking you what's in them, so answer me!"

"Salt fish."

"And in those trunks there?" The warrior rode up to the next wagon and kicked the side.

"Hooves," snapped Paulie Dahlberg. "And there, in the back, are buffalo skins."

"So I see." The lance-corporal waved his hand, smacked his lips at his horse, rode up to the vanguard and peered into Yarpen's wagon.

"And who is that woman lying there?"

Triss Merigold smiled weakly, raised herself to her elbow and traced a short, complicated sign with her hand.

"Who am I?" she asked in a quiet voice. "But you can't see me at all."

The soldier winked nervously, shuddered slightly.

"Salt fish," he said, convinced, lowering the canvas. "All is in order. And this child?"

"Dried mushrooms," said Ciri, looking at him impudently. The soldier fell silent, frozen with his mouth open.

"What's that?" he asked after a while, frowning. "What?"

"Have you concluded your inspection, warrior?" Wenck showed cool interest as he rode up on the other side of the cart. The soldier could barely look away from Ciri's green eyes.

"I have concluded it. Drive on, and may the gods guide you. But be on your guard. Two days ago, the Scoia'tael wiped out an entire mounted patrol up by Badger Ravine.

It was a strong, large command. It's true that Badger Ravine is far from here but elves travel through the forest faster than the wind. We were ordered to round them up, but how do you catch an elf? It's like trying to catch the wind—"

"Good, enough, we're not interested," the commissar interrupted him brusquely. "Time presses and we still have a long journey ahead of us."

"Fare you well then. Hey, follow me!"

"You heard, Geralt?" snarled Yarpen Zigrin, watching the patrol ride away. "There are bloody Squirrels in the vicinity. I felt it. I've got this tingling feeling in my back all the time as if some archer was already aiming at me. No, damn it, we can't travel blindly as we've been doing until now, whistling away, dozing and sleepily farting. We have to know what lies ahead of us. Listen, I've an idea."

Ciri pulled her chestnut up sharply, and then launched into a gallop, leaning low in the saddle. Geralt, engrossed in conversation with Wenck, suddenly sat up straight.

"Don't run wild!" he called. "No madness, girl! Do you want to break your neck? And don't go too far—"

She heard no more – she had torn ahead too fiercely. She had done it on purpose, not wanting to listen to the daily cautions. Not too quickly, not too fiercely, Ciri! *Pah-pah*. Don't go too far! *Pah-pah-pah*. Be careful! *Pah-pah! Exactly as if I were a child*, she thought. *And I'm almost thirteen and have a swift chestnut beneath me and a sharp sword across my back. And I'm not afraid of anything!*

And it's spring!

"Hey, careful, you'll burn your backside!"

Yarpen Zigrin. Another know-it-all. *Pah-pah!*

Further, further, at a gallop, along the bumpy path, through the green, green grasses and bushes, through the silver puddles, through the damp golden sand, through the feathery ferns. A frightened fallow deer disappeared into the woods, flashing the black and white lantern of its tail and rump as it skipped away. Birds soared up from the trees – colourful jays and bee-eaters, screaming black magpies with their funny tails. Water splashed beneath her horse's hooves in the puddles and the clefts.

Further, even further! The horse, which had been trudging sluggishly behind the wagon for too long, carried her joyously and briskly; happy to be allowed speed, it ran fluidly, muscles playing between her thighs, damp mane thrashing her face. The horse extended its neck as Ciri gave it free rein. *Further, dear horse, don't feel the bit, further, at the gallop, at the gallop, sharp, sharp! Spring!*

She slowed and glanced back. There, alone at last. Far away at last. No one was going to tell her off anymore, remind her of something, demand her attention, threaten that this would be the end of such rides. Alone at last, free, at ease and independent.

Slower. A light trot. After all, this wasn't just a fun ride, she also had responsibilities. Ciri was, after all, a mounted foray now, a patrol, an advance guard. *Ha*, she thought, looking around, *the safety of the entire convoy depends on me now. They're all waiting impatiently for me to return and report: the way is clear and passable, I didn't see anyone – there are no traces of wheels or hooves. I'll report it, and thin Master Wenck with his cold, blue eyes will nod his head gravely, Yarpen Zigrin will bare his yellow, horse teeth, Paulie Dahlberg will shout: "Well done, little one!" and Geralt will smile faintly. He'll smile, although he very rarely smiles recently.*

Ciri looked around and took a mental note. Two felled birches – no problem. A heap of branches – nothing the wagons couldn't pass. A cleft washed out by the rain – a small obstacle, the wheels of the first wagon will run over it, the others will follow in the ruts. A huge clearing – a good place for a rest . . .

Traces? What traces can there be here? There's no one here. There's the forest. There are birds screeching amidst fresh, green leaves. A red fox runs leisurely across the path . . . And everything smells of spring.

The track broke off halfway up the hill, disappeared in the sandy ravine, wound through the crooked pines which clung to the slopes. Ciri abandoned the path and, wanting to scrutinise the area from a height, climbed the steep slope. And so she could touch the wet, sweet-smelling leaves . . .

She dismounted, threw the reins over a snag in a tree and slowly strolled among the junipers which covered the hill. On the other side of the hill was an open space, gaping in the thick of the forest like a hole bitten out of the trees – left, no doubt, after a fire which had raged here a very long time ago, for there was no sign of blackened or charred remains, everywhere was green with low birches and little fir trees. The trail, as far as the eye could see, seemed clear and passable.

And safe.

What are they afraid of? she thought. *The Scoia'tael?*

But what was there to be afraid of? I'm not frightened of elves. I haven't done anything to them.

Elves. The Squirrels. Scoia'tael.

Before Geralt had ordered her to leave, Ciri had managed to take a look at the corpses in the fort. She remembered one in particular – his face covered by hair stuck together with darkened blood, his neck unnaturally twisted and bent. Pulled back in a ghastly, set grimace, his upper lip revealed teeth, very white and very tiny, non-human. She remembered the elf's boots, ruined and reaching up to the knees, laced at the bottom and fastened at the top with many wrought buckles.

Elves who kill humans and die in battles themselves. Geralt says you have to remain neutral . . . And Yarpen says you have to behave in such a way that you don't have to ask for forgiveness . . .

She kicked a molehill and, lost in thought, dug her heel into the sand.

Who and whom, whom and what should one forgive?

The Squirrels kill humans. And Nilfgaard pays them for it. Uses them. Incites them. Nilfgaard.

Ciri had not forgotten – although she very much wanted to forget – what had happened in Cintra. The wandering, the despair, the fear, the hunger and the pain. The apathy and torpor, which came later, much later when the druids from Transriver had found her and taken her in. She remembered it all as though through a mist, and she wanted to stop remembering it.

But it came back. Came back in her thoughts, into her dreams. Cintra. The thundering of horses and the savage cries, corpses, flames . . . And the black knight in his winged helmet . . . And later . . . Cottages in Trans-

189

river . . . A flame-blackened chimney amongst charred ruins . . . Next to it, by an unscathed well, a black cat licking a terrible burn on its side. A well . . . A sweep . . . A bucket . . .

A bucket full of blood.

Ciri wiped her face, looked down at her hand, taken aback. Her palm was wet. The girl sniffed and wiped the tears with her sleeve.

Neutrality? Indifference? She wanted to scream. *A witcher looking on indifferently? No! A witcher has to defend people. From the leshy, the vampire, the werewolf. And not only from them. He has to defend people from every evil. And in Transriver I saw what evil is.*

A witcher has to defend and save. To defend men so that they aren't hung on trees by their hands, aren't impaled and left to die. To defend fair girls from being spread-eagled between stakes rammed into the ground. Defend children so they aren't slaughtered and thrown into a well. Even a cat burned alive in a torched barn deserves to be defended. That's why I'm going to become a witcher, that's why I've got a sword, to defend people like those in Sodden and Transriver – because they don't have swords, don't know the steps, half-turns, dodges and pirouettes. No one has taught them how to fight, they are defenceless and helpless in face of the werewolf and the Nilfgaardian marauder. They're teaching me to fight so that I can defend the helpless. And that's what I'm going to do. Never will I be neutral. Never will I be indifferent.

Never!

She didn't know what warned her – whether it was the sudden silence which fell over the forest like a cold shadow, or a movement caught out of the corner of her eye. But she reacted in a flash, instinctively – with a reaction she had learnt in the woods of Transriver when, escaping from Cintra, she had raced against death. She fell to the ground, crawled under a juniper bush and froze, motionless. *Just let the horse not neigh*, she thought.

On the other side of the ravine something moved again; she saw a silhouette show faintly, hazily amidst the leaves. An elf peered cautiously from the thicket. Having thrown the hood from his head, he looked around for a moment, pricked up his ears and then, noiselessly and swiftly, moved along the ridge. After him, two more leaned out. And then others moved. Many of them. In single file. About half were on horseback – these rode slowly, straight in their saddles, focused and alert. For a moment she saw them all clearly and precisely as, in utter silence, they flowed across a bright breach in the wall of trees, framed against the background of the sky – before they disappeared, dissolved in the shimmering shadows of the wild forest. They vanished without a rustle or a sound, like ghosts. No horse tapped its hoof or snorted, no branch cracked under foot or hoof. The weapons slung across them did not clang.

They disappeared but Ciri did not move. She lay flat on the ground under the juniper bush, trying to breathe as quietly as possible. She knew that a frightened bird or animal could give her away, and a bird or animal could be frightened by any sound or movement – even the slightest, the most careful. She got up only when the woods had grown perfectly calm and the magpies chattered again among the trees where the elves had disappeared.

She rose only to find herself in a strong grip. A black

leather glove fell across her mouth, muffled the scream of fear.

"Be quiet."

"Geralt?"

"Quiet, I said."

"You saw them?"

"I did."

"It's them . . ." she whispered. "The Scoia'tael. Isn't it?"

"Yes. Quick back to the horses. Watch your feet."

They rode carefully and silently down the slope without returning to the trail; they remained in the thicket. Geralt looked around, alert. He did not allow her to ride independently; he did not give her the chestnut's reins; he led the horse himself.

"Ciri," he said suddenly. "Not a word about what we saw. Not to Yarpen, not to Wenck. Not to anybody. Understand?"

"No," she grunted, lowering her head. "I don't understand. Why shouldn't I say anything? They have to be warned. Whose side are we on, Geralt? Whose side are we against? Who's our friend and who's our enemy?"

"We'll part with the convoy tomorrow," he said after a moment's silence. "Triss is almost recovered. We'll say goodbye and go our own way. We have problems of our own, our own worries and our own difficulties. Then, I hope, you'll finally stop dividing the inhabitants of this world into friends and enemies."

"We're to be . . . neutral? Indifferent, is that right? And if they attack . . ."

"They won't."

"And if—"

"Listen to me." He turned to her. "Why do you think that such a vital load of gold and silver, King Henselt's secret aid for Aedirn, is being escorted by dwarves and not humans? I saw an elf watching us from a tree yesterday. I heard them pass by our camp during the night. The Scoia'tael will not attack the dwarves, Ciri."

"But they're here," she muttered. "They are. They're moving around, surrounding us . . ."

"I know why they're here. I'll show you."

He turned the horse abruptly and threw the reins to her. She kicked the chestnut with her heels and moved away faster, but he motioned for her to stay behind him. They cut across the trail and reentered the wild forest. The witcher led, Ciri following in his tracks. Neither said anything. Not for a long time.

"Look." Geralt held back his horse. "Look, Ciri."

"What is it?" she sighed.

"Shaerrawedd."

In front of them, as far as the woods allowed them to see, rose smoothly hewn blocks of granite and marble with blunt corners, worn away by the winds, decorated with patterns long leached out by the rains, cracked and shattered by frost, split by tree roots. Amongst the trunks broken columns flashed white, arcades, the remains of ornamental friezes entwined with ivy, and wrapped in a thick layer of green moss.

"This was . . . a castle?"

"A palace. The elves didn't build castles. Dismount, the horses won't manage in the rubble."

"Who destroyed it all? Humans?"

"No, they did. Before they left."

"Why?"

"They knew they wouldn't be coming back. It happened following their second clash with the humans, more than two hundred years ago. Before that, they used to leave towns untouched when they retreated. Humans used to build on the foundations left by the elves. That's how Novigrad, Oxenfurt, Wyzima, Tretogor, Maribor and Cidaris were built. And Cintra."

"Cintra?"

He confirmed it with a nod of the head, not taking his eyes off the ruins.

"They left," whispered Ciri, "but now they're coming back. Why?"

"To have a look."

"At what?"

Without a word he laid his hand on her shoulder and pushed her gently before him. They jumped down the marble stairs, climbing down holding on to the springy hazel, clusters of which had burst through every gap, every crevice in the moss-covered, cracked plates.

"This was the centre of the palace, its heart. A fountain."

"Here?" she asked, surprised, gazing at the dense thicket of alders and white birch trunks amongst the misshapen blocks and slabs. "Here? But there's nothing there."

"Come."

The stream feeding the fountain must have changed its course many times, patiently and constantly washing the marble blocks and alabaster plates which had sunk or fallen to form dams, once again changing the course of the current. As a result the whole area was divided up by shallow gullies. Here and there the water cascaded over the remains of the building, washing it clean of leaves, sand and litter. In these places, the marble, terracotta and mosaics were still as vibrant with colour, as fresh as if they had been lying there for three days, not two centuries.

Geralt leapt across the stream and went in amongst what remained of the columns. Ciri followed. They jumped off the ruined stairs and, lowering their heads, walked beneath the untouched arch of the arcade, half buried beneath a mound of earth. The witcher stopped and indicated with his hand. Ciri sighed loudly.

From rubble colourful with smashed terracotta grew an enormous rose bush covered with beautiful white-lilied flowers. Drops of dew as bright as silver glistened on the petals. The bush wove its shoots around a large slab of white stone and from it a sad, pretty face looked out at them; the downpours and snows had not yet managed to blur or wash away its delicate and noble features. It was a face which the chisels of plunderers digging out golden ornaments, mosaics and precious stones from the relief sculpture had not managed to disfigure.

"Aelirenn," said Geralt after a long silence.

"She's beautiful," whispered Ciri, grabbing him by the hand. The witcher didn't seem to notice. He stared at the sculpture and was far away, far away in a different world and time.

"Aelirenn," he repeated after a while. "Known as Eli-rena by dwarves and humans. She led them into battle two hundred years ago. The elders of the elves were against it, they knew they had no chance. That they would not be able to pick themselves up after the defeat. They wanted to save their people, wanted to survive. They decided to destroy their towns and retreat to the inaccessible, wild mountains . . . and to wait. Elves live a long time, Ciri. By our time scale they are almost eternal. They thought humans were something that would pass, like a drought, like a heavy winter, or a plague of locusts, after which comes rain, spring, a new harvest. They wanted to sit it out. Survive. They decided to destroy their towns and palaces, amongst them their pride – the beautiful Shaerrawedd. They wanted to weather out the storm, but Elirena . . . Elirena stirred up the young. They took up arms and followed her into their last desperate battle. And they were massacred. Mercilessly massacred."

Ciri did not say anything, staring at the beautiful, still face.

"They died with her name on their lips," the witcher continued quietly. "Repeating her challenge, her cry, they died for Shaerrawedd. Because Shaerrawedd was a symbol. They died for this stone and marble . . . and for Aelirenn. Just as she promised them, they died with dignity, heroically and honourably. They saved their honour but they brought nothing but ruin as a result, condemned their own race to annihilation. Their own people. You remember what Yarpen told you? Those who rule the world and those who die out? He explained it to you coarsely but truly. Elves live for a long time, but only their youngsters are fertile, only the young can have offspring. And practically all the elven youngsters had followed Elirena. They followed Aelirenn, the White Rose of Shaerrawedd. We are standing in the ruins of her palace, by the fountain whose waters she listened to in the evenings. And these . . . these were her flowers."

Ciri was silent. Geralt drew her to himself, put his arm around her.

"Do you know now why the Scoia'tael were here, do you see what they wanted to look at? And do you understand why the elven and dwarven young must not be allowed to be massacred once again? Do you understand why neither you nor I are permitted to have a hand in this massacre? These roses flower all year round. They ought to have grown wild by now, but they are more beautiful than any rose in a tended garden. Elves continue to come to Shaerrawedd, Ciri. A variety of elves. The impetuous and the foolish ones for whom the cracked stone is a symbol as well as the sensible ones for whom these immortal, forever reborn flowers are a symbol. Elves who understand that if this bush is torn from the ground and the earth burned out, the roses of Shaerrawedd will never flower again. Do you understand?"

She nodded.

"Do you understand what this neutrality is, which stirs you so? To be neutral does not mean to be indifferent or insensitive. You don't have to kill your feelings. It's enough to kill hatred within yourself. Do you understand?"

"Yes," she whispered. "I understand. Geralt, I . . . I'd like to take one . . . One of these roses. To remind me. May I?"

"Do," he said after some hesitation. "Do, in order to remember. Let's go now. Let's return to the convoy."

Ciri pinned the rose under the lacing of her jerkin. Suddenly she cried out quietly, lifted her hand. A trickle of blood ran from her finger down her palm.

"Did you prick yourself?"

"Yarpen . . ." whispered the girl, looking at the blood filling her life-line. "Wenck . . . Paulie . . ."

"What?"

"Triss!" she shouted with a piercing voice which was not hers, shuddered fiercely and wiped her face with her arm. "Quick, Geralt! We've got to help! To the horses, Geralt!"

"Ciri! What's happening?"

"They're dying!"

She galloped with her ear almost touching the horse's neck and spurred her mount on, kicking with her heels and shouting. The sand of the forest path flew beneath the hooves. She heard screaming in the distance, and smelt smoke.

Coming straight at them, blocking the path, raced two horses dragging a harness, reins and a broken shaft behind them. Ciri did not hold her chestnut back and shot past them at full speed, flakes of froth skimming across her face. Behind her she heard Roach neigh and Geralt's curses as he was forced to a halt.

She tore around a bend in the path in to a large glade.

The convoy was in flames. From thickets, flaming arrows flew towards the wagons like fire birds, perforating the canvas and digging into the boards. The Scoia'tael attacked with war-cries and yells.

Ciri, ignoring Geralt's shouts from behind her, directed her horse straight at the first two wagons brought to the fore. One was lying on its side and Yarpen Zigrin, axe in one hand, crossbow in the other, stood next to it. At his feet, motionless, with her blue dress hitched halfway up her thighs, lay . . .

"Triiiiiisss!" Ciri straightened in the saddle, thumping her horse with her heels. The Scoia'tael turned towards her and arrows whistled past the girl's ears. She shook her head without slowing her gallop. She heard Geralt shout, ordering her to flee into the woods. She did not intend to obey. She leaned down and bolted straight towards the archers shooting at her. Suddenly she smelt the overpowering scent of the white rose pinned to her jerkin.

"Triiiiisss!"

The elves leaped out of the way of the speeding horses. Ciri caught one lightly with her stirrup. She heard a sharp buzz, her steed struggled, whinnied and threw itself to the side. Ciri saw an arrow dug deep, just below the withers, right by her thigh. She tore her feet from the stirrups, jumped up, squatted in the saddle, bounced off strongly and leaped.

She fell softly on the body of the overturned wagon, used her hands to balance herself and jumped again, landing with bent knees next to Yarpen, who was roaring and brandishing his axe. Next to them, on the second wagon, Paulie Dahlberg was fighting while Regan, leaning back and bracing his legs against the board, was struggling to hold on to the harnessed horses. They neighed wildly, stamped their hooves and yanked at the shaft in fear of the fire devouring the canvas.

She rushed to Triss, who lay amongst the scattered barrels and chests, grabbed her by her clothes and started to drag her towards the overturned wagon. The enchantress moaned, holding her head just above the ear. Right by Ciri's side, hooves suddenly clattered and horses snorted – two elves, brandishing their swords, were pressing the madly fighting Yarpen hard. The dwarf spun like a top and agilely deflected the blows directed against him with his axe. Ciri heard curses, grunts and the whining clang of metal.

Another span of horses detached itself from the flaming convoy and rushed towards them, dragging smoke and flames behind it and scattering burning rags. The wagon-man hung inertly from the box and Yannick Brass stood next to him, barely keeping his balance. With one hand he wielded the reins, with the other he was cutting himself away from two elves galloping one at each side of the wagon. A third Scoia'tael, keeping up with the harnessed horses, was shooting arrow after arrow into their sides.

"Jump!" yelled Yarpen, shouting over the noise. "Jump, Yannick!"

Ciri saw Geralt catch up with the speeding wagon and with a short, spare slash of his sword swipe one of the elves from his saddle while Wenck, riding up on the opposite side, hewed at the other, the elf shooting the horses. Yannick threw the reins down and jumped off – straight under the third Scoia'tael's horse. The elf stood in his stirrups and slashed at him with his sword. The dwarf fell. At that moment the flaming wagon crashed into those still fighting, parting and scattering them. Ciri barely managed to pull Triss out from beneath the crazed horses' hooves at the last moment. The swingle-tree tore away with a crack, the wagon leaped into the air, lost a wheel and overturned, scattering its load and smouldering boards everywhere.

Ciri dragged the enchantress under Yarpen's overturned wagon. Paulie Dahlberg, who suddenly found himself next to her, helped, while Geralt covered them both, shoving Roach between them and the charging Scoia'tael. All around the wagon, battle seethed: Ciri heard shouting, blades clashing, horses snorting, hooves clattering. Yarpen, Wenck and Geralt, surrounded on all sides by the elves, fought like raging demons.

The fighters were suddenly parted by Regan's span as he struggled in the coachman's box with a halfling wearing a lynx fur hat. The halfling was sitting on Regan, trying to jab him with a long knife.

Yarpen deftly leaped onto the wagon, caught the half-ling by the neck and kicked him overboard. Regan gave a piercing yell, grabbed the reins and lashed the horses. The span jerked, the wagon rolled and gathered speed in a flash.

"Circle, Regan!" roared Yarpen. "Circle! Go round!"

The wagon turned and descended on the elves again, parting them. One of them sprang up, grabbed the right lead-horse by the halter but couldn't stop him; the impetus threw him under the hooves and wheels. Ciri heard an excruciating scream.

Another elf, galloping next to them, gave a back-handed swipe with his sword. Yarpen ducked, the blade rang against the hoop supporting the canvas and the momentum carried the elf forward. The dwarf hunched abruptly and vigorously swung his arm. The Scoia'tael yelled, stiffened in the saddle and tumbled to the ground. A martel protruded between his shoulder blades.

"Come on then, you whoresons!" Yarpen roared, whirling his axe. "Who else? Chase a circle, Regan! Go round!"

Regan, tossing his bloodied mane of hair, hunched in the box amidst the whizzing of arrows, howled like the damned, and mercilessly lashed the horses on. The span dashed in a tight circle, creating a moving barricade belching flames and smoke around the overturned wagon beneath which Ciri had dragged the semi-conscious, battered magician.

Not far from them danced Wenck's horse, a mouse-coloured stallion. Wenck was hunched over; Ciri saw the white feathers of an arrow sticking out of his side. Despite the wound, he was skilfully hacking his way past two elves on foot attacking him from both sides. As Ciri watched, another arrow struck him in the back. The commissar collapsed forward onto his horse's neck but remained in the saddle. Paulie Dahlberg rushed to his aid.

Ciri was left alone.

She reached for her sword. The blade which throughout her training had leaped out from her back in a flash would not let itself be drawn for anything; it resisted her, stuck in its scabbard as if glued in tar. Amongst the whirl seething around her, amongst moves so swift that they blurred in front of her eyes, her sword seemed strangely, unnaturally slow; it seemed ages would pass before it could be fully drawn. The ground trembled and shook. Ciri suddenly realised that it was not the ground. It was her knees.

Paulie Dahlberg, keeping the elf charging at him at bay with his axe, dragged the wounded Wenck along the ground. Roach flitted past, beside the wagon, and Geralt threw himself at the elf. He had lost his headband and his hair streamed out behind him with his speed. Swords clashed.

Another Scoia'tael, on foot, leaped out from behind the wagon. Paulie abandoned Wenck, pulled himself upright and brandished his axe. Then froze.

In front of him stood a dwarf wearing a hat adorned

with a squirrel's tail, his black beard braided into two plaits. Paulie hesitated.

The black-beard did not hesitate for a second. He struck with both arms. The blade of the axe whirred and fell, slicing into the collar-bone with a hideous crunch. Paulie fell instantly, without a moan; it looked as if the force of the blow had broken both his knees.

Ciri screamed.

Yarpen Zigrin leaped from the wagon. The black-bearded dwarf spun and cut. Yarpen avoided the blow with an agile half-turn dodge, grunted and struck fero-ciously, chopping in to black-beard – throat, jaw and face, right up to the nose. The Scoia'tael bent back and col-lapsed, bleeding, pounding his hands against the ground and tearing at the earth with his heels.

"Geraaaalllllttt!" screamed Ciri, feeling something move behind her. Sensing death behind her.

There was only a hazy shape, caught in a turn, a move and a flash but the girl – like lightning – reacted with a diagonal parry and feint taught her in Kaer Morhen. She caught the blow but had not been standing firmly enough, had been leaning too far to the side to receive the full force. The strength of the strike threw her against the body of the wagon. Her sword slipped from her hand.

The beautiful, long-legged elf wearing high boots standing in front of her grimaced fiercely and, tossing her hair free of her lowered hood, raised her sword. The sword flashed blindingly, the bracelets on the Squirrel's wrists glittered.

Ciri was in no state to move.

But the sword did not fall, did not strike. Because the

elf was not looking at Ciri but at the white rose pinned to her jerkin.

"Aelirenn!" shouted the Squirrel loudly as if wanting to shatter her hesitation with the cry. But she was too late. Geralt, shoving Ciri away, slashed her broadly across the chest with his sword. Blood spurted over the girl's face and clothes, red drops spattered on the white petals of the rose.

"Aelirenn . . ." moaned the elf shrilly, collapsing to her knees. Before she fell on her face, she managed to shout one more time. Loudly, lengthily, despairingly:

"Shaerraweeeeedd!"

Reality returned just as suddenly as it had disappeared. Through the monotonous, dull hum which filled her ears, Ciri began to hear voices. Through the flickering, wet curtain of tears, she began to see the living and the dead.

"Ciri," whispered Geralt who was kneeling next to her. "Wake up."

"A battle . . ." she moaned, sitting up. "Geralt, what—"

"It's all over. Thanks to the troops from Ban Gleán which came to our aid."

"You weren't . . ." she whispered, closing her eyes, "you weren't neutral . . ."

"No, I wasn't. But you're alive. Triss is alive."

"How is she?"

"She hit her head falling out of the wagon when Yarpen tried to rescue it. But she's fine now. Treating the wounded."

Ciri cast her eyes around. Amidst the smoke from the last wagons, burning out, silhouettes of armed men flickered. And all around lay chests and barrels. Some of were shattered and the contents scattered. They had contained ordinary, grey field stones. She stared at them, astounded.

"Aid for Demavend from Aedirn." Yarpen Zigrin, standing nearby, ground his teeth. "Secret and exceptionally important aid. A convoy of special significance!"

"It was a trap?"

The dwarf turned, looked at her, at Geralt. Then he looked back at the stones pouring from the barrels and spat.

"Yes," he confirmed. "A trap."

"For the Squirrels?"

"No."

The dead were arranged in a neat row. They lay next to each other, not divided – elves, humans and dwarves. Yannick Brass was amongst them. The dark-haired elf in the high boots was there. And the dwarf with his black, plaited beard, glistening with dried blood. And next to them . . .

"Paulie!" sobbed Regan Dahlberg, holding his brother's head on his knees. "Paulie! Why?"

No one said anything. No one. Even those who knew why. Regan turned his contorted face, wet with tears, towards them.

"What will I tell our mother?" he wailed. "What am I going to say to her?"

No one said anything.

Not far away, surrounded by soldiers in the black and gold of Kaedwen, lay Wenck. He was breathing with difficulty and every breath forced bubbles of blood to his lips. Triss knelt next to him and a knight in shining armour stood over them both.

"Well?" asked the knight. "Lady enchantress? Will he live?"

"I've done everything I can." Triss got to her feet, pinched her lips. "But . . ."

"What?"

"They used this." She showed him an arrow with a strange head to it and struck it against a barrel standing by them. The tip of the arrow fell apart, split into four barbed, hook-like needles. The knight cursed.

"Fredegard . . ." Wenck uttered with difficulty. "Fredegard, listen—"

"You mustn't speak!" said Triss severely. "Or move! The spell is barely holding!"

"Fredegard," the commissar repeated. A bubble of blood burst on his lips and another immediately appeared in its place. "We were wrong . . . Everyone was wrong. It's not Yarpen . . . We suspected him wrongly . . . I vouch for him. Yarpen did not betray . . . Did not betr—"

"Silence!" shouted the knight. "Silence, Vilfrid! Hey, quick now, bring the stretcher! Stretcher!"

"No need," the magician said hollowly, gazing at Wenck's lips where no more bubbles appeared. Ciri turned away and pressed her face to Geralt's side.

Fredegard drew himself up. Yarpen Zigrin did not look at him. He was looking at the dead. At Regan Dahlberg, still kneeling over his brother.

"It was necessary, Zigrin," said the knight. "This is war. There was an order. We had to be sure . . ."

Yarpen did not say anything. The knight lowered his eyes.

"Forgive us," he whispered.

The dwarf slowly turned his head, looked at him. At Geralt. At Ciri. At them all. The humans.

"What have you done to us?" he asked bitterly. "What have you done to us? What have you made of us?"

No one answered him.

The eyes of the long-legged elf were glassy and dull. Her contorted lips were frozen in a soundless cry.

Geralt put his arms around Ciri. Slowly, he unpinned the white rose, spattered with dark stains, from her jerkin and, without a word, threw it on the Squirrel's body.

"Farewell," whispered Ciri. "Farewell, Rose of Shaerrawedd. Farewell and . . ."

"And forgive us," added the witcher.

They roam the land, importunate and insolent, nominating themselves the stalkers of evil, vanquishers of werewolves and exterminators of spectres, extorting payment from the gullible and, on receipt of their ignoble earnings, moving on to dispense the same deceit in the near vicinity. The easiest access they find at cottages of honest, simple and unwitting peasants who readily ascribe all misfortune and ill events to spells, unnatural creatures and monsters, the doings of windsprites or evil spirits. Instead of praying to the gods, instead of bearing rich offerings to the temple, such a simpleton is ready to give his last penny to the base witcher, believing the witcher, the godless changeling, will turn around his fate and save him from misfortune.

Anonymous, *Monstrum*, or *Description of the Witcher*

I have nothing against witchers. Let them hunt vampires. As long as they pay taxes.

Radovid III the Bold, King of Redania

If you thirst for justice, hire a witcher.

Graffiti on the wall of the Faculty of Law, University of Oxenfurt

CHAPTER FIVE

"Did you say something?"

The boy sniffed and pushed his over-sized velvet hat, a pheasant's feather hanging rakishly to the side, back from his forehead.

"Are you a knight?" he repeated, gazing at Geralt with wide eyes as blue as the sky.

"No," replied the witcher, surprised that he felt like answering. "I'm not."

"But you've got a sword! My daddy's one of King Foltest's knights. He's got a sword, too. Bigger than yours!"

Geralt leaned his elbows on the railing and spat into the water eddying at the barge's wake.

"You carry it on your back," the little snot persisted. The hat slipped down over his eyes again.

"What?"

"The sword. On your back. Why have you got the sword on your back?"

"Because someone stole my oar."

The little snot opened his mouth, demanding that the impressive gaps left by milk teeth be admired.

"Move away from the side," said the witcher. "And shut your mouth or flies will get in."

The boy opened his mouth even wider.

"Grey-haired yet stupid!" snarled the little snot's mother, a richly attired noblewoman, pulling her offspring away by the beaver collar of his cloak. "Come here, Everett! I've told you so many times not to be familiar with the passing rabble!"

Geralt sighed, gazing at the outline of islands and islets looming through the morning mist. The barge, as ungainly as a tortoise, trudged along at an appropriate speed – that being the speed of a tortoise – dictated by the lazy Delta current. The passengers, mostly merchants and peasants, were dozing on their baggage. The witcher unfurled the scroll once more and returned to Ciri's letter.

. . . I sleep in a large hall called a Dormitorium and my bed is terribly big, I tell you. I'm with the Intermediary Girls. There are twelve of us but I'm most friendly with Eurneid, Katye and Iola the Second. Whereas today I Ate Broth and the worst is that sometimes we have to Fast and get up very early at Dawn. Earlier than in Kaer Morhen. I will write the rest tomorrow for we shall presently be having Prayers. No one ever prayed in Kaer Morhen, I wonder why we have to here. No doubt because this is a Temple.

Geralt. Mother Nenneke has read and said I must not write Silly Things and write clearly without mistakes. And about what I'm studying and that I feel well and healthy. I feel well and am healthy if unfortunately Hungry, but Soone be Dinner. And Mother Nenneke also said write that prayer has never harmed anybody yet, neither me nor, certainly, you.

Geralt, I have some free time again, I will write therefore that I am studying. To read and write correct Runes. History. Nature. Poetry and Prose. To express myself well in the Common Speech and in the Elder Speech. I am best at the Elder Speech, I can also write Elder Runes. I will write something for you and you will see for yourself. Elaine blath, Feainnewedd. That meant: Beautiful flower, child of the Sun. You see for yourself that I can. And also—

Now I can write again for I have found a new quill for the old one broke. Mother Nenneke read this and praised me that it was correct. That I am obedient, she told me to write, and that you should not worry. Don't worry, Geralt.

Again I have some time so I will write what happened. When we were feeding the turkey hens, I, Iola and Katye, One Enormous Turkey attacked us, a red neck it had and was Terrible Horrible. First it attacked Iola and then it wanted to attack me but I was not afraid because it was smaller and slower than the Pendulum anyway. I dodged and did a pirouette and walloped it twice with a switch until it Made Off. Mother Nenneke does not allow me to carry My Sword here, a pity, for I would have shown that Turkey what I learned in Kaer Morhen. I already know that in the Elder Runes it would be written Caer a'Muirehen and that it means Keep of the Elder Sea. So no doubt that is why there are Shells and

*Snails there as well as Fish imprinted on the stones.
And Cintra is correctly written Xin'trea. Whereas
my name comes from Zireael for that means Swallow and that means that . . .*

"Are you busy reading?"

He raised his head.

"I am. So? Has anything happened? Someone noticed
something?"

"No, nothing," replied the skipper, wiping his hands on
his leather jerkin. "There's calm on the water. But there's
a mist and we're already near Crane Islet—"

"I know. It's the sixth time I've sailed this way, Boatbug, not counting the return journeys. I've come to know
the trail. My eyes are open, don't worry."

The skipper nodded and walked away to the prow,
stepping over travellers' packages and bundles stacked
everywhere. Squeezed in amidships, the horses snorted
and pounded their hooves on the deck-boards. They were
in the middle of the current, in dense fog. The prow of the
barge ploughed the surface of water lilies, parting their
clumps. Geralt turned back to his reading.

*. . . that means I have an elven name. But I am not,
after all, an elf. Geralt, there is also talk about the
Squirrels here. Sometimes even the Soldiers come
and ask questions and say that we must not treat
wounded elves. I have not squealed a word to anyone about what happened in spring, don't worry.
And I also remember to practise, don't think otherwise. I go to the park and train when I have time. But
not always, for I also have to work in the kitchen or*

in the orchard like all the girls. And we also have a terrible amount of studying to do. But never mind, I will study. After all, you too studied in the Temple, Mother Nenneke told me. And she also told me that just any idiot can brandish a sword but a witcher-girl must be wise.

Geralt, you promised to come. Come.
    Your Ciri

PS Come, come.
PS II. Mother Nenneke told me to end with Praise be to Great Melitele, may her blessing and favour always go with you. And may nothing happen to you.
    Ciri

I'd like to go to Ellander, he thought, putting away the letter. *But it's dangerous. I might lead them to— These letters have got to end. Nenneke makes use of temple mail but still . . . Damn it, it's too risky.*

"Hmmm . . . Hm . . ."

"What now, Boatbug? We've passed Crane Islet."

"And without incident, thank the gods," sighed the skipper. "Ha, Geralt, I see this is going to be another peaceful trip. Any moment now the mist is going to clear and when the sun peeps through, the fear is over. The monster won't show itself in the sunlight."

"That won't worry me in the least."

"So I should think." Boatbug smiled wryly. "The company pays you by the trip. Regardless whether something happens or not a penny falls into your pouch, doesn't it?"

"You ask as if you didn't know. What is this – envy talking? That I earn money standing leaning against the side, watching the lapwings? And what do you get paid for? The same thing. For being on board. When everything is going smoothly you haven't got anything to do. You stroll from prow to stern, grinning at the women or trying to entice merchants to have a drink. I've been hired to be on board too. Just in case. The transport is safe because a witcher is on board. The cost of the witcher is included in the price of the trip, right?"

"Well, that certainly is true," sighed the skipper. "The company won't lose out. I know them well. This is the fifth year I sail the Delta for them from Foam to Novigrad, from Novigrad to Foam. Well, to work, witcher, sir. You go on leaning against the side and I'll go for a stroll from prow to stern."

The mist thinned a little. Geralt extracted another letter from his bag, one he had recently received from a strange courier. He had already read it about thirty times.

Dear friend . . .

The witcher swore quietly, looking at the sharp, angular, even runes drawn with energetic sweeps of the pen, faultlessly reflecting the author's mood. He felt once again the desire to try to bite his own backside in fury. When he was writing to the enchantress a month ago he had spent two nights in a row contemplating how best to begin. Finally, he had decided on "Dear friend." Now he had his just deserts.

Dear friend, your unexpected letter – which I received not quite three years after we last saw each other – has given me much joy. My joy is all the greater as various rumours have been circulating about your sudden and violent death. It is a good thing that you have decided to disclaim them by writing to me; it is a good thing, too, that you are doing so so soon. From your letter it appears that you have lived a peaceful, wonderfully boring life, devoid of all sensation. These days such a life is a real privilege, dear friend, and I am happy that you have managed to achieve it.

I was touched by the sudden concern which you deigned to show as to my health, dear friend. I hasten with the news that, yes, I now feel well; the period of indisposition is behind me, I have dealt with the difficulties, the description of which I shall not bore you with.

It worries and troubles me very much that the unexpected present you received from Fate brings you worries. Your supposition that this requires professional help is absolutely correct. Although your description of the difficulty – quite understandably – is enigmatic, I am sure I know the Source of the problem. And I agree with your opinion that the help of yet another magician is absolutely necessary. I feel honoured to be the second to whom you turn. What have I done to deserve to be so high on your list?

Rest assured, my dear friend; and if you had the intention of supplicating the help of additional magicians, abandon it because there is no need. I leave without delay, and go to the place which you

217

indicated in an oblique yet, to me, understandable way. It goes without saying that I leave in absolute secrecy and with great caution. I will surmise the nature of the trouble on the spot and will do all that is in my power to calm the gushing source. I shall try, in so doing, not to appear any worse than other ladies to whom you have turned, are turning or usually turn with your supplications. I am, after all, your dear friend. Your valuable friendship is too important to me to disappoint you, dear friend.

Should you, in the next few years, wish to write to me, do not hesitate for a moment. Your letters invariably give me boundless pleasure.

Your friend Yennefer

The letter smelled of lilac and gooseberries.

Geralt cursed.

He was torn from his reverie by the movement on deck and a rocking of the barge that indicated they were changing course. Some of the passengers crowded starboard. Skipper Boatbug was yelling orders from the bow; the barge was slowly and laboriously turning towards the Temerian shore, leaving the fairway and ceding right of way to two ships looming through the mist. The witcher watched with curiosity.

The first was an enormous three-masted galliass at least a hundred and forty yards long, carrying an amaranth flag with a silver eagle. Behind it, its forty oars rhythmically hard at work, glided a smaller, slim galley adorned with a black ensign with gold-red chevron.

"Ooohh, what huge dragons," said Boatbug standing

next to the witcher. "They're pushing a heck of a wave, the way they're ploughing the river."

"Interesting," muttered Geralt. "The galliass is sailing under the Redanian flag but the galley is from Aedirn."

"From Aedirn, very much so," confirmed the skipper. "And it carries the Governor of Hagge's pennon. But note, both ships have sharp keels, near on four yards' draught. That means they're not sailing to Hagge itself – they wouldn't cross the rapids and shallows up the river. They're heading to Foam or White Bridge. And look, there are swarms of soldiers on the decks. These aren't merchants. They're war ships, Geralt."

"Someone important is on that galliass. They've set up a tent on deck."

"That's right, that's how the nobles travel." Boatbug nodded, picking his teeth with a splinter peeled from the barge's side. "It's safer by river. Elven commandos are roaming the forests. There's no knowing which tree an arrow's going to come flying from. But on the water there's no fear. Elves, like cats, don't like water. They prefer dwelling in brushwood . . ."

"It's got to be someone really important. The tent is rich."

"That's right, could be. Who knows, maybe King Vizimir himself is favouring the river with his presence? All sorts of people are travelling this way now . . . And while we're at it, in Foam you asked me to keep my ears open in case anyone was interested in you, asking about you. Well, that weakling there, you see him?"

"Don't point, Boatbug. Who is he?"

"How should I know? Ask him yourself, he's coming over. Just look at his stagger! And the water's as still as a mirror, pox on it; if it were to swell just a little he'd probably be on all fours, the oaf."

The "oaf" turned out to be a short, thin man of uncertain age, dressed in a large, woollen and none-too-clean cloak pinned in place with a circular brass brooch. Its pin, clearly lost, had been replaced by a crooked nail with a flattened head. The man approached, cleared his throat and squinted with his myopic eyes.

"Hmm . . . Do I have the pleasure of speaking to Geralt of Rivia, the witcher?"

"Yes, sir. You do."

"Allow me to introduce myself. I am Linus Pitt, Master Tutor and Lecturer in Natural History at the Oxenfurt Academy."

"My very great pleasure."

"Hmm . . . I've been told that you, sir, are on commission from the Malatius and Grock Company to protect this transport. Apparently from the danger of some monster attack. I wonder what this 'monster' could be."

"I wonder myself." The witcher leaned against the ship's side, gazing at the dark outline of the marshy meadows on the Temerian riverbank looming in the mist. "And have come to the conclusion that I have most likely been hired as a precaution against an attack from a Scoia'tael commando force said to be roaming the vicinity. This is my sixth journey between Foam and Novigrad and no aeschna has shown itself—"

"Aeschna? That's some kind of common name. I would rather you used the scientific terminology. Hmm . . . aeschna . . . I truly do not know which species you have in mind—"

"I'm thinking of a bumpy and rough-skinned monster

four yards in length resembling a stump overgrown with algae and with ten paws and jaws like cut-saws."

"The description leaves a lot to be desired as regards scientific precision. Could it be one of the species of the *Hyphydridae* family?"

"I don't exclude the possibility," sighed Geralt. "The aeschna, as far as I know, belongs to an exceptionally nasty family for which no name can be abusive. The thing is, Master Tutor, that apparently a member of this unsympathetic clan attacked the Company's barge two weeks ago. Here, on the Delta, not far from where we are."

"He who says this" – Linus Pitt gave a screeching laugh – "is either an ignoramus or a liar. Nothing like that could have happened. I know the fauna of the Delta very well. The family *Hyphydridae* does not appear here at all. Nor do any other quite so dangerous predatory species. The considerable salinity and atypical chemical composition of the water, especially during high tide—"

"During high tide," interrupted Geralt, "when the incoming tide wave passes the Novigrad canals, there is no water – to use the word precisely – in the Delta at all. There is a liquid made up of excrement, soapsuds, oil and dead rats."

"Unfortunately, unfortunately." The Master Tutor grew sad. "Degradation of the environment . . . You may not believe it, but of more than two thousand species of fish living in this river only fifty years ago, not more than nine hundred remain. It is truly sad."

They both leaned against the railing and stared into the murky green depths. The tide must have already been coming in because the stench of the water was growing stronger. The first dead rats appeared.

"The white-finned bullhead has died off completely." Linus Pitt broke the silence. "The mullet has died, as have the snakehead, the kithara, the striped loach, the redbelly dace, the long-barbel gudgeon, the king pickerel . . ."

At a distance of about twenty yards from the ship's side, the water surged. For a moment, both men saw a twenty-pound or more specimen of the king pickerel swallowing a dead rat and disappearing into the depths, having gracefully flashed its tail fin.

"What was that?" The Master Tutor shuddered.

"I don't know." Geralt looked at the sky. "A penguin maybe?"

The scholar glanced at him and bit his lips.

"In all certainty it was not, however, your mythical aeschna! I have been told that witchers possess considerable knowledge about some rare species. But you, you not only repeat rumours and tales, you are also mocking me in a most crude manner . . . Are you listening to me at all?"

"The mist isn't going to lift," said Geralt quietly.

"Huh?"

"The wind is still weak. When we sail into the arm of the river, between the islets, it will be even weaker. It is going to be misty right up to Novigrad."

"I'm not going to Novigrad. I get off at Oxenfurt," declared Pitt dryly. "And the mist? It is surely not so thick as to render navigation impossible; what do you think?"

The little boy in the feathered hat ran past them and leaned far out, trying, with his stick, to fish out a rat bouncing against the boat. Geralt approached and tore the stick from him.

"Scram. Don't get near the side!"

"Muuuummyyyy!"

"Everett! Come here immediately!"

The Master Tutor pulled himself up and glared at the witcher with piercing eyes.

"It seems you really do believe we are in some danger?"

"Master Pitt," said Geralt as calmly as he could, "two weeks ago something pulled two people off the deck of one of the Company's barges. In the mist. I don't know what it was. Maybe it was your hyphydra or whatever its name is. Maybe it was a long-barbel gudgeon. But I think it was an aeschna."

The scholar pouted. "Conjecture," he declared, "should always be based on solid scientific foundations, not on rumours and gossip. I told you, the hyphydra, which you persist in calling an aeschna, does not appear in the waters of the Delta. It was wiped out a good half-century ago, due – incidentally – to the activity of individuals such as yourself who are prepared to kill anything that does not instantly look right, without forethought, tests, observation or considering its ecological niche."

For a moment, Geralt felt a sincere desire to tell the scholar where he could put the aeschna and its niche, but he changed his mind.

"Master Tutor," he said calmly, "one of those pulled from the deck was a young pregnant girl. She wanted to cool her swollen feet in the water. Theoretically, her child could, one day, have become chancellor of your college. What do you have to say to such an approach to ecology?"

"It is unscientific; it is emotional and subjective. Nature is governed by its own rules and although these rules are cruel and ruthless, they should not be amended. It is a struggle for survival!" The Master Tutor leaned over the railing and spat into the water. "And nothing can justify the extermination of a species, even a predatory one. What do you say to that?"

"I say that it's dangerous to lean out like that. There might be an aeschna in the vicinity. Do you want to try out the aeschna's struggle for survival on your own skin?"

Linus Pitt let go of the railing and abruptly jumped away. He turned a little pale but immediately regained his self-assurance and pursed his lips again.

"No doubt you know a great deal about these fantastical aeschna, witcher?"

"Certainly less than you. So maybe we should make use of the opportunity? Enlighten me, Master Tutor, expound a little upon your knowledge of aquatic predators. I'll willingly listen, and the journey won't seem so long."

"Are you making fun of me?"

"Not at all. I would honestly like to fill in the gaps in my education."

"Hmmm . . . If you really . . . Why not? Listen then to me. The *Hyphydridae* family, belonging to the *Amphipoda* order, includes four species known to science. Two live exclusively in tropical waters. In our climate, on the other hand, one can come across – though very rarely now – the not-so-large *Hyphydra longicauda* and the somewhat larger *Hyphydra marginata*. The biotope of both species is stagnant water or water which flows very slowly. The species are, indeed, predatory, preferring to feed on warm-blooded creatures . . . Have you anything to add?"

"Not right now. I'm listening with bated breath."

"Yes, hmm . . . Mention can also be found, in the great books, of the subspecies *Pseudohyphydra*, which lives in the marshy waters of Angren. However, the learned Bumbler of Aldersberg recently proved that this is an entirely different species, one from the *Mordidae* family. It feeds exclusively on fish and small amphibians. It has been named *Ichthyovorax bumbleri*."

"The monster's lucky," smiled the witcher. "That's the third time he was named."

"How come?"

"The creature you're talking about is an ilyocoris, called a cinerea in Elder Speech. And if the learned Bumbler states that it feeds exclusively on fish then I assume he has never bathed in a lake with an ilyocoris. But Bumbler is right on one account: the aeschna has as much in common with a cinerea as I do with a fox. We both like to eat duck."

"What cinerea?" The Master Tutor bridled. "The cinerea is a mythical creature! Indeed, your lack of knowledge disappoints me. Truly, I am amazed—"

"I know," interrupted Geralt. "I lose a great deal of my charm when one gets to know me better. Nevertheless I will permit myself to correct your theories a little further, Master Pitt. So, aeschnae have always lived in the Delta and continue to do so. Indeed, there was a time when it seemed that they had become extinct. For they lived off those small seals—"

"River porpoises," corrected the Master Tutor. "Don't be an ignoramus. Don't mistake seals for—"

"—they lived off porpoises and the porpoises were killed off because they looked like seals. They provided

225

seal-like skins and fat. Then, later, canals were dug out in the upper reaches of the river, dams and barriers built. The current grew weaker; the Delta got silted up and overgrown. And the aeschna underwent mutation. It adapted."

"Huh?"

"Humans have rebuilt its food chain. They supplied warm-blooded creatures in the place of porpoises. Sheep, cattle, swine began to be transported across the Delta. The aeschnae learned in a flash that every barge, raft or barque on the Delta was, in fact, a large platter of food."

"And the mutation? You spoke of mutation!"

"This liquid manure" – Geralt indicated the green water – "seems to suit the aeschna. It enhances its growth. The damn thing can become so large, apparently, that it can drag a cow off a raft with no effort whatsoever. Pulling a human off a deck is nothing. Especially the deck of one of these scows the Company uses to transport passengers. You can see for yourself how low it sits in the water."

The Master Tutor quickly backed away from the ship's side, as far as the carts and baggage allowed.

"I heard a splash!" he gasped, staring at the mist between the islets. "Witcher! I heard—"

"Calm down. Apart from the splashing you can also hear oars squeaking in rowlocks. It's the customs officers from the Redanian shore. You'll see them in a moment and they'll cause more of a commotion than three, or even four, aeschnae."

Boatbug ran past. He cursed obscenely as the little boy in the feathered hat got under his feet. The passengers and messengers, all extremely nervous, were going through their possessions trying to hide any smuggled goods.

After a little while, a large boat hit the side of the barge and four lively, angry and very noisy individuals jumped on board. They surrounded the skipper, bawled threateningly in an effort to make themselves and their positions seem important, then threw themselves enthusiastically at the baggage and belongings of the travellers.

"They check even before we land!" complained Boatbug, coming up to the witcher and the Master Tutor. "That's illegal, isn't it? After all, we're not on Redanian soil yet. Redania is on the right bank, half a mile from here!"

"No," contradicted the Master Tutor. "The boundary between Redania and Temeria runs through the centre of the Pontar current."

"And how the shit do you measure a current? This is the Delta! Islets, shoals and skerries are constantly changing its layout – the Fairway is different every day! It's a real curse! Hey! You little snot! Leave that boathook alone or I'll tan your arse black and blue! Honourable lady! Watch your child! A real curse!"

"Everett! Leave that alone or you'll get dirty!"

"What's in that chest?" shouted the customs officers. "Hey, untie that bundle! Whose is that cart? Any currency? Is there any currency, I say? Temerian or Nilfgaardian money?"

"That's what a customs war looks like," Linus Pitt commented on the chaos with a wise expression on his face. "Vizimir forced Novigrad to introduce the *ius stapulae*. Foltest of Temeria retaliated with a retortive, absolute *ius stapulae* in Wyzima and Gors Velen. That was a great blow for Redanian merchants so Vizimir increased the tax on Temerian products. He is defending the Redanian economy. Temeria is flooded with cheap goods coming from Nilfgaardian manufactories. That's why the customs officers are so keen. If too many Nilfgaardian goods were to cross the border, the Redanian economy would collapse. Redania has practically no manufactories and the craftsmen wouldn't be able to cope with competition."

"In a nutshell," smiled Geralt, "Nilfgaard is slowly taking over with its goods and gold that which it couldn't take with arms. Isn't Temeria defending itself? Hasn't Foltest blocked his southern borders?"

"How? The goods are coming through Mahakam, Brugge, Verden and the ports in Cidaris. Profit is all the merchants are interested in, not politics. If King Foltest were to block his borders, the merchants' guilds would raise a terrible outcry—"

"Any currency?" snarled an approaching customs officer with bloodshot eyes. "Anything to declare?"

"I'm a scholar!"

"Be a prince if you like! I'm asking what you're bringing in?"

"Leave them, Boratek," said the leader of the group, a tall, broad-shouldered customs officer with a long, black moustache. "Don't you recognise the witcher? Greetings, Geralt. Do you know him? Is he a scholar? So you're going to Oxenfurt, are you, sir? With no luggage?"

"Quite so. To Oxenfurt. With no luggage."

The customs officer pulled out an enormous handkerchief and wiped his forehead, moustache and neck.

"And how's it going today, Geralt?" he asked. "The monster show itself?"

"No. And you, Olsen, seen anything?"

"I haven't got time to look around. I'm working."

"My daddy," declared Everett, creeping up without a sound, "is one of King Foltest's knights! And he's got an even bigger moustache than you!"

"Scram, kid," said Olsen, then sighed heavily. "Got any vodka, Geralt?"

"No."

"But I do." The learned man from the Academy, pulling a flat skin from his bag, surprised them all.

"And I've got a snack," boasted Boatbug looming up as if from nowhere. "Smoked burbot!"

"And my daddy—"

"Scarper, little snot."

They sat on coils of rope in the shade of the carts parked amidships, sipping from the skin and devouring the burbot in turn. Olsen had to leave them momentarily when an argument broke out. A dwarven merchant from Mahakam was demanding a lower tax and trying to convince the customs officers that the furs he was bringing in were not silver fox but exceptionally large cats. The mother of the nosey and meddlesome Everett, on the other hand, did not want to undergo an inspection at all, shrilly evoking her husband's rank and the privileges of nobility.

The ship, trailing braids of gathered nenuphars, water lilies and pond-weed at its sides, slowly glided along the wide strait amongst shrub-covered islets. Bumble bees buzzed menacingly amongst the reeds, and tortoises whistled from time to time. Cranes, standing on one leg, gazed at the water with stoical calm, knowing there was no point in getting worked up – sooner or later a fish would swim up of its own accord.

"And what do you think, Geralt?" Boatbug uttered,

licking the burbot's skin clean. "Another quiet voyage? You know what I'd say? That monster's no fool. It knows you're lying in ambush. Hearken to this – at home in our village, there was a river and in that river lived an otter which would creep into the yard and strangle hens. It was so crafty that it never crept in when Father was home, or me and my brothers. It only showed up when Grandpa was left by himself. And our grandpa, hearken, was a bit feeble in the head and paralysis had taken his legs. It was as if the otter, that son-of-a-bitch, knew. Well then, one day our pa—"

"Ten per cent *ad valorem*!" yelled the dwarven merchant from amidships, waving the fox skin about. "That's how much I owe you and I'm not going to pay a copper more!"

"Then I'll confiscate the lot!" roared Olsen angrily. "And I'll let the Novigrad guards know so you'll go to the clink together with your 'Valorem'! Boratek, charge him to the penny! Hey, have you left anything for me? Have you guzzled it down to the dregs?"

"Sit down, Olsen." Geralt made room for him on the ropes. "Stressful job you've got, I see."

"Ah, I've had it up to my ears," sighed the customs officer, then took a swig from the skin and wiped his moustache. "I'm throwing it in, I'm going back to Aedirn. I'm an honest Vengerberger who followed his sister and brother-in-law to Redania but now I'm going back. You know what, Geralt? I'm set on enlisting in the army. They say King Demavend is recruiting for special troops. Half a year's training in a camp and then it's a soldier's pay, three times what I get here, bribes included. This burbot's too salty."

"I've heard about this special army," confirmed Boatbug. "It's getting ready for the Squirrels because the
regular army can't deal with the elven commandos. They
particularly want half-elves to enlist, I hear. But that camp
where they teach them to fight is real hell apparently.
They leave fifty-fifty, some to get soldier's pay, some to
the burial ground, feet first."

"And so it should be," said the customs officer. "The
special army, skipper, isn't just any old unit. It's not some
shitty shield-bearers who just need to be shown which
end of the javelin pricks. A special army has to know how
to fight like nobody's business!"

"So you're such a fierce warrior, are you, Olsen? And
the Squirrels, aren't you afraid of them? That they'll spike
your arse with arrows?"

"Big deal! I know how to draw a bow too. I've already
fought Nilfgaard, so elves are nothing to me."

"They say," Boatbug said with a shudder, "if someone
falls into their hands alive, the Scoia'taels' . . . It's better
they hadn't been born. They'll be tortured horrifically."

"Ah, do yourself a favour and shut your face, skipper.
You're babbling like a woman. War is war. You whack
the enemy in the backside, and they whack you back.
Captured elves aren't pampered by our men either, don't
you worry."

"The tactic of terror." Linus Pitt threw the burbot's
head and backbone overboard. "Violence breeds violence. Hatred has grown into hearts . . . and has poisoned
kindred blood . . ."

"What?" Olsen grimaced. "Use a human language!"

"Hard times are upon us."

"So they are, true," agreed Boatbug. "There's sure to

be a great war. Every day the sky is thick with ravens, they smell the carrion already. And the seeress Ithlin foretold the end of the world. White Light will come to be, the White Chill will then follow. Or the other way round, I've forgotten how it goes. And people are saying signs were also visible in the sky—"

"You keep an eye on the fairway, skipper, 'stead of the sky, or this skiff of yours is going to end up in the shallows. Ah, we're already level with Oxenfurt. Just look, you can see the Cask!"

The mist was clearly less dense now so that they could see the hillocks and marshy meadows of the right bank and, rising above them, a part of the aqueduct.

"That, gentlemen, is the experimental sewage purification plant," boasted the Master Tutor, refusing his turn to drink. "A great success for science, a great achievement for the Academy. We repaired the old elven aqueduct, canals and sediment trap and we're already neutralising the sewers of the university, town and surrounding villages and farms. What you call the Cask is a sediment trap. A great success for science—"

"Heads down, heads down!" warned Olsen, ducking behind the rail. "Last year, when that thing exploded, the shit flew as far as Crane Islet."

The barge sailed in between islands and the squat tower of the sediment trap and the aqueduct disappeared in the mist. Everyone sighed with relief.

"Aren't you sailing straight by way of the Oxenfurt arm, Boatbug?" asked Olsen.

"I'm putting in at Acorn Bay first. To collect fish traders and merchants from the Temerian side."

"Hmm . . ." The customs officer scratched his neck.

"At the Bay . . . Listen, Geralt, you aren't in any conflict with the Temerians by any chance, are you?"

"Why? Was someone asking about me?"

"You've guessed it. As you see, I remember you asked me to keep an eye out for anyone interested in you. Well, just imagine, the Temerian Guards have been enquiring about you. The customs officers there, with whom I have a good understanding, told me. Something smells funny here, Geralt."

"The water?" Linus Pitt was afraid, glancing nervously at the aqueduct and the great scientific success.

"That little snotrag?" Boatbug pointed to Everett who was still milling around nearby.

"I'm not talking about that." The customs officer winced. "Listen, Geralt, the Temerian customs men said these Guards were asking strange questions. They know you sail with the Malatius and Grock barges. They asked . . . if you sail alone. If you have— Bloody hell, just don't laugh! They were going on about some underage girl who has been seen in your company, apparently."

Boatbug chuckled. Linus Pitt looked at the witcher with eyes filled with the distaste which befitted someone looking at a white-haired man who has drawn the attention of the law on account of his preference for underage girls.

"That's why," Olsen hawked, "the Temerian customs officers thought it might be some private matters being settled, into which the Guards had been drawn. Like . . . Well, the girl's family or her betrothed. So the officers cautiously asked who was behind all this. And they found out. Well, apparently it's a nobleman with a tongue ready as a chancellor's, neither poor nor miserly, who calls himself . . . Rience, or something like that. He's got a red mark on his left cheek as if from a burn. Do you know anyone like that?"

Geralt got up.

"Boatbug," he said. "I'm disembarking in Acorn Bay."

"How's that? And what about the monster?"

"That's your problem."

"Speaking of problems," interrupted Olsen, "just look starboard, Geralt. Speak of the devil."

From behind an island, from the swiftly lifting mist, loomed a lighter. A black burgee dotted with silver lilies fluttered lazily from its mast. The crew consisted of several men wearing the pointed hats of Temerian Guards.

Geralt quickly reached into his bag and pulled out both letters – the one from Ciri and the one from Yennefer. He swiftly tore them into tiny shreds and threw them into the river. The customs officer watched him in silence.

"Whatever are you doing, may I ask?"

"No. Boatbug, take care of my horse."

"You want to . . ." Olsen frowned. "You intend to—"

"What I intend is my business. Don't get mixed up in this or there'll be an incident. They're sailing under the Temerian flag."

"Bugger their flag." The customs officer moved his cutlass to a more accessible place on his belt and wiped his enamelled gorget, an eagle on a red background, with his sleeve. "If I'm on board carrying out an inspection, then this is Redania. I will not allow—"

"Olsen," the witcher interrupted, grabbing him by the sleeve, "don't interfere, please. The man with a burned face isn't on the lighter. And I have to know who he is and what he wants. I've got to see him face to face."

"You're going to let them put you in the stocks? Don't be a fool! If this is a private settling of scores, privately commissioned revenge, then as soon as you get past the islet, on the Whirl, you'll fly overboard with an anchor round your neck. You'll be face to face all right, but it'll be with crabs at the bottom of the river!"

"They're Temerian Guards, not bandits."

"Is that so? Then just look at their mugs! Besides, I'll know instantly who they really are. You'll see."

The lighter, approaching rapidly, reached the barge. One of the Guards threw the rope over while another attached the boathook to the railing.

"I be the skipper!" Boatbug blocked the way as three men leaped on deck. "This is a ship belonging to the Malatius and Grock Company! What . . ."

One of the men, stocky and bald, pushed him brusquely aside with his arm, thick as the branch of an oak.

"A certain Gerald, called Gerald of Rivia!" he thundered, measuring the skipper with his eyes. "Is such a one on board?"

"No."

"I am he." The witcher stepped over the bundles and packages and drew near. "I am Geralt, and called Geralt. What is this about?"

"I arrest you in the name of the law." The bald man's eyes skimmed over the passengers. "Where's the girl?"

"I'm alone."

"You lie!"

"Hold it, hold it." Olsen emerged from behind the witcher's back and put his hand on his shoulder. "Keep calm, no shouting. You're too late, Temerians. He has already been arrested and in the name of the law at that. I caught him. For smuggling. I'm taking him to the guardhouse in Oxenfurt according to orders."

"What's that?" The bald man frowned. "And the girl?"

"There is no girl here, nor has there been."

The Guards looked at each other in uncertain silence. Olsen grinned broadly and turned up his black moustache.

"You know what we'll do?" he snorted. "Sail with us to Oxenfurt, Temerians. We and you are simple folk, how are we to know the ins and outs of law? The commandant of the Oxenfurt guardhouse is a wise and worldly man, he'll judge the matter. You know our commandant, don't you? Because he knows yours, the one from the Bay, very well. You'll present your case to him . . . Show him your orders and seals . . . You do have a warrant with all the necessary seals, don't you, eh?"

The bald man just stared grimly at the customs officer.

"I don't have the time or the inclination to go to Oxenfurt!" he suddenly bawled. "I'm taking the rogue to our shore and that's that! Stran, Vitek! Get on with it, search the barge! Find me the girl, quick as a flash!"

"One minute, slow down." Olsen was not perturbed by the yelling and drew out his words slowly and distinctly. "You're on the Redanian side of the Delta, Temerians. You don't have anything to declare, by any chance, do you? Or any contraband? We'll have a look presently. We'll do a search. And if we do find something then you will have to take the trouble to go to Oxenfurt for a while, after all. And we, if we wish to, we can always find something. Boys! Come here!"

"My daddy," squeaked Everett all of a sudden, appearing at the bald man's side as if from nowhere, "is a knight! He's got an even bigger blade than you!"

In a flash, the bald man caught the boy by his beaver collar and snatched him up from the deck, knocking his feathered hat off. Wrapping his arm around the boy's waist he put the cutlass to his throat.

"Move back!" he roared. "Move back or I'll slash the brat's neck!"

"Evereeeeett!" howled the noblewoman.

"Curious methods," said the witcher slowly, "you Temerian Guards use. Indeed, so curious that it makes it hard to believe you're Guards."

"Shut your face!" yelled the bald one, shaking Everett, who was squealing like a piglet. "Stran, Vitek, get him! Fetter him and take him to the lighter! And you, move back! Where's the girl, I'm asking you? Give her to me or I'll slaughter this little snot!"

"Slaughter him then," drawled Olsen giving a sign to his men and pulling out his cutlass. "Is he mine or something? And when you've slaughtered him, we can talk."

"Don't interfere!" Geralt threw his sword on the deck and, with a gesture, held back the customs officers and Boatbug's sailors. "I'm yours, liar-guard, sir. Let the boy go."

"To the lighter!" The bald man retreated to the side of the barge without letting Everett go, and grabbed a rope. "Vitek, tie him up! And all of you, to the stern! If any of you move, the kid dies!"

"Have you lost your mind, Geralt?" growled Olsen.

"Don't interfere!"

"Evereeeett!"

The Temerian lighter suddenly rocked and bounced away from the barge. The water exploded with a splash and two long green, coarse paws bristling with spikes like the limbs of a praying mantis, shot out. The paws grabbed the Guard holding the boathook and, in the wink of an eye, dragged him under water. The bald Guard howled savagely, released Everett, and clung onto the ropes which dangled from the lighter's side. Everett plopped into the already-reddening water. Everybody – those on the barge and those on the lighter – started to scream as if possessed.

Geralt tore himself away from the two men trying to bind him. He thumped one in the chin, then threw him overboard. The other took a swing at the witcher with an iron hook, but faltered and drooped into Olsen's hands with a cutlass buried to the hilt in his ribs.

The witcher leaped over the low railing. Before the water – thick with algae – closed in over his head, he heard Linus Pitt, the Lecturer of Natural History at the Academy of Oxenfurt, shout, "What is that? What species? No such animal exists!"

He emerged just by the Temerian lighter, miraculously avoiding the fishing spear which one of baldy's men was jabbing at him. The Guard didn't have time to strike him again before he splashed into the water with an arrow in his throat. Geralt, catching hold of the dropped spear, rebounded with his legs against the side of the boat, dived into the seething whirlpool and forcefully jabbed at something, hoping it was not Everett.

"It's impossible!" he heard the Master Tutor's cries. "Such an animal can't exist! At least, it shouldn't!"

I agree with that last statement entirely, thought the witcher, jabbing the aeschna's armour, bristling with its hard bumps. The corpse of the Temerian Guard was bouncing up and down inertly in the sickle-shaped jaws of the monster, trailing blood. The aeschna swung its flat tail violently and dived to the bottom, raising clouds of silt.

He heard a thin cry. Everett, stirring the water like a little dog, had caught hold of baldy's legs as he was trying to climb on to the lighter by the ropes hanging down the side. The ropes gave way and both the Guard and the boy disappeared with a gurgle under the surface of the water. Geralt threw himself in their direction and dived. The fact that he almost immediately came across the little boy's beaver collar was nothing but luck. He tore Everett from the entangled algae, swam out on his back and, kicking with his legs, reached the barge.

"Here, Geralt! Here!" He heard cries and shouts, each louder than the other: "Give him here!", "The rope! Catch hold of the rope!", "Pooooox!", "The rope! Geraaalt!", "With the boathook, with the boathook!", "My booyyyy!"

Someone tore the boy from his arms and dragged him upwards. At the same moment, someone else caught Geralt from behind, struck him in the back of the head, covered him over with his bulk and pushed him under the water. Geralt let go of the fishing spear, turned and caught his assailant by the belt. With his other hand he tried to grab him by the hair but in vain. It was baldy.

Both men emerged, but only for an instant. The Temerian lighter had already moved a little from the barge and both Geralt and baldy, locked in an embrace, were in between them. Baldy caught Geralt by the throat; the witcher dug a thumb in his eye. The Guard yelled, let go and swam away. Geralt could not swim – something was holding him by the leg and dragging him into the depths. Next to him, half a body bounced to the surface like a cork. And then he knew what was holding him; the information Linus Pitt yelled from the barge deck was unnecessary.

"It's an anthropod! Order *Amphipoda*! Group Mandi-bulatissimae!"

Geralt violently thrashed his arms in the water, trying to yank his leg from the aeschna's claws as they pulled him towards the rhythmical snap of its jaws. The Master Tutor was correct once again. The jaws were anything but small.

"Grab hold of the rope!" yelled Olsen. "The rope, grab it!"

A fishing spear whistled past the witcher's ear and plunged with a smack into the monster's algae-ridden armour as it surfaced. Geralt caught hold of the shaft, pressed down on it, bounced forcefully away, brought his free leg in and kicked the aeschna violently. He tore himself away from the spiked paws, leaving his boot, a fair part of his trousers and a good deal of skin behind. More fishing spears and harpoons whizzed through the air, most of them missing their mark. The aeschna drew in its paws, swished its tail and gracefully dived into the green depths.

Geralt seized the rope which fell straight onto his face. The boathook, catching him painfully in the side, caught him by the belt. He felt a tug, rode upwards and, taken up by many hands, rolled over the railing and tumbled on deck dripping with water, slime, weeds and blood. The passengers, barge crew and customs officers crowded around him. Leaning over the railings, the dwarf with the fox furs and Olsen were firing their bows. Everett, wet and green with algae, his teeth clattering, sobbed in his mother's arms explaining to everybody that he hadn't meant to do it.

"Geralt!" Boatbug yelled at his ear, "are you dead?"

"Damn it . . ." The witcher spat out seaweed. "I'm too old for this sort of thing . . . Too old . . ."

Nearby, the dwarf released his bowstring and Olsen roared joyously.

"Right in the belly! Ooh-ha-ha! Great shot, my furry friend! Hey, Boratek, give him back his money! He deserves a tax reduction for that shot!"

"Stop . . ." wheezed the witcher, attempting in vain to stand up. "Don't kill them all, damn it! I need one of them alive!"

"We've left one," the customs officer assured him. "The bald one who was bickering with me. We've shot the rest. But baldy is over there, swimming away. I'll fish him out right away. Give us the boathooks!"

"Discovery! A great discovery!" shouted Linus Pitt, jumping up and down by the barge side. "An entirely new species unknown to science! Absolutely unique! Oh, I'm so grateful to you, witcher! As of today, this species is going to appear in books as . . . As *Geraltia maxiliosa pitti*!"

"Master Tutor," Geralt groaned, "if you really want

ANDRZEJ SAPKOWSKI

to show me your gratitude, let that damn thing be called
Everetia."

"Just as beautiful," consented the scholar. "Oh, what
a discovery! What a unique, magnificent specimen! No
doubt the only one alive in the Delta—"

"No," uttered Boatbug suddenly and grimly. "Not the
only one. Look!"

The carpet of water lilies adhering to the nearby islet
trembled and rocked violently. They saw a wave and then
an enormous, long body resembling a rotting log, swiftly
paddling its many limbs and snapping its jaws. The bald
man looked back, howled horrifically and swam away,
stirring up the water with his arms and legs.

"What a specimen, what a specimen," Pitt quickly
noted, thrilled to no end. "Prehensile cephalic limbs, four
pairs of chelae . . . Strong tail-fan . . . Sharp claws . . ."

The bald man looked back again and howled even
more horribly. And the *Everetia maxiliosa pitti* extended
its prehensile cephalic limbs and swung its tail-fan vigorously. The bald man surged the water in a desperate,
hopeless attempt to escape.

"May the water be light to him," said Olsen. But he did
not remove his hat.

"My daddy," rattled Everett with his teeth, "can swim
faster than that man!"

"Take the child away," growled the witcher.

The monster spread its claws, snapped its jaws. Linus
Pitt grew pale and turned away.

Baldy shrieked briefly, choked and disappeared below
the surface. The water throbbed dark red.

"Pox." Geralt sat down heavily on the deck. "I'm too
old for this sort of thing . . . Far, far too old . . ."

242

BLOOD OF ELVES

*   *   *

What can be said? Dandelion simply adored the town of Oxenfurt.

The university grounds were surrounded by a wall and around this wall was another ring – that of the huge, loud, breathless, busy and noisy townlet. The wooden, colourful town of Oxenfurt with its narrow streets and pointed roofs. The town of Oxenfurt which lived off the Academy, off its students, lecturers, scholars, researchers and their guests, who lived off science and knowledge, off what accompanies the process of learning. In the town of Oxenfurt, from the by-products and chippings of theory, practice, business and profit were born.

The poet rode slowly along a muddy, crowded street, passing workshops, studios, stalls, shops small and large where, thanks to the Academy, tens of thousands of articles and wonderful things were produced and sold which were unattainable in other corners of the world where their production was considered impossible, or pointless. He passed inns, taverns, stands, huts, counters and portable grills from which floated the appetising aromas of elaborate dishes unknown elsewhere in the world, seasoned in ways not known elsewhere, with garnishes and spices neither known of nor used anywhere else. This was Oxenfurt, the colourful, joyful, noisy and sweet-smelling town of miracles into which shrewd people, full of initiative, had turned dry and useless theories drawn little by little from the university. It was also a town of amusements, constant festivities, permanent holidays and incessant revelry. Night and day the streets resounded with music, song, and the clinking of chalices and tankards, for it is well known that nothing is such thirsty work as the

243

acquisition of knowledge. Although the chancellor's orders forbade students and tutors to drink and play before dusk, drinking and playing took place around the clock in Oxenfurt, for it is well known that if there is anything that makes men thirstier than the acquisition of knowledge it is the full or partial prohibition of drinking.

Dandelion smacked his lips at his bay gelding and rode on, making his way through the crowds roaming the streets. Vendors, stall-holders and travelling charlatans advertised their wares and services loudly, adding to the confusion which reigned all around them.

"Squid! Roast squid!"

"Ointment for all spots'n'boils! Only sold here! Reliable, miraculous ointment!"

"Cats, mouse-catching, magic cats! Just listen, my good people, how they miaow!"

"Amulets! Elixirs! Philtres, love potions, guaranteed aphrodisiacs! One pinch and even a corpse will regain its vigour! Who'll buy, who'll buy?"

"Teeth extracted! Almost painless! Cheap, very cheap!"

"What do you mean by cheap?" Dandelion was curious as he bit into a stick-skewered squid as tough as a boot.

"Two farthings an hour!"

The poet shuddered and spurred his gelding on. He looked back surreptitiously. Two people who had been following in his tracks since the town hall stopped at the barber-shop pretending to ponder over the price of the barber's services displayed on a chalkboard. Dandelion did not let himself be deceived. He knew what really interested them.

He rode on. He passed the enormous building of the

bawdy-house The Rosebud, where he knew refined services either unknown or simply unpopular in other corners of the world were offered. For some time his rational mind struggled against his character and that desire to enter for an hour. Reason triumphed. Dandelion sighed and rode on towards the university trying not to look in the direction of the taprooms from which issued the sounds of merriment.

Yes, what more can be said – the troubadour loved the town of Oxenfurt.

He looked around once more. The two individuals had not made use of the barber's services, although they most certainly should have. At present they were standing outside a musical instrument shop, pretending to ponder over the clay ocarinas. The shopkeeper was falling over himself praising his goods and counting on making some money. Dandelion knew there was nothing to count on.

He directed his horse towards the Philosophers' Gate, the main gate to the Academy. He dealt swiftly with the formalities, which consisted of signing into a guest book and someone taking his gelding to the stables.

Beyond the Philosophers' Gate a different world greeted him. The college land was excluded from the ordinary infrastructure of town buildings; unlike the town it was not a place of dogged struggle for every square yard of space. Everything here was practically as the elves had left it. Wide lanes – laid with colourful gravel – between neat, eye-pleasing little palaces, open-work fences, walls, hedges, canals, bridges, flower-beds and green parks had been crushed in only a few places by some huge, crude mansion constructed in later, post-elven times. Everything was clean, peaceful and dignified – any kind of trade or paid service was forbidden here, not to mention entertainment or carnal pleasures.

Students, absorbed in large books and parchments, strolled along the lanes. Others, sitting on benches, lawns and in flower-beds, repeated their homework to each other, discussed or discreetly played at evens or odds, leapfrog, pile-up or other games demanding intelligence. Professors engrossed in conversation or debate also strolled here with dignity and decorum. Younger tutors milled around with their eyes glued to the backsides of female students. Dandelion ascertained with joy that, since his day, nothing had changed in the Academy.

A breeze swept in from the Delta carrying the faint scent of the sea and the somewhat stronger stink of hydrogen sulphide from the direction of the grand edifice of the Department of Alchemy which towered above the canal. Grey and yellow linnets warbled amongst the shrubs in the park adjacent to the students' dormitories, while an orangutan sat in the poplar having, no doubt, escaped from the zoological gardens in the Department of Natural History.

Not wasting any time, the poet marched briskly through the labyrinth of lanes and hedges. He knew the University grounds like the back of his hand – and no wonder, considering he had studied there for four years, then had lectured for a year in the Faculty of Trouvereship and Poetry. The post of lecturer had been offered to him when he had passed his final exams with full marks, to the astonishment of professors with whom he had earned the reputation of lazybones, rake and idiot during his studies. Then, when, after several years of roaming around the country with his lute, his fame as a minstrel had spread far and wide, the Academy had taken great pains to have him visit and give guest lectures. Dandelion yielded to their requests only sporadically, for his love of wandering was constantly at odds with his predilection for comfort, luxury and a regular income. And also, of course, with his liking for the town of Oxenfurt.

He looked back. The two individuals, not having purchased any ocarinas, pipes or violins, strode behind him at a distance, paying great attention to the treetops and façades.

Whistling lightheartedly the poet changed direction and made towards the mansion which housed the Faculty of Medicine and Herbology. The lane leading to the faculty swarmed with female students wearing characteristic pale green cloaks. Dandelion searched intently for familiar faces.

"Shani!"

A young medical student with dark red hair cropped just below her ears raised her head from a volume on anatomy and got up from her bench.

"Dandelion!" She smiled, squinting her happy, hazel eyes. "I haven't seen you for years! Come on, I'll introduce you to my friends. They adore your poems—"

"Later," muttered the bard. "Look discreetly over there, Shani. See those two?"

"Snoops." The medical student wrinkled her upturned nose and snorted, amazing Dandelion – not for the first time – with how easily students could recognise secret agents, spies and informers. Students' aversion to the secret service was legendary, if not very rational. The university grounds were extraterritorial and sacred, and students and lecturers were untouchable while there – and the service, although it snooped, did not dare to bother or annoy academics.

"They've been following me since the market place," said Dandelion, pretending to embrace and flirt with the medical student. "Will you do something for me, Shani?"

"Depends what." The girl tossed her shapely neck like a frightened deer. "If you've got yourself into something stupid again . . ."

"No, no," he quickly reassured her. "I only want to pass on some information and can't do it myself with these shits stuck to my heels—"

"Shall I call the lads? I've only got to shout and you'll have those snoops off your back."

"Oh, come on. You want a riot to break out? The row over the bench ghetto for non-humans has just about ended and you can't wait for more trouble? Besides, I loathe violence. I'll manage the snoops. However, if you could . . ."

He brought his lips closer to the girl's hair and took a while to whisper something. Shani's eyes opened wide.

"A witcher? A real witcher?"

"Quiet, for the love of gods. Will you do that, Shani?"

"Of course." The medical student smiled readily. "Just out of curiosity to see, close up, the famous—"

"Quieter, I asked you. Only remember: not a word to anyone."

"A physician's secret." Shani smiled even more beautifully and Dandelion was once more filled with the desire to finally compose a ballad about girls like her – not too pretty but nonetheless beautiful, girls of whom one dreams at night when those of classical beauty are forgotten after five minutes.

"Thank you, Shani."

"It's nothing, Dandelion. See you later. Take care."

Duly kissing each other's cheeks, the bard and the medical student briskly moved off in opposite directions – she towards the faculty, he towards Thinkers' Park.

He passed the modern, gloomy Faculty of Technology building, dubbed the "Deus ex machina" by the students, and turned on to Guildenstern Bridge. He did not get far. Two people lurked around a corner in the lane, by the flower-bed with a bronze bust of the first chancellor of the Academy, Nicodemus de Boot. As was the habit of all snoops in the world, they avoided meeting others' eyes and, like all snoops in the world, they had coarse, pale faces. These they tried very hard to furnish with an intelligent expression, thanks to which they resembled demented monkeys.

"Greetings from Dijkstra," said one of the spies. "We're off."

"Likewise," the bard replied impudently. "Off you go."

The spies looked at each other then, rooted to the spot, fixed their eyes on an obscene word which someone had scribbled in charcoal on the plinth supporting the chancellor's bust. Dandelion sighed.

"Just as I thought," he said, adjusting the lute on his shoulder. "So am I going to be irrevocably forced to accompany you somewhere, gentlemen? Too bad. Let's go then. You go first, I'll follow. In this particular instance, age may go before beauty."

*   *   *

Dijkstra, head of King Vizimir of Redania's secret service, did not resemble a spy. He was far from the stereotype which dictated that a spy should be short, thin, rat-like, and have piercing eyes forever casting furtive glances from beneath a black hood. Dijkstra, as Dandelion knew, never wore hoods and had a decided preference for bright coloured clothing. He was almost seven foot tall and probably only weighed a little under two quintals. When he crossed his arms over his chest – which he did with habitual pleasure – it looked as if two cachalots had prostrated themselves over a whale. As far as his features, hair colour and complexion were concerned, he looked like a freshly scrubbed pig. Dandelion knew very few people whose appearance was as deceptive as Dijkstra's – because this porky giant who gave the impression of being a sleepy, sluggish moron, possessed an exceptionally keen mind. And considerable authority. A popular saying at King Vizimir's court held that if Dijkstra states it is noon yet darkness reigns all around, it is time to start worrying about the fate of the sun.

At present, however, the poet had other reasons to worry.

"Dandelion," said Dijkstra sleepily, crossing the cachalots over the whale, "you thick-headed halfwit. You unmitigated dunce. Do you have to spoil everything you touch? Couldn't you, just once in your life, do something right? I know you can't think for yourself. I know you're almost forty, look almost thirty, think you're just over twenty and act as though you're barely ten. And being aware of this, I usually furnish you with precise instructions. I tell you what you have to do, when you have to do it and how you're to go about it. And I regularly get the impression that I'm talking to a stone wall."

"I, on the other hand," retorted the poet, feigning insolence, "regularly have the impression that you talk simply to exercise your lips and tongue. So get to the point, and eliminate the figures of speech and fruitless rhetoric. What are you getting at this time?"

They were sitting at a large oak table amongst bookshelves crammed with volumes and piled with rolls of parchment, on the top floor of the vice-chancellor's offices, in leased quarters which Dijkstra had amusingly named the Faculty of Most Contemporary History and Dandelion called the Faculty of Comparative Spying and Applied Sabotage. There were, including the poet, four present – apart from Dijkstra, two other people took part in the conversation. One of these was, as usual, Ori Reuven, the aged and eternally sniffing secretary to the chief of Redanian spies. The other was no ordinary person.

"You know very well what I'm getting at," Dijkstra replied coldly. "However, since you clearly enjoy playing the idiot I won't spoil your game and will explain using simple words. Or maybe you'd like to make use of this privilege, Philippa?"

Dandelion glanced at the fourth person present at the meeting, who until then had remained silent. Philippa Eilhart must have only recently arrived in Oxenfurt, or was perhaps intending to leave at once, since she wore neither a dress nor her favourite black agate jewellery nor any sharp makeup. She was wearing a man's short jacket, leggings and high boots – a "field" outfit as the poet called it. The enchantress's dark hair, usually loose and worn in a picturesque mess, was brushed smooth and tied back at the nape of her neck.

"Let's not waste time," she said, raising her even eyebrows. "Dandelion's right. We can spare ourselves the rhetoric and slick eloquence which leads nowhere when the matter at hand is so simple and trivial."

"Ah, even so." Dijkstra smiled. "Trivial. A dangerous Nilfgaardian agent, who could now be trivially locked away in my deepest dungeon in Tretogor, has trivially escaped, trivially warned and frightened away by the trivial stupidity of two gentlemen known as Dandelion and Geralt. I've seen people wander to the scaffolds over lesser trivialities. Why didn't you inform me about your ambush, Dandelion? Did I not instruct you to keep me informed about all the witcher's intentions?"

"I didn't know anything about Geralt's plans," Dandelion lied with conviction. "I told you that he went to Temeria and Sodden to hunt down this Rience. I also told you that he had returned. I was convinced he had given up. Rience had literally dissolved into thin air, the witcher didn't find the slightest trail, and this – if you remember – I also told you—"

"You lied," stated the spy coldly. "The witcher did find Rience's trail. In the form of corpses. That's when he decided to change his tactics. Instead of chasing Rience, he decided to wait for Rience to find *him*. He signed up to the Malatius and Grock Company barges as an escort. He did so intentionally. He knew that the Company would advertise it far and wide, that Rience would hear of it and then venture to try something. And so Rience did. The strange, elusive Master Rience. The insolent, self-assured Master Rience who does not even bother to use aliases or false names. Master Rience who, from a mile off, smells of Nilfgaardian chimney smoke. And of being a renegade sorcerer. Isn't that right, Philippa?"

The magician neither affirmed nor denied it. She remained silent, watching Dandelion closely and intently. The poet lowered his eyes and hawked hesitantly. He did not like such gazes.

Dandelion divided women – including magicians – into very likeable, likeable, unlikeable and very unlikeable. The very likeable reacted to the proposition of being bedded with joyful acquiescence, the likeable with a happy smile. The unlikeable reacted unpredictably. The very unlikeable were counted by the troubadour to be those to whom the very thought of presenting such a proposition made his back go strangely cold and his knees shake.

Philippa Eilhart, although very attractive, was decidedly very unlikeable.

Apart from that, Philippa Eilhart was an important figure in the Council of Wizards, and King Vizimir's trusted court magician. She was a very talented enchantress. Word had it that she was one of the few to have mastered the art of polymorphy. She looked thirty. In truth she was probably no less than three hundred years old.

Dijkstra, locking his chubby fingers together over his belly, twiddled his thumbs. Philippa remained silent. Ori Reuven coughed, sniffed and wriggled, constantly adjusting his generous toga. His toga resembled a professor's but did not look as if it had been presented by a senate. It looked more as if it had been found on a rubbish heap.

"Your witcher, however," suddenly snarled the spy, "underestimated Master Rience. He set a trap but – demonstrating a complete lack of common sense – banked on Rience troubling himself to come in person. Rience, according to the witcher's plan, was to feel safe. Rience wasn't to smell a trap anywhere, wasn't to spy Master Dijkstra's subordinates lying in wait for him. Because, on the witcher's instructions, Master Dandelion had not squealed to Master Dijkstra about the planned ambush. But according to the instructions received, Master Dandelion was duty bound to do so. Master Dandelion had clear, explicit instructions in this matter which he deigned to ignore."

"I am not one of your subordinates." The poet puffed up with pride. "And I don't have to comply with your instructions and orders. I help you sometimes but I do so out of my own free will, from patriotic duty, so as not to stand by idly in face of the approaching changes—"

"You spy for anyone who pays you," Dijkstra interrupted coldly. "You inform on anyone who has something on you. And I've got a few pretty good things on you, Dandelion. So don't be saucy."

"I won't give in to blackmail!"

"Shall we bet on it?"

"Gentlemen." Philippa Eilhart raised her hand. "Let's be serious, if you please. Let's not be diverted from the matter in hand."

"Quite right." The spy sprawled out in the armchair. "Listen, poet. What's done is done. Rience has been warned and won't be duped a second time. But I can't let anything like this happen in the future. That's why I want to see the witcher. Bring him to me. Stop wandering around town trying to lose my agents. Go straight to Geralt and bring him here, to the faculty. I have to talk to him. Personally, and without witnesses. Without the noise and publicity which would arise if I were to arrest the witcher. Bring him to me, Dandelion. That's all I require of you at present."

"Geralt has left," the bard lied calmly. Dijkstra glanced at the magician. Dandelion, expecting an impulse to sound out his mind, tensed but he did not feel anything. Philippa was watching him, her eyes narrowed, but nothing indicated that she was using spells to verify his truthfulness.

"Then I'll wait until he's back," sighed Dijkstra, pretending to believe him. "The matter I want to see him about is important so I'll make some changes to my schedule and wait for the witcher. When he's back, bring him here. The sooner the better. Better for many people."

"There might be a few difficulties," Dandelion grimaced, "in convincing Geralt to come here. He – just imagine it – harbours an inexplicable aversion to spies. Although to all intents and purposes he seems to understand it is a job like any other, he feels repulsion for those who execute it. Patriotic reasons, he's wont to say, are one thing, but the spying profession attracts only out-and-out scoundrels and the lowest—"

"Enough, enough." Dijkstra waved his hand carelessly. "No platitudes, please, platitudes bore me. They're so crude."

"I think so, too," snorted the troubadour. "But the witcher's a simple soul, a straightforward honest simpleton in his judgement, nothing like us men-of-the-world. He simply despises spies and won't want to talk to you for anything in the world, and as for helping the secret services, there's no question about it. And you haven't got anything on him."

"You're mistaken," said the spy. "I do. More than one

thing. But for the time being that brawl on the barge near Acorn Bay is enough. You know who those men who came on board were? They weren't Rience's men."

"That's not news to me," said the poet casually. "I'm sure they were a few scoundrels of the likes of which there is no shortage in the Temerian Guards. Rience has been asking about the witcher and no doubt offering a nice sum for any news about him. It's obvious that the witcher is very important to him. So a few crafty dogs tried to grab Geralt, bury him in some cave and then sell him to Rience, dictating their conditions and trying to bargain as much out of him as possible. Because they would have got very little, if anything at all, for mere information."

"My congratulations on such perspicacity. The witcher's, of course, not yours – it would never have occurred to you. But the matter is more complex than you think. My colleagues, men belonging to King Foltest's secret service, are also, as it turns out, interested in Master Rience. They saw through the plan of those – as you called them – crafty dogs. It is they who boarded the barge, they who wanted to grab the witcher. Perhaps as bait for Rience, perhaps for a different end. At Acorn Bay, Dandelion, the witcher killed Temerian agents. Their chief is very, very angry. You say Geralt has left? I hope he hasn't gone to Temeria. He might never return."

"And that's what you have on him?"

"Indeed. That's what I have. I can pacify the Temerians. But not for nothing. Where has the witcher gone, Dandelion?"

"Novigrad," the troubadour lied without thinking. "He went to look for Rience there."

"A mistake, a mistake," smiled the spy, pretending not

to have caught the lie. "You see what a shame it is he didn't overcome his repulsion and get in touch with me. I'd have saved him the effort. Rience isn't in Novigrad. Whereas there's no end of Temerian agents there. Probably all waiting for the witcher. They've caught on to something I've known for a long time. Namely, that Geralt, the witcher from Rivia, can answer all kinds of questions if he's asked in the right manner. Questions which the secret services of each of the Four Kingdoms are beginning to ask themselves. The arrangement is simple: the witcher comes here, to the department, and gives me the answers to these questions. And he'll be left in peace. I'll calm the Temerians and guarantee his safety."

"What questions are you talking about? Maybe I can answer them?"

"Don't make me laugh, Dandelion."

"Yet," Philippa Eilhart said suddenly, "perhaps he can? Maybe he can save us time? Don't forget, Dijkstra, our poet is mixed up to his ears in this affair and we've got him here but we haven't got the witcher. Where is the child seen with Geralt in Kaedwen? The girl with ashen hair and green eyes? The one Rience asked you about back in Temeria when he caught and tortured you? Eh, Dandelion? What do you know about the girl? Where has the witcher hidden her? Where did Yennefer go when she received Geralt's letter? Where is Triss Merigold hiding, and why is she hiding?"

Dijkstra did not stir, but his swift glance at the magician showed Dandelion that the spy was taken aback. The questions Philippa had raised had clearly been asked too soon. And directed to the wrong person. The questions appeared rash and careless. The trouble was that Philippa

Eilhart could be accused of anything but rashness and carelessness.

"I'm very sorry," he said slowly, "but I don't know the answer to any of the questions. I'd help you if I could. But I can't."

Philippa looked him straight in the eyes.

"Dandelion," she drawled. "If you know where that girl is, tell us. I assure you that all that I and Dijkstra care about is her safety. Safety which is being threatened."

"I have no doubt," lied the poet, "that's all you care about. But I really don't know what you're talking about. I've never seen the child you're so interested in. And Geralt—"

"Geralt," interrupted Dijkstra, "never confided in you, never said a word even though, no doubt, you inundated him with questions. Why do you think that might be, Dandelion? Could it be that this simple soul, this simpleton who despises spies, sensed who you really are? Leave him alone, Philippa, it's a waste of time. He knows shitall, don't be taken in by his cocksure expressions and ambiguous smirks. He can help us in only one way. When the witcher emerges from his hide-out, he'll get in touch with him, no one else. Just imagine, he considers him to be a friend."

Dandelion slowly raised his head.

"Indeed," he confirmed. "He considers me to be such. And just imagine, Dijkstra, that it's not without reason. Finally accept the fact and draw your conclusions. Have you drawn them? Right, so now you can try blackmail."

"Well, well," smiled the spy. "How touchy you are on that point. But don't sulk, poet. I was joking. Blackmail between us comrades? Out of the question. And believe me, I don't wish that witcher of yours any ill nor am I thinking of harming him. Who knows – maybe I'll even come to some understanding with him, to the advantage of us both? But in order for that to happen I've got to see him. When he appears, bring him to me. I ask you sincerely, Dandelion, very sincerely. Have you understood how sincerely?"

The troubadour snorted. "I've understood how sincerely."

"I'd like to believe that's true. Well, go now. Ori, show our troubadour to the door."

"Take care." Dandelion got to his feet. "I wish you luck in your work and your personal life. My regards, Philippa. Oh, and Dijkstra! Those agents traipsing after me. Call them off."

"Of course," lied the spy. "I'll call them off. Is it possible you don't believe me?"

"Nothing of the kind," lied the poet. "I believe you."

Dandelion stayed on the Academy premises until evening. He kept looking around attentively but didn't spot any snoops following him. And that was precisely what worried him most.

At the Faculty of Trouvereship he listened to a lecture on classical poetry. Then he slept sweetly through a seminar on modern poetry. He was woken up by some tutors he knew and together they went to the Department of Philosophy to take part in a long-enduring stormy dispute on "The essence and origins of life." Before it had even grown dark, half of the participants were outright drunk while the rest were preparing for blows, out-shouting each other and creating a hullabaloo hard to describe. All this proved handy for the poet.

He slipped unseen into the garret, clambered out by the window vent, slid down by way of the gutter onto the roof of the library, and – nearly breaking his leg – jumped across onto the roof of the dissecting theatre. From there he got into the garden adjacent to the wall. Amidst the dense gooseberry bushes he found a hole which he himself had made bigger when a student. Beyond the hole lay the town of Oxenfurt.

He merged into the crowd, then quickly sneaked down the backstreets, dodging like a hare chased by hounds. When he reached the coach house he waited a good half hour, hidden in the shadows. Not spotting anything suspicious, he climbed the ladder to the thatch and leaped onto the roof of the house belonging to Wolfgang Amadeus Goatbeard, a brewer he knew. Gripping the moss-covered roof tiles, he finally arrived at the window of the attic he was aiming for. An oil lamp was burning inside the little room. Perched precariously on the guttering, Dandelion knocked on the lead frames. The window was not locked and gave way at the slightest push.

"Geralt! Hey, Geralt!"

"Dandelion? Wait . . . Don't come in, please . . ."

"What's that, don't come in? What do you mean, don't come in?" The poet pushed the window. "You're not alone or what? Are you bedding someone right now?"

Neither receiving nor waiting for an answer he clambered onto the sill, knocking over the apples and onions lying on it.

"Geralt . . ." he panted and immediately fell silent. Then cursed under his breath, staring at the light green robes of a medical student strewn across the floor. He opened his mouth in astonishment and cursed once more. He could have expected anything. But not this.

"Shani." He shook his head. "May the—"

"No comments, thank you very much." The witcher sat down on the bed. And Shani covered herself, yanking the sheet right up to her upturned nose.

"Well, come in then." Geralt reached for his trousers. "Since you're coming by way of the window, this must be important. Because if it isn't I'm going to throw you straight back out through it."

Dandelion clambered off the sill, knocking down the rest of the onions. He sat down, pulling the high-backed, wooden chair closer with his foot. The witcher gathered Shani's clothes and his own from the floor. He looked abashed and dressed in silence. The medical student, hiding behind him, was struggling with her shirt. The poet watched her insolently, searching in his mind for similes and rhymes for the golden colour of her skin in the light of the oil lamp and the curves of her small breasts.

"What's this about, Dandelion?" The witcher fastened the buckles on his boots. "Go on."

"Pack your bags," he replied dryly. "Your departure is imminent."

"How imminent?"

"Exceptionally."

"Shani . . ." Geralt cleared his throat. "Shani told me about the snoops following you. You lost them, I understand?"

"You don't understand anything."

"Rience?"

"Worse."

261

"In that case I really don't understand . . . Wait. The Redanians? Tretogor? Dijkstra?"

"You've guessed."

"That's still no reason—"

"It's reason enough," interrupted Dandelion. "They're not concerned about Rience anymore, Geralt. They're after the girl and Yennefer. Dijkstra wants to know where they are. He's going to force you to disclose it to him. Do you understand now?"

"I do now. And so we're fleeing. Does it have to be through the window?"

"Absolutely. Shani? Will you manage?"

The student of medicine smoothed down her robe.

"It won't be my first window."

"I was sure of that." The poet scrutinised her intently, counting on seeing a blush worthy of rhyme and metaphor. He miscalculated. Mirth in her hazel eyes and an impudent smile were all he saw.

A big grey owl glided down to the sill without a sound. Shani cried out quietly. Geralt reached for his sword.

"Don't be silly, Philippa," said Dandelion.

The owl disappeared and Philippa Eilhart appeared in its place, squatting awkwardly. The magician immediately jumped into the room, smoothing down her hair and clothes.

"Good evening," she said coldly. "Introduce me, Dandelion."

"Geralt of Rivia. Shani of Medicine. And that owl which so craftily flew in my tracks is no owl. This is Philippa Eilhart from the Council of Wizards, at present in King Vizimir's service and pride of the Tretogor court. It's a shame we've only got one chair in here."

"It's quite enough." The enchantress made herself comfortable in the high-backed chair vacated by Dandelion, and cast a smouldering glance over those present, fixing her eyes somewhat longer on Shani. The medical student, to Dandelion's surprise, suddenly blushed.

"In principle, what I've come about is the sole concern of Geralt of Rivia," Philippa began after a short pause. "I'm aware, however, that to ask anybody to leave would be tactless, and so . . ."

"I can leave," said Shani hesitantly.

"You can't," muttered Geralt. "No one can until the situation's made clear. Isn't that so, my lady?"

"Philippa to you," smiled the enchantress. "Let's throw formalities aside. And no one has to go – no one's presence bothers me. Astonishes me, at most, but what to do? – life is an endless train of surprises . . . as one of my friends says . . . As our mutual friend says, Geralt. You're studying medicine, are you, Shani? What year?"

"Third," grunted the girl.

"Ah," Philippa Eilhart was looking not at her but at the witcher, "seventeen, what a beautiful age. Yennefer would give a lot to be that age again. What do you reckon, Geralt? Because I'll ask her when I get the chance."

The witcher smiled nastily.

"I've no doubt you will ask. I've no doubt you'll follow the question with a commentary. I've no doubt it'll amuse you no end. Now come to the point, please."

"Quite right." The magician nodded, growing serious. "It's high time. And you haven't got much time. Dandelion has, no doubt, already informed you that Dijkstra has suddenly acquired the wish to see and talk to you to establish the location of a certain girl. Dijkstra has orders from King Vizimir in this matter and so I think he will be very insistent that you reveal this place to him."

"Of course. Thank you for the warning. Only one thing puzzles me a little. You say Dijkstra received instructions from the king. And you didn't receive any? After all, you hold a prominent seat in Vizimir's council."

"Indeed." The magician was not perturbed by the gibe. "I do. I take my responsibilities seriously, and they consist of warning the king against making mistakes. Sometimes – as in this particular instance – I am not allowed to tell the king outright that he is committing a mistake, or to dissuade him from a hasty action. I simply have to render it impossible for him to make a mistake. You understand what I'm saying?"

The witcher confirmed with a nod. Dandelion wondered whether he really did understand, because he knew that Philippa was lying through her teeth.

"So I see," said Geralt slowly, proving that he understood perfectly well, "that the Council of Wizards is also interested in my ward. The wizards wish to find out where my ward is. And they want to get to her before Vizimir or anybody else does. Why, Philippa? What is it about my ward? What makes her so very interesting?"

The magician's eyes narrowed. "Don't you know?" she hissed. "Do you know so little about her? I wouldn't like to draw any hasty conclusions but such a lack of knowledge would indicate that your qualifications as her guardian amount to nothing. In truth, I'm surprised that being so unaware and so lacking in information, you decided to look after her. And not only that – you decided to deny the right to look after her to others, others who have both the qualifications and the right. And, on top of that, you ask why? Careful, Geralt, or your arrogance will be the end of you. Watch out. And guard that child, damn it! Guard that girl as though she's the apple of your eye! And if you can't do so yourself, ask others to!"

For a moment Dandelion thought the witcher was going to mention the role undertaken by Yennefer. He would not be risking anything, and would flatten Philippa's arguments. But Geralt said nothing. The poet guessed why. Philippa knew everything. Philippa was warning him. And the witcher understood her warning.

He concentrated on observing their eyes and faces, wondering whether by any chance something in the past had tied the two together. Dandelion knew that similar duels of words and allusions – demonstrating a mutual fascination – waged between the witcher and enchantresses very often ended in bed. But observation, as usual, gave him nothing. There was only one way to find out whether something had tied the witcher to anyone – one had to enter through the window at the appropriate moment.

"To look after someone," the enchantress continued after a while, "means to take upon oneself the responsibility for the safety of a person unable to assure that safety for herself. If you expose your ward . . . If she comes to any misfortune, the responsibility falls on you, Geralt. Only you."

"I know."

"I'm afraid you still know too little."

"So enlighten me. What makes so many people suddenly want to free me from the burden of that responsibility, want to take on my duties and care for my ward? What does the Council of Wizards want from Ciri? What do Dijkstra and King Vizimir want from her? What do the Temerians want from her? What does a certain Rience, who has already murdered three people in Sodden and Temeria who were in touch with me and the girl two years ago, want from her? Who almost murdered Dandelion trying to extract information about her? Who is this Rience, Philippa?"

"I don't know," said the magician. "I don't know who Rience is. But, like you, I'd very much like to find out."

"Does this Rience" – Shani unexpectedly said – "have a third-degree burn on his face? If so, then I know who he is. And I know where he is."

In the silence which fell, the first drops of rain knocked on the gutter outside the window.

Murder is always murder, regardless of motive or circumstance. Thus those who murder or who prepare to murder are malefactors and criminals, regardless of who they may be: kings, princes, marshals or judges. None who contemplates and commits violence has the right to consider himself better than an ordinary criminal. Because it is in the nature of all violence to lead inevitably to crime.
Nicodemus de Boot, *Meditations on Life, Happiness and Prosperity*

CHAPTER SIX

"Let us not commit a mistake," said Vizimir, King of Redania, sliding his ringed fingers through the hair at his temples. "We can't afford to make a blunder or mistake now."

Those assembled said nothing. Demavend, ruler of Aedirn, sprawled in his armchair staring at the tankard of beer resting on his belly. Foltest, the Lord of Temeria, Pontar, Mahakam and Sodden, and recently Senior Protector of Brugge, presented his noble profile to everyone by turning his head towards the window. At the opposite side of the table sat Henselt, King of Kaedwen, running his small, piercing eyes – glistening from a face as bearded as a brigand's – over the other participants of the council. Meve, Queen of Lyria, toyed pensively with the enormous rubies in her necklace, occasionally twisting her beautiful full lips into an ambiguous grimace.

"Let us not commit a mistake," repeated Vizimir, "because a mistake could cost us too much. Let us make use of the experience of others. When our ancestors landed on

269

the beaches five hundred years ago the elves also hid their heads in the sand. We tore the country away from them piece by piece, and they retreated, thinking all the while that *this* would be the last border, that we would encroach no further. Let us be wiser! Because now it is our turn. Now we are the elves. Nilfgaard is at the Yaruga and I hear: 'So, let them stay there'. I hear: 'They won't come any further'. But they will, you'll see. So I repeat, let us not make the same mistake as the elves!"

Raindrops knocked against the window panes and the wind howled eerily. Queen Meve raised her head. She thought she heard the croaking of ravens and crows, but it was only the wind. The wind and rain.

"Do not compare us to the elves," said Henselt of Kaedwen. "You dishonour us with such a comparison. The elves did not know how to fight – they retreated before our ancestors and hid in the mountains and forests. The elves did not treat our ancestors to a Sodden. But we showed the Nilfgaardians what it means to pick a quarrel with us. Do not threaten us with Nilfgaard, Vizimir, don't sow the seeds of propaganda. Nilfgaard, you say, is at the Yaruga? I say that Nilfgaard is sitting as quiet as a church mouse beyond the river. Because we broke their spine at Sodden. We broke them militarily, and above all we broke their morale. I don't know whether it is true that Emhyr var Emreis was, at the time, against aggression on such a scale, that the attack on Cintra was the work of some party hostile to him – I take it that if they had defeated us, he would be applauding, and distributing privileges and endowments amongst them. But after Sodden it suddenly turns out he was against it, and that everything which occurred was due to his marshals' insubordination.

And heads fell. The scaffolds flowed with blood. These are certain facts, not rumours. Eight solemn executions, and many more modest ones. Several apparently natural yet mysterious deaths, a good many cases of people suddenly choosing to retire. I tell you, Emhyr fell into a rage and practically finished off his own commanders. So who will lead their army now? The sergeants?"

"No, not the sergeants," said Demavend of Aedirn coldly. "It will be young and gifted officers who have long waited for such an opportunity and have been trained by Emhyr for an equally long time. Those whom the older marshals stopped from taking command, prevented from being promoted. The young, gifted commanders about whom we already hear. Those who crushed the uprisings in Metinna and Nazair, who rapidly broke up the rebels in Ebbing. Commanders who appreciate the roles of outflanking manoeuvres, of far-reaching cavalry raids, of swift infantry marches and of landing operations from the sea. They use the tactics of crushing assaults in specific directions, they use the newest siege techniques instead of relying on the uncertainties of magic. They must not be underestimated. They are itching to cross the Yaruga and prove that they have learned from the mistakes of their old marshals."

"If they have truly learned anything," Henselt shrugged, "they will not cross the Yaruga. The river estuary on the border between Cintra and Verden is still controlled by Ervyll and his three strongholds: Nastrog, Rozrog and Bodrog. They cannot be seized just like that – no new technology is going to help them there. Our flank is defended by Ethain of Cidaris's fleet, and thanks to it we control the shore. And also thanks to the pirates of Skellige. Jarl Crach an Craite, if you remember, didn't sign a truce with Nilfgaard, and regularly bites them, attacking and setting fire to their maritime settlements and forts in the Provinces. The Nilfgaardians have nicknamed him Tirth ys Muire, Sea Boar. They frighten children with him!"

"Frightening Nilfgaardian children," smiled Vizimir wryly, "will not ensure our safety."

"No," agreed Henselt. "Something else will. Without control of the estuary or the shore and with a flank exposed, Emhyr var Emreis will be in no position to ensure provisions reach any detachments he might care to send across the Yaruga. What swift marches, what cavalry raids? Ridiculous. The army will come to a standstill within three days of crossing the river. Half will lay siege to the stronghold and the rest will be slowly dispersed to plunder the region in search of fodder and food. And when their famed cavalry has eaten most of its own horses, we'll give them another Sodden. Damn it, I'd like them to cross the river! But don't worry, they won't."

"Let us say," Meve of Lyria said suddenly, "that they do not cross the Yaruga. Let us say that Nilfgaard will simply wait. Now let us consider: who would that suit, them or us? Who can let themselves wait and do nothing and who can't?"

"Exactly!" picked up Vizimir. "Meve, as usual, does not say much but she hits the nail on the head. Emhyr has time on his hands, gentlemen, but we don't. Can't you see what is happening? Three years ago, Nilfgaard disturbed a small stone on the mountainside and now they are calmly waiting for an avalanche. They can simply wait while new stones keep pouring down the slope. Because, to some, that first small stone looked like a boulder which would be impossible to move. And since it turned out that a mere touch sufficed to set it rolling, others appeared for whom an avalanche would prove convenient. From the Grey Mountains to Bremervoord, elven commandos rove the forests – this is no longer a small group of guerrilla fighters, this is war. Just wait and we'll see the free elves of Dol Blathanna rising to fight. In Mahakam the dwarves are rebelling, the dryads of Brokilon are growing bolder and bolder. This is war, war on a grand scale. Civil war. Domestic. Our own. While Nilfgaard waits . . . Whose side do you think time is on? The Scoia'tael commandos have thirty- or forty-year-old elves fighting for them. And they live for three hundred years! They have time, we don't!"

"The Scoia'tael," admitted Henselt, "have become a real thorn in the backside. They're paralysing my trade and transport, terrorising the farmers . . . we have to put an end to this!"

"If the non-humans want war, they will get it," threw in Foltest of Temeria. "I have always been an advocate of mutual agreement and co-existence but if they prefer a test of strength then we will see who is the stronger. I am ready. I undertake to put an end to the Squirrels in Temeria and Sodden within six months. Those lands have already run with elven blood once, shed by our ancestors. I consider the blood-letting a tragedy, but I do not see an alternative – the tragedy will be repeated. The elves have to be pacified."

"Your army will march against the elves if you give the order," nodded Demavend. "But will it march against humans? Against the peasantry from which you muster your infantry? Against the guilds? Against the free towns? Speaking of the Scoia'tael, Vizimir described only one stone in the avalanche. Yes, yes, gentlemen, do not gape at me like that! Word is already going round the villages and towns that on the lands already taken by the Nilfgaard, peasants, farmers and craftsmen are having an easier life, freer and richer, and that merchants' guilds have more privileges . . . We are inundated with goods from Nilfgaardian manufactories. In Brugge and Verden their coin is ousting local currency. If we sit and do nothing we will be finished, at odds with our neighbours, embroiled in conflict, tangled up in trying to quell rebellions and riots, and slowly subdued by the economic strength of the Nilfgaardians. We will be finished, suffocating in our own stuffy parochial corner because – understand this – Nilfgaard is cutting off our route to the South and we have to develop, we have to be expansive, otherwise there won't be enough room here for our grandchildren!"

Those gathered said nothing. Vizimir of Redania sighed deeply, grabbed one of the chalices standing on the table and took a long draught. Rain battered against the windows throughout the prolonged silence, and the wind howled and pounded against the shutters.

"All the worries of which we talk," said Henselt finally, "are the work of Nilfgaard. It is Emhyr's emissaries who are inciting the non-humans, spreading propaganda and calling for riots. It is they who are throwing gold around and promising privileges to corporations and guilds, assuring barons and dukes they will receive high positions in the provinces they plan to create in place of our kingdoms. I don't know what it's like in your countries, but in Kaedwen we've been inundated with clerics, preachers, fortune-tellers and other shitty mystics all appearing out of the blue, all preaching the end of the world . . ."

"It's the same in my country," agreed Foltest. "Damn it, for so many years there was peace. Ever since my grandfather showed the clerics their place and decimated their ranks, those who remained stuck to useful tasks. They studied books and instilled knowledge in children, treated the sick, took care of the poor, the handicapped and the homeless. They didn't get mixed up in politics. And now all of a sudden they've woken up and are yelling nonsense to the rabble – and the rabble is listening and believes they know, at last, why their lives are so hard. I put up with it because I'm less impetuous than my grandfather and less sensitive about my royal authority and dignity than he was. What sort of dignity or authority would it be, anyway, if it could be undermined by the squealings of some deranged fanatic? But my patience is coming to an end. Recently the main topic of preaching has been of a Saviour who will come from the south. From the south! From beyond the Yaruga!"

"The White Flame," muttered Demavend. "White Chill will come to be, and after it the White Light. And then the world will be reborn through the White Flame and the White Queen . . . I've heard it, too. It's a travesty of the prophecy of Ithlinne aep Aevenien, the elven seeress. I gave orders to catch one cleric who was going on about it in the Vengerberg market place and the torturer asked him politely and at length how much gold the prophet had received from Emhyr for doing it . . . But the preacher only prattled on about the White Flame and the White Queen . . . the same thing, to the very end."

"Careful, Demavend," grimaced Vizimir. "Don't

make any martyrs. That's exactly what Emhyr is after. Catch all the Nilfgaardian agents you please, but do not lay hands on clerics, the consequences are too unpredictable. They still are held in regard and have an important influence on people. We have too much trouble with the Squirrels to risk riots in our towns or war against our own peasants."

"Damn it!" snorted Foltest, "let's not do this, let's not risk that, we mustn't this, we mustn't that . . . Have we gathered here to talk about all we can't do? Is that why you dragged us all to Hagge, Demavend, to cry our hearts out and bemoan our weakness and helplessness? Let us finally do something! Something must be done! What is happening has to be stopped!"

"I've been saying that from the start." Vizimir pulled himself up. "I propose action."

"What sort of action?"

"What can we do?"

Silence fell again. The wind blustered, the shutters banged against the castle wall.

"Why," said Meve suddenly, "are you all looking at me?"

"We're admiring your beauty," Henselt mumbled from the depths of his tankard.

"That too," seconded Vizimir. "Meve, we all know you can find a solution to everything. You have a woman's intuition, you're a wise wo—"

"Stop flattering me." The Queen of Lyria clasped her hands in her lap and fixed her gaze on the darkened tapestries with their depictions of hunting scenes. Hounds, extended in a leap, were turning their muzzles up towards the flanks of a fleeing white unicorn. *I've never seen a live unicorn*, thought Meve. *Never. And I probably never will.*

"The situation in which we find ourselves," she said after a while, tearing her eyes away from the tapestry, "reminds me of long, winter evenings in Rivian Castle. Something always hung in the air. My husband would be contemplating how to get his hands on yet another maid-of-honour. The marshal would be working out how to start a war which would make him famous. The wizard would imagine he was king. The servants wouldn't feel like serving, the jester would be sad, gloomy and excruciatingly dull, the dogs would howl with melancholy and the cats sleep, careless of any mice that might be scuttling around on the table. Everybody was waiting for something. Everyone was scowling at me. And I . . . then I . . . I showed them. I showed them all what I was capable of, in a way that made the very walls shake and the local grizzly bears wake in their winter lairs. And any silly thoughts disappeared from their heads in a trice. Suddenly everyone knew who ruled."

No one uttered a word. The wind howled a little louder. The guards on the buttresses outside hailed each other casually. The patter of drops on the panes in the lead window frames grew to a frenzied staccato.

"Nilfgaard is watching and waiting," continued Meve slowly, toying with her necklace. "Nilfgaard is observing us. Something is hanging in the air, silly thoughts are springing up in many heads. So let us show them what we are capable of. Let us show them who is really king here. Let us shake the walls of this great castle plunged into a winter torpor!"

"Eradicate the Squirrels," said Henselt quickly. "Start

a huge joint military operation. Treat the non-humans to a blood bath. Let the Pontar, Gwenllech and Buina flow with elven blood from source to estuary!"

"Send a penal expedition to smother the free elves of Dol Blathanna," added Demavend, frowning. "March an interventionary force into Mahakam. Allow Ervyll of Verden a chance, at last, to get at the dryads in Brokilon. Yes, a blood bath! And any survivors – to the reservations!"

"Set Crach an Craite at the Nilfgaardian shores," picked up Vizimir. "Support him with Ethain of Cidaris's fleet, let them go ravaging from the Yaruga to Ebbing! A show of strength—"

"Not enough." Foltest shook his head. "All of that is still not enough. We need . . . I know what we need."

"So tell us!"

"Cintra."

"What?"

"To take Cintra back from the Nilfgaardians. Let us cross the Yaruga, be the first to attack. Now, while they don't expect it. Let us throw them out, back beyond the Marnadal."

"How? We've just said that it's impossible for an army to cross the Yaruga—"

"Impossible for Nilfgaard. But we have control of the river. We hold the estuary in our grasp, and the supply routes, and our flank is protected by Skellige, Cidaris and the strongholds in Verden. For Nilfgaard, getting forty or fifty thousand men across the river is a considerable effort. We can get far more across to the left bank. Don't gape, Vizimir. You wanted something to put an end to the waiting? Something spectacular? Something which will make us true kings again? That something is Cintra. Cintra will bind us and our rule together because Cintra is a symbol. Remember Sodden! If it were not for the massacre of that town and Calanthe's martyrdom, there would not have been such a victory then. The forces were equal – no one counted on our crushing them like that. But our armies threw themselves at their throats like wolves, like rabid dogs, to avenge the Lioness of Cintra. And there are those whose fury was not quelled by the blood spilt on the field of Sodden. Remember Crach an Craite, the Wild Boar of the Sea!"

"That is true," nodded Demavend. "Crach swore bloody vengeance on Nilfgaard. For Eist Tuirseach, killed at Marnadal. And for Calanthe. If we were to strike at the left bank, Crach would back us up with all the strength of Skellige. By the gods, this has a chance at success! I back Foltest! Let us not wait, let us strike first, let us liberate Cintra and chase those sons-of-bitches beyond the Amell pass!"

"Slow down," snarled Henselt. "Don't be in such a hurry to tug the lion's whiskers, because this lion is not dead yet. That is for starters. Secondly, if we are the first to strike, we will put ourselves in the position of aggressors. We will be breaking the truce to which we all put our seals. We will not be backed by Niedamir and his League, we will not be backed by Esterad Thyssen. I don't know how Ethain of Cidaris will react. An aggressive war will also be opposed by our guilds, merchants, nobles . . . And above all, the wizards. Do not forget the wizards!"

"The wizards won't back an assault on the left bank," confirmed Vizimir. "The peace agreement was the work of Vilgefortz of Roggeveen. It is well known that his plan was for the armistice to gradually turn into permanent peace. Vilgefortz will not back a war. And the Chapter, believe me, will do whatever Vilgefortz wishes. After Sodden he has become the most important person in the Chapter – let other magicians say what they will, Vilgefortz plays first fiddle there."

"Vilgefortz, Vilgefortz," bridled Foltest. "He has grown too large for us, that magician. Taking into account Vilgefortz's and the Chapter's plans – plans which I am not acquainted with anyway, and which I do not understand at that – is beginning to annoy me. But there is a way around that, too, gentlemen. What if it were Nilfgaard who was the aggressor? At Dol Angra for example? Against Aedirn and Lyria? We could arrange that somehow . . . could stage some tiny provocation . . . A border incident caused by them? An attack on a border fort, let us say? We will, of course, be prepared – we will react decisively and forcefully, with everybody's full acceptance, including that of Vilgefortz and the entire Chapter of Wizards. And when Emhyr var Emreis turns his eyes from Sodden and Transriver, the Cintrians will demand their country back – all those the emigrants and refugees who are gathering themselves in Brugge under Vissegerd's leadership. Nearly eight thousand of them are armed. Could there be a better spearhead? They live in the hope of regaining the country they were forced to flee. They are burning to fight. They are ready to strike the left bank. They await only the battle cry."

"The battle cry," bore out Meve, "and the promise that we will back them up. Because Emhyr can command eight thousand men at his border garrison; with that strength he won't even have to send for relief troops. Vissegerd knows this very well and won't move until he has the assurance that your armies, Foltest, reinforced by Redanian corps, will disembark on the left bank at his heels. But above all Vissegerd is waiting for the Lion Cub of Cintra. Apparently the queen's granddaughter survived the slaughter. Allegedly, she was seen amongst the refugees, but the child mysteriously disappeared. The emigrants persist in their search for her . . . Because they need someone of royal blood to sit on their regained throne. Someone of Calanthe's blood."

"Nonsense," said Foltest coldly. "More than two years have passed. If the child has not been found by now, she's dead. We can forget that myth. Calanthe is no more and there is no Lion Cub, no royal blood to whom the throne belongs. Cintra . . . will never again be what it was during the Lioness's lifetime. Obviously, we cannot say that to Vissegerd's emigrants."

"So you are going to send Cintrian guerrillas to their deaths?" Meve narrowed her eyes. "In the line of attack? Not telling them that Cintra can only be reborn as a vassal country under your protectorship? You are proposing, to all of us, an attack on Cintra for your own gain? You have suborned Sodden and Brugge for yourself, are sharpening your teeth on Verden and now you have caught a whiff of Cintra, is that right?"

"Admit it, Foltest," snapped Henselt. "Is Meve right? Is that why you are inciting us to this affair?"

"Come on, leave it." The ruler of Temeria furrowed his noble brow and bristled angrily. "Don't make me out as some conqueror dreaming of an empire. What are you talking about? Sodden and Brugge? Ekkehard of Sodden was my mother's half-brother. Are you surprised that following his death the Free States brought the crown to me, his relative? Blood not water! And yes, Venzlav of Brugge paid me homage as a vassal – but without coercion! He did it to protect his country because, on a fine day, he can see Nilfgaardian lances flashing on the left bank of the Yaruga!"

"And we are talking about the left bank," drawled out the Queen of Lyria. "The bank we are to strike. And the left bank is Cintra. Destroyed, burned out, ruined, decimated and occupied . . . but still Cintra. The Cintrians won't bring you their crown, Foltest, nor will they pay you homage. Cintra will not agree to be a vassal state. Blood, not water!"

"Cintra, if we . . . When we liberate it, it should become our joint protectorate," said Demavend of Aedirn. "Cintra is at the mouth of the Yaruga, in too important a strategic position to allow ourselves to lose control over it."

"It has to be a free country," objected Vizimir. "Free, independent and strong. A country which will be an iron gateway, a bulwark to the north, and not a strip of burned ground over which the Nilfgaardian cavalry will be able to gather speed!"

"Is it possible to rebuild such a Cintra? Without Calanthe?"

"Don't get all worked up, Foltest," pouted Meve. "I've already told you, the Cintrians will never accept a protectorate or foreign blood on their throne. If you try to force yourself on them as their lord, the tables will be turned. Vissegerd will again prepare his troops for battle, but this time under Emhyr's wings. And one day those detachments are going to assail us in the vanguard of a Nilfgaardian onslaught. As the spear point, as you just vividly described it."

"Foltest knows that," snorted Vizimir. "That's why he's searching so hard for this Lion Cub, for Calanthe's granddaughter. Don't you understand? Blood not water, the crown through marriage. It's enough for him to find the girl and force her to marry—"

"Are you out of your mind?" choked out the King of Temeria. "The Lion Cub is dead! I'm not looking for the girl at all, but if I were . . . It has not even occurred to me to force her to do such a thing—"

"You wouldn't have to force her," interrupted Meve, smiling charmingly. "You are still a strapping, handsome man, cousin. And Calanthe's blood runs through the Lion Cub. Very hot blood. I knew Cali when she was young. When she saw a fellow she liked, she leaped up and down so fast that if you put dry twigs beneath her feet they would have caught real fire. Her daughter, Pavetta, the Lion Cub's mother, was exactly the same. So, no doubt, the Lion Cub has not fallen far from the apple tree. A bit of effort, Foltest, and the girl would not be long in resisting. That is what you are counting on, admit it."

"Of course he's counting on it," chuckled Demavend. "Our king has thought up a cunning little plan for himself! We assail the left bank and before we realise it our Foltest will have found the girl, won her heart and have a young wife whom he will place on the throne of Cintra while her people cry for joy and pee in their knickers for happiness. For they will have their queen, blood of the blood and flesh of the flesh of Calanthe. They will have a queen . . . albeit one who comes with a king. King Foltest."

"What rubbish!" yelled Foltest, turning red then white in turn. "What's got into you? There's not a grain of sense in your prattling!"

"There is a whole lot of sense," said Vizimir dryly. "Because I know that someone is searching for the child very earnestly. Who, Foltest?"

"It's obvious! Vissegerd and the Cintrians!"

"No, it's not them. At least, not just them. Someone else is, too. Someone who is leaving a trail of corpses behind them. Someone who does not shrink from blackmail, bribery or torture . . . While we are on the subject, is a gentleman by the name of Rience in any of your services? Ah, I see from your expressions that either he isn't or you won't admit it – which comes to the same thing. I repeat: they are searching for Calanthe's granddaughter, and searching in such a way as to make you think twice about their intentions. Who is looking for her, I ask?"

"Hell!" Foltest thumped his fist on the table. "It's not me! It never occurred to me to marry some child for some throne! After all, I—"

"After all, you have been secretly sleeping with the Baroness La Valette for the past four years." Meve smiled again. "You love each other like two turtle doves and just wait for the old baron to finally kick the bucket. What are you staring at? We all know about it. What do you think we pay our spies for? But for the throne of Cintra, cousin, many a king would be prepared to sacrifice his personal happiness—"

"Hold on." Henselt scratched his beard with a rasp. "Many a king, you say. Then leave Foltest in peace for a moment. There are others. In her time, Calanthe wanted to give her granddaughter's hand to Ervyll of Verden's son. Ervyll, too, might have caught a whiff of Cintra. And not just him . . ."

"Hmm . . ." muttered Vizimir. "True. Ervyll has three sons . . . And what about those present here who also have male descendants? Huh? Meve? Are you not, by any chance, pulling wool over our eyes?"

"You can count me out." The Queen of Lyria smiled even more charmingly. "It is true, two of my offspring are roaming the world – the fruits of delightful abandon – if they have not been brought to the gallows yet. I doubt that either of them would suddenly desire to be king. They were neither predisposed nor inclined that way. Both were even stupider than their father, may he rest in peace. Whoever knew my deceased husband will understand what I mean."

"That's a fact," agreed the King of Redania. "I knew him. Are your sons really more stupid? Damn it, I thought it wasn't possible to get any more stupid . . . Forgive me, Meve . . ."

"It's nothing, Vizimir."

"Who else has sons?"

"You do, Henselt."

"My son is married!"

"And what is poison for? For the throne of Cintra, as someone here so wisely said, many would sacrifice their personal happiness. It would be worth it!"

"I will not permit such insinuations! And leave me alone! Others have sons, too!"

"Niedamir of Hengfors has two. And is a widower

himself. And he isn't old. And don't forget Esterad Thyssen of Kovir."

"I would count those out." Vizimir shook his head. "The Hengfors League and Kovir are planning a dynastic union with each other. They are not interested in Cintra or the south. Hmm . . . But Ervyll of Verden . . . It's not so far from him."

"There is someone else who is just as near," remarked Demavend suddenly.

"Who?"

"Emhyr var Emreis. He is not married. And he is younger than you, Foltest."

"Bloody hell." The King of Redania frowned. "If that were true . . . Emhyr would bugger us without grease! It's obvious that the people and nobility of Cintra will follow Calanthe's blood. Imagine what would happen if Emhyr were to get his hands on the Lion Cub? Damn it, that's all we need! Queen of Cintra, and Empress of Nilfgaard!"

"Empress!" snorted Henselt. "You exaggerate, Vizimir. What does Emhyr need the girl for, what the hell does he need to get married for? The throne of Cintra? Emhyr already has Cintra! He conquered the country and made it a province of Nilfgaard! He's got his whole butt on the throne and still has enough room to wriggle about!"

"Firstly," noted Foltest, "Emhyr grips Cintra by law, or rather by an aggressor's lawlessness. If he had the girl and married her, he could rule legally. You understand? Nilfgaard bound in marriage to Calanthe's blood is no longer Nilfgaard the invader, at which the entire north bares its teeth. It is Nilfgaard the neighbour whom one has to take into account. How would you want to force such a Nilfgaard beyond Marnadal, beyond the Amell

passes? Attacking a kingdom whose throne is legally occupied by the Lion Cub, granddaughter of the Lioness of
Cintra? Pox! I don't know who's looking for that child.
I'm not looking for her. But I declare that now I'm going
to start to. I still believe the girl is dead, but we can't take
the risk. It looks as if she is too important. If she survived
then we must find her!"

"And shall we decide now who she will marry when
we find her?" Henselt grimaced. "Such matters should
not be left to chance. We could, for that matter, hand her
over to Vissegerd's guerrillas as a battle standard, tied to
a long pole – they could carry her before the front line
as they attack the left bank. But if the recaptured Cintra
is to be useful to us all . . . Surely you see what I mean?
If we attack Nilfgaard and retrieve Cintra, the Lion Cub
can be put on the throne. But the Lion Cub can have only
one husband. One who will look after our interests at the
mouth of the Yaruga. Who of those present is going to
volunteer?"

"Not me," joked Meve. "I waive the privilege."

"I wouldn't exclude those who aren't present here,"
said Demavend seriously. "Neither Ervyll, nor Niedamir,
nor the Thyssens. And bear in mind that Vissegerd could
surprise you and put the standard attached to a long pole
to unexpected use. You've heard about morganatic marriages? Vissegerd is old and as ugly as cow's dung but
with enough decoctions of absinthe and damiana down
her throat, the Lion Cub might unexpectedly fall in love
with him! Is King Vissegerd included in our plans?"

"No," muttered Foltest, "not in mine."

"Hmm . . ." Vizimir hesitated. "Nor in mine. Vissegerd is a tool, not a partner, that's the role he is to play in

our plans for attacking Nilfgaard – that and no other. Besides, if the one who is so earnestly seeking the Lion Cub is indeed Emhyr var Emreis, we cannot take the risk."

"Absolutely not," seconded Foltest. "The Lion Cub cannot fall into Emhyr's hands. She cannot fall into anybody's— Into the wrong hands . . . Alive."

"Infanticide?" Meve grimaced. "An ugly solution, my kings. Unworthy. And surely unnecessarily drastic. First of all, let us find the girl – because we still don't have her. And when we have found her, give her to me. I'll keep her in some castle in the mountains for a couple of years, and marry her off to one of my knights. When you see her again, she will already have two children and a belly out to here."

"Leading to, if I count correctly, at least three future eventual pretenders and usurpers?" Vizimir nodded. "No, Meve. It is ugly, indeed, but the Lion Cub, if she has survived, must now die. For reasons of state. Gentlemen?"

The rain hammered against the windows. The gale howled among the towers of Hagge castle.

The kings grew silent.

"Vizimir, Foltest, Demavend, Henselt and Meve," repeated the marshal. "They met in a secret council in Hagge Castle on the Pontar. They conferred in privacy."

"How symbolic," said the slender, black-haired man wearing an elk tunic marked with the imprints of armour and rust stains, without looking round. "After all, it was at Hagge, not forty years ago, that Virfuril defeated Medell's armies, strengthened his control over the Pontar Valley and established today's borders between Aedirn and

Temeria. And today Demavend, Virfuril's son, invites Foltest, Medell's son, to Hagge, summoning Vizimir of Tretogor, Henselt of Ard Carraigh and the merry widow Meve of Lyria to complete the set. They are meeting now and holding council in secrecy. Can you guess what they are discussing, Coehoorn?"

"I can," the marshal replied succinctly. He did not say a word more. He knew that the man with his back turned hated anyone to display any eloquence or comment on obvious facts in his presence.

"They did not invite Ethain of Cidaris." The man in the elk tunic turned away from the window, clasped his hands behind his back and strolled slowly from the window to the table and then back again. "Nor Ervyll of Verden. They did not invite Esterad Thyssen or Niedamir. Which means they are either very sure of themselves, or very unsure. They did not invite anyone from the Chapter of Wizards. Which is interesting, and significant. Coehoorn, try to see to it that the wizards learn of this council. Let them know that their monarchs do not treat them as equals. It seems to me that the wizards of the Chapter have had some doubts in this respect. Disperse them."

"It's an order."

"Any news from Rience?"

"None."

The man paused at the window and stood there for a long while gazing at the hills drenched in rain. Coehoorn waited, restlessly clenching and unclenching his fist around the pommel of his sword. He was afraid he would be forced to listen to a long monologue. The marshal knew that the man standing at the window considered his monologues a conversation, and viewed conversation as a privilege and proof of trust. He knew this, but still didn't like listening to the monologues.

"How do you find the country, Governor? Have you grown to like your new province?"

He shuddered, taken unawares. He did not expect the question. But he did not ponder the answer for long. Insincerity and indecisiveness could cost him a great deal.

"No, your Highness. I haven't. That country is so . . . gloomy."

"It was different once," the man replied without looking round. "And it will be different again. You will see. You will still see a beautiful, happy Cintra, Coehoorn. I promise you. But don't be saddened, I shan't keep you here long. Someone else will take over the governorship of the province. I'll be needing you in Dol Angra. You'll leave immediately once the rebellion is quashed. I need someone responsible in Dol Angra. Someone who will not allow himself to be provoked. The merry widow of Lyria or Demavend . . . will want to provoke us. You'll take the young officers in hand. Cool their hot heads. You will let yourselves be provoked only when I give the order. No sooner."

"Yes, sir!"

The clatter of arms and spurs and the sound of raised voices came from the antechamber. Someone knocked on the door. The man in the elk tunic turned away from the window and nodded his head in consent. The marshal bowed a little and left.

The man returned to the table, sat down and lowered his head over some maps. He studied them for a long time then finally rested his brow on his interlocked hands. The enormous diamond in his ring sparkled in the candlelight as if a thousand flames.

"Your Highness?" The door squeaked faintly.

The man did not change his position. But the marshal noticed that his hands twitched. He spotted it by the flash of the diamond. He closed the door carefully and quietly behind him.

"News, Coehoorn? From Rience maybe?"

"No, your Highness. But good news. The rebellion in the province has been quelled. We have broken up the rebels. Only a few managed to escape to Verden. And we've caught their leader, Duke Windhalm of Attre."

"Good," said the man after a while, still not raising his head from his hands. "Windhalm of Attre . . . Order him to be beheaded. No . . . Not beheaded. Executed in some other way. Spectacularly, lengthily and cruelly. And publicly, it goes without saying. A terrifying example is necessary. Something that will frighten others. Only please, Coehoorn, spare me the details. You don't have to bother with a vivid description in your report. I take no pleasure from it."

The marshal nodded, then swallowed hard. He too found no pleasure in it. No pleasure whatsoever. He intended to leave the preparation and performance of the execution to the specialists, and he did not have the least intention of asking those specialists for details. And, above all, he did not intend to be there.

"You will be present at the execution." The man raised his head, picked a letter up from the table and broke the seal. "Officially. As the Governor of the Province of Cintra. You will stand in for me. I don't intend to watch it. That's an order, Coehoorn."

"Yes, sir!" The marshal did not even try to hide his embarrassment and discomfort. The man who had given the order did not allow anything to be kept from him. And rarely did anyone succeed in doing so.

The man glanced at the open letter and almost immediately threw it into the fire, into the hearth.

"Coehoorn."

"Yes, your Highness?"

"I am not going to wait for Rience's report. Set the magicians to work and have them prepare a telecommunication link with their point of contact in Redania. Let them pass on my verbal orders, which must immediately be sent to Rience. The order is to run as follows: Rience is to stop pussyfooting around, and to stop playing with the witcher. Else it could end badly. No one toys with the witcher. I know him, Coehoorn. He is too clever to lead Rience to the Trail. I repeat, Rience is to organise the assassination immediately, to take the witcher out of the game at once. He's to kill him, and then disappear, bide his time and await my orders. If he comes across the enchantress's trail before that he is to leave her alone. Not a hair on Yennefer's head is to be harmed. Have you remembered that, Coehoorn?"

"Yes, sir."

"The communiqué is to be coded and firmly secured against any magical deciphering. Forewarn the wizards about this. If they bungle it, if any undesirables learn of my order, I will hold them responsible."

"Yes, sir." The marshal hawked and pulled himself up straight.

"What else, Coehoorn?"

"The count . . . He is here already, your Highness. He came at your command."

"Already?" He smiled. "Such speed is worthy of admiration. I hope he didn't exhaust that black horse of his everyone envies so much. Have him come in."

"Am I to be present during the conversation, your Highness?"

"Of course, Governor of Cintra."

Summoned from the antechambers, the knight entered the chamber with an energetic, strong and noisy stride, his black armour grating. He stopped short, drew himself up proudly, threw his wet, muddy black cloak back from his shoulder, and laid his hand on the hilt of his mighty sword. He leaned his black helmet, adorned with wings of a bird of prey, on his hip. Coehoorn looked at the knight's face. He saw there the hard pride of a warrior, and impudence. He did not see any of the things that should have been visible in the face of one who had spent the past two years incarcerated in a place from which – as everything had indicated – he would only leave for the scaffold. A faint smile touched the marshal's lips. He knew that the disdain for death and crazy courage of youngsters stemmed from a lack of imagination. He knew that perfectly well. He had once been such a youngster himself.

The man sitting at the table rested his chin on his interlaced fingers and looked at the knight intently. The youngster pulled himself up taut as a string.

"In order for everything to be perfectly clear," the man behind the table addressed him, "you should understand that the mistake you made in this town two years ago has not been forgiven. You are getting one more chance. You are getting one more order. My decision as to your ulti-mate fate depends on the way in which you carry it out."

The young knight's face did not twitch, and nor did a single feather on the wings adorning the helmet at his hip.

"I never deceive anyone, I never give anyone false illusions," continued the man. "So let it be known that, naturally, the prospect of saving your neck from the executioner's axe exists only if you do not make a mistake this time. Your chances of a full pardon are small. Your chances of my forgiving and forgetting are . . . non-existent."

The young knight in the black armour did not flinch this time either, but Coehoorn detected the flash in his eyes. *He doesn't believe him*, he thought. *He doesn't believe him and is deluding himself. He is making a great mistake.*

"I command your full attention," continued the man behind the table. "Yours, too, Coehoorn, because the orders I am about to give concern you too. They come in a moment, for I have to give some thought to their substance and delivery."

Marshal Menno Coehoorn, Governor of the Province of Cintra and future Commander-in-Chief of the Dol Angra army, lifted his head and stood to attention, his hand on the pommel of his sword. The same attitude was assumed by the knight in black armour with the bird-of-prey-winged helmet. They both waited. In silence. Patiently. The way one should wait for orders, the substance and presentation of which were being pondered by the Emperor of Nilfgaard, Emhyr var Emreis, Deithwen

Addan yn Carn aep Morvudd, the White Flame Dancing on the Grave-Mounds of Enemies.

Ciri woke.

She was lying, or rather half-sitting, with her head resting high on several pillows. The compresses on her forehead had grown warm and only slightly damp. She threw them off, unable to bear their unpleasant weight and their stinging against her skin. She found it hard to breathe. Her throat was dry and her nose almost completely blocked with clots of blood. But the elixirs and spells had worked – the pain which had exploded within her skull and dimmed her sight a few hours ago had disappeared and given way to a dull throbbing and a sensation of pressure on her temples.

Carefully she touched her nose with the back of her hand. It was no longer bleeding.

What a strange dream I had, she thought. *The first dream for many days. The first where I wasn't afraid. The first which wasn't about me. I was an . . . observer. I saw everything as if from above, from high up . . . As if I were a bird . . . A night bird . . .*

A dream in which I saw Geralt.

In the dream it was night. And the rain, which furrowed the surface of the canal, spattered on the shingle roofs and thatches of sheds, glistened on the planks of foot-bridges and the decks of boats and barges . . . And Geralt was there. Not alone. There was a man with him in a funny hat with a feather, limp from the damp. And a slim girl in a green cloak with a hood . . . All three were walking slowly and carefully along a wet foot-bridge . . . *And I saw them from above. As if I were a bird. A night bird . . .*

Geralt had stopped short. "Is it still far?" he had asked. "No," the slim girl had answered, shaking the water off her green cloak. "We're almost there . . . Hey, Dandelion, don't lag behind or you'll get lost in these cul-de-sacs . . . And where the hell is Philippa? I saw her a moment ago, she was flying alongside the canal . . . What foul weather . . . Let's go. Lead on, Shani. And between you and me, where do you know this charlatan from? What have you got to do with him?"

"I sometimes sell him medicaments looted from the college workshop. What are you staring at me like that for? My stepfather can barely pay for my tuition . . . I sometimes need a little money . . . And the charlatan, having real medicaments, treats people . . . Or at least he doesn't poison them . . . Well, let's get going."

Strange dream, thought Ciri. *Shame I woke up. I'd like to have seen what was going to happen . . . I'd like to know what they were doing there. Where they were going . . .*

From the chamber next door came the sound of voices, the voices which had woken her. Mother Nenneke was speaking quickly, clearly worked up, agitated and angry. "You betrayed my trust," she was saying. "I shouldn't have allowed it. I might have guessed that your dislike of her would lead to disaster. I shouldn't have allowed you to— Because, after all, I know you. You're ruthless, you're cruel, and to make matters worse, it turns out you're also irresponsible and careless. You're torturing that child mercilessly, forcing her to try things which she can't possibly do. You've no heart.

"You really have no heart, Yennefer."

Ciri pricked up her ears, wanting to hear the enchantress's reply, her cold, hard and melodious voice. Wanting to hear how she reacted, how she sneered at the high priestess, how she ridiculed her over-protectiveness. She wanted to hear her say what she usually said – that using magic is no joke, that it isn't an occupation for young ladies made of porcelain, for dolls blown from thin glass. But Yennefer answered quietly, so quietly that the girl could neither understand nor even make out the individual words.

I'll fall asleep, she thought, carefully and delicately feeling her nose, which was still tender, painful and blocked with clotted blood. *I'll go back to my dream. I'll see what Geralt is doing there, in the night, in the rain, by the canal . . .*

Yennefer was holding her by the hand. They were both walking down a long, dark corridor, between stone columns or, perhaps, statues. Ciri could not make out their forms in the thick darkness. But there was someone there, in that darkness, someone hiding and observing them as they walked. She heard whispers, quiet as the rustle of the wind.

Yennefer was holding her by the hand, walking briskly and assuredly, full of decisiveness, so much so that Ciri could barely keep up with her. Doors opened before them in succession, one after another. An infinite number of doors with gigantic, heavy leaves opened up before them noiselessly.

The darkness thickened. Ciri saw yet another great door in front of her. Yennefer did not slow her stride but Ciri suddenly knew that this door would not open of its own accord. And she suddenly had an overwhelming certainty that this door must not be opened. That she must not go through it. That, behind this door, something was waiting for her . . .

She stopped short, tried to pull away, but Yennefer's hand was strong and unyielding and unrelentingly dragged her forward. And Ciri finally understood that she had been betrayed, deceived, sold out. That, ever since the first meeting, from the very beginning, from the first day, she had been no more than a marionette, a puppet on a string. She tugged harder, tore herself away from that grip. The darkness undulated like smoke and the whispering in the dark, all of a sudden, died away. The magician took a step forward, stopped, turned round and looked at her.

If you're afraid, turn back.

That door mustn't be opened. You know that.

I do.

But you're still leading me there.

If you're afraid, turn back. You still have time to turn back. It's not too late.

And you?

For me, it is.

Ciri looked around. Despite the omnipresent darkness she saw the door which they had passed through – and a long, distant vista. And there, from a distance, from the darkness, she heard . . .

The clatter of hooves. The grating of black armour. And the flutter of the wings of a bird of prey. And the voice. That quiet voice, boring into her skull . . .

You have made a mistake. You mistook the stars reflected in the surface of the lake at night for the heavens.

She woke and lifted her head abruptly, displacing the compress, fresh because it was still cool and wet. She was drenched in sweat; the dull pain was ringing and throbbing in her temples again. Yennefer was sitting beside her on the bed. Her head was turned away so that Ciri did not see her face. She saw only the tempest of black hair.

"I had a dream . . ." whispered Ciri. "In the dream . . ."

"I know," the magician said in a strange voice not her own. "That's why I'm here. I'm beside you."

Beyond the window, in the darkness, the rain rustled in the leaves of the trees.

"Damn it," snarled Dandelion, shaking water from the brim of his hat, soggy from the rain. "It's a veritable fortress, not a house. What's that fraud frightened of, fortifying himself like that?"

Boats and barges moored to the bank rocked lazily on water furrowed by the rain, bumping against each other, creaking and rattling their chains.

"It's the port," explained Shani. "There's no shortage of thugs and scum, both local and just passing through. Quite a few people visit Myhrman, bringing money . . . Everybody knows that. And that he lives alone. So he's secured himself. Are you surprised?"

"Not in the least." Geralt looked at the mansion built on stakes dug into the bottom of the canal some ten yards from the shore. "I'm trying to work out how to get to that islet, to that waterside cottage. We'll probably have to borrow one of those boats on the quiet—"

"No need," said the student of medicine. "There's a drawbridge."

"And how are you going to persuade that charlatan to

lower it? Besides, there's also the door, and we didn't bring a battering ram with us—"

"Leave it to me."

An enormous grey owl landed soundlessly on the deck's railing, fluttered its wings, ruffled its feathers and turned into Philippa Eilhart, equally ruffled and wet.

"What am I doing here?" the magician mumbled angrily. "What am I doing here with you, damn it? Balancing on a wet bar . . . And on the edge of betraying the state. If Dijkstra finds out I was helping you . . . And on top of it all, this endless drizzle! I hate flying in the rain. Is this it? This is Myhrman's house?"

"Yes," confirmed Geralt. "Listen, Shani, we'll try . . ."

They bunched together and started whispering, concealed in the dark under the eaves of a hut's reed roof. A strip of light fell on the water from the tavern on the opposite side of the canal. Singing, laughter and yelling resounded. Three bargemen rolled out on to the shore. Two were arguing, tugging, shoving each other and repeatedly swearing the same curses to the point of boredom. The third, leaning against a stake, was peeing into the canal and whistling. He was out of tune.

Dong, metallically reverberated the iron sheet tied by a strap to a pole by the deck. *Dong*.

The charlatan Myhrman opened a tiny window and peered out. The lantern in his hand only blinded him, so he set it aside.

"Who the devil is ringing at this time of the night?" he bawled furiously. "Whack yourself on that empty head of yours, you shit, you lame dick, when you get the urge to knock! Get out, get lost, you old soaks, right now! I've

300

got my crossbow at the ready here! Does one of you want six inches of crossbow bolt in their arse?"

"Master Myhrman! It's me, Shani!"

"Eh?" The charlatan leaned out further. "Miss Shani? Now, in the night? How come?"

"Lower the bridge, Master Myhrman! I've brought you what you asked for!"

"Right now, in the dark? Couldn't you do it during the day, miss?"

"Too many eyes here, during the day." A slim outline in a green cloak loomed on the deck. "If word gets out about what I'm bringing you they'll throw me out of the Academy. Lower the bridge, I'm not going to stand around in the rain, I'm soaked!"

"You're not alone, miss," the charlatan noted suspiciously. "You usually come alone. Who's there with you?"

"A friend, a student like me. Was I supposed to come alone, at night, to this forsaken neighbourhood of yours? What, you think I don't value my maidenhood or something? Let me in, damn it!"

Muttering under his breath, Myhrman released the stopper on the winch and the bridge creaked down, hitting the planks of the deck. The old fraud minced to the door and pulled back the bolts and locks. Without putting his crossbow aside, he carefully peered out.

He didn't notice the fist clad in a black silver-studded glove as it flew towards the side of his head. But although the night was dark, the moon was new and the sky overcast, he suddenly saw ten thousand dazzlingly bright stars.

* * *

Toublanc Michelet drew the whetstone over the blade of his sword once more, looking totally engrossed in this activity.

"So we are to kill one man for you." He set the stone aside, wiped the blade with a piece of greased rabbit skin and closely examined the blade. "An ordinary fellow who walks around the streets of Oxenfurt by himself, without a guard, an escort or bodyguards. Doesn't even have any knaves hanging about. We won't have to clamber into any castles, town halls, mansion houses or garrisons to get at him . . . Is that right, honourable Rience? Have I understood you correctly?"

The man with a face disfigured by a burn nodded, narrowing his moist eyes with their unpleasant expression a little.

"On top of that," Toublanc continued, "after killing this fellow we won't be forced to remain hidden somewhere for the next six months because no one is going to chase or follow us. No one is going to set a posse or reward seekers on us. We won't get drawn into any blood feuds or vendettas. In other words, Master Rience, we're to finish off an ordinary, common fool of no importance to you?"

The man with the scar did not reply. Toublanc looked at his brothers sitting motionless and stiff on the bench. Rizzi, Flavius and Lodovico, as usual, said nothing. In the team they formed, it was they who killed, Toublanc who talked. Because only Toublanc had attended the Temple school. He was as efficient at killing as his brothers but he could also read and write. And talk.

"And in order to kill such an ordinary dunce, Master Rience, you're hiring not just any old thug from the port but us, the Michelet brothers? For a hundred Novigrad crowns?"

"That is your usual rate," drawled the man with the scar, "correct?"

"Incorrect," contradicted Toublanc coldly. "Because we're not for the killing of ordinary fools. But if we do . . . Master Rience, this fool you want to see made a corpse is going to cost you two hundred. Two hundred untrimmed, shining crowns with the stamp of the Novigrad mint on them. Do you know why? Because there's a catch here, honourable sir. You don't have to tell us what it is, we can manage without that. But you will pay for it. Two hundred, I say. You shake on that price and you can consider that no-friend of yours dead. You don't want to agree, find someone else for the job."

Silence fell in the cellar reeking of mustiness and soured wine. A cockroach, briskly moving its limbs, scudded along the dirt floor. Flavius Michelet, moving his leg in a flash, flattened it with a crunch – hardly changing his position and not changing his expression in the least.

"Agreed," said Rience. "You get two hundred. Let's go."

Toublanc Michelet, professional killer from the age of fourteen, did not betray his surprise with so much as the flicker of an eyelid. He had not counted on being able to bargain for more than a hundred and twenty, a hundred and fifty at the most. Suddenly he was sure that he had named too low a price for the snag hidden in his latest job.

Charlatan Myhrman came to on the floor of his own room. He was lying on his back, trussed up like a sheep.

The back of his head was excruciatingly painful and he recalled that, in falling, he had thumped his head on the door-frame. The temple, where he had been struck, also hurt. He could not move because his chest was being heavily and mercilessly crushed by a high boot fastened with buckles. The old fraud, squinting and wrinkling up his face, looked up. The boot belonged to a tall man with hair as white as milk. Myhrman could not see his face – it was hidden in a darkness not dispersed by the lantern standing on the table.

"Spare my life . . ." he groaned. "Spare me, I swear by the gods . . . I'll hand you my money . . . Hand you everything . . . I'll show you where it's hidden . . ."

"Where's Rience, Myhrman?"

The charlatan shook at the sound of the voice. He was not a fearful man; there were not many things of which he was afraid. But the voice of the white-haired man contained them all. And a few others in addition.

With a superhuman effort of the will, he overcame the fear crawling in his viscera like some foul insect.

"Huh?" He feigned astonishment. "What? Who? What did you say?"

The man bent over and Myhrman saw his face. He saw his eyes. And the sight made his stomach slip right down to his rectum.

"Don't beat about the bush, Myhrman, don't twist up your tail." The familiar voice of Shani, the medical student, came from the shadows. "When I was here three days ago, here, in this high-backed chair, at this table, sat a gentleman in a cloak lined with musk-rat. He was drinking wine, and you never entertain anybody – only the best of friends. He flirted with me, brazenly urged me to go dancing at the Three Little Bells. I even had to slap his hand because he was starting to fondle me, remember? And you said: 'Leave her alone, Master Rience, don't frighten her, I needs must be on good terms with the little academic and do business'. And you both chuckled, you and your Master Rience with the burned face. So don't start playing dumb now because you're not dealing with someone dumber than yourself. Talk while you're still being asked politely."

Oh, you cocksure little student, thought the charlatan. *You treacherous creep, you red-haired hussy, I'm going to find you and pay you back . . . Just let me get myself out of this.*

"What Rience?" he yelped, writhing, trying in vain to free himself from the heel pressing down on his breastbone. "And how am I to know who he is and where he is? All sorts come here, what am I—?"

The white-haired man leaned over further, slowly pulling the dagger from his other boot while pressing down harder on the charlatan's chest with his first.

"Myrhman," he said quietly, "believe me or don't – as you like. But if you don't immediately tell me where Rience is . . . If you don't immediately reveal how you contact him . . . Then I will feed you, piece by piece, to the eels in the canal. Starting with your ears."

There was something in the white-haired man's voice which made the charlatan believe his every word. He stared at the stiletto blade and knew that it was sharper than the knives with which he punctured ulcers and boils. He started to shake so hard that the boot resting on his chest bounced nervously. But he did not say anything. He could not say anything. Not for the time being. Because if

Rience were to return and ask why he had betrayed him, Myhrman would have to be able to show him why. *One ear*, he thought, *one ear I have to endure. Then I'll tell him . . .*

"Why waste time and mess about with blood?" A woman's soft alto suddenly resounded from the semi-darkness. "Why risk him twisting the truth and lying? Allow me to take care of him my way. He'll talk so fast he'll bite his own tongue. Hold him down."

The charlatan howled and struggled against his fetters but the white-haired man crushed him to the floor with his knee, grabbed him by the hair and twisted his head. Someone knelt down next to them. He smelled perfume and wet bird feathers, felt the touch of fingers on his temple. He wanted to scream but terror choked him – all he managed was a croak.

"You want to scream already?" The soft alto right next to his ear purred like a cat. "Too soon, Myhrman, too soon. I haven't started yet. But I will in a moment. If evolution has traced any groove at all in your brain then I'm going to plough it somewhat deeper. And then you'll see what a scream can really be."

"And so," said Vilgefortz, having heard the report, "our kings have started to think independently. They have started to plan independently, in an amazingly short time evolving from thinking on a tactical level to a strategic one? Interesting. Not so long ago – at Sodden – all they could do was gallop around with savage cries and swords raised at the van of their company without even looking around to check their company hadn't by chance been left behind, or wasn't galloping in an entirely different direction. And today, there they are – in Hagge Castle – deciding the fate of the world. Interesting. But to be honest, I expected as much."

"We know," confirmed Artaud Terranova. "And we remember, you warned us about it. That's why we're telling you about it."

"Thank you for remembering," smiled the wizard, and Tissaia de Vries was suddenly sure that he had already been aware of each of the facts just presented to him, and had been for a long time. She did not say a word. Sitting upright in her armchair, she evened up her lace cuffs as the left fell a little differently from the right. She felt Terranova's unfavourable gaze and Vilgefortz's amused eyes on her. She knew that her legendary pedantry either annoyed or amused everybody. But she did not care in the least.

"What does the Chapter say to all this?"

"First of all," retorted Terranova, "we would like to hear your opinion, Vilgefortz."

"First of all," smiled the wizard, "let us have something to eat and drink. We have enough time – allow me to prove myself a good host. I can see you are frozen through and tired from your journeys. How many changes of portals, if I may ask?"

"Three." Tissaia de Vries shrugged.

"It was nearer for me," added Artaud. "Two proved enough. But still complicated, I must admit."

"Such foul weather everywhere?"

"Everywhere."

"So let us fortify ourselves with good fare and an old red wine from Cidaris. Lydia, would you be so kind?"

Lydia van Bredevoort, Vilgefortz's assistant and personal secretary, appeared from behind the curtain like an ethereal phantom and smiled with her eyes at Tissaia de Vries. Tissaia, controlling her face, replied with a pleasant smile and bow of her head. Artaud Terranova stood up and bowed with reverence. He, too, controlled his expression very well. He knew Lydia.

Two servants, bustling around and rustling their skirts, swiftly laid out the tableware, plates and platters. Lydia van Bredevoort, delicately conjuring up a tiny flame between her thumb and index finger, lit the candles in the candelabras. Tissaia saw traces of oil paint on her hand. She filed it in her memory so later, after supper, she could ask the young enchantress to show her her latest work. Lydia was a talented artist.

They supped in silence. Artaud Terranova did not stint himself and reached without embarrassment for the platters and – probably a little too frequently, and without his host's encouragement – clanged the silver top of the carafe of red wine. Tissaia de Vries ate slowly, devoting more attention to arranging her plates, cutlery and napkins symmetrically – although, in her opinion, they still lay irregularly and hurt her predilection for order and her aesthetic sensibility – than to the fare. She drank sparingly. Vilgefortz ate and drank even more sparingly. Lydia, of course, did not drink or eat at all.

The candle flames undulated in long red and golden whiskers of fire. Drops of rain tinkled against the stained glass of the windows.

"Well, Vilgefortz," said Terranova finally, rummaging in a platter with his fork in search of an adequately fatty piece of game. "What is your position regarding our monarchs' behaviour? Hen Gedymdeith and Francesca sent us here because they want to know your opinion. Tissaia and I are also interested. The Chapter wants to assume a unanimous stand in this matter. And, should it come to action, we also want to act unanimously. So what do you advise?"

"It flatters me greatly" – with a gesture, Vilgefortz thanked Lydia, who was offering to put more broccoli on his plate – "that my opinion in this matter should be decisive for the Chapter."

"No one said that." Artaud poured himself some more wine. "We're going to make a collective decision anyway, when the Chapter meets. But we wish to let everybody have the opportunity to express themselves beforehand so we can have an idea of all the various views. We're listening, therefore."

If we've finished supping, let us go through into the workshop, Lydia proposed telepathically, smiling with her eyes. Terranova looked at her smile and quickly downed what he had in his chalice. To the dregs.

"Good idea." Vilgefortz wiped his fingers on a napkin. "We'll be more comfortable there. My protection against magical eavesdropping is stronger there, too. Let us go. You can bring the carafe, Artaud."

"I won't say no. It's my favourite vintage."

They went through to the workshop. Tissaia could not stop herself from casting an eye over the workbench weighed down with retorts, crucibles, test-tubes, crystals and numerous magical utensils. All were enveloped in a screening spell, but Tissaia de Vries was an Archmage – there was no screen she could not penetrate. And she was a little curious as to what the mage had been doing of late. She worked out the configuration of the recently

309

used apparatus in a flash. It served for the detection of persons who had disappeared while enabling a psychic vision by means of the "crystal, metal, stone" method. The wizard was either searching for someone or resolving a theoretical, logistical problem. Vilgefortz of Roggeveen was well known for his love of solving such problems.

They sat down in carved ebony armchairs. Lydia glanced at Vilgefortz, caught the sign transmitted by his eye and immediately left. Tissaia sighed imperceptibly.

Everyone knew that Lydia van Bredevoort was in love with Vilgefortz of Roggeveen, that she had loved him for years with a silent, relentless and stubborn love. The wizard, it is to be understood, also knew about this but pretended not to. Lydia made it easier for him by never betraying her feelings to him – she never took the slightest step or made the slightest gesture, transmitted no sign by thought and, even if she could speak, would never have said a word. She was too proud. Vilgefortz, too, did nothing because he did not love Lydia. He could, of course, simply have made her his lover, tied her to him even more strongly and, who knows, maybe even made her happy. There were those who advised him to do so. But Vilgefortz did not. He was too proud and too much a man of principle. The situation, therefore, was hopeless but stable, and this patently satisfied them both.

"So." The young wizard broke the silence. "The Chapter are racking their brains about what to do about the initiatives and plans of our kings? Quite unnecessarily. Their plans must simply be ignored."

"I beg your pardon?" Artaud Terranova froze with the chalice in his left hand, the carafe in his right. "Did I understand you correctly? We are to do nothing? We're to let—"

"We already have," interrupted Vilgefortz. "Because no one asked us for our permission. And no one will. I repeat, we ought to pretend that we know nothing. That is the only rational thing to do."

"The things they have thought up threaten war, and on a grand scale at that."

"The things they have thought up have been made known to us thanks to enigmatic and incomplete information, which comes from a mysterious and highly dubious source. So dubious that the word 'disinformation' stubbornly comes to mind. And even if it were true, their designs are still at the planning stage and will remain so for a long while yet. And if they move beyond that stage . . . Well, then we will act accordingly."

"You mean to say," Terranova screwed up his face, "we will dance to the tune they play?"

"Yes, Artaud." Vilgefortz looked at him and his eyes flashed. "You will dance to the tune they play. Or you will take leave of the dance-floor. Because the orchestra's podium is too high for you to climb up there and tell the musicians to play some other tune. Realise that at last. If you think another solution is possible, you are making a mistake. You mistake the stars reflected in the surface of the lake at night for the heavens."

The Chapter will do as he says, disguising his order as advice, thought Tissaia de Vries. *We are all pawns on his chess board. He's moved up, grown, obscured us with his brightness, subordinated us to him. We're pawns in his game. A game the rules of which we do not know.*

Her left cuff had once again arranged itself differently from the right. The enchantress adjusted it with care.

"The kings' plans are already at the stage of practical realisation," she said slowly. "In Kaedwen and Aedirn an offensive against the Scoia'tael has begun. The blood of young elves is flowing. It is reaching the point of persecution and pogroms against non-humans. There is talk of an attack on the free elves of Dol Blathanna and the Grey Mountains. This is mass murder. Are we to say to Gedymdeith and Enid Findabair that you advise us to stand idly by, to watch and do nothing? Pretending we can't see anything?"

Vilgefortz turned his head towards her. *Now you're going to change tactics*, thought Tissaia. *You're a player, you can hear which way the dice roll on the table. You're going to change tactics. You're going to strike a different note.*

Vilgefortz did not lower his eyes from hers.

"You are right," he said curtly. "You are right, Tissaia. War with Nilfgaard is one thing but we must not look on idly at the massacre of non-humans and do nothing. I suggest we call a convention, a general convention of everyone up to and including Masters of the Third Degree, including those who have been sitting on royal councils since Sodden. At the convention we will make them see reason and order them to keep their monarchs in check."

"I second this proposition," said Terranova. "Let us call a convention and remind them to whom they owe first loyalty. Note that even some members of our Council now advise kings. The kings are served by Carduin, Philippa Eilhart, Fercart, Radcliffe, Yennefer—"

At the last name Vilgefortz twitched internally. But

Tissaia de Vries was an Archmage. Tissaia sensed the thought, the impulse leaping from the workbench and magical apparatus to the two volumes lying on the table. Both books were invisible, enveloped in magic. The magician focused herself and penetrated the screen.

Aen Ithlinnespeath, the prophecy foretold by Ithlinne Aegli aep Aevenien, the elven seeress. The prophecy of the end of civilisation, the prophecy of annihilation, destruction and the return of barbarianism which are to come with the masses of ice pressing down from the borders of the eternal freeze. And the other book . . . Very old . . . Falling apart . . . *Aen Hen Ichaer* . . . The Elder Blood . . . The Blood of Elves?

"Tissaia? And what do you think?"

"I second it." The enchantress adjusted her ring which had turned the wrong way round. "I second Vilgefortz's plan. Let us call a convention. As soon as possible."

Metal, stone, crystal, she thought. *Are you looking for Yennefer? Why? And what does she have to do with Ithlin's prophecy? Or with the Elder Blood of the Elves? What are you brewing, Vilgefortz?*

I'm sorry, said Lydia van Bredevoort telepathically, coming in without a sound. The wizard stood up.

"Forgive me," he said, "but this is urgent. I've been waiting for this letter since yesterday. It will only take a minute."

Artaud yawned, muffled a belch and reached for the carafe. Tissaia looked at Lydia. Lydia smiled. With her eyes. She could not do so any other way.

The lower half of Lydia van Bredevoort's face was an illusion.

Four years ago, on Vilgefortz's – her master's – recommendation, Lydia had taken part in experiments concerning the properties of an artefact found amongst the excavations of an ancient necropolis. The artefact turned out to be cursed. It activated only once. Of the five wizards taking part in the experiment, three died on the spot. The fourth lost his eyes, both hands and went mad. Lydia escaped with burns, a mangled jaw and a mutation of the larynx and throat which, to this day, effectively resisted all efforts at regeneration. A powerful illusion was therefore drawn so that people did not faint at the sight of Lydia's face. It was a very strong, very efficiently placed illusion, difficult for even the Chosen Ones to penetrate.

"Hmm . . ." Vilgefortz put the letter aside. "Thank you, Lydia."

Lydia smiled. *The messenger is waiting for a reply*, she said.

"There will be no reply."

I understand. I have given orders to prepare chambers for your guests.

"Thank you. Tissaia, Artaud, I apologise for the short delay. Let us continue. Where were we?"

Nowhere, thought Tissaia de Vries. *But I'm listening carefully to you. Because at some stage you'll finally mention the thing which really interests you.*

"Ah," began Vilgefortz slowly. "Now I know what I wanted to say. I'm thinking about those members of the Council who have had the least experience. Fercart and Yennefer. Fercart, as far as I know, is tied to Foltest of Temeria and sits on the king's council with Triss Merigold. But who is Yennefer tied to? You said, Artaud, that she is one of those who are serving kings."

"Artaud exaggerated," said Tissaia calmly. "Yennefer is living in Vengerberg so Demavend sometimes turns to her for help, but they do not work together all the time. It cannot be said for certain that she is serving Demavend."

"How is her sight? Everything is all right, I hope?"

"Yes. Everything's all right."

"Good. Very good. I was worried . . . You know, I wanted to contact her but it turned out she had left. No one knew where for."

Stone, metal, crystal, thought Tissaia de Vries. "Everything that Yennefer wears is active and cannot be detected using psychic visions. You won't find her that way, my dear. If Yennefer does not wish anyone to know where she is, no one will find out.

"Write to her," she said calmly, straightening out her cuffs. "And send the letter in the ordinary way. It will get there without fail. And Yennefer, wherever she is, will reply. She always does."

"Yennefer," threw in Artaud, "frequently disappears, sometimes for entire months. The reasons tend to be quite trivial . . ."

Tissaia looked at him, pursing her lips. The wizard fell silent. Vilgefortz smiled faintly.

"Precisely," he said. "That is just what I thought. At one time she was closely tied to . . . a certain witcher. Geralt, if I'm not mistaken. It seems it wasn't just an ordinary passing affair. It appeared Yennefer was quite strongly involved . . ."

Tissaia de Vries sat up straight and gripped the armrests of her chair.

"Why are you asking about that? They're personal matters. It is none of our business."

"Of course." Vilgefortz glanced at the letter lying discarded on the pulpit. "It is none of our business. But I'm not being guided by unhealthy curiosity but concern about the emotional state of a member of the Council. I am wondering about Yennefer's reaction to the news of . . . of Geralt's death. I presume she would get over it, come to terms with it, without falling into a depression or exaggerated mourning?"

"No doubt, she would," said Tissaia coldly. "Especially as such news has been reaching her every now and again – and always proving to be a rumour."

"That's right," confirmed Terranova. "This Geralt, or whatever he's called, knows how to fend for himself. And why be surprised? He is a mutant, a murdering machine, programmed to kill and not let himself be killed. And as for Yennefer, let us not exaggerate her alleged emotions. We know her. She does not give in to emotions. She toyed with the witcher, that's all. She was fascinated with death, which this character constantly courts. And when he finally brings it onto himself, that will be the end of it."

"For the time being," remarked Tissaia de Vries dryly, "the witcher is alive."

Vilgefortz smiled and once more glanced at the letter lying in front of him.

"Is that so?" he said. "I don't think so."

Geralt flinched a little and swallowed hard. The initial shock of drinking the elixir had passed and the second stage was beginning to take effect, as indicated by a faint but unpleasant dizziness which accompanied the adaptation of his sight to darkness.

The adaptation progressed quickly. The deep darkness

of the night paled; everything around him started to take on shades of grey, shades which were at first hazy and unclear then increasingly contrasting, distinct and sharp. In the little street leading to the canal bank which, a moment ago, had been as dark as the inside of a tar barrel, Geralt could now make out the rats roaming through the gutters, and sniffing at puddles and gaps in the walls.

His hearing, too, had been heightened by the witchers' decoction. The deserted tangle of lanes where, only a moment ago, there had been the sound of rain against guttering, began to come to life, to throb with sounds. He heard the cries of cats fighting, dogs barking on the other side of the canal, laughter and shouting from the taprooms and inns of Oxenfurt, yelling and singing from the bargemen's tavern, and the distant, quiet warble of a flute playing a jaunty tune. The dark, sleepy houses came to life as well – Geralt could make out the snoring of slumbering people, the thuds of oxen in enclosures, the snorting of horses in stables. From one of the houses in the depths of the street came the stifled, spasmodic moans of a woman in the throes of lovemaking.

The sounds increased, grew louder. He now made out the obscene lyrics of the carousing songs, learned the name of the moaning woman's lover. From Myhrman's homestead on the canal came the broken, uncoordinated gibberish of the charlatan who had been put, by Philippa Eilhart's treatment, into a state of complete and, no doubt, permanent idiocy.

Dawn was approaching. It had finally stopped raining, a wind started up which blew the clouds away. The sky in the east was clearly paling.

317

The rats in the lane suddenly grew uneasy, scattered in all directions and hid amongst the crates and rubbish.

The witcher heard footsteps. Four or five men; he could not as yet say exactly how many. He looked up but did not see Philippa.

Immediately he changed tactics. If Rience was amongst those approaching he had little chance of grabbing him. He would first have to fight his escort and he did not want to do so. Firstly, as he was under the influence of the elixir, those men would have to die. Secondly, Rience would then have the opportunity to flee.

The footsteps grew nearer. Geralt emerged from the shadows.

Rience loomed out of the lane. The witcher recognised the sorcerer instantly and instinctively, although he had never seen him before. The burn, a gift from Yennefer, was masked by the shadow of his hood.

He was alone. His escort did not reveal themselves, remaining hidden in the little street. Geralt immediately understood why. Rience knew who was waiting for him by the charlatan's house. Rience had suspected an ambush, yet he had still come. The witcher realised why. And that was even before he had heard the quiet grating of swords being drawn from their scabbards. *Fine*, he thought. *If that's what you want, fine*.

"It is a pleasure hunting for you," said Rience quietly. "You appear where you're wanted of your own accord."

"The same can be said of you," calmly retorted the witcher. "You appeared here. I wanted you here and here you are."

"You must have pushed Myhrman hard to tell you about the amulet, to show you where it is hidden. And how to activate it to send out a message. But Myhrman didn't know that the amulet informs and warns at the same time, and so he could not have told you even if roasted on red coals. I have distributed a good many of these amulets. I knew that sooner or later you would come across one of them."

Four men emerged from around a corner of the little street. They moved slowly, deftly and noiselessly. They still kept to the areas of darkness and wielded their drawn swords in such a way as not to be betrayed by a flash of blades. The witcher, obviously, saw them clearly. But he did not reveal the fact. *Fine, murderers*, he thought. *If that's what you want, that's what you'll get.*

"I waited," continued Rience without moving from the spot, "and here you are. I intend to finally rid the earth of your burden, you foul changeling."

"You intend? You overrate yourself. You are nothing but a tool. A thug hired by others to deal with their dirty work. Who hired you, stooge?"

"You want to know too much, mutant. You call me a stooge? And do you know what you are? A heap of dung on the road which has to be removed because someone prefers not to soil their boots. No, I am not going to disclose who that person is to you, although I could. But I will tell you something else so you have something to think about on your way to hell. I already know where to find the little bastard you were looking after. And I know where to find that witch of yours, Yennefer. My patrons don't care about her but I bear the whore a personal grudge. As soon as I've finished with you, I'm going after her. I'll see to it that she regrets her tricks with fire. Oh, yes, she is going to regret them. For a very long time."

"You shouldn't have said that." The witcher smiled nastily, feeling the euphoria of battle aroused by the elixir, reacting with adrenalin. "Before you said that, you still had a chance to live. Now you don't."

A powerful oscillation of his witcher's medallion warned him of a sudden assault. He jumped aside and, drawing his sword in a flash, deflected and annihilated the violent, paralysing wave of magical energy directed at him with his rune-covered blade. Rience backed away, raised his arm to make a move but at the last moment took fright. Not attempting a second spell, he swiftly retreated down the lane. The witcher could not run after him – the four men who thought they were concealed in the shadows threw themselves at him. Swords flashed.

They were professionals. All four of them. Experienced, skilled professionals working as a team. They came at him in pairs, two on the left, two on the right. In pairs – so that one always covered the other's back. The witcher chose those on the left. On top of the euphoria produced by the elixir came fury.

The first thug attacked with a feint from dextra only to jump aside and allow the man behind him to execute a deceptive thrust. Geralt spun in a pirouette, evaded and passed by them and with the very tip of his sword slashed the other one from behind across the occiput, shoulders and back. He was angry and hit hard. A fountain of blood spurted on the wall.

The first man backed away with lightning speed, making room for the next pair. These separated for the attack, slashing their swords from two directions in such a way that only one blow could be parried, the other having to meet its aim. Geralt did not parry and, whirling in a pirouette, came between them. In order not to collide, they both had to break their teamed rhythm, their rehearsed steps. One of them managed to turn in a soft, feline feint and leaped away dextrously. The other did not have time. He lost his balance and stumbled backwards. The witcher, turning in a reverse pirouette, used his momentum to slash him across the lower back. He was angry. He felt his sharp witcher's blade sever the spine. A terrifying howl echoed down the streets. The two remaining men immediately attacked him, showering him with blows which he parried with the greatest of difficulties. He went into a pirouette and tore himself from beneath the flashing blades. But instead of leaning his back against the wall and defending himself, he attacked.

They were not expecting it, did not have time to leap away and apart. One of them countered but the witcher evaded the counter-attack, spun, slashed from behind – blindly – counting on the rush of air. He was angry. He aimed low, at the belly. And hit his mark. He heard a stifled cry but did not have time to look back. The last of the thugs was already at his side, already striking a nasty sinistra with a quarte. Geralt parried at the last moment, statically, without a turn, with a quarte from dextra. The thug, making use of the impetus of the parry, unwound like a spring and slashed from a half-turn, wide and hard. Too hard. Geralt was already spinning. The killer's blade, considerably heavier than the witcher's, cut the air and the thug had to follow the blow. The impetus caused him to turn. Geralt slipped out of the half-turn just beside him, very close. He saw his contorted face, his horrified eyes. He was angry. He struck. Short but powerful. And sure. Right in the eyes.

He heard Shani's terrified scream as she tried to pull herself free of Dandelion on the bridge leading to the charlatan's house.

Rience retreated into the depths of the lane, raising and spreading both arms in front of him, a magical light already beginning to exude from them. Geralt grasped his sword with both hands and without second thoughts ran towards him. The sorcerer's nerves could not take it. Without completing his spell, he began to run away, yelling incomprehensibly. But Geralt understood. He knew that Rience was calling for help. Begging for help.

And help arrived. The little street blazed with a bright light and on the dilapidated, sullied walls of a house, flared the fiery oval of a portal. Rience threw himself towards it. Geralt jumped. He was furious.

Toublanc Michelet groaned and curled up, clutching his riven belly. He felt the blood draining from him, flowing rapidly through his fingers. Not far from him lay Flavius. He had still been twitching a moment ago, but now he lay motionless. Toublanc squeezed his eyelids shut, then opened them. But the owl sitting next to Flavius was clearly not a hallucination – it did not disappear. He groaned again and turned his head away.

Some wench, a young one judging by her voice, was screaming hysterically.

"Let me go! There are wounded there! I've got to . . . I'm a medical student, Dandelion! Let me go, do you hear?"

"You can't help them," replied Dandelion in a dull voice. "Not after a witcher's sword . . . Don't even go there. Don't look . . . I beg you, Shani, don't look."

Toublanc felt someone kneel next to him. He detected the scent of perfume and wet feathers. He heard a quiet, gentle, soothing voice. It was hard to make out the words, the annoying screams and sobs of the young wench interfered. Of that . . . medical student. But if it was the medical student who was yelling then who was kneeling next to him? Toublanc groaned.

". . . be all right. Everything will be all right."

"The son . . . of . . . a . . . bitch," he grunted. "Rience . . . He told us . . . An ordinary fool . . . But it . . . was a witcher . . . Caa . . . tch . . . Heee . . . elp . . . My . . . guts . . ."

"Quiet, quiet, my son. Keep calm. It's all right. It doesn't hurt anymore. Isn't that right, it doesn't hurt? Tell me who called you up here? Who introduced you to Rience? Who recommended him? Who got you into this? Tell me, please, my son. And then everything will be all right. You'll see, it'll be all right. Tell me, please."

Toublanc tasted blood in his mouth. But he did not have the strength to spit it out. His cheek pressing into the wet earth, he opened his mouth and blood poured out.

He no longer felt anything.

"Tell me," the gentle voice kept repeating. "Tell me, my son."

Toublanc Michelet, professional murderer since the age of fourteen, closed his eyes and smiled a bloodied smile. And whispered what he knew.

And when he opened his eyes, he saw a stiletto with a narrow blade and a tiny golden hilt.

"Don't be frightened," said the gentle voice as the point of the stiletto touched his temple. "This won't hurt."

Indeed, it did not hurt.

*   *   *

He caught up with the sorcerer at the last moment, just in front of the portal. Having already thrown his sword aside, his hands were free and his fingers, extended in a leap, dug into the edge of Rience's cloak. Rience lost his balance; the tug had bent him backwards, forcing him to totter back. He struggled furiously, violently ripped the cloak from clasp to clasp and freed himself. Too late.

Geralt spun him round by hitting him in the shoulder with his right hand, then immediately struck him in the neck under the ear with his left. Rience reeled but did not fall. The witcher, jumping softly, caught up with him and forcefully dug his fist under his ribs. The sorcerer moaned and drooped over the fist. Geralt grabbed him by the front of his doublet, spun him and threw him to the ground. Pressed down by the witcher's knee, Rience extended his arm and opened his mouth to cast a spell. Geralt clenched his fist and thumped him from above. Straight in the mouth. His lips split like blackcurrants.

"You've already received a present from Yennefer," he uttered in a hoarse voice. "Now you're getting one from me."

He struck once more. The sorcerer's head bounced up; blood spurted onto the witcher's forehead and cheeks. Geralt was slightly surprised – he had not felt any pain but had, no doubt, been injured in the fight. It was his blood. He did not bother nor did he have time to look for the wound and take care of it. He unclenched his fist and walloped Rience once more. He was angry.

"Who sent you? Who hired you?"

Rience spat blood at him. The witcher struck him yet again.

"Who?"

The fiery oval of the portal flared more strongly; the light emanating from it flooded the entire lane. The witcher felt the power throbbing from the oval, had felt it even before his medallion had begun to oscillate violently, in warning.

Rience also felt the energy streaming from the portal, sensed help approaching. He yelled, struggling like an enormous fish. Geralt buried his knees in the sorcerer's chest, raised his arm, forming the Sign of Aard with his fingers, and aimed at the flaming portal. It was a mistake.

No one emerged from the portal. Only power radiated from it and Rience had taken the power.

From the sorcerer's outstretched fingers grew six-inch steel spikes. They dug into Geralt's chest and shoulder with an audible crack. Energy exploded from the spikes. The witcher threw himself backwards in a convulsive leap. The shock was such that he felt and heard his teeth, clenched in pain, crunch and break. At least two of them.

Rience attempted to rise but immediately collapsed to his knees again and began to struggle to the portal on all fours. Geralt, catching his breath with difficulty, drew a stiletto from his boot. The sorcerer looked back, sprang up and reeled. The witcher was also reeling but he was quicker. Rience looked back again and screamed. Geralt gripped the knife. He was angry. Very angry.

Something grabbed him from behind, overpowered him, immobilised him. The medallion on his neck pulsated acutely; the pain in his wounded shoulder throbbed spasmodically.

Some ten paces behind him stood Philippa Eilhart.

From her raised arms emanated a dull light – two streaks, two rays. Both were touching his back, squeezing his arms with luminous pliers. He struggled, in vain. He could not move from the spot. He could only watch as Rience staggered up to the portal, which pulsated with a milky glow.

Rience, in no hurry, slowly stepped into the light of the portal, sank into it like a diver, blurred and disappeared. A second later, the oval went out, for a moment plunging the little street into impenetrable, dense, velvety blackness.

Somewhere in the lanes fighting cats yowled. Geralt looked at the blade of the sword he had picked up on his way towards the magician.

"Why, Philippa? Why did you do it?"

The magician took a step back. She was still holding the knife which a moment earlier had penetrated Toublanc Michelet's skull.

"Why are you asking? You know perfectly well."

"Yes," he agreed. "Now I know."

"You're wounded, Geralt. You can't feel the pain because you're intoxicated with the witchers' elixir but look how you're bleeding. Have you calmed down sufficiently for me to safely approach and take a look at you? Bloody hell, don't look at me like that! And don't come near me. One more step and I'll be forced to . . . Don't come near me! Please! I don't want to hurt you but if you come near—"

"Philippa!" shouted Dandelion, still holding the weeping Shani. "Have you gone mad?"

"No," said the witcher with some effort. "She's quite sane. And knows perfectly well what she's doing. She knew all along what she was doing. She took advantage of us. Betrayed us. Deceived—"

"Calm down," repeated Philippa Eilhart. "You won't understand and you don't have to understand. I did what I had to do. And don't call me a traitor. Because I did this precisely so as not to betray a cause which is greater than you can imagine. A great and important cause, so important that minor matters have to be sacrificed for it without second thoughts, if faced with such a choice. Geralt, damn it, we're nattering and you're standing in a pool of blood. Calm down and let Shani and me take care of you."

"She's right!" shouted Dandelion, "you're wounded, damn it! Your wound has to be dressed and we've got to get out of here! You can argue later!"

"You and your great cause . . ." The witcher, ignoring the troubadour, staggered forward. "Your great cause, Philippa, and your choice, is a wounded man, stabbed in cold blood once he told you what you wanted to know, but what I wasn't to find out. Your great cause is Rience, whom you allowed to escape so that he wouldn't by any chance reveal the name of his patron. So that he can go on murdering. Your great cause is those corpses which did not have to be. Sorry, I express myself poorly. They're not corpses, they're minor matters!"

"I knew you wouldn't understand."

"Indeed, I don't. I never will. But I do know what it's about. Your great causes, your wars, your struggle to save the world . . . Your end which justifies the means . . . Prick up your ears, Philippa. Can you hear those voices, that yowling? Those are cats fighting for a great cause. For indivisible mastery over a heap of rubbish. It's no joking matter – blood is being spilled and clumps of fur are flying. It's war. But I care incredibly little about either of these wars, the cats' or yours."

"That's only what you imagine," hissed the magician. "All this is going to start concerning you – and sooner than you think. You're standing before necessity and choice. You've got yourself mixed up in destiny, my dear, far more than you've bargained for. You thought you were taking a child, a little girl, into your care. You were wrong. You've taken in a flame which could at any moment set the world alight. Our world. Yours, mine, that of the others. And you will have to choose. Like I did. Like Triss Merigold. Choose, as your Yennefer had to. Because Yennefer has already chosen. Your destiny is in her hands, witcher. You placed it in those hands yourself."

The witcher staggered. Shani yelled and tore herself away from Dandelion. Geralt held her back with a gesture, stood upright and looked straight into the dark eyes of Philippa Eilhart.

"My destiny," he said with effort. "My choice . . . I'll tell you, Philippa, what I've chosen. I won't allow you to involve Ciri in your dirty machinations. I am warning you. Whoever dares harm Ciri will end up like those four lying there. I won't swear an oath. I have nothing by which to swear. I simply warn you. You accused me of being a bad guardian, that I don't know how to protect the child. I will protect her. As best I can. I will kill. I will kill mercilessly . . ."

"I believe you," said the magician with a smile. "I believe you will. But not today, Geralt. Not now. Because in a minute you're going to faint from loss of blood. Shani, are you ready?"

No one is born a wizard. We still know too little about genetics and the mechanisms of heredity. We sacrifice too little time and means on research. Unfortunately, we constantly try to pass on inherited magical abilities in, so to say, a natural way. Results of these pseudo-experiments can be seen all too often in town gutters and within temple walls. We see too many of them, and too frequently come across morons and women in a catatonic state, dribbling seers who soil themselves, seeresses, village oracles and miracle-workers, cretins whose minds are degenerate due to the inherited, uncontrolled Force.

These morons and cretins can also have offspring, can pass on abilities and thus degenerate further. Is anyone in a position to foresee or describe how the last link in such a chain will look?

Most of us wizards lose the ability to procreate due to somatic changes and dysfunction of the pituitary gland. Some wizards – usually women – attune to magic while still maintaining efficiency of the gonads. They can conceive and give birth – and have the audacity to consider this happiness and a blessing. But I repeat: no one is born a wizard. And no one should be born one! Conscious of the gravity of what I write, I answer the question posed at the Congress in Cidaris. I answer most emphatically: each one of us must decide what she wants to be – a wizard or a mother.

I demand all apprentices be sterilised. Without exception.

Tissaia de Vries, *The Poisoned Source*

CHAPTER SEVEN

"I'm going to tell you something," said Iola the Second suddenly, resting the basket of grain on her hip. "There's going to be a war. That's what the duke's greeve who came to fetch the cheeses said."

"A war?" Ciri shoved her hair back from her forehead. "With who? Nilfgaard?"

"I didn't hear," the novice admitted. "But the greeve said our duke had received orders from King Foltest himself. He's sending out a call to arms and all the roads are swarming with soldiers. Oh dear! What's going to happen?"

"If there's going to be a war," said Eurneid, "then it'll most certainly be with Nilfgaard. Who else? Again! Oh gods, that's terrible!"

"Aren't you exaggerating a bit with this war, Iola?" Ciri scattered some grains for the chickens and guinea-hens crowding around them in a busy, noisy whirl. "Maybe it's only another raid on the Scoia'tael?"

"Mother Nenneke asked the greeve the same thing,"

declared Iola the Second. "And the greeve said that no,
this time it wasn't about the Squirrels. Castles and citadels
have apparently been ordered to store supplies in case of
a siege. But elves attack in forests, they don't lay siege to
castles! The greeve asked whether the Temple could give
more cheese and other things. For the castle stores. And
he demanded goose feathers. They need a lot of goose
feathers, he said. For arrows. To shoot from bows, understand? Oh, gods! We're going to have masses of work!
You'll see! We'll be up to our ears in work!"

"Not all of us," said Eurneid scathingly. "Some aren't
going to get their little hands dirty. Some of us only work
two days a week. They don't have any time for work because they are, apparently, studying witchery. But in actual fact they're probably only idling or skipping around
the park thrashing weeds with a stick. You know who I'm
talking about, Ciri, don't you?"

"Ciri will leave for the war no doubt," giggled Iola
the Second. "After all, she is apparently the daughter
of a knight! And herself a great warrior with a terrible
sword! At last she'll be able to cut real heads off instead
of nettles!"

"No, she is a powerful wizard!" Eurneid wrinkled her
little nose. "She's going to change all our enemies into
field mice. Ciri! Show us some amazing magic. Make
yourself invisible or make the carrots ripen quicker. Or
do something so that the chickens can feed themselves.
Well, go on, don't make us ask! Cast a spell!"

"Magic isn't for show," said Ciri angrily. "Magic is
not some street market trick."

"But of course, of course," laughed the novice. "Not

for show. Eh, Iola? It's exactly as if I were hearing that hag Yennefer talk!"

"Ciri is getting more and more like her," appraised Iola, sniffing ostentatiously. "She even smells like her. Huh, no doubt some magical scent made of mandrake or ambergris. Do you use magical scents, Ciri?"

"No! I use soap! Something you rarely use!"

"Oh ho." Eurneid twisted her lips. "What sarcasm, what spite! And what airs!"

"She never used to be like this," Iola the Second puffed up. "She became like this when she started spending time with that witch. She sleeps with her, eats with her, doesn't leave her side. She's practically stopped attending lessons at the Temple and no longer has a moment to spare for us!"

"And we have to do all the work for her! Both in the kitchen and in the garden! Look at her little hands, Iola! Like a princess!"

"That's the way it is!" squeaked Ciri. "Some have brains, so they get a book! Others are feather-brained, so they get a broom!"

"And you only use a broom for flying, don't you? Pathetic wizard!"

"You're stupid!"

"Stupid yourself!"

"No, I'm not!"

"Yes, you are! Come on, Iola, don't pay any attention to her. Sorceresses are not our sort of company."

"Of course they aren't!" yelled Ciri and threw the basket of grain on the ground. "Chickens are your sort of company!"

The novices turned up their noses and left, passing through the horde of cackling fowl.

Ciri cursed loudly, repeating a favourite saying of Vesemir's which she did not entirely understand. Then she added a few words she had heard Yarpen Zigrin use, the meanings of which were a total mystery to her. With a kick, she dispersed the chickens swarming towards the scattered grain, picked up the basket, turned it upside down, then twirled in a witcher's pirouette and threw the basket like a discus over the reed roof of the henhouse. She turned on her heel and set off through the Temple park at a run.

She ran lightly, skilfully controlling her breath. At every other tree she passed, she made an agile half-turn leap, marking slashes with an imaginary sword and immediately following them with dodges and feints she had learned. She jumped deftly over the fence, landing surely and softly on bent knees.

"Jarre!" she shouted, turning her head up towards a window gaping in the stone wall of the tower. "Jarre, are you there? Hey! It's me!"

"Ciri?" The boy leaned out. "What are you doing here?"

"Can I come up and see you?"

"Now? Hmm . . . Well, all right then . . . Please do."

She flew up the stairs like a hurricane, catching the novice unexpectedly just as, with his back turned, he was quickly adjusting his clothes and hiding some parchments on the table under other parchments. Jarre ran his fingers through his hair, cleared his throat and bowed awkwardly. Ciri slipped her thumbs into her belt and tossed her ashen fringe.

"What's this war everybody's talking about?" she fired. "I want to know!"

"Please, have a seat."

She cast her eyes around the chamber. There were four large tables piled with large books and scrolls. There was only one chair. Also piled high.

"War?" mumbled Jarre. "Yes, I've heard those rumours . . . Are you interested in it? You, a g—? No, don't sit on the table, please, I've only just got all the documents in order . . . Sit on the chair. Just a moment, wait, I'll take those books . . . Does Lady Yennefer know you're here?"

"No."

"Hmm . . . Or Mother Nenneke?"

Ciri pulled a face. She knew what he meant. The sixteen-year-old Jarre was the high priestess's ward, being prepared by her to be a cleric and chronicler. He lived in Ellander where he worked as a scribe at the municipal tribunal, but he spent more time in Melitele's sanctuary than in the town, studying, copying and illuminating volumes in the Temple library for whole days and sometimes even nights. Ciri had never heard it from Nenneke's lips but it was well known that the high priestess absolutely did not want Jarre to hang around her young novices. And vice-versa. But the novices, however, did sneak keen glances at the boy and chatted freely, discussing the various possibilities presented by the presence on the Temple grounds of something which wore trousers. Ciri was amazed because Jarre was the exact opposite of everything which, in her eyes, should represent an attractive male. In Cintra, as she remembered, an attractive man was one whose head reached the ceiling, whose shoulders were as broad as a doorway, who swore like a dwarf, roared like a buffalo and stank at thirty paces of horses, sweat and beer, regardless of what time of day or night it was. Men who did not correspond to this description were not recognised by Queen Calanthe's chambermaids as worthy of sighs and gossip. Ciri had also seen a number of different men – the wise and gentle druids of Angren, the tall and gloomy settlers of Sodden, the witchers of Kaer Morhen. Jarre was different. He was as skinny as a stick-insect, ungainly, wore clothes which were too large and smelled of ink and dust, always had greasy hair and on his chin, instead of stubble, there were seven or eight long hairs, about half of which sprang from a large wart. Truly, Ciri did not understand why she was so drawn to Jarre's tower. She enjoyed talking to him. The boy knew a great deal and she could learn much from him. But recently, when he looked at her, his eyes had a strange, dazed and cloying expression.

"Well." She grew impatient. "Are you going to tell me or not?"

"There's nothing to say. There isn't going to be any war. It's all gossip."

"Aha," she snorted. "And so the duke is sending out a call to arms just for fun? The army is marching the highways out of boredom? Don't twist things, Jarre. You visit the town and castle, you must know something!"

"Why don't you ask Lady Yennefer about it?"

"Lady Yennefer has more important things to worry about!" Ciri spat, but then immediately had second thoughts, smiled pleasantly and fluttered her eyelashes. "Oh, Jarre, tell me, please! You're so clever! You can talk so beautifully and learnedly, I could listen to you for hours! Please, Jarre!"

The boy turned red and his eyes grew unfocused and bleary. Ciri sighed surreptitiously.

"Hmm . . ." Jarre shuffled from foot to foot and moved his arms undecidedly, evidently not knowing what to do with them. "What can I tell you? It's true, people are gossiping in town, all excited by the events in Dol Angra . . . But there isn't going to be a war. That's for sure. You can believe me."

"Of course, I can," she snorted. "But I'd rather know what you base this certainty on. You don't sit on the duke's council, as far as I know. And if you were made a voivode yesterday, then do tell me about it. I'll congratulate you."

"I study historical treatises," Jarre turned crimson, "and one can learn more from them than sitting on a council. I've read *The History of War* by Marshal Pelligram, Duke de Ruyter's *Strategy*, Bronibor's *The Victorious Deeds of Redania's Gallant Cavalrymen* . . . And I know enough about the present political situation to be able to draw conclusions through analogy. Do you know what an analogy is?"

"Of course," lied Ciri, picking a blade of grass from the buckle of her shoe.

"If the history of past wars" – the boy stared at the ceiling – "were to be laid over present political geography, it is easy to gauge that minor border incidents, such as the one in Dol Angra, are fortuitous and insignificant. You, as a student of magic, must, no doubt, be acquainted with the present political geography?"

Ciri did not reply. Lost in thought, she skimmed

through the parchments lying on the table and turned a few pages of the huge leather-bound volume.

"Leave that alone. Don't touch it." Jarre was worried. "It's an exceptionally valuable and unique work."

"I'm not going to eat it."

"Your hands are dirty."

"They're cleaner than yours. Listen, do you have any maps here?"

"I do, but they're hidden in the chest," said the boy quickly, but seeing Ciri pull a face, he sighed, pushed the scrolls of parchment off the chest, lifted the lid and started to rummage through the contents. Ciri, wriggling in the chair and swinging her legs, carried on flicking through the book. From between the pages suddenly slipped a loose page with a picture of a woman, completely naked with her hair curled into ringlets, entangled in an embrace with a completely naked bearded man. Her tongue sticking out, the girl spent a long time turning the etching around, unable to make out which way up it should be. She finally spotted the most important detail in the picture and giggled. Jarre, walking up with an enormous scroll under his arm, blushed violently, took the etching from her without a word and hid it under the papers strewn across the table.

"An exceptionally valuable and unique work," she gibed. "Are those the analogies you're studying? Are there any more pictures like that in there? Interesting, the book is called *Healing and Curing*. I'd like to know what diseases are cured that way."

"You can read the First Runes?" The boy was surprised and cleared his throat with embarrassment. "I didn't know . . ."

"There's still a lot you don't know." She turned up her nose. "And what do you think? I'm not just some novice feeding hens for eggs. I am . . . a wizard. Well, go on. Show me that map!"

They both knelt on the floor, holding down the stiff sheet, which was stubbornly trying to roll up again, with their hands and knees. Ciri finally weighed down one corner with a chair leg and Jarre pressed another down with a hefty book entitled *The Life and Deeds of Great King Radovid*.

"Hmm . . . This map is so unclear! I can't make head or tail of it . . . Where are we? Where is Ellander?"

"Here." He pointed. "Here is Temeria, this space. Here is Wyzima, our King Foltest's capital. Here, in Pontar Valley, lies the duchy of Ellander. And here . . . Yes, here is our Temple."

"And what's this lake? There aren't any lakes around here."

"That isn't a lake. It's an ink blot . . ."

"Ah. And here . . . This is Cintra. Is that right?"

"Yes. South of Transriver and Sodden. This way, here, flows the River Yaruga, flowing into the sea right at Cintra. That country, I don't know if you know, is now dominated by the Nilfgaardians—"

"I do know," she cut him short, clenching her fist. "I know very well. And where is this Nilfgaard? I can't see a country like that here. Doesn't it fit on this map of yours, or what? Get me a bigger one!"

"Hmm . . ." Jarre scratched the wart on his chin. "I don't have any maps like that . . . But I do know that Nilfgaard is somewhere further towards the south . . . There, more or less there. I think."

"So far?" Ciri was surprised, her eyes fixed on the place on the floor which he indicated. "They've come all the way from there? And on the way conquered those other countries?"

"Yes, that's true. They conquered Metinna, Maecht, Nazair, Ebbing, all the kingdoms south of the Amell Mountains. Those kingdoms, like Cintra and Upper Sodden, the Nilfgaardians now call the Provinces. But they didn't manage to dominate Lower Sodden, Verden and Brugge. Here, on the Yaruga, the armies of the Four Kingdoms held them back, defeating them in battle—"

"I know, I studied history." Ciri slapped the map with her open palm. "Well, Jarre, tell me about the war. We're kneeling on political geography. Draw conclusions through analogy and through anything you like. I'm all ears."

The boy blushed, then started to explain, pointing to the appropriate regions on the map with the tip of a quill.

"At present, the border between us and the South – dominated by Nilfgaard – is demarcated, as you can see, by the Yaruga River. It constitutes an obstacle which is practically insurmountable. It hardly ever freezes over, and during the rainy season it can carry so much water that its bed is almost a mile wide. For a long stretch, here, it flows between precipitous, inaccessible banks, between the rocks of Mahakam . . ."

"The land of dwarves and gnomes?"

"Yes. And so the Yaruga can only be crossed here, in its lower reaches, in Sodden, and here, in its middle reaches, in the valley of Dol Angra . . ."

"And it was exactly in Dol Angra, that inci— Incident?"

"Wait. I'm just explaining to you that, at the moment, no army could cross the Yaruga River. Both accessible valleys, those along which armies have marched for centuries, are very heavily manned and defended, both by us and by Nilfgaard. Look at the map. Look how many strongholds there are. See, here is Verden, here is Brugge, here the Isles of Skellige . . ."

"And this, what is this? This huge white mark?"

Jarre moved closer; she felt the warmth of his knee.

"Brokilon Forest," he said, "is forbidden territory. The kingdom of forest dryads. Brokilon also defends our flank. The dryads won't let anyone pass. The Nilfgaardians either . . ."

"Hmm . . ." Ciri leaned over the map. "Here is Aedirn . . . And the town of Vengerberg . . . Jarre! Stop that immediately!"

The boy abruptly pulled his lips away from her hair and went as red as a beetroot.

"I do not wish you to do that to me!"

"Ciri, I—"

"I came to you with a serious matter, as a wizard to a scholar," she said icily and with dignity, in a tone of voice which exactly copied that of Yennefer. "So behave!"

The "scholar" blushed an even deeper shade and had such a stupid expression on his face that the "wizard" could barely keep herself from laughing. He leaned over the map once more.

"All this geography of yours," she continued, "hasn't led to anything yet. You're telling me about the Yaruga River but the Nilfgaardians have, after all, already crossed to the other side once. What's stopping them now?"

"That time," hawked Jarre, wiping the sweat which

had all of a sudden appeared on his brow, "they only had Brugge, Sodden and Temeria against them. Now, we're united in an alliance. Like at the battle of Sodden. The Four Kingdoms. Temeria, Redania, Aedirn and Kaedwen . . ."

"Kaedwen," said Ciri proudly. "Yes, I know what that alliance is based on. King Henselt of Kaedwen offers special, secret aid to King Demavend of Aedirn. That aid is transported in barrels. And when King Demavend suspects someone of being a traitor, he puts stones in the barrels. Sets a trap—"

She broke off, recalling that Geralt had forbidden her to mention the events in Kaedwen. Jarre stared at her suspiciously.

"Is that so? And how can you know all that?"

"I read about it in a book written by Marshal Pelican," she snorted. "And in other analogies. Tell me what happened in Dol Angra or whatever it's called. But first, show me where it is."

"Here. Dol Angra is a wide valley, a route leading from the south to the kingdoms of Lyria and Rivia, to Aedirn, and further to Dol Blathanna and Kaedwen . . . And through Pontar Valley to us, to Temeria."

"And what happened there?"

"There was fighting. Apparently. I don't know much about it, but that's what they're saying at the castle."

"If there was fighting," frowned Ciri, "there's a war already! So what are you talking about?"

"It's not the first time there's been fighting," clarified Jarre, but the girl saw that he was less and less sure of himself. "Incidents at the border are very frequent. But they're insignificant."

"And how come?"

"The forces are balanced. Neither we nor the Nilf-gaardians can do anything. And neither of the sides can give their opponent a *casus belli*—"

"Give what?"

"A reason for war. Understand? That's why the armed incidents in Dol Angra are most certainly fortuitous matters, probably attacks by brigands or skirmishes with smugglers . . . In no way can they be the work of regular armies, neither ours nor those of Nilfgaard . . . Because that would be precisely a *casus belli* . . ."

"Aha. Jarre, tell me—"

She broke off. She raised her head abruptly, quickly touched her temples with her fingers and frowned.

"I've got to go," she said. "Lady Yennefer is calling me."

"You can hear her?" The boy was intrigued. "At a distance? How . . ."

"I've got to go," she repeated, getting to her feet and brushing the dust off her knees. "Listen, Jarre. I'm leaving with Lady Yennefer, on some very important matters. I don't know when we'll be back. I warn you they are secret matters which concern only wizards, so don't ask any questions."

Jarre also stood up. He adjusted his clothing but still did not know what to do with his hands. His eyes glazed over sickeningly.

"Ciri . . ."

"What?"

"I . . . I . . ."

"I don't know what you're talking about," she said

impatiently, glaring at him with her huge, emerald eyes. "Nor do you, obviously. I'm off. Take care, Jarre."

"Goodbye . . . Ciri. Have a safe journey. I'll . . . I'll be thinking of you . . ."

Ciri sighed.

"I'm here, Lady Yennefer!"

She flew into the chamber like a shot from a catapult and the door thumped open, slamming against the wall. She could have broken her legs on the stool standing in her way but Ciri jumped over it deftly, gracefully executed a half-pirouette feigning the slash of a sword, and joyfully laughed at her successful trick. Despite running briskly, she did not pant but breathed evenly and calmly. She had mastered breath control to perfection.

"I'm here!" she repeated.

"At last. Get undressed, and into the tub. Quick."

The enchantress did not look round, did not turn away from the table, looked at Ciri in the mirror. Slowly. She combed her damp, black curls which straightened under the pressure of the comb only to spring back a moment later into shiny waves.

The girl unbuckled her boots in a flash, kicked them off, freed herself of her clothes and with a splash landed in the tub. Grabbing the soap, she started to energetically scrub her forearms.

Yennefer sat motionless, staring at the window and toying with her comb. Ciri snorted, spluttered and spat because soap had got into her mouth. She tossed her head wondering whether a spell existed which could make washing possible without water, soap and wasting time.

The magician put the comb aside but, lost in thought,

kept gazing through the window at the swarms of ravens and crows croaking horrifically as they flew east. On the table, next to the mirror and an impressive array of bottled cosmetics, lay several letters. Ciri knew that Yennefer had been waiting for them a long time and that the day on which they were to leave the Temple depended on her receiving these letters. In spite of what she had told Jarre, the girl had no idea where and why they were leaving. But in those letters . . .

Splashing with her left hand so as to mislead, she arranged the fingers of her right in a gesture, concentrated on a formula, fixed her eyes on the letters and sent out an impulse.

"Don't you even dare," said Yennefer, without turning around.

"I thought . . ." She cleared her throat. "I thought one of them might be from Geralt . . ."

"If it was, I'd have given it to you." The magician turned in her chair and sat facing her. "Are you going to be long washing?"

"I've finished."

"Get up, please."

Ciri obeyed. Yennefer smiled faintly.

"Yes," she said, "you've finished with childhood. You've rounded out where necessary. Lower your hands. I'm not interested in your elbows. Well, well, don't blush, no false shyness. It's your body, the most natural thing in the world. And the fact that you're developing is just as natural. If your fate had turned out differently . . . If it weren't for the war, you'd have long been the wife of some duke or prince. You realise that, don't you? We've discussed matters concerning your gender often enough and in enough detail for you to know that you're already a woman. Physiologically, that is to say. Surely you've not forgotten what we talked about?"

"No. I haven't."

"When you visit Jarre I hope there aren't any problems with your memory either?"

Ciri lowered her eyes, but only momentarily. Yennefer did not smile.

"Dry yourself and come here," she said coolly. "No splashing, please."

Wrapped in a towel, Ciri sat down on the small chair at the magician's knees. Yennefer brushed the girl's hair, every now and again snipping off a disobedient wisp with a pair of scissors.

"Are you angry with me?" asked the girl reluctantly. "For, for . . . going to the tower?"

"No. But Nenneke doesn't like it. You know that."

"But I haven't . . . I don't care about Jarre in the least." Ciri blushed a little. "I only . . ."

"Exactly," muttered the enchantress. "You only. Don't play the child because you're not one anymore, let me remind you. That boy slobbers and stammers at the sight of you. Can't you see that?"

"That's not my fault! What am I supposed to do?"

Yennefer stopped combing Ciri's hair and measured her with a deep, violet gaze.

"Don't toy with him. It's base."

"But I'm not toying with him! I'm only talking to him!"

"I'd like to believe," the enchantress said as she snipped her scissors, cutting yet another wisp of hair which would not allow itself to be styled for anything in the world, "that during these conversations, you remember what I asked you."

"I remember, I remember!"

"He's an intelligent and bright boy. One or two inadvertent words could lead him on the right track, to matters he should know nothing about. No one, absolutely no one must find out who you are."

"I remember," repeated Ciri. "I haven't squealed a word to anyone, you can be sure of that. Tell me, is that why we have to leave so suddenly? Are you afraid that someone's going to find out I'm here? Is that why?"

"No. There are other reasons."

"Is it because . . . there might be a war? Everybody's talking about another war! Everybody's talking about it, Lady Yennefer."

"Indeed," the magician confirmed coolly, snipping her scissors just above Ciri's ear. "It's a subject which belongs to the so-called interminable category. There's been talk about wars in the past, there is talk now and there always will be. And not without reason – there have been wars and there will be wars. Lower your head."

"Jarre said . . . that there's not going to be a war with Nilfgaard. He spoke of some sort of analogies . . . Showed me a map. I don't know what to think myself anymore. I don't know what these analogies are, probably something terribly clever . . . Jarre reads various learned books and knows it all, but I think . . ."

"It interests me, what you think, Ciri."

"In Cintra . . . That time . . . Lady Yennefer, my grandmother was much cleverer than Jarre. King Eist was clever, too. He sailed the seas, saw everything, even a narwhal and sea serpent, and I bet he also saw many an analogy. And so what? Suddenly they appeared, the Nilfgaardians . . ."

Ciri raised her head and her voice stuck in her throat. Yennefer put her arms around her and hugged her tightly.

"Unfortunately," she said quietly, "unfortunately, you're right, my ugly one. If the ability to make use of experience and draw conclusions decided, we would have forgotten what war is a long time ago. But those whose goal is war have never been held back, nor will be, by experience or analogy."

"So . . . It's true, after all. There is going to be a war. Is that why we have to leave?"

"Let's not talk about it. Let's not worry too soon."

Ciri sniffed.

"I've already seen a war," she whispered. "I don't want to see another. Never. I don't want to be alone again. I don't want to be frightened. I don't want to lose everything again, like that time. I don't want to lose Geralt . . . or you, Lady Yennefer. I don't want to lose you. I want to stay with you. And him. Always."

"You will." The magician's voice trembled a little. "And I'm going to be with you, Ciri. Always. I promise you."

Ciri sniffed again. Yennefer coughed quietly, put down the scissors and comb, got to her feet and crossed over to the window. The ravens were still croaking in their flight towards the mountains.

"When I arrived here," the lady magician suddenly said in her usual, melodious, slightly mocking voice. "When we first met . . . You didn't like me."

Ciri did not say anything. *Our first meeting*, she

thought. *I remember. I was in the Grotto with the other girls. Hrosvitha was showing us plants and herbs. Then Iola the First came in and whispered something in Hrosvitha's ear. The priestess grimaced with animosity. And Iola the First came up to me with a strange expression on her face.* "Get yourself together, Ciri," *she said*, "and go the refectory, quick. Mother Nenneke is summoning you. Someone has arrived."

Strange, meaningful glances, excitement in their eyes. And whispers. Yennefer. "Magician Yennefer. Quick, Ciri, hurry up. Mother Nenneke is waiting. And she is waiting."

I knew immediately, thought Ciri, *that it was her. Because I'd seen her. I'd seen her the night before. In my dream.*

Her.

I didn't know her name then. She didn't say anything in my dream. She only looked at me and behind her, in the darkness, I saw a closed door . . .

Ciri sighed. Yennefer turned and the obsidian star on her neck glittered with a thousand reflections.

"You're right," admitted the girl seriously, looking straight into the magician's violet eyes. "I didn't like you."

"Ciri," said Nenneke, "come closer. This is Lady Yennefer from Vengerberg, Mistress of Wizardry. Don't be frightened. Lady Yennefer knows who you are. You can trust her."

The girl bowed, interlocking her palms in a gesture of full respect. The enchantress, rustling her long, black dress, approached, took Ciri by the chin and quite offhandedly lifted her head, turning it right and left. The girl felt anger and rebellion rising within her – she was not used to being treated this way. And at the same time, she experienced a burning envy. Yennefer was very beautiful. Compared to the delicate, pale and rather common comeliness of the priestesses and novices who Ciri saw every day, the magician glowed with a conscious, even demonstrative loveliness, emphasised and accentuated in every detail. Her raven-black locks cascading down her shoulders shone, reflected the light like the feathers of a peacock, curling and undulating with every move. Ciri suddenly felt ashamed, ashamed of her grazed elbows, chapped hands, broken nails, her ashen, stringy hair. All of a sudden, she had an overwhelming desire to possess what Yennefer had – a beautiful, exposed neck and on it a lovely black velvet ribbon with a lovely glittering star. Regular eyebrows, accentuated with charcoal, and long eyelashes. Proud lips. And those two mounds which rose with every breath, hugged by black cloth and white lace . . .

"So this is the famous Surprise." The magician twisted her lips a little. "Look me in the eyes, girl."

Ciri shuddered and hunched her shoulders. No, she did not envy Yennefer that one thing – did not desire to have it or even look at it. Those eyes, violet, deep as a fathomless lake, strangely bright, dispassionate and malefic. Terrifying.

The magician turned towards the stout high priestess. The star on her neck flamed with reflections of the sun beaming through the window into the refectory.

"Yes, Nenneke," she said. "There can be no doubt. One just has to look into those green eyes to know that there

350

is something in her. High forehead, regular arch of the brows, eyes set attractively apart. Narrow nose. Long fingers. Rare hair pigment. Obvious elven blood, although there is not much of it in her. An elven great-grandfather or great-grandmother. Have I guessed correctly?"

"I don't know her family tree," the high priestess replied calmly. "It didn't interest me."

"Tall for her age," continued the magician, still appraising Ciri with her eyes. The girl was boiling over with fury and annoyance, struggling with an overpowering desire to scream defiantly, scream her lungs out, stamp her feet and run off to the park, on the way knocking over the vase on the table and slamming the door so as to make the plaster crumble from the ceiling.

"Not badly developed." Yennefer did not take her eyes off her. "Has she suffered any infectious diseases in childhood? Ha, no doubt you didn't ask her about that either. Has she been ill since she's been here?"

"No."

"Any migraines? Fainting? Inclination to catch cold? Painful periods?"

"No. Only those dreams."

"I know." Yennefer gathered the hair from her cheek. "He wrote about that. It appears from his letter that in Kaer Morhen they didn't try out any of their . . . experiments on her. I would like to believe that's true."

"It is. They gave her only natural stimulants."

"Stimulants are never natural!" The magician raised her voice. "Never! It is precisely the stimulants which may have aggravated her symptoms in . . . Damn it, I never suspected him of such irresponsibility!"

"Calm down." Nenneke looked at her coldly and, all

of a sudden, somehow oddly without respect. "I said they were natural and absolutely safe. Forgive me, dear, but in this respect I am a greater authority than you. I know it is exceedingly difficult for you to accept someone else's authority but in this case I am forced to inflict it on you. And let there be no more talk about it."

"As you wish." Yennefer pursed her lips. "Well, come on, girl. We don't have much time. It would be a sin to waste it."

Ciri could barely keep her hands from shaking; she swallowed hard and looked inquiringly at Nenneke. The high priestess was serious, as if sad, and the smile with which she answered the unspoken question was unpleasantly false.

"You're going with Lady Yennefer now," she said. "Lady Yennefer is going to be looking after you for a while."

Ciri bowed her head and clenched her teeth.

"You are no doubt baffled," continued Nenneke, "that a Mistress of Wizardry is suddenly taking you into her care. But you are a reasonable girl, Ciri. You can guess why. You have inherited certain . . . attributes from your ancestors. You know what I am talking about. You used to come to me, after those dreams, after the nocturnal disturbances in the dormitory. I couldn't help you. But Lady Yennefer—"

"Lady Yennefer," interrupted the magician, "will do what is necessary. Let us go, girl."

"Go," nodded Nenneke, trying, in vain, to make her smile at least appear natural. "Go, child. Remember it is a great privilege to have someone like Lady Yennefer look after you. Don't bring shame on the Temple and us, your mentors. And be obedient."

I'll escape tonight, Ciri made up her mind. *Back to Kaer Morhen. I'll steal a horse from the stables and that's the last they'll see of me. I'll run away!*

"Indeed you will," said the magician under her breath.

"I beg your pardon?" the priestess raised her head. "What did you say?"

"Nothing, nothing," smiled Yennefer. "You just thought I did. Or maybe I thought I did? Just look at this ward of yours, Nenneke. Furious as a cat. Sparks in her eyes; just wait and she'll hiss. And if she could flatten her ears, she would. A witcher-girl! I'll have to take her firmly in hand, file her claws."

"Be more understanding." The high priestess's features visibly hardened. "Please, be kind-hearted and understanding. She really is not who you take her to be."

"What do you mean by that?"

"She's not your rival, Yennefer."

For a moment they measured each other with their eyes, the enchantress and the priestess, and Ciri felt the air quiver, a strange, terrible force between them growing in strength. This lasted no more than a fraction of a second, after which the force disappeared and Yennefer burst out laughing, lightheartedly and sweetly.

"I forgot," she said. "Always on his side, aren't you, Nenneke? Always worrying about him. Like the mother he never had."

"And you're always against him," smiled the priestess. "Bestowing him with strong feelings, as usual. And defending yourself as hard as you can not to call the feelings by their rightful name."

Once again, Ciri felt fury rise up somewhere in the pit of her stomach, and her temples throbbed with spite and rebellion. She remembered how many times and under what circumstances she had heard that name. Yennefer. A name which caused unease, a name which was the symbol of some sinister secret. She guessed what that secret was.

They're talking quite openly in front of me, without any restraint, she thought, feeling her hands start to shake with anger once more. *They're not bothered about me at all. Ignoring me completely. As if I were a child. They're talking about Geralt in front of me, in my presence, but they can't because I . . . I am . . .*

Who?

"You, on the other hand, Nenneke," retorted the magician, "are amusing yourself, as usual, analysing other people's emotions, and on top of that interpreting them to suit yourself!"

"And putting my nose into other people's business?"

"I didn't want to say that." Yennefer tossed her black locks, which gleamed and writhed like snakes. "Thank you for doing so for me. And now let us change the subject, please, because the one we were discussing is exceptionally silly – disgraceful in front of our young pupil. And as for being understanding, as you ask . . . I will be. But kind-hearted – with that, there might be a problem because, after all, it is widely thought I don't possess any such organ. But we'll manage somehow. Isn't that right, Surprise?"

She smiled at Ciri and, despite herself, despite her anger and annoyance, Ciri had to respond with a smile.

Because the enchantress's smile was unexpectedly pleasant, friendly and sincere. And very, very beautiful.

She listened to Yennefer's speech with her back ostentatiously turned, pretending to bestow her full attention on the bumble bee buzzing in the flower of one of the hollyhocks growing by the temple wall.

"No one asked me about it," she mumbled.

"What didn't anybody ask you about?"

Ciri turned in a half-pirouette and furiously whacked the hollyhock with her fist. The bumble bee flew away, buzzing angrily and ominously.

"No one asked me whether I wanted you to teach me!"

Yennefer rested her fists on her hips; her eyes flashed.

"What a coincidence," she hissed. "Imagine that – no one asked me whether I wanted to teach you either. Besides, wanting has got nothing to do with it. I don't apprentice just anybody and you, despite appearances, might still turn out to be a nobody. I was asked to check how things stand with you. To examine what is inside you and how that could endanger you. And I, though not unreluctantly, agreed."

"But I haven't agreed yet!"

The magician raised her arm and moved her hand. Ciri experienced a throbbing in her temples and a buzzing in her ears, as if she were swallowing but much louder. She felt drowsy, and an overpowering weakness, tiredness stiffened her neck and softened her knees.

Yennefer lowered her hand and the sensation instantly passed.

"Listen to me carefully, Surprise," she said. "I can easily cast a spell on you, hypnotise you, or put you in a trance. I can paralyse you, force you to drink an elixir, strip you naked, lay you out on the table and examine you for hours, taking breaks for meals while you lie there, looking at the ceiling, unable to move even your eyeballs. That is what I would do with just any snotty kid. I do not want to do that to you because one can see, at first glance, that you are an intelligent and proud girl, that you have character. I don't want to put you or myself to shame. Not in front of Geralt. Because he is the one who asked me to take care of your abilities. To help you deal with them."

"He asked you? Why? He never said anything to me! He never asked me—"

"You keep going back to that," cut in the magician. "No one asked for your opinion, no one took the trouble to check what you want or don't want. Could you have given cause for someone to consider you a contrary, stubborn, snotty kid, whom it is not worth asking questions like that? But I'm going to take the risk and am going to ask something no one has ever asked you. Will you allow yourself to be examined?"

"And what will it involve? What are these tests? And why . . ."

"I have already explained. If you haven't understood, that's too bad. I have no intention of polishing your perception or working on your intelligence. I can examine a sensible girl just as well as a stupid one."

"I'm not stupid! And I understood everything!"

"All the better."

"But I'm not cut out to be a magician! I haven't got any abilities! I'm never going to be a magician nor want to be one! I'm destined for Geralt . . . I'm destined to be a witcher! I've only come here for a short period! I'm going back to Kaer Morhen soon . . ."

"You are persistently staring at my neckline," said Yennefer icily, narrowing her violet eyes a little. "Do you see anything unusual there or is it just plain jealousy?"

"That star . . ." muttered Ciri. "What's it made of? Those stones move and shine so strangely . . ."

"They pulsate," smiled the magician. "They are active diamonds, sunken in obsidian. Do you want to see them close up? Touch them?"

"Yes . . . No!" Ciri backed away and angrily tossed her head, trying to dispel the faint scent of lilac and gooseberries emanating from Yennefer. "I don't. Why should I? I'm not interested! Not a bit! I'm a witcher! I haven't got any magical abilities! I'm not cut out to be a magician, surely that's clear because I'm . . . And anyway . . ."

The magician sat on the stone bench under the wall and concentrated on examining her fingernails.

". . . and anyway," concluded Ciri, "I've got to think about it."

"Come here. Sit next to me."

She obeyed.

"I've got to have time to think about it," she said hesitantly.

"Quite right." Yennefer nodded, still gazing at her nails. "It is a serious matter. It needs to be thought over."

Both said nothing for a while. The novices strolling through the park glanced at them with curiosity, whispered, giggled.

"Well?"

"Well what?"

"Have you thought about it?"

Ciri leaped to her feet, snorted and stamped.

"I . . . I . . ." she panted, unable to catch her breath from anger. "Are you making fun of me? I need time! I need to think about it! For longer! For a whole day . . . And night!"

Yennefer looked her in the eyes and Ciri shrivelled under the gaze.

"The saying goes," said the magician slowly, "that the night brings solutions. But in your case, Surprise, the only thing night can bring is yet another nightmare. You will wake up again, screaming and in pain, drenched in sweat. You will be frightened again, frightened of what you saw, frightened of what you won't be able to remember. And there will be no more sleep that night. There will be fear. Until dawn."

The girl shuddered, lowered her head.

"Surprise." Yennefer's voice changed imperceptibly. "Trust me."

The enchantress's shoulder was warm. The black velvet of her dress asked to be touched. The scent of lilac and gooseberries intoxicated delightfully. Her embrace calmed and soothed, relaxed, tempered excitement, stilled anger and rebellion.

"You'll submit to the tests, Surprise."

"I will," she answered, understanding that she did not really have to reply. Because it was not a question.

"I don't understand anything anymore," said Ciri. "First you say I've got abilities because I've got those dreams. But you want to do tests and check . . . So how is it? Do I have abilities or don't I?"

"That question will be answered by the tests."

"Tests, tests." She pulled a face. "I haven't got any abilities, I tell you. I'd know if I had them, wouldn't I? Well, but . . . If, by some sheer chance, I had abilities, what then?"

"There are two possibilities," the magician informed her with indifference as she opened the window. "Your abilities will either have to be extinguished or you will have to learn how to control them. If you are gifted and want to, I can try to instil in you some elementary knowledge of magic."

"What does 'elementary' mean?"

"Basic."

They were alone in the large chamber next to the library in an unoccupied side wing of the building, which Nenneke had allocated to the lady magician. Ciri knew that this chamber was used by guests. She knew that Geralt, whenever he visited the Temple, stayed right here.

"Are you going to want to teach me?" She sat on the bed and skimmed her hand over the damask eiderdown. "Are you going to want to take me away from here? I'm never going to leave with you!"

"So I'll leave alone," said Yennefer coldly, untying the straps of her saddlebags. "And I assure you, I'm not going to miss you. I did tell you that I'll educate you only if you decide you want to. And I can do so here, on the spot."

"How long are you going to edu— Teach me for?"

"As long as you want." The magician leaned over, opened the chest of drawers, pulled out an old leather bag, a belt, two boots trimmed with fur and a clay demijohn in a wicker basket. Ciri heard her curse under her breath while smiling, and saw her hide the finds back in the drawers. She guessed whose they were. Who had left them there.

"What does that mean, as long as I want?" she asked. "If I get bored or don't like the work—"

"We'll put an end to it. It's enough that you tell me. Or show me."

"Show you? How?"

"Should we decide on educating you, I will demand absolute obedience. I repeat: absolute. If, on the other hand, you get tired of it, it will suffice for you to disobey. Then the lessons will instantly cease. Is that clear?"

Ciri nodded and cast a fleeting glance of her green eyes at the magician.

"Secondly," continued Yennefer, unpacking her saddle-bags, "I will demand absolute sincerity. You will not be allowed to hide anything from me. Anything. So if you feel you have had enough, it will suffice for you to lie, pretend, feign or close in on yourself. If I ask you something and you do not answer sincerely, that will also indicate an instant end to our lessons. Have you understood?"

"Yes," muttered Ciri. "And that . . . sincerity . . . Does that work both ways? Will I be able to . . . ask you questions?"

Yennefer looked at her and her lips twisted strangely.

"Of course," she answered after a while. "That goes without saying. That will be the basis of the learning and protection I aim to give you. Sincerity works both ways. You are to ask me questions. At any time. And I will answer. Sincerely."

"Any question?"

"Any question."

"As of now?"

"Yes. As of now."

"What is there between you and Geralt, Lady Yennefer?"

Ciri almost fainted, horrified at her own impertinence, chilled by the silence which followed the question.

The enchantress slowly approached her, placed her hands on her shoulders, looked her in the eyes from up close – and deeply.

"Longing," she answered gravely. "Regret. Hope. And fear. Yes, I don't think I have omitted anything. Well, now we can get on with the tests, you little green-eyed viper. We will see if you're cut out for this. Although after your question I would be very surprised if it turned out you aren't. Let's go, my ugly one."

Ciri bridled.

"Why do you call me that?"

Yennefer smiled with the corners of her lips.

"I promised to be sincere."

Ciri, annoyed, pulled herself up straight and wriggled in her hard chair which, after many hours of sitting, hurt her backside.

"Nothing's going to come of it!" she snarled, wiping her charcoal-smeared fingers on the table. "After all this, nothing . . . Nothing works out for me! I'm not cut out to be a magician! I knew that right from the start but you didn't want to listen to me! You didn't pay any attention!"

Yennefer raised her eyebrows.

"I didn't want to listen to you, you say? That's interesting. I usually devote my attention to every sentence uttered in my presence and note it in my memory. The one condition being that there be at least a little sense in the sentence."

"You're always mocking me." Ciri grated her teeth. "And I just wanted to tell you . . . Well, about these abilities. You see in Kaer Morhen, in the mountains . . . I couldn't form a single witcher Sign. Not one!"

"I know."

"You know?"

"I know. But that doesn't mean anything."

"How's that? Well . . . But that's not all!"

"I'm listening in suspense."

"I'm not cut out for it. Can't you understand that? I'm . . . I'm too young."

"I was younger than you when I started."

"But I'm sure you weren't . . ."

"What do you mean, girl? Stop stuttering! At least one full sentence, please."

"Because . . ." Ciri lowered her head and blushed. "Because Iola, Myrrha, Eurneid and Katye – when we were having dinner – laughed at me and said that witchcraft doesn't have access to me and that I'm not going to perform any magic because . . . Because I'm . . . a virgin, that means—"

"I know what it means, believe it or not," interrupted the magician. "No doubt you'll see this as another spiteful piece of mockery but I hate to tell you that you are talking a lot of rubbish. Let us get back to the test."

"I'm a virgin!" repeated Ciri aggressively. "Why the tests? Virgins can't do magic!"

"I can't see a solution," Yennefer leaned back in her chair. "So go out and lose your virginity if it gets in your way so much. But be quick about it if you please."

"Are you making fun of me?"

"You've noticed?" The magician smiled faintly. "Congratulations. You've passed the preliminary test in perspicacity. And now for the real test. Concentrate, please. Look: there are four pine trees in this picture. Each one has a different number of branches. Draw a fifth to fit in with the other four and to fit in this space here."

"Pine trees are silly," decreed Ciri, sticking out her tongue and drawing a slightly crooked tree with her charcoal. "And boring! I can't understand what pine trees have to do with magic? What? Lady Yennefer! You promised to answer my questions!"

"Unfortunately," sighed the magician, picking up the sheet of paper and critically appraising the drawing, "I think I'm going to regret that promise. What do pine trees have in common with magic? Nothing. But you've drawn it correctly, and on time. In truth, excellent for a virgin."

"Are you laughing at me?"

"No. I rarely laugh. I really need to have a good reason to laugh. Concentrate on the next page, Surprise. There are rows of stars, circles, crosses and triangles drawn on it, a different number of each shape in each row. Think and answer: how many stars should there be in the last row?"

"Stars are silly!"

"How many?"

"Three!"

Yennefer did not say anything for a long time. She stared at a detail on the carved wardrobe door known only to her. The mischievous smile on Ciri's lips started slowly to disappear until finally it disappeared altogether, without a trace.

"No doubt you were curious to learn," said the magician very slowly, not ceasing to admire the wardrobe, "what would happen if you gave me a senseless and stupid reply. You thought perhaps that I might not notice because I am not in the least interested in your answers? You thought wrongly. You believed, perhaps, that I would simply accept that you are stupid? You were wrong. But if you are bored of being tested and wanted, for a change, to test me . . . Well, that has clearly worked, hasn't it? Either way, this test is concluded. Return the paper."

"I'm sorry, Lady Yennefer." The girl lowered her head. "There should, of course, be . . . one star there. I'm very sorry. Please don't be angry with me."

"Look at me, Ciri."

The girl raised her eyes, astonished. Because for the first time the magician had called her by her name.

"Ciri," said Yennefer. "Know that, despite appearances, I get angry just as rarely as I laugh. You haven't made me angry. But in apologising you have proved I wasn't wrong about you. And now take the next sheet of paper. As you can see there are five houses on it. Draw the sixth . . ."

"Again? I really can't understand why—"

". . . the sixth house." The lady magician's voice changed dangerously and her eyes flashed with a violet glow. "Here, in this space. Don't make me repeat myself, please."

After apples, pine trees, stars, fishes and houses, came the turn of labyrinths through which she had to quickly find a path, wavy lines, blots which looked like squashed cockroaches, and mosaics which made her go cross-eyed and set her head spinning. Then there was a shining ball on a piece of string at which she had to stare for a long time. Staring at it was as dull as dish-water and Ciri kept falling asleep. Yennefer, surprisingly, did not care even though a few days earlier she had scolded her grimly for napping over one of the cockroach blots.

Poring over the tests had made her neck and back ache and day by day they grew more painful. She missed movement and fresh air and, obliged to be sincere, she immediately told Yennefer. The magician took it easily, as if she had been expecting this for a long time.

For the next two days they both ran through the park, jumped over ditches and fences under the amused or pitying eyes of the priestesses and novices. They exercised and practised their balance walking along the top of the wall which encircled the orchard and farm buildings. Unlike the training in Kaer Morhen, though, the exercises with Yennefer were always accompanied by theory. The magician taught Ciri how to breathe, guiding the movement of her chest and diaphragm with strong pressure from her hand. She explained the rules of movement, how muscles and bones work, and demonstrated how to rest, release tension and relax.

During one such session of relaxation, stretched out on the grass and gazing at the sky, Ciri asked a question which was bothering her. "Lady Yennefer? When are we finally going to finish the tests?"

"Do they bore you so much?"

"No . . . But I'd like to know whether I'm cut out to be a magician."

"You are."

"You know that already?"

"I knew from the start. Few people can detect the activity of my star. Very few. You noticed it straight away."

"And the tests?"

"Concluded. I already know what I wanted to about you."

"But some of the tasks . . . They didn't work out very well. You said yourself that . . . Are you really sure? You're not mistaken? You're sure I have the ability?"

"I'm sure."

"But—"

"Ciri." The enchantress looked both amused and impatient. "From the moment we lay down in the meadow, I have been talking to you without using my voice. It's called telepathy, remember that. And as you no doubt noticed, it has not made our talking together any more difficult."

"Magic" – Yennefer, her eyes fixed on the sky above the hills, rested her hands on the pommel of her saddle – "is, in some people's opinion, the embodiment of Chaos. It is a key capable of opening the forbidden door. The door behind which lurk nightmares, fear and unimaginable horrors, behind which enemies hide and wait, destructive powers, the forces of pure Evil capable of annihilating not only the one who opens the door but with them the entire world. And since there is no lack of those who try to open the door, someone, at some point, is going to make a mistake and then the destruction of the world will be forejudged and inevitable. Magic is, therefore, the revenge and the weapon of Chaos. The fact that, following the Conjunction of the Spheres, people have learned to use magic, is the curse and undoing of the world. The undoing of mankind. And that's how it is, Ciri. Those who believe that magic is Chaos are not mistaken."

Spurred on by its mistress's heels, the magician's black stallion neighed lengthily and slowly made his way into the heather. Ciri hastened her horse, followed in Yennefer's tracks and caught up with her. The heather reached to their stirrups.

"Magic," Yennefer continued after a while, "is, in some people's opinion, art. Great, elitist art, capable of creating beautiful and extraordinary things. Magic is a talent granted to only a chosen few. Others, deprived of talent, can only look at the results of the artists' works with admiration and envy, can admire the finished work while feeling that without these creations and without this talent the world would be a poorer place. The fact that, following the Conjunction of the Spheres, some chosen few discovered talent and magic within themselves, the fact that they found Art within themselves, is the blessing of beauty. And that's how it is. Those who believe that magic is art are also right."

On the long bare hill which protruded from the heath like the back of some lurking predator lay an enormous boulder supported by a few smaller stones. The magician guided her horse in its direction without pausing her lecture.

"There are also those according to whom magic is a science. In order to master it, talent and innate ability alone are not enough. Years of keen study and arduous work are essential; endurance and self-discipline are necessary. Magic acquired like this is knowledge, learning, the limits of which are constantly stretched by enlightened and vigorous minds, by experience, experiments and practice. Magic acquired in such a way is progress. It is the plough, the loom, the watermill, the smelting furnace, the winch and the pulley. It is progress, evolution, change. It is constant movement. Upwards. Towards improvement. Towards the stars. The fact that following the Conjunction of the Spheres we discovered magic will, one day, allow us to reach the stars. Dismount, Ciri."

Yennefer approached the monolith, placed her palm on the coarse surface of the stone and carefully brushed away the dust and dry leaves.

"Those who consider magic to be a science," she continued, "are also right. Remember that, Ciri. And now come here, to me."

The girl swallowed and came closer. The enchantress put her arm around her.

"Remember," she repeated, "magic is Chaos, Art and Science. It is a curse, a blessing and progress. It all depends on who uses magic, how they use it, and to what purpose. And magic is everywhere. All around us. Easily accessible. It is enough to stretch out one's hand. See? I'm stretching out my hand."

The cromlech trembled perceptibly. Ciri heard a dull, distant noise and a rumble coming from within the earth. The heather undulated, flattened by the gale which suddenly gusted across the hill. The sky abruptly turned dark, covered with clouds scudding across it at incredible speed. The girl felt drops of rain on her face. She narrowed her eyes against the flash of lightning which suddenly flared across the horizon. She automatically huddled up to the enchantress, against her black hair smelling of lilac and gooseberries.

"The earth which we tread. The fire which does not go out within it. The water from which all life is born and without which life is not possible. The air we breathe. It is enough to stretch out one's hand to master them, to subjugate them. Magic is everywhere. It is in air, in water, in earth and in fire. And it is behind the door which the Conjunction of the Spheres has closed on us. From there, from behind the closed door, magic sometimes extends its hand to us. For us. You know that, don't you? You have already felt the touch of that magic, the touch of the hand from behind that door. That touch filled you with fear. Such a touch fills everyone with fear. Because there is Chaos and Order, Good and Evil in all of us. But it is possible and necessary to control it. This has to be learnt. And you will learn it, Ciri. That is why I brought you here, to this stone which, from time immemorial, has stood at the crossing of veins of power pulsating with force. Touch it."

The boulder shook, vibrated, and with it the entire hill vibrated and shook.

"Magic is extending its hand towards you, Ciri. To you, strange girl, Surprise, Child of the Elder Blood, the Blood of Elves. Strange girl, woven into Movement and Change, into Annihilation and Rebirth. Destined and destiny. Magic extends its hand towards you from behind the closed door, towards you, a tiny grain of sand in the workings of the Clock of Fate. Chaos extends its talons towards you, still uncertain if you will be its tool or an obstacle in its design. That which Chaos shows you in your dreams is this very uncertainty. Chaos is afraid of you, Child of Destiny. But it wants you to be the one who feels fear."

There was a flash of lightning and a long rumble of thunder. Ciri trembled with cold and dread.

"Chaos cannot show you what it really is. So it is showing you the future, showing you what is going to happen. It wants you to be afraid of the coming days, so that fear of what is going to happen to you and those closest to you will start to guide you, take you over completely. That is why Chaos is sending you those dreams. Now, you are going to show me what you see in your dreams. And you are going to be frightened. And then you will forget and master your fear. Look at my star, Ciri. Don't take your eyes from it!"

A flash. A rumble of thunder.

"Speak! I command you!"

Blood. Yennefer's lips, cut and crushed, move silently, flow with blood. White rocks flitter past, seen from a gallop. A horse neighs. A leap. Valley, abyss. Screaming. Flight, an endless flight. Abyss . . .

In the depth of the abyss, smoke. Stairs leading down.

Va'esse deireádh aep eigean . . . Something is coming to an end . . . What?

Elaine blath, Feainnewedd . . . Child of the Elder Blood? Yennefer's voice seems to come from somewhere afar, is dull, awakens echoes amidst the stone walls dripping with damp. Elaine blath—

"Speak!"

The violet eyes shine, burn in the emaciated, shrivelled face, blackened with suffering, veiled with a tempest of dishevelled, dirty black hair. Darkness. Damp. Stench. The excruciating cold of stone walls. The cold of iron on wrists, on ankles . . .

Abyss. Smoke. Stairs leading down. Stairs down

which she must go. Must because . . . Because something is coming to an end. Because Tedd Deireádh, the Time of End, the Time of the Wolf's Blizzard is approaching. The Time of the White Chill and White Light . . .

The Lion Cub must die! For reasons of state!

"Let's go," says Geralt. "Down the stairs. We must. It must be so. There is no other way. Only the stairs. Down!"

His lips are not moving. They are blue. Blood, blood everywhere . . . The whole stairs in blood . . . Mustn't slip . . . Because the witcher trips just once . . . The flash of a blade. Screams. Death. Down. Down the stairs.

Smoke. Fire. Frantic galloping, hooves thundering. Flames all around. "Hold on! Hold on, Lion Cub of Cintra!"

The black horse neighs, rears. "Hold on!"

The black horse dances. In the slit of the helmet adorned with the wings of a bird of prey shine and burn merciless eyes.

A broad sword, reflecting the glow of the fire, falls with a hiss. Dodge, Ciri! Feign! Pirouette, parry! Dodge! Dodge! Too slooooowwww!

The blow blinds her with its flash, shakes her whole body, the pain paralyses her for a moment, dulls, deadens, and then suddenly explodes with a terrible strength, sinks its cruel, sharp fangs into her cheek, yanks, penetrates right through, radiates into the neck, the shoulders, chest, lungs . . .

"Ciri!"

She felt the coarse, unpleasant, still coolness of stone on her back and head. She did not remember sitting down. Yennefer was kneeling next to her. Gently, but decisively, she straightened her fingers, pulled her hand away from her cheek. The cheek throbbed, pulsated with pain.

"Mama . . ." groaned Ciri. "Mama . . . How it hurts! Mama . . ."

The magician touched her face. Her hand was as cold as ice. The pain stopped instantly.

"I saw . . ." the girl whispered, closing her eyes, "the things I saw in the dreams . . . A black knight . . . Geralt . . . And also . . . You . . . I saw you, Lady Yennefer!"

"I know."

"I saw you . . . I saw how—"

"Never more. You will never see that again. You won't dream about it anymore. I will give you the force to push those nightmares away. That is why I have brought you here, Ciri – to show you that force. Tomorrow, I am going to start giving it to you."

Long, arduous days followed, days of intensive study and exhausting work. Yennefer was firm, frequently stern, sometimes masterfully formidable. But she was never boring. Previously, Ciri could barely keep her eyes open in the Temple school and would sometimes even doze off during a lesson, lulled by the monotonous, gentle voice of Nenneke, Iola the First, Hrosvitha or some other teacher. With Yennefer, it was impossible. And not only because of the timbre of the lady magician's voice and the short, sharply accentuated sentences she used. The most important element was the subject of her studies. The study of magic. Fascinating, exciting and absorbing study.

Ciri spent most of the day with Yennefer. She returned to the dormitory late at night, collapsed into bed like a log and fell asleep immediately. The novices complained that she snored very loudly and tried to wake her. In vain.

Ciri slept deeply.

With no dreams.

"Oh, gods." Yennefer sighed in resignation and, ruffling her black hair with both hands, lowered her head. "But it's so simple! If you can't master this move, what will happen with the harder ones?"

Ciri turned away, mumbled something in a raspy voice and massaged her stiff hand. The magician sighed once more.

"Take another look at the etching. See how your fingers should be spread. Pay attention to the explanatory arrows and runes describing how the move should be performed."

"I've already looked at the drawing a thousand times! I understand the runes! Vort, cáelme. Ys, veloë. Away from oneself, slowly. Down, quickly. The hand . . . like this?"

"And the little finger?"

"It's impossible to position it like that without bending the ring finger at the same time!"

"Give me your hand."

"Ouuuch!"

"Not so loud, Ciri, otherwise Nenneke will come running again, thinking that I'm skinning you alive or frying you in oil. Don't change the position of your fingers. And now perform the gesture. Turn, turn the wrist! Good. Now shake the hand, relax the fingers. And repeat. No, no! Do you know what you did? If you were to cast a real spell like that, you'd be wearing your hand in splints for a month! Are your hands made of wood?"

"My hand's trained to hold a sword! That's why!"

"Nonsense. Geralt has been brandishing his sword for his whole life and his fingers are agile and . . . mm-mm . . . very gentle. Continue, my ugly one, try again. See? It's enough to want to. It's enough to try. Once more. Good. Shake your hand. And once again. Good. Are you tired?"

"A little . . ."

"Let me massage your hand and arm. Ciri, why aren't you using the ointment I gave you? Your hands are as rough as crocodile skin . . . But what's this? A mark left by a ring, am I right? Was I imagining it or did I forbid you to wear any jewellery?"

"But I won the ring from Myrrha playing spinning tops! And I only wore it for half a day—"

"That's half a day too long. Don't wear it anymore, please."

"I don't understand, why aren't I allowed—"

"You don't have to understand," the magician said cutting her short, but there was no anger in her voice. "I'm asking you not to wear any ornaments like that. Pin a flower in your hair if you want to. Weave a wreath for your hair. But no metal, no crystals, no stones. It's important, Ciri. When the time comes, I will explain why. For the time being, trust me and do as I ask."

"You wear your star, earrings and rings! And I'm not allowed? Is that because I'm . . . a virgin?"

"Ugly one," Yennefer smiled and stroked her on the head, "are you still obsessed with that? I have already explained to you that it doesn't matter whether you are or not. Not in the least. Wash your hair tomorrow; it needs it, I see."

"Lady Yennefer?"

"Yes."

"May I . . . As part of the sincerity you promised . . . May I ask you something?"

"You may. But, by all the gods, not about virginity, please."

Ciri bit her lip and did not say anything for a long time.

"Too bad," sighed Yennefer. "Let it be. Ask away."

"Because, you see . . ." Ciri blushed and licked her lips, "the girls in the dormitory are always gossiping and telling all sorts of stories . . . About Belleteyn's feast and others like that . . . And they say I'm a snotty kid, a child because it's time . . . Lady Yennefer, how does it really work? How can one know that the time has come . . ."

". . . to go to bed with a man?"

Ciri blushed a deep shade of crimson. She said nothing for a while then raised her eyes and nodded.

"It's easy to tell," said Yennefer, naturally. "If you are beginning to think about it then it's a sign the time has come."

"But I don't want to!"

"It's not compulsory. You don't want to, then you don't."

"Ah." Ciri bit her lip again. "And that . . . Well . . . Man . . . How can you tell it's the right one to . . ."

". . . go to bed with?"

"Mmmh."

"If you have any choice at all," the enchantress twisted

her lips in a smile, "but don't have much experience, you first appraise the bed."

Ciri's emerald eyes turned the shape and size of saucers.

"How's that . . . The bed?"

"Precisely that. Those who don't have a bed at all, you eliminate on the spot. From those who remain, you eliminate the owners of any dirty or slovenly beds. And when only those who have clean and tidy beds remain, you choose the one you find most attractive. Unfortunately, the method is not a hundred per cent foolproof. You can make a terrible mistake."

"You're joking?"

"No. I'm not joking, Ciri. As of tomorrow, you are going to sleep here with me. Bring your things. From what I hear, too much time is wasted in the novices' dormitory on gabbling, time which would be better spent resting and sleeping."

After mastering the basic positions of the hands, the moves and gestures, Ciri began to learn spells and their formulae. The formulae were easier. Written in Elder Speech, which the girl already knew to perfection, they sank easily into her memory. Nor did she have any problems enunciating the frequently complicated intonations. Yennefer was clearly pleased and, from day to day, was becoming more pleasant and sympathetic. More and more frequently, taking breaks in the studies, both gossiped and joked about any old thing; both even began to amuse themselves by delicately poking fun at Nenneke who often "visited" their lectures and exercises – bristling and puffed up like a brooding hen

– ready to take Ciri under her protective wing, to protect and save her from the magician's imagined severity and the "inhuman tortures" of her education.

Obeying instructions, Ciri moved to Yennefer's chamber. Now they were together not only by day but also by night. Sometimes, their studies would take place during the night – certain moves, formulae and spells could not be performed in daylight.

The magician, pleased with the girl's progress, slowed the speed of her education. They had more free time. They spent their evenings reading books, together or separately. Ciri waded through Stammelford's *Dialogues on the Nature of Magic*, Giambattista's *Forces of the Elements* and Richert and Monck's *Natural Magic*. She also flicked through – because she did not manage to read them in their entirety – such works as Jan Bekker's *The Invisible World* and Agnes of Glanville's *The Secret of Secrets*. She dipped into the ancient, yellowed *Codex of Mirthe, Ard Aercane*, and even the famous, terrible *Dhu Dwimmermorc*, full of menacing etchings.

She also reached for other books which had nothing to do with magic. She read *The History of the World* and *A Treatise on Life*. Nor did she leave out lighter works from the Temple library. Blushing, she devoured Marquis La Creahme's *Gambols* and Anna Tiller's *The King's Ladies*. She read *The Adversities of Loving* and *Time of the Moon*, collections of poems by the famous troubadour Dandelion. She shed tears over the ballads of Essi Daven, subtle, infused with mystery, and collected in a small, beautifully bound volume entitled *The Blue Pearl*.

She made frequent use of her privilege to ask questions. And she received answers. More and more frequently, however, she was the one being questioned. In the beginning it had seemed that Yennefer was not at all interested in her lot, in her childhood in Cintra or the later events of war. But in time her questions became more and more concrete. Ciri had to reply and did so very unwillingly because every question the magician asked opened a door in her memory which she had promised herself never to open, which she wanted to keep forever locked. Ever since she had met Geralt in Sodden, she had believed she had begun "another life," that the other life – the one in Cintra – had been irrevocably wiped out. The witchers in Kaer Morhen never asked her about anything and, before coming to the temple, Geralt had even prevailed upon her not to say a word to anyone about who she was. Nenneke, who of course knew about everything, saw to it that to the other priestesses and the novices Ciri was exceptionally ordinary, an illegitimate daughter of a knight and a peasant woman, a child for whom there had been no place either in her father's castle or her mother's cottage. Half of the novices in Melitele's Temple were just such children.

And Yennefer too knew the secret. She was the one who "could be trusted." Yennefer asked. About it. About Cintra.

"How did you get out of the town, Ciri? How did you slip past the Nilfgaardians?"

Ciri did not remember. Everything broke off, was lost in obscurity and smoke. She remembered the siege, saying goodbye to Queen Calanthe, her grandmother; she remembered the barons and knights forcibly dragging her away from the bed where the wounded, dying Lioness of Cintra lay. She remembered the frantic escape through flaming streets, bloody battle and the horse falling. She remembered the black rider in a helmet adorned with the wings of a bird of prey.

And nothing more.

"I don't remember. I really don't remember, Lady Yennefer."

Yennefer did not insist. She asked different questions. She did so gently and tactfully and Ciri grew more and more at ease. Finally, she started to speak herself. Without waiting to be asked, she recounted her years as a child in Cintra and on the Isles of Skellige. About how she learned about the Law of Surprise and that fate had decreed her to be the destiny of Geralt of Rivia, the white-haired witcher. She recalled the war, her exile in the forests of Transriver, her time among the druids of Angren and the time spent in the country. How Geralt had found her there and taken her to Kaer Morhen, the Witchers' Keep, thus opening a new chapter in her short life.

One evening, of her own initiative, unasked, casually, joyfully and embellishing a great deal, she told the enchantress about her first meeting with the witcher in Brokilon Forest, amongst the dryads who had abducted her and wanted to force her to stay and become one of them.

"Oh!" said Yennefer on listening to the story, "I'd give a lot to see that – Geralt, I mean. I'm trying to imagine the expression on his face in Brokilon, when he saw what sort of Surprise destiny had concocted for him! Because he must have had a wonderful expression when he found out who you were?"

Ciri giggled and her emerald eyes lit up devilishly.

"Oh, yes!" she snorted. "What an expression! Do you want to see? I'll show you. Look at me!"

Yennefer burst out laughing.

That laughter, thought Ciri watching swarms of black birds flying eastwards, *that laughter, shared and sincere, really brought us together, her and me. We understood – both she and I – that we can laugh and talk together about him. About Geralt. Suddenly we became close, although I knew perfectly well that Geralt both brought us together and separated us, and that that's how it would always be.*

Our laughter together brought us closer to each other.

As did the events two days later. In the forest, on the hills. She was showing me how to find . . .

"I don't understand why I have to look for these . . . I've forgotten what they're called again . . ."

"Intersections," prompted Yennefer, picking off the burrs which had attached themselves to her sleeve as they crossed the scrubs. "I am showing you how to find them because they're places from which you can draw the force."

"But I know how to draw the force already! And you taught me yourself that the force is everywhere. So why are we roaming around in the bushes? After all, there's a great deal of force in the Temple!"

"Yes, indeed, there is a fair amount there. That's exactly why the Temple was built there and not somewhere else. And that's why, on Temple grounds, drawing it seems so easy to you."

"My legs hurt! Can we sit down for a while?"

"All right, my ugly one."

"Lady Yennefer?"

"Yes?"

"Why do we always draw the force from water veins? Magical energy, after all, is everywhere. It's in the earth, isn't it? In air, in fire?"

"True."

"And earth . . . Here, there's plenty of earth around here. Under our feet. And air is everywhere! And should we want fire, it's enough to light a bonfire and . . ."

"You are still too weak to draw energy from the earth. You still don't know enough to succeed in drawing anything from air. And as for fire, I absolutely forbid you to play with it. I've already told you, under no circumstances are you allowed to touch the energy of fire!"

"Don't shout. I remember."

They sat in silence on a fallen dry tree trunk, listening to the wind rustling in the tree tops, listening to a woodpecker hammering away somewhere close by. Ciri was hungry and her saliva was thick from thirst, but she knew that complaining would not get her anywhere. In the past, a month ago, Yennefer had reacted to such complaints with a dry lecture on how to control such primitive instincts; later, she had ignored them in contemptuous silence. Protesting was just as useless and produced as few results as sulking over being called "ugly one."

The magician plucked the last burr from her sleeve. *She's going to ask me something in a moment*, thought Ciri, *I can hear her thinking about it. She's going to ask about something I don't remember again. Or something I don't want to remember. No, it's senseless. I'm not going to answer. All of that is in the past, and there's no returning to the past. She once said so herself.*

"Tell me about your parents, Ciri."

"I can't remember them, Lady Yennefer."

"Please try to."

"I really don't remember my papa . . ." she said in a quiet voice, succumbing to the command. "Except . . . Practically nothing. My mama . . . My mama, I do. She had long hair, like this . . . And she was always sad . . . I remember . . . No, I don't remember anything . . ."

"Try to remember, please."

"I can't!"

"Look at my star."

Seagulls screamed, diving down between the fishing boats where they caught scourings and tiny fish emptied from the crates. The wind gently fluttered the lowered sails of the drakkars, and smoke, quelled by drizzle, floated above the landing-stage. Triremes from Cintra were sailing into the port, golden lions glistening on blue flags. Uncle Crach, who was standing next to her with his hand – as large as the paw of a grizzly bear – on her shoulder, suddenly fell to one knee. Warriors, standing in rows, rhythmically struck their shields with their swords.

Along the gang-plank towards them came Queen Calanthe. Her grandmother. She who was officially called Ard Rhena, the Highest Queen, on the Isles of Skellige. But Uncle Crach an Craite, the Earl of Skellige, still kneeling with bowed head, greeted the Lioness of Cintra with a title which was less official but considered by the islanders to be more venerable.

"Hail, Modron."

"Princess," said Calanthe in a cold and authoritative

voice, without so much as a glance at the earl, "come here. Come here to me, Ciri."

Her grandmother's hand was as strong and hard as a man's, her rings cold as ice.

"Where is Eist?"

"The King . . ." stammered Crach. "Is at sea, Modron. He is looking for the remains . . . And the bodies. Since yesterday . . ."

"Why did he let them?" shouted the queen. "How could he allow it? How could you allow it, Crach? You're the Earl of Skellige! No drakkar is allowed to go out to sea without your permission! Why did you allow it, Crach?"

Uncle Crach bowed his head even lower.

"Horses!" said Calanthe. "We're going to the fort. And tomorrow, at dawn, I am setting sail. I am taking the princess to Cintra. I will never allow her to return here. And you . . . You have a huge debt to repay me, Crach. One day I will demand repayment."

"I know, Modron."

"If I do not claim it, she will do so." Calanthe looked at Ciri. "You will repay the debt to her, Earl. You know how."

Crach an Craite got to his feet, straightened himself and the features of his weatherbeaten face hardened. With a swift move, he drew from its sheath a simple, steel sword devoid of ornaments and pulled up the sleeve on his left arm, marked with thickened white scars.

"Without the dramatic gestures," snorted the queen. "Save your blood. I said: one day. Remember!"

"Aen me Gláeddyv, zvaere a'Bloedgeas, Ard Rhena, Lionors aep Xintra!" Crach an Craite, the Earl of the Isles of Skellige, raised his arms and shook his sword. The warriors roared hoarsely and beat their weapons against their shields.

"I accept your oath. Lead the way to the fort, Earl."

Ciri remembered King Eist's return, his stony, pale face. And the queen's silence. She remembered the gloomy, horrible feast at which the wild, bearded sea wolves of Skellige slowly got drunk in terrifying silence. She remembered the whispers. "Geas Muire . . . Geas Muire!"

She remembered the trickles of dark beer poured onto the floor, the horns smashed against the stone walls of the hall in bursts of desperate, helpless, senseless anger. "Geas Muire! Pavetta!"

Pavetta, the Princess of Cintra, and her husband, Prince Duny. Ciri's parents. Perished. Killed. Geas Muire, the Curse of the Sea, had killed them. They had been swallowed up by a tempest which no one had foreseen. A tempest which should not have broken out . . .

Ciri turned her head away so that Yennefer would not see the tears swelling in her eyes. *Why all this*, she thought. *Why these questions, these recollections? There's no returning to the past. There's no one there for me anymore. Not my papa, nor my mama, nor my grandmother, the one who was Ard Rhena, the Lioness of Cintra. Uncle Crach an Craite, no doubt, is also dead. I haven't got anybody anymore and am someone else. There's no returning . . .*

The magician remained silent, lost in thought.

"Is that when your dreams began?" she asked suddenly.

"No," Ciri reflected. "No, not then. Not until later."

"When?"

The girl wrinkled her nose.

"In the summer . . . The one before . . . Because the following summer there was the war already . . ."

"Aha. That means the dreams started after you met Geralt in Brokilon?"

She nodded. *I'm not going to answer the next question*, she decided. But Yennefer did not ask anything. She quickly got to her feet and looked at the sun.

"Well, that's enough of this sitting around, my ugly one. It's getting late. Let's carry on looking. Keep your hand held loosely in front of you, and don't tense your fingers. Forward."

"Where am I to go? Which direction?"

"It's all the same."

"The veins are everywhere?"

"Almost. You're going to learn how to discover them, to find them in the open and recognise such spots. They are marked by trees which have dried up, gnarled plants, places avoided by all animals. Except cats."

"Cats?"

"Cats like sleeping and resting on intersections. There are many stories about magical animals but really, apart from the dragon, the cat is the only creature which can absorb the force. No one knows why a cat absorbs it and what it does with it . . . What's the matter?"

"Oooo . . . There, in that direction! I think there's something there! Behind that tree!"

"Ciri, don't fantasise. Intersections can only be sensed by standing over them . . . Hmmm . . . Interesting. Extraordinary, I'd say. Do you really feel the pull?"

"Really!"

"Let's go then. Interesting, interesting . . . Well, locate it. Show me where."

"Here! On this spot!"

"Well done. Excellent. So you feel delicate cramps in your ring finger? See how it bends downwards? Remember, that's the sign."

"May I draw on it?"

"Wait, I'll check."

"Lady Yennefer? How does it work with this drawing of the force? If I gather force into myself then there might not be enough left down below. Is it right to do that? Mother Nenneke taught us that we mustn't take anything just like that, for the fun of it. Even the cherry has to be left on its tree for the birds, so that it can simply fall."

Yennefer put her arm around Ciri, kissed her gently on the hair at her temple.

"I wish," she muttered, "others could hear what you said. Vilgefortz, Francesca, Terranova . . . Those who believe they have exclusive right to the force and can use it unreservedly. I wish they could listen to the little wise ugly one from Melitele's Temple. Don't worry, Ciri. It's a good thing you're thinking about it but believe me, there is enough force. It won't run out. It's as if you picked one single little cherry from a huge orchard."

"Can I draw on it now?"

"Wait. Oh, it's a devilishly strong pocket. It's pulsating violently. Be careful, ugly one. Draw on it carefully and very, very slowly."

"I'm not frightened! Pah-pah! I'm a witcher. Ha! I feel it! I feel . . . Ooouuuch! Lady . . . Ye . . . nnnne . . . feeeeer . . ."

"Damn it! I warned you! I told you! Head up! Up, I say! Take this and put it to your nose or you'll be covered in blood! Calmly, calmly, little one, just don't faint. I'm

beside you. I'm beside you . . . daughter. Hold the handkerchief. I'll just conjure up some ice . . ."

There was a great fuss about that small amount of blood.
Yennefer and Nenneke did not talk to each other for a
week.

For a week, Ciri lazed around, read books and got
bored because the magician had put her studies on hold.
The girl did not see her for entire days – Yennefer disappeared somewhere at dawn, returned in the evening,
looked at her strangely and was oddly taciturn.

After a week, Ciri had had enough. In the evening,
when the enchantress returned, she went up to her without
a word and hugged her hard.

Yennefer was silent. For a very long time. She did not
have to speak. Her fingers, clasping the girl's shoulders
tightly, spoke for her.

The following day, the high priestess and the lady magician made up, having talked for several hours.

And then, to Ciri's great joy, everything returned to
normal.

"Look into my eyes, Ciri. A tiny light. The formula,
please!"

"Aine verseos!"

"Good. Look at my hand. The same move and disperse
the light in the air."

"Aine aen aenye!"

"Excellent. And what gesture comes next? Yes, that's
the one. Very good. Strengthen the gesture and draw.
More, more, don't stop!"

"Oooouuuch . . ."

"Keep your back straight! Arms by your side! Hands loose, no unnecessary moves with your fingers. Every move can multiply the effect. Do you want a fire to burst out here? Strengthen it, what are you waiting for?"

"Oouuch, no . . . I can't—"

"Relax and stop shaking! Draw! What are you doing? There, that's better . . . Don't weaken your will! That's too fast, you're hyperventilating! Unnecessarily getting hot! Slower, ugly one, calmer. I know it's unpleasant. You'll get used to it."

"It hurts . . . My belly . . . Down here—"

"You're a woman, it's a typical reaction. Over time you'll harden yourself against it. But in order to harden yourself you have to practise without any painkillers blocking you. It really is necessary, Ciri. Don't be afraid of anything, I'm alert and screening you. Nothing can happen to you. But you have to endure the pain. Breathe calmly. Concentrate. The gesture, please. Perfect. And take the force, draw it, pull it in . . . Good, good . . . Just a bit more . . ."

"O . . . O . . . Oooouuuch!"

"There, you see? You can do it, if you want to. Now watch my hand. Carefully. Perform the same movement. Fingers! Fingers, Ciri! Look at my hand, not the ceiling! Now, that's good, yes, very good. Tie it up. And now turn it around, reverse the move and now issue the force in the form of a stronger light."

"Eeeee . . . Eeeeek . . . Aiiiieee . . ."

"Stop moaning! Control yourself! It's just a cramp! It'll stop in a moment! Fingers wider, extinguish it, give it back, give it back from yourself! Slower, damn it, or your blood vessels will burst again!"

"Eeeeeek!"

"Too abrupt, ugly one, still too abrupt. I know the force is bursting out but you have to learn to control it. You mustn't allow outbursts like the one a moment ago. If I hadn't insulated you, you would have caused havoc here. Now, once more. We're starting right from the beginning. Move and formula."

"No! Not again! I can't!"

"Breathe slowly and stop shaking. It's plain hysteria this time, you don't fool me. Control yourself, concentrate and begin."

"No, please, Lady Yennefer . . . It hurts . . . I feel sick . . ."

"Just no tears, Ciri. There's no sight more nauseating than a magician crying. Nothing arouses greater pity. Remember that. Never forget that. One more time, from the beginning. Spell and gesture. No, no, this time without copying me. You're going to do it by yourself. So, use your memory!"

"Aine verseos . . . Aine aen aenye . . . Oooouuuuch!"

"No! Too fast!"

Magic, like a spiked iron arrow, lodged in her. Wounded her deeply. Hurt. Hurt with the strange sort of pain oddly associated with bliss.

To relax, they once again ran around the park. Yennefer persuaded Nenneke to take Ciri's sword out of storage and so enabled the girl to practise her steps, dodges and attacks – in secret, of course, to prevent the other priestesses and novices seeing her. But magic was omnipresent. Ciri learned how – using simple spells and focusing her will – to relax her muscles, combat cramps, control adrenalin, how to master her aural labyrinth and its nerve, how to slow or speed her pulse and how to cope without oxygen for short periods.

The lady magician knew a surprising amount about a witcher's sword and "dance." She knew a great deal about the secrets of Kaer Morhen; there was no doubt she had visited the Keep. She knew Vesemir and Eskel. Although not Lambert and Coën.

Yennefer used to visit Kaer Morhen. Ciri guessed why – when they spoke of the Keep – the eyes of the enchantress grew warm, lost their angry gleam and their cold, indifferent, wise depth. If the words had befitted Yennefer's person, Ciri would have called her dreamy, lost in memories.

Ciri could guess the reason.

There was a subject which the girl instinctively and carefully avoided. But one day, she got carried away and spoke out. About Triss Merigold. Yennefer, as if casually, as if indifferently, asking as if banal, sparing questions, dragged the rest from her. Her eyes were hard and impenetrable.

Ciri could guess the reason. And, amazingly, she no longer felt annoyed.

Magic was calming.

"The so-called Sign of Aard, Ciri, is a very simple spell belonging to the family of psychokinetic magic which is based on thrusting energy in the required direction. The force of the thrust depends on how the will of the person throwing it is focused and on the expelled force. It can be considerable. The witchers adapted the spell, making use of the fact that it does not require knowledge of a magical formula – concentration and the gesture are enough. That's why they called it a Sign. Where they got the name from, I don't know, maybe from the Elder Speech – the word 'ard', as you know, means 'mountain', 'upper' or 'the highest'. If that is truly the case then the name is very misleading because it's hard to find an easier psychokinetic spell. We, obviously, aren't going to waste time and energy on something as primitive as the witchers' Sign. We are going to practise real psychokinesis. We'll practise on . . . Ah, on that basket lying under the apple tree. Concentrate."

"Ready."

"You focus yourself quickly. Let me remind you: control the flow of the force. You can only emit as much as you draw. If you release even a tiny bit more, you do so at the cost of your constitution. An effort like that could render you unconscious and, in extreme circumstances, could even kill you. If, on the other hand, you release everything you draw, you forfeit all possibility of repeating it, and you will have to draw it again and, as you know, it's not easy to do and it is painful."

"Ooooh, I know!"

"You mustn't slacken your concentration and allow the energy to tear itself away from you of its own accord. My Mistress used to say that emitting the force must be like blowing a raspberry in a ballroom; do it gently, sparingly, and with control. And in such a way that you don't let those around you to know it was you. Understood?"

"Understood!"

"Straighten yourself up. Stop giggling. Let me remind you that spells are a serious matter. They are cast with grace and pride. The motions are executed fluently but with restraint. With dignity. You do not pull faces, grimace or stick your tongue out. You are handling a force of nature, show Nature some respect."

"All right, Lady Yennefer."

"Careful, this time I'm not screening you. You are an independent spell-caster. This is your debut, ugly one. You saw that demi-john of wine in the chest of drawers? If your debut is successful, your mistress will drink it tonight."

"By herself?"

"Novices are only allowed to drink wine once they are qualified apprentices. You have to wait. You're smart, so that just means another ten years or so, not more. Right, let's start. Arrange your fingers. And the left hand? Don't wave it around! Let it hang loose or rest it on your hip. Fingers! Good. Right, release."

"Aaaah . . ."

"I didn't ask you to make funny noises. Emit the energy. In silence."

"Haa, ha! It jumped! The basket jumped! Did you see?"

"It barely twitched. Ciri, sparingly does not mean weakly. Psychokinesis is used with a specific goal in mind. Even witchers use the Sign of Aard to throw their opponent off his feet. The energy you emitted would not knock their hat off their head! Once more, a little stronger. Go for it!"

"Ha! It certainly flew! It was all right that time, wasn't it, Lady Yennefer?"

"Hmmm . . . You'll run to the kitchen afterwards and pinch a bit of cheese to go with our wine . . . That was almost right. Almost. Stronger still, ugly one, don't be frightened. Lift the basket from the ground and throw it hard against the wall of that shack, make feathers fly. Don't slouch! Head up! Gracefully, but with pride! Be bold, be bold! Oh, bloody hell!"

"Oh, dear . . . I'm sorry, Lady Yennefer . . . I probably . . . probably used a bit too much . . ."

"A little bit. Don't worry. Come here. Come on, little one."

"And . . . and the shack?"

"These things happen. There's no need to take it to heart. Your debut, on the whole, should be viewed as a success. And the shack? It wasn't too pretty. I don't think anyone will miss its presence in the landscape. Hold on, ladies! Calm down, calm down, why this uproar and commotion, nothing has happened! Easy, Nenneke! Really, nothing has happened. The planks just need to be cleared away. They'll make good firewood!"

During the warm, still afternoons the air grew thick with the scent of flowers and grass, pulsating with peace and silence, broken by the buzz of bees and enormous beetles. On afternoons like this Yennefer carried Nenneke's wicker chair out into the garden and sat in it, stretching her legs out in front of her. Sometimes she studied books, sometimes read letters which she received by means of strange couriers, usually birds. At times she simply sat gazing into the distance. With one hand, and lost in thought, she ruffled her black, shiny locks, with the other she stroked Ciri's head as she sat on the grass, snuggled up to the magician's warm, firm thigh.

"Lady Yennefer?"

"I'm here, ugly one."

"Tell me, can one do anything with magic?"

"No."

"But you can do a great deal, am I right?"

"You are." The enchantress closed her eyes for a moment and touched her eyelids with her fingers. "A great deal."

"Something really great . . . Something terrible! Very terrible?"

"Sometimes even more so than one would have liked."

"Hmm . . . And could I . . . When will I be able to do something like that?"

"I don't know. Maybe never. Would that you don't have to."

Silence. No words. Heat. The scent of flowers and herbs.

"Lady Yennefer?"

"What now, ugly one?"

"How old were you when you became a wizard?"

"When I passed the preliminary exams? Thirteen."

"Ha! Just like I am now! And how . . . How old were you when . . . No, I won't ask about that—"

"Sixteen."

"Aha . . ." Ciri blushed faintly and pretended to be suddenly interested in a strangely formed cloud hovering over the temple towers. "And how old were you . . . when you met Geralt?"

"Older, ugly one. A bit older."

"You still keep on calling me ugly one! You know how I don't like it. Why do you do it?"

"Because I'm malicious. Wizards are always malicious."

"But I don't want to . . . don't want to be ugly. I want to be pretty. Really pretty, like you, Lady Yennefer. Can I, through magic, be as pretty as you one day?"

"You . . . Fortunately you don't have to . . . You don't need magic for it. You don't know how lucky you are."

"But I want to be really pretty!"

"You are really pretty. A really pretty ugly one. My pretty little ugly one . . ."

"Oh, Lady Yennefer!"

"Ciri, you're going to bruise my thigh."

"Lady Yennefer?"

"Yes."

"What are you looking at like that?"

"At that tree. That linden tree."

"And what's so interesting about it?"

"Nothing. I'm simply feasting my eyes on it. I'm happy that . . . I can see it."

"I don't understand."

"Good."

Silence. No words. Humid.

"Lady Yennefer!"

"What now?"

"There's a spider crawling towards your leg! Look how hideous it is!"

"A spider's a spider."

"Kill it!"

"I can't be bothered to bend over."

"Then kill it with magic!"

"On the grounds of Melitele's Temple? So that Nenneke can throw us out head first? No, thank you. And now be quiet. I want to think."

"And what are you thinking about so seriously? Hmm. All right, I'm not going to say anything now."

"I'm beside myself with joy. I was worried you were going to ask me another one of your unequal grand questions."

"Why not? I like your unequal grand answers!"

"You're getting impudent, ugly one."

"I'm a wizard. Wizards are malicious and impudent."

No words. Silence. Stillness in the air. Close humidity as if before a storm. And silence, this time broken by the distant croaking of ravens and crows.

"There are more and more of them." Ciri looked upwards. "They're flying and flying . . . Like in autumn . . . Hideous birds . . . The priestesses say that it's a bad sign . . . An omen, or something. What is an omen, Lady Yennefer?"

"Look it up in *Dhu Dwimmermorc*. There's a whole chapter on the subject."

Silence.

"Lady Yennefer . . ."

"Oh, hell. What is it now?"

"It's been so long, why isn't Geralt . . . Why isn't he coming?"

"He's forgotten about you, no doubt, ugly one. He's found himself a prettier girl."

"Oh, no! I know he hasn't forgotten! He couldn't have! I know that, I know that for certain, Lady Yennefer!"

"It's good you know. You're a lucky ugly one."

"I didn't like you," she repeated.

Yennefer did not look at her as she stood at the window

with her back turned, staring at the hills looming black in the east. Above the hills, the sky was dark with flocks of ravens and crows.

In a minute she's going to ask why I didn't like her, thought Ciri. *No, she's too clever to ask such a question. She'll dryly draw my attention to my grammar and ask when I started using the past tense. And I'll tell her. I'll be just as dry as she is, I'll parody her tone of voice, let her know that I, too, can pretend to be cold, unfeeling and indifferent, ashamed of my feelings and emotions. I'll tell her everything. I want to, I have to tell her everything. I want her to know everything before we leave Melitele's Temple. Before we part to finally meet the one I miss. The one she misses. The one who no doubt misses us both. I want to tell her that . . .*

I'll tell her. It's enough for her to ask.

The magician turned from the window and smiled. She did not ask anything.

They left the following day, early in the morning. Both wore men's travelling clothes, cloaks, hats and hoods which hid their hair. Both were armed.

Only Nenneke saw them off. She spoke quietly and at length with Yennefer, then they both – the magician and the priestess – shook each other's hand, hard, like men. Ciri, holding the reins of her dapple-grey mare, wanted to say goodbye in the same way, but Nenneke did not allow it. She embraced her, hugged her and gave her a kiss. There were tears in her eyes. In Ciri's, too.

"Well," said the priestess finally, wiping her eye with the sleeve of her robe, "now go. May the Great Melitele protect you on your way, my dears. But the goddess has a great many things on her mind, so look after yourselves too. Take care of her, Yennefer. Keep her safe, like the apple of your eye."

"I hope" – the magician smiled faintly – "that I'll manage to keep her safer."

Across the sky, towards Pontar Valley, flew flocks of crows, croaking loudly. Nenneke did not look at them.

"Take care," she repeated. "Bad times are approaching. It might turn out to be true, what Ithlinne aep Aevenien knew, what she predicted. The Time of the Sword and Axe is approaching. The Time of Contempt and the Wolf's Blizzard. Take care of her, Yennefer. Don't let anyone harm her."

"I'll be back, Mother," said Ciri, leaping into her saddle. "I'll be back for sure! Soon!"

She did not know how very wrong she was.

The story continues in...

THE TIME OF CONTEMPT

Book TWO of the Witcher
Keep reading for a sneak peek!

extras

orbit

meet the author

ANDRZEJ SAPKOWSKI was born in 1948 in Poland. He studied economy and business, but the success of his fantasy cycle about the sorcerer Geralt of Rivia turned him into a bestselling writer. He is now one of Poland's most famous and successful authors.

if you enjoyed
BLOOD OF ELVES
look out for
THE TIME OF CONTEMPT
Book 2 of the Witcher

by

Andrzej Sapkowski

Geralt is a witcher: guardian of the innocent; protector of those in need; a defender, in dark times, against some of the most frightening creatures of myth and legend. His task, now, is to protect Ciri. A child of prophecy, she will have the power to change the world for good or for ill—but only if she lives to use it.

A coup threatens the Wizard's Guild.

War breaks out across the lands.

A serious injury leaves Geralt fighting for his life...

...and Ciri, in whose hands the world's fate rests, has vanished...

CHAPTER ONE

When talking to youngsters entering the service, Aplegatt usually told them that in order to make their living as mounted messengers two things would be necessary: a head of gold and an arse of iron.

A head of gold is essential, Aplegatt instructed the young messengers, since in the flat leather pouch strapped to his chest beneath his clothing the messenger only carries news of less vital importance, which could without fear be entrusted to treacherous paper or manuscript. The really important, secret tidings – those on which a great deal depended – must be committed to memory by the messenger and only repeated to the intended recipient. Word for word; and at times those words are far from simple. Difficult to pronounce, let alone remember. In order to memorise them and not make a mistake when they are recounted, one has to have a truly golden head.

And the benefits of an arse of iron, oh, every messenger will swiftly learn those for himself. When the moment comes for him to spend three days and nights in the saddle, riding a hundred or even two hundred miles along roads or sometimes, when necessary, trackless terrain, then it is needed. No, of course you don't sit in the saddle without respite; sometimes you dismount and rest. For a man can bear a great deal, but a horse less. However, when it's time to get back in the saddle after resting, it's as though your arse were shouting, 'Help! Murder!'

'But who needs mounted messengers now, Master Aplegatt?' young people would occasionally ask in astonishment. 'Take

Vengerberg to Vizima; no one could knock that off in less than four – or even five – days, even on the swiftest steed. But how long does a sorcerer from Vengerberg need to send news to a sorcerer from Vizima? Half an hour, or not even that. A messenger's horse may go lame, but a sorcerer's message always arrives. It never loses its way. It never arrives late or gets lost. What's the point of messengers, if there are sorcerers everywhere, at every kingly court? Messengers are no longer necessary, Master Aplegatt.'

For some time Aplegatt had also been thinking he was no longer of any use to anyone. He was thirty-six and small but strong and wiry, wasn't afraid of hard work and had – naturally – a head of gold. He could have found other work to support himself and his wife, to put a bit of money by for the dowries of his two as yet unmarried daughters and to continue helping the married one whose husband, the sad loser, was always unlucky in his business ventures. But Aplegatt couldn't and didn't want to imagine any other job. He was a royal mounted messenger and that was that.

And then suddenly, after a long period of being forgotten and humiliatingly idle, Aplegatt was once again needed. And the highways and forest tracks once again echoed to the sound of hooves. Just like the old days, messengers began to travel the land bearing news from town to town.

Aplegatt knew why. He saw a lot and heard even more. It was expected that he would immediately erase each message from his memory once it had been given, that he would forget it so as to be unable to recall it even under torture. But Aplegatt remembered. He knew why kings had suddenly stopped communicating with the help of magic and sorcerers. The news that the messengers were carrying was meant to remain a secret from them. Kings had suddenly stopped trusting sorcerers; stopped confiding their secrets in them.

Aplegatt didn't know what had caused this sudden cooling off in the friendship between kings and sorcerers and wasn't overly concerned about it. He regarded both kings and magic-users as incomprehensible creatures, unpredictable in their deeds – particularly when times were becoming hard. And the fact that times were now hard could not be ignored, not if one travelled across the land from castle to castle, from town to town, from kingdom to kingdom.

There were plenty of troops on the roads. With every step one came across an infantry or cavalry column, and every commander you met was edgy, nervous, curt and as self-important as if the fate of the entire world rested on him alone. The cities and castles were also full of armed men, and a feverish bustle went on there, day and night. The usually invisible burgraves and castellans now ceaselessly rushed along walls and through courtyards, angry as wasps before a storm, yelling, swearing and issuing orders and kicks. Day and night, lumbering columns of laden wagons rolled towards strongholds and garrisons, passing carts on their way back, moving quickly, unburdened and empty. Herds of frisky three-year-old mounts taken straight out of stables kicked dust up on the roads. Ponies not accustomed to bits nor armed riders cheerfully enjoyed their last days of freedom, giving stable boys plenty of extra work and other road users no small trouble.

To put it briefly, war hung in the hot, still air.

Aplegatt stood up in his stirrups and looked around. Down at the foot of the hill a river sparkled, meandering sharply among meadows and clusters of trees. Forests stretched out beyond it, to the south. The messenger urged his horse on. Time was running out.

He'd been on the road for two days. The royal order and mail had caught up with him in Hagge, where he was resting after returning from Tretogor. He had left the stronghold by night, galloping along the highway following the left bank of the Pontar, crossed the border with Temeria before dawn, and now, at noon of the following day, was already at the bank of the Ismena. Had King Foltest been in Vizima, Aplegatt would have delivered him the message that night. Unfortunately, the king was not in the capital; he was residing in the south of the country, in Maribor, almost two hundred miles from Vizima. Aplegatt knew this, so in the region of the White Bridge he left the westward-leading road and rode through woodland towards Ellander. He was taking a risk. The Scoia'tael* continued to roam the forests, and woe betide anyone who fell into their hands or came within arrowshot. But a royal messenger had to take risks. Such was his duty.

He crossed the river without difficulty – it hadn't rained since June and the Ismena's waters had fallen considerably. Keeping to the edge of the forest, he reached the track leading southeast from Vizima, towards the dwarven foundries, forges and settlements in the Mahakam Mountains. There were plenty of carts along the track, often being overtaken by small mounted units. Aplegatt sighed in relief. Where there were lots of humans, there weren't any Scoia'tael. The campaign against the guerrilla elves had endured in Temeria for a year and, being harried in the forests, the Scoia'tael commandos had divided up into smaller groups. These smaller groups kept well away from well-used roads and didn't set ambushes on them.

---

* The Scoia'tael – commonly known as the Squirrels – are non-human guerrillas. Predominantly elves, their ranks also include halflings and dwarves, and they are so named due to their habit of attaching squirrel tails to their caps or clothing. Allied with Nilfgaard, motivated by the racism of men, they fight all humans in the Northern Kingdoms.

Before nightfall he was already on the western border of the duchy of Ellander, at a crossroads near the village of Zavada. From here he had a straight and safe road to Maribor: forty-two miles of hard, well-frequented forest track, and there was an inn at the crossroads. He decided to rest his horse and himself there. Were he to set off at daybreak he knew that, even without pushing his mount too hard, he would see the silver and black pennants on the red roofs of Maribor Castle's towers before sundown.

He unsaddled his mare and groomed her himself, sending the stable boy away. He was a royal messenger, and a royal messenger never permits anyone to touch his horse. He ate a goodly portion of scrambled eggs with sausage and a quarter of a loaf of rye bread, washed down with a quart of ale. He listened to the gossip. Of various kinds. Travellers from every corner of the world were dining at the inn.

Aplegatt learned there'd been more trouble in Dol Angra; a troop of Lyrian cavalry had once again clashed with a mounted Nilfgaardian unit. Meve, the queen of Lyria, had loudly accused Nilfgaard of provocation – again – and called for help from King Demavend of Aedirn. Tretogor had seen the public execution of a Redanian baron who had secretly allied himself with emissaries of the Nilfgaardian emperor, Emhyr. In Kaedwen, Scoia'tael commandos, amassed into a large unit, had orchestrated a massacre in Fort Leyda. To avenge the massacre, the people of Ard Carraigh had organised a pogrom, murdering almost four hundred non-humans residing in the capital.

Meanwhile the merchants travelling from the south described the grief and mourning among the Cintran emigrants gathered in Temeria, under the standard of Marshal Vissegerd. The dreadful news of the death of Princess Cirilla, the Lion Cub, the last of the bloodline of Queen Calanthe, had been confirmed.

Some even darker, more foreboding gossip was told. That in

several villages in the region of Aldersberg cows had suddenly begun to squirt blood from their udders while being milked, and at dawn the Virgin Bane, harbinger of terrible destruction, had been seen in the fog. The Wild Hunt, a spectral army galloping across the firmament, had appeared in Brugge, in the region of Brokilon Forest, the forbidden kingdom of the forest dryads; and the Wild Hunt, as is generally known, always heralds war. And a spectral ship had been spotted off Cape Bremervoord with a ghoul on board: a black knight in a helmet adorned with the wings of a bird of prey ...

The messenger stopped listening; he was too tired. He went to the common sleeping chamber, dropped onto his pallet and fell fast asleep.

He arose at daybreak and was a little surprised as he entered the courtyard – he was not the first person preparing to leave, which was unusual. A black gelding stood saddled by the well, while nearby a woman in male clothing was washing her hands in the trough. Hearing Aplegatt's footsteps she turned, gathered her luxuriant black hair in her wet hands, and tossed it back. The messenger bowed. The woman gave a faint nod.

As he entered the stable he almost ran into another early riser, a girl in a velvet beret who was just leading a dapple grey mare out into the courtyard. The girl rubbed her face and yawned, leaning against her horse's withers.

'Oh my,' she murmured, passing the messenger, 'I'll probably fall asleep on my horse ... I'll just flake out ... Auuh ...'

'The cold'll wake you up when you give your mare free rein,' said Aplegatt courteously, pulling his saddle off the rack. 'Godspeed, miss.'

The girl turned and looked at him, as though she had only then noticed him. Her eyes were large and as green as emeralds. Aplegatt threw the saddlecloth over his horse.

'I wished you a safe journey,' he said. He wasn't usually talkative or effusive but now he felt the need to talk to someone, even if this someone was just a sleepy teenager. Perhaps it was those long days of solitude on the road, or possibly that the girl reminded him a little of his middle daughter.

'May the gods protect you,' he added, 'from accidents and foul weather. There are but two of you, and womenfolk at that ... And times are ill at present. Danger lurks everywhere on the highways.'

The girl opened her green eyes wider. The messenger felt his spine go cold, and a shudder passed through him.

'Danger ...' the girl said suddenly, in a strange, altered voice. 'Danger comes silently. You will not hear it when it swoops down on grey feathers. I had a dream. The sand ... The sand was hot from the sun.'

'What?' Aplegatt froze with the saddle pressed against his belly. 'What say you, miss? What sand?'

The girl shuddered violently and rubbed her face. The dapple grey mare shook its head.

'Ciri!' shouted the black-haired woman sharply from the courtyard, adjusting the girth on her black stallion. 'Hurry up!'

The girl yawned, looked at Aplegatt and blinked, appearing surprised by his presence in the stable. The messenger said nothing.

'Ciri,' repeated the woman, 'have you fallen asleep in there?'

'I'm coming, Madam Yennefer.'

By the time Aplegatt had finally saddled his horse and led it out into the courtyard there was no sign of either woman or girl. A cock crowed long and hoarsely, a dog barked, and a cuckoo called from among the trees. The messenger leapt into the saddle. He suddenly recalled the sleepy girl's green eyes and her strange words. *Danger comes silently? Grey feathers? Hot sand? The maid was probably not right in the head*, he

412

thought. *You come across a lot like that these days; deranged girls spoiled by vagabonds or other ne'er-do-wells in these times of war ... Yes, definitely deranged. Or possibly only sleepy, torn from her slumbers, not yet fully awake. It's amazing the poppycock people come out with when they're roaming around at dawn, still caught between sleep and wakefulness ...*

A second shudder passed through him, and he felt a pain between his shoulder blades. He massaged his back with a fist.

Weak at the knees, he spurred his horse on as soon as he was back on the Maribor road, and rode away at a gallop. Time was running out.

The messenger did not rest for long in Maribor – not a day had passed before the wind was whistling in his ears again. His new horse, a roan gelding from the Maribor stable, ran hard, head forward and its tail flowing behind. Roadside willows flashed past. The satchel with the diplomatic mail pressed against Aplegatt's chest. His arse ached.

'Oi! I hope you break your neck, you blasted gadabout!' yelled a carter in his wake, pulling in the halter of his team, startled by the galloping roan flashing by. 'See how he runs, like devils were licking his heels! Ride on, giddy-head, ride; you won't outrun Death himself!'

Aplegatt wiped an eye, which was watering from the speed.

The day before he had given King Foltest a letter, and then recited King Demavend's secret message.

'Demavend to Foltest. All is prepared in Dol Angra. The disguised forces await the order. Estimated date: the second night after the July new moon. The boats are to beach on the far shore two days later.'

Flocks of crows flew over the highway, cawing loudly. They flew east, towards Mahakam and Dol Angra, towards

Vengerberg. As he rode, the messenger silently repeated the confidential message the king of Temeria had entrusted to him for the king of Aedirn.

'Foltest to Demavend. Firstly: let us call off the campaign. The windbags have called a council. They are going to meet and debate on the Isle of Thanedd. This council may change much. Secondly: the search for the Lion Cub can be called off. It is confirmed. The Lion Cub is dead.'

Aplegatt spurred on his horse. Time was running out.

if you enjoyed
BLOOD OF ELVES

look out for

KINGS OF THE WYLD

by

Nicholas Eames

GLORY NEVER GETS OLD.

Clay Cooper and his band were once the best of the best, the most feared and renowned crew of mercenaries this side of the Heartwyld.

Their glory days long past, the mercs have grown apart and grown old, fat, drunk, or a combination of the three. Then an ex-bandmate turns up at Clay's door with a plea for help—the kind of mission that only the very brave or the very stupid would sign up for.

It's time to get the band back together.

"It's Rose."

They had finished eating, set their bowls aside. He should have put them in the basin, Clay knew, got them soaking so they wouldn't be such a chore to clean later, but it suddenly seemed like he couldn't leave the table just now. Gabriel had come in the night, from a long way off, to say something. Best to let him say it and be done.

"Your daughter?" Clay prompted.

Gabe nodded slowly. His hands were both flat on the table. His eyes were fixed, unfocused, somewhere between them. "She is... *willful*," he said finally. "Impetuous. I wish I could say she gets it from her mother, but..." That smile again, just barely. "You remember I was teaching her to use a sword?"

"I remember telling you that was a bad idea," said Clay.

A shrug from Gabriel. "I just wanted her to be able to protect herself. You know, stick 'em with the pointy end and all that. But she wanted more. She wanted to be..." he paused, searching for the word, "...great."

"Like her father?"

Gabriel's expression turned sour. "Just so. She heard too many stories, I think. Got her head filled with all this nonsense about being a hero, fighting in a band."

And from whom could she have heard all that? Clay wondered.

"I know," said Gabriel, perceiving his thoughts. "Partly my fault, I won't deny it. But it wasn't just me. Kids these days... they're obsessed with these mercenaries, Clay. They worship them. It's unhealthy. And most of these mercs aren't even in real bands! They just hire a bunch of nameless goons to do their fighting while they paint their faces and parade around with shiny swords and fancy armour. There's even one guy—I shit you not—who rides a manticore into battle!"

"A manticore?" asked Clay, incredulous.

Gabe laughed bitterly. "I know, right? Who the fuck *rides* a manticore? Those things are dangerous! Well, I don't need to tell you."

He didn't, of course. Clay had a nasty-looking puncture scar on his right thigh, testament to the hazards of tangling with such monsters. A manticore was nobody's pet, and it certainly wasn't fit to ride. As if slapping wings and a poison-barbed tail on a lion made it somehow a *fine* idea to climb on its back!

"They worshipped us, too," Clay pointed out. "Well *you*, anyway. And Ganelon. They tell the stories, even still. They sing the songs."

The stories were exaggerated, naturally. The songs, for the most part, were wildly inaccurate. But they persisted. Had lasted long after the men themselves had outlived who (or what) they'd been.

We were giants once.

"It's not the same," Gabriel persisted. "You should see the crowds gather when these bands come to town, Clay. People screaming, women crying in the streets."

"That sounds horrible," said Clay, meaning it.

Gabriel ignored him, pressing on. "Anyhow, Rose wanted to learn the sword, so I indulged her. I figured she'd get bored of it sooner or later, and that if she was going to learn, it might as well be from me. And also it made her mother mad as hell."

It would have, Clay knew. Her mother, Valery, despised violence and weapons of any kind, along with those who used either toward any end whatsoever. It was partly because of Valery that Saga had dissolved all those years ago.

"Problem was," said Gabriel, "she was good. Really good, and that's not just a father's boasts. She started out sparring against kids her age, but when they gave up getting their asses whooped she went out looking for street fights, or wormed her way into sponsored matches."

"The daughter of Golden Gabe himself," Clay mused. "Must've been quite the draw."

"I guess so," his friend agreed. "But then one day Val saw the bruises. Lost her mind. Blamed me, of course, for everything. She put her foot down—you know how she gets—and for a while Rose stopped fighting, but…" He trailed off, and Clay saw his jaw clamp down on something bitter. "After her mother left, Rosie and I…didn't get along so well, either. She started going out again. Sometimes she wouldn't come home for days. There were more bruises, and a few nastier scrapes besides. She chopped her hair off—thank the Holy Tetrea her mother was gone by then, or mine would've been next. And then came the cyclops."

"Cyclops?"

Gabriel looked at him askance. "Big bastards, one huge eye right here on their head?"

Clay leveled a glare of his own. "I know what a cyclops is, asshole."

"Then why did you ask?"

"I didn't…" Clay faltered. "Never mind. What *about* the cyclops?"

Gabriel sighed. "Well, one settled down in that old fort north of Ottersbrook. Stole some cattle, some goats, a dog, and then killed the folks that went looking for 'em. The courtsmen had their hands full, so they were looking for someone to clear the beast out for them. Only there weren't any mercs around at the time—or none with the chops to take on a cyclops, anyway. Somehow my name got tossed into the pot. They even sent someone round to ask if I would, but I told them no. Hell, I don't even own a sword anymore!"

Clay cut in again, aghast. "What? What about *Vellichor*?"

Gabriel's eyes were downcast. "I...uh...sold it."

"I'm sorry?" Clay asked, but before his friend could repeat himself he put his own hands flat on the table, for fear they would ball into fists, or snatch one of the bowls nearby and smash it over Gabriel's head. He said, as calmly as he could manage, "For a second there I thought you said that *you sold Vellichor*. As in the sword entrusted to you by the Archon himself as he lay dying? The sword he used to carve a fucking doorway from his world to ours. *That* sword? You sold *that sword*?"

Gabriel, who had slumped deeper into his chair with every word, nodded. "I had debts to pay, and Valery wanted it out of the house after she found out I taught Rose to fight," he said meekly. "She said it was dangerous."

"She—" Clay stopped himself. He leaned back in his chair, kneading his eyes with the palms of his hands. He groaned, and Griff, sensing his frustration, groaned himself from his mat in the corner. "Finish your story," he said at last.

Gabriel continued. "Well, needless to say, I refused to go after the cyclops, and for the next few weeks it caused a fair bit of havoc. And then suddenly word got around that someone had gone out and killed it." He smiled, wistful and sad. "All by herself."

"Rose," Clay said. Didn't make it a question. Didn't need to.

Gabriel's nod confirmed it. "She was a celebrity overnight. Bloody Rose, they called her. A pretty good name, actually."

It is, Clay agreed, but didn't bother saying so. He was still fuming about the sword. The sooner Gabe said whatever it was he'd come here to say, the sooner Clay could tell his oldest, dearest friend to get the hell out of his house and never come back.

"She even got her own band going," Gabe went on. "They

managed to clear out a few nests around town: giant spiders, some old carrion wyrm down in the sewer that everyone forgot was still alive. But I hoped—" he bit his lip "—I still hoped, even then, that she might choose another path. A better path. Instead of following mine." He looked up. "Until the summons came from the Republic of Castia, asking every able sword to march against the Heartwyld Horde."

For a heartbeat Clay wondered at the significance of that. Until he remembered the news he'd heard earlier that evening. An army of twenty thousand, routed by a vastly more numerous host; the survivors surrounded in Castia, doubtless wishing they had died on the battlefield rather than endure the atrocities of a city under siege.

Which meant that Gabriel's daughter was dead. Or she would be, when the city fell.

Clay opened his mouth to speak, to try to keep the heartbreak from his voice as he did so. "Gabe, I—"

"I'm going after her, Clay. And I need you with me." Gabriel leaned forward in his chair, the flame of a father's fear and anger alight in his eyes. "It's time to get the band back together."

THE TIME OF CONTEMPT

By Andrzej Sapkowski

The Last Wish
Sword of Destiny
Blood of Elves
The Time of Contempt
Baptism of Fire
The Tower of Swallows
The Lady of the Lake

The Malady and Other Stories:
An Andrzej Sapkowski Sampler (e-only)

THE TIME OF CONTEMPT

ANDRZEJ SAPKOWSKI

Translated by David French

www.orbitbooks.net

Cover design by Lauren Panepinto
Cover illustration by Bartłomiej Gaweł, Paweł Mielniczuk, Marcin Błaszczak,
   Arkadiusz Matyszewski, Marian Chomiak
Cover copyright © 2013 by Hachette Book Group, Inc.

Originally published in Polish as *Czas Pogardy*

Orbit
Hachette Book Group
1290 Avenue of the Americas, New York, NY 10104
HachetteBookGroup.com

First U.S. Edition: August 2013
Published by arrangement with Agence de l'Est Literary Agency
First published in Great Britain in 2013 by Gollancz
An imprint of the Orion Publishing Group
Orion House, 5 Upper St Martin's Lane, London WC2H 9EA
A Hachette UK Company

Orbit is an imprint of Hachette Book Group, Inc. The Orbit name and logo are trademarks of Little, Brown Book Group Limited.

The Hachette Speakers Bureau provides a wide range of authors for speaking events. To find out more, go to www.hachettespeakersbureau.com or call (866) 376-6591.

The publisher is not responsible for websites (or their content) that are not owned by the publisher.

Library of Congress Control Number: 2013940461
ISBN: 978-0-316-21913-6

20 19 18

LSC-C

Printed in the United States of America

Blood on your hands, Falka,
Blood on your dress.
Burn, burn, Falka, and die,
Die in agony for your crimes!

*Vedymins, called witchers among the Nordlings (q.v.), a mysterious
and elite caste of warrior-priests, probably an offshoot of the druids
(q.v.). In the folk consciousness, they are endowed with magical powers
and superhuman abilities; v. were said to fight evil spirits, monsters and
all manner of dark forces. In reality, since they were unparalleled in
their ability to wield weapons, v. were used by the rulers of the north
in the tribal fighting they waged with each other. In combat v. fell into
a trance, brought on, it is believed, by autohypnosis or intoxicating
substances, and fought with pure energy, being utterly invulnerable to
pain or even grave wounds, which reinforced the superstitions about
their superhuman powers. The theory, according to which v. were said
to have been the products of mutation or genetic engineering, has not
found confirmation. V. are the heroes of numerous Nordling tales (cf. F.
Delannoy, Myths and Legends of the Nordlings).*

Effenberg and Talbot
Encyclopaedia Maxima Mundi, Vol. XV

CHAPTER ONE

When talking to youngsters entering the service, Aplegatt usually told them that in order to make their living as mounted messengers two things would be necessary: a head of gold and an arse of iron.

A head of gold is essential, Aplegatt instructed the young messengers, since in the flat leather pouch strapped to his chest beneath his clothing the messenger only carries news of less vital importance, which could without fear be entrusted to treacherous paper or manuscript. The really important, secret tidings – those on which a great deal depended – must be committed to memory by the messenger and only repeated to the intended recipient. Word for word; and at times those words are far from simple. Difficult to pronounce, let alone remember. In order to memorise them and not make a mistake when they are recounted, one has to have a truly golden head.

And the benefits of an arse of iron, oh, every messenger will swiftly learn those for himself. When the moment comes for him to spend three days and nights in the saddle, riding a hundred or even two hundred miles along roads or sometimes, when necessary, trackless terrain, then it is needed. No, of course you don't sit in the saddle without respite; sometimes you dismount and rest. For a man can bear a great deal, but a horse less. However, when it's time to get back in the saddle after resting, it's as though your arse were shouting, 'Help! Murder!'

'But who needs mounted messengers now, Master Aplegatt?' young people would occasionally ask in astonishment. 'Take Vengerberg to Vizima; no one could knock that off in less than four – or even five – days, even on the swiftest steed. But how long does a sorcerer from Vengerberg need to send news to a sorcerer from Vizima? Half an hour, or not even that. A messenger's horse may go lame, but a sorcerer's message always arrives. It never loses its way.

3

It never arrives late or gets lost. What's the point of messengers, if there are sorcerers everywhere, at every kingly court? Messengers are no longer necessary, Master Aplegatt.'

For some time Aplegatt had also been thinking he was no longer of any use to anyone. He was thirty-six and small but strong and wiry, wasn't afraid of hard work and had – naturally – a head of gold. He could have found other work to support himself and his wife, to put a bit of money by for the dowries of his two as yet unmarried daughters and to continue helping the married one whose husband, the sad loser, was always unlucky in his business ventures. But Aplegatt couldn't and didn't want to imagine any other job. He was a royal mounted messenger and that was that.

And then suddenly, after a long period of being forgotten and humiliatingly idle, Aplegatt was once again needed. And the highways and forest tracks once again echoed to the sound of hooves. Just like the old days, messengers began to travel the land bearing news from town to town.

Aplegatt knew why. He saw a lot and heard even more. It was expected that he would immediately erase each message from his memory once it had been given, that he would forget it so as to be unable to recall it even under torture. But Aplegatt remembered. He knew why kings had suddenly stopped communicating with the help of magic and sorcerers. The news that the messengers were carrying was meant to remain a secret from them. Kings had suddenly stopped trusting sorcerers; stopped confiding their secrets in them.

Aplegatt didn't know what had caused this sudden cooling off in the friendship between kings and sorcerers and wasn't overly concerned about it. He regarded both kings and magic-users as incomprehensible creatures, unpredictable in their deeds – particularly when times were becoming hard. And the fact that times were now hard could not be ignored, not if one travelled across the land from castle to castle, from town to town, from kingdom to kingdom.

There were plenty of troops on the roads. With every step one came across an infantry or cavalry column, and every commander you met was edgy, nervous, curt and as self-important as if the fate of the entire world rested on him alone. The cities and castles were also full of armed men, and a feverish bustle went on there, day and night. The usually invisible burgraves and castellans now ceaselessly rushed along walls and through courtyards, angry as wasps before a storm, yelling, swearing and issuing orders and kicks. Day and night, lumbering columns of laden wagons rolled towards strongholds and garrisons, passing carts on their way back, moving quickly, unburdened and empty. Herds of frisky three-year-old mounts taken straight out of stables kicked dust up on the roads. Ponies not accustomed to bits nor armed riders cheerfully enjoyed their last days of freedom, giving stable boys plenty of extra work and other road users no small trouble.

To put it briefly, war hung in the hot, still air.

Aplegatt stood up in his stirrups and looked around. Down at the foot of the hill a river sparkled, meandering sharply among meadows and clusters of trees. Forests stretched out beyond it, to the south. The messenger urged his horse on. Time was running out.

He'd been on the road for two days. The royal order and mail had caught up with him in Hagge, where he was resting after returning from Tretogor. He had left the stronghold by night, galloping along the highway following the left bank of the Pontar, crossed the border with Temeria before dawn, and now, at noon of the following day, was already at the bank of the Ismena. Had King Foltest been in Vizima, Aplegatt would have delivered him the message that night. Unfortunately, the king was not in the capital; he was residing in the south of the country, in Maribor, almost two hundred miles from Vizima. Aplegatt knew this, so in the region of the White Bridge he left the westward-leading road and rode through woodland towards Ellander. He was taking a risk. The Scoia'tael* continued to roam the forests, and woe betide anyone who fell into their hands or came within arrowshot. But a royal messenger had to take risks. Such was his duty.

He crossed the river without difficulty – it hadn't rained since

---

* The Scoia'tael – commonly known as the Squirrels – are non-human guerrillas. Predominantly elves, their ranks also include halflings and dwarves, and they are so named due to their habit of attaching squirrel tails to their caps or clothing. Allied with Nilfgaard, motivated by the racism of men, they fight all humans in the Northern Kingdoms.

June and the Ismena's waters had fallen considerably. Keeping to the edge of the forest, he reached the track leading south-east from Vizima, towards the dwarven foundries, forges and settlements in the Mahakam Mountains. There were plenty of carts along the track, often being overtaken by small mounted units. Aplegatt sighed in relief. Where there were lots of humans, there weren't any Scoia'tael. The campaign against the guerrilla elves had endured in Temeria for a year and, being harried in the forests, the Scoia'tael commandos had divided up into smaller groups. These smaller groups kept well away from well-used roads and didn't set ambushes on them.

Before nightfall he was already on the western border of the duchy of Ellander, at a crossroads near the village of Zavada. From here he had a straight and safe road to Maribor: forty-two miles of hard, well-frequented forest track, and there was an inn at the crossroads. He decided to rest his horse and himself there. Were he to set off at daybreak he knew that, even without pushing his mount too hard, he would see the silver and black pennants on the red roofs of Maribor Castle's towers before sundown.

He unsaddled his mare and groomed her himself, sending the stable boy away. He was a royal messenger, and a royal messenger never permits anyone to touch his horse. He ate a goodly portion of scrambled eggs with sausage and a quarter of a loaf of rye bread, washed down with a quart of ale. He listened to the gossip. Of various kinds. Travellers from every corner of the world were dining at the inn.

Aplegatt learned there'd been more trouble in Dol Angra; a troop of Lyrian cavalry had once again clashed with a mounted Nilfgaardian unit. Meve, the queen of Lyria, had loudly accused Nilfgaard of provocation – again – and called for help from King Demavend of Aedirn. Tretogor had seen the public execution of a Redanian baron who had secretly allied himself with emissaries of the Nilfgaardian emperor, Emhyr. In Kaedwen, Scoia'tael commandos, amassed into a large unit, had orchestrated a massacre in Fort Leyda. To avenge the massacre, the people of Ard Carraigh had organised a pogrom, murdering almost four hundred non-humans residing in the capital.

Meanwhile the merchants travelling from the south described

the grief and mourning among the Cintran emigrants gathered in Temeria, under the standard of Marshal Vissegerd. The dreadful news of the death of Princess Cirilla, the Lion Cub, the last of the bloodline of Queen Calanthe, had been confirmed.

Some even darker, more foreboding gossip was told. That in several villages in the region of Aldersberg cows had suddenly begun to squirt blood from their udders while being milked, and at dawn the Virgin Bane, harbinger of terrible destruction, had been seen in the fog. The Wild Hunt, a spectral army galloping across the firmament, had appeared in Brugge, in the region of Brokilon Forest, the forbidden kingdom of the forest dryads; and the Wild Hunt, as is generally known, always heralds war. And a spectral ship had been spotted off Cape Bremervoord with a ghoul on board: a black knight in a helmet adorned with the wings of a bird of prey ...

The messenger stopped listening; he was too tired. He went to the common sleeping chamber, dropped onto his pallet and fell fast asleep.

He arose at daybreak and was a little surprised as he entered the courtyard – he was not the first person preparing to leave, which was unusual. A black gelding stood saddled by the well, while nearby a woman in male clothing was washing her hands in the trough. Hearing Aplegatt's footsteps she turned, gathered her luxuriant black hair in her wet hands, and tossed it back. The messenger bowed. The woman gave a faint nod.

As he entered the stable he almost ran into another early riser, a girl in a velvet beret who was just leading a dapple grey mare out into the courtyard. The girl rubbed her face and yawned, leaning against her horse's withers.

'Oh my,' she murmured, passing the messenger, 'I'll probably fall asleep on my horse ... I'll just flake out ... Auuh ...'

'The cold'll wake you up when you give your mare free rein,' said Aplegatt courteously, pulling his saddle off the rack. 'Godspeed, miss.'

The girl turned and looked at him, as though she had only then noticed him. Her eyes were large and as green as emeralds. Aplegatt threw the saddlecloth over his horse.

7

'I wished you a safe journey,' he said. He wasn't usually talkative or effusive but now he felt the need to talk to someone, even if this someone was just a sleepy teenager. Perhaps it was those long days of solitude on the road, or possibly that the girl reminded him a little of his middle daughter.

'May the gods protect you,' he added, 'from accidents and foul weather. There are but two of you, and womenfolk at that . . . And times are ill at present. Danger lurks everywhere on the highways.'

The girl opened her green eyes wider. The messenger felt his spine go cold, and a shudder passed through him.

'Danger . . .' the girl said suddenly, in a strange, altered voice. 'Danger comes silently. You will not hear it when it swoops down on grey feathers. I had a dream. The sand . . . The sand was hot from the sun.'

'What?' Aplegatt froze with the saddle pressed against his belly. 'What say you, miss? What sand?'

The girl shuddered violently and rubbed her face. The dapple grey mare shook its head.

'Ciri!' shouted the black-haired woman sharply from the court-yard, adjusting the girth on her black stallion. 'Hurry up!'

The girl yawned, looked at Aplegatt and blinked, appearing sur-prised by his presence in the stable. The messenger said nothing.

'Ciri,' repeated the woman, 'have you fallen asleep in there?'

'I'm coming, Madam Yennefer.'

By the time Aplegatt had finally saddled his horse and led it out into the courtyard there was no sign of either woman or girl. A cock crowed long and hoarsely, a dog barked, and a cuckoo called from among the trees. The messenger leapt into the saddle. He suddenly recalled the sleepy girl's green eyes and her strange words. *Danger comes silently? Grey feathers? Hot sand? The maid was probably not right in the head*, he thought. *You come across a lot like that these days; deranged girls spoiled by vagabonds or other ne'er-do-wells in these times of war . . . Yes, definitely deranged. Or possibly only sleepy, torn from her slumbers, not yet fully awake. It's amazing the poppycock people come out with when they're roaming around at dawn, still caught between sleep and wakefulness . . .*

A second shudder passed through him, and he felt a pain between his shoulder blades. He massaged his back with a fist.

Weak at the knees, he spurred his horse on as soon as he was back on the Maribor road, and rode away at a gallop. Time was running out.

The messenger did not rest for long in Maribor – not a day had passed before the wind was whistling in his ears again. His new horse, a roan gelding from the Maribor stable, ran hard, head forward and its tail flowing behind. Roadside willows flashed past. The satchel with the diplomatic mail pressed against Aplegatt's chest. His arse ached.

'Oi! I hope you break your neck, you blasted gadabout!' yelled a carter in his wake, pulling in the halter of his team, startled by the galloping roan flashing by. 'See how he runs, like devils were licking his heels! Ride on, giddy-head, ride; you won't outrun Death himself!'

Aplegatt wiped an eye, which was watering from the speed.

The day before he had given King Foltest a letter, and then recited King Demavend's secret message.

'Demavend to Foltest. All is prepared in Dol Angra. The disguised forces await the order. Estimated date: the second night after the July new moon. The boats are to beach on the far shore two days later.'

Flocks of crows flew over the highway, cawing loudly. They flew east, towards Mahakam and Dol Angra, towards Vengerberg. As he rode, the messenger silently repeated the confidential message the king of Temeria had entrusted to him for the king of Aedirn.

'Foltest to Demavend. Firstly: let us call off the campaign. The windbags have called a council. They are going to meet and debate on the Isle of Thanedd. This council may change much. Secondly: the search for the Lion Cub can be called off. It is confirmed. The Lion Cub is dead.'

Aplegatt spurred on his horse. Time was running out.

The narrow forest track was blocked with wagons. Aplegatt slowed down and trotted unhurriedly up to the last wagon in the long column. He saw he could not force his way through the obstruction, but nor could he think about heading back; too much time would be lost. Venturing into the boggy thicket and riding around the obstruction was not an attractive alternative either, particularly since darkness was falling.

'What's going on?' he asked the drivers of the last wagon in the column. They were two old men, one of whom seemed to be dozing and the other showing no signs of life. 'An attack? Scoia'tael? Speak up! I'm in a hurry ...'

Before either of the two old men had a chance to answer, screams could be heard from the head of the column, hidden amongst the trees. Drivers leapt onto their wagons, lashing their horses and oxen to the accompaniment of choice oaths. The column moved off ponderously. The dozing old man awoke, moved his chin, clucked at his mules and flicked the reins across their rumps. The moribund old man came to life too, drew his straw hat back from his eyes and looked at Aplegatt.

'Mark him,' he said. 'A hasty one. Well, laddie, your luck's in. You've joined the company right on time.'

'Aye,' said the other old man, motioning with his chin and urging the mules forward. 'You are timely. Had you come at noon, you'd have come to a stop like us and waited for a clear passage. We're all in a hurry, but we had to wait. How can you ride on, when the way is closed?'

'The way closed? Why so?'

'There's a cruel man-eater in these parts, laddie. He fell on a knight riding along the road with nowt but a boy for company. They say the monster rent the knight's head right off – helmet and all – and spilt his horse's gizzards. The boy made good his escape and said it was a fell beast, that the road was crimson with gore—'

'What kind of monster is it?' asked Aplegatt, reining in his horse in order to continue talking to the wagoners as they drove on. 'A dragon?'

'Nay, it's no dragon,' said the one in the straw hat. ''Tis said to be a manticore, or some such. The boy said 'tis a flying beast, awful huge. And vicious! We reckoned he would devour the knight and

10

fly away, but no! They say he settled on the road, the whoreson, and was sat there, hissing and baring its fangs ... Yea, and the road all stopped up like a corked-up flagon, for whoever drove up first and saw the fiend left his wagon and hastened away. Now the wagons are backed up for a third of a league, and all around, as you see, laddie, thicket and bog. There's no riding around or turning back. So here we stood ...'

'Such a host!' snorted the horseman. 'And they were standing by like dolts when they ought to've seized axe and spear to drive the beast from the road, or slaughter it.'

'Aye, a few tried,' said the old wagoner, driving on his mules, for the column was now moving more quickly. 'Three dwarves from the merchants' guard and, with them, four recruits who were heading to the stronghold in Carreras to join the army. The monster carved up the dwarves horribly, and the recruits –'

'– bolted,' finished the other old man, after which he spat rapturously. The gob flew a long way ahead of him, expertly falling into the space between the mules' rumps. 'Bolted, after barely setting their eyes on the manticore. One of them shat his britches, I hear. Oh, look, look, laddie. That's him! Yonder!'

'What are you blathering on about?' asked Aplegatt, somewhat annoyed. 'You're pointing out that shitty arse ? I'm not interested—'

'Nay! The monster! The monster's corpse! They're lifting it onto a wagon! D'you see?'

Aplegatt stood in his stirrups. In spite of the gathering darkness and the crowd of onlookers he saw the great tawny body being lifted up by soldiers. The monster's bat-like wings and scorpion tail dragged inertly along the ground. Cheering, the soldiers lifted the corpse higher and heaved it onto a wagon. The horses harnessed to it, clearly disturbed by the stench of the carcass and the blood, neighed and tugged at the shaft.

'Move along!' the sergeant shouted at the old men. 'Keep moving! Don't block the road!'

The greybeard drove his mules on, the wagon bouncing over the rutted road. Aplegatt, urging on his horse with his heel, drew alongside.

11

'Looks like the soldiers have put paid to the beast.'

'Not a bit of it,' rejoined the old man. 'When the soldiers arrived, all they did was yell and order people around. "Stand still! Move on!" and all the rest of it. They were in no haste to deal with the monster. They sent for a witcher.'

'A witcher?'

'Aye,' confirmed the second old man. 'Someone recalled he'd seen a witcher in the village, and they sent for him. A while later he rode past us. His hair was white, his countenance fearful to behold, and he bore a cruel blade. Not an hour had passed than someone called from the front that the road would soon be clear, for the witcher had dispatched the beast. So at last we set off; which was just about when you turned up, laddie.'

'Ah,' said Aplegatt absentmindedly. 'All these years I've been scouring these roads and never met a witcher. Did anyone see him defeat the monster?'

'I saw it!' called a boy with a shock of tousled hair, trotting up on the other side of the wagon. He was riding bareback, steering a skinny, dapple grey nag using a halter. 'I saw it all! I was with the soldiers, right at the front!'

'Look at him, snot-nosed kid,' said the old man driving the wagon. 'Milk not dried on his face, and see how he mouths off. Looking for a slap?'

'Leave him, father,' interrupted Aplegatt. 'We'll reach the crossroads soon and I'm riding to Carreras, so first I'd like to know how the witcher got on. Talk, boy.'

'It was like this,' he began quickly, still trotting alongside the wagon. 'That witcher comes up to the officer. He says his name's Geralt. The officer says it's all the same to him, and it'd be better if he made a start. Shows him where the monster is. The witcher moves closer and looks on. The monster's about five furlongs or more away, but he just glances at it and says at once it's an uncommon great manticore and he'll kill it if they give him two hundred crowns.'

'Two hundred crowns?' choked the other old man. 'Had he gone cuckoo?'

'The officer says the same, only his words were riper. So the witcher says that's how much it will cost and it's all the same to him; the monster can stay on the road till Judgement Day. The officer says he won't pay that much and he'll wait till the beast flies off by itself. The witcher says it won't because it's hungry and pissed off. And if it flies off, it'll be back soon because that's its hunting terri–terri– territor—'

'You whippersnapper, don't talk nonsense!' said the old man driving the cart, losing his temper, unsuccessfully trying to clear his nose into the fingers he was holding the reins with. 'Just tell us what happened!'

'I *am* telling you! The witcher goes, "The monster won't fly away, he'll spend the entire night eating the dead knight, nice and slow, because the knight's in armour and it's hard to pick out the meat." So some merchants step up and try making a deal with the witcher, by hook or by crook, that they'll organise a whip-round and give him five score crowns. The witcher says that beast's a manticore and is very dangerous, and they can shove their hundred crowns up their arses, he won't risk his neck for it. So the officer gets pissed off and says tough luck, it's a witcher's fate to risk his neck, and that a witcher is perfectly suited to it, like an arse is perfectly suited to shitting. But I can see the merchants get afeared the witcher would get angry and head off, because they say they'll pay seven score and ten. So then the witcher gets his sword out and heads off down the road towards where the beast's sitting. And the officer makes a mark behind him to drive away magic, spits on the ground and says he doesn't know why the earth bears such hellish abominations. One of the merchants says that if the army drove away monsters from roads instead of chasing elves through forests, witchers wouldn't be needed and that—'

'Don't drivel,' interrupted the old man. 'Just say what you saw.'

'I saw,' boasted the boy, 'the witcher's horse, a chestnut mare with a white blaze.'

'Blow the mare! Did you see the witcher kill the monster?'

'Err ...' stammered the boy. 'No I didn't ... I got pushed to the back. Everybody was shouting and the horses were startled, when—'

'Just what I said,' declared the old man contemptuously. 'He didn't see shite, snotty-nosed kid.'

'But I saw the witcher coming back!' said the boy, indignantly. 'And the officer, who saw it all, he was as pale as a ghost and said quietly to his men it was magic spells or elven tricks and that a normal man couldn't wield a sword that quickly ... While the witcher ups and takes the money from the merchants, mounts his mare and rides off.'

'Hmm,' murmured Aplegatt. 'Which way was he headed? Along the road to Carreras? If so, I might catch him up, just to have a look at him ...'

'No,' said the boy. 'He took the road to Dorian from the crossroads. He was in a hurry.'

The Witcher seldom dreamed at all, and he never remembered those rare dreams on waking. Not even when they were nightmares – and they were usually nightmares.

This time it was also a nightmare, but at least the Witcher remembered some of it. A distinct, clear image had suddenly emerged from a swirling vortex of unclear but disturbing shapes, of strange but foreboding scenes and incomprehensible but sinister words and sounds. It was Ciri, but not as he remembered her from Kaer Morhen. Her flaxen hair, flowing behind her as she galloped, was longer – as it had been when they first met, in Brokilon. When she rode by he wanted to shout but no words came. He wanted to run after her, but it was as if he were stuck in setting pitch to half-way up his thighs. And Ciri seemed not to see him and galloped on, into the night, between misshapen alders and willows waving their boughs as if they were alive. He saw she was being pursued. That a black horse was galloping in her tracks, and on it a rider in black armour, wearing a helmet decorated with the wings of a bird of prey.

He couldn't move, he couldn't shout. He could only watch as the winged knight chased Ciri, caught her hair, pulled her from the saddle and galloped on, dragging her behind him. He could only watch Ciri's face contort with pain, watch her mouth twist into a soundless cry. *Awake!* he ordered himself, unable to bear the nightmare. *Awake! Awake at once!*

He awoke.

He lay motionless for a long while, recalling the dream. Then he rose. He drew a pouch from beneath his pillow and quickly counted out some ten-crown coins. One hundred and fifty for yesterday's manticore. Fifty for the fogler he had been commissioned to kill by the headman of a village near Carreras. And fifty for the werewolf some settlers from Burdorff had driven out of hiding for him.

Fifty for a werewolf. That was plenty, for the work had been easy. The werewolf hadn't even fought back. Driven into a cave from which there was no escape, it had knelt down and waited for the sword to fall. The Witcher had felt sorry for it.

But he needed the money.

Before an hour had passed he was ambling down the streets of the town of Dorian, looking for a familiar lane and sign.

The wording on the sign read: 'Codringher and Fenn, legal consultation and services'. But Geralt knew only too well that Codringher and Fenn's trade had little in common with the law, while the partners themselves had a host of reasons to avoid any kind of contact either with the law or its enforcers. He also seriously doubted if any of the clients who showed up in their chambers knew what the word 'consultation' meant.

There was no entrance on the ground floor of the small building; there was only a securely bolted door, probably leading to a coach house or a stable. In order to reach the door one had to venture around the back of the building, enter a muddy courtyard full of ducks and chickens and, from there, walk up some steps before proceeding down a narrow gallery and along a cramped, dark corridor. Only then did one find oneself before a solid, studded mahogany door, equipped with a large brass knocker in the form of a lion's head.

Geralt knocked, and then quickly withdrew. He knew the mechanism mounted in the door could shoot twenty-inch iron spikes through holes hidden among the studs. In theory the spikes were only

15

released if someone tried to tamper with the lock, or if Codringher or Fenn pressed the trigger mechanism, but Geralt had discovered, many times, that all mechanisms are unreliable. They only worked when they ought not to work, and vice versa.

There was sure to be a device in the door – probably magic – for identifying guests. Having knocked, as today, no voice from within ever plied him with questions or demanded that he speak. The door opened and Codringher was standing there. Always Codringher, never Fenn.

'Welcome, Geralt,' said Codringher. 'Enter. You don't need to flatten yourself against the doorframe, I've dismantled the security device. Some part of it broke a few days ago. It went off quite out of the blue and drilled a few holes in a hawker. Come right in. Do you have a case for me?'

'No,' said the Witcher, entering the large, gloomy anteroom which, as usual, smelled faintly of cat. 'Not for you. For Fenn.'

Codringher cackled loudly, confirming the Witcher's suspicions that Fenn was an utterly mythical figure who served to pull the wool over the eyes of provosts, bailiffs, tax collectors and any other individuals Codringher detested.

They entered the office, where it was lighter because it was the topmost room and the solidly barred windows enjoyed the sun for most of the day. Geralt sat in the chair reserved for clients. Opposite, in an upholstered armchair behind an oaken desk, lounged Codringher; a man who introduced himself as a 'lawyer', a man for whom nothing was impossible. If anyone had difficulties, troubles, problems, they went to Codringher. And would quickly be handed proof of his business partner's dishonesty and malpractice. Or he would receive credit without securities or guarantees. Or find himself the only one, from a long list of creditors, to exact payment from a business which had declared itself bankrupt. He would receive his inheritance even though his rich uncle had threatened he wouldn't leave them a farthing. He would win an inheritance case when even the most determined relatives unexpectedly withdrew their claims. His son would leave the dungeon, cleared even of charges based on irrefutable evidence, or would be released due to the sudden absence of any such proof. For, when Codringher and Fenn were involved, if there had been proof it would mysteriously disappear, or the witnesses would vie to retract their earlier testimonies. A dowry hunter courting their daughter would suddenly direct his affections towards another. A wife's lover or daughter's seducer would suffer a complicated fracture of three members – including at least one upper one – in an unfortunate accident. Or a fervent enemy or other extremely inconvenient individual would stop doing him harm; as a rule they were never seen or heard of again. Yes, if someone had a problem they could always ride to Dorian, run swiftly to Codringher and Fenn and knock at the mahogany door. Codringher, the 'lawyer', would be standing in the doorway, short, spare and grizzled, with the unhealthy pallor of a person who seldom spent time in the fresh air. Codringher would lead them into his office, sit down in his armchair, lift his large black and white tomcat onto his lap and stroke it. The two of them – Codringher and the tomcat – would measure up the client with identical, unpleasant, unsettling expressions in their yellowish-green eyes.

'I received your letter,' said Codringher, while he and the tomcat weighed the Witcher up with their yellowish-green gaze. 'Dandelion also visited. He passed through Dorian a few weeks ago and told me a little about your concerns. But he said very little. Really too little.'

'Indeed? You astonish me. That's the first time I've heard that Dandelion didn't say too much.'

'Dandelion,' said Codringher unsmilingly, 'said very little because he knew very little. He said even less than he knew because you'd forbidden him to speak about certain issues. Where does your lack of trust come from? Especially towards a professional colleague?'

This visibly annoyed Geralt. Codringher would probably have pretended not to notice, but he couldn't because of the cat. It opened its eyes wide, bared its white fangs and hissed almost silently.

'Don't annoy my cat,' said the lawyer, stroking the animal to calm it. 'Did it bother you to be called a colleague? But it's true. I'm also a witcher. I also save people from monsters and from monstrous difficulties. And I also do it for money.'

'There are certain differences,' muttered Geralt, still under the tomcat's unpleasant gaze.

'There are,' agreed Codringher. 'You are an anachronistic witcher, and I'm a modern witcher, moving with the spirit of the times. Which is why you'll soon be out of work and I'll be doing well. Soon there won't be any strigas, wyverns, endriagas or werewolves left in the world. But there'll always be whoresons.'

'But it's mainly the whoresons you get out of difficulties, Codringher. Paupers with difficulties can't afford your services.'

'Paupers can't afford your services either. Paupers can never afford anything, which is precisely why they're called paupers.'

'Astonishingly logical of you. And so original it takes the breath away.'

'The truth always has that effect. And it's the truth that being a bastard is the basis and mainstay of our professions. Except your business is almost a relic and mine is genuine and growing in strength.'

'All right, all right. Let's get down to our business.'

'About time,' said Codringher, nodding his head and stroking his cat, which had arched its back and was now purring loudly, sinking its claws into his knee. 'And we'll sort these things out in order of importance. The first issue: the fee, my friend, is two hundred and fifty Novigrad crowns. Do you have that kind of money? Or perhaps you number yourself among the paupers with difficulties?'

'First let's establish whether you've done enough to deserve a sum like that.'

'Decide for yourself,' said the lawyer coldly, 'and be quick about it. Once you feel convinced, lay the money on the table. Then we'll move on to other, less important matters.'

Geralt unfastened a purse from his belt and threw it, with poor grace and a clink of coins, onto the desk. The tomcat jumped off Codringher's lap with a bound and ran away. The lawyer dropped the purse in a drawer without checking the contents.

'You alarmed my cat,' he said with undisguised reproach.

'I do beg your pardon. I thought the clink of money was the last thing that could scare it. Tell me what you uncovered.'

'That Rience,' began Codringher, 'who interests you so much, is quite a mysterious character. I've been able to ascertain that he was a student at the school for sorcerers in Ban Ard for two years. They threw him out after catching him thieving. Recruiting officers from the Kaedwen secret service were waiting outside the school, as usual, and Rience allowed himself to be recruited. I was unable to determine what he did for the Kaedwen secret service, but sorcerers' rejects are usually trained as killers. Does that fit?'

'Like a glove. Go on.'

'My next information comes from Cintra. Rience served time in the dungeons there, during Queen Calanthe's reign.'

'What for?'

'For debts, would you believe? He didn't stay long though, because someone bought him out after paying off the debts along with the interest. The transaction took place through a bank, with the anonymity of the benefactor preserved. I tried to uncover the identity of this benefactor but admitted defeat after checking four banks in turn. Whoever bought Rience out was a pro. And cared a great deal about preserving their anonymity.'

Codringher fell silent and then coughed loudly, pressing a handkerchief to his mouth.

'And suddenly, as soon as the war was over, Mr Rience showed up in Sodden, Angren and Brugge,' he continued after a moment, wiping his lips and looking down at the handkerchief. 'Changed beyond recognition, at least as regards his behaviour and the quantities of cash he had to throw around. Because, as far as his identity went, the brazen son of a bitch didn't bother with secrecy: he continued to use the name "Rience". And as Rience he began to search intensively for a certain party; to be precise a young, female party. He visited the druids from the Angren Circle, the ones who looked after war orphans. One druid's body was found some time later in a nearby forest, mutilated, bearing the marks of torture. Rience showed up afterwards in Riverdell—'

'I know,' interrupted Geralt. 'I know what he did to the Riverdell peasant family. And I was expecting more for my two hundred and fifty crowns. Up to now, your only fresh information has been

19

about the sorcerers' school and the Kaedwen secret service. I know the rest. I know Rience is a ruthless killer. I know he's an arrogant rogue who doesn't even bother to use aliases. I know he's working for somebody. But for whom, Codringher?'

'For some sorcerer or other. It was a sorcerer who bought him out of that dungeon. You told me yourself – and Dandelion confirmed it – that Rience uses magic. Real magic, not the tricks that some expellee from the academy might know. So someone's backing him, they're equipping him with amulets and probably secretly training him. Some officially practising sorcerers have secret pupils and factotums like him for doing illegal or dirty business. In sorcerers' slang it's described as "having someone on a leash".'

'Were he on a magician's leash Rience would be using camouflaging magic. But he doesn't change his name or face. He hasn't even got rid of the scar from the burn Yennefer gave him.'

'That confirms precisely that he's on a leash,' said Codringher, coughing and wiping his lips again with his handkerchief, 'because magical camouflage isn't camouflage at all; only dilettantes use stuff like that. Were Rience hiding under a magical shield or illusory mask, it would immediately set off every magical alarm, and there are currently alarms like that at practically every city gate. Sorcerers never fail to detect illusory masks. Even in the biggest gathering of people, in the biggest throng, Rience would attract all of their attention, as if flames were shooting out of his ears and clouds of smoke out of his arse. So I repeat: Rience is in the service of a sorcerer and is operating so as not to draw the attention of other sorcerers to himself.'

'Some say he's a Nilfgaardian spy.'

'I know. For example, Dijkstra, the head of the Redania secret service, thinks that. Dijkstra is seldom wrong, so one can only assume he's right this time, too. But having one role doesn't rule out the other. A sorcerer's factotum may be a Nilfgaardian spy at the same time.'

'You're saying that a sanctioned sorcerer is spying for Nilfgaard through Rience?'

'Nonsense,' coughed Codringher, looking intently into his

20

handkerchief. 'A sorcerer spying for Nilfgaard? Why? For money? Risible. Counting on serious power under the rule of the victorious Emperor Emhyr? Even more ludicrous. It's no secret that Emhyr var Emreis keeps his sorcerers on a short leash. Sorcerers in Nilfgaard are treated about the same as, let's say, stablemen. And they have no more power than stablemen either. Would any of our headstrong mages choose to fight for an emperor who would treat them as a stable boy? Philippa Eilhart, who dictates addresses and edicts to Vizimir of Redania? Sabrina Glevissig, who interrupts the speeches of Henselt of Kaedwen, banging her fist on the table and ordering the king to be silent and listen? Vilgefortz of Roggeveen, who recently told Demavend of Aedirn that, for the moment, he has no time for him?'

'Get to the point, Codringher. What does any of that have to do with Rience?'

'It's simple. The Nilfgaardian secret service is trying to get to a sorcerer by getting their factotum to work for them. From what I know, Rience wouldn't spurn the Nilfgaardian florin and would probably betray his master without a second thought.'

'Now *you're* talking nonsense. Even our headstrong mages know when they're being betrayed and Rience, were he exposed, would dangle from a gibbet. If he was lucky.'

'You're acting like a child, Geralt. You don't hang exposed spies – you make use of them. You stuff them with disinformation and try to make double agents out of them—'

'Don't bore this child, Codringher. Neither the arcana of intelligence work nor politics interest me. Rience is breathing down my neck, and I want to know why and on whose orders. On the orders of some sorcerer, it would appear. So who is it?'

'I don't know yet. But I soon will.'

'Soon,' muttered the Witcher, 'is too late for me.'

'I in no way rule that out,' said Codringher gravely. 'You've landed in a dreadful pickle, Geralt. It's good you came to me; I know how to get people out of them. I already have, essentially.'

'Indeed?'

'Indeed,' said the lawyer, putting his handkerchief to his lips and coughing. 'For you see, my friend, in addition to the sorcerer, and possibly also Nilfgaard, there is a third party in the game. I was visited, and mark this well, by agents from King Foltest's secret service. They had a problem: the king had ordered them to search for a certain missing princess. When finding her turned out not to be quite so simple, those agents decided to enlist a specialist in such thorny problems. While elucidating the case to the specialist, they hinted that a certain witcher might know a good deal about the missing princess. That he might even know where she was.'

'And what did the specialist do?'

'At first he expressed astonishment. It particularly astonished him that the aforementioned witcher had not been deposited in a dungeon in order to find out – in the traditional manner – everything he knew, and even plenty of what he didn't know but might invent in order to satisfy his questioners. The agents replied that they had been forbidden to do that. Witchers, they explained, have such a sensitive nervous system that they immediately die under torture when, as they described quite vividly, a vein bursts in their brains. Because of that, they had been ordered to hunt the witcher. This task had also turned out to be taxing. The specialist praised the agents' good sense and instructed them to report back in two weeks.'

'And did they?'

'I'll say they did. This specialist, who already regarded you as a client, presented the agents with hard evidence that Geralt the Witcher has never had and could never have anything in common with the missing princess. For the specialist had found witnesses to the death of Princess Cirilla; granddaughter of Calanthe, daughter of Queen Pavetta. Cirilla died three years ago in a refugee camp in Angren. Of diphtheria. The child suffered terribly before her death. You won't believe it, but the Temerian agents had tears in their eyes as they listened to my witnesses' accounts.'

'I have tears in my eyes too. I presume these Temerian agents could not – or would not – offer you more than two hundred and fifty crowns?'

'Your sarcasm pains my heart, Witcher. I've got you out of a pickle, and you, rather than thank me, wound my heart.'

22

'I thank you and I beg your pardon. Why did King Foltest order his agents to search for Ciri, Codringher? What were they ordered to do, should they have found her?'

'Oh, but you are slow-witted. Kill her, of course. She is considered a pretender to the throne of Cintra, for which there are other plans.'

'It doesn't add up, Codringher. The Cintran throne was burnt to the ground along with the royal palace, the city and the rest of the country. Nilfgaard rules there now. Foltest is well aware of that; and other kings too. How, exactly, can Ciri pretend to a throne that doesn't exist?'

'Come,' said Codringher, getting up, 'let us try to find an answer to that question together. In the meanwhile, I shall give you proof of my trust ... What is it about that portrait that interests you so much?'

'That it's riddled with holes, as though a woodpecker had been pecking at it for a few seasons,' said Geralt, looking at a painting in a gilt frame hanging on the wall opposite the lawyer's desk, 'and that it portrays a rare idiot.'

'It's my late father,' said Codringher, grimacing a little. 'A rare idiot indeed. I hung his portrait there so as to always have him before my eyes. As a warning. Come, Witcher.'

They went out into the corridor. The tomcat, which had been lying in the middle of the carpet, enthusiastically licking a rear paw extended at a strange angle, vanished into the darkness of the corridor at the sight of the witcher.

'Why don't cats like you, Geralt? Does it have something to do with the—'

'Yes,' he interrupted, 'it does.'

One of the mahogany panels slid open noiselessly, revealing a secret passage. Codringher went first. The panel, no doubt set in motion by magic, closed behind them but did not plunge them into darkness. Light reached them from the far end of the secret passage.

It was cold and dry in the room at the end of the corridor, and the oppressive, stifling smell of dust and candles hung in the air.

'You can meet my partner, Geralt.'

'Fenn?' smiled the Witcher. 'You jest.'

23

'Oh, but I don't. Admit it, you suspected Fenn didn't exist!'

'Not at all.'

A creaking could be heard from between the rows of bookcases and bookshelves that reached up to the low vaulted ceiling, and a moment later a curious vehicle emerged. It was a high-backed chair on wheels. On the chair sat a midget with a huge head, set directly on disproportionately narrow shoulders. The midget had no legs.

'I'd like to introduce Jacob Fenn,' said Codringher, 'a learned legist, my partner and valued co-worker. And this is our guest and client –'

'– the Witcher, Geralt of Rivia,' finished the cripple with a smile. 'I guessed without too much difficulty. I've been working on the case for several months. Follow me, gentlemen.'

They set off behind the creaking chair into the labyrinth of book-cases, which groaned beneath a weight of printed works that even the university library of Oxenfurt would have been proud to have in its collection. The incunabula, judged Geralt, must have been collected by several generations of Codringhers and Fenns. He was pleased by the obvious show of trust, and happy to finally have the chance to meet Fenn. He did not doubt, however, that the figure of Fenn, though utterly genuine, was also partially fictitious. The ficti-tious Fenn, Codringher's infallible alter ego, was supposedly often seen abroad, while the chair-bound, learned legist probably never left the building.

The centre of the room was particularly well lit, and there stood a low pulpit, accessible from the chair on wheels and piled high with books, rolls of parchment and vellum, great sheets of paper, bottles of ink, bunches of quills and innumerable mysterious utensils. Not all of them were mystifying. Geralt recognised moulds for forging seals and a diamond grater for removing the text from official docu-ments. In the centre of the pulpit lay a small ball-firing repeating arbalest, and next to it huge magnifying glasses made of polished rock crystal peeped out from under a velvet cloth. Magnifying glasses of that kind were rare and cost a fortune.

'Found anything new, Fenn?'

'Not really,' said the cripple, smiling. His smile was pleasant and

24

very endearing. 'I've reduced the list of Rience's potential paymasters to twenty-eight sorcerers ...'

'Let's leave that for the moment,' Codringher interrupted quickly. 'Right now something else is of interest to us. Enlighten Geralt as to the reasons why the missing princess of Cintra is the object of extensive search operations by the agents of the Four Kingdoms.'

'The girl has the blood of Queen Calanthe flowing in her veins,' said Fenn, seeming astonished to be asked to explain such obvious matters. 'She is the last of the royal line. Cintra has considerable strategic and political importance. A vanished pretendress to the crown remaining beyond the sphere of influence is inconvenient, and may be dangerous were she to fall under the wrong influence. For example, that of Nilfgaard.'

'As far as I recall,' said Geralt, 'Cintran law bars women from succession.'

'That is true,' agreed Fenn and smiled once more. 'But a woman may always become someone's wife and the mother of a male heir. The Four Kingdoms' intelligence services learned of Rience's feverish search for the princess and were convinced that's what it's all about. It was thus decided to prevent the princess from becoming a wife or a mother. Using simple but effective means.'

'But the princess is dead,' said Codringher, seeing the change the smiling midget's words had evoked on Geralt's face. 'The agents learned of it and have called off their hunt.'

'Only for now,' said the Witcher, working hard to remain calm and sound unemotional. 'The thing about falsehoods is that they usually come to light. What's more, the royal agents are only one of the parties participating in this game. The agents – you said yourselves – were tracking Ciri in order to confound the other hunters' plans. Those others may be less susceptible to disinformation. I hired you to find a way of guaranteeing the child's safety. So what do you propose?'

'We have a certain notion,' said Fenn, glancing at his partner but seeing no instructions to remain silent in his expression. 'We want to circulate the news – discretely but widely – that neither Princess

Cirilla nor any of her male heirs will have any right to the throne of Cintra.'

'In Cintra, the distaff side does not inherit,' explained Codringher, fighting another coughing fit. 'Only the spear side does.'

'Precisely,' confirmed the learned legist. 'Geralt said so himself a moment ago. It's an ancient law, which even that she-devil Calanthe was unable to revoke – though not for want of trying.'

'She tried to nullify the law using intrigue,' said Codringher with conviction, wiping his lips with a handkerchief. 'Illegal intrigue. Explain, Fenn.'

'Calanthe was the only daughter of King Dagorad and Queen Adalia. After her parents' death she opposed the aristocracy, who only saw her as the wife of the new king.

'She wanted to reign supreme. At most, for the sake of formality and to uphold the dynasty, she agreed to the institution of a prince consort who would reign with her, but have as much importance as a straw doll. The old houses defied this. Calanthe had three choices: a civil war; abdication in favour of another line; or marriage to Roegner, Prince of Ebbing. She chose the third option and she ruled the country ... but at Roegner's side. Naturally, she didn't allow herself to be subjugated or bundled off to join the womenfolk. She was the Lioness of Cintra. But it was Roegner who was the formal ruler – though none ever called him "the Lion".'

'So Calanthe,' Codringher took up, 'tried very hard to fall pregnant and produce a son. Nothing came of it. She bore a daughter, Pavetta, and miscarried twice after which it became clear she would have no more children. All her plans had fallen through. There you have a woman's fate. A ravaged womb scuppers her lofty ambitions.'

Geralt scowled.

'You are execrably crude, Codringher.'

'I know. The truth was also crude. For Roegner began looking around for a young princess with suitably wide hips, preferably from a family of fertility proven back to her great-great-grandmother. And Calanthe found herself on shaky ground. Every meal, every glass of wine could contain death, every hunt might end with an unfortunate accident. There is much to suggest that at the moment

26

the Lioness of Cintra took the initiative, Roegner died. The pox was raging across the country, and the king's death surprised no one.'

'I begin to understand,' said the Witcher, seemingly dispassionately, 'what news you plan to circulate discreetly but widely. Ciri will be named the granddaughter of a poisoner and husband-killer?'

'Don't get ahead of yourself, Geralt. Go on, Fenn.'

'Calanthe had saved her own life,' said the cripple, smiling, 'but the crown was further away than ever. When, after Roegner's death, the Lioness tried to seize absolute power, the aristocracy once again strongly opposed this violation of the law and tradition. A king was meant to sit on Cintra's throne, not a queen. The solution was eventually made clear: as soon as young Pavetta began to resemble a woman in any way, she should be married off to someone suitable to become the new king. A second marriage for the barren queen wasn't an option. The most the Lioness of Cintra could hope for was the role of queen mother. To cap it all, Pavetta's husband could turn out to be someone who might totally remove his mother-in-law from power.'

'I'm going to be crude again,' warned Codringher. 'Calanthe delayed marrying off Pavetta. She wrecked the first marital project when the girl was ten and the second when she was thirteen. The aristocracy demanded that Pavetta's fifteenth birthday would be her last as a maiden. Calanthe had to agree; but first she achieved what she had been counting on. Pavetta had remained a maiden too long. She'd finally got the itch, and so badly that she was knocked up by the first stray to come along; and he was an enchanted monster to boot. There were some kind of supernatural circumstances too, some prophecies, sorcery, promises ... Some kind of Law of Surprise? Am I right, Geralt? What happened next you probably recall. Calanthe brought a witcher to Cintra, and the witcher stirred up trouble. Not knowing he was being manipulated, he removed the curse from the monstrous Urcheon, enabling his marriage to Pavetta. In so doing, the witcher also made it possible for Calanthe to retain the throne. Pavetta's marriage to a monster – even a now unenchanted one – was such a great shock to the noblemen that they could suddenly accept the marriage of the Lioness to Eist Tuirseach. For the jarl of the Isles of Skellige seemed better than the stray Urcheon. Thus, Calanthe continued to rule the country. Eist, like all islanders, gave the Lioness of Cintra too much respect to oppose her in anything, and kingly duties simply bored him. He handed over his rule whole-sale to her. And Calanthe, stuffing herself with medicaments and elixirs, dragged her husband into bed day and night. She wanted to reign until the end of her days. And, if not as queen mother, then as the mother of her own son. As I've already said, great ambitions, but—'

'You've already said it. Don't repeat yourself.'

'It was too late. Queen Pavetta, wife of the weird Urcheon, was wearing a suspiciously loose-fitting dress even during the marriage ceremony. Calanthe, resigned, changed her plans; if she couldn't rule through her son, let it be Pavetta's son. But she gave birth to a daughter. A curse, or what? Queen Pavetta could still have had a child though. I mean would have been able to. For a mysterious accident occurred. Pavetta and the weird Urcheon perished in an unexplained maritime disaster.'

'Aren't you implying too much, Codringher?'

'I'm trying to explain the situation, nothing more. Calanthe was devastated after Pavetta's death, but not for long. Her granddaughter was her final hope. Pavetta's daughter, Cirilla. Ciri; a little devil incarnate, roaring around the royal palace. She was the apple of some people's eyes, particularly the older folk because she was so like Calanthe had been as a child. To others ... she was a changeling, the daughter of the monstrous Urcheon, the girl to whom some witcher or other was also claiming rights. And now we're getting to the nub of the matter: Calanthe's little darling, clearly being groomed as her successor, treated almost as a second incarnation, the Lion Cub of the Lioness's blood, was already viewed by some as bereft of any right to the throne. Cirilla was ill-born. Pavetta's marriage had been a misalliance. She had mixed royal blood with the inferior blood of a stray of unknown origin.'

'Crafty, Codringher. But it wasn't like that. Ciri's father wasn't inferior in any way. He was a prince.'

'What are you saying? I didn't know that. From which kingdom?'

'One of the southern ones … From Maecht … ? Yes, indeed, from Maecht.'

'Interesting,' mumbled Codringher. 'Maecht has been a Nilfgaardian march for a long time. It's part of the Province of Metinna.'

'But it's a kingdom,' interrupted Fenn. 'A king reigns there.'

'Emhyr var Emreis rules there,' Codringher cut him off. 'Whoever sits on that throne does so by the grace and will of Emhyr. But while we're on the subject, find out who Emhyr made king. I can't recall.'

'Right away,' said the cripple, pushing the wheels of his chair and creaking off in the direction of a bookcase. He took down a thick roll of scrolls and began looking at them, discarding them on the floor after checking them. 'Hmm … Here it is. The Kingdom of Maecht. Its coat of arms presents quarterly, azure and gules, one and four two fishes argent, two and three a crown of the same—'

'To hell with heraldry, Fenn. The king, who is the king?'

'Hoët the Just. Chosen by means of election …'

'By Emhyr of Nilfgaard,' postulated Codringher coldly.

'… nine years ago.'

'Not that one,' said the lawyer, counting quickly. 'He doesn't concern us. Who was before him?'

'Just a moment. Here it is. Akerspaark. Died—'

'Died of acute pneumonia, his lungs having been pierced by the dagger of Emhyr's hit men or Hoët the Just,' said Codringher, once again displaying his perspicacity. 'Geralt, does Akerspaark ring any bells for you? Could he be Urcheon's father?'

'Yes,' said the Witcher after a moment's thought. 'Akerspaark. I recall that's what Duny called his father.'

'Duny?'

'That was his name. He was a prince, the son of that Akerspaark—'

'No,' interrupted Fenn, staring at the scrolls. 'They are all mentioned here. Legitimate sons: Orm, Gorm, Torm, Horm and Gonzalez. Legitimate daughters: Alia, Valia, Nina, Paulina, Malvina and Argentina …'

'I take back the slander spread about Nilfgaard and Hoët the Just,' announced Codringher gravely. 'Akerspaark wasn't murdered, he

29

bonked himself to death. I presume he had bastards too, Fenn?'

'Indeed. Aplenty. But I see no Duny here.'

'I didn't expect you to see him. Geralt, your Urcheon was no prince. Even if that boor Akerspaark really did sire him on the side, he was separated from the rights to such a title by – aside from Nilfgaard – a bloody long queue of legitimate Orms, Gorms and other Gonzalezes and their own, probably abundant, offspring. From a technical point of view Pavetta committed a misalliance.'

'And Ciri, being the child of a misalliance, has no rights to the throne?'

'Bullseye.'

Fenn creaked up to the pulpit, pushing the wheels of his chair.

'That is an argument,' he said, raising his huge head. 'Purely an argument. Don't forget, Geralt, we are neither fighting to gain the crown for Princess Cirilla, nor to deprive her of it. The rumour we're spreading is meant to show that the girl can't be used to seize Cintra. That if anyone makes an attempt of that kind, it will be easy to challenge, to question. The girl will cease to be a major piece in this political game; she'll be an insignificant pawn. And then ...'

'They'll let her live,' completed Codringher unemotionally.

'How strong is your argument,' asked Geralt, 'from the formal point of view?'

Fenn looked at Codringher and then at the Witcher.

'Not that strong,' he admitted. 'Cirilla is still Calanthe, albeit somewhat diluted. In normal countries she might have been removed from the throne, but these circumstances aren't normal. The Lioness's blood has political significance ...'

'Blood ...' said Geralt, wiping his forehead. 'What does "Child of the Elder Blood" mean, Codringher?'

'I don't understand. Has anyone used such a term with reference to Cirilla?'

'Yes.'

'Who?'

'Never mind who. What does it mean?'

'Luned aep Hen Ichaer,' said Fenn suddenly, pushing off from the pulpit. 'It would literally be not *Child*, but *Daughter* of the Elder

30

Blood. Hmm ... Elder Blood ... I've come across that expression. I don't remember exactly ... I think it concerns some sort of elven prophecy. In some versions of Itlina's prophecy, the older ones, it seems to me there are mentions of the Elder Blood of the Elves, or Aen Hen Ichaer. But we don't have the complete text of that prophecy. We would have to ask the elves—'

'Enough,' interrupted Codringher coldly. 'Not too many of these matters at one time, Fenn, not too many irons in the fire, not too many prophecies or mysteries. That's all for now, thank you. Farewell, and fruitful work. Geralt, if you would, let's go back to the office.'

'Too little, right?' the Witcher asked to be sure, when they had returned and sat down in their chairs, the lawyer behind his desk, and he facing him. 'Too low a fee, right?'

Codringher lifted a metal star-shaped object from the desk and turned it over in his fingers several times.

'That's right, Geralt. Rootling around in elven prophecies is an infernal encumbrance for me; a waste of time and resources. The need to search out contacts amongst the elves, since no one aside from them is capable of understanding their writings. Elven manuscripts, in most cases, mean tortuous symbolism, acrostics, occasionally even codes. The Elder Speech is always, to put it mildly, ambiguous and, when written down, may have as many as ten meanings. The elves were never inclined to help humans who wanted to fathom their prophecies. And in today's times, when a bloody war against the Squirrels is raging in the forests, when pogroms are taking place, it's dangerous to approach them. Doubly dangerous. Elves may take you for a provocateur, while humans may accuse you of treachery ...'

'How much, Codringher?'

The lawyer was silent for a moment, still playing with the metal star.

'Ten per cent,' he said finally.

'Ten per cent of what?'

'Don't mock me, Witcher. The matter is becoming serious. It's becoming ever less clear what this is all about, and when no one

31

knows what something's about it's sure to be all about money. In which case a percentage is more agreeable to me than an ordinary fee. Give me ten per cent of what you'll make on this, minus the sum already paid. Shall we draw up a contract?'

'No. I don't want you to lose out. Ten per cent of nothing gives nothing, Codringher. My dear friend, I won't be making anything out of this.'

'I repeat, don't mock me. I don't believe you aren't acting for profit. I don't believe that, behind this, there isn't some ...'

'I'm not particularly bothered what you believe. There won't be any contract. Or any percentages. Name your fee for gathering the information.'

'Anyone else I would throw out of here,' said Codringher, coughing, 'certain they were trying to pull the wool over my eyes. But noble and naive disinterestedness, my anachronistic Witcher, strangely suits you. It's your style, it's so wonderfully and pathetically outmoded to let yourself be killed for nothing ...'

'Let's not waste time. How much, Codringher?'

'The same again. Five hundred in total.'

'I'm sorry,' said Geralt, shaking his head, 'I can't afford a sum like that. Not right now at least.'

'I repeat the proposition I laid before you at the beginning of our acquaintance,' said the lawyer slowly, still playing with the star. 'Come and work for me and you will. You will be able to afford information and other luxuries besides.'

'No, Codringher.'

'Why not?'

'You wouldn't understand.'

'This time you're wounding not my heart, but my professional pride. For I flatter myself, believing that I generally understand everything. Being a downright bastard is the basis of our professions, but you insist on favouring the anachronistic version over the modern one.'

The Witcher smiled.

'Bullseye.'

Codringher coughed violently once again, wiped his lips, looked down at his handkerchief, and then raised his yellow-green eyes.

'You took a good look at the list of sorcerers and sorceresses lying on the pulpit? At the list of Rience's potential paymasters?'

'Indeed.'

'I won't give you that list until I've checked it thoroughly. Don't be influenced by what you saw there. Dandelion told me Philippa Eilhart probably knows who's running Rience, but she didn't let you in on it. Philippa wouldn't protect any old sucker. It's an important character running that bastard.'

The Witcher said nothing.

'Beware, Geralt. You're in grave danger. Someone's playing a game with you. Someone is accurately predicting your movements, if not actually controlling them. Don't give in to arrogance and self-righteousness. Whoever's playing with you is no striga or werewolf. It's not the brothers Michelet. It's not even Rience. The Child of the Elder Blood, damn it. As if the throne of Cintra, sorcerers, kings and Nilfgaard weren't enough, now there are elves. Stop playing this game, Witcher. Get yourself out of it. Confound their plans by doing what no one expects. Break off that crazy bond; don't allow yourself to be linked to Cirilla. Leave her to Yennefer; go back to Kaer Morhen and keep your head down. Hole yourself up in the mountains, and I'll root around in elven manuscripts, calmly, unhurriedly and thoroughly. And when I have some information about the Child of the Elder Blood, when I have the name of the sorcerer who's involved in it, you'll get the money together and we'll do a swap.'

'I can't wait. The girl's in danger.'

'That's true. But I know you're considered an obstacle on the way to her. An obstacle to be ruthlessly removed. Thus, you are in danger too. They'll set about getting the girl once they've finished you off.'

'Or when I leave the game, withdraw and hole up in Kaer Morhen. I've paid you too much, Codringher, for you to be giving me advice like that.'

The lawyer turned the steel star over in his fingers.

'I've been busily working for some time, for the sum you paid

33

me today, Witcher,' he said, suppressing a cough. 'The advice I'm giving you has been thoroughly considered. Hide in Kaer Morhen; disappear. And then the people who are looking for Cirilla will get her.'

Geralt squinted and smiled. Codringher didn't blench. 'I know what I'm talking about,' he said, impervious to the look and the smile. 'Your Ciri's tormentors will find her and do with her what they will. And meanwhile, both she and you will be safe.'

'Explain, please. And make it quick.'

'I've found a certain girl. She's from the Cintra nobility, a war orphan. She's been through refugee camps, and is currently measuring cloth in ells and cutting it out, having been taken in by a Brugge draper. There is nothing remarkable about her, aside from one thing. She is quite similar in likeness to a certain miniature of the Lion Cub of Cintra ... Fancy a look?'

'No, Codringher. No, I don't. And I can't permit a solution like that.'

'Geralt,' said the lawyer, closing his eyes. 'What drives you? If you want to save Ciri ... I wouldn't have thought you could afford the luxury of contempt. No, that was badly expressed. You can't afford the luxury of spurning contempt. A time of contempt is approaching, Witcher, my friend, a time of great and utter contempt. You have to adapt. What I'm proposing is a simple solution. Someone will die, so someone else can live. Someone you love will survive. A girl you don't know, and whom you've never seen, will die—'

'And who am I free to despise?' interrupted the Witcher. 'Am I to pay for what I love with contempt for myself? No, Codringher. Leave the girl in peace; may she continue to measure cloth. Destroy her portrait. Burn it. And give me something else for the two hundred and fifty hard-earned crowns which you threw into a drawer. I need information. Yennefer and Ciri have left Ellander. I'm certain you know that. I'm certain you know where they are headed. And I'm certain you know who's chasing them.'

Codringher drummed his fingers on the table and coughed.

'The wolf, heedless of warnings, wants to carry on hunting,' he said. 'He doesn't see he's being hunted, and he's heading straight for some tasty kippers hung up as bait by a real hunter.'

'Don't be trite. Get to the point.'

'If you wish. It's not difficult to guess that Yennefer is riding to the Conclave of Mages, called at the beginning of July in Garstang on the Isle of Thanedd. She is cleverly staying on the move and not using magic, so it's hard to locate her. A week ago she was still in Ellander, and I calculate that in three or four days she will reach the city of Gors Velen; from there Thanedd is a stone's throw. On the way to Gors Velen she has to ride through the hamlet of Anchor. Were you to set off immediately you would have a chance of catching those who are pursuing her. Because someone is pursuing her.'

'They wouldn't, by any chance,' said Geralt, smiling hideously, 'be royal agents?'

'No,' said the lawyer, looking at the metal star he was playing with. 'They aren't agents. Neither is it Rience, who's cleverer than you, because after the ruckus with the Michelets he's crawled into a hole somewhere and he's keeping his head down. Three hired thugs are after Yennefer.'

'I presume you know them?'

'I know them all. Which is why I suggest something to you: leave them alone. Don't ride to Anchor. And I'll use all the contacts and connections I possess. I'll try to bribe the thugs and reword the contract. In other words, I'll set them on Rience. If I succeed . . .'

He broke off suddenly and swung an arm powerfully. The steel star whirred through the air and slammed with a thud into the portrait, right into the forehead of Codringher senior, cutting a hole in the canvas and embedding itself almost halfway into the wall.

'Not bad, eh?' grinned the lawyer. 'It's called an orion. A foreign invention. I've been practising for a month; I never miss now. It might come in useful. This little star is unerring and lethal at thirty feet, and it can be hidden in a sleeve or stuck behind a hatband. Orions have been part of the Nilfgaardian secret service equipment for a year now. Ha, ha, if Rience is spying for Nilfgaard, it would be amusing if they found him with an orion in his temple . . . What do you say to that?'

'Nothing. That's your business. Two hundred and fifty crowns are lying in your drawer.'

'Sure,' said Codringher, nodding. 'I treat your words to mean you're giving me a free hand. Let's be silent for a moment, Geralt. Let's honour Rience's imminent death with a minute's silence. Why the hell are you frowning? Have you no respect for the majesty of death?'

'I do. Too great a respect to listen to idiots mocking it. Have you ever thought about your own death, Codringher?'

The lawyer coughed heavily and looked for a long time at the handkerchief in front of his mouth. Then he raised his eyes.

'Of course,' he said quietly. 'I have. Intensively, at that. But my thoughts are nothing to do with you, Witcher. Will you ride to Anchor?'

'I will.'

'Ralf Blunden, a.k.a. the Professor. Heimo Kantor. Little Yaxa. Do those names mean anything to you?'

'No.'

'All three are pretty handy with a sword. Better than the Michelets. So I would suggest a more reliable, long-range weapon. These Nilfgaardian throwing stars, for example. I'll sell you a few if you like. I've plenty of them.'

'No thanks. They're impractical. Noisy in flight.'

'The whistling has a psychological element. They're capable of paralysing their victim with fear.'

'Perhaps. But they can also warn them. I'd have time to dodge it.'

'If you saw it being thrown at you, you could. I know you can dodge an arrow or a quarrel ... But from behind—'

'From behind as well.'

'Bullshit.'

'Let's try a wager,' said Geralt coldly. 'I'll turn my face to the portrait of your dullard of a father, and you throw an orion at me. Should you hit me, you win. Should you not, you lose. Should you lose, you'll decipher those elven manuscripts. You'll get hold of information about the Child of the Elder Blood. Urgently. And on credit.'

'And if I win?'

'You'll still get that information but you'll pass it on to Yennefer. She'll pay. You won't be left out of pocket.'

Codringher opened the drawer and took out another orion.

'You don't expect me to accept the wager.' It was a statement, not a question.

'No,' smiled the Witcher. 'I'm sure you'll accept it.'

'A daredevil, I see. Have you forgotten? I don't have any scruples.'

'I haven't forgotten. After all, the time of contempt is approaching, and you keep up with progress and the zeitgeist. But I took your accusations of anachronistic naivety to heart, and this time I'll take a risk, though not without hope of profit. What's it to be then? Is the bet on?'

'Yes.' Codringher took hold of the steel star by one of its arms and stood up. 'Curiosity always won out over good sense in me, not to mention unfounded mercy. Turn around.'

The Witcher turned around. He glanced at the face on the portrait riddled with holes and with the orion sticking into it. And then he closed his eyes.

The star whistled and thudded into the wall four inches from the frame of the portrait.

'Damn and blast!' roared Codringher. 'You didn't even flinch, you whoreson!'

Geralt turned back and smiled. Quite hideously.

'Why should I have flinched? I could hear you aiming to miss.'

The inn was empty. A young woman with dark rings under her eyes sat on a bench in the corner. Bashfully turned away to one side, she was breastfeeding a child. A broad-shouldered fellow, perhaps her husband, dozed alongside, his back resting against the wall. Someone else, whose features Aplegatt couldn't make out in the gloom of the inn, sat in the shadows behind the stove.

The innkeeper looked up, saw Aplegatt, noticed his attire and the badge with the arms of Aedirn on his chest, and his face immediately darkened. Aplegatt was accustomed to welcomes like that. As a royal messenger he was absolute entitled to a mount. The royal decrees were explicit – a messenger had the right to demand a fresh horse in every town, village, inn or farmyard – and woe betide anyone who refused. Naturally, the messenger left his own horse, and signed a receipt for the new one; the owner could appeal to the magistrate and receive compensation. But you never knew. Thus a messenger was always looked upon with dislike and anxiety; would he demand a horse or not? Would he take our Golda, never to be seen again? Or our Beauty, reared from a foal? Our pampered Ebony? Aplegatt had seen sobbing children clinging to their beloved playmate as it was being led out of the stable, saddled, and more than once had looked into the faces of adults, pale with the sense of injustice and helplessness.

'I don't need a fresh horse,' he said brusquely. It seemed to him the innkeeper sighed with relief.

'I'll only have a bite to eat; the road's given me an appetite,' added the messenger. 'Anything in the pot?'

'There's some gruel left over. I'll serve you d'reckly. Sit you down. Needing a bed? Night's falling.'

Aplegatt thought it over. He had met Hansom two days before. He knew the messenger and they had exchanged messages as ordered. Hansom took the letters and the message for King Demavend and galloped off through Temeria and Mahakam to Vengerberg. Aplegatt, meanwhile, having received the messages for King Vizimir of Redania, rode towards Oxenfurt and Tretogor. He had over three hundred miles to cover.

'I'll eat and be on my way,' he declared. 'The moon is full and the road is level.'

'As you will.'

The gruel he was served was thin and tasteless, but the messenger paid no attention to such trifles. At home, he enjoyed his wife's cooking, but on the road he made do with whatever came his way. He slowly slurped it, clumsily gripping the spoon in fingers made numb from holding the reins.

A cat that had been snoozing on the stove bench suddenly lifted its head and hissed.

'A royal messenger?'

38

Aplegatt shuddered. The question had been asked by the man sitting in the shadows, who now emerged to stand beside him. His hair was as white as milk. He had a leather band stretched across his forehead and was wearing a silver-studded leather jacket and high boots. The pommel of the sword slung across his back glistened over his right shoulder.

'Where does the road take you?'

'Wherever the royal will sends me,' answered Aplegatt coldly. He never answered any other way to questions of that nature.

The white-haired man was silent for some time, looking searchingly at the messenger. He had an unnaturally pale face and strange, dark eyes.

'I imagine,' he finally said, in an unpleasant, somewhat husky voice, 'the royal will orders you to make haste? Probably in a hurry to get off, are you?'

'What business is it of yours? Who are you to hasten me?'

'I'm no one,' said the white-haired man, smiling hideously, 'and I'm not hurrying you. But if I were you I'd leave here as quickly as possible. I wouldn't want anything ill to befall you.'

Aplegatt also had a tried and tested answer to comments like that. Short and blunt. Not aggressive, calm; but emphatically reminding the listener who the royal messenger served and what was risked by anyone who dared touch him. But there was something in the white-haired man's voice that stopped Aplegatt from giving his usual answer.

'I must let my horse rest, sir. An hour, maybe two.'

'Indeed,' nodded the white-haired man, upon which he lifted his head, seeming to listen to the sounds which reached him from outside. Aplegatt also pricked up his ears but heard only crickets.

'Then rest,' said the white-haired man, straightening the sword belt which passed diagonally across his chest. 'But don't go out into the courtyard. Whatever happens, don't go out.'

Aplegatt refrained from further questions. He felt instinctively it would be better not to. He bent over his bowl and resumed fishing out the few bits of pork floating in the gruel. When he looked up the white-haired one was no longer in the room.

A moment later a horse neighed and hooves clattered in the courtyard.

Three men entered the inn. On seeing them the innkeeper began wiping the beer mug he was holding more quickly. The woman with the baby moved closer to her slumbering husband and woke him with a poke. Aplegatt grabbed the stool where he had laid his belt and short sword and pulled it a little closer.

The men went over to the bar, casting keen glances at the guests and sizing them up. They walked slowly, their spurs and weapons jangling.

'Welcome, good sirs,' said the innkeeper, clearing his throat. 'How may I serve you?'

'With vodka,' said one of them, short and stocky with long arms like an ape's, furnished with two Zerrikan sabres hanging crossed on his back. 'Fancy a drop, Professor?'

'With the utmost pleasure,' responded the other man, straightening a pair of gold-framed glasses made of bluish-coloured crystal, which were perched on his hooked nose. 'As long as the liquor hasn't been adulterated with any additives.'

The innkeeper poured. Aplegatt noticed that his hands were trembling slightly. The men leaned back against the bar and unhurriedly drank from the earthenware cups.

'My dear innkeeper,' began the one in the glasses suddenly. 'I conjecture that two ladies rode through here not long ago, speeding their way towards Gors Velen?'

'All sorts ride through here,' mumbled the innkeeper.

'You could not have missed the aforementioned ladies,' said the bespectacled one slowly. 'One is black-haired and exceedingly fair. She rides a black gelding. The other is younger, fair-haired and green-eyed and journeys on a dappled grey mare. Have they been here?'

'No,' interrupted Aplegatt, suddenly going cold, 'they haven't.'

Grey-feathered danger. Hot sand …

'A messenger?'

Aplegatt nodded.

'Travelling from where to where?'

40

'From where and to where the royal fortune sends me.'

'Have your travels adventitiously crossed the path of the women on the road about whom I enquired?'

'No.'

'Your denial is too swift,' barked the third man, as tall and thin as a beanpole. His hair was black and glistened as if covered in grease. 'And it seems to me you weren't trying especially hard to remember.'

'Let it drop, Heimo,' said the bespectacled man, waving his hand. 'He's a messenger. Don't vex yourself. What is this station's name, innkeeper?'

'Anchor.'

'What is the proximity of Gors Velen?'

'Beg pardon?'

'How many miles?'

'Can't say I've ever measured it. But it'll be a three-day journey ...'

'On horseback?'

'By cart.'

'Hey,' called the stocky one suddenly in a hushed voice, straightening up and looking out onto the courtyard through the wide-open door. 'Have a butchers, Professor. Who would that be? Isn't it that ... ?'

The man in glasses also looked out at the courtyard, and his face suddenly tightened.

'Yes,' he hissed. 'It's indisputably him. It appears fortune smiles on us.'

'Will we wait till he comes in?'

'He won't. He saw our horses.'

'He knows we're—'

'Silence, Yaxa. He's saying something.'

'You have a choice,' a slightly gruff but powerful voice resounded from the courtyard, a voice which Aplegatt recognised at once. 'One of you will come out and tell me who hired you. Then you may ride away without any trouble. Or all three of you may come out. I'm waiting.'

41

'Whoreson ...' growled the black-haired man. 'He knows. What do we do?'

The bespectacled man put his mug down on the bar with a slow movement.

'We do what we're paid to do.'

He spat on his palm, flexed his fingers and drew his sword. At the sight of it the two other men also bared their blades. The innkeeper opened his mouth to shout but quickly shut it on seeing the cold eyes peering above the blue glasses.

'Nobody moves,' hissed the bespectacled man. 'And keep schtum. Heimo, when it all kicks off, endeavour to get behind him. Very well, boys, good luck. Out we go.'

It began at once. Groans, the stamping of feet, the crash of blades. And then a scream of the kind that makes one's hair stand on end.

The innkeeper blanched, the woman with the dark rings under her eyes screamed too, clutching her suckling to her breast. The cat behind the stove leapt to its feet and arched its back, its tail fluffing up like a brush. Aplegatt slid into the corner on his stool. He had his short sword in his lap but didn't draw it.

Once again the thudding of feet across boards and the whistle and clang of blades came from the courtyard.

'You ...' shouted someone wildly, but even though it ended with a vile insult, there was more despair in it than fury. 'You ...'

The whistle of a blade. And immediately after it a high, penetrating scream shredded the air. A thud as if a heavy sack of grain had hit the ground. The clatter of hooves from the hitching post and the neighing of terrified horses.

A thud on the boards once more and the quick, heavy steps of a man running. The woman with the baby clung to her husband, and the innkeeper pressed his back against the wall. Aplegatt drew his short sword, still hiding the weapon beneath the table. The running man was heading straight for the inn, and it was clear he would soon appear in the doorway. But before he did, a blade hissed.

The man screamed and lurched inside. It seemed as though he would fall across the threshold, but he didn't. He took several staggering, laboured steps forward and only then did he topple, falling heavily into the middle of the chamber, throwing up the dust gathered between the floorboards. He fell on his face, inertly, pinning his arms underneath him, his legs bent at the knee. The crystal glasses fell to the floorboards with a clatter and shattered into tiny blue pieces. A dark, gleaming puddle began to spread from beneath the body.

No one moved. Or cried out.

The white-haired man entered the inn.

He deftly sheathed the sword he was holding into the scabbard on his back. He approached the bar, not even gracing the body lying on the floor with a glance. The innkeeper cringed.

'Those evil men . . .' said the white-haired one huskily, 'those evil men are dead. When the bailiff arrives, it may turn out there was a bounty on their heads. He should do with it as he sees fit.'

The innkeeper nodded eagerly.

'It may turn out,' said the white-haired man a moment later, 'that their comrades or cronies may ask what befell these evil men. Tell them the Wolf bit them. The White Wolf. And add that they should keep glancing over their shoulders. One day they'll look back and see the Wolf.'

When, after three days, Aplegatt reached the gates of Tretogor, it was well after midnight. He was furious because he'd wasted time at the moat and shouted himself hoarse – the guards were sleeping sinfully and had been reluctant to open the gate. He got it all off his chest and cursed them painstakingly and comprehensively back to the third generation. He then overheard with pleasure as the commander of the watch – now awake – added totally new details to the charges he had levelled against the soldiers' mothers, grandmothers and great-grandmothers. Of course, gaining access to King Vizimir was out of the question. That actually suited him, as he was counting on sleeping until matins and the morning bell. He was wrong. Instead of being shown to his billet he was rushed to the guardhouse. Waiting for him there was not the king but the other one, immense and fat. Aplegatt knew him; it was Dijkstra, confidant of the King of Redania. Dijkstra – the messenger knew – was authorised to receive messages meant exclusively for the king's ears. Aplegatt handed him the letters.

'Do you have a spoken message?'

'Yes, sire.'

'Speak.'

'Demavend to Vizimir,' recited Aplegatt, closing his eyes. 'Firstly: the disguised troops are ready for the second night after the July new moon. Take care that Foltest does not let us down. Secondly: I will not grace the conclave of the devious old windbags in Thanedd with my presence, and I advise you to do the same. Thirdly: the Lion Cub is dead.'

Dijkstra grimaced and drummed his fingers on the table.

'Here are letters for King Demavend. And a spoken message ... Prick up your ears and pay attention. Repeat this to your king, word for word. Only to him, to no one else. No one, do you understand?'

'I do, sire.'

'The message runs thus: Vizimir to Demavend. You must hold back the disguised troops. There has been a betrayal. The Flame has mustered an army in Dol Angra and is only waiting for an excuse. Now repeat.'

Aplegatt repeated it.

'Good,' Dijkstra nodded. 'You will leave at sunup.'

'I've been on the road for five days, Your Excellency,' said the messenger, rubbing his rump. 'Might I but sleep to the morning ... Will you permit it?'

'Does now your king, Demavend, sleep at night? Do I sleep? You deserve a punch in the face for the question alone, laddie. You will be given vittles, then stretch out a while on the hay. But you ride at dawn. I've ordered a pure-bred young stallion for you. It'll bear you like the wind. And don't make faces. Take this purse with an extra gratuity, so as not to call Vizimir a skinflint.'

'Thank you, sire.'

'Be careful in the forests by the Pontar. Squirrels have been seen there. But there's no shortage of ordinary brigands in those parts anyway.'

'Oh, I know, sire. Oh, what I did see three days past ...'

'What did you see?'

Aplegatt quickly reported the events in Anchor. Dijkstra listened, his powerful forearms lying crossed on his chest.

'The Professor ...' he said lost in thought. 'Heimo Kantor and Little Yaxa. Dispatched by a witcher. In Anchor, on the road to Gors Velen; in other words the road to Thanedd and Garstang ... And the Lion Cub is dead?'

'What's that, sire?'

'It's of no concern.' Dijkstra raised his head. 'At least not to you. Rest. And at dawn you ride.'

Aplegatt ate what he was brought, lay for a while without sleeping a wink, and was outside the gate by daybreak. The stallion was indeed swift, but skittish. Aplegatt didn't like horses like that.

Something itched unbearably on his back, between his left shoulder blade and his spine. A flea must have bitten him when he was resting in the stable. But there was no way to scratch it.

The stallion danced and neighed. The messenger spurred him and he galloped away. Time was short.

'Gar'ean,' Cairbre hissed, peering from behind a branch, from where he was observing the road. 'En Dh'oine aen evall a strsede!'

Toruviel leapt to her feet, seizing and belting on her sword, and poked Yaevinn in the thigh with the toe of her boot. He had been dozing, leaning against the wall of a hollow, and when he sprang up he scorched his hand as he pushed off from the hot sand.

'Que suecc's?'

'A rider on the road.'

'One?' said Yaevinn, lifting his bow and quiver. 'Cairbre? Only one?'

'Only one. He's getting closer.'

'Let's fix him then. It'll be one less Dh'oine.'

'Forget it,' said Toruviel, grabbing him by the sleeve. 'Why bother? We were supposed to carry out reconnaissance and then join the commando. Are we to murder civilians on the road? Is that what fighting for freedom is about?'

'Precisely. Stand aside.'

'If a body's left on the road, every passing patrol will raise the alarm. The army will set out after us. They'll stake out the fords, and we might have difficulty crossing the river!'

'Few people ride along this road. We'll be far away before anyone finds the body.'

'That rider's already far away,' said Cairbre from the tree. 'You should have shot instead of yapping. You won't hit him now. He's a good two hundred paces away.'

'With my sixty-pounder?' Yaevinn stroked his bow. 'And a thirty-inch arrow? And anyway, that's never two hundred paces. It's hundred and fifty, tops. Mire, que spar aen'le.'

'Yaevinn, forget it …'

'Thaess aep, Toruviel.'

The elf turned his hat around so the squirrel's tail pinned to it wouldn't get in the way, quickly and powerfully drew back his bow-string, right to his ear, and then aimed carefully and shot.

Aplegatt did not hear the arrow. It was a 'silent' arrow, specially fledged with long, narrow grey feathers, its shaft fluted for increased stiffness and weight reduction. The three-edged, razor-sharp arrow hit the messenger in the back with great force, between his left shoulder blade and his spine. The blades were positioned at an angle – and as they entered his body, the arrow rotated and bored in like a screw, mutilating the tissue, cutting through blood vessels and shattering bone. Aplegatt lurched forward onto his horse's neck and slid to the ground, limp as a sack of wool.

The sand on the road was hot, heated up so much by the sun that it was painful to the touch. The messenger didn't feel it. He died at once.

To say I knew her would be an exaggeration. I think that, apart from the Witcher and the enchantress, no one really knew her. When I saw her for the first time she did not make a great impression on me at all, even in spite of the quite extraordinary accompanying circumstances. I have known people who said that, right away, from the very first encounter, they sensed the foretaste of death striding behind the girl. To me she seemed utterly ordinary, though I knew that ordinary she was not; for which reason I tried to discern, discover – sense – the singularity in her. But I noticed nothing and sensed nothing. Nothing that could have been a signal, a presentiment or a harbinger of those subsequent, tragic events. Events caused by her very existence. And those she caused by her actions.

Dandelion, *Half a Century of Poetry*

CHAPTER TWO

Right by the crossroads, where the forest ended, nine posts were driven into the ground. Each was crowned by a cartwheel, mounted flat. Above the wheels teemed crows and ravens, pecking and tearing at the corpses bound to the rims and hubs. Owing to the height of the posts and the great number of birds, one could only imagine what the unidentifiable remains lying on top of the wheels might be. But they were bodies. They couldn't have been anything else.

Ciri turned her head away and wrinkled her nose in disgust. The wind blew from the posts and the sickening stench of rotting corpses drifted above the crossroads.

'Wonderful scenery,' said Yennefer, leaning out of the saddle and spitting on the ground, forgetting that a short time earlier she had fiercely scolded Ciri for doing the same thing. 'Picturesque and fragrant. But why do this here, at the edge of the wilderness? They usually set things like that up right outside the city walls. Am I right, good people?'

'They're Squirrels, noble lady,' came the hurried explanation from one of the wandering traders they had caught up with at the crossroads. He was guiding the piebald horse harnessed to his fully laden cart. 'Elves. There, on those posts. And that's why the posts are by the forest. As a warning to other Squirrels.'

'Does that mean,' said the enchantress, looking at him, 'that captured Scoia'tael are brought here alive ... ?'

'Elves, m'lady, seldom let themselves be taken alive,' interrupted the trader. 'And even if the soldiers catch one they take them to the city, because civilised non-humans dwell there. When they've watched Squirrels being tortured in the town square, they quickly lose interest in joining them. But if any elves are killed in combat, their bodies are taken to a crossroads and hung on posts like this. Sometimes they're brought from far away and by the time they get here they reek—'

'To think,' snapped Yennefer, 'we have been forbidden from necromantic practices out of respect for the dignity of death and mortal remains; on the grounds that they deserve reverence, peace, and a ritual and ceremonial burial . . .'

'What are you saying, m'lady?'

'Nothing. We're leaving, Ciri, let's get away from this place. Ugh, I feel as though the stench were sticking to me.'

'Yuck. Me too,' said Ciri, trotting around the trader's cart. 'Let's gallop, yes?'

'Very well . . . Ciri! Gallop, but don't break your neck!'

They soon saw the city; surrounded by walls, bristling with towers with glistening, pointed roofs. And beyond the city was the sea; grey-green, sparkling in the morning sun, flecked here and there with the white dots of sails. Ciri reined in her horse at the edge of a sandy drop, stood up in her stirrups and greedily breathed in the wind and the scent.

'Gors Velen,' said Yennefer, riding up and stopping at her side. 'We finally made it. Let's get back on the road.'

They rode off down the road at a canter, leaving several ox carts and people walking, laden down with faggots, behind them.

Once they had overtaken them all and were alone, though, the enchantress slowed and gestured for Ciri to stop.

'Come closer,' she said. 'Closer still. Take the reins and lead my horse. I need both hands.'

'What for?'

'I said take the reins, Ciri.'

Yennefer took a small, silver looking glass from her saddlebags, wiped it and then whispered a spell. The looking glass floated out of her hand, rose up and remained suspended above her horse's neck, right before the enchantress's face.

Ciri let out a sigh of awe and licked her lips.

The enchantress removed a comb from her saddlebags, took off

50

her beret and combed her hair vigorously for the next few minutes. Ciri remained silent. She knew she was forbidden to disturb or distract Yennefer while she combed her hair. The arresting and apparently careless disarray of her wavy, luxuriant locks was the result of long, hard work and demanded no little effort.

The enchantress reached into her saddlebags once more. She attached some diamond earrings to her ears and fastened bracelets on both wrists. She took off her shawl and undid a few buttons on her blouse, revealing her neck and a black velvet ribbon decorated with an obsidian star.

'Ha!' said Ciri at last, unable to hold back. 'I know why you're doing that! You want to look nice because we're going to the city! Am I right?'

'Yes, you are.'

'What about me?'

'What *about* you?'

'I want to look nice, too! I'll do my hair—'

'Put your beret on,' said Yennefer sharply, eyes still fixed on the looking glass floating above the horse's ears, 'right where it was before. And tuck your hair underneath it.'

Ciri snorted angrily but obeyed at once. She had long ago learned to distinguish the timbre and shades of the enchantress's voice. She had learned when she could get into a discussion and when it was wiser not to.

Yennefer, having at last arranged the locks over her forehead, took a small, green, glass jar out of her saddlebags.

'Ciri,' she said more gently. 'We're travelling in secret. And the journey's not over yet. Which is why you have to hide your hair under your beret. There are people at every gate who are paid for their accurate and reliable observation of travellers. Do you understand?'

'No!' retorted Ciri impudently, reining back the enchantress's black stallion. 'You've made yourself beautiful to make those gate watchmen's eyes pop out! Very secretive, I must say!'

'The city to whose gates we are heading,' smiled Yennefer, 'is Gors Velen. I don't have to disguise myself in Gors Velen; quite

51

the contrary, I'd say. With you it's different. You ought not to be remembered by anyone.'

'The people who'll be staring at you will see me too!'

The enchantress uncorked the jar, which gave off the scent of lilac and gooseberries. She stuck her index finger in and rubbed a little of it under her eyes.

'I doubt,' she said, still smiling mysteriously, 'whether anyone will notice you.'

A long column of riders and wagons stood before the bridge, and travellers crowded around the gatehouse, waiting for their turn to be searched. Ciri fumed and growled, angry at the prospect of a long wait. Yennefer, however, sat up straight in the saddle and rode at a trot, looking high over the heads of the travellers – they parted swiftly for her and made room, bowing in respect. The guards in hauberks also noticed the enchantress at once and gave her free passage, liberally handing out blows with their spear shafts to the stubborn or the overly slow.

'This way, this way, noble lady,' called one of the guards, staring at Yennefer and flushing. 'Come through here, I entreat you. Make way, make way, you churls!'

The hastily summoned officer of the watch emerged from the guardhouse sullen and angry, but at the sight of Yennefer he blushed, opened his eyes and his mouth wide and made a low bow.

'I humbly welcome you to Gors Velen, Your Ladyship,' he mumbled, straightening up and staring. 'I am at your command ... May I be of any service to you? Perhaps an escort? A guide? Should I summon anyone?'

'That will not be necessary,' replied Yennefer, straightening up in her saddle and looking down at him. 'My stay in the city shall be brief. I am riding to Thanedd.'

'Of course, ma'am,' said the soldier, shifting from foot to foot and unable to tear his eyes from the enchantress's face. The other guards also stared. Ciri proudly pulled her shoulders back and raised her head, only to realise no one was looking at her. It was as if she didn't exist.

'Yes, ma'am,' repeated the officer of the guard. 'To Thanedd, yes

'... For the conclave. I understand, very well. Then I wish you—'

'Thank you,' said the enchantress, spurring her horse, clearly uninterested in whatever the officer wanted to wish her. Ciri followed her. The guardsmen bowed to Yennefer as she rode by, but none of them paid Ciri so much as a glance.

'They didn't even ask your name,' she muttered, catching up with Yennefer and carefully guiding her horse between the ruts worn into the muddy road. 'Did you put a spell on them?'

'Not on them. On myself.'

The enchantress turned back and Ciri sighed. Yennefer's eyes burnt with a violet light and her face radiated with beauty. Dazzling beauty. Provocative. Dangerous. And unnatural.

'The little green jar,' Ciri realised. 'What was in it?'

'Glamarye. An elixir. Or rather a cream for special occasions. Ciri, must you ride into every puddle in the road?'

'I'm trying to clean my horse's fetlocks.'

'It hasn't rained for a month. That's slops and horse piss, not water.'

'Aha ... Tell me, why did you use that elixir? Did it matter so much to you to—'

'This is Gors Velen,' interrupted Yennefer. 'A city that owes much of its prosperity to sorcerers and enchantresses. Actually, if I'm honest, chiefly to enchantresses. You saw for yourself how enchantresses are treated here. And I had no desire to introduce myself or prove who I am. I preferred to make it obvious at first glance. We turn left after that red house. We'll walk, Ciri. Slow your horse down or you'll trample a child.'

'But why did we come *here* then?'

'I just told you.'

Ciri snorted, thinking hard, then pursed her lips and dug her heels hard into her horse. Her mare skittered, almost colliding with a passing horse and cart. The carter got up from his seat, ready to unleash a stream of professional abuse at her, but on seeing Yennefer sat down quickly and began a thorough analysis of the state of his clogs.

'Try to bolt like that once more,' enunciated Yennefer, 'and we'll get cross. You're behaving like an adolescent goat. You're embarrassing me.'

'I figured it out. You want to put me in some school or orphanage, don't you? I don't want to go!'

'Be quiet. People are staring.'

'They're staring at you, not at me! I don't want to go to school! You promised me you'd always be with me, and now you're planning to leave me all by myself! I don't want to be alone!'

'You won't be alone. There are plenty of girls your age at the school. You'll have lots of friends.'

'I don't want any friends. I want to be with you and ... I thought we'd—'

Yennefer suddenly turned to face her.

'What did you think?'

'I thought we were going to see Geralt,' said Ciri, tossing her head provocatively. 'I know perfectly well what you've been thinking about the entire journey. And why you were sighing at night—'

'Enough,' hissed the enchantress, and the sight of her glaring eyes made Ciri bury her face in her horse's mane. 'You've overstepped the mark. May I remind you that the moment when you could defy me has passed for ever? You only have yourself to blame and now you have to be obedient. You'll do as I say. Understood?'

Ciri nodded.

'Whatever I say will be the best for you. Always. Which is why you will obey me and carry out my instructions. Is that clear? Rein in your horse. We're here.'

'That's the school?' grunted Ciri, looking up at the magnificent facade of a building. 'Is that—?'

'Not another word. Dismount. And mind your manners. This isn't the school. It's in Aretuza, not in Gors Velen. This is a bank.'

'Why do we need a bank?'

'Think about it. And dismount, as I said. Not in a puddle! Leave your horse; that's the servant's job. Take off your gloves. You don't go into a bank wearing riding gloves. Look at me, Ciri. Straighten your beret. And your collar. Stand up straight. And if you don't know what to do with your hands then don't do anything with them!'

Ciri sighed.

The servants who poured out of the entrance and assisted them – falling over each other as they bowed – were dwarves. Ciri looked at them with interest. Although they were all short, sturdy and bearded, in no way did they resemble her companion Yarpen Zigrin or his 'lads'. These servants looked grey: identically uniformed and unremarkable. They were subservient, too, which could never be said about Yarpen and his lads.

They went inside. The magic elixir was still working, so Yennefer's appearance immediately caused a great commotion. More dwarves bustled and bowed, and there were further obsequious welcomes and declarations of readiness to serve, which only subsided on the appearance of a fat, opulently attired and white-bearded dwarf.

'My dear Yennefer!' boomed the dwarf, jingling a golden chain which dangled from a powerful neck and fell to considerably below his white beard. 'What a surprise! And what an honour! Please, please come to my office. And you lot; don't stand there staring. To work, to your abacuses. Wilfli, bring a bottle of Castel de Neuf to my office. Which vintage ... ? You know what vintage. Be quick, jump to it! This way, this way, Yennefer. It's an unalloyed joy to see you. You look ... Oh, dammit, you look drop-dead gorgeous!'

'As do you,' the enchantress smiled. 'You're keeping well, Giancardi.'

'Naturally. Please, come through to my office. But no, no, you go first. You know the way after all, Yennefer.'

It was a little dark but pleasantly cool in the office, and the air held a scent Ciri remembered from Jarre the scribe's tower: the smell of ink and parchment and dust covering the oak furniture, tapestries and old books.

'Sit down, please,' said the banker, pulling a heavy armchair away from the table for Yennefer, and throwing Ciri a curious glance. 'Hmm ...'

'Give her a book, Molnar,' said the enchantress carelessly, noticing his look. 'She adores books. She'll sit at the end of the table and won't disturb us. Will you, Ciri?'

Ciri did not deign to reply.

'A book, hmm, hmm,' said the dwarf solicitously, going over to a chest of drawers. 'What have we here? Oh, a ledger ... No, not that. Duties and port charges ... Not that either. Credit and reimbursement? No. Oh, how did that get here? God only knows ... But this will probably be just the thing. There you go, miss.'

The book bore the title *Physiologus* and was very old and very tattered. Ciri carefully opened the cover and turned several pages. The book immediately caught her interest, since it concerned mysterious monsters and beasts and was full of illustrations. For the next few moments, she tried to divide her interest between the book and the conversation between the enchantress and the dwarf.

'Do you have any letters for me, Molnar?'

'No,' said the banker, pouring wine for Yennefer and himself. 'No new ones have arrived. I delivered the last ones a month ago, using our usual method.'

'I received them, thank you. Did anyone show interest in those letters, by any chance?'

'No one here,' smiled Molnar Giancardi. 'But your suspicions are not unwarranted, my dear. The Vivaldi Bank informed me, confidentially, that several attempts were made to track the letters. Their branch in Vengerberg also uncovered an attempt to track all transactions of your private account. A member of the staff proved to be disloyal.'

The dwarf broke off and looked at the enchantress from beneath his bushy eyebrows. Ciri listened intently. Yennefer said nothing and toyed with her obsidian star.

'Vivaldi,' said the banker, lowering his voice, 'couldn't or didn't want to conduct an investigation into the case. The corrupt, disloyal clerk fell, drunk, into a ditch and drowned. An unfortunate accident. Pity. Too quick, too hasty ...'

'No use crying over spilt milk,' the enchantress pouted. 'I know who was interested in my letters and account; the investigation at Vivaldi's wouldn't have produced any revelations.'

'If you say so ...' Giancardi ruffled his beard. 'Are you going to Thanedd, Yennefer? To the General Mages' Conclave?'

'Indeed.'

'To determine the fate of the world?'

'Let's not exaggerate.'

'Various rumours are doing the rounds,' said the dwarf coldly. 'And various things are happening.'

'What might they be, if it's not a secret?'

'Since last year,' said Giancardi, stroking his beard, 'strange fluctuations in taxation policy have been observed ... I know it doesn't interest you ...'

'Go on.'

'Poll tax and winter billeting tax, both of which are levied directly by the military authorities, have been doubled. Every merchant and entrepreneur also has to pay their "tenth groat" into the royal treasury. This is an entirely new tax: one groat on every noble of turnover. In addition, dwarves, gnomes, elves and halflings are paying increased poll and chimney tax. If they engage in trade or manufacturing they are also charged with a compulsory "non-human" donation of ten per hundred groats. In this way, I hand over sixty per cent of my income to the treasury. My bank, including all its branches, gives the Four Kingdoms six hundred marks a year. For your information, that's almost three times as much as a wealthy duke or earl pays in levy on an extensive estate.'

'Are humans not also charged with making the donation for the army?'

'No. Only the winter billeting tax and poll tax.'

'That means,' the enchantress nodded, 'that the dwarves and other non-humans are financing the campaign being waged against the Scoia'tael in the forests. I expected something like that. But what do taxes have to do with the conclave on Thanedd?'

'Something always happens after your conclaves,' muttered the banker. 'Something *always* happens. This time, I hope it will finally be the opposite. I'm counting on your conclave *stopping* things from happening. I'd be very happy, for example, if these strange price rises were to stop.'

'Be precise.'

The dwarf leaned back in his chair and linked his fingers across his beard-covered belly.

57

'I've worked for a good many years in this profession,' he said. 'Sufficiently long to be able to connect certain price fluctuations with certain facts. And recently the prices of precious stones have risen sharply. Because there's a demand for them.'

'Isn't cash usually exchanged for gemstones to avoid losses based on fluctuations in exchange rates and parities of coinage?'

'That too. But gemstones have one other considerable virtue. A pouch of diamonds weighing a few ounces, which can fit inside a pocket, corresponds in value to some fifty marks. The same sum in coins weighs twenty-five pounds and would fill a fair-sized sack. It is considerably quicker and easier to run away with a pouch in one's pocket than with a sack over one's shoulder. And one has one's hands free, which is of no small import. One can hold onto one's wife with one hand and, if needs must, punch someone with the other.'

Ciri snorted quietly, but Yennefer immediately quietened her with a fierce look.

'Which means' – she looked up – 'that some people are preparing, well in advance, to run away. But where to, I wonder?'

'The far north tops the list. Hengfors, Kovir and Poviss. Firstly because it is indeed far away, and secondly because those countries are neutral and are on good terms with Nilfgaard.'

'I see,' said the enchantress, a nasty smile on her lips. 'So it's diamonds into your pocket, grab the wife and head for the north ... Not too premature? Oh, never mind. So tell me: what else is getting dearer?'

'Boats.'

'What?'

'Boats,' repeated the dwarf, grinning. 'All the boat builders from the coast are building boats, their orders placed by quartermasters from King Foltest's army. The quartermasters pay well and keep placing new orders. Invest in boats, Yennefer, if you have any spare capital. It's a gold mine. You can build a boat from bark and reeds, make out a bill for a barque made of first-rate pine and split the profit with the quartermaster ...'

'Don't joke, Giancardi. Tell me what it's about.'

'Those boats,' said the banker casually, looking at the ceiling, 'are transported south. To Sodden and Brugge, to the River Yaruga. But from what I hear they aren't used for catching fish on the river. They're being hidden in the forest, on the east bank. It's said the army are spending hours on embarkation and disembarkation drills. But it's not for real yet.'

'Aha,' said Yennefer, biting her lip. 'And why are some people in such a rush to lend a hand? Yaruga is in the south.'

'There's some understandable anxiety,' muttered the dwarf, glancing over at Ciri, 'that Emperor Emhyr var Emreis will not be overjoyed when he hears that the aforementioned boats have been launched. Some people think it is sure to infuriate him, and then it'll be better to be as far as possible from the Nilfgaardian border ... Hell, at least until the harvest. Once the harvest's in I'll sigh with relief. If something's going to happen, it'll happen before the harvest.'

'Before the crops are in the granaries,' said Yennefer slowly.

'That's right. It's hard to graze horses on stubble, and strongholds with full granaries can endure long sieges. The weather is favourable for farmers and the harvest looks promising ... yes, the weather is exceptionally beautiful. The sun's hot, so cats and dogs alike are hoping it'll soon rain cats and dogs ... And the Yaruga in Dol Angra is very shallow. It's easy to ford it. In both directions.'

'Why Dol Angra?'

'I hope,' said the banker, stroking his beard and fixing the sorceress with a penetrating glance, 'I can trust you.'

'You've always been able to, Giancardi. Nothing has changed.'

'Dol Angra,' said the dwarf slowly, 'means Lyria and Aedirn, who have a military alliance with Temeria. You surely don't think that Foltest, who's buying the boats, intends to use them for his own ends, do you?'

'No,' said the enchantress slowly. 'I don't. Thank you for the information, Molnar. Who knows, perhaps you're right. Perhaps at the conclave we'll somehow manage to influence the fate of the world and the people living in it.'

'Don't forget about the dwarves,' snorted Giancardi. 'Or their banks.'

'We'll try not to. Since we're on the subject …'

'I'm all ears.'

'I have some expenses, Molnar. And should I take something from my account at the Vivaldi Bank, someone is bound to drown again, so …'

'Yennefer,' interrupted the dwarf. 'You have unlimited credit with me. The pogrom in Vengerberg took place long ago. Perhaps you have forgotten, but I never will. None of the Giancardi family will forget. How much do you need?'

'One thousand five hundred Temerian orens, transferred to the branch of the Cianfanelli Bank in Ellander, in favour of the Temple of Melitele.'

'Consider it done. A nice transfer; donations to temples aren't taxed. What else?'

'What are the annual fees for the school at Aretuza?'

Ciri listened carefully.

'One thousand two hundred Novigrad crowns,' said Giancardi. 'And then you have to add the matriculation fee; around two hundred for a new novice.'

'It's bloody gone up.'

'Everything has. They don't skimp on novices though; they live like queens at Aretuza. And half the city lives off them: tailors, shoemakers, confectioners, suppliers—'

'I know. Pay two thousand into the school's account. Anonymously. With a note that it's the registration fee and payment of the annual fees for one novice.'

The dwarf put down his quill, looked at Ciri and smiled in understanding. Ciri, pretending to leaf through the book, listened intently.

'Will that be all, Yennefer?'

'And three hundred Novigrad crowns for me, in cash. I'll need at least three dresses for the conclave on Thanedd.'

'Why cash? I'll give you a banker's draft for five hundred. The prices of imported fabric have risen damnably, and you don't dress in wool or linen, after all. And should you need anything – for yourself or for the future pupil at Aretuza – my shops and storehouses are at your disposal.'

'Thank you. What interest rate shall we say?'

'Interest?' said the dwarf, looking up. 'You paid the Giancardi family in advance, Yennefer. In Vengerberg. Let's talk no more about it.'

'I don't like debts of this kind, Molnar.'

'Neither do I. But I'm a merchant, a business-dwarf. I know what an obligation is. I know its value. So I repeat, let's speak no more about it. You may consider the favours you've asked of me sorted. And the favour you didn't ask about, too.'

Yennefer raised an eyebrow.

'A certain witcher I consider family,' chuckled Giancardi, 'visited the city of Dorian recently. I was informed he ran up a debt of a hundred crowns with a moneylender there. The said moneylender works for me. I'll cancel the debt, Yennefer.'

The enchantress glanced at Ciri and made a sour grimace.

'Molnar,' she said coldly, 'don't stick your fingers in a door with broken hinges. I doubt he still holds me dear, and if he learns about any debts being cancelled he'll hate my guts. You know him, don't you? Honour is an obsession with him. Was he in Dorian a long time ago?'

'Some ten days ago. Then he was seen in Little Marsh. I'm informed he went from there to Hirundum, since he had a commission from the farmers there. Some kind of monster to kill, as usual ...'

'And, as usual, they'll be paying him peanuts for killing it.' Yennefer's voice changed a little. 'Which, as usual, will barely cover the cost of medical treatment should he be mauled by the monster. Business as usual. If you really want to do something for me, Molnar, get involved. Contact the farmers from Hirundum and raise the bounty. Give him enough to live on.'

'Business as usual,' snorted Giancardi. 'And if he eventually finds out about it?'

Yennefer fixed her eyes on Ciri, who was watching and listening now, not even attempting to feign interest in *Physiologus*.

'And from whom,' she muttered, 'might he find out?'

Ciri lowered her gaze. The dwarf smiled meaningfully and stroked his beard.

61

'Will you be heading towards Hirundum before setting off for Thanedd? Just by chance, of course?'

'No,' said the enchantress, turning away. 'I won't. Change the subject, Molnar.'

Giancardi stroked his beard again and looked at Ciri. She lowered her head, cleared her throat and fidgeted in her chair.

'Quite,' he said. 'Time to change the subject. But your charge is clearly bored by that book, and by our conversation. And my next topic will bore her even more, I suspect; the fate of the world; the fate of the dwarves of this world; the fate of their banks. What a boring subject for girls, for future graduates of Aretuza ... Let her spread her wings a little, Yennefer. Let her take a walk around the city—'

'Oh, yes!' cried Ciri.

The enchantress looked annoyed and was opening her mouth to protest, but suddenly changed tack. Ciri wasn't certain, but she suspected the faint wink that accompanied the banker's suggestion influenced her decision.

'Let the girl have a look at the wonders of the ancient city of Gors Velen,' added Giancardi, smiling broadly. 'She deserves a little freedom before Aretuza. And we'll chat about certain issues of a ... hmm ... personal nature. No, I'm not suggesting the girl goes alone, even though it's a safe city. I'll assign her a companion and guardian. One of my younger clerks ...'

'Forgive me, Molnar,' said Yennefer, ignoring the smile, 'but I'm not convinced that, in the present times and even in a safe city, the presence of a dwarf ...'

'It didn't even occur to me,' said Giancardi indignantly, 'to send her with a dwarf. The clerk I have in mind is the son of a respected merchant, every inch a human, if you'll excuse the expression. Did you think I only employ dwarves? Hey, Wifli! Summon Fabio, and look lively!'

'Ciri.' The enchantress walked over to her, bending forward slightly. 'Make sure there's no funny business, nothing I'll have to be ashamed of. And keep schtum, got it? Promise me you'll watch your words and deeds. Don't just nod. Promises are made aloud.'

'I promise, Yennefer.'

'And glance at the sun from time to time. You're to be back at noon. Punctually. And should ... no, I don't imagine anyone will recognise you. But should you notice someone observing you too intently ...'

The enchantress put her hand in her pocket and pulled out a small piece of chrysoprase marked with runes, ground and polished into the shape of an hourglass.

'Put that in your pouch and don't lose it. In case of emergencies ... do you recall the spell? Just use it discreetly; activation emits a powerful echo, and the amulet transmits waves when it's in use. Should there be someone nearby who's sensitive to magic, you'll reveal yourself to them rather than remain hidden. Ah, and take this ... should you wish to buy something.'

'Thank you, madam.' Ciri put the amulet and coins into her pouch and looked with interest at the boy who had rushed into the office. He was freckled, and his wavy, chestnut hair fell onto the high collar of his grey clerk's uniform.

'Fabio Sachs,' said Giancardi by way of introduction. The boy bowed courteously.

'Fabio, this is Madam Yennefer, our honoured guest and respected client. And this young lady, her ward, wishes to visit our city. You shall be accompanying her and acting as her guide and guardian.'

The boy bowed once more, this time towards Ciri.

'Ciri,' said Yennefer coldly. 'Please stand up.'

She stood up, slightly taken aback, for she knew the custom well enough to know it wasn't expected of her. And she understood at once what Yennefer had seen. The clerk might look the same age as Ciri, but he was a head shorter.

'Molnar,' said the enchantress. 'Who is taking care of whom? Couldn't you assign someone of slightly more substantial dimensions to this task?'

The boy blushed and looked at his superior questioningly. Giancardi nodded his head in assent. The clerk bowed a third time.

'Your Highness,' he began, fluently and confidently. 'I may not be tall, but you can rely on me. I know the city, the suburbs and the surroundings very well. I shall look after this young lady to the best of my ability. And if I, Fabio Sachs the Younger, son of Fabio Sachs, do something to the best of my ability, then ... many an older boy would not better it.'

Yennefer looked at him for a while and then turned towards the banker.

'Congratulations, Molnar,' she said. 'You know how to choose your staff. You will have cause to be grateful to your young clerk in the future. It's true: the purest gold rings truest when you strike it. Ciri, I entrust you into the care of Fabio, son of Fabio, in absolute confidence, since he is a serious, trustworthy man.'

The boy blushed to the roots of his chestnut hair. Ciri felt herself blushing, too.

'Fabio,' said the dwarf, opening a small chest and rummaging around in its clinking contents, 'here's half a noble and three – two – five-groat pieces, in the event the young lady requests anything. Should she not, you shall return it. Very well, you may go.'

'By noon, Ciri,' reminded Yennefer. 'And not a moment later.'

'I remember, I remember.'

'My name is Fabio,' said the boy, as soon as they'd run down the stairs and out into the busy street. 'And you're Ciri, right?'

'Yes.'

'What would you like to see in Gors Velen, Ciri? The main street? Goldsmiths' alley? The seaport? Or maybe the market square and the market?'

'Everything.'

'Hmm ...' mused the boy seriously. 'We've only got till noon ... It would be best to go to the market square. It's market day today; you can see heaps of amazing things! But first we'll go up onto the wall, where there's a view of the entire bay and the famous Isle of Thanedd. How does that sound?'

'Let's go.'

Carts rumbled past, horses and oxen plodded, coopers rolled barrels along the noisy street, and everyone was in a hurry. Ciri was a little bewildered by the bustle and commotion; she clumsily stepped off the wooden footpath and ended up ankle-deep in mud and muck.

Fabio tried to take her arm, but she pulled away.

'I don't need any help to walk!'

'Hmm ... of course not. Let's go then. We're in the main street here. It's called Kardo Street and connects the two gates: the main gate and the sea gate. You get to the town hall that way. Do you see the tower with the gold weathervane? That's the town hall. And there, where that colourful sign's hanging, that's a tavern called The Unlaced Corset. But we won't, ah ... won't be going there. We're going over there. We'll take a short cut through the fish market in Winding Street.'

They turned into a narrow street and came out into a small square squeezed between some buildings. It was full of stalls, barrels and vats, all strongly smelling of fish. The market was full of bustle and noise, with the stallholders and customers alike trying to outshout the seagulls circling above. There were cats sitting at the foot of the wall, pretending that the fish didn't interest them in the least.

'Your mistress,' said Fabio suddenly, weaving his way between the stalls, 'is very strict.'

'I know.'

'She isn't a close relative, is she? It's obvious right away.'

'Is it? How can you tell?'

'She's very beautiful,' said Fabio, with the cruel, casual frankness of a young person. Ciri turned away abruptly. But before she could treat Fabio to a stinging comment about his freckles or his height, the boy was pulling her between handcarts, barrels and stalls, explaining all the time that the bastion towering above the square was called the Thief's Bastion, that the stones used for its construction came from the seabed and that the trees growing at its foot were called plantains.

'You're very quiet, Ciri,' he suddenly said.

'Me?' Ciri pretended to be astonished. 'Not at all! I'm just listening carefully to what you're saying. It's all really interesting, you know? And I just wanted to ask you ...'

'Fire away.'

'Is it far to ... to the city of Aretuza?'

'It isn't far at all. Aretuza isn't even a city. We'll go up on the wall and I'll show you. Look, the steps are over there.'

The wall was high and the steps steep. Fabio was sweating and panting, and no small wonder, because he never stopped talking while they climbed. Ciri learned that the wall surrounding the city of Gors Velen was a recent construction, much more recent than the city itself, which had been built long before by the elves. She also found out it was thirty-five feet high and that it was a so-called casemate wall, made of hewn stones and unfired brick, because that type of construction was the most resistant to blows from battering rams.

At the top they were greeted and fanned by a fresh sea wind. Ciri breathed it in joyfully after the heavy, stagnant stuffiness of the city. She rested her elbows on the top of the wall, looking down over the harbour dotted with colourful sails.

'What's that, Fabio? That mountain?'

'That's the Isle of Thanedd.'

The island seemed very close, and it didn't resemble an island. It looked like the base of a gigantic stone column stuck into the seabed, a huge ziggurat encircled by a spirally twisting road and zigzagging steps and terraces. The terraces were green with groves and gardens, and protruding from the greenery – which clung to the rocks like swallows' nests – rose soaring white towers and the ornate domes of groups of buildings framed by cloisters. The buildings gave no clue at all that they had been constructed from stone. They seemed to have been carved directly from the mountain's rocky slopes.

'All of this was built by elves,' explained Fabio. 'It's said they did it with the help of magic. However, for as long as anyone can remember, Thanedd has belonged to sorcerers. Near the summit, where you can see those gleaming domes, is Garstang Palace. The great Conclave of Mages will begin there in a few days. And there, look, on the very top. That solitary tower with battlements is Tor Lara, the Tower of Gulls ...'

'Can you get there overland? I can see it's very close.'

'Yes, you can. There's a bridge connecting the bay to the island. We can't see it because the trees are in the way. Do you see those red roofs at the foot of the mountain? That's Loxia Palace. The bridge

66

ends there. You have to pass through Loxia to reach the road to the upper terraces . . .'

'And those lovely cloisters and little bridges? And those gardens? How do they stay on the rock without falling off . . . ? What is that palace?'

'That's Aretuza, the place you were asking about. The famous school for young enchantresses is there.'

'Oh,' said Ciri, moistening her lips, 'it's there . . . Fabio?'

'Yes.'

'Do you ever see the young enchantresses who attend the school? The school at Aretuza?'

The boy looked at her, clearly astonished.

'No, never! No one sees them! They aren't allowed to leave the island or visit the city. And no one has access to the school. Even the burgrave and the bailiff can only travel as far as Loxia if they have business for the enchantresses. It's on the lowest level.'

'That's what I thought.' Ciri nodded, staring at Aretuza's shimmering roofs. 'It's not a school. It's a prison. On an island, on a rock, above a cliff. Quite simply: a prison.'

'I suppose it is,' admitted Fabio after a moment's thought. 'It's pretty difficult to get out of there . . . But no, it's not like being in prison. The novices are girls, after all. They need protecting—'

'From what?'

'Er . . .' the boy stammered. 'I mean, you know what . . .'

'No, I don't.'

'Oh . . . I think . . . Look, Ciri, no one locks them up in the school by force. They must want to be there . . .'

'Of course,' smiled Ciri mischievously. 'If they want to, they can stay in that prison. If they didn't, they wouldn't allow themselves to be locked up there. There's nothing to it. You'd just have to choose the right moment to make a break for it. But you'd have to do it before you end up there, because once you went in it would be too late . . .'

'What? Run away? Where would they run to—?'

'They,' she interrupted, 'probably wouldn't have anywhere to go, the poor things. Fabio? Where's that town . . . Hirundum?'

67

The boy looked at her in surprise.

'Hirundum's not a city,' he said. 'It's a huge farm. There are orchards and gardens there which supply vegetables and fruit to all the towns and cities in the area. There are also fishponds where they breed carp and other fish.'

'How far is it from here to Hirundum? Which way is it? Show me.'

'Why do you want to know?'

'Just show me, will you?'

'Do you see that road leading westwards? Where those wagons are? That's the road to Hirundum. It's about fifteen miles away, through forests all the way.'

'Fifteen miles,' repeated Ciri. 'Not far, if you've got a good horse ... Thank you, Fabio.'

'What are you thanking me for?'

'Never mind. Now take me to the town square. You promised.'

'Let's go.'

Ciri had never before seen such a crush and hubbub as there was in the market square in Gors Velen. The noisy fish market they'd walked through a little earlier seemed like a quiet temple compared to this place. It was absolutely huge, but still so crowded that Ciri assumed they would only be able to look at it from a distance. There would be no chance of actually getting into it. Fabio, however, bravely forced his way into the seething crowd, pulling her along by the hand. Ciri felt dizzy at once.

The market traders bellowed, the customers bellowed even louder, and children lost in the crowd howled and wailed. Cattle lowed, sheep bleated, and poultry clucked and quacked. Dwarven craftsmen doggedly banged their hammers onto sheets of metal, cursing foully whenever they interrupted their hammering to take a drink. Pipes, fiddles and dulcimers could be heard from various parts of the square; apparently some minstrels and musicians were performing. To cap it all, someone hidden in the crowd was blowing a brass trumpet incessantly. That someone was clearly not a musician.

Dodging a pig that trotted past with a piercing squeal, Ciri fell against a cage of chickens. A moment later, she was jostled by a passer-by and trod on something soft that meowed. She jumped back and barely avoided being trampled on by a huge, smelly, revolting, fearsome-looking beast, shoving people aside with its shaggy flanks. 'What was that?' she groaned, trying to regain her balance. 'Fabio?'

'A camel. Don't be afraid.'

'I'm not afraid! The thought of it!'

Ciri looked around curiously. She watched halflings at work creating ornate wineskins from goat's hide in full view of the public, and she was delighted by the beautiful dolls on display at a stall run by a pair of half-elves. She looked at wares made of malachite and jasper, which a gruff, gloomy gnome was offering for sale. She inspected the swords in a swordsmith's workshop with interest and the eye of an expert. She watched girls weaving wicker baskets and concluded that there was nothing worse than work.

The horn blower stopped blowing. Someone had probably killed him.

'What smells so delicious round here?'

'Doughnuts,' said Fabio, feeling the pouch. 'Do you wish to eat one?'

'I wish to eat two.'

The vendor handed them three doughnuts, took the five-groat piece and gave them four coppers in change, one of which he broke in half. Ciri, slowly regaining her poise, watched the operation of the coin being broken while voraciously devouring the first doughnut.

'Is that,' she asked, getting started on the second, 'where the expression "not worth a broken groat" comes from?'

'That's right,' said Fabio, swallowing his doughnut. 'There aren't any smaller coins than groats. Don't people use half-groats where you come from?'

'No.' Ciri licked her fingers. 'Where I come from we used gold ducats. And anyway all that breaking business was stupid and pointless.'

'Why?'

'Because I wish to eat a third doughnut.'

The plum-jam-filled doughnuts acted like the most miraculous elixir. Ciri was now in a good mood, and the teeming square had stopped terrifying her and had even begun to please her. Now she didn't let Fabio drag her behind him, but pulled him into the biggest crowd herself, towards a place where someone on a makeshift rostrum built of barrels was addressing the crowd. The speaker was fat and a bit past it. Ciri recognised him as a wandering priest by his shaved head and greyish-brown robes. She had seen his kind before, as they would occasionally visit the Temple of Melitele in Ellander. Mother Nenneke never referred to them as anything other than 'fanatical chumps'.

'There is but one law in the world!' roared the podgy priest. 'Divine law! The whole of nature is subject to that law, the whole of earth and everything that lives on the earth! And spells and magic are contrary to that law! Thus are sorcerers damned, and close is the day of wrath when fire will pour from the heavens and destroy their vile island! Then down will come the walls of Loxia, Aretuza and Garstang, where those pagans are gathering to hatch their intrigues! Those walls will tumble down ...'

'And we'll have to build the sodding things again,' muttered a journeyman bricklayer in a lime-spattered smock standing next to Ciri.

'I admonish you all, good and pious people,' yelled the priest. 'Don't believe the sorcerers, don't turn to them for advice or aid! Be beguiled neither by their beautiful looks nor their clever speech, for verily I do say to you that those magicians are like whitened graves, beautiful on the outside but full of putrefaction and rotten bones on the inside!'

'See what a powerful gob 'e 'as on 'im?' remarked a young woman with a basket full of carrots. 'E's 'aving a go at the magicians, coz 'e's jealous of 'em and that's that.'

'Course he is,' said the bricklayer. 'Look at his noggin, he's bald as an egg, and that belly hangs down to his knees. On the other hand, sorcerers are handsome; they don't get fat or bald ... And sorceresses, well, they're just gorgeous ...'

'Only because they've sold their souls to the devil for their beauty!' yelled a short individual with a shoemaker's hammer stuck into his belt.

70

'Fool of a cobbler! Were it not for the ladies of Aretuza, you'd long since have gone begging! Thanks to them you've got food in your belly!'

Fabio pulled Ciri by the sleeve, and they plunged once more into the crowd, which carried them towards the middle of the square. They heard the pounding of a drum and loud shouting, calling for silence. The crowd had no intention of being quiet, but it didn't bother the town crier on the wooden platform in the least. He had a powerful, trained voice and knew how to use it.

'Let it be known,' he bellowed, unfurling a roll of parchment, 'that Hugo Ansbach of halfling stock is outlawed, for he gave lodgings and victuals to those villainous elves called Squirrels. The same applies to Justin Ingvar, a blacksmith of dwarven stock, who forged arrowheads for those wrongdoers. Thus does the burgrave announce that both are wanted and orders them to be hunted down. Whosoever seizes them will earn a reward of fifty crowns. Any who gives them victuals or shelter shall be considered an accomplice to their crime and shall suffer the same punishment. And should they be apprehended in a village or hamlet, the entire village or hamlet will pay a fine—'

'But who,' shouted someone in the crowd, 'would give a halfling shelter? They should be hunted on their farms, and when they're found, all those non-humans should be slung into the dungeons!'

'To the gallows, not the dungeons!'

The town crier began to read further announcements issued by the burgrave and town council, and Ciri lost interest. She was just about to extricate herself from the crowd when she suddenly felt a hand on her bottom. A totally non-accidental, brazen and extremely skilled hand.

The crush ought to have prevented her from turning around to look, but in Kaer Morhen Ciri had learned how to manoeuvre in places that were difficult to move around in. She turned around, causing something of a disturbance. The young priest with the shaved head standing right behind her smiled an arrogant, rehearsed smile. 'Right, then,' said that smile, 'what are we going to do now? You'll blush sweetly and that'll be the end of it, won't it?'

It was clear the priest had never had to deal with one of Yennefer's pupils.

'Keep your hands to yourself, baldy!' yelled Ciri, white with rage. 'Grab your own arse, you ... You whitewashed tomb!'

Taking advantage of the fact that the priest was pinned in by the crowd and couldn't move, she intended to kick him, but Fabio prevented that, hurriedly pulling her well away from the priest and the site of the incident. Seeing that she was trembling with rage, he treated her to a few fritters dusted with caster sugar, at the sight of which Ciri immediately calmed down and forgot about the incident. From where they were standing by the stall they had a view of a scaffold with a pillory, but with no criminal in it. The scaffold itself was decorated with garlands of flowers and was being used by a group of wandering minstrels, dressed up like parrots, sawing away vigorously at violins and playing flutes and bagpipes. A young black-haired woman in a sequined waistcoat sang and danced, shaking a tambourine and merrily stamping tiny slippers.

To bite a witch beside a path,
Some vipers did contrive.
The snakes all perished one by one,
The witch is still alive.

The crowd gathered around the scaffold laughed heartily and clapped along. The fritter seller threw another batch into the hot oil. Fabio licked his fingers and tugged Ciri away by the sleeve.

There were innumerable stalls and delicious foods were being offered everywhere. They each ate a cream bun, then shared a smoked eel, which they followed with something very strange, which had been fried and impaled on a skewer. After that, they stopped by some barrels of sauerkraut and pretended to be tasting it, as if intending to buy a large quantity. When they had eaten their fill but then didn't buy anything the stallholder called them 'a pair of little shits'.

They walked on. Fabio bought a small basket of bergamot pears with the rest of the money. Ciri looked up at the sky but decided it still wasn't noon.

'Fabio? What are those tents and booths over there, by the wall?'

'Sideshows. Want to see?'

'Yes.'

There was a crowd of men in front of the first tent, shuffling about excitedly. The sounds of a flute floated out from inside.

'The black-skinned Leila ...' read Ciri, struggling to decipher the lopsided, crooked writing on the flap, 'reveals all the secrets of her body in the dance ... What nonsense! What kind of secrets ...?'

'Come on, let's go,' said Fabio, urging her on and blushing slightly. 'Oh, look, this is more interesting. There's a clairvoyant here who'll tell your fortune. I've still got two groats. That should be enough—'

'Waste of money,' snorted Ciri. 'Some prophecy it'll be, for two groats! To predict the future you have to be a prophetess. Divination is a great gift. Even among enchantresses, no more than one in a hundred has that kind of ability—'

'A fortune-teller predicted,' interrupted the boy, 'that my eldest sister would get married and it came true. Don't make faces, Ciri. Come on, let's have our fortunes told ...'

'I don't want to get married. I don't want my fortune told. It's hot and that tent stinks of incense. I'm not going in. Go in yourself, if you want, and I'll wait. I just don't understand why you want a prophecy. What would you like to know?'

'Well ...' stammered Fabio. 'Mostly, it's ... it's if I'm going to travel. I'd like to travel. And see the whole world ...'

He will, thought Ciri suddenly, feeling dizzy. *He'll sail on great white sailing ships ... He'll sail to countries no one has seen before him ... Fabio Sachs, explorer. He'll give his name to a cape, to the very furthest point of an as-yet unnamed continent. When he's fifty-four, married with a son and three daughters, he'll die far from his home and his loved ones ... of an as-yet unnamed disease ...*

'Ciri! What's the matter with you?'

She rubbed her face. She felt as though she were coming up through water, rising to the surface from the bottom of a deep, ice-cold lake.

'It's nothing ...' she mumbled, looking around and coming back

73

to herself. 'I felt dizzy ... It's because of this heat. And because of that incense from the tent ...'

'Because of that cabbage, more like,' said Fabio seriously. 'We oughtn't to have eaten so much. My belly's gurgling too.'

'There's nothing wrong with me!' snapped Ciri, lifting her head briskly and actually feeling better. The thoughts that had flown through her mind like a whirlwind dissipated and were lost in oblivion. 'Come on, Fabio. Let's go.'

'Do you want a pear?'

'Course I do.'

A group of teenage boys were playing spinning tops for money. The top, carefully wound up with string, had to be set spinning with a deft tug, like cracking a whip, to make it follow a circular path around a course drawn with chalk. Ciri had beaten most of the boys in Skellige and all the novices at the Temple of Melitele at spinning tops. So she was toying with the thought of joining the game and relieving the urchins not only of their coppers, but also of their patched britches, when her attention was suddenly caught by some loud cheering.

At the very end of a row of tents and booths stood a curious semicircular enclosure squeezed between the foot of the wall and some stone steps. It was formed from sheets of canvas stretched over six-foot poles. There was an entrance between two of the poles, blocked by a tall, pockmarked man wearing a jerkin and striped trousers tucked into sailor's boots. A small group of people milled around in front of him, and folk would throw a few coppers into the pockmarked man's hand and then disappear behind the canvas. The pockmarked man was dropping the money into a large sack, which he jingled as he shouted hoarsely.

'Roll up, roll up! Over here! You will see, with your own eyes, the most frightful creature the gods ever created! Horror of horrors! A live basilisk, the venomous terror of the Zerrikan deserts, the devil incarnate, an insatiable man-eater! You've never seen such a monster, folks. Freshly caught, brought from beyond the seas in a coracle. Come and see this vicious, live basilisk with your own eyes, because you'll never see one again. Not never, not nowhere! Last chance! Here, behind me, for a mere fifteen groats. Just ten groats for women with children!'

'Ha,' said Ciri, shooing wasps away from the pears. 'A basilisk? A live one? This I must see. I've only seen them in books. Come on, Fabio.'

'I haven't got any more money ...'

'But I have. I'll pay for you. Come on, in we go.'

'That'll be six,' said the pockmarked man, looking down at the four coppers in his palm. '*Three* five-groat pieces each. Only women with children get in cheap.'

'He,' replied Ciri, pointing at Fabio with a pear, 'is a child. And I'm a woman.'

'Only women carrying children,' growled the pockmarked man. 'Go on, chuck in two more five-groat pieces, clever little miss, or scram and let other people through. Make haste, folks! Only three more empty spaces!'

Inside the canvas enclosure townspeople were milling around, forming a solid ring around a stage constructed of wooden planks. On the stage stood a wooden cage covered with a carpet. Having let in the final spectators, the pockmarked man jumped onto the stage, seized a long pole and used it to pull the carpet away. The air filled with the smell of offal mixed with an unpleasant reptilian stench. The spectators rumbled and stepped back a little.

'You are being sensible, good people,' said the pockmarked man. 'Not too close, for it may be perilous!'

Inside the cage, which was far too cramped for it, lay a lizard. It was covered in dark, strangely shaped scales and curled up into a ball. When the pockmarked man knocked the cage with his pole, the reptile writhed, grated its scales against the bars, extended its long neck and let out a piercing hiss, revealing sharp, white fangs, which contrasted vividly with the almost black scales around its maw. The spectators exhaled audibly. A shaggy little dog in the arms of a woman who looked like a stallholder yapped shrilly.

'Look carefully, good people,' called the pockmarked man. 'And be glad that beasts like this don't live near our city! This monstrous basilisk is from distant Zerrikania! Don't come any closer because, though it's secure in a cage, its breath alone could poison you!'

Ciri and Fabio finally pushed their way through the ring of spectators.

'The basilisk,' continued the pockmarked man on stage, resting on the pole like a guard leaning on his halberd, 'is the most venomous beast in the world! For the basilisk is the king of all the serpents! Were there more basilisks, this world would disappear without a trace! Fortunately, it is a most rare monster; it only ever hatches from an egg laid by a cockerel. And you know yourselves that not every cockerel can lay an egg, but only a knavish one who presents his rump to another cockerel in the manner of a mother hen.'

The spectators reacted with general laughter to this superior – or possibly posterior – joke. The only person not laughing was Ciri. She didn't take her eyes off the creature, which, disturbed by the noise, was writhing and banging against the bars of the cage, biting them and vainly trying to spread its wings in the cramped space.

'An egg laid by a cockerel like that,' continued the pockmarked man, 'must be brooded by a hundred and one venomous snakes! And when the basilisk hatches from the egg –'

'That isn't a basilisk,' said Ciri, chewing a bergamot pear. The pockmarked man looked at her, askance.

'– when the basilisk hatches, I was saying,' he continued, 'then it devours all the snakes in the nest, imbibing their venom without suffering any harm from it. It becomes so swollen with venom itself that it is able to kill not only with its teeth, not only with its touch, but with its breath alone! And when a mounted knight ups and stabs a basilisk with his spear, the poison runs up the shaft, killing both rider and horse outright!'

'That's the falsest lie,' said Ciri aloud, spitting out a pip.

'It's the truest truth!' protested the pockmarked man. 'He kills them; he kills the horse and its rider!'

'Yeah, right!'

'Be quiet, miss!' shouted the market trader with the dog. 'Don't interfere! We want to marvel and listen!'

'Ciri, stop it,' whispered Fabio, nudging her in the ribs. Ciri snorted at him, reaching into the basket for another pear.

'Every animal,' said the pockmarked man, raising his voice against the murmur which was intensifying among the spectators, 'flees the basilisk as soon as it hears its hiss. Every animal, even a dragon – what am I saying? – even a cockrodile, and a cockrodile is awfully dreadful, as anyone who's seen one knows. The one and only animal that doesn't fear the basilisk is the marten. The marten, when it sees the monster in the wilderness, runs as fast as it can into the forest, looks for certain herbs known only to it and eats them. Then the basilisk's venom is harmless, and the marten can bite it to death ...'

Ciri snorted with laughter and made a long-drawn-out, extremely rude noise with her lips.

'Hey, little know-it-all!' burst out the pockmarked man. 'If it's not to your liking, you know where the door is! No one's forcing you to listen or look at the basilisk!'

'That's no basilisk!'

'Oh, yeah? So what is it, Miss Know-It-All?'

'It's a wyvern,' said Ciri, throwing away the pear stalk and licking her fingers. 'It's a common wyvern. Young, small, starving and dirty. But a wyvern, that's all. Vyverne, in the Elder Speech.'

'Oh, look at this!' shouted the pockmarked man. 'What a clever clogs! Shut your trap, because when I—'

'I say,' spoke up a fair-haired young man in a velvet beret and a squire's doublet without a coat of arms. He had a delicate, pale girl in an apricot dress on his arm. 'Not so fast, my good animal catcher! Do not threaten the noble lady, for I will readily tan your hide with my sword. And furthermore, something smacks of trickery here!'

'What trickery, young sir knight?' choked the pockmarked man. 'She's lying, the horri— I meant to say, the high-born young lady is in error. It *is* a basilisk!'

'It's a wyvern,' repeated Ciri.

'What do you mean, a Vernon! It's a basilisk! Just look how menacing it is, how it hisses, how it bites at its cage! Look at those teeth! It's got teeth, I tell you, like—'

'Like a wyvern,' scowled Ciri.

'If you've taken leave of your senses,' said the pockmarked man, fixing her with a gaze that a real basilisk would have been proud of, 'then come closer! Step up, and let it breathe on you! You laughed at its venom. Now let's see you croak! Come along, step up!'

'Not a problem,' said Ciri, pulling her arm out of Fabio's grasp and taking a step forward.

'I shan't allow it!' cried the fair-haired squire, dropping his apricot companion's arm and blocking Ciri's way. 'It cannot be! You are risking too much, fair lady.'

Ciri, who had never been addressed like that before, blushed a little, looked at the young man and fluttered her eyelids in a way she had tried out numerous times on the scribe Jarre.

'There's no risk whatsoever, noble knight,' she smiled seductively, in spite of all Yennefer's warnings, and reminders about the fable of the simpleton gazing foolishly at the cheese. 'Nothing will happen to me. That so-called poisonous breath is claptrap.'

'I would, however, like to stand beside you,' said the youth, putting his hand on the hilt of his sword. 'To protect and defend ... Will you allow me?'

'I will,' said Ciri, not knowing why the expression of rage on the apricot maiden's face was causing her such pleasure.

'It is I who shall protect and defend her!' said Fabio, sticking his chest out and looking at the squire defiantly. 'And I shall stand with her too!'

'Gentlemen.' Ciri puffed herself up with pride and stuck her nose in the air. 'A little more dignity. Don't shove. There'll be room enough for everyone.'

The ring of spectators swayed and murmured as she bravely approached the cage, followed so closely by the boys that she could almost feel their breath on her neck. The wyvern hissed furiously and struggled, its reptilian stench assaulting their noses. Fabio gasped loudly, but Ciri didn't withdraw. She drew even closer and held out a hand, almost touching the cage. The monster hurled itself at the bars, raking them with its teeth. The crowd swayed once more and someone cried out.

'Well?' Ciri turned around, hands proudly on her hips. 'Did I die? Has that so-called venomous monster poisoned me? He's no more a basilisk than I'm a—'

She broke off, seeing the sudden paleness on the faces of Fabio and the squire. She turned around quickly and saw two bars of the cage parting under the force of the enraged lizard, tearing rusty nails out of the frame.

'Run!' she shouted at the top of her voice. 'The cage is breaking!'

The crowd rushed, screaming, for the door. Several of them tried to tear their way through the canvas sheeting, but they only managed to entangle themselves and others in it, eventually collapsing into a struggling, yelling mass of humanity. Just as Ciri was trying to jump out of the way the squire seized her arm, and the two of them staggered, tripped and fell to the ground, taking Fabio down with them. Anxious yaps came from the stallholder's shaggy little dog, colourful swearwords from the pockmarked man and piercing shrieks from the disorientated apricot maiden.

The bars of the cage broke with a crack and the wyvern struggled free. The pockmarked man jumped down from the stage and tried to restrain it with his pole, but the writhing monster knocked it out of his hand with one blow of its claws and lashed him with its spiny tail, transforming his pockmarked cheek into a bloody pulp. Hissing and spreading its tattered wings, the wyvern flew down from the stage; its sights were set on Ciri, Fabio and the squire, who were trying to get to their feet. The apricot maiden fainted and fell flat on her back. Ciri tensed, preparing to jump, but realised she wouldn't make it.

They were saved by the shaggy little dog who, still yapping shrilly, broke free from its owner's arms – she had fallen and become entangled in her own six skirts – and lunged at the monster. The wyvern hissed, rose up, pinned the cur down with its talons, twisted its body with a swift, serpentine movement and sank its teeth into the dog's neck. The dog howled wildly.

The squire struggled to his knees and reached down to his side, but didn't find his hilt. Ciri had been too quick for him. She had drawn his sword from its scabbard in a lightning-fast movement and leapt into a half-turn. The wyvern rose, the dog's severed head hanging in its sharp-toothed jaws.

It seemed to Ciri that all the movements she had learned in Kaer Morhen were performing themselves, almost without her conscious will or participation. She slashed the astonished wyvern in the belly and immediately spun away to avoid it. The lunging lizard fell to the sand spurting blood. Ciri jumped over it, skilfully avoiding its swishing tail. Then, with a sure, accurate and powerful blow, she hacked into the monster's neck, jumped back, and made an instinctive – but now unnecessary – evasive manoeuvre, and then struck again at once, this time chopping through its backbone. The wyvern writhed briefly in pain and then stopped moving; only its serpentine tail continued to thrash and slap the ground, raining sand all around.

Ciri quickly shoved the bloodied sword into the squire's hand.

'Danger over!' she shouted to the fleeing crowd and the spectators still trying to extricate themselves from the canvas sheeting. 'The monster's dead! This brave knight has killed him dead ...'

She suddenly felt a tightening in her throat and a whirling in her stomach; everything went black. Something hit her in the bottom with tremendous force, making her teeth snap together. She looked around blankly. The thing that had struck her was the ground.

'Ciri ...' whispered Fabio, kneeling beside her. 'What's the matter? By the gods, you're as white as a sheet ...'

'It's a pity,' she muttered, 'you can't see yourself.'

People crowded around. Several of them prodded the wyvern's body with sticks and pokers. A few of them began dressing the pockmarked man's wounds. The rest cheered the heroic squire: the fearless dragon killer, the only person to keep a cool head, and prevent a massacre. The squire revived the apricot maiden, still staring somewhat dumbstruck at the blade of his sword which was covered with smeared streaks of drying blood.

'My hero ...' said the apricot maiden, coming to and throwing her arms around the squire's neck. 'My saviour! My darling!'

'Fabio,' said Ciri weakly, seeing the city constables pushing through the crowd. 'Help me get up and get us out of here. Quickly.'

'Poor children ...' said a fat townswoman in a cap as she watched them sneak away from the crowd. 'Oh, you were lucky. Were it not for this valiant young knight, your mothers would be sorely grieving!'

'Find out who that young squire serves!' shouted a craftsman in a leather apron. 'That deed deserves a knightly belt and spurs!'

'And to the pillory with the animal catcher! He deserves a thrashing! Bringing a monster like that into the city, among people …'

'Water, and quickly! The maiden's fainted again!'

'My darling Foo-Foo!' the stallholder suddenly howled, as she leaned over what was left of the shaggy little dog. 'My poor little sweetheart! Someone, please! Catch that wench, that rascal who infuriated the dragon! Where is she? Someone grab her! It wasn't the animal catcher; she's to blame for all this!'

The city constables, helped by numerous volunteers, began to shove their way through the crowd and look around. Ciri had overcome her dizziness.

'Fabio,' she whispered. 'Let's split up. We'll meet up in a bit in that alleyway we came along. Go. And if anyone stops you to ask, you don't know me or anything about me.'

'But … Ciri—'

'Go!'

She squeezed Yennefer's amulet in her fist and murmured the activation spell. It started working in an instant, and there was no time to lose. The constables, who had been forcing their way through the crowd towards her, stopped, confused.

'What the bloody hell?' said one of them in astonishment, looking, it would have seemed, straight at Ciri. 'Where is she? I just saw her …'

'There, over there!' yelled another, pointing the wrong way.

Ciri turned around and walked away, still a little dazed and weakened by the rush of adrenaline and the activation of the amulet. The amulet was working perfectly; no one could see her and no one was paying any attention to her. Absolutely no one. As a consequence she was jostled, stamped on and kicked innumerable times before she finally extricated herself from the crowd. By some miracle she escaped being crushed by a chest thrown from a cart. She almost had an eye poked out by a pitchfork. Spells, it turned out, had their good and bad sides, and as many advantages as disadvantages.

The amulet's effects did not last long. Ciri was not powerful enough to control it or extend the time the spell was active. Fortunately, the spell wore off at the right moment, just as she left the crowd and saw Fabio waiting for her in the alley.

'Oh my,' said the boy. 'Oh my goodness, Ciri. You're here. I was worried . . .'

'You needn't have been. Come on, quickly. Noon has passed. I've got to get back.'

'You were pretty handy with that monster.' The boy looked at her in admiration. 'You moved like lightning! Where did you learn to do that?'

'What? The squire killed the wyvern.'

'That's not true. I saw—'

'You didn't see anything! Please, Fabio, not a word to anyone. Anyone. And particularly not to Madam Yennefer. Oh, I'd be in for it if she found out . . .'

She fell silent.

'Those people were right.' She pointed behind her, towards the market square. 'I provoked the wyvern . . . It was all my fault . . .'

'No, it wasn't,' retorted Fabio firmly. 'That cage was rotten and bodged together. It could have broken any second: in an hour, tomorrow, the next day . . . It's better that it happened now, because you saved—'

'The squire did!' yelled Ciri. 'The squire! Will you finally get that into your head? I'm telling you, if you grass me up, I'll turn you into a . . . a . . . well something horrible! I know spells! I'll turn you into—'

'Stop,' someone called out behind them. 'That's quite enough of that!'

One of the women walking behind them had dark, smoothly combed hair, shining eyes and thin lips. She had a short mauve camaka cape trimmed with dormouse fur thrown over her shoulders.

'Why aren't you in school, novice?' she asked in a cold, resonant voice, eyeing Ciri with a penetrating gaze.

'Wait, Tissaia,' said the other woman, who was younger, tall and fair-haired, and wore a green dress with a plunging neckline. 'I don't know her. I don't think she's—'

'Yes, she is,' interrupted the dark-haired woman. 'I'm certain she's one of your girls, Rita. You can't know them all. She's one of the ones who sneaked out of Loxia during the confusion when we were moving dormitories. And she'll admit as much in a moment. Well, novice, I'm waiting.'

'What?' frowned Ciri.

The woman pursed her thin lips and straightened her cuffs. 'Who did you steal that amulet of concealment from? Or did someone give it to you?'

'What?'

'Don't test my patience. Name, class, and the name of your preceptress. Quickly!'

'What?'

'Are you acting dumb, novice? Your name! What is your name?'

Ciri clenched her teeth together and her eyes flared with a green glow.

'Anna Ingeborga Klopstock,' she muttered brazenly.

The woman raised a hand and Ciri immediately realised the full extent of her error. Only once had Yennefer, wearied by Ciri's endless complaining, showed her how a paralysing spell worked. The sensation had been extremely unpleasant. It was the same this time, too.

Fabio yelled weakly and lunged towards her, but the fair-haired woman seized him by the collar and held him fast. The boy struggled but the woman's grip was like iron. Ciri couldn't budge an inch either. She felt as though she were slowly becoming rooted to the spot. The dark-haired woman leaned over her and fixed her with her shining eyes.

'I do not approve of corporal punishment,' she said icily, straightening her cuffs once more. 'But I'll do my best to have you flogged, novice. Not for disobedience, nor for theft, nor for truancy. Not because you are wearing non-regulation clothing. Not for being in the company of a boy and not even for talking to him about matters you are forbidden to speak of. You will be flogged for not recognising an arch-mistress.'

'No!' shrieked Fabio. 'Don't harm her, noble lady! I'm a clerk in Mr Molnar Giancardi's bank, and this young lady is—'

'Shut up!' yelled Ciri. 'Shut—' The gagging spell was cast quickly and brutally. She tasted blood in her mouth.

'Well?' the fair-haired woman urged Fabio, releasing the boy and tenderly smoothing his ruffled collar. 'Speak. Who is this haughty young maid?'

Margarita Laux-Antille emerged from the pool with a splash, spraying water everywhere. Ciri couldn't stop herself looking. She had seen Yennefer naked on several occasions and hadn't imagined anyone could have a more shapely figure. She was wrong. Even marble statues of goddesses and nymphs would have blushed at the sight of Margarita Laux-Antille undressed.

The enchantress took a pail of cold water and poured it over her breasts, swearing lewdly and then shaking herself off.

'You, girl.' She beckoned to Ciri. 'Be so good as to hand me a towel. And please stop being angry with me.'

Ciri snorted quietly, still piqued. When Fabio had revealed who she was, the enchantresses had dragged her half the length of the city, making a laughing stock of her. Naturally, the matter was cleared up instantly in Giancardi's bank. The enchantresses apologised to Yennefer, asking for their behaviour to be excused. They explained that the Aretuza novices had been temporarily moved to Loxia because the school's rooms had been turned into accommodation for the participants of the mages' conclave. Taking advantage of the confusion around the move, several novices had slipped out of Thanedd and played truant in the city. Margarita Laux-Antille and Tissaia de Vries, alarmed by the activation of Ciri's amulet, had mistaken her for one of their truants.

The enchantresses apologised to Yennefer, but none of them thought of apologising to Ciri. Yennefer, listening to the apologies, simply looked at her and Ciri could feel her ears burning with shame. But it was worse for Fabio; Molnar Giancardi admonished him so severely the boy had tears in his eyes. Ciri felt sorry for him but was also proud of him; Fabio kept his promise and didn't breathe a word about the wyvern.

Yennefer, it turned out, knew Tissaia and Margarita very well.

84

The enchantresses invited her to the Silver Heron, the best and most expensive inn in Gors Velen, where Tissaia de Vries was staying, delaying her trip to the island for reasons known only to herself. Margarita Laux-Antille, who, it turned out, was the rectoress of Aretuza, had accepted the older enchantress's invitation and was temporarily sharing the apartment with her. The inn was truly luxurious; it had its own bathhouse in the cellars, which Margarita and Tissaia had hired for their exclusive use, paying extortionate sums of money for it. Yennefer and Ciri, of course, were encouraged to use the bathhouse too. As a result, all of them had been soaking in the pool and perspiring in the steam by turns for several hours, gossiping the entire time.

Ciri gave the enchantress a towel. Margarita pinched her gently on the cheek. Ciri snorted again and dived with a splash into the rosemary-perfumed water of the pool.

'She swims like a young seal,' laughed Margarita, stretching out beside Yennefer on a wooden lounger, 'and is as shapely as a naiad. Will you give her to me, Yenna?'

'That's why I brought her here.'

'Which class shall I put her in? Does she know the basics?'

'She does, but she can start at the beginning like everyone else. It won't do her any harm.'

'That would be wise,' said Tissaia de Vries, busily correcting the arrangement of cups on the marble tabletop, which was covered in a thin layer of condensation. 'That would be wise indeed, Yennefer. The girl will find it easier if she begins with the other novices.'

Ciri hauled herself out of the pool and sat on the edge, wringing her hair out and splashing her feet in the water. Yennefer and Margarita gossiped lazily, wiping their faces from time to time with cloths soaked in cold water. Tissaia, modestly swathed in a sheet, didn't join in the conversation, and gave the impression of being utterly absorbed in tidying the objects on the table.

'My humble apologies, noble ladies,' called the innkeeper suddenly, unseen, from above. 'Please forgive my daring to disturb, but ... an officer wishes to talk to Madam de Vries urgently. Apparently the matter will brook no delay!'

Margarita Laux-Antille giggled and winked at Yennefer, upon which they pulled the towels from their hips and assumed exotic and extremely provocative poses.

'Let the officer enter,' shouted Margarita, trying not to laugh. 'Welcome. We're ready.'

'Children,' sighed Tissaia de Vries, shaking her head. 'Cover yourself, Ciri.'

The officer came in, but the enchantresses' prank misfired. The officer wasn't embarrassed at the sight of them, and didn't blush, gape or goggle, because the officer was a woman. A tall, slender woman with a thick, black plait and a sword at her side.

'Madam,' said the woman stiffly, her hauberk clanking as she gave Tissaia de Vries a slight bow, 'I report the execution of your instructions. I would like to ask for permission to return to the garrison.'

'You may,' replied Tissaia curtly. 'Thank you for the escort and your help. Have a safe journey.'

Yennefer sat up on her lounger, looking at the black, gold and red rosette on the soldier's shoulder.

'Do I know you?'

The warrior bowed stiffly and wiped her sweat-covered face. It was hot in the bathhouse, and she was wearing a hauberk and leather tunic.

'I often used to visit Vengerberg, Madam Yennefer,' she said. 'My name is Rayla.'

'Judging by the rosette, you serve in King Demavend's special units.'

'Yes, madam.'

'Your rank?'

'Captain.'

'Very good.' Margarita Laux-Antille laughed. 'I note with pleasure that Demavend's army has finally begun to award commissions to soldiers with balls.'

'May I withdraw?' said the soldier, standing up straight and resting her hand on the hilt of her sword.

'You may.'

'I sensed hostility in your voice, Yenna,' said Margarita a moment later. 'What do you have against the captain?'

Yennefer stood up and took two goblets from the table.

'Did you see the posts by the crossroads?' she asked. 'You must have seen them, must have smelled the stench of rotting corpses. Those posts are their idea and their work. She and her subordinates from the special units. They're a gang of sadists!'

'There's a war on, Yennefer. Rayla must have seen her comrades-in-arms falling, alive, into the Squirrels' clutches many times. Then hung by their arms from trees as target practice. Blinded, castrated, with their feet burnt in campfires. Falka herself wouldn't have been ashamed of the atrocities committed by the Scoia'tael.'

'The methods of the special units are remarkably similar to those of Falka. But that's not the point, Rita. I'm not getting sentimental about the fate of elves and I know what war is. I know how wars are won, too. They're won by soldiers who fight for their countries and homes with conviction and sacrifice. Not by soldiers like her, by mercenaries fighting for money who are unable and unwilling to sacrifice themselves. They don't even know what sacrifice is. And if they do, they despise it.'

'To hell with her, her dedication and her contempt. What does it matter to us? Ciri, throw something decent on, pop upstairs and fetch us another carafe. I feel like getting drunk today.'

Tissaia de Vries sighed, shaking her head. It didn't escape Margarita's attention.

'Fortunately,' she giggled, 'we aren't at school any longer, mistress dear. We can do what we want now.'

'Even in the presence of a future novice?' asked Tissaia scathingly. 'When I was rectoress at Aretuza—'

'We remember, we remember,' interrupted Yennefer with a smile, 'and even if we'd prefer to forget, we never will. Go and fetch that carafe, Ciri.'

Upstairs, waiting for the carafe, Ciri witnessed the officer depart with her squad of four soldiers. She watched their posture, expressions, clothing and arms in fascination and admiration. Right then Rayla, the captain with the black plait, was arguing with the innkeeper.

'I'm not going to wait until daybreak! And I couldn't give a damn if the gates are locked. I want to leave immediately. I know the inn has its own postern in the stables. I order it to be opened!'

'But the regulations—'

'I don't give a damn about the regulations! I'm carrying out the orders of Arch-Mistress de Vries!'

'All right, all right, captain. Don't shout. I'll open up ...'

The postern, it turned out, was in a narrow, securely gated passageway, leading straight beyond the city walls. Before Ciri took the carafe from the servant's hands, she saw the postern being opened and Rayla and her unit riding out, into the night.

Ciri was deep in thought.

'Oh, at last,' said Margarita cheerfully, though it was unclear whether she was referring to the sight of Ciri or the carafe she was carrying. Ciri put the carafe on the table – very clearly wrongly, because Tissaia de Vries repositioned it at once. When Yennefer poured, she spoiled the entire arrangement too, and Tissaia had to put it right again. Imagining Tissaia as a teacher filled Ciri with dread.

Yennefer and Margarita returned to their interrupted conversation, not sparing the contents of the carafe. Ciri realised it wouldn't be long before she would have to go and get a fresh one. She pondered, listening to the enchantresses' discussion.

'No, Yenna.' Margarita shook her head. 'You aren't up to speed, I see. I've dumped Lars. That's history. Elaine deireadh, as the elves would say.'

'And that's why you want to get drunk?'

'That's one of the reasons,' confirmed Margarita Laux-Antille. 'I'm sad. I can't hide it. I was with him for four years, after all. But I had to dump him. It was hopeless ...'

'Particularly,' snorted Tissaia de Vries, staring at the golden wine as she swilled it around her cup, 'since Lars was married.'

'I consider that of no importance,' said the enchantress, shrugging. 'All the attractive men of a certain age and who interest me are married. I can't help that. Lars loved me and, I would add, loved me for quite some time ... Ah, what can I say? He wanted too much. He jeopardised my freedom, and the thought of monogamy makes me sick. And after all, I was only following your example, Yenna. Do you remember that conversation in Vengerberg? When you decided to break up with that witcher of yours? I advised you then to think twice. I told you, you can't find love in the street. But you were right. Love is love, and life is life. Love passes ...'

'Don't listen to her, Yennefer,' said Tissaia coldly. 'She's bitter and full of regrets. Do you know why she's not going to the banquet at Aretuza? Because she's ashamed to show up alone, without the man she's been involved with for four years. The man people envied her for. Who she lost because she was unable to value his love.'

'Perhaps we could talk about something else,' suggested Yennefer in an apparently carefree but slightly altered voice. 'Ciri, pour us some wine. Oh hell, that carafe's small. Be so kind as to bring us another.'

'Bring two,' laughed Margarita, 'and as a reward you'll get a sip and be able to sit with us; you won't have to strain your ears from a distance. Your education can begin here, right now, before you join me at Aretuza.'

'Education!' Tissaia raised her eyes to the ceiling. 'By the gods!'

'Oh, do be quiet, beloved mistress,' said Margarita, slapping a hand against her wet thigh, pretending to be angry. 'I'm the rectoress of the school now! You didn't manage to flunk me during the final exams!'

'I regret that.'

'I do, too! Just imagine, I'd have a private practice now, like Yenna. I wouldn't have to sweat with novices. I wouldn't have to wipe the noses of the blubbering ones or lock horns with the cheeky ones. Ciri, listen to me and learn. An enchantress always takes action. Wrongly or rightly; that is revealed later. But you should act, be brave, seize life by the scruff of the neck. Believe me, little one, you should only regret inactivity, indecisiveness, hesitation. You shouldn't regret actions or decisions, even if they occasionally end in sadness and regret. Look at that serious lady sitting there pulling faces and pedantically correcting everything in sight. That's Tissaia de Vries, arch-mistress, who has educated dozens of enchantresses. Teaching them how to act. Teaching them that indecision—'

'Enough, Rita.'

'Tissaia's right,' said Yennefer, still staring into the corner of the bathhouse. 'Stop. I know you're feeling low because of Lars, but don't moralise. The girl still has time for that kind of learning. And she won't receive it in school. Ciri, go and get another carafe.'

Ciri stood up. She was completely dressed.

And her mind was utterly made up.

'What?' Yennefer shrieked. 'What do you mean she's gone?'

'She ordered me ...' mumbled the innkeeper, pale, with his back pressed against the wall. 'She ordered me to saddle a horse ...'

'And you obeyed her? Rather than ask us?'

'Madam! How was I to know? I was sure she was leaving on your orders ... It never once occurred to me—'

'You damned fool!'

'Take it easy, Yennefer,' said Tissaia, pressing a hand against her forehead. 'Don't succumb to your emotions. It's night. They won't let her through the gate.'

'She ordered the postern opened ...' whispered the innkeeper.

'And was it?'

'Because of the conclave, madam,' said the innkeeper, lowering his eyes, 'the city is full of sorcerers ... People are afraid. No one dares to get in their way ... How could I refuse her? She spoke just like you do, madam, in exactly the same tone, and she looked the same way ... No one even dared to look her in the eye, never mind ask a question ... She was like you ... The spitting image ... She even ordered a quill and ink and wrote a letter.'

'Hand it over!'

Tissaia de Vries was quicker, and read aloud:

Madam Yennefer,

Forgive me. I'm riding to Hirundum because I want to see Geralt. I want to see him before I start school. Forgive my dis-obedience, but I must. I know you'll punish me, but I don't want

to regret my indecision and hesitation. If I'm to have regrets, let them be for deeds and actions. I'm an enchantress. I seize life by the scruff of the neck. I'll return when I can.
    Ciri

'Is that all?'
'There's also a postscript.'

Tell Madam Rita she won't have to wipe my nose at school.

Margarita Laux-Antille shook her head in disbelief as Yennefer cursed. The innkeeper flushed and opened his mouth. He'd heard many curses in his life, but never that one.

The wind blew from the land towards the sea. Waves of cloud drifted over the moon, suspended over the forest. The road to Hirundum was plunged into darkness making galloping too dangerous. Ciri slowed to a trot, but she didn't consider slowing to a walk. She was in a hurry.

The growling of an approaching storm could be heard in the distance, and from time to time the horizon was lit up by a flash of lightning, revealing the toothed saw of treetops against the dusk.

She reined in her horse. She was at a junction; the road forked and both forks looked identical.

Why hadn't Fabio said anything about a fork in the road? And anyway, I never get lost. After all, I always know which way to walk or ride ...

So why don't I know which road to take now?

A huge shape glided silently past her head and Ciri felt her heart in her throat. The horse neighed, kicked and galloped off, choosing the right-hand fork. After a moment, she reined it in.

'It was just an owl,' she panted, trying to calm herself and the horse. 'Just an ordinary bird ... There's nothing to be afraid of ...'

The wind grew stronger, and the dark clouds completely covered the moon. But before her, in the vista of the road, in the hole gaping among the trees, it was light. She rode faster, the sand flying up from the horse's hooves.

A little later she had to stop. In front of her was a cliff and the sea, from which the familiar black cone of the island rose up. The lights of Garstang, Loxia and Aretuza could not be seen from where she was. She could only see the soaring, solitary tower which crowned Thanedd.

Tor Lara.

A blinding bolt of lightning connected the overcast sky to the pinnacle of the tower, and a moment later it thundered. Tor Lara glowered at her, its windows become red eyes. For a second it seemed a fire was burning inside the tower.

Tor Lara ... The Tower of Gulls ... *Why does its name fill me with such dread?*

The gale tossed the trees around. The branches whispered. Ciri screwed up her eyes, and dust and leaves struck her cheek. She turned the snorting, skittering horse back, having regained her orientation. The Isle of Thanedd faced north, so she must have ridden westwards. The sandy road lay in the dusk like a bright, white ribbon. She set off again at a gallop.

Ciri suddenly saw some riders in a flash of lightning. Dark, vague, moving shapes on both sides of the road. It thundered once more and she heard a cry.

'Gar'ean!'

Without thinking, she spurred her horse, reined it back, turned around and galloped away. Behind her there were shouts, whistles, neighing and the thudding of hooves.

'Gar'ean! Dh'oine!'

Galloping, the thud of hooves, the rush of the wind. Darkness, with the white trunks of roadside birches flashing by. Lightning. A thunderclap. And, in its light, two riders trying to block her way. One reached out, trying to grab her reins. He had a squirrel's tail attached to his hat. Ciri kicked her horse with her heels, clinging to its neck, the speed pulling her over to one side. Lightning. Behind her rose shouting, whistling and a clap of thunder.

'Spar'le, Yaevinn!'

Gallop, gallop! Quicker, horse! Lightning. Thunder. A fork in the road. *To the left! I never lose my way!* Another fork. *To the right! Gallop, horse! Faster, faster!*

The road went uphill, sand under the horse's hooves. The horse, even though it was being spurred on, slowed ...

She looked around at the top of the hill. Another lightning flash lit up the road. It was totally empty. She listened hard but only heard the wind whistling in the leaves. It thundered again.

There's no one here. Squirrels ... it's just a memory from Kaedwen. The Rose of Shaerrawedd ... I imagined it. There isn't a living soul here. No one's chasing me ...

The wind struck her. *The wind's blowing from the land,* she thought, *and I can feel it on my right cheek ...*

I'm lost.

Lightning. It lit up the surface of the sea against the black cone of the Isle of Thanedd. And Tor Lara. The Tower of Gulls. The tower that was drawing Ciri like a magnet ... *But I don't want to go to that tower. I'm riding to Hirundum. I must see Geralt.*

Lightning flashed again.

A black horse stood between her and the cliff. And on it sat a knight in a helmet adorned with the wings of a bird of prey. Its wings suddenly flapped, the bird took flight ...

Cintra!

Paralysing fear. Her hands gripping the reins tightly. Lightning. The black knight spurred his horse. He had a ghastly mask instead of a face. The wings flapped ...

The horse set off at a gallop without needing to be urged. Darkness illuminated by lightning. The forest was coming to an end. The splash and squelch of swamp under the horse's hooves. Behind her the swish of a raptor's wings. Closer and closer ... Closer ...

A furious gallop, her eyes watering from their speed. Lightning sliced the sky, and in its flash Ciri saw alders and willows on either side of the road. But they weren't trees. They were the servants of the Alder King. Servants of the black knight, who was galloping after her, with raptor's wings swishing on his helmet. Misshapen monsters on both sides of the road stretched their gnarled arms towards her; they laughed insanely, the black jaws of their hollows opening wide. Ciri flattened herself against the horse's neck. Branches whistled, lashed her and tore at her clothes. The distorted trunks creaked and the hollow jaws snapped, howling with scornful laughter ...

The Lion Cub of Cintra! Child of the Elder Blood!

The black knight was right behind her; Ciri felt his hand trying to seize her long hair. The horse, urged on by her cries, leapt forward, cleared an unseen obstacle with a powerful bound, crashed through reeds, stumbled ...

She reined it in, leaning back in the saddle, and turned the snorting horse back. She screamed wildly, furiously. She yanked her sword from its scabbard and whirled it above her head. *This is Cintra no longer! I'm no longer a child! I'm no longer helpless! I won't allow it ...*

'I forbid it! You will not touch me again! You will never touch me!'

Her horse landed in the water with a splash and a squelch, belly-deep. Ciri leaned forward, cried out, urged her mount on with her heels and struggled back onto the causeway again. *Ponds*, she thought. *Fabio talked about fishponds. It's Hirundum. I've made it. I never lose my way ...*

Lightning. Behind her the causeway, ahead of her a black wall of forest cutting into the sky like a saw blade. And no one there. Silence broken only by the howling of the gale. Somewhere on the marsh she could hear a frightened duck quacking.

Nobody. There is no one on the causeway. No one's following me. It was a phantom, a nightmare. Memories from Cintra. I only imagined it.

A small light in the distance. A lighthouse. Or a fire. *It's a farm. Hirundum. It's close now. Only one more effort ...*

Flashes of lightning. One. Another. Yet another. Each without a thunderclap. The wind suddenly dropped. The horse neighs, tosses its head and rears up.

Against the black sky appears a milky, quickly brightening ribbon, writhing like a serpent. The wind hits the willows once more, throwing up clouds of leaves and dry grass.

The distant lights vanish. They disappear and blur in the deluge of the million blue sparks which suddenly light up the entire swamp.

The horse snorts, whinnies and charges frantically across the causeway. Ciri struggles to remain in the saddle.

The vague, ghastly shapes of riders become visible in the ribbon sliding across the sky. As they come closer and closer, they can be seen ever more clearly. Buffalo horns and ragged crests sway on their helmets, and cadaverous masks show white beneath them. The riders sit on horses' skeletons, cloaked in ragged caparisons. A fierce gale howls among the willows, blades of lightning slash the black sky. The wind moans louder and louder. No, it's not the wind. It's ghostly singing.

The ghostly cavalcade turns and hurtles straight at her. The hooves of the spectral horses stir up the glow of the will o' the wisps suspended above the swamps. At the head of the cavalcade gallops the King of the Wild Hunt. A rusty helmet sways above his skull-like face, its gaping eye sockets burning with a livid flame. A ragged cloak flutters. A necklace, as empty as an old peapod, rattles against the rusty cuirass, a necklace which, it is said, once contained precious stones, which fell out during the frenzied chase across the heavens. And became stars . . .

It isn't true! It doesn't exist! It's a nightmare, a phantom, an illusion! I'm only imagining this!

The King of the Wild Hunt spurs on his skeleton steed and erupts in wild, horrifying laughter.

O, Child of the Elder Blood! You belong to us! You are ours! Join our procession, join our hunt! We will race, race unto the very end, unto eternity, unto the very end of existence! You are ours, starry-eyed daughter of chaos! Join us; learn the joy of the hunt! You are ours. You are one of us! Your place is among us!

'No!' she cries. 'Be gone! You are corpses!'

The King of the Wild Hunt laughs, the rotten teeth snapping above his rusted gorget. The skull's eye sockets glitter lividly.

Yes, we are corpses. But you are death.

Ciri clung to the horse's neck. She didn't have to urge her horse on. Sensing the pursuing apparitions behind her, the steed thundered across the causeway at a breakneck gallop.

*

The halfling Bernie Hofmeier, a Hirundum farmer, lifted his shock of curly locks, listening to the sound of the distant thunder.

'It's a dangerous thing,' he said, 'a storm like this without any rain. Lightning will strike somewhere and then you've got a fire on your hands ...'

'A little rain would come in handy,' sighed Dandelion, tightening up the pegs of his lute, 'because you could cut the air with a knife ... My shirt's stuck to my back and the mosquitoes are biting ... But I reckon it'll blow over. The storm has been circling, circling, but for a while there's been lightning somewhere in the north. Over the sea, I think.'

'It's hitting Thanedd,' confirmed the halfling, 'the highest point in the area. That tower on the island, Tor Lara, attracts lightning like nobody's business. It looks like it's on fire during a decent storm. It's a wonder it doesn't fall apart ...'

'It's magic,' said the troubadour with conviction. 'Everything on Thanedd is magic, even the rock itself. And sorcerers aren't afraid of thunderbolts. What am I saying? Did you know, Bernie, that they can even catch thunderbolts?'

'Get away! You're lying, Dandelion.'

'May the lightning strike me—' the poet broke off, anxiously looking up at the sky. 'May a goose nip me if I'm lying. I'm telling you, Hofmeier, sorcerers catch thunderbolts. I've seen it with my own eyes. Old Gorazd, the one who was killed on Sodden Hill, once caught a thunderbolt in front of my very eyes. He took a long, thin piece of metal, he hooked one end of it onto the top of his tower, and the other—'

'You should put the other end in a bottle,' suddenly squeaked Hofmeier's son, who was hanging around on the veranda. He was a tiny little halfling with a thick mop of hair as curly as a ram's fleece. 'In a glass demijohn, like the ones Daddy makes wine in. The lightning whizzes down the wire into the demijohn—'

'Get inside, Franklin!' yelled the farmer. 'Time for bed, this minute! It'll be midnight soon and there's work to be done tomorrow! And just you wait till I catch you, spouting off about demijohns and wires. The strap'll be out for you! You won't be able to sit down

96

for the next two Sundays! Petunia, get him out of here! And bring us more beer!'

'You've had quite enough,' said Petunia Hofmeier angrily, gathering up her son from the veranda. 'You've already put away a skinful.'

'Stop nagging. Just look out for the Witcher's coming. A guest ought to be offered hospitality.'

'When the Witcher arrives I'll bring some. For him.'

'Stingy cow,' muttered Hofmeier so that his wife didn't hear. 'All her kin, the Biberveldts from Knotweed Meadow, every last one of them is a tight-fisted, stingy, skinflint ... But the Witcher's taking his time. He went over to the ponds and disappeared. 'E's a strange one. Did you see how he looked at the girls, at Cinia and Tangerine, when they were playing in the yard of an evening? He had a strange look about him. And now ... I can't help feeling he went away to be by himself. And he took shelter with me because my farm's out of the way, far from the others. You know him best, Dandelion, you say ...'

'Do I know him?' said the poet, swatting a mosquito on his neck, plucking his lute and staring at the black outlines of willows by the pond. 'No, Bernie. I don't know him. I don't think anyone knows him. But something's happening to him, I can see it. Why did he come here, to Hirundum? To be nearer the Isle of Thanedd? And yesterday, when I suggested we both ride to Gors Velen, from where you can see Thanedd, he refused without a second thought. What's keeping him here? Did you give him some well-paid contracts?'

'Not a chance,' muttered the halfling. 'To be honest, I don't believe there was ever a monster here at all. That kid who drowned in the pond might have got cramp. But everyone started yelling that it was a drowner or a kikimora and we ought to call a witcher ... And they promised him such a paltry purse it's shameful. And what does he do? He's been roaming around the causeway for three nights; he sleeps during the day or sits saying nothing, like a straw man, watching the children and the house ... Strange. Peculiar, I'd say.'

'And you'd be right.'

Lightning flashed, lighting up the farmyard and the farm buildings. For a moment, the ruins of the elven palace at the end of the causeway flashed white. A few seconds later, a clap of thunder rolled over the ponds. A sudden wind got up, and the trees and reeds by the pond whispered and bent. The surface of the water rippled, went dull and then ruffled up the leaves of the water lilies.

'The storm seems to be coming towards us,' said the farmer, looking up at the sky. 'Perhaps the sorcerers used magic to drive it from the island. They say at least two hundred of them have turned up on Thanedd ... What do you think, Dandelion, what will they be debating on that island of theirs? Will any good come of it?'

'For us? I doubt it,' said the troubadour, strumming the lute strings with his thumb. 'Those conclaves usually mean a fashion show, lots of gossiping, and a good chance for backbiting and infighting. Arguments about whether to make magic more universal, or make it more elite. Quarrels between those who serve kings and those who prefer to bring pressure to bear on kings from afar ...'

'Ha,' said Bernie Hofmeier. 'Seems to me that during the conclave there'll be as much thunder and lightning on Thanedd as there is during a storm.'

'Perhaps. But of what interest is it to us?'

'To you, none,' said the halfling gloomily. 'Because all you do is pluck away at your lute and screech. You look at the world around and see only rhymes and notes. But just last Sunday some horsemen trampled my cabbages and turnips. Twice. The army are chasing the Squirrels, the Squirrels are evading the army and running from them, and they both use the same road through my cabbage patch ...'

'Do not grieve for the cabbage when the forest is burning,' recited the poet.

'You, Dandelion,' said Bernie Hofmeier, frowning at him. 'When you come out with stuff like that I don't know whether to cry, laugh or kick your arse. I kid you not! And I'm telling you, a wretched time has come. There are stakes and gibbets by the highways, corpses in the fields and by forest tracks. Gorblimey, the country must have looked like this in Falka's times. And how can anyone live here? During the day, the king's men come and threaten to put us in the stocks for helping the Squirrels; at night the elves show up, and just try turning them down! They poetically promise that we'll see the night sky glow red. They're so poetic you could throw up. But anyhow, with them both we're caught between two fires ...'

'And are you counting on the mages' conclave changing anything?'

'That I am. You said yourself that two factions are battling it out among the mages. It was sometimes thus, that the sorcerers held the kings back and put an end to wars and disturbances. After all, it was the sorcerers who made peace with Nilfgaard three years since. Mebbe this time too ...'

Bernie Hofmeier fell silent and listened carefully. Dandelion silenced the resonating strings with his hand.

The Witcher emerged from the gloom on the causeway. He walked slowly towards the house. Lightning flashed once more. By the time it thundered, the Witcher was already with them on the veranda.

'Well, Geralt?' asked Dandelion, by way of ending the awkward silence. 'Did you track the fiend down?'

'No. It isn't a night for tracking. It's a turbulent night. Uneasy ... I'm tired, Dandelion.'

'Well, sit down, relax.'

'You misunderstood me.'

'Indeed,' muttered the halfling, looking at the sky and listening. 'A turbulent night, something ill is hanging in the air ... The animals are restless in the barn ... And screams can be heard in that wind ...'

'The Wild Hunt,' said the Witcher softly. 'Close the shutters securely, Mr Hofmeier.'

'The Wild Hunt?' said Bernie, terrified. 'Spectres?'

'Never fear. It'll pass by high up. It always passes by high during the summer. But the children may wake, for the Hunt brings nightmares. Better close the shutters.'

'The Wild Hunt,' said Dandelion, glancing anxiously upwards, 'heralds war.'

'Poppycock. Superstitions.'

'Wait! A short time before the Nilfgaardian attack on Cintra—'

'Silence!' the Witcher gestured him to be quiet and sat up straight with a jerk, staring into the darkness.

'What the ... ?'

'Horsemen.'

'Hell,' hissed Hofmeier, springing up from the bench. 'At night it can only be Scoia'tael ...'

'A single horse,' the Witcher interrupted, picking his sword up from the bench. 'A single, real horse. The rest are the spectres of the Hunt ... Damn, it can't be ... in the summer?'

Dandelion had also leapt to his feet but was too ashamed to run away, because neither Geralt nor Bernie was preparing to flee. The Witcher drew his sword and ran towards the causeway, and the half-ling rushed after him without a second thought, armed with a pitch-fork. Lightning flashed once more, and a galloping horse came into view on the causeway. Behind the horse came something vague, an irregular cloud, a whirl, a phantom, woven from the gloom and glow. Something that caused panicky fear and a revolting, gut-wrenching dread.

The Witcher yelled, lifting his sword. The rider saw him, spurred the horse on and looked back. The Witcher yelled again. The thun-der boomed.

There was a flash, but it wasn't lightning this time. Dandelion crouched by the bench and would have crawled under it had it not been too low. Bernie dropped the pitchfork. Petunia Hofmeier, who had run out of the house, shrieked.

A blinding flash materialised into a transparent sphere, and inside it loomed a shape, assuming contours and shapes at frightening speed. Dandelion recognised it at once. He knew those wild, black curls and the obsidian star on a velvet ribbon. What he didn't know and had never seen before was the face. It was a face of rage and fury, the face of the goddess of vengeance, destruction and death.

Yennefer raised a hand and screamed a spell. Spirals shot from her hands with a hiss, showering sparks, cutting the night sky and reflect-ing thousands of sparkles on the surface of the ponds. The spirals penetrated the cloud that was chasing the lone rider like lances. The cloud seethed, and it seemed to Dandelion that he could hear ghastly cries, that he could see the vague, nightmarish silhouettes of spectral horses. He only saw it for a split second, because the cloud suddenly contracted, clustered up into a ball and shot upwards into the sky, lengthening and dragging a tail behind it like a comet's as it sped away. Darkness fell, only lit by the quivering glare of the lamp being held by Petunia Hofmeier.

The rider came to a halt in the yard in front of the house, slithered down from the saddle, and took some staggering steps. Dandelion realised who it was immediately. He had never seen the slim, flaxen-haired girl before. But he knew her at once.

'Geralt . . .' said the girl softly. 'Madam Yennefer . . . I'm sorry . . . I had to. You know, I mean . . .'

'Ciri,' said the Witcher. Yennefer took a step towards the girl, but then stopped. She said nothing.

Who will the girl choose? wondered Dandelion. *Neither of them – the Witcher nor the enchantress – will take a step nor make a gesture. Which will she approach first? Him? Or her?*

Ciri did not walk to either of them. She was unable to decide. Instead of moving, she fainted.

The house was empty. The halfling and his entire family had left for work at daybreak. Ciri pretended to be asleep but she heard Geralt and Yennefer go out. She slipped out from the sheets, dressed quickly and stole silently out of the room, following them to the orchard.

Geralt and Yennefer turned to face the causeway between the ponds, which were white and yellow with water lilies. Ciri hid behind a ruined wall and watched them through a crack. She had imagined that Dandelion, the famous poet whose work she had read count-less times, was still asleep. But she was wrong. The poet Dandelion wasn't asleep. And he caught her in the act.

'Hey,' he said, coming up unexpectedly and chuckling. 'Is it polite to eavesdrop and spy on people? More discretion, little one. Let them be together for a while.'

Ciri blushed, but then immediately narrowed her lips.

'First of all, I'm not your little one,' she hissed haughtily. 'And second of all, I'm not really disturbing them, am I?'

Dandelion grew a little serious.

'I suppose not,' he said. 'It seems to me you might even be helping them.'

'How? In what way?'

'Don't kid me. That was very cunning yesterday, but you didn't fool me. You pretended to faint, didn't you?'

'Yes, I did,' she muttered, turning her face away. 'Madam Yennefer realised but Geralt didn't ...'

'They carried you into the house together. Their hands were touching. They sat by your bed almost until morning but they didn't say a word to each other. They've only decided to talk now. There, on the causeway, by the pond. And you've decided to eavesdrop on what they're saying ... And watch them through a hole in the wall. Are you so desperate to know what they're doing there?'

'They aren't doing anything there,' said Ciri, blushing slightly. 'They're talking a little, that's all.'

'And you,' said Dandelion, sitting down on the grass under an apple tree and leaning back against the trunk, having first checked whether there were any ants or caterpillars on it. 'You'd like to know what they're talking about, wouldn't you?'

'Yes ... No! And anyway ... Anyway, I can't hear anything. They're too far away.'

'I'll tell you,' laughed the bard. 'If you want.'

'And how are you supposed to know?'

'Ha, ha. I, my dear Ciri, am a poet. Poets know everything about things like this. I'll tell you something else; poets know more about this sort of thing than the people involved do.'

'Of course you do!'

'I give you my word. The word of a poet.'

'Really? Well then ... Tell me what they're talking about? Tell me what it all means!'

'Look through that hole again and tell me what they're doing.'

'Hmm ...' Ciri bit her lower lip, then leaned over and put her eye closer to the hole. 'Madam Yennefer is standing by a willow ... She's plucking leaves and playing with her star. She isn't saying anything and isn't even looking at Geralt ... And Geralt's standing beside her. He's looking down and he's saying something. No, he isn't. Oh, he's pulling a face ... What a strange expression ...'

'Childishly simple,' said Dandelion, finding an apple in the grass, wiping it on his trousers and examining it critically. 'He's asking her to forgive him for his various foolish words and deeds. He's apologising to her for his impatience, for his lack of faith and hope, for his obstinacy, doggedness. For his sulking and posing; which are unworthy of a man. He's apologising to her for things he didn't understand and for things he hadn't wanted to understand—'

'That's the falsest lie!' said Ciri, straightening up and tossing the fringe away from her forehead with a sudden movement. 'You're making it all up!'

'He's apologising for things he's only now understood,' said Dandelion, staring at the sky, and he began to speak with the rhythm of a balladeer. 'For what he'd like to understand, but is afraid he won't have time for ... And for what he will never understand. He's apologising and asking for forgiveness ... Hmm, hmm ... Meaning, conscience, destiny? Everything's so bloody banal ...'

'That's not true!' Ciri stamped. 'Geralt isn't saying anything like that! He's not even speaking. I saw for myself. He's standing with her and saying nothing ...'

'That's the role of poetry, Ciri. To say what others cannot utter.'

'It's a stupid role. And you're making everything up!'

'That is also the role of poetry. Hey, I hear some raised voices coming from the pond. Have a quick look, and see what's happening there.'

'Geralt,' said Ciri, putting her eye once more to the hole in the wall, 'is standing with his head bowed. And Yennefer's yelling at him. She's screaming and waving her arms. Oh dear ... What can it mean?'

'It's childishly simple.' Dandelion stared at the clouds scudding across the sky. 'Now she's saying sorry to him.'

Thus do I take you, to have and to hold, for the most wondrous and terrible of times, for the best and the worst of times, by day and by night, in sickness and in health. For I love you with all my heart and swear to love you eternally, until death do us part.

Traditional marriage vows

We know little about love. Love is like a pear. A pear is sweet and has a distinct shape. Try to define the shape of a pear.

Dandelion, *Half a Century of Poetry*

CHAPTER THREE

Geralt had reason to suspect – and had long suspected – that sorcerers' banquets differed from the feasts of ordinary mortals. He never suspected, however, that the differences could be so great or so fundamental.

The offer of accompanying Yennefer to the banquet preceding the sorcerers' conclave surprised but did not dumbfound him, since it was not the first such proposal. Previously, when they lived together and things were good between them, Yennefer had wanted to attend assemblies and conclaves with him at her side. At that time, he steadfastly refused. He was convinced he would be treated by the sorcerers at best as a freak and a spectacle, and at worst as an intruder and a pariah. Yennefer scoffed at his fears, but had never insisted. Since in other situations she was capable of insisting until the house shook and windows shattered, that had confirmed Geralt's belief that his decision had been right.

This time he agreed. Without a second thought. The offer came after a long, frank and emotional conversation. After a conversation which had brought them closer again, consigned the old conflicts to the shadows and to oblivion, and melted the ice of resentment, pride and stubbornness. After their conversation on the causeway in Hirundum, Geralt would have agreed to any – absolutely any – proposition of Yennefer's. He would not even have declined had she suggested they walked into hell to drink a cup of boiling tar with some fiery demons.

And on top of it there was Ciri, without whom neither that conversation nor that meeting could have happened. Ciri, in whom – according to Codringher – some unknown sorcerer had taken an interest. Geralt expected his presence at the convocation to provoke that sorcerer and force his hand. But he didn't tell Yennefer a single word about it.

They rode straight from Hirundum to Thanedd: Geralt, Yennefer, Ciri and Dandelion. First they stopped at the immense palace complex of Loxia, at the south-eastern foot of the mountain. The palace was already teeming with delegates to the conclave and their companions but accommodation was immediately found for Yennefer. They spent the entire day in Loxia. Geralt whiled away the day talking to Ciri. Dandelion ran around collecting and spreading gossip, and the enchantress measured and chose clothes. When evening finally came, the Witcher and Yennefer joined the colourful procession heading towards Aretuza and the palace, where the banquet was due to take place. And now, in Aretuza, Geralt knew surprise and astonishment, even though he'd vowed to himself he wouldn't be surprised by anything and nothing would astonish him.

The palace's huge central hall had been constructed in the shape of a letter 'T'. The long side had narrow and extremely tall windows, reaching almost to the tops of the columns that supported the ceiling. The ceiling was so high it was difficult to make out the details of the frescoes decorating it, in particular the gender of the naked figures, which were their most common motif. The windows were of stained glass, which must have cost an absolute fortune, but in spite of that a draught could be felt distinctly in the hall. Geralt was initially surprised the candles didn't go out, but on closer inspection he understood why. The candelabras were magical, and possibly even illusory. In any case, they gave plenty of light, incomparably more than candles would have.

When they entered, a good hundred people were already there. The hall, the Witcher estimated, could have held at least three times as many, even if the tables had been arranged in a semicircle in the centre, as was customary. But there was no traditional semicircle. It appeared they would be banqueting standing up, doggedly wandering along walls adorned with tapestries, garlands and pennants, all waving in the draught. Rows of long tables had been arranged under the tapestries and garlands, and the tables were piled high with elaborate dishes served on even more elaborate table settings, among elaborate flower arrangements and extraordinary ice carvings. On closer examination, Geralt noted there was considerably more elaboration than food.

'There's no fare,' he stated in a glum voice, smoothing down the short, black, silver-braided, narrow-waisted tunic Yennefer had dressed him in. Tunics like that – the latest fashion – were called doublets. The Witcher had no idea where the name came from. And no desire to find out.

Yennefer didn't react. Geralt wasn't expecting her to, knowing well that the enchantress was not generally inclined to react to statements of that kind. But he didn't give up. He continued to complain. He simply felt like moaning.

'There's no music. It's draughty as hell. There's nowhere to sit down. Are we going to eat and drink standing up?'

The enchantress gave him a meaningful, violet glance.

'Indeed,' she said, surprisingly calmly. 'We shall be eating standing up. You should also know that stopping too long by the food table is considered an indiscretion.'

'I shall try to behave,' he muttered. 'Particularly since I observe there isn't much to stop by.'

'Drinking in an unrestrained way is also considered a breach of etiquette,' said Yennefer, continuing her instructions and paying absolutely no attention to his grizzling. 'Avoiding conversations is considered an inexcusable indiscretion—'

'And if that beanpole in those ridiculous pantaloons points me out to his two girlfriends,' he interrupted, 'is that considered a faux pas?'

'Yes. But a minor one.'

'What are we going to be doing, Yen?'

'Circulating around the hall, greeting people, paying them compliments, engaging in conversation ... Stop tugging your doublet and flattening your hair.'

'You wouldn't let me wear a headband ...'

'Your headband's pretentious. Well then, take my arm and let's go. Standing near the entrance is considered a faux pas.'

They wandered through the hall, which was gradually filling up with guests. Geralt was ravenously hungry but quickly realised Yennefer hadn't been joking. It became clear that the etiquette observed by mages did indeed demand that one eat and drink very little, and do it with a nonchalant air. To cap it all, every stop at the food table carried with it social obligations. Someone would notice you, express their joy

109

at the fact and then approach and offer their greetings, which were as effusive as they were disingenuous. After the compulsory air kisses or unpleasantly weak handshakes, after the insincere smiles and even less sincere, although well-concocted, compliments, followed a brief and tediously banal conversation about nothing.

The Witcher looked around eagerly, searching for familiar faces, mainly in the hope he wasn't the only person present who didn't belong to this magical fraternity. Yennefer had assured him he wouldn't be, but in spite of that he couldn't see anyone who wasn't a member of the Brotherhood, or at least he was unable to recognise anyone.

Pageboys carrying trays weaved among the guests, serving wine. Yennefer didn't drink at all. The Witcher wanted to get tight, but couldn't. Instead, he found his doublet was. Under the arms.

Skilfully steering Geralt with her arm, the enchantress pulled him away from the table and led him into the middle of the hall, to the very centre of general interest. His resistance counted for nothing. He realised what this was all about. It was quite simply a display.

Geralt knew what to expect, so with stoical calm he endured the glances of the enchantresses, brimming with insalubrious curiosity, and the enigmatic smirks of the sorcerers. Although Yennefer assured him that propriety and tact forbade the use of magic at this kind of event, he didn't believe the mages were capable of restraining themselves, particularly since Yennefer was provocatively thrusting him into the limelight. And he was right not to believe. He felt his medallion vibrating several times, and the pricking of magical impulses. Some sorcerers, or more precisely some enchantresses, brazenly tried to read his thoughts. He was prepared for that, knew what was happening, and knew how to respond. He looked at Yennefer walking alongside him, at white-and-black-and-diamond Yennefer, with her raven hair and violet eyes, and the sorcerers trying to sound him out became unsettled and disorientated; confronted with his blissful satisfaction, they were clearly losing their composure and poise. *Yes*, he answered in his thoughts, *you're not mistaken. There is only she, Yennefer, at my side, here and now, and only she matters. Here and now. And what she was long ago, where she was long ago and who she was with long ago doesn't have any, doesn't*

110

have the slightest, importance. Now she's with me, here, among you all. With me, with no one else. That's what I'm thinking right now, thinking only about her, thinking endlessly about her, smelling the scent of her perfume and the warmth of her body. And you can all choke on your envy.

The enchantress squeezed his forearm firmly and moved closer to his side.

'Thank you,' she murmured, guiding him towards the tables once again. 'But without such excessive ostentation, if you don't mind.'

'Do you mages always take sincerity for ostentation? Is that why you don't believe in sincerity, even when you read it in someone's mind?'

'Yes. That *is* why.'

'But you still thank me?'

'Because I believe you,' she said, squeezing his arm even tighter and picking up a plate. 'Give me a little salmon, Witcher. And some crab.'

'These crabs are from Poviss. They were probably caught a month ago; and it's really hot right now. Aren't you worried ... ?'

'These crabs,' she interrupted, 'were still creeping along the seabed this morning. Teleportation is a wonderful invention.'

'Indeed,' he concurred. 'It ought to be made more widely available, don't you think?'

'We're working on it. Come on, give me some. I'm hungry.'

'I love you, Yen.'

'I said drop the ostentation ...' she broke off, tossed her head, drew some black curls away from her cheek and opened her violet eyes wide. 'Geralt! It's the first time you've ever said that!'

'It can't be. You're making fun of me.'

'No, no I'm not. You used only to think it, but today you said it.'

'Is there such a difference?'

'A huge one.'

'Yen ...'

'Don't talk with your mouth full. I love you too. Haven't I ever told you? Heavens, you'll choke! Lift your arms up and I'll thump you in the back. Take some deep breaths.'

111

'Yen ...'

'Keep breathing, it'll soon pass.'

'Yen!'

'Yes. I'm repaying sincerity with sincerity.'

'Are you feeling all right?'

'I was waiting,' she said, squeezing lemon on the salmon. 'It wouldn't have been proper to react to a declaration made as a thought. I was waiting for the words. I was able to reply, so I replied. I feel wonderful.'

'What's up?'

'I'll tell you later. Eat. This salmon is delicious, I swear on the Power, absolutely delicious.'

'May I kiss you? Right now, here, in front of everyone?'

'No.'

'Yennefer!' A dark-haired sorceress passing alongside freed her arm from the crook of her companion's elbow and came closer. 'So you made it? Oh, how divine! I haven't seen you for ages!'

'Sabrina!' said Yennefer, displaying such genuine joy that anyone apart from Geralt might have been deceived. 'Darling! How wonderful!'

The enchantresses embraced gingerly and kissed each other beside their ears and their diamond and onyx earrings. The two enchantresses' earrings, resembling miniature bunches of grapes, were identical; but the whiff of fierce hostility immediately floated in the air.

'Geralt, if I may. This is a school friend of mine, Sabrina Glevissig of Ard Carraigh.'

The Witcher bowed and kissed the raised hand. He had already observed that all enchantresses expected to be greeted by being kissed on the hand, a gesture which awarded them the same status as princesses, to put it mildly. Sabrina Glevissig raised her head, her earrings shaking and jingling. Gently, but ostentatiously and impudently.

'I've been so looking forward to meeting you, Geralt,' she said with a smile. Like all enchantresses, she didn't recognise any 'sirs', 'Your Excellencies' or other forms of address used among the nobility. 'You can't believe how delighted I am. You've finally stopped hiding him from us, Yenna. Speaking frankly, I'm amazed you put it off for so long. You have absolutely nothing to be ashamed of.'

'I agree,' replied Yennefer nonchalantly, narrowing her eyes a little and ostentatiously tossing her hair back from her own earrings. 'Gorgeous blouse, Sabrina. Simply stunning. Isn't it, Geralt?'

The Witcher nodded and swallowed. Sabrina Glevissig's blouse, made of black chiffon, revealed absolutely everything there was to reveal, and there was plenty of it. Her crimson skirt, gathered in by a silver belt with a large rose-shaped buckle, was split up the side, in keeping with the latest fashion. Fashion demanded it be split half-way up the thigh, but Sabrina wore hers split to halfway up her hip. And a very nice hip at that.

'What's new in Kaedwen?' asked Yennefer, pretending not to see what Geralt was looking at. 'Is your King Henselt still wasting energy and resources chasing the Squirrels through the forests? Is he still thinking about a punitive expedition against the elves from Dol Blathann?'

'Let's give politics a rest,' smiled Sabrina. Her slightly too-long nose and predatory eyes made her resemble the classic image of a witch. 'Tomorrow, at the Council, we'll be politicking until it comes out of our ears. And we'll hear plenty of moralising, too. About the need for peaceful coexistence ... About friendship ... About the necessity to adopt a loyal position regarding the plans and ambitions of our kings ... What else shall we hear, Yennefer? What else are the Chapter and Vilgefortz preparing for us?'

'Let's give politics a rest.'

Sabrina Glevissig gave a silvery laugh, echoed by the gentle jingling of her earrings.

'Indeed. Let's wait until tomorrow. Tomorrow ... Everything will become clear tomorrow. Oh, politics, and those endless debates, what an awful effect they have on the complexion. Fortunately, I have an excellent cream. Believe me, darling, wrinkles disappear like morning mist ... Shall I give you the formula?'

'Thank you, darling, but I don't need it. Truly.'

'Oh, I know. I always envied your complexion at school. How many years is it now, by the gods?'

Yennefer pretended she was returning a greeting to someone passing alongside, while Sabrina smiled at the Witcher and joyously thrust out everything the black chiffon wasn't hiding. Geralt swallowed again, trying not to look too blatantly at her pink nipples, only too visible beneath the transparent material. He glanced timidly at Yennefer. The enchantress smiled, but he knew her too well. She was incandescent.

'Oh, forgive me,' said Yennefer suddenly. 'I can see Philippa over there; I just have to talk to her. Come with me, Geralt. Bye-bye, Sabrina.'

'Bye, Yenna,' said Sabrina Glevissig, looking the Witcher in the eyes. 'Congratulations again on your ... taste.'

'Thank you,' said Yennefer, her voice suspiciously cold. 'Thank you, darling.'

Philippa Eilhart was accompanied by Dijkstra. Geralt, who'd once had a fleeting contact with the Redanian spy, ought in principle to have been pleased; he had finally met someone he knew, who – like he – didn't belong to the fraternity. Yet he wasn't glad at all.

'How lovely to see you, Yenna,' said Philippa, giving Yennefer an air kiss. 'Greetings, Geralt. You both know Count Dijkstra, don't you?'

'Who doesn't?' said Yennefer, bowing her head and proffering her hand to Dijkstra. The spy kissed it with reverence. 'I'm delighted to see you again, Your Excellency.'

'It's a joy for me to see you again, Yennefer,' replied the chief of King Vizimir's secret service. 'Particularly in such agreeable company. Geralt, my respects come from the bottom of my heart ...'

Geralt, refraining from telling Dijkstra *his* respect came from the heart of his bottom, shook the proffered hand – or rather tried to. Its dimensions exceeded the norm which made shaking it practically impossible.

The gigantic spy was dressed in a light beige doublet, unbuttoned informally. He clearly felt at ease in it.

'I noticed,' said Philippa, 'you talking to Sabrina.'

'That's right,' snorted Yennefer. 'Have you seen what she's wearing? You'd either have to have no taste or no shame to ... She's bloody older than me by at least— Never mind. And as if she still had anything to show! The revolting cow!'

'Did she try to question you? Everyone knows she spies for Henselt of Kaedwen.'

'You don't say?' said Yennefer, faking astonishment, which was rightly considered an excellent joke.

'And you, Your Excellency, are you enjoying our celebration?' asked Yennefer, after Philippa and Dijkstra had stopped laughing.

'Extraordinarily,' said King Vizimir's spy, giving a courtly bow.

'If we presume,' said Philippa, smiling, 'that the Count is here on business, such an assurance is extremely complimentary. And, like every similar compliment, not very sincere. Only a moment ago, he confessed he'd prefer a nice, murky atmosphere, the stink of flaming brands and scorched meat on a spit. He also misses a traditional table swimming in spilt sauce and beer, which he could bang with his beer mug to the rhythm of a few filthy, drunken songs, and which he could gracefully slide under in the early hours, to fall asleep among hounds gnawing bones. And, just imagine, he remains deaf to my arguments extolling the superiority of our way of banqueting.'

'Indeed?' said the Witcher, looking at the spy more benignly. 'And what were those arguments, if I might ask?'

This time his question was clearly treated as an excellent joke, because both enchantresses began laughing at the same time.

'Oh, you men,' said Philippa. 'You don't understand anything. How can you show off your dress or your figure if you're hiding behind a table in the gloom and smoke?'

Geralt, unable to find the words, merely bowed. Yennefer squeezed his arm gently.

'Oh,' she said. 'I see Triss Merigold over there. I just have to exchange a few words with her . . . Excuse me for abandoning you. Take care, Philippa. We will certainly find an opportunity for a chat today. Won't we, Your Excellency?'

'Undoubtedly,' said Dijkstra, smiling and bowing low. 'At your service, Yennefer. Your wish is my command.'

They went over to Triss, who was shimmering in shades of blue and pale green. On seeing them, Triss broke off her conversation with two sorcerers, smiled radiantly and hugged Yennefer; the ritual of kissing the air near each other's ears was repeated. Geralt took the proffered hand, but decided to act contrary to the rules of etiquette; he embraced the chestnut-haired enchantress and kissed her on her soft cheek, as downy as a peach. Triss blushed faintly.

The sorcerers introduced themselves. One of them was Drithelm of Pont Vanis, the other his brother, Detmold. They were both in the service of King Esterad of Kovir. Both proved to be taciturn and both moved away at the first opportunity that presented itself.

'You were talking to Philippa and Dijkstra of Tretogor,' observed Triss, playing with a lapis-lazuli heart set in silver and diamonds, which hung around from her neck. 'You know who Dijkstra is, of course?'

'Yes, we do,' said Yennefer. 'Did he talk to you? Did he try to get anything out of you?'

'He tried,' said the enchantress, smiling knowingly and giggling. 'Quite subtly. But Philippa was doing a good job throwing him off his stride. And I thought they were on better terms.'

'They're on excellent terms,' Yennefer warned her gravely. 'Be careful, Triss. Don't breathe a word to him about – about you know who.'

'I know. I'll be careful. And by the way ...' Triss lowered her voice. 'How's she doing? Will I be able to see her?'

'If you finally decide to run classes at Aretuza,' smiled Yennefer, 'you'll be able to see her very often.'

'Ah,' said Triss, opening her eyes widely. 'I see. Is Ciri ... ?'

'Be quiet, Triss. We'll talk about it later. Tomorrow. After the Council.'

'Tomorrow?' said Triss, smiling strangely. Yennefer frowned, but before she had time to ask a question, a slight commotion suddenly broke out in the hall.

'They're here,' said Triss, clearing her throat. 'They've finally arrived.'

'Yes,' confirmed Yennefer, tearing her gaze from her friend's eyes. 'They're here. Geralt, at last you'll have a chance to meet the members of the Chapter and the High Council. If the opportunity

116

presents itself I'll introduce you, but it won't hurt if you know who's who beforehand.'

The assembled sorcerers parted, bowing with respect at the personages entering the hall. The first was a middle-aged but vigorous man in extremely modest woollen clothing. At his side strode a tall, sharp-featured woman with dark, smoothly combed hair.

'That is Gerhart of Aelle, also known as Hen Gedymdeith, the oldest living sorcerer,' Yennefer informed Geralt in hushed tones. 'The woman walking beside him is Tissaia de Vries. She isn't much younger than Hen, but is not afraid of using elixirs to hide it.'

Behind the couple walked an attractive woman with very long, dark golden hair, and a grey-green dress decorated with lace, which rustled as she moved.

'Francesca Findabair, also called Enid an Gleanna, the Daisy of the Valleys. Don't goggle, Witcher. She is widely considered to be the most beautiful woman in the world.'

'Is she a member of the Chapter?' he whispered in astonishment. 'She looks very young. Is that also thanks to magical elixirs?'

'Not in her case. Francesca is a pure-blooded elf. Observe the man escorting her. He's Vilgefortz of Roggeveen and he really is young. But incredibly talented.'

In the case of sorcerers, as Geralt knew, the term 'young' covered any age up to and including a hundred years. Vilgefortz looked thirty-five. He was tall and well-built, wore a short jerkin of a knightly cut – but without a coat of arms, naturally. He was also fiendishly handsome. It made a great impression, even considering that Francesca Findabair was flowing gracefully along at his side, with her huge, doe eyes and breathless beauty.

'That short man walking alongside Vilgefortz is Artaud Terranova,' explained Triss Merigold. 'Those five constitute the Chapter—'

'And that girl with a strange face, walking behind Vilgefortz?'

'That's his assistant, Lydia van Bredevoort,' said Yennefer coldly. 'A meaningless individual, but looking her directly in the face is considered a serious faux pas. Take note of those three men bringing up the rear; they're all members of the Council. Fercart of Cidaris, Radcliffe of Oxenfurt and Carduin of Lan Exeter.'

'Is that the whole Council? In its entirety? I thought there were more of them.'

'The Chapter numbers five, and there are another five in the Council. Philippa Eilhart is another Council member.'

'The numbers still don't add up,' he said, shaking his head. Triss giggled.

'Haven't you told him? Do you really not know, Geralt?'

'Know what, exactly?'

'That Yennefer's also a member of the Council. Ever since the Battle of Sodden. Haven't you boasted about it to him yet, darling?'

'No, darling,' said the enchantress, looking her friend straight in the eyes. 'For one thing, I don't like to boast. For another, there's been no time. I haven't seen Geralt for ages, and we have a lot of catching up to do. There's already a long list. We're going through it point by point.'

'I see,' said Triss hesitantly. 'Hmm ... After such a long time I understand. You must have lots to talk about ...'

'Talking,' smiled Yennefer suggestively, giving the Witcher another smouldering glance, 'is way down the list. Right at the very bottom, Triss.'

The chestnut-haired enchantress was clearly discomfited and blushed faintly.

'I see,' she said, playing in embarrassment with her lapis-lazuli heart.

'I'm so glad you do. Geralt, bring us some wine. No, not from that page. From that one, over there.'

He complied, sensing at once a note of compulsion in her voice. As he took the goblets from the tray the page was carrying, he discreetly observed the two enchantresses. Yennefer was speaking quickly and quietly, while Triss Merigold was listening intently, with her head down. When he returned, Triss had gone. Yennefer didn't show any interest in the wine, so he placed the two unwanted goblets on a table.

'Sure you didn't go a bit too far?' he asked coldly. Yennefer's eyes flared violet.

'Don't try to make a fool out of me. Did you think I don't know about you and her?'

'If that's what you—'

'That's precisely what,' she said, cutting him off. 'Don't make stupid faces, and refrain from comments. And above all, don't try to lie to me. I've known Triss longer than I've known you. We like each other. We understand each other wonderfully and will always do so, irrespective of various minor . . . incidents. Just then it seemed to me she had some doubts. So I put her right, and that's that. Let's not discuss it any further.'

He didn't intend to. Yennefer pulled her curls back from her cheek.

'Now I shall leave you for a moment; I must talk to Tissaia and Francesca. Have some more food, because your stomach's rumbling. And be vigilant. Several people are sure to accost you. Don't let them walk all over you and don't tarnish my reputation.'

'You can be sure of that.'

'Geralt?'

'Yes.'

'A short while ago you expressed a desire to kiss me here, in front of everyone. Do you still hold to that?'

'I do.'

'Just try not to smudge my lipstick.'

He glanced at the assembly out of the corner of his eye. They were watching the kiss, but not intrusively. Philippa Eilhart, standing nearby, with a group of young sorcerers, winked at him and feigned applause.

Yennefer pulled her mouth away from his and heaved a deep sigh.

'A trifling thing, but pleasing,' she purred. 'All right, I'm going. I'll be right back. And later, after the banquet . . . Hmm . . .'

'I beg your pardon?'

'Please don't eat anything containing garlic.'

After she had gone the Witcher abandoned convention, unfastened his doublet, drank both goblets of wine and tried to get down to some serious eating. Nothing came of it.

'Geralt.'

'Your Excellency.'

'Lay off the titles,' frowned Dijkstra. 'I'm no count. Vizimir ordered me to introduce myself like that, so as not affront courtiers or sorcerers with my peasant origins. So, how's it going impressing people with your outfit and your figure? And pretending to have fun?'

'I don't have to pretend. I'm not here in a professional capacity.'

'That's interesting,' smiled the spy, 'but confirms the general opinion, that says you're special; one of a kind. Because everyone else is here in a professional capacity.'

'That's what I was afraid of,' said Geralt, also deeming it appropriate to smile. 'I guessed I'd be one of a kind. Meaning out of place.'

The spy inspected the nearby dishes and then picked up and devoured the large, green pod of a vegetable unfamiliar to Geralt.

'By the way,' he said, 'thank you for the Michelet brothers. Plenty of people in Redania sighed with relief when you hacked the four of them to death in the port in Oxenfurt. I laughed out loud when the university physician who was summoned to the investigation concluded – after examining the wounds – that someone had used a scythe blade mounted upright.'

Geralt didn't comment. Dijkstra put another pod into his mouth.

'It's a pity,' he continued, chewing, 'that after dispatching them you didn't report to the mayor. There was a bounty on them, dead or alive. A considerable one.'

'Too many problems with my tax return already,' said the Witcher, also deciding to sample a green pod, which turned out to taste like soapy celery. 'Besides, I had to get away quickly, because ... But I'm probably boring you, Dijkstra. You know everything, after all.'

'Not a bit of it,' smiled the spy. 'I really don't. Where would I learn such things from, anyway?'

'From the reports of, oh, I don't know, Philippa Eilhart.'

'Reports, tales, rumours. I have to listen to them; it's my job. But at the same time, my job forces me to sift every detail through a very fine sieve. Recently, just imagine, I heard that someone hacked the infamous Professor and his two comrades to death. It happened outside an inn in Anchor. The person who did it was also in too much of a hurry to collect the bounty.'

Geralt shrugged.

'Rumours. Sift them through a fine sieve and you'll see what remains.'

'I don't have to. I know what will remain. Most often, it's a deliberate attempt at disinformation. Ah, and while we're on the subject of disinformation, how is little Cirilla doing? Poor, sickly little girl, so prone to diphtheria? She's healthy, I trust?'

'Drop it, Dijkstra,' replied the Witcher coldly, looking the spy straight in the eye. 'I know you're here in a professional capacity, but don't be overzealous.'

The spy chortled and two passing sorceresses looked at him in astonishment. And with interest.

'King Vizimir,' said Dijkstra, his chuckle over, 'pays me an extra bonus for every mystery I solve. My zealousness guarantees me a decent living. You can laugh, but I have a wife and children.'

'I don't see anything funny about it. Work to support your wife and children, but not at my expense, if you don't mind. It seems to me there's no shortage of mysteries and riddles in this hall.'

'Quite. The whole of Aretuza is one great riddle. You must have noticed. Something's in the air, Geralt. And, for the sake of clarity, I don't mean the candelabras.'

'I don't get it.'

'I believe you. Because I don't get it either. And I'd like very much to. Wouldn't you? Oh, I beg your pardon. Because you're sure to know it all too. From the reports of, oh, I don't know, the enchanting Yennefer of Vengerberg. But just think, there were times when I would pick up scraps of information from the enchanting Yennefer too. Ah, where are the snows of yesteryear?'

'I really don't know what you mean, Dijkstra. Could you express your thoughts more lucidly? Do your best. On condition you're not doing it out of professional considerations. Forgive me, but I have no intention of earning you an extra bonus.'

'Think I'm trying to trick you dishonourably?' scowled the spy. 'To get information out of you using deceit? You're being unfair, Geralt. It simply interests me whether you see the same patterns in this hall that are so obvious to me.'

'So what's so obvious to you?'

'Doesn't the total absence of crowned heads – which is blatantly apparent at this gathering – surprise you?'

'It doesn't surprise me in the least,' said Geralt, finally managing to stab a marinated olive with a toothpick. 'I'm sure kings prefer traditional banquets, seated at a table, which one can gracefully slide beneath in the early hours. And what's more ...'

'What is more?' asked Dijkstra, putting four olives – which he had unceremoniously extracted from the bowl with his fingers – into his mouth.

'What is more,' said the Witcher, looking at the small crowd passing through the hall, 'the kings didn't bother to make the effort. They sent an army of spies in their stead. Both members of the fraternity and not. Probably in order to find out what's really in the air here.'

Dijkstra spat the olive stones out onto the table, took a long fork from the silver tray and used it to rummage around in a deep, crystal bowl.

'And Vilgefortz,' he said, continuing to rummage, 'made sure no spy was absent. He has all the royal spies in one pot. Why would Vilgefortz want all the royal spies in one pot, Witcher?'

'I have no idea. And it interests me little. I told you I'm here as a private individual. I'm – how shall I put it? – outside the pot.'

King Vizimir's spy fished a small octopus out of the bowl and examined it in disgust.

'People eat these?' he said, shaking his head in fake sympathy, and then turning towards Geralt.

'Listen to me carefully, Witcher,' he said quietly. 'Your convictions about privacy, your certainty that you don't care about anything and that you couldn't possibly care about anything ... they perturb me and that inclines me to take a gamble. Do you like a flutter?'

'Be precise, please.'

'I suggest a wager,' said Dijkstra, raising the fork with the octopus impaled on it. 'I venture that in the course of the next hour, Vilgefortz will ask you to join him in a long conversation. I venture that during this conversation he will prove to you that you aren't here as a private individual and you *are* in his pot. Should I be wrong, I'll eat this shit in front of you, tentacles and all. Do you accept the wager?'

'What will I have to eat, should I lose?'

'Nothing,' said Dijkstra and quickly looked around. 'But should you lose, you'll report the entire content of your conversation with Vilgefortz to me.'

The Witcher was silent for a while, and looked calmly at the spy. 'Farewell, Your Excellency,' he said at last. 'Thank you for the chat. It was educational.'

Dijkstra was somewhat annoyed.

'Would you say so—?'

'Yes, I would,' interrupted Geralt. 'Farewell.'

The spy shrugged his shoulders, threw the octopus and fork into the bowl, turned on his heel and walked away. Geralt didn't watch him go. He slowly moved to the next table, led by the desire to get his hands on some of the huge pink and white prawns piled up on a silver platter among lettuce leaves and quarters of lime. He had an appetite for them but, still feeling curious eyes on him, wanted to consume the crustaceans in a dignified manner, without losing face. He approached extravagantly slowly, picking at delicacies from the other dishes cautiously and with dignity.

Sabrina Glevissig stood at the next table, deep in conversation with a flame-haired enchantress he didn't know. The redhead wore a white skirt and a blouse of white georgette. The blouse, like that of Sabrina's, was totally transparent, but had several strategically placed appliqués and embroideries. The appliqués – noticed Geralt – had an interesting quality: they became opaque and then transparent by turns.

The enchantresses were talking, sustaining themselves with slices of langouste. They were conversing quietly in the Elder Speech. And although they weren't looking at him, they were clearly talking about him. He discreetly focused his sensitive witcher hearing, pretending to be utterly absorbed by the prawns.

'... with Yennefer?' enquired the redhead, playing with a pearl necklace, coiled around her neck like a dog's collar. 'Are you serious, Sabrina?'

'Absolutely,' answered Sabrina Glevissig. 'You won't believe it, but it's been going on for several years. And I'm surprised indeed he can stand that vile toad.'

'Why be surprised? She's put a spell on him. She has him under a charm. Think I've never done that?'

'But he's a witcher! They can't be bewitched. Not for so long, at any rate.'

'It must be love then,' sighed the redhead. 'And love is blind.'

'He's blind, more like,' said Sabrina, grimacing. 'Would you believe, Marti, that she dared to introduce me to him as an old school friend? Bloody hell, she's older than me by ... Oh, never mind. I tell you, she's hellishly jealous about that Witcher. Little Merigold only smiled at him and that hag bawled her out and sent her packing in no uncertain terms. And right now ... Take a look. She's standing there, talking to Francesca, without ever taking her eyes off her Witcher.'

'She's afraid,' giggled the redhead, 'that we'll have our way with him, even if only for tonight. Are you up for it, Sabrina? Shall we try? He's a fit lad, not like those conceited weaklings of ours with all their complexes and pretensions ...'

'Don't talk so loud, Marti,' hissed Sabrina. 'Don't look at him and don't grin. Yennefer's watching us too. And stay classy. Do you really want to seduce him? That would be in bad taste.'

'Hmm, you're right,' agreed Marti after a moment's thought. 'But what if he suddenly came over and suggested it himself?'

'In that case,' said Sabrina Glevissig, glancing at the Witcher with a predatory, coal-black eye. 'I'd give it to him without a second thought, even lying on a rock.'

'I'd even do it lying on a hedgehog,' sniggered Marti.

The Witcher, staring at the tablecloth, hid his foolish expression behind a prawn and a lettuce leaf, extremely pleased to have the mutation of his blood vessels which prevented him from blushing.

'Witcher Geralt?'

He swallowed the prawn and turned around. A sorcerer who looked familiar smiled faintly, touching the embroidered facings of his purple doublet.

'Dorregaray of Vole. But we are acquainted. We met ...'

'I remember. Excuse me; I didn't recognise you right away. Glad to ...'

The sorcerer smiled a little more broadly, taking two goblets from a tray being carried by a pageboy.

'I've been watching you for some time,' he said, handing one of the glasses to Geralt. 'You've told everyone Yennefer has introduced you to that you're enjoying yourself. Is that duplicity or a lack of criticism?'

'Courtesy.'

'Towards them?' said Dorregaray, indicating the banqueters with a sweeping gesture. 'Believe me, it's not worth the effort. They're a vain, envious and mendacious bunch; they don't appreciate your courtesy. Why, they treat it as sarcasm. With them, Witcher, you have to use their own methods. Be obsessive, arrogant and rude, and then at least you'll impress them. Will you drink a glass of wine with me?'

'The gnat's piss they serve here?' smiled Geralt pleasantly. 'With the greatest revulsion. Well, but if you like it ... then I'll force myself.'

Sabrina and Marti, listening intently from their table, snorted noisily. Dorregaray sized them both up with a contemptuous glance, turned, clinked his goblet against the Witcher's and smiled, this time genuinely.

'A point to you,' he admitted freely. 'You learn quickly. Where the hell did you acquire that wit, Witcher? On the road you insist on roaming around, hunting endangered species? Your good health. You may laugh, but you're one of the few people in this hall I feel like proposing such a toast to.'

'Indeed?' said Geralt, delicately slurping the wine and savouring the taste. 'In spite of the fact I make my living slaughtering endangered species?'

'Don't try to trip me up,' said the sorcerer, slapping him on the back. 'The banquet has only just begun. A few more people are sure to accost you, so ration out your scathing ripostes more sparingly. But as far as your profession is concerned ... You, Geralt, at least have enough dignity not to deck yourself out with trophies. But take a good look around. Go on, forget convention for a moment; they like people to stare at them.'

The Witcher obediently fixed his gaze on Sabrina Glevissig's breasts.

'Look,' said Dorregaray, seizing him by the sleeve and pointing at a sorceress walking past, tulle fluttering. 'Slippers made from the skin of the horned agama. Had you noticed?'

He nodded, ingenuously, since he'd only noticed what her transparent tulle blouse *wasn't* covering.

'Oh, if you please, rock cobra,' said the sorcerer, unerringly spotting another pair of slippers being paraded around the hall. The fashion, which had shortened hemlines to a span above the ankle, made his task easier. 'And over there ... White iguana. Salamander. Wyvern. Spectacled caiman. Basilisk ... Every one of those reptiles is an endangered species. Can't people bloody wear shoes of calfskin or pigskin?'

'Going on about leather, as usual, Dorregaray?' asked Philippa Eilhart, stopping beside them. 'And tanning and shoemaking? What vulgar, tasteless subjects.'

'People find a variety of things tasteless,' said the sorcerer grimacing contemptuously. 'Your dress has a beautiful trim, Philippa. Diamond ermine, if I'm not mistaken? Very tasteful. I'm sure you're aware this species was exterminated twenty years ago owing to its beautiful pelt?'

'Thirty,' corrected Philippa, stuffing the last of the prawns – which Geralt hadn't been quick enough to eat – into her mouth one after the other. 'I know, I know, the species would surely have come back to life, had I instructed my dressmaker to trim my dress with bunches of raw flax. I considered it. But the colours wouldn't have matched.'

'Let's go to that table over there,' suggested the Witcher easily. 'I saw a large bowl of black caviar there. And, since the shovelnose sturgeon has almost totally died out, we ought to hurry.'

'Eating caviar in your company? I've dreamed about that,' said Philippa, fluttering her eyelashes and smelling enticingly of cinnamon and muskroot as she slipped her arm into his. 'Let's not hang around. Will you join us, Dorregaray? You won't? Well, see you later and enjoy yourself.'

The sorcerer snapped his fingers and turned away. Sabrina Glevissig and her redheaded friend watched them walk away with looks more venomous than the endangered rock cobra's.

'Dorregaray,' murmured Philippa, unashamedly snuggling up to Geralt, 'spies for King Ethain of Cidaris. Be on your guard. That reptiles and skin talk of his is the prelude to being interrogated. And Sabrina Glevissig was listening closely –'

'– because she spies for Henselt of Kaedwen,' he finished. 'I know; you mentioned it. And that redhead, her friend—'

'She's no redhead – it's dyed. Haven't you got eyes? That's Marti Södergren.'

'Who does she spy for?'

'Marti?' Philippa laughed, her teeth flashing behind her vividly painted lips. 'Not for anyone. Marti isn't interested in politics.'

'Outrageous! I thought everyone here was a spy.'

'Many of them are,' said the enchantress, narrowing her eyes. 'But not everyone. Not Marti Södergren. Marti is a healer. And a nymphomaniac. Oh, damn, look! They've scoffed all the caviar! Down to the last egg; they've licked the plate clean! What are we going to do now?'

'Now,' smiled Geralt innocently, 'you'll announce that something's in the air. You'll say I have to reject neutrality and make a choice. You'll suggest a wager. I daren't even imagine what the prize might be. But I know I'll have to do something for you should I lose.'

Philippa Eilhart was quiet for a long time, her eyes fixed on his.

'I should have guessed,' she said quietly. 'Dijkstra couldn't restrain himself, could he? He made you an offer. And I warned him you detest spies.'

'I don't detest spies. I detest spying. And I detest contempt. Don't propose any wagers to me, Philippa. Of course I can sense something in the air. And it can hang there, for all I care. It doesn't affect or interest me.'

'You already told me that. In Oxenfurt.'

'I'm glad you haven't forgotten. You also recall the circumstances, I trust?'

'Very clearly. Back then I didn't reveal to you who Rience – or

127

whatever his name is – was working for. I let him get away. Oh, you were so angry with me ...'

'To put it mildly.'

'Then the time has come for me to be exonerated. I'll give you Rience tomorrow. Don't interrupt and don't make faces. This isn't a wager à la Dijkstra. It's a promise, and I keep my promises. No, no questions, please. Wait until tomorrow. Now let's concentrate on caviar and trivial gossip.'

'There's no caviar.'

'One moment.'

She looked around quickly, waved a hand and mumbled a spell. The silver dish in the shape of a leaping fish immediately filled with the roe of the endangered shovelnose sturgeon. The Witcher smiled.

'Can one eat one's fill of an illusion?'

'No. But snobbish tastes can be pleasantly titillated by it. Have a try.'

'Hmm ... Indeed ... I'd say it's tastier than the real thing ...'

'And it's not at all fattening,' said the enchantress proudly, squeezing lemon juice over a heaped teaspoon of caviar. 'May I have another goblet of white wine?'

'At your service. Philippa?'

'Yes.'

'I'm told etiquette precludes the use of spells here. Wouldn't it be safer, then, to conjure up the illusion of the taste of caviar alone, without the caviar? Just the sensation? You'd surely be able to ...'

'Of course I would,' said Philippa Eilhart, looking at him through her crystal goblet. 'The construction of such a spell is easy as pie. But were you only to have the sensation of taste, you'd lose the pleasure the activity offers. The process, the accompanying ritual movements, the gestures, the conversation and eye contact which accompanies the process ... I'll entertain you with a witty comparison. Would you like that?'

'Please do. I'm looking forward to it.'

'I'd also be capable of conjuring the sensation of an orgasm.'

Before the Witcher had regained the power of speech, a short, slim sorceress with long, straight, straw-coloured hair came over to him. He recognised her at once – she was the one in the horned agama skin slippers and the green tulle top, which didn't even cover a minor detail like the small mole above her left breast.

'I'm sorry,' she said, 'but I have to interrupt your little flirting session, Philippa. Radcliffe and Detmold would like to talk to you for a moment. It's urgent.'

'Well, if it's like that, I'm coming. Bye, Geralt. We'll continue our flirting later!'

'Ah,' said the blonde, sizing him up. 'Geralt. The Witcher, the man Yennefer lost her head over? I've been watching you and wondering who you might be. It was tormenting me terribly.'

'I know that kind of torment,' he replied, smiling politely. 'I'm experiencing it right now.'

'Do excuse the gaffe. I'm Keira Metz. Oh, caviar!'

'Be careful. It's an illusion.'

'Bloody hell, you're right!' said the sorceress, dropping the spoon as though it was the tail of a black scorpion. 'Who was so barefaced . . . You? Can you create fourth-level illusions?'

'I,' he lied, continuing to smile, 'am a master of magic. I'm pretending to be a witcher to remain incognito. Do you think Yennefer would bother with an ordinary witcher?'

Keira Metz looked him straight in the eyes and scowled. She was wearing a medallion in the form of an ankh cross; silver and set with zircon.

'A drop of wine?' he suggested, trying to break the awkward silence. He was afraid his joke hadn't been well received.

'No thank you . . . O fellow master,' said Keira icily. 'I don't drink. I can't. I plan to get pregnant tonight.'

'By whom?' asked the fake-redheaded friend of Sabrina Glevissig, who was dressed in a transparent, white, georgette blouse, decorated with cleverly positioned details, walking over to them. 'By whom?' she repeated, innocently fluttering her long eyelashes.

Keira turned and gave her an up-and-down glare, from her white iguana slippers to her pearl-encrusted tiara.

'What business is it of yours?'

'It isn't. Professional curiosity. Won't you introduce me to your companion, the famous Geralt of Rivia?'

'With great reluctance. But I know I won't be able to fob you off. Geralt, this is Marti Södergren, seductress. Her speciality is aphrodisiacs.'

'Must we talk shop? Oh, have you left me a little caviar? How kind of you.'

'Careful,' chorused Keira and the Witcher. 'It's an illusion.'

'So it is!' said Marti Södergren, leaning over and wrinkling her nose, after which she picked up a goblet and looked at the traces of crimson lipstick on it. 'Ah, Philippa Eilhart. I should have known. Who else would have dared to do something so brazen? That revolting snake. Did you know she spies for Vizimir of Redania?'

'And is a nymphomaniac?' risked the Witcher. Marti and Keira snorted in unison.

'Is that what you were counting on, fawning over her and flirting with her?' asked the seductress. 'If so, you ought to know someone's played a mean trick on you. Philippa lost her taste for men some time ago.'

'But perhaps you're really a woman?' asked Keira Metz, pouting her glistening lips. 'Perhaps you're only pretending to be a man, my fellow master of magic? To remain incognito? Do you know, Marti, he confessed a moment ago that he likes to pretend.'

'He likes to and knows how to,' smiled Marti spitefully. 'Right, Geralt? A while back I saw you pretending to be hard of hearing and unable to understand the Elder Speech.'

'He has endless vices,' said Yennefer coldly, walking over and imperiously linking arms with the Witcher. 'He has practically nothing but vices. You're wasting your time, ladies.'

'So it would seem,' agreed Marti Södergren, still smiling spitefully. 'Here's hoping you enjoy the party, then. Come on, Keira, let's have a goblet of something ... alcohol-free. Perhaps I'll also decide to have a try tonight.'

'Phew,' he exclaimed, once they'd gone. 'Right on time, Yen. Thank you.'

'You're thanking me? Not sincerely, I should imagine. There are precisely eleven women in this hall flashing their tits through transparent blouses. I leave you for just half an hour, and I catch you talking to two of them –'

Yennefer broke off and looked at the fish-shaped dish.

'– and eating illusions,' she finished. 'Oh, Geralt, Geralt. Come with me. I can introduce you to several people who are worth knowing.'

'Would one of them be Vilgefortz?'

'Interesting,' said the enchantress, squinting, 'that you should ask about him. Yes, Vilgefortz would like to meet you and talk to you. I warn you that the conversation may appear banal and frivolous, but don't let that deceive you. Vilgefortz is an expert, exceptionally intelligent old hand. I don't know what he wants from you, but stay vigilant.'

'I will,' he sighed. 'But I can't imagine your wily old fox is capable of surprising me. Not after what I've been through here. I've been mauled by spies and jumped by endangered reptiles and ermines. I've been fed non-existent caviar. Nymphomaniacs with no interest in men have questioned my manhood. I've been threatened with rape on a hedgehog, menaced by the prospect of pregnancy, and even of an orgasm, but one without any of the ritual movements. Ugh ...'

'Have you been drinking?'

'A little white wine from Cidaris. But there was probably an aphrodisiac in it ... Yen? Are we going back to Loxia after the conversation with Vilgefortz?'

'No, we aren't.'

'I beg your pardon?'

'I want to spend the night in Aretuza. With you. An aphrodisiac, you say? In the wine? How fascinating ...'

'Oh heavens, oh heavens,' sighed Yennefer, stretching and throwing a thigh over the Witcher's. 'Oh heavens, oh heavens. I haven't made love for so long ... For so very long.'

Geralt disentangled his fingers from her curls without responding. Firstly, her statement might have been a trap; he was afraid there might be a hook hidden in the bait. Secondly, he didn't want to wipe away with words the taste of her delight, which was still on his lips.

'I haven't made love to a man who declared his love to me and to whom I declared my love for a very long time,' she murmured a moment later, when it was clear the Witcher wasn't taking the bait. 'I forgot how wonderful it can be. Oh heavens, oh heavens.'

She stretched even more vigorously, reaching out with her arms and seizing the corners of the pillow in both hands, so that her breasts, now flooded in moonlight, took on curves that made themselves felt as a shudder in the Witcher's lower back. He hugged her, and they both lay still, spent, their ardour cooled.

Outside their chamber cicadas chirped and from far off quiet voices and laughter could also be heard, testimony that the banquet still wasn't over, in spite of the late hour.

'Geralt?'

'Yes, Yen?'

'Tell me.'

'About the conversation with Vilgefortz? Now? I'll tell you in the morning.'

'Right now, if you please.'

He looked at the writing desk in the corner of the chamber. On it were various books and other objects which the novice who had been temporarily rehoused to accommodate Yennefer in Loxia had been unable to take with her. A plump ragdoll in a ruffled dress, lovingly placed to lean up against the books and crumpled from frequent cuddling, was also there. She didn't take the doll, he thought, to avoid exposing herself to her friends' teasing in a Loxia dormitory. She didn't take her doll with her. And she probably couldn't fall asleep without it tonight.

The doll stared at him with button eyes. He looked away.

When Yennefer had introduced him to the Chapter, he'd observed the sorcerers' elite intently. Hen Gedymdeith only gave him a tired glance; it was apparent the banquet had already exhausted the old man. Artaud Terranova bowed with an ambiguous grimace, shifting his eyes from him to Yennefer, but immediately became serious when he realised others were watching him. The blue, elven eyes of Francesca Findabair were as inscrutable and hard as glass. The Daisy of the Valleys smiled when he was introduced to her. That smile, although incredibly beautiful, filled the Witcher with dread. During the introductions Tissaia de Vries, although apparently preoccupied with her sleeves and jewellery, which seemed to required endless straightening, smiled at him considerably less beautifully but with considerably more sincerity. And it was Tissaia who immediately struck up a conversation with him, referring to one of his noble witcher deeds which he, incidentally, could not recall and suspected she had invented.

And then Vilgefortz joined the conversation. Vilgefortz of Roggeveen, a sorcerer of imposing stature, with noble and beautiful features and a sincere and honest voice. Geralt knew he could expect anything from people who looked like that.

They spoke briefly, sensing plenty of anxious eyes on them. Yennefer looked at the Witcher. A young sorceress with friendly eyes, constantly trying to hide the bottom of her face behind a fan, was looking at Vilgefortz. They exchanged several conventional comments, after which Vilgefortz suggested they continue their conversation in private. It seemed to Geralt that Tissaia de Vries was the only person surprised by this proposition.

'Have you fallen asleep, Geralt?' muttered Yennefer, shaking him out of his musings. 'You're meant to be telling me about your conversation.'

The doll looked at him from the writing desk with its button gaze. He looked away again.

'As soon as we entered the cloister,' he began a moment later, 'that girl with the strange face ...'

'Lydia van Bredevoort. Vilgefortz's assistant.'

'Yes, that's right, you said. Just a meaningless person. So, when we entered the cloister that meaningless person stopped, looked at him and asked him something. Telepathically.'

'It wasn't an indiscretion. Lydia can't use her voice.'

'I guessed as much. Because Vilgefortz didn't answer her using telepathy. He replied ...'

'Yes, Lydia, that's a good idea,' answered Vilgefortz. 'Let's take a walk through the Gallery of Glory. You'll have the opportunity to take a look at the history of magic, Geralt of Rivia. I have no doubt you're familiar with it, but now you'll have the chance to become acquainted with its visual history, too. If you're a connoisseur of painting, please don't be horrified. Most of them are the work of the enthusiastic students of Aretuza. Lydia, be so good as to lighten the gloom around here a little.'

Lydia van Bredevoort passed her hand through the air, and it immediately became lighter in the corridor.

The first painting showed an ancient sailing craft being hurled around by whirlpools among reefs protruding from the surf. A man in white robes stood on the prow of the ship, his head encircled by a bright halo.

'The first landing,' guessed the Witcher.

'Indeed,' Vilgefortz confirmed. 'The Ship of Outcasts. Jan Bekker is bending the Power to his will. He calms the waves, proving that magic need not be evil or destructive but may save lives.'

'Did that event really take place?'

'I doubt it,' smiled the sorcerer. 'It's more likely that, during the first journey and landing, Bekker and the others were hanging over the side, vomiting bile. After the landing which, by a strange twist of fate, was successful, he was able to overcome the Power. Let's go on. Here we see Jan Bekker once more, forcing water to gush from the rock, in the very spot where the first settlement was established. And here, if you please, Bekker – surrounded by settlers – drives away the clouds and holds back a tempest to save the harvest.'

'And here? What event is shown in this painting?'

'The identification of the Chosen Ones. Bekker and Giambattista put the children of the settlers through a magical test as they arrived, in order to reveal Sources. The selected children were taken from their parents and brought to Mirthe, the first seat of the mages. Right now, you are looking at a historical moment. As you can see, all the children are terrified, and only that determined brown-haired girl is holding a hand out to Giambattista with a completely trusting smile. She became the famous Agnes of Glanville, the first woman to become an enchantress. The woman behind her is her mother. You can see sadness in her expression.'

'And this crowd scene?'

'The Novigradian Union. Bekker, Giambattista and Monck are

concluding a pact with rulers, priests and druids. A pact of non-aggression codifying the separation of magic and state. Dreadful kitsch. Let's go on. Here we see Geoffrey Monck setting off up the Pontar, which at that time was still called Aevon y Pont ar Gwennelen, the River of Alabaster Bridges. Monck sailed to Loc Muinne, to persuade the elves there to adopt a group of Source children, who were to be taught by elven sorcerers. It may interest you to know that among those children was a little boy, who came to be known as Gerhart of Aelle. You met him a moment ago. That little boy is now called Hen Gedymdeith.'

'This,' said the Witcher, looking at the sorcerer, 'is just calling out for a battle scene. After all, several years after Monck's successful expedition, the forces of Marshal Raupenneck of Tretogor carried out a pogrom in Loc Muinne and Est Haemlet, killing all of the elves, regardless of age or sex. And a war began, ending with the massacre at Shaerrawedd.'

'And your impressive knowledge of history,' Vilgefortz smiled once again, 'will remind you, however, that no sorcerer of any note took part in those wars. For which reason the subject did not inspire any of the novices to paint a work to commemorate it. Let's move on.'

'Very well. What event is shown in this canvas? Oh, I know. It's Raffard the White reconciling the feuding kings and putting an end to the Six Years' War. And here we have Raffard refusing to accept the crown. A beautiful, noble gesture.'

'Do you think so?' said Vilgefortz, tilting his head. 'Well, in any case, it was a gesture with the weight of precedent behind it. Raffard did, however, accept the position of first adviser so became the de facto ruler, since the king was an imbecile.'

'The Gallery of Glory ...' muttered the Witcher, walking up to the next painting. 'And what do we have here?'

'The historical moment when the first Chapter was installed and the Law enacted. From the left you see seated: Herbert Stammelford, Aurora Henson, Ivo Richert, Agnes of Glanville, Geoffrey Monck and Radmir of Tor Carnedd. This, if I'm to be honest, also cries out for a battle scene to complete it. For soon after, those who refused to acknowledge the Chapter and submit to the Law were wiped out in a brutal war. Raffard the White died, among others. But historical treatises remain silent about it, so as not to spoil a beautiful legend.'

'And here ... Hmm ... Yes, a novice probably painted this. And a very young one, at that ...'

'Undoubtedly. It's an allegory, after all. I'd call it an allegory of triumphant womanliness. Air, water, earth and fire. And four famous enchantresses, all masters at wielding the forces of those elements. Agnes of Glanville, Aurora Henson, Nina Fioravanti and Klara Larissa de Winter. Look at the next – and more effective – painting. Here you also see Klara Larissa opening the academy for girls here, in the building where we now stand. And those are por-traits of renowned Aretuza graduates. This shows a long history of triumphant womanhood and the growing feminisation of the pro-fession: Yanna of Murivel, Nora Wagner, her sister Augusta, Jada Glevissig, Leticia Charbonneau, Ilona Laux-Antille, Carla Demetia Crest, Yiolenta Suarez, April Wenhaver ... And the only surviving one: Tissaia de Vries ...'

They continued. The silk of Lydia van Bredevoort's dress whis-pered softly, and the whisper contained a menacing secret.

'And that?' Geralt stopped. 'What is this dreadful scene?'

'The martyrdom of the sorcerer Radmir, flayed alive during the Falka rebellion. In the background burns the town of Mirthe, which Falka had ordered to be consumed by flame.'

'For which act Falka herself was soon consumed by flame. At the stake.'

'That is a widely known fact; Temerian and Redanian children still play at burning Falka on Saovine's Eve. Let's go back, so that you may see the other side of the gallery ... Ah, I see you have a question.'

'I'm wondering about the chronology. I know, naturally, how elixirs of youth work, but the simultaneous appearance of living people and long dead ones in these paintings ...'

'You mean: you are astonished that you met Hen Gedymdeith and Tissaia de Vries at the banquet, but Bekker, Agnes of Glanville, Stammelford or Nina Fioravanti are not with us?'

'No. I know you're not immortal—'

'What is death?' interrupted Vilgefortz. 'To you?'

'The end.'

'The end of what?'

'Existence. It seems to me we've moved from art history to philosophy.'

'Nature doesn't know the concept of philosophy, Geralt of Rivia. The pathetic – ridiculous – attempts which people undertake to try to understand nature are typically termed philosophy. The results of such attempts are also considered philosophy. It's as though a cabbage tried to investigate the causes and effects of its existence, called the result of these reflections "an eternal and mysterious conflict between head and root", and considered rain an unfathomable causative power. We, sorcerers, don't waste time puzzling out what nature is. We know what it is; for we are nature ourselves. Do you understand?'

'I'm trying to, but please talk more slowly. Don't forget you're talking to a cabbage.'

'Have you ever wondered what happened when Bekker forced the water to gush from the rock? It's generally put very simply: Bekker tamed the Power. He forced the element to be obedient. He subdued nature; controlled it ... What is your relationship to women, Geralt?'

'I beg your pardon?'

Lydia van Bredevoort turned with a whisper of silk and froze in anticipation. Geralt saw she was holding a wrapped-up painting under one arm. He had no idea where the picture had come from, since Lydia had been empty-handed a moment before. The amulet around his neck vibrated faintly.

Vilgefortz smiled.

'I enquired,' he repeated, 'as to your views concerning the relationship between men and women.'

'Regarding what respect of that relationship?'

'Can obedience, in your opinion, be forced upon women? I'm talking about real women, of course, not just the female of the species. Can a real woman be controlled? Overcome? Made to surrender to your will? And if so, how? Answer me.'

*

137

The ragdoll didn't take her eyes off them. Yennefer looked away.

'Did you answer?'

'Yes, I did.'

With her left hand, the enchantress squeezed his elbow, and with her right squeezed his fingers, which were touching her breasts.

'How?'

'You surely know.'

'You've understood,' said Vilgefortz a moment later. 'And you've probably always understood. And thus you will also understand that if the concept of will and submission, of commands and obedience, and of male ruler and servant woman will perish and disappear, then unity will be achieved. A community merging into a single entity will be achieved. All will be as one. And if something like that were to occur, death would lose its meaning. Jan Bekker, who was water gushing from the rock, is present there in the banqueting hall. To say that Bekker died is like saying that water has died. Look at that painting.'

Geralt looked.

'It's unusually beautiful,' he said after a moment. At once he felt a slight vibration of his witcher's medallion.

'Lydia,' smiled Vilgefortz, 'thanks for your acknowledgement. And I congratulate you on your taste. The landscape depicts the meeting between Cregennan of Lod and Lara Dorren aep Shiadhal, the legendary lovers, torn apart and destroyed by the time of contempt. He was a sorcerer and she was an elf, one of the elite of Aen Saevherne, or the Knowing Ones. What might have been the beginning of reconciliation was transformed into tragedy.'

'I know that story. I always treated it as a fairytale. What really happened?'

'That,' said the sorcerer, becoming serious, 'nobody knows. I mean almost nobody. Lydia, hang up your picture over here. Geralt, have a look at another of Lydia's impressive works. It's a portrait of Lara Dorren aep Shiadhal taken from an ancient miniature.'

'Congratulations,' said the Witcher, bowing to Lydia van Bredevoort, finding it hard to keep his voice from quavering. 'It's a true masterpiece.'

His tone didn't quaver, even though Lara Dorren aep Shiadhal looked at him from the portrait with Ciri's eyes.

'What happened after that?'

'Lydia remained in the gallery. The two of us went out onto the terrace. And he enjoyed himself at my expense.'

'This way, Geralt, if you would. Step only on the dark slabs, please.'

The sea roared below, and the Isle of Thanedd stood in the white foam of the breakers. The waves broke against the walls of Loxia, directly beneath them. Loxia sparkled with lights, as did Aretuza. The stone block of Garstang towering above them was black and lifeless, however.

'Tomorrow,' said the sorcerer, following the Witcher's gaze, 'the members of the Chapter and the Council will don their traditional robes: the flowing black cloaks and pointed hats known to you from ancient prints. We will also arm ourselves with long wands and staffs, thus resembling the wizards and witches parents frighten children with. That is the tradition. We will go up to Garstang in the company of several other delegates. And there, in a specially prepared chamber, we will debate. The other delegates will await our return and our decisions in Aretuza.'

'Are the smaller meetings in Garstang, behind closed doors, also traditional?'

'But of course. It's a long tradition and one which has come about through practical considerations. Gatherings of mages are known to be tempestuous and have led to very frank exchanges of views. During one of them, ball lightning damaged Nina Fioravanti's coiffure and dress. Nina reinforced the walls of Garstang with an incredibly powerful aura and an anti-magic blockade, which took her a year to prepare. From that day on, no spells have worked in Garstang and the discussions have proceeded altogether more peacefully. Particularly when it is remembered to remove all bladed weapons from the delegates.'

'I see. And that solitary tower on the very summit above Garstang. What is it? Some kind of important building?'

'It is Tor Lara, the Tower of Gulls. A ruin. Is it important? It probably is.'

'Probably?'

The sorcerer leaned on the banisters.

'According to elvish tradition, Tor Lara is connected by a portal to the mysterious, still undiscovered Tor Zireael, the Tower of Swallows.'

'According to tradition? You haven't managed to find the portal? I don't believe you.'

'You are right not to. We discovered the portal, but it was necessary to block it. There were protests. Everyone was itching to conduct experiments; everyone wanted the fame of being the first to discover Tor Zireael, the mythical seat of elven mages and sages. But the portal is irreversibly warped and transports people chaotically. There were casualties, so it was blocked up. Let's go, Geralt, it's getting cold. Carefully. Only walk on the dark slabs.'

'Why only the dark ones?'

'These buildings are in ruins. Damp, erosion, strong winds, the salt air; they all have a disastrous effect on the walls. Repairs would cost too much, so we make use of illusion instead of workmen. Prestige, you understand.'

'It doesn't apply to everything.'

The sorcerer waved a hand and the terrace vanished. They were standing over a precipice, over an abyss bristling far below with the teeth of rocks jutting from the foam. They were standing on a narrow belt of dark slabs, stretched like a tightrope between the rocky ledge of Aretuza and the pillar holding up the terrace.

Geralt had difficulty keeping his balance. Had he been a man and not a witcher, he would have failed. But even he was rattled. His sudden movement could not have escaped the attention of the sorcerer, and his reaction must also have been visible. The wind rocked him on the narrow footbridge, and the abyss called to him with a sinister roaring of the waves.

'You're afraid of death,' noted Vilgefortz with a smile. 'You are afraid, after all.'

*

140

The ragdoll looked at them with button eyes.

'He tricked you,' murmured Yennefer, cuddling up to the Witcher. 'There was no danger. He's sure to have protected you and himself with a levitational field. He wouldn't have taken the risk ... What happened then?'

'We went to another wing of Aretuza. He led me to a large chamber, which was probably the office of one of the teachers, or even the rectoress. We sat by a table with an hourglass on it. The sand was trickling through it. I could smell the fragrance of Lydia's perfume and knew she had been in the chamber before us ...'

'And Vilgefortz?'

'He asked me a question.'

'Why didn't you become a sorcerer, Geralt? Weren't you ever attracted by the Art? Be honest.'

'I will. I was.'

'Why, then, didn't you follow the voice of that attraction?'

'I decided it would be wiser to follow the voice of good sense.'

'Meaning?'

'Years of practice in the witcher's trade have taught me not to bite off more than I can chew. Do you know, Vilgefortz, I once knew a dwarf who, as a child, dreamed of being an elf. What do you think; would he have become one had he followed the voice of attraction?'

'Is that supposed to be a comparison? A parallel? If so, it's utterly ill-judged. A dwarf could not become an elf. Not without having an elf for its mother.'

Geralt remained silent for a long time.

'I get it,' he finally said. 'I should have guessed. You've been having a root around in my life history. To what purpose, if you don't mind?'

'Perhaps,' smiled the sorcerer faintly. 'I'm dreaming of a painting in the Gallery of Glory. The two of us seated at a table and on a brass plaque the title: *Vilgefortz of Roggeveen entering into a pact with Geralt of Rivia.*'

'That would be an allegory,' said the Witcher, 'with the title: *Knowledge Triumphing Over Ignorance.* I'd prefer a more realistic

141

painting, entitled: *In Which Vilgefortz Explains To Geralt What This Is All About.*'

Vilgefortz brought the tips of his fingers together in front of his mouth.

'Isn't it obvious?'

'No.'

'Have you forgotten? The painting I'm dreaming about hangs in the Gallery of Glory, where future generations, who know perfectly well what it's all about, what event is depicted in the picture, can look at it. On the canvas, Vilgefortz and Geralt are negotiating and concluding an agreement, as a result of which Geralt, following the voice – not of some kind of attraction or predilection, but a genuine vocation – finally joined the ranks of mages. This brings to an end his erstwhile and not particularly sensible existence, which has no future whatsoever.'

'Just think,' said the Witcher after a lengthy silence, 'that not so long ago I believed that nothing more could astonish me. Believe me, Vilgefortz, I'll remember this banquet and this pageant of incredible events for a long time. Worthy of a painting, indeed. The title would be: *Geralt Leaving the Isle of Thanedd, Shaking with Laughter.*'

'I don't understand,' said the sorcerer, leaning forward a little. 'You lost me with the floweriness of your discourse, so liberally sprinkled with sophisticated words.'

'The causes of the misunderstanding are clear to me. We differ too much to understand each other. You are a mighty sorcerer from the Chapter, who has achieved oneness with nature. I'm a wanderer, a witcher, a mutant, who travels the world and slays monsters for money –'

'That floweriness,' interrupted the sorcerer, 'has been supplanted by banality.'

'– We differ too greatly,' said Geralt, not allowing himself to be interrupted, 'and the minor fact that my mother was, by accident, a sorceress, is unable to erase that difference. But just out of curiosity: who was *your* mother?'

'I have no idea,' said Vilgefortz calmly. The Witcher immediately fell silent.

'Druids from the Kovir Circle,' said the sorcerer a moment later, 'found me in a gutter in Lan Exeter. They took me in and raised me. To be a druid, of course. Do you know what a druid is? It's a kind of mutant, a wanderer, who travels the world and bows to sacred oaks.'

The Witcher said nothing.

'And later,' continued Vilgefortz, 'my gifts revealed themselves during certain druidical rituals. Gifts which clearly and undeniably pointed to my origins. I was begat by two people, evidently unplanned, and at least one of them was a sorcerer.'

Geralt said nothing.

'The person who discovered my modest abilities was, of course, a sorcerer, whom I met by accident,' continued Vilgefortz calmly. 'He offered me a tremendous gift: the chance of an education and of self-improvement, with a view to joining the Brotherhood of Sorcerers.'

'And you,' said the Witcher softly, 'accepted the offer.'

'No,' said Vilgefortz, his voice becoming increasingly cold and unpleasant. 'I rejected it in a rude – even boorish – way. I unloaded all my anger on the old fool. I wanted him to feel guilty; he and his entire magical fraternity. Guilty, naturally, for the gutter in Lan Exeter; guilty that one or two detestable conjurers – bastards without hearts or human feelings – had thrown me into that gutter at birth, and not before, when I wouldn't have survived. The sorcerer, it goes without saying, didn't understand; wasn't concerned by what I told him. He shrugged and went on his way, by doing so branding himself and his fellows with the stigma of insensitive, arrogant, whoresons, worthy of the greatest contempt.'

Geralt said nothing.

'I'd had a gutful of druids,' said Vilgefortz. 'So I gave up my sacred oak groves and set off into the world. I did a variety of things. I'm still ashamed of some of them. I finally became a mercenary. My life after that unfolded, as you might imagine, predictably. Victorious soldier, defeated soldier, marauder, robber, rapist, murderer, and finally a fugitive fleeing the noose. I fled to the ends of the world. And there, at the end of the world, I met a woman. A sorceress.'

'Be careful,' whispered the Witcher, and his eyes narrowed. 'Be careful, Vilgefortz, that the similarities you're desperately searching for don't lead you too far.'

'The similarities are over,' said the sorcerer without lowering his gaze, 'since I couldn't cope with the feelings I felt for that woman. I couldn't understand her feelings, and she didn't try to help me with them. I left her. Because she was promiscuous, arrogant, spiteful, unfeeling and cold. Because it was impossible to dominate her, and her domination of me was humiliating. I left her because I knew she was only interested in me because my intelligence, personality and fascinating mystery obscured the fact that I wasn't a sorcerer, and it was usually only sorcerers she would honour with more than one night. I left her because … because she was like my mother. I suddenly understood that what I felt for her was not love at all, but a feeling which was considerably more complicated, more powerful but more difficult to classify: a mixture of fear, regret, fury, pangs of conscience and the need for expiation, a sense of guilt, loss, and hurt. A perverse need for suffering and atonement. What I felt for that woman was hate.'

Geralt remained silent. Vilgefortz was looking to one side.

'I left her,' he said after a while. 'And then I couldn't live with the emptiness which engulfed me. And I suddenly understood it wasn't the absence of a woman that causes that emptiness, but the lack of everything I had been feeling. It's a paradox, isn't it? I imagine I don't need to finish; you can guess what happened next. I became a sorcerer. Out of hatred. And only then did I understand how stupid I was. I mistook stars reflected in a pond at night for those in the sky.'

'As you rightly observed, the parallels between us aren't completely parallel,' murmured Geralt. 'In spite of appearances, we have little in common, Vilgefortz. What did you want to prove by telling me your story? That the road to wizardly excellence, although winding and difficult, is available to anyone? Even – excuse my parallel – to bastards or foundlings, wanderers or witchers—'

'No,' the sorcerer interrupted. 'I didn't mean to prove this road is open to all, because that's obvious and was proved long ago. Neither was there a need to prove that certain people simply have no other path.'

'And so,' smiled the Witcher, 'I have no choice? I have to enter into a pact with you, a pact which should someday become the subject of a painting, and become a sorcerer? On account of genetics alone? Give me a break. I know a little about the theory of heredity. My father, as I discovered with no little difficulty, was a wanderer, a churl, a troublemaker and a swashbuckler. My genes on the spear side may be dominant over the genes on the distaff side. The fact that I can swash a buckler pretty well seems to confirm that.'

'Indeed,' the sorcerer derisively smiled. 'The hourglass has almost run its course, and I, Vilgefortz of Roggeveen, master of magic, member of the Chapter, am still discoursing – not unpleasantly – with a churl and swashbuckler, the son of a churl, a swashbuckler and a wanderer. We are talking of matters which, as everyone knows, are typical fireside debate subjects beloved of churlish swashbucklers. Subjects like genetics, for example. How do you even know that word, my swashbuckling friend? From the temple school in Ellander, where they teach the pupils to read and write just twenty-four runes? Whatever induced you to read books in which words like that and other, similar ones can be found? Where did you perfect your rhetoric and eloquence? And why did you do it? To converse with vampires? Oh, my genetic wanderer, upon whom Tissaia de Vries deigned to smile. Oh, my Witcher, my swashbuckler, who fascinates Philippa Eilhart so much her hands tremble. At the recollection of whom Triss Merigold blushes crimson. Not to mention the effect you have on Yennefer of Vengerberg.'

'Perhaps it's as well you aren't going to mention her. Indeed, so little sand remains in the hourglass I can almost count the grains. Don't paint any more pictures, Vilgefortz. Tell me what this is all about. Tell me using simple words. Imagine we're sitting by the fire, two wanderers, roasting a piglet which we just stole, trying and failing to get drunk on birch juice. Just a simple question. Answer it. As one wanderer to another.'

'What is the simple question?'

'What kind of pact are you proposing? What agreement are we to conclude? Why do you want me in your pot? In this cauldron, which, it seems to me, is starting to boil? What else is hanging in the air here – apart from candelabras?'

'Hmm,' the sorcerer pondered, or pretended to. 'The question is not simple, but I'll try to answer it. But not as a wanderer to a wanderer. I'll answer ... as one hired swashbuckler to another, similar, swashbuckler.'

'Suits me.'

'Then listen, comrade swashbuckler. Quite a nasty scrap is brewing. A bloody fight for life or death, with no mercy shown. One side will triumph, and the other will be pecked apart by ravens. I put it to you, comrade: join the side with the better chance. Join us. Forget the others, spit on them with utter contempt, because they don't stand a chance. What's the point of perishing with them? No, no, comrade, don't scowl at me. I know what you want to say. You want to say you're neutral. That you don't give a shit about any of them, that you'll simply sit out the slaughter, hunkered down in Kaer Morhen, hidden in the mountains. That's a bad idea, comrade. Everything you love will be with us. If you don't join us, you'll lose everything. And then you'll be consumed by emptiness, nothingness and hatred. You'll be destroyed by the approaching time of contempt. So be sensible and join the right side when the time comes to choose. And it will come. Trust me.'

'It's incredible,' the Witcher smiled hideously, 'how much my neutrality outrages everybody. How it makes me subject to offers of pacts and agreements, offers of collaboration, lectures about the necessity to make choices and join the right side. Let's put an end to this conversation, Vilgefortz. You're wasting your time. I'm not an equal partner for you in this game. I can't see any chance of the two of us ending up in a painting in the Gallery of Glory. Particularly not in a battle scene.'

The sorcerer said nothing.

'Set out on your chessboard,' said Geralt, 'the kings, queens, elephants and rooks, and don't worry about me, because I mean as much on your chessboard as the dust on it. It's not my game. You say I'll have to choose? I say you're wrong. I won't choose. I'll respond to events. I'll adapt to what others choose. That's what I've always done.'

'You're a fatalist.'

'That's right. Although that's yet another word I ought not to know. I repeat: it's not my game.'

'Really?' said Vilgefortz, leaning across the table. 'In this game, Witcher, on the chessboard, stands a black horse. It's tied to you by bonds of destiny. For good or ill. You know who I'm talking about, don't you? And I'm sure you don't want to lose her, do you? Just know there's only one way not to lose her.'

The Witcher's eyes narrowed.

'What do you want from that child?'

'There's only one way for you to find out.'

'I'm warning you. I won't let anyone harm her—'

'There's only one way you could prevent that. I offered you that option, Geralt of Rivia. Think over my offer. You have the entire night. Think, as you look up at the sky. At the stars. And don't mistake them with their reflection in a pond. The sand has run out.'

'I'm afraid for Ciri, Yen.'

'There's no need.'

'But ...'

'Trust me,' she said, hugging him. 'Trust me, please. Don't worry about Vilgefortz. He's a wily old fox. He wanted to trick you, to provoke you. And he was partly successful. But it's not important. Ciri is in my care, and she'll be safe in Aretuza. She'll be able to develop her abilities here, and no one will interfere with that. No one. But forget about her becoming a witcher. She has other talents. And she's destined for other work. You can trust me.'

'I trust you.'

'That's significant progress. And don't worry about Vilgefortz. Tomorrow will explain many matters and solve many problems.'

Tomorrow, he thought. *She's hiding something from me. And I'm afraid to ask what. Codringher was right. I've got mixed up in a dreadful mess, but now there's no way out. I have to wait and see what tomorrow – which is supposed to explain everything – will bring. I have to trust her. I know something's going to happen. I'll wait. And adapt to the situation.*

He looked at the writing desk.

'Yen?'

'I'm here.'

'When you were a pupil at Aretuza ... When you slept in a chamber like this ... Did you have a doll you couldn't sleep without? Which you put on the writing desk during the day?'

'No,' said Yennefer, moving suddenly. 'I didn't have a doll of any kind. Don't ask me about that, Geralt. Please, don't ask me.'

'Aretuza,' he whispered, looking around. 'Aretuza on the Isle of Thanedd. It'll become her home. For so many years ... When she leaves here she'll be a mature woman ...'

'Stop that. Don't think about it and don't talk about it. Instead ...'

'What, Yen?'

'Love me.'

He embraced her. And touched her. And found her. Yennefer, in some astonishing way hard and soft at the same time, sighed loudly. The words they had uttered broke off, perished among the sighs and quickened breaths, ceased to have any meaning and were dissipated. So they remained silent, and focused on the search for one another, on the search for the truth. They searched for a long time, lovingly and very thoroughly, fearful of needless haste, recklessness and nonchalance. They searched vigorously, intensively and passionately, fearful of needless self-doubt and indecision. They searched cautiously, fearful of needless tactlessness.

They found one another, conquered their fear and, a moment later, found the truth, which exploded under their eyelids with a terrible, blinding clarity, tore apart the lips pursed in determination with a moan. Then time shuddered spasmodically and froze, everything vanished, and touch became the only functioning sense.

An eternity passed, reality returned and time shuddered once more and set off again, slowly, ponderously, like a great, fully laden cart. Geralt looked through the window. The moon was still hanging in the sky, although what had just happened ought in principle to have struck it down from the sky.

'Oh heavens, oh heavens,' said Yennefer much later, slowly wiping a tear from her cheek.

They lay still among the dishevelled sheets, among thrills, among steaming warmth and waning happiness and among silence, and all around whirled vague darkness, permeated by the scent of the night and the voices of cicadas. Geralt knew that, in moments like this, the enchantress's telepathic abilities were sharpened and very powerful, so he thought about beautiful matters and beautiful things. About things which would give her joy. About the exploding brightness of the sunrise. About fog suspended over a mountain lake at dawn. About crystal waterfalls, with salmon leaping up them, gleaming as though made of solid silver. About warm drops of rain hitting burdock leaves, heavy with dew.

He thought for her and Yennefer smiled, listening to his thoughts. The smile quivered on her cheek along with the crescent shadows of her eyelashes.

'A home?' asked Yennefer suddenly. 'What home? Do you have a home? You want to build a home? Oh ... I'm sorry. I shouldn't ...'

He was quiet. He was angry with himself. As he had been thinking for her, he had accidentally allowed her to read a thought about herself.

'A pretty dream,' said Yennefer, stroking him lightly on the shoulder. 'A home. A house built with your own hands, and you and I in that house. You would keep horses and sheep, and I would have a little garden, cook food and card wool, which we would take to market. With the pennies earned from selling the wool and various crops we would buy what we needed; let's say some copper cauldrons and an iron rake. Every now and then, Ciri would visit us with her husband and three children, and Triss Merigold would occasionally look in, to stay for a few days. We'd grow old together, beautifully and with dignity. And should I ever get bored, you would play for me in the evening on your homemade bagpipes. Playing the bagpipes – as everyone knows – is the best remedy for depression.'

The Witcher said nothing. The enchantress cleared her throat softly.

'I'm sorry,' she said, a moment later. He got up on an elbow, leaned across and kissed her. She moved suddenly, and hugged him. Wordlessly.

'Say something.'

'I wouldn't like to lose you, Yen.'

'But you have me.'

'The night will end.'

'Everything ends.'

No, he thought. *I don't want it to be like that. I'm tired. Too tired to accept the perspective of endings which are beginnings, and starting everything over again. I'd like . . .*

'Don't talk,' she said, quickly placing her fingers on his lips. 'Don't tell me what you'd like and what you desire. Because it might turn out I won't be able to fulfil your desires, and that causes me pain.'

'What do you desire, Yen? What do you dream about?'

'Only about achievable things.'

'And about me?'

'I already have you.'

He remained quiet for a long time, waiting until she broke the silence.

'Geralt?'

'Mm?'

'Love me, please.'

At first, satiated with each other, they were both full of fantasy and invention, creative, imaginative and craving for the new. As usual, it quickly turned out it was at once too much and too little. They understood it simultaneously and once more made love to one another.

When Geralt had recovered his senses, the moon was still in its place. The cicadas were playing wildly, as though they also wanted to conquer anxiety and fear with madness and abandon. From a nearby window in the left wing of Aretuza, someone craving sleep yelled out, fulminating sternly and demanding quiet. From a window on the other side someone else, clearly with a more artistic soul, applauded enthusiastically and congratulated them.

'Oh, Yen . . .' whispered the Witcher reproachfully.

'I had a reason . . .' She kissed him and then buried her cheek in the pillow. 'I had a reason to scream. So I screamed. It shouldn't be suppressed. It would be unhealthy and unnatural. Hold me, please.'

The Lara Portal, also known as **Benavent's Portal**, *after its discoverer. Located on the Isle of Thanedd, on the uppermost floor of the Tower of Gulls. A fixed portal, periodically active. Principles of functioning: unknown. Destination: unknown, but probably skewed, owing to damage. Numerous forks or dispersions possible. Important information: a chaotic and lethally dangerous portal. All experimentation categorically forbidden. Magic may not be used in the Tower of Gulls or in close proximity to it, particularly not teleportational magic. In exceptional cases, the Chapter will examine applications for permission to enter Tor Lara and for inspections of the portal. Applications should be supported by evidence of research work already in progress and of specialisation in the subject area.*

Bibliography: Geoffrey Monck, The Magic of the Elder Folk; *Immanuel Benavent*, The Portal of Tor Lara; *Nina Fioravanti*, The Theory and Practice of Teleportation; *Ransant Alvaro*, The Gates of Mystery.

Prohibita (list of banned artefacts),
Ars Magica, Edition LVIII

CHAPTER FOUR

In the beginning there was only pulsating, shimmering chaos, a cascade of images and a whirling abyss of sounds and voices. Ciri saw a tower reaching up to the sky with thunderbolts dancing across the roof. She heard the cry of a raptor and suddenly *became* it. She was flying with enormous speed and beneath her was a stormy sea. She saw a small button-eyed doll and suddenly *was* that doll, and all around her teemed the darkness, pulsing with the sounds of cicadas. She saw a large black and white tomcat and suddenly *was* that cat, surrounded by a sombre house, darkened wood panelling and the smell of candles and old books. Several times, she heard someone call her name; summon her. She saw silver salmon leaping up waterfalls, heard the sound of rain drumming against leaves. And then she heard Yennefer's strange, long-drawn-out scream. And it was that scream that woke her, pulled her out of the chasm of timelessness and chaos.

Now, vainly trying to recall the dream, she could only hear the soft sounds of lute and flute, the jingling of a tambourine, singing and laughter. Dandelion and the group of minstrels he had chanced upon continued to have the time of their lives in the chamber at the end of the corridor.

A shaft of moonlight shone through the window, somewhat lightening the gloom and making the chamber in Loxia resemble a dream world. Ciri threw off the sheet. She was bathed in sweat and her hair was stuck to her forehead. It had taken her a long time to fall asleep the night before; it had been stuffy, even though the window had been wide open. She knew what had caused it. Before leaving with Geralt, Yennefer had encircled the chamber with protective charms. Ostensibly it was in order to prevent anyone from entering, though Ciri suspected their true purpose was to stop her leaving.

She was, quite simply, a prisoner. Yennefer, although clearly happy to be back with Geralt, had neither forgiven nor forgotten Ciri's wilful and reckless flight to Hirundum, even though it had led to her reunion with Geralt.

The meeting with Geralt itself had filled Ciri with sadness and disappointment. The Witcher had been taciturn, tense, restless and demonstrably insincere. Their conversation had faltered and limped along, losing its way in sentences and questions which suddenly broke off. The Witcher's eyes and thoughts kept running away from her and fleeing into the distance. Ciri knew where they were running to.

Dandelion's soft, mournful singing and the music he raised from the lute's strings, murmuring like a stream flowing over pebbles, drifted to her from the chamber at the end of the corridor. She recognised it as the melody the bard had started composing some days before. The ballad – as Dandelion had boasted several times – bore the title *Elusive* and was intended to earn the poet first place at the annual bard's tournament due to take place in the later autumn at Vartburg Castle. Ciri listened carefully to the words.

O'er glistening roofs you float
Through lily-strewn rivers you dive
Yet one day I will know your truths
If only I am still alive ...

Hooves thundered, riders galloped in the night, and on the horizon the sky bloomed with the glow of many fires. A bird of prey screeched and spread its wings, taking flight. Ciri plunged into sleep once more, hearing people calling her name over and over. Once it was Geralt, once Yennefer, once Triss Merigold, finally – several times – a sad, slim, fair-haired girl she didn't recognise, who looked out at her from a miniature, framed in horn and brass.

Then she saw a black and white cat, and a moment later, she again *was* that cat, and seeing with its eyes. She was in a strange, dark house. She saw great shelves of books, and a lectern lit by several candlesticks, with two men sitting at it, poring over scrolls. One of the men was coughing and wiping his lips with a handkerchief. The second, a midget with a huge head, sat on a chair on wheels. He had no legs.

'Extraordinary ...' sighed Fenn, running his eyes over the decaying parchment. 'It's hard to believe ... Where did you get these documents?'

'You wouldn't believe me if I told you,' Codringher coughed. 'Have you only now realised who Cirilla, Princess of Cintra, really is? The Child of the Elder Blood; the last offshoot of that bloody tree of hatred! The last branch and, on it, the last poisoned apple ...'

'The Elder Blood ... So far back in time ... Pavetta, Calanthe, Adalia, Elen, Fiona ...'

'And Falka.'

'By the gods, but that's impossible. Firstly, Falka had no children! Secondly, Fiona was the legitimate daughter of —'

'Firstly, we know nothing about Falka's youth. Secondly, Fenn, don't make me laugh. You know, of course, that I'm overcome with spasms of mirth at the sound of the word "legitimate". I believe that document, because in my opinion it's authentic and speaks the truth. Fiona, Pavetta's great-great-grandmother, was the daughter of Falka, that monster in human form. Damn it, I don't believe in all those insane predictions, prophecies and other poppycock, but when I now recall the Ithlinne forecasts ...'

'Tainted blood?'

'Tainted, contaminated, accursed; it can be understood in various ways. And according to legend, if you recall, it was Falka who was accursed – because Lara Dorren aep Shiadhal had put a curse on her mother—'

'Those are just stories, Codringher.'

'You're right: stories. But do you know when stories stop being stories? The moment someone begins to believe in them. And someone believes in the story of the Elder Blood. In particular, in the part that says *from Falka's blood will be born an avenger who will destroy the old world and build a new one on its ruins.*'

'And Cirilla is supposed to be that avenger?'

'No. Not Cirilla. Her son.'

'And Cirilla is being hunted by –'

'– Emhyr var Emreis, Emperor of Nilfgaard,' finished Codringher coldly. 'Now do you understand? Cirilla, irrespective of her will, is to become the mother of the heir to the throne. Mother to an arch-prince; the Arch-Prince of Darkness, the descendant and avenger of that she-devil Falka. The destruction and the subsequent rebuilding of the world is meant – it seems to me – to proceed in a guided and controlled way.'

The cripple said nothing for a long time.

'Don't you think,' he finally asked, 'we should tell Geralt about this?'

'Geralt?' sneered Codringher. 'Who? You mean that simpleton who, not so long ago, tried to persuade me he doesn't work for gain? Oh, I believe that; he doesn't work for his own gain. But for someone else's. And unwittingly, as a matter of fact. Geralt is hunting Rience; Rience may be on a leash but Geralt doesn't even know there's a collar around his neck. Should I inform him? And so help the people planning to capture this golden-egg laying hen, in order to blackmail Emhyr or ingratiate themselves with him? No, Fenn. I'm not that stupid.'

'The Witcher's on a leash? But who's holding it?'

'Think.'

'Bitch!'

'You said it. The only person who can influence him. Whom he trusts. But I don't trust her and never have. So I'm going to join the game myself.'

'It's a dangerous one, Codringher.'

'There aren't any safe games. Games are either worth a candle or they aren't. Fenn, old man, don't you understand what has fallen into our hands? A golden hen, which will lay for us – and no one else – and it'll be huge egg, with a rich, yellow yolk ...'

Codringher coughed violently. When he removed the handkerchief from his mouth there were flecks of blood on it.

'Gold won't cure that,' said Fenn, looking at the handkerchief in his partner's hand. 'Nor give me back my legs ...'

'Who knows?'

Somebody knocked at the door. Fenn fidgeted nervously in his wheeled chair.

'Are you expecting anyone, Codringher?'

'I am. The men I'm sending to Thanedd. To fetch our golden hen.'

'Don't open it,' Ciri screamed. 'Don't open the door! Death stands behind it! Don't open the door!'

'All right, all right, I'm just coming,' called Codringher, pulling back the bolts, then turning to his meowing cat. 'And you'll sit quietly, you accursed little beast ...'

He broke off. The men in the doorway were not the ones he had been expecting. Instead, three characters he did not know were standing there.

'The Honourable Mr Codringher?'

'The master's away on business,' said the lawyer, assuming the expression of a halfwit and speaking with a slightly squeaky voice. 'I am the master's butler. The name is Dullord, Mikael Dullord. How may I serve your honourable selves?'

'You cannot,' said one of the individuals, a tall half-elf. 'Since your master is not here, we'll just leave a letter and a message. Here is the letter.'

'I will pass it on without fail,' said Codringher, playing the role of a simple lackey perfectly; bowing subserviently and holding out a hand to take a scroll of parchment tied up with a red cord. 'And the message?'

The cord binding the scroll unwound like a striking snake, lashing and curling itself tightly around his wrist. The tall man jerked hard. Codringher lost his balance and lurched forward, instinctively thrusting his left hand towards the half-elf's chest to stop himself from falling against him. As he fell he was unable to avoid the dagger which was rammed into his belly. He cried out breathlessly and jerked backwards, but the magic cord around his wrist held fast. The half-elf pulled Codringher towards him and stabbed again.

157

This time the whole of Codringher's weight bore down on the blade.

'That's the message and greetings from Rience,' hissed the tall half-elf, pulling the dagger upwards powerfully and gutting the lawyer like a fish. 'Go to hell, Codringher. Straight to hell.'

Codringher's breath rasped. He felt the dagger blade grate and crunch against his ribs and sternum. He slumped onto the floor, curling up into a ball. He wanted to shout, to warn Fenn, but was only able to screech, and the screech was immediately drowned in a gush of blood.

The tall half-elf stepped over the body and was followed inside by the other two. They were humans.

Fenn was ready for them.

The bowstring thwacked, and one of the thugs crashed onto his back, struck directly in the forehead by a steel ball. Fenn shoved himself backwards in his chair, trying desperately to reload the arbalest with his shaking hands.

The tall man leapt towards him, knocking over the chair with a powerful kick. The midget rolled among the papers strewn over the floor. Waving his small hands and the stumps of his legs helplessly, he resembled a mutilated spider.

The half-elf kicked the arbalest out of Fenn's reach. Paying no attention to the cripple's attempts to struggle away, he hurriedly looked through the documents lying on the lectern. His attention was caught by a miniature in a horn and brass frame, showing a fair-haired girl. He picked it up with the scrap of paper attached to it.

The second thug ignored the one who had been hit by the arbalest ball and came closer. The half-elf raised his eyebrows questioningly. The thug shook his head.

The half-elf picked up several documents from the lectern, tucking them away in his coat, along with the miniature. He then took a handful of quills from the inkwell and set light to them with one of the candlesticks. He turned them around slowly, allowing the fire take good hold and then threw them onto the lectern among the scrolls of parchment, which immediately burst into flames.

Fenn screamed.

The tall half-elf took a bottle of ink remover from the burning table, stood over the midget thrashing around on the floor and emptied the contents over him. Fenn gave a tormented howl. The other thug swept an armful of scrolls from a bookshelf and threw them over the cripple.

The fire on the lectern had just reached the ceiling. A second, smaller bottle of solvent exploded with a roar, the flames licking the bookshelves. The scrolls, rolls and files began to blacken, curl up and catch fire. Fenn wailed. The tall half-elf stepped back from the burning pulpit, twisted up a second piece of paper and lit it. The second thug threw another armful of vellum scrolls on the cripple.

Fenn screamed.

The half-elf stood over him, holding the burning brand.

Codringher's black and white cat alighted on a nearby wall. In its yellow eyes danced the reflection of the fire, which had transformed the pleasant night into this horrific parody of day. People were screaming. *Fire! Fire! Water!* People ran towards the building. The cat froze, watching them with astonishment and contempt. Those idiots were clearly heading towards the fiery abyss, from which it had only just managed to extricate itself.

Turning away, unconcerned, Codringher's cat went back to licking its bloodstained paws.

Ciri awoke covered in sweat, with her hands painfully gripping the sheets. Everything was quiet, and the soft darkness was pierced by a dagger-like shaft of moonlight.

A fire. An inferno. Blood. A nightmare ... I don't remember, I don't remember anything ...

She took a deep breath of the crisp night air. The sense of stuffiness had vanished. She knew why.

The protective charms had stopped working.

Something's happened, thought Ciri. She jumped out of bed and quickly dressed. She belted on her dagger. She didn't have a sword any more; Yennefer had taken it from her, giving it to Dandelion for safekeeping. The poet must have gone to sleep, and it was silent in Loxia. Ciri was already wondering whether to go and wake him when she felt a strong pulse and a rush of blood in her ears.

The shaft of moonlight coming through the window became a road. At the end of the road, far away, was a door. The door opened and Yennefer stood there.

'Come with me.'

Other doors opened behind the sorceress's back. One after the other. An endless succession. The black shapes of columns crystallised from the darkness. *Not columns – perhaps they're statues ... I'm dreaming*, thought Ciri, *I don't believe my eyes. I'm dreaming. That isn't a road. It's light, a shaft of light. I can't go along that ...*

'Come with me.'

She obeyed.

Had it not been for the foolish scruples of the Witcher, and his impractical principles, many subsequent events would have run their course quite differently. Many events would probably have not taken place at all. And the history of the world would have unfolded in an alternative way.

But the history of the world unfolded as it unfolded, the sole cause of which was that the Witcher had scruples. When he awoke in the morning with the need to relieve himself, he didn't do what any other man would have done; he didn't go out onto the balcony and piss into a flowerpot of nasturtiums. He had scruples. He dressed quietly without waking Yennefer, who was sleeping deeply, motionless and barely breathing. He left the chamber and went out to the garden.

The banquet was still in progress but, as the sounds indicated, only in a fragmentary form. The lights were still burning in the ballroom windows, illuminating the atrium and beds of peonies. The Witcher went a little further in, among some dense bushes, where he stared at the lightening sky. The horizon was already burning with the purple streaks of dawn.

As he slowly returned, pondering important matters, his medallion vibrated powerfully. He held it in his hand, feeling the vibrations penetrate his entire body. There was no doubt; someone in

Aretuza had cast a spell. Geralt listened carefully and heard some muffled shouts, and a clattering and pounding coming from the cloister in the palace's left wing.

Anyone else would have turned on their heels at once and walked briskly back to where they'd come from, pretending they hadn't heard anything. And then perhaps the history of the world would have unfolded differently. But the Witcher had scruples and was accustomed to acting according to foolish, impractical principles.

When he ran into the cloister and the corridor, he saw that a fight was in progress. Several tough-looking men in grey jerkins were in the act of overpowering a short sorcerer who had been thrown to the ground. The fight was being directed by Dijkstra, chief of Vizimir, King of Redania's intelligence service. Before Geralt was able to take any action he was overpowered himself; two other heavies in grey pinned him to a wall, and a third held the three-pronged blade of a partisan against his chest.

All the heavies had breastplates emblazoned with the Redanian eagle.

'That's called "being in the shit",' explained Dijkstra quietly, approaching him. 'And you, Witcher, seem to have an inborn talent for falling into it. Stand there nice and peacefully and try not to attract anyone's attention.'

The Redanians finally overpowered the short sorcerer and lifted him up, holding him by his arms. It was Artaud Terranova, a member of the Chapter.

The light which made the details visible emanated from an orb suspended above Keira Metz's head – a sorceress with whom Geralt had been chatting at the banquet the previous evening. He barely recognised her; she had exchanged her flowing tulle for severe male clothing, and she had a dagger at her side.

'Handcuff him,' she ordered curtly. A set of handcuffs made of a bluish metal clinked in her hand.

'Don't you dare put those on me!' yelled Terranova. 'Don't you dare, Metz! I am a member of the Chapter!'

'You were. Now you're a common traitor. And you will be treated as such.'

'And you're a lousy whore, who—'

Keira took a step back, swayed her hips and punched him in the face with all her strength. The sorcerer's head jerked backwards so hard that for a moment Geralt thought it would be torn from his trunk. Terranova lolled in the arms of the men holding him, blood streaming from his nose and mouth. The sorceress didn't strike him a second time, though her fist was raised. The Witcher saw the flash of brass knuckles on her fingers. He wasn't surprised. Keira was very lightly built, and a blow like that couldn't have been dealt with a bare fist.

He didn't move. The thugs were holding him tightly, and the point of the partisan was pressing against his chest. Geralt wasn't sure if he would have moved, had he been free, or whether he would have known what to do.

The Redanians snapped the handcuffs around the sorcerer's wrists, which were twisted behind his back. Terranova cried out, struggled, bent over and retched and Geralt realised what the handcuffs were made of. It was an alloy of iron and dimeritium, a rare metal characterised by its inhibition of magical powers. The inhibition was accompanied by a set of rather unpleasant side effects for sorcerers.

Keira Metz raised her head, pulling her hair back from her forehead. And then she saw him.

'What the bloody hell is he doing here? How did he get here?'

'He just stepped in,' answered Dijkstra unemotionally. 'He's got a talent for putting his foot in it. What shall I do with him?'

Keira's face darkened and she stamped several times with the high heel of her boot.

'Guard him. I don't have time now.'

She walked quickly away, followed by the Redanians who were dragging Terranova behind them. The shining orb floated behind the sorceress, although it was already dawn and quickly becoming light. On a signal from Dijkstra, the thugs released Geralt. The spy came closer and looked the Witcher in the eyes.

'Don't try anything.'

'What's happening here? What—?'

'And don't utter a word.'

Keira Metz returned a short time later; but not alone. She was accompanied by a flaxen-haired sorcerer, introduced to Geralt on the previous day as Detmold of Ban Ard. At the sight of the Witcher, he cursed and smacked his fist into his palm.

'Shit! Is he the one Yennefer's taken a liking to?'

'Yes, that's him,' said Keira. 'Geralt of Rivia. The problem is, I don't know about Yennefer ...'

'I don't know either,' said Detmold, shrugging his shoulders. 'In any case, he's mixed up in this now. He's seen too much. Take him to Philippa; she'll decide. Put him in handcuffs.'

'There's no need,' said Dijkstra with a languid air. 'I'll answer for him. I'll take him to where he ought to be.'

'Excellent,' nodded Detmold, 'because we have no time for him. Come on, Keira, it's a mess up there ...'

'Oh, but aren't they anxious?' muttered the Redanian spy, watching them walk away. 'It's lack of experience, nothing more. And coups d'état and putsches are like green beet soup. They're best served cold. Let's go, Geralt. And remember: peacefully and with dignity. Don't make a scene. And don't make me regret not having you handcuffed or tied up.'

'What's happening, Dijkstra?'

'Haven't you guessed yet?' said the spy, walking beside him, with the three Redanian heavies bringing up the rear. 'Tell me straight, Witcher. How did you wind up here?'

'I was worried about the nasturtiums wilting.'

'Geralt,' said Dijkstra, frowning at him. 'You've fallen head first into the shit. You've swum upwards, and you're holding your head above the surface, but your feet still aren't touching the bottom. Someone's offering you a helping hand, at the risk of falling in and getting covered in it himself. So drop the foolish jokes. Yennefer made you come here, did she?'

'No. Yennefer's still asleep in a warm bed. Does that reassure you?'

The huge spy turned suddenly, seized the Witcher by the arms and shoved him against the wall of the corridor.

163

'No, it doesn't reassure me, you bloody fool,' he hissed. 'Haven't you got it yet, you idiot, that decent sorcerers who are faithful to kings aren't asleep tonight? That they didn't go to bed at all? Only traitors who have sold out to Nilfgaard are asleep in their warm beds. Traitors, who were preparing a putsch of their own, but for a later date. They didn't know their plans had been rumbled and their intentions second-guessed. And as you can see, they're being dragged out of those warm beds, getting smacked in the teeth with knuckledusters, and having dimeritium bracelets wrapped around their wrists. The traitors are finished. Get it? If you don't want to go down with them, stop playing the fool! Did Vilgefortz manage to recruit you yesterday evening? Or perhaps Yennefer already did. Talk! And fast, before your mouth is flooded with shit!'

'Green beet soup, Dijkstra,' reminded Geralt. 'Take me to Philippa. Peacefully and with dignity. And without causing a scene.'

The spy released him and took a step back.

'Let's go,' he said coldly. 'Up these stairs. But this conversation isn't over yet. I promise you.'

It was bright from the light of lanterns and magical orbs floating beneath the column which supported the vaulting, at the point where four corridors joined. The place was heaving with Redanians and sorcerers. Among the latter were two members of the Council: Radcliffe and Sabrina Glevissig. Sabrina, like Keira Metz, was dressed in grey men's apparel. Geralt realised it was possible to identify the different factions within the putsch by their uniforms.

Triss Merigold crouched on the floor, hunched over a body which was lying in a pool of blood. Geralt recognised the body as that of Lydia van Bredevoort. He knew her by her hair and silk dress. He couldn't have recognised her by her face because it was no longer a face. It was a horrifying, macabre skull, with shining teeth exposed halfway up the cheeks, and a distorted, sunken jaw, the bones badly knitted together.*

---

* The lower part of Lydia van Bredevoort's face, as seen in society and her portraits, was actually an illusion. Experiments on a mysterious artefact had left her with burns, and throat and larynx mutations.

'Cover her up,' said Sabrina Glevissig softly. 'When she died, the illusion vanished ... I said bloody cover her up with something!'

'How did it happen, Radcliffe?' asked Triss, withdrawing her hand from the gilded haft of the dagger which was embedded beneath Lydia's sternum. 'How could it have happened? This was supposed to be bloodless!'

'She attacked us,' muttered the sorcerer and lowered his head. 'She attacked us as Vilgefortz was being escorted out. There was a scuffle ... I have no idea ... It's her own dagger.'

'Cover her face!' said Sabrina, suddenly turning away. She saw Geralt, and her predatory eyes shone like anthracite.

'How did he get here?'

Triss leapt to her feet and sprang towards the Witcher. Geralt saw her hand right in front of his face. Then he saw a flash, and everything faded into darkness. He couldn't see. He felt a hand on his collar and a sharp tug.

'Hold him up or he'll fall,' said Triss, her voice unnatural, feigning anger. She jerked him again, pulling him towards her for a moment.

'Forgive me,' she whispered hurriedly. 'I had to do that.'

Dijkstra's men held him fast.

He moved his head around, activating his other senses. There were movements in the corridors and the air rippled, carrying scents with it. And voices. Sabrina Glevissig swore; Triss mollified her. The Redanians, reeking of an army barracks, dragged the limp body across the floor, rustling the silk of the dress. Blood. The smell of blood. And the smell of ozone; the scent of magic. Raised voices. Footsteps. The nervous clattering of heels.

'Hurry up! It's all taking too long! We ought to be in Garstang by now!'

That was Philippa Eilhart. Sounding anxious.

'Sabrina, find Marti Södergren quickly. Drag her out of bed, if necessary. Gedymdeith's in a bad way. I think it's a heart attack. Have Marti see to him but don't say anything to her or to whoever she's sleeping with. Triss, find Dorregaray, Drithelm and Carduin and bring them to Garstang.'

'What for?'

165

'They represent the kings. Ethain and Esterad are to be informed about our operation and its consequences. You'll be taking them ... Triss, you have blood on your hand! Whose is it?'

'Lydia's.'

'Damn it. When? How?'

'Is it important how?' said a cold, calm voice. The voice of Tissaia de Vries. The rustle of a dress. Tissaia was in a ball gown, not a rebel uniform. Geralt listened carefully but could not hear the jingling of dimeritium handcuffs.

'Are you pretending to be worried?' repeated Tissaia. 'Concerned? When revolts are organised, when armed thugs are deployed at night, you have to expect casualties. Lydia is dead. Hen Gedymdeith is dying. A moment ago I saw Artaud with his face carved up. How many more casualties will there be, Philippa Eilhart?'

'I don't know,' answered Philippa resolutely. 'But I'm not backing down.'

'Of course not. You don't back down from anything.'

The air vibrated, and heels thudded on the floor in a familiar rhythm. Philippa walked towards him. He remembered the nervous rhythm of her footsteps when they were walking through the hall at Aretuza together, to feast on caviar. He recalled the scent of cinnamon and muskroot. Now, that scent was mixed with the smell of baking soda. Geralt had no intention of participating in any kind of coup or putsch, but wondered whether – had he decided to – he would have thought about cleaning his teeth beforehand.

'He can't see you, Phil,' said Dijkstra nonchalantly. 'He can't see anything and didn't see anything. The one with the beautiful hair blinded him.'

He heard Philippa's breath and sensed every one of her movements but moved his head around awkwardly, simulating helplessness. The enchantress was not to be fooled.

'Don't bother pretending, Geralt. Triss may have darkened your eyes but she didn't take away your mind. How the hell did you end up here?'

'I dropped in. Where's Yennefer?'

'Blessed are they who do not know,' said Philippa, in a voice devoid of mockery. 'For they will live longer. Be grateful to Triss. It was a soft spell; the blindness will soon pass. And you didn't see anything you weren't meant to. Guard him, Dijkstra. I'll be right back.'

There was a disturbance again. And voices. Keira Metz's resonant soprano, Radcliffe's nasal bass. The clatter of heavy Redanian boots. And Tissaia de Vries's raised voice.

'Let her go! How could you? How could you do that to her?'

'She's a traitress!' responded Radcliffe's nasal voice.

'I will never believe that!'

'Blood's thicker than water,' said Philippa Eilhart, coldly. 'And Emperor Emhyr has promised the elves freedom. As well as their own, independent state. Here, in these lands. After the humans have been slaughtered, naturally. And that was sufficient for her to betray us without a second thought.'

'Answer!' said Tissaia de Vries forcefully. 'Answer her, Enid!'

'Answer, Francesca.'

The clinking of dimeritium handcuffs. The singsong, elven lilt of Francesca Findabair, the Daisy of the Valleys, the most beautiful woman in the world.

'Va vort a me, Dh'oine. N'aen te a dice'n.'

'Will that suffice, Tissaia?' barked Philippa. 'Will you believe me now? You, me, all of us, are – and always were – Dh'oine, humans, to her. And she, Aen Seidhe, has nothing to say to humans. And you, Fercart? What did Vilgefortz and Emhyr promise you, that made you choose treachery?'

'Go to hell, you debauched slut.'

Geralt held his breath, but this time didn't hear the sound of brass knuckles hitting bone. Philippa was more composed than Keira. Or she didn't have any brass knuckles.

'Radcliffe, take the traitors to Garstang! Detmold, give your arm to Arch-Mistress de Vries. Go. I'll join you soon.'

Footsteps. The scent of cinnamon and muskroot.

'Dijkstra.'

'I'm here, Phil.'

167

'Your men are no longer needed here. They may return to Loxia.'

'Are you absolutely sure—'

'To Loxia, Dijkstra!'

'Yes, Your Grace.' There was scorn in the spy's voice. 'The lackeys can leave. They've done their bidding. Now it is a private matter for the mages. And thus I, without further ado, will leave Your Grace's beautiful presence. I didn't expect gratitude for my help or my contribution to your putsch, but I am certain that Your Grace will keep me in her gracious memory.'

'Forgive me, Sigismund. Thank you for your help.'

'Not at all. It was my pleasure. Hey, Voymir, get your men. I want five to stay with me. Take the others downstairs and board *The Spada*. But do it quietly, on tiptoe, without any fuss, commotion or fireworks. Use side corridors. Don't breathe a word of this in Loxia or in the harbour. That's an order!'

'You didn't see anything, Geralt,' said Philippa Eilhart in a whisper, wafting cinnamon, muskroot and baking soda onto the Witcher. 'You didn't hear anything. You never spoke to Vilgefortz. Dijkstra will take you to Loxia now. I'll try to find you when ... when it's all over. I promised you as much yesterday and I'll keep my word.'

'What about Yennefer?'

'I'd say he's obsessed,' said Dijkstra, returning and shuffling his feet. 'Yennefer, Yennefer ... It's getting tedious. Don't bother yourself with him, Phil. There are more important things to do. Was the expected item found on Vilgefortz?'

'Indeed. Here, this is for you.'

'Oh!' The rustle of paper being unwrapped. 'Oh my, oh my! Excellent! Duke Nitert. Splendid! Baron—'

'Discreetly; no names. And please don't start the executions immediately after your return to Tretogor. Don't incite a premature scandal.'

'Don't worry. The lads on this list – so greedy for Nilfgaardian gold – are safe. At least for the moment. They'll become my sweet little puppets. I'll be able to pull their strings, and later we'll put those strings around their sweet little necks ... Just out of curiosity, were there any other lists? Any traitors from Kaedwen, from Temeria, from Aedirn? I'd be delighted to take a look. Just a glimpse ...'

'I know you would. But it's not your business. Radcliffe and Sabrina Glevissig were given those lists, and they'll know what to do with them. And now I must go. I'm in a hurry.'

'Phil?'

'Yes.'

'Restore the Witcher's sight so he doesn't trip on the stairs.'

The banquet in the Aretuza ballroom was still in progress, but it had become more traditional and relaxed. The tables had been pushed aside, and the sorcerers and enchantresses had brought in armchairs, chairs and stools they'd found in other rooms and were lounging in them and amusing themselves in various ways. Most of their amusements were vulgar. A large group, crowded around a bulky cask of rotgut, were carousing, talking and erupting into laughter from time to time. Those who not long before had been delicately spearing exquisite morsels with little silver forks were now unceremoniously chewing mutton ribs held in both hands. Several of them were playing cards, ignoring the rest. Others were asleep. A couple were kissing passionately in the corner, and the ardour they were displaying indicated it wouldn't stop there.

'Just look at them, Witcher,' said Dijkstra, leaning over the banisters of the cloister and looking down at the sorcerers. 'How merrily they play. Just like children. And meanwhile, their Council has just nicked almost their entire Chapter and are trying them for treason, for cuddling up to Nilfgaard. Look at that couple. They'll be soon looking for a secluded corner, and before they've finish bonking, Vilgefortz will have hanged. Oh, what a strange world it is ...'

'Be quiet, Dijkstra.'

The path leading to Loxia was cut into the slopes of the mountain in a zigzag of steps. The steps connected terraces, which were decorated with neglected hedges, flowerbeds and yellowing agaves in flowerpots. Dijkstra stopped at one of the terraces they passed and walked over to a wall with a row of stone chimeras' heads. Water was trickling from their jaws. The spy leaned over and took a long drink.

The Witcher approached the balustrade. The sea glimmered gold, and the sky was even more kitsch in colour than it was in the paintings filling the Gallery of Glory. Below, he could see the squad of Redanians who had been ordered to leave Aretuza. They were heading for the harbour in well-ordered formation, just crossing a bridge linking the two sides of a rocky cleft.

His attention was suddenly caught by a colourful, lone figure, conspicuous because it was moving quickly. And moving in the opposite direction to the Redanians. Uphill, towards Aretuza.

'Right,' said Dijkstra, urging him on with a cough. 'It's time we were going.'

'Go yourself, if you're in such a hurry.'

'Yeah, right,' scowled the spy. 'And you'll go back up there to rescue your beloved Yennefer. And stir up trouble like a tipsy gnome. We're heading for Loxia, Witcher. Are you kidding yourself or something? Do you think I got you out of Aretuza because of some long-hidden love for you? Well I didn't. I got you out of there because I need you.'

'For what?'

'Are you having me on? Twelve young ladies from Redania's finest families are pupils at Aretuza. I can't risk a conflict with the honourable rectoress, Margarita Laux-Antille. But the rectoress won't give me Cirilla, the Princess of Cintra, the girl Yennefer brought to Thanedd. She'll give her to *you*, however. When you ask her.'

'What gave you the ridiculous idea that I'll ask for her?'

'The ridiculous assumption that you want to make sure Cirilla will be safe. She'll be safe in my care, in King Vizimir's care. In Tretogor. She isn't safe on Thanedd. Refrain from making any sarcastic comments. Yes, I know the kings didn't have the most wonderful plans for her at the beginning. But that has changed. Now it's become clear that Cirilla – alive, safe and in good health – may be worth more in the coming war than ten regiments of heavy horse. Dead, she's not worth a brass farthing.'

'Does Philippa Eilhart know what you're planning?'

'No, she doesn't. She doesn't even know I know the girl's in Loxia. My erstwhile beloved Phil may put on airs and graces, but Vizimir is still the King of Redania. I carry out his orders, and I don't give a shit what the sorcerers are plotting. Cirilla will board *The Spada* and sail to Novigrad, from where she'll travel to Tretogor. And she'll be safe. Do you believe me?'

The Witcher leaned over towards one of the chimera heads and drank some of the water trickling from its monstrous maw.

'Do you believe me?' repeated Dijkstra, standing over him.

Geralt stood up, wiped his mouth, and punched him in the jaw with all his strength. The spy staggered but didn't go down. The nearest Redanian leapt forward, intending to seize the Witcher, but grabbed thin air, and immediately sat down, spitting blood and one of his teeth. Then all the others jumped him. There was a chaotic confusion and crush, which was exactly what the Witcher had been hoping for.

One of the Redanians slammed head first into the gargoyle, and the water trickling from its jaws turned red. Another caught the heel of the Witcher's fist in the windpipe and doubled up as though his genitals had been ripped out. A third, smacked in the eye, fell back with a groan. Dijkstra seized the Witcher in a bearlike grip, and Geralt kicked him hard in the ankle with his heel. The spy howled and cavorted hilariously on one leg.

Another heavy tried to strike the Witcher with his short sword but slashed only the air. Geralt caught hold of his elbow in one hand and his wrist in the other. He spun him around, knocking over two others who were trying to get up. The thug he was holding was strong and had no intention of releasing his sword. So Geralt tightened his grip and the man's arm broke with a crack.

Dijkstra, still hopping on one leg, seized a partisan from the ground, hoping to pin the Witcher to the wall with its three-pronged blade. Geralt dodged, seized the shaft in both hands and used the principle – well known to scholars – of the lever. The spy, seeing the bricks and mortar of the wall looming, dropped the partisan but was too late to prevent his crotch slamming into the chimera's head.

Geralt used the partisan to knock another thug off his feet and then held the shaft against the ground and broke it with a kick, shortening it to the length of a sword. He tried out the makeshift club, first by hitting Dijkstra – who was sitting astride the chimera – and then by quietening the moans of the bruiser with the broken arm. The seams of his doublet had burst under both arms some time before, and the Witcher was feeling considerably better.

The last brute on his feet also attacked with a partisan, expecting its length to offer him an advantage. Geralt hit him between the eyebrows, and the bruiser sat down hard on the pot holding the agave. Another of the Redanians – who was unusually stubborn – clung to the Witcher's thigh and bit him painfully. This angered the Witcher, who deprived the rodent of his ability to bite with a powerful kick.

Dandelion arrived on the steps out of breath, saw what was happening and went as white as a ghost.

'Geralt!' he yelled a moment later. 'Ciri's disappeared! She isn't here!'

'I expected as much,' answered the Witcher, bashing the next Redanian, who was refusing to lie down quietly, with his club. 'But you really make a body wait, Dandelion. I told you yesterday that you were to leg it to Aretuza if anything happened! Have you brought my sword?'

'Both of them!'

'The other one is Ciri's, you idiot.' Geralt whacked the heavy trying to get up from the agave pot.

'I don't know much about swords,' panted the poet. 'Stop hitting them, by the gods! Can't you see the Redanian eagle? They're King Vizimir's men! This is treachery and rebellion. You could end up in a dungeon for that ...'

'On the scaffold,' mumbled Dijkstra, drawing a dagger and staggering closer. 'You'll both be for the scaffold ...'

He wasn't able to say anything else because he collapsed on all fours, struck on the side of the head with the stump of the partisan's shaft.

'Broken on the wheel,' pictured Dandelion gloomily. 'After being rent with red-hot pincers ...'

The Witcher kicked the spy in the ribs. Dijkstra flopped over on one side like a felled elk.

'. . . then our bodies quartered,' continued the poet.

'Stop that, Dandelion. Give me both swords and get away from here as quickly as possible. Flee from the island. As far away as you can!'

'What about you?'

'I'm going back up. I have to save Ciri . . . And Yennefer. Dijkstra, lie there nicely and get your hands off that dagger!'

'You won't get away with this,' panted the spy. 'I'll send my men after you . . . I'll get you . . .'

'No you won't.'

'Oh, I will. I've got fifty men on *The Spada* . . .'

'And is there a barber surgeon among them?'

'Eh?'

Geralt came up behind the spy, bent down, seized him by the foot and jerked it, twisting the foot quickly and very powerfully. There was a cracking sound. Dijkstra howled and fainted. Dandelion screamed as if it had been his own ankle.

'I don't much care what they do to me after I've been quartered,' muttered the Witcher.

It was quiet in Aretuza. Only a few diehards remained in the ballroom, but now they had too little energy to make a racket. Geralt avoided it, not wanting to be noticed.

He had some difficulty finding the chamber where he'd spent the night with Yennefer. The palace corridors were a veritable labyrinth and all looked alike.

The ragdoll looked at him with its button eyes.

He sat down on the bed, clutching his head. There was no blood on the chamber floor. But a black dress was draped over the back of a chair. Yennefer had changed. Into men's clothes, the uniform of the conspirators?

Or they'd dragged her out in her underwear. In dimeritium handcuffs.

*

Marti Södergren, the healer, was sitting in the window alcove. Hearing his footsteps, she raised her head. Her cheeks were wet with tears.

'Hen Gedymdeith is dead,' she said in a faltering voice. 'It was his heart. I couldn't do a thing ... Why did they call me so late? Sabrina hit me. She hit me in the face. Why? What has happened?'

'Have you seen Yennefer?'

'No, I haven't. Leave me. I want to be alone.'

'Show me the shortest way to Garstang. Please.'

Above Aretuza were three terraces covered with shrubs. Beyond them, the mountain slopes became sheer and inaccessible. Garstang loomed up above the precipice. At its foot the palace was a dark, uniformly smooth block of stone growing out of the rocks. Only the marble and stained-glass windows of its upper storey sparkled and the metal roofs of its domes shone like gold in the sun.

The paved road leading to Garstang and on to the summit wound around the mountain like a snake. There was another, shorter, route: a stairway linking the terraces, which vanished into the black maw of a tunnel just beneath Garstang. It was this stairway that Marti Södergren pointed out to the Witcher.

Immediately beyond the tunnel was a bridge joining the two sides of the precipice. Beyond the bridge, the stairway climbed steeply upwards and curved, vanishing around a bend. The Witcher quickened his pace.

The balustrade was decorated with small statues of fauns and nymphs which gave the impression of being alive. They were moving. The Witcher's medallion began to vibrate intensively.

He rubbed his eyes. The statues were not in fact moving but metamorphosing, transforming from smooth-surfaced carvings to porous, shapeless masses of stone, eroded by strong winds and salt. And an instant later they renewed themselves once more.

He knew what that meant. The illusion disguising Thanedd was becoming unstable and weakening. The bridge was also partly illusory. A chasm with a waterfall roaring at its foot was visible through the hole-riddled camouflage.

There were no dark slabs to indicate a safe way across. He crossed the bridge tentatively, careful of every step, cursing to himself at the time he was wasting. When he reached the far side of the chasm, he heard running footsteps.

He knew who it was at once. Running down the steps towards him was Dorregaray, the sorcerer in the service of King Ethain of Cidaris. He recalled the words of Philippa Eilhart. The sorcerers who represented neutral kings had been invited to Garstang as observers. But Dorregaray was hurtling down the steps at such a speed that it appeared his invitation had suddenly been revoked.

'Dorregaray!'

'Geralt?' panted the sorcerer. 'What are you doing here? Don't stay here. Run away! Get down to Aretuza quickly!'

'What has happened?'

'Treachery!'

'What?'

Dorregaray suddenly shuddered and coughed strangely, then toppled forwards and fell onto the Witcher. Before Geralt could catch hold of him he spotted the grey fletching of an arrow sticking out of his back. He and the sorcerer swayed in an embrace. That movement saved the Witcher's life as a second, identical, arrow, rather than piercing his throat, slammed into the grotesquely grinning face of a stone faun, knocking off its nose and part of its cheek. The Witcher released Dorregaray and ducked down behind the balustrade. The sorcerer collapsed onto him.

There were two archers, and both had squirrels' tails in their hats. One remained at the top of the staircase, pulling his bowstring back, while the other drew his sword and hurtled down the stairway, several steps at a time. Geralt pushed Dorregaray aside and leapt to his feet, drawing his sword. An arrow sang, but the Witcher interrupted the song, deflecting the arrowhead with a quick blow of his sword. The other elf, already close, hesitated for a moment on seeing the arrow deflected. But only for a moment. He came at the Witcher, swinging his blade and ready to strike. Geralt made a short parry, obliquely, so that the elf's sword slid across his. The elf lost his balance, the Witcher spun around smoothly and slashed him across the side of the neck below his ear. Just once. Once was enough.

The archer at the top of the stairway bent his bow again but did not have time to release the string. Geralt saw a flash. The elf screamed, spread out his arms and fell forwards, tumbling down the steps. The back of his jerkin was on fire.

Another sorcerer ran down the steps. On seeing the Witcher, he stopped and raised a hand. Geralt didn't waste time with explanations but flattened himself on the ground as a fiery lightning bolt flew over him with a hiss, pulverising a statue of a faun.

'Stop!' he yelled. 'It's me, the Witcher!'

'Damn it,' the sorcerer panted, running over to Geralt, who could not remember him from the banquet. 'I took you for one of those elven thugs ... How is Dorregaray? Is he still alive?'

'I think so ...'

'Quickly, to the other side of the bridge!'

They dragged Dorregaray across. And luck was on their side, because in their haste they paid no attention to the wavering and vanishing illusion. No one was pursuing them, but the sorcerer nonetheless extended a hand, chanting a spell, and sent a lightning bolt to destroy the bridge. The stones crashed down the walls of the abyss.

'That ought to hold them back,' he said.

The Witcher wiped away the blood pouring from Dorregaray's mouth.

'He has a punctured lung. Can you help him?'

'*I* can,' said Marti Södergren, hauling herself up the steps from the tunnel leading from Aretuza. 'What's happening, Carduin? Who shot him?'

'Scoia'tael,' said the sorcerer, wiping his forehead with a sleeve. 'There's a battle raging in Garstang. Bloody rabble. They're all as bad as each other! Philippa handcuffed Vilgefortz during the night, and Vilgefortz and Francesca Findabair brought Squirrels to the island! And Tissaia de Vries ... She's stirred everything up!'

'Be clearer, Carduin!'

'I'm not hanging around here talking! I'm fleeing to Loxia, and from there I'm going to teleport to Kovir. Everyone in Garstang

176

can go ahead and slaughter each other! It's all meaningless now! It's war! This mayhem was concocted by Philippa to allow the kings to start a war with Nilfgaard! Meanwhile Meve of Lyria and Demavend of Aedirn have provoked Nilfgaard! Do you understand that?'

'No,' said Geralt. 'And we don't want to understand it. Where's Yennefer?'

'Stop it, you two!' screamed Marti Södergren, attending to Dorregaray. 'Help me! Hold him! I can't pull the arrow out!'

They helped her. Dorregaray groaned and trembled, and then the steps shook. At first Geralt thought it was the magic of Marti's healing spells. But it was Garstang. The stained-glass windows suddenly exploded and flames could be seen flickering inside the palace. Smoke was billowing out.

'They're still fighting,' said Carduin, grinding his teeth. 'It's hot down there, one spell after another . . .'

'Spells? In Garstang? But there's an anti-magic aura there!'

'It was Tissaia's doing. She suddenly decided whose side she was on. She took down the blockade, removed the aura and neutralised the dimeritium. Then everyone went for each other! Vilgefortz and Terranova on one side, Philippa and Sabrina on the other . . . The columns cracked and the vaulting collapsed . . . And then Francesca opened the entrance to the cellars, and those elven devils suddenly leapt out . . . We told them that we were neutral, but Vilgefortz only laughed. Before we had time to build a shield, Drithelm had been shot in the eye, and Rejean had been spitted like a hedgehog . . . I didn't wait to see what happened after that. Marti, are you going to be much longer? We have to get out of here!'

'Dorregaray won't be able to walk,' said the healer, wiping her bloody hands on her white ball gown. 'Teleport us, Carduin.'

'From here? You must be insane. It's too close to Tor Lara. The Lara portal gives out emanations which warp any attempts at teleportation. You can't teleport from here!'

'He can't walk! I have to stay with him—'

'Well stay, then!' Carduin stood up. 'And enjoy yourself! Life is dear to me! I'm going back to Kovir! Kovir is neutral!'

'Splendid,' said the Witcher, spitting and watching the sorcerer disappear into the tunnel. 'Friendship and solidarity! But I can't stay with you either, Marti. I have to go to Garstang. Your neutral comrade smashed up the bridge. Is there another way?'

Marti Södergren sniffed. Then she raised her head and nodded.

He was at the foot of the wall in Garstang when Keira Metz landed on his head.

The way he'd been shown by the healer led through some hanging gardens linked by winding steps. The steps were covered in dense ivy and vines and the vegetation made climbing difficult but it also gave cover. He managed to get to the foot of the palace wall undetected and had been looking for a way in when Keira had fallen on him, and the two of them tumbled into some blackthorn bushes.

'I've lost a tooth,' said the sorceress, gloomily, lisping slightly. She was dishevelled, dirty and covered in plaster and soot. There was a large bruise on her cheek.

'And I think I've broken my leg,' she added, spitting blood. 'Is that you, Witcher? Did I land on you? How come?'

'I was wondering the same thing myself.'

'Terranova threw me out of a window.'

'Can you stand?'

'No, I can't.'

'I want to get inside. Unnoticed. Which way is it?'

'Are all witchers,' said Keira, spitting blood again, groaning, and trying to prop herself up on an elbow, 'insane? There's a battle going on in Garstang! It's kicking off so badly the plaster's falling off the ceiling! Are you looking for trouble?'

'No. I'm looking for Yennefer.'

'Oh!' said Keira, giving up her struggles and lying on her back. 'I wish someone would love me like that. Carry me.'

'Another time, perhaps. I'm in a bit of a hurry.'

'Carry me, I said! I'll show you the way into Garstang. I have to get that son of a bitch Terranova. Well, what are you waiting for? You won't find the way yourself, and even if you did, those fucking elves would finish you off ... I can't walk, but I'm still capable of casting a few spells. If anyone gets in our way they'll regret it.'

She cried out when he picked her up.

'Sorry.'

'Don't worry,' she said, wrapping her arms around his neck. 'It's that leg. Did you know you still smell of her perfume? No, not that way. Turn back and go uphill. It's the second entrance on the Tor Lara side. There may not be any elves there . . . Ouch! Gently, damn it!'

'Sorry. How did the Scoia'tael get here?'

'They were hidden in the cellars. Thanedd is as hollow as a nutshell and there's a huge cavern under it; you could sail a ship in if you knew how. Someone must have told them the way— Ouuuch! Be careful! Stop jolting me!'

'Sorry. So the Squirrels came here by sea? When?'

'God knows when. It might have been yesterday, or a week ago. We were preparing to strike at Vilgefortz, and Vilgefortz at us. Vilgefortz, Francesca, Terranova and Fercart . . . They conned us good and proper. Philippa thought they were planning a slow seizure of power in the Chapter, and to put pressure on the kings . . . But they were planning to finish us off during the Conclave . . . Geralt, it's too painful . . . It's my leg . . . Put me down for a second. Ouuuch!'

'Keira, it's an open fracture. The blood's seeping through your trousers.'

'Shut up and listen. Because it's about your Yennefer. We entered Garstang and went into the debating chamber. There's an anti-magic blockade there, but it doesn't affect dimeritium, so we felt safe. There was an argument. Tissaia and the neutrals yelled at us and we yelled at them. And Vilgefortz just said nothing and smiled . . .'

'I repeat: Vilgefortz is a traitor! He's in cahoots with Emhyr of Nilfgaard, and he's inveigled others into the plot! He broke the Law, he betrayed us and the kings . . .'

'Slow down, Philippa. I know the grace and favour Vizimir surrounds you with mean more to you than the solidarity of the

Brotherhood. The same applies to you, Sabrina, for you play an identical role in Kaedwen. Keira Metz and Triss Merigold represent the interests of Foltest of Temeria, and Radcliffe is a tool of Demavend of Aedirn—'

'What does that have to do with it, Tissaia?'

'The kings' interests don't have to correspond to ours. I know perfectly well what it's all about. The kings have begun the extermination of elves and other non-humans. Perhaps you, Philippa, regard that as legitimate. Perhaps you, Radcliffe, think it appropriate to help Demavend's forces in their hunt for the Scoia'tael. But I am opposed to it. And it doesn't surprise me that Enid Findabair is also against it. But that is not sufficient to call it treachery. Let me finish! I know perfectly well what your kings were planning. I know they want to unleash a war. The measures which were meant to prevent that war may be seen as treachery by Vizimir, but not by me. If you wish to judge Vilgefortz and Francesca; do the same to me!'

'What war do you speak of? My king, Esterad of Kovir, will not support any acts of aggression against the Nilfgaardian Empire! Kovir is, and will remain, neutral!'

'You are a member of the Council, Carduin! Not Kovir's ambassador!'

'Look who's talking, Sabrina.'

'Enough!' Philippa slammed her fist down on the table. 'I shall satisfy your curiosity, Carduin. You ask who is preparing a war? Nilfgaard. They intend to attack and destroy us. But Emhyr var Emreis remembers Sodden Hill and has decided to protect himself by removing the mages from the game first. With this in mind, he made contact with Vilgefortz of Roggeveen. He bought him with promises of power and honour. Yes, Tissaia. Vilgefortz, hero of Sodden, sold us out to become the governor and ruler of all the conquered territories of the north. Vilgefortz, helped by Terranova and Fercart, shall rule the provinces which will be established in place of the conquered kingdoms. It is he who will wield the Nilfgaardian scourge over the people who inhabit those lands and will begin toiling as the Empire's slaves. And Francesca Findabair, Enid an Gleanna, will become queen of the land of the free elves. It will, of course, be a Nilfgaardian protectorate, but it will suffice for the elves so long as Emperor Emhyr will give them a free hand to murder humans. The elves desire nothing so much as to murder Dh'oine.'

'That is a serious accusation. Which means the proof will also have to be as weighty. But before you throw your proof onto the scale, Philippa Eilhart, be aware of my stance. Proof may be fabricated. Actions and their motives may be misinterpreted. But nothing can change existing facts. You have broken the unity and solidarity of the Brotherhood, Philippa Eilhart. You have handcuffed members of the Chapter like criminals. So do not dare to offer me a position in the new Chapter which your gang of traitors – who have sold out to the kings, rather than to Nilfgaaard – intend to create. We are separated by death and blood. The death of Hen Gedymdeith. And the blood of Lydia van Bredevoort. You spilled that blood with contempt. You were my best pupil, Philippa Eilhart. I was always proud of you. But now I have nothing but contempt for you.'

Keira Metz was as pale as parchment.

'It's been quieter in Garstang for some time now,' she whispered. 'It's coming to an end ... They are chasing each other through the palace. There are five floors and seventy-six chambers and halls. That's plenty of room for a chase ...'

'You were going to tell me about Yennefer. Be quick. I'm worried you'll faint.'

'Yennefer? Oh, yes ... Everything was going according to plan until Yennefer suddenly appeared. And brought that medium into the hall ...'

'Who?'

'A girl, aged perhaps fourteen. Very fair hair and huge, green eyes ... She began to prophesy before we'd had time to look at her properly. She talked of the events in Dol Angra. No one had any doubt she was speaking the truth. She was in a trance, and in a trance no one lies.'

'Last night,' said the medium, 'armed forces in Lyrian livery and carrying Aedirnian standards committed acts of aggression against the Empire of Nilfgaard. Glevitzingen, a border outpost in Dol Angra, was attacked. King Demavend's heralds informed the people of the surrounding villages that Aedirn is taking control of the entire country from today. The entire population was incited to rise up against Nilfgaard—'

'That is impossible! It's nothing but vile provocation!'

'You utter that word easily, Philippa Eilhart,' said Tissaia de Vries calmly. 'But do not deceive yourself; your cries will not break her trance. Speak on, child.'

'Emperor Emhyr var Emreis has given the order to answer blows with blows. Nilfgaardian forces entered Lyria and Aedirn at dawn today.'

'And thus,' laughed Tissaia, 'our kings have shown what judicious, enlightened and peace-loving rulers they are. And some of our mages have proved which cause they really serve. Those who might have prevented this imperialist war have been prudently clamped in dimeritium handcuffs and are facing trumped-up charges—'

'That is nothing but a pack of lies!'

'Fuck the lot of you!' roared Sabrina Glevissig suddenly. 'Philippa! What is this all about? What was the purpose of that brawl in Dol Angra? Hadn't we agreed not to begin too soon? Why couldn't that fucking Demavend restrain himself? Why did that slut Meve . . .'

'Silence, Sabrina!'

'No, no. Let her speak,' said Tissaia de Vries, raising her head. 'Let her speak of Henselt of Kaedwen's army, which is concentrated on the border. Let her speak of Foltest of Temeria's forces, which no doubt are already launching the boats which have been hidden in undergrowth by the Yaruga. Let her speak of the expeditionary force under the command of Vizimir of Redania, standing ready on the Pontar. Philippa, did you think we were both blind and deaf?'

'It's nothing but an enormous bloody provocation! King Vizimir—'

'King Vizimir,' interrupted the fair-haired medium in an unemotional voice, 'was murdered yesterday evening. Stabbed by an assassin. Redania no longer has a king.'

'Redania has not had a king for a very long time,' said Tissaia de

Vries, rising to her feet. 'The Most Honourable Philippa Eilhart, the worthy successor of Raffard the White, ruled in Redania. A person prepared to sacrifice tens of thousands of beings in order to gain absolute power.'

'Do not listen to her!' yelled Philippa. 'Do not listen to that medium! She's a tool, an unthinking tool ... Who do you serve, Yennefer? Who instructed you to bring that monster here?'

'I did,' said Tissaia de Vries.

'What happened next? What happened to the girl? To Yennefer?'

'I don't know,' said Keira, closing her eyes. 'Tissaia suddenly lifted the blockade. With one spell. I'd never seen anything like it in my life. She stunned and blocked us, then freed Vilgefortz and the others ... And then Francesca opened the entrance to the cellars and suddenly Garstang was swarming with Scoia'tael. They were being led by a freak in armour wearing a winged, Nilfgaardian helmet. Helped by that character with the mark on his face. He knew how to cast spells. And shield himself with magic ...'

'Rience.'

'Perhaps. I don't know. It was hot ... The ceiling caved in. Spells and arrows were flying everywhere; it was a massacre ... Fercart was among their dead, Drithelm and Radcliffe among ours. Marquard, Rejean and Bianca d'Este were killed ... Triss Merigold was hurt. Sabrina was wounded ... When Tissaia saw their bodies she understood her mistake, tried to protect us, tried to calm Vilgefortz and Terranova ... But Vilgefortz ridiculed and laughed at her. Then she lost her head and fled. Oh, Tissaia ... So many dead ...'

'What happened to the girl and to Yennefer?'

'I don't know,' said the sorceress, coughing and spitting blood. She was breathing very shallowly and with obvious difficulty. 'I passed out after one of the explosions. The one with the scar and his elves overpowered me. Terranova beat me black and blue and then threw me out of a window.'

'It isn't just your leg, Keira. You've got some broken ribs.'

'Don't leave me.'

'I have to. I'll come back for you.'

'Yeah, right.'

At first, there was only shimmering chaos, the pulsing of shadows, a confusion of dark and light, and a choir of incoherent voices emerging from the abyss. Suddenly the voices became stronger and, from all around, the screaming and the roaring exploded. The brightness amongst the darkness became a fire consuming the tapestries, seeming to shoot streams of sparks from the walls, the balustrades and the columns supporting the ceiling.

Ciri choked on the smoke and realised it was no longer a dream.

She tried to stand, propping herself up on her arms. Her hand came to rest on something wet, and she looked down. She was kneeling in a pool of blood. Beside her lay a motionless body. The body of an elf. She knew at once.

'Get up.'

Yennefer was standing beside her. She was holding a dagger.

'Mistress Yennefer ... Where are we? I don't remember ...'

The enchantress seized her by the hand.

'I'm with you, Ciri.'

'Where are we? Why is everything on fire? Who's that ... lying there?'

'I told you once, a long time ago, that chaos is reaching out to seize you. Do you remember? No, you probably don't. That elf reached out to get you. I had to kill him using a knife, as his paymasters are just waiting for one of us to reveal ourselves by using magic. And it will happen, but not yet ... Are you totally conscious?'

'Those sorcerers ...' whispered Ciri. 'The ones in the great hall ... What did I say to them? And why did I say it? I didn't want to at all ... But I couldn't stop myself! Why? Why, Mistress Yennefer?'

'Be quiet, my ugly little duckling. I made a mistake. No one's perfect.'

A roar and a terrifying scream resounded from below.

'Come on. Quickly. There's no time.'

They ran along the corridor. The smoke became thicker and thicker. It choked them, blinded them. The walls shook from the explosion.

184

'Ciri.' Yennefer stopped at a junction in the corridors and squeezed the girl's hand tightly. 'Listen to me now. Listen carefully. I have to stay here. Do you see those stairs? Go down them ...'

'No! Don't leave me all alone!'

'I have to. I repeat: go down those stairs. To the very bottom. There'll be a door and, beyond it a long corridor. At the end of the corridor is a stable and a single, saddled horse. Only one. Lead it out and mount it. It's a trained horse; it serves messengers riding to Loxia. It knows the way; just spur it on. When you get to Loxia find Margarita. She will look after you. Don't let her out of your sight—'

'Mistress Yennefer! No! I don't want to be alone!'

'Ciri,' said the enchantress softly. 'I once told you that everything I do is for your own good. Trust me. Trust me, I beg you. Now run for it.'

Ciri was already on the steps when she heard Yennefer's voice once more. The enchantress was standing beside a column, resting her forehead against it.

'I love you, my daughter,' she said indistinctly. 'Run.'

They trapped her halfway down the stairs. At the bottom there were two elves with squirrels' tails in their hats and, at the top, a man dressed in black. Without thinking, Ciri jumped over the banisters and fled down a side corridor. They ran after her. She was quicker and would have escaped them with ease had the corridor not ended in a window.

She looked through the window. A stone ledge – about two spans wide – ran along the wall. Ciri swung a leg over the windowsill and climbed out. She moved away from the window and pressed her back to the wall. The sea glistened in the distance.

One of the elves leaned out through the window. He had very fair hair and green eyes and wore a silk kerchief around his neck. Ciri moved quickly along the ledge towards the next window. But the man dressed in black was looking out of it. His eyes were dark and intense, and he had a reddish mark on his cheek.

'We've got you, wench!'

She looked down. She could see a courtyard far below her. There was a narrow bridge linking two cloisters above the courtyard, about ten feet below the ledge she was standing on. Except it was not a bridge. It was the remains of a bridge. A narrow, stone footbridge with the remains of a shattered balustrade.

'What are you waiting for?' shouted the one with the scar. 'Get out there and grab her!'

The fair-haired elf stepped gingerly out onto the ledge, pressing his back against the wall. He reached out to grab her. He was getting closer.

Ciri swallowed. The stone footbridge – the remains of the footbridge – was no narrower than the seesaw at Kaer Morhen, and she had landed on that dozens of times. She knew how to cushion her fall and keep her balance. The witchers' seesaw was only four feet off the ground, however, while the stone footbridge spanned such a long drop that the slabs of the courtyard looked smaller than the palm of her hand.

She jumped, landed, tottered and kept her balance by catching hold of the shattered balustrade. With sure steps, she reached the cloister. She couldn't resist it; she turned around and showed her pursuers her middle finger, a gesture she had been taught by the dwarf Yarpen Zigrin. The man with the scar swore loudly.

'Jump!' he shouted at the fair-haired elf standing on the ledge. 'After her!'

'You're insane, Rience,' said the elf coldly. 'Jump yourself.'

As usual, her luck didn't last. She was caught as she ran down from the cloister and slipped behind a wall into a blackthorn bush. She was caught and held fast in an extremely strong grip by a short, podgy man with a swollen nose and a scarred lip.

'Got you,' he hissed. 'Got you, poppet!'

Ciri struggled and howled because the hands gripping her shoulders transfixed her with a sudden paroxysm of overwhelming pain. The man chuckled.

'Don't flap your wings, little bird, or I'll singe your feathers. Let's have a good look at you. Let's have a look at this chick that's worth so much to Emhyr var Emreis, Imperator of Nilfgaard. And to Vilgefortz.'

Ciri stopped trying to escape. The short man licked his scarred lip.

'Interesting,' he hissed again, leaning over towards her. 'They say you're so precious, but I wouldn't even give a brass farthing for you. How appearances deceive. Ha! My treasure! What if, not Vilgefortz, not Rience, not that gallant in the feathered helmet, but old Terranova gave you to Emhyr as a present? Would Emhyr look kindly on old Terranova? What do you say to that, little clairvoyant? You can see the future, after all!'

His breath stank unbearably. Ciri turned her head away, grimacing. He misread the movement.

'Don't snap your beak at me, little bird! I'm not afraid of little birds. But should I be, perhaps? Well, false soothsayer? Bogus oracle? Should I be afraid of little birds?'

'You ought to be,' whispered Ciri, feeling giddy, a sudden cold sensation overcoming her.

Terranova laughed, throwing his head back. His laugh became a howl of pain. A huge, grey owl had swooped down noiselessly and sunk its talons into his eyes. The sorcerer released Ciri, tore the owl off with a desperate movement and then fell to his knees, clutching his face. Blood poured between his fingers. Ciri screamed and stepped back. Terranova removed his bloodied, mucus-covered fingers from his face and began to chant a spell in a wild, cracked voice. He was not quick enough. A vague shape appeared behind his back, and a witcher's blade whistled in the air and severed his neck at the base of his skull.

'Geralt!'

'Ciri.'

'This isn't the time for tenderness,' said the owl from the top of the wall, transforming into a dark-haired woman. 'Flee! The squirrels will be here soon!'

Ciri freed herself from Geralt's arms and looked up in astonishment. The owl-woman sitting on top of the wall looked ghastly. She

187

was blackened, ragged and smeared in ash and blood.

'You little monster,' said the owl-woman, looking down at her. 'For your inopportune augury I ought to ... But I made your Witcher a promise, and I always keep my promises. I couldn't give you Rience, Geralt. In exchange I'm giving you her. Alive. Flee, both of you!'

Cahir Mawr Dyffryn aep Ceallach was furious. He had seen the girl he had been ordered to capture, but only for a moment. Then, before he had been able to act, the insane sorcerers unleashed such an inferno in Garstang that no action was possible. Cahir lost his bearings among the smoke and flames, blindly stumbling along corridors, running up and down stairs and through cloisters, and cursing Vilgefortz, Rience, himself and the entire world.

He happened upon an elf who told him the girl had been seen outside the palace, fleeing along the road to Aretuza. And then fortune smiled upon Cahir. The Scoia'tael found a saddled horse in the stable.

'Run, Ciri, run. They're close. I'll stop them, you run. Fast as you can! Just like you used to on the assault course!'

'Are you abandoning me too?'

'I'll be right behind you. But don't look back!'

'Give me my sword, Geralt.'

He looked at her. Ciri stepped back involuntarily. She had never seen him with an expression like that before.

'If you had a sword, you might have to kill with it. Can you do it?'

'I don't know. Give me my sword.'

'Run. And don't look back.'

Horses' hooves thudded on the road. Ciri looked back. And she froze, paralysed with fear.

She was being pursued by a black knight in a helmet decorated with raptor wings. The wings whooshed, and the black cloak streamed behind him. Horseshoes sent up sparks from the cobblestones.

She was unable to move.

The black horse burst through the roadside bushes, and the knight shouted loudly. Cintra was in that cry. The night, slaughter, blood and conflagration were in that cry. Ciri overcame her overwhelming fear and darted away. She leapt over a hedge and plunged into a small courtyard with a fountain. There was no way out; it was encircled by smooth, high walls. She could hear the horse snorting behind her. She turned, stumbled backwards and shuddered as she felt a hard, unyielding wall behind her. She was trapped.

The bird of prey flapped its wings, taking flight. The black knight urged his horse on and jumped the hedge separating him from the courtyard. Hooves thudded on the slabs, and the horse slipped, skidded and sat back on its haunches. The knight swayed in the saddle and toppled over. The horse regained its footing but the knight fell off, his armour clattering on the stones. He was on his feet immediately, though, and quickly trapped Ciri, who was pinned into a corner.

'You will not touch me!' she screamed, drawing her sword. 'You will never touch me again!'

The knight moved slowly towards her, rising up like a huge, black tower. The wings on his helmet moved to and fro and whispered.

'You will not escape me now, o Lion Cub of Cintra,' he said, and his cruel eyes burned in the slit of his helmet. 'Not this time. This time you have nowhere to run, o reckless maiden.'

'You will not touch me,' she repeated in a voice of stifled horror, her back pressed against the stone wall.

'I have to. I am carrying out orders.'

As he held out his hand to seize her, Ciri's fear subsided, to be replaced by savage fury. Her tense muscles, previously frozen in terror, began to work like springs. All the moves she had learned in Kaer Morhen performed themselves, smoothly and fluidly. Ciri jumped; the knight lunged towards her but was unprepared for the pirouette which spun her effortlessly out of reach of his hands. Her sword whined and stung, striking unerringly between the plates of his armour. The knight staggered and dropped to one knee as a stream of scarlet blood spurted from beneath his spaulder. Screaming fiercely, Ciri whirled around him with another pirouette and struck

189

the knight again, this time directly on the bell of his helmet, knocking him down onto his other knee. Fury and madness had utterly blinded her, and she saw nothing except the loathsome wings. The black feathers were strewn in all directions. One wing fell off, and the other was resting on the bloodied spaulder. The knight, still vainly trying to get up from his knees, tried to seize her sword in his armoured glove and grunted painfully as the witcher blade slashed through the chainmail sleeve into his hand. The next blow knocked off his helmet, and Ciri jumped back to gather momentum for the last, mortal blow.

She did not strike.

There was no black helmet, no raptor's wings, whose whistling had tormented her in her nightmares. There was no black knight of Cintra. There was a pale, dark-haired young man with stupefyingly blue eyes and a mouth distorted in a grimace of fear, kneeling in a pool of blood. The black knight of Cintra had fallen beneath the blows of her sword, had ceased to exist. Only hacked-up feathers remained of the forbidding wings. The terrified, cowering young man bleeding profusely was no one. She did not know him; she had never seen him before. He meant nothing to her. She wasn't afraid of him, nor did she hate him. And neither did she want to kill him.

She threw her sword onto the ground.

She turned around, hearing the cries of the Scoia'tael approaching fast from Garstang. She knew that in a moment they would trap her in the courtyard. She knew they would catch up with her on the road. She had to be quicker than them. She ran over to the black horse, which was clattering its horseshoes on the paved ground, and urged it into a gallop with a cry, leaping into the saddle in full flight.

'Leave me ...' groaned Cahir Mawr Dyffryn aep Ceallach, pushing away the elves who were trying to lift him up with his good hand. 'I'm fine. It's just a scratch ... After her. Get the girl ...'

One of the elves screamed, and blood spurted into Cahir's face. Another Scoia'tael reeled and fell to his knees, his fingers clutching his mutilated belly. The remaining elves leapt back and scattered all around the courtyard, swords flashing.

They had been attacked by a white-haired fiend, who had fallen on them from a wall, from a height that would have broken a normal man's legs. It ought to have been impossible to land gently, whirl in an impossibly fast pirouette, and a split second later begin killing. But the white-haired fiend had done it. And the killing had begun.

The Scoia'tael fought fiercely. They had the advantage, but they had no chance. A massacre was played out before Cahir's eyes, wide with terror. The fair-haired girl, who had wounded him a moment earlier, had been fast, had been unbelievably lithe, had been like a mother cat defending her kittens. But the white-haired fiend who had fallen amongst the Scoia'tael was like a Zerrikan tiger. The fair-haired maid of Cintra, who for some unknown reason had not killed him, seemed insane. The white-haired fiend was not insane. He was calm and cold. And killed calmly and coldly.

The Scoia'tael had no chance. Their corpses piled up on the slabs of the courtyard. But they did not yield. Even when only two of them remained, they did not run away, but attacked the white-haired fiend once more. The fiend hacked off the arm of one of them above the elbow as Cahir watched. He hit the other elf with an apparently light, casual blow, which nonetheless threw him backwards. It tipped him over the lip of the fountain and hurled him into the water. The water brimmed over the edge of the basin in ripples of crimson.

The elf with the severed arm knelt by the fountain, staring vacantly at the blood gushing from the stump. The white-haired fiend seized him by the hair and cut his throat with a rapid slash of his sword.

When Cahir opened his eyes the fiend was standing over him.

'Don't kill me ...' he whispered, giving up his efforts to rise from the ground, now slippery with blood. His hand, slashed by the fair-haired girl, had gone numb and did not hurt.

'I know who you are, Nilfgaardian,' said the white-haired fiend, kicking the helmet with the hacked-up wings. 'You have been pursuing her doggedly and long. But now you will harm her no more.'

'Don't kill me ...'

'Give me one reason. Just one. Make haste.'

'It was I ...' whispered Cahir. 'It was I who got her out of Cintra. From the fire ... I rescued her. I saved her life ...'

When he opened his eyes, the fiend was no longer there. Cahir was alone in the courtyard with the bodies of the elves. The water in the fountain soughed, spilling over the edge of the basin, washing away the blood on the ground. Cahir fainted.

At the foot of the tower stood a building which seemed to be a single, large hall, or perhaps some kind of peristyle. The roof over the peristyle, probably illusory, was full of holes. It was supported by columns and pilasters carved in the shape of scantily clad caryatids with generous breasts. The same kinds of caryatids supported the arch of the entrance through which Ciri had vanished. Beyond the doorway, Geralt noticed some steps leading upwards. Towards the tower.

The Witcher cursed under his breath. He did not understand why she had fled there. He had seen her horse fall as he rushed after her along the tops of the walls. He saw her leap nimbly to her feet, but instead of running along the winding road encircling the peak, she had suddenly rushed uphill, towards the solitary tower. Only later did he notice the elves on the road. Those elves – busy shooting arrows at some men running uphill – saw neither Ciri nor himself. Reinforcements were arriving from Aretuza.

He intended to follow Ciri up the steps when he heard a sound. From above. He quickly turned around. It was not a bird.

Vilgefortz flew down through a hole in the roof, his wide sleeves swishing, and slowly alighted on the floor.

Geralt stood in front of the entrance to the tower, drew his sword and heaved a sigh. He had sincerely hoped that the dramatic, concluding fight would be played out between Vilgefortz and Philippa Eilhart. He didn't have the least bit of interest in this kind of drama.

Vilgefortz brushed down his jerkin, straightened his cuffs, looked at the Witcher and read his mind.

'Infernal drama,' he sighed. Geralt made no comment.

'Did she go into the tower?'

He made no answer. The sorcerer nodded his head.

'So we have an epilogue then,' he said coldly. 'The denouement that draws the play to a close. Or is it perhaps fate? Do you know where those steps lead? To Tor Lara. To the Tower of Gulls. There is no way out of there. It's all over.'

Geralt stepped back between two of the caryatids holding up the doorway, in order to protect his flanks.

'Yes indeed,' he drawled, keeping his eyes on the sorcerer's hands. 'It's all over. Half of your accomplices are dead. The bodies of the elves who were brought to Thanedd are piled up all the way to Garstang. The others ran away. Sorcerers and Dijkstra's men are arriving from Aretuza. The Nilfgaardian who was supposed to take Ciri has probably bled to death already. And Ciri is up there in the tower. No way out of there? I'm glad to hear it. That means there's only one way in. The one I'm blocking.'

Vilgefortz bridled.

'You're incorrigible. You are still incapable of assessing the situation correctly. The Chapter and Council have ceased to exist. The forces of Emperor Emhyr are marching north. Deprived of the mages' assistance and advice, the kings are as helpless as children. In the face of Nilfgaard, their kingdoms are tumbling like sandcastles. I proposed this to you yesterday and repeat it today: join the victors. Spit on the losers.'

'It is you who's lost. You were only a tool to Emhyr. He wanted Ciri, which is why he sent that character with the wings on his helmet. I wonder what Emhyr will do to you when you report this fiasco.'

'You're shooting wildly, Witcher. And you're wide of the mark, naturally. What if I told you that Emhyr is my tool?'

'I wouldn't believe you.'

'Geralt, be sensible. Do you really want to play at theatrics, play out the banal final battle between good and evil? I repeat my proposition of yesterday. It is by no means too late. You can still make a choice. You can join the right side—'

'Join the side I thinned out a little today?'

'Don't grin. Your demonic smiles make no impression on me. Those few elves you hacked down? Artaud Terranova? Trifles, meaningless details. They can be waved aside.'

'But of course. I know your philosophy. Death has no meaning, right? Particularly other people's?'

'Don't be trite. It's a pity about Artaud but, well, too bad. Let's call it ... settling old scores. After all, I tried to kill you twice. Emhyr grew impatient, so I sent some assassins after you. Each time I did it with genuine reluctance. You see, I still hope they'll paint a picture of us one day.'

'Abandon that hope, Vilgefortz.'

'Put away your sword. Let's go up into Tor Lara together. We'll reassure the Child of the Elder Blood, who is sure to be dying of fright up there somewhere. And then let's leave. Together. You'll be by her side. You will see her destiny fulfilled. And Emperor Emhyr? Emperor Emhyr will get what he wanted. Because I forgot to tell you that although Codringher and Fenn are dead, their work and ideas are still alive and doing very well, thank you.'

'You are lying. Leave this place before I spit on *you*.'

'I really have no desire to kill you. I kill with reluctance.'

'Indeed? What about Lydia van Bredevoort?'

The sorcerer sneered.

'Speak not that name, Witcher.'

Geralt gripped the hilt of his sword tightly and smiled scornfully.

'Why did Lydia have to die, Vilgefortz? Why did you order her death? She was meant to distract attention from you, wasn't she? She was meant to give you time to become resistant to dimeritium, to send a telepathic signal to Rience, wasn't she? Poor Lydia, the artist with the damaged face. Everyone knew she was expendable. Everyone knew that except her.'

'Be silent.'

'You murdered Lydia, wizard. You used her. And now you want to use Ciri? With my help? No. You will not enter Tor Lara.'

The sorcerer took a step back. Geralt tensed up, ready to jump and strike. Vilgefortz did not raise his hand, however, but simply held it out to one side. A stout, two-yard staff suddenly materialised in his hand.

'I know,' he said, 'what hinders you from making a sensible

assessment of the situation. I know what complicates and obstructs your attempts at making a correct prediction of the future. Your arrogance, Geralt. I will disabuse you of arrogance. And I will do so with the help of this magic staff here.'

The Witcher squinted and raised his blade a little.

'I'm trembling with impatience.'

A few weeks later, having been healed by the dryads and the waters of Brokilon, Geralt wondered what mistakes he had made during the fight. And came to the conclusion he hadn't made any. His only mistake was made before the fight. He ought to have fled before it even began.

The sorcerer was fast, his staff flickering in his hands like lightning. Geralt's astonishment was even greater when, during a parry, the staff and sword clanged metallically. But there was no time for astonishment. Vilgefortz attacked, and the Witcher had to contort himself using body-swerves and pirouettes. He was afraid to parry. The bloody staff was made of iron; and magical to boot.

Four times, he found himself in a position from which he was able to counterattack and deliver a blow. Four times, he struck. To the temple, to the neck, under the arm, to the thigh. Each blow ought to have been fatal. But each one was parried.

No human could have parried blows like that. Geralt slowly began to understand. But it was already too late.

He didn't see the blow that finally caught him. The impact drove him against the wall. He rebounded from it but was unable to jump aside or dodge. The blow had knocked the breath out of him. He was caught by a second blow, this time on the shoulder, and once again flew backwards, smashing his head against a protruding caryatid's breast on one of the pilasters. Vilgefortz leapt closer, swung the staff and thumped him in the belly, below the ribs. Very hard. Geralt doubled up and was then hit on the side of the head. His knees suddenly went weak and crumpled beneath him. And the fight was over. In principle.

He feebly tried to protect himself with his sword. The blade, caught between the wall and the pilaster, broke under a blow with a shrill, vibrating whine. He tried to protect his head with his left hand, but the staff fell with enough force to break his forearm. The pain utterly blinded him.

'I could smash your brain out through your ears,' said Vilgefortz from far away. 'But this was supposed to be a lesson. You were mistaken, Witcher. You mistook the stars reflected in a pond at night for the sky. Oh, are you vomiting? Good. Concussion. Bleeding from the nose? Excellent. Well, I shall see you later. One day. Perhaps.'

Now Geralt could see nothing and hear nothing. He was sinking, submerging into something warm. He thought Vilgefortz had gone. He was astonished, then, when a fierce blow from the iron staff struck his thigh, smashing the shaft of his femur.

If anything occurred after that, he did not remember it.

'Hang in there, Geralt. Don't give up,' repeated Triss Merigold endlessly. 'Hang in there. Don't die ... Please don't die ...'

'Ciri ...'

'Don't talk. I'll soon get you out of here. Hold on ... Damn I'm too weak, by the gods ...'

'Yennefer ... I have to—'

'You don't have to do anything! You can't do anything! Hang in there. Don't give up ... Don't faint ... Don't die, please ...'

She dragged him across the floor, which was littered with bodies. He saw his chest and belly covered in blood, which was streaming from his nose. He saw his leg. It was twisted at a strange angle and seemed much shorter than the intact one. He didn't feel any pain. He felt cold. His entire body was cold, numb and foreign. He wanted to puke.

'Hold on, Geralt. Help is coming from Aretuza. It'll soon be here ...'

'Dijkstra ... If Dijkstra gets his hands on me ... I'm finished ...'

Triss swore. Desperately.

She dragged him down the steps, his broken leg and arm bouncing down them. The pain returned. It bored into his guts and his temples, and it radiated all the way to his eyes, to his ears, to the top of his head. He didn't scream. He knew screaming would bring him relief, but he didn't scream. He just opened his mouth, which also brought him relief.

He heard a roar.

At the top of the stair stood Tissaia de Vries. Her hair was dishevelled, her face covered in dust. She raised both her hands, and her palms flamed. She screamed a spell and the flames dancing on her fingers hurtled downwards in the form of a blinding sphere, roaring with fire. The Witcher heard the clatter of walls crashing down below and the dreadful cries of people being burnt.

'No, Tissaia!' screamed Triss in desperation. 'Don't do it!'

'They will not enter here,' said the arch-mistress, without turning her head. 'This is Garstang, on the Isle of Thanedd. No one invited those royalist lackeys, who carry out the orders of their short-sighted kings!'

'You're killing them!'

'Be silent, Triss Merigold! The attack on the unity of the Brotherhood has failed. The island is still ruled by the Chapter! The kings should keep their hands off the Chapter's business! This is our conflict and we shall resolve it ourselves! We will resolve our business and then put an end to this senseless war, for it is we, sorcerers, who bear the responsibility for the fate of the world!'

A ball of lightning shot from her hands, and the redoubled echo of the explosion roared among the columns and stone walls.

'Begone!' she screamed again. 'You will not enter this place! Begone!'

The screaming from below subsided. Geralt understood that the attackers had withdrawn from the stairway, had beaten a retreat. Tissaia's outline blurred in front of his eyes. It wasn't magic. He was losing consciousness.

'Run, Triss Merigold,' the enchantress's words came from far away, as if from behind a wall. 'Philippa Eilhart has already fled; she flew away on owl's wings. You were her accomplice in this wicked conspiracy and I ought to punish you. But there has been enough blood, death and misfortune! Begone! Go to Aretuza and join your allies! Teleport away. The portal in the Tower of Gulls no longer exists. It was destroyed along with the tower. You can teleport without fear. Wherever you wish. To your King Foltest, for instance, for whom you betrayed the Brotherhood!'

'I will not leave Geralt ...' groaned Triss. 'He cannot fall into the hands of the Redanians ... He's gravely injured ... He has internal bleeding, and I have no more strength! I don't have the strength to open the portal! Tissaia! Help me please!'

Darkness. Bitter cold. From far away, from behind a stone wall, the voice of Tissaia de Vries:

'I shall help you.'

Evertsen Peter, b. 1234, confidant of Emperor Emhyr Deithwen and one of the true authors of the Empire's might. The chief chamberlain of the army during the time of the Northern Wars (q.v.), from 1290 imperial treasurer of the crown. In the final period of Emhyr's rule, he was raised to the rank of coadjutor of the Empire. During the rule of Emperor Morvran Voor he was falsely accused of misappropriation of funds, found guilty, imprisoned and died in 1301 in Winneburg Castle. Posthumously rehabilitated by Emperor Jan Calveit in 1328.

Effenberg and Talbot, *Encyclopaedia Maxima Mundi,*
Volume V

May Ye All Wail, for the Destroyer of Nations is upon us. Your lands shall they trample and divide with rope. Your cities razed shall be, their dwellers expelled. The bat, owl and raven your homes shall infest, and the serpent will therein make its nest . . .

Aen Ithlinnespeath

CHAPTER FIVE

The captain of the squad reined back his mount, removed his helmet and used his fingers to comb his thinning hair, which was matted with sweat.

'Journey's over,' he repeated, seeing the troubadour's questioning gaze.

'What? How d'you mean?' said Dandelion, astonished. 'Why?'

'We aren't going any further. Do you see? The river you see glinting down there is the Ribbon. We were only told to escort you to the Ribbon. That means it's time we were off.'

The rest of the troops stopped behind them, but none of the soldiers dismounted. They were all looking around nervously. Dandelion shielded his eyes with a hand and stood up in the stirrups.

'Where can you see that river?'

'I said it's down there. Ride down the ravine and you'll be there in no time.'

'You could at least escort me to the bank,' protested Dandelion, 'and show me the ford ...'

'There's nothing much to show. Since May the weather's been baking hot, so the water level's dropped. There isn't much water in the Ribbon. Your horse won't have any problem crossing it ...'

'I showed your commander the letter from King Venzlav,' said the troubadour, puffing up. 'He read the contents and I heard him order you to escort me to the very edge of Brokilon. And you're going to abandon me here in this thicket? What'll happen if I get lost?'

'You won't get lost,' muttered another soldier gloomily, who had come closer but had not so far spoken. 'You won't have time to get lost. A dryad's arrow will find you first.'

'What cowardly simpletons,' Dandelion sneered. 'I see you're afraid of the dryads. But Brokilon only begins on the far bank of the

201

Ribbon. The river is the border. We haven't crossed it yet.'

'Their border,' explained the leader, looking around, 'extends as far as their arrows do. A powerful bow shot from that bank will send an arrow right to the edge of the forest and still have enough impetus to pierce a hauberk. You insisted on going there. That's your business, it's your hide. But life is dear to me. I'm not going any further. I'd rather shove my head in a hornets' nest!'

'I've explained to you,' said Dandelion, pushing his hat back and sitting up in the saddle, 'that I'm riding to Brokilon on a mission. I am, it may be said, an ambassador. I do not fear dryads. But I would like you to escort me to the bank of the Ribbon. What'll happen if brigands rob me in that thicket?'

The gloomy soldier laughed affectedly.

'Brigands? Here? In daylight? You won't meet a soul here during the day. Latterly, the dryads have been letting arrows fly at anyone who appears on the bank of the Ribbon, and they're not above venturing deeper into our territory either. No, no need to be afraid of brigands.'

'That's true,' agreed the captain. 'A brigand would have to be pretty stupid to be riding along the Ribbon during the day. And we're not idiots. You're riding alone, without armour or weapons, and you don't look, forgive me, anything like a fighting man. You can see that a mile off. That may favour you. But if those dryads see us, on horseback and armed, you won't be able to see the sun for arrows.'

'Ah, well. There's nothing else for it.' Dandelion patted his horse's neck and looked down towards the ravine. 'I shall have to ride alone. Farewell, soldiers. Thank you for the escort.'

'Don't be in such a rush,' said the gloomy soldier, looking up at the sky. 'It'll be evening soon. Set off when the haze starts rising from the water. Because, you know ...'

'What?'

'An arrow's not so sure in the fog. If fate smiles on you, the dryads might miss. But they seldom miss ...'

'I told you—'

'All right, all right. I've got it. You're going to them on some kind of mission. But I'll tell you something else. They don't care whether

202

it's a mission or a church procession. They'll let fly at you, and that's that.'

'You insist on frightening me, do you?' said the poet snootily. 'What do you take me for, a court scribbler? I, my good men, have seen more battlegrounds than the lot of you. And I know more about dryads than you. If only that they never fire without warning.'

'It once was thus, you're right,' said the leader quietly. 'Once they gave warnings. They shot an arrow into a tree trunk or into the road, and that marked the border that you couldn't cross. If a fellow turned back right then, he could get out in one piece. But now it's different. Now they shoot to kill at once.'

'Why such cruelty?'

'Well,' muttered the soldier, 'it's like this. When the kings made a truce with Nilfgaard, they went after the elven gangs with a will. You can tell they're putting the screws on, for there isn't a night that survivors don't flee through Brugge, seeking shelter in Brokilon. And when our boys hunt the elves, they sometimes mix it with the dryads too, those who come to the elves' aid from the far side of the Ribbon. And our army has also been known to go too far ... Get my drift?'

'Yes,' said Dandelion, looking at the soldier intently and shaking his head. 'When you were hunting the Scoia'tael you crossed the Ribbon. And you killed some dryads. And now the dryads are taking their revenge in the same way. It's war.'

'That it is. You took the words right out of my mouth. War. It was always a fight to kill – never to let live – but now it's worse than ever. There's a fierce hatred between them and us. I'll say it one more time: if you don't have to, don't go there.'

Dandelion swallowed.

'The whole point,' he said, sitting tall in the saddle and working hard to assume a resolute expression and strike a dashing pose, 'is that I *do* have to. And I'm going. Right now. Evening or no evening, fog or no fog. Duty calls.'

The years of practice paid off. The troubadour's voice sounded beautiful and menacing, austere and cold. It rang with iron and valour. The soldiers looked at him in unfeigned admiration.

203

'Before you set off,' said the leader, unfastening a flat, wooden canteen from his saddle, 'neck down some vodka, minstrel, sir. Have a good old swig ...'

'It'll make the dying easier,' added the gloomy one, morosely.

The poet sipped from the canteen.

'A coward,' he declared with dignity, when he'd stopped coughing and had got his breath back, 'dies a hundred times. A brave man dies but once. But Dame Fortune favours the brave and holds cowards in contempt.'

The soldiers looked at him in even greater admiration. They didn't know and couldn't have known that Dandelion was quoting from a heroic epic poem. Moreover, from one written by someone else.

'I shall repay you for the escort with this,' said the poet, removing a jingling, leather pouch from his bosom. 'Before you return to the fort, before you're once again embraced by strict mother-duty, stop by at a tavern and drink my health.'

'Thank you, sir,' said the leader, blushing somewhat. 'You are generous, although we— Forgive us for leaving you alone, but ...'

'It's nothing. Farewell.'

The bard adjusted his hat to a jaunty angle over his left ear, prodded his horse with his heels and headed into the ravine, whistling 'The Wedding Party at Bullerlyn', a well-known and extremely indecent cavalry song.

'The cornet in the fort said he was a freeloader, a coward and a knobhead. But he's a valiant, military gentleman, even if he is a poetaster.' The voice of the gloomy soldier was carried to Dandelion's ears.

'Truly spoken,' responded the captain. 'He isn't faint-hearted, you couldn't say that. He didn't even bat an eyelid, I noticed. And on top of that, he's whistling, can you hear? Ho, ho ... Heard what he said? That he's an embarrassador. You can be sure they don't make any old bugger an embarrassador. You've got to have your head screwed on to be made an embarrassador ...'

Dandelion quickened his pace in order to get away as quickly as possible. He didn't want to sabotage the reputation he'd just earned himself. And he knew, with his mouth drying up in terror, that he wouldn't be able to whistle for much longer.

The ravine was sombre and damp, and the wet clay and carpet of rotten leaves lying on it muffled the thudding of his dark bay gelding's hooves. He'd called the horse 'Pegasus'. Pegasus walked slowly, head hanging down. He was one of those rare specimens of horse who could never care less.

The forest had come to an end, but a wide, reedy meadow still separated Dandelion from the banks of the river, which was marked by a belt of alders. The poet reined Pegasus in. He looked around carefully but didn't see anything. He listened out intently but only heard the singing of frogs.

'Well, boy,' he croaked. 'It's do or die. Gee up.'

Pegasus lifted his head a little and stuck up his ears, which normally hung down, questioningly.

'You heard right. Off you go.'

The gelding set off reluctantly, the boggy ground squelching beneath his hooves. Frogs fled with long hops. A duck took flight a few paces in front of them, fluttering and quacking, briefly stopping the troubadour's heart, after which it began pounding very hard and very rapidly. Pegasus showed no interest in the duck whatsoever.

'The hero rode ...' mumbled Dandelion, wiping the cold sweat from the nape of his neck with a handkerchief taken from inside his jerkin, 'rode fearlessly through the wilderness, heedless of the leaping lizards and flying dragons ... He rode and rode ... Until he reached a vast expanse of water ...'

Pegasus snorted and stopped. They were by the river, among reeds and bulrushes, which stood taller than his stirrups. Dandelion wiped his sweaty forehead and tied the handkerchief around his neck. He had been staring at the alder thicket on the far bank until his eyes watered. He saw nothing and no one. The surface of the water rippled from waterweed being swayed by the current, while overhead turquoise and orange kingfishers flitted past. The air twinkled with swarming insects. Fish gulped down mayflies, leaving huge rings on the surface of the water.

Everywhere, as far as the eye could see, there were beaver lodges

– piles of cut branches, and felled and gnawed tree trunks – being washed by the lazy current.

There's an astonishing abundance of beavers here, thought the poet. *And no small wonder. No one bothers those bloody tree-chewers. Neither robbers, hunters nor forest beekeepers venture into this region; not even those interfering fur trappers would dare set their snares here. The ones who tried would have got an arrow through the throat, and the crayfish would have nibbled on them in the ooze by the riverbank. And I, the idiot, am forcing my way out here of my own free will; here, by the Ribbon, over which hangs a cadaverous stench, a stench which even the scent of sweet flag and mint cannot mask . . .*

He sighed heavily.

Pegasus slowly planted his forelegs into the water, lowered his muzzle towards the surface, drank long, and then turned his head and looked at Dandelion. The water dripped from his muzzle and nostrils. The poet nodded, sighed once more and sniffed loudly.

'The hero gazed on the maelstrom,' he quietly declaimed, trying not to let his teeth chatter. 'He gazed on it and travelled on, for his heart knew not trepidation.'

Pegasus lowered his head and ears.

'Knew not trepidation, I said.'

Pegasus shook his head, jingling the rings on his reins and bit. Dandelion dug a heel into his side. The gelding entered the water with pompous resignation.

The Ribbon was shallow but very overgrown. Before they had reached the centre of the current, Pegasus was dragging long plaits of waterweed. The horse walked slowly and with effort, trying to shake the annoying pondweed off with every step.

The rushes and alders of the far bank were close. So close that Dandelion felt his stomach sinking low, very low, right down to the saddle itself. He knew that in the centre of the river, entangled in the waterweed, he was an excellent target; a sitting duck. In his mind's eye he could already see bows bending, bowstrings being pulled back and sharp arrowheads being aimed at him.

He squeezed the horse's sides with his calves, but Pegasus was having none of it. Instead of picking up speed, he stopped and lifted his tail. Balls of dung splashed into the water. Dandelion gave a long groan.

'The hero,' he muttered, closing his eyes, 'was unable to cross the raging rapids. He fell in action, pierced by many missiles. He was hidden for ages long in the azure depths, rocked by jade-green algae. All traces of him vanished. Only horse shit remained, borne by the current to the distant sea ...'

Pegasus, clearly relieved, headed jauntily towards the bank without any encouragement, and when he reached the bank, and was finally free of waterweed, even took the liberty of breaking into a canter, utterly soaking Dandelion's trousers and boots. The poet didn't notice it, though, since the vision of arrows aimed at his belly hadn't left him for a moment, and dread crept down his neck and back like a huge, cold, slimy leech. For beyond the alders, less than a hundred paces away, beyond the vivid green band of riverside grass, rose up a vertical, black, menacing wall of trees.

It was Brokilon.

On the bank, a few steps downstream, lay the white skeleton of a horse. Nettles and bulrushes had grown through its ribcage. Some other – smaller – bones, which didn't come from a horse, were also lying there. Dandelion shuddered and looked away.

Squelching and splashing, the gelding, urged on by Dandelion, hauled himself out of the riverside swamp, the mud smelling unpleasantly. The frogs stopped croaking for a moment. It all went very quiet. Dandelion closed his eyes. He stopped declaiming and improvising. His inspiration and daring had evaporated. Only cold, revolting fear remained; an intense sensation, but one utterly bereft of creative impulses.

Pegasus perked up his floppy ears and dispassionately shambled towards the Forest of the Dryads. Called by many the Forest of Death.

I've crossed the border, thought the poet. *Now it will all be settled. While I was by the river and in the water, they could be magnanimous. But not now. Now I'm an intruder. Just like that one ... I might end up a skeleton, too; a warning for people to heed ... If there are dryads here at all. If they're watching me ...*

He recalled watching shooting tournaments, competitions and archery displays at country markets. Straw targets and mannequins, studded or torn apart by arrowheads. *What does a man feel when he's hit by an arrow? The impact? Pain? Or perhaps ... nothing?*

There were either no dryads nearby, or they hadn't made up their minds what to do with this lone rider, because the poet rode up to the forest petrified with fear but in one piece. Entry to the trees was barred by a dense tangle of scrub and fallen trunks, bristling with roots and branches, but in any case Dandelion didn't have the slightest intention of riding up to the very edge, much less of heading deeper into the forest. He was capable of making himself take risks – but not of committing suicide.

He dismounted very slowly and fastened the reins to a protruding root. He didn't usually do that; Pegasus wasn't inclined to wander away from his master. Dandelion was not certain, however, how the horse would react to the whistle and whir of arrows. Up until now he had tried not to expose either Pegasus or himself to sounds of that kind.

He removed a lute from the saddle's pommel. It was a unique, magnificent instrument with a slender neck. *This was a present from a she-elf,* he recalled, stroking the inlaid wood. *It might end up returning to the Elder Folk ... Unless the dryads leave it by my dead body ...*

Close by lay an old tree, blown down in a gale. The poet sat down on the trunk, rested the lute on his knee, licked his lips and wiped his sweaty hands on his trousers.

The day was drawing to a close. A haze rose from the Ribbon, forming a grey-white shroud enveloping the meadows. It was cooler now. The honking of cranes sounded and died away, leaving only the croaking of frogs.

Dandelion plucked the strings. Once, then twice, then a third time. He twisted the pegs, tuned the lute and began to play. And a moment later, to sing.

Yviss, m'evelienn vente cáelm en tell
Elaine Ettariel Aep cór me lode deith ess'viell
Yn blath que me darienn

208

Aen minne vain tegen a me
Yn toin av muirednn que dis eveigh e aep llea ...

The sun vanished behind the trees. It immediately became dark in
the shade of Brokilon's mighty trees.

Ueassan Lamm feainne renn, ess'ell,
Elaine Ettariel,
Aep cor ...

He didn't hear – but he felt – somebody's presence.
'N'te mirę daetre. Sh'aente vort.'
'Don't shoot ...' he whispered, obediently not looking around.
'N'aen aespar a me ... I come in peace ...'
'N'ess a tearth. Sh'aente.'
He obeyed, although his fingers had turned cold and numb on the
strings, and he had difficulty making any sound whatsoever emerge
from his throat. But there was no hostility in the dryad's voice and
he was a professional, dammit.

Ueassan Lamm feainne renn, ess'ell,
Elaine Ettariel,
Aep cor aen tedd teviel e gwen
Yn blath que me darienn
Ess yn e evellien a me
Que shaent te cáelm a'vean minne me striscea ...

This time he took the liberty of glancing over his shoulder.
Whatever was crouching by the tree trunk, very near, resembled a
bush entwined in ivy. But it wasn't a bush. Bushes didn't have such
large, shining eyes.

Pegasus snorted softly, and Dandelion knew that behind him in
the darkness someone was stroking his horse's muzzle.

'Sh'aente vort,' requested the dryad squatting behind him once
again. Her voice was like the pattering of rain on leaves.

'I ...' he began. 'I am ... The comrade of the witcher Geralt ... I

know that Geralt— That Gwynbleidd is among you in Brokilon. I
have come ...'

'N'te dice'en. Sh'aente, va.'

'Sh'aent,' gently asked a second dryad from behind him, virtually
in unison with a third. And maybe a fourth. He couldn't be certain.

'Yea, sh'aente, taedh,' said the thing that a moment earlier the
poet had taken to be a birch sapling standing a few paces in front of
him, in a silvery, girlish voice. 'Ess'laine ... Taedh ... Sing ... Sing
some more about Ettariel ... Yes?'

He did as she asked.

To adore you, is all my life
Fair Ettariel
Let me keep, then, the treasure of memories
And the magical flower;
A pledge and sign of your love.
Silvered by drops of dew as if by tears ...

This time he heard steps approaching.

'Dandelion.'

'Geralt!'

'Yes, it's me. You can stop that racket now.'

'How did you find me? How did you know I was in Brokilon?'

'Triss Merigold ... Bloody hell ...' said Dandelion. He tripped
again and would have fallen, had a passing dryad not seized him in a
dextrous and astonishingly powerful grip for one so slight.

'Gar'ean, táedh,' she warned in silver tones. 'Va cáelm.'

'Thank you. It's awfully dark here ... Geralt? Where are you?'

'Here. Don't lag behind.'

Dandelion quickened his pace, stumbled once more and almost
fell on the Witcher, who had stopped in the dark in front of him.
The dryads passed by them silently.

'It's hellishly dark ... Is it much further?'

'No. We'll soon be at the camp. Who, apart from Triss, knows
I'm hiding here? Did you let it slip to anyone?'

'I had to tell King Venzlav. I needed safe conduct through Brugge. You wouldn't believe the times we live in ... I also had to have permission for the expedition to Brokilon. But anyway, Venzlav knows you and likes you ... He appointed me an envoy. Just imagine. I'm sure he'll keep it secret, I asked him to. Don't get annoyed now, Geralt ...'

The Witcher came closer. Dandelion couldn't see the expression on his face, only the white hair and bristles of several days' beard growth, which was visible even in the dark.

'I'm not annoyed,' said the Witcher, placing his hand on Dandelion's shoulder. It seemed as though his voice, which up until then had been cold, was somewhat changed. 'I'm glad you're here, you whoreson.'

'It's so cold here,' said Dandelion, shuddering and making the branches they were sitting on creak under him. 'We could get a fire going—'

'Don't even think about it,' muttered the Witcher. 'Have you forgotten where you are?'

'Are you serious ... ?' The troubadour glanced around timidly. 'Oh. No fire, right?'

'Trees hate fire. And they do too.'

'Dammit. Are we going to sit here and freeze? And in the bloody dark? I can't see my hand in front of my face ...'

'Keep it by your side then.'

Dandelion sighed, hunched forward and rubbed his arms. He heard the Witcher beside him breaking some thin twigs in his fingers.

A small green light suddenly flared up in the dark, first of all dim and faint, then quickly becoming brighter. After the first one, many others began to glimmer around them, moving and dancing like fireflies or will-o'-the-wisps above a marsh. The forest suddenly came to life with a shimmering of shadows, and Dandelion began to see the silhouettes of the dryads surrounding them. One of them approached and put something on the ground near them, which looked like a hot, glowing tangle of plants. The poet reached a hand out carefully and took hold of it. The green glow was totally cold.

211

'What is it, Geralt?'

'Rotten wood and a special kind of moss. It only grows here in Brokilon. And only they know how to weave it all together to make it give off light. Thank you, Fauve.'

The dryad did not answer, but neither did she go away, remaining squatting alongside the pair. She had a garland on her brow, and her long hair fell to her shoulders. Her hair looked green in the light and may actually have been green. Dandelion knew that dryads' hair could be of the weirdest colours.

'Taedh,' she said melodically, raising her flashing eyes to the troubadour. Her fine-featured face was crossed diagonally by two parallel dark stripes of painted camouflage. 'Ess've vort shaente aen Ettariel? Shaente a'vean vort?'

'No ... Later perhaps,' he answered politely, carefully searching for words in the Elder Speech. The dryad sighed and leaned over, gently stroking the neck of the lute, which was lying nearby. She rose nimbly to her feet. Dandelion watched her as she disappeared into the forest towards the others, whose shadows showed faintly in the dim light of the small green lanterns.

'I trust I didn't offend her, did I?' he asked softly. 'They have their own dialect, and I don't know polite expressions ...'

'Check whether you've got a knife in your guts,' said the Witcher, with neither mockery nor humour in his voice. 'Dryads react to insults by sticking a knife in your belly. Don't worry, Dandelion. I'd say they're willing to forgive you a good deal more than slips of the tongue. The concert you gave at the edge of the forest was clearly to their liking. Now you're ard táedh, "the great bard". They're waiting for the next part of 'The Flower of Ettariel'. Do you know the rest? It's not your ballad, after all.'

'It's my translation. I also embellished it somewhat with elven music. Didn't you notice?'

'No.'

'As I thought. Fortunately, dryads are more receptive to art. I read somewhere that they're exceptionally musical. Which is why I came up with my cunning plan. For which, incidentally, you haven't yet praised me.'

'My congratulations,' said the Witcher after a moment's silence. 'It was indeed cunning. And fortune smiled on you, as usual. They shoot accurately at two hundred paces. They don't usually wait until someone crosses onto their bank of the river and begins to sing. They are very sensitive to unpleasant smells. So when the corpse falls into the Ribbon and gets carried away by the current, they don't have to put up with the stench.'

'Oh, whatever,' said the poet, clearing his throat and swallowing. 'The most important thing is I pulled it off and found you. Geralt, how did you ...'

'Do you have a razor?'

'Eh? Of course I do.'

'Lend it to me tomorrow morning. This beard of mine is driving me insane.'

'Didn't the dryads have any? Hmm ... I guess not, they don't have much need for them, do they? Of course, I'll lend it to you. Geralt?'

'What?'

'I don't have any grub with me. Should ard táedh, the great bard, hold out any hopes of supper when visiting dryads?'

'They don't eat supper. Never. And the guards on Brokilon's border don't eat breakfast either. You'll have to survive until noon. I've already got used to it.'

'But when we get to their capital, the famous, Duen Canell, concealed in the very heart of the forest ...'

'We'll never get there, Dandelion.'

'What? I thought ... But you— I mean they've given you sanctuary. After all ... they tolerate ...'

'You've chosen the right word.'

They both said nothing for a long time.

'War,' said the poet finally. 'War, hatred and contempt. Everywhere. In everyone's hearts.'

'You're being poetic.'

'But that's what it's like.'

'Precisely. Right, tell me your news. Tell me what's been happening in the world while they've been tending to me here.'

213

'First,' said Dandelion, coughing softly, 'tell me what really happened in Garstang.'

'Didn't Triss tell you?'

'Yes, she did. But I'd like to hear your version.'

'If you know Triss's version, you know a more complete and probably more faithful version already. Tell me what's happened since I've been here.'

'Geralt,' whispered Dandelion. 'I don't know what happened to Yennefer and Ciri ... No one does. Triss doesn't either ...'

The Witcher shifted suddenly, making the branches creak.

'Did I ask you about Ciri or Yennefer?' he said in a different voice. 'Tell me about the war.'

'Don't you know anything? Hasn't any news reached you here?'

'Yes, it has. But I want to hear everything from you. Speak, please.'

'The Nilfgaardians,' began the bard after a moment's silence, 'attacked Lyria and Aedirn. Without declaring war. The reason was supposedly an attack by Demavend's forces on some border fort in Dol Angra, which happened during the mages' conclave on Thanedd. Some people say it was a setup. That they were Nilfgaardians disguised as Demavend's soldiers. We'll probably never find out what really happened. In any case, Nilfgaard's retaliation was swift and overwhelming; the border was crossed by a powerful army, which must have been concentrated in Dol Angra for weeks, if not months. Spalla and Scala, the two Lyrian border strongholds, were captured right away, in just three days. Rivia was prepared for a siege lasting months but capitulated after two days under the pressure of the guilds and the merchants who were promised that, should the town open its gates and pay a ransom, it wouldn't be sacked ...'

'Was the promise kept?'

'Yes.'

'Interesting.' The Witcher's voice changed again a little. 'Promises being kept in these times? I won't mention that, in the past, no one would have dreamed of making promises like that, because no one would have expected them. Craftsmen and merchants never opened the gates of strongholds, they defended them; each guild had its own tower or machicolations.'

'Money has no fatherland, Geralt. The merchants don't care whose rule they make their money under. And the Nilfgaardian palatine doesn't care who he levies taxes on. Dead merchants don't make money or pay taxes.'

'Go on.'

'After the capitulation of Rivia the Nilfgaardian Army headed northwards at great speed, almost without encountering any resistance. The armies of Demavend and Meve withdrew, unable to form a front in the deciding battle. The Nilfgaardians reached Aldersberg. In order to prevent the stronghold being blockaded, Demavend and Meve decided to join battle. The positions of their armies could have been better ... Bugger it, if there were more light here I'd draw you—'

'Don't draw anything. And keep it brief. Who won?'

'Have you heard, sir?' said a reeve, out of breath and sweating, pushing through the group gathered around the table. 'A messenger has arrived from the field! We have triumphed! The battle is won! Victory! It is our day, our day! We have vanquished our foe, we have beaten him into the ground!'

'Silence,' scowled Evertsen. 'My head is splitting from your cries. Yes, I've heard, I've heard. We've vanquished the foe. It is our day, it is our field and it is also our victory. What a sensation.'

The bailiffs and reeves fell silent and looked at their superior in astonishment.

'Do you not rejoice, Chamberlain, sir?'

'That I do. But I'm able to do it quietly.'

The reeves were silent and looked at one another. *Young pups,* thought Evertsen. *Overexcited young whippersnappers. Actually, I'm not surprised at them. But for heaven's sake, there, on the hill, even Menno Coehoorn and Elan Trahe, forsooth, even the grizzly bearded General Braibant, are yelling, jumping for joy and slapping each other's backs in congratulation. Victory! It is our day! But who else's day could it have been? The kingdoms of Aedirn and Lyria only managed to mobilise three thousand horse and ten thousand foot, of which one-fifth had already been blockaded in the first days of the invasion, cut off in its forts and strongholds. Part of the remaining army had to withdraw to protect its flanks, threatened by far-reaching raids by light horse and diversionary strikes by units of Scoia'tael. The remaining five or six thousand – including no more than twelve hundred knights – joined battle on the fields outside Aldersberg. Coehoorn sent an army of thirteen thousand to attack them, including ten armoured companies, the flower of the Nilfgaard knighthood. And now he's overjoyed, he's yelling, he's thwacking his mace against his thigh and calling for beer ... Victory! What a sensation.*

With a sudden movement, he gathered together the maps and papers lying on the table, lifted his head and looked around.

'Listen carefully,' he said brusquely to the reeves. 'I shall be issuing instructions.'

His subordinates froze in anticipation.

'Each one of you,' he began, 'heard Field Marshal Coehoorn's speech yesterday, to his officers. I would like to point out, gentlemen, that what the marshal said to his men does not apply to you. You are to execute other assignments and orders. My orders.'

Evertsen pondered for a moment and wiped his forehead.

'"War to the castles, peace to the villages," Coehoorn said to his commanders yesterday. You know that principle,' he added at once. 'You learned it in officer training. That principle applied until today; from tomorrow you're to forget it. From tomorrow a different principle applies, which will now be the battle cry of the war we are waging. The battle cry and my orders run: War on everything alive. War on everything that can burn. You are to leave scorched earth behind you. From tomorrow, we take war beyond the line we will withdraw behind after signing the treaty. We are withdrawing, but there is to be nothing but scorched earth beyond that line. The kingdoms of Rivia and Aedirn are to be reduced to ashes! Remember Sodden! The time of revenge is with us!'

Evertsen cleared his throat loudly.

'Before the soldiers leave the earth scorched behind them,' he said to the listening reeves, 'your task will be to remove from that earth and that land everything you can, anything that may increase the riches of our fatherland. You, Audegast, will be responsible for loading and transporting all harvested and stored crops. Whatever is still in the fields and what Coehoorn's gallant knights don't destroy is to be taken.'

'I have too few men, Chamberlain, sir—'

'There will be enough slaves. Put them to work. Marder and you ... I've forgotten your name ...?'

'Helvet. Evan Helvet, Chamberlain, sir.'

'You'll be responsible for livestock. Gather it into herds and drive it to the designated points for quarantine. Beware of rot-foot and other diseases. Slaughter any sick or suspect specimens and burn the carcasses. Drive the rest south along the designated routes.'

'Yes, sir.'

And now a special task, thought Evertsen, scrutinising his subordinates. *To whom shall I entrust it? They're all striplings, milk still wet on their cheeks, they've seen little, they've experienced nothing ... Oh, I miss those old, hardened bailiffs of mine. Wars, wars, always wars ... Soldiers are always falling, and in great numbers, but the losses among bailiffs, even though much fewer in number, are more telling. You don't see the deficit among the active troops, because fresh recruits always keep replacing them, for every man wants to be a soldier. But who wants to be a bailiff or a reeve? Who, when asked by their sons on returning home what they did during the war, wants to say he measured bushels of grain, counted stinking pelts and weighed wax as he led a convoy of carts laden with spoils along rutted roads, covered in ox shit, and drove herds of lowing and bleating beasts, swallowing dust and flies and breathing in the stench ...?*

A special mission. The foundry in Gulet, with its huge furnaces. The puddling furnaces, the zinc ore foundry and the huge ironworks in Eysenlaan, annual production of five hundred hundredweight. The foundries and wool manufactories in Aldersberg. The maltings, distilleries, weaving mills and dyeworks in Vengerberg ...

Dismantle and remove. Thus ordered Emperor Emhyr, the White Flame Dancing on the Barrows of his Enemies. As simple as that. Dismantle and remove, Evertsen.

An order's an order. It must be carried out.

That leaves the most important things. The ore mines and their yield.

217

*Coinage. Valuables. Works of art. But I'll take care of that myself. In
person.*

Alongside the black columns of smoke which were visible on the
horizon rose other plumes. And yet others. The army was imple-
menting Coehoorn's orders. The Kingdom of Aedirn had become
a land of fires.

A long column of siege engines trundled along the road, rumbling and throwing up clouds of dust. Towards Aldersberg, which
was still holding out. And towards Vengerberg, King Demavend's
capital.

Peter Evertsen looked and counted and calculated. And added up
the money. Peter Evertsen was the grand chamberlain of the Empire;
during the war the army's chief bailiff. He had held that position for
twenty-five years. Figures and calculations; they were his life.

A mangonel costs five hundred florins, a trebuchet two hundred,
an onager at least a hundred and fifty, the simplest ballista eighty.
A trained crew requires nine and a half florins of monthly pay. The
column heading for Vengerberg, including horses, oxen and minor
tackle, is worth at least three hundred marks. Sixty florins can be
struck from a mark of pure ore weighing half a pound. The annual
yield of a mine is five or six thousand marks ...

The siege column was overtaken by some light cavalry. Evertsen
recognised them as the Duke of Winneburg's tactical company, one
of those redeployed from Cintra, by the designs on its pennants.
Yes, he thought, *they have something to be pleased about. The battle
won, the army from Aedirn routed. Reserves will not be deployed in a
heavy battle against the regular army. They will be pursuing forces in
retreat, wiping out scattered, leaderless groups. They will murder, pil-
lage and burn. They're pleased because it promises to be a pleasant, jolly
little war. A little war that isn't exhausting. And doesn't leave you dead.*

Evertsen was calculating.

*The tactical company combines ten ordinary companies and numbers
two thousand horse. Although the Winneburgians will probably not take
part in any large battles now, no fewer than a sixth of their number will
fall in skirmishes. Then there will be camps and bivouacs, rotten victuals, filth, lice, mosquitoes, contaminated water. Then the inevitable*

will come: typhus, dysentery and malaria, which will kill no fewer than
a quarter. To that you should include an estimate for unpredictable
occurrences, usually around one-fifth of the total. Eight hundred will
return home. No more. And probably far fewer.

Cavalry companies continued to pass along the road; and infantry
corps followed the cavalry. These, in turn, were followed by marching longbowmen in yellow jerkins and round helmets, crossbowmen
in flat kettle hats, pavisiers and pikemen. Beyond them marched
shield bearers, veterans from Vicovaro and Etolia armoured like
crabs, then a colourful hodgepodge: hirelings from Metinna, mercenaries from Thurn, Maecht, Gheso and Ebbing ...

The troops marched briskly in spite of the intense heat, and the
dust stirred up by their heavy boots billowed above the road. Drums
pounded, pennants fluttered, and the blades of pikes, lances, halberds and guisarmes swayed and glittered. The soldiers marched
jauntily and cheerfully. This was a victorious army. An undefeated
army. *Onward, lads, forward, into battle! On Vengerberg! Destroy our*
foe! Avenge Sodden! Enjoy this merry little war, stuff our money bags
with loot and then home. And then home!

Evertsen watched. And calculated.

'Vengerberg fell after a week-long siege,' finished Dandelion. 'It
may surprise you, but the guilds courageously defended their towers
and the sections of wall assigned to them until the very end. So the
entire garrison and all the townspeople were slaughtered; it must
have been around six thousand people. When news of it got out, a
great flight began. Defeated regiments and civilians began to flee to
Temeria and Redania en masse. Crowds of fugitives headed along
the Pontar Valley and the passes of Mahakam. But not all of them
managed to escape. Mounted Nilfgaardian troops followed them
and cut off their escape ... You know what I'm driving at?'

'No, I don't. I don't know much about ... I don't know much
about war, Dandelion.'

'I'm talking about captives. About slaves. They wanted to take
as many prisoners as possible. It's the cheapest form of labour for
Nilfgaard. That's why they pursued the fugitives so doggedly. It

219

was a huge manhunt, Geralt. Easy pickings. Because the army had run away, and no one was left to defend the fleeing civilians.'

'No one?'

'Almost no one.'

'We won't make it in time ...' Villis wheezed, looking around. 'We won't get away ... Damn it, the border is so close ... So close ...'

Rayla stood up in her stirrups, and looked at the road winding among the forested hills. The road, as far as the eye could see, was strewn with people's abandoned belongings, dead horses, and with wagons and handcarts pushed to the side of the road. Behind them, beyond the forests, black columns of smoke rose into the sky. Screams and the intensifying sounds of battle could be heard ever closer.

'They're wiping out the rearguard ...' Villis wiped the soot and sweat from his face. 'Can you hear it, Rayla? They've caught up with the rearguard, and they're putting them to the sword! We'll never make it!'

'We're the rearguard now,' said the mercenary drily. 'Now it's our turn.'

Villis blenched, and one of the soldiers standing close by gave a loud sigh. Rayla tugged at the reins, and turned around her mount, which was snorting loudly and barely able to lift its head.

'There's no chance of our getting away,' she said calmly. 'The horses are ready to drop. They'll catch up with us and slaughter us before we make it to the pass.'

'Let's dump everything and hide among the trees,' said Villis, not looking at her. 'Individually, every man for himself. Maybe some of us will manage to ... survive.'

Rayla didn't answer, but indicated the mountain pass with a glance and a wave of her head, then the road and the rearmost ranks of the long column of refugees trudging towards the border. Villis understood. He cursed bitterly, leapt from his saddle, staggered and leaned on his sword.

'Dismount!' he yelled to the soldiers hoarsely. 'Block the road with anything you can! What are you staring at? Your mother bore you once and you only die once! We're the army! We're the rear-guard! We have to hold back our pursuers, delay them ...'

He fell silent.

'Should we delay the pursuers, the people will manage to cross into Temeria, to cross the mountains,' ended Rayla, also dismounting. 'There are women and children among them. What are you gawping at? It's our trade. This is what we're paid for, remember?'

The soldiers looked at one another. For a moment Rayla thought they would actually run away, that they would rouse their wet and exhausted horses for a last, desperate effort, that they would race past the column of fugitives, towards the pass – and safety. She was wrong. She had misjudged them.

They upset a cart on the road. They quickly built a barricade. A makeshift barricade. Not very high. And absolutely ineffectual.

They didn't have to wait long. Two horses, snorting and stumbling, lurched into the ravine, strewing flecks of froth around. Only one of them bore a rider.

'Blaise!'

'Ready yourselves ...' The mercenary slid from the saddle into a soldier's arms. 'Ready yourselves, dammit ... They're right behind me ...'

The horse snorted, skittered a few paces sideways, fell back on its haunches, collapsed heavily on its side, kicked, stretched its neck out, and uttered a long neigh.

'Rayla ...' wheezed Blaise, looking away. 'Give me ... Give me something. I've lost my sword ...'

Rayla, looking at the smoke from fires rising into the sky, gestured with her head to an axe leaning against the overturned cart. Blaise seized the weapon and staggered. The left leg of his trousers was soaked in blood.

'What about the others, Blaise?'

'They were slaughtered,' the mercenary groaned. 'Every last man. The entire troop ... Rayla, it's not Nilfgaard ... It's the Squirrels ... It was the elves who overhauled us. The Scoia'tael are in front, ahead of the Nilfgaardians.'

One of the soldiers wailed piercingly, and another sat down heavily on the ground, burying his face in his hands. Villis cursed, tightening the strap of his cuirass.

'To your positions!' yelled Rayla. 'Behind the barricade! They won't take us alive! I swear to you!'

Villis spat, then tore the three-coloured, black, gold and red rosette of King Demavend's special forces from his spaulder, throwing it into the bushes. Rayla, cleaning and polishing her own badge, smiled wryly.

'I don't know if that'll help, Villis. I don't know.'

'You promised, Rayla.'

'I did. And I'll keep my promise. To your positions, boys! Grab your crossbows and longbows!'

They didn't have to wait long.

After they had repelled the first wave, there were only six of them left alive. The battle was short but fierce. The soldiers mobilised from Vengerberg fought like devils and were every bit as savage as the mercenaries. Not one of them fell into the hands of the Scoia'tael alive. They chose to die fighting. And they died shot through by arrows; died from the blows of lance and sword. Blaise died lying down, stabbed by the daggers of two elves who pounced on him, dragging him from the barricade. Neither of the elves got up again. Blaise had a dagger too.

The Scoia'tael gave them no respite. A second group charged. Villis, stabbed with a lance for the third time, fell to the ground.

'Rayla!' he screamed indistinctly. 'You promised!'

The mercenary, dispatching another elf, swung around.

'Farewell, Villis,' she said, placing the point of her sword beneath his sternum and pushing hard. 'See you in hell!'

A moment later, she stood alone. The Scoia'tael encircled her from all sides. The soldier, smeared with blood from head to foot, raised her sword, whirled around and shook her black plait. She stood among the elves, terrible and hunched like a demon. The elves retreated.

'Come on!' she screamed savagely. 'What are you waiting for? You will not take me alive! I am Black Rayla!'

'Glaeddyv vort, beanna,' responded a beautiful, fair-haired elf in a calm voice. He had the face of a cherub and the large, cornflower-blue eyes of a child. He had emerged from the surrounding group of Scoia'tael, who were still hanging back hesitantly. His snow-white horse snorted, tossed its head powerfully up and down and energetically pawed at the bloodstained sand of the road.

'Glaeddyv vort, beanna,' repeated the rider. 'Throw down your sword, woman.'

The mercenary laughed horribly and wiped her face with her cuff, smearing sweat mixed with dust and blood.

'My sword cost too much to be thrown away, elf!' she cried. 'If you want to take it you will have to break my fingers! I am Black Rayla! What are you waiting for?'

She did not have to wait long.

'Did no one come to relieve Aedirn?' asked the Witcher after a long pause. 'I understood there were alliances. Agreements about mutual aid ... Treaties ...'

'Redania,' said Dandelion, clearing his throat, 'is in disarray after Vizimir's death. Did you know King Vizimir was murdered?'

'Yes, I did.'

'Queen Hedwig has assumed power, but bedlam has broken out across the land. And terror. Scoia'tael and Nilfgaardian spies are being hunted. Dijkstra raged through the entire country; the scaffolds were running with blood. Dijkstra is still unable to walk so he's being carried in a sedan chair.'

'I can imagine it. Did he come after you?'

'No. He could have, but he didn't. Oh, but never mind. In any case, Redania – plunged into chaos itself – was incapable of raising an army to support Aedirn.'

'And Temeria? Why didn't King Foltest of Temeria help Demavend?'

'When the fighting began in Dol Angra,' said Dandelion softly, 'Emhyr var Emreis sent an envoy to Vizima ...'

*

'Blast!' hissed Bronibor, staring at the closed doors. 'What are they spending so long debating? Why did Foltest abase himself so, to enter negotiations? Why did he give an audience to that Nilfgaardian dog at all? He ought to have been executed and his head sent back to Emhyr! In a sack!'

'By the gods, voivode,' choked the priest Willemer. 'He is an envoy, don't forget! An envoy's person is sacrosanct and inviolable! It is unfitting—'

'Unfitting? I'll tell you what's unfitting! It is unfitting to stand idly by and watch as the invader wreaks havoc in countries we are allied to! Lyria has already fallen and Aedirn is falling! Demavend will not hold Nilfgaard off by himself! We ought to dispatch an expeditionary force to Aedirn immediately. We ought to relieve Demavend with an assault on the Yaruga's left bank! There are few forces there. Most of the regiments have been redeployed to Dol Angra! And we're standing here debating! We're yapping instead of fighting! And on top of that we are playing host to a Nilfgaardian envoy!'

'Quite, voivode,' said Duke Hereward of Ellander, giving the old warrior a scolding look. 'This is politics. You have to be able to look a little further than a horse's muzzle and a lance. The envoy must be heard. Emperor Emhyr had reason to send him here.'

'Of course he had reason,' snarled Bronibor. 'Right now, Emhyr is crushing Aedirn and knows that if we cross the border, bringing Redania and Kaedwen with us, we'll defeat him and throw him back beyond Dol Angra, to Ebbing. He knows that were we to attack Cintra, we'd strike him in his soft underbelly and force him to fight on two fronts! That is what he fears! So he's trying to intimidate us, to stop us from intervening. That is the mission the Nilfgaardian envoy came here with. And no other!'

'Then we ought to hear out the envoy,' repeated the duke, 'and take a decision in keeping with the interests of our kingdom. Demavend unwisely provoked Nilfgaard and has suffered the consequences. And I'm in no hurry to die for Vengerberg. What is happening in Aedirn is no concern of ours.'

'Not our concern? What, by a hundred devils, are you drivelling on about? You consider it other people's business that the Nilfgaardians are in Aedirn and Lyria, on the right bank of the Yaruga, when only Mahakam separates us from them? You don't have an ounce of common sense ...'

'Enough of this feuding,' warned Willemer. 'Not another word. The king is coming out.'

The chamber doors opened. The members of the Royal Council rose, scraping their chairs. Many of the seats were vacant. The crown hetman and most of the commanders were with their regiments: in the Pontar Valley, in Mahakam and by the Yaruga. The chairs which were usually occupied by sorcerers were also vacant. Sorcerers ... *Yes*, thought Willemer, the priest, *the places occupied by sorcerers here, at the royal court in Vizima, will remain vacant for a long time. Who knows, perhaps for ever?*

King Foltest crossed the hall quickly and stood by his throne but did not sit down. He simply leaned over, resting his fists on the table. He was very pale.

'Vengerberg is under siege,' said the King of Temeria softly, 'and will fall any day now. Nilfgaard is pushing northwards relentlessly. The surrounded troops continue to fight, but that will change nothing. Aedirn is lost. King Demavend has fled to Redania. The fate of Queen Meve is unknown.'

The Council was silent.

'In a few days, the Nilfgaardians will take our eastern border, by which I mean the mouth of the Pontar Valley,' Foltest went on, still very softly. 'Hagge, Aedirn's last fortress, will not withstand them for long, and Hagge is on our eastern border. And on our southern border ... something very unfortunate has occurred. King Ervyll of Verden has sworn fealty to Emperor Emhyr. He has surrendered and opened the strongholds at the mouth of the Yaruga. Nilfgaardian garrisons are already installed in Nastrog, Rozrog and Bodrog, which were supposed to have protected our flank.'

The Council was silent.

'Owing to that,' continued Foltest, 'Ervyll has retained his royal title, but Emhyr is his sovereign. Verden remains a kingdom but, de facto, is now a Nilfgaardian province. Do you understand what that means? The situation has turned about face. The Verdenian strongholds and the mouth of the Yaruga are in Nilfgaard's hands. I cannot attempt to cross the river. And I cannot weaken the army stationed there by forming a corps which could enter Aedirn and support Demavend's forces. I cannot do that. Responsibility for my country and my subjects rests on me.'

The Council was silent.

'Emperor Emhyr var Emreis, the imperator of Nilfgaard,' said the king, 'has offered me a proposition ... an agreement. I have accepted that proposition. I shall now present this proposition to you. And you, when you have heard me out, will understand ... Will agree that— Will say ...'

The Council was silent.

'You will say ...' concluded Foltest. 'You will say I am bringing you peace.'

'So Foltest crumbled,' muttered the Witcher, breaking another twig in his fingers. 'He struck a deal with Nilfgaard. He left Aedirn to its fate ...'

'Yes,' agreed the poet. 'However, he sent his army to the Pontar Valley and occupied and manned the stronghold at Hagge. And the Nilfgaardians didn't march into the Mahakam pass or cross the Yaruga in Sodden. They didn't attack Brugge, which, after its capitulation and Ervyll's fealty, they have in their clutches. That was without doubt the price of Temeria's neutrality.'

'Ciri was right,' whispered the Witcher. 'Neutrality ... Neutrality is always contemptible.'

'What?'

'Nothing. But what about Kaedwen, Dandelion? Why didn't Henselt of Kaedwen come to Demavend and Meve's aid? They had a pact, after all; they were bound by an alliance. But even if Henselt, following Foltest's example, pisses on the signatures and seals on documents, and the royal word means nothing to him, he cannot be stupid, can he? Doesn't he understand that after the fall of Aedirn and the deal with Temeria, it will be his turn; that he's next on the Nilfgaardian list? Kaedwen ought to support Demavend out of good sense. There may no longer be faith nor truth in the world, but surely good sense still exists. What say you, Dandelion? Is there still good sense in the world? Or do only contemptibility and contempt remain?'

Dandelion turned his head away. The green lanterns were close. They were surrounding them in a tight ring. He hadn't noticed it earlier, but now he understood. All the dryads had been listening in to his story.

'You say nothing,' said Geralt, 'which means that Ciri was right. That Codringher was right. You were all right. Only I, the naive, anachronistic and stupid witcher, was wrong.'

Centurion Digod, known by the nickname Half-Gallon, opened the tent flap and entered, panting heavily and snarling angrily. The decurions jumped to their feet, assuming military poses and expressions. Zyvik dextrously threw a sheepskin over the small barrel of vodka standing among the saddles, before the eyes of the centurion had time to adjust to the gloom. Not to save themselves from punishment, because Digod wasn't actually a fervent opponent of drinking on duty or in the camp, but more in order to save the barrel. The centurion's nickname had not come about by accident; the story went that, in favourable conditions, he was capable of knocking back half a gallon of hooch, vigorously and with impressive speed. The centurion could polish off a standard soldier's quart mug as if it were a gill, in one draught, and seldom got his ears wet doing it.

'Well, Centurion, sir?' asked Bode, the bowmen's decurion. 'What have the top brass decided? What are our orders? Are we crossing the border? Tell us!'

'Just a moment,' grunted Half-Gallon. 'What bloody heat ... I'll tell you everything in a moment. But first, give me something to drink because my throat's bone dry. And don't tell me you haven't got any; I can smell the vodka in this tent a mile off. And I know where it's coming from. From under that there sheepskin.'

Zyvik, muttering an oath, took out the barrel. The decurions crowded together in a tight group and clinked cups and tin mugs.

227

'Aaaah,' said the centurion, wiping his whiskers and eyes. 'Ooooh, that's foul stuff. Keep pouring, Zyvik.'

'Come on, tell us quickly,' said Bode, becoming impatient. 'What orders? Are we marching on the Nilfgaardians or are we going to hang around on the border like a bunch of spare pricks at a wedding?'

'Itching for a scrap?' Half-Gallon wheezed lengthily, spat, and sat down hard on a saddle. 'In a hurry to get over the border, towards Aedirn? You can't wait, eh? What fierce wolf cubs you are, doing nothing but standing there growling, baring your fangs.'

'That's right,' said old Stahler coldly, shuffling from one foot to the other. His legs were as crooked as a spider's, which befitted an old cavalryman. 'That's right, Centurion, sir. This is the fifth night we've slept in our boots, at the ready. And we want to know what's happening. Is it a scrap or back to the fort?'

'We're crossing the border,' announced Half-Gallon brusquely. 'Tomorrow at dawn. Five brigades, with the Dun Banner leading the way. And now pay attention, because I'm going to tell you what was told to us centurions and warrant officers by the voivode and the Honourable Margrave Mansfeld of Ard Carraigh, who'd come straight from the king. Prick up your ears, because I won't tell you twice. And they're unusual orders.'

The tent fell silent.

'The Nilfgaardians have passed through Dol Angra,' said the centurion. 'They crushed Lyria, and reached Aldersberg in four days, where they routed Demavend's army in a decisive battle. Right away, after only six days' siege, they took Vengerberg by means of treachery. Now they're heading swiftly northwards, driving the armies back from Aedirn towards the Pontar Valley and Dol Blathanna. They're heading towards us, towards Kaedwen. So the orders for the Dun Banner are as follows: cross the border and march hard south, straight for the Valley of the Flowers. We have three days to get to the River Dyfne. I repeat, three days, which means we'll be marching at a trot. And, when we get there, not a step across the Dyfne. Not a single step. Shortly after, the Nilfgaardians will show up on the far bank. We do not, heed my words well, engage them. In no way, understood? Even if they try to cross the river, we're only to show them ... show them our colours. That it's us, the Kaedwen Army.'

Although it seemed impossible, the silence in the tent grew even more palpable.

'What?' mumbled Bode finally. 'We aren't to fight the Nilfgaardians? Are we going to war or not? What's this all about, Centurion, sir?'

'That's our orders. We aren't going to war, but ...' Half-Gallon scratched his neck ' ... but to give fraternal help. We're crossing the border to give protection to the people of Upper Aedirn ... Wait, what am I saying ... Not from Aedirn, but from Lormark. That's what the Honourable Margrave Mansfeld said. Yes, and he said that Demavend has suffered a defeat. He's tripped up and is lying flat on his face, because he governed poorly and his politics were crap. So that's the end of him and the end of the whole of Aedirn with him. Our king lent Demavend a pretty penny because he gave him help. One cannot allow wealth like that to be lost, so now it's time to get that money back with interest. Neither can we let our compatriots and brothers from Lormark be taken prisoner by Nilfgaard. We have to, you know, liberate them. For those are our ancient lands: Lormark. They were once under Kaedwen rule and now they shall return to its rule. All the way to the River Dyfne. That's the agreement Our Grace, King Henselt, has concluded with Emhyr of Nilfgaard. Agreements or no agreements, the Dun Banner is to station itself by the river. Do you understand?'

No one answered. Half-Gallon grimaced and waved a hand.

'Ah, sod the lot of you. You don't understood shit, I see. But don't worry yourselves, because I didn't either. For His Majesty the King, the margraves, the voivodes and nobles are there to think. And we're the army! We have to follow orders: get to the River Dyfne in three days, stop there and stand like a wall. And that's it. Pour, Zyvik.'

'Centurion, sir ...' stammered Zyvik. 'And what will happen ... What will happen if the army of Aedirn resists? Or bars the road? After all, we're passing through their country armed. What then?'

'Should our compatriots and brothers,' continued Stahler spitefully, 'the ones we're supposedly liberating ... Should they begin to shoot arrows at us or throw stones? Eh?'

'We are to be on the banks of the Dyfne in three days,' said Half-Gallon forcefully. 'And no later. Whoever tries to delay or stop us is clearly an enemy. And our enemies can be cut to ribbons. But heed my words well! Listen to the orders! Burn no villages, nor cottages. Take no goods from anyone. Do not plunder. Rape no women! Make sure you and your men remember this, for should anyone break this order, they will hang. The voivode must have repeated this ten times: we aren't fucking invading, we're coming to give a helping hand! Why are you grinning, Stahler? It's a bloody order! And now get to your units on the double. Get 'em all on their feet. The horses and tack are to shine like the full moon! In the afternoon, all companies are to fall in for inspection; the voivode himself will be drilling them. If I have to be ashamed of one of the platoons, the decurion will remember me. Oh yes, he'll remember! You have your orders!'

Zyvik was the last to leave the tent. Squinting in the bright sunlight, he watched the commotion which had taken over the camp. Decurions were rushing to their units, centurions were running about and cursing, and noblemen, cornets and pages were getting under each other's feet. The heavy cavalry from Ban Ard was trotting around the field, stirring up clouds of dust. The heat was horrendous.

Zyvik quickened his pace. He passed four bards from Ard Carraigh who had arrived the previous day and were sitting in the shadow cast by the margrave's richly decorated tent. The bards were just composing a ballad about the victorious military operation, about the prowess of the king, the prudence of the commanders and the bravery of the humble foot soldier. As usual, to save time, they were doing it before the operation.

'*Our brothers greeted us, they greeted us with breaaad and salt ...*' sang one of the bards, trying out his lyrics. '*They greeted their saviours and liberators, they greeted them with breaaad and salt ...* Hey, Hrafhir, think up a clever rhyme for "salt".'

The second bard suggested a rhyme. Zyvik did not hear what it was.

The platoon, camped among some willows by a pond, leapt up on seeing him.

'Make ready!' roared Zyvik, standing a good way back, so that the smell of his breath would not influence the morale of his subordinates. 'Before the sun rises another four fingers there'll be a full inspection! Everything's to be shining like the sun. Arms, tack, trappings and your mounts. There will be an inspection, and if I have to be ashamed of one of you before the centurion, I'll tear that soldier's legs off. Look lively!'

'We're going into battle,' guessed cavalryman Kraska, tucking his shirt quickly into his trousers. 'Are we going into battle, Decurion, sir?'

'What do you think? Or maybe we're off to a dance, to a Lammas party? We're crossing the frontier. The entire Dun Banner sets off tomorrow at dawn. The centurion didn't say in what array, but we know our platoon will be leading as usual. Now look lively, move your arses! Hold on, come back. I'll say this right now, because there'll be no time later. It won't be a typical little war, lads. The honourable gentlemen have thought up some modern idiocy. Some kind of liberation, or some such. We aren't going to fight the enemy, but we're heading towards our, what was it, eternal lands, to bring, you know, fraternal help. Now pay attention to what I say: you're not to touch the folk of Aedirn, not to loot—'

'What?' said Kraska, mouth agape. 'What do you mean, don't loot? And what are we going to feed our horses on, Decurion, sir?'

'You can loot fodder for the horses, but nothing else. Don't cut anyone up, don't burn any cottages down, don't destroy any crops ... Shut your trap, Kraska! This isn't a village gathering. It's the fucking army! Carry out the orders or you hang! I said: don't kill, don't murder, and don't—'

Zyvik broke off and pondered.

'And if you rape any women, do it on the quiet. Out of sight,' he finished a moment later.

*

'They shook hands,' finished Dandelion, 'on the bridge on the River Dyfne. Margrave Mansfeld of Ard Carraigh and Menno Coehoorn, the commander-in-chief of the Nilfgaardian armies from Dol Angra. They shook hands over the bleeding, dying Kingdom of Aedirn, sealing a criminal division of the spoils. The most despicable gesture history has ever known.'

Geralt remained silent.

'On the subject of despicableness,' he said, surprisingly calmly, a moment later, 'what about the sorcerers, Dandelion? The ones from the Chapter and the Council.'

'Not one of them remained with Demavend,' began the poet, soon after, 'while Foltest drove all those who had served him out of Temeria. Philippa is in Tretogor, helping Queen Hedwig to bring the chaos reigning in Redania under control. With her is Triss and three others, whose names I can't recall. Several of them are in Kaedwen. Many of them escaped to Kovir and Hengfors. They chose neutrality, because Esterad Thyssen and Niedamir, as you know, were, and are, neutral.'

'I know. What about Vilgefortz? And the people who stuck by him?'

'Vilgefortz has disappeared. It was expected he would surface in Aedirn after its capture, as Emhyr's viceroy ... But there's no trace of him. Neither of him nor any of his accomplices. Apart from ...'

'Go on, Dandelion.'

'Apart from one sorceress, who has become a queen.'

Filavandrel aep Fidhail waited for the answer in silence. The queen, who was staring out of the window, was also silent. The window looked out onto the gardens which, not so long ago, had been the pride and delight of the previous ruler of Dol Blathanna, the governor of the despot from Vengerberg. Fleeing before the arrival of the Free Elves, who were coming in the vanguard of Emperor Emhyr's army, the human governor had managed to take most of the valuables from the ancient elven palace, and even some of the furniture. But he could not take the gardens. So he destroyed them.

'No, Filavandrel,' said the queen finally. 'It is too early for that, much too early. Let us not think about extending our borders, for at present we are not even certain of their exact positions. Henselt of Kaedwen has no intention of abiding by the agreement and withdrawing from the Dyfne. Our spies inform us he has by no means abandoned his thoughts of aggression. He may attack us any day.'

'So we have achieved nothing.'

The queen slowly held out a hand. An Apollo butterfly, which had flown in through the window, alighted on her lace cuff, folding and unfolding its pointed wings.

'We've achieved more,' said the queen softly, in order not to frighten away the butterfly, 'than we could have hoped for. We have finally recovered our Valley of the Flowers after a hundred years—'

'I would not name it thus.' Filavandrel smiled sadly. 'Now, after the armies have passed through, it should be called the Valley of the Ashes.'

'We have our own country once more,' finished the queen, looking at the butterfly. 'We are a people again, no longer outcasts. And the ash will nourish the soil. In spring the valley will blossom anew.'

'That is too little, Daisy. It is ever too little. We've come down a station or two. Not long ago we boasted we would push the humans back to the sea, whence they came. And now we have narrowed our borders and ambitions to Dol Blathann ...'

'Emhyr Deithwen gave us Dol Blathanna as a gift. What do you expect from me, Filavandrel? Am I to demand more? Do not forget that even in receiving gifts there should be moderation. Particularly when it concerns gifts from Emhyr, because he gives nothing for nothing. We must keep the lands he gave us. And the powers at our disposal are barely sufficient to retain Dol Blathanna.'

'Let us then withdraw our commandos from Temeria, Redania and Kaedwen,' suggested the white-haired elf. 'Let us withdraw all Scoia'tael forces who are fighting the humans. You are now queen, Enid, and they will obey your orders. Now that we have our own small scrap of land, there is no sense in their continuing to fight. Their duty is to return and defend the Valley of the Flowers. Let them fight as a free people in defence of their own borders. Right now they are falling like bandits in the forests!'

The elf bowed her head.

'Emhyr has not permitted that,' she whispered. 'The commandos are to fight on.'

'Why? To what end?' said Filavandrel aep Fidhail, sitting up abruptly.

'I will say more. We are not to support nor to help the Scoia'tael. This was the condition set by Foltest and Henselt. Temeria and Kaedwen will respect our rule in Dol Blathanna, but only if we officially condemn the Squirrels' aggression and distance ourselves from them.'

'Those children are dying, Daisy. They are dying every day, perishing in an unequal contest. As a direct result of these secret pacts with Emhyr, humans will attack the commandos and crush them. They are our children, our future! Our blood! And you tell me we should dissociate ourselves from them? Que'ss aen me dicette, Enid? Vorsaeke'llan? Aen vaine?'

The butterfly took flight, flapping its wings, and flew towards the window, then spun around, caught by currents of hot summer air. Francesca Findabair, known as Enid an Gleanna, once a sorceress and presently the Queen of Aen Seidhe, the Free Elves, raised her head. Tears glistened in her beautiful blue eyes.

'The commandos,' she repeated softly, 'must continue to fight. They must disrupt the human kingdoms and hinder their preparations for war. That is the order of Emhyr and I may not oppose Emhyr. Forgive me, Filavandrel.'

Filavandrel aep Fidhail looked at her and bowed low.

'I forgive you, Enid. But I do not know if they will.'

'Did not one sorcerer think the matter over a second time? Even when Nilfgaard was slaughtering and burning in Aedirn, did none of them abandon Vilgefortz or join Philippa?'

'Not one.'

Geralt was silent for a long time.

'I can't believe,' he said finally, very softly, 'I can't believe none of them left Vilgefortz when the real causes and effects of his treachery came to light. I am – as is generally known – a naive, stupid and anachronistic witcher. But I still cannot believe that the conscience of not one sorcerer was pricked.'

Tissaia de Vries penned her practised, decorative signature beneath the final sentence of the letter. After lengthy reflection, she also added an ideogram signifying her true name alongside. A name no one knew. A name she had not used for a very long time. Not since she became an enchantress.

Skylark.

She put her pen down, very carefully, very precisely, across the sheet of parchment. For a long while she sat motionless, staring at the red orb of the setting sun. Then she stood up and walked over to the window. For some time she looked at the roofs of houses. Houses in which ordinary people were at that moment going to bed, tired by their ordinary, human lives and hardship; full of ordinary human anxiety about their fates, about tomorrow. The enchantress glanced at the letter lying on the table. At the letter addressed to ordinary people. The fact that most ordinary people couldn't read was of no significance.

She stood in front of the looking glass. She straightened her hair. She smoothed her dress. She brushed a non-existent speck from her puffed sleeve. She straightened the ruby necklace on her breast.

The candlesticks beneath the looking glass stood unevenly. Her servant must have moved them while she was cleaning.

Her servant. An ordinary woman. An ordinary human with eyes full of fear about what was happening. An ordinary human, adrift in these times of contempt. An ordinary human, searching in her – in an enchantress – for hope and certainty about tomorrow ...

An ordinary human whose trust she had betrayed.

The sound of steps, the pounding of heavy soldiers' boots, drifted up from the street. Tissaia de Vries did not even twitch, did not even turn to face the window. It was unimportant to her whose steps they were. Royal soldiers? A provost with orders to arrest the traitress? Hired assassins? Vilgefortz's hit men? She could not care less.

The steps faded into the distance.

The candlesticks beneath the looking glass stood out of kilter.

The enchantress straightened them and corrected the position of a tablecloth, so that its corner was exactly in the centre, symmetrically aligned with the candlesticks' quadrangular bases. She unfastened the gold bracelets from her wrists and placed them perfectly evenly on the smoothed cloth. She examined the tablecloth critically but could not find the tiniest fault. Everything was lying evenly and neatly. As it should have lain before.

She opened the drawer in the dresser and took out a short knife with a bone handle.

Her face was proud and fixed. Expressionless.

It was quiet in the house. So quiet, the sound of a wilted petal falling on the tabletop could be heard.

The sun, as red as blood, slowly sank below the roofs of the houses.

Tissaia de Vries sat down on the chair by the table, blew out a candle, straightened the quill lying across the letter one more time and severed the arteries in both wrists.

The fatigue caused by the daylong journey had made itself felt. Dandelion awoke and realised he had probably fallen asleep during the story, dropping off in mid-sentence. He shifted and almost rolled off the pile of branches. Geralt was no longer lying alongside him to balance the makeshift bed.

'Where did I ...' he said, coughing. He sat up. 'Where did I get to? Ah, the sorcerers ... Geralt? Where are you?'

'Here,' said the Witcher, barely visible in the gloom. 'Go on, please. You were just going to tell me about Yennefer.'

'Listen,' said the poet, knowing perfectly well he'd had absolutely no intention of even mentioning the person in question. 'I really know nothing ...'

'Don't lie. I know you.'

'If you know me so well,' said the troubadour, beginning to bristle, 'why the bloody hell are you making me speak? Since you know me through and through, you ought to know why I'm keeping my counsel, why I'm not repeating the gossip I've heard! You also ought to be able to guess what the gossip is and why I want to spare you it!'

'Que suecc's?' said one of the dryads sleeping nearby, on being woken by his raised voice.

'I beg your pardon,' said the Witcher softly.

Almost all of the green lanterns of Brokilon were out; only a few of them still glimmered gently.

'Geralt,' said Dandelion, interrupting the silence. 'You've always maintained that you don't get involved, that nothing matters to you ... She may have believed that. She believed that when she began this game with Vilgefortz—'

'Enough,' said Geralt. 'Not another word. When I hear the word "game" I feel like killing someone. Oh, give me that razor. I want to have that shave at last.'

'Now? It's still dark ...'

'It's never too dark for me. I'm a freak.'

After the Witcher had snatched the pouch of toiletries from him and headed off towards the stream, Dandelion realised he had shaken off all drowsiness. The sky was already lightening with the promise of dawn. He got up and walked into the forest, carefully stepping over the dryads, who were sleeping cuddled together.

'Are you one of those who had a hand in this?'

He turned around suddenly. The dryad leaning against a pine tree had hair the colour of silver, visible even in the half-light of the dawn.

'A most deplorable sight,' she said, folding her arms across her chest. 'Someone who has lost everything. You know, minstrel, it is interesting. Once, I thought it was impossible to lose everything, that something always remains. Always. Even in times of contempt, when naivety is capable of backfiring in the cruellest way, one cannot lose everything. But he ... he lost several pints of blood, the ability to walk properly, the partial use of his left hand, his witcher's sword, the woman he loves, the daughter he had gained by a miracle, his faith ... Well, I thought, he must have been left with something. But I was wrong. He has nothing now. Not even a razor.'

Dandelion remained silent. The dryad did not move.

'I asked if you had a hand in this,' she began a moment later. 'But I think there was no need. It's obvious you had a hand in it. It's

237

obvious you are his friend. And if someone has friends, and he loses everything in spite of that, it's obvious the friends are to blame. For what they did, or for what they didn't do.'

'What could I have done?' he whispered. 'What could I have done?'

'I don't know,' answered the dryad.

'I didn't tell him everything ...'

'I know.'

'I'm not guilty of anything.'

'Yes, you are.'

'No! I am not ...'

He jumped to his feet, making the branches of his makeshift bed creak. Geralt sat beside him, rubbing his face. He smelled of soap.

'Aren't you?' he asked coolly. 'I wonder what else you dreamed about. That you're a frog? Calm down. You aren't. Did you dream that you're a chump? Well, that dream might have been prophetic.'

Dandelion looked all around. They were completely alone in the clearing.

'Where is she? Where are they?'

'On the edge of the forest. Get ready, it's time you left.'

'Geralt, I spoke with a dryad a moment ago. She was talking in the Common Speech without an accent and told me ...'

'None of the dryads in that group spoke the Common Speech without an accent. You dreamed it, Dandelion. This is Brokilon. Many things can be dreamed here.'

A lone dryad was waiting for them at the edge of the forest. Dandelion recognised her at once – it was the one with the greenish hair who had brought them light during the night and encouraged him to continue singing. The dryad raised a hand, instructing them to stop. In her other hand she was holding a bow with an arrow nocked. The Witcher put his hand on the troubadour's shoulder and squeezed it hard.

'Is something going on?' whispered Dandelion.

'Indeed. Be quiet and don't move.'

The dense fog hanging over the Ribbon valley stifled voices and sounds, but not so much that Dandelion was unable to hear the splash of water and the snorting of horses. Riders were crossing the river.

'Elves,' he guessed. 'Scoia'tael? They're fleeing to Brokilon, aren't they? An entire commando unit ...'

'No,' muttered Geralt, staring into the fog. The poet knew the Witcher's eyesight and hearing were incredibly acute and sensitive, but he was unable to guess if his assessment was based on vision or hearing. 'It isn't a commando unit. It's what's left of one. Five or six riders, three riderless horses. Stay here, Dandelion. I'm going over there.'

'Gar'ean,' said the green-haired dryad in warning, raising her bow. 'Nfe va, Gwynbleidd! Ki'rin!'

'Thaess aep, Fauve,' replied the Witcher unexpectedly brusquely. 'M'aespar que va'en, ell'ea? Go ahead and shoot. If not, lock me up and don't try to frighten me, because there's nothing you can frighten me with. I must talk to Milva Barring, and I will do so whether you like it or not. Stay there, Dandelion.'

The dryad lowered her head. Her bow too.

Nine horses emerged from the fog, and Dandelion saw that indeed only six of them were bearing riders. He saw the shapes of dryads emerging from the undergrowth and heading to meet them. He noticed that three riders had to be helped to dismount and had to be supported in order to walk towards the trees of Brokilon and safety. The other dryads stole like wraiths across the hillside, which was covered with wind-fallen trees, and vanished into the fog hanging above the Ribbon. A shout, the neighing of horses and the splash of water came from the opposite bank. It also seemed to the poet that he could hear the whistle of arrows. But he was not certain.

'They were being pursued ...' he muttered. Fauve turned around, gripping her bow.

'You sing a song, taedh,' she snapped. 'N'te shaent a'minne, not about Ettariel. No, my darling. The time is not right. Now is time to kill, yes. Such a song, yes!'

'I,' he stammered, 'am not to blame for what is happening ...'

The dryad was silent for a moment and looked to one side.

239

'Also not I,' she said and quickly disappeared into the undergrowth.

The Witcher was back before an hour had passed. He was leading two saddled horses: Pegasus and a bay mare. The mare's saddlecloth bore traces of blood.

'She's one of the elves' horses, isn't she? One of those who crossed the river?'

'Yes,' replied Geralt. His face and voice were changed and unfamiliar. 'The mare belongs to the elves. But she will be serving me for the moment. And when I have the chance, I'll exchange her for a horse that knows how to carry a wounded rider and, when its rider falls, remains by him. It's clear this mare wasn't taught to do that.'

'Are we leaving?'

'You're leaving,' said the Witcher, throwing the poet Pegasus's reins. 'Farewell, Dandelion. The dryads will escort you a couple of miles upstream so you won't fall into the hands of the soldiers from Brugge, who are probably still hanging around on the far bank.'

'What about you? Are you staying here?'

'No. I'm not.'

'You've learned something. From the Squirrels. You know something about Ciri, don't you?'

'Farewell, Dandelion.'

'Geralt ... Listen to me—'

'Listen to what?' shouted the Witcher, before his voice suddenly faltered. 'I can't leave— I can't just leave her to her fate. She's completely alone ... She cannot be left alone, Dandelion. You'll never understand that. No one will ever understand that, but I know. If she remains alone, the same thing will happen to her as once happened to me ... You'll never understand that ...'

'I do understand. Which is why I'm coming with you.'

'You're insane. Do you know where I'm headed?'

'Yes, I do. Geralt, I— I haven't told you everything. I'm ... I feel guilty. I didn't do anything; I didn't know what to do. But now I know. I want to go with you. I want to be by your side. I never told you ... about Ciri and the rumours that are circulating. I met some acquaintances from Kovir, and they in turn had heard the reports of some envoys who had returned from Nilfgaard ... I imagine those rumours may even have reached the Squirrels' ears. That you've already heard everything from those elves who crossed the Ribbon. But let ... let me tell you ...'

The Witcher stood thinking for a long time, his arms hanging limply at his sides.

'Get on your horse,' he finally said, his voice sounding different. 'You can tell me on the way.'

That morning there was an unusual commotion in Loc Grim Palace, the imperator's summer residence. All the more unusual since commotions, emotions or excitement were not at all customary for the Nilfgaardian nobility and demonstrating anxiety or excitement was regarded as a sign of immaturity. Behaviour of that kind was treated by the Nilfgaardian noblemen as highly reprehensible and contemptible, to such an extent that even callow youths, from whom few would have demanded greater maturity, were expected to refrain from any displays of animation.

That morning, though, there were no young men in Loc Grim. Young men wouldn't have had any reason to be in Loc Grim. Stern, austere aristocrats, knights and courtiers were filling the palace's enormous throne room, every one of them dressed in ceremonial courtly black, enlivened only by white ruffs and cuffs. The men were accompanied by a small number of equally stern, austere ladies, whom custom permitted to brighten the black of their costume with a little modest jewellery. They all pretended to be dignified, stern and austere. But they were all extremely excited.

'They say she's ugly. Skinny and ugly.'

'But she allegedly has royal blood.'

'Illegitimate?'

'Not a bit of it. Legitimate.'

'Will she ascend to the throne?'

'Should the imperator so decide ...'

'By thunder, just look at Ardal aep Dahy and Count de Wett ... Look at their faces; as though they'd drunk vinegar ...'

'Be quiet, Your Excellency ... Do their expressions surprise you?

241

If the rumours are true, Emhyr will be giving the ancient houses a slap in the face. He will humiliate them—'

'The rumours won't be true. The imperator won't wed that foundling! He couldn't possibly ...'

'Emhyr will do whatever he wants. Heed your words, Your Excellency. Be careful of what you say. There have been people who said Emhyr couldn't do this or that. And they all ended up on the scaffold.'

'They say he has already signed a decree concerning an endowment for her. Three hundred marks annually, can you imagine?'

'And the title of princess. Have any of you seen her yet?'

'She was placed under the care of Countess Liddertal on her arrival and her house was cordoned off by the guard.'

'They have entrusted her to the countess, in order that she may instil some idea of manners in the little chit. They say your princess behaves like a farm girl ...'

'What's so strange about that? She comes from the north, from barbaric Cintra—'

'Which makes the rumours about a marriage to Emhyr all the more unlikely. No, no, it's utterly beyond the pale. The imperator is to marry de Wett's youngest daughter, as planned. He will not marry that usurper!'

'It is high time he finally married somebody. For the sake of the dynasty ... It is high time we had a little archduke ...'

'Then let him be wed, but not to that stray!'

'Quiet, don't gush. I give you my word, noble lords, that that marriage will not happen. What purpose could such a match serve?'

'It's politics, Countess. We are waging a war. That bond would have political and strategic significance ... The dynasty of which the princess is a member has legal titles and confirmed feudatory rights to the lands on the Lower Yarra. Were she to become the imperator's spouse ... Ha, it would be an excellent move. Just look over there, at King Esterad's envoys; how they whisper ...'

'So you support this outlandish relationship, Duke? Or you've simply been counselling Emhyr, is that it?'

'It's my business, Margrave, what I do or don't support. And I would advise you not to question the imperator's decisions.'

'Has he already made his decision then?'

'I doubt it.'

'You are in error then, to doubt it.'

'What do you mean by that, madam?'

'Emhyr has sent Baroness Tarnhann away from the court. He has ordered her to return to her husband.'

'He's broken off with Dervla Tryffin Broinne? It cannot be! Dervla has been his favourite for three years . . .'

'Now she has been expelled from the court.'

'It's true. They say the golden-haired Dervla kicked up an awful fuss. Four royal guardsmen had to manhandle her into the carriage . . .'

'Her husband will be overjoyed . . .'

'I doubt that.'

'By the Great Sun! Emhyr has broken off with Dervla? He's broken off with her for that foundling? For that savage from the North?'

'Quiet . . . Quiet, for heaven's sake!'

'Who supports this? Which faction supports this?'

'Be quiet, I said. They're looking at us—'

'That wench – I mean princess – is said to be ugly . . . When the imperator sees her . . .'

'Are you trying to say he hasn't seen her yet?'

'He hasn't had time. He only returned from Darn Ruach an hour ago.'

'Emhyr never had a liking for ugly women. Aine Dermott, Clara aep Gwydolyn Gor . . . And Dervla Tryffin Broinne was a true beauty.'

'Perhaps the foundling will grow pretty with time . . .'

'After she's been given a good scrubbing? They say princesses from the north seldom wash—'

'Heed your words. You may be speaking about the imperator's spouse!'

'She is still a child. She is no more than fourteen.'

'I say again, it would be a political union . . . Purely formal . . .'

'Were that the case, the golden-haired Dervla would remain at court. The foundling from Cintra would politically and formally ascend the throne beside Emhyr ... But in the evening Emhyr would give her a tiara and the crown jewels to play with and would visit Dervla's bedchamber ... At least until the chit attained an age when she could safely bear him a child.'

'Hmm ... Yes, you may have something there. What is the name of the ... princess?'

'Xerella, or something of the kind.'

'Not a bit of it. She is called ... Zirilla. Yes, I think it's Zirilla.'

'A barbarous name.'

'Be quiet, damn it ...'

'And show a little dignity. You're squabbling like unruly children!'

'Heed your words! Be careful that I do not treat them as an affront!'

'If you're demanding satisfaction, you know where to find me, Margrave!'

'Silence! Be quiet! The imperator ...'

The herald did not have to make a special effort. One blow of his staff on the floor was sufficient for the black-bereted heads of the aristocrats and knights to bow down like ears of corn blown in the wind. The silence in the throne room was so complete that the herald did not have to raise his voice especially, either.

'Emhyr var Emreis, Deithwen Addan yn Carn aep Monrudd!'

The White Flame Dancing on the Barrows of his Foes. He marched down the double file of noblemen with his usual brisk step, vigorously waving his right hand. His black costume was identical to that of the courtiers, aside from the lack of a ruff. The imperator's dark hair – largely unkempt as usual – was kept reasonably neat by a narrow gold band, and the imperial chain of office glistened on his neck.

The Emhyr sat down on the throne quite carelessly, placing an elbow on the armrest and his chin in his hand. He did not throw a leg over the other armrest, signifying that etiquette still applied. None of the bowed heads rose by even an inch.

The imperator cleared his throat loudly without changing his position. The courtiers breathed again and straightened up. The herald struck his staff on the floor once again.

'Cirilla Fiona Elen Riannon, the Queen of Cintra, the Princess of Brugge and Duchess of Sodden, heiress of Inis Ard Skellig and Inis An Skellig, and suzerain of Attre and Abb Yarra!'

All eyes turned towards the doors, where the tall and dignified Stella Congreve, Countess of Liddertal, was standing. Alongside the countess walked the holder of all those impressive titles. Skinny, fair-haired, extremely pale, somewhat stooped, in a long, blue dress. A dress in which she very clearly felt awkward and uncomfortable.

Emhyr Deithwen sat up on his throne, and the courtiers immediately bowed low again. Stella Congreve nudged the fair-haired girl very gently, and the two of them filed between the double row of bowing aristocrats, all members of the leading houses of Nilfgaard. The girl walked stiffly and hesitantly. *She'll stumble*, thought the countess.

Cirilla Fiona Elen Riannon stumbled.

Ugly, scrawny little thing, thought the countess, as she neared the throne. *Clumsy and, what's more, rather bovine. But I shall make her a beauty. I shall make her a queen, Emhyr, just as you ordered.*

The White Flame of Nilfgaard watched them from his position on the throne. As usual, his eyes were somewhat narrowed and the hint of a sneer played on his lips.

The Queen of Cintra stumbled a second time. The imperator placed an elbow on the armrest of the throne and touched his cheek with his hand. He was smiling. Stella Congreve was close enough to recognise that smile. She froze in horror. *Something is not right,* she thought, *something is not right. Heads will fall. By the Great Sun, heads will fall . . .*

She regained her presence of mind and curtseyed, making the girl follow suit.

Emhyr var Emreis did not rise from the throne. But he bowed his head slightly. The courtiers held their breath.

'Your Majesty,' said Emhyr. The girl cowered. The imperator was not looking at her. He was looking at the noblemen gathered in the hall.

'Your Majesty,' he repeated. 'I'm glad to be able to welcome you to my palace and my country. I give you my imperial word that the day is close when all the titles belonging to you will return to you, along with the lands which are your legal inheritance, which legally and incontrovertibly belong to you. The usurpers, who lord it over your estates, have declared war on me. They attacked me, stating that they were defending your just rights. May the entire world know that you are turning to me – not to them – for help. May the entire world know that here, in my land, you enjoy the reverence and royal name deserving of a queen, while among my enemies you were merely an outcast. May the entire world know that in my country you are safe, while my enemies not only denied you your crown, but even made attempts on your life.'

The Emperor of Nilfgaard fixed his gaze on the envoys of Esterad Thyssen, the King of Kovir, and on the ambassador of Niedamir, the King of the Hengfors League.

'May the entire world know the truth, and among them also the kings who pretended not to know where rightness and justice lay. And may the entire world know that help will be given to you. Your enemies and mine will be defeated. Peace will reign once again in Cintra, in Sodden and Brugge, in Attre, on the Isles of Skellige and at the mouth of the Yarra Delta, and you will ascend the throne to the joy of your countrymen and every one to whom justice is dear.'

The girl in the blue dress lowered her head even further.

'Before that happens,' said Emhyr, 'you will be treated with the respect due to you, by me and by all of my subjects. And since the flame of war still blazes in your kingdom, as evidence of the honour, respect and friendship of Nilfgaard, I endow you with the title of Duchess of Rowan and Ymlac, lady of the castle of Darn Rowan, where you will now travel, in order to await the arrival of more peaceful, happier times.'

Stella Congreve struggled to control herself, not allowing even a trace of astonishment to appear on her face. *He's not going to keep her with him,* she thought, *but is sending her to Darn Rowan, to the end of the world; somewhere he never goes. He has no intention of courting this girl. He isn't considering a quick marriage. He doesn't even want to see*

246

her. Why, then, has he got rid of Dervla? What is this all about?

She recovered and quickly took the princess by the hand. The audience was over. The emperor didn't look at them as they were leaving the hall. The courtiers bowed.

Once they had left Emhyr var Emreis slung a leg over the armrest of his throne.

'Ceallach,' he said. 'To me.'

The seneschal stopped in front of the emperor at the distance decreed by etiquette and bowed.

'Closer,' said Emhyr. 'Come closer, Ceallach. I shall speak quietly. And what I say is meant for your ears only.'

'Your Highness.'

'What else is planned for today?'

'Receiving accrediting letters and granting a formal exequatur to the envoy of King Esterad of Kovir,' recited the seneschal rapidly. 'Appointing viceroys, prefects and palatines in the new provinces and palatinates. Ratifying the title of Count and appanage of—'

'We shall grant the envoy his exequatur and receive him in a private audience. Postpone the other matters until tomorrow.'

'Yes, Your Royal Highness.'

'Inform the Viscount of Eiddon and Skellen that immediately after the audience with the ambassador they are to report to the library. In secret. You are also to be there. And bring that celebrated mage of yours, that soothsayer ... What was his name?'

'Xarthisius, Your Highness. He lives in a tower outside the city—'

'Where he lives is of no interest to me. Send for him. He is to be brought to my apartments. Quietly, with a minimum of fuss, clandestinely.'

'Your Highness ... Is it wise, for that astrologer—'

'That is an order, Ceallach.'

'Yes, sir.'

Before three hours had passed, all of those summoned were present in the imperial library. The summons didn't surprise Vattier de Rideaux, the Viscount of Eiddon. Vattier was the chief of military intelligence. Vattier was often summoned by Emhyr; they were at war, after all. Neither did the summons surprise Stefan Skellen

– also known as Tawny Owl – who served the imperator as coroner and as the authority on special services and operations. Nothing ever surprised Tawny Owl.

The third person summoned, however, was astonished to be asked to attend. Particularly since the emperor addressed him first.

'Master Xarthisius.'

'Your Imperial Highness.'

'I must establish the whereabouts of a certain individual. An individual who has either gone missing or is being hidden. Or is perhaps imprisoned. The sorcerers I previously gave this task to failed me. Will you undertake it?'

'At what distance is this individual – may this individual be – residing?'

'If I knew that, I wouldn't need your witchcraft.'

'I beg your forgiveness, Your Imperial Highness ...' stammered the astrologer. 'The point is that great distances hinder astromancy, they practically preclude it ... Hum, hum ... And should this individual be under magical protection ... I can try, but—'

'Keep it brief, master.'

'I need time ... And ingredients for the spells ... If the alignment of stars is auspicious, then ... Hum, hum ... Your Imperial Highness, what you request is an exacting task ... I need time—'

Much more of this and Emhyr will order him to be stuck on a spike, thought Tawny Owl. *If the wizard doesn't stop jabbering ...*

'Master Xarthisius,' interrupted the imperator surprisingly politely, even gently. 'You will have everything you need at your disposal. Including time. Within reason.'

'I shall do everything in my power,' declared the astrologer. 'But I shall only be able to determine the approximate location ... I mean the region or radius—'

'I beg your pardon?'

'Astromancy ...' stammered Xarthisius. 'At great distances astromancy only permits approximate localisations ... Very approximate, with considerable tolerance ... With very considerable tolerance. I truly know not whether I will be able—'

'You will be able, master,' drawled the imperator and his dark

248

eyes flashed balefully. 'I am utterly confident in your abilities. And as far as tolerance is concerned, the less is yours, the greater will be mine.'

Xarthisius cowered.

'I must know the precise birth date of this individual,' he mumbled. 'To the hour; if possible ... An object which belonged to the individual would also be invaluable ...'

'Hair,' said Emhyr quietly. 'Would hair suffice?'

'Oooh!' said the astrologer, brightening up. 'Hair! That would expedite things considerably ... Ah, and if I could also have faeces or urine ...'

Emhyr's eyes narrowed menacingly and the wizard cowered and made a low bow.

'I humbly apologise, Your Imperial Highness ...' he grunted. 'Please forgive me ... Of course ... Indeed, hair will suffice ... Will absolutely suffice ... When might I be given it?'

'It will be supplied to you today, along with the date and hour of birth. I won't keep you any longer, master. Return to your tower and start examining the constellations.'

'May the Great Sun keep you ever in its care, Your Imperial—'

'Yes, yes. You may withdraw.'

Now for us, thought Tawny Owl. *I wonder what's in store for us.*

'Should anyone,' said the imperator slowly, 'breathe a word of what is about to be said, they will be quartered. Vattier!'

'Yes, Your Highness.'

'How did that ... *princess* ... end up here? Who was involved?'

'She came from the stronghold in Nastrog,' said the chief of intelligence. 'She was escorted here by guardsmen commanded by ...'

'That's not what I bloody mean! How did that girl end up in Nastrog, in Verden? Who had her brought to the stronghold? Who is currently the commandant there? Is it the man who sent the report? Godyvron something?'

'Godyvron Pitcairn,' said Vattier de Rideaux quickly, 'was of course informed about Rience and Count Cahir aep Ceallach's mission. Three days after the events on the Isle of Thanedd, two people showed up in Nastrog. To be precise: one human and the other a half-blood elf. It was they who, citing the names Rience and Count Cahir, handed the princess over to Godyvron.'

'Aha,' said the imperator, smiling, and Tawny Owl felt a shiver running down his back. 'Vilgefortz vouched he would capture Cirilla on Thanedd. Rience assured me of the same. Cahir Mawr Dyffryn aep Ceallach received clear orders in this matter. And so, three days after the scandal on the island, Cirilla is brought to Nastrog on the River Yarra; not by Vilgefortz, nor Rience, nor Cahir, but by a human and a half-elf. Did it not occur to Godyvron to arrest them?'

'No. Shall he be punished for it, Your Highness?'

'No.'

Tawny Owl swallowed. Emhyr was silent, rubbing his forehead, and the huge diamond in his ring shone like a star. A moment later, the imperator looked up.

'Vattier.'

'Your Highness?'

'Mobilise all your subordinates. Order them to arrest Rience and Count Cahir. I presume the two of them are residing in territories as yet unoccupied by our forces. You will use Scoia'tael or Queen Enid's elves to achieve that end. Take the two captives to Darn Ruach and subject them to torture.'

'What information is required, Your Highness?' said Vattier de Rideaux, narrowing his eyes and pretending not notice the paleness on the face of Seneschal Ceallach.

'None. Later, when they're softened up a little, I shall ask them personally. Skellen!'

'Yes, sire.'

'That old fool Xarthisius; if that jabbering copromancer manages to determine what I've ordered him to, then you will organise a search for a certain individual in the area he indicates. You will receive a description. It's possible that the astrologer will indicate a region under our control, and then you will mobilise everyone responsible for that region. The entire civilian and military apparatus. It is a matter of the highest priority. Is that understood?'

'Yes, sire. May I ... ?'

'No, you may not. Sit down and listen, Tawny Owl. Xarthisius will probably not come up with anything. The individual I have ordered him to search for is probably in foreign territory and under magical protection. I'd give my head that the individual I'm looking for is in the same place as our good friend, the sorcerer Vilgefortz of Roggeveen, who has mysteriously vanished. That is also why, Skellen, you will assemble and prepare a special unit, which you will personally command. Use the best men you have. They are to be ready for everything ... and not superstitious. I mean not afraid of magic.'

Tawny Owl raised his eyebrows.

'Your unit,' concluded Emhyr, 'will be charged with attacking and capturing the hideout of Vilgefortz, former good friend and ally that he was, the whereabouts of which is currently unknown to me, and which is probably quite well camouflaged and defended.'

'Yes, sire,' said Tawny Owl emotionlessly. 'I presume that the individual being sought, whom they will probably find there, is not to be harmed.'

'You presume correctly.'

'What about Vilgefortz?'

'He can be ...' The emperor smiled cruelly. 'In his case he *ought* to be harmed, once and for all. Terminally harmed. This also applies to any other sorcerers you happen to find in his hideout. Without exception.'

'Yes, sire. Who is responsible for finding Vilgefortz's hideout?'

'You are, Tawny Owl.'

Stefan Skellen and Vattier de Rideaux exchanged glances. Emhyr leaned back in his chair.

'Is everything clear? If so ... What is it, Ceallach?'

'Your Highness ...' whined the seneschal, to whom no one had paid any attention up until that moment. 'I beg you for mercy ...'

'There is no mercy for traitors. There is no mercy for those who oppose my will.'

'Cahir ... My son ...'

'Your son ...' said Emhyr, narrowing his eyes. 'I don't yet know what your son is guilty of. I would like to hope that he is only guilty

251

of stupidity and ineptitude and not of treachery. If that is the case he will only be beheaded and not broken on the wheel.'

'Your Highness! Cahir is not a traitor ... Cahir could not have—'

'Enough, Ceallach, not another word. The guilty will be punished. They attempted to deceive me and I will not forgive them for that. Vattier, Skellen, in one hour, report for your signed instructions, orders and authorisations. You will then set about executing your tasks at once. And one more thing: I trust I do not have to add that the poor girl you saw in the throne room a short while ago is to remain to everyone Cirilla, Queen of Cintra and Duchess of Rowan. To everyone. I order you to treat it as a state secret and a matter of the gravest national importance.'

All those present looked at the imperator in astonishment. Deithwen Addan yn Carn aep Morvudd smiled faintly.

'Have you not understood? Instead of the real Cirilla of Cintra I've been sent some kind of dolt. Those traitors probably told themselves that I would not recognise her. But I will know the real Ciri. I would know her at the end of the world and in the darkness of hell.'

The behaviour of the unicorn is greatly mystifying. *Although exceptionally timid and fearful of people, if it should chance upon a
maiden who has not had carnal relations with a man it will at once
run to her, kneel before her and, without any fear whatsoever, lay
its head in her lap. It is said that in the dim and distant past there
were maidens who made a veritable practice of this. They remained
unmarried and in abstinence for many years in order to be employed
by hunters as a lure for unicorns. It soon transpired, however, that
the unicorn only approached youthful maidens, paying absolutely
no attention to older ones. Being a wise creature, the unicorn indub-
itably knows that remaining too long in the state of maidenhood is
suspicious and counter to the natural order.*

Physiologus

CHAPTER SIX

The heat woke her. It burnt her skin like a torturer's glowing irons. She could barely move her head, for something held it fast. She pulled away and howled in pain, feeling the skin over her temple tear and split. She opened her eyes. The boulder on which she had been resting her head was dark brown from dry, congealed blood. She touched her temple and felt the remains of a hard, cracked scab under her fingers. The scab, which had been stuck to the boulder and then torn from it when she moved her head, now dripped blood and plasma. Ciri cleared her throat, hawked and spat out sand mixed with thick, sticky saliva. She raised herself on her elbows and then sat up, looking around.

She was completely surrounded by a greyish-red, stony plain, scored by ravines and faults, with mounds of stones and huge, strangely shaped rocks. High above the plain hung an enormous, golden, burning sun, turning the entire sky yellow, distorting visibility with its blinding glare and making the air shimmer.

Where am I?

She gingerly touched her gashed, swollen forehead. It hurt. It hurt intensely. *I must have taken quite a tumble,* she thought. *I must have slid a fair way along the ground.* Her attention turned to her torn clothing and she discovered other sources of pain: in her back, in her shoulder and in her hips. When she hit the ground she had become covered in dust, sharp sand and grit. It was in her hair, ears, mouth and even her eyes, which were smarting and watering. Her hands and elbows, grazed to the raw flesh, were also stinging.

She slowly and cautiously straightened her legs and groaned once more, for her left knee reacted to movement with an intense, dull ache. She examined it through her undamaged trousers but did not find any swelling. When she breathed in, she felt a worrying stabbing in her side, and her attempts to bend her trunk almost made her scream, shooting her through with a sharp spasm which she felt in her lower back. *I'm good and bruised,* she thought. *But I don't think I've broken anything. If I'd broken a bone, it would hurt much more. I'm in one piece, just a bit knocked about. I'll be able to get up. So I'll get up.*

Crouching forward awkwardly, making deliberate movements, she very slowly manoeuvred herself into a position which would protect her injured knee. Then she went onto all fours, groaning and hissing. Finally, after what seemed an eternity, she stood up. Only to fall heavily onto the rock, as the dizziness which blurred her vision instantly took her legs from under her. Sensing a sudden wave of nausea, she lay down on one side. The searing rock stung like red-hot coals.

'I'll never get up ...' she sobbed. 'I can't ... I'll burn up in this sun ...'

A growing, loathsome, intractable pain throbbed in her head. Each movement made the pain more intense, so Ciri stopped moving for a moment. She covered her head with an arm, but the heat soon became unbearable. She knew she would have to hide from it. Fighting the overpowering resistance of her aching body. Screwing her eyes up against the shooting pain in her temples, she crawled on all fours towards a large boulder, sculpted by the wind to resemble a strange mushroom, whose shapeless cap gave a little shade at its foot. She curled up in a ball, coughing and sniffing.

She lay there for a long time, until the sun assaulted her once again with its scorching heat as it wandered across the sky. She moved around to the other side of the boulder, only to find it made no difference. The sun was at its zenith and the stone mushroom gave practically no shade. She pressed her hands to her temples, which were exploding with pain.

She was woken by a shivering which gripped her entire body. The sun's fiery ball had lost its blinding golden glow. Now, hanging lower in the sky above the serrated, jagged rocks, it was orange. The heat had eased off.

Ciri sat up with difficulty and looked around. Her headache was less intense and was no longer blinding her. She touched her head and discovered that the heat had dried the blood on her temple, turning it into a hard, smooth crust. Her entire body still hurt, though, and it seemed to her there was not a single place free of pain. She hawked, sand grating between her teeth, and tried to spit. Unsuccessfully. She leaned back against the mushroom-shaped boulder, which was still hot from the sun. *At last the heat has broken,* she thought. *Now, with the sun sinking in the west, it's bearable, and soon . . .*

Soon, night will fall.

She shuddered. *Where the hell am I? How do I get out of here? And which way? Which way should I go? Or perhaps I should stay in one place and wait until they find me. They must be looking for me. Geralt. Yennefer. They won't just leave me here . . .*

She tried to spit again, and again she could not. And then she understood.

Thirst.

She remembered. Back then, during her escape, she had been tortured by thirst. There had been a wooden canteen tied to the saddle of the black horse she had been riding when she was escaping towards the Tower of Gulls; she remembered it distinctly. But she had been unable to unfasten it or take it with her; she'd had no time. And now it was gone. Now everything was gone. There was nothing save sharp, scalding stones, save a scab on her temple that pulled her skin tight, save the pain in her body and her parched throat, which she couldn't even give relief to by swallowing.

I can't stay here. I have to go and find water. If I don't find water I'll die.

She tried to stand, cutting her fingers on the stone mushroom. She got up. She took a step. And with a howl she toppled over onto her hands and knees, her back arching as spasms of nausea gripped her. Cramps and dizziness seized her so intensively she had to lie down.

I'm helpless. And alone. Again. Everyone has betrayed me, abandoned me, left me all alone. Just like before . . .

Ciri felt invisible pincers squeezing her throat, felt the muscles in her jaw tensing to the point of pain, felt her cracked lips begin to quiver. *There is no more dreadful sight than a weeping enchantress,* rang Yennefer's words in her head.

But wait ... No one will see me here ... No one at all ...

Curled up in a ball beneath the stone mushroom, Ciri sobbed uncontrollably in a dry, dreadful lament. Without tears.

When she opened her swollen, gummed-up eyelids, she realised the heat had diminished even more, and the sky – which a short time before had still been yellow – had taken on its characteristic cobalt colour and was astonishingly clear, shot with thin, white strips of cloud. The sun's disc had reddened and sunk lower but was still pouring its undulating, pulsating heat down on the desert. Or perhaps the heat was radiating upwards from the hot stones?

She sat up to find that the pain inside her skull and bruised body had stopped tormenting her. That right now it was nothing in comparison to the terrible suffering growing in her stomach and the cruel itch in her dry throat, which forced her to cough.

Don't give up, she thought. *I can't give up. Just like in Kaer Morhen, I have to get up, defeat the enemy, fight, suppress the pain and weakness inside me. I have to get up and walk. At least I know the direction now. The sun is setting in the west. I have to walk, I have to find water and something to eat. I have to. Or I'll die. This is a desert. I landed in a desert. The thing I entered in the Tower of Gulls was a magical portal, a magical device, which can transport people great distances ...*

The portal in Tor Lara was a strange one. When she ran up to the top floor there was nothing, not even any windows, only bare, mould-covered walls. And on one of the walls burnt an irregular oval filled with an iridescent gleam. She hesitated, but the portal drew her on, summoned her; literally invited her. And there was no other way out; only that shining oval. She'd closed her eyes and stepped inside.

Afterwards, there was a blinding light and a furious vortex, a blast which took her breath away and squeezed her ribs. She remembered the flight through silence, cold and emptiness, then a bright light and she was choking on air. Above her had been blue and down below a vague greyness ...

The vortex spat her out in mid-flight, as a young eagle drops a fish which is too heavy for it. When she smashed against the rock, she lost consciousness. She didn't know for how long.

I read about portals in the temple, she recalled, shaking the sand from her hair. *Some books mentioned teleportation portals, which were either distorted or chaotic. They transported people towards random destinations and threw them out in random places. The portal in the Tower of Gulls must have been one of those. It threw me out somewhere at the end of the world. I have no idea where. No one is going to look for me here and no one will find me. If I stay here I'll die.*

She stood up. Summoning up all her strength and bracing herself against the boulder, she took the first step. Then a second. Then a third.

The first steps made her aware that the buckles of her right shoe had been torn off, and the flapping upper made walking impossible. She sat down, this time intentionally and deliberately, and carried out an inspection of her clothes and equipment. While she concentrated on this task, she forgot about her exhaustion and pain.

The first thing she discovered was the dagger. She had forgotten about it, and the sheath had slid around to her back. Next to the dagger, as usual, was a small pouch on a strap. It had been a present from Yennefer. It contained 'things a lady always ought to have'. Ciri untied it. Unfortunately, a lady's standard equipment had not foreseen the situation she was now in. The pouch contained a tortoiseshell comb, a knife and a combination knife and nail file, a packed, sterilised tampon made from linen fabric and a small jade casket containing hand ointment.

Ciri rubbed the ointment into her cracked face and lips at once, then greedily licked the ointment from her lips. Without much thought, she went on to lick out the entire box, revelling in its greasiness and the tiny amount of soothing moisture. The chamomile, ambergris and camphor used to perfume the ointment made it taste disgusting, but they acted as stimulants.

She strapped the shoe to her ankle with a strip she had ripped from her sleeve, stood up and stamped several times to test it. She unpacked and unfurled the tampon, making a wide headband from it to protect her injured temple and sunburnt forehead.

She stood, adjusted her belt, shifted the dagger nearer to her left hip and instinctively drew it from its sheath, checking the blade with her thumb. It was sharp. She knew it would be.

I'm armed, she thought. *I'm a witcher. No, I won't die here. Hunger? I can endure it. In the Temple of Melitele, it was occasionally necessary to fast for up to two days. But water ... I have to find water. I'll keep walking until I find some. This accursed desert must finish eventually. If it were a very large desert, I would know something about it. I would have noticed it on the maps I used to look at with Jarre. Jarre ... I wonder what he's doing now ...*

I'll set off, she decided. *I'll walk towards the west. I can see where the sun sets. It's the only certain direction. After all, I never lose my way. I always know which way to go. I'll walk all night if I have to. I'm a witcher. When I get my strength back, I'll run like I used to on the Trail at Kaer Morhen. That way I'll get to the edge of the desert quicker. I'll hold out. I have to hold out ... Ha, I bet Geralt's often been in deserts like this one, if not in even worse ones ...*

Off I go.

After the first hour of walking, nothing in the landscape had changed. There was still nothing at all around her apart from stones; greyish-red, sharp, shifting underfoot, forcing her to be cautious. There were scrawny bushes, dry and thorny, reaching out to her from clefts in the rocks with their contorted branches. Ciri stopped at the first bush she encountered, expecting to find leaves or young shoots which she would be able to suck and chew. But the bush only had sharp thorns which cut her fingers. It didn't even have any branches suitable to break off and use as a stick. The second and third bushes were no different and she ignored all the rest, passing by them without stopping.

Dusk fell quickly. The sun sank over the jagged horizon, and the sky lit up red and purple. As darkness fell, it became cold. At first, she greeted it with gladness, for the coolness soothed her sunburnt skin. Soon after, however, it became even colder and Ciri's teeth began to chatter. She walked quicker, hoping that a vigorous pace would warm her up, but the effort revived the pain in her side and knee. She began to limp. On top of that, the sun had completely sunk below the horizon and it was rapidly becoming dark. The moon was new, and the stars twinkling in the sky were no help. Ciri was soon unable to see the ground in front of her. She fell down several times, painfully grazing the skin on her wrists. Twice she caught her feet in clefts in the rocks, and only her well-drilled reactions as she was falling saved her from twisting or breaking an ankle. She realised it was no good. Walking in the dark was impossible.

She sat down on a flat basalt slab, feeling overwhelming despair She had no idea if she was heading in the right direction and had long since lost sight of the point where the sun had disappeared over the horizon. There was now no sign whatsoever of the glow which had guided her during the first hours after nightfall. Around her was nothing but velvety, impenetrable blackness. And bitter cold. Cold which paralysed, which bit at the joints, forcing her to stoop and tuck her head down into her painfully hunched shoulders. Ciri began to miss the sun, even though she knew its return would mean another onslaught of unbearable heat descending upon the rocks. Heat which would prevent her from continuing her journey. Once again, she felt the urge to cry rising in her throat and a wave of desperation and hopelessness overcoming her. But this time the desperation and hopelessness transformed into fury.

'I will not cry!' she screamed in the darkness. 'I am a witcher! I am ...'

An enchantress.

Ciri lifted her hands and pressed her palms against her temples. *The Power is everywhere. It's in the water, in the air, in the earth ...*

She quickly stood up, held her hands in front of her, and then slowly and hesitantly took a few steps, feverishly searching for an underground spring. She was fortunate. Almost immediately, she felt a familiar rushing sound, a throbbing in her ears and the energy emanating from a water vein hidden deep within the earth. She imbibed the Power with cautious inhalations, which she gradually released, knowing she was weak and that, in her state, a sudden shortage of oxygen to the brain might render her unconscious and thwart all her efforts. The energy slowly filled her up, giving her a familiar, momentary euphoria. Her lungs began to work more strongly and more quickly. Ciri brought her accelerated breathing under control; too much oxygen to the brain too rapidly could also have fatal consequences.

She'd done it.

First the aching, she thought. *First the paralysing pain in my shoulders and thighs. Then the cold. I have to raise my body temperature ...*

She gradually recalled the gestures and spells. She performed and uttered some of them too hurriedly and was instantly seized by cramps and convulsions. A sudden spasm and dizziness made her weak at the knees. She sat down on a basalt slab, stilled her shaking hands and brought her fractured, irregular breathing back under control.

She repeated the formulas, forcing herself to be calm and exact, to concentrate and totally focus her will. And this time the result was immediate. She rubbed the warmth sweeping through her into her thighs and neck. She stood up, feeling the exhaustion vanish and her aching muscles relax.

'I'm an enchantress!' she cried in triumph, holding her arms up high. 'Come, immortal light! I summon you! Aen'drean va, eveigh Aine!'

A small, warm sphere of light floated from her hands like a butterfly, casting shifting mosaics of shadow on the stones. Moving her hand slowly, she stabilised the sphere, guiding it so that it was hanging in front of her. It was not the best idea; the light blinded her. She tried to move the sphere behind her back but again with a disappointing result. It cast her own shadow in front of her, making visibility worse. Ciri slowly moved the shining sphere to the side and suspended it just above her right shoulder. Although the sphere was nowhere as good as the real, magical Aine, the girl was extremely proud of her achievement.

'Ha!' she said proudly. 'It's a pity Yennefer can't see this!'

She began to march jauntily and vigorously, striding quickly and confidently, choosing where to step in the flickering and indistinct chiaroscuro cast by the sphere. As she walked, she tried to recall other spells, but none of them seemed suitable or useful in this situation. Furthermore, some of them were very draining, and she was a little afraid of them, not wanting to use them without an obvious need. Unfortunately, she did not know any which would have been able to create water or food. She knew spells like that existed, but didn't know how to cast any of them.

The hitherto lifeless desert came to life in the light of her magical sphere. Ungainly, glossy beetles and hairy spiders scuttled away to avoid being stepped on. A small reddish-yellow scorpion, pulling its segmented tail behind it, scurried swiftly across her path, disappearing into a crack in the rocks. A long-tailed, green lizard, rustling over the stones, vanished into the gloom. Rodents resembling large mice ran nimbly away from her, leaping high on their hind legs. Several times she saw eyes reflected in the dark, and once she heard a blood-curdling hiss issuing from a pile of rocks. If she'd had thoughts of catching something edible, the hissing completely discouraged her from groping around among the rocks. She began to watch her step more cautiously, and in her mind's eye she saw the illustrations she had studied in Kaer Morhen. Giant scorpions. Scarletias. Frighteners. Wights. Lamias. Crab spiders. Desert-dwelling monsters. She walked on, looking around more timidly and listening out intently, gripping the hilt of her dagger in her sweaty palm.

After several hours, the shining sphere grew faint and the circle of light it was casting shrank and became vague. Ciri, beginning to find it hard to concentrate, uttered the spell again. For a few seconds, the ball pulsated more brightly but soon after darkened and faded once more. The effort made her dizzy. Then she staggered and black and red spots danced in front of her eyes. She sat down hard, crunching the grit and loose stones beneath her.

The sphere finally went out completely. Ciri did not try any more spells; the exhaustion, emptiness and lack of energy she felt inside precluded any chance of success.

A vague glow arose on the horizon, far ahead of her. *I've gone the wrong way*, she realised in horror. *I've muddled everything ... I was heading towards the west at first, and now the sun's going to rise directly in front of me, which means ...*

She felt overwhelming fatigue and sleepiness, which not even the bitter cold could frighten away. *I won't fall asleep*, she decided. *I can't fall asleep ... I just cannot ...*

263

She was woken by fierce cold and growing brightness, and brought back to her senses by the gut-wrenching pain in her belly and the dry, nagging, burning sensation in her throat. She tried to stand up. She couldn't. Her stiff, painful limbs failed her. Groping around her with her hands, she felt moisture under her fingers.

'Water ...' she croaked. 'Water!'

Shaking all over, she got up onto her hands and knees and then lowered her mouth to the basalt slabs, frantically using her tongue to collect the drops which had gathered on the smooth rock and sucking up the moisture from hollows in the boulder's uneven surface. There was almost half a handful of dew in one of them, which she lapped up with sand and grit, not daring to spit. She looked around.

Carefully, so as not to waste even the tiniest quantity, she used her tongue to gather the glistening drops hanging on the thorns of a stunted shrub, which had mysteriously managed to grow between the rocks. Her dagger was lying on the ground. She could not remember drawing it. The blade was lustreless from a thin layer of dew. She scrupulously and precisely licked the cold metal.

Overcoming the pain which made her whole body stiffen, she crawled on, searching out the moisture on other rocks. But the golden disc of the sun had already burst above the rocky horizon, flooding the desert with blinding, yellow light and instantly drying them. Ciri joyfully greeted the burgeoning warmth, although she was aware that soon she would be mercilessly scorched and longing for the cool of the night again.

She turned away from the glaring orb. The sun was shining in the east. But she had to head towards the west. She had to.

The rapidly intensifying heat soon became unbearable. By noon, it had exhausted her so much that, whether she liked it or not, she had to change her route in order to look for shade. She finally found some protection: a large boulder, shaped like a mushroom. She crawled under it.

And then she saw something lying among the rocks. It was the jade casket which had contained hand ointment but was now licked clean.

She couldn't find the strength inside to cry.

*

Hunger and thirst overcame her exhaustion and resignation. Staggering, she set off once more. The sun still beat down.

Far away on the horizon, beyond the shimmering veil of heat, she saw something which might have been a mountain range. An extremely distant mountain range.

After night fell, she expended immense effort on generating the Power, but only managed to conjure up the magical sphere after several attempts, and those tired her out to such a degree she was unable to go on. She had consumed all her energy and failed to cast the warming and relaxing spells in spite of repeated attempts. Conjuring up the light gave her courage and raised her spirit, but the cold weakened her. The piercing, bitter cold kept her shivering until dawn, as she waited impatiently for the sunrise. She removed her dagger from its sheath and placed it carefully on a rock so that the dew would condense on the metal. She was absolutely exhausted, but the hunger and thirst drove sleep away. She held out until dawn. It was still dark when she began greedily to lick the dew from the blade. When it grew light, she immediately got on all fours in order to search for more moisture in hollows and crevices.

She heard a hiss.

A large colourful lizard sitting on a nearby rocky ledge opened its toothless jaws at her, ruffled its impressive crest, puffed itself up and lashed the rock with its tail. In front of the lizard she saw a tiny, water-filled crevice.

At first Ciri retreated in horror, but she was quickly seized by desperation and savage fury. Groping around with her trembling hands, she grabbed an angular piece of rock.

'It's my water!' she howled. 'It's mine!'

She hurled the rock. And missed. The lizard jumped on its long-clawed feet and disappeared nimbly into a rocky labyrinth. Ciri flattened herself against the abandoned rock and sucked the rest of the water from the cleft. And then she saw it.

Beyond the rock, in a circular depression, lay seven eggs, all partly protruding from the reddish sand. The girl wasted no time. She fell onto the nest on her knees, seized one of the eggs and sank her teeth

265

into it. The leathery shell burst and collapsed in her hand, the sticky gunk running into her sleeve. Ciri sucked the egg empty and licked her arm. She had difficulty swallowing and couldn't taste anything at all.

She ate every egg and remained on her hands and knees, sticky, dirty, covered in sand, with yolk stuck in her teeth, feverishly digging around in the sand and emitting inhuman, sobbing noises. She froze.

Sit up straight, princess! Don't rest your elbows on the table! Be careful how you serve yourself from the dish! You're dirtying the lace on your sleeves! Wipe your mouth with a napkin and stop slurping! By the gods, has no one ever taught that girl any table manners? Cirilla!

Ciri burst into tears, her head resting on her knees.

She endured the march until noon, when the heat defeated her and forced her to rest. She dozed for a long time, hidden in the shade beneath a rocky shelf. It wasn't cool in the shade, but it was better than the scorching sun. Eventually her thirst and hunger frightened sleep away again.

The distant range of mountains seemed to be on fire and sparkling in the sun's rays. *There might be snow lying on those mountain peaks,* she thought. *There might be ice. There might be streams. I have to get there. I have to get there fast.*

She walked for almost the entire night. She decided to navigate using the night sky. The whole sky was bedecked in stars and Ciri regretted not paying attention during lessons; not wanting to study the atlases of the constellations in the temple library. Naturally enough, she knew the most important of them: the Seven Goats, the Jug, the Sickle, the Dragon and the Winter Maiden, but those were hanging high in the sky, and would have been difficult to navigate by. She finally managed to select one bright star from the twinkling throng, which she thought was indicating the right direction. She didn't know what it was called, so she christened it herself. She named it the Eye.

*

She walked. The mountain range she was heading towards did not get the slightest bit closer; it was still as far away as it had been the previous day. But it pointed the way.

As she walked, she looked around intently. She found another lizard's nest, containing four eggs. She spotted a green plant, no longer than her little finger, which had miraculously managed to grow between the rocks. She tracked down a large brown beetle. And a thin-legged spider.

She ate everything.

At noon, she vomited up everything she had eaten and then fainted. When she came to, she found a patch of shade and lay, curled up in a ball, her hands clutching her painful belly.

She began to march again at sunset. She moved painfully stiffly. She fell down again and again but got up each time and continued walking.

She kept walking. She had to keep walking.

Evening. Rest. Night. The Eye showed her the way. Marching until she reached the point of utter exhaustion, which came well before sunrise. Rest. Fitful sleep. Hunger. Cold. The absence of magical energy; a disaster when she tried to conjure up light and warmth. Her thirst only intensified by licking the dew from the dagger's blade and the rocks in the early hours.

When the sun rose she fell asleep in the growing warmth. She was woken by the searing heat. She stood up and continued on her way.

She fainted after less than an hour's march. When she came to the sun was at its zenith, and the heat was unbearable. She didn't have the strength to look for shade. She didn't have the strength to get to her feet. But she did.

She walked on. She didn't give in. She walked for almost the entire following day, and part of the night.

Once again, she slept through the worst of the heat, curled up in a ball beneath a sloping boulder which was partly buried in the sand. Her sleep had been fitful and exhausting; she had dreamed of water.

Water which could be drunk. Huge, white waterfalls framed in haze and rainbows. Gurgling streams. Small forest springs shaded by ferns with their roots in the water. Palace fountains smelling of wet marble. Mossy wells and full buckets spilling over ... drops of water falling from melting icicles ... Water. Cold, refreshing water, cold enough to make your teeth sting, but with such a wonderful, incomparable taste ...

She awoke, leapt to her feet and began to walk back the way she had come. She turned around, staggering and falling. She had to go back! She had passed water on the way! She had passed a stream, gushing amongst the rocks! How could she be so foolish!

She came to her senses.

The heat subsided; evening was approaching. The setting sun indicated the way west. The mountains. The sun could not be – could not possibly be – at her back. Ciri chased away the visions and choked back her sobs. She turned around and began to march.

She walked the entire night, but very slowly. She did not get far. She was dropping off to sleep as she walked, dreaming of water. The rising sun found her sitting on a rock, staring at the dagger's blade and her naked forearm.

Blood is a liquid, after all. It can be drunk.

She drove away the hallucinations and nightmares. She licked the dew-covered dagger and began to walk.

She fainted. She came around, seared by the sun and the baking stones.

Before her, beyond a shimmering heat haze, she saw the jagged, serrated mountain range.

Closer. Significantly closer.

But she had no more strength. She sat up.

The dagger in her hand reflected the sunlight and burnt hot. It was sharp. She knew that.

Why do you torture yourself? said the calm, pedantic voice of the enchantress, Tissaia de Vries. *Why do you condemn yourself to suffering? It's time you put an end to it!*

No. I won't give in.

You will not endure this. Do you know how you die from thirst? Any moment now you will lose your mind, and then it will be too late. Then you won't be able to end it all.

No. I won't give in. I will endure it.

She sheathed the dagger. She stood up, staggered and fell down. She stood up again, staggered and began to march.

Above her, high in the yellow sky, she saw a vulture.

When she came to again, she couldn't remember having fallen. She couldn't remember how long she had been lying there. She looked up at the sky. Two more vultures had joined the first one wheeling above her. She didn't have enough strength to get up.

She realised this was the end. She accepted it calmly. Almost with relief.

Something touched her.

It nudged her gently and cautiously on the shoulder. After such a long period of solitude, after so long surrounded by lifeless, motion-less rocks, the touch made her jerk up, in spite of her exhaustion. It made her attempt to jump to her feet. Whatever had touched her snorted and sprang back, stamping its feet noisily.

Ciri sat up with difficulty, rubbing the encrusted corners of her eyes with her knuckles.

I've gone mad, she thought.

Several paces in front of her stood a horse. She blinked. It wasn't an illusion. It really was a horse. A young horse, not much more than a foal.

She was now fully awake. She licked her cracked lips and cleared her throat involuntarily. The horse jumped and ran some distance away, its hooves grating over the loose stones. It moved very strangely, and its coat was also unusual – neither dun nor grey. Perhaps the effect was just an illusion, created by the sunlight shining behind it.

The horse snorted and took a few steps towards her. Now she could see it better. Well enough to notice, in addition to its unchar-acteristic coat colour, the strange peculiarities in its build: the small head, the extremely slender neck, the very thin pasterns and the long, thick tail. The horse stood and looked at her, holding its muzzle in profile. Ciri let out a quiet sigh.

A horn, at least two spans long, protruded from the horse's domed forehead.

An impossible impossibility, thought Ciri, coming to her senses and gathering her thoughts. *There are no unicorns in the world; they've died out. There wasn't even a unicorn in the witcher's tome in Kaer Morhen! I've only read about them in* The Book of Myths *in the temple ... Oh, and there was an illustration of a unicorn in that* Physiologus *I looked through in Mr Giancardi's bank ... But the unicorn in that illustration was more like a goat than a horse. It had shaggy fetlocks and a goat's beard, and its horn must have been two ells long ...*

She was astonished that she could remember everything so well; incidents that seemed to have happened hundreds of years before. Suddenly her head spun and pain twisted her insides. She groaned and curled up in a ball. The unicorn snorted and took a step towards her, then stopped and raised its head high. Ciri suddenly recalled what the books had said about unicorns.

'Please come closer ...' she croaked, trying to sit up. 'You may, because I am ...'

The unicorn snorted, leapt backwards and galloped away, waving its tail vigorously. But after a moment it stopped, tossed its head, pawed the ground with a hoof and whinnied loudly.

'That's not true!' she whined in despair. 'Jarre only kissed me once and that doesn't count! Come back!'

The effort of speaking blurred her vision and she slumped down onto the rock. When she finally managed to raise her head, the unicorn was once more close by. Looking at her inquisitively, it lowered its head and snorted softly.

'Don't be afraid of me ...' she whispered. 'You don't have to ... You can see I'm dying ...'

The unicorn neighed, shaking its head. Ciri fainted.

When she awoke again she was alone. Aching, stiff, thirsty, hungry, and all alone. The unicorn had been a mirage, an illusion, a dream.

And had vanished like a dream. She understood that, accepted it, but still felt regret and despair as though the creature really had existed, had been with her and had abandoned her. Just like everyone had abandoned her.

She tried to stand but could not. She rested her face on the rocks. Very slowly, she reached to one side and felt the hilt of her dagger.

Blood is a liquid. I have to drink.

She heard the clatter of hooves and a snorting.

'You've come back ...' she whispered, raising her head. 'Have you really come back?'

The unicorn snorted loudly. She saw its hooves, close by. Right beside her. They were wet. They were literally dripping with water.

Hope gave her strength, filled her with euphoria. The unicorn led and Ciri followed him, still not certain if she was in a dream. When exhaustion overcame her she fell to all fours. And then crawled.

The unicorn led her among some rocks to a shallow ravine with a sandy bottom. Ciri used the last of her strength to crawl, but she kept going. Because the sand was wet.

The unicorn stopped above a hollow which was visible in the sand, whinnied and pawed powerfully with his hoof; once, twice, three times. She understood. She crawled closer, helping him. She burrowed, breaking her fingernails, digging, pushing the sand aside. She may have sobbed as she did so, but she wasn't certain. When a muddy liquid appeared at the bottom of the hollow, she pressed her mouth to it at once, lapping up the water muddy with sand, so voraciously that the liquid disappeared. It took immense effort for Ciri to control herself. She used the dagger to dig deeper, then sat up and waited. She felt the sand crunching between her teeth and trembled with impatience, but waited until the hollow filled with water again. And then she drank. She drank long.

The third time, she let the water settle somewhat and then drank about four sand-free, sludgy mouthfuls. And then she remembered the unicorn.

'You must be thirsty too, little horse,' she said. 'But you can't drink mud. No horse ever drank mud.'

271

The unicorn neighed.

Ciri deepened the hollow, reinforcing the sides with stones.

'Wait, little horse. Let it settle a little ...'

'Little Horse' snorted, stamped his hooves and turned his head away.

'Don't be cross. Drink.'

The unicorn cautiously brought its muzzle towards the water.

'Drink, Little Horse. It isn't a dream. It's real water.'

At first Ciri tarried, not wanting to move away from the spring. She had just invented a new way of drinking by pressing a handkerchief she had soaked in the deepened hollow to her mouth, which allowed her to filter out most of the sand and mud. But the unicorn kept insisting; neighing, stamping, running away and returning again. He was calling her to start walking and was indicating the way. After long consideration, Ciri did as he suggested. The animal was right. It was time to go, to go towards the mountains, to get out of the desert. She set off after the unicorn, looking around and making a precise mental note of the spring's location. She didn't want to lose her way, should she ever have to return there.

They travelled together throughout the day. The unicorn, who now answered to Little Horse, led the way. He was a strange little horse. He bit and chewed dry stalks which no normal horse or even a starving goat would have touched. And when he caught a column of large ants wandering among the rocks, he began to eat them too. At first Ciri looked on in astonishment, but then joined in the feast herself. She was hungry.

The ants were dreadfully sour, but possibly because of that they didn't make her nauseous. Aside from that, the ants were in plentiful supply and she was able to get her stiff jaws moving again. The unicorn ate the ants whole while she contented herself with their abdomens, spitting out hard pieces of their chitinous carapaces.

They went on. The unicorn discovered several clumps of yellowed thistles and ate them with relish. This time Ciri did not join him. But when Little Horse found some lizard's eggs in the sand, she ate and he watched her. They continued on their way. Ciri noticed a clump of thistles and pointed them out to Little Horse. After a while, Little Horse drew her attention to a huge, black scorpion with a long tail, which must have measured a span and a half. Ciri trampled the hideous creature. Seeing that she was not interested in eating the scorpion, the unicorn ate it himself, and soon after pointed out another lizard's nest.

It was, it turned out, quite an effective collaboration.

They walked on.

The mountain range was getting closer and closer.

When it was very dark, the unicorn stopped. He slept standing up. Ciri, who was familiar with horses, initially tried to persuade him to lie down; she would have been able to sleep lying on him and benefit from his warmth. But it came to nothing. Little Horse grew cross and walked away, remaining aloof. He refused to behave in the classical way, as described in the learned books; he clearly did not have the slightest intention of resting his head in her lap. Ciri was full of doubts. She even wondered if the books were lying about unicorns and virgins, but there was also another possibility. The unicorn was clearly a foal and, as a young animal, may not have known anything about virgins. She rejected the possibility of Little Horse being able to sense, or take seriously, those few strange dreams she had once had. Who would ever take dreams seriously?

He was somewhat of a disappointment to her. They had been wandering for two days and nights, but he had not found any more water, even though he had been searching for it. Several times he stopped, twisted his head, moved his horn around, and then trotted off, rummaging in rocky clefts or rooting about in the sand with his hooves. He found ants and he found ants' eggs and larvae. He found a lizard's nest. He found a colourful snake, which he deftly trampled to death. But he did not find any water.

Ciri noticed that the unicorn roamed around; he didn't keep to a straight course. She came to the reasonable conclusion that the creature did not live in the desert at all. He had strayed there. Just as she had.

The ants, which they were beginning to find in abundance, contained some sour juice, but Ciri began to think more and more seriously about returning to the spring. Should they go even further and not find any water, her strength might not hold out. The heat was still terrible and the march exhausting.

She was just about to explain as much to Little Horse when he suddenly gave a long-drawn-out neigh, waved his tail and galloped off between some jagged rocks. Ciri followed him, eating ants' bodies as she walked.

The considerable expanse between the rocks was occupied by a wide sandy hollow. There was a distinct dip in the centre.

'Ha!' said Ciri, pleased. 'You're a clever pony, Little Horse. You've found another spring. There's got to be water in there!'

The unicorn gave a long snort, circling the hollow at a gentle trot. Ciri came closer. The hollow was large; at least twenty feet wide. It described a precise, regular circle resembling a funnel, as regular as if someone had pressed a gigantic egg into the sand. Ciri suddenly realised that such a regular shape could not have come about by accident. But by then it was too late.

Something moved at the bottom of the crater and Ciri was hit in the face by a sudden shower of sand and small stones. She leapt back, lost her balance and realised she was sliding downwards. The fountains of stones that were shooting out weren't only hitting her – they were also striking the edges of the pit, and the edges were crumbling in waves and sliding towards the bottom. She screamed and floundered like a drowning swimmer, vainly trying to find a foothold. She realised immediately that sudden movements only worsened her situation, making the sand subside more quickly. She turned over on her back, dug in with her heels, and spread her arms out wide. The sand at the bottom shifted and undulated, and she saw some brown, hooked pincers, at least a yard long, emerging from it. She screamed again, this time much louder.

The hail of stones suddenly stopped raining down on her, flying instead towards the opposite edge of the pit. The unicorn reared, neighing frenziedly, and the edge collapsed beneath him. He tried to struggle free from the shifting sand, but in vain; he was getting more and more bogged down and slipping more and more quickly towards the bottom. The dreadful pincers snapped violently. The unicorn neighed in despair, and thrashed around, helplessly striking the slipping sand with his forehooves. His back legs were completely stuck. When he had slid to the very bottom of the pit, he was caught by the horrible pincers of the creature which was concealed in the centre.

Hearing a frenzied wail of agony, Ciri screamed and charged downwards, wresting her dagger from its sheath. When she reached the bottom, she realised her mistake. The monster was hidden deep, and the dagger thrusts didn't even touch it through the layers of sand. On top of that the unicorn, held fast in the monstrous pincers and being dragged into the sandy trap, was frantic with pain and squealing, blindly pounding away with its forehooves and risking fracturing its limbs.

Witcher dances and tricks were useless here. But there was one quite simple spell. Ciri summoned the Power and struck using telekinesis.

A cloud of sand flew up into the air, uncovering the hidden monster, which had latched itself onto the squealing unicorn's thigh. Ciri yelled in horror. She had never seen anything so revolting in her entire life; not in illustrations, nor in any witcher books. She would have been incapable of imagining anything so hideous.

The monster was a dirty grey colour, plump and pot-bellied like a blood-gorged louse, and the narrow segments of its barrel-shaped torso were covered with sparse bristles. It appeared not to have any legs, but its pincers were almost the same length as its entire body.

Deprived of its sandy refuge the creature immediately released the unicorn and began to bury itself with a rapid, urgent wriggling of its bloated body. It performed this manoeuvre extremely ably, and the unicorn, struggling to escape from the trap, helped it by pushing mounds of sand downwards. Ciri was seized by fury and the lust for revenge. She threw herself at the monstrosity, now barely visible beneath the sand, and thrust her dagger into its domed back.

She attacked it from behind, prudently keeping away from the snapping pincers, which, it transpired, the monster was able to extend quite far backwards. She stabbed again, and the creature continued to bury itself at astonishing speed. But it was not burying itself in the sand to escape. It was doing so to attack. It only had to wriggle twice more in order to cover itself completely. Once hidden, it violently propelled out waves of stones, burying Ciri up to mid-thigh. She struggled to free herself and lunged backwards, but there was nowhere to escape; she was still in a crater of loose sand, where each movement pulled her downwards. The sand at the bottom bulged in a wave, which glided towards her, and from the wave emerged the clashing, cruelly hooked pincers.

She was rescued by Little Horse. Slipping down to the bottom of the crater, he used his hooves to strike the bulge of sand which betrayed the presence of the monster hidden just beneath the surface. The savage kicks uncovered the grey back and the unicorn lowered its head and stabbed the monster with its horn, striking at the precise point where the head, with its flailing pincers, was attached to the pot-bellied thorax. Seeing that the pincers of the monster, now pinned against the ground, were helplessly raking the sand, Ciri leapt forward and thrust the dagger deep into its wriggling body. She jerked the blade out and struck again. And again. The unicorn shook its horn free and drove its forehooves down powerfully onto the barrel-shaped body.

The trampled monster was no longer trying to bury itself. It had stopped moving entirely. A greenish liquid darkened the sand around it.

They climbed out of the crater with great difficulty. Ciri ran a few paces away and collapsed on the sand, breathing heavily and shaking under the waves of adrenaline which were assaulting her larynx and temples. The unicorn walked in circles around her. He was moving awkwardly. Blood dripped from the wound on his thigh, and ran down his leg onto his fetlock, leaving a red trail as he walked. Ciri got up onto her hands and knees and was violently sick. After a moment she stood up, swayed, and then staggered over to the unicorn, but Little Horse wouldn't let her touch him. He ran away, lay down and rolled on the ground. Then he cleaned his horn, stabbing it into the sand several times.

Ciri also cleaned and wiped the blade of her dagger, still glancing anxiously at the nearby crater. The unicorn stood up, whinnied and then walked over to her.

'I'd like to look at your wound, Little Horse.'

Little Horse neighed and shook his horned head.

'It's up to you. If you can walk, we'll set off. We'd better not stay here.'

Soon after, another vast sandbar appeared in their way, dotted all over with pits, which were hollowed out in the sand almost to the edge of the surrounding rocks. Ciri looked at them in horror; some of the craters were at least twice as big as the one in which they had fought for their lives.

They weren't brave enough to cross the sandbar by weaving their way between the craters. Ciri was convinced they were traps for careless creatures, and the monsters with the pincers lurking in them were only dangerous to the victims that fell in. By being cautious and staying away from the hollows, one could conceivably cut across the sandy ground without fear that one of the monsters would emerge and pursue them. She was sure there was no risk, but she preferred not to find out. The unicorn was clearly of the same opinion; he snorted and ran off, drawing her away from the sandbar. They made their journey longer by giving the dangerous terrain a wide berth, sticking close to the rocks and the hard, stony ground, through which none of the beasts would have been capable of digging.

As she walked, Ciri never took her eyes off the pits. Several times, she saw fountains of sand shooting up from the deadly traps; the monsters were deepening and repairing their lairs. Some of the craters were so close to each other that the stones flung out by one monster ended up in other craters, disturbing the creatures hidden at the bottom, and then a terrible cannonade would begin, with sand whizzing and blasting around like hail.

Ciri wondered what the sand monsters ate in this arid, desolate wilderness. She didn't have to wait long to find out; a dark object flew out of one of the nearby pits in a wide arc, falling close to them with a thump. After a moment's hesitation, she ran down onto the sand from the rocks. The object that had flown out of the crater was a rodent, resembling a rabbit. At least it looked like rabbit fur. For the body was shrunken; as hard and dry as a bone and as light and hollow as a pea pod. There wasn't a drop of blood in it. Ciri shuddered; now she knew what the monsters preyed on.

The unicorn neighed a warning. Ciri looked up. There was no crater in the near vicinity, and the sand was flat and smooth. And then, before her eyes, the smooth, flat sand suddenly bulged and the bulge began to glide quickly towards her. She threw the shrivelled carcass down and hurried back to the rocks.

The decision to steer clear of the sandbar turned out to have been very sensible.

They went on, skirting around even the smallest patches of sand, treading only on rocky ground.

The unicorn walked slowly, limping. The cuts on his thigh continued to bleed. But he still refused to allow her to approach him and examine the wound.

The sandbar narrowed considerably and began to meander. The fine, loose sand was replaced by coarse grit and then larger stones. They had not seen any pits for a long time now, so they decided to follow the path marked out by the remains of the sandbar. Ciri, although once again wearied by thirst and hunger, began to walk faster. There was hope. The rocky shoal was not what it seemed. It was actually the bed of a river with its source in the mountains. There was no water in the river, but it led to some springs which, although they were too small and produced too little water to fill the watercourse, were large enough to drink from.

She walked more quickly but then had to slow down because the unicorn could not keep pace with her. He was walking with visible difficulty, limping, dragging his leg, and planting his hoof awkwardly. When evening came, he lay down. He didn't get up when she approached him. This time he let her examine the wound.

278

There were two cuts, one on each side of his extremely swollen, angrily red thigh. Both cuts were inflamed, both were still bleeding and a sticky, foul-smelling pus was dripping along with the blood.

The monster had been venomous.

The next day it was even worse. The unicorn could barely walk. In the evening, he lay down on the rocks and refused to get up. When she knelt down beside him, he swung his head and horn towards the wounded thigh and neighed. There was suffering in the neighing.

The pus oozed more and more intensively and the smell was repulsive. Ciri took out her dagger. The unicorn whinnied shrilly, tried to stand and then collapsed rump first on the stone.

'I don't know what to do ...' she sobbed, looking at the blade. 'I really don't know ... I'm sure I should cut open the wound and squeeze out the pus and the venom ... But I don't know how. I might harm you even more.'

The unicorn tried to lift its head. It neighed. Ciri sat down on the rocks, clutching her head in her hands.

'They didn't teach me how to tend wounds,' she said bitterly. 'They taught me how to kill, telling me that's how I could save people. It was one big lie, Little Horse. They deceived me.'

Night was falling and it was quickly becoming dark. The unicorn was lying down, and Ciri was thinking frantically. She had collected some thistles and dry stalks, which grew in abundance on the banks of the dried-up riverbed, but Little Horse didn't want to eat them. He laid his head lifelessly on the rocks, no longer trying to lift it. All he could do was blink. Froth appeared on his muzzle.

'I can't help you, Little Horse,' she said in a stifled voice. 'I don't have anything ...'

Except magic.

I'm an enchantress.

She stood up and held out a hand. Nothing happened. She needed a great deal of magical energy, but there wasn't a trace of any here. She hadn't expected that. It astonished her.

But wait, there are water veins everywhere!

She took a few paces, first in one direction and then in the other.

She began to walk around in a circle. She stepped backwards.

Nothing.

'You damned desert!' she shouted, shaking her fists. 'There's nothing in you! No water and no magic! And magic was supposed to be everywhere! That was a lie too! Everybody deceived me, everybody!'

The unicorn neighed.

Magic is everywhere. It's in water, in the earth, in the air . . .

And in fire.

Ciri slammed her fist angrily against her forehead. It hadn't occurred to her earlier perhaps because, among the bare rocks, there hadn't even been anything to burn. But now she had a supply of dry thistles and stalks, and in order to create a tiny spark she ought only to need the tiny amount of energy she could still feel inside . . .

She gathered more sticks, arranged them in a heap and piled dry thistles around them. She cautiously put her hand in.

'Aenye!'

The pile of sticks glowed brightly, a flame flickered, then flared up, set the leaves on fire, consumed them and shot upwards. Ciri threw on more dry stalks.

What now? she thought, looking at the flame coming back to life. *Now to gather the energy. But how? Yennefer has forbidden me from touching fire energy . . . But I don't have a choice! Or any time! I have to act now; the sticks and leaves are burning fast . . . the fire will go out . . . Fire . . . how beautiful it is, how warm . . .*

She didn't know when or how it happened. As she stared at the flames she suddenly felt a pounding in her temples. She clutched her breast, feeling as though her ribcage would burst. A pain throbbed in her belly, her crotch and her nipples, which instantly transformed into horrifying pleasure. She stood up. No, she didn't stand up. She floated up.

The Power filled her like molten lead. The stars in the sky danced like stars reflected on the surface of a pond. The Eye, burning in the west, exploded with light. She took that light and with it the Force.

'Hael, Aenye!'

The unicorn neighed in a frenzy and tried to spring up, pushing with its forehooves. Ciri's arm rose automatically, her hand formed a gesture involuntarily, and her mouth shouted out the spell of its own accord. Bright, undulating light streamed from her fingers. The fire roared with great flames.

The waves of light streaming from her hand touched the unicorn's injured thigh, converging and penetrating.

'I wish you to be healed! That is my wish! Vess'hael, Aenye!'

The Power exploded inside her and she was filled with a wild euphoria. The fire shot upwards, and everything became bright around her. The unicorn raised his head, neighed and then suddenly leapt up from the ground, taking a few awkward paces. He bent his neck, swung his head towards his thigh, quivered his nostrils and snorted as if in disbelief. He neighed loud and long, kicked his hooves, swished his tail and galloped around the fire.

'I've healed you!' cried Ciri proudly. 'I've healed you! I'm a sorceress! I managed to draw the power from the fire! And I have that power! I can do anything I want!'

She turned away. The blazing fire roared, shooting sparks.

'We don't have to look for any more springs! We don't have to drink scooped-up mud any longer! I have the power now! I feel the power that's in this fire! I'll make rain fall on this accursed desert! I'll make it gush from the rocks! I'll make flowers grow here! Grass! Cabbages! I can do anything now! Anything!'

She lifted both arms, screaming out spells and chanting invocations. She didn't understand them, didn't remember when she had learnt them – or even if she'd *ever* learnt them. That was unimportant. She felt power, felt strength, was burning with fire. She was the fire. She trembled with the power that had pervaded her.

The night sky was suddenly riven by a slash of lightning. A wind whipped up among the rocks and thistles. The unicorn gave a long neigh and reared up. The fire roared upwards, exploding. The sticks and stems had charred long before; now the rock itself was afire. But Ciri paid no attention to it. She felt power. She saw only the fire. She heard only the fire.

You can do anything, whispered the flames. *You are in possession*

281

of our power. You can do anything. The world is at your feet. You are
great. You are mighty.

There was a figure among the flames. A tall, young woman with
long, straight, coal-black hair. The woman smiled, wildly, cruelly,
and the fire writhed and danced around her.

You are mighty! Those that harmed you did not know who they had
challenged! Avenge yourself! Make them pay! Make them all pay! Let
them tremble with fear at your feet, teeth chattering, not daring to look
you in the face! Let them beg for mercy but do not grant it to them! Make
them pay! Make them pay for everything! Revenge!

Behind the black-haired woman there was fire and smoke and,
in the smoke, rows of gallows, rows of sharpened stakes, scaffolds,
mountains of corpses. They were the corpses of Nilfgaardians,
of those who had captured and plundered Cintra and killed King
Eist and her grandmother Calanthe, of those who had murdered
people in the streets of the city. A knight in black armour swung
on a gibbet. The noose creaked and crows fought each other to
peck at his eyes through his winged helmet's visor. Other gibbets
stretched away towards the horizon, and on them hung Scoia'tael,
those who killed Paulie Dahlberg in Kaedwen, and those who'd
pursued Ciri on the Isle of Thanedd. The sorcerer Vilgefortz
danced on a towering stake, his beautiful, fraudulently noble
face contorted and blue-black with suffering. The sharpened,
bloodstained point of the stake protruded from his collarbone ...
Other sorcerers from Thanedd were kneeling on the ground,
their hands tied behind their backs and sharpened stakes awaiting
them ...

Stakes piled high with bundles of firewood rose up all the way
to the burning horizon, marked by ribbons of smoke. Chained
to the nearest stake was ... Triss Merigold. Beyond her was
Margarita Laux-Antille ... Mother Nenneke ... Jarre ... Fabio
Sachs ...

No. No. No.

Yes, screamed the black-haired woman. *Death to them all! Take*
your revenge on all of them. Despise them! They all harmed you or wanted
to harm you! Or perhaps they will want to harm you in the future! Hold

them in contempt, for at last the time of contempt is here! Contempt,
revenge and death! Death to the entire world! Death, destruction and
blood!

There is blood on your hand, blood on your dress . . .

They betrayed you! Tricked you! Harmed you! Now you have the
power, so take revenge!

Yennefer's mouth was cut and torn, pouring blood; her hands and
feet were shackled, fastened to the wet, dirty walls of a dungeon
by heavy chains. The mob around the scaffold shrieked, the poet
Dandelion laid his head on the block, the blade of the executioner's
axe flashed above him. The street urchins crowded beneath the scaffold unfolded a kerchief to be spattered with blood . . . The screaming of the mob drowned out the noise of the blow, so powerful it
made the scaffold shudder . . .

They betrayed you! They deceived and tricked you! To them you were
a pawn, just a puppet on a stick! They used you! They condemned you
to hunger, to the burning sun, to thirst, to misery and to loneliness! The
time of contempt and revenge is come! You have the power! You are
mighty! Let the whole world cower before thee! Let the whole world
cower before the Elder Blood!

Now the witchers were being led onto the scaffold: Yesemir,
Eskel, Coen, Lambert. And Geralt . . . Geralt was staggering, covered in blood . . .

'No!'

Fire surrounded her, and beyond the wall of flames was a furious
neighing. Unicorns were rearing, shaking their heads and dashing
their hooves against the ground. Their manes were like tattered
battle flags, their horns were as long and sharp as swords. The unicorns were huge, as huge as warhorses, much bigger than her Little
Horse. *Where had they come from? Where had so many of them come*
from? The flame shot upwards with a roar. The black-haired woman
raised her hands, and they were covered in blood. The heat billowed
her hair.

Let it burn, Falka, let it all burn!

'Go away! Be gone! I don't want you! I don't want your power!'

Let it burn, Falka, let it burn!

283

'I don't want to!'

You do! You desire this! Desire and lust seethe in you like a flame! The pleasure is enslaving you! It is might! It is force! It is power! The most delicious of the world's pleasures!

Lightning. Thunder. Wind. The thudding of hooves and the neighing of unicorns galloping with abandon around the fire.

'I don't want that power! I don't want it! I relinquish it!'

She didn't know if the fire had gone out or if her eyes had clouded over as she slumped to the ground, feeling the first drops of rain on her face.

The being should be divested of its beingness. It cannot be allowed to exist. The being is dangerous. Confirmation?

Negative. The being did not summon the Power for itself. It did it to save Ihuarraquax. The being feels sympathy. Thanks to the being, Ihuarraquax is once more among us.

But the being has the Power. Should it wish to make use of it . . .

It will not be able to use it. Never. It relinquished it. It relinquished the Power. Utterly. The Power disappeared. It is most curious . . .

We will never understand these beings.

We do not need to understand them! We will remove existence from the being. Before it is too late. Confirmation?

Negative. Let us leave this place. Let us leave the being. Let us leave it to its fate.

She did not know how long she lay on the rocks, trembling, staring at the changing colours of the sky. It was by turns dark and light, cold and hot, and she lay powerless, dried out like that dead rodent's carcass sucked dry and thrown from the crater.

She did not think about anything. She was alone. She was empty. Now she had nothing and she felt nothing inside. There was no thirst, hunger, fatigue or fear. Everything had vanished, even the will to survive. She was one great, cold, dreadful void. She felt that void with all her being, with every cell of her body.

She felt blood on her inner thighs. She did not care. She was empty. She had lost everything.

The colour of the sky was changing. She did not move. Was there any point in moving in such a void?

She did not move when hooves thudded around her, when horse-shoes clanged. She did not react to the loud cries and calls, to the excited voices, to the horses' snorts. She did not move when hard, powerful hands seized her. When she was lifted, she drooped limply. She did not react to the jerking or the shaking, to the harsh, aggressive questions. She did not understand them and did not want to understand.

She was empty and indifferent. She reacted indifferently to water being splashed on her face. When a canteen was put to her mouth, she did not choke. She drank. Indifferently.

Neither did she care later. She was hauled up onto a saddle. Her crotch was tender and painful. She was shivering so she was wrapped in a blanket. She was numb and limp, on the verge of fainting, so she was fastened by a belt to the rider sitting behind her. The rider stank of sweat and urine. She did not care.

There were riders all around. Many riders. Ciri looked at them indifferently. She was empty. She had lost everything. Nothing mattered any longer.

Nothing.

Not even the fact that the knight in command of the riders wore a helmet decorated with the wings of a raptor.

When the fire was lit at the foot of the criminal's pyre and the flames began to engulf her, she began to hurl abuse at the knights, barons, sorcerers and lord councillors gathered in the square; using such words that terror seized them all. Although at first only damp logs were placed on the pyre, in order that the she-devil would not perish quickly and would know the full agony of fire, now came the order to throw on more dry sticks and put an end to the torture as quickly as possible. However, a veritable demon had entered the accursed one; for although she was already sizzling well, she uttered no cries of anguish, but instead began to hurl even more awful abuse. 'An avenger will be born of my blood,' she cried. 'From my tainted Elder Blood will be born the avenger of the nations and of the world! He will avenge my torment! Death, death and vengeance to all of you and your kin!' Only this much was she able to cry out before the flame consumed her. Thus perished Falka; such was her punishment for spilling innocent blood.

Roderick de Novembre, *The History of the World,*
Volume II

CHAPTER SEVEN

'Look at her. Sunburnt and covered in cuts. She's an outcast. She's drinking like a fish and is as ravenous as a wolf. She came out of the east, I tell you. She crossed Korath. She crossed the Frying Pan.'

'Rubbish! No one survives the Frying Pan. She's come out of the west, down from the mountains, along the course of the Suchak. She barely touched the edge of Korath and that was enough for her. We found her lying in a heap on the ground, almost lifeless.'

'The desert also drags on for miles to the west. So where did she walk from?'

'She didn't walk, she'd been riding. Who knows how far? There were hoof prints by her. Her horse must have thrown her in the Suchak valley, and that's why she's battered and bruised.'

'Why is she so important to Nilfgaard, I wonder? When the prefect sent us off on that search party, I thought some important noblewoman had gone missing. But her? An ordinary slummock, a shabby drudge, and dazed and mute to boot. I really don't know, Skomlik, if we've found the one we're after ...'

'That's 'er. But ordinary she is not. Had she been ordinary, we'd have found her dead.'

'It was a close thing. There's no doubt the rain saved her. The oldest grandfathers can't recall rain in the Frying Pan, dammit. Clouds always pass by Korath ... Even when it rains in the valleys, not a single drop falls there!'

'Look at her wolfing down that food. It's as if she'd had nothing in her gob for a week ... Hey, you, slut! Like that pork fat? And that dry bread?'

'Ask her in Elven. Or in Nilfgaardian. She doesn't understand Common Speech. She's some kind of elven spawn ...'

'She's a simpleton, not right in the head. When I lifted her onto the horse this morning, it was like holding a wooden doll.'

'Don't you have eyes?' asked the powerful, balding one they called Skomlik, baring his teeth. 'What kind of Trappers are you, if you haven't rumbled her yet? She's neither stupid, nor simple. She's pretending. She's a strange and cunning little bird.'

'So why's she so important to Nilfgaard? They've promised a reward. There are patrols rushing around all over the place ... Why?'

'That I don't know. Though it might be an idea to ask her ... A whip across the back might encourage her ... Ha! Did you mark how she looked at me? She understands everything, she's listening carefully. Hey, wench! I'm Skomlik, a hunter. Also called a Trapper. And this, look here, is a whip. Also called a knout! Want to keep the skin on your back? Then let's hear it—'

'Enough! Silence!'

A loud, stern order, tolerating no opposition, came from another campfire, where a knight and his squire were sitting.

'Getting bored, Trappers?' asked the knight menacingly. 'Then get down to some work. The horses need grooming. My armour and weapons need cleaning. Go to the forest for wood. And do not touch the girl! Do you understand, you churls?'

'Indeed, noble Sir Sweers,' muttered Skomlik. His comrades looked sheepish.

'To work! Carry out my orders!'

The Trappers made themselves busy.

'Fate has really punished us with that arsehole,' muttered one of them. 'Oh, that the prefect put us under the command of that fucking knight—'

'Full of himself,' muttered another quietly, glancing around stealthily. 'And, after all, it was us Trappers what found the girl ... We had the hunch to ride into the Suchak valley.'

'Right enough. We deserve the credit, but His Lordship will take the bounty. We'll barely see a groat ... They'll toss us a florin. "There you go, be grateful for your lord's generosity, Trapper".'

'Shut your traps,' hissed Skomlik. 'He might hear you ...'

Ciri found herself alone by the fire. The knight and squire looked at her inquisitively, but said nothing.

The knight was a middle-aged but still robust man with a scarred face. When riding, he wore a helmet with birds' wings, but they were not the wings Ciri had first seen in her nightmares and later on the Isle of Thanedd. He was not the Black Knight of Cintra. But he was a Nilfgaardian knight. When he issued orders, he spoke the Common Speech fluently, but with a marked accent, similar to that of the Elves. However, he spoke with his squire (a boy not much older than Ciri) in a language resembling the Elder Speech, but harder and less melodious. It had to be Nilfgaardian. Ciri, who spoke the Elder Speech well, understood most of the words. But she didn't let on that she understood. The Nilfgaardian knight and his squire had peppered her with questions during the first stop, at the edge of the desert known as the Frying Pan or Korath. She hadn't answered then, because she had been indifferent and stupefied. Befuddled. A few days into the ride, when they had left the rocky ravines and rode down into green valleys, Ciri had already fully recovered her faculties. At last she began to notice the world around her and react to it, albeit apathetically. But she continued to ignore questions, so the knight stopped speaking to her at all. He appeared not to pay her any attention. Only the ruffians – the ones calling themselves Trappers – took an interest in her. And they also tried to question her. Aggressively.

But the Nilfgaardian in the winged helmet swiftly took them to task. It was clear who was the master and who was the servant.

Ciri pretended to be a simple mute, but she listened intently. She slowly began to understand her situation. She had fallen into Nilfgaard's hands. Nilfgaard had hunted her and found her, no doubt having located the route the chaotic portal in Tor Lara had transported her along. The winged knight and the Trappers had achieved what neither Yennefer nor Geralt had been able to do.

What had happened to Yennefer and Geralt on Thanedd? Where was she? She feared the worst. The Trappers and their leader, Skomlik, spoke a simple, slovenly version of the Common Speech, but without a Nilfgaardian accent. The Trappers were ordinary men, but were serving the knight from Nilfgaard. They were looking forward to the thought of the bounty the prefect would pay them for finding Ciri. In florins.

The only countries which used florins and where the people served Nilfgaardians were the Provinces in the far south, administered by imperial prefects.

The following day, during a stop by the bank of a stream, Ciri began to consider her chances of escaping. Magic might help her. She cautiously tried the most simple spell, a mild telekinesis. But her fears were confirmed. She didn't have even a trace of magical energy. Having foolishly played with fire, her magical abilities had deserted her utterly.

She became indifferent once more. To everything. She became withdrawn and sank into apathy, where she remained for a long while.

Until the day the Blue Knight blocked their path across the moorland.

'Oh dear, oh dear,' muttered Skomlik, looking at the horsemen barring their way. 'This means trouble. They're Varnhagens from the stronghold in Sarda ...'

The horsemen came closer. At their head, on a powerful grey, rode a giant of a man in a glittering blue, enamelled suit of armour. Close behind him rode a second armoured horseman, while two more in simple, dun costumes – clearly servants – brought up the rear.

The Nilfgaardian in the winged helmet rode out to meet them, reining in his bay in a dancing trot. His squire fingered the hilt of his sword and turned around in the saddle.

'Stay back and guard the girl,' he barked to Skomlik and his Trappers. 'And don't interfere!'

'I ain't that stupid,' said Skomlik softly, as soon as the squire had ridden away. 'I ain't so stupid as to interfere in a feud between the lords of Nilfgaard ...'

'Will there be a fight, Skomlik?'

'Bound to be. There's an ancestral vendetta and blood feud between the Sweers and the Varnhagens. Dismount. Guard the wench, because she's our best asset and our profit. If we're lucky, we'll get the entire bounty that's on her head.'

'The Varnhagens are sure to be hunting the girl too. If they overcome us, they'll take her from us ... And there's only four of us ...'

'Five,' said Skomlik, flashing his teeth. 'One of the camp followers from Sarda is a mucker of mine, if I'm not mistaken. You'll see; the benefits from this ruckus will come to us, not to Their Lordships ...'

The knight in the blue armour reined in his grey. The winged knight came to a halt facing him. The Blue Knight's companion trotted up and stopped behind him. His strange helmet was decorated with two straps of leather hanging from the visor, resembling two long whiskers or walrus tusks. Across his saddle, Two Tusks held a menacing-looking weapon somewhat resembling the spontoons carried by the guardsmen from Cintra, but with a considerably shorter shaft and a longer blade.

The Blue Knight and the Winged Knight exchanged a few words. Ciri could not make out what they were saying, but their tone left her in no doubt. They were not words of friendship. The Blue Knight suddenly sat up straight in the saddle, pointed fiercely at Ciri, and said something loudly and angrily. In answer, the Winged Knight cried out just as angrily and shook his fist in his armoured glove, clearly sending the Blue Knight on his way.

And then it began.

The Blue Knight dug his spurs into his grey and charged forward, yanking his battleaxe from a holder by his saddle. The Winged Knight spurred on his bay, pulling his sword from its scabbard. Before the armoured knights came together in battle, however, Two Tusks attacked, urging his horse into a gallop with the shaft of his spontoon. The Winged Knight's squire leapt on him, drawing his sword, but Two Tusks rose up in the saddle and thrust the spontoon straight into the squire's chest. The long blade penetrated his gorget and hauberk with a crack, the squire groaned loudly and thudded to the ground, grasping the spontoon, which was thrust in as far as the crossguard.

The Blue Knight and the Winged Knight collided with a crash and a thud. The battleaxe was more lethal but the sword was quicker.

The Blue Knight was hit in the shoulder and a piece of his enamelled spaulder flew off to one side, spinning, its strap flapping behind it. The knight shuddered in the saddle and streaks of crimson glistened on the blue armour. The impact pushed the warriors apart. The Winged Nilfgaardian turned his bay back, but then Two Tusks fell upon him, raising his sword to strike two-handed. The Winged Knight tugged at his reins and Two Tusks, steering his horse with his legs, galloped past. The Winged Knight managed to strike him in passing, however. Ciri saw the metal plate of the rerebrace deform and blood spurt out from beneath the metal.

The Blue Knight was already coming back, swinging his battle-axe and screaming. The two knights exchanged thundering blows at full tilt and then drew apart. Two Tusks fell on the Winged Knight once more; their horses collided and their swords clanged. Two Tusks slashed the Winged Knight, destroying his rerebrace and rondel. The Winged Knight straightened up and struck a powerful blow from the right into the side of Two Tusk's breastplate. Two Tusks swayed in the saddle. The Winged Knight stood in his stirrups and struck another mighty blow, between the dented and cloven pauldron and the helmet. The blade of the broad sword cut into the metal with a clang and became caught. Two Tusks tensed up and shuddered. The horses came together, stamping their hooves and gnashing their teeth on their bits. The Winged Knight braced himself against his pommel and pulled his sword out of Two Tusks's body. Two Tusks toppled from his saddle and crashed under the horses' hooves. The sound of horseshoes striking and twisting armour rang out as he was trampled by his own mount.

The Blue Knight turned his grey and attacked, lifting his battle-axe. The wound to his hand impeded his efforts to control his horse. The Winged Knight noticed this and stole up deftly from the right, standing in his stirrups to deliver a terrible blow. The Blue Knight caught the blow on his battleaxe and knocked the sword out of the Winged Knight's hand. The horses crashed together once more. The Blue Knight was immensely strong; the heavy axe in his hand rose and fell like a twig. A blow thudded on the Winged Knight's armour, making the bay sit down on its haunches. The Winged Knight swayed, but remained in the saddle. Before the battleaxe had time to fall again, he released the reins and twisted his left hand, seizing a heavy angular mace hanging from a leather sword knot, and hit the Blue Knight savagely on the helmet. The helmet rang like a bell and now it was the turn of the Blue Knight to sway in his saddle. The horses squealed, trying to bite each other and not wanting to separate.

The Blue Knight, although clearly dazed by the blow from the mace, managed to strike again with his battleaxe, hitting his opponent in the breastplate with a thud. It seemed an absolute miracle that they were both able to stay in the saddle, but it was simply owing to their high pommels and cantles. Blood dripped down the sides of both horses; particularly conspicuous on the grey's light coat. Ciri looked on in horror. She had been taught to fight in Kaer Morhen, but she could not imagine how she could have faced either of those two strongmen. Or parry even one of their powerful blows.

The Blue Knight seized the helve of the battleaxe, which was plunged deeply into the Winged Knight's breastplate, in both hands. He bent forward and heaved, trying to push his opponent out of the saddle. The Winged Knight struck him hard with the mace; once, twice, three times. Blood spurted from the peak of the helmet, splashing onto the blue armour and the grey's neck. The Winged Knight spurred his bay away, the impetus of the horse wrenching the axe's blade from his breastplate. The Blue Knight, swaying in the saddle, released the helve. The Winged Knight transferred the mace to his right hand, rode up, and struck with a vicious blow, shoving the Blue Knight's head against his horse's neck. Taking the reins of the grey in his free hand, the Nilfgaardian struck again with his mace. The blue suit of armour rang like a cast-iron pot and blood gushed from the misshapen helmet. One more blow and the Blue Knight fell head first under the grey's hooves. The grey trotted away, but the Winged Knight's bay, evidently specially trained, trampled the fallen knight with a clatter. The Blue Knight was still alive, evidenced by his desperate cries of pain. The bay continued to trample him with such force that the wounded Winged Knight could not stay in the saddle and fell alongside him with a thud.

'They've finished each other off, dammit,' grunted the Trapper who was holding Ciri.

'Noble knights. The plague and the pox on them all,' spat another.

The Blue Knight's servants were watching from a distance. One of them wheeled his horse around.

'Stop right there, Remiz!' yelled Skomlik. 'Where are you going? To Sarda? In a hurry to get to the gallows?'

The servants came to a halt. One of them looked over, shielding his eyes with his hand.

'Is that you, Skomlik?'

'Yes, it is! Get over here, Remiz, don't worry! Knightly spats aren't our business!'

Ciri had suddenly had enough of inaction. She nimbly tore herself free from the Trapper holding her, set off at a run, caught hold of the Blue Knight's grey, and with one leap was in the saddle with the high pommel.

She might have managed her escape had not the servants from Sarda been mounted and on fresh horses. They caught up with her without difficulty and snatched the reins from her. She jumped off and sprinted towards the forest, but the horsemen caught her once again. One of them seized her by the hair in full flight, then pulled and dragged her behind him. Ciri screamed, hanging from his arm. The horseman threw her down at Skomlik's feet. The knout swished, and Ciri howled and curled up in a ball, protecting her head with her hands. The whip swished again, cutting into the backs of her hands. She rolled away, but Skomlik jumped after her, kicked her, and then pinned her down with his boot.

'Trying to escape, you viper?'

The knout swished. Ciri howled. Skomlik kicked her again and lashed her with the knout.

'Stop hitting me!' she screamed, cowering.

'So you can talk, bitch! Cat let go of your tongue? I'll teach you—'

'Control yourself, Skomlik!' shouted one of the Trappers. 'Do you want to beat the life out of her or what? She's worth too much to waste!'

'Bloody hell,' said Remiz, dismounting. 'Is she the one Nilfgaard's spent a week searching for?'

'That's right.'

'Ha! All the garrisons are hunting for her. She's some kind of important personage to Nilfgaard. They say a mighty sorceror divined that she must be somewhere in the area. That's what they were saying in Sarda, at least. Where did you find her?'

'In the Frying Pan.'

'That's not possible!'

'It is, it is,' said Skomlik angrily, frowning. 'We've got her and the reward's ours. Why are you standing around like statues? Bind the little bird and get her up in the saddle! Let's scram, boys! Look lively!'

'I think the Honourable Sweers,' said one of the Trappers, 'is still breathing ...'

'But not for long. Curse him! We're riding straight to Amarillo, boys. To the prefect. We'll deliver the wench to him and pick up the bounty.'

'To Amarillo?' Remiz scratched the back of his head, and looked at the scene of the recent fight. 'And right into the hangman's hands? What will you tell the prefect? That the knights battered each other to death and you're all in one piece? When the whole story comes out the prefect will have you hanged, and send us back to Sarda under guard ... And then the Varnhagens will take the bounty. You might want to head for Amarillo, but I'd rather disappear into the forest ...'

'You're my brother-in-law, Remiz,' said Skomlik. 'And even though you're a son of a bitch for beating my sister you're still a mate. So I'll save your skin. We're going to Amarillo, I said. The prefect knows there's a feud between the Sweers and the Varnhagens. They met and did each other in. That's normal for them. What could we have done? And we – heed my words – found the wench afterwards. We did, the Trappers. You're a Trapper now, too, Remiz. The prefect hasn't got a bloody clue how many of us set off with Sweers. He won't count us up ...'

'Haven't you forgotten something, Skomlik?' asked Remiz in a slow drawl, looking at the other servant from Sarda.

Skomlik turned around slowly, then as quick as a flash pulled out a knife and thrust it hard into the servant's throat. The servant rasped and then collapsed on the ground.

'I don't forget about anything,' said the Trapper coldly. 'We're all in it together. There are no witnesses, and not too many heads to divide the bounty amongst either. To horse, boys, and on to Amarillo! There's a fair distance between us and the bounty, so let's not hang around!'

After leaving a dark, wet, beech forest, they saw a village at the foot of the mountain: a dozen or so thatched cottages inside the ring of a low stockade enclosing a bend in a small river.

The wind carried the scent of smoke. Ciri wiggled her numb fingers, which were fastened by a leather strap to the pommel. She was numb all over; her buttocks ached unbearably and she was being tormented by a full bladder. She'd been in the saddle since daybreak. She had not rested during the night, since she had been forced to sleep with her hands fastened to the wrists of two Trappers lying on either side of her. Each time she moved, the Trappers reacted with curses and threats to beat her.

'It's a village,' said one of them.

'I can see that,' responded Skomlik.

They rode down the slope, their horses' hooves crunching through the tall, dry grass. They soon found themselves on a bumpy track leading straight to the village, towards a wooden bridge and a gate in the stockade.

Skomlik reined back his horse and stood up in his stirrups.

'What village is this? I've never stopped here. Remiz, do you know these parts?'

'Years ago,' said Remiz, 'this village was called White River. But when the unrest began, some locals joined the rebels. Then the Varnhagens of Sarda put it to the torch, murdered the villagers or took them prisoner. Now only Nilfgaardian settlers live here, all newcomers. And the village has been renamed Glyswen. These settlers are fierce, nasty people. I'm telling you, let's not dally. We should ride on.'

'We have to let the horses rest,' protested one of the Trappers, 'and feed them. And my belly's rumbling like I've swallowed a brass band. Why worry about the settlers? They're just rabble. Scum. We'll wave the prefect's order in front of their noses. I mean, the prefect's a Nilfgaardian like them. You watch, they'll bow down before us.'

'I can just see that,' growled Skomlik. 'Has anyone seen a Nilfgaardian bow? Remiz, is there an inn in this 'ere Glyswen?'

'Yes. The Varnhagens didn't burn it down.'

Skomlik turned around in the saddle and looked at Ciri.

'We'll have to untie her,' he said. 'We can't risk anyone recognising her ... Give her a mantle. And a hood for her head ... Hey there! Where you going, you slummock?'

'I have to go into the bushes—'

'I'll give you bushes, you slut! Squat by the track! And mark: don't breathe a word in the village. Don't start getting clever! One squeak and I'll slit your throat. If I don't get any florins for you, no one's getting any.'

They approached at a walk, the horses' hooves thudding on the bridge. Right away, some settlers armed with lances emerged from behind the stockade.

'They're guarding the gate,' muttered Remiz. 'I wonder why.'

'Me too,' Skomlik muttered back, raising himself in his stirrups. 'They're guarding the gate, and the stockade's down by the mill. You could drive a wagon through there ...'

They rode closer and reined in their horses.

'Greetings, gentlemen!' called out Skomlik jovially, but somewhat unnaturally. 'Good day to you.'

'Who are you?' asked the tallest of the settlers brusquely.

'We, mate, are the army,' lied Skomlik, leaning back in the saddle. 'In the service of His Lordlyship, the prefect of Amarillo.'

The settler slid his hand down the shaft of his lance and scowled at Skomlik. He clearly couldn't recall when he and the Trapper had become mates.

'His Lordship the prefect sent us here,' Skomlik continued to lie, 'to learn how his countrymen, the good people of Glyswen, are faring. His Lordlyship sends his greetings and enquires if the people of Glyswen need any kind of help.'

'We're getting by,' said the settler. Ciri noticed he spoke the Common Speech in a similar way to the Winged Knight, with the same accent, as though he was trying to imitate Skomlik's lazy speech pattern. 'We've got used to looking after ourselves.'

'The prefect will be pleased to hear it. Is the inn open? We're parched . . .'

'It's open,' said the settler grimly. 'For the moment.'

'For the moment?'

'For the moment. For we'll soon be pulling it down. The rafters and planks will serve us for a granary. The inn's no use to anyone. We toil in the fields and don't visit the inn. The inn only serves travellers, mostly of a sort that aren't to our liking. Some of that kind are drinking there now.'

'Who's that?' asked Remiz, blanching somewhat. 'Not from the stronghold in Sarda, by any chance? Not the Honourable Varnhagens?'

The settler grimaced and moved his lips around, as though intending to spit.

'Unfortunately not. They're the Lords Barons' militiamen. The Nissirs.'

'The Nissirs?' frowned Skomlik. 'Where did they come from? Under whose command?'

'Their commander is tall and black-haired, with whiskers like a catfish.'

'Eh!' Skomlik turned to his companions. 'We're in luck. We only know one like that, don't we? It's sure to be our old comrade "Trust Me" Vercta. Remember him? And what are the Nissirs doing here, mate?'

'The Lords Nissir,' explained the settler grimly, 'are bound for Tyffi. They honoured us with a visit. They're moving

300

a prisoner. They've caught one of those of Rats.'

'Of course they have,' snorted Remiz. 'And why not the Nilfgaardian emperor?'

The settler frowned and tightened his grip on the shaft of his lance. His companions murmured softly.

'Go to the inn, sirs,' said the settler, the muscles in his jaw working, 'and talk to the Lords Nissir, your comrades. You claim to be in the prefect's service, so ask the Lords Nissirs why they're taking the criminal to Tyffi, rather than impaling him on a stake right here, right now, as the prefect ordered. And remind the Lords Nissirs, your comrades, that the prefect is in command here, not the Baron of Tyffi. We already have the oxen yoked up and the stake sharpened. If the Lords Nissirs don't want to, we'll do the necessary. Tell them that.'

'I'll tell them. Rely on me,' said Skomlik, winking meaningfully at his comrades. 'Farewell, gentlemen.'

They set off at a walk between the cottages. The village appeared deserted; there was not a soul around. An emaciated pig was rooting around by one of the fences and some dirty ducks were splashing around in the mud. A large black tomcat crossed the riders' path.

'Ugh, ugh, bloody cat,' said Remiz, leaning over, spitting and making a sign with his fingers to protect himself from black magic. 'He ran across our path, the son of a bitch!'

'I hope he chokes on a mouse!'

'What was it?' said Skomlik, turning back.

'A cat. As black as pitch. He crossed our path, ugh, ugh.'

'To hell with him,' said Skomlik, looking all around. 'Just look how empty it is. But I saw the people in their cottages, watching. And I saw a lance blade glint in that doorway.'

'They're guarding their womenfolk,' laughed the man who had wished ill on the cat. 'The Nissirs are in the village! Did you hear what that yokel was saying? It's obvious they don't like them.'

'And no wonder. Trust Me and his company never pass up a chance. They'll get what's coming to them one day, those Lords Nissirs. The barons call them "keepers of the peace", and that's what they're paid to do. To keep order and guard the roads. But try

301

whispering "Nissir" near a peasant's ear, and you'll see. He'll shit his pants in fear. But they'll get their comeuppance. They'll slaughter one too many calf, rape one too many wench, and the peasants will tear them apart with their pitchforks. You'll see. Did you notice their fierce expressions by those gates? They're Nilfgaardian settlers. You don't want to mess with them ... Ah, and here's the inn ...'

They urged the horses on.

The inn had a slightly sunken, very mossy thatched roof. It stood some distance from the cottages and farm buildings, although it marked the central point of the entire area encircled by the dilapidated stockade; the place where the two roads passing through the village crossed. In the shadow cast by the only large tree in the vicinity were two enclosures; one for cattle and the other for horses. In the latter stood five or six unsaddled horses. On the steps leading up to the door sat two individuals in leather jerkins and pointed fur hats. They were both nursing earthenware mugs, and between them stood a bowl full of bones picked clean of meat.

'Who are you?' yelled one of them at the sight of Skomlik and his company dismounting. 'What do you want? Be off with you! This inn is occupied by the forces of law and order!'

'Don't holler, Nissir, don't holler,' said Skomlik, pulling Ciri down from the saddle. 'And get that door open, because we want to go inside. Your commander, Vercta, is a friend of ours.'

'I don't know you!'

'Because you're naught but a stripling. Me and Trust Me served together years ago, before Nilfgaard came into power here.'

'Well, if you say so ...' The fellow hesitated, letting go of his sword hilt. 'You'd better come inside. It's all the same to me ...'

Skomlik shoved Ciri and another Trapper grabbed her by the collar. They went inside.

It was gloomy and stuffy, and smelled of smoke and baking. The inn was almost empty – only one of the tables was occupied, standing in a stream of light coming through a small window with some kind of animal skin stretched across it. A small group of men were sitting at the table. The innkeeper was bustling around in the background by the fireplace, clinking beer mugs.

'Good cheer to you, Nissirs!' boomed Skomlik.

'We don't shake hands with any old brigands,' growled a member of the company sitting by the window, who then spat on the floor. Another stopped him with a gesture.

'Take it easy,' he said. 'They're mates, don't you recognise them? That's Skomlik and his Trappers. Welcome, welcome!'

Skomlik brightened up and walked towards the table, but stopped on seeing his companions staring at the wooden post holding up the roof timbers. At its base, on a stool, sat a slim, fair-haired youth, strangely erect and stiff. Ciri saw that his unnatural position derived from the fact that his hands were twisted behind him and tied together, and his neck was attached to the post by a leather strap.

'May the pox seize me,' loudly sighed one of the Trappers, the one holding Ciri by the collar, 'Just look, Skomlik. It's Kayleigh!'

'Kayleigh?' Skomlik tilted his head. 'Kayleigh the Rat? Can't be!'

One of the Nissirs sitting at the table, a fat man with hair shorn in an exotic topknot, gave a throaty laugh.

'Might just be,' he said, licking a spoon. 'It is Kayleigh, in all his foulness. It was worth getting up at daybreak. We're certain to get half a mark of florins of good imperial coin for him.'

'You've nabbed Kayleigh. Well, well,' frowned Skomlik. 'So that Nilfgaardian peasant was telling the truth—'

'Thirty florins, dammit,' sighed Remiz. 'Not a bad sum ... Is Baron Lutz of Tyffi paying?'

'That's right,' confirmed the other Nissir, black-haired and black-moustached. 'The Honourable Baron Lutz of Tyffi, our lord and benefactor. The Rats robbed his steward on the highway; he was so enraged he offered a bounty. And we, Skomlik, will get it; trust me. Ha, just look, boys, how his nose is out of joint! He doesn't like it that we nabbed the Rat and not him, even though the prefect ordered the gang to be tracked down!'

'Skomlik the Trapper,' said the fat man with the topknot, pointing his spoon at Ciri, 'has also caught something. Do you see, Vercta? Some girl or other.'

'I see,' said the black-moustached man, flashing his teeth. 'What's this, Skomlik? Are you feeling the pinch so much you kidnap children for the ransom? What scruff is this?'

'Mind your own business!'

'Who's touchy?' laughed the one with the topknot. 'We only want to check she's not your daughter.'

'His daughter?' laughed Vercta, the one with the black moustache. 'Chance would be a fine thing. You need balls to sire a daughter.'

The Nissirs roared with laughter.

'Fuck off, you dolts!' yelled Skomlik, puffed up. 'All I'll tell you is this, Vercta. Before Sunday's past you might be surprised to hear who people will be talking about. You and your Rat, or me and my prize. And we'll see who's the more generous: your baron or the imperial prefect of Amarillo!'

'You can kiss my arse,' declared Vercta contemptuously, and went back to slurping his soup. 'You, your prefect, your emperor and the whole of Nilfgaard, trust me. And don't get crabby. I'm well aware Nilfgaard's been hunting some girl for a week, so hard you can't see the road for dust. I know there's a bounty on her. But I don't give a monkey's. I have no intention of serving the Nilfgaardians and I curse them. I serve Baron Lutz now. I answer to him; no one else.'

'Unlike you,' rasped Skomlik, 'your baron kisses the Nilfgaardian hand and licks Nilfgaardian boots. Which means you don't have to. So it's easy for you to talk.'

'Easy, now,' said the Nissir in a placatory manner. 'That wasn't against you; trust me. It's fine that you found the wench Nilfgaard's searching for, and I'm glad you'll get the reward and not those bloody Nilfgaardians. And you serve the prefect? No one chooses his own master; it's them that chooses, ain't it? Come on, sit down with us, we'll have a drink since we're all here together.'

'Aye, why not,' agreed Skomlik. 'But first give us a bit of twine. I'll tie the wench to the post next to your Rat, all right?'

The Nissirs roared with laughter.

'Look at 'im, the terror of the borderland!' cackled the fat one with the topknot. 'The armed forces of Nilfgaard! Bind 'er up, Skomlik, bind 'er up good and tight. But use an iron chain, because your important captive is likely to break her bonds and smash your face in before she escapes. She looks so dangerous, I'm trembling!'

Even Skomlik's companions snorted with suppressed laughter. The Trapper flushed, twisted his belt, and walked over to the table.

'Just to be sure she won't make a run for it—'

'Do as you bloody want,' interrupted Vercta, breaking bread. 'If you want to talk, sit down and get a round in. And hang the wench up by her feet from the ceiling, if you wish. I couldn't give a shit. It's just bloody funny, Skomlik. Perhaps she *is* an important prisoner to you and your prefect, but to me she's a skinny, frightened kid. Want to tie her up? She can barely stand, never mind escape; trust me. What are you afraid of?'

'I'll tell you what I'm afraid of,' said Skomlik, pursing his lips. 'This is a Nilfgaardian settlement. The settlers didn't exactly greet us with bread and salt, and they said they've already got a stake sharpened for your Rat. And the law's with them, because the prefect issued an edict that any brigands that are caught should be punished on the spot. If you don't give them their prisoner, they're ready to sharpen a stake for you too.'

'Oh dear, oh dear,' said the fat man with the topknot. 'They're only fit to scare birds, the rascals. They'd better not interfere with us, because blood will be spilt.'

'We won't give them the Rat,' added Vercta. 'He's ours and he's going to Tyffi. And Baron Lutz will put the whole case to rights with the prefect. Let's not waste our breath. Sit you down.'

The Trappers, sliding their sword belts around, were happy to join the Nissirs' table, yelling at the innkeeper and pointing in unison at Skomlik as their sponsor. Skomlik kicked a stool towards the post, yanked Ciri by the arm and pushed her so hard she fell over, banging her shoulder against the knee of the boy who was tied to the post.

'Sit there,' he snarled. 'And don't you dare move, or I'll thrash you like a dog.'

'You louse,' growled the stripling, looking at him through half-closed eyes. 'You fucking ...'

Ciri didn't know most of the words which erupted from the boy's angry, scowling mouth, but from the change coming over Skomlik's face she realised they must have been extremely filthy and offensive. The Trapper blanched with rage, took a swing, hit the boy in the face, then seized him by his long, fair hair and shoved him, banging the back of his head against the post.

'Hey!' called out Vercta, getting up from the table. 'What's going on over there?'

'I'll knock the mangy Rat's teeth out!' roared Skomlik. 'I'll tear his legs from his arse!'

'Come here and stop your screeching,' said the Nissir, sitting down, draining his mug of beer in a single draught and wiping his moustache. 'You can knock your prisoner around all you like, but hands off ours. And you, Kayleigh, don't play the hero. Sit still and ponder over the scaffold that Baron Lutz is having built. The list of punishments the hangman's going to perform on you is already written, trust me, and measures three ells. Half the town's already placing bets about how far down the list you'll make it. So save your strength, Rat. I'm going to put a small sum on that you won't let me down and you'll hold out at least to castration.'

Kayleigh spat and turned his head away, as much as the strap around his neck would allow. Skomlik hauled up his belt, threw Ciri a baleful glance, sitting perched on the stool, then joined the company at the table, cursing, since all that remained in the jug of beer the innkeeper had brought them were streaks of froth.

'How did you catch Kayleigh?' he asked, indicating to the innkeeper that he wanted to extend the order. 'And alive? Because I can't believe you knocked off the other Rats.'

'To tell the truth,' answered Vercta, critically examining what he had just picked from his nose, 'we were lucky. He was all alone. He'd left the gang and nipped over to New Forge for a night with his girlfriend. The village headman knew we weren't far away and sent word. We got there before sun-up and collared him in the hay; he didn't even squeal.'

'And we all had some sport with his wench,' cackled the fat one with the topknot. 'If Kayleigh hadn't satisfied her that night, there was no harm done. We satisfied her so thoroughly in the morning she couldn't move her arms or legs!'

306

'Well, I tell you, you're incompetent fools,' declared Skomlik loudly and derisively. 'You fucked away a pretty penny, you thick-heads. Instead of wasting time on the wench, you ought to have heated up a branding iron and made the Rat tell you where his gang were spending the night. You could've had the lot of 'em. Giselher, Reef and the rest. The Varnhagens of Sarda offered twenty florins for Giselher a year ago. And for that whore, what's her name ... Mistle, wasn't it? The prefect would give even more after what she did to his nephew at Druigh, when the Rats fleeced that convoy.'

'You, Skomlik,' grimaced Vercta, 'were either born stupid, or a hard life has driven all the good sense out of your head. There are six of us. Do you expect me to take on the whole gang with six men, or what? And we won't miss out on the bounty, either. Baron Lutz will warm Kayleigh's heels in the dungeons. He'll take his time, trust me. Kayleigh will sing, he'll betray their hideouts and base, then we'll go there in force and number, we'll surround the gang, and pick them out like crayfish from a sack.'

'Yeah, right. They'll be waiting for you. They'll find out you've got Kayleigh and lie low in their other hideouts and in the rushes. No, Vercta, you have to stare the truth in the face: you fucked up. You traded the reward for a woman. That's you all over ... nothing but fucking on your mind.'

'You're the fucker!' Vercta jumped up from the table. 'If you're in such a hurry, go after the Rats with your heroes yourself! But beware, because taking on the Rats, Your Honourable Nilfgaardian Lackeyship, isn't the same as catching young wenches!'

The Nissirs and Trappers began to trade insults with each other. The innkeeper quickly brought them more beer, snatching the empty jug from the hand of the fat one with the topknot, who was aiming it at Skomlik. The beer quickly took the heat out of the quarrel, cooled their throats and calmed their tempers.

'Bring us victuals!' yelled the fat one to the innkeeper. 'Scrambled egg and sausage. Beans, bread and cheese!'

'And beer!'

'What are you goggling at, Skomlik? We're in the money today! We fleeced Kayleigh of his horse, his pouch, his trinkets,

307

his sword, his saddle and sheepskin, and we sold everything to the dwarves!'

'We sold his wench's red shoes as well. And her beads!'

'Ho, ho, enough to buy a few rounds, indeed! Glad to hear it!'

'Why are you so glad? We've got beer money, not you. All you can do is wipe the snot from your prisoner's nose or pluck lice from her! The size of the purse reflects the class of prisoner, ha, ha!'

'You sons of bitches!'

'Ha, ha, sit down. I was jesting, shut your trap!'

'Let's drink to settle our differences! The drinks are on us!'

'Where's that scrambled egg, innkeeper, a plague on you! Quickly!'

'And bring us that beer!'

Huddled on the stool, Ciri raised her head, meeting Kayleigh's furious green eyes staring at her from under his tousled fringe of fair hair. A shudder passed through her. Kayleigh's face, though not unattractive, was evil, very evil. Ciri could see that this boy, although not much older than her, was capable of anything.

'The gods must have sent you to me,' whispered the Rat, piercing her with his green stare. 'Just think. I don't believe in them, but they sent you. Don't look around, you little fool. You have to help me ... Listen carefully, scumbag ...'

Ciri huddled down even more and lowered her head.

'Listen,' hissed Kayleigh, indeed flashing his teeth like a rat. 'In a moment, when the innkeeper passes, you'll call him ... Listen to me, by the devil ...'

'No,' she whispered. 'They'll beat me ...'

Kayleigh's mouth twisted, and Ciri realised that being beaten by Skomlik was by no means the worst thing she might encounter. Although Skomlik was huge, and Kayleigh thin and bound, she sensed instinctively which of them she ought to fear more.

'If you help me,' whispered the Rat, 'I'll help you. I'm not alone. I've got comrades who don't abandon a friend in need ... Get it? And when my comrades arrive, when it all kicks off, I can't stay tied up to this post. Those scoundrels will carve me up ... Listen carefully, dammit. I'll tell you what you're to do ...'

Ciri lowered her head even further. Her lips quivered.

The Trappers and the Nissirs were devouring the scrambled eggs, and smacking their lips like wild boars. The innkeeper stirred something in a cauldron and brought another jug of beer and a loaf of rye bread to the table.

'I'm hungry,' squeaked Ciri obediently, blanching slightly. The innkeeper stopped, looked at her in a friendly way, and then looked around at the revellers.

'Can I give her some food, sir?'

'Bugger off!' yelled Skomlik indistinctly, flushing and spitting scrambled eggs. 'Get away from her, you bloody spit-turner, before I wrench your legs off! None of that! And you sit still, you gadabout, or I'll—'

'Hey, Skomlik, are you sodding crazy, or what?' interrupted Vercta, struggling to swallow a slice of bread piled high with onions. 'Look at him, boys, the skinflint. He stuffs himself on other people's money, but stints on a young girl. Give her a bowl, innkeeper. I'm paying, and I decide who gets it and who doesn't. And if anyone doesn't like it, he may get a smack in his bristly chops.'

Skomlik flushed even more, but said nothing.

'That's reminded me,' added Vercta. 'We must feed the Rat, so he won't collapse on the road, or the baron would flay us alive, trust me. The wench can feed him. Hey, innkeeper! Knock up some grub for them! And you, Skomlik, what are you grumbling about? What's not to your liking?'

'She needs to be watched,' said the Trapper, nodding at Ciri, 'because she's a strange kind of bird. Were she a normal wench, then Nilfgaard wouldn't be chasing after her, nor the prefect offering a reward ...'

'We can soon find out if she's ordinary or not,' chuckled the fat one with the topknot. 'We just need to look between her legs! How about it, boys? Shall we take her to the barn for a while?'

'Don't you dare touch her!' snapped Skomlik. 'I won't allow it!'

'Oh, really? Like we're going to ask you!'

'I'm putting the bounty and my head on the line, to deliver her there in one piece! The prefect of Amarillo—'

'Fuck your prefect. We're paying for your drinks and you're denying us some fun? Hey, Skomlik, don't be a cheapskate! And you won't get into trouble, never fear, nor will you miss out on the reward! You'll deliver her in one piece. A wench isn't a fish bladder, it doesn't pop from being squeezed!'

The Nissirs burst into loud chuckles. Skomlik's companions chimed in. Ciri shuddered, went pale and raised her head. Kayleigh smiled mockingly.

'Understand now?' he hissed from his faintly smiling mouth. 'When they get drunk, they'll start on you. They'll rape you. We're in the same boat. Do what I told you. If I escape, you will too ...'

'Grub up!' called the innkeeper. He didn't have a Nilfgaardian accent. 'Come and get it, miss!'

'A knife,' whispered Ciri, taking the bowl from him.

'What?'

'A knife. And fast.'

'If it's not enough, take more!' said the innkeeper unnaturally, sneaking a glance at the diners and putting more groats into the bowl. 'Be off with you.'

'A knife.'

'Be off or I'll call them ... I can't ... They'll burn down the inn.'

'A knife.'

'No. I feel sorry for you, missy, but I can't. I can't, you have to understand. Go away ...'

'No one,' she said, repeating Kayleigh's words in a trembling voice, 'will get out of here alive. A knife. And fast. And when it all starts, get out of here.'

'Hold the bowl, you clod!' yelled the innkeeper, turning to shield Ciri with his body. He was pale and his jaws were chattering slightly. 'Nearer the frying pan.'

She felt the cold touch of a kitchen knife, which he was sliding into her belt, covering the handle with her jacket.

'Very good,' hissed Kayleigh. 'Sit so that you're covering me. Put the bowl on my lap. Take the spoon in your left hand and the knife in your right. And cut through the twine. Not there, idiot. Under my elbow, near the post. Be careful, they're watching.'

310

Ciri's throat went dry. She lowered her head almost to the bowl.

'Feed me and eat yourself.' The green eyes staring from half-closed lids hypnotised her. 'And keep cutting. As if you meant it, little one. If I escape, you will too . . .'

True, thought Ciri, cutting through the twine. The knife smelled of iron and onion, and the blade was worn down from frequent sharpening. *He's right. Do I know where those scoundrels will take me? Do I know what that Nilfgaardian prefect wants from me? Maybe a torturer's waiting for me in Amarillo, or perhaps the wheel, gimlets and pincers. Red-hot irons . . . I won't let them lead me like a lamb to the slaughter. Better to take a chance . . .*

A tree stump came crashing in through the window, taking the frame and broken glass with it. It landed on the table, wreaking havoc among the bowls and mugs. The tree stump was followed by a young woman with close-cropped fair hair in a red doublet and high, shiny boots reaching above the knee. Crouching on the table, she whirled a sword around her head. One of the Nissirs, the slowest, who hadn't managed to get up or jump out of the way, toppled over backwards with the bench, blood spurting from his mutilated throat. The girl rolled nimbly off the table, making room for a boy in a short, embroidered sheepskin jacket to jump in through the window.

'It's the Raaats!!' yelled Vercta, struggling with his sword, which was entangled in his belt.

The fat one with the topknot drew his weapon, jumped towards the girl who was kneeling on the floor, and swung. But the girl, even though she was on her knees, deftly parried the blow, spun away, and the boy in the sheepskin jacket who had jumped in after her slashed the Nissir hard across the temple. The fat man fell to the floor, suddenly as limp as a palliasse.

The inn door was kicked open and two more Rats burst inside. The first was tall and dark, dressed in a studded kaftan and a scarlet headband. He sent two Trappers to opposite corners with swift blows of his sword and then squared off with Vercta. The second, broad-shouldered and fair-haired, ripped open Remiz, Skomlik's brother-in-law, with a sweeping blow. The others rushed to escape, heading for the kitchen door. But the Rats were already entering that

311

way too; a dark-haired girl in fabulously coloured clothes suddenly erupted from the kitchen. She stabbed one of the Trappers with a rapid thrust, forced back another with a moulinet, and then hacked the innkeeper down before he had time to identify himself.

The inn was full of uproar and the clanging of swords. Ciri hid behind the post.

'Mistle!' shouted Kayleigh, tearing apart the partially cut twine and struggling with the strap still binding his neck to the post. 'Giselher! Reef! Over here!'

The Rats were busy fighting, though, and only Skomlik heard Kayleigh's cry. The Trapper turned around and prepared to thrust, intending to pin the Rat to the post. Ciri reacted instinctively, like lightning, as she had during the fight with the wyvern in Gors Velen and on Thanedd. All the moves she had learnt in Kaer Morhen happened automatically, almost without her conscious control. She jumped out from behind the post, whirled into a pirouette, fell on Skomlik and struck him powerfully with her hip. She was too small and lightly built to shove the hefty Trapper back, but she was able to disrupt the rhythm of his movement. And draw his attention towards her.

'You bitch!'

Skomlik took a swing, his sword wailing through the air. Once again, Ciri's body instinctively made a graceful evasive manoeuvre and the Trapper almost lost his balance, lunging after his thrusting blade. Swearing foully, he struck again, putting all his strength behind the blow. Ciri dodged nimbly, landing surely on her left foot, and whirled into a pirouette in the other direction. Skomlik slashed again, but again was unable to make contact.

Vercta suddenly fell between them, spattering them both with blood. The Trapper stepped back and looked around. He was surrounded by dead bodies. And by the Rats, who were approaching from all sides with drawn swords.

'Don't move,' said the dark one in the red headband, finally releasing Kayleigh. 'It looks like he really wants to hack that girl to death. I don't know why. Nor why he hasn't managed to yet. But let's give him a chance, seeing as he wants it so much.'

'Let's give her a chance too, Giselher,' said the broad-shouldered one. 'Let it be a fair fight. Give her some hardware, Iskra.'

Ciri felt the hilt of a sword in her hand. It was a little too heavy for her.

Skomlik panted furiously, and lunged at her, brandishing his blade in a flashing moulinet. He was slow. Ciri dodged the blows which began raining down on her using quick feints and half turns, without even attempting to parry them. Her sword merely served her as a counterweight for her evasive manoeuvres.

'Incredible,' laughed the girl with the close-cropped hair. 'She's an acrobat!'

'She's fast,' said the colourful girl who had given Ciri the sword. 'Fast as a she-elf. Hey, you, fatty! Perhaps you'd prefer one of us? You're getting no change out of her!'

Skomlik withdrew, looked around, then suddenly leapt forward, trying to stab Ciri with a thrust like a heron seizing its prey. Ciri avoided the thrust with a short feint and spun away. For a second she saw a swollen, pulsating vein on Skomlik's neck. She knew that in that position he wouldn't be able to avoid the blow or parry it. She knew where and how to strike.

But she did not strike.

'That's enough.'

She felt a hand on her shoulder. The girl in the colourful costume shoved her aside, and at the same time two other Rats – the one in the short sheepskin coat and the close-cropped one – pushed Skomlik into the corner of the inn, blocking him in with their swords.

'Enough of this lark,' repeated the flamboyantly dressed girl, turning Ciri towards herself. 'It's going on too long. And you're to blame, miss. You could've killed him, but you didn't. I don't think you'll live long.'

Ciri shuddered, looking into the huge, dark, almond-shaped eyes, seeing the teeth exposed in a smile. Teeth so small they made the smile seem ghoulish. Neither the eyes nor the teeth were human. The colourful girl was an elf.

'Time to run,' said Giselher, the one in the scarlet headband, sharply. He was clearly the leader. 'It's indeed taking too long! Mistle, finish off the bastard.'

The close-cropped girl approached, raising her sword.

'Mercy!' screamed Skomlik, falling on his knees. 'Spare my life! I have young children ... Very young ...'

The girl struck savagely, twisting at the hips. Blood splashed the whitewashed wall in a wide, irregular arc of crimson flecks.

'I can't stand little children,' said the close-cropped girl, wiping blood off the fuller with a quick movement of her fingers.

'Don't just stand there, Mistle,' urged the one in the scarlet head-band. 'To horse! We must fly! It's a Nilfgaardian settlement; we don't have any friends here!'

The Rats sped out of the inn. Ciri didn't know what to do, but she didn't have time to think. Mistle, the close-cropped one, pushed her towards the door.

Outside the inn, among pieces of broken beer mugs and chewed bones, lay the bodies of the Nissirs who had been guarding the entrance. Settlers armed with lances were running up from the village, but at the sight of the Rats bursting out of the inn they disappeared among the cottages.

'Can you ride?' yelled Mistle at Ciri.

'Yes ...'

'So let's go. Grab a horse and ride! There's a bounty on our heads and this is a Nilfgaardian village! They're all grabbing bows and spears! Jump on and follow Giselher! Keep to the middle of the track and stay away from the cottages!'

Ciri hurdled a low fence, seized the reins of one of the Trappers' horses, jumped into the saddle, and slapped the horse on the rump with the flat of the sword, which had never left her hand. She set off at a swift gallop, overtaking Kayleigh and the flamboyant elf they called Iskra. She raced with the Rats towards the mill. She saw a man with a crossbow emerging from behind one of the cottages, aiming at Giselher's back.

'Cut him down!' she heard from behind her. 'Have him, girl!'

Ciri leaned back in the saddle, forcing the galloping horse to change direction with a tug of the reins and pressure from her heels, and swung her sword. The man with the crossbow turned around at the last moment and she saw his face contorted in terror. Ciri's arm, which was raised to strike, hesitated for a moment, which was enough for the galloping horse to carry her past him. She heard the clang of the bowstring being released. Her horse squealed, its croup twitched and it reared up. Ciri jumped, wrenching her feet from the stirrups and landed nimbly, dropping into a crouch. Iskra, galloping up, leaned out of the saddle to swing powerfully, and slashed the crossbowman across the back of his head. He fell to his knees, toppled forward and fell headlong into a puddle, splashing mud. The wounded horse neighed and thrashed around beside him, finally rushing off between the cottages, kicking vigorously.

'You idiot!' yelled the she-elf, passing Ciri at full pelt. 'You bloody idiot!'

'Jump on!' screamed Kayleigh, riding over to her. Ciri ran up and seized the outstretched hand. The impetus jerked her, her shoulder joint creaking, but she managed to jump onto the horse and cling to the fair-haired Rat. They galloped off, overtaking Iskra. The elf turned back, pursuing one more crossbowman, who had thrown down his weapon and fled towards some barn doors. Iskra caught him with ease. Ciri turned her head away. She heard the mutilated crossbowman howl briefly and savagely, like an animal.

Mistle caught them up, pulling a saddled riderless horse behind her. She shouted something which Ciri didn't hear properly, but understood at once. She let go of Kayleigh, jumped onto the ground at full speed, and ran over to the horse, which was dangerously close to some buildings. Mistle threw her the reins, looked around and shouted a warning. Ciri turned around just in time to avoid the treacherous thrust of a spear, dealt by a stocky settler who had appeared from behind a pigsty, with a nimble half turn.

What happened later haunted her dreams for a long time after. She remembered everything, every movement. The half turn which saved her from the spear blade placed her in an ideal position. The spearman was leaning well forward, unable either to jump away or to protect himself with the spear shaft he was holding in both hands. Ciri thrust flat, spinning the opposite way in a half turn. For a moment, she saw a mouth open to scream in a face with the bristle of several days of beard growth. She saw the forehead lengthened by a bald patch, fair-skinned above the line where a cap or hat had protected it from the sun. And then everything she saw was blotted out by a fountain of blood.

She was still holding the horse by the reins, but the horse shied, howling, and thrashed around, knocking her to her knees. Ciri did not release the reins. The wounded man moaned and wheezed, thrashing about convulsively among the straw and muck, and blood spurted from him as though from a stuck pig. She felt her gorge rising.

Right alongside, Iskra reined back her horse. Seizing the reins of the still stamping, riderless horse, she tugged, pulling Ciri – still clutching the reins – up onto her feet.

'Into the saddle!' she yelled. 'Get out of here!'

Ciri fought back nausea and jumped into the saddle. There was blood on the sword, which she was still holding. She struggled to overcome the desire to throw the weapon as far away as she could.

Mistle rushed out from between some cottages, chasing two men. One of them managed to get away, leaping over a fence, but the second, hit by a short thrust, fell to his knees, clutching his head in both hands.

Mistle and Iskra leapt into a gallop, but a moment later pulled up their horses, bracing themselves in their stirrups, because Giselher and the other Rats were returning from near the mill. Behind them rushed a pack of armed settlers, yelling loudly to summon up their courage.

'After us!' yelled Giselher, riding past at full speed. 'After us, Mistle! To the river!'

Mistle, leaning over to one side, tugged on her reins, turned her horse back and galloped after him, clearing some low wattle fences. Ciri pressed her face against her horse's mane and set off after her. Iskra galloped along beside her. The speed blew her beautiful, dark hair around, revealing a small, pointed ear decorated with a filigree earring.

The man wounded by Mistle was still kneeling in the middle of the road, rocking back and forth and holding his bloody head in both hands. Iskra wheeled her horse around, galloped up to him and struck downwards with her sword, powerfully, with all her strength. The wounded man wailed. Ciri saw his severed fingers fly up like woodchips from a chopping block and fall onto the ground like fat, white grubs.

She barely overcame the urge to vomit.

Mistle and Kayleigh waited for them by a gap in the stockade; the rest of the Rats were already far away. The foursome set off in a hard, fast gallop, and hurtled across the river, splashing water which spurted up above the horses' heads. Leaning forward, pressing their cheeks against the horses' manes, they climbed up a sandy slope and then flew across a meadow, purple with lupines. Iskra, riding the fastest horse, took the lead.

They raced into a forest, into damp shade, between the trunks of beeches. They had caught up with Giselher and the others, but they only slowed for a moment. After crossing the forest and reaching moorland, they once again set off at a gallop. Soon Ciri and Kayleigh had been left behind, the Trappers' horses unable to keep pace with the beautiful, pedigree mounts the Rats were riding. Ciri had an additional difficulty; she could barely reach the big horse's stirrups, and at a gallop was unable to adjust the stirrup leathers. She could ride without stirrups as well as she could with, but knew that in that position she would not be able to endure a gallop for long.

Fortunately, after a few minutes, Giselher slowed the pace and stopped the leading group, letting Ciri and Kayleigh catch up with them. Ciri slowed to a trot. She still couldn't shorten the stirrup leathers, since there were no holes in the straps. Without slowing, she swung her right leg over the pommel and switched to side-saddle.

Mistle, seeing the girl's riding position, burst out laughing.

'Do you see, Giselher? She isn't only an acrobat, she's a circus rider, too! Eh, Kayleigh, where did you happen upon this she-devil?'

Iskra, reining back her beautiful chestnut, skin still dry and raring to gallop on, rode over, pushing against Ciri's dapple grey. The horse neighed and stepped back, tossing its head. Ciri tightened the reins, leaning back in the saddle.

'Do you know the reason you're still alive, you cretin?' snarled the elf, pulling her hair away from her forehead. 'The peasant you so mercifully spared released the trigger too soon, so he hit the horse and not you. Otherwise you'd have a quarrel sticking into your back up to its fletchings! Why do you carry that sword?'

'Leave her alone, Iskra,' said Mistle, stroking the sweaty neck of her mount. 'Giselher, we have to slow down or we'll ride the horses into the ground! I mean, no one's chasing us right now.'

'I want to cross the Velda as quickly as possible,' said Giselher. 'We'll rest on the far bank. Kayleigh, how's your horse?'

'He'll hold out. He's no racehorse, but he's a powerful beast.'

'All right, let's go.'

'Hold on,' said Iskra. 'What about this chit?'

Giselher looked back, straightened his scarlet headband, and rested his gaze on Ciri. His face and its expression somewhat resembled Kayleigh's; the same malevolent grimace, the same narrowed eyes, the thin, protruding lower jaw. He was older than the fair-haired Rat, though, and the bluish shadow on his cheeks was evidence that he was already shaving.

'Yeah, true,' he said brusquely. 'What about you, wench?'

Ciri lowered her head.

'She helped me,' chimed in Kayleigh. 'If it hadn't been for her, that lousy Trapper would have nailed me to the post . . .'

'The villagers saw her escaping with us,' added Mistle. 'She cut one of them down and I doubt he survived. They're settlers from Nilfgaard. If the girl falls into their hands, they'll club her to death. We can't leave her.'

Iskra snorted angrily but Giselher gestured to her to be quiet.

'She can ride with us,' he decided, 'as far as Velda. Then we'll see. Ride your horse normally, maid. If you don't manage to keep up, we won't look back. Understood?'

Ciri nodded eagerly.

'Talk, girl. Who are you? Where are you from? What's your name? Why were you travelling under escort?'

Ciri lowered her head. During the ride she'd had time to try to invent a story. And she had thought up several. But the leader of the Rats didn't look like someone who would believe any of them.

'Right,' pressed Giselher. 'You've been riding with us for a few hours. You're taking breaks with us, but I haven't even heard the sound of your voice. Are you dumb?'

Fire shot upwards in flames amid a shower of sparks, flooding the ruins of the shepherd's cottage in a wave of golden light. As if obedient to Giselher's order, the fire lit up Ciri's face, in order more easily to uncover the lies and insincerity in it. *But I can't tell them the truth*, Ciri thought in desperation. *They're robbers. Brigands. If they find out about the Nilfgaardians, that the Trappers caught me for the bounty, they may want to claim it for themselves. And anyway, the truth is too far-fetched for them to believe.*

'We got you out of the settlement,' continued the gang leader slowly. 'We brought you here, to one of our hideouts. We gave you food. You're sitting at our campfire. So tell us who you are.'

'Leave her be,' said Mistle suddenly. 'When I look at you, Giselher, I see a Nissir, a Trapper or one of those Nilfgaardian sons of bitches. And I feel as if I'm being interrogated, chained to a tor-turer's bench in a dungeon!'

'Mistle's right,' said the fair-haired boy in the short sheepskin jacket. Ciri shuddered to hear his accent. 'The girl clearly doesn't want to say who she is, and it's her right. I didn't say much when I joined you, either. I didn't want you to know I'd been one of those Nilfgaardian bastards—'

'Don't talk rubbish, Reef.' Giselher waved a hand. 'It was differ-ent with you. And you, Mistle, you're wrong. It's not an interroga-tion. I want her to say who she is and where she's from. When I find out, I'll point out the way home, and that's all. How can I do that if I don't know ...?'

'You don't know anything,' said Mistle, turning to look at him. 'Not even if she has a home. And I'm guessing she doesn't. The Trappers picked her up on the road because she was alone. That's typical of those cowards. If you send her on her way she won't survive in the mountains. She'll be torn apart by wolves or die of hunger.'

'What shall we do with her, then?' asked the broad-shouldered one in an adolescent bass, jabbing a stick at the burning logs. 'Dump her outside some village or other?'

'Excellent idea, Asse,' sneered Mistle. 'Don't you know what peasants are like? They're short of labourers. They'll put her to work grazing cattle, after first injuring one of her legs so she won't be able to run away. At night, she'll be treated as nobody's property; in other words she'll be anybody's. You know how she'll have to pay for her board and lodgings. Then in spring she'll get childbed fever giving birth to somebody's brat in a dirty pigsty.'

'If we leave her a horse and a sword,' drawled Giselher, without taking his eyes off Ciri, 'I wouldn't like to be the peasant who tried to injure her leg. Or tried knocking her up. Did you see the jig she danced in the inn with that Trapper, the one Mistle finished off? He was stabbing at thin air. And she was dancing like it was nothing ... Ha, it's true, I'm more interested in where she learnt tricks like that than in her name or family. I'd love to know—'

'Tricks won't save her,' suddenly chipped in Iskra, who up until then had been busy sharpening her sword. 'She only knows how to dance. To survive, you have to know how to kill, and she doesn't.'

'I think she does,' grinned Kayleigh. 'When she slashed that guy across the neck, the blood shot up six foot in the air ...'

'And she almost fainted at the sight of it,' the elf snorted.

'Because she's still a child,' interjected Mistle. 'I think I can guess who she is and where she learnt those tricks. I've seen girls like her before. She's a dancer or an acrobat from some wandering troupe.'

'Since when have we been interested in dancers and acrobats? Dammit, it's almost midnight and I'm getting sleepy. Enough of this idle chatter. We need a good night's sleep, to be in New Forge by twilight. The village headman there – I don't think you need reminding – shopped Kayleigh to the Nissirs. So the entire village ought to see the night sky glow red. And the girl? She's got a horse, she's got a sword. She earned both of them fairly and squarely. Let's give her a bit of grub and a few pennies. For saving Kayleigh. And then let her go where she wants to. Let her take care of herself ...'

'Fine,' said Ciri, pursing her lips and standing up. A silence fell, only interrupted by the crackling of the fire. The Rats looked at her curiously, in anticipation.

'Fine,' she repeated, astonished at the strange sound of her own voice. 'I don't need you, I didn't ask for anything ... And I don't want to stay with you! I'll leave—'

'So you aren't dumb,' said Giselher sombrely. 'Not only can you speak, you're cocky, with it.'

'Look at her eyes,' snorted Iskra. 'Look how she holds her head. She's a raptor! A young falcon!'

'You want to go,' said Kayleigh. 'Where to, if I may ask?'

'What do you care?' screamed Ciri, and her eyes blazed with a green light. 'Do I ask you where you're going? I couldn't care less! And I don't care about you! You're no use to me! I can cope ... I'll manage! By myself!'

'By yourself?' repeated Mistle, smiling strangely. Ciri fell silent and lowered her head. The Rats also fell silent.

'It's night,' said Giselher finally. 'No one rides at night. And no one rides alone, girl. Anyone who's alone is sure to die. There are blankets and furs over there, by the horses. Take what you need. Nights in the mountains are cold. Why are you goggling your green eyes at me? Prepare yourself a bed and go to sleep. You need to rest.'

After a moment of thought, she did as he said. When she returned, carrying a blanket and a fur wrap, the Rats were no longer sitting around the campfire. They were standing in a semicircle, and the red gleam of the flames was reflected in their eyes.

'We are the Rats of the Marches,' said Giselher proudly. 'We can sniff out booty a mile away. We aren't afraid of traps. And there's nothing we can't bite through. We're the Rats. Come over here, girl.'

She did as she was told.

'You don't have anything,' added Giselher, handing her a belt set with silver. 'Take this at least.'

'You don't have anyone or anything,' said Mistle, smiling, throwing a green, satin tunic over her shoulders and pressing an embroidered blouse into her hands.

'You don't have anything,' said Kayleigh, and the gift from him was a small stiletto in a sheath sparkling with precious stones. 'You are all alone.'

'You don't have anyone,' Asse repeated after him. Ciri was given an ornamental pendant.

321

'You don't have any family,' said Reef in his Nilfgaardian accent, handing her a pair of soft, leather gloves. 'You don't have any family or ...'

'You will always be a stranger,' completed Iskra seemingly carelessly, placing a beret with pheasant's feathers on Ciri's head with a swift and unceremonious movement. 'Always a stranger and always different. What shall we call you, young falcon?'

Ciri looked her in the eyes.

'Gvalch'ca.'

The elf laughed.

'When you finally start speaking, you speak in many languages, Young Falcon! Let it be then. You shall bear a name of the Elder Folk, a name you have chosen for yourself. You will be Falka.'

Falka.

She couldn't sleep. The horses stamped and snorted in the darkness, and the wind soughed in the crowns of the fir trees. The sky sparkled with stars. The Eye, for so many days her faithful guide in the rocky desert, shone brightly. The Eye pointed west, but Ciri was no longer certain if that was the right way. She wasn't certain of anything any longer.

She couldn't fall asleep, although for the first time in many days she felt safe. She was no longer alone. She had made a makeshift bed of branches out of the way, some distance from the Rats, who were sleeping on the fire-warmed clay floor of the ruined shepherd's hut. She was far from them, but felt their closeness and presence. She was not alone.

She heard some quiet steps.

'Don't be afraid.'

It was Kayleigh.

'I won't tell them Nilfgaard's looking for you,' whispered the fair-haired Rat, kneeling down and leaning over her. 'I won't tell them about the bounty the prefect of Amarillo has promised for you. You saved my life in the inn. I'll repay you for it. With something nice. Right now.'

He lay down beside her, slowly and cautiously. Ciri tried to get

322

up, but Kayleigh pressed her down onto her bed with a strong and firm, though not rough, movement. He placed his fingers gently on her mouth. Although he needn't have. Ciri was paralysed with fear, and she couldn't have uttered a cry from her tight, painfully dry throat even if she had wanted to. But she didn't want to. The silence and darkness were better. Safer. More familiar. She was covered in terror and shame. She groaned.

'Be quite, little one,' whispered Kayleigh, slowly unlacing her shirt. Slowly, with gentle movements, he slid the material from her shoulders, and pulled the edge of the shirt above her hips. 'And don't be afraid. You'll see how nice it is.'

Ciri shuddered beneath the touch of the dry, hard, rough hand. She lay motionless, stiff and tense, full of an overpowering fear which took her will away, and an overwhelming sense of revulsion, which assailed her temples and cheeks with waves of heat. Kayleigh slipped his left arm beneath her head, pulled her closer to him, trying to dislodge the hand which was tightly gripping the lap of her shirt and vainly trying to pull it downwards. Ciri began to shake.

She sensed a sudden commotion in the surrounding darkness, felt a shaking, and heard the sound of a kick.

'Mistle, are you insane?' snarled Kayleigh, lifting himself up a little.

'Leave her alone, you swine.'

'Get lost. Go to bed.'

'Leave her alone, I said.'

'Am I bothering her, or something? Is she screaming or struggling? I just want to cuddle her to sleep. Don't interfere.'

'Get out of here or I'll cut you.'

Ciri heard the grinding of a knife in a metal sheath.

'I'm serious,' repeated Mistle, looming indistinctly in the dark above them. 'Get lost and join the boys. Right now.'

Kayleigh sat up and swore under his breath. He stood up without a word and walked quickly away.

Ciri felt the tears running down her cheeks, quickly, quicker and quicker, creeping like wriggling worms among the hair by her ears. Mistle lay down beside her, and covered her tenderly with the fur.

But she didn't pull the dishevelled shirt down. She left it as it had been. Ciri began to shake again.

'Be still, Falka. It's all right now.'

Mistle was warm, and smelled of resin and smoke. Her hand was smaller than Kayleigh's; more delicate, softer. More pleasant. But its touch stiffened Ciri once more, once more gripped her entire body with fear and revulsion, clenched her jaw and constricted her throat. Mistle lay close to her, cradling her protectively and whispering soothingly, but at the same time, her small hand relentlessly crept like a warm, little snail, calmly, confidently, decisively. Certain of its way and its destination. Ciri felt the iron pincers of revulsion and fear relaxing, releasing their hold; she felt herself slipping from their grip and sinking downwards, downwards, deep, deeper and deeper, into a warm and wet well of resignation and helpless submissiveness. A disgusting and humiliatingly pleasant submissiveness.

She moaned softly, desperately. Mistle's breath scorched her neck. Her moist, velvet lips tickled her shoulder, her collarbone, very slowly sliding lower. Ciri moaned again.

'Quiet, Falcon,' whispered Mistle, gently sliding her arm under her head. 'You won't be alone now. Not any more.'

The next morning, Ciri arose with the dawn. She carefully slipped out from under the fur, without waking Mistle, who was sleeping with parted lips and her forearm covering her eyes. She had goose flesh on her arm. Ciri tenderly covered the girl. After a moment's hesitation, she leaned over and kissed Mistle gently on her close-cropped hair, which stuck up like a brush. She murmured in her sleep. Ciri wiped a tear from her cheek.

She was no longer alone.

The rest of the Rats were also asleep; one of them was snoring, another farted just as loudly. Iskra lay with her arm across Giselher's chest, her luxuriant hair in disarray. The horses snorted and stamped, and a woodpecker drummed the trunk of a pine with a short series of blows.

Ciri ran down to a stream. She spent a long time washing, trembling from the cold. She washed with violent movements of her shaking hands, trying to wash off what was no longer possible to wash off. Tears ran down her cheeks.

Falka.

The water foamed and soughed on the rocks, and flowed away into the distance; into the fog.

Everything was flowing away into the distance. Into the fog.

Everything.

They were outcasts. They were a strange, mixed bag created by war, misfortune and contempt. War, misfortune and contempt had brought them together and thrown them onto the bank, the way a river in flood throws and deposits drifting, black pieces of wood smoothed by stones onto its banks.

Kayleigh had woken up in smoke, fire and blood, in a plundered stronghold, lying among the corpses of his adoptive parents and siblings. Dragging himself across the corpse-strewn courtyard, he came across Reef. Reef was a soldier from a punitive expedition, which Emperor Emhyr var Emreis had sent to crush the rebellion in Ebbing. He was one of the soldiers who had captured and plundered the stronghold after a two-day siege. Having captured it, Reef's comrades abandoned him, although Reef was still alive. Caring for the wounded was not a custom among the killers of the Nilfgaardian special squads.

At first, Kayleigh planned to finish Reef off. But Kayleigh didn't want to be alone. And Reef, like Kayleigh, was only sixteen years old.

They licked their wounds together. Together they killed and robbed a tax collector, together they gorged themselves on beer in a tavern, and later, as they rode through the village on stolen horses, they scattered the rest of the stolen money all around them, laughing their heads off.

Together, they ran from the Nissirs and Nilfgaardian patrols.

Giselher had deserted from the army. It was probably the army of the lord of Gheso who had allied himself with the insurgents from Ebbing. Probably. Giselher didn't actually know where the press gang had dragged him to. He had been dead drunk at the time.

When he sobered up and received his first thrashing from the drill sergeant, he ran away. At first, he wandered around by himself, but after the Nilfgaardians crushed the insurrectionary confederation the forests were awash with other deserters and fugitives. The fugitives quickly formed up into gangs. Giselher joined one of them.

The gang ransacked and burnt down villages, attacking convoys and transports, and then dwindled away in desperate escapes from the Nilfgaardian cavalry troops. During one of those flights, the gang happened upon some forest elves in a dense forest and met with destruction; met with invisible death, hissing down on them in the form of grey arrows flying from all sides. One of the arrows penetrated Giselher's shoulder and pinned him to a tree. The next morning, the one who pulled the arrow and dressed his wound was Aenyeweddien.

Giselher never found out why the elves had condemned Aenyeweddien to banishment, for what misdeed they had condemned her to death; since it was a death sentence for a free elf to be alone in the narrow strip of no-man's-land dividing the free Elder Folk from the humans. The solitary elf was sure to perish should she fail to find a companion.

Aenyeweddien found a companion. Her name, meaning 'Child of the Fire' in loose translation, was too difficult and too poetic for Giselher. He called her Iskra.

Mistle came from a wealthy, noble family from the city of Thurn in North Maecht. Her father, a vassal of Duke Rudiger, joined the insurrectionary army, was defeated and vanished without trace. When the people of Thurn were escaping from the city at the news of an approaching punitive expedition by the notorious Pacifiers of Gemmera, Mistle's family also fled, but Mistle got lost in the panic-stricken crowd. The elegantly dressed and delicate maiden, who had been carried in a sedan chair from early childhood, was unable to keep pace with the fugitives. After three days of solitary wandering, she fell into the hands of the manhunters who were following the Nilfgaardians. Girls younger than seventeen were in demand. As long as they were untouched. The manhunters didn't touch Mistle, not once they'd checked she really was untouched. Mistle spent the entire night following the examination sobbing.

In the valley of the River Velda, the caravan of manhunters was routed and massacred by a gang of Nilfgaardian marauders. All the manhunters and male captives were killed. Only the girls were spared. The girls didn't know why they had been spared. Their ignorance did not last long.

Mistle was the only one to survive. She was pulled out of the ditch where she had been thrown naked, covered in bruises, filth, mud and congealed blood, by Asse, the son of the village blacksmith, who had been hunting the Nilfgaardians for three days, insane with the desire for revenge for what the marauders had done to his father, mother and sisters, which he'd had to watch, hidden in a hemp field.

They all met one day during the celebrations of Lammas, the Festival of the Harvest, in one of the villages in Gheso. At the time, war and misery had not especially afflicted the lands on the upper Velda – the villages were celebrating the beginning of the Month of the Sickle traditionally, with a noisy party and dance.

They didn't take long to find each other in the merry crowd. Too much distinguished them. They had too much in common. They were united by their love of gaudy, colourful, fanciful outfits, of stolen trinkets, beautiful horses, and of swords – which they didn't even unfasten when they danced. They stood out because of their arrogance and conceit, overconfidence, mocking truculence and impetuousness.

And their contempt.

They were children of the time of contempt. And they had nothing but contempt for others. For them, only force mattered. Skill at wielding weapons, which they quickly acquired on the high roads. Resoluteness. Swift horses and sharp swords.

And companions. Comrades. Mates. Because the one who is alone will perish; from hunger, from the sword, from the arrow, from makeshift peasant clubs, from the noose, or in flames. The one who is alone will perish; stabbed, beaten or kicked to death, defiled, like a toy passed from hand to hand.

They met at the Festival of the Harvest. Grim, black-haired, lanky Giselher. Thin, long-haired Kayleigh, with his malevolent eyes and mouth set in a hateful grimace. Reef, who still spoke with a Nilfgaardian accent. Tall, long-legged Mistle, with cropped, straw-coloured hair sticking up like a brush. Big-eyed and colourful Iskra, lithe and ethereal in the dance, quick and lethal in a fight, with her narrow lips and small, elven teeth. Broad-shouldered Asse with fair, curly down on his chin.

Giselher became the leader. And they christened themselves the Rats. Someone had called them that and they took a liking to it.

They plundered and murdered, and their cruelty became legendary.

At first the Nilfgaardian prefects ignored them. They were certain that – following the example of other gangs – they would quickly fall victim to the massed ranks of furious peasantry, or that they would destroy or massacre each other themselves when the quantity of loot they collected would make cupidity triumph over criminal solidarity. The prefects were right with respect to other gangs, but were mistaken when it came to the Rats. Because the Rats, the children of contempt, scorned spoils. They attacked, robbed and killed for entertainment, and they handed out the horses, cattle, grain, forage, salt, wood tar and cloth stolen from military transports in the villages. They paid tailors and craftsmen handfuls of gold and silver for the things they loved most of all: weapons, costumes and ornaments. The recipients fed and watered them, put them up and hid them. Even when whipped raw by the Nilfgaardians and Nissirs, they did not betray the Rats' hideouts or favoured routes.

The prefects offered a generous reward; and at the beginning, there were people who were tempted by Nilfgaardian gold. But at night, the informers' cottages were set on fire, and the people escaping from the inferno died on the glittering blades of the spectral riders circling in the smoke. The Rats attacked like rats. Quietly, treacherously, cruelly. The Rats adored killing.

The prefects used methods which had been tried and tested against other gangs; several times they tried to install a traitor among the Rats. Unsuccessfully. The Rats didn't accept anyone. The close-knit and loyal group of six created by the time of contempt didn't want strangers. They despised them.

Until the day a pale-haired, taciturn girl, as agile as an acrobat,

328

appeared. A girl about whom the Rats knew nothing.

Aside from the fact that she was as they had once been; like each one of them. Lonely and full of bitterness, bitterness for what the time of contempt had taken from her.

And in times of contempt anyone who is alone must perish.

Giselher, Kayleigh, Reef, Iskra, Mistle, Asse and Falka. The prefect of Amarillo was inordinately astonished when he learnt that the Rats were now operating as a gang of seven.

'Seven?' said the prefect of Amarillo in astonishment, looking at the soldier in disbelief. 'There were seven of them, not six? Are you certain?'

'May I live and breathe,' muttered the only soldier to escape the massacre in one piece.

His wish was quite apt; his head and half of his face were swathed in dirty, bloodstained bandages. The prefect, who was no stranger to combat, knew that the sword had struck the soldier from above and from the left – with the very tip of the blade. An accurate blow, precise, demanding expertise and speed, aimed at the right ear and cheek; a place unprotected by either helmet or gorget.

'Speak.'

'We were marching along the bank of the Velda towards Thurn,' the soldier began. 'We had orders to escort one of Chamberlain Evertsen's transports heading south. They attacked us by a ruined bridge, as we were crossing the river. One wagon got bogged down, so we unharnessed the horses from another to haul it out. The rest of the convoy went on and I stayed behind with five men and the bailiff. That's when they jumped us. The bailiff, before they killed him, managed to shout that it was the Rats, and then they were on top of us ... And put paid to every last man. When I saw what was happening ...'

'When you saw what was happening,' scowled the prefect, 'you spurred on your horse. But too late to save your skin.'

'That seventh one caught up with me,' said the soldier, lowering his head. 'That seventh one, who I hadn't seen at the beginning. A young girl. Not much more than a kid. I thought the Rats had left her at the back because she was young and inexperienced ...'

The prefect's guest slipped out of the shadow from where he had been sitting.

'It was a girl?' he asked. 'What did she look like?'

'Just like all the others. Painted and done up like a she-elf, colourful as a parrot, dressed up in baubles, in velvet and brocade, in a hat with feathers—'

'Fair-haired?'

'I think so, sir. When I saw her, I rode hard, thinking I'd at least bring one down to avenge my companions; that I'd repay blood with blood ... I stole up on her from the right, to make striking easier ... How she did it, I don't know. But I missed her. As if I was striking an apparition or a wraith ... I don't know how that she-devil did it. I had my guard up but she struck through it. Right in the kisser ... Sire, I was at Sodden, I was at Aldersberg. And now I've got a souvenir for the rest of my life from a tarted-up wench ...'

'Be thankful you're alive,' grunted the prefect, looking at his guest. 'And be thankful you weren't found carved up by the river crossing. Now you can play the hero. Had you'd legged it without putting up a fight, had you reported the loss of the cargo without that souvenir, you'd soon be hanging from a noose and clicking your heels together! Very well. Dismissed. To the field hospital.'

The soldier left. The prefect turned towards his guest.

'You see for yourself, Honourable Sir Coroner, that military service isn't easy here. There's no rest; our hands are full. You there, in the capital, think all we do in the province is fool around, swill beer, grope wenches and take bribes. No one thinks about sending a few more men or a few more pennies, they just send orders: give us this, do that, find that, get everyone on their feet, dash around from dawn to dusk ... While my head's splitting from my own troubles. Five or six gangs like the Rats operate around here. True, the Rats are the worst, but not a day goes by—'

'Enough, enough,' said Stefan Skellen, pursing his lips. 'I know what your bellyaching is meant to achieve, Prefect. But you're wasting your time. No one will release you from your orders. Don't count on it. Rats or no Rats, gangs or no gangs, you are to continue with the search. Using all available means, until further notice. That is an imperial order.'

'We've been looking for three weeks,' the prefect said with a grimace. 'Without really knowing who or what we're looking for: an apparition, a ghost or a needle in a haystack. And what's the result? Only that a few men have disappeared without trace, no doubt killed by rebels or brigands. I tell you once more, coroner, if we've not found your girl yet, we'll never find her. Even if someone like her were around here, which I doubt. Unless—'

The prefect broke off and pondered, scowling at the coroner.

'That wench ... That seventh one riding with the Rats ...'

Tawny Owl waved a hand dismissively, trying to make his gesture and facial expression appear convincing.

'No, Prefect. Don't expect easy solutions. A decked out half-elf or some other female bandit in brocade is certainly not the girl we're looking for. It definitely isn't her. Continue the search. That's an order.'

The prefect became sullen and looked through the window.

'And about that gang,' added Stefan Skellen, the Coroner of Imperator Emhyr, sometimes known as Tawny Owl, in a seemingly indifferent voice, 'about those Rats, or whatever they're called ... Take them to task, Prefect. Order must prevail in the Province. Get to work. Catch them and hang them, without ceremony or fuss. All of them.'

'That's easy to say,' muttered the prefect. 'But I shall do everything in my power to, please assure the imperator of that. I think, nonetheless, that it would be worth taking that seventh girl with the Rats alive just to be sure—'

'No,' interrupted Tawny Owl, making sure not to let his voice betray him. 'Without exception, hang them all. All seven of them. We don't want to hear any more about them. Not another word.'

The story continues in...

BAPTISM OF FIRE

Book THREE of the Witcher
Keep reading for a sneak peek!

extras

orbit

meet the author

ANDRZEJ SAPKOWSKI was born in 1948 in Poland. He studied economy and business, but the success of his fantasy cycle about the sorcerer Geralt of Rivia turned him into a bestselling writer. He is now one of Poland's most famous and successful authors.

if you enjoyed
THE TIME OF CONTEMPT

look out for

BAPTISM OF FIRE
Book 3 of the Witcher

by

Andrzej Sapkowski

The Wizard's Guild has been shattered by a coup and, in the uproar, Geralt was seriously injured. The Witcher is supposed to be a guardian of the innocent, a protector of those in need, a defender against powerful and dangerous monsters that prey on men in dark times.

But now that dark times have fallen upon the world, Geralt is helpless until he has recovered from his injuries.

extras

*While war rages across all of the lands, the future of magic is
under threat and those sorcerers who survive are determined to
protect it. It's an impossible situation in which to find one girl
- Ciri, the heiress to the throne of Cintra, has vanished - until a
rumor places her in the Niflgaard court, preparing to marry the
Emperor.*

Injured or not, Geralt has a rescue mission on his hands.

CHAPTER ONE

Birds were chirping loudly in the undergrowth.

The slopes of the ravine were overgrown with a dense, tangled mass of brambles and barberry; a perfect place for nesting and feeding. Not surprisingly, it was teeming with birds. Greenfinches trilled loudly, redpolls and whitethroats twittered, and chaffinches gave out ringing 'vink-vink's every now and then. *The chaffinch's call signals rain*, thought Milva, glancing up at the sky. There were no clouds. *But chaffinches always warn of the rain. We could do with a little rain.*

Such a spot, opposite the mouth of a ravine, was a good place for a hunter, giving a decent chance of a kill – particularly here in Brokilon Forest, which was abundant with game. The dryads, who controlled extensive tracts of the forest, rarely hunted and humans dared to venture into it even less often. Here, a hunter greedy for meat or pelts became the quarry himself. The Brokilon dryads showed no mercy to intruders. Milva had once discovered that for herself.

No, Brokilon was not short of game. Nonetheless, Milva had been waiting in the undergrowth for more than two hours and nothing had crossed her line of sight. She couldn't hunt on the move; the drought which had lasted for more than a month had lined the forest floor with dry brush and leaves, which rustled and crackled at every step. In conditions like these, only standing still and unseen would lead to success, and a prize.

An admiral butterfly alighted on the nock of her bow. Milva didn't shoo it away, but watched it closing and opening its wings. She also looked at her bow, a recent acquisition which she still wasn't tired of admiring. She was a born archer and loved a good weapon. And she was holding the best of the best.

Milva had owned many bows in her life. She had learned to shoot using ordinary ash and yew bows, but soon gave them up for composite reflex bows, of the type elves and dryads used. Elven bows were shorter, lighter and more manageable and, owing to the laminated composition of wood and animal sinew, much 'quicker' than yew bows. An arrow shot with them reached the target much more swiftly and along a flatter arc, which considerably reduced the possibility of its being blown off course. The best examples of such weapons, bent fourfold, bore the elven name of *zefhar*, since the bow's shape formed that rune. Milva had used zefhars for several years and couldn't imagine a bow capable of outclassing them.

But she had finally come across one. It was, of course, at the Seaside Bazaar in Cidaris, which was renowned for its diverse selection of strange and rare goods brought by sailors from the most distant corners of the world; from anywhere a frigate or galleon could reach. Whenever she could, Milva would visit the bazaar and look at the foreign bows. It was there she bought the bow she'd thought would serve her for many years. She had thought the zefhar from Zerrikania, reinforced with polished antelope horn, was perfect. For just a year. Twelve months later, at the same market stall, owned by the same trader, she had found another rare beauty.

The bow came from the Far North. It measured just over five feet, was made of mahogany, had a perfectly balanced riser and flat, laminated limbs, glued together from alternating layers of fine wood, boiled sinew and whalebone. It differed from the other composite bows in its construction and also in its price; which is what had initially caught Milva's attention. When, however, she picked up the bow and flexed it, she paid the price the trader was asking without hesitation or haggling. Four hundred Novigrad crowns. Naturally, she didn't have such a titanic sum on her; instead she had given up her Zerrikanian zefhar, a bunch of sable pelts, a small, exquisite elven-made medallion, and a coral cameo pendant on a string of river pearls.

But she didn't regret it. Not ever. The bow was incredibly light and, quite simply, perfectly accurate. Although it wasn't long it had an impressive kick to its laminated wood and sinew limbs. Equipped with a silk and hemp bowstring stretched between its precisely curved limbs, it generated fifty-five pounds of force from a twenty-four-inch draw. True enough, there were bows that could generate eighty, but Milva considered that excessive. An arrow shot from her whalebone fifty-fiver covered a distance of two hundred feet in two heartbeats, and at a hundred paces still had enough force to impale a stag, while it would pass right through an unarmoured human. Milva rarely hunted animals larger than red deer or heavily armoured men.

The butterfly flew away. The chaffinches continued to make a racket in the undergrowth. And still nothing crossed her line of sight. Milva leant against the trunk of a pine and began to think back. Simply to kill time.

Her first encounter with the Witcher had taken place in July, two weeks after the events on the Isle of Thanedd and the outbreak of war in Dol Angra. Milva had returned to Brokilon after a fortnight's absence; she was leading the remains of a Scoia'tael commando defeated in Temeria during an attempt to make their way into war-torn Aedirn. The Squirrels had wanted to join the uprising incited by the elves in Dol Blathanna. They had failed, and would have perished had it not been for Milva. But they'd found her, and refuge in Brokilon.

Immediately on her arrival, she had been informed that Aglaïs needed her urgently in Col Serrai. Milva had been a little taken aback. Aglaïs was the leader of the Brokilon healers, and the deep valley of Col Serrai, with its hot springs and caves, was where healings usually took place.

She responded to the call, convinced it concerned some elf who had been healed and needed her help to re-establish contact with his commando. But when she saw the wounded witcher and learned what it was about, she was absolutely furious. She ran from the cave with her hair streaming behind her and offloaded all her anger on Aglaïs.

'He saw me! He saw my face! Do you understand what danger that puts me in?'

'No, no I don't understand,' replied the healer coldly. 'That is Gwynbleidd, the Witcher, a friend of Brokilon. He has been here for a fortnight, since the new moon. And more time will pass before he will be able to get up and walk normally. He craves tidings from the world; news about those close to him. Only you can supply him with that.'

'Tidings from the world? Have you lost your mind, dryad? Do you know what is happening in the world now, beyond the borders of your tranquil forest? A war is raging in Aedirn! Brugge, Temeria and Redania are reduced to havoc, hell, and much slaughter! Those who instigated the rebellion on Thanedd are being hunted high and low! There are spies and an'givare – informers – everywhere; it's sometimes sufficient to let slip a single word, make a face at the wrong moment, and you'll meet the hangman's red-hot iron in the dungeon! And you want me to creep around spying, asking questions, gathering information? Risking my neck? And for whom? For some half-dead witcher? And who is he to me? My own flesh and blood? You've truly taken leave of your senses, Aglaïs.'

'If you're going to shout,' interrupted the dryad calmly, 'let's go deeper into the forest. He needs peace and quiet.'

Despite herself, Milva looked over at the cave where she had seen the wounded witcher a moment earlier. *A strapping lad,* she had thought, *thin, yet sinewy . . . His hair's white, but his belly's as flat as a young man's; hard times have been his companion, not lard and beer . . .*

'He was on Thanedd,' she stated; she didn't ask. 'He's a rebel.'

'I know not,' said Aglaïs, shrugging. 'He's wounded. He needs help. I'm not interested in the rest.'

Milva was annoyed. The healer was known for her taciturnity. But Milva had already heard excited accounts from dryads in the eastern marches of Brokilon; she already knew the details of the events that had occurred a fortnight earlier. About the chestnut-haired sorceress who had appeared in Brokilon in a burst of magic; about the cripple with a broken arm and leg she had been dragging with her. A cripple who had turned out to be the Witcher, known to the dryads as Gwynbleidd: the White Wolf.

At first, according to the dryads, no one had known what steps to take. The mutilated witcher screamed and fainted by turns, Aglaïs had applied makeshift dressings, the sorceress cursed and wept. Milva did not believe that at all: who has ever seen a sorceress weep? And later the order came from Duén Canell, from the silver-eyed Eithné, the Lady of Brokilon. Send the sorceress away, said the ruler of the Forest of the Dryads. And tend to the Witcher.

And so they did. Milva had seen as much. He was lying in a cave, in a hollow full of water from the magical Brokilon springs. His limbs, which had been held in place using splints and put in traction, were swathed in a thick layer of the healing climbing plant – conynhaela – and turfs of knitbone. His hair was as white as milk. Unusually, he was conscious: anyone being treated with conynhaela normally lay lifeless and raving as the magic spoke through them . . .

'Well?' the healer's emotionless voice tore her from her reverie. 'What is it going to be? What am I to tell him?'

'To go to hell,' snapped Milva, lifting her belt, from which hung a heavy purse and a hunting knife. 'And you can go to hell, too, Aglaïs.'

'As you wish. I shall not compel you.'

'You are right. You will not.'

She went into the forest, among the sparse pines, and didn't look back. She was angry.

Milva knew about the events which had taken place during the first July new moon on the Isle of Thanedd; the Scoia'tael talked about it endlessly. There had been a rebellion during the Mages' Conclave on the island. Blood had been spilt and heads had rolled. And, as if on a signal, the armies of Nilfgaard had attacked Aedirn and Lyria and the war had begun. And in Temeria, Redania and Kaedwen it was all blamed on the Squirrels. For one thing, because a commando of Scoia'tael had supposedly come to the aid of the rebellious mages on Thanedd. For another, because an elf or possibly half-elf had supposedly stabbed and killed Vizimir, King of Redania. So the furious humans had gone after the Squirrels with a vengeance. The fighting was raging everywhere and elven blood was flowing in rivers . . .

Ha, thought Milva, *perhaps what the priests are saying is true after all and the end of the world and the day of judgement are close at hand? The world is in flames, humans are preying not only on elves but on other humans too. Brothers are raising knives against brothers . . . And the Witcher is meddling in politics . . . and joining the rebellion. The Witcher, who is meant to roam the world and kill monsters eager to harm humans! No witcher, for as long as anyone can remember, has ever allowed himself to be drawn into politics or war. Why, there's even the tale about a foolish king who carried water in a sieve, took a hare as a messenger, and appointed a witcher as a palatine. And yet here we have the Witcher, carved up in a rebellion against the kings and forced to escape punishment in Brokilon. Perhaps it truly is the end of the world!*

'Greetings, Maria.'

She started. The short dryad leaning against a pine had eyes and hair the colour of silver. The setting sun gave her head a halo against the background of the motley wall of trees. Milva dropped to one knee and bowed low.

'My greetings to you, Lady Eithné.'

The ruler of Brokilon stuck a small, crescent-shaped, golden knife into a bast girdle.

'Arise,' she said. 'Let us take a walk. I wish to talk with you.'

They walked for a long time through the shadowy forest; the delicate, silver-haired dryad and the tall, flaxen-haired girl. Neither of them broke the silence for some time.

'It is long since you were at Duén Canell, Maria.'

'There was no time, Lady Eithné. It is a long road to Duén Canell from the River Ribbon, and I . . . But of course you know.'

'That I do. Are you weary?'

'The elves need my help. I'm helping them on your orders, after all.'

'At my request.'

'Indeed. At your request.'

'And I have one more.'

'As I thought. The Witcher?'

'Help him.'

Milva stopped and turned back, breaking an overhanging twig of honeysuckle with a sharp movement, turning it over in her fingers before flinging it to the ground.

'For half a year,' she said softly, looking into the dryad's silvery eyes, 'I have risked my life guiding elves from their decimated commandos to Brokilon . . . When they are rested and their wounds healed, I lead them out again . . . Is that so little? Haven't I done enough? Every new moon, I set out on the trail in the dark of the night. I've begun to fear the sun as much as a bat or an owl does . . .'

'No one knows the forest trails better than you.'

'I will not learn anything in the greenwood. I hear that the Witcher wants me to gather news, by moving among humans. He's a rebel, the ears of the an'givare prick up at the sound of his name. I must be careful not to show myself in the cities. And what if someone recognises me? The memories still endure, the blood is not yet dry . . . for there was a lot of blood, Lady Eithné.'

'A great deal.' The silver eyes of the old dryad were alien, cold; inscrutable. 'A great deal, indeed.'

'Were they to recognise me, they would impale me.'

'You are prudent. You are cautious and vigilant.'

'In order to gather the tidings the Witcher requests, it is necessary to shed vigilance. It is necessary to ask. And now it is dangerous to demonstrate curiosity. Were they to capture me—'

'You have contacts.'

'They would torture me. Until I died. Or grind me down in Drakenborg—'

'But you are indebted to me.'

Milva turned her head away and bit her lip.

'It's true, I am,' she said bitterly. 'I have not forgotten.'

She narrowed her eyes, her face suddenly contorted, and she clenched her teeth tightly. The memory shone faintly beneath her eyelids; the ghastly moonlight of that night. The pain in her ankle suddenly returned, held tight by the leather snare, and the pain in her joints, after they had been cruelly wrenched. She heard again the soughing of leaves as the tree shot suddenly upright ... Her screaming, moaning; the desperate, frantic, horrified struggle and the invasive sense of fear which flowed over her when she realised she couldn't free herself ... The cry and fear, the creak of the rope, the rippling shadows; the swinging, unnatural, upturned earth, upturned sky, trees with upturned tops, pain, blood pounding in her temples ...

And at dawn the dryads, all around her, in a ring ... The distant silvery laughter ... *A puppet on a string! Swing, swing, marionette, little head hanging down* ... And her own, unnatural, wheezing cry. And then darkness.

'Indeed, I have a debt,' she said through clenched teeth. 'Indeed, for I was a hanged man cut from the noose. As long as I live, I see, I shall never pay off that debt.'

'Everyone has some kind of debt,' replied Eithné. 'Such is life, Maria Barring. Debts and liabilities, obligations, gratitude, payments ... Doing something for someone. Or perhaps for ourselves? For in fact we are always paying ourselves back and not someone else. Each time we are indebted we pay off the debt to ourselves. In each of us lies a creditor and a debtor at once and the art is for the reckoning to tally inside us. We enter the world as a minute part of the life we are given, and from then on we are ever paying off debts. To ourselves. For ourselves. In order for the final reckoning to tally.'

'Is this human dear to your, Lady Eithné? That ... that witcher?'

'He is. Although he knows not of it. Return to Col Serrai, Maria Barring. Go to him. And do what he asks of you.'

BAPTISM OF FIRE

BAPTISM OF FIRE

ANDRZEJ SAPKOWSKI

Translated by David French

www.orbitbooks.net

Then the soothsayer spake thus to the witcher: 'This counsel I shall give you: don hobnailed boots and take an iron staff. Walk in your hobnailed boots to the end of the world, tap the road in front of you with the staff, and let your tears fall. Go through fire and water, do not stop, do not look back. And when your boots are worn out, when your iron staff is worn down, when the wind and the sun have dried your eyes such that not a single tear will fall from them, then you will find what you are searching for, what you love, at the end of the world. Perhaps.'

And the witcher walked through fire and water, never looking back. But he took neither hobnailed boots nor a staff. He took only his witcher's sword. He obeyed not the words of the soothsayer. And rightly so, for she was wicked.

Flourens Delannoy, *Tales and Legends*

BAPTISM OF FIRE

CHAPTER ONE

Birds were chirping loudly in the undergrowth.

The slopes of the ravine were overgrown with a dense, tangled mass of brambles and barberry; a perfect place for nesting and feeding. Not surprisingly, it was teeming with birds. Greenfinches trilled loudly, redpolls and whitethroats twittered, and chaffinches gave out ringing 'vink-vink's every now and then. *The chaffinch's call signals rain*, thought Milva, glancing up at the sky. There were no clouds. *But chaffinches always warn of the rain. We could do with a little rain.*

Such a spot, opposite the mouth of a ravine, was a good place for a hunter, giving a decent chance of a kill – particularly here in Brokilon Forest, which was abundant with game. The dryads, who controlled extensive tracts of the forest, rarely hunted and humans dared to venture into it even less often. Here, a hunter greedy for meat or pelts became the quarry himself. The Brokilon dryads showed no mercy to intruders. Milva had once discovered that for herself.

No, Brokilon was not short of game. Nonetheless, Milva had been waiting in the undergrowth for more than two hours and nothing had crossed her line of sight. She couldn't hunt on the move; the drought which had lasted for more than a month had lined the forest floor with dry brush and leaves, which rustled and crackled at every step. In conditions like these, only standing still and unseen would lead to success, and a prize.

An admiral butterfly alighted on the nock of her bow. Milva didn't shoo it away, but watched it closing and opening its wings. She also looked at her bow, a recent acquisition which she still wasn't tired of admiring. She was a born archer and loved a good weapon. And she was holding the best of the best.

Milva had owned many bows in her life. She had learned to shoot using ordinary ash and yew bows, but soon gave them up for composite reflex bows, of the type elves and dryads used. Elven bows were shorter, lighter and more manageable and, owing to the laminated composition of wood and animal sinew, much 'quicker' than yew bows. An arrow shot with them reached the target much more swiftly and along a flatter arc, which considerably reduced the possibility of its being blown off course. The best examples of such weapons, bent fourfold, bore the elven name of *zefhar*, since the bow's shape formed that rune. Milva had used zefhars for several years and couldn't imagine a bow capable of outclassing them.

But she had finally come across one. It was, of course, at the Seaside Bazaar in Cidaris, which was renowned for its diverse selection of strange and rare goods brought by sailors from the most distant corners of the world; from anywhere a frigate or galleon could reach. Whenever she could, Milva would visit the bazaar and look at the foreign bows. It was there she bought the bow she'd thought would serve her for many years. She had thought the zefhar from Zerrikania, reinforced with polished antelope horn, was perfect. For just a year. Twelve months later, at the same market stall, owned by the same trader, she had found another rare beauty.

The bow came from the Far North. It measured just over five feet, was made of mahogany, had a perfectly balanced riser and flat, laminated limbs, glued together from alternating layers of fine wood, boiled sinew and whalebone. It differed from the other composite bows in its construction and also in its price; which is what had initially caught Milva's attention. When, however, she picked up the bow and flexed it, she paid the price the trader was asking without hesitation or haggling. Four hundred Novigrad crowns. Naturally, she didn't have such a titanic sum on her; instead she had given up her Zerrikanian zefhar, a bunch of sable pelts, a small, exquisite elven-made medallion, and a coral cameo pendant on a string of river pearls.

But she didn't regret it. Not ever. The bow was incredibly light and, quite simply, perfectly accurate. Although it wasn't long it had an impressive kick to its laminated wood and sinew limbs. Equipped with a silk and hemp bowstring stretched between its

2

precisely curved limbs, it generated fifty-five pounds of force from a twenty-four-inch draw. True enough, there were bows that could generate eighty, but Milva considered that excessive. An arrow shot from her whalebone fifty-fiver covered a distance of two hundred feet in two heartbeats, and at a hundred paces still had enough force to impale a stag, while it would pass right through an unarmoured human. Milva rarely hunted animals larger than red deer or heavily armoured men.

The butterfly flew away. The chaffinches continued to make a racket in the undergrowth. And still nothing crossed her line of sight. Milva leant against the trunk of a pine and began to think back. Simply to kill time.

Her first encounter with the Witcher had taken place in July, two weeks after the events on the Isle of Thanedd and the outbreak of war in Dol Angra. Milva had returned to Brokilon after a fortnight's absence; she was leading the remains of a Scoia'tael commando defeated in Temeria during an attempt to make their way into war-torn Aedirn. The Squirrels had wanted to join the uprising incited by the elves in Dol Blathanna. They had failed, and would have perished had it not been for Milva. But they'd found her, and refuge in Brokilon.

Immediately on her arrival, she had been informed that Aglaïs needed her urgently in Col Serrai. Milva had been a little taken aback. Aglaïs was the leader of the Brokilon healers, and the deep valley of Col Serrai, with its hot springs and caves, was where healings usually took place.

She responded to the call, convinced it concerned some elf who had been healed and needed her help to re-establish contact with his commando. But when she saw the wounded witcher and learned what it was about, she was absolutely furious. She ran from the cave with her hair streaming behind her and offloaded all her anger on Aglaïs.

'He saw me! He saw my face! Do you understand what danger that puts me in?'

'No, no I don't understand,' replied the healer coldly. 'That is

3

Gwynbleidd, the Witcher, a friend of Brokilon. He has been here for a fortnight, since the new moon. And more time will pass before he will be able to get up and walk normally. He craves tidings from the world; news about those close to him. Only you can supply him with that.'

'Tidings from the world? Have you lost your mind, dryad? Do you know what is happening in the world now, beyond the borders of your tranquil forest? A war is raging in Aedirn! Brugge, Temeria and Redania are reduced to havoc, hell, and much slaughter! Those who instigated the rebellion on Thanedd are being hunted high and low! There are spies and an'givare – informers – everywhere; it's sometimes sufficient to let slip a single word, make a face at the wrong moment, and you'll meet the hangman's red-hot iron in the dungeon! And you want me to creep around spying, asking questions, gathering information? Risking my neck? And for whom? For some half-dead witcher? And who is he to me? My own flesh and blood? You've truly taken leave of your senses, Aglaïs.'

'If you're going to shout,' interrupted the dryad calmly, 'let's go deeper into the forest. He needs peace and quiet.'

Despite herself, Milva looked over at the cave where she had seen the wounded witcher a moment earlier. *A strapping lad*, she had thought, *thin, yet sinewy . . . His hair's white, but his belly's as flat as a young man's; hard times have been his companion, not lard and beer . . .*

'He was on Thanedd,' she stated; she didn't ask. 'He's a rebel.'

'I know not,' said Aglaïs, shrugging. 'He's wounded. He needs help. I'm not interested in the rest.'

Milva was annoyed. The healer was known for her taciturnity. But Milva had already heard excited accounts from dryads in the eastern marches of Brokilon; she already knew the details of the events that had occurred a fortnight earlier. About the chestnut-haired sorceress who had appeared in Brokilon in a burst of magic; about the cripple with a broken arm and leg she had been dragging with her. A cripple who had turned out to be the Witcher, known to the dryads as Gwynbleidd: the White Wolf.

At first, according to the dryads, no one had known what steps to take. The mutilated witcher screamed and fainted by turns, Aglaïs

4

had applied makeshift dressings, the sorceress cursed and wept. Milva did not believe that at all: who has ever seen a sorceress weep? And later the order came from Duén Canell, from the silver-eyed Eithné, the Lady of Brokilon. Send the sorceress away, said the ruler of the Forest of the Dryads. And tend to the Witcher.

And so they did. Milva had seen as much. He was lying in a cave, in a hollow full of water from the magical Brokilon springs. His limbs, which had been held in place using splints and put in traction, were swathed in a thick layer of the healing climbing plant – conynhaela – and turfs of knitbone. His hair was as white as milk. Unusually, he was conscious: anyone being treated with conynhaela normally lay lifeless and raving as the magic spoke through them . . .

'Well?' the healer's emotionless voice tore her from her reverie. 'What is it going to be? What am I to tell him?'

'To go to hell,' snapped Milva, lifting her belt, from which hung a heavy purse and a hunting knife. 'And you can go to hell, too, Aglaïs.'

'As you wish. I shall not compel you.'

'You are right. You will not.'

She went into the forest, among the sparse pines, and didn't look back. She was angry.

Milva knew about the events which had taken place during the first July new moon on the Isle of Thanedd; the Scoia'tael talked about it endlessly. There had been a rebellion during the Mages' Conclave on the island. Blood had been spilt and heads had rolled. And, as if on a signal, the armies of Nilfgaard had attacked Aedirn and Lyria and the war had begun. And in Temeria, Redania and Kaedwen it was all blamed on the Squirrels. For one thing, because a commando of Scoia'tael had supposedly come to the aid of the rebellious mages on Thanedd. For another, because an elf or pos- sibly half-elf had supposedly stabbed and killed Vizimir, King of Redania. So the furious humans had gone after the Squirrels with a vengeance. The fighting was raging everywhere and elven blood was flowing in rivers . . .

Ha, thought Milva, *perhaps what the priests are saying is true after all and the end of the world and the day of judgement are close at hand?*

5

The world is in flames, humans are preying not only on elves but on other humans too. Brothers are raising knives against brothers . . . And the Witcher is meddling in politics . . . and joining the rebellion. The Witcher, who is meant to roam the world and kill monsters eager to harm humans! No witcher, for as long as anyone can remember, has ever allowed himself to be drawn into politics or war. Why, there's even the tale about a foolish king who carried water in a sieve, took a hare as a messenger, and appointed a witcher as a palatine. And yet here we have the Witcher, carved up in a rebellion against the kings and forced to escape punishment in Brokilon. Perhaps it truly is the end of the world!

'Greetings, Maria.'

She started. The short dryad leaning against a pine had eyes and hair the colour of silver. The setting sun gave her head a halo against the background of the motley wall of trees. Milva dropped to one knee and bowed low.

'My greetings to you, Lady Eithné.'

The ruler of Brokilon stuck a small, crescent-shaped, golden knife into a bast girdle.

'Arise,' she said. 'Let us take a walk. I wish to talk with you.'

They walked for a long time through the shadowy forest; the delicate, silver-haired dryad and the tall, flaxen-haired girl. Neither of them broke the silence for some time.

'It is long since you were at Duén Canell, Maria.'

'There was no time, Lady Eithné. It is a long road to Duén Canell from the River Ribbon, and I . . . But of course you know.'

'That I do. Are you weary?'

'The elves need my help. I'm helping them on your orders, after all.'

'At my request.'

'Indeed. At your request.'

'And I have one more.'

'As I thought. The Witcher?'

'Help him.'

Milva stopped and turned back, breaking an overhanging twig of honeysuckle with a sharp movement, turning it over in her fingers before flinging it to the ground.

6

'For half a year,' she said softly, looking into the dryad's silvery eyes, 'I have risked my life guiding elves from their decimated commandos to Brokilon . . . When they are rested and their wounds healed, I lead them out again . . . Is that so little? Haven't I done enough? Every new moon, I set out on the trail in the dark of the night. I've begun to fear the sun as much as a bat or an owl does . . .'

'No one knows the forest trails better than you.'

'I will not learn anything in the greenwood. I hear that the Witcher wants me to gather news, by moving among humans. He's a rebel, the ears of the an'givare prick up at the sound of his name. I must be careful not to show myself in the cities. And what if someone recognises me? The memories still endure, the blood is not yet dry . . . for there was a lot of blood, Lady Eithné.'

'A great deal.' The silver eyes of the old dryad were alien, cold; inscrutable. 'A great deal, indeed.'

'Were they to recognise me, they would impale me.'

'You are prudent. You are cautious and vigilant.'

'In order to gather the tidings the Witcher requests, it is necessary to shed vigilance. It is necessary to ask. And now it is dangerous to demonstrate curiosity. Were they to capture me—'

'You have contacts.'

'They would torture me. Until I died. Or grind me down in Drakenborg—'

'But you are indebted to me.'

Milva turned her head away and bit her lip.

'It's true, I am,' she said bitterly. 'I have not forgotten.'

She narrowed her eyes, her face suddenly contorted, and she clenched her teeth tightly. The memory shone faintly beneath her eyelids; the ghastly moonlight of that night. The pain in her ankle suddenly returned, held tight by the leather snare, and the pain in her joints, after they had been cruelly wrenched. She heard again the soughing of leaves as the tree shot suddenly upright . . . Her screaming, moaning; the desperate, frantic, horrified struggle and the invasive sense of fear which flowed over her when she realised she couldn't free herself . . . The cry and fear, the creak of the rope, the rippling shadows; the swinging, unnatural, upturned earth,

7

upturned sky, trees with upturned tops, pain, blood pounding in her temples . . .

And at dawn the dryads, all around her, in a ring . . . The distant silvery laughter . . . *A puppet on a string! Swing, swing, marionette, little head hanging down* . . . And her own, unnatural, wheezing cry. And then darkness.

'Indeed, I have a debt,' she said through clenched teeth. 'Indeed, for I was a hanged man cut from the noose. As long as I live, I see, I shall never pay off that debt.'

'Everyone has some kind of debt,' replied Eithné. 'Such is life, Maria Barring. Debts and liabilities, obligations, gratitude, payments . . . Doing something for someone. Or perhaps for ourselves? For in fact we are always paying ourselves back and not someone else. Each time we are indebted we pay off the debt to ourselves. In each of us lies a creditor and a debtor at once and the art is for the reckoning to tally inside us. We enter the world as a minute part of the life we are given, and from then on we are ever paying off debts. To ourselves. For ourselves. In order for the final reckoning to tally.'

'Is this human dear to your, Lady Eithné? That . . . that witcher?'

'He is. Although he knows not of it. Return to Col Serrai, Maria Barring. Go to him. And do what he asks of you.'

In the valley, the brushwood crunched and a twig snapped. A magpie gave a noisy, angry 'chacker-chacker', and some chaffinches took flight, flashing their white wing bars and tail feathers. Milva held her breath. At last.

Chacker-chacker, called the magpie. Chacker-chacker-chacker. Another twig cracked.

Milva adjusted the worn, polished leather guard on her left forearm, and placed her hand through the loop attached to her gear. She took an arrow from the flat quiver on her thigh. Out of habit, she checked the arrowhead and the fletchings. She bought shafts at the market – choosing on average one out of every dozen offered to her – but she always fletched them herself. Most ready-made arrows in circulation had too-short fletchings arranged straight along the shaft, while Milva only used spirally fletched arrows, with the fletchings never shorter than five inches.

She nocked the arrow and stared at the mouth of the ravine, at a green spot of barberry among the trees, heavy with bunches of red berries. The chaffinches had not flown far and began their trilling again. *Come on, little one*, thought Milva, raising the bow and drawing the bowstring. *Come on. I'm ready.*

But the roe deer headed along the ravine, towards the marsh and springs which fed the small streams flowing into the Ribbon. A young buck came out of the ravine. A fine specimen, weighing in – she estimated – at almost four stone. He lifted his head, pricked up his ears, and then turned back towards the bushes, nibbling leaves.

With his back toward her, he was an easy victim. Had it not been for a tree trunk obscuring part of the target, Milva would have fired without a second thought. Even if she were to hit him in the belly, the arrow would penetrate and pierce the heart, liver or lungs. Were she to hit him in the haunch, she would destroy an artery, and the animal would be sure to fall in a short time. She waited, without releasing the bowstring.

The buck raised his head again, stepped out from behind the trunk and abruptly turned round a little. Milva, holding the bow at full draw, cursed under her breath. A shot face-on was uncertain; instead of hitting the lung, the arrowhead might enter the stomach. She waited, holding her breath, aware of the salty taste of the bowstring against the corner of her mouth. That was one of the most important, quite invaluable, advantages of her bow; were she to use a heavier or inferior weapon, she would never be able to hold it fully drawn for so long without tiring or losing precision with the shot.

Fortunately, the buck lowered his head, nibbled on some grass protruding from the moss and turned to stand sideways. Milva exhaled calmly, took aim at his chest and gently released her fingers from the bowstring.

She didn't hear the expected crunch of ribs being broken by the arrow, however. For the buck leapt upwards, kicked and fled,

9

accompanied by the crackling of dry branches and the rustle of leaves being shoved aside.

Milva stood motionless for several heartbeats, petrified like a marble statue of a forest goddess. Only when all the noises had subsided did she lift her hand from her cheek and lower the bow. Having made a mental note of the route the animal had taken as it fled, she sat down calmly, resting her back against a tree trunk. She was an experienced hunter, she had poached in the lord's forests from a child. She had brought down her first roe deer at the age of eleven, and her first fourteen-point buck on the day of her fourteenth birthday – an exceptionally favourable augury. And experience had taught that one should never rush after a shot animal. If she had aimed well, the buck would fall no further than two hundred paces from the mouth of the ravine. Should she have been off target – a possibility she actually didn't contemplate – hurrying might only make things worse. A badly injured animal, which wasn't agitated, would slow to a walk after its initial panicked flight. A frightened animal being pursued would race away at breakneck speed and would only slow down once it was over the hills and far away.

So she had at least half an hour. She plucked a blade of grass, stuck it between her teeth and drifted off in thought once again. The memories came back.

When she returned to Brokilon twelve days later, the Witcher was already up and about. He was limping somewhat and slightly dragging one hip, but he was walking. Milva was not surprised – she knew of the miraculous healing properties of the forest water and the herb conynhaela. She also knew Aglaïs's abilities and on several occasions had witnessed the astonishingly quick return to health of wounded dryads. And the rumours about the exceptional resistance and endurance of witchers were also clearly no mere myths either.

She did not go to Col Serrai immediately on her arrival, although the dryads hinted that Gwynbleidd had been impatiently awaiting her return. She delayed intentionally, still unhappy with her mission and wanting to make her feelings clear. She escorted the Squirrels back to their camp. She gave a lengthy account of the incidents on the road and warned the dryads about the plans to seal the border on the Ribbon by humans. Only when she was rebuked for the third time did Milva bathe, change and go to the Witcher.

He was waiting for her at the edge of a glade by some cedars. He was walking up and down, squatting from time to time and then straightening up with a spring. Aglaïs had clearly ordered him to exercise.

'What news?' he asked immediately after greeting her. The coldness in his voice didn't deceive her.

'The war seems to be coming to an end,' she answered, shrugging. 'Nilfgaard, they say, has crushed Lyria and Aedirn. Verden has surrendered and the King of Temeria has struck a deal with the Nilfgaardian emperor. The elves in the Valley of Flowers have established their own kingdom but the Scoia'tael from Temeria and Redania have not joined them. They are still fighting . . .'

'That isn't what I meant.'

'No?' she said, feigning surprise. 'Oh, I see. Well, I stopped in Dorian, as you asked, though it meant going considerably out of my way. And the highways are so dangerous now . . .'

She broke off, stretching. This time he didn't hurry her.

'Was Codringher,' she finally asked, 'whom you asked me to visit, a close friend of yours?'

The Witcher's face did not twitch, but Milva knew he understood at once.

'No. He wasn't.'

'That's good,' she continued easily. 'Because he's no longer with us. He went up in flames along with his chambers; probably only the chimney and half of the façade survived. The whole of Dorian is abuzz with rumours. Some say Codringher was dabbling in black magic and concocting poisons; that he had a pact with the devil, so the devil's fire consumed him. Others say he'd stuck his nose and his fingers into a crack he shouldn't have, as was his custom. And it wasn't to somebody's liking, so they bumped him off and set everything alight, to cover their tracks. What do you think?'

She didn't receive a reply, or detect any emotion on his ashen face. So she continued, in the same venomous, arrogant tone of voice.

11

'It's interesting that the fire and Codringher's death occurred during the first July new moon, exactly when the unrest on the Isle of Thanedd was taking place. As if someone had guessed that Codringher knew something about the disturbances and would be asked for details. As if someone wanted to stop his trap up good and proper in advance, strike him dumb. What do you say to that? Ah, I see you won't say anything. You're keeping quiet, so I'll tell you this: your activities are dangerous, and so is your spying and questioning. Perhaps someone will want to shut other traps and ears than Codringher's. That's what I think.'

'Forgive me,' he said a moment later. 'You're right. I put you at risk. It was too dangerous a task for a—'

'For a woman, you mean?' she said, jerking her head back, flicking her still wet hair from her shoulder with a sudden movement. 'Is that what you were going to say? Are you playing the gentleman all of a sudden? I may have to squat to piss, but my coat is lined with wolf skin, not coney fur! Don't call me a coward, because you don't know me!'

'I do,' he said in a calm, quiet voice, not reacting to her anger or raised voice. 'You are Milva. You lead Squirrels to safety in Brokilon, avoiding capture. Your courage is known to me. But I recklessly and selfishly put you at risk—'

'You're a fool!' she interrupted sharply. 'Worry about yourself, not about me. Worry about that young girl!'

She smiled disdainfully. Because this time his face did change. She fell silent deliberately, waiting for further questions.

'What do you know?' he finally asked. 'And from whom?'

'You had your Codringher,' she snorted, lifting her head proudly. 'And I have my own contacts. The kind with sharp eyes and ears.'

'Tell me, Milva. Please.'

'After the fighting on Thanedd,' she began, after waiting a moment, 'unrest erupted everywhere. The hunt for traitors began, particularly for any sorcerers who supported Nilfgaard and for the other turncoats. Some were captured, others vanished without trace. You don't need much nous to guess where they fled to and under whose wings they're hiding. But it wasn't just sorcerers and traitors who were hunted. A Squirrel commando led by the famous Faoiltiarna also helped the mutinous sorcerers in the rebellion on Thanedd. So now he's wanted. An order has been issued that every elf captured should be tortured and interrogated about Faoiltiarna's commando.'

'Who's Faoiltiarna?'

'An elf, one of the Scoia'tael. Few have got under the humans' skin the way he has. There's a hefty bounty on his head. But they're seeking another too. A Nilfgaardian knight who was on Thanedd. And also for a . . .'

'Go on.'

'The an'givare are asking about a witcher who goes by the name of Geralt of Rivia. And about a girl named Cirilla. Those two are to be captured alive. It was ordered on pain of death: if either of you is caught, not a hair on your heads is to be harmed, not a button may be torn from her dress. Oh! You must be dear to their hearts for them to care so much about your health . . .'

She broke off, seeing the expression on his face, from which his unnatural composure had abruptly disappeared. She realised that however hard she tried, she was unable to make him afraid. At least not for his own skin. She unexpectedly felt ashamed.

'Well, that pursuit of theirs is futile,' she said gently, with just a faintly mocking smile on her lips. 'You are safe in Brokilon. And they won't catch the girl alive either. When they searched through the rubble on Thanedd, all the debris from that magical tower which collapsed— Hey, what's wrong with you?'

The Witcher staggered, leant against a cedar, and sat down heavily near the trunk. Milva leapt back, horrified by the pallor which his already whitened face had suddenly taken on.

'Aglaïs! Sirssa! Fauve! Come quickly! Damn, I think he's about to keel over! Hey, you!'

'Don't call them . . . There's nothing wrong with me. Speak. I want to know . . .'

Milva suddenly understood.

'They found nothing in the debris!' she cried, feeling herself go

13

pale too. 'Nothing! Although they examined every stone and cast spells, they didn't find . . .'

She wiped the sweat from her forehead and held back with a gesture the dryads running towards them. She seized the Witcher by his shoulders and leant over him so that her long hair tumbled over his pale face.

'You misunderstood me,' she said quickly, incoherently; it was difficult to find the right words among the mass which were trying to tumble out. 'I only meant— You understood me wrongly. Because I . . . How was I to know she is so . . . No . . . I didn't mean to. I only wanted to say that the girl . . . That they won't find her, because she disappeared without a trace, like those mages. Forgive me.'

He didn't answer. He looked away. Milva bit her lip and clenched her fists.

'I'm leaving Brokilon again in three days,' she said gently after a long, very long, silence. 'The moon must wane a little and the nights become a little darker. I shall return within ten days, perhaps sooner. Shortly after Lammas, in the first days of August. Worry not. I shall move earth and water, but I shall find out everything. If anyone knows anything about that maiden, you'll know it too.'

'Thank you, Milva.'

'I'll see you in ten days . . . Gwynbleidd.'

'Call me Geralt,' he said, holding out a hand. She took it without a second thought. And squeezed it very hard.

'And I'm Maria Barring.'

A nod of the head and the flicker of a smile thanked her for her sincerity. She knew he appreciated it.

'Be careful, please. When you ask questions, be careful who you ask.'

'Don't worry about me.'

'Your informers . . . Do you trust them?'

'I don't trust anyone.'

'The Witcher is in Brokilon. Among the dryads.'

'As I thought,' Dijkstra said, folding his arms on his chest. 'But I'm glad it's been confirmed.'

14

He remained silent for a moment. Lennep licked his lips. And waited.

'I'm glad it's been confirmed,' repeated the head of the secret service of the Kingdom of Redania, pensively, as though he were talking to himself. 'It's always better to be certain. If only Yennefer were with him . . . There isn't a witch with him, is there, Lennep?'

'I beg your pardon?' the spy started. 'No, Your Lordship. There isn't. What are your orders? If you want him alive, I'll lure him out of Brokilon. But if you'd prefer him dead . . .'

'Lennep,' said Dijkstra, raising his cold, pale blue eyes towards the agent. 'Don't be overzealous. In our trade, officiousness never pays and should always be viewed with suspicion.'

'Sire,' said Lennep, blanching somewhat. 'I only—'

'I know. You only asked about my orders. Well, here they are: leave the Witcher alone.'

'Yes, sire. And what about Milva?'

'Leave her alone, too. For now.'

'Yes, sire. May I go?'

'You may.'

The agent left, cautiously and silently closing the oak door behind him. Dijkstra remained silent for a long time, staring at the towering pile of maps, letters, denunciations, interrogation reports and death sentences in front of him.

'Ori.'

The secretary raised his head and cleared his throat. He said nothing.

'The Witcher is in Brokilon.'

Ori Reuven cleared his throat again, involuntarily glancing under the table, towards his boss's leg. Dijkstra noticed the look.

'That's right. I won't let him get away with that,' he barked. 'I couldn't walk for two weeks because of him. I lost face with Philippa, forced to whimper like a dog and beg her for a bloody spell, otherwise I'd still be hobbling. I can't blame anyone but myself; I underestimated him. But the worst thing is that I can't get my own back and tan his witcher's hide! I don't have the time, and anyway, I can't use my own men to settle private scores! That's right isn't it, Ori?'

15

'Ahem . . .'

'Don't grunt at me. I know. But, hell, power tempts! How it beguiles, invites to be made use of! How easy it is to forget, when one has it! But if you forget once, there's no end to it . . . Is Philippa Eilhart still in Montecalvo?'

'Yes.'

'Take a quill and an inkwell. I'll dictate a letter to her. I shall begin . . . Damn it, I can't concentrate. What's that bloody racket, Ori? What's happening in the square?'

'Some students are throwing stones at the Nilfgaardian envoy's residence. We paid them to do so, hem, hem, if I'm not mistaken.'

'Oh. Very well. Close the window. And have the lads throw stones at the dwarf Giancardi's bank, tomorrow. He refused to reveal the details of some accounts.'

'Giancardi, hem, hem, donated a considerable sum of money to the military fund.'

'Ha. Then have them throw stones at the banks that didn't donate.'

'They all did.'

'Oh, you're boring me, Ori. Write, I said. Darling Phil, the sun of my . . . Blast, I keep forgetting. Take a new sheet of paper. Ready?'

'Of course, hem, hem.'

'Dear Philippa. Mistress Triss Merigold is sure to be worried about the witcher she teleported from Thanedd to Brokilon, which she kept so secret that even I didn't know anything. It hurt me terribly. Please reassure her: the Witcher is doing well now. He has even begun to send female emissaries from Brokilon to search for traces of Princess Cirilla, the young girl you're so interested in. Our good friend Geralt clearly doesn't know Cirilla is in Nilfgaard, where she's preparing for her wedding to Imperator Emhyr. It's important to me that the Witcher lies low in Brokilon, which is why I'll do my best to ensure the news reaches him. Have you got that?'

'Hem, hem . . . the news reaches him.'

'New paragraph! It puzzles me . . . Ori, wipe the bloody quill! We're writing to Philippa, not to the royal council. The letter must look neat! New paragraph. It puzzles me why the Witcher hasn't tried to make contact with Yennefer. I refuse to believe that his passion,

16

which was verging on obsession, has petered out so suddenly, irrespective of learning his darling's political objectives. On the other hand, if Yennefer is the one who handed Cirilla over to Emhyr, and if there's proof of it, I would gladly make sure the Witcher was furnished with it. The problem would solve itself, I'm certain, and the faithless, black-haired beauty would be on very shaky ground. The Witcher doesn't like it when anyone touches his little girl, as Artaud Terranova discovered on Thanedd in no uncertain terms. I would like to think, Phil, that you don't have any evidence of Yennefer's betrayal and you don't know where she is hiding. It would hurt me greatly to discover this is the latest secret being concealed from me. I have no secrets from you . . . What are you sniggering about, Ori?'

'Oh, nothing, hem, hem.'

'Write! I have no secrets from you, Phil, and I count on reciprocity. With my deepest respect, et cetera, et cetera. Give it here, I'll sign it.'

Ori Reuven sprinkled the letter with sand. Dijkstra made himself more comfortable, interlacing his fingers over his stomach and twiddling his thumbs.

'That Milva, the Witcher's spy,' he asked. 'What can you tell me about her?'

'She is engaged at present, hem, hem' – his secretary coughed – 'in escorting the remnants of Scoia'tael units defeated by the Temerian Army to Brokilon. She rescues elves from hunts and traps, enabling them to rest and regroup into combat commandos . . .'

'Refrain from supplying me with common knowledge,' interrupted Dijkstra. 'I'm familiar with Milva's activities, and will eventually make use of them. Otherwise I would have sold her out to the Temerians long since. What can you tell me about Milva herself? As a person?'

'She comes, if I'm not mistaken, from some godforsaken village in Upper Sodden. Her true name is Maria Barring. Milva is a nickname the dryads gave her. In the Elder Speech it means—'

'Red Kite,' interrupted Dijkstra. 'I know.'

'Her family have been hunters for generations. They are forest dwellers, and feel most comfortable in the greenwood. When old

17

Barring's son was trampled to death by an elk, the old man taught his daughter the forest crafts. After he passed away, her mother married again. Hem, hem . . . Maria didn't get on with her step-father and ran away from home. She was sixteen at the time, if I'm not mistaken. She headed north, living from hunting, but the lords' gamekeepers didn't make her life easy, hunting and harrying her as though she were fair game. So she began to poach in Brokilon and it was there, hem, hem, that the dryads got hold of her.'

'And instead of finishing her off, they took her in,' Dijkstra muttered. 'Adopted her, if you will . . . And she repaid their kindness. She struck a pact with the Hag of Brokilon, old silver-eyed Eithné. Maria Barring is dead; long live Milva . . . How many human expeditions had come unstuck by the time the forces in Verden and Kerack cottoned on? Three?'

'Hem, hem . . . Four, if I'm not mistaken . . .' Ori Reuven was always hoping he wasn't mistaken, although in fact his memory was infallible. 'All together, it was about five score humans, those who'd gone after dryad scalps most savagely. And it took them a long time to catch on, because Milva occasionally carried someone out of the slaughter on her own back, and whoever she'd rescued would praise her courage to the skies. It was only after the fourth time, in Verden, if I'm not mistaken, that someone caught on. "Why is it?" the shout suddenly went up, hem, hem, "that the guide who bands humans together to fight the dryads always gets out in one piece?" And the cat was out of the bag. The guide *was* leading them. But into a trap, right into the shooting range of the dryads waiting in ambush . . .'

Dijkstra slid an interrogation report to the edge of his desk, because the parchment still seemed to reek of the torture chamber.

'And then,' he concluded, 'Milva vanished into Brokilon like the morning mist. And it's still difficult to find volunteers for expeditions against the dryads in Verden. Old Eithné and young Red Kite were carrying out pretty effective purges. And they dare say that we, humans, invented all the dirty tricks. On the other hand . . .'

'Hem, hem?' coughed Ori Reuven, surprised by his boss's sudden – and then continuing – silence.

'On the other hand, they may have finally begun to learn from us,' said the spy coldly, looking down at the denunciations, interrogation reports and death sentences.

Milva grew anxious when she couldn't see blood anywhere near where the buck had disappeared. She suddenly recalled that he had jumped just as she had fired her arrow. Had jumped or was about to; it amounted to the same thing. He had moved and the arrow might have hit him in the belly. Milva cursed. A shot to the belly was a disgrace for any hunter! Urgh, the very thought of it!

She quickly ran over to the slope of the ravine, looking carefully among the brambles, moss and ferns. She was hunting for her arrow. It was equipped with four blades so sharp they could shave the hairs on your forearm. Fired from a distance of fifty paces the arrow must have passed right through the animal.

She searched, she found it and sighed in relief, then spat three times, happy with her luck. She needn't have worried; it was better than she had imagined. The arrow was not covered in sticky, foul-smelling stomach contents. Neither did it bear traces of bright, pink, frothy blood from the lungs. What covered the shaft was dark red and viscous. The arrow had gone through the heart. Milva didn't have to creep or stalk; she had been spared a long walk following the deer's tracks. The buck had to be lying in the undergrowth, no more than a hundred paces from the clearing, in a spot that would be surely indicated by the blood. And after being shot through the heart, he would have started bleeding after a few paces, so she knew she would easily find the trail.

She picked it up after ten paces and followed it, once again losing herself in her reverie.

She kept the promise she had given the Witcher. She returned to Brokilon five days after the Harvest Festival – five days after the new moon – which marked the beginning of the month of August for people, and for elves, Lammas, the seventh and penultimate savaed of the year.

She crossed the Ribbon at daybreak with five elves. The

19

commando she was leading had initially numbered nine riders, but the soldiers from Brugge were following them the whole time. Three furlongs before the river they were hot on their trail, pressing hard, and only abandoned their efforts when they reached the Ribbon, with Brokilon looming up in the dawn mists on the far bank. The soldiers were afraid of Brokilon and that alone saved the commando. They made it across. Exhausted and wounded. But not all of them.

She had news for the Witcher, but thought that Gwynbleidd was still in Col Serrai. She had intended to see him around noon, after a good long sleep so she was astonished when he suddenly emerged from the fog like a ghost. He sat down beside her without a word, watching as she made herself a makeshift bed by spreading a blanket over a heap of branches.

'You're in a hurry, Witcher,' she scoffed. 'I'm ready to drop. I've been in the saddle all day and all night, my backside's numb, and my trousers are soaked up to my belt, for we crept our way through the wetlands at dawn like a pack of wolves . . .'

'Please. Did you learn anything?'

'Yes I did,' she snorted, unlacing and pulling off her drenched, clinging boots. 'Without much difficulty, because everybody's talking about it. You never told me your young girl was such a personage! I'd thought she was your stepdaughter, some sort of waif and stray, a star-crossed orphan. And who does she turn out to be? A Cintran princess! Well! And perhaps you're a prince in disguise?'

'Tell me, please.'

'The kings won't get their hands on her now, for your Cirilla, it turns out, fled straight from Thanedd to Nilfgaard; probably with those treacherous mages. And Imperator Emhyr received her there with all ceremony. And do you know what? He's said to be thinking of marrying her. Now let me rest. We can talk after I've slept, if you want.'

The Witcher said nothing. Milva hung her wet footwraps on a forked branch, positioned so that the rising sun's rays would fall on them, and tugged at her belt buckle.

'I want to get undressed,' she growled. 'Why are you still hanging about? You can't have expected happier news, can you? You're in no danger; no one's asking after you, the spies have stopped being interested in you. And your wench has escaped from the clutches of the kings and will be declared Imperatoress . . .'

'Is that information reliable?'

'Nothing is certain these days,' she yawned, sitting down on her bed, 'apart from the fact that the sun journeys across the heavens from the east to the west. But what people are saying about the Nilfgaardian Imperator and the Princess of Cintra seems to be true. It's all anyone's talking about.'

'Why this sudden interest?'

'You really don't know? She's said to be bringing Emhyr a goodly acreage of land in her dowry! And not just Cintra, but land on this side of the Yaruga too! Ha, and she'll be my Lady as well, for I'm from Upper Sodden, and the whole of Sodden, it turns out, is her fiefdom! So if I bring down a buck in her forests and they lay hands on me, I can be hung on her orders . . . Oh, what a rotten world! And a pox on it, I can't keep my eyes open . . .'

'Just one more question. Did they capture any sorceresses— I mean did they capture anyone from that pack of treacherous sorcerers?'

'No. But one enchantress, they say, took her own life. Soon after Vengerberg fell and the Kaedwen Army entered Aedirn. No doubt out of distress, or fear of torture—'

'There were riderless horses in the commando you brought here. Would the elves give me one?'

'Oh, in a hurry, I see,' she muttered, wrapping herself in the blanket. 'I think I know where you're planning to . . .'

She fell silent, astonished by the expression on his face before she realised that the news she had brought was not at all happy. She saw that she understood nothing, nothing at all. Suddenly, unexpectedly, unawares, she felt the urge to sit down by his side, bombard him with questions, listen to him, learn more, perhaps offer counsel . . . She urgently ground her knuckles into the corners of her eyes. *I'm exhausted,* she thought, *death was breathing down my neck all night. I have to rest. And anyway, why should I be bothered by his sorrows and cares? What does he matter to me? And that wench? To hell with him and with her! A pox on it, all this has driven the sleep from me...*

The Witcher stood up.

'Will the elves give me a horse?' he repeated.

'Take whichever you please,' she said a moment later. 'But don't let them see you. They gave us a good hiding by the ford, blood was spilt ... And don't touch the black; he's mine ... What are you waiting for?'

'Thank you for your help. For everything.'

She didn't answer.

'I'm indebted to you. How shall I pay you back?'

'How? By getting out of my sight!' she cried, raising herself on an elbow and tugging sharply at the blanket. 'I ... I have to sleep! Take a horse ... and go ... To Nilfgaard, to hell, to all the devils. Makes no difference to me! Go away and leave me in peace!'

'I'll pay back what I owe,' he said quietly. 'I won't forget. It may happen that one day you'll be in need of help. Or support. A shoulder to lean on. Then call out, call out in the night. And I'll come.'

The buck lay on the edge of the slope, which was spongy from gushing springs and densely overgrown with ferns, his neck contorted, with a glassy eye staring up at the sky. Milva saw several large ticks bored into his light brown belly.

'You'll have to find yourselves some other blood, vermin,' she muttered, rolling up her sleeves and drawing a knife. 'Because this is going cold.'

With a swift and practised movement, she slit the skin from sternum to anus, adroitly running the blade around the genitalia. She cautiously separated the layer of fat, up to her elbows in blood. She severed the gullet and pulled the entrails out. She cut open the stomach and gall bladder, hunting for bezoars. She didn't believe in their magical qualities, but there was no shortage of fools who did and would pay well for them.

She lifted the buck and laid him on a nearby log, his slit belly pointing downwards, letting the blood drain out. She wiped her hands on a bunch of ferns.

She sat down by her quarry.

'Possessed, insane Witcher,' she said softly, staring at the crowns of the Brokilon pines looming a hundred feet above her. 'You're heading for Nilfgaard to get your wench. You're heading to the end of the world, which is all in flames, and you haven't even thought about supplying yourself with victuals. I know you have someone to live for. But do you have anything to live on?'

Naturally enough, the pines didn't comment or interrupt her monologue.

'I don't think,' Milva said, using her knife to scrape the blood out from beneath her fingernails, 'you have the slightest chance of getting your young girl back. You won't make it to the Yaruga, never mind Nilfgaard. I don't think you'll even make it to Sodden. I think you're fated to die. It's written on your fierce face, it's staring through your hideous eyes. Death will catch up with you, O mad Witcher, it'll catch up with you soon. But thanks to this little buck at least it won't be death by starvation. It may not be much, but it's something. That's what I think.'

Dijkstra sighed to himself at the sight of the Nilfgaardian ambassador entering the audience chamber. Shilard Fitz-Oesterlen, Imperator Emhyr var Emreis's envoy, was accustomed to conducting conversations in diplomatic language, and adored larding his sentences with pompous linguistic oddities, comprehensible only to diplomats and scholars. Dijkstra had studied at the Academy of Oxenfurt, and although he had not been awarded the title of Master of Letters, he knew the basics of bombastic scholarly jargon. However, he was reluctant to use it, since he hated with a vengeance pomposity and all forms of pretentious ceremony.

'Greetings, Your Excellency.'

'Your Lordship,' Shilard Fitz-Oesterlen said, bowing ceremoniously. 'Ah, please forgive me. Perhaps I ought to say: Your Grace the Duke? Your Highness the Regent? Secretary of State? 'Pon my word, offices are falling on you like hailstones, such that I really don't know how to address you so as not to breach protocol.'

'"Your Majesty" would be best,' Dijkstra replied modestly. 'You are aware after all, Your Excellency, that the king is judged by his court. And you are probably aware that when I shout: "Jump!" the court in Tretogor asks: "How high?"'

The ambassador knew that Dijkstra was exaggerating, but not inordinately. Prince Radovid was still a minor, Queen Hedwig distraught by her husband's tragic death, and the aristocracy intimidated, stupefied, at variance and divided into factions. Dijkstra was the *de facto* governor of Redania and could have taken any rank he pleased with no difficulty. But Dijkstra had no desire to do so.

'Your Lordship deigned to summon me,' the ambassador said a moment later. 'Passing over the Foreign Minister. To what do I owe this honour?'

'The minister,' Dijkstra said, looking up at the ceiling, 'resigned from the post owing to his poor state of health.'

The ambassador nodded gravely. He knew perfectly well that the Foreign Minister was languishing in a dungeon and, being a coward and a fool, had doubtless told Dijkstra everything about his collusion with the Nilfgaardian secret service during the demonstration of torture instruments preceding his interrogation. He knew that the network established by Vattier de Rideaux, head of the imperial secret service, had been crushed, and all its threads were in Dijkstra's hands. He also knew that those threads led directly to his person. But his person was protected by immunity and protocol forced them to play this game to the bitter end. Particularly following the curious, encoded instructions recently sent to the embassy by Vattier and Coroner Stephan Skellen, the imperial agent for special affairs.

'Since his successor has not yet been named,' Dijkstra continued, 'it is my unpleasant duty to inform you that Your Excellency is now deemed *persona non grata* in the Kingdom of Redania.'

The ambassador bowed.

'I regret,' he said, 'that the distrust that resulted in the mutual recall of ambassadors are the consequence of matters which, after all, directly concern neither the Kingdom of Redania nor the Nilfgaardian Empire. The Empire has not undertaken any hostile measures against Redania.'

'Apart from a blockade against our ships and goods at the mouth of the Yaruga and the Skellige Islands. And apart from arming and supporting gangs of Scoia'tael.'

'Those are insinuations.'

'And the concentration of imperial forces in Verden and Cintra? The raids on Sodden and Brugge by armed gangs? Sodden and Brugge are under Temerian protection; we in turn are in alliance with Temeria, Your Excellency, which makes an attack on Temeria an attack on us. In addition, there are matters which directly concern Redania: the rebellion on the Isle of Thanedd and the criminal assassination of King Vizimir. And the question of the role the Empire played in those incidents.'

'*Quod attinet* the incident on Thanedd,' the ambassador said, spreading his arms, 'I have not been empowered to express an opinion. His Imperial Highness Emhyr var Emreis is unaware of the substance of the private feuds of your mages. I regret the fact that our protests are achieving minimal success in the face of the propaganda which seeks to suggest something else. Propaganda disseminated, I dare say, not without the support of the highest authorities of the Kingdom of Redania.'

'Your protests greatly astonish and surprise me,' Dijkstra said, smiling faintly. 'Since the Imperator in no way conceals the presence of the Cintran princess at his court, after she was abducted from the very same Thanedd.'

'Cirilla, *Queen* of Cintra,' Shilard Fitz-Oesterlen corrected him with emphasis, 'was not abducted, but sought asylum in the Empire. That has nothing to do with the incident on Thanedd.'

'Indeed?'

'The incident on Thanedd,' the ambassador continued, his countenance stony, 'aroused the Imperator's horror. And the murderous attack on the life of King Vizimir, carried out by a madman, evoked his sincere and intense abomination. However, the vile rumour being disseminated among the common people is an even greater abomination, which dares to search for the instigators of these crimes in the Empire.'

'The capture of the actual instigators,' Dijkstra said slowly, 'will put an end to the rumours, one would hope. And their capture and the meting out of justice to them is purely a matter of time.'

'*Justitia fundamentum regnorum*,' admitted Shilard Fitz-Oesterlen gravely. 'And *crimen horribilis non potest non esse punibile*. I affirm that His Imperial Majesty also wishes this to happen.'

'The Imperator has it in his power to fulfil that wish,' Dijkstra threw in casually, folding his arms. 'One of the leaders of the conspiracy, Enid an Gleanna, until recently the sorceress Francesca Findabair, is playing at being queen of the elven puppet state in Dol Blathanna, by the imperial grace.'

'His Imperial Majesty,' said the ambassador, bowing stiffly, 'cannot interfere in the doings of Dol Blathanna, recognised by all its neighbouring powers as an independent kingdom.'

'But not by Redania. For Redania, Dol Blathanna remains part of the Kingdom of Aedirn. Although together with the elves and Kaedwen you have dismantled Aedirn – although not a stone remains of Lyria – you are striking those kingdoms too swiftly from the map of the world. It's too soon, Your Excellency. However, this is neither the time nor the place to discuss it. Let Francesca Findabair play at reigning for now; she'll get her comeuppance. And what of the other rebels and King Vizimir's assassins? What about Vilgefortz of Roggeveen, what about Yennefer of Vengerberg? There are grounds to believe they both fled to Nilfgaard following the collapse of the rebellion.'

'I assure you that is not so,' said the ambassador, raising his head. 'But were it true, they would not escape punishment.'

'They did not wrong you, thus their punishment does not rest with you. Imperator Emhyr would prove his sincere desire for justice, which after all is *fundamentum regnorum*, by handing the criminals over to us.'

'One may not deny the validity of your request,' admitted Shilard Fitz-Oesterlen, feigning an embarrassed smile. 'However, *primo*, those individuals are not in the Empire. And *secundo*, had they even reached it, there exists an impediment. Extradition is carried out on the basis of a judgment of the law, each case decided upon by the Imperial Council. Bear in mind, Your Lordship, that the breaking of diplomatic ties by Redania is a hostile act; it would be difficult to expect the Council to vote in favour of the extradition of persons seeking asylum, were a hostile country to demand that extradition. It would be an unprecedented matter . . . Unless . . .'

'Unless what?'

'A precedent were established.'

'I do not understand.'

'Were the Kingdom of Redania prepared to hand one of his subjects to the Imperator, a common criminal who had been captured here, the Imperator and his Council would have grounds to reciprocate this gesture of good will.'

Dijkstra said nothing for a long time, giving the impression he was either dozing or thinking.

'Whom do you have in mind?'

'The name of the criminal . . .' said the ambassador, pretending to recall it. He finally searched for a document in his saffian portfolio. 'Forgive me, *memoria fragilis est*. Here it is. A certain Cahir Mawr Dyffryn aep Ceallach. Serious gravamina weigh on him. He is being sought for murder, desertion, *raptus puellae*, rape, theft and forging documents. Fleeing from the Imperator's wrath, he escaped abroad.'

'To Redania? He chose a long route.'

'Your Lordship,' said Shilard Fitz-Oesterlen, smiling faintly, 'does not limit his interests only to Redania, after all. There is not a shadow of doubt in my mind that were the criminal to be seized in any of the allied kingdoms, Your Lordship would hear of it from the reports of numerous . . . friends.'

'What did you say the name of the felon was?'

'Cahir Mawr Dyffryn aep Ceallach.'

Dijkstra fell silent again, pretending to be searching in his memory.

'No,' he said finally. 'No one of that name has been apprehended.'

'Indeed?'

'Regrettably, my *memoria* is not *fragilis* in such cases, Your Excellency.'

'I regret it too,' Shilard Fitz-Oesterlen responded icily. 'Particularly since the mutual extradition of criminals seems to be impossible to

27

carry out in such circumstances. I shall not weary Your Lordship any longer. I wish you good health and good fortune.'

'Likewise. Farewell, Your Excellency.'

The ambassador left, after several elaborate, ceremonial bows.

'You can kiss *sempiternum meam*, you sly old devil,' Dijkstra muttered, folding his arms. 'Ori!'

His secretary, red in the face from suppressing his cough, emerged from behind a curtain.

'Is Philippa still in Montecalvo?'

'Yes, hem, hem. Mistresses Laux-Antille, Merigold and Metz are with her.'

'War may break out in a day or two, the border on the Yaruga will soon go up in flames, and they've hidden themselves in some godforsaken castle! Take a quill and write. Darling Phil . . . Oh, bugger!'

'I've written: "Dear Philippa".'

'Good. Continue. It may interest you that the freak in the plumed helmet, who disappeared from Thanedd as mysteriously as he appeared, is called Cahir Mawr Dyffryn and is the son of Seneschal Ceallach. This strange individual is being sought not only by us, but also, it would appear, by the secret service of Vattier de Rideaux and the men of that son-of-a-bitch . . .'

'Mistress Philippa, hem, hem, does not like expressions of that kind. I have written: "that scoundrel".'

'Let it be: that scoundrel Stephan Skellen. You know as well as I do, dear Phil, that the imperial secret service is urgently hunting only those agents and emissaries who got under Emhyr's skin. Those who, instead of carrying out their orders or dying, betrayed him and their orders alike. The case thus appears quite curious, since we were certain that this Cahir's orders concerned the capture of Princess Cirilla and her delivery to Nilfgaard.

'New paragraph: I would like to discuss in person the strange, but well-founded suspicions this matter has evoked in me, and the somewhat astonishing, but reasonable theories I have arrived at. With my deepest respect et cetera, et cetera.'

*

28

Milva rode south, as the crow flies, first along the banks of the Ribbon, through Burn Stump, and then, having crossed the river, through marshy gorges covered in a soft, bright green carpet of hair-cap moss. She guessed that the Witcher, not knowing the terrain as well as she did, would not risk crossing onto the human-controlled bank. Taking a short cut across a huge bend in the river, which curved towards Brokilon, there was a chance she might catch up with him in the region of the Ceann Treise Falls. Were she to ride hard and not take a break, she even stood a chance of overtaking him.

The chirruping chaffinches hadn't been mistaken. The sky had clouded over considerably to the south. The air had become dense and heavy, and the mosquitoes and horseflies extremely annoying.

When she rode into the wetlands, thick with hazel hung with still-green nuts and leafless, blackish buckthorn, she felt a presence. She didn't hear it. She felt it. And so she knew it must be elves.

She reined in her horse, so the bowmen concealed in the under-growth could have a good look at her. She also held her breath. In the hope that she hadn't happened upon quick-tempered ones.

A fly buzzed over the buck, which was slung over the horse's rump.

A rustling. A soft whistling. She whistled back. The Scoia'tael emerged from the brush soundlessly and only then did Milva breathe freely again. She knew them. They belonged to Coinneach Dá Reo's commando.

'Hael,' she said, dismounting. 'Que'ss va?'

'Ne'ss,' an elf whose name she couldn't recall replied coldly. 'Caemm.'

Other elves were encamped in the nearby clearing. There were at least thirty of them, more than there should be in Coinneach's com-mando. This surprised Milva; in recent times, Squirrel units were more likely to shrink than grow in size. In recent times, commandos had become groups of bloodied, nervy ragamuffins who could barely stand or stay upright in the saddle. This commando was different.

'Cead, Coinneach,' she greeted the approaching commander.

'Ceadmil, sor'ca.'

Sor'ca. Little sister. It's how she was addressed by those she was friendly with, when they wanted to express their respect and affection. And that they were indeed many, many more winters older than she. At first, she had only been Dh'oine – human – to the elves. Later, when she had begun helping them regularly, they called her Aen Woedbeanna, 'woman of the forest'. Still later, when they knew her better, they called her – following the dryads' example – Milva, or Red Kite. Her real name, which she only revealed to those she was closest to, responding to similar gestures received from them, didn't suit the elves – they pronounced it Mear'ya, with a hint of a grimace, as though in their speech it carried negative connotations. Then they would immediately switch to 'sor'ca'.

'Where are you headed?' asked Milva, looking around more intently, but still not seeing any wounded or ill elves. 'To Eight-Mile? To Brokilon?'

'No.'

She refrained from further questions; she knew them too well. It was enough to glance several times at their motionless, hardened faces, at the exaggerated, pointed calm with which they were preparing their tackle and weapons. One close look into their deep, fathomless eyes was enough. She knew they were going into battle.

To the south the sky was darkening, becoming overcast.

'And where are you headed, sor'ca?' asked Coinneach, then quickly glanced at the buck slung over her horse and smiled faintly.

'South,' she said coldly, putting him right. 'Towards Drieschot.'

The elf stopped smiling.

'Along the human bank?'

'At least as far as Ceann Treise,' she said, shrugging. 'When I reach the falls I'll definitely go back over to the Brokilon side, because . . .'

She turned around, hearing the snorting of horses. Fresh Scoia'tael were joining the already unusually large commando. Milva knew these new ones even better.

'Ciaran!' she shouted softly, without attempting to hide her astonishment. 'Toruviel! What are you doing here? I've only just led you to Brokilon, and you're already—'

'Ess'creasa, sor'ca,' Ciaran aep Dearbh said gravely. The bandage swathed around his head was stained with oozing blood.

'We have no choice,' Toruviel repeated. She dismounted cautiously using one arm, in order to protect the other one, which was still bent in a sling. 'News has come. We may not remain in Brokilon, when every bow counts.'

'If I had known,' Milva said, pouting, 'I wouldn't have bothered. I wouldn't have risked my neck at the ford.'

'News came last night,' explained Toruviel quietly. 'We could not . . . We cannot leave our comrades in arms at a time like this. We cannot. Understand that, sor'ca.'

The sky had darkened even more. This time Milva clearly heard thunder in the distance.

'Don't ride south, sor'ca,' Coinneach Dá Reo pleaded. 'There's a storm coming.'

'What can a storm do to. . . ?' She broke off and looked at him intently. 'Ah! So that kind of tidings have reached you, have they? It's Nilfgaard, is it? They are crossing the Yaruga in Sodden? They are striking Brugge? And that's why you're marching?'

He did not answer.

'Yes, just like it was in Dol Angra,' she said, looking into his dark eyes. 'Once again the Nilfgaardian Imperator has you sowing mayhem with fire and sword on the humans' rear lines. And then he will make peace with the kings and they will slaughter you all. You will burn in the very fire you are starting.'

'Fire purges. And hardens. It must be passed through. Aenyell'hael, ell'ea, sor'ca? In your tongue: a baptism of fire.'

'I prefer another kind of fire,' Milva said, untying the buck and throwing it down onto the ground at the feet of the elves. 'The kind that crackles under the spit. Have it, so you won't fall from hunger on the march. It's of no use to me now.'

'Aren't you riding south?'

'I am.'

I'm going south, she thought, *and quickly. I have to warn that fool of a witcher, I have to warn him about what kind of a turmoil he's getting himself into. I have to make him turn back.*

31

'Don't go, sor'ca.'

'Give me a break, Coinneach.'

'A storm is coming from the south,' the elf repeated. 'A great tempest is coming. And a great fire. Hide in Brokilon, little sister, don't ride south. You've done enough for us, you cannot do any more now. And you do not have to. We have to. Ess'tedd, esse creasa! It is time we left. Farewell.'

The air around them was heavy and dense.

The teleprojective spell was complicated; they had to cast it together, joining their hands and thoughts. Even then, it turned out to be a devilishly great effort. Because the distance was considerable too.

Philippa Eilhart's tightly closed eyelids twitched, Triss Merigold panted and there were beads of sweat on Keira Metz's high forehead. Only on Margarita Laux-Antille's face was there no sign of fatigue.

It suddenly became very bright in the poorly lit chamber and a mosaic of flashes danced across the dark wood panelling. A sphere glowing with a milky light was suspended over the round table. Philippa Eilhart chanted the end of the spell and the sphere descended away from her onto one of the twelve chairs positioned around the table. A vague shape appeared inside the sphere. The image shimmered, as the projection was not very stable. But it quickly became more defined.

'Bloody hell,' Keira muttered, wiping her forehead. 'Haven't they heard of glamarye or beautifying spells down in Nilfgaard?'

'Apparently not,' said Triss out of the corner of her mouth. 'They don't seem to have heard of fashion either.'

'Or of make-up,' Philippa said softly. 'But now hush. And don't stare at her. We must stabilise the projection and welcome our guest. Intensify me, Rita.'

Margarita Laux-Antille repeated the spell's formula and Philippa's movements. The image shimmered several times, lost its foggy vagueness and unnatural gleam, and its contours and colours sharpened. The sorceresses could now look at the shape on the other side of the table even more closely. Triss bit her lip and winked at Keira conspiratorially.

The woman in the projection had a pale face with poor complexion, dull, expressionless eyes, thin bluish lips and a somewhat hooked nose. She was wearing a strange, conical and slightly crumpled hat. Dark, not very fresh-looking hair fell from beneath the soft brim. The impressions of unattractiveness and seediness were complemented by her shapeless, black, baggy robes, embroidered on the shoulders with frayed silver thread. The embroidery depicted a half-moon within a circle of stars. It was the only decoration worn by the Nilfgaardian sorceress.

Philippa Eilhart stood up, trying not display her jewellery, lace or cleavage too ostentatiously.

'Mistress Assire,' she said. 'Welcome to Montecalvo. We are immensely pleased that you have agreed to accept our invitation.'

'I did it out of curiosity,' the sorceress from Nilfgaard said, in an unexpectedly pleasant and melodious voice, straightening her hat involuntarily. Her hand was slim, marked by yellow spots, her fingernails broken and uneven, and clearly bitten.

'Only out of curiosity,' she repeated. 'The consequences of which may yet prove catastrophic for me. I would ask for an explanation.'

'I shall provide one forthwith,' Philippa nodded, giving a sign to the other sorceresses. 'But first, however, allow me to call forth projections of the other participants of this gathering and make some introductions. Please be patient for a moment.'

The sorceresses linked hands again and together began the incantations once more. The air in the chamber hummed like a taut wire as a glowing fog flowed down from behind the panels on the ceiling, filling the room with a shimmer of shadows. Spheres of pulsing light hung above three of the unoccupied chairs and the outlines of shapes became visible. The first one to appear was Sabrina Glevissig, in a turquoise dress with a provocatively plunging neckline and a large, lace, standing-up collar, beautifully framing her coiffured hair, which was held in a diamond tiara. Next to her Sheala de Tancarville emerged from the hazy light of the projection, dressed in black velvet sewn with pearls and with her neck draped with silver fox furs. The enchantress from Nilfgaard nervously licked her thin lips.

Just you wait for Francesca, thought Triss. *When you see Francesca, you black rat, your eyes will pop out of your head.*

Francesca Findabair did not disappoint. Not by her lavish dress, the colour of bull's blood, nor with her majestic hairstyle, nor her ruby necklace, nor her doe eyes ringed with provocative elven make-up.

'Welcome, ladies,' Philippa said, 'to Montecalvo Castle, whither I have invited you to discuss certain issues of considerable importance. I bemoan the fact that we are meeting in the form of teleprojection. But neither the time, nor the distances dividing us, nor the situation we all find ourselves in permitted a face-to-face meeting. I am Philippa Eilhart, the lady of this castle. As the initiator of this meeting and the hostess, I shall perform the introductions. On my right is Margarita Laux-Antille, the rectoress of the academy in Aretuza. On my left is Triss Merigold of Maribor and Keira Metz of Carreras. Continuing, Sabrina Glevissig of Ard Carraigh. Sheala de Tancarville of Creyden in Kovir. Francesca Findabair, also known as Enid an Gleanna, the present queen of the Valley of Flowers. And finally Assire var Anahid of Vicovaro the Nilfgaardian Empire. And now—'

'And now I bid farewell!' Sabrina Glevissig screamed, pointing a heavily beringed hand at Francesca. 'You have gone too far, Philippa! I have no intention of sitting at the same table as that bloody elf – even as an illusion! The blood on the walls and floors of Garstang has not even faded! And she spilt that blood! She and Vilgefortz!'

'I would request you observe etiquette,' Philippa said, gripping the edge of the table with both hands. 'And keep calm. Listen to what I have to say, I ask for nothing more. When I finish, each of you shall decide whether to stay or leave. The projection is voluntary, it may be interrupted at any moment. All I ask is that those who decide to leave keep this meeting secret.'

'I knew it!' Sabrina jumped up so suddenly that for a moment she moved out of the projection. 'A secret meeting! Clandestine arrangements! To put it bluntly: a conspiracy! And it's quite clear against whom it is directed. Are you mocking us, Philippa? You demand that we keep a secret from our kings and comrades, whom you did not condescend to invite. And there sits Enid Findabair – reigning in Dol Blathanna by the grace of Emhyr var Emreis – the queen of the elves, who are actively providing Nilfgaard with armed support. If that were not enough, I notice with astonishment that we are joined by a Nilfgaardian sorceress. Since when did the mages of Nilfgaard stop professing blind obedience and slavish servility to imperial rule? Secrets? What secrets, I am asking! If she is here, it is with the permission of Emhyr! By his order! As his eyes and ears!'

'I repudiate that,' Assire var Anahid said calmly. 'No one knows that I am taking part in this meeting. I was asked to keep it secret, which I have done and will continue to do. For my own sake, as much as yours. For were it to come to light, I would not survive. That's the servility of the Empire's mages for you. We have the choice of servility or the scaffold. I took a risk. I did not come here as a spy. I can only prove it in one way: through my own death. It would be sufficient for the secrecy that our hostess is appealing for to be broken. It would be sufficient for news of our meeting to go beyond these walls, for me to lose my life.'

'Betrayal of the secret could have unpleasant consequences for me, too,' Francesca said, smiling charmingly. 'You have a wonderful opportunity for revenge, Sabrina.'

'My revenge will come about in other ways, elf,' said Sabrina, and her black eyes flashed ominously. 'Should the secret come to light, it won't be through my fault or through my carelessness. By no means mine!'

'Are you suggesting something?'

'Of course,' interrupted Philippa Eilhart. 'Of course Sabrina is. She is subtly reminding you about my collaboration with Sigismund Dijkstra. As though she didn't have any contact with King Henselt's spies!'

'There is a difference,' Sabrina barked. 'I wasn't Henselt's lover for three years! Nor that of his spies, for that matter!'

'Enough of this! Be quiet!'

'I concur,' Sheala de Tancarville suddenly said in a loud voice. 'Be quiet, Sabrina. That's enough about Thanedd, enough about spying and extramarital affairs. I did not come here to take part in arguments or to listen to old grudges and insults being bandied about. Nor am I interested in being your mediator. And if I was invited with that intention, I declare that those efforts were in vain. Indeed, I have my suspicions that I am participating in vain and without purpose, that I am wasting time, which I only wrested with difficulty from my scholarly work. I shall, however, refrain from presuppositions. I propose that we give the floor to Philippa Eilhart. Let us discover the aim of this gathering. Let us learn the roles we are expected to play here. Then we shall decide – without unnecessary emotion – whether to continue with the performance or let the curtain fall. The discretion we have been asked for binds us all. Along with the measures that I, Sheala de Tancarville, will personally take against the indiscreet.'

None of the sorceresses moved or spoke. Triss did not doubt Sheala's warning for a second. The recluse from Kovir was not one to make hollow threats.

'We give you the floor, Philippa. And I ask the honourable assembly to remain quiet until she indicates that she has finished.'

Philippa Eilhart stood up, her dress rustling.

'Distinguished sisters,' she said. 'Our situation is grave. Magic is under threat. The tragic events on Thanedd, to which my thoughts return with regret and reluctance, proved that the effects of hundreds of years of apparently peaceful cooperation could be laid waste in an instant, as self-interest and inflated ambitions came to the fore. We now have discord, disorder, mutual hostility and mistrust. Events are beginning to get out of control. In order to regain control, in order to prevent a cataclysm happening, the helm of this storm-tossed ship must be grasped by strong hands. Mistress Laux-Antille, Mistress Merigold, Mistress Metz and I have discussed the matter and we are in agreement. It is not enough to re-establish the Chapter and the Council, which were destroyed on Thanedd. In any case, there is no one left to rebuild the two institutions, no guarantee that should they be rebuilt they would not be infected with the disease that destroyed the previous ones. An utterly new, secret organisation should be founded which will exclusively serve matters of magic. Which will do everything to prevent a cataclysm. For if magic were to perish, our world would perish with it. Just as happened many centuries ago, the world without magic and the progress it brings with it will be plunged into chaos and darkness; will drown in blood and barbarity. We invite the ladies present here to take part in our initiative: to actively participate in the work proposed by this secret assembly. We took the decision to summon you here in order to hear your opinions on this matter. With this, I have finished.'

'Thank you,' Sheala de Tancarville said, nodding. 'If you will allow, ladies, I shall begin. My first question, dear Philippa, is: why me? Why have I been summoned here? Many times have I refused to have my candidature to the Chapter put forward, and I resigned my seat on the Council. Firstly, my work absorbs me. Secondly, I am ever of the opinion that there are others in Kovir, Poviss and Hengfors more worthy of these honours. So I ask why *I* have been invited here, and not Carduin. Not Istredd of Aedd Gynvael, not Tugdual or Zangenis?'

'Because they are men,' replied Philippa. 'This organisation will consist exclusively of women. Mistress Assire?'

'I withdraw my question,' the Nilfgaardian enchantress smiled. 'It was coincident with the substance of Mistress De Tancarville's. The answer satisfies me.'

'It smacks to me of female chauvinism,' Sabrina Glevissig said with a sneer. 'Particularly coming from your lips, Philippa, after your change in . . . sexual orientation. I have nothing against men. I'd go further; I adore men and I cannot imagine life without them. But . . . after a moment's reflection . . . Yours is actually a reasonable proposal. Men are psychologically unstable, too prone to emotions; not to be relied upon in moments of crisis.'

'That's right,' Margarita Laux-Antille admitted calmly. 'I often compare the results of the novices from Aretuza with those of the boys from the school in Ban Ard, and the comparisons are invariably to the girls' credit. Magic requires patience, delicacy, intelligence, prudence, and perseverance, not to mention the humble, but calm, endurance of defeat and failure. Ambition is the undoing of men. They always want what they know to be impossible and unattainable. And they are unaware of the attainable.'

'Enough, enough, enough,' Sheala interrupted her, making no effort to hide a smile. 'There is nothing worse than chauvinism underpinned by scholarship. You ought to be ashamed, Rita. Nonetheless . . . Yes, I also consider the proposed single-sex structure of this . . . convent or perhaps, if you will, this lodge, justified. As we have heard, it concerns the future of magic, and magic is too important a matter to entrust its fate to men.'

'If I may,' came the melodious voice of Francesca Findabair, 'I should like to cut these digressions about the natural and undeniable domination of our sex short for a moment, and focus on matters concerning the proposed initiative, the goal of which is still not entirely clear to me. For the moment chosen is not accidental and gives food for thought. A war is being waged. Nilfgaard has crushed the northern kingdoms and nailed them down. Is there not then, concealed beneath the vague slogans I have heard here, the understandable desire to reverse that state of affairs? To crush and nail down Nilfgaard? And then to tan the hides of the insolent elves? If that is so, my dear Philippa, we shall not find common grounds for agreement.'

'Is that the reason I have been invited here?' Assire var Anahid asked. 'I do not pay much attention to politics, but I know that the imperial army is seizing the advantage over your armies in this war. Apart from Mistresses Francesca and de Tancarville, who represents a neutral kingdom, all of you ladies represent kingdoms which are hostile to the Nilfgaardian Empire. How am I to understand these words of magical solidarity? As an incitement to treachery? I'm sorry, but I cannot see myself in such a role.'

On finishing her speech, Assire leant forward, as though touching something which was outside the frame of the projection. It seemed to Triss she could hear miaowing.

'She's even got a cat,' Keira Metz whispered. 'And I bet it's black . . .'

'Quiet,' hissed Philippa. 'My dear Francesca, most esteemed Mistress Assire. Our initiative is intended to be utterly apolitical; that is its fundamental premise. We shall not be guided by interests of race, kingdoms, kings or imperators, but by the interests of magic and its future.'

'While putting magic first,' Sabrina Glevissig said and smiled sneeringly, 'I hope we will not forget, though, about the interests of sorceresses. We know, after all, how sorcerers are treated in Nilfgaard. We can sit here chatting away apolitically, but when Nilfgaard triumphs and we end up under imperial rule, we shall all look like . . .'

Triss shifted anxiously, Philippa sighed almost inaudibly. Keira lowered her head, Sheala pretended to be straightening her boa. Francesca bit her lip. Assire var Anahid's face did not twitch, but a faint blush appeared on it.

'It will be bad for all of us, is what I meant to say,' Sabrina finished quickly. 'Philippa, Triss and I, all three of us were on Sodden Hill. Emhyr will seek revenge for that defeat, for Thanedd, for all our activities. But that is only one of the reservations that the declared political neutrality of this convent arouses in me. Does participation in it mean immediate resignation from the active – and indeed political – service we presently offer to our kings? Or are we to remain in that service and serve two masters: magic and kingly rule?'

'When someone tells me he is politically neutral,' Francesca smiled, 'I always ask which politics he specifically has in mind.'

'And I know he definitely isn't thinking about the one he engages in,' Assire var Anahid added, looking at Philippa.

'I am politically neutral,' Margarita Laux-Antille chimed in, lifting her head, 'and my school is politically neutral. I have in mind every type, kind and class of politics which exists!'

'Dear ladies,' Sheala said, having remained silent for some time. 'Remember you are the dominant sex. So don't behave like little girls, fighting over a tray of sweetmeats. The principium proposed by Philippa is clear, at least to me, and I still have too little cause to consider you any less intelligent. Outside this chamber be who you want, serve who you wish, as faithfully as you want. But when the convent meets, we shall focus exclusively on magic and its future.'

'That is precisely how I imagine it,' Philippa Eilhart agreed. 'I know there are many problems, and that there are doubts and uncertainties. We shall discuss them during the next meeting, in which we shall all participate; not in the form of projections or illusions, but in person. Your presence will be treated not as a formal act of accession to the convent, but as a gesture of good will. We shall decide together whether a convent of this kind will be founded at all, then. Together. All of us. With equal rights.'

'All of us?' Sheala repeated. 'I see empty seats and I presume they were not put here inadvertently.'

'The convent ought to number twelve sorceresses. I would like the candidate for one of those empty seats to be proposed and presented to us at our next meeting by Mistress Assire. There must be at least one more worthy sorceress in the Nilfgaardian Empire. I leave the second place for you to fill, Francesca, so that you will not feel alone as the only pureblood elf. The third . . .'

Enid an Gleanna raised her head.

'I would like two places. I have two candidates.'

'Do any of you have any objections to this request? If not, then I concur. Today is the fifth day of August, the fifth day after the new moon. We shall meet again on the second day after the full moon, sisters dear, in fourteen days.'

'Just a moment,' Sheala de Tancarville interrupted. 'One place still remains empty. Who is to be the twelfth sorceress?'

'That is precisely the first problem the lodge will have to solve,' Philippa said, smiling mysteriously. 'In two weeks' time I shall tell you who ought to take their place in the twelfth seat. And then we shall ponder over how to get that person to take it up. My choice will astonish you. Because it is not an ordinary person, most esteemed sisters. It is death or life, destruction or rebirth, chaos or order. Depending on how you look at it.'

The entire village had poured out of their houses to watch the gang pass through. Tuzik also joined them. He had work to do, but he couldn't resist it. In recent days, people had been talking a great deal about the Rats. A rumour was even going around that they had all been caught and hanged. The rumour had been false, though, the evidence of which was ostentatiously and unhurriedly parading in front of the whole village at this very moment.

'Impudent scoundrels,' someone behind Tuzik whispered, and it was a whisper full of admiration. 'Ambling down the main street . . .'

'Decked out like wedding guests . . .'

'And what horses! You don't even see Nilfgaardians with horses like that!'

'Ha, they're nicked. Nobody's horses are safe from them. And you can offload them everywhere nowadays. But they keep the best for 'emselves . . .'

'That one up the front, look, that's Giselher . . . Their leader.'

'And next to him, on the chestnut, it's that she-elf . . . they call her Iskra . . .'

A cur came scuttling out from behind a fence, barking furiously, scurrying around near the fore hooves of Iskra's mare. The elf shook her luxurious mane of dark hair, turned her horse around, leant down to the ground and lashed the dog with a knout. The cur howled and spun on the spot three times, as Iskra spat on it. Tuzik muttered a curse between clenched teeth.

The people standing close by continued to whisper, discreetly pointing out the various Rats as they passed through the village. Tuzik listened, because he had to. He knew the gossip and tales as well as the others, and easily recognised the one with the long, tousled, straw-coloured hair, eating an apple, as Kayleigh, the broad-shouldered one as Asse, and the one in the embroidered sheepskin jerkin as Reef.

Two girls, riding side by side and holding hands, brought up the rear of the procession. The taller of the two, riding a bay, had her hair shorn as though recovering from the typhus, her jacket was unbuttoned, her lacy blouse gleamed white beneath it, and her neck-lace, bracelets and earrings flashed brightly.

'That shaven-headed one is Mistle . . .' someone near Tuzik said. 'Dripping with trinkets, just like a Yule tree.'

'They say she's killed more people than she's seen springs . . .'

'And the other one? On the roan? With the sword across her back?'

'Falka, they call her. She's been riding with the Rats since the summer. She also s'pposed to be a nasty piece of work . . .'

That nasty piece of work, Tuzik guessed, wasn't much older than

41

his daughter, Milena. The flaxen hair of the young bandit tumbled from beneath her velvet beret decorated with an impudently jiggling bunch of pheasant feathers. Around her neck glowed a poppy-red silk kerchief, tied up in a fanciful bow.

A sudden commotion had broken out among the villagers who had poured out in front of their cottages. For Giselher, the one riding at the head of the gang, had reined in his horse, and with a careless gesture thrown a clinking purse at the foot of Granny Mykita, who was standing leaning on a cane.

'May the Gods protect you, gracious youth!' wailed Granny Mykita. 'May you enjoy good health, O our benefactor, may you—'

A peal of laughter from Iskra drowned out the crone's mumbling. The elf threw a jaunty leg over her pommel, reached into a pouch and vigorously scattered a handful of coins among the crowd. Reef and Asse followed her lead, a veritable silver rain showering down on the dusty road. Kayleigh, giggling, threw his apple core into the figures scrambling to gather up the money.

'Our benefactors!'

'Our bold young hawks!'

'May fate be kind to you!'

Tuzik didn't run after the others, didn't drop to his knees to scrabble in the sand and chicken shit for coins. He stood by the fence, watching the girls pass slowly by.

The younger of the two, the one with the flaxen hair, noticed his gaze and expression. She let go of the short-haired girl's hand, spurred her horse and rode straight for him, pressing him against the fence and almost getting her stirrup caught. Her green eyes flashed and he shuddered, seeing so much evil and cold hatred in them.

'Let him be, Falka,' the other girl called, needlessly.

The green-eyed bandit settled for pushing Tuzik against the fence, and rode off after the Rats, without even looking back.

'Our benefactors!'

'Young hawks!'

Tuzik spat.

In the early evening, men in black uniforms arrived in the village. They were forbidding-looking horsemen from the fort near Fen

42

Aspra. Their hooves thudded, their horses neighed and their weapons clanked. When asked, the village headman and other peasants lied through their teeth, and sent the pursuers on a false trail. No one asked Tuzik. Fortunately.

When he returned from the pasture and went into his garden, he heard voices. He recognised the twittering of Zgarba the carter's twin girls, the cracking falsettos of his neighbour's adolescent boys. And Milena's voice. *They're playing*, he thought. He turned the corner beyond the woodshed. And froze in his tracks.

'Milena!'

Milena, his only surviving daughter, the apple of his eye, had hung a piece of wood across her back on a string, like a sword. She'd let her hair down, attached a cockerel's feather to her woollen hat, and tied her mother's kerchief around her neck. In a bizarre, fanciful bow.

Her eyes were green.

Tuzik had never beaten his daughter before, never raised his hand against her.

That was the first time.

Lightning flashed on the horizon and thunder rumbled. A gust of wind raked across the surface of the Ribbon.

There's going to be a storm, thought Milva, *and after the storm the rain will set in. The chaffinches weren't mistaken.*

She urged her horse on. She would have to hurry if she wanted to catch up with the Witcher before the storm broke.

I have met many military men in my life. I have known marshals, generals, commanders and governors, the victors of numerous campaigns and battles. I've listened to their stories and recollections. I've seen them poring over maps, drawing lines of various colours on them, making plans, thinking up strategies. In those paper wars everything worked, everything functioned, everything was clear and everything was in exemplary order. That's how it has to be, explained the military men. The army represents discipline and order above all. The army cannot exist without discipline and order.

So it is all the stranger that real wars – and I have seen several real wars – have as much in common with discipline and order as a whorehouse with a fire raging through it.

Dandelion, *Half a Century of Poetry*

CHAPTER TWO

The crystalline clear water of the Ribbon brimmed over the edge of the drop in a smooth, gentle arc, falling in a soughing and frothing cascade among boulders as black as onyx. It broke up on them and vanished in a white foam, from where it spilt into a wide pool which was so transparent that every pebble and every green strand of waterweed swaying in the current could be seen in the variegated mosaic of the riverbed.

Both banks were overgrown with carpets of knotgrass, through which dippers bustled, proudly flashing the white ruffles on their throats. Above the knotgrass, bushes shimmered green, brown and ochre against spruce trees which looked as though they had been sprinkled with silver.

'Indeed,' Dandelion sighed. 'It's beautiful here.'

A large, dark bull trout attempted to jump the lip of the waterfall. For a moment it hung in the air, flexing its fins and flicking its tail, and then fell heavily into the seething foam.

The darkening sky to the south was split by a forked ribbon of lightning and the dull echo of distant thunder rumbled over the wall of trees. The Witcher's bay mare danced, jerked her head and bared her teeth, trying to spit out the bit. Geralt tugged the reins hard and the mare skittered backwards, dancing hooves clattering on the stones.

'Whoa! Whoaaa! Do you see her, Dandelion? Damned ballerina! I'm getting rid of this bloody beast the first chance I get! Strike me down, if I don't swap her for a donkey!'

'See that happening anytime soon?' said the poet, scratching the itching mosquito bites on the nape of his neck. 'This valley's savage landscape indeed offers unparalleled aesthetic impressions, but for a change I'd be happy to gaze on a less aesthetic tavern. I've spent almost a week admiring nothing but romantic nature, breathtaking panoramas and distant horizons. I miss the indoors. Particularly the kind where they serve warm victuals and cold beer.'

'You'll have to carry on missing them a bit longer,' said the Witcher, turning around in the saddle. 'That I miss civilisation a little too may alleviate your suffering. As you know, I was stuck in Brokilon for exactly thirty-six days . . . and nights too, when romantic nature was freezing my arse, crawling across my back and sprinkling dew on my nose— Whoaaa! Pox on you! Will you stop sulking, you bloody nag?'

'It's the horseflies biting her. The bugs are getting vicious and bloodthirsty, because a storm's approaching. The thunder and lightning's getting more frequent to the south.'

'So I see,' the Witcher said, looking at the sky and reining in his skittish horse. 'And the wind's coming from a different direction, too. It smells of the sea. The weather's changing, without a doubt. Let's ride. Urge on that fat gelding of yours, Dandelion.'

'My steed is called Pegasus.'

'Of course, what else? Know what? Let's think up a name for my elven nag. Mmm . . .'

'Why not Roach?' mocked the troubadour.

'Roach,' agreed the Witcher. 'Nice.'

'Geralt?'

'Yes.'

'Have you ever had a horse that wasn't called Roach?'

'No,' answered the Witcher after a moment's thought. 'I haven't. Spur on that castrated Pegasus of yours, Dandelion. We've a long road ahead of us.'

'Indeed,' grunted the poet. 'Nilfgaard . . . How many miles away, do you reckon?'

'Plenty.'

'Will we make it before winter?'

'We'll ride to Verden first. We have to discuss . . . certain matters there.'

'What matters? You'll neither discourage me nor get rid of me. I'm coming along! That is my last word.'

'We shall see. As I said, we ride to Verden.'

'Is it far? Do you know these lands?'

'Yes I do. We are at Ceann Treise Falls and in front of us there's a place called Seventh Mile. Those are the Owl Hills beyond the river.'

'And we're heading south, downriver? The Ribbon joins the Yaruga near the stronghold at Bodrog . . .'

'We're heading south, but along the other bank. The Ribbon bends towards the west and we'll go through the forest. I want to get to a place called Drieschot, or the Triangle. The borders of Verden, Brugge and Brokilon meet there.'

'And from there?'

'Along the Yaruga. To the mouth. And to Cintra.'

'And then?'

'And then we'll see. If at all possible, force that idle Pegasus of yours to go a little quicker.'

A downpour caught them as they were crossing, right in the middle of the river. First a strong wind got up, with hurricane-force gusts blowing their hair and mantles around and lashing their faces with leaves and branches torn from the trees along the banks. They urged on their horses with shouts and kicks of their heels, stirring up the water as they headed for the bank. Then the wind suddenly dropped and they saw a grey curtain of rain gliding towards them. The surface of the Ribbon turned white and boiling, as though someone were hurling great handfuls of gravel at the river.

Having reached the bank, drenched to the skin, they hurried to hide in the forest. The branches created a dense, green roof over their heads, but it was not a roof capable of protecting them from such a downpour. The rain lashed intensely and forced down the leaves, and was soon pouring on them almost as hard as it had in the open.

They wrapped themselves up in their mantles, put up their hoods and kept moving. It became dark among the trees, the only light coming from the increasingly frequent flashes of lightning. The thunder followed, with long, deafening crashes. Roach shied, stamped her hooves and skittered around. Pegasus remained utterly calm.

'Geralt!' Dandelion yelled, trying to outshout a peal of thunder which was crashing through the forest like a gigantic wagon. 'We have to stop! Let's shelter somewhere!'

'Where?' he shouted back. 'Ride on!'

And they rode on.

After some time the rain visibly eased off, the strong wind once again soughed in the branches, and the crashes of thunder stopped boring into their ears. They rode out onto a track among a dense alder grove, then into a clearing. A towering beech tree stood in the middle. Beneath its boughs, on a thick, wide carpet of brown leaves and beechnuts, stood a wagon harnessed to a pair of mules. A wagoner sat on the coachman's seat pointing a crossbow at them. Geralt swore. His curse was drowned out by a clap of thunder.

'Put the bow down, Kolda,' said a short man in a straw hat, turning from the trunk of a beech tree, hopping on one leg and fastening his trousers. 'They're not the ones we're waiting for. But they are customers. Don't frighten away customers. We don't have much time, but there's always time to trade!'

'What the bloody hell?' muttered Dandelion behind Geralt's back.

'Over here, Master Elves!' the man in the hat called over. 'Don't you worry, no harm will come your way. N'ess a tearth! Va, Seidhe. Ceadmil! We're mates, right? Want to trade? Come on, over here, under this tree, out of the rain!'

Geralt wasn't surprised by the wagoner's mistake. Both he and Dandelion were wrapped in grey elven mantels. He was also wearing a jerkin decorated with the kind of leafy pattern elves favoured, given to him by the dryads, was riding a horse with typical elven trappings and a decorated bridle. His face was partially hidden by his hood. As far as the foppish Dandelion was concerned, he was regularly mistaken for an elf or half-elf, particularly since he had begun wearing his hair shoulder-length and taken up the habit of occasionally curling it with tongs.

'Careful,' Geralt muttered, dismounting. 'You're an elf. So don't open your trap if you don't have to.'

'Why?'

'Because they're hawkers.'

Dandelion hissed softly. He knew what that meant.

Money made the world go round, and supply was driven by demand. The Scoia'tael roaming the forests gathered saleable booty that was useless to them, while suffering from a shortage of equipment and weapons themselves. That was how forest trading began. And how a class of humans who earned their living from this kind of trade sprang up. The wagons of profiteers who traded with the Squirrels began appearing clandestinely on forest tracks, paths, glades and clearings. The elves called them *hav'caaren*, an untranslatable word, but one which was associated with rapacious greed. Among humans the term 'hawker' became widespread, and the connotations were even more hideous than usual, because the traders themselves were so awful. Cruel and ruthless, they stopped at nothing, not even killing. A hawker caught by the army could not count on mercy. Hence he was not in the habit of showing it himself. If they came across anyone who might turn them in, hawkers would reach for a crossbow or a knife without a second thought.

So they were out of luck. It was fortunate the hawkers had taken them for elves. Geralt pulled his hood down over his eyes and began to wonder what would happen if the hav'caaren saw through the masquerade.

'What foul weather,' said the trader, rubbing his hands. 'It's pouring like the sky was leaking! Awful tedd, ell'ea? But what to do, there's no bad weather for doing business. There's only bad goods and bad money, innit! You know what I'm saying?'

Geralt nodded. Dandelion grunted something from under his hood. Luckily for them, the elves' contemptuous dislike of conversing with humans was generally known and came as no surprise. The wagoner did not put the crossbow down, however, which was not a good sign.

'Who are you with? Whose commando?' the hawker asked, unconcerned, as any serious trader would be, by the reticence of his customers. 'Coinneach Dá Reo's? Or Angus Bri-Cri's? Or maybe Riordain's? I heard Riordain put some royal bailiffs to the sword.

They were travelling home after they'd done their duty, collecting a levy. And they had it in coinage, not grain. I don't take wood tar nor grain in payment, nor blood-stained clothing, and if we're talking furs, only mink, sable or ermine. But what I like most is common coinage, precious stones and trinkets! If you have them we can trade! I only have first-class goods! Evelienn; vara en ard scedde, ell'ea, you know what I mean? I've got everything. Take a look.'

The trader went over to the wagon and pulled back the edge of the wet tarpaulin. They saw swords, bows, bunches of arrows and saddles. The hawker rooted around among them and took out an arrow. The arrowhead was serrated and sawn through.

'You won't find any other traders selling this,' he said boastfully. 'They'd shit themselves if they were to touch 'em. You'd be torn apart by horses if you were caught with arrows like that. But I know what you Squirrels like. Customer comes first, and you've got to take a risk when you barter, as long as there's a profit from it! I've got barbed arrowheads at . . . nine orens a dozen. Naev'de aen tvedeane, ell'ea, got it, Seidhe? I swear I'm not fleecing you, I don't make much myself, I swear on my little children's heads. And if you take three dozen straight away, I'll knock a bit off the price. It's a bargain, I swear, a sheer bargain— Hey, Seidhe, hands off my wagon!'

Dandelion nervously withdrew his hand from the tarpaulin and pulled his hood further down over his face. Once again, Geralt quietly cursed the bard's irrepressible curiosity.

'Mir'me vara,' mumbled Dandelion, raising his hand in a gesture of apology. 'Squaess'me.'

'No harm done,' said the hawker, grinning. 'But no looking in there, because there's other goods in the wagon too. Not for sale, those, not for Seidhe. A special order, ha, ha. But that's enough rabbiting . . . Show us the colour of your money.'

Here we go, thought Geralt, looking at the wagoner's nocked crossbow. He had reason to believe the quarrel's tip was barbed too – just like the arrows he'd been so proudly shown moments before – and would, after entering the belly, exit through the back in three or sometimes four places, turning the victim's internal organs into a very messy goulash.

'N'ess tedd,' he said, trying to speak in a singsong way. 'Tearde. Mireann vara, va'en vort. We'll trade when we return from the commando. Ell'ea? Understood, Dh'oine?'

'Understood,' the hawker said, spitting. 'Understood that you're skint. You'd like the goods, you just don't have the readies. Be off with you! And don't come back, because I'm meeting important parties here. It'll be safer if they don't clap eyes on you. Go to—'

He broke off, hearing the snorting of a horse.

'Damn it!' he snarled. 'It's too late! They're here! Hoods down, elves! Don't move and button your lips! Kolda, you ass, put that crossbow down and fast!'

The heavy rain, thunder and the carpet of leaves had dampened the thudding of hooves, which meant the riders had been able to ride up undetected and surround the beech tree in an instant. They weren't Scoia'tael. Squirrels didn't wear armour, and the metal helmets, spaulders and hauberks of the eight horsemen surrounding the tree were glistening in the rain.

One of the horsemen approached at a walk and towered over the hawker like a mountain. He was of impressive height and was mounted on a powerful warhorse. A wolf skin was draped over his armoured shoulders and his face was obscured by a helmet with a broad, protruding nose-guard reaching down to his lower lip. The stranger was holding a menacing-looking war hammer.

'Rideaux!' he called huskily.

'Faoiltiarna!' replied the trader in a slightly quavering voice.

The horseman came even closer and leant forward. Water poured down from his steel nose-guard straight onto his vambrace and the balefully glistening point of the hammer.

'Faoiltiarna!' the hawker repeated, bowing low. He removed his hat and the rain immediately plastered his thinning hair to his head. 'Faoiltiarna! I'm your man; I know the password and the countersign . . . I've been with Faoiltiarna, Your Lordship . . . Here I am, as arranged . . .'

'And those men, who are they?'

'My escort,' the hawker said, bowing even lower. 'You know, elves . . .'

'The prisoner?'

'On the wagon. In a coffin.'

'In a coffin?' The thunder partially drowned the furious roar of the horseman. 'You won't get away with this! Viscount de Rideaux gave clear instructions that the prisoner was to be handed over alive!'

'He's alive, he's alive,' the trader gibbered hurriedly. 'As per orders . . . Shoved into a coffin, but alive . . . The coffin wasn't my idea, Your Lordship. It was Faoiltiarna's . . .'

The horseman rapped the hammer against his stirrup, as a sign. Three other horsemen dismounted and pulled the tarpaulin off the wagon. When they had thrown various saddles, blankets and bunches of harnesses onto the ground, Geralt actually saw a coffin made of fresh pine, lit by a flash of lightning. He didn't look too closely, however. He felt a tingling in the tips of his fingers. He knew what was about to happen.

'What's all this, Your Lordship?' the hawker said, looking at the goods lying on the wet leaves. 'You're chucking all my gear out of the wagon.'

'I'll buy it all. Along with the horse and cart.'

'Aaah,' a repulsive grin crept over the trader's bristly face. 'Now you're talking. That'll be . . . Let me think . . . Five hundred, if you'll excuse me, Your Nobleness, if we're talking Temerian currency. If it's your florins, then it'll be forty-five.'

'That's cheap,' snorted the horseman, smiling eerily behind his nose-guard. 'Come closer.'

'Watch out, Dandelion,' hissed the Witcher, imperceptibly unfastening the buckle of his mantle. It thundered once more.

The hawker approached the horseman, naively counting on the deal of his life. And in a way it was the deal of his life, not the best, perhaps, but certainly the last. The horseman stood in his stirrups and drove the point of the hammer down with great force onto the hawker's bald crown. The trader dropped without a sound, shuddered, flapped his arms and scraped the wet carpet of leaves with his heels. One of the men rummaging around on the wagon threw a leather strap around the wagoner's neck and pulled it tight; the other leapt forward and stabbed him with a dagger.

One of the horsemen raised his crossbow quickly to his shoulder and took aim at Dandelion. But Geralt already had a sword – one of those thrown from the wagon – in his hand. Seizing the weapon halfway down the blade, he flung it like a javelin and hit the crossbowman, who fell off the horse with an expression of utter astonishment on his face.

'Run, Dandelion!'

Dandelion caught up with Pegasus and leapt for the saddle with a desperate bound. The jump was a tad too desperate, however, and the poet was a tad too inexperienced. He didn't hang onto the pommel and tumbled to the ground on the other side of the horse. And that saved his life, as the blade of the attacking horseman's sword cut through the air above Pegasus's ears with a hiss. The gelding shied, jerked, and collided with the attacker's horse.

'They aren't elves!' yelled the horseman in the helmet with the nose-guard, drawing his sword. 'Take them alive! Alive!'

One of the men who had jumped down from the wagon hesitated on hearing the order. Geralt, however, had already drawn his own sword and didn't hesitate for a second. The fervour of the other two men was somewhat cooled by the fountain of blood which spurted over them. He took advantage of the situation and cut one of them down. But the horsemen were already charging at him. He ducked under their swords, parried their blows, dodged aside and suddenly felt a piercing pain in his right knee. He could feel himself keeling over. He wasn't hurt; the injured leg, which had been treated in Brokilon, had simply crumpled under him without warning.

The foot soldier aiming for him with the butt of a battle-axe suddenly groaned and lurched forward, as though someone had shoved him hard in the back. Before he fell, the Witcher saw an arrow with long fletchings sticking out of his assailant's side, driven in to halfway up the shaft. Dandelion yelled; a thunderclap drowned out his cry.

Geralt, who was hanging on to one of the cartwheels, saw a fair-haired girl with a drawn bow dashing out of an alder grove. The horsemen saw her too. They couldn't fail to see her, because at that moment one of them tumbled backwards over his horse's croup,

55

his throat transformed into a scarlet pulp by an arrow. The remaining three, including the leader in the helmet with the nose-guard, assessed the danger immediately and galloped towards the archer, hiding behind their horses' necks. They thought the horses' necks represented sufficient protection against the arrows. They were mistaken.

Maria Barring, also known as Milva, drew her bow. She took aim calmly, the bowstring pressed against her cheek.

The first of her attackers screamed and slid off his horse. One foot caught in the stirrup and he was trampled beneath the horse's iron-shod hooves. Another arrow hurled the second from his saddle. The third man, the leader, who was already close, stood in the saddle and raised his sword to strike. Milva did not even flinch. Fearlessly looking straight at her attacker, she bent her bow and shot an arrow right into his face from a distance of five paces, striking just to the side of the steel nose-guard and jumping aside as she shot. The arrow passed right through his skull, knocking off his helmet. The horse did not slow its gallop. The horseman, now lacking a helmet and a considerable part of his skull, remained in the saddle for a few seconds, then slowly tipped over and crashed into a puddle. The horse neighed and ran on.

Geralt struggled to his feet and massaged his leg which, though painful, for a wonder seemed to be functioning normally. He could stand on it without difficulty and walk. Next to him, Dandelion hauled himself up, throwing off the corpse with a mutilated throat which was weighing down on him. The poet's face was the colour of quicklime.

Milva came closer, pulling an arrow from a dead man as she approached.

'Thank you,' the Witcher said. 'Dandelion, say thank you. This is Maria Barring, or Milva. It's thanks to her we're alive.'

Milva yanked an arrow from another of the dead bodies and examined the bloody arrowhead. Dandelion mumbled incoherently, bent over in a courtly – but somewhat quavering – bow, then dropped to his knees and vomited.

'Who's that?' the archer asked, wiping the arrowhead on some wet leaves and replacing it in her quiver. 'A comrade of yours, Witcher?'

'Yes. His name's Dandelion. He's a poet.'

'A poet,' Milva watched the troubadour wracked by attacks of dry retching and then looked up. 'That I can understand. But I don't quite understand why he's puking here, instead of writing rhymes in a quiet spot somewhere. But I suppose that's none of my business.'

'It is yours, in a sense. You saved his skin. And mine too.'

Milva wiped her rain-splashed face, with the imprint of the bowstring still visible on it. Although she had shot several arrows, there was only one imprint; the bowstring pressed against the same place each time.

'I was already in the alder grove when you started talking to the hawker,' she said. 'I didn't want the scoundrel to see me, for there was no need. And then those others arrived and the slaughter began. You messed a few of them up very nicely. You know how to swing a sword, I'll give you that. Even if you are a cripple. You should have stayed in Brokilon till your peg healed instead of making it worse. You might limp for the rest of your life. You realise that, don't you?'

'I'll survive.'

'I reckon you will, too. I followed you to warn you, and to make you turn back. Your quest won't come to anything. There's a war raging in the south. The Nilfgaardian Army are marching on Brugge from Drieschot.'

'How do you know?'

'Just look at them,' the girl said, making a sweeping gesture and pointing at the bodies and the horses. 'I mean, they're Nilfgaardians! Can't you see the suns on their helmets? The embroidery on their saddlecloths? Pack up your things, and we'll take to our heels; more of them may arrive any moment. These were mounted scouts.'

'I don't think they were just scouts,' he said, shaking his head. 'They were after something.'

'What might that be, just out of interest?'

'That,' he said, pointing at the pinewood coffin lying in the wagon, now darkened from the rain. It wasn't raining as hard as it had been during the short battle, and it had stopped thundering. The storm was moving north. The Witcher picked up his sword from among the leaves and jumped onto the wagon, quietly cursing because his knee still hurt.

'Help me get it open.'

'What do you want with a stiff . . . ?' Milva broke off, seeing the holes bored into the lid. 'Bloody hell! Was the hawker lugging a live person around in here?'

'It's some kind of prisoner,' Geralt said, levering the lid open. 'The trader was waiting for these Nilfgaardians, to hand him over to them. They exchanged passwords and countersigns . . .'

The lid tore off with the sound of splitting wood, revealing a man with a gag over his mouth, his arms and legs fastened to the sides of the coffin by leather straps. The Witcher leant over. He took a good look. And again, this time more intently. And swore.

'Well I never,' he drawled. 'What a surprise. Who would have thought it?'

'Do you know him, Witcher?'

'By sight.' He smiled hideously. 'Put the knife away, Milva. Don't cut his bonds. It seems this is an internal Nilfgaardian matter. We shouldn't get involved. Let's leave him as he is.'

'Am I hearing right?' Dandelion asked, joining in from behind. He was still pale, but curiosity had overcome his other emotions. 'Are you planning to leave him tied up in the forest? I'm guessing you've recognised someone you have a bone to pick with, but he's a prisoner, by the Gods! He was the prisoner of the men who jumped us and almost killed us. And the enemy of our enemy . . .'

He broke off, seeing the Witcher removing a knife from his boot-top. Milva coughed quietly. The captive's dark blue eyes, previously screwed up against the rain, widened. Geralt leant over and cut the strap fastened around the prisoner's left arm.

'Look, Dandelion,' he said, seizing the captive's wrist and raising his now-free arm. 'Do you see the scar on his hand? Ciri did that. On the Isle of Thanedd, a month ago. He's a Nilfgaardian. He came to Thanedd specifically to abduct Ciri and she wounded him, defending herself from being captured.'

'But it all came to nothing anyway,' muttered Milva. 'I sense

58

something doesn't add up here. If he kidnapped your Ciri for Nilfgaard, how did he end up in this coffin? Why was that hawker handing him over to the Nilfgaardians? Take that gag off him, Witcher. Perhaps he'll tell us something.'

'I have no desire to listen to him,' he said flatly. 'My hand is itching to stab him through the heart, with him lying there looking at me. It's all I can do to restrain myself. And if he opens his mouth, I know I won't be able to hold back. I haven't told you everything.'

'Don't hold back then.' Milva shrugged her shoulders. 'Stick him, if he's such a villain. But do it quickly, because time's getting on. As I said, the Nilfgaardians will be here soon. I'm going to get my horse.'

Geralt straightened up and released the captive's hand. The man immediately loosened the gag and spat it out of his mouth. But he said nothing. The Witcher threw his knife onto the man's chest.

'I don't know what sins you committed for them to trap you in this chest, Nilfgaardian,' he said. 'And I don't care. I'll leave you this blade. Free yourself. Wait here for your own people, or escape into the forest, it's up to you.'

The captive said nothing. Tied up and lying in that wooden crate, he looked even more miserable and defenceless than he had on Thanedd – and Geralt had seen him there on his knees, wounded and trembling with fear in a pool of blood. He also looked considerably younger now. The Witcher wouldn't have put him at more than twenty-five.

'I spared your life on the island,' he said. 'And I'm doing it again. But it's the last time. The next time we meet I'll kill you like a dog. Remember that. If you persuade your comrades to pursue us, take the coffin with you. It'll come in useful. Let's go, Dandelion.'

'Make haste!' Milva shouted, turning away at full gallop from the westward track. 'But not that way! Into the trees, by thunder, into the trees!'

'What's going on?'

'A large group of riders are heading towards us from the Ribbon! It's Nilfgaard! What are you staring at? To horse, before they're upon us!'

*

The battle for the village had been going on for an hour and wasn't showing any signs of finishing soon. The infantry, holding out behind stone walls, fences and upturned wagons, had repulsed three attacks by the cavalry, who came charging at them from the causeway. The width of the causeway did not permit the horsemen to gain enough momentum for a frontal attack, but allowed the foot soldiers to concentrate their defence. As a result, waves of cavalry repeatedly foundered on the barricades, behind which the desperate but fierce soldiers were shooting a hail of quarrels and arrows into the mounted throng. The cavalry seethed and teemed under this assault, and then the defenders rushed out at them in a rapid counter-attack, fighting furiously with battle-axes, guisarmes and studded flails. The cavalry retreated to the ponds, leaving human and equine corpses behind, while the infantry concealed themselves among the barricades and hurled filthy insults at the enemy. After a while, the cavalry formed up and attacked once again.

And again.

'Who do you think's fighting whom?' Dandelion asked once more, but indistinctly, as he was trying to soften and chew a piece of hard tack he had scrounged from Milva.

They were sitting on the very edge of the cliff, well hidden among juniper shrubs. They were able to watch the battle without being afraid anyone would notice them. Actually, they could do nothing but watch. They had no choice: a battle was raging in front of them and a forest fire was raging behind them.

'It's easy to identify them,' Geralt said, reluctantly responding to Dandelion's question. 'They're Nilfgaardian horsemen.'

'And the infantry?'

'The infantry aren't Nilfgaardian.'

'The horsemen are regular cavalrymen from Verden,' said Milva, until then sombre and strangely taciturn. 'They have the Verdenian checkerboard emblem sewn onto their tunics. And the ones in the village are the Bruggian regular infantry. You can tell by their banners.'

Indeed, encouraged by another small victory, the infantrymen

60

raised their green standard – with a white cross moline – above the entrenchment. Geralt had been watching intently, but hadn't noticed the standard before. It must have gone missing at the start of the battle.

'Are we staying here for much longer?' Dandelion asked.

'Oh dear,' muttered Milva 'Here he goes. Take a look around! Whichever way you turn, it looks pretty shitty, doesn't it?

Dandelion didn't have to look or turn around. The entire horizon was striped with columns of smoke. It was thickest to the north and the west, where the armies had set fire to the forests. Smoke was also rising into the sky in many places to the south, where they had been heading when the battle had barred their way. And during the hour they had spent on the hill, smoke had also started rising to the east.

'However,' the archer began a moment later, looking at Geralt, 'I'd really like to know what you intend doing now, Witcher. Behind us we've got Nilfgaard and a burning forest, and you can see for yourself what's in front of us. So what are your plans?'

'My plans haven't changed. I'll wait for this scrap to finish and then I'll head south. Towards the Yaruga.'

'I think you've lost your mind.' Milva scowled. 'Can't you see what's happening? It's as clear as the nose on your face that it's not some leaderless band of mercenaries, but something called war. Nilfgaard and Verden are on the march. They're sure to have crossed the Yaruga in the south and probably the whole of Brugge and possibly Sodden are in flames—'

'I have to get to the Yaruga.'

'Excellent. And what then?'

'I'll find a boat, I'll sail downstream and try to make it to the delta. Then a ship— I mean, hell, some ships must still sail from there—'

'To Nilfgaard?' she snorted. 'So the plans haven't changed?'

'You don't have to go with me.'

'No, I don't. And praise the Gods for that, because I don't have a death wish. I'm not afraid, but mind you: getting yourself killed is no claim to fame.'

'I know,' he replied calmly. 'I know from experience. I wouldn't be heading that way if I didn't have to. But I have to, so I'm going. Nothing's going to stop me.'

'Ah,' she said, looking him up and down. 'Listen to this hero, his voice like someone scraping a sword across a shield. If Imperator Emhyr could hear you, I'm sure he'd be shitting his britches in terror. "To my side, guards, to my side, my imperial regiments, oh woe is me, the Witcher's heading for Nilfgaard in a rowing boat, soon he'll be here to take my crown and life from me! I'm doomed!"'

'Give over, Milva.'

'I won't! It's time someone finally told you the truth to your face. Fuck me with a mangy rabbit if I've ever seen a stupider clod! You're going to snatch your maid from Emhyr? The same maid Emhyr has got lined up as his Imperatoress? The girl he snatched from Thanedd? Emhyr's got long hands. They don't let go of what they seize. The kings stand no chance against him, but still you fancy yours?'

He didn't answer.

'You're heading for Nilfgaard,' Milva repeated, shaking her head in mock sympathy. 'To fight the Imperator and rescue his fiancée. But have you thought about what might happen? When you get there, when you find Ciri in her imperial apartments, all dressed in gold and silk, what will you say to her? Follow me, my darling. What do you want with an imperial throne? We'll live together in a shack and eat bark during the lean season. Look at yourself, you lame scruff. You even got your coat and boots from the dryads, stripped from some elf who died of his wounds in Brokilon. And do you know what'll happen when your maid sees you? She'll spit in your eye and scorn you. She'll order the imperial guard to throw you out on your ear and set the dogs on you!'

Milva was speaking louder and louder and she was almost shouting by the end of her tirade. Not only from anger, but also to be heard over the intensifying noise of battle. Down below, scores – or even hundreds – of throats were roaring. Another attack descended on the Bruggian infantry. But this time from two sides simultaneously. Verdenians dressed in greyish-blue tunics adorned with a chequered pattern galloped along the causeway, while a powerful cavalry force in black cloaks dashed out from behind the ponds, striking the defenders' flank.

'Nilfgaard,' said Milva tersely.

This time the Bruggian infantry had no chance. The cavalry forced their way through the barricades and ripped the defenders apart with their swords. The standard with the cross fell. Some of the infantrymen laid down their arms and surrendered; others tried to escape towards the trees. But as they ran a third unit emerged from the trees and attacked; a mixed band of light cavalry.

'The Scoia'tael,' Milva said, getting to her feet. 'Now do you understand what's going on, Witcher? Do you get it? Nilfgaard, Verden and the Squirrels all at once. War. Like it was in Aedirn a month ago.'

'It's a raid,' Geralt said, shaking his head. 'A plundering raid. Only horsemen, no infantry . . .'

'The infantry are capturing forts and their garrisons. Where do you think those plumes of smoke are coming from? Smokehouses?'

The bestial, dreadful screams of people fleeing only to be caught and slaughtered by the Squirrels drifted up from the village. Smoke and flames belched from the roofs of the cottages. A strong wind was swiftly spreading the fire from one thatched roof to another.

'Look at that village going up in smoke,' muttered Milva. 'And they'd only just finished rebuilding it after the last war. They sweated for two years to put up the foundations and it'll burn down in a few seconds. That's a lesson to be learned!'

'What lesson would that be?' asked Geralt brusquely.

She didn't answer. The smoke from the burning village rose up to the top of the cliff, stung their eyes and made them water. They could hear the screams from the inferno. Dandelion suddenly went as white as a sheet.

The captives were driven into a huddle, surrounded by a ring of soldiers. On the order of a knight in a black-plumed helmet the horsemen began to slash and stab the unarmed villagers. They were trampled by horses as they fell. The ring tightened. The screams which reached the cliff top no longer resembled sounds made by humans.

'And you want to travel south?' asked the poet, looking meaningfully at the Witcher. 'Through these fires? Where these butchers come from?'

'Seems to me,' Geralt replied reluctantly, 'that we don't have a choice.'

'Yes, we do,' Milva said. 'I can lead you through the forests to the Owl Hills and back to Ceann Treise. And Brokilon.'

'Through those burning forests? Through more skirmishes like this?'

'It's safer than the road south. It's no more than fourteen miles to Ceann Treise and I know which paths to take.'

The Witcher looked down at the village perishing in the flames. The Nilfgaardians had dealt with the captives and the cavalry had formed up in marching order. The motley band of Scoia'tael set off along the highway leading east.

'I'm not going back,' he retorted. 'But you can escort Dandelion to Brokilon.'

'No!' the poet protested, although he still hadn't regained his normal colour. 'I'm going with you.'

Milva shrugged, picked up her quiver and bow, took a step towards the horses and then suddenly turned around.

'Devil take it!' she snapped. 'I've been saving elves from death for too long. I can't just let someone go to his death! I'll lead you to the Yaruga, you crazy fools. But by the eastern route, not the southern one.'

'The forests are burning there too.'

'I'll lead you through the fire. I'm used to it.'

'You don't have to, Milva.'

'Too right I don't. Now to horse! And get a bloody move on!'

They didn't get far. The horses had difficulty moving through the undergrowth and along the overgrown tracks, and they didn't dare use roads; the hoofbeats and clanking could be heard everywhere, betraying the presence of armed forces. Dusk surprised them among brush-covered ravines, so they stopped for the night. It wasn't raining and the sky was bright from the glow of fires.

They found a fairly dry place, wrapped themselves in their mantles and blankets and sat down. Milva went off to search the surrounding area. As soon as she moved away, Dandelion gave vent to the long-suppressed curiosity that the Brokilonian archer had aroused in him.

'That's a comely girl if ever there was one,' he murmured. 'You're lucky when it comes to the female of the species, Geralt. She's tall and curvaceous, and walks as though she were dancing. A little too slim in the hips for my taste, and a little too sturdy in the shoulders, but she's very womanly . . . And those two little apples in the front, ho, ho . . . Almost bursting out of her blouse—'

'Shut it, Dandelion.'

'I happened to bump against her by accident on the road,' the poet dreamed on. 'A thigh, I tell you, like marble. Methinks you weren't bored during that month in Brokilon—'

Milva, who had just returned from her patrol, heard his theatrical whispering and noticed their expressions.

'Are you talking about me, poet? What are you staring at as soon as my back's turned? Has a bird shat on me?'

'We're amazed by your archery skills.' Dandelion grinned. 'You wouldn't find much competition at an archery tournament.'

'Yes, yes, I've heard it all before, and the rest.'

'I've read,' Dandelion said, winking tellingly at Geralt, 'that the best archeresses can be found among the Zerrikanian steppe clans. I gather that some even cut off their left breast, so it won't interfere when they draw the bow. Their breast, they say, gets in the way of the bowstring.'

'Some poet must have dreamed that up,' Milva snorted. 'He sits down and writes twaddle like that, dipping his quill in a chamber pot, and foolish people believe it. Think I use my tits to shoot with, do you? You pull the bowstring back to your kisser, standing side on, like this. Nothing snags on the bowstring. All that talk of cutting off a tit is hogwash, thought up by some layabout with nothing but women's bodies on the brain.'

'Thank you for your kind words about poets and poetry. And the archery lesson. Good weapon, a bow. You know what? I think the

65

arts of war will develop in that direction. People are going to fight at a distance in the wars of the future. They'll invent a weapon with such a long range that the two sides will be able to kill each other while completely out of eyeshot.'

'Twaddle,' Milva said bluntly. 'A bow's a good thing, but war's all about man against man, a sword's length apart, the stouter one smashing the weaker one's head in. That's how it's always been and that's how it'll always be. And once that finishes, all wars will finish. But for now, you've seen how wars are fought. You saw it in that village, by the causeway. And that's enough idle talk. I'm going to have another look around. The horses are snorting as though a wolf was sniffing around . . .'

'Comely, oh yes.' Dandelion followed her with his gaze. 'Mmm . . . Going back to the village by the causeway and what she told you when we were sitting on the cliff— Don't you think there's something in what she says?'

'About?'

'About . . . Ciri,' the poet stammered slightly. 'Our beautiful, sharp-shooting wench seems not to understand the relationship between you and Ciri, and thinks, it seems to me, that you intend to woo her away from the Nilfgaardian Imperator. That that's the real motive behind your expedition to Nilfgaard.'

'So in that regard she's totally wrong. But what's she right about?'

'Take it easy, keep your cool. Nonetheless stare the truth in the face. You took Ciri under your wing and consider yourself her guardian, but she's no ordinary girl. She's a princess, Geralt. Without beating about the bush, she's in line for the throne. For the palace. And the crown. Maybe not necessarily the Nilfgaardian crown. I don't know if Emhyr is the best husband for her—'

'Precisely. You don't know.'

'And do *you*?'

The Witcher wrapped himself up in a blanket.

'You're heading, quite naturally, towards a conclusion,' he said. 'But don't bother; I know what you're thinking. "There's no point saving Ciri from a fate she's been doomed to since the day of her birth. Because Ciri, who doesn't need saving at all, will be quite ready to order the imperial guard to throw us down the stairs. Let's forget about her." Right?'

Dandelion opened his mouth, but Geralt didn't let him speak.

'"After all,' he continued in an even harsher voice, 'the girl wasn't abducted by a dragon or an evil wizard, nor did pirates seize her for the ransom money. She's not locked in a tower, a dungeon or a cage; she's not being tortured or starved. Quite the opposite; she sleeps on damask, eats from silverware, wears silks and lace, is bedecked with jewellery and is just waiting to be crowned. In short, she's happy. Meanwhile some witcher who, by some unfortunate fate happened upon her, has taken it upon himself to disrupt, spoil, destroy and crush that happiness beneath the rotten old boots he pulled off some dead elf." Right?'

'That's not what I was thinking,' Dandelion muttered.

'He wasn't talking to you,' Milva said, suddenly looming up from the darkness and after a moment's hesitation sitting down beside the Witcher. 'That was for me. It was my words that upset him. I spoke in anger, without thinking . . . Forgive me, Geralt. I know what it's like when a claw scratches an open wound. Come on, don't fret. I won't do it any more. Do you forgive me? Or should I say sorry by kissing you?'

Not waiting either for an answer or permission she grabbed him powerfully by the neck and kissed him on the cheek. He squeezed her shoulder hard.

'Slide nearer.' He coughed. 'And you too, Dandelion. We'll be warmer together.'

They said nothing for a long time. Clouds scudded across a sky bright with firelight, obscuring the twinkling stars.

'I want to tell you something,' Geralt said at last. 'But promise you won't laugh.'

'Out with it.'

'I had some strange dreams. In Brokilon. At first I thought they were ravings; something wrong with my head. You know, I got a good beating on Thanedd. But I keep having the same dream. Always the same one.'

Dandelion and Milva said nothing.

67

'Ciri,' he began a moment later, 'isn't sleeping in a palace beneath a brocade canopy. She's riding a horse through a dusty village . . . the villagers are pointing at her. They're calling her by a name I don't recognise. Dogs are barking. She's not alone. There are others with her. There's a crop-haired girl, who's holding Ciri's hand . . . and Ciri's smiling at her but I don't like that smile. I don't like her heavy make-up . . . But the thing I like least is that she leaves a trail of death.'

'So where is the girl?' Milva mused, snuggling up to him like a cat. 'Not in Nilfgaard?'

'I don't know,' he said with difficulty. 'But I've had the same dream several times. The problem is I don't believe in dreams like that.'

'Well, you're a fool. I do.'

'I don't *know* it,' he repeated. 'But I can *feel* it. There's fire ahead of her and death behind her. I have to make haste.'

It began to rain at dawn. Not like the previous day, when the storm had been accompanied by a brief but strong downpour. The sky turned grey and took on a leaden patina. It began to spit with rain; a fine, even and drenching drizzle.

They rode east. Milva led the way. When Geralt pointed out to her that the Yaruga was to the south, the archer growled and reminded him she was the guide and knew what she was doing. He said nothing after that. After all, the most important thing was that they were under way. The direction wasn't so important.

They rode in silence, wet, chilled to the bone, and hunched over their saddles. They kept to footpaths, stole along forest tracks, cut across highways. They disappeared into the undergrowth at the sound of thudding hooves of cavalry tramping along the roads. They gave a wide berth to the uproar of battle. They rode past villages engulfed in flames, past smoking and glowing rubble, and past settlements and hamlets which had been razed to black squares of burnt earth and the acrid stench of rain-soaked charred embers. They startled flocks of crows feeding on corpses. They passed groups and columns of peasants bent beneath bundles, fleeing from war and conflagration, dazed, responding to questions with nothing but a fearful, uncomprehending and mute raising of their eyes, emptied by misfortune and horror.

They rode east, amidst fire and smoke, amidst drizzle and fog, and the tapestry of war unfolded in front of their eyes. So many sights.

There was a black silhouette of a crane projecting among the ruins of a burnt-out village, with a naked corpse dangling from it head downwards. Blood from the mutilated crotch and belly dripped down onto its chest and face, to hang like icicles from its hair. The Rune of Ard was visible on its back. Carved with a knife.

'An'givare,' Milva said, throwing her wet hair off her neck. 'The Squirrels were here.'

'What does an'givare mean?'

'Informer.'

There was a grey horse, saddled in a black caparison. It was walking unsteadily around the edge of the battlefield, wandering between piles of corpses and broken spears stuck into the ground, whinnying quietly and pitifully, dragging its entrails behind it, dangling from its mutilated belly. They couldn't finish it off, for on the battlefield – apart from the horse – there were also marauders robbing corpses.

There was a spread-eagled girl, lying near a burnt-out farmyard, naked, bloody, staring at the sky with glazed eyes.

'They say war's a male thing,' Milva growled. 'But they have no mercy on women; they have to have their fun. Fucking heroes; damn them all.'

'You're right. But you won't change it.'

'I already have. I ran away from home. I didn't want to sweep the cottage and scrub the floors. I wasn't going to wait until they arrived and put the cottage to the torch, spread me out on the very same floor and . . .' She broke off, and spurred her horse forward.

And later there was a tar house. Here Dandelion puked up everything he'd eaten that day: some hard tack and half a stockfish.

In the tar house some Nilfgaardians – or perhaps Scoia'tael – had dealt with a group of captives. It was impossible even to guess at the exact size of the group. Because during the carnage they had not only used arrows, swords and lances, but also woodmen's tools they'd found there: axes, drawknives and crosscut saws.

There were other scenes of war, but Geralt, Dandelion and Milva didn't remember them. They had discarded them from their memories.

They had become indifferent.

Over the next two days they didn't even cover twenty miles. It continued to rain. The earth, absorbent after the summer drought, sucked up water like a sponge, and the forest tracks were transformed into muddy slides. Fog and haze prevented them from spotting the smoke from fires, but the stench of burning buildings told them the armies were still close at hand and were still setting light to anything that would catch fire.

They didn't see any fugitives. They were alone in the forest. Or so they thought.

Geralt was the first to hear the snorting of the horse following in their tracks. With a stony countenance, he turned Roach back. Dandelion opened his mouth, but Milva gestured him to remain silent, and removed her bow from where it hung by her saddle.

The rider following them emerged from the brush. He saw they were waiting for him and reined back his horse, a chestnut colt. They stood in a silence broken only by the beating of the rain.

'I forbade you from riding after us,' the Witcher finally said.

The Nilfgaardian, whom Dandelion had last seen lying in a coffin, looked down at his horse's wet mane. The poet barely recognised him, as he was now dressed in a hauberk, leather tunic and cloak, no doubt stripped from one of the horsemen killed by the wagon. However, he remembered the young face, which hadn't grown much more stubble since the adventure under the beech tree.

'I forbade it,' the Witcher repeated.

'You did,' the young man finally agreed. He spoke without a Nilfgaardian accent. 'But I must.'

Geralt dismounted, handing the reins to the poet. And drew his sword.

'Get down,' he said calmly. 'You've equipped yourself with some

70

hardware, I see. Good. There was no way I could kill you then, while you were unarmed. Now it's different. Dismount.'

'I'm not fighting you. I don't want to.'

'So I imagine. Like all your fellow countrymen, you prefer another kind of fight. Like in that tar house, which you must have ridden past, following our trail. Dismount, I said.'

'I am Cahir Mawr Dyffryn aep Ceallach.'

'I didn't ask you to introduce yourself. I ordered you to dismount.'

'I will not. I don't want to fight you.'

'Milva.' The Witcher nodded at the archer. 'Be so kind as to shoot his horse from under him.'

'No!' the Nilfgaardian raised an arm, before Milva had time to nock her arrow. 'Please don't. I'm dismounting.'

'That's better. Now draw your sword, son.'

The young man folded his arms across his chest.

'Kill me, if you want. If you prefer, order the she-elf to shoot me. I'm not fighting you. I am Cahir Mawr Dyffryn . . . son of Ceallach. I want . . . I want to join you.'

'I must have misheard. Say that again.'

'I want to join you. You're riding to search for the girl. I want to help you. I have to help you.'

'He's a madman.' Geralt turned to Milva and Dandelion. 'He's taken leave of his senses. We're dealing with a madman.'

'He'd suit the company,' muttered Milva. 'He'd suit it perfectly.'

'Think his proposition over, Geralt,' Dandelion mocked. 'After all, he's a Nilfgaardian nobleman. Perhaps with his help it'll be easier for us to get to—'

'Keep your tongue in check,' the Witcher interrupted the poet sharply. 'As I said, draw your sword, Nilfgaardian.'

'I am not going to fight. And I am not a Nilfgaardian. I come from Vicovaro, and my name is—'

'I'm not interested in your name. Draw your weapon.'

'No.'

'Witcher.' Milva leant down from the saddle and spat on the ground. 'Time's flying and the rain's falling. The Nilfgaardian doesn't want to fight, and although you're pulling a stern face, you won't cut him to pieces in cold blood. Do we have to hang about here all fucking day? I'll stick an arrow in his chestnut's underbelly and let's be on our way. He won't catch up on foot.'

Cahir, son of Ceallach, was by his chestnut colt in one bound, jumped into the saddle and galloped back the way he'd come, yelling at his steed to go faster. The Witcher watched him riding off for a moment then mounted Roach. In silence. Without looking back.

'I'm getting old,' he mumbled some time later, after Roach had caught up with Milva's black. 'I'm starting to develop scruples.'

'Aye, it can happen with old 'uns,' said the archer, looking at him in sympathy. 'A decoction of lungwort can help. But for now put a cushion on your saddle.'

'Scruples,' Dandelion explained gravely, 'are not the same as piles, Milva. You're confusing the terms.'

'Who could understand your smart-arsed chatter? You never stop jabbering, it's the only thing you know! Come on, let's ride!'

'Milva,' the Witcher asked a moment later, protecting his face from the rain, which stabbed against it as they galloped. 'Would you have killed the horse under him?'

'No,' she confessed reluctantly. 'The horse hadn't done anything. But that Nilfgaardian— Why in hell is he stalking us? Why does he say he has to?'

'Devil take me if I know.'

It was still raining when the forest suddenly came to an end and they rode onto a highway winding between the hills from the south to the north. Or the other way around, depending on your point of view. What they saw on the highway didn't surprise them. They had already seen similar sights. Overturned and gutted wagons, dead horses, scattered bundles, saddlebags and baskets. And ragged shapes, which not long before had been people, frozen into strange poses.

They rode closer, without fear, because it was apparent that the slaughter had not taken place that day. They had come to recognise such things; or perhaps to sense them with a purely animalistic instinct, which the last days had awoken and sharpened in them.

They had also learned to search through battlefields, because occasionally – though not often – they had managed to find a little food or a sack of fodder among the scattered objects.

They stopped by the last wagon of a devastated column. It had been pushed into the ditch, and was resting on the hub of a shattered wheel. Beneath the wagon lay a stout woman with an unnaturally twisted neck. The collar of her tunic was covered with rain-washed streaks of coagulated blood from her torn ear, from which an earring had been ripped. The sign on the tarpaulin pulled over the wagon read: 'Vera Loewenhaupt and Sons'. There was no sign of the sons.

'They weren't peasants,' Milva said through pursed lips. 'They were traders. They came from the south, wending from Dillingen towards Brugge, and were caught here. It's not good, Witcher. I thought we could turn south at this point, but now I truly have no idea what to do. Dillingen and the whole of Brugge is sure to be in Nilfgaardian hands, so we won't make it to the Yaruga this way. We'll have to go east, through Turlough. There are forests and wildernesses there, the army won't go that way.'

'I'm not going any further east,' Geralt protested. 'I have to get to the Yaruga.'

'You'll get there,' she replied, unexpectedly calm. 'But by a safer route. If we head south from here, you'll fall right into the Nilfgaardians' jaws. You won't gain anything.'

'I'll gain time,' he snapped, 'by heading east I'm just wasting it. I told you, I can't afford to—'

'Quiet,' Dandelion said suddenly, steering his horse around. 'Be quiet for a moment.'

'What is it?'

'I can hear . . . singing.'

The Witcher shook his head. Milva snorted.

'You're hearing things, poet.'

'Quiet! Shut up! I'm telling you, someone's singing! Can't you hear it?'

Geralt lowered his hood; Milva also strained to listen and a moment later glanced at the Witcher and nodded silently.

The troubadour's musical ear hadn't let him down. What had

seemed impossible turned out to be true. Here they were, standing in the middle of a forest, in the drizzle, on a road strewn with corpses, and they could hear singing. Someone was approaching from the south, singing jauntily and gaily.

Milva tugged the reins of her black, ready to flee, but the Witcher gestured to her to wait. He was curious. Because the singing they could hear wasn't the menacing, rhythmic, booming, massed singing of marching infantry, nor a swaggering cavalry song. The singing, which was becoming louder all the time, didn't arouse any anxiety.

Quite the opposite.

The rain drummed on the foliage. They began to make out the words of the song. It was a merry song, which seemed strange, unnatural and totally out of place in this landscape of death and war.

Look how the wolf dances in the holt.
Teeth bared, tail waving, leaping like a colt.
Oh, why does he prance like one bewitched?
The frolicking beast simply hasn't been hitched!
Oom-pah, oom-pah, oom-pah-pah!

Dandelion suddenly laughed, took his lute from under his wet mantle, and – ignoring the hissing from the Witcher and Milva – strummed the strings and joined in at the top of his voice:

Look how the wolf is dragging his paws.
Head drooping, tail hanging, clenching his jaws.
Oh, why is the beast in such a sorry state?
He's either proposed or he's married his mate!

'Ooh-hoo-ha!' came the roared response from many voices close by.

Thunderous laughter burst out, then someone whistled piercingly through their fingers, after which a strange but colourful company came walking around a bend in the highway, marching in single file, splashing mud with rhythmic steps of their heavy boots.

74

'Dwarves,' Milva said under her breath. 'But they aren't Scoia'tael. They don't have plaited beards.'

There were six of them, dressed in short, hooded capes, shimmering with countless shades of grey and brown, the kind which were usually worn by dwarves in foul weather. Capes like that, as Geralt knew, had the quality of being totally waterproof, which was achieved by the impregnation of wood tar over many years, not to mention dust from the highway and the remains of greasy food. These practical garments passed from fathers to oldest sons; as a result they were used exclusively by mature dwarves. And a dwarf attains maturity when his beard reaches his waist, which usually occurs at the age of fifty-five.

None of the approaching dwarves looked young. But none looked old either.

'They're leading some humans,' muttered Milva, indicating to Geralt with a movement of her head a small group emerging from the forest behind the company of dwarves, 'who must be fugitives, because they're laden down with goods and chattels.'

'The dwarves aren't exactly travelling light themselves,' Dandelion added.

Indeed, each dwarf was heaving a load that many humans and horses would soon have collapsed under. In addition to the ordinary sacks and saddlebags, Geralt noticed iron-bound chests, a large copper cauldron and something that looked like a small chest of drawers. One of them was even carrying a cartwheel on his back.

The one walking at the front wasn't carrying anything. He had a small battle-axe in his belt, on his back was a long sword in a scabbard wrapped in tabby cat skins, and on his shoulder sat a green parrot with wet, ruffled feathers. The dwarf addressed them.

'Greetings!' he roared, after coming to a halt in the middle of the road and putting his hands on his hips. 'These days it's better to meet a wolf in the forest than a human. And if you do have such bad luck, you're more likely to be greeted with an arrow in the chest than a kind word! But whoever greets someone with a song or music must be a sound fellow! Or a sound wench; my apologies to the good lady! Greetings. I'm Zoltan Chivay.'

'I'm Geralt,' the Witcher introduced himself after a moment's hesitation. 'The singer is Dandelion. And this is Milva.'

''Kin' 'ell!' the parrot squawked.

'Shut your beak,' Zoltan Chivay growled at the bird. 'Excuse me. This foreign bird is clever but vulgar. I paid ten thalers for the freak. He's called Field Marshal Windbag. And while I'm at it, this is the rest of my party. Munro Bruys, Yazon Varda, Caleb Stratton, Figgis Merluzzo and Percival Schuttenbach.'

Percival Schuttenbach wasn't a dwarf. From beneath his wet hood, instead of a matted beard, stuck out a long, pointed nose, unerringly identifying its owner as one of the old and noble race of gnomes.

'And those,' Zoltan Chivay said, pointing at the small group of humans, who had stopped and were huddled together, 'are fugitives from Kernow. As you can see, they're women and children. There were more, but Nilfgaard seized them and their fellows three days ago, put some of them to the sword and scattered the others. We came across them in the forest and now we're travelling together.'

'It's bold of you,' the Witcher ventured, 'to be marching along the highway, singing as you go.'

'I don't reckon,' the dwarf said, wiggling his beard, 'that weeping as we go would be any better. We've been marching through the woods since Dillingen, quietly and out of sight, and after the army passed we joined the highway to make up time.' He broke off and looked around the battlefield.

'We've grown accustomed to sights like this,' he said, pointing at the corpses. 'Beyond Dillingen and the Yaruga there's nothing but dead bodies on the roads . . . Were you with this lot?'

'No. Nilfgaard put some traders to the sword.'

'Not Nilfgaard,' said the dwarf, shaking his head and looking at the dead with an indifferent expression. 'Scoia'tael. The regular army don't bother pulling arrows out of corpses. And a good arrowhead costs half a crown.'

'He knows his prices,' Milva muttered.

'Where are you headed?'

'South,' Geralt answered immediately.

'I advise you against it,' Zoltan Chivay said, and shook his head again. 'It's sheer hell, fire and slaughter there. Dillingen is taken for sure, the Nilfgaardians are crossing the Yaruga in greater and greater numbers; any moment now they'll flood the whole valley on the right bank. As you see, they're also in front of us, to the north. They're heading for the city of Brugge. So the only sensible direction to escape is east.'

Milva glanced knowingly at the Witcher, who refrained from comment.

'And that's where we're headed; east,' Zoltan Chivay continued. 'The only chance is to hide behind the frontline, and wait until the Temerian Army finally start out from the River Ina in the east. Then we plan to march along forest tracks until we reach the hills. Turlough, then the Old Road to the River Chotla in Sodden, which flows into the Ina. We can travel together, if you wish. If it doesn't bother you that we make slow progress. You're mounted and I realise our refugees slow the pace down.'

'It doesn't seem to bother you, though,' Milva said, looking at him intently. 'A dwarf, even fully laden, can march thirty miles a day. Almost the same as a mounted human. I know the Old Road. Without those refugees you'd reach the Chotla in about three days.'

'They are women and children,' Zoltan Chivay said, sticking out his beard and his belly. 'We won't leave them to their fate. Would you suggest we do anything else, eh?'

'No,' the Witcher said. 'No, we wouldn't.'

'I'm pleased to hear it. That means my first impressions didn't deceive me. So what's it to be? Do we march as one company?'

Geralt looked at Milva and the archer nodded.

'Very well,' Zoltan Chivay said, noticing the nod. 'So let's head off, before some raiding party chances upon us on the highway. But first— Yazon, Munro, search the wagons. If you find anything useful there, get it stowed away, and pronto. Figgis, check if our wheel fits that little wagon, it'll be just right for us.'

'It fits!' yelled the one who'd been lugging the cartwheel. 'Like it was made for it!'

'You see, muttonhead? And you were so surprised when I made you take that wheel and carry it! Put it on! Help him, Caleb!'

In an impressively short time the wagon of the dead Vera Loewenhaupt had been equipped with a new wheel, stripped of its tarpaulin and inessential elements, and pulled out of the ditch and onto the road. All their goods were heaved onto it in an instant. After some thought, Zoltan Chivay also ordered the children to be loaded onto the wagon. The instruction was carried out reluctantly; Geralt noticed that the children's mothers scowled at the dwarves and tried to keep their distance from them.

With visible distaste, Dandelion watched two dwarves trying on articles of clothing removed from some corpses. The remaining dwarves rummaged around among the wagons, but didn't consider anything to be worth taking. Zoltan Chivay whistled through his fingers, signalling that the time for looting was over, and then he looked over Roach, Pegasus and Milva's black with an expert eye.

'Saddle horses,' he said, wrinkling his nose in disapproval. 'In other words: useless. Figgis and Caleb, to the shaft. We'll be hauling in turn. Maaaaarch!'

Geralt was certain the dwarves would quickly discard the wagon the moment it got well and truly stuck in soft, boggy ground, but he was mistaken. They were as strong as oxen, and the forest tracks leading east turned out to be grassy and not too swampy, even though it continued to rain without letting up. Milva became gloomy and grumpy, and only broke her silence to express the conviction that the horses' softened hooves would split at any moment. Zoltan Chivay licked his lips in reply, examined the hooves in question and declared himself a master at roasting horsemeat, which infuriated Milva.

They kept to the same formation, the core of which was formed by the wagon hauled on a shift system. Zoltan marched in front of the wagon. Next to him, on Pegasus, rode Dandelion, bantering with the parrot. Geralt and Milva rode behind them, and at the back trudged the six women from Kernow.

The leader was usually Percival Schuttenbach, the long-nosed gnome. No match for the dwarves in terms of height or strength, he was their equal in stamina and considerably superior in agility. During the march he never stopped roaming around and rummaging in bushes; then he would pull ahead and disappear, only to appear and with nervous, monkey-like gestures signal from a considerable distance away that everything was in order and that they could continue. Occasionally he would return and give a rapid report about the obstacles on the track. Whenever he did, he would have a handful of blackberries, nuts or strange – but clearly tasty – roots for the four children sitting on the wagon.

Their pace was frightfully slow and they spent three days marching along forest tracks. They didn't happen upon any soldiers; they saw no smoke or the glow of fires. They were not alone, however. Every so often Percival spotted groups of fugitives hiding in the forests. They passed several such groups, hurriedly, because the expressions of the peasants armed with pitchforks and stakes didn't encourage them to try to make friends. There was nonetheless a suggestion to try to negotiate and leave the women from Kernow with one of the groups, but Zoltan was against it and Milva backed him up. The women were in no hurry at all to leave the company either. This was all the stranger since they treated the dwarves with such obvious, fearful aversion and reserve, hardly ever spoke, and kept out of the way during every stop.

Geralt ascribed the women's behaviour to the tragedy they had experienced a short time before, although he suspected that their aversion may have been due to the dwarves' casual ways. Zoltan and his company cursed just as filthily and frequently as the parrot called Field Marshal Windbag, but had a wider repertoire. They sang dirty songs, which Dandelion enthusiastically joined in with. They spat, blew their noses on their fingers and gave thunderous farts, which usually prompted laughs, jokes and competition. They only went into the bushes for major bodily needs; with the minor ones they didn't even bother moving very far away. This finally enraged Milva, who gave Zoltan a good telling-off when one morning he pissed on the still warm ashes of the campfire, totally oblivious to his audience. Having been dressed down, Zoltan was unperturbed and announced that shamefully concealing that kind of activity was only common among two-faced, perfidious people who were likely to be informers, and could be identified as such by doing just that.

This eloquent explanation made no impression on the archer. The dwarves were treated to a rich torrent of abuse, with several very specific threats, which was effective, since they all obediently began to go into the bushes. To avoid laying themselves open to the appellation of 'perfidious informers', however, they went in a group.

The new company, nevertheless, changed Dandelion utterly. He got on famously with the dwarves, particularly when it turned out that some of them had heard of him and even knew his ballads and couplets. Dandelion dogged Zoltan's company. He wore a quilted jacket he had weaselled out of the dwarves, and his crumpled hat with a feather was replaced by a swashbuckling marten-fur cap. He sported a broad belt with brass studs, into which he had stuck a cruel-looking knife he had been given. This knife pricked him in the side each time he tried to lean over. Fortunately, he quickly mislaid it and wasn't given another.

They wandered through the dense forests covering the hillsides of Turlough. The forests seemed deserted; there were no traces of any wild animals, for they had apparently been frightened away by the armies and fugitives. There was nothing to hunt, but they weren't immediately threatened by hunger. The dwarves were lugging along a large quantity of provisions. As soon as they were finished, however – and that occurred quickly, because there were many mouths to feed – Yazon Varda and Munro Bruys vanished soon after dark, taking an empty sack with them. When they returned at dawn, they had two sacks, both full. In one was fodder for the horses, in the other barley groats, flour, beef jerky, an almost entire cheese, and even a huge haggis: a delicacy in the form of a pig's stomach stuffed with offal and pressed between two slats, the whole resembling a pair of bellows.

Geralt guessed where the haul had come from. He didn't comment right away, but bided his time until a moment when he was alone with Zoltan, and then asked him politely if he saw nothing indecent in robbing other fugitives, who were no less hungry than them, after all, and fighting for survival just like them. The dwarf answered gravely that indeed, he was very ashamed of it, but unfortunately, such was his character.

'Unbridled altruism is a huge vice of mine,' he explained. 'I simply have to do good. I am a sensible dwarf, however, and know that I'm unable to do everyone good. Were I to attempt to be good to everyone, to the entire world and to all the creatures living in it, it would be a drop of fresh water in the salt sea. In other words, a wasted effort. Thus, I decided to do specific good; good which would not go to waste. I'm good to myself and my immediate circle.'

Geralt asked no further questions.

At one of the camps, Geralt and Milva chatted at length with Zoltan Chivay, the incorrigible and compulsive altruist. The dwarf was well informed about how the military activities were proceeding. At least, he gave that impression.

'The attack,' he said, frequently quietening down Field Marshal Windbag, who was screeching obscenities, 'came from Drieschot, and began at dawn on the seventh day after Lammas. Nilfgaard marched with its allies, the Verdenian Army, since Verden, as you know, is now an imperial protectorate. They moved swiftly, putting all the villages beyond Drieschot to the torch and wiping out the Bruggian Army which was garrisoned there. The Nilfgaardian infantry marched on the fortress in Dillingen from the other side of the Yaruga. They crossed the river in a totally unexpected place. They built a pontoon bridge. Only took them half a day, can you believe it?'

'It's possible to believe anything,' muttered Milva. 'Were you in Dillingen when it started?'

'Thereabouts,' the dwarf replied evasively. 'When news of the attack reached us, we were already on the way to the city of Brugge. The highway was an awful shambles, it was teeming with fugitives, some of them fleeing from the south to the north, others from the north to the south. They jammed up the highway, so we got stuck. And Nilfgaard, as it turned out, were both behind us and in front of us. The forces that had left Drieschot must have split up. I reckon a large cavalry troop had headed north-east, towards Brugge.'

'So the Nilfgaardians are already north of Turlough. It appears we're stuck between two forces, right in the middle. And safe.'

'Right in the middle, yes,' the dwarf agreed. 'But not safe. The imperial troops are flanked by the Squirrels, Verdenian volunteers and various mercenaries, who are even worse than the Nilfgaardians. It was them as burnt down Kernow and almost seized us later; we barely managed to leg it into the woods. So we shouldn't poke our noses out of the forest. And we should remain on guard. We'll make it to the Old Road, then downstream by the River Chotla to the Ina, and at the Ina we're sure to bump into the Temerian Army. King Foltest's men must have shaken off their surprise and begun standing up to the Nilfgaardians.'

'If only,' Milva said, looking at the Witcher. 'But the problem is that urgent and important matters are driving us on to the south. We pondered heading south from Turlough, towards the Yaruga.'

'I don't know what matters are driving you to those parts,' Zoltan said, glowering suspiciously at them. 'They must indeed be greatly urgent and important to risk your necks for them.'

He paused and waited, but neither of them was in a hurry to explain. The dwarf scratched his backside, hawked and spat.

'It wouldn't surprise me,' he said finally, 'if Nilfgaard had both banks of the Yaruga right up to the mouth of the Ina in their grasp. And where exactly on the Yaruga do you need to be?'

'Nowhere specific,' Geralt decided to reply. 'As long as we reach the river. I want to take a boat up to the delta.'

Zoltan looked at him and laughed. Then stopped immediately when he realised it hadn't been a joke.

'I have to admit,' he said a moment later, 'you've got quite some route in mind. But get rid of those pipe dreams. The whole of south Brugge is in flames. They'll impale you before you reach the Yaruga, or drive you to Nilfgaard in fetters. However, were you by some miracle to reach the river, there'd be no chance of sailing to the delta. That pontoon bridge spanning the river from Cintra to the Bruggian bank? They guard it day and night; nothing could get through that part of the river, except perhaps a salmon. Your urgent and important matters will have to lose their urgency and importance. You haven't got a prayer. That's how I see it.'

Milva's glance testified that she shared his opinion. Geralt didn't comment. He felt terrible. The slowly healing bone in his left forearm and his right knee still gnawed with the invisible fangs of a dull, nagging pain, made worse by effort and the constant damp. He was also being troubled by overwhelming, disheartening, exceptionally unpleasant feelings, alien feelings he had never experienced before and was unable to deal with.

Helplessness and resignation.

After two days, it stopped raining and the sun came out. The forests breathed forth mists and quickly dissipating fog, and birds began to vigorously make up for the silence forced on them by the constant rain. Zoltan cheered up and ordered a long break, after which he promised a quicker march and that they would reach the Old Road in a day at most.

The women from Kernow draped all the surrounding branches with the black and grey of drying clothing, and then, dressed only in their shifts, hid shamefacedly in the bushes and prepared food. The children charged around naked, disturbing the dignified calm of the steaming forest in elaborate ways. Dandelion slept off his tiredness. Milva vanished.

The dwarves took their rest seriously. Figgis Merluzzo and Munro Bruys went off hunting mushrooms. Zoltan, Yazon Varda, Caleb Stratton and Percival Schuttenbach sat down near the wagon and without taking a breather played Barrel, their favourite card game, which they devoted every spare minute to, including the previous wet evenings.

The Witcher occasionally sat down to join them and watch them play, as he did during this break. He was still unable to understand the complicated rules of this typical dwarven game, but was fascinated by the amazing, intricate workmanship of the cards and the drawings of the figures. Compared to the cards humans played with, the dwarves' cards were genuine works of art. Geralt was once again convinced that the advanced technology of the bearded folk was not limited to the fields of mining and metallurgy. The fact that in this specific, card-playing field the dwarves' talents hadn't helped them to monopolise the market was because cards were still less popular among humans than dice, and human gamblers attached little import-ance to aesthetics. Human card players, whom the Witcher had had several opportunities to observe, always played with greasy cards, so dirty that before cards were placed on the table they had to be laboriously peeled away from the fingers. The court cards were painted so carelessly that distinguishing the lady from the knave was only possible because the knave was mounted on a horse. Which actually looked more like a crippled weasel.

Mistakes of that kind were impossible with the dwarves' cards. The crowned king was really regal, the lady comely and curvaceous, and the halberd-wielding knave jauntily moustachioed. The colour cards were called, in Dwarven Speech, the *hraval*, *vaina* and *ballet*, but Zoltan and company used the Common Speech and human names when they played.

The sun shone warmly, the forest steamed, and Geralt watched.

The fundamental principle of dwarven Barrel was something resembling an auction at a horse fair, both in its intensity and the volume of the bidders' voices. The pair declaring the highest 'price' would endeavour to win as many tricks as possible, which the rival pair had to impede at all costs. The game was played noisily and heatedly, and a sturdy staff lay beside each player. These staffs were seldom used to beat an opponent, but were often brandished.

'Look what you've done! You plonker! You bonehead! Why did you open with spades instead of hearts? Think I was leading hearts just for the fun of it? Why, I ought to take my staff and knock some sense into you!'

'I had four spades up to the knave, so I was planning to make a good contract!'

'Four spades, 'course you did! Including your own member, which you counted when you looked down at your cards. Use your loaf, Stratton, we're not at university! We're playing cards here! And remember that when the fool has the cards and doesn't blunder, he'll even beat the sage, by thunder. Deal, Varda.'

'Contract in diamonds.'

'A small slam in diamonds!'

'The king led diamonds, but lost his crown, fled the kingdom with his trousers down. A double in spades!'

'Barrel!'

'Wake up, Caleb. That was a double with a Barrel! What are you bidding?'

'A big slam in diamonds!'

'No bid. Aaagh! What now? No one's Barrelling? Chickened out, laddies? You're leading, Varda. Percival, if you wink at him again, I'll whack you so hard in the kisser your eyes'll be screwed up till next winter.'

'Knave.'

'Lady!'

'And the king on the lady! The lady's shafted! I'll take her and, ha, ha, I've got another heart, kept for a rainy day! Knave, a ten and another—'

'And a trump! If you can't play a trump, you'd better take a dump. And diamonds! Zoltan? Grabbed you where it hurts!'

'Do you see him, fucking gnome. Pshaw, I'm gonna take my staff to him . . .'

Before Zoltan could use his stick, a piercing cry was heard from the forest.

Geralt was the first to his feet. He swore as he ran, pain shooting through his knee. Zoltan Chivay rushed after him, seizing his sword wrapped in tabby cat skins from the wagon. Percival Schuttenbach and the rest of the dwarves ran after them, armed with sticks, while Dandelion, who'd been woken by the screaming, brought up the rear. Figgis and Munro leapt out of the forest from one side. Throwing down their baskets of mushrooms, the two dwarves gathered up the scattering children and pulled them away. Milva appeared from nowhere, drawing an arrow from her quiver while running and showing the Witcher where the scream had come from. There was no need. Geralt saw and heard, and now knew what it was all about.

One of the children was screaming. She was a freckled, little girl with plaits, aged about nine. She stood petrified, a few paces from a pile of rotten logs. Geralt was with her in an instant. He seized her under the arms, interrupting her terrified shrieking, and watched the movement among the logs out of the corner of his eye. He quickly withdrew and bumped into Zoltan and his dwarves. Milva, who had also seen something moving, nocked her arrow and took aim.

'Don't shoot,' Geralt hissed. 'Get this kid out of here, fast. And you, get back. But nice and easy. Don't make any sudden movements.'

At first it seemed to them that the movement had come from one of the rotten logs, as though it was intending to crawl out of the sunlit woodpile and look for shade among the trees. It was only when they looked closer that they saw features which were atypical for a log: in particular, four pairs of thin legs with knobbly joints sticking up from the furrowed, speckled, segmented crayfish-like shell.

'Easy does it,' Geralt said quietly. 'Don't provoke it. Don't let its apparent sluggishness deceive you. It isn't aggressive, but it moves like lightning. If it feels threatened it may attack and there's no antidote for its venom.'

The creature slowly crawled onto a log. It looked at the humans and the dwarves, slowly turning its eyes, which were set on stalks. It was barely moving. It cleaned the ends of its legs, lifting them up one by one and carefully nibbling them with its impressive-looking, sharp mandibles.

'There was such an uproar,' Zoltan declared emotionlessly, appearing beside the Witcher, 'I thought it was something really worrying. Like a cavalryman from a Verdenian reserve troop. Or a military prosecutor. And what is it? Just an overgrown creepy-crawly. You have to admit, nature takes on some pretty curious forms.'

'Not any longer,' Geralt replied. 'The thing that's sitting there is an eyehead. A creature of Chaos. A dying, post-conjunction relic, if you know what I'm talking about.'

'Of course I do,' the dwarf said, looking him in the eyes. 'Although I'm not a witcher, nor an authority on Chaos and creatures like that. Well, I'm very curious to see what the Witcher will do with this post-conjunction relic. Or to be more precise, I'm wondering *how* the Witcher will do it. Will you use your sword or do you prefer my sihil?'

'Nice weapon,' Geralt said, glancing at the sword, which Zoltan

86

had drawn from its lacquered scabbard wrapped in tabby cat skins. 'But it won't be necessary.'

'Interesting,' Zoltan repeated. 'So are we just going to stand here looking at each other? Just wait until that relic feels threatened? Or should we withdraw and ask some Nilfgaardians for help? What do you suggest, monster slayer?'

'Fetch the ladle and the cauldron lid from the wagon.'

'What?'

'Don't question his authority, Zoltan,' Dandelion chipped in.

Percival Schuttenbach scurried off to the wagon and soon returned with the requested objects. The Witcher winked at the company and then began to beat the ladle against the lid with all his strength.

'Stop it! Stop it!' Zoltan Chivay screamed a moment later, covering his ears with his hands. 'You'll break the fucking ladle! The beast's run off! He's gone, for pox's sake!'

'Oh yes,' Percival said, delighted. 'Did you see him? On my life, he showed a clean pair of heels! Not that he has any!'

'The eyehead,' Geralt explained calmly, handing back the slightly dented kitchen utensils to the dwarves, 'has remarkably delicate, sensitive hearing. It doesn't have any ears, but hears, so to speak, with its entire body. In particular it can't bear metallic noises. It feels them as a pain . . .'

'Even in the arse,' Zoltan interrupted. 'I know, because it pained me too when you started whacking that lid. If the monster has more sensitive hearing than I do, he has my sympathy. Sure he won't be back? He won't rustle up some mates?'

'I don't imagine many of its mates are left on this earth. That specimen is certain not to be back in these parts for a long time. There's nothing to be afraid of.'

'I'm not going to talk about monsters,' the dwarf said, looking glum. 'But your concerto for brass instruments must have been heard as far away as the Skellige Islands, so it's possible some music lovers might be heading this way. And we'd better not be around when they come. Strike camp, boys! Hey, ladies, get clad and count up the children! We're moving out, and quickly!'

*

When they stopped for the night, Geralt decided to clear up a few issues. This time Zoltan Chivay hadn't sat down to play Barrel, so there was no difficulty leading him away to a secluded place for a frank, man-to-man conversation. He got straight to the point.

'Out with it. How do you know I'm a witcher?'

The dwarf winked at him and smiled slyly.

'I might boast about my perspicacity. I could say I noticed your eyes changing after dusk and in full sunlight. I could show that I'm a dwarf-of-the-world and that I've heard this and that about Geralt of Rivia. But the truth is much more banal. Don't scowl. You can keep things to yourself, but your friend the bard sings and jabbers; he never shuts his trap. That's how I know about your profession.'

Geralt refrained from asking another question. And rightly so.

'It's like this,' Zoltan continued. 'Dandelion told me everything. He must have sensed we value sincerity, and, after all, he didn't have to sense our friendly disposition to you, because we don't hide our dispositions. So in short: I know why you're in a hurry to go south. I know what important and urgent matters are taking you to Nilfgaard. I know who you're planning to seek. And not just from the poet's gossip. I lived in Cintra before the war and I heard tales of the Child of Destiny and the white-haired witcher to whom the child was granted.'

Geralt did not respond this time either.

'The rest,' the dwarf said, 'is just a question of observation. You let that crusty monstrosity go, even though you're a witcher and it's your professional duty to exterminate monsters like that. But the beast didn't do your Surprise any harm, so you spared it and just drove it away by banging on a cauldron lid. Because you're no longer a witcher; you're a valiant knight, who is hastening to rescue his kidnapped and oppressed maiden.

'Why don't you stop glaring at me,' he added, still not hearing an answer or an explanation. 'You're constantly sniffing out treachery; fearful of how this secret – now it's out – may turn against you. Don't fret. We're all going to the Ina, helping each other, supporting each other. The challenge you have in front of you is the same one we face: to survive and stay alive. In order for this noble mission to continue. Or live an ordinary life, but so as not to be ashamed at the hour of death. You think you've changed. That the world has changed. But look; the world's the same as it's always been. Quite the same. And you're the same as you used to be. Don't fret.

'But drop your idea about heading off alone,' Zoltan continued his monologue, unperturbed by the Witcher's silence, 'and about a solo journey south, through Brugge and Sodden to the Yaruga. You'll have to search for another way to Nilfgaard. If you want, I can advise you—'

'Don't bother,' Geralt said, rubbing his knee, which had been hurting incessantly for several days. 'Don't bother, Zoltan.'

He found Dandelion watching the Barrel-playing dwarves. He took the poet by the sleeve and led him off to the forest. Dandelion realised at once what it was all about; one glance at the Witcher's face was enough.

'Babbler,' Geralt said quietly. 'Windbag. Bigmouth. I ought to shove your tongue in a vice, you blockhead. Or put a bit between your teeth.'

The troubadour said nothing, but his expression was haughty.

'When news got out that I'd started to associate with you,' the Witcher continued, 'some sensible people were surprised by our friendship. It astonished them that I let you travel with me. They advised me to abandon you in a desert, to rob you, strangle you, throw you into a pit and bury you in dung. Indeed, I regret I didn't follow their advice.'

'Is it such a secret who you are and what you're planning to do?' Dandelion suddenly said, losing his temper. 'Are we to keep the truth from everybody and pretend all the time? Those dwarves . . . We're all one company now . . .'

'I don't have a company,' the Witcher snapped. 'I don't have one, and I don't want to have one. I don't need one. Do you get it?'

'Of course he gets it,' Milva said from behind him. 'And I get it too. You don't need anyone, Witcher. You show it often enough.'

'I'm not fighting a private war,' he said, turning around suddenly. 'I don't need a company of daredevils, because I'm not going to Nilfgaard to save the world or to bring down an evil empire. I'm going to get Ciri. And that's why I can go alone. Forgive me if that sounds unkind, but the rest of it doesn't concern me. And now leave me. I want to be alone.'

When he turned around a moment later, he discovered that only Dandelion had walked away.

'I had that dream again,' he said abruptly. 'Milva, I'm wasting time. I'm wasting time! She needs me. She needs help.'

'Talk,' she said softly. 'Get it out. No matter how frightening it is, get it out.'

'It wasn't frightening. In my dream . . . She was dancing. She was dancing in some smoky barn. And she was – hell's bells – happy. There was music playing, someone was yelling . . . The entire barn was shaking from shouting and music . . . And she was dancing, dancing, clicking her heels . . . And on the roof of that bloody barn, in the cold, night air . . . death was dancing too. Milva . . . Maria . . . She needs me.'

Milva turned her face away.

'Not just her,' she whispered. Quietly, so he wouldn't hear.

At the next stop, the Witcher demonstrated his interest in Zoltan's sword, the sihil, which he had glanced at during the adventure with the eyehead. Without hesitation, the dwarf unwrapped the weapon from its catskins and drew it from its lacquered scabbard.

The sword measured a little over three feet, but didn't weigh much more than two pounds. The blade, which was decorated along much of its length with mysterious runes, had a bluish hue and was as sharp as a razor. In the right hands, it could have been used to shave with. The twelve-inch hilt, wound around with criss-crossed strips of lizard skin, had a cylindrical brass cap instead of a spherical pommel and its crossguard was very small and finely crafted.

'A fine piece of work,' Geralt said, making a quick, hissing moulinet followed by a thrust from the left and then a lightning transition to a high seconde parry and then laterally into prime. 'Indeed, a nice bit of ironmongery.'

'Phew!' Percival Schuttenbach snorted. 'Bit of ironmongery! Take a better look at it, because you'll be calling it a horseradish root next.'

'I had a better sword once.'

'I don't dispute that,' Zoltan said, shrugging his shoulders. 'Because it was sure to have come from our forges. You witchers know how to wield a sword, but you don't make them yourselves. Swords like that are only forged by dwarves, in Mahakam under Mount Carbon.'

'Dwarves smelt the steel,' Percival added, 'and forge the laminated blades. But it's us, the gnomes, who do the finishing touches and the sharpening. In our workshops. Using our own, gnomish technology, as we once made our gwyhyrs, the best swords in the world.'

'The sword I wield now,' Geralt said, baring the blade, 'comes from the catacombs of Craag An in Brokilon. It was given to me by the dryads. It's a first-class weapon, but it's neither dwarven nor gnomish. It's an elven blade, at least one or maybe two hundred years old.'

'He doesn't know what he's talking about!' the gnome called, picking up the sword and running his fingers over it. 'The details are elven, I give you that. The hilt, crossguard and pommel. The etching, engraving, chasing and other decorative elements. But the blade was forged and sharpened in Mahakam. And it's true that it was made several centuries ago, because it's obvious that the steel is mediocre and the workmanship primitive. Now, hold Zoltan's sihil against it; do you see the difference?'

'Yes I do. And I have the impression mine's just as well made.'

The gnome snorted and waved a hand. Zoltan smiled superciliously.

'The blade,' he explained in a patronising voice, 'should cut, not make an impression, and it shouldn't be judged on first impressions either. The point is that your sword is a typical composition of steel and iron, while my sihil's blade was forged from a refined alloy containing graphite and borax . . .'

'It's a modern technique!' Percival burst out, a little excited, since the conversation was moving inevitably towards his field of expertise. 'The blade's construction and composition, numerous laminates in its soft core, edged with hard – not soft – steel . . .'

'Take it easy,' the dwarf said, reining him in. 'You won't make a metallurgist out of him, Schuttenbach, so don't bore him with details. I'll explain it in simple terms. It's incredibly difficult to sharpen good, hard, magnetite steel, Witcher. Why? Because it's hard! If you don't have the technology, as we dwarves once did not, and you humans still don't have, but you want a sharp sword, you forge soft steel edges, which are more malleable, onto a hardened core. Your Brokilonian sword is made using just such a simplified method. Modern dwarven blades are made the opposite way around: with a soft core and hard edges. The process is time-consuming and, as I said, demands advanced technology. But as a result you get a blade which will cut a batiste scarf tossed up in the air.'

'Is your sihil capable of a trick like that?'

'No' The dwarf smiled. 'The swords sharpened to that degree are few and far between, and not many of them ever left Mahakam. But I guarantee that the shell of that knobbly old crab wouldn't have put up much resistance against it. You could have sliced him up without breaking a sweat.'

The discussion about swords and metallurgy continued for some time. Geralt listened with interest, shared his own experiences, added some extra information, asked about this and that and then examined and tried out Zoltan's sihil. He had no idea that the following day he would have the opportunity to add practice to the theory he had acquired.

The first indication that humans were living in the area was the neatly stacked cord of firewood standing among woodchips and tree bark by the track, spotted by Percival Schuttenbach, who was walking at the head of the column.

Zoltan stopped the procession and sent the gnome ahead to scout. Percival vanished and after half an hour hurried back, excited and out of breath and gesticulating from a long way off. He reached them, but instead of giving his report, grabbed his long nose in his fingers and blew it powerfully, making a sound resembling a shepherd's horn.

'Don't frighten away the game,' Zoltan Chivay barked. 'And talk. What lies ahead of us?'

'A settlement,' the gnome panted, wiping his fingers on the tails of his many-pocketed kaftan. 'In a clearing. Three cottages, a barn, a few mud and straw huts . . . There's a dog running around in the farmyard and the chimney's smoking. Someone's preparing food there. Porridge. And made with milk.'

'You mean you went into the kitchen?' Dandelion laughed. 'And peered into the pot? How do you know it's porridge?'

The gnome looked at him with an air of superiority and Zoltan snarled angrily.

'Don't insult him, poet. He can sniff out grub a mile away. If he says it's porridge, it's porridge. Still, I don't like the sound of this.'

'Why's that? I like the sound of porridge. I'd be happy to try some.'

'Zoltan's right,' Milva said. 'And you keep quiet, Dandelion, because this isn't poetry. If the porridge is made with milk that means there's a cow. And a peasant who sees fires burning will take his cow and disappear into the forest. Why didn't this one? Let's duck into the forest and give it a wide berth. There's something fishy about this.'

'Not so fast, not so fast,' the dwarf muttered. 'There'll be plenty of time to flee. Perhaps the war's over. Perhaps the Temerian Army has finally moved out. What do we know, stuck in this forest? Perhaps the decisive battle's over, perhaps Nilfgaard's been repulsed, perhaps the front's already behind us, and the peasants are returning home with their cows. We ought to examine this and find out what's behind it. Figgis and Munro; you two stay here and keep your eyes peeled. We'll do a bit of reconnaissance. If it's safe, I'll make a call like a sparrow hawk.'

'Like a sparrow hawk?' said Munro Bruys, anxiously moving his chin. 'Since when did you know anything about mimicking bird calls, Zoltan?'

'That's the whole point. If you hear a strange, unrecognisable sound, you'll know it's me. Percival, lead on. Geralt, will you come with us?'

'We'll all go,' Dandelion said, dismounting. 'If it's a trap we'll be safer in a bigger group.'

'I'll leave you the Field Marshal,' Zoltan said, removing the parrot from his shoulder and passing him to Figgis Merluzzo. 'This ugly bird might suddenly start effing and blinding at the top of his voice and then our silent approach will go to fuck. Let's go.'

Percival quickly led them to the edge of the forest, into dense elder shrubs. The ground fell away slightly beyond the shrubs, where they saw a large pile of uprooted tree stumps. Beyond them there was a broad clearing. They peered out cautiously.

The gnome's account had been accurate. There really were three cottages, a barn and several sod-roofed mud and straw huts in the middle of the clearing. A huge puddle of muck glistened in the farm-yard. The buildings and a small, untended plot were surrounded by a low, partly fallen down fence, on the other side of which a scruffy dog was barking. Smoke was rising from the roof of one of the cottages, creeping lazily over the sunken turfs.

'Indeed,' Zoltan whispered, sniffing, 'that smoke smells good. Particularly since my nostrils are used to the stench of burnt-down houses. There are no horses or guards around, which is good, because I bore in mind that some rabble might be resting up and cooking a meal here. Mmm, I'd say it's safe.'

'I'll take a look,' volunteered Milva.

'No,' the dwarf protested. 'You look too much like a Squirrel. If they see you they might get frit, and humans can be unpredictable when they're startled. Yazon and Caleb will go. But keep your bow at the ready; you can cover them if needs be. Percival, leg it over to the others. You lot be prepared, in case we have to sound the retreat.'

Yazon Varda and Caleb Stratton cautiously left the thicket and headed towards the buildings. They walked slowly, looking around intently.

The dog smelled them right away, started barking furiously, then ran around the farmyard, not reacting to the dwarves' clucking and whistling. The door to the cottage opened. Milva raised her bow and drew back the bowstring in a single movement. And then immediately slackened it.

A short, stout girl with long plaits came rushing out. She shouted something, waving her arms. Yazon Varda spread his arms and

94

shouted something back. The girl continued to bawl something. They could hear the sound but were unable to make out what she was saying.

But the words must have reached Yazon and Caleb, who made an about-turn and hurried back towards the elder shrubs. Milva drew her bow again and swept around with the arrowhead, searching for a target.

'What the devil's going on?' Zoltan rasped. 'What's happening? What are they running away from? Milva?'

'Shut your trap,' the archer hissed, still taking aim at each cottage and hut in turn. But she couldn't find anyone to shoot. The girl with the plaits disappeared into her cottage and shut the door behind her.

The dwarves were sprinting as though the Grim Reaper was on their heels. Yazon yelled something – or possibly cursed. Dandelion suddenly blanched.

'He's saying . . . Oh, Gods!'

'What . . .' Zoltan broke off, for Yazon and Caleb had made it back, red in the face. 'What is it? Spit it out!'

'The plague . . .' Caleb gasped. 'Smallpox . . .'

'Did you touch anything?' Zoltan Chivay asked, stepping back nervously and almost knocking Dandelion over. 'Did you touch anything in the farmyard?'

'No . . . The dog wouldn't let us near . . .'

'May the fucking mutt be praised,' Zoltan said, raising his eyes heavenwards. 'May the Gods give it a long life and a heap of bones higher than Mount Carbon. That girl, the plump one, did she have blisters?'

'No. She's healthy. The infected ones are in the last cottage, her in-laws. And a lot of people have already died, she said. Blimey, Zoltan, the wind was blowing right towards us!'

'That's enough teeth chattering,' Milva said, lowering her bow. 'If you didn't touch any infected people, you've got nothing to worry about. If it's true what she says about the pox. Maybe the girl just wanted to scare you away.'

'No,' Yazon replied, still breathing heavily. 'There was a pit behind the hut . . . with bodies in it. The girl doesn't have the strength to bury the dead, so she throws them into the pit . . .'

'Well,' Zoltan said, sniffing. 'That's your porridge, Dandelion. But I've slightly lost my appetite for it. Let's get out of here; and fast.'

The dog in the farmyard began barking again.

'Get down,' the Witcher hissed, dropping into a crouch.

A group of horsemen came riding out from a gap in the trees on the other side of the clearing. Whistling and whooping, they circled the farmstead at a gallop and then burst into the yard. The riders were armed, but weren't in identical uniforms. Quite the contrary, in fact – they were all dressed differently and haphazardly, and their weaponry and tackle gave the impression of being assembled at random. And not in an armoury, but on a battlefield.

'Thirteen,' Percival Schuttenbach said, making a quick tally.

'Who are they?'

'Neither Nilfgaard, nor any other regulars,' came Zoltan's assessment. 'Not Scoia'tael. I think they're volunteers. A random mob.'

'Or marauders.'

The horsemen were yelling and cavorting around the farmyard. One of them hit the dog with a spear shaft and it bolted. The girl with the plaits ran outside, shouting. But this time her warning had no effect or wasn't taken seriously. One of the horseman galloped up, seized the girl by one of her plaits, pulled her away from the doorway and dragged her through the puddle of muck. The others jumped off their horses to assist the first, dragging the girl to the end of the farmyard. They tore her shift off her and threw her down onto a pile of rotten straw. The girl fought back ferociously, but she had no chance. Only one of the marauders didn't join in the fun; he guarded the horses, which were tied to the fence. The girl gave a long, piercing scream. Then a short, pained one. They heard nothing after that.

'Warriors!' Milva said, jumping to her feet. 'Fucking heroes!'

'They aren't afraid of the pox,' Yazon Varda said, shaking his head.

'Fear,' Dandelion muttered, 'is a human quality. There's nothing human in them any longer.'

'Apart from their innards,' Milva rasped, carefully nocking an arrow, 'which I shall now prick.'

'Thirteen,' Zoltan Chivay repeated gravely. 'And they're all mounted. You'll knock off one or two and the rest will have us surrounded. And anyway, it might be an advance party. The devil knows what kind of bigger force they belong to.'

'Do you expect me to stand by and watch?'

'No,' Geralt said, straightening his headband and the sword on his back. 'I've had enough of standing by and watching. I'm fed up with my own helplessness. But first we have to stop them from getting away. See the one holding the horses? When I get there, knock him out of the saddle. And if you can, take out another. But only when I get down there.'

'That leaves eleven,' the archer said, turning to face him.

'I can count.'

'You've forgotten about the smallpox,' Zoltan Chivay muttered. 'If you go down there, you'll come back infected . . . Bollocks to that, Witcher! You're putting us all at risk . . . For fuck's sake, *she's* not the girl you're looking for!'

'Shut up, Zoltan. Go back to the wagon and hide in the forest.'

'I'm coming with you,' Milva declared hoarsely.

'No. Cover me from here, you'll be helping more if you do that.'

'What about me?' Dandelion asked. 'What should I do?'

'The same as usual. Nothing.'

'You're insane . . .' Zoltan snarled. 'Taking on the entire band? What's got into you? Want to play the hero, rescuing fair maidens?'

'Shut up.'

'Go to hell! No, wait. Leave your sword. There's a whole bunch of them, so it'd be better if you didn't have to swing twice. Take my sihil. One blow is enough.'

The Witcher took the dwarf's weapon without a word or a moment's hesitation. He pointed out the marauder guarding the horses one more time. And then hopped over the tree stumps and moved quickly towards the cottages.

The sun was shining. Grasshoppers scattered in front of him.

The man guarding the horses saw him and pulled a spear from its place by his saddle. He had very long, unkempt hair, falling onto a torn hauberk, patched up with rusty wire. He was wearing brand-new – clearly stolen – boots with shiny buckles.

The guard yelled and another marauder appeared from behind the fence. He was carrying a sword slung from a belt around his neck and was just buttoning his britches. Geralt was quite close by now. He could hear the guffawing of the men amusing themselves with the girl on the pile of straw. He took some deep breaths and each one intensified his blood lust. He could have calmed himself down, but didn't want to. He wanted to have some fun himself.

'And who might you be? Stop!' the long-haired man shouted, hefting the spear in his hand. 'What do you want here?'

'I've done enough standing and watching.'

'Whaaat?'

'Does the name Ciri mean anything to you?'

'I'll—'

The marauder was unable to finish his sentence. A grey-fletched arrow hit him in the middle of his chest and threw him from the saddle. Before he hit the ground, Geralt could hear the next arrow whistling. The second soldier caught the arrowhead in the abdomen, low, right between the hands buttoning up his fly. He howled like an animal, bent double and lurched back against the fence, knocking over and breaking some of the pickets.

Before the others had managed to come to their senses and pick up their weapons, the Witcher was among them. The dwarven blade glittered and sang. There was a savage craving for blood in the song of the feather-light, razor-sharp steel. The bodies and limbs offered almost no resistance. Blood splashed onto his face; he had no time to wipe it off.

Even if the marauders were thinking about putting up a fight, the sight of falling corpses and blood gushing in streams effectively discouraged them. One of them, who had his trousers around his knees since he hadn't even had time to pull them up, was slashed in the carotid artery and tumbled onto his back, comically swinging his still unsatisfied manhood. The second, nothing but a stripling, covered his head with both hands, which the sihil severed at the wrists. The remaining men took flight, dispersing in various directions. The Witcher pursued them, softly cursing the pain that was once again pulsing through his knee. He hoped the leg wouldn't buckle under him.

He managed to pin two of them against the fence. They tried to defend themselves by holding up their swords. Paralysed by terror, their defence was woeful. The Witcher's face was once again spattered with blood from arteries slashed open by the dwarven blade. But the remaining men made use of the time and managed to get away; they were already mounted. One of then fell, however, hit by an arrow, wriggling and squirming like a fish emptied from a net. The last two spurred their horses into a gallop. But only one of them managed to escape, because Zoltan Chivay had suddenly appeared in the farmyard. The dwarf swung his axe around his head and threw it, hitting one of the fleeing men in the centre of the back. The marauder screamed and tumbled from the saddle, legs kicking. The last one pressed himself tight to his horse's neck, cleared the pit full of dead bodies and galloped towards the gap in the trees.

'Milva!' the Witcher and the dwarf both yelled.

The archer was already running towards them. Now she stopped, frozen, with legs apart. She let her nocked bow fall and then began to lift it up slowly, higher and higher. They didn't hear the twang of the bowstring, neither did Milva change her position or even twitch. They only saw the arrow when it dipped and hurtled downwards. The horseman lurched sideways out of the saddle, the feathered shaft protruding from a shoulder. But he didn't fall. He straightened up and with a cry urged his horse into a faster gallop.

'What a bow,' Zoltan Chivay grunted in awe. 'What a shot!'

'What a shot, my arse,' the Witcher said, wiping blood from his face. 'The whoreson's got away and he'll be back with a bunch of his mates.'

'She hit him! And it must have been two hundred paces!'

'She could have aimed at the horse.'

'The horse isn't guilty of anything,' Milva panted with anger, walking over to them. She spat and watched the horseman disappear into the forest. 'I missed the good-for-nothing, because I was a mite out of breath . . . Ugh, you rat, running away with my arrow! I hope it brings you bad luck!'

The neighing of a horse could be heard from the gap in the trees, and immediately afterwards the dreadful cry of a man being killed.

'Ho, ho!' Zoltan said, looking at the archer in awe. 'He didn't get very far! Your arrows are damned effective! Poisoned? Or enchanted perhaps? Because even if the good-for-nothing had caught the small-pox, the plague wouldn't have taken its toll so quickly!'

'It wasn't me,' Milva said, looking knowingly at the Witcher. 'Nor the smallpox. But I think I know who it was.'

'I think I do too,' the dwarf said, chewing his moustache with a canny smile on his face. 'I've noticed you keep looking back, and I know someone's secretly following us. On a chestnut colt. I don't know who he is, but since it doesn't bother you . . . It's none of my business.'

'Particularly since a rearguard can have its uses,' Milva said, looking at Geralt meaningfully. 'Are you certain that Cahir's your enemy?'

The Witcher didn't reply. He gave Zoltan his sword back.

'Thanks. It cuts nicely.'

'In the right hands,' the dwarf said, grinning. 'I've heard tales about witchers, but to fell eight in less than two minutes . . .'

'It's nothing to brag about. They didn't know how to defend themselves.'

The girl with the plaits raised herself onto her hands and knees, stood up, staggered, and then tried ineffectually to pull down her torn shift with trembling hands. The Witcher was astonished to see that she was in no way similar to Ciri, when a moment earlier he would have sworn they were twins. The girl wiped her face with an uncoordinated movement, and moved unsteadily towards the cot-tage. Straight through the puddle of muck.

'Hey, wait,' Milva called. 'Hey, you . . . Need any help? Hey!'

The girl didn't even look towards her. She stumbled over the threshold, almost falling, then grabbed the door jamb. And slammed the door behind her.

'Human gratitude knows no boundaries,' the dwarf commented. Milva jerked around, her face hardened.

'What does she have to be grateful for?'

'Exactly,' the Witcher added. 'What for?'

'For the marauders' horses,' Zoltan said, not lowering his gaze. 'She can slaughter them for their meat; she won't have to kill the cow. She's clearly resistant to smallpox and now she doesn't have to fear hunger. She'll survive. And in a few days, when she gathers her thoughts, she'll understand that thanks to you she avoided a longer frolic and these cottages being burnt to the ground. Let's get out of here before the plague blows our way . . . Hey, Witcher, where are you going? To get a token of gratitude?'

'To get a pair of boots,' Geralt said coldly, stooping down over the long-haired marauder, whose dead eyes stared heavenwards. 'These look right for me.'

They ate horsemeat for several days. The boots with the shiny buckles were quite comfortable. The Nilfgaardian called Cahir was still riding in their tracks on his chestnut colt, but the Witcher had stopped looking back.

He had finally fathomed the arcana of Barrel and even played a hand with the dwarves. He lost.

They didn't speak about the incident in the forest clearing. There was nothing to say.

Mandrake, or Love Apple, is a class of plant from the Mandragora *or nightshade family, a group including herbaceous, stemless plants with parsnip-like roots, in which a similarity to the human form may be observed; the leaves are arranged in a rosette.* **M.** autumnalis *or* officinalis, *is cultivated on a small scale in Vicovaro, Rowan and Ymlac, rarely found in the wild. Its berries, which are green and later turn yellow, are eaten with vinegar and pepper, while its leaves are consumed raw. The root of the* **m.***, which is a valued ingredient in medicine and herb lore, long ago had great import in superstitions, particularly among the Nordlings; human effigies (called alruniks or alraunes) were carved from it and kept in homes as revered talismans. They were believed to offer protection from illnesses, to bring good fortune during trials, and to ensure fertility and uncomplicated births. The effigies were clad in dresses which were changed at each new moon.* **M.** *roots were bought and sold, with prices reaching as much as sixty florins. Bryony roots (q.v.) were used as substitutes. According to superstition,* **m.** *was used for making spells, magical philtres and poisons. This belief returned during the period of the witch hunts. The charge of the criminal use of* **m.** *was made, for example, during the trial of Lucretia Vigo (q.v.). The legendary Philippa Alhard (q.v.) was also said to have used* **m.** *as a poison.*

Effenberg and Talbot, *Encyclopaedia Maxima Mundi,*
Volume IX

CHAPTER THREE

The Old Road had changed somewhat since the last time the Witcher had travelled along it. Once a level highway paved with slabs of basalt, built by elves and dwarves centuries before, it had now become a potholed ruin. In some places the holes were so deep that they resembled small quarries. The pace of the march dropped since the dwarves' wagon wove between the potholes with extreme difficulty, frequently becoming stuck.

Zoltan Chivay knew the reason for the road's desperate state of disrepair. Following the last war with Nilfgaard, he explained, the need for building materials had increased tremendously. People had recalled that the Old Road was an almost inexhaustible source of dressed stone. And since the neglected road, built in the middle of nowhere and leading nowhere, had long ago lost its importance for transport and served few people, it was vandalised without mercy or restraint.

'Your great cities,' the dwarf complained, accompanied by the parrot's screeched expletives, 'were without exception built on dwarven and elven foundations. You built your own foundations for your smaller castles and towns, but you still use our stones for the walls. And yet you never stop repeating that it's thanks to you – humans – that the world progresses and develops.'

Geralt did not comment.

'But you don't even know how to destroy things wisely,' Zoltan griped, ordering yet another attempt to pull a wheel out of a hole. 'Why can't you remove the stones gradually, from the edges of the road? You're like children! Instead of eating a doughnut systematically, you gouge the jam out with a finger and then throw away the rest because it's not sweet any more.'

Geralt explained patiently that political geography was to blame for everything. The Old Road's western end lay in Brugge, the eastern end in Temeria and the centre in Sodden, so each kingdom destroyed its own section at its own discretion. In response, Zoltan obscenely stated where he'd happily shove all the kings and listed some imaginative indecencies he would commit regarding their politics, while Field Marshal Windbag added his own contribution to the subject of the kings' mothers.

The further they went, the worse it became. Zoltan's comparison with a jam doughnut turned out to be less than apt; the road was coming to resemble a suet pudding with all the raisins gouged out. It looked as though the inevitable moment was approaching when the wagon would shatter or become totally and irreversibly stuck. They were saved, however, by the same thing that had destroyed the road. They happened upon a track heading towards the southeast, worn down and compacted by the heavy wagons which had been used to transport the pillaged stone. Zoltan brightened up, for he recognised that the track led unerringly to one of the forts on the Ina, on whose bank he was hoping to meet the Temerian Army. The dwarf solemnly believed that, as during the previous war, a crushing counter-attack by the northern kingdoms would be launched from Sodden on the far side of the Ina, following which the survivors of Nilfgaard's thoroughly decimated forces would scurry back across the Yaruga.

And indeed, the change in their trek's direction once again brought them closer to the war. During the night a great light suddenly flared up in front of them, while during the day they saw columns of smoke marking the horizon to the south and the east. Since they were still uncertain who was attacking and burning and who was being attacked and burnt they proceeded cautiously, sending Percival Schuttenbach far ahead to reconnoitre.

They were astonished one morning to be overtaken by a riderless horse, the chestnut colt. The green saddlecloth embroidered with Nilfgaardian symbols was stained with dark streaks of blood. There was no way of knowing if it was the blood of the horseman who had been killed near the hawker's wagon or if it had been spilt later, when the horse had acquired a new owner.

'Well, that takes care of the problem,' Milva said, glancing at Geralt. 'If it ever really was a problem.'

'The biggest problem is we don't know who knocked the rider from the saddle,' Zoltan muttered. 'And whether that someone is following our trail and the trail of our erstwhile, unusual rearguard.'

'He was a Nilfgaardian,' Geralt said between clenched teeth. 'He spoke almost without an accent, but runaway peasants could have recognised it . . .'

Milva turned to face him.

'You ought to have finished him off, Witcher,' she said softly. 'He would have had a kinder death.'

'He got out of that coffin,' Dandelion said, nodding, looking meaningfully at Geralt, 'just to rot in some ditch.'

And that was the epitaph for Cahir, son of Ceallach, the Nilfgaardian who insisted he wasn't a Nilfgaardian. He was not talked about any longer. Since Geralt – in spite of repeated threats – seemed to be in no hurry to part with the skittish Roach, Zoltan Chivay mounted the chestnut. The dwarf's feet didn't reach the stirrups, but the colt was mild-mannered and let himself be ridden.

During the night the horizon was bright with the glow of fires and during the day ribbons of smoke rose into the sky, soiling the blue. They soon came upon some burnt-out buildings, with flames still creeping over the charred beams and ridges. Alongside the smouldering timbers sat eight ragged figures and five dogs, all busily gnawing the remains of the flesh from a bloated, partly charred horse carcass. At the sight of the dwarves the feasters fled in a panic. Only one man and one dog remained, who no threats were capable of tearing away from the carrion on the arched spine and ribs. Zoltan and Percival tried to question the man, but learned nothing. He only whimpered, trembled, tucked his head into his shoulders and choked on the scraps torn from the bones. The dog snarled and bared its teeth up to its gums. The horse's carcass stank repulsively.

They took a risk and didn't leave the road, and soon reached the next smouldering remains. A sizeable village had been burnt down and a skirmish must have taken place nearby, because they saw a fresh burial mound directly behind the smoking ruins. And at a certain distance beyond the mound a huge oak tree stood by the crossroads. The tree was hung with acorns.

And human corpses.

'We ought to take a look,' Zoltan Chivay decided, putting an end to the discussion about the risks and the danger. 'Let's go closer.'

'Why the bloody hell,' Dandelion asked, losing his temper, 'do you want to look at those corpses, Zoltan? To despoil them? I can see from here they don't even have boots.'

'Fool. It's not their boots I'm interested in but the military situation. I want to know of the developments in the theatre of war. What's so funny? You're just a poet, and you don't know what strategy is.'

'You're in for a surprise. I do.'

'Nonsense. You wouldn't know strategy from your own arse, even if your life depended on it.'

'Indeed, I wouldn't. I'll leave half-arsed strategies to dwarves. The same applies to strategies dangling from oak trees.'

Zoltan dismissed him with a wave and tramped over to the tree. Dandelion, who had never been able to rein in his curiosity, urged Pegasus on and trotted after him. A moment later Geralt decided to follow them. And then noticed that Milva was riding behind him.

The crows feeding on the carcasses took flight, cawing and flapping their wings noisily. Some of them flew off towards the forest, while others merely alighted on the mighty tree's higher branches, intently observing Field Marshal Windbag, who was coarsely defaming their mothers from the dwarf's shoulder.

The first of the seven hanged humans had a sign on his chest reading: 'Traitor'. The second was described as a 'Collaborator', the third as an 'Elven Nark' and the fourth as a 'Deserter'. The fifth was a woman in a torn and bloodied shift, described as a 'Nilfgaardian Whore'. Two of the corpses weren't bearing signs, which suggested at least some of the victims had been hanged by chance.

'Look,' Zoltan Chivay said cheerfully, pointing at the signs. 'Our army passed by this way. Our brave boys have taken the initiative and repulsed the enemy. And they had time, as we can see, for relaxation and wartime entertainment.'

'And what does that mean for us?'

'That the front has moved and the Temerian Army are between us and the Nilfgaardians. We're safe.'

'And the smoke ahead of us?'

'That's our boys,' the dwarf declared confidently. 'They're burning down villages where Squirrels were given rest or vittles. We're behind the front line now, I'm telling you. The southern way heads from the crossroads to Armeria, a fortress lying in a fork of the Chotla and the Ina. The road looks decent, we can take it. We needn't be afraid of Nilfgaardians now.'

'Where there's smoke, there's fire,' Milva said. 'And where there's fire you can get your fingers burnt. I reckon it's stupid to head towards the flames. It's also stupid to travel along a road, when the cavalry could be on us in an instant. Let's disappear into the trees.'

'The Temerians or an army from Sodden passed through here,' the dwarf insisted. 'We're behind the front line. We can march along the highway without fear; if we come across an army it'll be ours.'

'Risky,' said the archer, shaking her head. 'If you're such an old hand, Zoltan, you must know that Nilfgaard usually sends advance parties a long way ahead. Perhaps the Temerians were here. But we have no idea what's in front of us. The sky's black from smoke to the south. That fortress of yours in Armeria is probably burning right now. Which means we aren't behind the front line, but right on it. We may run into the army, marauders, leaderless bands of rogues, or Squirrels. Let's head for the Chotla, but along forest tracks.'

'She's right,' Dandelion concurred. 'I don't like the look of that smoke either. And even if Temeria is on the offensive, there may still be advance Nilfgaardian squadrons in front of us. The Nilfgaardians are fond of long-distance raids. They attack the rear lines, link up with the Scoia'tael, wreak havoc and ride back. I remember what happened in Upper Sodden during the last war. I'm also in favour of travelling through the forest. We have nothing to fear there.'

'I wouldn't be so sure,' Geralt said, pointing to the last corpse who, although he was dangling high up, had bloody stumps instead of feet. They looked like they had been raked by talons until all that was left was protruding bones. 'Look. That's the work of ghouls.'

'Ghouls?' Zoltan Chivay said, retreating and spitting on the ground. 'Flesh-eaters?'

'Naturally. We have to beware in the forest at night.'

'Fuuuckiiin' 'ell!' Field Marshal Windbag screeched.

'You took the words right out of my mouth, birdie,' Zoltan Chivay said, frowning. 'Well, we're in a pretty pickle. What's it to be, then? Into the forest, where there's ghouls, or along the road, where there's armies and marauders?'

'Into the forest,' Milva said with conviction. 'The denser the better. I prefer ghouls to humans.'

They marched through the forest, at first cautious, on edge, reacting with alarm to every rustle in the undergrowth. Soon, however, they regained their poise, their good humour and their previous speed. They didn't see any ghouls, or the slightest trace of their presence. Zoltan joked that spectres and any other demons must have heard about the approaching armies, and if the fiends had happened to see the marauders and Verdenian volunteers in action, then – seized with terror – they would have hidden in their most remote and inaccessible lairs, where they were now cowering and trembling, fangs chattering.

'And they're guarding the she-ghouls, their wives and their daughters,' Milva snapped. 'The monsters know that a soldier on the march won't even pass up a sheep. And if you hung a woman's shift on a willow tree, a knothole would be enough for those heroes.' She looked pointedly at the women and children from Kernow, who were still with the group.

Dandelion, who had been full of vigour and good humour for quite some time, tuned his lute and began to compose a fitting couplet about willows, knotholes and lascivious warriors, and the dwarves and the parrot outdid each other in supplying ideas for rhymes.

*

'O,' Zoltan stated.

'What? Where?' Dandelion asked, standing up in his stirrups and looking down into the ravine in the direction the dwarf was pointing. 'I can't see anything!'

'O.'

'Don't drivel like your parrot! What do you mean "oh"?'

'It's a stream,' Zoltan calmly explained. 'A right-bank tributary of the Chotla. It's called the O.'

'Ey . . .'

'Not a bit of it!' Percival Schuttenbach laughed. 'The A joins the Chotla upstream, some way from here. That's the O, not the A.'

The ravine, along the bottom of which flowed the stream with the uncomplicated name, was overgrown with nettles taller than the marching dwarves, smelled intensively of mint and rotten wood and resounded with the unremitting croaking of frogs. It also had steep sides, which turned out to be fatal. Vera Loewenhaupt's wagon, which from the beginning of the journey had valiantly born the adversities of fate and overcome every obstacle, lost out in its clash with the stream by the name of 'O'. It slipped from the hands of the dwarves leading it downwards, bounced on down to the very bottom of the ravine and was smashed to matchwood.

"Kin' . . . 'ell!' Field Marshal Windbag squawked, a counterpoint to the massed cry of Zoltan and his company.

'To tell the truth,' Dandelion concluded, scrutinising the remains of the vehicle and the scattered possessions, 'perhaps it's for the best. That bloody wagon of yours only slowed down the march. There were constant problems with it. Look at it realistically, Zoltan. We were just lucky that no one was following us. If we'd had to suddenly run for it we'd have had to abandon the wagon along with all of your belongings, which we can now at least salvage.'

The dwarf seethed and grunted angrily into his beard, but Percival Schuttenbach unexpectedly backed up the troubadour. The support, as the Witcher observed, was accompanied by several conspiratorial winks. The winks were meant to be surreptitious, but the lively expression of the gnome's little face revealed everything.

'The poet's right,' Percival repeated, contorting his face and wink-ing. 'We're a muddy stone's throw from the Chotla and the Ina. Fen Carn's in front of us; not a road to be seen. It would have been arduous with a wagon. And should we meet the Temerian Army by the Ina, with our load . . . we might be in trouble.'

Zoltan pondered this, sniffing.

'Very well,' he said finally, looking at the remains of the wagon being washed by the O's lazy current. 'We'll split up. Munro, Figgis, Yazon and Caleb will stay here. The rest of us will continue on our way. We'll have to saddle the horses with our sacks of vittles and small tackle. Munro, do you know what to do? Got spades?'

'Yes.'

'Just don't leave the merest trace! And mark the spot well and remember it!'

'Rest assured.'

'You'll catch up with us easily,' Zoltan said, throwing his ruck-sack and sihil over his shoulder and adjusting the battle-axe in his belt. 'We'll be heading down the O and then along the Chotla to the Ina. Farewell.'

'I wonder,' Milva mumbled to Geralt when the depleted unit had set off, sent on its way by the waving of the four dwarves who were remaining behind, 'I wonder what they have in those chests that needs burying in secret.'

'It's not our business.'

'I can't imagine,' Dandelion said, *sotto voce*, cautiously steering Pegasus between the fallen trees, 'that there were spare trousers in those chests. They're pinning their hopes on that load. I talked with them enough to work out how the land lies and what might be con-cealed in those coffers.'

'And what might be concealed in them, in your opinion?'

'Their future,' the poet said, looking around to check no one could hear. 'Percival's a stone polisher and cutter by trade, and wants to open his own workshop. Figgis and Yazon are smiths, they've been talking about a forge. Caleb Stratton plans to marry, but his fiancée's parents have already driven him away once as a penniless bum. And Zoltan . . .'

112

'That's enough, Dandelion. You're gossiping like an old woman. No offence, Milva.'

'None taken.'

The trees thinned out beyond the stream and the dark, boggy strip of ancient woodland. They rode into a clearing with low birch woods and dry meadows. In spite of that they made slow progress. Following the example of Milva, who right away had lifted the freckled girl with the plaits onto her saddle, Dandelion also put a child on Pegasus, while Zoltan put a couple on his chestnut colt and walked alongside, holding the reins. But the pace didn't increase, since the women from Kernow were unable to keep up.

It was almost evening when, after nearly an hour of roaming through ravines and gorges, Zoltan Chivay stopped, exchanged a few words with Percival Schuttenbach, and then turned to the rest of the company.

'Don't yell and don't laugh at me,' he said, 'but I reckon we're lost. I don't bloody know where we are or which way to go.'

'Don't talk drivel,' Dandelion said, irritated. 'What do you mean you don't know? After all, we're following the course of the river. And down there in the ravine is your O. Right?'

'Right. But look which way it's flowing.'

'Oh bugger. That's impossible!'

'No, it's not,' Milva said gloomily, patiently pulling dry leaves and pine needles from the hair of the freckled girl who was riding in front of her. 'We're lost among the ravines. The stream twists and turns. We're on a meander.'

'But it's still the O,' Dandelion insisted. 'If we follow the river, we can't get lost. Little rivers are known to meander, I admit, but ultimately they all invariably flow into something bigger. That is the way of the world.'

'Don't play the smart-arse, singer,' Zoltan said, wrinkling his nose. 'And shut your trap. Can't you see I'm thinking?'

'No. There's nothing to suggest it. I repeat, let's keep to the course of the stream, and then . . .'

'That'll do,' Milva snapped. 'You're a townie. Your world is bounded by walls. Perhaps your worldly wisdom is of some use there. Take a look around! The valley's furrowed by ravines with steep, overgrown banks. How do you think we'll follow the course of the stream? Down the side of a gorge into thickets and bogs, up the other side and down again and up again, pulling our horses by the reins? After two ravines you'll be so short of breath you'll be flat on your back halfway up a slope. We're leading women and children, Dandelion. And the sun'll be setting directly.'

'I noticed. Very well, I'll keep quiet. And listen to what the experienced forest trackers come up with.'

Zoltan Chivay cuffed the cursing parrot around the head, twisted a tuft of his beard around a finger and tugged it in anger.

'Percival?'

'We know the rough direction,' the gnome said, squinting up at the sun, which was suspended just above the treetops. 'So the first conception is this: blow the stream, turn back, leave these ravines for dry land and go through Fen Carn, between the rivers, all the way to the Chotla.'

'And the second conception?'

'The O's shallow. Even though it's carrying more water than usual after the recent rains, it can be forded. We'll cut off the meanders by wading through the stream each time it blocks our way. By holding a course according to the sun, we'll come right out at the fork of the Chotla and the Ina.'

'No,' the Witcher suddenly broke in. 'I suggest we drop the second idea right away. Let's not even think about it. On the far bank we'll end up in one of the Mealybug Moors sooner or later. It's a vile place, and I strongly advise we keep well away from it.'

'Do you know these parts, then? Ever been there before? Do you know how we can get out of here?'

The Witcher remained silent for a while.

'I've only been there once,' he said, wiping his forehead. 'Three years ago. But I entered from the other side. I was heading for Brugge and wanted to take a short cut. How I got out I don't remember. I was carried out on a wagon half-dead.'

The dwarf looked at him for a while, but asked no more questions.

They returned in silence. The women from Kernow had difficulty walking. They were stumbling and using sticks for support, but none of them uttered a word of complaint. Milva rode alongside the Witcher, holding up the girl with the plaits, who was asleep on the saddle in front of her.

'I think,' she suddenly began, 'that you got carved up in that wilderness, three years ago. By some monster, I understand. You have a dangerous job, Geralt.'

'I don't deny it.'

'I remember what happened then,' Dandelion boasted from behind. 'You were wounded, some merchant got you out and then you found Ciri in Riverdell. Yennefer told me about it.'

At the sound of that name Milva smiled faintly. It did not escape Geralt's notice. He decided to give Dandelion a good dressing down at the next camp for his untrammelled chatter. Knowing the poet, he couldn't count on any results, particularly since Dandelion had probably already blabbed everything he knew.

'Perhaps it wasn't such a good idea,' said the archer after a while, 'that we didn't cross to the far bank, towards the wilderness. If you found the girl then . . . The elves say that sometimes lightning can strike twice. They call it . . . Bugger, I've forgotten. The noose of fate?'

'The loop,' he corrected her. 'The loop of fate.'

'Uurgh!' Dandelion said, grimacing. 'Can't you stop talking about nooses and loops? A she-elf once divined that I would say farewell to this vale of tears on the scaffold, with the help of the deathsman. Admittedly I don't believe in that type of tawdry fortune-telling, but a few days ago I dreamed I was being hanged. I awoke in a muck sweat, unable to swallow or catch my breath. So I listen with reluctance to discussions about gibbets.'

'I'm not talking to you, I'm talking to the Witcher,' Milva riposted. 'So don't flap your ears and nothing horrible will fall into them. Well then, Geralt? What have you got to say about that loop of fate? If we go to the wilderness, perhaps time will repeat itself.'

'That's why it's good we've turned back,' he replied brusquely. 'I don't have the slightest desire to repeat that nightmare.'

*

'There's no two ways about it.' Zoltan nodded, looking around. 'You've led us to a pretty charming place, Percival.'

'Fen Carn,' the gnome muttered, scratching the tip of his long nose. 'Meadow of the Barrows . . . I've always wondered how it got its name . . .'

'Now you know.'

The broad valley in front of them was already shrouded in evening mist from which, as far as the eye could see, protruded thousands of burial mounds and moss-covered monoliths. Some of the boulders were ordinary, shapeless lumps of stone. Others, smoothly hewn, had been sculpted into obelisks and menhirs. Still others, standing closer to the centre of this stone forest, were formed into dolmens, cairns and cromlechs, in a way that ruled out any natural processes.

'Indeed,' the dwarf repeated, 'a charming place to spend the night. An elven cemetery. If my memory doesn't fail me, Witcher, some time ago you mentioned ghouls. Well, you ought to know, I can sense them among these kurgans. I bet there's everything here. Ghouls, graveirs, spectres, wights, elven spirits, wraiths, apparitions; the works. They're hunkered down there and do you know what they're whispering? "We won't have to go looking for supper, because it's come right to us."'

'Perhaps we ought to go back,' Dandelion suggested in a whisper. 'Perhaps we should get out of here, while there's still some light.'

'That's what I think too.'

'The womenfolk can't go any further,' Milva said angrily. 'The kids are ready to drop. The horses have stopped. You were the one driving us on, Zoltan. "Let's keep going, just another half a mile," you kept repeating. "Just another furlong," you said. And now what? Two more furlongs back the way we came? Crap. Cemetery or no cemetery, we're stopping for the night, the first place we find.'

'That's right,' the Witcher said in support, dismounting. 'Don't panic. Not every necropolis is crawling with monsters and apparitions. I've never been to Fen Carn before, but if it were really dangerous I'd have heard about it.'

No one, not even Field Marshal Windbag, commented. The

women from Kernow retrieved their children and sat down in a tight group, silent and visibly frightened. Percival and Dandelion tethered the horses and let them graze on the lush grass. Geralt, Zoltan and Milva approached the edge of the meadow, to look at the burial ground drowning in the fog and the gathering gloom.

'To cap it all, the moon's completely full,' the dwarf muttered. 'Oh dear, there'll be a ghastly feast tonight, I can feel it, oh, the demons will make our lives miserable . . . But what's that glow to the south? A fire?'

'What else? Of course it is,' the Witcher confirmed. 'Someone's torched someone else's roof over their head again. Know what, Zoltan? I think I feel safer here in Fen Carn.'

'I'll feel like that too, but only when the sun comes up. As long as the ghouls let us see out the night.'

Milva rummaged in her saddlebag and took out something shiny.

'A silver arrowhead,' she said. 'Kept for just such an occasion. It cost me five crowns at the market. That ought to kill a ghoul, right, Witcher?'

'I don't think there are any ghouls here.'

'You said yourself,' Zoltan snapped, 'that ghouls had been chewing that corpse on the oak tree. And where there's a cemetery, there are ghouls.'

'Not always.'

'I'll take your word for it. You're a witcher, a specialist; so you'll defend us, I hope. You chopped up those marauders pretty smartly . . . Is it harder fighting ghouls than marauders?'

'Incomparably. I said stop panicking.'

'And will it be any good for a vampire?' Milva asked, screwing the silver arrowhead onto a shaft and checking it for sharpness with her thumb. 'Or a spectre?'

'It may be.'

'An ancient dwarven incantation in ancient dwarven runes is engraved on my sihil,' Zoltan growled, drawing his sword, 'If just one ghoul approaches at a blade's length, it won't forget me. Right here, look.'

'Ah,' Dandelion, who had just joined them, said with interest. 'So those are some of the famous secret runes of the dwarves. What does the engraving say?'

'"Confusion to the whores' sons!"'

'Something moved among the stones,' Percival Schuttenbach suddenly yelled. 'It's a ghoul, it's a ghoul!'

'Where?'

'Over there! It's hid itself among the boulders!'

'One?'

'I saw one!'

'He must be seriously hungry, since he's trying to get his teeth into us before nightfall,' the dwarf said, spitting on his hands and gripping the hilt of his sihil tightly. 'Ha! He'll soon find out gluttony will be his ruin! Milva, you stick an arrow in his arse and I'll cut his gizzard open!'

'I can't see anything there,' Milva hissed, with the fletchings already touching her chin. 'Not a single weed between the stones is trembling. Sure you weren't seeing things, gnome?'

'Not a chance,' Percival protested. 'Do you see that boulder that looks like a broken table? The ghoul hid behind it.'

'You lot stay here,' Geralt said, quickly drawing his sword from the scabbard on his back. 'Guard the womenfolk and keep an eye on the horses. If the ghouls attack, the animals will panic. I'll go and find out what it was.'

'You aren't going by yourself,' Zoltan firmly stated. 'Back there in the clearing I let you go alone. I chickened out because of the smallpox. And two nights running I haven't slept for shame. Never again! Percival, where are you off to? To the rear? You claim to have seen the phantom, so now you're going in the vanguard. Don't be afeared, I'm coming with you.'

They headed off cautiously between the barrows, trying not to disturb the weeds – which were knee-high to Geralt and waist-high to the dwarf and the gnome. As they approached the dolmen that Percival had pointed out they artfully split up, cutting off the ghoul's potential escape route. But the strategy turned out to be unnecessary. As Geralt had expected, his witcher medallion didn't even quiver; betrayed no sign of anything monstrous nearby.

'There's no one here,' Zoltan confirmed, looking around. 'Not a soul. You must have imagined it, Percival. It's a false alarm. You put the wind up us for no reason. You truly deserve my boot up your arse for that.'

'I saw it!' the gnome said indignantly. 'I saw it hopping about among the stones! It was skinny and dressed all in black like a tax collector . . .'

'Be quiet, you foolish gnome, or I'll . . .'

'What's that strange odour?' Geralt suddenly asked. 'Can you smell it?'

'Indeed,' the dwarf said, nose extended like a pointer. 'What a pong.'

'Herbs,' Percival said, sniffling with his sensitive, two-inch-long nose. 'Wormwood, basil, sage, aniseed . . . Cinnamon? What the blazes?'

'What do ghouls smell of, Geralt?'

'Rotting corpses,' the Witcher said, taking a quick look around and searching for footprints in the grass. Then with a few swift steps he returned to the sunken dolmen and tapped gently against the stone with the flat of his sword.

'Get out,' he said through clenched teeth. 'I know you're in there. Be quick, or I'll poke a hole in you.'

A soft scraping could be heard from a cleverly concealed cavity beneath the stones.

'Get out,' Geralt repeated. 'You're perfectly safe.'

'We won't touch a hair on your head,' Zoltan added sweetly, raising his sihil above the hollow and rolling his eyes menacingly. 'Out with you!'

Geralt shook his head and made a clear sign for the dwarf to withdraw. Once again there was a scratching from the cavity under the dolmen and once again they were aware of the intense aroma of herbs and spices. A moment later they saw a grizzled head and then a face embellished with a nobly aquiline nose, belonging by no means to a ghoul but to a slim, middle-aged man. Percival hadn't been wrong. The man did indeed somewhat resemble a tax collector.

'Is it safe to come out?' he asked, raising black eyes beneath slightly greying eyebrows towards Geralt.

'Yes, it is.'

The man scrambled out of the hole, brushed down his black robes – which were tied around the waist with some kind of apron – and straightened a linen bag, causing another wave of the herbal aroma.

'I suggest you put away your weapons, gentlemen,' he declared in a measured voice, running his eyes over the group of wanderers surrounding him. 'They won't be necessary. I, as you can see, bear no blade. I never do. Neither do I have anything on me that might be termed attractive booty. My name is Emiel Regis. I come from Dillingen. I'm a barber-surgeon.'

'Indeed,' Zoltan Chivay grimaced a little. 'A barber-surgeon, alchemist or herbalist. No offence, my dear sir, but you smell seriously like an apothecary's shop.'

Emiel Regis smiled strangely, with pursed lips, and spread his arms apologetically.

'The scent betrayed you, master barber-surgeon,' Geralt said, replacing his sword in its sheath. 'Did you have any particular reason to hide from us?'

'Any particular reason?' the man asked, turning his black eyes towards him. 'No. I was just taking general precautions. I was simply afraid of you. These are difficult times.'

'True.' The dwarf nodded and pointed towards the glow of fire lighting up the sky. 'Difficult times. I surmise that you are a fugitive, as we are. It intrigues me, however, that although you've fled far from your native Dillingen, you're hiding all alone among these kurgans. Well, people's fates are various, particularly during difficult times. We were afraid of you and you of us. Fear makes one imagine things.'

'You have nothing to fear from me,' the man who was claiming to be Emiel Regis said, without taking his eyes off them, 'I hope I can count on reciprocity.'

'My, my,' Zoltan said, grinning broadly. 'You don't take us for robbers, do you? We, master barber-surgeon, are fugitives. We are travelling to the Temerian border. You may join us if you wish. The more the merrier . . . and safer, and a physician may come in handy. We have women and children in the party. Among the stinking medicaments I can smell about you, would you have a remedy for blisters?'

'I ought to have something,' the barber-surgeon said softly. 'Glad to be of assistance. But as far as travelling together is concerned . . . Thank you for the offer, but I'm not running away, gentlemen. I wasn't fleeing from Dillingen to escape the war. I live here.'

'Come again?' the dwarf said, frowning and taking a step back. 'You live here? Here, in this burial ground?'

'In the burial ground? No. I have a cottage not far from here. Apart from my house and shop in Dillingen, you understand. But I spend my summers here every year, from June to September, from Midsummer to the Equinox. I gather healing herbs and roots, from which I distil medicines and elixirs in my cottage . . .'

'But you know about the war in spite of your reclusive solitude far from the world and people.' Geralt pointed out. 'Who do you get your news from?'

'From the refugees who pass this way. There's a large camp less than two miles from here, by the River Chotla. A good few hundred fugitives – peasants from Brugge and Sodden – are gathered there.'

'And what about the Temerian Army?' Zoltan asked with interest. 'Are they on the move?'

'I know nothing about that.'

The dwarf swore and then glowered at the barber-surgeon.

'So you simply live here, Master Regis,' he drawled, 'and stroll among the graves of an evening. Aren't you afraid?'

'What ought I to be afraid of?'

'This here gentleman,' Zoltan pointed at Geralt, 'is a witcher. He saw evidence of ghouls not long ago. Corpse eaters, get it? And you don't have to be a witcher to know that ghouls hang around in cemeteries.'

'A witcher,' the barber-surgeon said, and looked at Geralt with obvious interest. 'A monster killer. Well, well. Fascinating. Didn't you explain to your comrades, Master Witcher, that this necropolis is over five hundred years old? Ghouls aren't fussy about what they eat, but they don't chew five-hundred-year-old bones. There aren't any ghouls here.'

'I feel a lot better knowing that,' Zoltan Chivay said, looking around. 'Well, master physician, come over to our camp. We have some cold horsemeat. You won't refuse it, will you?'

Regis looked at him long and hard.

'My thanks,' he said finally. 'But I have a better idea. Come to my place. My summer abode is more of a shack than a cottage, and a small one at that. You'll have no choice but to sleep under the stars. But there's a spring nearby and a hearth where you can warm up your horsemeat.'

'We'll gladly take you up on your invitation,' the dwarf said, bowing. 'Perhaps there really aren't any ghouls here, but the thought of spending a night in the burial ground doesn't do much for me. Let's go, I'll introduce you to the rest of our company.'

When they reached the camp the horses snorted and stamped their hooves on the ground.

'Stand a little downwind, Master Regis,' Zoltan Chivay said, casting the physician a telling glance. 'The smell of sage frightens our horses, and in my case, I'm ashamed to admit, reminds me unpleasantly of teeth being pulled.'

'Geralt,' Zoltan muttered, as soon as Emiel Regis had disappeared behind the flap covering the entrance to the cottage. 'Let's keep our eyes open. There's something fishy about that stinking herbalist.'

'Anything specific?'

'I don't like it when people spend their summers near cemeteries, never mind cemeteries a long way from human dwellings. Do herbs really not grow in more pleasant surroundings? That Regis looks like a grave robber to me. Barber-surgeons, alchemists and the like exhume corpses from boneyards, in order to perform various excrements on them.'

'Experiments. But fresh corpses are needed for practices of that kind. This cemetery is very old.'

'True,' the dwarf said, scratching his chin and watching the women from Kernow making their beds under some hagberry shrubs growing by the barber-surgeon's shack. 'So perhaps he steals buried treasure from these barrows?'

'Ask him,' Geralt said, shrugging. 'You accepted the invitation to stay at his homestead at once, without hesitation, and now you've suddenly become as suspicious as an old maid being paid a compliment.'

'Er . . .' Zoltan mumbled, somewhat tongue-tied. 'There's something in that. But I'd like to have a gander at what he keeps in that hovel of his. You know, just to be on the safe side . . .'

'So follow him in and pretend you want to borrow a fork.'

'Why a fork?'

'Why not?'

The dwarf gave Geralt an old-fashioned look and finally made up his mind. He hurried over to the cottage, knocked politely on the door jamb and entered. He remained inside for some little time, and then suddenly appeared in the doorway.

'Geralt, Percival, Dandelion, step this way. Come and see something interesting. Come on, without further ado, Master Regis has invited us in.'

The interior of the cottage was dark and dominated by a warm, intoxicating aroma that made the nose tickle, mainly coming from the bunches of herbs and roots hanging from all the walls. The only items of furniture were a simple cot – also strewn with herbs – and a rickety table cluttered with innumerable glass, pottery and ceramic vials. The room was illuminated by the dim glow of burning coals in a curious, pot-bellied stove, resembling a bulging hourglass. The stove was surrounded by a spidery lattice of shining pipes of various diameters, bent into curves and spirals. Beneath one of the pipes stood a wooden pail into which a liquid was dripping.

At the sight of the stove Percival Schuttenbach first stared goggle-eyed, then gaped, and finally sighed and leapt up in the air.

'Ho, ho, ho!' he called, unable to conceal his delight. 'What do I see? That's an absolutely authentic athanor coupled to an alembic! Equipped with a rectifying column and a copper condenser! A beautiful apparatus! Did you build it yourself, master barber-surgeon?'

'Indeed,' Emiel Regis admitted modestly. 'My work involves producing elixirs, so I have to distil, extract the fifth essence, and also . . .'

He broke off, seeing Zoltan Chivay catching a drop falling from the end of the pipe and licking his finger. The dwarf sighed and a look of indescribable bliss appeared on his ruddy face.

Dandelion couldn't resist and also had a go, tasting and moaning softly.

'The fifth essence,' he confirmed, smacking his lips. 'And I suspect the sixth and even the seventh.'

'Well ...' The barber-surgeon smiled faintly. 'As I said: a distillate.'

'Moonshine,' Zoltan corrected him gently. 'And what moonshine! Try some, Percival.'

'But I'm not an expert in organic chemistry,' the gnome answered absentmindedly, examining the details of the alchemical furnace's construction. 'It's doubtful I would be familiar with the ingredients ...'

'It is a distillate of mandrake,' Regis said, dispelling any doubt. 'Enriched with belladonna. And fermented starch mass.'

'You mean mash?'

'One could also call it that.'

'May I request a cup of some kind?'

'Zoltan, Dandelion,' the Witcher said, folding his arms on his chest. 'Are you deaf? It's mandrake. The moonshine is made of mandrake. Leave that copper alone.'

'But dear Master Geralt,' the alchemist said, digging a small graduated flask out from between some dust-covered retorts and demijohns, and meticulously polishing it with a rag. 'There's nothing to be afraid of. The mandrake is appropriately seasoned and the proportions carefully selected and precisely weighed out. I only add five ounces of mandrake to a pound of mash, and only half a dram of belladonna ...'

'That's not the point,' the Witcher said, looking at Zoltan. The dwarf understood at once, grew serious and cautiously withdrew from the still. 'The point is not how many drams you add, Master Regis, but how much a dram of mandrake costs. It's too dear a tipple for us.'

'Mandrake,' Dandelion whispered in awe, pointing at the small heap of sugar beet-like roots piled up in the corner of the shack. 'That's mandrake? Real mandrake?'

'The female form' – the alchemist nodded – 'grows in large clumps in the very cemetery where we chanced to meet. Which is also why I spend my summers here.'

The Witcher looked knowingly at Zoltan. The dwarf winked. Regis gave a half-suppressed smile.

'Gentlemen, please, I warmly invite you to sample it, if you wish. I appreciate your moderation, but in the current situation there's little chance of me taking the elixirs to war-torn Dillingen. It all would have gone to waste anyway, so let's not talk about the price. My apologies, but I only have one drinking vessel.'

'That should do,' Zoltan said, picking up the flask and carefully scooping up moonshine from the pail. 'Your good health, Master Regis. Ooooh . . .'

'Please forgive me,' the barber-surgeon said, smiling again. 'The quality of the distillate probably leaves a lot to be desired . . . It's actually unfinished.'

'It's the best unfinished product I've ever tasted,' Zoltan said, gasping. 'Your turn, poet.'

'Aaaah . . . Oh, mother of mine! Excellent! Have a sip, Geralt.'

'Give it to our host,' the Witcher said, bowing slightly towards Emiel Regis. 'Where are your manners, Dandelion?'

'Please forgive me, gentlemen,' the alchemist said, acknowledging the gesture, 'but I never permit myself any stimulants. My health isn't what it was. I've been forced to give up many . . . pleasures.'

'Not even a sip?'

'It's a principle,' Regis explained calmly. 'I never break any principles once I've adopted them.'

'I admire and envy you your resoluteness,' Geralt said, sipping a little from the flask and then, after a moment's hesitation, draining it in one. The tears trickling from his eyes interfered a little with the taste of the moonshine. An invigorating warmth spread through his stomach.

'I'll go and get Milva,' he offered, handing the flask to the dwarf. 'Don't polish it all off before we get back.'

Milva was sitting near the horses, bantering with the freckled girl she had been carrying on her saddle all day. When she heard about Regis's hospitality she initially shrugged, but in the end didn't need much persuading.

When they entered the shack they found the company carrying out an inspection of the stored mandrake roots.

'I've never seen it before,' Dandelion confessed, turning a bulbous root around in his fingers. 'Indeed, it does somewhat resemble a man.'

'A man twisted by lumbago, perhaps,' Zoltan added. 'And that one's the spitting image of a pregnant woman. And that one, if you'll excuse me, looks just like a couple busy bonking.'

'You lot only think of one thing,' Milva sneered, boldly drinking from the full flask and then coughing loudly into a fist. 'Bloody hell . . . Powerful stuff, that hooch! Is it really made from love apples? Ha, so we're drinking a magic potion! That doesn't happen every day. Thank you, master barber-surgeon.'

'The pleasure is all mine.'

The flask, kept topped up, circulated around the company, prompting good humour, verve and garrulousness.

'The mandrake, I hear, is a vegetable with great magical powers,' Percival Schuttenbach said with conviction.

'Yes, indeed,' Dandelion confirmed. He then emptied the flask, shuddered and resumed talking. 'There's no shortage of ballads written on the subject. It's well known that sorcerers use mandrake in elixirs, which help them preserve their eternal youth and sorceresses make an ointment, which they call glamarye. If an enchantress applies such ointment she becomes so beautiful and enchanting it makes your eyes pop out of your head. You also ought to know that mandrake is a powerful aphrodisiac and is used in love magic, particularly to break down female resistance. That's the explanation of mandrake's folk name: love apple. It's a herb used to pander lovers.'

'Blockhead,' Milva commented.

'And I heard,' the gnome said, downing the contents of the flask, 'that when mandrake root is pulled from the ground the plant cries and wails as though it were alive.'

'Why,' Zoltan said, filling the flask from the pail, 'if it only wailed! Mandrake, they say, screams so horribly it can send you up the wall, and moreover it screams out evil spells and showers curses on whoever uproots it. You can pay with your life taking a risk like that.'

'That sounds like a cloth-headed fairy-tale,' Milva said, taking the flask from him and drinking deeply. She shuddered and added: 'It's impossible for a plant to have such powers.'

'It's an infallible truth!' the dwarf called heatedly. 'But sagacious herbalists have found a way of protecting themselves. Having found a mandrake, you must tie one end of a rope to the root and the other end to a dog . . .'

'Or a pig,' the gnome broke in.

'Or a wild boar,' Dandelion added gravely.

'You're a fool, poet. The whole point is for the mutt or swine to pull the mandrake out of the ground, for then the vegetable's curses and spells fall on the said creature, while the herbalist – hiding safely, far away in the bushes – gets out in one piece. Well, Master Regis? Am I talking sense?'

'An interesting method,' the alchemist admitted, smiling mysteriously. 'Interesting mainly for its ingenuity. The disadvantage, however, is its extreme complexity. For in theory the rope ought to be enough, without the draught animal. I wouldn't suspect mandrake of having the ability of knowing who or what's pulling the rope. The spells and curses should always fall on the rope, which after all is cheaper and less problematic to use than a dog, not to mention a pig.'

'Are you jesting?'

'Wouldn't dream of it. I said I admire the ingenuity. Because although the mandrake, contrary to popular opinion, is incapable of casting spells or curses, it is – in its raw state – an extremely toxic plant, to the extent that even the earth around the root is poisonous. Sprinkling the fresh juice onto the face or on a cut hand, why, even breathing in its fumes, may all have fatal consequences. I wear a mask and gloves, which doesn't mean I have anything against the rope method.'

'Mmmm . . .' the dwarf pondered. 'But what about that horrifying scream the plucked mandrake makes? Is that true?'

'The mandrake doesn't have vocal chords,' the alchemist explained calmly, 'which is fairly typical for plants, is it not? However, the toxin secreted by the root has a powerful hallucinogenic effect. The voices, screams, whispers and other sounds are nothing more than hallucinations produced by the poisoned central nervous system.'

'Ha, I clean forgot,' Dandelion said, having just drained the flask and letting out a suppressed burp, 'that mandrake is extremely poisonous! And I was holding it! And now we're guzzling this tincture with abandon . . .'

'Only the fresh mandrake root is toxic,' Regis said, calming him down. 'Mine is seasoned and suitably prepared, and the distillate has been filtered. There is no need for alarm.'

'Of course there isn't,' Zoltan agreed. 'Moonshine will always be moonshine, you can even distil it from hemlock, nettles, fish scales and old bootlaces. Give us the glass, Dandelion, there's a queue forming here.'

The flask, kept topped up, circulated around the company. Everybody was sitting comfortably on the dirt floor. The Witcher hissed and swore, and shifted his position, because the pain shot through his knee again as he sat. He caught sight of Regis looking at him intently. 'Is that a fresh injury?'

'Not really. But it's tormenting me. Do you have any herbs capable of soothing the pain?'

'That all depends on the class of pain,' the barber-surgeon said, smiling slightly. 'And on its causes. I can detect a strange odour in your sweat, Witcher. Were you treated with magic? Were you given magic enzymes and hormones?'

'They gave me various medicaments. I had no idea they could still be smelled in my sweat. You've got a bloody sensitive nose, Regis.'

'Everybody has their good points. To even out the vices. What ailment did they use magic to treat you with?'

'I broke my arm and the shaft of my thighbone.'

'How long ago?'

'A little over a month.'

'And you're already walking? Remarkable. The dryads of Brokilon, I presume?'

'How can you tell?'

'Only the dryads have medicaments capable of rebuilding bone tissue so quickly. I can see dark marks on the backs of your hands. They're the places where the tendrils of the conynhaela and the symbiotic shoots of knitbone entered. Only dryads know how to use conynhaela, and knitbone doesn't grow outside Brokilon.'

'Well done. Admirable deduction skills. Though something else interests me. My thighbone and forearm were broken, but the strong pain is in the knee and elbow.'

'That's typical,' the barber-surgeon nodded. 'The dryads' magic reconstructed your damaged bone, but simultaneously caused a minor upheaval in your nerve trunks. It's a side effect, felt most intensely in the joints.'

'What do you advise?'

'Unfortunately, nothing. You'll continue to predict rainy weather unerringly for a long time to come. The pains will grow stronger in the winter. However, I wouldn't recommend that you take powerful painkilling drugs. Particularly steer clear of narcotics. You're a witcher and in your case it's absolutely to be avoided.'

'I'll treat myself with your mandrake, then,' the Witcher said, raising the full flask, which Milva had just handed him. He took a deep swallow and hacked until tears filled his eyes. 'Bloody hell! I'm feeling better already.'

'I'm not certain,' Regis said, smiling through pursed lips, 'that you're treating the right illness. I'd also like to remind you that one should treat causes, not symptoms.'

'Not in the case of this witcher,' Dandelion snorted, now a little flushed and eavesdropping on their conversation. 'Booze is just right for him and his worries.'

'It ought to do you good, too,' Geralt said, giving the poet a chilling stare. 'Particularly if it paralyses your tongue.'

'I wouldn't especially count on that.' The barber-surgeon smiled again. 'Belladonna is one of the preparation's ingredients, which means a large number of alkaloids, including scopolamine. Before the mandrake puts you to sleep, you're all sure to give me a display of eloquence.'

'A display of what?' Percival asked.

'Talkativeness. My apologies. Let's use simpler words.'

Geralt mouth twisted into a fake smile.

'That's right,' he said. 'It's easy to adopt an affected style and start using words like that every day. Then people take the speaker for an arrogant buffoon.'

'Or an alchemist,' Zoltan Chivay said, filling the flask from the pail once more.

'Or a witcher,' Dandelion snorted, 'who's read a lot to impress a certain enchantress. Nothing attracts enchantresses like an elaborate tale, gentlemen. Am I right, Geralt? Go on, spin us a yarn . . .'

'Sit out your turn, Dandelion,' the Witcher cut in coldly. 'The alkaloids in this hooch are acting on you too quickly. They've loosened your tongue.'

'It's time you gave up your secrets, Geralt,' Zoltan grimaced. 'Dandelion hasn't told us much we didn't know. You can't help it if you're a walking legend. They re-enact stories of your adventures in puppet theatres. Like the story about you and an enchantress by the name of Guinevere.'

'Yennefer,' Regis corrected in hushed tones. 'I saw that one. It was the story of a hunt for a genie, if my memory serves me correctly.'

'I was present during that hunt,' Dandelion boasted. 'We had some laughs, I can tell you . . .'

'Tell them all,' Geralt said, getting up. 'Tell them while you're sipping the moonshine and embellishing the story suitably. I'm taking a walk.'

'Hey,' the dwarf said, nettled. 'No need to get offended . . .'

'You misunderstand, Zoltan. I'm going to relieve my bladder. Why, it even happens to walking legends.'

The night was as cold as hell. The horses stamped and snorted, and steam belched from their nostrils. Bathed in moonlight, Regis's shack seemed utterly as if it could have come from a fairy-tale. It could have been a witch's cottage. Geralt fastened his trousers.

Milva, who had left soon after him, coughed hesitantly. Her long shadow drew level with his.

'Why are you delaying going back?' she asked. 'Did they really annoy you?'

'No,' he replied.

'Then why the hell are you standing here by yourself in the moonlight?'

'I'm counting.'

'Huh?'

'Twelve days have passed since I set out from Brokilon, during which I've travelled around sixty miles. Rumour has it that Ciri's in Nilfgaard, the capital of the Empire. Which is around two and half thousand miles from here. Simple arithmetic tells me that at this rate I'll get there in a year and four months. What do you say to that?'

'Nothing,' Milva said, shrugging and coughing again. 'I'm not as good at reckoning as you. I don't know how to read or write at all. I'm a foolish, simple country girl. No company for you. Nor someone to talk to.'

'Don't say that.'

'It's the truth, though,' she said, turning away abruptly. 'Why did you tally up the days and miles? For me to advise you? Cheer you up? Chase away your fear, suppress the remorse that torments you worse than the pain in your broken peg? I don't know how! You need another. The one Dandelion was talking about. Intelligent, educated. Your beloved.'

'Dandelion's a prattler.'

'That he is. But he occasionally prattles sense. Let's go back, I want to drink some more.'

'Milva?'

'What?'

'You never told me why you decided to ride with me.'

'You never asked.'

'I'm asking now.'

'It's too late now. I don't know any more.'

*

131

'Oh, you're back at last,' Zoltan said, pleased to see them, his voice now sounding quite different. 'And we, just imagine, have decided that Regis will continue on our journey with us.'

'Really?' The Witcher looked intently at the barber-surgeon. 'What's behind this sudden decision?'

'Master Zoltan,' Regis said, without lowering his gaze, 'has made me aware that Dillingen has been engulfed by a much more serious war than I understood from the refugees' accounts. A return to those parts is totally out of the question, and remaining in this wilderness doesn't seem wise. Or travelling alone, for that matter.'

'And we, although you don't know us at all, look like people you could travel with safely. Was one glance enough for you?'

'Two,' the barber-surgeon replied with a faint smile. 'One at the women you're looking after. And the other at their children.'

Zoltan belched loudly and scraped the flask against the bottom of the pail.

'Appearances can be deceptive,' he sneered. 'Perhaps we intend to sell the women into slavery. Percival, do something with this apparatus. Loosen a valve a little or something. We want to drink more and it's taking for ever to drip out.'

'The condenser can't keep up. The liquor will be warm.'

'Not a problem. The night's cool.'

The lukewarm moonshine greatly stimulated the conversation. Dandelion, Zoltan and Percival were all ruddy-cheeked, and their voices had altered even more – in the case of the poet and the gnome one could now say that they were almost on the verge of gibbering. Ravenous, the company were chewing cold horsemeat and nibbling horseradish roots they had found in the cottage – which made their eyes water, because the horseradish was as bracing as the hooch. And added passion to the discussion.

Regis gave an expression of astonishment when it turned out that the final destination of the trek was not the enclave of the Mahakam massif, the eternal and secure home of the dwarves. Zoltan, who had become even more garrulous than Dandelion, declared that under no circumstances would he ever return to Mahakam, and unburdened himself of his animosity to its ruling regime, particularly regarding the politics and absolute rule of Brouver Hoog, the Elder of Mahakam and all the dwarven clans.

'The old fart!' he roared, and spat into the hearth of the furnace. 'To look at him you wouldn't know if he was alive or stuffed. He almost never moves, which is just as well, because he farts every time he does. You can't understand a word he's saying because his beard and whiskers are stuck together with dried borscht. But he lords it over everyone and everything, and everyone has to dance to his tune . . .'

'It would be difficult to claim, however, that Hoog's policies are poor,' Regis interrupted. 'For, owing to his decisive measures, the dwarves distanced themselves from the elves and don't fight along-side the Scoia'tael any more. And thanks to that the pogroms have ceased. Thanks to that there have been no punitive expeditions to Mahakam. Prudence in their dealings with humans is bearing fruit.'

'Bollocks,' Zoltan said, drinking from the flask. 'In the case of the Squirrels, the old fossil wasn't interested in prudence, it was because too many youngsters were abandoning work in the mines and the forges and joining the elves to sample freedom and manly adventures in the commandos. When the phenomenon grew to the size of a problem, Brouver Hoog took the punks in hand. He couldn't care less about the humans being killed by the Squirrels, and he made light of the repression falling on the dwarves because of that – including your infamous pogroms. He didn't give a damn and doesn't give a damn about them, because he considers the dwarves who've settled in the cities apostates. And as regards punitive expeditions to Mahakam – don't make me laugh, my dears. There's no threat and never has been, because none of the kings would dare lay a finger on Mahakam. I'll go further: even the Nilfgaardians, were they to manage to take control of the valleys surrounding the massif, wouldn't dare touch Mahakam. Do you know why? I'll tell you: Mahakam is steel; and not just any old steel. There's coal there, there's magnetite ore, boundless deposits. Everywhere else it's just bog ore.'

'And they have expertise and technology in Mahakam,' Percival

Schuttenbach interposed. 'Metallurgy and smelting! Enormous furnaces, not some pathetic smelteries. Trip hammers and steam hammers . . .'

'There you go, Percival, neck that,' Zoltan said, handing the gnome the now full flask, 'before you bore us to death with your technology and engineering. Everyone knows about it. But not everyone knows Mahakam exports steel. To the kingdoms, but to Nilfgaard too. And should anyone lay a finger on us, we'll wreck the workshops and flood the mines. And then you humans will continue fighting, but with oaken staves, flint blades and asses' jawbones.'

'You say you have it in for Brouver Hoog and the regime in Mahakam,' the Witcher observed, 'but you've suddenly started saying "we".'

'I certainly have,' the dwarf confirmed heatedly. 'There is something like solidarity, isn't there? I admit that pride also plays its part, because we're cleverer than those stuck-up elves. You can't deny it, can you? For a few centuries the elves pretended there weren't any humans at all. They gazed up at the sky, smelled the flowers, and at the sight of a human averted their vulgarly bedaubed eyes. But when that strategy turned out to be ineffective they suddenly roused themselves and took up arms. They decided to kill and be killed. And we? The dwarves? We adapted. No, we didn't subordinate ourselves to you, don't get that into your heads. We subordinated you. Economically.'

'To tell the truth,' Regis chipped in, 'it was easier for you to adapt than it was for the elves. Land and territory is what integrates elves. In your case it's the clan. Wherever your clan is, that's your homeland. Even if an exceptionally short-sighted king were to attack Mahakam, you'd flood the mines and head off somewhere else without any regrets. To other, distant mountains. Or perhaps to human cities instead.'

'And why not? It's not a bad life in your cities.'

'Even in the ghettoes?' Dandelion asked, gasping after a swig of distillate.

'And what's wrong with living in a ghetto? I'd prefer to live among my own. What do I need with assimilation?'

134

'As long as they let us near the guilds,' Percival said, wiping his nose on his sleeve.

'They will eventually,' the dwarf said with conviction. 'And if they don't we'll just bodge our way through, or we'll found our own guilds; and healthy competition will decide.'

'So it would be safer in Mahakam than in the cities, then,' Regis observed. 'The cities could go up in flames any second. It would be more judicious to see out the war in the mountains.'

'Anyone who wishes to can do just that,' Zoltan said, replenishing the flask from the pail. 'Freedom is dearer to me, and you won't find that in Mahakam. You have no idea how the old bugger governs. He recently took it upon himself to regulate what he calls "community issues". For example: whether you can wear braces or not. Whether you should eat carp right away or wait until the jelly sets. Whether playing the ocarina is in keeping with our centuries-old dwarven traditions or is a destructive influence of rotten and decadent human culture. How many years you have to work before submitting an application for a permanent wife. Which hand you should wipe your arse with. How far away from the mines you're allowed to whistle. And other issues of vital importance. No, boys, I'm not going to return to Mount Carbon. I have no desire to spend my life at the coalface. Forty years underground, assuming firedamp doesn't blow you up first. But we've got other plans now, haven't we, Percival? We've already secured ourselves a future . . .'

'A future, a future . . .' the gnome said and emptied the graduated flask. He cleared his nose and looked at the dwarf with a now slightly glazed expression. 'Don't count our chickens, Zoltan. Because they might still nab us and then our future's the gibbet . . . Or Drakenborg.'

'Shut your trap,' the dwarf snapped, looking menacingly at him. 'You're blabbing!'

'Scopolamine,' Regis mumbled softly.

The gnome was rambling. Milva was gloomy. Zoltan, having forgotten that he'd already done so, told everyone about Hoog, the old fart and the Elder of Mahakam. Geralt listened, having forgotten he'd already heard it once. Regis also listened and even added comments, utterly unperturbed by the fact that he was the only sober individual in a now very drunk party. Dandelion strummed away on his lute and sang.

No wonder that comely ladies are all so stuck-up
For the taller the tree, the harder it is to get up.

'Idiot,' Milva commented. Dandelion was undeterred.

Simply treat a maiden as you would a tree
Whip out your chopper and one-two-three . . .

'A cup . . .' Percival Schuttenbach jabbered. 'A goblet, I mean . . . Carved from a single piece of milk opal . . . This big. I found it on the summit of Montsalvat. Its rim was set with jasper and the base was of gold. A sheer marvel . . .'

'Don't give him any more spirits,' Zoltan Chivay said.

'Hold on, hold on,' Dandelion said, becoming interested, also slurring his words somewhat. 'What happened to that legendary goblet?'

'I exchanged it for a mule. I needed a mule, in order to transport a load . . . Corundum and crystalline carbon. I had . . . Err . . . Lots of it . . . Hic . . . A load, I mean, a heavy load, couldn't have moved it without a mule . . . Why the hell did I need that goblet?'

'Corundum? Carbon?'

'Yeah, what you call rubies and diamonds. Very . . . hic . . . handy . . .'

'So I imagine.'

'. . . for drill bits and files. For bearings. I had lots of them . . .'

'Do you hear, Geralt?' Zoltan said. He waved a hand and although seated, almost fell over. 'He's little, so he got pissed quickly. He's dreaming about a shitload of diamonds. Careful now, Percival, that your dream doesn't come true! Or at least half. And I don't mean the half about diamonds!'

'Dreams, dreams,' Dandelion mumbled once more. 'And you,

Geralt? Have you dreamed of Ciri again? Because you ought to know, Regis, that Geralt has prophetic dreams! Ciri is the Child of Destiny, and Geralt is bound to her by bonds of fate, which is why he sees her in his dreams. You also ought to know that we're going to Nilfgaard to take back Ciri from Imperator Emhyr, who abducted her and wants to marry her. But he can whistle for it, the bastard, because we'll rescue her before he knows it! I'd tell you something else, boys, but it's a secret. A dreadful, deep, dark secret . . . Not a word, understood? Not one!'

'I haven't heard anything,' Zoltan assured him, looking impudently at the Witcher. 'I think an earwig crawled into my ear.'

'There's a veritable plague of earwigs,' Regis agreed, pretending to be poking around in his ear.

'We're going to Nilfgaard . . .' Dandelion said, leaning against the dwarf to keep his balance, which turned out to be a bad idea. 'Which is a secret, just like I told you. It's a secret mission!'

'And ingeniously concealed indeed,' the barber-surgeon nodded, glancing at Geralt, who was now white with rage. 'Not even the most suspicious individual would ever guess the aim of your journey by analysing the direction you are headed.'

'Milva, what is it?'

'Don't talk to me, you drunken fool.'

'Hey, she's crying! Hey, look . . .'

'Go to hell, I said!' the archer raised her voice, wiping away the tears. 'Or I'll smack you between the eyes, you fucking poetaster . . . Give me the glass, Zoltan . . .'

'I've mislaid it . . .' the dwarf mumbled. 'Oh, here it is. Thanks, master barber-surgeon . . . And where the hell is Schuttenbach?'

'He went outside. Some time ago. Dandelion, I recall you promised you'd tell me the story of the Child of Destiny.'

'All right, all right, Regis. I'll just have a swig . . . and I'll tell you everything . . . About Ciri, and about the Witcher . . . In detail . . .'

'Confusion to the whores' sons!'

'Be quiet, dwarf! You'll wake up the kids outside the cottage!'

'Calm down, archeress. There you go, drink that.'

'Ah, well.' Dandelion looked around the shack with a slightly vacant stare. 'If the Countess de Lettenhove could see me like this . . .'

'Who?'

'Never mind. Bloody hell, this moonshine really does loosen the tongue . . . Geralt, shall I pour you another one? Geralt!'

'Leave him be,' Milva said. 'Let him sleep.'

The barn on the edge of the village was pounding with music. The rhythm seized them before they arrived, filling them with excitement. They began to sway involuntarily in their saddles as their horses walked up, firstly to the rhythm of the dull boom of the drum and double bass, and then, when they were closer, to the beat of the melody being played by the fiddles and the pipes. The night was cold, the moon shone full and in its glow the barn, illuminated by the light shining through gaps in the planks, looked like a fairy-tale enchanted castle.

A clamour and a bright glow, broken up by the shadows of cavorting couples, flooded out from the doorway of the barn.

When they entered the music fell silent, dissolving in a long-drawn-out discord. The dancing, sweating peasants parted, leaving the dirt floor, and grouped together by the walls and posts. Ciri, walking alongside Mistle, saw the eyes of the young women, wide with fear; noticed the hard, determined glances of the men and lads, ready for anything. She heard the growing whispering and growling, louder than the cautious skirling of the bagpipes, than the fading insect-like droning of violins and fiddles. Whispering. The Rats . . . The Rats . . . Robbers . . .

'Fear not,' Giselher said loudly, chucking a plump and chinking purse towards the dumbstruck musicians. 'We've come here to make merry. The village fair is open to anyone, isn't it?'

'Where's the beer?' Kayleigh asked, shaking a pouch. 'And where's the hospitality?'

'And why is it so quiet here?' Iskra asked, looking around. 'We came down from the mountains for a dance. Not for a wake!'

One of the peasants finally broke the impasse, and walked over to Giselher with a clay mug overflowing with froth. Giselher took it with a bow, drank from it, and courteously and decorously thanked him. Several peasants shouted enthusiastically. But the others remained silent.

'Hey, fellows,' Iskra called again. 'I see that you need livening up!' A heavy oak table, laden with clay mugs, stood against one wall of the barn. The she-elf clapped her hands and nimbly jumped onto it. The peasants quickly gathered up the mugs. With a vigorous kick Iskra cleared the ones they were too slow to remove.

'Very well, musicians,' she said, putting her fists on her hips and shaking her hair. 'Show me what you can do. Music!'

She quickly tapped out a rhythm with her heels. The drum repeated the rhythm and the double bass and oboe followed. The pipes and fiddles took up the tune, quickly embellishing it, challenging Iskra to adjust her steps and tempo. The she-elf, gaudily dressed and as light as a butterfly, adapted to it with ease and began moving rhythmically. The peasants began to clap.

'Falka!' Iskra called, narrowing her eyes, which were intensified by heavy make-up. 'You're swift with a sword! And in the dance? Can you keep step with me?'

Ciri freed herself from Mistle's arm, untied the scarf from around her neck and took off her beret and jacket. With a single bound she was on the table beside the she-elf. The peasants cheered enthusiastically, the drum and double bass boomed and the bagpipes wailed plaintively.

'Play, musicians!' Iskra yelled. 'With verve! And passion!'

With her hands on her hips and an upturned head, the she-elf tapped her feet, cut a caper, and beat out a quick, rhythmic staccato with her heels. Ciri, bewitched by the rhythm, copied the steps. The she-elf laughed, hopped and changed the tempo. Ciri shook her hair from her forehead with a sudden jerk of her head and copied Iskra's movements perfectly. The two girls stepped in unison, each the mirror image of the other. The peasants yelled and applauded. The fiddles and violins sang a piercing song, tearing the measured, solemn rumbling of the double bass and keening of the bagpipes to shreds.

They danced, both as straight as a poker, arms akimbo, touching each other's elbows. The iron on their heels beat out the rhythm, the table shook and trembled, and dust whirled in the light of tallow candles and torches.

'Faster!' Iskra urged on the musicians. 'Look lively!'

It was no longer music, it was a frenzy.

'Dance, Falka! Abandon yourself to it!'

Heel, toe, heel, toe, heel, step forward and jump, shoulders swinging, fists on hips, heel, heel. The table shakes, the light shimmers, the crowd sways, everything sways, the entire barn is dancing, dancing, dancing . . . The crowd yells, Giselher yells, Asse yells, Mistle laughs, claps, everyone claps and stamps, the barn shudders, the earth shudders, the world is shaken to its foundations. The world? What world? There's no world now, there's nothing, only the dance, the dance . . . Heel, toe, heel . . . Iskra's elbow . . . Fever pitch, fever pitch . . . Only the wild playing of the fiddles, pipes, double bass and bagpipes, the drummer raises and lowers his drumsticks but he is now superfluous, they beat the rhythm out by themselves. Iskra and Ciri, their heels, until the table booms and rocks, the entire barn booms and rocks . . . The rhythm, the rhythm is them, the music is them, they are the music. Iskra's dark hair flops on her forehead and shoulders. The fiddles' strings play a passionate tune, reaching fever pitch. Blood pounds in their temples.

Abandon. Oblivion.

I am Falka. I have always been Falka! Dance, Iskra! Clap, Mistle! The violins and pipes finish the melody on a strident, high chord, and Iskra and Ciri mark the end of the dance with a simultaneous bang of their heels, their elbows still touching. They are both panting, quivering, het up, they suddenly cling to each other, they hug, they share their sweat, their heat and their happiness with each other. The barn explodes with one great bellow and the clapping of dozens of hands.

'Falka, you she-devil,' Iskra pants. 'When we grow tired of robbery, we'll go out into the world and earn a living as dancers . . .'

Ciri also pants. She is unable to say a single word. She just laughs spasmodically. A tear runs down her cheek.

A sudden shout in the crowd, a disturbance. Kayleigh shoves a burly peasant hard, the peasant shoves Kayleigh back, the two of them are caught in the press, raised fists fly. Reef jumps in and a dagger flashes in the light of a torch.

'No! Stop!' Iskra cries piercingly. 'No brawling! This is a night of dance!' She takes Ciri by the hand. They drop from the table to the floor. 'Musicians, play! Whoever wants to show us their paces, join us! Well, who's feeling brave?'

The double bass booms monotonously, the long-drawn-out wailing of the bagpipes cuts in, to be joined by the high, piercing song of the fiddles. The peasants laugh, nudge one another, overcoming their reserve. One – broad-shouldered and fair-haired – seizes Iskra. A second – younger and slimmer – bows hesitantly in front of Ciri. Ciri haughtily tosses her head, but soon smiles in assent. The lad closes his hands around her waist and Ciri places her hands on his shoulders. The touch shoots through her like a flaming arrowhead, filling her with throbbing desire.

'Look lively, musicians!'

The barn shudders from the noise, vibrates with the rhythm and the melody.

Ciri dances.

A vampire, or upir, is a dead person brought to life by Chaos.
*Having lost its first life, a **v**. enjoys its second life during the night*
hours. It leaves its grave by the light of the moon and only under its
light may it act, assailing sleeping maidens or young swains, who it
wakes not, but whose blood it sucks.

Physiologus

The peasants consumed garlic in great abundance and for greater
certainty hung strings of garlic around their necks. Some, women-
folk in particular, stopped up their orifices with whole bulbs of
garlic. The whole hamlet stank of garlic horrendus, so the peasants
believed they were safe and that the vampire was incapable of doing
them harm. Mighty was their astonishment, however, when the
vampire who flew to their hamlet at midnight was not in the least
afraid and simply began to laugh, gnashing his teeth in delight and
jeering at them.

'It is good,' he said, 'that you have spiced yourselves, for I shall
soon devour you and seasoned meat is more to my taste. Apply also
salt and pepper to yourselves, and forget not the mustard.'

Sylvester Bugiardo, Liber Tenebrarum,
or The Book of Fell but Authentic Cases
never Explained by Science

The moon shines bright,
The vampire alights
Swish, swish goes his cloak . . .
Maiden, are you not afeared?

Folk song

CHAPTER FOUR

As usual, the birds filled the grey and foggy dawn with an explosion of chirruping in anticipation of the sunrise. As usual, the first members of the party ready to set off were the taciturn women from Kernow and their children. Emiel Regis turned out to be equally swift and energetic, joining the others with a travelling staff and a leather bag over one shoulder. The rest of the company, who had drained the still during the night, were not quite so lively. The cool of the morning roused and revived the revellers, but failed to thwart the effects of the mandrake moonshine. Geralt awoke in a corner of the shack with his head in Milva's lap. Zoltan and Dandelion lay in each other's arms on a pile of mandrake roots, snoring so powerfully that they were making the bundles of herbs hanging on the walls flutter. Percival was discovered outside, curled up in a ball under a hagberry bush, covered by the straw mat Regis normally used to wipe his boots on. The five of them betrayed distinct – but varied – symptoms of fatigue and they all went to soothe their raging thirst at the spring.

However, by the time the mists had dissipated and the red ball of the sun was blazing in the tops of the pines and larches of Fen Carn the company were already on their way, marching briskly among the barrows. Regis took the lead, followed by Percival and Dandelion, who kept each other's spirits up by singing a two-part ballad about three sisters and an iron wolf. After them trudged Zoltan Chivay, leading the chestnut colt by the reins. The dwarf had found a knobbly ashen staff in the barber-surgeon's yard, which he was now using to whack all the menhirs they passed and wish the long-deceased elves eternal rest, while Field Marshal Windbag – who was sitting on his shoulder – puffed up his feathers and occasionally squawked; reluctantly, indistinctly and somewhat half-heartedly.

Milva turned out to be the least tolerant to the mandrake distillate. She marched with visible difficulty, was sweaty, pale and acted like a bear with a sore head, not even responding to the twittering of the little girl with the plaits who was riding in the black's saddle. Geralt thus made no attempt to strike up a conversation, not being in the best of shape himself.

The fog and the adventures of the iron wolf sung in loud – though somewhat morning-after – voices meant that they happened upon a small group of peasants suddenly and without warning. The peasants, however, had heard them much earlier and were waiting, standing motionless among the monoliths sunk into the ground, their grey homespun coats camouflaging them perfectly. Zoltan Chivay barely avoided whacking one of them with his staff, having mistaken him for a tombstone.

'Yo-ho-ho!!' he shouted. 'Forgive me, good people! I didn't notice you. A good day to you! Greetings!'

The dozen peasants murmured an answer to his greeting in an incoherent chorus, grimly scrutinising the company. The peasants were clutching shovels, picks and six-foot pointed stakes.

'Greetings,' the dwarf repeated. 'I presume you're from the camp by the Chotla. Am I right?'

Rather than answering, one of the peasants pointed out Milva's horse to the rest of them.

'That black one,' he said. 'See it?'

'The black,' affirmed another and licked his lips. 'Oh, yes, the black. Should do the job.'

'Eh?' Zoltan said, noticing their expressions and gestures. 'Are you referring to our black steed? What about it? It's a horse, not a giraffe, there's nothing to be astonished about. What are you up to, my good fellows, in this burial ground?'

'And you?' the peasant asked, looking askance at the company. 'What are *you* doing here?'

'We've bought this land,' the dwarf said, looking him straight in the eye and hitting a menhir with his staff, 'and we're pacing it out, to check we haven't been swindled on the acreage.'

'And we're hunting a vampire!'

'What?'

'A vampire,' the oldest peasant repeated emphatically, scratching his forehead beneath a felt cap stiff with grime. 'He must have his lair somewhere here, curse him. We have sharpened these here aspen stakes, and now we shall find the scoundrel and run him through, so he will never rise again!'

'And we've holy water in a pot the priest gave us!' another peasant called cheerfully, pointing to the vessel. 'We'll sprinkle it on the bloodsucker, make things hot for him!'

'Ha, ha,' Zoltan Chivay said, with a smile. 'I see it's a proper hunt; full scale and well organised. A vampire, you say? Well, you're in luck, good fellows. We have a vampire specialist in our company, a wi . . .'

He broke off and swore under his breath, because the Witcher had kicked him hard in the ankle.

'Who saw the vampire?' Geralt asked, hushing his companions with a telling glance. 'Why do you think you should be looking for him here?'

The peasants whispered among themselves.

'No one saw him,' the peasant in the felt cap finally admitted. 'Or heard him. How can you see him when he flies at night, in the dark? How can you hear him when he flies on bat's wings, without a sound?'

'We didn't see the vampire,' added another, 'but there are signs of his ghastly practices. Ever since the moon's been full, the fiend's murdered one of our number every night. He's already torn two people apart, ripped them to shreds. A woman and a stripling. Horrors and terrors! The vampire tore the poor wretches to ribbons and drank all their blood! What are we to do? Stand idly by for a third night?'

'But who says the culprit is a vampire, and not some other predator? Whose idea was it to root around in this burial ground?'

'The venerable priest told us to. He's a learned and pious man, and thanks be to the Gods he arrived in our camp. He said at once that a vampire was plaguing us. As punishment, for we've neglected our prayers and church donations. Now he's reciting prayers and carrying out all kinds of exorcismums in the camp, and ordered us to search for the tomb where the undead fiend sleeps during the day.'

'What, here?'

'And where would a vampire's grave be, if not in a burial ground? And anyway it's an elven burial ground and every toddler knows that elves are a rotten, godless race, and every second elf is condemned to damnation after death! Elves are to blame for everything!'

'Elves and barber-surgeons,' said Zoltan, nodding his head seriously. 'That's true. Every child knows that. That camp you were talking about, is it far from here?'

'Why, no . . .'

'Don't tell them too much, Father,' said an unshaven peasant with a shaggy fringe, the one who had previously been unfriendly. 'The devil only knows who they are; they're a queer-looking band. Come on, let's get to work. Let them give us the horse and they can go on their way.'

'Right you are,' the older peasant said. 'Let's not dilly-dally, time's getting on. Hand over the horse. That black one. We need it to search for the vampire. Get that kid off the saddle, lassie.'

Milva, who had been staring at the sky with a blank expression all along, looked at the peasant and her features hardened dangerously.

'Talking to me, yokel?'

'What do you think? Give us the black, we need it.'

Milva wiped her sweaty neck and gritted her teeth, and the expression in her tired eyes became truly ferocious.

'What's this all about, good people?' the Witcher asked, smiling and trying to defuse the tense situation. 'Why do you need this horse? The one you are so politely requesting?'

'How else are we going to find the vampire's grave? Everybody knows you have to ride around a cemetery on a black colt, as it will stop by the vampire's grave and will not be budged from it. Then you have to dig up the vampire and stab him with an aspen stake. Don't argue with us, for we're desperate. It's a matter of life and death here. We have to have that black horse!'

'Will another colour do?' Dandelion asked placatingly, holding out Pegasus's reins to the peasant.

'Not a chance.'

'Pity for you, then,' Milva said through clenched teeth. 'Because I'm not giving you my horse.'

'What do you mean you won't? Didn't you hear what we said, wench? We have to have it!'

'You might. But I don't have to give it to you.'

'We can solve this amicably,' Regis said in a kind voice. 'If I understand rightly, Miss Milva is reluctant to hand over her horse to a stranger . . .'

'You could say that,' the archer said, and spat heartily. 'I cringe at the very thought.'

'Both the wolves have eaten much and the sheep have not been touched,' the barber-surgeon recited calmly. 'Let Miss Milva mount the horse herself and carry out the necessary circuit of the necropolis.'

'I'm not going to ride around the graveyard like an idiot!'

'And no one's asking you to, wench!' said the one with the shaggy fringe. 'This requires a bold and strong blade; a maid's place is in the kitchen, bustling around the stove. A wench may come in handy later, true enough, because a virgin's tears are very useful against a vampire; for if you sprinkle a vampire with them he burns up like a firebrand. But the tears must be shed by a pure and untouched wench. And you don't quite look the part, love. So you're not much use for anything.'

Milva took a quick step forward and her right fist shot out as fast as lightning. There was a crack and the peasant's head lurched backwards, which meant his bristly throat and chin created an excellent target. The girl took another step and struck straight ahead with the heel of her open hand, increasing the force of the blow with a twist of her hips and shoulders. The peasant staggered backwards, tripped over his own feet and keeled over, banging the back of his head with an audible thud against the menhir.

'Now you see what use I am,' the archer said, in a voice trembling with fury, rubbing her fist. 'Who's the blade now, and whose place is in the kitchen? Truly, there's nothing like a fist-fight, which clears everything up. The bold and strong one is still on his feet,

149

and the pussy and the milksop is lying on the ground. Am I right, yokels?'

The peasants didn't hurry to answer, but looked at Milva with their mouths wide open. The one in the felt cap knelt down by the one on the ground and slapped him gently on his cheek. In vain.

'Killed,' he wailed, raising his head. 'Dead. How could you, wench? How could you just up and kill a man?'

'I didn't mean to,' Milva whispered, lowering her hands and blenching frightfully. And then she did something no one expected.

She turned away, staggered, rested her forehead against the menhir and vomited violently.

'What's up with him?'

'Slight concussion,' the barber-surgeon replied, standing up and fastening his bag. 'His skull's in one piece. He's already regained consciousness. He remembers what happened and he knows his own name. That's a good sign. Miss Milva's intense reaction was, fortunately, groundless.'

The Witcher looked at the archer, who was sitting at the foot of the menhir with her eyes staring into the distance.

'She isn't a delicate maiden, prone to that sort of emotion,' he muttered. 'I'd be more inclined to blame yesterday's hooch.'

'She's puked before,' Zoltan broke in softly. 'The day before yesterday, at the crack of dawn. While everyone was still asleep. I think it's because of those mushrooms we scoffed in Turlough. My guts gave me grief for two days.'

Regis looked at the Witcher from under his greying eyebrows with a strange expression on his face, smiled mysteriously, and wrapped himself in his black, woollen cloak. Geralt went over to Milva and cleared his throat.

'How do you feel?'

'Rough. How's the yokel?'

'He'll be fine. He's come round. But Regis won't let him get up. The peasants are making a cradle and we'll carry him to the camp between two horses.'

'Take mine.'

'We're using Pegasus and the chestnut. They're more docile. Get up, it's time we hit the road.'

The enlarged company now resembled a funeral procession and crawled along at a funereal pace.

'What do you think about this vampire of theirs?' Zoltan Chivay asked the Witcher. 'Do you believe their story?'

'I didn't see the victims. I can't comment.'

'It's a pack of lies,' Dandelion declared with conviction. 'The peasants said the dead had been torn apart. Vampires don't do that. They bite into an artery and drink the blood, leaving two clear fang marks. The victim quite often survives. I've read about it in a respectable book. There were also illustrations showing the marks of vampire bites on virgins' swanlike necks. Can you confirm that, Geralt?'

'What do you want me to confirm? I didn't see those illustrations. I'm not very clued up about virgins, either.'

'Don't scoff. You can't be a stranger to vampire bite marks. Ever come across a case of a vampire ripping its victim to shreds?'

'No. That never happens.'

'In the case of higher vampires – never, I agree,' Emiel Regis said softly. 'From what I know alpors, katakans, moolas, bruxas and nosferats don't mutilate their victims. On the other hand, fleders and ekimmas are pretty brutal with their victims' remains.'

'Bravo,' Geralt said, looking at him in genuine admiration. 'You didn't leave out a single class of vampire. Nor did you mention any of the imaginary ones, which only exist in fairy-tales. Impressive knowledge indeed. You must also know that ekimmas and fleders are never encountered in this climate.'

'What happened, then?' Zoltan snorted, swinging his ashen staff. 'Who mutilated that woman and that lad in this climate, then? Or did they mutilate themselves in a fit of desperation?'

'The list of creatures that may have been responsible is pretty long. Beginning with a pack of feral dogs, quite a common affliction during times of war. You can't imagine what dogs like that are capable of. Half the supposed victims of chaotic monsters can actually be chalked up to packs of wild farmyard curs.'

'Does that mean you rule out monsters?'

'Not in the least. It may have been a striga, a harpy, a graveir, a ghoul . . .'

'Not a vampire?'

'Unlikely.'

'The peasants mentioned some priest or other,' Percival Schuttenbach recalled. 'Do priests know much about vampires?'

'Some are expert on a range of subjects, to quite an advanced level, and their opinions are worth listening to, as a rule. Sadly, that doesn't apply to all of them.'

'Particularly the kind that roam around forests with fugitives,' the dwarf snorted. 'He's most probably some kind of hermit, an illiterate anchorite from the wilderness. He dispatched a peasant expedition to your burial ground, Regis. Have you never noticed a single vampire while you were gathering mandrake there? Not even a tiny one? A teeny-weeny one?'

'No, never,' the barber-surgeon gave a faint smile. 'But no wonder. A vampire, as you've just heard, flies in the dark on bat's wings, without making a sound. He's easy to miss.'

'And easy to see one where it isn't and has never been,' Geralt confirmed. 'When I was younger, I wasted my time and energy several times chasing after delusions and superstitions which had been seen and colourfully described by an entire village, including the headman. Once I spent two months living in a castle which was supposedly haunted by a vampire. There was no vampire. But they fed me well.'

'No doubt, however, you have experienced cases when the rumours about vampires were well founded,' Regis said, not looking at the Witcher. 'In those cases, I presume, your time and energy were not wasted. Did the monsters die by your sword?'

'It has been known.'

'In any event,' Zoltan said, 'the peasants are in luck. I think we'll wait in that camp for Munro Bruys and the lads, and a rest won't do you any harm either. Whatever killed the woman and the boy,

I don't fancy its chances when the Witcher turns up in the camp.'

'While we're at it,' Geralt said, pursing his lips, 'I'd rather you didn't bruit who I am and what my name is. That particularly applies to you, Dandelion.'

'As you wish,' the dwarf nodded. 'You must have your reasons. Lucky you've forewarned us, because I can see the camp.'

'And I can hear it,' Milva added, breaking a lengthy silence. 'They're making a fearful racket.'

'The sound we can hear,' Dandelion said, playing the wiseacre, 'is the everyday symphony of a refugee camp. As usual, scored for several hundred human throats, as well as no fewer bovine, ovine and anserine ones. The solo parts are being performed by women squabbling, children bawling, a cock crowing and, if I'm not mistaken, a donkey, who someone's poked in the backside with a thistle. The title of the symphony is: *A human community fights for survival.*'

'The symphony, as usual, can be heard *and* smelled,' Regis observed, quivering the nostrils of his noble nose. 'This community – as it fights for survival – gives off the delicious fragrance of boiled cabbage, a vegetable without which survival would apparently be impossible. The characteristic olfactory accent is also being created by the effects of bodily functions, carried out in random places, most often on the outskirts of the camp. I've never understood why the fight for survival manifests itself in a reluctance to dig latrines.'

'To hell with your smart-arsed chatter,' said Milva in annoyance. 'Three dozen fancy words when three will do: it stinks of shit and cabbage!'

'Shit and cabbage always go hand in hand,' Percival Schuttenbach said pithily. 'One drives the other. It's perpetuum mobile.'

No sooner had they set foot in the noisy and foul-smelling camp, among the campfires, wagons and shelters, than they became the centre of interest of all the fugitives gathered there, of which there must have been at least two hundred, possibly even more. The interest bore fruit quickly and remarkably; someone suddenly screamed, someone else suddenly bellowed, someone suddenly flung their arms around someone else's neck, someone began to laugh wildly, and someone else to sob wildly. There was a huge commotion. At first it was difficult to work out what was happening among the cacophony of men, women and children screaming, but finally all was explained. Two of the women from Kernow who had been travelling with them had found, respectively, a husband and a brother, whom they had believed to be dead or to missing without trace in the turmoil of war. The delight and tears seemed to be never-ending.

'Something so banal and melodramatic,' Dandelion said with conviction, indicating the moving scene, 'could only happen in real life. If I tried to end one of my ballads like that, I would be ribbed mercilessly.'

'Undoubtedly,' Zoltan confirmed. 'Nonetheless, banalities like these gladden the heart, don't they? One feels more cheerful when fortune gives one something, rather than only taking. Well, we've got rid of the womenfolk. We guided them and guided them and finally got them here. Come on, no point hanging around.'

For a moment, the Witcher felt like suggesting they delay their departure. He was counting on one of the women deciding it would be fitting to express a few words of gratitude and thanks to the dwarf. He abandoned that idea, though, when he saw no sign of it happening. The women, overjoyed at being reunited with their loved ones, had completely forgotten about Geralt and his company.

'What are you waiting for?' Zoltan said, looking at him keenly. 'To be covered in blossom out of gratitude? Or anointed with honey? Let's clear off; there's nothing for us here.'

'You're absolutely right.'

They didn't get far. A squeaky little voice stopped them in their tracks. The freckle-faced little girl with the plaits had caught them up. She was out of breath and had a large posy of wild flowers in her hand.

'Thank you,' she squeaked, 'for looking after me and my little brother and my mummy. For being kind to us and all that. I picked these flowers for you.'

'Thank you,' Zoltan Chivay said.

'You're kind,' the little girl added, sticking the end of her plait into her mouth. 'I don't believe what auntie said at all. You aren't filthy little burrowing midgets. And you aren't a grey-haired misfit from hell. And you, Uncle Dandelion, aren't a gobbling turkey. Auntie wasn't telling the truth. And you, Auntie Maria, aren't a slapper with a bow and arrow. You're Auntie Maria and I like you. I picked the prettiest flowers for you.'

'Thank you,' Milva said in a slightly altered voice.

'We all thank you,' Zoltan echoed. 'Hey, Percival, you filthy little burrowing midget, give the child some token as a farewell present. A souvenir. Have you got a spare stone in one of your pockets?'

'I have. Take this, little miss. It's beryllium aluminium cyclosilicate, popularly known as . . .'

'An emerald,' the dwarf finished off the sentence. 'Don't confuse the child, she won't remember anyway.'

'Oh, how pretty! And how green! Thank you very, very much!'

'Enjoy it and may it bring you fortune.'

'And don't lose it,' Dandelion muttered. 'Because that little pebble's worth as much as a small farm.'

'Get away,' Zoltan said, adorning his cap with the cornflowers the girl had given him. 'It's only a stone, nothing special. Take care of yourself, little miss. Let's go and sit down by the ford to wait for Bruys, Yazon Varda and the others. They ought to stroll by any time now. Strange they haven't shown up yet. I forgot to get the bloody cards off 'em. I bet they're sitting somewhere and playing Barrel!'

'The horses need feeding,' Milva said. 'And watering. Let's go towards the river.'

'Perhaps we'll happen upon some home-cooked fare,' Dandelion added. 'Percival, take a gander around the camp and put your hooter to use. We'll eat where the food is tastiest.'

To their slight amazement, the way down to the river was fenced off and under guard. The peasants guarding the watering place were demanding a farthing per horse. Milva and Zoltan were incandescent, but Geralt, hoping to avoid a scene and the publicity it would lead to, calmed them down, while Dandelion contributed a few coins he dug from the depths of his pocket.

Soon after Percival Schuttenbach showed up, dour and cross.

155

'Found any grub?'

The gnome cleared his nose and wiped his fingers on the fleece of a passing sheep.

'Yes. But I don't know if we can afford it. They expect to be paid for everything here and the prices will take your breath away. Flour and barley groats are a crown a pound. A plate of thin soup's two nobles. A pot of weatherfish caught in the Chotla costs the same as a pound of smoked salmon in Dillingen . . .'

'And fodder for the horses?'

'A measure of oats costs a thaler.'

'How much?' the dwarf yelled. 'How much?'

'How much, how much,' Milva snapped. 'Ask the horses how much. They'll peg it if we make them nibble grass! And there isn't any here anyway.'

There was no way of debating self-evident facts. Attempts at hard bargaining with the peasant selling oats didn't achieve anything either. He relieved Dandelion of the last of his coins, and was also treated to a few insults from Zoltan, which didn't bother him in the slightest. But the horses enthusiastically stuck their muzzles into the nosebags.

'Daylight bloody robbery!' the dwarf yelled, unloading his anger by aiming blows of his staff at the wheels of passing wagons. 'Incredible that they let us breathe here for nothing, and don't charge a ha'penny for each inhalation! Or a farthing for a dump!'

'Higher physiological needs,' Regis declared in utter seriousness, 'have a price. Do you see the tarpaulin stretched between those sticks? And the peasant standing alongside? He's peddling the charms of his own daughter. Price open to negotiation. A moment ago I saw him accepting a chicken.'

'I predict a bad end for your race, humans,' Zoltan Chivay said grimly. 'Every sentient creature on this earth, when it falls into want, poverty and misfortune, usually cleaves to his own. Because it's easier to survive the bad times in a group, helping one another. But you, humans, you just wait for a chance to make money from other people's mishaps. When there's hunger you don't share out your food, you just devour the weakest ones. This practice works among

156

wolves, since it lets the healthiest and strongest individuals survive. But among sentient races selection of that kind usually allows the biggest bastards to survive and dominate the rest. Come to your own conclusions and make your own predictions.'

Dandelion forcefully protested, giving examples of even greater scams and self-seeking among the dwarves, but Zoltan and Percival drowned him out, simultaneously and loudly imitating with their lips the long-drawn-out sounds which accompany farting, by both races considered an expression of disdain for one's adversary's arguments in a dispute.

The sudden appearance of a small group of peasants led by their friend the vampire hunter, the old chap in the felt cap, brought an end to the quarrel.

'It's about Cloggy,' one of the peasants said.

'We aren't buying anything,' the dwarf and the gnome snapped in unison.

'The one whose head you split open,' another peasant quickly explained. 'We were planning to get him married off.'

'We've got nothing against that,' Zoltan said angrily. 'We wish him and his new bride all the best. Good health, happiness and prosperity.'

'And lots of little Cloggies,' Dandelion added.

'Just a moment,' the peasant said. 'You may laugh, but how are we to get him hitched? For ever since you whacked him in the head he's been totally dazed, and can't tell day from night.'

'It isn't that bad,' Milva grunted, eyes fixed on the ground. 'He seems to be doing better. That is, much better than he was early this morning.'

'I've got no idea how Cloggy was early this morning,' the peasant retorted. 'But I just saw him standing in front of an upright thill saying what a beauty she was. But never mind. I'll say it briefly: pay up the blood money.'

'What?'

'When a knight kills a peasant he must pay blood money. So says the law.'

'I'm not a knight!' Milva yelled.

157

'That's one thing,' Dandelion said in her defence. 'And for another, it was an accident. And for a third, Cloggy's alive, so blood money's out of the question. The most you can expect is compensation, namely redress. But for a fourth, we're penniless.'

'So hand over your horses.'

'Hey,' Milva said, her eyes narrowing malevolently. 'You must be out of your mind, yokel. Mind you don't go too far.'

'Motherrfuccckkerr!' Field Marshal Windbag squawked.

'Ah, the bird's hit the nail on the head,' Zoltan Chivay drawled, tapping his axe, which was stuck into his belt. 'You ought to know, tillers of the soil, that I also don't have the best opinion about the mothers of individuals who think of nothing but profit, even if they plan to make money out of their mate's cracked skull. Be off with you, people. If you go away forthwith, I promise I won't come after you.'

'If you don't want to pay, let the authorities arbitrate.'

The dwarf ground his teeth and was just reaching for his battle-axe when Geralt seized him by the elbow.

'Calm down. How do you want to solve this problem? By killing them all?'

'Why kill them right away? It's enough to cripple them good and proper.'

'That's enough, darn it,' the Witcher hissed, and then turned to the peasant. 'These authorities you were talking about; who are they?'

'Our camp elder, Hector Laabs, the headman from Breza, one of the villages that was burnt down.'

'Lead us to him, then. We'll come to some agreement.'

'He's busy at present,' the peasant announced. 'He's sitting in judgement on a witch. There, do you see that crowd by the maple? They've caught a hag who was in league with a vampire.'

'Here we go again,' Dandelion snorted, spreading his arms. 'Did you hear that? When they aren't digging up cemeteries they're hunting witches, supposedly vampires' accomplices. Folks, perhaps instead of ploughing, sowing and harvesting, you'll become witchers.'

'Joke as much as you like,' the peasant said, 'and laugh all you want, but there's a priest here and priests are more trustworthy than witchers. The priest said that vampires always carry out their practices in league with witches. The witch summons the vampire and points out the victim to him, then blinds everyone's eyes so they won't see anything.'

'And it turned out it was indeed like that,' a second one added. 'We were harbouring a treacherous hag among us. But the priest saw through her witchcraft and now we're going to burn her.'

'What else,' the Witcher muttered. 'Very well, we'll take a look at your court. And we'll talk to the elder about the accident that befell the unfortunate Cloggy. We'll think about suitable compensation. Right, Percival? I'll wager that we'll find another pebble in one of your pockets. Lead on, good people.'

The procession set off towards a spreading maple. The ground beneath it was indeed teeming with excited people. The Witcher, having purposely slowed his pace, tried to strike up a conversation with one of the peasants, who looked reasonably normal.

'Who's this witch they've captured? Was she really engaged in black magic?'

'Well, sir,' the peasant mumbled, 'I couldn't say. That wench is a waif, a stranger. To my mind, she's not quite right in the head. Grown-up, but still only plays with the nippers, as if she was a child herself; ask her something and she won't say a word. Everyone says she consorted with a vampire and hexed people.'

'Everyone except the suspect,' said Regis, who until then had been walking quietly beside the Witcher. 'Because she, if asked, wouldn't utter a word. I'm guessing.'

There was not enough time for a more detailed investigation, because they were already under the maple. They made their way through the crowd, not without the help of Zoltan and his ashen staff.

A girl of about sixteen had been tied to the rack of a wagon laden with sacks, her arms spread wide apart. The girl's toes barely reached the ground. Just as they arrived, her shift and blouse were torn away to reveal thin shoulders. The captive reacted by

159

rolling her eyes and loosing a foolish combination of giggling and sobbing.

A fire had been started directly alongside the wagon. Someone had fanned the coals well and someone else had used pincers to place some horseshoes in the glowing embers. The excited cries of the priest rose above the crowd.

'Vile witch! Godless female! Confess the truth! Ha, just look at her, people, she's overindulged in some devilish herbs! Just look at her! Witchery is written all over her countenance!'

The priest who spoke those words was thin and his face was as dark and dry as a smoked fish. His black robes hung loosely on his skinny frame. A sacred symbol glistened on his neck. Geralt didn't recognise which deity it represented, and anyway he wasn't an expert. The pantheon, which in recent times had been growing quickly, did not interest him much. The priest must, however, have belonged to one of the newer religious sects. The older ones were concerned with more useful matters than catching girls, tying them to wagons and inciting superstitious mobs against them.

'Since the dawn of time woman has been the root of all evil! The tool of Chaos, the accomplice in a conspiracy against the world and the human race! Woman is governed only by carnal lust! That is why she so willingly serves demons, in order to slake her insatiable urges and her unnatural wantonness!'

'We'll soon learn more about women,' Regis muttered. 'This a phobia, in a pure clinical form. The devout man must often dream about a *vagina dentata*.'

'I'll wager it's worse,' Dandelion murmured. 'I'm absolutely certain that even when he's awake he dreams about a regular toothless one. And the semen has affected his brain.'

'But it's this feeble-minded girl who will have to pay for it.'

'Unless we can find someone,' Milva growled, 'who'll stop that black-robed ass.'

Dandelion looked meaningfully and hopefully at the Witcher, but Geralt avoided his gaze.

'And of what, if not female witchery, are our current calamities and misfortunes the result?' the priest continued to yell. 'For no one else but the sorceresses betrayed the kings on the Isle of Thanedd and concocted the assassination of the King of Redania! Indeed, no one else but the elven witch of Dol Blathanna is sending Squirrels after us! Now you see to what evil the familiarity with sorceresses has led us! And the tolerance of their vile practices! Turning a blind eye to their wilfulness, their impudent hubris, their wealth! And who is to blame? The kings! The vainglorious kings renounced the Gods, drove away the priests, took away their offices and seats on councils, and showered the loathsome sorceresses with honours and gold! And now we all suffer the consequences!'

'Aha! There lies the rub,' Dandelion said. 'You were wrong, Regis. It was all about politics and not vaginas.'

'And about money,' Zoltan Chivay added.

'Verily,' the priest roared, 'I say unto you, before we join battle with Nilfgaard, let us first purge our own house of these abominations! Scorch this abscess with a white-hot iron! Subject it to a baptism of fire! We shall not allow any woman who dabbles in witchcraft to live!'

'We shall not allow it! Burn her at the stake!' yelled the crowd.

The girl who was bound to the wagon laughed hysterically and rolled her eyes.

'All right, all right, easy does it,' said a lugubrious peasant of immense size who until that moment had been silent, and around whom was gathered a small group of similarly silent men and several grim-faced women. 'We've only heard squawking so far. Everyone's capable of squawking, even crows. We expect more from you, venerable father, than we would from a crow.'

'Do you refute my words, Elder Laabs? The words of a priest?'

'I'm not refitting anything,' the giant replied, then he spat on the ground and hitched up a pair of coarse britches. 'That wench is an orphan and a stray, no family of mine. If it turns out that she is in league with a vampire, take her and kill her. But while I'm the elder of this camp, only the guilty will be punished here. If you want to punish her, first establish her guilt.'

'That I shall!' the priest screamed, giving a sign to his stooges, the same ones who had previously put the horseshoes into the fire. 'I'll show you incontrovertibly! You, Laabs, and everyone else present here!'

His stooges brought out a small, blackened cauldron with a curved handle from behind the wagon and set it on the ground.

'Here is the proof!' the priest roared, kicking the cauldron over. A thin liquid spilt onto the ground, depositing some small pieces of carrots, some strips of unrecognisable greens and several small bones onto the sand. 'The witch was brewing a magic concoction! An elixir which enabled her to fly through the air to her vampire-lover. To have immoral relations with him and hatch more iniquities! I know the ways and deeds of sorcerers and I know what that decoct is made of! The witch boiled up a cat alive!'

The crowd oohed and aahed in horror.

'Ghastly,' Dandelion said, shuddering. 'Boiling a creature alive? I felt sorry for the girl, but she went a bit too far . . .'

'Shut your gob,' Milva hissed.

'Here is the proof!' the priest yelled, holding up a small bone he had removed from the steaming puddle. 'Here is the irrefutable proof! A cat's bone!'

'That's a bird's bone,' Zoltan Chivay said coldly, squinting. 'It's a jay's, I would say, or a pigeon's. The girl cooked herself some broth, and that's that!'

'Silence, you pagan imp!' the priest roared. 'Don't blaspheme, or the Gods will punish you at the hands of the pious! The brew came from a cat, I tell you!'

'From a cat! Without doubt a cat!' the peasants surrounding the priest yelled. 'The wench had a cat! A black cat! Everyone knew she did! It followed her around everywhere! And where is that cat now? It's gone! Gone into the pot!'

'Cooked! Boiled up as a potion!'

'Right you are! The witch has cooked up the cat into a potion!'

'No other proof is needed! Into the fire with the witch! But first torture her! Let her confess everything!'

"Kin' 'ell!' Field Marshal Windbag squawked.

'It's a shame about that cat,' Percival Schuttenbach suddenly said in a loud voice. 'It was a fine beast, sleek and fat. Fur shining like anthracite, eyes like two chrysoberyls, long whiskers, and a tail as thick as a mechanical's tool! Everything you could want in a cat. He must have caught plenty of mice!'

The peasants fell silent.

'And how would you know, Master Gnome?' someone asked. 'How do you know what the cat looked like?'

Percival Schuttenbach cleared his nose and wiped his fingers on a trouser leg.

'Because he's sitting over there on a cart. Right behind you.'

The peasants all turned around at once, muttering as they observed the cat sitting on a pile of bundles. The cat, meanwhile, utterly unconcerned about being the centre of attention, stuck a hind leg up in the air and got down to licking his rump.

'Thus it has turned out,' Zoltan Chivay said, breaking the silence, 'that your irrefutable proof is a load of crap, reverend. What will the next proof be? Perhaps a she-cat? That would be good. Then we'll put them together, they'll produce a litter and not a single rodent will come within half an arrow's shot of the granary.'

Several peasants snorted, and several others, including Elder Laabs, cackled openly. The priest turned purple with rage.

'I will remember you, blasphemer!' he roared, pointing a finger at the dwarf. 'O heathen kobold! O creature of darkness! How did you come to be here? Perhaps you are in collusion with the vampire? Just wait; we'll punish the witch and then we'll inter-rogate you! But first we'll try the witch! Horseshoes have already been put on the coals, so we'll see what the sinner reveals when her hideous skin starts to sizzle! I tell you she will confess to the crimes of witchcraft herself. And what more proof is there than a confession?'

'Oh, she will, she will,' Hector Laabs said. 'And were red-hot horseshoes placed against the soles of your feet, reverend, you would surely even confess to immoral coition with a mare. Ugh! You're a godly man, but you sound like a rascal!'

'Yes, I'm a godly man!' the priest bellowed, outshouting the inten-sifying murmurs of the peasants. 'I believe in divine judgement! And in a divine trial! Let the witch face trial by ordeal . . .'

'Excellent idea,' the Witcher interrupted loudly, stepping out from the crowd.

The priest glared at him. The peasants stopped muttering and stared at him with mouths agape.

'Trial by ordeal,' Geralt repeated to complete silence from the crowd, 'is utterly certain and utterly just. The verdicts of trial by ordeal are also accepted by secular courts and have their own principles. These rules say that in the case of a charge against a woman, child, old or otherwise enfeebled person a defence counsel may represent them. Am I right, Elder Laabs? So, I hereby offer myself in that role. Mark off the circle. Whomsoever is certain of the girl's guilt and is not afraid of trial of ordeal should step forward and do battle with me.'

'Ha!' the priest called, still glaring at him. 'Don't be too cunning, noble stranger. Throwing down the gauntlet? It's clear at once you are a swordsman and a killer! You wish to conduct a trial of ordeal with your criminal sword?'

'If the sword doesn't suit you, your reverence,' Zoltan Chivay announced in a drawling voice, standing alongside Geralt, 'and if you object to this gentleman, perhaps I would be more suitable. By all means, may the girl's accuser take up a battle-axe against me.'

'Or challenge me at archery,' Milva said, narrowing her eyes and also stepping forward. 'A single arrow each at a hundred paces.'

'Do you see, people, how quickly defenders of the witch are springing up?' the priest screamed, and then turned away and contorted his face into a cunning smile. 'Very well, you good-for-nothings, I invite all three of you to the trial by ordeal which will soon take place. We shall establish the hag's guilt, and test your virtue at one and the same time! But not using swords, battle-axes, lances or arrows! You know, you say, the rules? I also know them! See the horseshoes in the coals, glowing white-hot? Baptism of fire! Come, O minions of witchcraft! Whomsoever removes a horseshoe from the fire, brings it to me and betrays no marks of burning, will have proven that the witch is innocent. If, though, the trial of ordeal reveals something else, then it shall be death to all of you and to her! I have spoken!'

The hostile rumble of Elder Laabs and his group was drowned out by the enthusiastic cries of most of the people gathered behind the priest. The mob had already scented excellent sport and entertainment. Milva looked at Zoltan, Zoltan at the Witcher, and the Witcher first at the sky and then at Milva.

'Do you believe in the Gods?' he asked in hushed tones.

'Yes, I do,' the archer snapped back softly, looking at the glowing coals. 'But I don't think they'll want to be bothered by red-hot horseshoes.'

'It's no more than three paces from the fire to that bastard,' Zoltan hissed through clenched teeth. 'I'll get through it somehow, I worked in a foundry . . . But if you wouldn't mind praying to your Gods for me. . .'

'One moment,' Emiel Regis said, placing a hand on the dwarf's shoulder. 'Please withhold your prayers.'

The barber-surgeon walked over to the fire, bowed to the priest and the audience, then stooped rapidly and put his hand into the hot coals. The crowd screamed as one, Zoltan cursed and Milva dug her fingers into Geralt's arm. Regis straightened up, calmly looked down at the white-hot horseshoe he was holding, and walked unhurriedly over to the priest. The priest took a step back, bumping into the peasants standing behind him.

'This was the idea, if I'm not mistaken, your reverence.' Regis said, holding up the horseshoe. 'Baptism of fire? If so, I believe the divine judgement is unambiguous. The girl is innocent. Her defenders are innocent. And I, just imagine, am also innocent.'

'Sh . . . sh . . . show me your hand . . .' the priest mumbled. 'Is it not burnt?'

The barber-surgeon smiled his usual smile, with pursed lips, then moved the horseshoe to his left hand, and showed his right hand, totally unharmed, first to the priest, and then, holding it up high, to everyone else. The crowd roared.

'Whose horseshoe is it?' Regis asked. 'Let the owner take it back.'

No one came forward.

'It's a devilish trick!' the priest bellowed. 'You are a sorcerer yourself, or the devil incarnate!'

165

Regis threw the horseshoe onto the ground and turned around.

'Carry out an exorcism on me then,' he suggested coldly. 'You are free to do so. But the trial of ordeal has taken place. I have heard, though, that to question its verdict is heresy.'

'Perish. Be gone!' the priest shrieked, waving an amulet in front of the barber-surgeon's nose and tracing cabbalistic signs with his other hand. 'Be gone to the abyss of hell, devil! May the earth be riven asunder beneath you . . .'

'That is enough!' Zoltan shouted angrily. 'Hey, people! Elder Laabs! Do you intend to stand and watch this foolishness any longer? Do you intend . . . ?'

The dwarf's voice was drowned out by a piercing cry.

'Niiiilfgaaaaaard!'

'Cavalry from the west! Horsemen! Nilfgaard are attacking! Every man for himself!'

In one moment the camp was transformed into total pandemonium. The peasants charged towards their wagons and shelters, knocking each other down and trampling on each other. A single, great cry rose up into the sky.

'Our horses!' Milva yelled, making room around herself with punches and kicks. 'Our horses, Witcher! Follow me, quickly!'

'Geralt!' Dandelion shouted. 'Save me!'

The crowd separated them, scattered them like a great wave and carried Milva away in the blink of an eye. Geralt, gripping Dandelion by the collar, didn't allow himself to be swept away, for just in time he caught hold of the wagon which the girl accused of witchcraft was tied to. The wagon, however, suddenly lurched and moved off, and the Witcher and the poet fell to the ground. The girl jerked her head and began to laugh hysterically. As the wagon receded the laughter became quieter and was then lost among the uproar.

'They'll trample us!' Dandelion shouted from the ground. 'They'll crush us! Heeeelp!'

''Kiiin' 'ell!' Field Marshal Windbag squawked from somewhere out of sight.

Geralt raised his head, spat out some sand and saw a chaotic scene. Only four people did not panic, although to tell the truth one of

166

them simply had no choice. That was the priest, unable to move owing to his neck being held in the iron grip of Hector Laabs. The two other individuals were Zoltan and Percival. The gnome lifted up the priest's robe at the back with a rapid movement, and the dwarf, armed with the pincers, seized a red-hot horseshoe from the fire and dropped it down the saintly man's long johns. Freed from Laabs's grip, the priest shot straight ahead like a comet with a smoking tail, but his screams were drowned in the roar of the crowd. Geralt saw Laabs, the gnome and the dwarf about to congratulate one another on a successful ordeal by fire when another wave of panic-stricken peasants descended upon them. Everything disappeared in clouds of dust. The Witcher could no longer see anything, though neither did he have time to watch since he was busy rescuing Dandelion, whose legs had been swept from under him again by a stampeding hog. When Geralt bent down to lift the poet up, a hay rack was thrown straight on his back from a wagon rattling past. The weight pinned him to the ground, and before he was able to throw it off a dozen people ran across it. When he finally freed himself, another wagon overturned with a bang and a crash right alongside, and three sacks of wheaten flour – costing a crown a pound in the camp – fell onto him. The sacks split open and the world vanished in a white cloud.

'Get up, Geralt!' the troubadour yelled. 'Get on your blasted feet!'

'I can't,' the Witcher groaned, blinded by the precious flour, seizing in both hands his knee, which had been shot through by an overwhelming pain. 'Save yourself. Dandelion . . .'

'I won't leave you!'

Gruesome screams could be heard from the western edge of the camp, mixed up with the thud of iron-shod hooves and the neighing of horses. The screaming and tramping of hooves intensified suddenly, and the ringing, clanging and banging of metal striking against metal joined it.

'It's a battle!' the poet shouted. 'It's war!'

'Who's fighting who?' Geralt asked, trying desperately to clean the flour and chaff from his eyes. Not far away something was on fire, and they were engulfed by a wave of heat and a cloud of foul-smelling smoke. The hoofbeats rose in their ears and the earth shuddered. The first thing he saw in the cloud of dust were dozens of horses' fetlocks crashing up and down. All around him. He fought off the pain.

'Get under the wagon! Hide under the wagon, Dandelion, or they'll trample us!'

'Let's stay still . . .' the poet whimpered, flattened against the ground. 'Let's just lie here . . . I've heard a horse will never tread on a person lying on the ground . . .'

'I'm not sure,' Geralt exhaled, 'if every horse has heard that. Under the wagon! Quickly!'

At that moment one of the horses, unaware of human proverbs, kicked him in the side of the head as it thundered by. Suddenly all the constellations of the firmament flashed red and gold in the Witcher's eyes, and a moment later the earth and the sky were engulfed in impenetrable darkness.

The Rats sprang up, awoken by a long-drawn-out scream that boomed with an intensifying echo around the walls of the cave. Asse and Reef seized their swords and Iskra swore loudly as she banged her head on a rocky protrusion.

'What is it?' Kayleigh yelled. 'What's happening?'

It was dark in the cave even though the sun was shining outside – the Rats had been sleeping off a night spent in the saddle, fleeing from pursuers. Giselher shoved a brand into the glowing embers, lit it, held it up and walked over to where Ciri and Mistle were sleeping, as usual away from the rest of the gang. Ciri was sitting with her head down and Mistle had her arm around her.

Giselher lifted the flaming brand higher. The others also approached. Mistle covered Ciri's naked shoulders with a fur.

'Listen, Mistle,' the leader of the Rats said gravely. 'I've never interfered with what you two do in a single bed. I've never said a nasty or mocking word. I always try to look the other way and not notice. It's your business and your tastes, and nobody else's, as long as you do it discreetly and quietly. But this time you went a little too far.'

'Don't be stupid,' Mistle exploded. 'Are you trying to say that . . . ? She was screaming in her sleep! It was a nightmare!'

'Don't yell. Falka?'

Ciri nodded.

'Was your dream so dreadful? What was it about?'

'Leave her in peace!'

'Give it a rest, Mistle. Falka?'

'Someone, someone I once knew,' Ciri stammered, 'was being trampled by horses. The hooves . . . I felt them crushing me . . . I felt his pain . . . In my head and knee . . . I can still feel it. I'm sorry I woke you up.'

'Don't be sorry,' Giselher said, looking at Mistle's stern expression. 'You two deserve the apology. Forgive me. And the dream? Why, anybody could have dreamed that. Anybody.'

Ciri closed her eyes. She wasn't certain if Giselher was right.

He was awoken by a kick.

He was lying with his head against a wheel of the overturned cart, with Dandelion hunched up alongside him. He had been kicked by a foot soldier in a padded jacket and a round helmet. A second stood beside him. They were both holding the reins of horses, the saddles of which were hung with crossbows and shields.

'Bloody millers or what?'

The other soldier shrugged. Geralt saw that Dandelion couldn't take his eyes off the shields. Geralt himself had already noticed that there were lilies on them. The emblem of the Kingdom of Temeria. Other mounted crossbowmen – who were swarming around nearby – also bore the same arms. Most of them were busy catching horses and stripping the dead. The latter mainly wore black Nilfgaardian cloaks.

The camp was still a smoking ruin after the attack, but peasants who had survived and hadn't fled very far were beginning to reappear. The mounted crossbowmen with Temerian lilies were rounding them up with loud shouts.

Neither Milva, Zoltan, Percival nor Regis were anywhere to be seen.

The hero of the recent witchcraft trial, the black tomcat, sat alongside the cart, dispassionately looking at Geralt with his greenish-golden eyes. The Witcher was a little surprised, since ordinary cats couldn't bear his presence. He had no time to reflect on this unusual phenomenon, since one of the soldiers was prodding him with the shaft of his lance.

'Get up, you two! Hey, the grey-haired one has a sword!'

'Drop your weapon!' the other one shouted, attracting the attention of the rest. 'Drop your sword on the ground. Right now, or I'll stick you with my glaive.'

Geralt obeyed. His head was ringing.

'Who are you?'

'Travellers,' Dandelion said.

'Sure you are,' the soldier snorted. 'Are you travelling home? After fleeing from your standard and throwing away your uniforms? There are plenty of travellers like that in this camp, who've taken fright at Nilfgaard and lost the taste for army bread! Some of them are old friends of ours. From our regiment!'

'Those travellers can expect another trip now,' his companion cackled. 'A short one! Upwards on a rope!'

'We aren't deserters!' the poet yelled.

'We'll find out who you are. When you account for yourselves to the officer.'

A unit of light horse led by several armoured cavalrymen with splendid plumes on their helmets emerged from the ring of mounted crossbowmen.

Dandelion looked closely at the knights, brushed the flour off himself and tidied up his clothing, then spat on a hand and smoothed down his dishevelled hair.

'Geralt, keep quiet,' he forewarned. 'I'll parley with them. They're Temerian knights. They defeated the Nilfgaardians. They won't do anything to us. I know how to talk to the knighthood. You have to show them they aren't dealing with commoners, but with equals.'

'Dandelion, for the love of . . .'

'Never fear, everything will be fine. I have a lot of experience in talking to the knighthood and the nobility; half of Temeria know me. Hey, out of our way, servants, step aside! I wish to speak with your superiors!'

The soldiers looked on hesitantly, and then raised their couched lances and made room. Dandelion and Geralt moved towards the knights. The poet strode proudly, bearing a lordly expression which was somewhat out of place considering his frayed and flour-soiled tunic.

'Stop!' one of the armoured men yelled at him. 'Not another step! Who are you?'

'Who should I tell?' Dandelion said, putting his hands on his hips. 'And why? Who are these well-born lords, that they oppress innocent travellers?'

'You don't ask the questions, riffraff! You answer them!'

The troubadour inclined his head and looked at the coats of arms on the knights' shields and tabards.

'Three red hearts on a golden field,' he observed. 'That means you are an Aubry. There's a three-pointed label on the shield's chief, so you must be the eldest son of Anzelm Aubry. I know your pater well, good Sir Knight. And you, strident Sir Knight, what do you have on your silver shield? A black stripe between two gryphons' heads? The Papebrock family's coat of arms, if I'm not mistaken, and I am rarely mistaken in matters of this kind. The stripe, they say, illustrates the acuity possessed by that family's members.'

'Will you bloody stop,' Geralt groaned.

'I'm the celebrated poet Dandelion!' the bard said, puffing himself up and paying no attention to the Witcher. 'No doubt you've heard of me? Lead me, then, to your commander, to the seigneur, for I'm accustomed to speaking with equals!'

The knights did not react, but their facial expressions became more and more uncongenial and their iron gloves gripped their decorated bridles more and more tightly. Dandelion clearly hadn't noticed.

'Well, what's the matter with you?' he asked haughtily. 'What are you staring at? Yes, I'm talking to you, Sir Black Stripe! Why are you making faces? Did someone tell you that if you narrow your eyes and stick your lower jaw out you look manly, doughty, dignified and

171

menacing? Well, they deceived you. You look like someone who hasn't had a decent shit for a week!'

'Seize them!' yelled the eldest son of Anzelm Aubry – the bearer of the shield with three hearts – to the foot soldiers. The Black Stripe from the Papebrock family spurred his steed.

'Seize them! Bind the blackguards!'

They walked behind the horses, pulled by ropes attaching their wrists to the pommels. They walked and occasionally ran, because the horsemen spared neither their mounts nor their captives. Dandelion fell over twice and was dragged along on his belly, yelling pathetically. He was stood up again and urged on roughly with the lance shaft. And then driven on once more. The dust choked and blinded them, making their eyes water and their noses tingle. Thirst parched their throats.

Only one thing was encouraging; the road they were being driven along was heading south. Geralt was thus journeying in the right direction at last and pretty quickly, at that. He wasn't happy, though. Because he had imagined the journey would be altogether different.

They arrived at their destination just as Dandelion had made himself hoarse from curses peppered with cries for mercy, while the pain in Geralt's elbow and knee had become sheer torment – so severe that the Witcher had begun to consider taking radical, or even desperate measures.

They reached a military camp organised around a ruined, half-burnt stronghold.

Beyond the ring of guards, hitching bars and smoking campfires they saw knights' tents adorned with pennants, surrounding a large and bustling field beyond a ruined and charred stockade. The field marked the end of their forced trek.

Seeing a horse trough, Geralt and Dandelion strained against their bonds. The horsemen were initially disinclined to let them go anywhere near the water, but Anzelm Aubry's son evidently recalled the supposed acquaintance of Dandelion and his father and deigned to be kind. They forced their way between the horses, and drank and washed their faces using their bound hands. A tug of the ropes soon brought them back to reality.

'Who've you brought me this time?' said a tall, slim knight in enamelled, richly gilded armour, rhythmically striking a mace against an ornamented tasset. 'Don't tell me it's more spies.'

'Spies or deserters,' Anzelm Aubry's son stated. 'We captured them in the camp by the Chotla, when we wiped out the Nilfgaardian foray. Clearly a suspicious element!'

The knight in the gilded armour snorted, looked intently at Dandelion, and then his young – but austere – face suddenly lit up.

'Nonsense. Untie them.'

'They're Nilfgaardian spies!' Black Stripe of the Papebrocks said indignantly. 'Particularly this one here, as insolent as a country cur. Says he's a poet, the rogue!'

'And he speaks the truth,' the knight in the gilded armour smiled. 'It's the bard Dandelion. I know him. Remove his bonds. And free the other one too.'

'Are you sure, My Lord?'

'That was an order, Knight Papebrock.'

'Didn't realise I could come in useful, did you?' said Dandelion to Geralt, while he rubbed his wrists, which were numb from the bonds. 'So now you do. My fame goes before me, I'm known and esteemed everywhere.'

Geralt didn't comment, being busy massaging his own wrists, his sore elbow and knee.

'Please forgive the overzealousness of these youngsters,' said the knight who had been addressed as a member of the nobility. 'They see Nilfgaardian spies everywhere, bring back a few suspicious-looking types every time they're sent out. I mean anybody who in any way stands out from the fleeing rabble. And you, Master Dandelion, stand out, after all. How did you end up by the Chotla, among those fugitives?'

'I was travelling from Dillingen to Maribor,' the poet lied with ease, 'when we were caught up in this hell, me and my . . . confrere. You're sure to know him. His name is . . . Giraldus.'

'But of course I do, I've read him,' the knight bragged. 'It's an honour for me, Master Giraldus. I am Daniel Etcheverry, Count of Garramone. Upon my word, Master Dandelion, much has changed since the times you sang at King Foltest's court.'

'Much indeed.'

'Who would have thought,' the count said, his face darkening, 'that it would come to this. Verden subjugated to Emhyr, Brugge practically defeated, Sodden in flames . . . And we're in retreat, in constant retreat . . . My apologies, I meant to say we are "executing tactical withdrawals". Nilfgaard are burning and pillaging everywhere. They have almost reached the banks of the Ina, have almost completed the sieges of the fortresses of Mayena and Razwan, and the Temerian Army continues its "tactical withdrawals". . .'

'When I saw the lilies on your shields by the Chotla,' Dandelion said, 'I thought the offensive was here.'

'A counter-attack,' Daniel Etcheverry corrected him, 'and reconnaissance in force. We crossed the Ina, put to the sword a few Nilfgaardian forays and Scoia'tael commandos who were lighting fires. You can see what remains of the garrison in Armeria, who we managed to free. But the forts in Carcano and Vidort were burnt to the ground . . . The entire south is soaked in blood, afire and dense with smoke . . . Oh, but I'm boring you. You know only too well what's happening in Brugge and Sodden. After all, you ended up wandering with fugitives from there. And my brave boys took you for spies! Please accept my apologies one more time. And my invitation to dinner. Some of the noblemen and officers will be delighted to meet you, Master Poets.'

'It is a genuine honour, My Lord,' said Geralt, bowing stiffly. 'But time is short. We must be away.'

'Oh, please don't be shy,' Daniel Etcheverry said, smiling. 'A standard, modest soldier's repast. Venison, grouse, sterlet, truffles . . .'

'To decline,' Dandelion said, swallowing and giving the Witcher a telling glance, 'would be a serious affront. Let us go without delay, My Lord. Is that your tent, the sumptuous one, in blue and gold?'

'No. That is the commander-in-chief's. Azure and gold are the colours of his fatherland.'

'Really?' Dandelion said in astonishment. 'I thought this was the Temerian Army. And that you were in command.'

'This is a regiment assigned to the Temerian Army. I am King Foltest's liaison officer, and a goodly number of the Temerian nobility are serving here with detachments, which bear lilies on their shields as a formality. But the main part of this corps consists of the subjects of another kingdom. Do you see the standard in front of the tent?'

'Lions,' Geralt said, stopping. 'Golden lions on a blue field. That's . . . That's the emblem . . .'

'Of Cintra,' the count averred. 'They are emigrants from the Kingdom of Cintra, at present occupied by Nilfgaard. Under the command of Marshal Vissegerd.'

Geralt turned back, intending to announce to the count that urgent matters were nonetheless compelling him to decline the venison, sterlet and truffles. He wasn't quick enough. He saw some men approaching, led by a well-built, big-bellied, grey-haired knight in a blue cloak with a gold chain over his armour.

'Here, Master Poets, is Marshal Vissegerd in person,' Daniel Etcheverry said. 'Allow me, Your Lordship, to introduce you to . . .'

'That won't be necessary,' Marshal Vissegerd interrupted hoarsely, looking piercingly at Geralt. 'We have already been introduced. In Cintra, at the court of Queen Calanthe. On the day of Princess Pavetta's betrothal. It was fifteen years ago, but I have a good memory. And you, you rogue of a witcher? Do you remember me?'

'Indeed, I do,' Geralt said nodding, obediently holding out his hands for the soldiers to bind.

Daniel Etcheverry, Count of Garramone, had tried to vouch for them when the infantrymen were sitting the trussed-up Geralt and Dandelion down on stools in the tent, and now, after the soldiers had left on the orders of Marshal Vissegerd, the count renewed his efforts.

'That is the poet and troubadour Dandelion, marshal,' he repeated. 'I know him. The whole world knows him. I consider it

175

unfitting to treat him thus. I pledge my knightly word he is not a Nilfgaardian spy.'

'Don't make such rash pledges,' Vissegerd snarled, without taking his eyes off the captives. 'Perhaps he is a poet, but if he was captured in the company of that blackguard, the Witcher, I wouldn't vouch for him. It seems to me you still have no idea what kind of bird we've ensnared.'

'The Witcher?'

'Indeed. Geralt, also known as the Wolf. The very same good-for-nothing who claimed the right to Cirilla, the daughter of Pavetta and the granddaughter of Calanthe; the very same Ciri about whom everyone is talking at present. You are too young, My Lord, to remember the time when that scandal was being widely discussed at many courts. But I, as it happens, was an eyewitness.'

'But what could link him to Princess Cirilla?'

'That scoundrel there,' Vissegerd said, pointing at Geralt, 'played his part in giving Pavetta, the daughter of Queen Calanthe, in marriage to Duny, a totally unknown stranger from the south. From that mongrel union was subsequently born Cirilla, the subject of their reprehensible conspiracy. For you ought to know that Duny, the bastard, had promised the girl to the Witcher in advance, as payment for facilitating his marriage. The Law of Surprise, do you see?'

'Not entirely. But speak on, My Lord Marshal.'

'The Witcher,' Vissegerd said, pointing a finger at Geralt once again, 'wanted to take the girl away after Pavetta's death, but Calanthe did not permit him, and drove him away. But he waited for a timely moment. When the war with Nilfgaard broke out and Cintra fell, he kidnapped Ciri, exploiting the confusion. He kept the girl hidden, although he knew we were searching for her. And finally he grew tired of her and sold her to Emhyr!'

'Those are lies and calumny!' Dandelion yelled. 'There is not a word of truth in it!'

'Quiet, fiddler, or I'll have you gagged. Put two and two together, My Lord. The Witcher had Cirilla and now Emhyr var Emreis has her. And the Witcher gets captured in the vanguard of a Nilfgaardian raid. What does that signify?'

Daniel Etcheverry shrugged his shoulders.

'What does it signify?' Vissegerd repeated, bending over Geralt. 'Well, you rascal? Speak! How long have you been spying for Nilfgaard, cur?'

'I do not spy for anybody.'

'I'll have your hide tanned!'

'Go ahead.'

'Master Dandelion,' the Count of Garramone suddenly interjected. 'It would probably be better if you set about explaining. The sooner, the better.'

'I would have done so before,' the poet exploded, 'but My Lord Marshal here threatened to gag me! We are innocent; those are all outright fabrications and vile slanders. Cirilla was kidnapped from the Isle of Thanedd, and Geralt was seriously wounded defending her. Anybody can confirm that. Every sorcerer who was on Thanedd. And Redania's secretary of state, Sigismund Dijkstra . . .'

Dandelion suddenly fell silent, recalling that Dijkstra was in no way suitable as a defence witness in the case; and neither were references to the mages of Thanedd likely to improve the situation to any great degree.

'What utter nonsense it is,' he continued loudly and quickly, 'to accuse Geralt of kidnapping Ciri in Cintra! Geralt found the girl when she was wandering around in Riverdell after the city had been sacked, and hid her, not from you, but from the Nilfgaardian agents who were pursuing her! I myself was captured by those agents and submitted to torture so that I would betray where Ciri was concealed! But I didn't breathe a word and those agents are now six feet under. They didn't know who they were up against!'

'Your valour,' the count interrupted, 'was in vain, however. Emhyr finally has Cirilla. As we are all aware, he means to marry her and make her Imperatrice of Nilfgaard. For the moment he has proclaimed her Queen of Cintra and the surrounding lands, causing us some problems by so doing.'

'Emhyr,' the poet declared, 'could place whoever he wanted on the Cintran throne. Ciri, whichever way you look at it, has a right to the throne.'

'A right?' Vissegerd bellowed, spraying Geralt with spittle. 'What fucking right? Emhyr may marry her; that is his choice. He may give her and the children he sires with her endowments and titles according to his whims and fancies. Queen of Cintra and the Skellige Islands? Duchess of Brugge? Countess Palatine of Sodden? By all means. Let us all bow down! And why not, I humbly ask, why not the Queen of the Sun and the Suzerain of the Moon? That accursed, tainted blood has no right to the throne! The entire female line of that family is accursed, all rotten vipers, beginning with Riannon! Like Cirilla's great-grandmother, Adalia, who lay with her own cousin; like her great-great-grandmother, Muriel the Impure, who debased herself with everyone! Incestuous bastards and mongrels emerge from that family on the distaff side, one after the other!'

'Speak more softly, My Lord Marshal,' Dandelion advised haughtily. 'The standard with the golden lions flutters before your tent, and you are prepared at any moment to proclaim Ciri's grand-mother, Calanthe, the Lioness of Cintra, in whose name the majority of your soldiers shed blood at the Battles of Marnadal and Sodden, a bastard. I would not be sure of the loyalty of your army, were you to do so.'

Vissegerd covered the distance separating him from Dandelion in two paces, seized the poet by the ruff and lifted him up from his chair. The marshal's face, which a moment before had only been flecked with red spots, now assumed the colour of deep, heraldic red. Geralt was just beginning to seriously worry about his friend when luckily an aide-de-camp burst into the tent, informing the marshal in an excited voice about urgent and important news brought by the scouts. Vissegerd shoved Dandelion back down onto the stool and exited.

'Phew . . .' the poet snuffled, twisting his head and neck around. 'Much more of that and he'd have throttled me . . . Could you loosen my bonds somewhat, My Lord?'

'No, Master Dandelion. I cannot.'

'Do you give credence to this balderdash? That we are spies?'

'My credence is neither here nor there. You will remain bound.'

'Very well,' Dandelion said, clearing his throat. 'What's got into your marshal? Why did he suddenly assault me like a falcon swooping on a woodcock?'

Daniel Etcheverry smiled wryly.

'When you alluded to the soldiers' loyalty you unwittingly rubbed salt in the wound, Master Poet.'

'What do you mean? What wound?'

'These soldiers sincerely lamented Cirilla's passing, when news of her death reached them. And then new information got out. It turned out that Calanthe's granddaughter was alive. That she was in Nilfgaard, in the good graces of Imperator Emhyr. Which led to mass desertion. Bear in mind that these men left their homes and families, and fled to Sodden and Brugge, and to Temeria, because they wanted to fight for Cintra, for Calanthe's blood. They wanted to liberate their country, to drive the invader from Cintra, so that Calanthe's descendant would regain the throne. And what has happened? Calanthe's blood is returning to the Cintran throne in triumph and glory . . .'

'As a puppet in the hands of Emhyr, who kidnapped her.'

'Emhyr will marry her. He wants to place her beside him on the imperial throne and validate her titles and fiefs. Is that how puppets are treated? Cirilla was seen at the imperial court by envoys from Kovir. They maintain that she did not give the impression of someone who had been kidnapped. Cirilla, the only heiress to Cintra's throne, is returning to that throne as an ally of Nilfgaard. That is the news that has spread among the soldiery.'

'Circulated by Nilfgaardian agents.'

'I'm aware of that.' The count nodded. 'But the soldiers aren't. When we catch deserters, we stretch their necks, but I understand them a little. They're Cintrans. They want to fight for their own – not Temerian – homes. Under their own banner. Under their own command, not the command of Temeria. They see that here, in this army, their golden lions have to bow the knee before the Temerian lilies. Vissegerd had eight thousand men, of which five thousand were native Cintrans; the rest consisted of Temerian reserve units and volunteer chivalry from Brugge and Sodden. At this moment the corps numbers six thousand. And all the deserters have been from Cintra. Vissegerd's army has been decimated even before the battle has begun. Do you understand what that means for him?'

'A serious loss of face. And maybe position.'

'Precisely. Should another few hundred desert, King Foltest will deprive him of his baton. Right now it's hard to call this corps "Cintran". Vissegerd is vacillating, wanting to put an end to the defection, which is why he's spreading rumours about the doubtful – but most certainly unlawful – descent of Cirilla and her ancestors.'

'Which you,' Geralt said, unable to stop himself, 'listen to with evident distaste, My Lord.'

'Have you noticed?' Daniel Etcheverry said, smiling faintly. 'Why, Vissegerd doesn't know my lineage . . . In short, I'm related to this Cirilla. Muriel, Countess of Garramone, known as the Beautiful Impure, Cirilla's great-great-grandmother, was also my great-great-grandmother. Legends about her love affairs circulate in the family to this day. However, I listen with distaste as Vissegerd imputes incestuous tendencies and promiscuity to my ancestor. But I do not react. Because I'm a soldier. Do you understand me sufficiently, gentlemen?'

'Yes,' Geralt said.

'No,' Dandelion said.

'Vissegerd is the commander of this corps, which forms part of the Temerian Army. And Cirilla in Emhyr's hands is a threat to the corps, and thus to the army, not to mention my king and my country. I have no intention of refuting the rumours being circulated about Cirilla by Vissegerd nor of challenging my commanding officer's authority. I even intend to support him in proving that Cirilla is a bastard with no rights to the throne. Not only will I not challenge the marshal – not only will I not question his decisions or orders – I shall actually support them. And execute them when necessary.'

The Witcher's mouth contorted into a smile.

'I think you understand now, don't you, Dandelion? Not for a moment did the count consider us spies, or he would not have given us such a thorough explanation. The count knows we're innocent. But he will not lift a finger when Vissegerd sentences us.'

'You mean . . . You mean we're . . .'

The count looked away.

'Vissegerd,' he said softly, 'is furious. You were unlucky to fall into his hands. Particularly you, Master Witcher. As for Master Dandelion, I shall try to . . .'

He was interrupted by the return of Vissegerd, still red-faced and panting like a bull. The marshal walked over to the table, slammed his mace onto the maps spread over it, then turned towards Geralt and bored his eyes into him. The Witcher did not avert his gaze.

'The wounded Nilfgaardian the scouts captured,' Vissegerd drawled, 'managed to tear his dressing off and bled to death on the way. He preferred to die, rather than contribute to the defeat and death of his countrymen. We wanted to use him, but he escaped, slipped through our fingers, leaving nothing on them but blood. He'd been well schooled. It's a pity that witchers don't instil such customs in royal children when they take them to be raised.'

Geralt remained silent, but still did not lower his eyes.

'Well, you monster. You freak of nature. You hell spawn. What did you teach Cirilla after kidnapping her? How did you bring her up? Everyone can see how! That snake-in-the-grass is alive, and is lounging on the Nilfgaardian throne, as if it were nothing! And when Emhyr takes her to his bed she's sure to spread her legs willingly, as if it were nothing too, the slut!'

'Your anger is getting the better of you,' Dandelion mumbled. 'Is it chivalrous, marshal, to blame a child for everything? A child that Emhyr took by force?'

'There are also ways against force! Chivalrous ones, noble ones! Were she really of royal blood, she would have found a way! She would have found a knife! A pair of scissors, a piece of broken glass. Why, even a bodkin! The bitch could have torn open the veins in her wrists with her own teeth! Or hanged herself with her own stockings!'

'I don't want to listen to you any longer, marshal,' Geralt said softly. 'I don't want to listen to you any longer.'

Vissegerd ground his teeth audibly and leant over.

'You don't want to,' he said, in a voice trembling with fury. 'That is fortunate, because I don't have anything more to say to you. Apart

181

from one thing. Back then, in Cintra, fifteen years ago, a great deal was said about destiny. At the time I thought it was nonsense. But it turned out to be your destiny, Witcher. Ever since that night your fate has been sealed, written in black runes among the stars. Ciri, daughter of Pavetta, is your destiny. And your death. Because of Ciri, daughter of Pavetta, you shall hang.'

The Brigade joined Operation Centaur as a unit assigned to the 4th Horse Cavalry. We received reinforcements in the form of three squads of Verdenian light horse, which I assigned to the Vreemde Battle Group. Following the example of the campaign in Aedirn, I created two more battle groups from the rest of the brigade, naming them Sievers and Morteisen, each comprising four squadrons.

We set out from the concentration area near Drieschot on the night of the fourth of August. The Groups' orders ran:

> Capture the Vidort-Carcano-Armeria territory; seize the crossing over the Ina; destroy any hostile troops encountered, but avoid significant points of resistance. Start fires, particularly at night, to light the way for the 4th Horse Cavalry. Induce panic among civilians and use their flight to block all of the arterial routes to the enemy's rear. Feign encirclement to drive the retreating enemy forces towards the actual encirclements. Carry out the elimination of selected groups of the civilian population and prisoners of war to cause terror, intensify panic, and undermine the enemy's morale.

The Brigade carried out the above mission with great soldierly devotion.

Elan Trahe,
*For Imperator and Fatherland. The glorious trail of fire
of the 7th Daerlanian Cavalry Brigade*

CHAPTER FIVE

Milva did not have time to reach the horses and save them. She was a witness to their theft, but a helpless one. First she was swept along by the frantic, panic-stricken crowd, then the road was obstructed by careering wagons, and finally she became stuck in a woolly, bleating flock of sheep, through which she had to force her way as though it were a snowdrift. Later, by the Chotla, only a leap into the tall rushes growing in the marshes by the bank saved her from the Nilfgaardians' swords as they ruthlessly cut down the fugitives crowded by the river, showing no mercy either to women or children. Milva jumped into the water and reached the other bank, partly wading and partly swimming on her back among the corpses being carried by the current.

And she took up the hunt. She remembered the direction in which the peasants who had stolen Roach, Pegasus, the chestnut colt and her own black had fled. And her priceless bow was still attached to her saddle. *Tough luck*, she thought, feet squelching in her wet boots as she ran, *the others will have to cope without me for now. I must get my damn bow and horse back!*

She freed Pegasus first. The poet's horse was ignoring the heels digging into his sides. He was paying no heed to the urgent shouts of the inexperienced rider and had no intention of galloping; instead he trotted slowly through the birch wood. The poor fellow was being left a long way behind the other horse thieves. When he heard and then saw Milva over his shoulder, he jumped off without a second thought and bolted into the undergrowth, holding up his britches with both hands. Milva did not pursue him, overcoming her seething desire to exact some serious revenge. She leapt into the saddle in full flight, landing heavily and making the strings of the lute fastened to the saddlebags twang. A skilled horsewoman, she managed

185

to force the gelding to gallop. Or rather, to the lumbering canter that Pegasus considered a gallop.

But even this pseudo-gallop was enough, for the horse thieves' escape had been slowed by another tricky mount. The Witcher's skittish Roach, the infuriating, sulky bay mare Geralt had so often sworn he'd exchange for another steed, whether it be an ass, a mule or even a billy goat. Milva caught up with the thieves just as Roach, irritated by a clumsy tug of the reins, had thrown her rider to the ground. The rest of the peasants had dismounted and were trying to get the frisky and excitable mare under control. They were so busy they only noticed Milva when she rode among them on Pegasus and kicked one of them in the face, breaking his nose. When he fell to the ground, howling and calling upon the Gods, she recognised him. It was Cloggy. A peasant who clearly had no luck in his dealings with people. Or, more particularly, with Milva.

Unfortunately, luck deserted Milva too. To be precise, it wasn't her luck that was to blame, more her own conceit and her conviction – based on shaky practical evidence – that she could beat up any brace of peasants she happened to meet, in whatever manner she chose. When she dismounted she was punched in the eye and found herself on the ground. She drew her knife, ready to spill some guts, but was hit over the head with a stout stick so hard that it broke, blinding her with bark and rotten wood. Stunned and blinded, she still managed to grab the knee of the peasant beating her with the remains of the stick, when he unexpectedly howled and keeled over. The other yelled too, bringing both hands up to protect his head. Milva rubbed her eyes and saw that he was protecting himself from a rain of blows from a knout, dealt by a man riding a grey horse. She sprang up, dealing a powerful kick to the neck of the prostrate peasant. The rustler wheezed and flailed his legs, leaving his loins unprotected. Milva took advantage of that at once, channelling all her anger into a well-aimed kick. The peasant curled up in a ball, clamped his hands on his crotch and howled so loudly leaves fell from the birch trees.

Meanwhile, the horseman on the grey was busy with Cloggy, whose nose was streaming blood, and with the other peasant – he

186

chased them away into the trees with blows from the knout. He returned in order to thrash the one on the ground, but reined in his horse; Milva had managed to catch her black and was holding her bow with an arrow already nocked. The bowstring was only pulled halfway back, but the arrowhead was pointing directly at the horseman's chest.

For a moment, they looked at each other: the horseman and the young woman. Then, with a slow movement, he pulled an arrow with long fletchings from his belt and threw it down at Milva's feet.

'I knew I'd have the chance to give you back your arrow, elf,' he said calmly.

'I'm not an elf, Nilfgaardian.'

'And I'm not a Nilfgaardian. Put that bow down, will you? If I wished you ill, I could have just stood by and watched those peasants kick you around.'

'The devil only knows,' she said through her teeth, 'who you are and what you wish for me. But thanks for saving me. And for my arrow. And for dealing with that good-for-nothing I didn't hit properly the other day.'

The roughed-up horse thief, still curled up in a ball, choked back his sobs, his face buried in the leaf litter. The horseman didn't even look at him. He looked at Milva.

'Catch the horses,' he said. 'We have to get away from the river, and fast too; the army's combing the forests on both banks.'

'*We* have to?' she said, grimacing and lowering her bow. 'Together? Since when were we comrades? Or a company?'

'I'll explain,' he said, steering his horse and grabbing the chestnut's reins, 'if you give me time.'

'The point is, I don't have any time. The Witcher and the others—'

'I know. But we won't save them by letting ourselves get killed or captured. Catch the horses and we'll flee into the forest. Hurry!'

His name's Cahir, Milva recalled, glancing at her companion, with whom she was now sitting in the pit left by a fallen tree. *A strange Nilfgaardian, who says he isn't a Nilfgaardian. Cahir.*

'We thought they'd killed you,' she muttered. 'The riderless chestnut came running past us . . .'

'I had a minor adventure,' he answered drily, 'with three brigands, as shaggy as werewolves. They ambushed me. The horse got away. The brigands didn't, but then they were on foot. Before I managed to get a new mount, I'd fallen far behind you. I only managed to catch up with you this morning. Right by the camp. I crossed the river down in the gully and waited on the far bank. I knew you'd head east.'

One of the horses concealed in the alder wood snorted and stamped its hooves. Dusk was falling. Mosquitoes whined annoyingly around their ears.

'It's quiet in the forest,' Cahir said. 'The armies have gone, the battle is over.'

'The slaughter's over, you mean.'

'Our cavalry . . .' he stammered and cleared his throat. 'The imperial cavalry attacked the camp, and then troops appeared from the south. I think it was the Temerian Army.'

'If the battle's over, we should go back. We should search for the Witcher, Dandelion and the others.'

'It would be better to wait until nightfall.'

'There's something horrible about this place,' she said softly, tightening her grip on the bow. 'It's such a bleak wilderness. It gives me the shivers. Apparently quiet, but there's always something rustling in the bushes . . . The Witcher said ghouls are attracted to battle-fields . . . And the peasants were telling stories about a vampire . . .'

'You aren't alone,' he replied under his breath. 'It's much more frightening when you're alone.'

'Indeed.' She nodded, empathising with him. 'After all you've been following us for almost a fortnight, all alone. You've been trudging after us, while surrounded by your people— You might say you're not a Nilfgaardian, but they're still yours, aren't they. Devil take me if I understand it; instead of going back to your own you're tracking the Witcher. Why?'

'It's a long story.'

*

When the tall Scoia'tael leant over him Struycken, who was bound to a pole, blinked in fear. It was said there was no such thing as an ugly elf, that every single one of them was comely, that they were born beautiful. And perhaps the legendary commander of the Squirrels had been born beautiful. But now that his face was gashed by a hideous diagonal scar deforming his forehead, eyebrow, nose and cheek, nothing remained of his elven good looks.

The elf with the disfigured physiognomy sat down on a fallen tree trunk.

'I am Isengrim Faoiltiarna,' he said, leaning over the captive once again. 'I've been fighting humans for four years and leading a commando for three. I have buried my brother, who fell in combat, four cousins and more than four hundred brothers in arms. In my struggle, I treat your imperator as my ally, as I have proved several times by passing intelligence to your spies, helping your agents and eliminating individuals selected by you.'

Faoiltiarna fell silent and made a sign with his gloved hand. The Scoia'tael standing alongside picked up a small birchbark canteen. The canteen gave off a sweet aroma.

'I considered and consider Nilfgaard an ally,' the elf with the scar repeated, 'which is why I did not, initially, believe my informant when he warned that a trap was being laid for me. That I would receive instructions for a private meeting with a Nilfgaardian emissary, and that I would be captured then. I didn't believe but, being cautious by nature, I turned up for the rendezvous a little earlier than expected and not alone. Much to my surprise and dismay, instead of the said emissary, there were six thugs waiting with a fishing net, ropes, a leather mask with a gag, and a straitjacket fastened with straps and buckles. Standard equipment used by your secret service during abductions I would say. Nilfgaard wanted to capture me, Faoiltiarna, alive, and transport me somewhere, gagged and securely fastened in a straitjacket. A curious affair, I would say. And one requiring some elucidation. I'm delighted that I managed to take alive at least one of the thugs who had been set on me – no doubt their leader – who will be able to furnish me with that elucidation.'

Struycken gritted his teeth and turned his head away, in order not to look at the elf's disfigured face. He preferred to look at the birch-bark canteen, and the two wasps buzzing around it.

'And now,' Faoiltiarna continued, wiping his sweaty neck with a scarf, 'let's have a little chat, Master Kidnapper. To make the conversation flow, let me clarify a few points. There is maple syrup in the canteen. Should our little chat not proceed in a spirit of mutual understanding and complete frankness, we shall copiously anoint your head with the aforementioned syrup, paying very close attention to your eyes and ears. Then we shall place you on an anthill, this one here to be precise, over which these charming, hardworking insects are scurrying. Let me add that this method has already proved its worth in the case of several Dh'oine and an'givare who evinced great stubbornness and a lack of candour.'

'I am in the imperial service!' the spy screamed, blanching. 'I am an officer of the imperial military intelligence, a subordinate of Lord Vattier de Rideaux, Viscount of Eiddon! My name is Jan Struycken! I protest—'

'What awful luck,' the elf interrupted him, 'that these red ants, greedy for maple syrup, have never heard of the viscount. Let us begin. I shall not ask who gave the order for my abduction, because it is obvious. So my first question shall be: where was I to be taken?'

The Nilfgaardian spy struggled against the ropes and jerked his head, for it seemed to him the ants were already crawling over his cheeks. But he remained silent.

'Too bad,' Faoiltiarna said, breaking the silence and gesturing to the elf with the canteen. 'Apply the syrup.'

'I was to transport you to Nastrog Castle in Verden!' Struycken yelled. 'On the orders of Viscount de Rideaux!'

'Thank you. And what awaited me there?'

'An interrogation . . .'

'What was I to be asked about?'

'About the events on Thanedd! Untie me, I beg you! I'll tell you everything!'

'Of course you will,' the elf sighed, stretching. 'Particularly since we've already made a start, and in matters like these that's usually the most difficult part. Continue.'

'I was ordered to make you confess where Vilgefortz and Rience are hiding! And Cahir Mawr Dyffryn, son of Ceallach!'

'How comical. A trap laid to ask me about Vilgefortz and Rience? Whatever would I know about them? What could link me with them? And Cahir? That's even more comical. I sent him to you, did I not? Just as you requested. In fetters. Are you saying the package didn't arrive?'

'The unit which was sent to the designated rendezvous point was slaughtered . . . Cahir was not among the dead . . .'

'Ah. And Lord Vattier de Rideaux became suspicious? But instead of sending another emissary to the commando and asking for an explanation, he immediately laid a trap for me. And ordered me dragged to Nastrog in chains and interrogated about the incidents on Thanedd.'

The spy said nothing.

'Didn't you get it?' the elf said and bent his head, bringing his hideous face towards Struycken. 'That was a question. And it ran: what's this all about?'

'I don't know . . . I don't know, I swear . . .'

Faoiltiarna beckoned with a hand and pointed. Struycken howled, thrashed around, swore on the Great Sun, pleaded his innocence, wept, tossed his head about and spat out the syrup, which had been thickly smeared over his face. Only when he was carried over to the anthill by four Scoia'tael did he decide to talk – although the consequences of speaking were potentially more dreadful than the ants.

'Sire . . . Should anyone find out about this, I'm dead meat . . . But I shall disclose it to you . . . I've seen confidential orders. I've eavesdropped . . . I'll tell you everything . . .'

'Of course you will.' The elf nodded. 'The record on the anthill is an hour and forty minutes, and belongs to a certain officer from King Demavend's special forces. But even he talked in the end. Very well, begin. Quickly, coherently and to the point.'

'The Imperator is certain he was betrayed on Thanedd. The traitor is Vilgefortz of Roggeveen, a sorcerer, and his assistant Rience. But mostly Cahir Mawr Dyffryn aep Ceallach. Vattier . . . Viscount Vattier is not certain whether you Scoia'tael also had a hand in the treachery, if only unwittingly . . . Which is why he ordered you to be seized and delivered in secret to Nastrog Castle . . . Lord Faoiltiarna, I've been working in the secret service for twenty years . . . Vattier de Rideaux is my third boss . . .'

'More coherently, please. And stop shaking. If you're frank with me, you'll still be able to serve a few more bosses.'

'Although it was kept absolutely confidential, I knew . . . I knew who Vilgefortz and Cahir were supposed to capture on the island. And it looked like they had succeeded. Because they brought that . . . you know . . . that princess from Cintra to Loc Grim. I thought they'd pulled it off and that Cahir and Rience would become barons, and that sorcerer a count at least . . . But instead the Imperator summoned Tawny Owl – I mean, Lord Skellen – and ordered him and Lord Vattier to capture Cahir . . . And Rience, and Vilgefortz . . . Anyone who might know anything about Thanedd and that incident was to be tortured . . . Including you . . . It didn't take much to guess, you know, that it was treachery. That a sham princess had been brought to Loc Grim . . .'

The spy struggled to breathe, nervously gasping for air through lips covered with maple syrup.

'Untie him,' Faoiltiarna ordered his Squirrels. 'And let him wash his face.'

The order was carried out immediately. A moment later the mastermind of the unsuccessful ambush was standing with head lowered before the legendary Scoia'tael commander. Faoiltiarna looked at him indifferently.

'Scrape the syrup thoroughly from your ears,' he finally said. 'Then prick them up and listen carefully, as befits a spy with many years' experience. I shall give you proof of my loyalty to the Imperator. I shall give you a thorough account of the matters that interest him. And you will repeat everything, word for word, to Vattier de Rideaux.'

The spy nodded eagerly.

'In the middle of Blathe, which according to your reckoning is the beginning of June,' the elf began, 'I was contacted by Enid an Gleanna, the sorceress also known as Francesca Findabair. Soon after, on her orders, a certain Rience came to my commando. He was said to be the factotum of Vilgefortz of Roggeveen, also a sorcerer. A plan of action was drawn up in utter secrecy, with the aim of eliminating a number of mages during the conclave on the Isle of Thanedd. The plan was presented as one having the full support of Imperator Emhyr, Vattier de Rideaux and Stephan Skellen; otherwise I should not have agreed to collaborate with Dh'oine – sorcerers or not – for I have seen too many entrapments in my life. The involvement of the Empire was confirmed by the arrival of a ship at Cape Bremervoord. On board was Cahir, son of Ceallach, equipped with special authorisation and orders. According to those orders I selected a special squad from the commando, which would be answerable only to Cahir. I was aware that they were trusted to capture and remove a . . . certain individual . . . from the island.'

'We sailed to Thanedd,' Faoiltiarna began again after a pause, 'on the ship which had brought Cahir. Rience had some amulets and he used them to surround the ship with a magical fog. We sailed into the caverns beneath the island. From there we proceeded to the catacombs under Garstang. There we realised at once that something wasn't right. Rience had received some telepathic signals from Vilgefortz. We knew we'd have to start fighting any minute. Fortunately, we were ready, because the moment we left the catacombs we were plunged into hell.'

The elf contorted his mutilated face, as though the recollection pained him.

'After our initial successes, matters became complicated. We were unable to eliminate all the royal sorcerers, and we took heavy casualties. Several mages who were party to the conspiracy also perished, while others began to save their skins and teleport away. All of a sudden Vilgefortz vanished, then Rience, and Enid an Gleanna soon followed suit. I treated that final disappearance as the conclusive signal for our withdrawal. I did not, however, give the order, but waited for the return of Cahir and his squad, who had set off at once to carry out their mission. When they did not return, we began to search for them.'

'No one,' Faoiltiarna said, looking the Nilfgaardian spy in the eyes, 'survived from that squad; they were all brutally slaughtered. We found Cahir on the steps leading to Tor Lara, a tower which exploded during the battle and ended up as a heap of rubble. He was wounded and unconscious; it was clear he had not accomplished the mission he had been assigned. There was no sign of his target anywhere and royal troops were already pouring out of Aretuza and Loxia. I knew there was no way Cahir could fall into their hands, because it would have been proof of Nilfgaard's active involvement in the operation. So we took him with us and fled back to the catacombs and then the caverns. We boarded the ship and sailed away. Twelve remained of my commando, most of them wounded.'

'The wind was at our backs. We landed to the west of Hirundum and hid in the forest. Cahir was trying to tear off his bandages and was yelling something about an insane girl with green eyes, about the Lion Cub of Cintra, about a witcher who had massacred his men, about the Tower of Gulls and a mage who flew like a bird. He demanded a horse and ordered us to return him to the island, citing the imperial orders, which under the circumstances I had to treat as the ravings of a madman. As we knew, war was already raging in Aedirn, so I considered it more important to swiftly rebuild my depleted commando and resume the fight against the Dh'oine.'

'Cahir was still with us when I found your secret order in a dead drop. I was astonished. Although Cahir had clearly not completed his mission, there was nothing to suggest he was guilty of treachery. But I did not ponder over it for long, judging that it was your business and that you ought to clear it up. Cahir put up no resistance to being tied up, he was calm and resigned. I ordered him to be placed in a coffin and with the help of a hawker acquaintance delivered to the location designated in the letter. I was not, I admit, inclined to further deplete my commando by providing an escort. I don't know who murdered your men at the rendezvous point. But only I knew where it was. So if this version of the totally random extermination of your unit doesn't suit you, search for traitors among your own, because only you and I knew the time and place.'

Faoiltiarna stood up.

'That is all. All the information I have given here is true. I would not supply you with anything more in the dungeons of Nastrog. The lies and confabulations with which I might try to satisfy the investigating officer and his torturers would actually do more harm than good. I do not know anything more. In particular I don't know Vilgefortz and Rience's whereabouts, and neither do I know if your suspicions of betrayal are justified. I also emphatically declare that I know nothing about the princess from Cintra, the genuine or the sham one. I have told you everything I know. I trust that neither Lord de Rideaux nor Stephan Skellen will want to set any more traps for me. The Dh'oine have been trying to capture and kill me for a long, long time, so I have adopted the custom of ruthless extermination of all trap setters. I shall not, in the future, investigate to check if one of the trap setters is, by chance, a subordinate of Vattier or Skellen. I do not have the time nor the desire to make such an investigation. Do I make myself clear?'

Struycken nodded and swallowed.

'Now take a horse, spy, and get the hell out of my forest.'

'You mean they were delivering you to the gallows?' Milva mumbled. 'Now I understand some of it, but not everything. Why, instead of holing up somewhere, are you following the Witcher? He's really got it in for you . . . And he's spared your life twice . . .'

'Three times.'

'I saw two of them. Though you weren't the one who beat the shit out of the Witcher on Thanedd, as I first thought, I don't think you ought to get in the way of his sword again. There's a lot about your feud I don't understand, but you saved me and you've got an honest face . . . So I'll tell you, Cahir, bluntly: when the Witcher talks about the men who took his Ciri to Nilfgaard, he grinds his teeth until sparks fly. And if you spat on him, he would steam.'

'Ciri,' he repeated. 'Sounds nice.'

'Didn't you know?'

'No. My people always called her Cirilla or the Lion Cub of Cintra . . . And when she was with me – for she was once . . . she didn't say a single word. Even though I saved her life.'

'Only the devil himself could grasp all this,' Milva said,

exasperated. 'Your fates are all entangled, Cahir, knotted and mixed up. It's too much for my head.'

'And what's your name?' he suddenly asked.

'Milva . . . Maria Barring. But call me Milva.'

'The Witcher's heading the wrong way, Milva,' he offered a moment later. 'Ciri isn't in Nilfgaard. The kidnappers didn't take her to Nilfgaard. If it was a kidnap at all.'

'What do you mean?'

'It's a long story.'

'By the Great Sun,' Fringilla said, standing in the doorway, tilting her head and looking in astonishment at her friend. 'What have you done to your hair, Assire?'

'I washed it,' Assire var Anahid replied coldly. 'And styled it. Come in and sit down. Get out of that chair, Merlin. Shoo!'

The sorceress sat down in the chair the black cat had reluctantly vacated, her eyes still fixed on her friend's coiffure.

'Stop staring,' Assire said, touching her bouffant and glistening curls. 'I decided to make a few changes. Why, I just took your lead.'

'I was always taken as an oddball and a rebel,' Fringilla Vigo chuckled. 'But when they see you in the academy or at court . . .'

'I'm seldom at court,' Assire cut her off, 'and the academy will have to get used to it. This is the thirteenth century. It's high time we challenged the superstition that dressing up is proof of an enchant-ress's flightiness and the superficiality of her mind.'

'Fingernails too,' Fringilla said, slightly narrowing her green eyes, which never, ever, missed anything. 'Whatever next, darling? I hardly recognise you.'

'A simple spell,' the enchantress replied coolly, 'ought to be enough to prove it's me and no doppelgänger. Cast the spell, if you must. And then let's move on to the matter in hand. I asked some-thing of you . . .'

Fringilla Vigo stroked the cat, which was rubbing himself against her calf, purring and arching his back, pretending it was a gesture of friendship and not a veiled hint that the black-haired sorceress should get up from the armchair.

'The same thing Seneschal Ceallach aep Gruffyd asked of you,' she said, without raising her head.

'Indeed,' Assire confirmed in hushed tones, 'Ceallach visited me, distraught, and asked me to intercede to save his son. Emhyr has ordered him to be captured, tortured and executed. Who else could he turn to except a relative? Mawr, Ceallach's wife and Cahir's mother, is my niece, my sister's youngest daughter. In spite of all that I didn't promise him anything. Because my hands are tied. Certain circumstances took place recently which do not permit me to draw attention to myself. I shall elucidate. But only after you've given me the information I asked you to gather.'

Fringilla Vigo furtively sighed with relief. She had been afraid her friend would want to get involved in the case of Cahir, son of Ceallach, which had 'gallows' written all over it. And equally afraid she would be asked for help she couldn't refuse.

'Around the middle of July,' she began, 'the entire court at Loc Grim had the opportunity to marvel at a fifteen-year-old girl, supposedly the Princess of Cintra, whom Emhyr insisted on referring to as "Your Majesty" during the audience and was treated so kindly there were even rumours of a quick marriage.'

'So I heard,' Assire said, stroking the cat, which had given up on Fringilla and was trying to occupy her own armchair instead. 'This doubtlessly political marriage is still talked about.'

'But more discreetly and not so often. For the Cintran was moved to Darn Rowan. Prisoners of state, as you know, are often kept in Darn Rowan. Potential imperatrices much less often.'

Assire didn't comment. She waited patiently, examining her freshly filed and varnished fingernails.

'You must remember,' Fringilla Vigo continued, 'how Emhyr summoned us all three years ago and ordered us to establish the whereabouts of a certain individual. Within the Northern Kingdoms. You must also recall how furious he became when we failed. Albrich – who explained it was impossible to detect anything from such a distance, never mind bypassing protective screens – was severely reprimanded. But that's not all. A week after the aforementioned audience in Loc Grim, when victory at Aldersberg was being celebrated, Emhyr noticed myself and Albrich in the castle chamber. And graced us with his conversation. The gist of his speech, only somewhat trivialising it, was: "You're all of you leeches, spongers and idlers. Your conjuring tricks cost me a fortune and there's nothing to show for it. The task which your entire lamentable academy failed to achieve was carried out in four days by an ordinary astrologist.'

Assire var Anahid snorted disdainfully and continued to stroke the cat.

'It was easy to discover,' Fringilla Vigo went on, 'that the miracle worker was none other than the infamous astrologist Xarthisius.'

'I take it the subject of the search was the Cintran candidate for the position of Imperatrice. Xarthisius found her. And then what? Was he appointed Secretary of State? Head of the Department of Unfeasible Affairs?'

'No. He was thrown into a dungeon the following week.'

'I fear I fail to understand what this has to do with Cahir, son of Ceallach.'

'Patience. Don't make me get ahead of myself. This is crucial.'

'I beg your pardon. Go on.'

'Do you remember what Emhyr gave us when we began our search three years ago?'

'A lock of hair.'

'Precisely,' Fringilla said, reaching for a small, leather purse. 'And this is it. A few blonde hairs belonging to a six-year-old girl. I kept the remnants. And it's worth your knowing that Stella Congreve, Countess of Liddertal, is looking after the Cintran princess who is being kept in isolation in Darn Rowan. Stella happens to be indebted to me for various reasons, so it was easy for me to come by a second lock of hair. And this is it. Somewhat darker, but hair darkens with age. Nonetheless, the locks belong to two totally different people. I've examined them and there is no doubt in this respect.'

'I had expected a revelation of this kind,' Assire var Anahid admitted, 'when I heard that the Cintran had been shut up in Darn Rowan. The astrologer either fouled up completely or is implicated in a conspiracy that planned to supply Emhyr with a bogus individual. A conspiracy which will cost Cahir aep Ceallach his head. Thank you, Fringilla. Everything is clear.'

'Not everything,' the sorceress said and shook her head of black hair. 'First of all, it wasn't Xarthisius who found the Cintran or took her to Loc Grim. The astrologist started on his horoscopes and astromancy *after* Emhyr realised he had a bogus princess and begun an intensive search for the real one. And the old fool ended up in the dungeon because of a simple mistake in his art or fraud. For he had established the whereabouts of the person Emhyr sought with a radial tolerance of approximately one hundred miles. And that region turned out to be a desert, a savage wilderness somewhere beyond the Tir Tochair massif and the riverhead of the Velda. Stephan Skellen, who was sent there, found nothing but scorpions and vultures.'

'I wouldn't have expected much more from Xarthisius. But that won't affect Cahir's fate. Emhyr is quick-tempered, but he never sentences anyone to torture or death just like that, without evidence. Someone, as you said yourself, made sure the bogus princess was taken to Loc Grim in place of the real one. Someone came up with a double. So there was a conspiracy and Cahir became mixed up in it. Possibly unwittingly. Which means he was used.'

'If that was the case, he would have been used until the goal was reached. He would personally have delivered the double to Emhyr. But Cahir has vanished without a trace. Why? His disappearance was sure to have aroused suspicions. Did he fear Emhyr would notice the deception at first glance? For he did. He couldn't fail to, after all he had a—'

'A lock of hair,' Assire cut in. 'A lock of hair from a six-year-old girl. Fringilla, Emhyr hasn't been hunting for that girl for three years, but for much longer. It looks as though Cahir has become embroiled in something very nasty, something which began when he was still riding a stick horse and pretending to be a knight. Mmm . . . Leave me those strands of hair. I'd like to test them both thoroughly.'

Fringilla Vigo nodded slowly and narrowed her green eyes.

'I will. But be cautious, Assire. Don't get mixed up in any dirty business, because it might draw attention to you. And at the beginning of the conversation you hinted that attention would be inconvenient to you. And promised you'd reveal why.'

Assire var Anahid stood up, walked over to the window and stared at the spires and pinnacles of Nilfgaard – the capital of the Empire, called the City of the Golden Towers – shimmering in the setting sun.

'You once told me and I remembered it,' she said, without turning around, 'that no borders should ever divide magic. That magic should have the highest values, be above all divisions. That what was needed was some kind of . . . secret organisation . . . Something like a convent or a lodge . . .'

'I am ready,' said Fringilla Vigo, Nilfgaardian sorceress, breaking the short silence. 'My mind is made up and I am ready. Thank you for your trust and the distinction. When and where will this lodge meet, my mysterious and enigmatic friend?'

Assire var Anahid, Nilfgaardian sorceress, turned away. The hint of a smile played on her lips.

'Soon,' she said. 'I'll explain everything to you soon. But first, before I forget . . . Give me the address of your milliner, Fringilla.'

'There isn't a single fire,' Milva whispered, staring at the dark bank beyond the river, gleaming in the moonlight, 'or a living soul there, I reckon. There were two hundred refugees in the camp. Has no one got off scot-free?'

'If the imperial troops won, they took them all captive,' Cahir whispered back. 'If your boys got the upper hand, they took the refugees with them when they moved on.'

They neared the riverbank and the reeds covering the marsh. Milva trod on something and sprang back, suppressing a scream, at the sight of a stiff arm, covered in leeches, sticking out of the mud.

'It's just a dead body,' Cahir muttered, grabbing her hand. 'One of ours. A Daerlanian.'

'Who is he?'

'One of the Seventh Daerlanian Cavalry Brigade. See the silver scorpion on his sleeve . . .'

'By the Gods. . .' The girl shuddered and gripped her bow tightly in her sweating fist. 'Did you hear that noise? What was it?'

'A wolf.'

'Or a ghoul . . . Or some other hell spawn. There must be a whole load of dead bodies in the camp . . . A pox on it, I'm not crossing that river at night!'

'Fine, we'll wait until dawn . . . Milva? What's that strange . . . ?'

'Regis . . .' the archer said, stifling a shout at the scent of worm-wood, sage, coriander and aniseed. 'Regis? Is that you?'

'Yes, it's me,' the barber-surgeon replied, noiselessly emerging from the gloom, 'I was worried about you. But you're not alone, I see.'

'Aye.' Milva released Cahir's arm, noticing he had already drawn his sword. 'I'm not alone and he's not alone any more. But that's a long story, as some people would say. Regis, what about the Witcher? And Dandelion? And the others? Do you know what's happened to them?'

'Indeed I do. Do you have horses?'

'Yes, they're hidden in the willows . . .'

'Then let's head southwards, down the Chotla. Without delay. We must reach Armeria before midnight.'

'What about the Witcher and the poet? Are they alive?'

'Yes. But they're in a bit of difficulty.'

'What kind of difficulty?'

'It's a long story.'

Dandelion groaned, trying to turn around and get into a slightly more comfortable position. It was, however, an impossible task for someone lying trussed up like a ham to be smoked in a pile of soft wood shavings and sawdust and.

'They didn't hang us right away,' he grunted. 'There's hope for us still. We aren't done for yet . . .'

'Would you mind shutting up?' the Witcher said, lying back calmly and looking up at the moon, visible through a hole in the roof of the woodshed. 'Do you know why Vissegerd didn't hang us right away? Because we're to be executed publicly, at dawn, while

201

the entire corps are mustered before moving out. For propaganda purposes.'

Dandelion did not respond to that. Geralt only heard him panting with worry.

'You still have a chance of dodging the drop,' he added, trying to reassure the poet. 'Vissegerd simply wants to exact his own private revenge on me; he hasn't got anything against you. Your friend the count will get you out of trouble, you'll see.'

'That's crap,' the bard replied, to the Witcher's astonishment calmly and quite reasonably. 'Crap, crap, crap. Don't treat me like a child. For one thing, two hanged men are better for propaganda purposes than one. For another, you don't let a witness to private revenge live. No, brother, they'll stretch us both.'

'That's enough, Dandelion. Lie there quietly and think up a plan.'

'What bloody plan?'

'Any bloody plan.'

The poet's idle chatter prevented the Witcher from gathering his thoughts, and he had no time to waste. He expected that men from Temerian military intelligence – some of whom must have been present in Vissegerd's corps – would burst into the woodshed at any moment. Intelligence officers would surely be interested in asking him about various aspects of the events in Garstang on the Isle of Thanedd. Geralt hardly knew any of the details, but he was confident that he would be feeling very, very poorly indeed before the agents accepted this. All his hopes depended on Vissegerd, blinded by the lust for revenge, not having made the Witcher's capture public. Intelligence officers might want to free the captives from the clutches of the furious marshal in order to take them to headquarters. Or, to be more precise, take whatever was left of them after the first round of interrogation.

The poet, meanwhile, had come up with a plan.

'Geralt! Let's pretend we know something important. That we really are spies or something like that. Then—'

'Dandelion, please.'

'No? So we could try to bribe the sentries. I have some money hidden away. Doubloons, sewn into the lining of my boot. For a rainy day . . . We'll summon the sentries . . .'

'Who'll take all you have and then beat you up for good measure.'

The poet grumbled, but stopped talking. From the field they heard shouts, the patter of hooves and – what was worse – the smell of army pea soup. At that moment, Geralt would have given all the sterlets and truffles in the world for a bowl of it. The sentries standing outside the shed were talking lazily, chuckling and, from time to time, hawking up and spitting. The sentries were professional soldiers, which could be discerned by their remarkable ability to communicate using sentences constructed entirely of pronouns and coarse expletives.

'Geralt?'

'What?'

'I wonder what's happened to Milva . . . And Zoltan, and Percival and Regis . . . Did you see them?'

'No. We can't rule out their being hacked to death or trampled by horses during the skirmish. The camp was knee-deep in corpses.'

'I can't believe,' Dandelion declared resolutely and with a note of hope in his voice, 'I can't believe that crafty buggers like Zoltan and Percival . . . Or Milva . . .'

'Stop deluding yourself. Even if they did survive, they won't help us.'

'Why not?'

'For three reasons. Firstly, they have their own problems. Secondly, we're lying tied up in a shed in the middle of a camp of several thousand soldiers.'

'And the third reason? You mentioned three.'

'Thirdly,' the Witcher replied in a tired voice, 'the monthly quota on miracles was used up when the woman from Kernow found her missing husband.'

'Over there,' the barber-surgeon said, indicating the small dots of campfires, 'is Fort Armeria, at present the camp of the Temerian Army concentrated at Mayena.'

'Are the Witcher and Dandelion being held prisoner there?'

Milva asked, standing up in her stirrups. 'Ha, then things are bad . . . There must be hordes of armed men and guards everywhere. Won't be easy sneaking in there.'

'You won't have to,' Regis responded, dismounting from Pegasus. The gelding gave a long snort and pulled his head away, clearly disgusted by the barber-surgeon's herbal odour, which made his nostrils tingle.

'You won't have to sneak in,' he repeated. 'I'll take care of it. You'll be waiting with the horses where the river's sparkling, do you see? Beneath the brightest star in the Seven Goats. The Chotla flows into the Ina there. Once I've got the Witcher out of trouble I'll point him in that direction. And that's where you'll meet.'

'How arrogant is that?' Cahir muttered to Milva when they came close to each other, dismounting. 'He'll get them out of trouble by himself, without anyone's help. Did you hear that? Who is he?'

'In truth, I don't know,' Milva muttered back. 'But when it comes to impossible tasks, I believe him. Yesterday, in front of my very eyes, he got a red-hot horseshoe out of a fire with his bare hands . . .'

'Is he a sorcerer?'

'No,' Regis answered from behind Pegasus, demonstrating his exceptionally sensitive hearing. 'But does it really matter who I am? After all, I haven't asked for your personal details.'

'I am Cahir Mawr Dyffryn aep Ceallach.'

'I thank you and am full of admiration.' The barber-surgeon's voice had a slight note of scorn. 'I heard almost no Nilfgaardian accent when you pronounced your Nilfgaardian surname.'

'I'm not—'

'Enough!' Milva cut him off. 'This isn't the time for arguing or hesitating. Regis, the Witcher's waiting to be rescued.'

'Not before midnight,' the barber-surgeon said coldly, looking up at the moon. 'So we have some time to talk. Who is this person, Milva?'

'That person,' the archer replied, a little angry and standing up for Cahir, 'rescued me from a tight spot. That person will tell the Witcher, when he meets him, that he's going in the wrong direction. Ciri's not in Nilfgaard.'

'A revelation indeed,' the barber-surgeon said, his voice softening. 'And its source, Sir Cahir, son of Ceallach?'

'It's a long story.'

Dandelion had been silent for a long time when one of the sentries suddenly stopped talking in the middle of a curse and the other rasped, or possibly groaned. Geralt knew there had been three on guard, so he listened intently, but the third didn't utter even the slightest sound.

The Witcher waited, holding his breath, but what came to his ears a moment later was not the creaking of the door to the woodshed being opened by their rescuers. Not in the least. He heard even, soft, choral snoring. The sentries were quite simply asleep on duty.

He breathed out, swore silently, and was just about to lose himself in thoughts about Yennefer when medallion around the Witcher's neck suddenly vibrated and the air was filled with the scent of wormwood, basil, coriander, sage, aniseed, and the devil only knew what else.

'Regis?' he whispered in disbelief, ineffectually trying to lift his head from the wood shavings.

'Regis,' Dandelion whispered back, moving around and rustling. 'No one else reeks like that . . . Where are you? I can't see you—'

'Be quiet!'

The medallion stopped vibrating, Geralt heard the poet's relieved sigh and immediately after the soft hiss of a blade cutting his ropes. A moment later Dandelion gave a moan of pain as his circulation returned, but dutifully tried to suppress it by sticking his fist into his mouth.

'Geralt,' the barber-surgeon said, his vague, wavering shadow materialising at the Witcher's side, and immediately began to cut his bonds. 'You'll have to get past the camp guard yourselves. Head towards the east and the brightest star in the Seven Goats. Straight to the Ina. Milva's waiting for you there with the horses.'

'Help me get up . . .'

He stood first on one leg and then on the other, biting his fist.

Dandelion's circulation was already back to normal. A moment later the Witcher was also ready for action.

'How are we going to get out?' the poet suddenly asked. 'The sentries at the door are snoring, but they may . . .'

'No, they won't,' Regis interrupted in a whisper. 'But be careful when you leave. It's a full moon and the field's lit by campfires. In spite of it being night the entire camp is bustling, but perhaps that's a good thing. The corporals of the guard are bored of challenging the sentries. Out you go. Good luck.'

'What about you?'

'Don't worry about me. Don't wait for me and don't look back.'

'But—'

'Dandelion,' the Witcher hissed. 'You've been told not to worry about him, got it?'

'Out you go,' Regis repeated. 'Good luck. Until the next time, Geralt.'

The Witcher turned around.

'Thank you for rescuing us,' he said. 'But it would be best if we never met again. Am I making myself clear?'

'Absolutely. Don't waste time.'

The sentries were sleeping as they had fallen, snoring and smacking their lips. Not one of them even twitched when Geralt and Dandelion squeezed out through the slightly open door. Neither did any of them react when the Witcher unceremoniously pulled the thick homespun capes from two of them.

'That's no ordinary sleep,' Dandelion whispered.

'Of course it isn't,' Geralt said. Hidden in the dark of the wood-shed's shadow, he looked around.

'I see.' The poet sighed. 'Is Regis a sorcerer?'

'No. No, not a sorcerer.'

'He took that horseshoe from the fire. Put the sentries to sleep . . .'

'Stop wittering and concentrate. We aren't free yet. Wrap that cape around you and let's cross the field. If anyone stops us we're pretending to be soldiers.'

'Right. If anything happens I'll say—'

'We're pretending to be stupid soldiers. Let's go.'

They crossed the field, keeping their distance from the soldiers crowded around glowing braziers and campfires. Soldiers were roaming about here and there; two more weren't conspicuous. They didn't arouse anyone's suspicions; no one questioned them or stopped them. They passed beyond the stockade quickly and without any difficulty.

Everything went smoothly; in fact, *too* smoothly. Geralt became anxious, since he instinctively sensed danger and his anxiety was growing – rather than diminishing – the further they moved from the centre of the camp. He repeated to himself that there was nothing strange in that: they hadn't drawn attention to themselves in the middle of a military camp that was busy even at night, and the only danger had been that of the alarm being raised, should someone notice the sleeping sentries at the door to the woodshed. Now, however, they were approaching the perimeter, where the sentries had – by necessity – to be vigilant. The fact that they were heading away from the centre of the camp could not be helping them. The Witcher recalled the plague of desertion in Vissegerd's corps and was certain the guards had orders to watch carefully for anyone trying to abandon the camp.

The moon was shining brightly enough for Dandelion not to have to grope his way. This amount of light meant the Witcher could see as well as during the day, which enabled them to avoid two sentry posts and wait in the bushes for a mounted patrol to pass. There was an alder grove directly in front of them, apparently outside the ring of sentry posts. Everything was still going smoothly. Too smoothly.

Their ignorance of military customs proved to be their undoing.

They were tempted by the low, dark clump of alders, because of the cover it offered. But since time immemorial there have always been soldiers who lie in the bushes when it is their turn to be on guard duty, while the ones who aren't asleep keep an eye both on the enemy and on their own bloody-minded officers, should any of the latter descend on them with an unexpected inspection.

Geralt and Dandelion had barely reached the alder grove before several dark shapes – and spear blades – loomed up in front of them.

'Password?'

'Cintra!' Dandelion blurted out without hesitation.

The soldiers chuckled as one.

'Really, boys,' one of them said, 'is that the best you can do? If only someone would come up with something original. But no, nothing but "Cintra". Missing home, are we? Well, the fee's the same as yesterday.'

Dandelion audibly ground his teeth. Geralt weighed up the situation and their chances. His assessment: decidedly crap.

'Come on,' the soldier said, hurrying them. 'If you want to get through, pay up and we'll turn a blind eye. And quickly, because the corporal of the guard will be here any second.'

''Owd on,' the poet said, changing his accent and mode of speech. 'I'll just sit down and get me boot off, because there's. . .'

He didn't manage to say anything else. Four soldiers threw him to the ground. Then two of them, each one seizing one of his legs between theirs, pulled off his boots. The one who'd asked for the password tore the lining from the inside of a bootleg. Something scattered around with a jingle.

'Gold!' the leader yelled. 'Pull the boots off the other one! And summon the corporal!'

However, there was no one to do any boot-pulling or summoning, because half the guard dropped on their knees to search for the doubloons scattered among the leaves while the other half immediately began fighting furiously over Dandelion's second boot. *It's now or never*, Geralt thought, punching the leader in the jaw and then kicking him in the side of his head as he fell. The soldiers who were searching for gold didn't even notice. Dandelion needed no encouragement to spring up and dash through the bushes, his footwraps flapping. Geralt ran after him.

'Help! Help!' the leader of the watch bellowed from the ground, his voice soon after joined by his comrades. 'Cooorporaaal!'

'You swine!' Dandelion yelled back as he fled. 'Knaves! You stole my money!'

'Save your breath, dolt! See that forest? Make for it.'

'Stop them! Stop theeem!'

They ran. Geralt swore furiously, hearing shouts, whistles, neighing and the thudding of hooves. Behind them. And in front of them.
His astonishment didn't last long; one careful look was enough.
What he had taken for a forest and a safe haven was an approaching
wall of cavalry, surging towards them like a wave.

'Stop, Dandelion!' he shouted, then turned back to the patrol galloping in their direction and whistled piercingly through his fingers.

'Nilfgaard!' he yelled at the top of his voice. 'Nilfgaard are coming!
Back to the camp! Get back to the camp, you fools! Sound the alarm!
Nilfgaard!'

The leading rider of the patrol pursuing them reined his horse to
a rapid stop, looked towards where Geralt had pointed, screamed in
terror and was about to turn back. But Geralt decided he had already
done enough for the Cintran lions and Temerian lilies. He leapt at
the soldier and dragged him from the saddle with a dextrous tug.

'Jump on, Dandelion! And hold tight!'

The poet didn't need to be told twice. The horse sagged a little
under the weight of an extra rider, but spurred on by two pairs
of heels was soon galloping hard. The approaching swarm of
Nilfgaardians now represented a much greater threat than Vissegerd
and his corps, so they galloped along the ring of sentry posts, trying
to escape from the area where the two armies would clash at any
moment. The Nilfgaardians were close, however, and had seen
them. Dandelion yelled, then Geralt looked around and saw the dark
wall of Nilfgaardian troops beginning to extend black tentacles of
pursuit. Without hesitating he steered the horse towards the camp,
overtaking the fleeing guards. Dandelion yelled once again, but this
time there was no need. The Witcher could also see the cavalry
charging at them from the camp. Having been alerted, Vissegerd's
corps had mounted at admirable speed. And Geralt and Dandelion
were caught in a trap.

There was no way out. The Witcher changed the direction of
their flight once more and urged from the horse all the speed it could
muster, trying to slip out of the dangerously narrowing gap between
hammer and anvil. When hope dawned that they might just make it,
the night air suddenly sang with a whistle of fletchings. Dandelion

yelled, this time very loudly indeed, and dug his fingers into Geralt's sides. The Witcher felt something warm dripping onto his neck.

'Hold on!' he shouted, catching the poet by his elbow and drawing him closer to his own back. 'Hold on, Dandelion!'

'They've killed me!' the poet howled, impressively loudly for a dead man. 'I'm bleeding! I'm dying!'

'Hold on!'

The hail of arrows and quarrels, which was raining down on both armies and had proved to be so disastrous for Dandelion, was also their salvation. The armies under fire seethed and lost momentum, and the gap between the front lines which had been about to draw together remained open just long enough for the heavily snorting horse to whisk the two riders out of the trap. Geralt mercilessly forced his steed to ride hard, for although the trees and safety were looming up in front of them, hooves continued to thunder behind them. The horse grunted and stumbled, but did not stop and they might have escaped had not Dandelion suddenly groaned and lurched backwards, dragging the Witcher out of the saddle with him. Geralt unintentionally tugged on the reins, the horse reared, and the two men tumbled to the ground among some very low pines. The poet thudded onto the dirt and lay still, groaning pathetically. His head and left shoulder were covered in blood, which glistened black in the moonlight.

Behind them, the armies collided with thuds, clangs and screams. But despite the raging battle, their Nilfgaardian pursuers hadn't forgotten about them. Three cavalrymen were galloping towards them.

The Witcher sprang up, feeling a swelling wave of cold fury and hatred inside him. He jumped out to meet their pursuers, drawing the horsemen's attention away from Dandelion. But not because he wanted to sacrifice himself for his friend. He wanted to kill.

The leading rider, who had pulled ahead, flew at him with a raised battle-axe, but had no way of knowing he was attacking a witcher. Geralt dodged the blow effortlessly and seized the Nilfgaardian leaning over in the saddle by his cloak, while the fingers of his other hand caught the soldier's broad belt. He pulled the rider from the saddle with a powerful wrench and fell on him, pinning him to the ground.

Only then did Geralt realise he had no weapon. He caught the man by the throat, but couldn't throttle him because of his iron gorget. The Nilfgaardian struggled, hit him with an armoured gauntlet and gashed his cheek. The Witcher smothered his opponent with his entire body, groped for the misericord in the broad belt, and jerked it out of its sheath. The man on the ground felt it and howled. Geralt fended off the arm with the silver scorpion on the sleeve that was still hitting him and raised the dagger to strike.

The Nilfgaardian screamed.

The Witcher plunged the misericord into his open mouth. Up to the hilt.

When he got to his feet, he saw horses without riders, bodies and a cavalry unit heading away towards the battle. The Cintrans from the camp had dispatched their Nilfgaardian pursuers, and had not even noticed the poet or the two men fighting on the ground in the gloom among the low pine trees.

'Dandelion! Where were you hit? Where's the arrow?'

'In my head . . . It's stuck in my head . . .'

'Don't talk nonsense! Bloody hell, you were lucky . . . It only grazed you . . .'

'I'm bleeding . . .'

Geralt removed his jerkin and tore off a shirtsleeve. The point of the quarrel had caught Dandelion above the ear, leaving a nasty-looking gash extending to his temple. The poet kept bringing his shaking hand up to the wound and then looking at the blood, which was profusely spattering his hands and cuffs. His eyes were vacant. The Witcher realised he was dealing with a person who, for the first time in his life, had been wounded and was in pain. Who, for the first time in his life, was seeing his own blood in such quantities.

'Get up,' he said, wrapping the shirtsleeve quickly and clumsily around the troubadour's head. 'It's nothing. Dandelion, it's only a scratch . . . Get up, we have to get out of here fast . . .'

The battle on the field raged on in the dark; the clatter of steel, neighing of horses and screams grew louder and louder. Geralt quickly caught two Nilfgaardian steeds, but it turned out one was sufficient. Dandelion managed to get up, but immediately sat down again, groaned and sobbed pitifully. The Witcher lifted him to his feet, shook him back to consciousness and hauled him into the saddle.

Geralt mounted behind the wounded poet and spurred the horse east, to where – above the already visible pale blue streaks of the dawn – hung the brightest star of the Seven Goats constellation.

'Dawn will be breaking soon,' Milva said, looking not at the sky but at the glistening surface of the river. 'The catfish are tormenting the small fry. But there's neither hide nor hair of the Witcher or Dandelion. Oh, I hope Regis didn't mess up—'

'Don't tempt fate,' Cahir muttered, adjusting the girth of the recovered chestnut colt.

Milva looked around for a piece of wood to knock on.

'. . . But it does seem to be like that . . . Whoever encounters your Ciri, it's as though they've put their head on the block . . . That girl brings misfortune . . . Misfortune and death.'

'Spit that out, Milva.'

She spat obediently, as superstition demanded.

'There's such a chill, I'm shivering . . . And I'm thirsty, but I saw another rotting corpse in the river near the bank. Phooey . . . I feel sick . . . I think I'm going to throw up . . .'

'There you go,' Cahir said, handing her a canteen. 'Drink that. And sit down close to me, I'll keep you warm.'

Another catfish struck a shoal of minnows in the shallows and they scattered near the surface in a silver hail. A bat or nightjar flashed past in a beam of moonlight.

'Who knows,' Milva muttered pensively, cuddling up to Cahir, 'what tomorrow will bring. Who'll cross that river and who'll perish.'

'What will be, will be. Drive those thoughts away.'

'Aren't you afraid?'

'I am. What about you?'

'I feel sick.'

There was a lengthy pause.

'Tell me, Cahir, when did you meet Ciri?'

'For the first time? Three years ago. During the fight for Cintra. I got her out of the city. I found her, beset by fire. I rode through the fire, through the flames and smoke, holding her in my arms. And she was like a flame herself.'

'And?'

'You can't hold a flame in your hands.'

'If it isn't Ciri in Nilfgaard,' she said after a long silence, 'then who is it?'

'I don't know.'

Drakenborg, the Redanian fortress converted into an internment camp for elves and other subversive elements, had some grim traditions, which had evolved during its three years of operation. One of those traditions was dawn hangings. Another was gathering all those under death sentences in a large, common cell, from which they were led out to the gallows at daybreak.

About a dozen of the condemned were grouped together in the cell, and every morning two, three – or occasionally four – of them were hanged. The others waited their turn. A long time. Sometimes as long as a week. The condemned were called Clowns. Because the mood around the death cell was always jolly. Firstly, at meals prisoners were served very thin, sour wine nicknamed 'Dijkstra Dry' in the camp, as it was no secret that they could enjoy it at the behest of the head of the Redanian secret service. Secondly, no one was dragged to the sinister, underground Wash House to be interrogated any longer, nor were the warders allowed to maltreat the convicts.

The tradition was also observed that night. It was merry in the cell being occupied by six elves, a half-elf, a halfling, two humans and a Nilfgaardian. Dijkstra Dry was poured onto a single, shared tin plate and lapped up without the use of the arms, since that method gave the greatest chance of at least some intoxication by the gnat's piss. Only one of the elves, a Scoia'tael from Iorweth's defeated commando, recently severely tortured in the Wash House, retained his composure and dignity and was busy carving the words 'Freedom Or Death' on a post. There were several hundred similar inscriptions on the posts around the cell. The remaining condemned convicts, also in keeping with tradition, sang the Clowns' Anthem over and

213

over again, a song composed in Drakenborg by an unknown author. Every convict learned the words in the barracks, as the song drifted to them at night from the condemned cell, knowing that the day would come when they would join the choir.

The Clowns dance on the scaffold
Rhythmically twitching and jerking
They sing their song
Of sadness and beauty
And the Clowns have all the fun
Every corpse will recall
When the stool's kicked away
And his eyes roll up to the sun.

The bolt rattled, the key grated in the lock and the Clowns stopped singing. Warders entering at dawn could only mean one thing: in a moment the choir would be depleted by several voices. The only question was: whose?

The warders entered together. All were carrying ropes to tie the hands of the convicts being led to the scaffold. One sniffed, shoved his cudgel under his arm, unrolled a scroll of parchment and cleared his throat.

'Echel Trogelton!'

'Traighlethan,' the elf from Iorweth's commando corrected him softly. He looked at the carved slogan once more and struggled to his feet.

'Cosmo Baldenvegg!'

The halfling swallowed loudly. Nazarian knew Baldenvegg had been imprisoned on charges of acts of sabotage, carried out on the instructions of the Nilfgaardian secret service. However, Baldenvegg had not admitted his guilt and stubbornly maintained he had stolen both cavalry horses on his own initiative to make some money, and that Nilfgaard had nothing to do with it. He had clearly not been believed.

'Nazarian!'

Nazarian stood up obediently and held his hands out for the

warders to bind. When the three of them were being led out, the rest of the Clowns took up the song.

> The Clowns dance on the scaffold
> Merrily twitching and jerking
> And the wind carries their song
> The chorus echoing all around . . .

The dawn glowed purple and red, heralding a beautiful, sunny day.

The Clowns' Anthem, thought Nazarian, *was misleading*. They could not dance a jaunty jig, since they were not hanged from a gibbet with a cross beam, but from ordinary posts sunk into the ground. They didn't have stools kicked from under them, but practical, low birch blocks, bearing the marks of frequent use. The song's anonymous author, who had been executed the previous year, could not have known that when he composed it. Like all the other convicts, he was only acquainted with the details shortly before his death. In Drakenborg the executions were never carried out in public. They were a just punishment and not sadistic vengeance. Those words were also attributed to Dijkstra.

The elf from Iorweth's commando shook the warders' hands off, stepped onto the block without hesitation and allowed the noose to be placed around his neck.

'Long li—'

The block was kicked out from under his feet.

The halfling required two blocks, which were placed one on top of the other. The alleged saboteur did not bother with any grandiloquent cries. His short legs kicked vigorously and then sagged against the post. His head lolled slackly on his shoulder.

When the warders seized Nazarian he suddenly changed his tune.

'I'll talk!' he croaked. 'I'll testify! I have important information for Dijkstra!'

'Bit late for that,' said Vascoigne, the deputy commander for political affairs at Drakenborg, who was assisting at the execution, doubtingly. 'The sight of the noose rouses the imagination in every second one of you!'

'I'm not making it up!' Nazarian appealed, struggling in the executioners' arms. 'I've got information!'

Less than an hour later Nazarian was sitting in a seclusion cell, delighting in the beauty of life. A messenger stood at readiness beside his horse, scratching his groin vigorously, and Vascoigne was reading and checking the report which was about to be sent to Dijkstra.

I humbly inform Your Lordship, that the felon by the name of Nazarian, sentenced for an assault on a royal official, has testified to the following: that acting on the orders of a certain Ryens, on the day of the July new moon this year, with two of his accomplices, the elven half-breed Schirrú and Millet, he did take part in the murder of the jurists Codringher and Fenn in the city of Dorian. Millet was killed there, but the half-breed Schirrú murdered the two jurists and set their house on fire. The felon Nazarian shifts all the blame onto the said Schirrú, denies and refutes any suggestion that he committed the murders, but that is probably owing to fear of the gallows. What may interest Your Lordship, however, is that prior to the crime against the jurists being committed, the said malefactors (that is Nazarian, the half-elf Schirrú and Millet) were hunting a witcher, a certain Gerald of Rivia, who had been holding secret meetings with the jurist Codringher. To what end, the felon Nazarian does not know, because neither the aforementioned Ryens, nor the half-elf Schirrú, did divulge the secret to him. But when Ryens was given the report concerning their collusions, he ordered the jurists to be destroyed.

The felon Nazarian further testified that his accomplice Schirrú stole some documents from the jurists, which were later delivered to Ryens at an inn called the Sly Fox in Carreras. What Ryens and Schirrú conversed about there is not known to Nazarian, but the following day the criminal trio travelled to Brugge where, on the fourth day after the new moon, they committed the abduction of a maiden from a red-brick house, on the door of which a pair of brass shears were affixed. Ryens drugged her with a magic potion, and the malefactors Schirrú and Nazarian conveyed her in great haste by carriage to the stronghold of Nastrog in Verden. And now a matter which I commend to Your Lordship's close attention: the malefactors handed the abducted maid over to the stronghold's Nilfgaardian commandant, assuring him that the said individual was Cyryla of Cintra. The commandant, as testified by the felon Nazarian, was greatly content with these tidings.

I dispatch the above in strict confidence to Your Lordship by messenger. I shall likewise send an exhaustive report of the interrogation, when the scribe has made a fair copy. I humbly request instructions from Your Lordship as to what to do with the felon Nazarian. Whether to order him stung with a bullwhip, so that he remembers more, or hang him according to regulations.

Your loyal servitor.

Vascoigne signed the report with a flourish, affixed a seal and summoned the messenger.

Dijkstra was acquainted with the contents of the report that evening; Philippa Eilhart by noon of the following day.

By the time the horse carrying the Witcher and Dandelion emerged from the riverside alders, Milva and Cahir were extremely agitated. They had heard the battle, as the water of the Ina carried the sounds a great distance.

As she helped lift the poet down from the saddle, Milva saw Geralt stiffening at the sight of the Nilfgaardian. However, she did not say anything – and neither did the Witcher – for Dandelion was moaning desperately and swooning. They laid him down on the sand, placing a folded-up cloak beneath his head. Milva had just set about changing the blood-soaked makeshift dressing when she felt a hand on her shoulder and smelled the familiar scent of wormwood, aniseed and other herbs. Regis, as was his custom, had appeared unexpectedly, out of thin air.

'Let me,' he said, pulling instruments and other paraphernalia from his sizeable medical bag, 'I'll take it from here.'

When the barber-surgeon peeled the dressing from the wound, Dandelion groaned pitifully.

'Relax,' Regis said, cleansing the wound. 'It's nothing. Only blood. Only a little blood . . . Your blood smells nice, poet.'

At precisely that moment the Witcher did something Milva would never have expected. He walked over to the horse and drew a long Nilfgaardian sword from the scabbard fastened under the saddle flap.

'Move away from him,' he snarled, standing over the barber-surgeon.

'The blood smells nice,' Regis repeated, not paying the slightest bit of attention to the Witcher. 'I can't detect in it the smell of infection, which with a head wound could have disastrous consequences. The main arteries and veins are intact . . . This will sting a little.'

Dandelion groaned and took a sharp intake of breath. The sword in the Witcher's hand vibrated and glistened with light reflected from the river.

'I'll put in a few stitches,' Regis said, continuing to ignore both the Witcher and his sword. 'Be brave, Dandelion.'

Dandelion was brave.

'Almost done here,' Regis said, setting about bandaging the victim's head. 'Don't you worry, Dandelion, you'll be right as rain. The wound's just right for a poet, Dandelion. You'll look like a war hero, with a proud bandage around your head, and the hearts of the maidens looking at you will melt like wax. Yes, a truly poetic wound. Unlike an abdominal wound for instance. Liver all cut up, kidneys and guts mangled, stomach contents and faeces pouring out, peritonitis . . . Right, that's done. Geralt, I'm all yours.'

He stood and the Witcher brought the sword up against his throat, as quick as lightning.

'Move away,' he snapped at Milva. Regis didn't twitch, even though the point of the sword was pressing gently against his neck. The archer held her breath, seeing the barber-surgeon's eyes glowing in the dark with a strange, cat-like light.

'Go on,' Regis said calmly. 'Thrust it in.'

'Geralt,' Dandelion spoke from the ground, totally alert. 'Are you utterly insane? He saved us from the gallows . . . And patched me up . . .'

'He saved us and the girl in the camp,' Milva recalled softly.

'Be quiet, all of you. You don't know what he is.'

The barber-surgeon did not move. And Milva suddenly saw what she ought to have seen long before: Regis did not cast a shadow.

'Indeed,' he said slowly. 'You don't know what I am. And it's time you did. My name is Emiel Regis Rohellec Terzieff-Godefroy. I have lived on this earth for four hundred and twenty-eight years according to your reckoning, or six hundred and forty-two years by the elven calendar. I'm the descendant of survivors, unfortunate beings imprisoned here after the cataclysm you call the Conjunction of the Spheres. I'm regarded, to put it mildly, as a monster. As a blood-sucking fiend. And now I've encountered a witcher, who earns his living eliminating creatures such as I. And that's it.'

'And that is enough,' Geralt said, lowering the sword. 'More than enough. Now scram, Emiel Regis Whatever-It-Was. Get out of here.'

'Astonishing.' Regis sneered. 'You're permitting me to leave? Me, who represents a danger to people? A witcher ought to make use of every opportunity to eliminate dangers of this kind.'

'Get lost. Make yourself scarce and do it fast.'

'To which far-flung corner should I make myself scarce?' Regis asked slowly. 'You're a witcher, after all. You know about me. When you've dealt with your problem, when you've sorted out whatever you need to sort out, you'll probably return to these parts. You know where I live, where I spend my time, how I earn my keep. Will you come after me?'

'It's possible. If there's a bounty. I am a witcher.'

'I wish you luck,' Regis said, fastening his bag and spreading his cape. 'Farewell. Ah, one more thing. How high would the price on my head have to be in order for you to bother? How high do you value me?'

'Bloody high.'

'You tickle my vanity. To be precise?'

'Fuck off, Regis.'

'I'm going. But first put a value on me. If you please.'

'I've usually taken the equivalent of a good saddle horse for an ordinary vampire. But you, after all, are not ordinary.'

'How much?'

'I doubt,' the Witcher said, his voice as cold as ice, 'I doubt whether anyone could afford it.'

'I understand and thank you,' the vampire said, smiling. This time he bared his teeth. At the sight, Milva and Cahir stepped back and Dandelion stifled a cry of horror.

'Farewell. Good luck.'

'Farewell, Regis. Same to you.'

Emiel Regis Rohellec Terzieff-Godefroy shook his cape, wrapped himself up in it with a flourish and vanished. He simply vanished.

'And now,' Geralt said, spinning around, the unsheathed sword still in his hand, 'it's your turn, Nilfgaardian . . .'

'No,' Milva interrupted angrily. 'I've had a bellyful of this. To horse, let's get out of here! Shouts carry over the water and before we know it someone will be hot on our trail!'

'I'm not going any further in his company.'

'Go on alone then!' she yelled, furious. 'The other way! I'm up to here with your moods, Witcher! You've driven Regis away, even though he saved your life, and that's your business. But Cahir saved me, so we're comrades! If he's an enemy to you, go back to Armeria. Suit yourself! Your mates are waiting for you there with a noose!'

'Stop shouting.'

'Well, don't just stand there. Help me get Dandelion onto the gelding.'

'You rescued our horses? Roach too?'

'*He* did,' she said, nodding towards Cahir. 'Let's be going.'

They forded the Ina. They rode along the right-hand bank, along-side the river, through shallow backwaters, through wetlands and old riverbeds, through swamps and marshes resounding with the croaking of frogs and the quacking of unseen mallards and gar-ganeys. The day exploded with red sunlight, blindingly sparkling on the surfaces of small lakes overgrown with water lilies, and they turned towards a point where one of the Ina's numerous branches flowed into the Yaruga. Now they were riding through tenebrous, gloomy forests, where the trees grew straight from the marsh, green with duckweed.

Milva led the way, riding beside the Witcher, busy giving him an account of Cahir's story in hushed tones. Geralt was as silent as the grave, never once looking back at the Nilfgaardian, who was riding behind them, helping the poet. Dandelion moaned a little from time to time, swore and complained that his head was hurting, but held out bravely, without slowing down the march. His mood had improved with the recovery of Pegasus and the lute fastened to the saddle.

Around noon they rode out once more into sunny wetlands, beyond which the broad, calm waters of the Great Yaruga stretched out. They forced their way through dried-up riverbeds and waded through shallows and backwaters. And happened upon an island, a dry spot among the marshes and tussocks of grass between the river's numerous offshoots. The island was overgrown with bushes and willows, and there were a few taller trees growing on it, bare, withered and white from cormorants' guano.

Milva was the first to notice a boat among the reeds, which must have been deposited there by the current. She was also the first to spot a clearing among the osiers, which was a perfect place for a rest.

They stopped, and the Witcher decided it was time to talk to the Nilfgaardian. Face to face and without witnesses.

'I spared your life on Thanedd. I felt sorry for you, whippersnapper. It's the biggest mistake I've ever made. Early this morning I let a higher vampire go, even though he is certain to have several human lives on his conscience. I ought to have killed him. But I couldn't be bothered with him, for I'm preoccupied with one thought: to get my hands on the people who harmed Ciri. I've sworn that those who've harmed her will pay for it with their blood.'

Cahir did not speak.

'Your revelations, which Milva has told me about, don't change anything. There's only one conclusion: you were unable to abduct

221

Ciri on Thanedd, despite your best efforts. Now you're trailing me, so that I can lead you to her. So that you can get your hands on her again, because then your imperator might spare you and not send you to the scaffold.'

Cahir said nothing. Geralt felt bad. Very bad.

'She cried out in the night because of you,' he snapped. 'You grew to nightmarish proportions in her child's eyes. But actually, you were – and are – only a tool, a wretched minion of your imperator. I don't know what you did to become a nightmare for her. And the worst thing is I don't understand why in spite of everything I can't kill you. I don't understand what's holding me back.'

'Perhaps,' Cahir said softly, 'that despite all the circumstances and appearances we have something in common, you and I.'

'You reckon?'

'Like you, I want to rescue Ciri. Like you, I don't care if that surprises or astonishes anybody. Like you, I have no intention of justifying my motives to anybody.'

'Is that all?'

'No.'

'Very well, go on.'

'Ciri,' the Nilfgaardian began slowly, 'is riding a horse through a dusty village. With six other young people. Among those people is a girl with close-cropped hair. Ciri is dancing on a table in a barn and is happy . . .'

'Milva has told you about my dreams.'

'No. She hasn't told me anything. Do you believe me?'

'No.'

Cahir lowered his head and ground his heel in the sand.

'I'd forgotten,' he said, 'that you can't believe me, can't trust me. I understand that. But like you I had one more dream. A dream you haven't told anyone about. Because I seriously doubt that you'd want to tell anyone about it.'

It could be said that Servadio was simply in luck. He had come to Loredo without intending to spy on anyone in particular. But the village wasn't called the Bandits' Lair for no reason. Loredo lay on the Bandits' Trail, and brigands and thieves from all the regions of the Upper Velda called in there, met up to sell or barter loot, to stock up with provisions and tackle, and relax and enjoy themselves in the select company of fellow criminals. The village had been burnt down several times, but the few permanent and more numerous temporary residents would rebuild it each time. They lived off the bandits, and did very well, thank you. And snoopers and narks like Servadio always had the opportunity to pick up some information there, which might be worth a few florins to the prefect.

This time Servadio was counting on more than just a few. Because the Rats were riding into the village.

They were led by Giselher and flanked by Iskra and Kayleigh. Behind them rode Mistle and the new, flaxen-haired girl they called Falka. Asse and Reef brought up the rear, pulling some riderless horses, doubtlessly stolen with intent to sell. The Rats were tired and dust-covered but bore themselves briskly in the saddle, enthusiastically responding to greetings from the various comrades and acquaintances they happened to see. After dismounting and being given beer, they immediately entered noisy negotiations with traders and fences. All of them except Mistle and the new, flaxen-haired one, who wore a sword slung across her back. These two set off among the stalls, which, as usual, covered the village green. Loredo had its market days and the range of goods on offer (with the visiting bandits in mind) was especially rich and varied then. Today was such a day.

Servadio cautiously followed the girls. In order to make any money, he had to have information, and in order to have information he had to eavesdrop.

The girls looked at colourful scarves, beads, embroidered blouses, saddlecloths and ornate browbands for their horses. They sifted through the goods, but didn't buy anything. Mistle kept a hand on the fair-haired girl's shoulder almost the whole time.

The snooper cautiously moved closer, pretending to be looking at the straps and belts on a leatherworker's stall. The girls were talking, but quietly. He couldn't hear them and was too afraid to approach them any closer. They might have noticed, grown suspicious.

Candyfloss was being sold at one of the stalls. The girls walked over, Mistle bought two sticks wrapped round with the snow-white sweetmeat and handed one to the flaxen-haired girl. She nibbled it delicately. A white strand stuck to her lip. Mistle wiped it off with a careful, tender movement. The flaxen-haired girl opened her emerald-green eyes widely, slowly licked her lips and smiled, cocking her head playfully. Servadio felt a shudder, a cold trickle running between his shoulder blades. He recalled the rumours going around about the two female bandits.

He was going to withdraw stealthily, since it was clear he wouldn't pick up any useful information. The girls weren't talking about anything important. However, not far away, where the senior members of various bandit gangs were gathered, Giselher, Kayleigh and the others were noisily quarrelling, haggling, and yelling, every now and then holding mugs under the tap of a small cask. Servadio was likely to learn more from them. One of the Rats might let something slip, if only a single word, betraying the gang's current plans, their route or their destination. Should he manage to eavesdrop and supply the information in time to the prefect's soldiers or the Nilfgaardian spies who showed a lively interest in the Rats, the reward was practically his for the taking. And were the prefect to set a successful trap thanks to his information, Servadio could count on a considerable injection of funds. *I'll buy the old lady a sheepskin coat*, he thought feverishly. *I'll finally get the kids some shoes and maybe some toys . . . And for me . . .*

The girls wandered between the stalls, licking and nibbling the candyfloss from the sticks. Servadio suddenly noticed they were being watched. And pointed at. He knew who was doing the pointing; footpads and horse thieves from the gang of Pinta, also known as Otterpelt.

The thieves exchanged several provocatively loud comments and cackled with glee. Mistle squinted and placed her hand on the flaxen-haired girl's shoulder.

'Turtle doves!' one of the thieves snorted. He was a beanpole with a moustache like a bunch of oakum. 'Look, they'll be billing and cooing next!' Servadio saw the flaxen-haired girl tense up and noticed that Mistle's grip on her shoulder tightened. The thieves all chuckled. Mistle turned around slowly and several of them stopped laughing. But the one with the oakum moustache was either too drunk or too lacking in imagination to take the hint.

'Maybe one of you needs a man?' he said, moving closer and making obscene, suggestive movements. 'All you need is a good shag, and you'll cure that kink in a flash! Hey! I'm talking to you, you—'

He didn't manage to touch her. The flaxen-haired girl coiled up like an attacking adder, and her sword flashed and struck before the candyfloss she released had hit the ground. The moustachioed thief staggered and gobbled like a turkey, the blood from his butchered neck gushing in a long stream. The girl coiled up again, was on him in two nimble steps and struck once more, a wave of gore splashing the stalls. The corpse toppled over, the sand around it immediately turning red. Someone screamed. A second thief leant over and drew a knife from his bootleg, but at the same moment slumped, struck by Giselher with the metal handle of his knout.

'One stiff's enough!' the Rats' leader yelled. 'That one's only got himself to blame; he didn't know who he was crossing! Back off, Falka!'

Only then did the flaxen-haired girl lower her sword. Giselher took out a purse and shook it.

'According to the laws of our brotherhood, I'm paying for the man who was killed. Fairly, according to his weight, a thaler for every pound of the lousy cadaver! And that'll put an end to the feud! Am I right, comrades? Pinto, what do you say?'

Iskra, Kayleigh, Reef and Asse stood behind their leader. They had faces of stone and held their hands on their sword hilts.

'That's fair,' Otterpelt replied, surrounded by his gang. He was a short, bow-legged man in a leather tunic. 'You're right, Giselher. The feud's over.'

Servadio swallowed, trying to melt into the crowd now gathering at the scene. He swiftly lost all interest in stalking the Rats or the flaxen-haired girl they called Falka. He decided that the reward promised by the prefect was not nearly as high as he'd thought.

Falka calmly sheathed her sword and looked around. Servadio was dumbstruck at the sudden change in her expression.

'My candyfloss,' the girl whined miserably, looking at her treat lying soiled in the sand. 'I dropped my candyfloss . . .'

Mistle hugged her.

'I'll buy you another.'

The Witcher sat on the sand among the willows, gloomy, angry and lost in thought. He was looking at the cormorants sitting on the shit-covered tree.

After their conversation, Cahir had vanished into the bushes and had not reappeared. Milva and Dandelion were looking for something to eat. They had managed to find a copper cauldron and a trug of vegetables under some nets in the boat which had been washed up by the current. They set a wicker trap they had found in the boat in a riverside channel, then waded near to the bank and began hitting the rushes with sticks in order to drive fish into it. The poet was now feeling better and was strutting around as proud as a peacock with his heroically bandaged head.

Geralt continued to brood and sulk.

Milva and Dandelion hauled the fish pot out and began to swear, for instead of the catfish and carp they had expected, all they saw was silvery fry wriggling around inside.

The Witcher stood up.

'Come over here, you two! Leave that trap and come here. I've got something to tell you.

'You're returning home,' he began bluntly when they came over, wet and stinking of fish. 'Head north, towards Mahakam. I'm going on by myself.'

'What?'

'Now we must go our separate ways. The party's over, Dandelion. You're going home to write poems. Milva will lead you through the forests . . . What's the matter?'

'Nothing's the matter,' Milva said, tossing her hair from her shoulder with a sudden movement. 'Nothing. Speak, Witcher. I'd like to hear what you're going to say.'

'I don't have anything else to say. I'll go south, crossing to the Yaruga's far bank. Through Nilfgaardian territory. It'll be a dangerous and long journey. And there's no time to waste. Which is why I'm going by myself.'

'Having got rid of the inconvenient baggage.' Dandelion nodded. 'The ball and chain slowing down your march and causing so many problems. In other words: me.'

'And me,' Milva added, glancing to one side.

'Listen,' Geralt said, now much more calmly. 'This is my own private matter. None of this concerns you. I don't want you to risk your necks for something that only concerns me.'

'It only concerns you,' Dandelion repeated slowly. 'You don't need anybody. Company impedes you and slows down your journey. You don't expect help from anybody and you have no intention of relying on anybody. Furthermore, you love solitude. Have I forgotten anything?'

'Naturally,' Geralt replied angrily. 'You've forgotten to swap your empty head for one with a brain. Had that arrow passed an inch to the right, you idiot, the rooks would be pecking out your eyes now. You're a poet and you've got an imagination; so try imagining a scene like that. I repeat: you're returning north, and I'm heading in the opposite direction. By myself.'

'Go on then,' Milva said, and sprang to her feet. 'I'm not going to plead with you. Go to hell, Witcher. Come on, Dandelion, let's cook something. I'm starving and listening to him makes me sick.'

Geralt turned his head away. He watched the green-eyed cormorants hanging their wings out to dry on the limbs of the guano-covered tree. He smelled the intense scent of herbs and swore furiously.

'You're trying my patience, Regis.'

The vampire, who had suddenly appeared out of thin air, was unconcerned, and sat down alongside the furious witcher.

'I have to change the poet's dressing,' he said calmly.

'Then go to him. But stay well away from me.'

Regis heaved a sigh, showing no intention of moving away.

'I was listening to your conversation with Dandelion and the archer,' he said, not without a hint of mockery in his voice. 'I have to

227

admit you've got a real talent for winning people over. Though the entire world seems to be out to get you, you disregard the comrades and allies wanting to help you.'

'The world turned upside down. A vampire's teaching me how to deal with humans. What do you know about humans, Regis? The only thing you know is the taste of their blood. Why am I still talking to you?'

'The world turned upside down,' the vampire admitted, deadpan. 'You are talking to me indeed. Perhaps you'd also like to listen to some advice?'

'No. No, I wouldn't. I don't need to.'

'True, I'd forgotten. Advice is superfluous to you, allies are super-fluous, you'll get by without any travelling companions. The goal of your expedition is, after all, personal and private. More than that, the nature of the goal demands that you accomplish it alone, in person. The risks, dangers, hardships and constant struggle with doubt must only burden you. For, after all, they are components of the penance, the expiation of guilt you want to earn. A baptism of fire, I'd say. You'll pass through fire, which burns, but also purges. And you'll do it alone. For were someone to support you in this, help you, take on even a scrap of that baptism of fire, that pain, that penance, they would, by the same token, impoverish you. They would deprive you of part of the expiation you desire, which would be owed to them for their involvement. After all, it should be your exclusive expiation. Only *you* have a debt to pay off, and you don't want to run up debts with other creditors at the same time. Is my logic correct?'

'Surprisingly so, considering you're sober. Your presence annoys me, vampire. Leave me alone with my expiation, please. And with my debt.'

'As you wish,' Regis said, arising. 'Sit and think. But I will give you some advice anyway. A sense of guilt, as well as the need for expiation, for a cleansing baptism of fire, aren't things you can claim an exclusive right to. Life differs from banking because it has debts which are paid off by running up debts with others.'

'Go away, please.'

'As you wish.'

The vampire walked off and joined Dandelion and Milva. While Regis changed the dressing the trio debated what to eat. Milva shook the fry from the fish pot and examined the catch critically.

'There's nothing for it,' she said. 'We'll have to skewer the little tiddlers on twigs and grill them over the embers.'

'No,' Dandelion demurred, shaking his freshly bandaged head, 'that isn't a good idea. There are too few of them, and they won't fill us up. I suggest we make soup.'

'Fish soup?'

'By all means. We have enough of these tiddlers and we have salt,' Dandelion said, counting out the list of ingredients on his fingers. 'We've acquired onions, carrots, parsley root and celery. And a cauldron. If we put it all together we end up with soup.'

'Some seasoning would come in handy.'

'Oh.' Regis smiled, reaching into his bag. 'No problem there. Basil, pimento, pepper, bay leaves, sage . . .'

'Enough, enough.' Dandelion raised his hand, stopping him. 'That'll do. We don't need mandrake in the soup. Right, let's get to work. Clean the fish, Milva.'

'Clean them yourself! Ha! Just because you've got a woman in the company, it doesn't mean she'll slave for you in the kitchen! I'll bring the water and start the fire. And you can get yourself covered in guts with those weatherfish.'

'They aren't weatherfish,' Regis said. 'They're chub, roach, ruff and silver bream.'

'Ah,' Dandelion said, unable to keep quiet. 'I see you know your fish.'

'I know lots of things,' Regis replied neutrally, without boasting. 'I've picked up this and that along the way.'

'If you're such a scholar,' Milva said, blowing on the fire again and getting to her feet, 'use your brain to get these tiddlers gutted. I'm getting the water.'

'Can you manage a full cauldron? Geralt, help her.'

'Course I can.' Milva snorted. 'And I don't need his help. He has his own – personal – issues. No one's to disturb him!'

Geralt turned his head away, pretending not to hear. Dandelion and the vampire skilfully prepared the small fry.

'This soup's going to be thin,' Dandelion said, hanging the cauldron over the fire. 'We could do with a bigger fish.'

'Will this do?' Cahir said, suddenly emerging from the willows carrying a three-pound pike by the gills. It was still flexing its tail and opening and closing its mouth.

'Oh! What a beauty! Where did you come by that, Nilfgaardian?'

'I'm not a Nilfgaardian. I come from Vicovaro and my name is Cahir—'

'All right, all right, we know all that. Now where did you get the pike?'

'I knocked up a tip-up using a frog as bait. I cast it into a hollow under the bank. The pike took it right away.'

'Experts to a man,' Dandelion said, shaking his bandaged head. 'Pity I didn't suggest steak, you would have conjured up a cow. But let's make a start on what we've got. Regis, chuck all the fry into the cauldron, heads and tails and all. And the pike needs to be nicely dressed. Know how to, Nilf— Cahir?'

'Yes.'

'Get to work then. Geralt, dammit, do you plan to sit there sulking for much longer? Peel the vegetables!'

The Witcher got up obediently and joined them, but stayed ostentatiously well away from Cahir. Before he had time to complain that there wasn't a knife, the Nilfgaardian – or possibly the Vicovarian – gave him his, taking another from his bootleg. Geralt took it, grunting his thanks.

The teamwork was carried out efficiently. The cauldron full of fingerlings and vegetables was soon bubbling and frothing. The vampire dextrously skimmed off the froth using a spoon Milva had whittled. Once Cahir had dressed and divided up the pike, Dandelion threw the predator's tail, fins, spine and toothed head into the cauldron and stirred.

'Mmm, it smells delicious. Once it's all boiled down, we'll strain off the waste.'

'What, through our footwraps?' Milva said with a grimace, as she

230

whittled another spoon. 'How can we strain it without a sieve?'

'But my dear Milva,' smiled Regis. 'Don't say that! We can easily replace what we don't have with what we do. It's purely a matter of invention and positive thinking.'

'Go to hell with your smart-arsed chatter, vampire.'

'We'll sieve it through my hauberk,' Cahir said. 'Not a problem, it can be rinsed out afterwards.'

'It should be rinsed out before, too,' Milva declared, 'or I won't eat it.'

The sieving was carried out efficiently.

'Now throw the pike into the broth, Cahir,' Dandelion instructed. 'Smells delicious. Don't add any more wood, it just needs to simmer. Geralt, where are you shoving that spoon! You don't stir it now!'

'Don't yell. I didn't know.'

'Ignorance' – Regis smiled – 'is no justification for ill-conceived actions. When one doesn't know or has doubts it's best to seek advice . . .'

'Shut up, vampire!' Geralt said, stood up and turned his back on them. Dandelion snorted.

'He's taken offence, look at him.'

'That's him all over,' Milva said, pouting. 'He's all talk. If he doesn't know what to do, he just talks and gets offended. Haven't you lot caught on yet?'

'A long time ago,' Cahir said softly.

'Add pepper,' Dandelion said, licking the spoon and smacking his lips. 'And some more salt. Ah, now it's just right. Take the cauldron off the heat. By thunder, it's hot! I don't have any gloves . . .'

'I have,' Cahir said.

'And I,' Regis said, seizing the cauldron from the other side, 'don't need any.'

'Right,' said the poet, wiping the spoon on his trousers. 'Well, company, be seated. Enjoy! Geralt, are you waiting for a special invitation? For a herald and a fanfare?'

They sat crowded around the cauldron on the sand and for a long time all that could be heard was dignified slurping, interrupted by blowing on spoons. After half of the broth had been eaten, the cautious fishing out of pieces of pike began, until finally their spoons were scraping against the bottom of the cauldron.

'Oh, I'm stuffed,' Milva groaned. 'It wasn't a bad idea with that soup, Dandelion.'

'Indeed,' Regis agreed. 'What do you say, Geralt?'

'I say "thank you",' the Witcher said, getting up with difficulty and rubbing his knee, which had begun to torment him again. 'Will that do? Or do you want a fanfare?'

'He's always like that,' the poet said, waving a hand. 'Take no notice of him. You're lucky, anyway. I was around when he was fighting with that Yennefer of his; the wan beauty with ebony hair.'

'Be discreet,' the vampire admonished Dandelion, 'and don't forget he has problems.'

'Problems,' said Cahir, stifling a burp, 'are there to be solved.'

'Of course they are,' Dandelion replied. 'But how?'

Milva snorted, making herself more comfortable on the hot sand. 'The vampire is a scholar. He's sure to know.'

'It's not about knowledge, but about the skilful examination of the circumstances,' Regis said calmly. 'And when the circumstances are examined, we come to the conclusion that we are facing an insoluble problem. The entire undertaking has no chance of success. The likelihood of finding Ciri amounts to zero.'

'But you can't say that,' Milva jibed. 'We should think positively and use inventigation. It's like it was with that sieve. If we don't have something, we find a replacement. That's how I see it.'

'Until recently,' the vampire continued, 'we thought Ciri was in Nilfgaard. Reaching the destination and rescuing her – or abducting her – seemed beyond our powers. Now, after hearing Cahir's revelations, we have no idea where Ciri is. It's hard to talk about invention when we have no idea where we should be directing it.'

'What are we to do, then?' Milva said, bridling. 'The Witcher insists on going south . . .'

'For him' – Regis laughed – 'the points of the compass have no great importance. It's all the same to him which one he chooses, as long as he's not idle. That is truly a witcher's principium. The world is full of evil, so it's sufficient to stride ahead, and destroy the Evil encountered on the way, in that way rendering a service to Good. The rest takes care of itself. To put it another way: being in motion is everything, the goal is nothing.'

'Baloney,' Milva commented. 'I mean, Ciri's his goal. How can you say she's nothing?'

'I was joking,' the vampire admitted, winking at Geralt's back, which was still turned away from them. 'And not very tactfully. I apologise. You're right, dear Milva. Ciri is our goal. And since we don't know where she is, it would make sense to find that out and direct our activities accordingly. The case of the Child of Destiny, I observe, is simply pulsating with magic, fate and other supernatural elements. And I know somebody who is extremely knowledgeable about such matters and will certainly help us.'

'Ah,' Dandelion said, delighted. 'Who's that? Where are they? Far from here?'

'Closer than the capital of Nilfgaard. In actual fact, really quite close. In Angren. On this bank of the Yaruga. I'm talking about the Druids' Circle, which has its seat in the forests of Caed Dhu.'

'Let's go without delay!'

'Don't any of you,' Geralt said, annoyed, 'think you should ask me my opinion?'

'You?' Dandelion said, turning around. 'But you haven't got a clue what you're doing. You even owe the soup you gobbled down to us. Were it not for us, you'd be hungry. We would be too, had we waited for you to act. That cauldron of soup was the result of cooperation. Of teamwork. The joint efforts of a fellowship united by a common goal. Get it, friend?'

'How could he get it?' Milva said, grimacing. 'He's just "me, me, by myself, all alone". A lone wolf! But you can see he's no hunter, that he's a stranger to the forest. Wolves don't hunt alone! Never! A lone wolf, ha, what twaddle, foolish townie nonsense. But he doesn't understand that!'

'Oh, he does, he does,' Regis cut in, smiling through pursed lips, as was his custom.

'He only looks stupid,' Dandelion confirmed. 'But I do keep hoping he'll finally decide to strain his grey matter. Perhaps he'll come to some useful conclusions. Perhaps he'll realise the only activity that's worth doing alone is wanking.'

Cahir Mawr Dyffryn aep Ceallach remained tactfully silent.

'The hell with all of you,' the Witcher finally said, sticking his spoon into his bootleg. 'The hell with all of you, you cooperative fellowship of idiots, united by a common goal which none of you understand. And the hell with me too.'

This time the others, following Cahir's example, also remained tactfully silent. Dandelion, Maria Barring, also known as Milva, and Emiel Regis Rohellec Terzieff-Godefroy.

'What a company I ended up with,' Geralt continued, shaking his head. 'Brothers in arms! A team of heroes! What have I done to deserve it? A poetaster with a lute. A wild and lippy half-dryad, half-woman. A vampire, who's about to notch up his fifth century. And a bloody Nilfgaardian who insists he isn't a Nilfgaardian.'

'And leading the party is the Witcher, who suffers from pangs of conscience, impotence and the inability to take decisions,' Regis finished calmly. 'I suggest we travel incognito, to avoid arousing suspicion.'

'Or raising a laugh,' Milva added.

The queen replied: 'Ask not me for mercy, but those whom you wronged with your magic. You had the courage to commit those deeds, now have courage when your pursuers and justice are close at hand. It is not in my power to pardon your sins.' Then the witch hissed like a cat and her sinister eyes flashed. 'My end is nigh,' she shrieked, 'but yours is too, O Queen. You shall remember Lara Dorren and her curse in the hour of your dreadful death. And know this: my curse will hound your descendants unto the tenth generation.' Seeing, however, that a doughty heart was beating in the queen's breast, the evil elven witch ceased to malign her, or try to frighten her with the curse, but began instead to whine for help and mercy like a bitch dog . . .

The Tale of Lara Dorren,
as told by the humans

. . . but her begging softened not the stony hearts of the Dh'oine, the merciless, cruel humans. So when Lara, now not begging for mercy for herself, but for her unborn child, caught hold of the carriage door, on the order of the queen the thuggish executioner struck with a sword and hacked off her fingers. And when a severe frost descended in the night, Lara breathed her last on the forested hilltop, giving birth to a tiny daughter, whom she protected with the remains of the warmth still flickering in her. And though she was surrounded by the blizzard, the night and the winter, spring suddenly bloomed on the hilltop and feainnewedd flowers blossomed. Even today do those flowers bloom in only two places: in Dol Blathanna and on the hilltop where Lara Dorren aep Shiadhal perished.

The Tale of Lara Dorren,
as told by the elves

CHAPTER SIX

'I asked you,' Ciri, who was lying on her back, snapped angrily. 'I asked you not to touch me.'

Mistle withdrew her hand and the blade of grass she had been tickling Ciri's neck with, stretched out beside her and gazed up at the sky, placing both hands under her shaven neck.

'You've been acting strangely of late, Young Falcon.'

'I just want you to stop touching me!'

'It's just for fun.'

'I know,' Ciri said through pursed lips. 'Just for fun. It's always been "just for fun". But I've stopped enjoying it, do you see? For me it's no fun any more!'

Mistle was silent for a long while, lying on her back and staring at the blue sky riven with ragged streaks of cloud. A hawk circled high above the trees.

'Your dreams,' she finally said. 'It's because of your dreams, isn't it? You wake almost every night screaming. What you once lived through now returns in your dreams. I'm no stranger to such things myself.'

Ciri did not answer.

'You've never told me anything about yourself,' Mistle said, breaking the silence once again. 'About what you've been through. Or where you're from. Or if you've left anyone behind . . .'

Ciri brought a hand up swiftly to her neck, but this time it was only a ladybird.

'There were a few people,' she said quietly, not looking at her companion. 'I mean, I thought there were . . . People who would find me even here, at the end of the world, if they only wanted to . . . Or if they were still alive. Oh, what do you want of me, Mistle? Do you want me to unbosom myself?'

'You don't have to.'

'Good. Because, surely, it'd just be for fun. Like everything else we share.'

'I don't understand,' Mistle said, turning her head away, 'why you don't leave, if being with me is so awful.'

'I don't want to be alone.'

'Is that all?'

'That is a lot.'

Mistle bit her lip. But before she had time to say anything, there was a whistle. They both sprang to their feet, brushing off pine needles, and ran to their horses.

'The fun's about to begin,' said Mistle, leaping into the saddle and drawing her sword. 'The fun you've come to enjoy more than anything, Falka. Don't think I haven't noticed.'

Ciri angrily kicked her horse with her heels. They hurtled along the side of a ravine at breakneck speed, already hearing the wild whooping of the remaining Rats rushing out of a thicket on the other side of the highway. The pincers of the ambush were closing.

The private audience was over. Vattier de Rideaux, Viscount of Eiddon, head of Imperator Emhyr var Emreis's military intelligence, left the library, bowing to the Queen of the Valley of Flowers even more politely than courtly protocol demanded. At the same time his bow was very cautious, and his movements deliberate and guarded; the imperial spy's eyes never left the two ocelots stretched out at the feet of the elven queen. The golden-eyed cats looked languorous and drowsy, but Vattier knew they weren't cuddly mascots but vigilant guards, ever ready to reduce anyone to a bloody pulp if they tried to come closer to the queen than protocol decreed.

Francesca Findabair, also called Enid an Gleanna, the Daisy of the Valleys, waited until the door was closed behind Vattier, and stroked the ocelots.

'Very well, Ida,' she said.

Ida Emean aep Sivney, elven sorceress, one of the free Aen Seidhe from the Blue Mountains, during the audience shrouded by an invisibility spell, materialised in a corner of the library, and smoothed down her dress and vermilion-red hair. The ocelots only reacted with a slight widening of their eyes. Like all cats, they could see what was invisible and could not be deceived by a simple spell.

'This parade of spies is beginning to annoy me,' Francesca said with a sneer, finding a more comfortable position on the ebony chair. 'Henselt of Kaedwen sent me a "consul" not long ago. Dijkstra dispatched a "trade mission" to Dol Blathanna. And now the arch-spy Vattier de Rideaux himself! Oh, and some time ago Stephan Skellen, the Grand Imperial Nobody, was creeping around too. But I didn't give him an audience. I'm the queen and Skellen's a nobody. He may hold a position, but he's a nobody nonetheless.'

'Stephan Skellen,' Ida Emean said slowly, 'visited us too, and was more fortunate. He spoke with Filavandrel and Vanadain.'

'And like Vattier with me, did he enquire about Vilgefortz, Yennefer, Rience and Cahir Mawr Dyffryn aep Ceallach?'

'Among other things. It may surprise you, but he was more interested in the original version of Ithlinne Aegli aep Aevenien's prophecy, particularly the parts about Aen Hen Ichaer, the Elder Blood. He was also curious about Tor Lara, the Tower of Gulls, and the legendary portal which once connected the Tower of Gulls to Tor Zireael, the Tower of Swallows. How typical of humans, Enid. To expect that, at a single nod, we shall unravel enigmas and mysteries for them which we have been endeavouring to solve for centuries.'

Francesca raised her hand and examined the rings adorning it.

'I wonder,' she said, 'whether Philippa knows about the strange preoccupation of Skellen and Vattier. And of Emhyr var Emreis, whom they both serve.'

'It would be risky to assume she doesn't,' Ida Emean replied, looking keenly at the queen, 'and to withhold what we know from Philippa and the entire lodge at the council in Montecalvo. It wouldn't show us in a very favourable light . . . And we want the lodge to come into being. We want to be trusted – we, elven sorceresses – and not to be suspected of playing a double game.'

'But we *are* playing a double game, Ida. And playing with fire: with the White Flame of Nilfgaard . . .'

'Fire burns,' Ida Emean said, raising her heavily made-up eyes at the queen, 'but it also purifies. It must be passed through. Risks have to be taken, Enid. The lodge ought to exist, ought to begin functioning. At full strength. Twelve sorceresses, including the one mentioned in the prophecy. Even if it is a game, let us rely on trust.'

'And if it's an entrapment?'

'You know the individuals involved better than I do.'

Enid an Gleanna thought for a while.

'Sheala de Tancarville,' she finally said, 'is a secretive recluse, without any loyalties. Triss Merigold and Keira Metz were loyal but they are now both emigrants, since King Foltest drove all the mages from Temeria. Margarita Laux-Antille cares for her school and nothing besides. Of course, at this moment the last three are heavily under Philippa's sway, and Philippa is an enigma. Sabrina Glevissig will not give up the political influence she has in Kaedwen, but will not betray the lodge either. She is too attracted by the power it can give her.'

'And what about Assire var Anahid? And the other Nilfgaardian, whom we shall meet in Montecalvo?'

'I know little about them.' Francesca smiled faintly. 'But once I see them I shall know more. As soon as I see how they are dressed.'

Ida Emean lowered her painted eyelids, but refrained from asking a question.

'This leaves us with the jade statuette,' she said a moment later. 'The still dubious and enigmatic jade figurine mentioned in the Ithlinnespeath, Ithlinne's Prophecy. I now deem it's time to allow her to express herself. And to tell her what she may expect. Shall I help you with the decompression?'

'No, I shall do it myself. You are familiar with reactions to unpacking. The fewer the witnesses, the less painful a blow it will be to her pride.'

Francesca Findabair checked one more time that the entire courtyard was thoroughly isolated from the rest of the palace by a protective field, which hid it from view and muffled its sounds. She lit three black candles planted in candlesticks equipped with parabolic mirrors. The candlesticks stood at points marked out by a circular mosaic pavement depicting the eight signs of Vicca, the elven zodiac, on the symbols indicating Belleteyn, Lammas and Yule. Inside the zodiac circle, the mosaic formed another, smaller circle, dotted with magic symbols and enclosing a pentagram. Francesca placed small, iron tripods on three symbols of the smaller circle, and then on each of them she carefully mounted three crystals. The cut of the crystals' bases corresponded to the form of the tripods' tops, which meant their placement could be nothing other than precise, but even so Francesca checked everything several times. She didn't want to leave anything to chance.

A fountain was trickling nearby, the water gushing from a marble jug held by a marble naiad. It fell into the pool in four streams and made the water lilies, between which goldfish darted, quiver.

Francesca opened a jewellery case, removed a small, waxy jade figurine from it, and placed it precisely at the centre of the pentagram. She withdrew, glanced once again at the grimoire lying on a table, took a deep breath, raised her hands and chanted a spell.

The candles burst into bright flame, the crystals' facets lit up and sparkled with streaks of light. Those streaks of light shot towards the figurine, which immediately changed colour from green to gold, and a moment later became transparent. The air shimmered with magical energy, which struck against the protective field. Sparks flew from one of the candles, shadows played on the floor, the mosaic came alive and the shapes in it transformed. Francesca did not lower her hands or interrupt the incantation.

The statuette grew at lightning speed, pulsating and throbbing, its structure and shape changing like a cloud of smoke crawling across the floor. The light shining from the crystals pierced the air; movement and congealing matter appeared in the streams of light. A moment later a human body suddenly manifested in the centre of the magical circles. It was the figure of a black-haired woman, lying inertly on the floor.

The candles bloomed with ribbons of smoke and the crystals went out. Francesca lowered her arms, relaxed her fingers and wiped the sweat from her forehead.

The black-haired woman on the floor curled up in a ball and began to scream.

'What is your name?' Francesca asked in a breathy voice.

The woman convulsed and howled, both hands clutching her belly.

'What is your name?'

'Ye . . . Yennef . . . Yennefeerrr!!! Aaaaaagh . . .'

The elf sighed with relief. The woman continued to squirm and howl, banging her fists against the floor and retching. Francesca waited patiently. And calmly. The woman – a moment earlier a jade figurine – was suffering, that was obvious. And normal. But her mind was undamaged.

'Well, Yennefer,' she said after a long pause, interrupting the groans. 'That ought to do, oughtn't it?'

Yennefer raised herself onto her hands and knees with obvious effort, wiped her nose with her wrist and looked around vacantly. Her gaze flitted over Francesca, as though the she-elf wasn't even in the courtyard, then came to rest – and brightened – at the sight of the fountain gushing water. Having crawled up to it with immense difficulty, Yennefer hauled herself over the lip and flopped into the pool with a splash. She choked, began to splutter, cough and spit, until finally, parting the water lilies, she waded to the marble naiad and sat down, leaning back against the pedestal of the statue. The water came up to her breasts.

'Francesca . . .' she mumbled, touching the obsidian star hanging from her neck and looking at the she-elf with a slightly clearer gaze. 'It's you . . .'

'It's me. What do you recall?'

'You packed me up . . . Hell's teeth, you packed me up, didn't you!'

'I packed you up and then unpacked you. What do you recall?'

'Garstang . . . Elves. Ciri. You. And the fifty tons suddenly landing on my head . . . Now I know what it was. Artefact compression . . .'

'Your memory's working. Good.'

Yennefer lowered her head and looked between her thighs, over which goldfish were darting.

'The water in the pool will need changing, Enid,' she mumbled. 'I just peed in it.'

'No matter.' Francesca smiled. 'But just see if there's any blood in the water. Compression has been known to damage the kidneys.'

'Only the kidneys?' Yennefer said, taking a cautious breath. 'I don't think there's a single undamaged organ in my body . . . At least that's how I feel. Hell's teeth, Enid, I really don't know what I did to deserve this . . .'

'Get out of the pool.'

'No. I like it here.'

'I know. It's called dehydration.'

'Degradation. Depredation! Why did you do it to me?'

'Get out, Yennefer.'

The sorceress stood up with difficulty, holding onto the marble naiad with both hands. She shook off the water lilies, with a sharp tug tore away her dripping dress and stood naked before the fountain, under the gushing streams. After rinsing herself down and drinking deeply, she stepped out of the pool, sat down on the edge, wrung out her hair and looked around.

'Where am I?'

'In Dol Blathanna.'

Yennefer wiped her nose.

'Do the hostilities on Thanedd continue?'

'No. They ended a month and a half ago.'

'I must have wronged you greatly,' Yennefer said a moment later. 'I must really have got under your skin, Enid. But you can consider us even. You've exacted a full revenge, if a little too sadistic. Couldn't you have just cut my throat?'

'Don't talk nonsense,' the elf said, making a face. 'I packed you up and got you out of Garstang to save your life. We'll come back to that, but a little later. Here, have this towel. And this sheet. You'll get a new dress after you've bathed – in a suitable place, in a tub full of warm water. You've done enough damage to my goldfish.'

*

243

Ida Emean and Francesca were drinking wine. Yennefer was drinking sugar water and carrot juice. In huge quantities.

'To sum up,' she said, after hearing Francesca's account. 'Nilfgaard has defeated Lyria, in an alliance with Kaedwen has dismantled Aedirn, burnt down Vengerberg, subjugated Verden, and is crushing Brugge and Sodden at this very moment. Vilgefortz has disappeared without a trace. Tissaia de Vries has committed suicide, and you've become queen of the Valley of Flowers. Imperator Emhyr has rewarded you with a crown and sceptre in exchange for my Ciri, whom he was hunting for so long, and whom he now has in his power and is using as he sees fit. You packed me up and have kept me in a box as a jade statuette for a month and a half. And no doubt expect me to thank you for it.'

'It would be polite,' Francesca Findabair replied coldly. 'On Thanedd there was a certain Rience, who had made it a point of honour to submit you to a slow and cruel death, and Vilgefortz offered to expedite it. Rience pursued you all over Garstang. But he didn't find you, because you were already a jade figurine safe in my cleavage.'

'And I was that figurine for forty-seven days.'

'Yes. While I, if asked, could always reply that Yennefer of Vengerberg was not in Dol Blathanna. Because the question referred to Yennefer, not a statuette.'

'What changed to induce you finally to unpack me?'

'A great deal changed. I shall explain forthwith.'

'First explain something else to me: the Witcher was also on Thanedd. Geralt. Remember, I introduced him to you in Aretuza. How is he?'

'Please remain calm. He's alive.'

'I *am* calm. Tell me, Enid.'

'In the space of an hour,' Francesca said, 'your Witcher did more than some manage in their entire lives. Put succinctly: he broke Dijkstra's leg, beheaded Artaud Terranova and slew ten Scoia'tael. Oh, I almost forgot: he also aroused Keira Metz's unhealthy passions.'

'Dreadful,' Yennefer said with a grimace. 'But Keira will have got over it by now, I imagine. I hope she doesn't hold a grudge against him. The fact that he didn't fuck her after inflaming her desire certainly resulted from lack of time, not lack of respect. Please put her mind at ease for me.'

'You'll have the chance to do that yourself,' the Daisy of the Valleys said coldly. 'And quite soon. Let's go back, though, to the issues about which you are lamely feigning indifference. Your Witcher was so fervid in his defence of Ciri that he acted very rashly. He attacked Vilgefortz. And Vilgefortz gave him a sound thrashing. The fact that he didn't kill him certainly resulted from lack of time, not lack of effort. Well? Are you still going to pretend you don't care?'

'No,' Yennefer said, her grimace no longer expressing scorn. 'No, Enid. I do care. Some people will soon learn how much. You can take my word for it.'

Francesca was no more concerned by Yennefer's threat than she had been by her mockery.

'Triss Merigold teleported what was left of the Witcher to Brokilon,' she stated. 'As far as I know, the dryads are still healing him. He is said to be recovering now, but it would be better if he didn't venture out of the forest. He's being tracked by Dijkstra's spies and the military intelligence services of all the kings. So are you, for that matter.'

'What did I do to deserve such attention? I didn't break anything of Dijkstra's . . . Oh, keep quiet and let me guess. I vanished without a trace from Thanedd. No one suspects I ended up in your pocket, shrunken down and packed up. Everybody is convinced I escaped to Nilfgaard with my fellow conspirators. Everybody apart from the real conspirators, naturally, but they won't be correcting that error. For a war is raging, and disinformation is a weapon whose blade must always be kept sharp. And now, forty-seven days later, comes your moment to use that weapon. My house in Vengerberg is burnt to the ground, and I'm being hunted. There's nothing left to do but join a Scoia'tael commando. Or join the fight for the elves' freedom in some other way.'

Yennefer sipped her carrot juice, and stared into the eyes of Ida Emean aep Sivney, who still remained peaceful and silent.

'Well, Mistress Ida, free lady of the Aen Seidhe from the Blue Mountains, have I correctly guessed what's in store for me? Why are you so tight-lipped?'

'Because I, Mistress Yennefer,' the red-headed she-elf answered, 'say nothing when I have nothing sensible to say. It's always better than to make unfounded speculations and disguise one's anxiety with idle talk. Enid, get to the point. Tell Mistress Yennefer what this is all about.'

'You have my undivided attention,' Yennefer said, touching the obsidian star hanging from its velvet ribbon. 'Speak, Francesca.'

The Daisy of the Valleys rested her chin on her interlocked hands.

'Today,' she announced, 'is the second night of the full moon. In a short while, we shall be teleporting to Montecalvo Castle, the seat of Philippa Eilhart. We shall be taking part in a session of an organisation that ought to interest you. After all, you were always of the opinion that magic represents the utmost value, superior to all disputes, conflicts, political choices, personal interests, grudges, sentiments and animosities. It will no doubt gladden you to hear that not long ago the foundations of an institution were laid down. Something like a secret lodge, brought into being exclusively to defend the interests of magic, meant to ensure that magic occupies the place it deserves in the hierarchy of the world. Exercising my privilege to recommend new members to this lodge, I took the liberty of proposing two candidates: Ida Emean aep Sivney and you.'

'What an unexpected honour,' Yennefer sneered. 'From magical oblivion straight to a secret, elite and omnipotent lodge, which stands above personal grudges and resentments. But am I suitable? Will I find sufficient strength of character to rid myself of my grudges against the people who took Ciri from me, cruelly beat a man who is dear to me, and packed—'

'I am certain,' the she-elf interrupted, 'that you will find sufficient strength of character, Yennefer. I know you and know you are not lacking in strength of that kind. Neither are you lacking in ambition, which ought to dispel your doubts about the honour and the advancement which has come your way. If you want, though, I'll tell you frankly: I'm recommending you to the lodge, because I consider

you a person who deserves it and who may render the cause a significant service.'

'Thank you,' Yennefer responded, the scornful smirk in no hurry
to disappear from her lips. 'Thank you, Enid. I truly feel the ambition, hubris and self-adoration filling me up. I'm ready to explode
at any moment. And that's before I even begin wondering why you
aren't recommending one more elf from Dol Blathanna or a she-elf
from the Blue Mountains instead of me.'

'You will find out why in Montecalvo,' Francesca replied coldly.

'I'd rather find out now.'

'Tell her,' Ida Emean muttered.

'It's because of Ciri,' Francesca said after a moment's thought,
raising her inscrutable eyes towards Yennefer. 'The lodge is interested in her, and no one knows the girl as well as you. You'll learn
the rest when we get there.'

'Agreed,' Yennefer said, vigorously scratching a shoulder blade.
Her skin, dried out by the compression, was still itching intolerably.
'Now tell me the names of the other members. Apart from you and
Philippa.'

'Margarita Laux-Antille, Triss Merigold and Keira Metz. Sheala
de Tancarville of Kovir. Sabrina Glevissig. And two sorceresses
from Nilfgaard.'

'An international women's republic?'

'Let's say.'

'They must still think I'm an accomplice of Vilgefortz. Will they
accept me?'

'They accepted me. The rest I leave to you. You will be asked
to give an account of your relationship with Ciri. From the very
beginning, which – thanks to your witcher – was fifteen years ago
in Cintra, and right up until the events of a month and a half ago.
Frankness and honesty will be absolutely paramount. And will confirm your loyalty to the lodge.'

'Who said there's anything to confirm? Isn't it too early to talk of
loyalty? I'm not even familiar with the statute or programme of this
new institution . . .'

'Yennefer,' the she-elf interjected, frowning slightly. 'I'm recommending you to the lodge. But I have no intention of forcing you to do anything. Particularly not to be loyal. You have a choice.'

'I think I know what it is.'

'And you would be right. But it is still a free choice. Speaking for myself, I still heartily encourage you to choose the lodge. Trust me; by doing so you'll be helping Ciri much more effectively than by plunging headlong into a whirl of events, which, I'm guessing, you would love to do. Ciri's life is in danger. Only our combined efforts can save her. When you have heard what is said in Montecalvo, you'll realise I was speaking the truth . . . Yennefer, I don't like the gleam in your eyes. Give me your word you will not try to escape.'

'No.' Yennefer shook her head, covering the star on the velvet ribbon with her hand. 'No, I will not, Francesca.'

'I must warn you, my dear. All Montecalvo's stationary portals have a distorting blockade. Anyone who tries to enter or leave without Philippa's permission will end up in a dungeon lined with dimeritium. You'll be unable to open your own teleportal without the appropriate components. I don't want to confiscate your star, because you have to be in full possession of your faculties. But if you try any tricks . . . Yennefer, I cannot allow— The lodge won't allow you to launch an insane, one-woman attempt to rescue Ciri and seek vengeance. I still have your matrix and the spell's algorithm. I'll shrink you and pack you into a jade statuette again. For several months this time. Or years, if necessary.'

'Thank you for the warning. But I still will not give you my word.'

Fringilla Vigo was putting on a brave face, but she was anxious and stressed. She herself had often reprimanded young Nilfgaardian mages for uncritically yielding to stereotypical opinions and notions. She herself had regularly ridiculed the crude image painted by gossip and propaganda of the typical sorceress from the North: artificially beautiful, arrogant, vain and spoiled to the limits of perversion, and often beyond them. Right now, though, the closer the sequence of teleportals brought her to Montecalvo Castle, the greater she was racked by uncertainty about what she would find when she arrived at the secret lodge meeting. And about what awaited her. Her untrammelled imagination offered up images of impossibly gorgeous women with diamond necklaces resting on naked breasts with rouged nipples, women with moist lips and eyes glistening from the effects of alcohol and narcotics. In her mind's eye Fringilla could already see the gathering becoming a wild and depraved orgy accompanied by frenzied music, aphrodisiacs, and slaves of both sexes using exotic accessories.

The final teleportal left her standing between two black marble columns, with dry lips, her eyes watering from the magic wind and her hand tightly clenching her emerald necklace, which filled the square neckline. Beside her materialised Assire var Anahid, also visibly agitated. Nevertheless, Fringilla had reason to suppose her friend was feeling uncomfortable owing to her new and unfamiliar outfit: a plain, but very elegant hyacinth dress, complemented with a small, modest alexandrite necklace.

Her anxiety was dispelled at once. It was cool and quiet in the large hall, which was lit by magical lanterns. There was no naked slave beating a drum, nor girls with sequinned pubic mounds dancing on the table. Neither was there the scent of hashish or Spanish fly in the air. Instead the Nilfgaardian enchantresses were welcomed by Philippa Eilhart, the lady of the castle; tastefully dressed, grave, courteous and businesslike. The others approached and introduced themselves and Fringilla sighed with relief. The sorceresses from the North were beautiful, colourful, and sparkled with jewellery, but there was no trace of intoxicating substances or nymphomania in their eyes, which were accentuated by understated make-up. Nor did any of them have naked breasts. Quite the opposite. Two of them had extremely modest gowns, fastened up to the neck: the severe Sheala de Tancarville, dressed in black, and the young Triss Merigold with her blue eyes and exquisite auburn hair. The dark-haired Sabrina Glevissig and the blondes Margarita Laux-Antille and Keira Metz all had low-cut necklines, only slightly more revealing than Fringilla's.

The wait for other participants was filled by polite conversation, during which all of them had the opportunity to say something about themselves. Philippa Eilhart's tactful comments and observations swiftly and adroitly broke the ice, although the only ice in the vicinity was on the food table, which was piled high with a mountain of oysters. No other ice could be discerned. Sheala de Tancarville, a scholar, immediately found a great deal of common ground with the scholar Assire var Anahid, while Fringilla quickly warmed towards the bubbly Triss Merigold. The conversation was accompanied by the greedy consumption of oysters. The only person not eating was Sabrina Glevissig, a true daughter of the Kaedwen forests, who took the liberty of expressing a scornful opinion about 'that slimy filth' and a yen for a slice of cold venison with plums. Philippa Eilhart, instead of reacting to the insult with haughty coolness, tugged on the bell pull and a moment later meat was brought in inconspicuously and noiselessly. Fringilla's astonishment was immense. *Well*, she thought, *it takes all sorts*.

The teleportal between the columns flared up and vibrated audibly. Utter amazement was painted on Sabrina Glevissig's face. Keira Metz dropped an oyster and a knife onto the ice. Triss stifled a gasp.

Three sorceresses emerged from the portal. Three she-elves. One with hair the colour of dark gold, one of vermilion and the third of raven black.

'Welcome, Francesca,' Philippa said. In her voice was none of the emotion being expressed by her eyes, which, though, she quickly narrowed. 'Welcome, Yennefer.'

'I was given the privilege of filling two seats,' the golden-haired newcomer addressed as Francesca said melodiously, undoubtedly noticing Philippa's astonishment. 'Here are my candidates. Yennefer of Vengerberg, who needs no introduction. And Mistress Ida Emean aep Sivney, an Aen Saevherne from the Blue Mountains.'

Ida Emean slightly inclined her head and her mass of red curls and rustled her floating daffodil-yellow dress.

'May I assume,' Francesca said, looking around, 'that we are all here now?'

'Only Vilgefortz is missing,' Sabrina Glevissig hissed quietly, but with unfeigned anger, looking askance at Yennefer.

'And the Scoia'tael hiding in the cellars,' Keira Metz muttered. Triss froze her with a look.

Philippa made the introductions. Fringilla watched Francesca Findabair with curiosity – Enid an Gleanna, the Daisy of the Valleys, the illustrious Queen of Dol Blathanna, the queen of the elves, who had not long before recovered their country. *The rumours about Francesca's beauty were not exaggerated*, thought Fringilla.

The red-headed and large-eyed Ida Emean clearly aroused everybody's interest, including both sorceresses from Nilfgaard. The free elves from the Blue Mountains maintained contact neither with humans nor with their own kind living closer to humans. The few Aen Saevherne – or Sages – among the free elves were an almost legendary enigma. Few – even among elves – could boast of a close relationship with the Aen Saevherne. Ida did not only stand out in the group by the colour of hair. There was not a single ounce of metal nor a carat of stone in her jewellery; she wore only pearls, coral and amber.

However, the source of the greatest emotions was, unsurprisingly, the third of the new arrivals: Yennefer, dressed in black and white and with raven-black hair, who was no elf despite first impressions. Her arrival in Montecalvo must have been an immense surprise, and a not entirely pleasant one. Fringilla felt an aura of antipathy and hostility emanating from some of the sorceresses.

While the Nilfgaardian sorceresses were being introduced to her, Yennefer let her violet eyes rest on Fringilla. They were tired and had dark circles around them, which even her make-up was unable to hide.

'We know each other,' she said, touching the obsidian star hanging from its velvet ribbon.

A heavy silence, pregnant with anticipation, suddenly descended on the chamber.

'We've already met,' Yennefer spoke again.

'I don't recall,' Fringilla said without looking away.

'I'm not surprised. But I have a good memory for faces and figures. I saw you from Sodden Hill.'

'In which case there can be no mistake,' Fringilla Vigo said and raised her head proudly, sweeping her eyes over all those present. 'I was at the Battle of Sodden.'

Philippa Eilhart forestalled a response.

'I was there too,' she said. 'And I also have many recollections. I don't think, however, that excessive straining of the memory or unnecessary rummaging around in it will bring us any benefit here, in this chamber. What we plan to undertake here will be better served by forgetting, forgiving and being reconciled with each other. Do you agree, Yennefer?'

The black-haired sorceress tossed her curly locks away from her forehead.

'When I finally learn what you're trying to do here,' she replied, 'I'll tell you what I agree with, Philippa. And what I don't agree with.'

'In that case it would be best if we began without delay. Please, would you take your places, ladies.'

The seats at the round table – apart from one – had place cards. Fringilla sat down beside Assire var Anahid, with the unnamed seat on her right separating her from Sheala de Tancarville, beyond whom Sabina Glevissig and Keira Metz took their places. On Assire's left sat Ida Emean, Francesca Findabair and Yennefer. Philippa Eilhart occupied the place exactly opposite Assire, with Margarita Laux-Antille on her right, and Triss Merigold on her left.

All of the chairs had armrests carved in the shape of sphinxes.

Philippa began. She repeated the welcome and immediately got down to business. Fringilla, to whom Assire had given a detailed report of the lodge's previous meeting, learned nothing new from the introduction. Neither was she surprised by the declarations made by all the sorceresses to join the lodge, nor the first contributions to the discussion. She was somewhat disconcerted, however, that those first voices related to the war the Empire was waging with the Nordlings, and in particular the operation in Sodden and Brugge which had been begun a short time before, during which the imperial forces had clashed with the Temerian Army. In spite of the lodge's statutory political neutrality, the sorceresses were unable to hide their views. Some were clearly anxious about the close proximity of

Nilfgaard. Fringilla had mixed feelings. She had assumed that such educated people would understand that the Empire was bringing culture, prosperity, order and political stability to the North. On the other hand, though, she didn't know how she would have reacted herself, were foreign armies approaching her home.

However, Philippa Eilhart had clearly heard enough discussion about military matters.

'No one is capable of predicting the outcome of this war,' she said. 'What is more, predictions of that kind are pointless. It's time we looked at this matter with a dispassionate eye. Firstly, war is not such a great evil. I'd be more afraid of the consequences of over-population, which at this stage of the growth of agriculture and industry would lead to famine. Secondly, war is an extension of the kings' politics. How many of those who are reigning now will be alive in a hundred years? None of them, that's obvious. How many dynasties will last? There's no way of predicting. In a hundred years, today's territorial and dynastic conflicts, today's ambitions and hopes will be dust in the history books. But if we don't protect ourselves, if we allow ourselves to be drawn into the war, nothing but dust will remain of us too. If, however, we look a little beyond the battle flags, if we close our ears to the cries of war and patriotism, we shall survive. And we must survive. We must, because we bear responsibility. Not towards kings and their local interests, focused on the concerns of one kingdom. We are responsible for the whole world. For progress. For the changes which accompany this progress. We are responsible for the future.'

'Tissaia de Vries would have expressed it differently,' Francesca Findabair said. 'She was always concerned with responsibility towards the common man. Not in the future, but here and now.'

'Tissaia de Vries is dead. Were she alive, she would be here among us.'

'No doubt,' the Daisy of the Valleys smiled. 'But I don't think she would have agreed with the theory that war is a remedy for famine and overpopulation. Pay attention to the language used here, honourable sisters. We are debating using the Common Speech, which is meant to ease understanding. But for me it's a foreign language;

one becoming more and more foreign. In the language of my mother the expression "the common man" does not exist, and "the common elf" would be a coinage. The late, lamented Tissaia de Vries was concerned with the fate of ordinary humans. To me, the fate of ordinary elves is no less important. I'd gladly applaud the idea of looking ahead and treating today as ephemera. But I'm sorry to state that today paves the way for tomorrow, and without tomorrow there won't be any future. For you, humans, perhaps the tears I shed over a lilac shrub burnt to ash during the turmoil of war are ridiculous. After all, there will always be lilac shrubs; if not that one, then another. And if there are no more lilac shrubs, well, there'll be acacia trees. Forgive my botanical metaphors. But kindly note that what is a matter of politics to you humans is a matter of physical survival to the elves.'

'Politics don't interest me,' Margarita Laux-Antille, the rectoress of the academy of magic, announced loudly. 'I simply do not wish my girls, whose education I've dedicated myself to, to be used as mercenaries, pulling the wool over their eyes with slogans about love for one's homeland. The homeland of those girls is magic; that's what I teach them. If someone involves my girls in a war, stands them on a new Sodden Hill, they will be lost, irrespective of the result on that battlefield. I understand your reservations, Enid, but we're here to discuss the future of magic, not issues of race.'

'We are here to discuss the future of magic,' Sabrina Glevissig repeated. 'But the future of magic is determined by the status of sorcerers. Our status. Our importance. The role we play in society. Trust, respect and credibility, general faith in our usefulness, faith that magic is indispensable. The alternative we face seems simple: either a loss of status and isolation in ivory towers, or service. Service even on the hills of Sodden, even as mercenaries . . .'

'Or as servants and errand girls?' Triss Merigold cut in, tossing her beautiful hair off her shoulder. 'With bent backs, ready to leap into action at every wag of the imperial finger? For that's the role we will be assigned by the *Pax Nilfgaardiana*, should Nilfgaard conquer us all.'

'If it does,' Philippa said with emphasis. 'Anyhow we won't have much choice. For we have to serve. But serve magic. Not kings or imperators, not their present politics. Not matters of racial integration, because they are also subject to today's political goals. Our lodge, my dear ladies, was not brought into being for us to adapt to today's politics and daily changes on the front line. Or to feverishly search for solutions appropriate to the situation at hand, changing the colour of our skin like chameleons. Our lodge must be active, but its assigned role should be quite the opposite. And carried out using all the means we have at our disposal.'

'If I understand correctly,' Sheala de Tancarville said, raising her head, 'you are persuading us to actively influence the course of events. By fair means or foul? Including illegal measures?'

'What laws do you speak of? The ones governing the rabble? The ones written in the codices, which we drew up and dictated to the royal jurists? We are only bound by one law. Our own!'

'I see.' The sorceress from Kovir smiled. 'We, then, shall actively influence the course of events. Should the kings' politics not be to our liking, we'll simply change it. Correct, Philippa? Or perhaps it's better to overthrow all those crowned asses at once; dethrone them and drive them out. And seize power at once?'

'In the past we crowned kings who were convenient to us. Unfortunately we did not put magic on the throne. We have never given magic absolute power. It's time we corrected that mistake.'

'You have yourself in mind, of course?' Sabrina Glevissig said, leaning across the table. 'On the Redanian throne, naturally? Her Majesty Philippa the First? With Dijkstra as prince consort?'

'I was not thinking about myself. Nor was I thinking about the Kingdom of Redania. I have in mind the Kingdom of the North, which the Kingdom of Kovir is today evolving into. An empire whose power will be equal to Nilfgaard's, thanks to which the currently oscillating scales of the world will finally come to rest in equilibrium. An empire ruled by magic, which we shall raise to the throne by marrying the Kovirian crown prince to a sorceress. Yes, you heard correctly, dear sisters; you are looking in the right direction. Yes, here, at this table, in this vacant seat, we shall place the lodge's twelfth sorceress. And then we shall put her on the throne.'

255

The silence that fell was broken by Sheala de Tancarville.

'An ambitious project indeed,' she said with a hint of derision in her voice. 'Truly worthy of us all, here seated. It absolutely justifies establishing a lodge of this kind. After all, less lofty tasks, even ones that are tottering on the brink of reality and feasibility, would be an affront to us. That would be like using an astrolabe to hammer in nails. No, no, it is best to set ourselves an utterly impossible task from the start.'

'Why call it impossible?'

'Have mercy, Philippa.' Sabrina Glevissig sighed. 'No king would ever wed a sorcereress. No society would accept a sorceress on the throne. An ancient custom stands in the way. A foolish one, perhaps, but it is there nevertheless.'

'There also exist,' Margarita Laux-Antille added, 'obstacles of what I would call a technical nature. The sorceress who joined the House of Kovir would have to comply with a large number of conditions, both from our point of view and that of the House of Kovir. Those conditions are mutually exclusive, they contradict each other in obvious ways. Don't you see that, Philippa? For us this person ought to be schooled in magic, utterly dedicated to magic, comprehending her role and capable of playing it deftly, imperceptibly and without arousing suspicion. Without direction or prompt, without any grey eminences standing in the shadows, against whom rebels always first direct their anger in a revolution. And Kovir itself, without any apparent pressure from us, must also choose her as the wife of the heir to the throne.'

'That is obvious.'

'So who do you think Kovir would select, given a free choice? A girl from a royal family, whose royal blood flows back many generations. A very young woman, suitable for a young prince. A girl who is fertile, because this is about a dynasty. Such prerequisites rule you out, Philippa. Rule me out, rule out Keira and Triss even, the youngest among us. They also rule out all the novices at my school, who are anyhow of little interest to us; they are but buds, the colour of whose petals are still unknown. It's unthinkable that any of them could occupy the twelfth, empty seat at this table. In other words, were Kovir to be afflicted with insanity and willing to marry their prince to a sorceress, we couldn't find a suitable woman. Who, then, is to be this Queen of the North?'

'A girl from a royal family,' Philippa calmly replied, 'in whose veins flows royal blood, the blood of several great dynasties. Very young and capable of producing offspring. A girl with exceptional magical and prophetic abilities, a carrier of the Elder Blood as the prophecies have heralded. A girl who will play her role with great aplomb without direction, prompt, sycophants or grey eminences, because that is what her destiny demands. A girl, whose true abilities are and will be known only to us: Cirilla, daughter of Princess Pavetta of Cintra, the granddaughter of the Queen Calanthe called the Lioness of Cintra. The Elder Blood, the Icy Flame of the North, the Destroyer and Restorer, whose coming was prophesied centuries ago. Ciri of Cintra, the Queen of the North. And her blood, from which will be born the Queen of the World.'

At the sight of the Rats bursting out of the ambush, two of the horsemen escorting the carriage immediately turned tail and sped away. But they didn't stand a chance. Giselher, helped by Reef and Iskra, cut off their escape and after a short fight hacked them to pieces. Kayleigh, Asse and Mistle fell on the other two, who were prepared to defend the carriage, and the four spotted horses harnessed to it, desperately. Ciri felt disappointment and overwhelming anger. They hadn't left anyone for her. It looked as though she would have no one to kill.

But there was still one horseman, riding in front of the carriage as an outrider, lightly armed, on a swift horse. He could have escaped, but hadn't. He turned back, swung his sword and dashed straight at Ciri.

She let him approach, even somewhat slowing her horse. When he struck, rising up in the stirrups, she leant far out from the saddle, skilfully ducking under his blade, then sat back up, pushing off hard against the stirrups. The horseman was quick and agile and managed to strike again. This time she parried obliquely, and when the sword slid away she struck the horseman in the hand from below with a short lunge, then swung her sword in a feint towards his face. He involuntarily covered his head with his left hand and she deftly turned the sword around in her hand and slashed him in the armpit, a cut she had practised for hours at Kaer Morhen. The Nilfgaardian slid from his saddle, fell to the ground, lifted himself up onto his knees, and howled like an animal, desperately trying to staunch the blood gushing from his severed arteries. Ciri watched him for a moment, as usual fascinated by the sight of a man fiercely fighting death with all his strength. She waited for him to bleed out. Then she rode off without looking back.

The ambush was over. The escort had been dispatched. Asse and Reef stopped the carriage, seizing the reins of the lead pair. The postilion, a young boy in colourful livery, having been pushed from the right lead horse, knelt on the ground, crying and begging for mercy. The coachman threw down the reins and also begged for his life, his hands placed together as though in prayer. Giselher, Iskra and Mistle cantered over to the carriage, and Kayleigh jumped off and jerked the door open. Ciri rode up and dismounted, still holding her blood-covered sword.

In the carriage sat a fat matron in an old-fashioned gown and bonnet, clutching a young and terribly pale girl in a black dress fastened up to the neck with a guipure lace collar. Ciri noticed she had a brooch pinned to her dress. A very pretty brooch.

'Oh, spotted horses!' Iskra called, looking at the rig. 'What beauties! We'll get a few florins for this four!'

'And the coachman and postilion,' Kayleigh said, grinning at the woman and the girl, 'will pull the carriage to town, once we've harnessed them up. And when we come to a hill, these two fine ladies will help!'

'Highwaymen, sirs!' the matron in the old-fashioned gown whimpered, clearly more horrified by Kayleigh's hideous smile than the bloody steel in Ciri's hand. 'I appeal to your honour! You surely will not outrage this young maiden.'

'Hey, Mistle,' Kayleigh called, smiling derisively, 'your honour's being appealed to!'

'Shut your gob.' Giselher grimaced, still mounted. 'Your jokes

258

don't make anyone laugh. And you, woman, calm down. We're the Rats. We don't fight women and we don't harm them. Reef, Iskra. Unharness the ponies! Mistle, catch our mounts; we're leaving!'

'We Rats don't fight with women.' Kayleigh grinned once more, staring at the ashen face of the girl in the black dress. 'We just have some fun with them occasionally, if they have a yen. Well, do you, young lady? You haven't got an itch between your legs, have you? Please don't be shy. Just nod your little head.'

'Show some respect!' the lady in the old-fashioned gown screamed, her voice faltering. 'How dare you talk like that to the Much Honoured Baron's daughter, brigand!'

Kayleigh roared with laughter, then bowed extravagantly.

'I beg for forgiveness. I didn't wish to offend. What, mayn't I even ask?'

'Kayleigh!' Iskra called. 'Come here and stop dallying! Help us unharness these horses! Falka! Move it!'

Ciri couldn't tear her eyes away from the coat of arms on the carriage doors: a silver unicorn on a black field. *A unicorn*, she thought. *I once saw a unicorn like that . . . When? In another life? Or perhaps it was only a dream.*

'Falka! What's the matter?'

I am Falka. But I wasn't always. Not always.

She gathered herself and pursed her lips. *I was unkind to Mistle*, she thought. *I upset her. I have to apologise somehow.*

She placed a foot on the carriage steps, staring at the brooch on the pale girl's dress.

'Hand it over,' she said bluntly.

'How dare you?' the matron choked. 'Do you know who you are speaking to? She is the noble-born daughter of the Baron of Casadei!'

Ciri looked around, making sure no one was listening.

'A Baron's daughter?' she hissed. 'A petty title. And even if the snot were a countess, she ought to curtsy before me, arse close to the ground and head low. Give me the brooch! What are you waiting for? Should I tear it off along with the bodice?'

*

259

The silence which fell at the table after Philippa's declaration was quickly replaced by an uproar. The sorceresses vied with each other to voice their astonishment and disbelief, demanding explanations. Some of them undoubtedly knew a great deal about the prophesied Queen of the North – Cirilla or Ciri – while for others the name was less familiar. Fringilla Vigo didn't know anything, but she had her suspicions and was lost in conjecture, mainly centred on a certain lock of hair. However, when she asked Assire in hushed tones, the sorceress said nothing and instructed her to remain silent too. Meanwhile, Philippa Eilhart took the floor once again.

'Most of us saw Ciri on Thanedd, where she delivered prophecy in a trance and caused a great deal of confusion. Some of us are close – or even very close – to her. I have you in mind, in particular, Yennefer. It's your turn to speak.'

When Yennefer was telling the assembly about Ciri, Triss Merigold looked attentively at her. Yennefer spoke calmly and without emotion, but Triss knew her too well and had known her for too long to be fooled. She had seen her in many situations, including stressful ones, which had exhausted her and led her to the verge of sickness, and occasionally into it. Now, without doubt, Yennefer found herself in such a situation again. She looked distressed, weary and ill.

The sorceress talked, and Triss, who knew both the story and the person it concerned, discreetly observed the audience. Particularly the two sorceresses from Nilfgaard. The utterly transformed Assire var Anahid, now dressed up but still feeling uncertain in her make-up and fashionable dress. And Fringilla Vigo, the younger, friendly, naturally graceful and modestly elegant one, with green eyes and hair as black as Yennefer's but less luxuriant, cut shorter and brushed down smoothly.

Neither of the Nilfgaardians gave the impression of being lost among the complexities of Ciri's story, even though Yennefer's account was lengthy and tangled, beginning with the infamous love affair between Pavetta of Cintra and the young man magically transformed into Urcheon. She recounted Geralt's role and the Law of Surprise, and the destiny linking the Witcher and Ciri. Yennefer talked about Ciri and Geralt meeting in Brokilon, about the war, about her being lost and found, and about Kaer Morhen. About Rience and the Nilfgaardian agents hunting the girl. About her education in the Temple of Melitele, and about Ciri's mysterious abilities.

They're listening with such inscrutable expressions, Triss thought, looking at Assire and Fringilla. *Like sphinxes. But they are clearly hiding something. I wonder what. Their astonishment? Since they couldn't have known who Emhyr had brought to Nilfgaard. Or is it that they've known all this for a long time, perhaps even better than we do? Yennefer will soon reach Ciri's arrival on Thanedd, and the prophecy she gave while in a trance, which sowed so much confusion. About the bloody fighting in Garstang, which left Geralt severely beaten and Ciri abducted.*

Then the dissembling will be over, Triss thought, *and the masks will fall. Everyone knows that Nilfgaard was behind the events on Thanedd. And when all eyes turn towards you, Nilfgaardians, you won't have a choice, you'll have to talk. And then certain matters will be explained and perhaps I shall find out more. Like how Yennefer managed to vanish from Thanedd, and why she suddenly appeared here, in Montecalvo, with Francesca. Who is Ida Emean, she-elf, Aen Saevherne from the Blue Mountains, and what role is she playing here? Why do I have the impression Philippa Eilhart reveals less than she knows, even though she declares her devotion and loyalty to magic, and not to Dijkstra . . . with whom she remains in unceasing contact?*

And perhaps I'll finally learn who Ciri really is. Ciri; the Queen of the North to them, but the flaxen-haired witcher-girl of Kaer Morhen to me. A girl I still think of as a younger sister.

Fringilla Vigo had heard something about witchers: individuals who earned their keep by killing monsters and beasts. She listened attentively to Yennefer's story and to the sound of her voice, and observed her face. She didn't let herself be deceived. The strong emotional relationship between Yennefer and Ciri – whom everyone found so fascinating – was clear as day. Interestingly enough, the relationship between the sorceress and the Witcher she had mentioned was equally clear and equally strong. Fringilla began to reflect on this, but was interrupted by raised voices.

She had already worked out that some of the assembled company had been in opposing camps during the rebellion on Thanedd, so was not at all surprised by the antipathy expressed in the form of biting comments, directed at Yennefer as she spoke. Just as an argument seemed inevitable, Philippa Eilhart cut it short by unceremoniously slapping the table, which made the cups jingle.

'Enough!' she shouted. 'Be quiet, Sabrina! Don't let her goad you, Francesca! That's quite enough about Thanedd and Garstang. It's history!'

History, Fringilla thought, with an astonishing sense of hurt. *But history, which they – even though they belonged to different camps – had a hand in. They made their mark. They knew what they were doing and why. And we, imperial sorceresses, don't know anything. We really are like errand girls, who know what they are being sent to do, but don't know why. It's good that this lodge is coming into being,* she deemed. *The devil only knows how it will end, but at least it's beginning, here and now.*

'Yennefer, continue,' Philippa summoned.

'I don't have anything else to say,' the black-haired sorceress answered through pursed lips. 'I repeat: Tissaia de Vries ordered me to bring Ciri to Garstang.'

'It's easy to blame the dead,' Sabrina Glevissig snarled, but Philippa quietened her with a sharp gesture.

'I didn't want to meddle in Aretuza's business,' Yennefer said, pale and clearly disturbed. 'I wanted to take Ciri and escape Thanedd. But Tissaia convinced me that the girl's appearance in Garstang would be a shock to many and that her prophecy would pour oil on troubled waters. I'm not blaming her, however, because I agreed with her then. Both of us made a mistake. Mine was greater, though. Had I left Ciri in Rita's care . . .'

'What's done cannot be undone,' Philippa interrupted. 'Anyone can make a mistake. Even Tissaia de Vries. When did Tissaia see Ciri for the first time?'

'Three days before the conclave began,' Margarita Laux-Antille replied. 'In Gors Velen. I also made her acquaintance then. And I knew she was a remarkable individual the moment I saw her!'

'Extremely remarkable,' said the previously silent Ida Emean aep Sivney. 'For the legacy of remarkable blood is concentrated in her. Hen Ichaer, the Elder Blood. Genetic material determining the carrier's uncommon abilities. Determining the great role she will play. That she *must* play.'

'Because that is what elven legends, myths and prophecies demand?' Sabrina Glevissig asked with a sneer. 'Since the very beginning, this whole matter has smacked of fairy-tales and fantasies! Now I have no doubts. My dear ladies, I suggest we discuss something important, rational and real for a change.'

'I bow before sober rationality; the power and source of your race's great superiority,' Ida Emean said, smiling faintly. 'Nonetheless, here, in the company of individuals capable of using a power which does not always lend itself to rational analysis or explanations, it seems somewhat improper to disregard the elves' prophecies. Neither our race nor our power draws its strength from rationality. In spite of that it has endured for tens of thousands of years.'

'The genetic material called the Elder Blood, of which we are talking, turned out to be a little less hardy, however,' Sheala de Tancarville observed. 'Even elven legends and prophecies, which I in no way disregard, consider the Elder Blood to be utterly atrophied. Extinct. Am I right, Mistress Ida? There is no more Elder Blood in the world. The last person in whose veins it flowed was Lara Dorren aep Shiadhal, and we all know the legend of Lara Dorren and Cregennan of Lod.'

'Not all of us,' Assire var Anahid said, speaking for the first time. 'I only studied your mythology cursorily and have never come across that legend.'

'It is not a legend,' Philippa Eilhart said, 'but a true story. And there is one among us who not only knows the tale of Lara and Cregennan very well, but also what came after, which will certainly interest you all. Would you take up the story, Francesca?'

'From what you say' – the queen of the elves smiled – 'it would seem you know this tale no less thoroughly than I do.'

'Quite possibly. But I would nonetheless ask you to tell it.'

'In order to test my honesty and loyalty to the lodge,' Enid an Gleanna said, nodding. 'Very well. I would ask you all to make yourselves comfortable, for the story will not be a short one.'

'The story of Lara and Cregennan is a true story, although today it is so overgrown with fairy-tale ornamentation it is difficult to recognise. There is also enormous variance between the legend's human and elven versions; chauvinism and racial hatred can be heard in both of them, though. Thus I shall refrain from embellishments and limit myself to dry facts. Cregennan of Lod was a sorcerer. Lara Dorren aep Shiadhal was an elven sorceress, an Aen Saevherne, a Sage, one of the carriers of the Elder Blood, which is even mysterious to we elves. The friendship – and later romance – between the two of them was at first joyfully acknowledged by both races, but there soon appeared opponents to their union. Sworn enemies to the idea of melding human and elven magic, who regarded it as betrayal. With the wisdom of hindsight, there were also feuds of a personal nature at work: jealousy and envy. Put simply: Cregennan was assassinated and Lara Dorren, hounded and hunted, died of exhaustion in a wilderness after giving birth to a daughter. The baby was saved by a miracle. She was taken in by Cerro, the Queen of Redania—'

'Only because she was terrified of the curse Lara cast when she refused to help and drove Lara out into the cold of winter,' Keira Metz said, butting in. 'Had Cerro not adopted the child, terrible calamities would have fallen on her and her entire family—'

'Those are precisely the fantastic ornaments Francesca has dispensed with,' Philippa Eilhart interrupted. 'Let us stick to facts.'

'The prophetic abilities of the Sages of the Elder Blood are facts,' Ida Emean said, raising her eyes towards Philippa. 'And the evocative motif of prophecy which appears in every version of the legend is food for thought.'

'It is now, and it was in the past,' Francesca confirmed. 'The rumours of Lara's curse never died away, and were even recalled seventeen years later when Riannon – the little girl Cerro had adopted – grew into a young woman whose beauty eclipsed even her mother's legendary looks. She bore the official title of Princess of Redania, and many ruling houses were interested in making a match with her. When Riannon finally chose Goidemar, the young King of Temeria, from among many suitors, it would not have taken much for rumours of the curse to thwart the marriage. However, the rumours only became common knowledge three years after their wedding. During the Falka Rebellion.'

Fringilla, who had never heard of Falka or the rebellion, raised her eyebrows. Francesca noticed it.

'For the northern kingdoms,' she explained, 'these are tragic and bloody events, which live on in the memory, though more than a century has passed. In Nilfgaard, with whom the North had almost no contact at that time, the matter is probably not known so I will take the liberty of briefly restating certain facts. Falka was the daughter of Vridank, the King of Redania, and the issue of a marriage he dissolved when he took a fancy to the beautiful Cerro – the same Cerro who later adopted Lara's child. A document survives, lengthily and circuitously stating the reasons for the divorce, but a surviving miniature of Vridank's first wife, an undoubtedly half-elf Kovirian noblewoman with predominantly human traits, says a lot more. It depicts her with the eyes of a deranged hermit, the hair of a drowned corpse and the mouth of a lizard. To cut a long story short: an ugly woman was sent back to Kovir with her year-old daughter, Falka. And soon after, the one and the other were both forgotten.'

'Falka,' Enid an Gleanna picked up after a while, 'gave cause to be remembered five-and-twenty years later, when she launched an uprising and murdered her own father, Cerro and two of her stepbrothers, allegedly with her own hands. The armed rebellion initially broke out as an attempt by the legally firstborn daughter, supported by some of the Temerian and Kovirian nobility, to gain the throne which was rightly hers. But it was soon transformed into a peasants' revolt of immense proportions. Both sides committed gruesome atrocities. Falka passed into legend as a bloodthirsty demon, although actually it is more likely she simply lost control of the situation and of the slogans displayed on the insurrectionary standards. "Death To Kings"; "Death To Sorcerers"; "Death To

Priests, Nobility, Gentry and Anybody Well-To-Do"; and soon after: "Death To Everyone and Everything", for it became impossible to curb the blood-drenched evil mob. Then the rebellion began to spread to other countries . . .'

'Nilfgaardian historians have written about that,' Sabrina Glevissig interrupted with a distinct sneer. 'And Mistresses Assire and Vigo have undoubtedly read it. Keep it brief, Francesca. Move on to Riannon and the Houtborg triplets.'

'But of course. Riannon, issue of Lara Dorren, adopted daughter of Cerro, now the wife of Goidemar, King of Temeria, was accidentally seized by Falka's rebels and imprisoned in Houtborg Castle. She was pregnant at the time of her capture. The castle was still under siege long after the rebellion had been suppressed and Falka executed, but Goidemar finally took it by storm and rescued his wife. And three children: two little girls, who were already walking, and a boy, who was learning to. Riannon had been driven insane. The furious Goidemar put all the captives on the rack and from the shreds of their testimonies, interspersed with groans, constructed a plausible picture.

'Falka, who had inherited her looks more from her elven grandmother than her mother, had generously bestowed her charms on all her officers in command, from the noblemen to ordinary captains and thugs; by so doing ensuring their faithfulness and loyalty to her. She finally fell pregnant and gave birth to a child, precisely at the same moment that Riannon – who was imprisoned in Houtborg – had twins. Falka ordered her infant to be raised with Riannon's children. As she was later alleged to have said, only queens were worthy of the honour of being wet nurses to her bastards, and a similar fate would await every queen and princess in the new order Falka would build following her victory.

'The problem was that no one, not even Riannon, knew which of the "triplets" was Falka's. It was surmised that it was most likely one of the girls, because Riannon had reputedly given birth to a girl and a boy. I repeat, most likely, since in spite of Falka's boast the children were suckled by ordinary, peasant wet nurses. Riannon could hardly remember anything when her insanity was finally cured. Yes, she gave birth. Yes, the triplets were occasionally brought to her bed and shown to her. But nothing more.

'Sorcerers were summoned to examine the triplets and establish which was which. Goidemar was so unwavering that he intended – after ascertaining which was Falka's bastard – to publicly execute the child. We could not allow it. After the uprising's suppression, unspeakable brutality had been inflicted on the captured rebels, and it was time to put an end to it. The execution of a child before its second birthday? Can you imagine? What legends would have sprung up! And anyway it had already been rumoured that Falka herself had been born a monster as a result of Lara Dorren's curse. Nonsense, of course, since Falka had been born before Lara had even met Cregennan. But few people could be bothered to count the years. Pamphlets and other ridiculous documents were written about it and published clandestinely in Oxenfurt Academy. But I will return to the examination Goidemar ordered us to carry out—'

'Us?' Yennefer asked, looking up. 'Who precisely was that?'

'Tissaia de Vries, Augusta Wagner, Leticia Charbonneau and Hen Gedymdeith,' Francesca said calmly. 'I was later added to that body. I was a young sorceress, but a pureblood elf. And my father . . . my biological father, who disowned me . . . he was a Sage. I knew what the Elder Blood gene was.'

'And that gene was found in Riannon, when you examined her and the king before studying the children,' Sheala de Tancarville stated. 'And in two of the children – although to different extents – which allowed Falka's bastard to be identified. How did you save the child from the king's wrath?'

'Very simply,' the she-elf smiled. 'By feigning ignorance. We told the king that the matter was complicated, that we were still doing tests, but that tests of that kind demanded time . . . A great deal of time. Goidemar, an irascible but fundamentally good and noble man, quickly cooled down and put no pressure on us while the triplets were growing and running around the palace, bringing joy to the royal couple and the entire court. Amavet, Fiona and Adela. The triplets were as alike as three sparrows. They were watched attentively, of course, and there were frequent suspicions, particularly if one of the children was getting up to mischief. Fiona once tipped the contents of a chamber pot from a window right onto the Great Constable. He called her "a demonic bastard" and kissed goodbye to his post. Sometime later Amavet smeared tallow on the stairs, and then, when a splint was put on the arm of a certain lady-in-waiting, she groaned something about "accursed blood" and soon afterwards said farewell to the court. More lowborn loudmouths made the acquaintance of the whipping post and the horsewhip. Thus everyone swiftly learned to hold their tongues. There was even a baron from an ancient family, who Adela shot in the backside with an arrow, who confined himself to—'

'That's enough about the children's pranks,' Philippa Eilhart interjected. 'When was Goidemar finally told the truth?'

'He was never told. He never asked, which suited us.'

'But you knew which of the children was Falka's bastard?'

'Of course. It was Adela.'

'Not Fiona?'

'No. Adela. She died of the plague. The demonic bastard, the accursed blood, the daughter of the diabolical Falka helped the priests in the infirmary beyond the castle walls during an epidemic – in spite of the king's protests. She caught the plague from the sick children she was treating and died. She was seventeen. A year later her pseudo-brother Amavet became romantically involved with Countess Anna Kameny and was murdered by assassins hired by her husband. The same year Riannon died, distraught and inconsolable after the death of two of her beloved children. Then Goidemar summoned us once more. For the King of Cintra, Coram, was showing an interest in the last of the famous triplets: Princess Fiona. He wanted her to marry his son, also Coram, but knew of the rumours and didn't want to go ahead with the match in case Fiona was indeed Falka's bastard. We staked our reputation on the fact that Fiona was a legitimate child. I don't know if he believed us, but the young couple grew to like each other and thus Riannon's daughter, Ciri's great-great-great-grandmother, became the Queen of Cintra.'

'Introducing your celebrated gene to the Coram dynasty.'

'Fiona,' Enid an Gleanna said calmly, 'was not a carrier of the Elder Blood gene, which we had begun to call the Lara gene.'

'What do you mean exactly?'

'Well, Amavet carried the Lara gene, so our experiment went on. For Anna Kameny, who inadvertently caused the death of both her lover and husband, gave birth to twins while still in mourning. A boy and a girl. Their father must have been Amavet, for the baby girl was a carrier. She was named Muriel.'

'Muriel the Impure?' Sheala de Tancarville asked in astonishment.

'She became that much later.' Francesca smiled. 'At first she was Muriel the Delightful. Indeed, she was a sweet, charming child. When she was fourteen they were already calling her Doe-Eyed Muriel. Many men drowned in those eyes. She was finally given in marriage to Robert, Count of Garramone.'

'And the boy?'

'Crispin. He wasn't a carrier, so he was of no interest to us. If my memory serves, he fell in combat somewhere, for his passion was warfare.'

'Just a moment,' Sabrina said, ruffling her hair vigorously. 'Wasn't Muriel the Impure the mother of Adalia the Seer?'

'Indeed,' Francesca confirmed. 'An interesting one, was Adalia. A powerful Source, excellent material for a sorceress. But she didn't want to be one, unfortunately. She preferred to be a queen.'

'And the gene?' Assire var Anahid asked. 'Did she bear it?'

'Interestingly not.'

'As I thought,' Assire said, nodding. 'Lara's gene can only be passed on inviolately down the female line. If the carrier is a man, the gene disappears in the second, or – at most – the third generation.'

'But wait—'

'It activates later, however,' Philippa Eilhart broke in. 'After all, Adalia, who didn't have the gene, was Calanthe's mother, and Calanthe, Ciri's grandmother, carried the Lara gene.'

'She was the first carrier after Riannon,' Sheala de Tancarville said, suddenly joining the discussion. 'You made a mistake, Francesca. There were two genes. One, the true gene, was latent, quiescent.

You were beguiled by Amavet's powerful, distinct gene. However, what Amavet had wasn't a gene, but an activator. Mistress Assire is right. The activator travelling down the male line was so faint in Adalia you didn't identify it at all. Adalia was Muriel's first child; her later-born definitely didn't have even a trace of the activator. Fiona's latent gene would probably also have vanished in her male descendants at most in the third generation. But it didn't, and I know why.'

'Bloody hell,' Yennefer hissed through her teeth.

'I'm lost,' Sabrina Glevissig declared. 'In this tangle of genetics and genealogy.'

Francesca drew a fruit bowl towards herself, held out a hand and murmured a spell.

'I apologise for this vulgar display of psychokinesis,' she said with a smile, making a red apple rise high above the table. 'But the fruit will help me demonstrate your mistake. Red apples are the Lara gene, the Elder Blood. Green apples represent the latent gene. Pomegranates are the pseudo-gene, the activator. Let us begin. This is Riannon, the red apple. Her son, Amavet, is the pomegranate. Amavet's daughter, Muriel, and his granddaughter, Adalia, are still pomegranates, the last of which is very faint. And here is Fiona's line, Riannon's daughter: a green apple. Her son, Corbett, the King of Cintra, is green. Dagorad, Corbett and Elen of Kaedwen's son, is green too. As you have observed, in two successive generations there are exclusively male descendants. The gene is very weak, and vanishes. So at the very bottom, here, we finish with a pomegranate and a green apple; Adalia, the Princess of Maribor, and Dagorad, the King of Cintra. And the couple's daughter was Calanthe. A red apple. The revived, powerful Lara gene.'

'Fiona's latent gene' – Margarita Laux-Antille nodded – 'met Amavet's activator gene through marital incest. Did no one notice their kinship? Did none of the royal heraldists or chroniclers pay any attention to this blatant incest?'

'It wasn't as blatant as it seems. After all, Anna Kameny didn't advertise that her twins were bastards, because her husband's family would have deprived her and her children of their coat of arms, titles and fortune. Of course there were persistent rumours, and not just among the peasantry. That's why they had to search for a husband for Calanthe, who was contaminated by incest, in distant Ebbing, beyond the rumours' reach.'

'Add two more red apples to your pyramid, Enid,' Margarita said. 'Now, as Mistress Assire has astutely indicated, we can see the reborn Lara gene moving smoothly down the female line.'

'Yes. Here is Pavetta, Calanthe's daughter. And Pavetta's daughter, Cirilla, the sole inheritor of the Elder Blood, carrier of the Lara gene.'

'The sole inheritor?' Sheala de Tancarville asked abruptly. 'You're very confident, Enid.'

'What do you mean by that?'

Sheala suddenly stood up, snapped her beringed fingers towards the fruit bowl and made the remaining fruit levitate, disrupting Francesca's model and transforming it into a multi-coloured confusion.

'This is what I mean,' she said coldly, pointing at the jumble of fruit. 'Here we have all of the possible genetic combinations and permutations. And we know as much as we can see here. Namely nothing. Your mistake backfired, Francesca, and it caused an avalanche of errors. The gene only reappeared by accident after a century, during which time we have no idea what may have occurred. Secret, hidden, hushed-up events. Premarital children, extramarital children, adoptive children – even changelings. Incest. The cross-breeding of races, the blood of forgotten ancestors returning in later generations. In short: a hundred years ago you had the gene within arm's reach, even in your hands. And it gave you the slip. That was a mistake, Enid, a terrible mistake! Too much confusion, too many accidents. Too little control, too little interference in the randomness of it all.'

'We weren't dealing,' Enid an Gleanna said through pursed lips, 'with rabbits, which we could pair off and put in a hutch.'

Fringilla, following Triss Merigold's gaze, noticed Yennefer's hands suddenly clenching her chair's carved armrests.

*

So this is what Yennefer and Francesca have in common, Triss thought feverishly, still avoiding her close friend's gaze. *Cynical duplicity. For, after all, pairing off and breeding turned out to be unavoidable. Indeed, their plans for Ciri and the Prince of Kovir, although apparently improbable, are actually quite realistic. They've done it before. They've placed whoever they wanted on thrones, created the marriages and dynasties they desired and which were convenient for them. Spells, aphrodisiacs and elixirs were all used. Queens and princesses suddenly entered bizarre – often morganatic – marriages, contrary to all plans, intentions and agreements. And later those who wanted children, but ought not to have them, were secretly given contraceptive agents. Those who didn't want children, but ought to have them, were given placebos of liquorice water instead of the promised agents. Which resulted in all of those improbable connections: Calanthe, Pavetta . . . and now Ciri. Yennefer was involved in this. And now she regrets it. She's right to. Damn it, were Geralt to find out . . .*

Sphinxes, Fringilla Vigo thought. *The sphinxes carved on the chairs' armrests. Yes, they ought to be the lodge's emblem. Wise, mysterious, silent. They are all sphinxes. They will easily achieve what they want. It's a trifle for them to marry Kovir off to that Ciri of theirs. They have the power to. They have the expertise. And the means. The diamond necklace around Sabrina Glevissig's neck is probably worth almost as much as the entire income of forested, rocky Kaedwen. They could easily carry out their plans. But there is one snag . . .*

Aha, Triss Merigold thought, *at last we've reached the topic we should have started with: the sobering and discouraging fact that Ciri is in Nilfgaard, in Emhyr's clutches. Far away from the plans being hatched here . . .*

'There is no question that Emhyr had been hunting for Cirilla for many years,' Philippa continued. 'Everyone assumed his goal was a political union with Cintra and control of the fiefdom which is her legal heritage. However, one cannot rule out that rather than politics it concerns the gene of the Elder Blood, which Emhyr wants to introduce to the imperial line. If Emhyr knows what we do, he may want

272

the prophecy to manifest itself in his dynasty, and the future Queen of the World to be born in Nilfgaard.'

'A correction,' Sabrina Glevissig interrupted. 'It's not Emhyr who wants it, but the Nilfgaardian sorcerers. They alone were capable of tracking down the gene and making Emhyr aware of its significance. I'm sure the Nilfgaardian ladies here present will want to confirm that and explain their role in the intrigue.'

'I am astonished,' Fringilla burst out, 'by your tendency to search for the threads of intrigue in distant Nilfgaard, while the evidence requires us to search for conspirators and traitors much closer to you.'

'An observation as blunt as it is apt,' Sheala de Tancarville said, silencing with a glance Sabrina, who was preparing a riposte. 'All the evidence suggests that the facts about the Elder Blood were leaked to Nilfgaard from us. Is it possible you've forgotten about Vilgefortz, ladies?'

'Not I,' Sabrina said, a flame of hatred flaring in her black eyes for a second. 'I have not forgotten!'

'All in good time,' Keira Metz said, flashing her teeth malevolently. 'But for the moment it's not about him, but about the fact that Emhyr var Emreis, Imperator of Nilfgaard, has Ciri – and thus the Elder Blood that is so important to us – in his grasp.'

'The Imperator,' Assire declared calmly, glancing at Fringilla, 'doesn't have anything in his grasp. The girl being held in Darn Rowan is not the carrier of any extraordinary gene. She's ordinary to the point of commonness. Beyond a shadow of doubt she is not Ciri of Cintra. She is not the girl the Imperator was seeking. For he was clearly seeking a girl who carries the gene; he even had some of her hair. I examined it and found something I didn't understand; now I do.'

'So Ciri isn't in Nilfgaard,' Yennefer said softly. 'She's not there.'

'She's not there,' Philippa Eilhart repeated gravely. 'Emhyr was tricked; a double was planted on him. I've known as much since yesterday. However, I'm pleased by Mistress Assire's disclosure. It confirms that our lodge is now functioning.'

Yennefer had great difficulty controlling the trembling of her hands and mouth. *Keep calm*, she told herself. *Keep calm; don't reveal anything; wait for an opportunity. Keep listening. Collect information. A sphinx. Be a sphinx.*

'So it was Vilgefortz,' Sabrina said, slamming her fist down on the table. 'Not Emhyr, but Vilgefortz. That charmer, that handsome scoundrel! He duped Emhyr and us!'

Yennefer calmed herself by breathing deeply. Assire var Anahid, the Nilfgaardian sorceress, feeling understandably uncomfortable in her tight-fitting dress, was talking about a young Nilfgaardian nobleman. Yennefer knew who it was and involuntarily clenched her fists. A black knight in a winged helmet, the nightmare from Ciri's hallucinations . . . She sensed Francesca and Philippa's eyes on her. However, Triss – whose gaze she was trying to attract – was avoiding her eyes. *Bloody hell*, Yennefer thought, trying hard to remain impassive, *I've landed myself in it. What bloody predicament have I tangled the girl up in? Shit, how will I ever be able to look the Witcher in the eye . . . ?*

'Thus, we'll have a perfect opportunity,' Keira Metz called in an excited voice, 'to rescue Ciri and strike at Vilgefortz at the same time. We'll scorch the ground beneath the rascal's arse!'

'Any scorching of ground must be preceded by the discovery of Vilgefortz's whereabouts,' Sheala de Tancarville, the sorceress from Kovir whom Yennefer had never felt much affection for, said mockingly. 'And no one's managed it so far. Not even some of the ladies sitting at this table, who have devoted both their time and their extraordinary abilities to looking for it.'

'Two of Vilgefortz's numerous hideouts have already been found,' Philippa Eilhart responded coldly. 'Dijkstra is searching intensively for the remaining ones, and I wouldn't write him off. Sometimes spies and informers succeed where magic fails.'

One of the agents accompanying Dijkstra looked into the dungeon, stepped back sharply, leant against the wall and went as white as a sheet, looking as though he would faint at any moment. Dijkstra made a mental note to transfer the milksop to office work. But when he looked into the cell himself, he changed his mind. He felt his bile rising. He couldn't embarrass himself in front of his subordinates, however. He unhurriedly removed a perfumed handkerchief from his pocket, held it against his nose and mouth, and leant over the naked corpse lying on the stone floor.

'Belly and womb cut open,' he diagnosed, struggling to maintain his calm and a cold tone. 'Very skilfully, as if by a surgeon's hand. The foetus was removed from the girl. She was alive when they did it, but it was not done here. Are all of them like that? Lennep, I'm talking to you.'

'No . . .' the agent said with a shudder, tearing his eyes away from the corpse. 'The others had been garrotted. They weren't pregnant . . . But we shall perform post-mortems . . .'

'How many were found, in total?'

'Apart from this one, four. We haven't managed to identify any of them.'

'That's not true,' Dijkstra countered from behind his handkerchief. 'I've already managed to identify this one. It's Jolie, the youngest daughter of Count Lanier. The girl who disappeared without a trace a year ago. I'll take a glance at the other ones.'

'Some of them are partially burnt,' Lennep said. 'They will be difficult to identify . . . But, sire, apart from this . . . we found . . .'

'Speak. Don't stammer.'

'There are bones in that well,' the agent said, pointing at a hole gaping in the floor. 'A large quantity of bones. We have not removed or examined them, but we can be sure they all belonged to young women. Were we to ask sorcerers for aid we might be able to identify them . . . and inform those parents who are still looking for their missing daughters . . .'

'Under no circumstances,' Dijkstra said, swinging around. 'Not a word about what's been found here. To anyone. Particularly not to any mages. I'm beginning to lose faith in them after what I've seen here. Lennep, have the upper levels been thoroughly searched? Has nothing been found that might help us in our quest?'

'Nothing, sire,' Lennep said and lowered his head. 'As soon as we received word, we rushed to the castle. But we arrived too late. Everything had burnt down. Consumed by a fearful conflagration.

'Magical, without any doubt. Only here, in the dungeons, did the spell not destroy everything. I don't know why . . .'

'But I do. The fuse wasn't lit by Vilgefortz, but by Rience or another of the sorcerer's factotums. Vilgefortz wouldn't have made such a mistake, he wouldn't have left anything but the soot on the walls. Oh yes, he knows that fire purifies . . . and covers tracks.'

'Indeed it does,' Lennep muttered. 'There isn't even any evidence that Vilgefortz was here at all . . .'

'Then fabricate some,' Dijkstra said, removing the handkerchief from his face. 'Must I teach you how it's done? I know that Vilgefortz was here. Did anything else survive in the dungeons apart from the corpses? What's behind that iron door?'

'Step this way, sire,' the agent said, taking a torch from one of the assistants. 'I will show you.'

There was no doubt that the magical spark which had been meant to turn everything in the dungeon to ashes had been placed right there, in the spacious chamber behind the iron door. An error in the spell had largely thwarted the plan, but the fire had still been power-ful and fierce. The flames had charred the shelves occupying one of the walls, destroyed and fused the glass vessels, turning everything into a stinking mass. The only thing left unaffected in the chamber was a table with a metal top and two curious chairs set into the floor. Curious, but leaving no doubt as to their function.

'They are constructed,' Lennep said swallowing, and pointing at the chairs and the clasps attached to them, 'so as to hold . . . the legs . . . apart. Wide apart.'

'Bastard,' Dijkstra snapped through clenched teeth. 'Damned bastard . . .'

'We found traces of blood, faeces and urine in the gutter beneath the wooden chair,' the agent continued softly. 'The steel one is brand new, most probably unused. I don't know what to make of it . . .'

'I do,' Dijkstra said. 'The steel one was constructed for somebody special. Someone that Vilgefortz suspected of special abilities.'

*

276

'In no way do I disregard Dijkstra or his secret service,' Sheala de Tancarville said. 'I know that finding Vilgefortz is only a matter of time. However, passing over the motif of personal vengeance which seems to fascinate some of you, I'll take the liberty of observing that it is not at all certain that Vilgefortz has Ciri.'

'If it's not Vilgefortz, then who? She was on the island. None of us, as far as I know, teleported her away from there. Neither Dijkstra nor any of the kings have her, we know that for sure. And her body wasn't found in the ruins of the Tower of Gulls.'

'Tor Lara,' Ida Emean said slowly, 'once concealed a very powerful teleportal. Could the girl have escaped Thanedd through that portal?'

Yennefer veiled her eyes with her eyelashes and dug her nails into the heads of the sphinxes on the chair's armrests. *Keep calm*, she thought. *Just keep calm.* She felt Margarita's eyes on her, but did not raise her head.

'If Ciri entered the teleportal in the Tower of Gulls,' the rectoress of Aretuza said in a slightly altered voice, 'I fear we can forget our plans and projects. We may never see Ciri again. The now-destroyed portal of Tor Lara was damaged. It's warped. Lethal.'

'What are we talking about here?' Sabrina exploded. 'In order to uncover the teleportal in the tower, in order to see it at all, would require fourth-level magic! And the abilities of a grandmaster would be necessary to activate the portal! I don't know if Vilgefortz is capable of that, never mind a fifteen-year-old filly. How can you even imagine something like that? Who is this girl, in your opinion? What potential does she hold?'

'Is it so important,' Stephan Skellen, also called Tawny Owl, the Coroner of Imperator Emhyr var Emreis said, stretching, 'what potential she holds, Master Bonhart? Or even if any? I'd rather she wasn't around at all. And I'm paying you a hundred florins to make my wish come true. If you want, examine her – after killing her or before, up to you. Either way the fee won't change, I give you my solemn word.'

'And were I to supply her alive?'

'It still won't.'

The man called Bonhart twisted his grey whiskers. He was of immense height, but as bony as a skeleton. His other hand rested on his sword the entire time, as though he wanted to hide the ornate pommel of the hilt from Skellen's eyes.

'Am I to bring you her head?'

'No,' Tawny Owl said, wincing. 'Why would I want her head? To preserve in honey?'

'As proof.'

'I'll take you at your word. You are well known for your reliability, Bonhart.'

'Thank you for the recognition,' the bounty hunter said, and smiled. At the sight of his smile, Skellen, who had twenty armed men waiting outside the tavern, felt a shiver running down his spine. 'Rarely received, although well deserved. I have to bring the barons and the lords Varnhagens the heads of all the Rats I catch or they won't pay. If you have no need of Falka's head, you won't, I imagine, have anything against my adding it to the set.'

'To claim the other reward? What about your professional ethics?'

'Honoured sir,' Bonhart said, narrowing his eyes, 'I am not paid for killing, but for the service I render by killing. A service I'll be rendering both you and the Varnhagens.'

'Fair enough,' Tawny Owl agreed. 'Do whatever you think's right. When can I expect you to collect the bounty money?'

'Soon.'

'Meaning?'

'The Rats are heading for the Bandit's Trail, with plans to winter in the mountains. I'll cut off their route. Twenty days, no more.'

'Are you certain of the route they're taking?'

'They've been seen near Fen Aspra, where they robbed a convoy and two merchants. They've been prowling near Tyffi. Then they stopped off at Druigh for one night, to dance at a village fair. They finally ended up in Loredo, where your Falka hacked a fellow to pieces, in such a fashion that they're still talking about it through chattering teeth. Which is why I asked what there is to this Falka.'

'Perhaps you and she are very much alike,' Stephan Skellen

mocked. 'But no, forgive me. After all, you don't take money for killing, but for services rendered. You're a true craftsman, Bonhart, a genuine professional. A trade, like any other? A job to be done? They pay for it, and everyone has to make a living? Eh?'

The bounty hunter looked at him long and hard. Until Tawny Owl's smirk finally vanished.

'Indeed,' he said. 'Everyone has to make a living. Some earn money doing what they've learned. Others do what they have to. But not many craftsmen have been as lucky in life as I am: they pay me for a trade I truly and honestly enjoy. Not even whores can say that.'

Yennefer welcomed Philippa's suggestion of a break for a bite to eat and to moisten throats dried out by speaking with relief, delight and hope. It soon turned out, however, that her hopes were in vain. Philippa quickly dragged away Margarita – who clearly wanted to talk to Yennefer – to the other end of the room, and Triss Merigold, who had drawn closer to her, was accompanied by Francesca. The she-elf unceremoniously controlled the conversation. Yennefer saw anxiety in Triss's cornflower-blue eyes, however, and was certain that even without witnesses it would have been futile to ask for help. Triss was undoubtedly already committed, heart and soul, to the lodge. And doubtlessly sensed that Yennefer's loyalty was still wavering.

Triss tried to cheer her up by assuring her that Geralt, safe in Brokilon, was returning to health thanks to the dryads' efforts. As usual, she blushed at the mention of his name. *He must have pleased her back then*, Yennefer thought, not without malice. *She had never known anyone like him before and she won't forget him in a hurry. And a good thing too.*

She dismissed the revelations with an apparently indifferent shrug of her shoulders. She wasn't concerned by the fact that neither Triss nor Francesca believed her indifference. She wanted to be alone, and wanted them to see that.

They did just that.

She stood at the far end of the food table, devoting herself to oysters. She ate cautiously, still in pain from her compression. She was reluctant to drink wine, not knowing how she might react.

'Yennefer?'

She turned around. Fringilla Vigo smiled faintly, looking down at the short knife Yennefer was gripping tightly.

'I can see and sense,' she said, 'that you'd rather prise me open than that oyster. Still no love lost?'

'The lodge,' Yennefer replied coolly, 'demands mutual loyalty. Friendship is not compulsory.'

'It isn't and shouldn't be,' the Nilfgaardian sorceress said, and looked around the chamber. 'Friendship is either the result of a lengthy process or is spontaneous.'

'The same goes for enmity,' Yennefer said, opening the oyster and swallowing the contents along with some seawater. 'Occasionally one happens to see another person for only a split second, right before going blind, and one takes a dislike to them instantly.'

'Oh, enmity is considerably more complicated,' Fringilla said, squinting. 'Imagine someone you don't know at all standing at the top of a hill, and ripping a friend of yours to shreds in front of your eyes. You neither saw them nor know them at all, but you still don't like them.'

'So it goes,' Yennefer said, shrugging. 'Fate has a way of playing tricks on you.'

'Fate,' Fringilla said quietly, 'is unpredictable indeed, like a mischievous child. Friends sometimes turn their backs on us, while an enemy comes in useful. You can, for example, talk to them face to face. No one tries to interfere, no one interrupts or eavesdrops. Everyone wonders what the two enemies could possibly be talking about. About nothing important. Why, they're mouthing platitudes and twisting the occasional barb.'

'No doubt,' Yennefer said, nodding, 'that's what everyone thinks. And they're absolutely right.'

'Which means it'll be even easier,' Fringilla said, quite relaxed, 'to bring up a particularly important and remarkable matter.'

'What matter would that be?'

'That of the escape attempt you're planning.'

Yennefer, who was opening another oyster, almost cut her finger. She looked around furtively, and then glanced at the Nilfgaardian from under her eyelashes. Fringilla Vigo smiled slightly.

'Be so kind as to lend me the knife. To open an oyster. Your oysters are excellent. It's not easy for us to get such good ones in the south. Particularly not now, during the wartime blockade . . . A blockade is a very bad thing, isn't it?'

Yennefer gave a slight cough.

'I've noticed,' Fringilla said, swallowing the oyster and reaching for another. 'Yes, Philippa's looking at us. Assire too, probably worrying about my loyalty to the lodge. My endangered loyalty. She's liable to think I'll yield to sympathy. Let us see . . . Your sweetheart was seriously injured. The girl you treat as a daughter has disappeared, is possibly being imprisoned . . . perhaps her life's in danger. Or perhaps she'll just be played as a card in a rigged game? I swear, I couldn't stand it. I'd flee at once. Please, take the knife back. That's enough oysters, I have to watch my figure.'

'A blockade, as you have deigned to observe,' Yennefer whispered, looking into the Nilfgaardian sorceress's eyes, 'is a very bad thing. Simply beastly. It doesn't allow one to do what one wants. But a blockade can be overcome, if one has . . . the means. Which I don't.'

'Do you expect me to give the means to you?' the Nilfgaardian asked, examining the rough shell of the oyster, which she was still holding. 'Oh no, not a chance. I'm loyal to the lodge, and the lodge, naturally, doesn't wish you to hurry to the aid of your loved ones. Furthermore, I'm your enemy. How could you forget that, Yennefer?'

'Indeed. How could I?'

'I would warn a friend,' Fringilla said quietly, 'that even if she were in possession of the components for teleportation spells, she wouldn't be able to break the blockade undetected. An operation of that kind demands time and is too conspicuous. An unobtrusive but energetic attractor is a little better. I repeat: a *little* better. Teleportation using an improvised attractor, as you are no doubt aware, is very risky. I would try to dissuade a friend from taking such a risk. But you aren't a friend.'

Fringilla spilt a sprinkling of seawater from the shell she was holding onto the table.

281

'And on that note, we'll end our banal conversation,' she said. 'The lodge demands mutual loyalty from us. Friendship, fortunately, isn't compulsory.'

'She teleported,' Francesca Findabair stated coldly and unemotionally, when the confusion caused by Yennefer's disappearance had calmed down. 'There's nothing to get het up about, ladies. And there's nothing we can do about it now. She's too far away. It's my mistake. I suspected her obsidian star masked the echo of spells—'

'How did she bloody do it?' Philippa yelled. 'She could muffle an echo, that isn't difficult. But how did she manage to open the portal? Montecalvo has a blockade!'

'I've never liked her,' Sheala de Tancarville said, shrugging her shoulders. 'I've never approved of her lifestyle. But I've never questioned her abilities.'

'She'll tell them everything!' Sabrina Glevissig yelled. 'Everything about the lodge! She'll fly straight to—'

'Nonsense,' Triss Merigold interrupted animatedly, looking at Francesca and Ida Emean. 'Yennefer won't betray us. She didn't escape to betray us.'

'Triss is right,' Margarita Laux-Antille added, backing her up. 'I know why she escaped and who she wants to rescue. I've seen them, she and Ciri, together. And I understand.'

'But I don't understand any of this!' Sabrina yelled and everything became heated again.

Assire var Anahid leant towards her friend.

'I won't ask why you did it,' she whispered. 'I won't ask how you did it. I'll only ask: where is she headed?'

Fringilla Vigo smiled faintly, stroking the carved head of the sphinx on the chair's armrest with her fingers.

'And how could I possibly know,' she whispered back, 'which coast these oysters came from?'

***Ithlina**, actually Ithlinne Aegli: daughter of Aevenien, the legendary elven healer, astrologist and soothsayer, famous for her predictions and prophecies, of which Aen Ithlinnespeath, Ithlina's Prophecy, is the best known. It has been written down many times and published in numerous forms. The Prophecy enjoyed great popularity at certain moments, and the commentaries, clues and clarifications appended to it adapted the text to contemporary events, which strengthened convictions about its great clairvoyance. In particular it is believed **I.** predicted the Northern Wars (1239– 1268), the Great Plagues (1268, 1272 and 1294), the bloody War of the Two Unicorns (1309–1318) and the Haak Invasion (1350). **I.** was also supposed to have prophesied the climatic changes observed from the end of the thirteenth century, known as the Great Frost, which superstition always claimed was a sign of the end of the world and linked to the prophesied coming of the Destroyer (q.v.). This passage from **I.**'s Prophecy gave rise to the infamous witch hunts (1272–76) and contributed to the deaths of many women and unfortunate girls mistaken for the incarnation of the Destroyer. Today **I.** is regarded by many scholars as a legendary figure and her 'prophecies' as very recently fabricated apocrypha, and a cunning literary fraud.*

Effenberg and Talbot,
Encyclopaedia Maxima Mundi, Volume X

CHAPTER SEVEN

The children gathered in a ring around the wandering storyteller Stribog showed their disapproval by making a dreadful, riotous uproar. Finally Connor, the blacksmith's son, the oldest, strongest and bravest of the children, and also the one who brought the storyteller a pot full of cabbage soup and potatoes sprinkled with scraps of fried bacon, stepped forward as the spokesman and exponent of the general opinion.

'How's that?' he yelled. 'What do you mean "that's your lot"? Is it fair to end the tale there? To leave us hungry for more? We want to know what happened next! We can't wait till you visit our village again, for it might be in six months or a whole year! Go on with the story!'

'The sun's gone down,' the old man replied. 'It's time for bed, young 'uns. When you start to yawn and grumble over your chores tomorrow, what will your parents say? I know what they'll say: "Old Stribog was telling them tales till past midnight, wearying the children's heads with songs, and didn't let them get to bed. So when he wends his way to the village again, don't give him nothing; no kasha, no dumplings, no bacon. Just drive him off, the old gimmer, because nothing comes from his tales but woe and trouble—"'

'They won't say that!' the children all shouted. 'Tell us more! Pleeease!'

'Mmm,' the old man mumbled, looking at the sun disappearing behind the treetops on the far bank of the Yaruga. 'Very well then. But here's the bargain: one of you's to hurry over to the cottage and fetch some buttermilk for me to moisten my throat. The rest of you, meanwhile, are to decide whose story I'll tell, for I shan't tell everyone's tale today, even were I to spin yarns till morning. You have to decide: who do I tell of now, and who another time.'

The children began to yell again, each trying to outshout the others.

'Silence!' Stribog roared, brandishing his stick. 'I told you to choose, not shriek like jays: skaak-skaak-skaak! What'll it be? Whose story shall I tell?'

'Yennefer's,' Nimue squeaked. She was the youngest in the audience, nicknamed 'Squirt' owing to her height, and was stroking a kitten that was asleep on her lap. 'Tell us what happened to the sorceress afterwards. How she used magic to flee from the cov-cov-coven on Bald Mountain to rescue Ciri. I'd love to hear that. I want to be a sorceress when I grow up!'

'No chance!' shouted Bronik, the miller's son. 'Wipe your nose first, Squirt. They don't take snot-noses for sorcerers' apprentices! And you, old man, don't talk about Yennefer, but about Ciri and the Rats, when they went a-robbing and beat up—'

'Quiet,' Connor said, glum and pensive. 'You're all stupid, and that's that. If we're to hear one thing more tonight, let there be some order. Tell us about the Witcher and his band, when the company set off from the Yaruga—'

'I want to hear about Yennefer,' Nimue squealed.

'Me too,' Orla, her elder sister, joined in. 'I want to hear about her love for the Witcher. How they doted on each other. But be sure it's a happy ending! Nowt about fighting, oh no!'

'Quiet, you silly thing, who cares about love? We want war and fighting!'

'And the Witcher's sword!'

'No, Ciri and the Rats!'

'Shut your traps,' Connor said and looked around fiercely. 'Or I'll get a stick and give you a thrashing, you little snots! I said: let there be some order. Let him carry on about the Witcher, when he was travelling with Dandelion and Milva—'

'Yes!' Nimue squealed again. 'I want to hear about Milva, about Milva! Because if the sorceresses don't take me, I'm going to be an archer!'

'So we've decided,' Connor said. 'Look at him nodding, nose dipping like a corncrake's . . . Hey, old man! Wake up! Tell us about

286

the Witcher, about Geralt the Witcher, I mean. When he formed his fellowship on the bank of the Yaruga.'

'But first,' Bronik interrupted, 'to salve our curiosity, tell us a little about the others. About what happened to them. Then it'll be easier for us to wait till you come back and continue the story. Just a little about Yennefer and Ciri. Please.'

'Yennefer' – Stribog giggled – 'flew from the enchanted castle, which was called Bald Mountain, using a spell. And she plopped straight into the ocean. Into the rough seas, among cruel rocks. But don't be afeared, it was a trifle for the enchantress. She didn't drown. She landed up on the Skellige Islands and found allies there. For you must know that a great fury arose in her against the Wizard Vilgefortz. Convinced he had kidnapped Ciri, she vowed to track him down, exact a terrible vengeance and free Ciri. And that's that. I'll tell you more another time.'

'And Ciri?'

'Ciri was still prowling with the Rats, calling herself "Falka". She had gained a taste for the robbers' life. For though no one knew it then, there was fury and cruelty in that girl. The worst of everything that hides in a person emerged from her and slowly got the upper hand. Oh, the witchers of Kaer Morhen made a great mistake by teaching her how to kill! And Ciri herself – dealing out death – didn't even suspect that the Grim Reaper was hot on her trail. For the terrible Bonhart was tracking her, hunting her. The meeting of these two, Bonhart and Ciri, was meant to be. But I shall recount their tale another time. For tonight you shall hear the tale of the Witcher.'

The children calmed down and crowded around the old man in a tight circle. They listened. Night was falling. The hemp shrubs, the raspberry bushes and hollyhocks growing near the cottage – friendly during the day – were suddenly transformed into an extraordinary, sinister forest. What was rustling there? Was it a mouse, or a terrible, fiery-eyed elf? Or perhaps a striga or a witch, hungry for children's flesh? Was it an ox stamping in the cowshed, or the hooves of cruel invaders' warhorses, crossing the Yaruga as they had a century before? Was that a nightjar flitting above the thatched roof, or perhaps a vampire, thirsty for blood? Or perhaps a beautiful sorceress, flying towards the distant sea with the aid of a magic spell?

'Geralt the Witcher,' the storyteller began, 'set out with his company towards the bogs and forests of Angren. And you must know that in those days there were truly wild forests in Angren, oh my, not like now, there aren't any forests like that left, unless in Brokilon . . . The company trekked eastwards, up the Yaruga, towards the wildernesses of the Black Forest. Things went well at first, but later, oh my . . . you'll learn what happened later . . .'

The tale of long-past, forgotten times unravelled and flowed. And the children listened.

The Witcher sat on a log at the top of a cliff from which unfolded a view over the wetlands and reed beds lining the bank of the Yaruga. The sun was sinking. Cranes soared up from the marshes, whooping, flying in a skein.

Everything's gone to pot, the Witcher thought, looking at the ruins of a woodman's shack and the thin ribbon of smoke rising from Milva's campfire. *Everything's fallen through. And it was going so well. My companions were strange, but at least they stood by me. We had a goal to achieve; close at hand, realistic, defined. Eastwards through Angren, towards Caed Dhu. It was going pretty well. But it had to get fucked up. Was it bad luck, or fate?*

The cranes sounded their bugle call.

Emiel Regis Rohellec Terzieff-Godefroy led the way, riding a Nilfgaardian bay captured by the Witcher near Armeria. The horse, although at first somewhat tetchy with the vampire and his herby smell, quickly became accustomed to him and didn't cause any more problems than Roach, who was walking alongside and was capable of bucking wildly if stung by a horsefly. Dandelion followed behind Regis and Geralt on Pegasus, with a bandaged head and a warlike mien. As he rode, the poet composed a heroic ballad, in whose melody and rhymes could be heard his recollections of their recent adventures. The song clearly implied that the author and performer had been the bravest of the brave during the adventures. Milva and Cahir Mawr Dyffryn aep Ceallach brought up the rear. Cahir was riding his recovered chestnut, pulling the grey laden with some of their modest accoutrement.

They finally left the riverside marshes, heading towards higher and drier, hilly terrain from which they could see the sparkling ribbon of the Great Yaruga to the south, and to the north the high, rocky approaches to the distant Mahakam massif. The weather was splendid, the sun was warm, and the mosquitoes had stopped biting and buzzing around their ears. Their boots and trousers had dried out. On the sunny slope brambles were black with fruit and the horses found grass to eat. The streams tumbling down from the hills flowed with crystal-clear water and were full of trout. When night fell, they were able to make a fire and even lie beside it. In short, everything was wonderful and their moods ought to have improved right away. But they didn't. The reason why became apparent at one of the first camps.

'Wait a moment, Geralt,' the poet began, looking around and clearing his throat. 'Don't rush back to the camp. Milva and I would like to talk to you in private. It's about . . . you know . . . Regis.'

'Ah,' the Witcher said, laying a handful of brushwood on the ground. 'So now you're afraid? It's a bit late for that.'

'Stop that,' Dandelion said with a grimace. 'We've accepted him as a companion; he's offered to help us search for Ciri. He saved my neck from the noose, which I shall never forget. But hell's bells, we are feeling something like fear. Does that surprise you? You've spent your entire life hunting and killing his like.'

'I did not kill him. And I'm not planning to. Does that declaration suffice? If it doesn't, even though my heart's brimming with sorrow for you, I can't cure you of your anxieties. Paradoxically, Regis is the only one among us capable of curing anything.'

'Stop that,' the troubadour repeated, annoyed. 'You aren't talking to Yennefer; you can drop the tortuous eloquence. Give us a simple answer to a simple question.'

'Then ask it. Without any tortuous eloquence.'

'Regis is a vampire. It's no secret what vampires feed on. What will happen when he gets seriously hungry? Yes, yes, we saw him eating fish soup, and since then he's been eating and drinking with us, as normal as anyone. But . . . will he be able to control his craving . . . Geralt, do I have to spell it out to you?'

'He controlled his blood lust, when gore was pouring from your head. He didn't even lick his fingers after he'd finished applying the dressing. And during the full moon, when we'd been drinking his mandrake moonshine and were sleeping in his shack, he had the perfect opportunity to get his hands on us. Have you checked for puncture marks on your swanlike neck?'

'Don't take the piss, Witcher,' Milva growled. 'You know more about vampires than we do. You're mocking Dandelion, so tell me. I was raised in the forest, I didn't go to school. I'm ignorant. But it's no fault of mine. It's not right to mock. I – I'm ashamed to say – am also a bit afraid of . . . Regis.'

'Not unreasonably,' Geralt said, nodding. 'He's a so-called higher vampire. He's extremely dangerous. Were he our enemy, I'd be afraid of him too. But, bloody hell, for reasons unknown to me, he's our companion. Right now, he's leading us to Caed Dhu, to the druids, who may be able to help me get information about Ciri. I'm desperate, so I want to seize the chance and certainly not give up on it. Which is why I've agreed to his vampiric company.'

'Only because of that?'

'No,' he answered, with a trace of reluctance. Then he finally decided to be frank. 'Not just that. He . . . he behaves decently. He didn't hesitate to act during that girl's trial at the camp by the Chotla. Although he knew it would unmask him.'

'He took that red-hot horseshoe from the fire,' Dandelion recalled. 'Why, he held it in his hand for a good few seconds without even flinching. None of us would be able to repeat that trick; not even with a roast potato.'

'He's invulnerable to fire.'

'What else is he capable of?'

'He can become invisible if he wishes. He can bewitch with his gaze, and put someone in a deep sleep. He did that to the guards in Vissegerd's camp. He can assume the form of a bat and fly. I presume he can only do those things at night, during a full moon, but I could be wrong. He's already surprised me a few times, so he might still have something up his sleeve. I suspect he's quite remarkable even among vampires. He imitates humans perfectly, and has done so for years. He baffles horses and dogs – which can sense his true nature – using the smell of the herbs he keeps with him at all times. Though my medallion doesn't react to him either, and it ought to. I tell you; he defies easy classification. Talk to him if you want to know more. He's our companion. There should be nothing left unsaid between us, particularly not mutual mistrust or fear. Let's get back to the camp. Help me with this brushwood.'

'Geralt?'

'Yes, Dandelion.'

'If . . . and I'm asking purely theoretically . . . If . . .'

'I don't know,' the Witcher replied honestly and frankly. 'I don't know if I'd be capable of killing him. I truly would prefer not to be forced to try.'

Dandelion took the Witcher's advice to heart, deciding to clear up the uncertainty and dispel their doubts. He began as soon as they set off. With his usual tact.

'Milva!' he suddenly called as they were riding, sneaking a glance at the vampire. 'Why don't you ride on ahead with your bow, and bring down a fawn or wild boar. I've had enough of damned black-berries and mushrooms, fish and mussels. I fancy eating a hunk of real meat for a change. How about you, Regis?'

'I beg your pardon?' the vampire said, lifting his head from the horse's neck.

'Meat!' the poet repeated emphatically. 'I'm trying to persuade Milva to go hunting. Fancy some fresh meat?'

'Yes, I do.'

'And blood. Would you like some fresh blood?'

'Blood?' Regis asked, swallowing. 'No. I'll decline the blood. But, if you have a taste for some, feel free.'

Geralt, Milva and Cahir observed an awkward, sepulchral silence.

'I know what this is about, Dandelion,' Regis said slowly. 'And let me reassure you. I'm a vampire, but I don't drink blood.'

The silence became as heavy as lead. But Dandelion wouldn't have been Dandelion if he had remained silent.

'You must have misunderstood me,' he said seemingly light-heartedly. 'I didn't mean . . .'

'I don't drink blood,' Regis interrupted. 'Haven't for many years. I gave it up.'

'What do you mean, gave it up?'

'Just that.'

'I really don't understand . . .'

'Forgive me. It's a personal matter.'

'But . . .'

'Dandelion,' the Witcher burst out, turning around in the saddle. 'Regis just told you to fuck off. He just said it more politely. Be so good as to shut your trap.'

However, the seeds of anxiety and doubts that had been sown now germinated and sprouted. When they stopped for the night, the ambience was still heavy and tense, which even Milva shooting down a plump barnacle goose by the river couldn't relieve. They covered the catch in clay, roasted and ate it, gnawing even the tiniest bones clean. They had sated their hunger, but the anxiety remained. The conversation was awkward despite Dandelion's titanic efforts. The poet's chatter became a monologue, so obviously apparent that even he finally noticed it and stopped talking. Only the sound of the horses crunching their hay disturbed the deathly silence around the campfire.

In spite of the late hour no one seemed to be getting ready for bed. Milva was boiling water in a pot above the fire and straightening the crumpled fletchings of her arrows in the steam. Cahir was repairing a torn boot buckle. Geralt was whittling a piece of wood. And Regis swept his eyes over all of them in turn.

'Very well,' he said at last. 'I see it is inevitable. It would appear I ought to have explained a few things to you long ago . . .'

'No one expects it of you,' Geralt said. He threw the stick he had been lengthily and enthusiastically carving into the fire and looked up. 'I don't need explanations. I'm the old-fashioned type. When I hold my hand out to someone and accept him as a comrade, it means more to me than a contract signed in the presence of a notary.'

'I'm old-fashioned too,' Cahir said, still bent over his boot.

'I don't know any other custom,' Milva said drily, placing another arrow in the steam rising up from the pot.

'Don't worry about Dandelion's chatter,' the Witcher added. 'He can't help it. And you don't have to confide in us or explain anything. We haven't confided in you either.'

'I nonetheless think' – the vampire smiled faintly – 'that you'd like to hear what I have to say, even though no one's forcing you to. I feel the need for openness towards the individuals I extend a hand to and accept as my comrades.'

This time no one said anything.

'I ought to begin by saying,' Regis said a moment later, 'that all fears linked to my vampiric nature are groundless. I won't attack anybody, nor will I creep around at night trying to sink my teeth into somebody's neck. And this does not merely concern my comrades, to whom my relationship is no less old-fashioned than theirs is to me. I don't touch blood. Not at all and never. I stopped drinking it when it became a problem for me. A serious problem, which I had difficulty solving.

'In fact, the problem arose and acquired negative characteristics in true textbook style,' he continued a moment later. 'Even during my youth I enjoyed . . . er . . . the pleasures of good company, in which respect I was no different to the majority of my peers. You know what it's like; you were young too. With humans, however, there exists a system of rules and restrictions: parental authority, guardians, superiors and elders – morals, ultimately. We have nothing like that. Youngsters have complete freedom and exploit it. They create their own patterns of behaviour. Stupid ones, you understand. It's real youthful foolishness. "Don't fancy a drink? And you call yourself a vampire?" "He doesn't drink? Don't invite him, he'll spoil the party!" I didn't want to spoil the party, and the thought of losing social approval terrified me. So I partied. Revelries and frolics, shindigs and booze-ups; every full moon we'd fly to a village and drink from anyone we found. The foulest, the worst class of . . . er . . . fluid. It made no difference to us whose it was, as long as there was . . . er . . . haemoglobin . . . It can't be a party without blood, after all! And I was terribly shy with vampire girls, too, until I'd had a drop.'

Regis fell silent, lost in thought. No one responded. Geralt felt a terrible urge to have a drink himself.

'It got rowdier and rowdier,' the vampire continued. 'And worse and worse as time went on. Occasionally I went on such benders that I didn't return to the crypt for three or four nights in a row. A tiny amount of fluid and I lost control, which, of course, didn't stop me from continuing the party. My friends? Well, you know what they're like. Some of them tried to make me see reason, so I took offence. Others were a bad influence, and dragged me out of the crypt to revels. Why, they even set me up with . . . er . . . playthings. And they enjoyed themselves at my expense.'

Milva, still busy restoring her arrows' flattened fletchings, murmured angrily. Cahir had finished repairing his boot and seemed to be asleep.

'Later on,' Regis continued, 'more alarming symptoms appeared. Parties and company began to play an absolutely secondary role. I noticed I could manage without them. Blood was all I needed, was all that mattered, even when it was . . .'

'Just you and your shadow?' Dandelion interjected.

'Worse than that,' Regis answered calmly. 'I don't even cast one.'

He was silent for a while.

'Then I met a special vampire girl. It might have been – I think it was – serious. I settled down. But not for long. She left me. So I began to double my intake. Despair and grief, as you know, are perfect excuses. Everyone thinks they understand. Even I thought I understood. But I was merely applying theory to practice. Am I boring you? I'll try to make it short. I finally began to do absolutely unacceptable things, the kind of things no vampire does. I flew under the influence. One night the boys sent me to the village to fetch some blood, and I missed my target: a girl who was walking to the well. I smashed straight into the well at top speed . . . The villagers almost beat me to death, but fortunately they didn't know how to go about it . . . They punctured me with stakes, chopped my head off, poured holy water all over me and buried me. Can you imagine how I felt when I woke up?'

'We can,' Milva said, examining an arrow. Everyone looked at her strangely. The archer coughed and looked away. Regis smiled faintly.

'I won't be long now,' he said. 'In the grave I had plenty of time to rethink things . . .'

'Plenty?' Geralt asked. 'How much?'

Regis looked at him.

'Professional curiosity? Around fifty years. After I'd regenerated I decided to pull myself together. It wasn't easy, but I did it. And I haven't drunk since.'

'Not at all?' Dandelion said, and stuttered. But his curiosity got the better of him. 'Not at all? Never? But . . . ?'

'Dandelion,' Geralt said, slightly raising his eyebrows. 'Get a grip and think. In silence.'

'I beg your pardon,' the poet grunted.

'Don't apologise,' the vampire said placatingly. 'And, Geralt, don't chasten him. I understand his curiosity. I – by which I mean I and my myth – personify all his human fears. One cannot expect a human to rid himself of them. Fear plays a no less important role in the human psyche than all the other emotions. A psyche without fears would be crippled.'

'But,' Dandelion said, regaining his poise, 'you don't frighten me. Does that make me a cripple?'

For a moment Geralt expected Regis to show his fangs and cure Dandelion of his supposed disability, but he was wrong. The vampire wasn't inclined towards theatrical gestures.

'I was talking about fears deeply lodged in the consciousness and the subconscious,' he explained calmly. 'Please don't be hurt by this metaphor, but a crow isn't afraid of a hat and coat hung on a stick, after it has overcome that fear and alighted on them. But when the wind jerks the scarecrow, the bird flees.'

'The crow's behaviour might be seen as a struggle for life,' Cahir observed from the darkness.

'Struggle, schmuggle.' Milva snorted. 'The crow isn't afraid of the scarecrow. It's afraid of men, because men throw stones and shoot at it.'

'A struggle for life.' Geralt nodded. 'But in human – not corvine – terms. Thank you for the explanation, Regis, we accept it whole-heartedly. But don't go rooting about in the depths of the human subconscious. Milva's right. The reasons people react in panic-stricken horror at the sight of a thirsty vampire aren't irrational, they are a result of the will to survive.'

'Thus speaks an expert,' the vampire said, bowing slightly towards him. 'An expert whose professional pride would not allow him to take money for fighting imaginary fears. The self-respecting witcher who only hires himself out to fight real, unequivocally dangerous evil. This professional will probably want to explain why a vampire is a greater threat than a dragon or a wolf. They have fangs too, don't forget.'

'Perhaps because the latter two use their fangs to stave off hunger or in self-defence, but never for fun or for breaking the ice or overcoming shyness towards the opposite sex.'

'People know nothing about that,' riposted Regis. 'You have known it for some time, but the rest of our company have only just discovered the truth. The remaining majority are deeply convinced that vampires do not drink for fun but feed on blood, and nothing but blood. Needless to say, human blood. Blood is a life-giving fluid; its loss results in the weakening of the body, the seeping away of a vital force. You reason thus: a creature that spills our blood is our deadly enemy. And a creature that attacks us for our blood, because it lives on it, is doubly evil. It grows in vital force at the expense of ours. For its species to thrive, ours must fade away. Ultimately a creature like that is repellent to you humans, for although you are aware of blood's life-giving qualities, it is disgusting to you. Would any of you drink blood? I doubt it. And there are people who grow weak or even faint at the sight of blood. In some societies women are considered unclean for a few days every month and they are isolated—'

'Among savages, perhaps,' Cahir interrupted. 'And I think only Nordlings grow faint at the sight of blood.'

'We've strayed,' the Witcher said, looking up. 'We've deviated from a straight path into a tangle of dubious philosophy. Do you think, Regis, that it would make a difference to humans were they to know you don't treat them as prey, but as a watering hole? Where do you see the irrationality of fears here? Vampires drink human blood; that particular fact cannot be challenged. A human treated by a vampire as a demijohn of vodka loses his strength, that's also clear. A totally drained human – so to speak – loses his vitality definitively. He dies. Forgive me, but the fear of death can't be lumped together with an aversion to blood. Menstrual or otherwise.'

'Your talk's so clever it makes my head spin,' Milva snorted. 'And all your wisdom comes down to what's under a woman's skirt. Woeful philosophers.'

'Let's cast aside the symbolism of blood for a moment,' Regis said. 'For here the myths really do have certain grounds in facts. Let's focus on those universally accepted myths with no grounds in fact. After all, everyone knows that if someone is bitten by a vampire and survives they must become a vampire themselves. Right?'

'Right,' Dandelion said. 'There's even a ballad—'

'Do you understand basic arithmetic?'

'I've studied all seven liberal arts, and was awarded a degree summa cum laude.'

'After the Conjunction of the Spheres there remained approximately one thousand two hundred higher vampires in your world. The number of teetotallers – because there is a considerable number of them – balances the number who drink excessively, as I did in my day. Generally, the statistically average vampire drinks during every full moon, for the full moon is a holy day for us, which we usually . . . er . . . celebrate with a drink. Applying the matter to the human calendar and assuming there are twelve full moons a year gives us the theoretical sum of fourteen thousand four hundred humans bitten annually. Since the Conjunction – once again calculating according to your reckoning – one thousand five hundred years have passed. A simple calculation will show that at the present moment, twenty-one million six hundred thousand vampires ought to exist in the world. If that figure is augmented by exponential growth . . .'

'That'll do.' Dandelion sighed. 'I don't have an abacus, but I can imagine the number. Actually I can't imagine it, and you're saying that infection from a bite is nonsense and a fabrication.'

'Thank you,' Regis said, bowing. 'Let's move on to the next myth, which states that a vampire is a human being who has died – but not completely. He doesn't rot or crumble to dust in the grave. He lies there as fresh as a daisy and ruddy-faced, ready to go forth and bite a victim. Where does that myth come from, if not from your subconscious and irrational aversion to your dearly departed? You surround the dead with veneration and memory, you dream of immortality, and in your myths and legends there's always someone being resurrected, conquering death. But were your esteemed late great-grandfather really to suddenly rise from the grave and order a beer, panic would ensue. And it doesn't surprise me. Organic matter, in which the vital processes have ceased, succumbs to degradation, which manifests itself very unpleasantly. The corpse stinks and dissolves into slime. The immortal soul, an indispensable element of your myths, abandons the stinking carcass in disgust and spirits away, forgive the pun. The soul is pure, and one can easily venerate it. But then you invented a revolting kind of spirit, which doesn't soar, doesn't abandon the cadaver, why, it doesn't even stink. That's repulsive and unnatural! For you, the living dead is the most revolting of revolting anomalies. Some moron even coined the term "the undead", which you're ever so keen to bestow on us.'

'Humans,' Geralt said, smiling slightly, 'are a primitive and superstitious race. They find it difficult to fully understand and appropriately name a creature that resurrects, even though it's had stakes pushed through it, had its head removed and been buried in the ground for fifty years.'

'Yes, indeed,' said the vampire, impervious to the derision. 'Your mutated race is capable of regenerating its fingernails, toenails, hair and epidermis, but is unable to accept the fact that other races are more advanced in that respect. That inability is not the result of your primitiveness. Quite the opposite: it's a result of egotism and a conviction in your own perfection. Anything that is more perfect than you must be a repulsive aberration. And repulsive aberrations are consigned to myths, for sociological reasons.'

'I don't understand fuck all,' Milva announced calmly, brushing the hair from her forehead with an arrow tip. 'I hear you're talking about fairy-tales, and even I know fairy-tales, though I'm a foolish wench from the forest. So it astonishes me that you aren't afraid of the sun, Regis. In fairy-tales sunlight burns a vampire to ash. Should I lump it together with the other fairy-tales?'

'Of course you should,' Regis confirmed. 'You believe a vampire is only dangerous at night, that the first rays of the sun turn him into ash. At the root of this myth, invented around primeval campfires, lies your heliophilia, by which I mean love of warmth; the circadian rhythm, which relies upon diurnal activity. For you the night is cold, dark, sinister, menacing, and full of danger. The sunrise, however, represents another victory in the fight for life, a new day, the continuation of existence. Sunlight carries with it light and the sun; and the sun's rays, which are invigorating for you, bring with them the destruction of hostile monsters. A vampire turns to ash, a troll succumbs to petrifaction, a werewolf turns back into a human, and a goblin flees, covering his eyes. Nocturnal predators return to their lairs and cease to be a threat. The world belongs to you until sunset. I repeat and stress: this myth arose around ancient campfires. Today it is only a myth, for now you light and heat your dwelling places. Even though you are still governed by the solar rhythm, you have managed to appropriate the night. We, higher vampires, have also moved some way from our primeval crypts. We have appropriated the day. The analogy is complete. Does this explanation satisfy you, my dear Milva?'

'Not in the slightest,' the archer replied, throwing the arrow away. 'But I think I've got it. I'm learning. I'll be learned one day. Sociolation, petrificology, werewolfation, crap-ology. In schools they lecture and birch you. It's more pleasant learning with you lot. My head hurts a bit, but my arse is still in one piece.'

'One thing is beyond question and is easy to observe,' Dandelion said. 'The sun's rays don't turn you into ash, Regis. The sun's warmth has as much effect on you as that red-hot horseshoe you so nimbly removed from the fire with your bare hands. Returning, however, to your analogies, for us humans the day will always remain the natural time for activity, and the night the natural time for rest. That is our physical structure. During the day, for example, we see better than at night. Except Geralt, who sees just as well at all times, but he's a mutant. Was it also a question of mutation among vampires?'

'One could call it that,' Regis agreed. 'Although I would argue that when mutation is spread over a sufficiently long period it ceases to be mutation and becomes evolution. But what you said about physical structure is apt. Adapting to sunlight was an unpleasant necessity for us. In order to survive, we had to become like humans in that respect. Mimicry, I'd call it. Which had its consequences. To use a metaphor: we lay down in the sick man's bed.'

'I beg your pardon?'

'There are reasons to believe that sunlight is lethal in the long run. There's a theory that in about five thousand years, at a conservative estimate, this world will only be inhabited by lunar creatures, which are active at night.'

'I'm glad I won't be around that long.' Cahir sighed, then yawned widely. 'I don't know about you, but the intensive diurnal activity is reminding me of the need for nocturnal sleep.'

'Me too,' the Witcher said, stretching. 'And there are only a few hours left until the dawning of the murderous sun. But before sleep overcomes us . . . Regis, in the name of science and the spread of knowledge, puncture some other myths about vampirism. Because I bet you've still got at least one.'

'Indeed.' The vampire nodded. 'I have one more. It's the last, but in no sense any less important. It is the myth behind your sexual phobias.'

Cahir snorted softly.

'I left this myth until the end,' Regis said, looking him up and down. 'I would have tactfully passed over it, but since Geralt has challenged me, I won't spare you. Humans are most powerfully influenced by fears with a sexual origin. The virgin fainting in the embrace of a vampire who drinks her blood. The young man falling prey to the vile practices of a female vampire running her lips over his body. That's how you imagine it. Oral rape. Vampires paralyse their victims with fear and force them to have oral sex. Or rather, a revolting parody of oral sex. And there is something disgusting about sex like that, which, after all, rules out procreation.'

'Speak for yourself,' the Witcher muttered.

'An act crowned not by procreation, but by sensual delight and death,' Regis continued. 'You have turned it into a baleful myth. You unconsciously dream of something like it, but shy away from offering it to your lovers. So it's done for you by the mythological vampire, who as a result swells to become a fascinating symbol of evil.'

'Didn't I say it?' Milva yelled, as soon as Dandelion had finished explaining to her what Regis had been talking about. 'It's all they ever have on their minds! It starts off brainy, but always comes back to humping!'

The distant trumpeting of cranes slowly died away.

The next day, the Witcher recalled, *we set off in much better humour. And then, utterly unexpectedly, war caught up with us again.*

They travelled through a practically deserted and strategically unimportant country covered in huge, dense forests, unappealing to invaders. Although Nilfgaard was close at last, and they were only separated from the imperial lands by the broad waters of the Great Yaruga, it was difficult terrain to cover. Their astonishment was all the greater because of that.

War appeared in a less spectacular way than it had in Brugge and Sodden, where the horizon had glowed with fires at night, and during the day columns of black smoke had slashed the blue sky. It was not so picturesque here in Angren. It was much worse. They suddenly saw a murder of crows circling over the forest with a horrible cawing, and soon after they happened upon some corpses. Although the bodies had been stripped of their clothing and were impossible to identify, they bore the infallible and clear marks of violent death. Those people had been killed in combat. And not

301

just killed. Most of the corpses were lying in the undergrowth, but some, cruelly mutilated, hung from trees by their arms or legs, lay sprawled on burnt-out pyres, or were impaled on stakes. And they stank. The whole of Angren had suddenly begun to reek with the monstrous, repulsive stench of barbarity.

It wasn't long before they had to hide in ravines and thick undergrowth, for to their left and right, and in front and behind them, the earth shook with cavalry horses' hooves, and more and more units passed their hideout, stirring up dust.

'Once again,' Dandelion said, shaking his head, 'once again we don't know who's fighting who and why. Once again we don't know who's behind us or who's ahead of us, or what direction they're headed. Who's attacking and who's retreating. The pox take it all. I don't know if I've ever told you, but I see it like this: war is no different to a whorehouse with a fire raging through it—'

'You have,' Geralt interrupted. 'A hundred times.'

'What are they fighting over?' the poet asked, spitting violently. 'Juniper bushes and sand? I mean, this exquisite country hasn't got anything else to offer.'

'There were elves among the bodies in the bushes,' Milva said. 'Scoia'tael commandos march this way, they always have. This is the route volunteers from Dol Blathanna and the Blue Mountains take when they head for Temeria. Someone wants to block their path. That's what I think.'

'It's likely,' Regis admitted, 'that the Temerian Army would try to ambush the Squirrels here. But I'd say there are too many soldiers in the area. I surmise the Nilfgaardians have crossed the Yaruga.'

'I surmise the same,' the Witcher said, grimacing a little as he looked at Cahir's stony countenance. 'The bodies we saw this morning carried the marks of Nilfgaardian combat methods.'

'They're all as bad as each other,' Milva snapped, unexpectedly taking the side of the young Nilfgaardian. 'And don't look daggers at Cahir, because now you're bound by the same, bizarre fate. He dies if he falls into the Blacks' clutches, and you escaped a Temerian noose a while back. So it's no use trying to find out which army is in front of us and which behind, who are our comrades, who are our enemies, who's good and who's evil. Now they're all our common foes, no matter what colours they're wearing.'

'You're right.'

'Strange,' Dandelion said, when the next day they had to hide in another ravine and wait for another cavalcade to pass. 'The army are rumbling over the hills, and yet woodmen are felling trees by the Yaruga as if nothing was happening. Can you hear it?'

'Perhaps they aren't woodmen,' Cahir wondered. 'Perhaps it's the army, and they're sappers.'

'No, they're woodmen,' Regis said. 'It's clear nothing is capable of interrupting the mining of Angren gold.'

'What gold?'

'Take a closer look at those trees,' the vampire said, once again assuming the tone of an all-knowing, patronising sage instructing mere mortals or the simple-minded. He often acquired that tone, which Geralt found somewhat irritating. 'Those trees,' Regis repeated, 'are cedars, sycamores and Angren pines. Very valuable material. There are timber ports all around here, from which logs are floated downstream. They're felling trees everywhere and axes are thudding away day and night. The war we can see and hear is beginning to make sense. Nilfgaard, as you know, has captured the mouth of the Yaruga, Cintra and Verden, as well as Upper Sodden. At this moment probably also Brugge and part of Lower Sodden. That means that the timber being floated from Angren is already supplying the imperial sawmills and shipyards. The northern kingdoms are trying to halt the process, while the Nilfgaardians, on the contrary, want to fell and float as much as possible.'

'And we, as usual, have found ourselves in a tight spot,' Dandelion said, nodding. 'Seeing as we have to get to Caed Dhu, right through the very centre of Angren and this timber war. Isn't there another bloody way?'

*

I asked Regis the same question, the Witcher recalled, staring at the sun setting over the Yaruga, *as soon as the thudding of hooves had faded into the distance, things had calmed down and we were finally able to continue our journey.*

'Another way to Caed Dhu?' the vampire pondered. 'Which avoids the hills and keeps out of the soldiers' way? Indeed, there is such a way. Not very comfortable and not very safe. And it's longer too. But I guarantee we won't meet any soldiers there.'

'Go on.'

'We can turn south and try to get across a low point in one of the Yaruga's meanders. Across Ysgith. Do you know Ysgith, Witcher?'

'Yes.'

'Have you ever ridden through those forests?'

'Of course.'

'The calm in your voice,' the vampire said, clearing his throat, 'would seem to signify you accept the idea. Well, there are five of us, including a witcher, a warrior and an archer. Experience, two swords and a bow. Too little to take on a Nilfgaardian raiding party, but it ought to be sufficient for Ysgith.'

Ysgith, the Witcher thought. *More than thirty square miles of bogs and mud, dotted with tarns. And murky forests full of weird trees dividing up the bogs. Some have trunks covered in scales. At the base they're as bulbous as onions, thinning towards the top, ending in dense, flat crowns. Others are low and misshapen, crouching on piles of roots twisted like octopuses, with beards of moss and shrivelled bog lichen hanging on their bare branches. Those beards sway, not from the wind though, but from poisonous swamp gas. Ysgith means mud hole. 'Stink hole' would be more appropriate.*

And the mud and bogs, the tarns and lakes overgrown with duckweed and pondweed teem with life. Ysgith isn't just inhabited by beavers, frogs, tortoises and water birds. It is swarming with much more dangerous creatures, armed with pincers, tentacles and prehensile limbs, which they use to catch, mutilate, drown and tear apart their prey. There are so many of these creatures that no one has ever been able to identify and classify them all. Not even witchers. Geralt

304

himself had rarely hunted in Ysgith and never in Lower Angren. The land was sparsely populated, and the few humans who lived on the fringes of the bogs were accustomed to treating the monsters as part of the landscape. They kept their distance, but it rarely occurred to them to hire a witcher to exterminate the monstrosities. Rarely, however, did not mean never. So Geralt knew Ysgith and its dangers.

Two swords and a bow, he thought. *And experience, my witcher's expertise. We ought to manage in a group. Especially when I'll be riding in the vanguard and keeping close watch on everything. On the rotten tree trunks, piles of weed, scrub, tussocks of grass; and the plants, orchids included. For in Ysgith even the orchids sometimes only look like plants, but are actually venomous crab spiders. I'll have to keep Dandelion on a short leash, and make sure he doesn't touch anything. Particularly since there's no shortage of plant life which likes to supplement its chlorophyll diet with morsels of meat. Plants whose shoots are as deadly as a crab spider's venom when they come into contact with skin. And the gas, of course. Not to mention poisonous fumes. We shall have to find a way to cover our mouths and noses . . .*

'Well?' Regis asked, pulling him out of his reverie. 'Do you accept the plan?'

'Yes, I do. Let's go.'

Something finally prompted me, the Witcher recalled, *not to talk to the rest of the company about the plan to cross Ysgith. And to ask Regis not to mention it either. I don't know why I was reluctant. Today, when everything is absolutely and totally screwed up, I might claim to have been aware of Milva's behaviour. Of the problems she was having. Of her obvious symptoms. But it wouldn't be true; I didn't notice anything, and what I did notice I ignored. Like a blockhead. So we continued eastwards, reluctant to turn towards the bogs.*

On the other hand it was good that we lingered, he thought, drawing his sword and running his thumb over the razor-sharp blade. *Had we headed straight for Ysgith then, I wouldn't have this weapon today.*

*

They hadn't seen or heard any soldiers since dawn. Milva led the way, riding far ahead of the rest of the company. Regis, Dandelion and Cahir were talking.

'I just hope those druids will deign to help us find Ciri,' the poet said worriedly. 'I've met druids and, believe me, they are unco-operative, tight-lipped, unfriendly, eccentric recluses. They might not talk to us at all, far less use magic to help us.'

'Regis knows one of the druids from Caed Dhu,' the Witcher reminded them.

'Are you sure the friendship doesn't go back three or four centuries?'

'It's considerably more recent than that,' the vampire assured them with a mysterious smile. 'Anyhow, druids enjoy longevity. They're always out in the open, in the bosom of primordial and unpolluted nature, which has a marvellous effect on the health. Breathe deeply, Dandelion, fill your lungs with forest air and you'll be healthy too.'

'I'll soon grow fur in this bloody wilderness,' Dandelion said sneeringly. 'When I sleep, I dream of inns, drinks and bathhouses. A primordial pox on this primordial nature. I really have my doubts about its miraculous effect on the health, particularly mental health. The said druids are the best example, because they're eccentric madmen. They're fanatical about nature and protecting it. I've witnessed them petitioning the authorities more times than I care to remember. Don't hunt, don't cut down trees, don't empty cesspits into rivers and other similar codswallop. And the height of idiocy was the visit of a delegation all arrayed in mistletoe wreathes to the court of King Ethain in Cidaris. I happened to be there . . .'

'What did they want?' Geralt asked, curious.

'Cidaris, as you know, is a kingdom where most people make a living from fishing. The druids demanded that the king order the use of nets with mesh of a specific size, and harshly punish anyone who used finer nets than instructed. Ethain's jaw dropped, and the mistletoers explained that limiting the size of mesh was the only way to protect fish stocks from depletion. The king led them out onto the terrace, pointed to the sea and told them how his bravest sailor had once sailed westwards for two months and only returned because supplies of fresh water had run out on his vessel, and there still wasn't a sign of land on the horizon. Could the druids, he asked, imagine the fish stocks in a sea like that being exhausted? By all means, the mistletoers confirmed. For though there was no doubt sea fishery would endure the longest as a means of acquiring food directly from nature, the time would come when fish would run out and hunger would stare them all in the face. Then it would be absolutely necessary to fish using nets with large mesh, to only catch fully grown specimens, and protect the small fry. Ethain asked when, in the druids' opinion, this dreadful time of hunger would occur, and they said in about two thousand years, according to their forecasts. The king bade them a courteous farewell and requested that they drop by in around a thousand years, when he would think it over. The mistletoers didn't get the joke and began to protest, so they were thrown out.'

'They're like that, those druids,' Cahir agreed. 'Back home, in Nilfgaard—'

'Got you!' Dandelion cried triumphantly. 'Back home, in Nilfgaard! Only yesterday, when I called you a Nilfgaardian, you leapt up as though you'd been stung by a hornet! Perhaps you could finally decide who you are, Cahir.'

'To you,' Cahir said, shrugging, 'I have to be a Nilfgaardian, for as I see nothing will convince you otherwise. However, for the sake of precision please know that in the Empire such a title is reserved exclusively for indigenous residents of the capital and its closest environs, lying by the lower reaches of the Alba. My family originates in Vicovaro, and thus—'

'Shut your traps!' Milva commanded abruptly and not very politely from the vanguard.

They all immediately fell silent and reined in their horses, having learned by now that it was a sign the girl had seen, heard or instinctively sensed something edible, provided it could be stalked and shot with an arrow. Milva had indeed raised her bow to shoot, but had not dismounted. That meant it was not about food. Geralt approached her cautiously.

'Smoke,' she said bluntly.

'I can't see it.'

'Sniff it then.'

The archer's sense of smell had not deceived her, even though the scent of smoke was faint. It couldn't have been the smoke from the conflagration behind them.

This smoke, Geralt observed, *smells nice. It's coming from a campfire on which something is being roasted.*

'Do we steer clear of it?' Milva asked quietly.

'After we've taken a look,' he replied, dismounting from his mare and handing the reins to Dandelion. 'It would be good to know what we're steering clear of. And who we have behind us. Come with me, Maria. The rest of you stay in your saddles. Be vigilant.'

From the brush at the edge of the forest unfolded a view of a vast clearing with logs piled up in even cords of wood. A very thin ribbon of smoke rose from between the woodpiles. Geralt calmed down somewhat, as nothing was moving in his field of vision and there was too little space between the woodpiles for a large group to be hiding there. Milva shared his opinion.

'No horses,' she whispered. 'They aren't soldiers. Woodmen, I'd say.'

'Me too. But I'll go and check. Cover me.'

When he approached, cautiously picking his way around the piles of logs, he heard voices. He came closer. And was absolutely amazed. But his ears hadn't let him down.

'Half a contract in diamonds!'

'Small slam in diamonds!'

'Barrel!'

'Pass. Your lead! Show your hand! Cards on the table! What the . . . ?'

'Ha-ha-ha! Just the knave and some low numbers. Got you right where it hurts! I'll make you suffer, before you get a small slam!'

'We'll see about that. My knave. What? It's been taken? Hey, Yazon, you really got fucked over!'

'Why didn't you play the lady, shithead? Pshaw, I ought to take my rod to you . . .'

The Witcher, perhaps, might still have been cautious; after all, various different individuals could have been playing Barrel, and many people might have been called Yazon. However, a familiar hoarse squawking interrupted the card players' excited voices.

"Uuuckkk . . . me!'

'Hello, boys,' Geralt said, emerging from behind the woodpile. 'I'm delighted to see you. Particularly as you're at full force again, including the parrot.'

'Bloody hell!' Zoltan Chivay said, dropping his cards in astonishment, then quickly leaping to his feet, so suddenly that Field Marshal Windbag, who was sitting on his shoulder, fluttered his wings and shrieked in alarm. 'The Witcher, as I live and breathe! Or is it a mirage? Percival, do you see what I see?'

Percival Schuttenbach, Munro Bruys, Yazon Varda and Figgis Merluzzo surrounded Geralt and seriously strained his right hand with their iron-hard grips. And when the rest of the company emerged from behind the logs, the shouts of joy increased accordingly.

'Milva! Regis!' Zoltan shouted, embracing them all. 'Dandelion, alive and kicking, even if your skull's bandaged! And what do you say, you bloody busker, about this latest melodramatic banality? Life, it turns out, isn't poetry! And do you know why? Because it's so resistant to criticism!'

'Where's Caleb Stratton?' Dandelion asked, looking around.

Zoltan and the others fell silent and grew solemn.

'Caleb,' the dwarf finally said, sniffing, 'is sleeping in a birch wood, far from his beloved peaks and Mount Carbon. When the Blacks overwhelmed us by the Ina, his legs were too slow and he didn't make it to the forest . . . He caught a sword across the head and when he fell they dispatched him with bear spears. But come on, cheer up, we've already mourned him and that'll do. We ought to be cheerful. After all, you got out of the madness in the camp in one piece. Why, the company's even grown, I see.'

Cahir inclined his head a little under the dwarf's sharp gaze, but said nothing.

'Come on, sit you down,' Zoltan invited. 'We're roasting a lamb here. We happened upon it a few days ago, lonely and sad. We stopped it from dying a miserable death from hunger or in a wolf's maw by slaughtering it mercifully and turning it into food. Sit down. And I'd like a few words with you, Regis. And Geralt, if you would.'

Two women were sitting behind the woodpile. One of them, who was suckling an infant, turned away in embarrassment at the sight of them approaching. Nearby, a young woman with an arm wrapped in none too clean rags was playing with two children on the sand. As soon as she raised her misty, blank eyes to him the Witcher recognised her.

'We untied her from the wagon, which was already in flames,' the dwarf explained. 'It almost finished the way that priest wanted. You know, the one who was after her blood. She passed through a baptism of fire, nonetheless. The flames were licking at her, scorching her to the raw flesh. We dressed her wounds as well as we could. We covered her in lard, but it's a bit messy. Barber-surgeon, if you would . . . ?'

'Right away.'

When Regis tried to peel off the dressing the girl whimpered, retreating and covering her face with her good hand. Geralt approached to hold her still, but the vampire gestured him to stop. He looked deeply into the girl's vacant eyes, and she immediately calmed down and relaxed. Her head drooped gently on her chest. She didn't even flinch when Regis carefully peeled off the dirty rag and smeared an intense and strange smelling ointment on her burnt arm.

Geralt turned his head, pointed with his chin at the two women and the two children, and then bored his eyes into the dwarf. Zoltan cleared his throat.

'We came across the two young 'uns and the women here in Angren,' he explained in hushed tones. 'They'd got lost during their escape. They were alone, fearful and hungry, so we took them on board, and we're looking after them. It just seemed to happen.'

'It just seemed to happen,' Geralt echoed, smiling faintly. 'You're an incorrigible altruist, Zoltan Chivay.'

'We all have our faults. I mean, you're still determined to rescue your girl.'

'Indeed. Although it's become more complicated than that . . . .'

310

'Because of that Nilfgaardian, who was tracking you and has now joined the company?'

'Partly. Zoltan, where are those fugitives from? Who were they fleeing? Nilfgaard or the Squirrels?'

'Hard to say. The kids know bugger all, the women aren't too talkative and get upset for no reason at all. If you swear near them or fart they go as red as beetroots . . . Never mind. But we've met other fugitives – woodmen – and they say the Nilfgaardians are prowling around here. It's our old friends, probably, the troop that came from the west, from across the Ina. But apparently there are also units here that arrived from the south. From across the Yaruga.'

'And who are they fighting?'

'It's a mystery. The woodmen talked of an army being commanded by a White Queen or some such. That queen's fighting the Blacks. It's said she and her army are even venturing onto the far bank of the Yaruga, taking fire and sword to imperial lands.'

'What army could that be?'

'No idea,' Zoltan said and scratched an ear. 'See, every day some company or other comes through, messing up the tracks with their hooves. We don't ask who they are, we just hide in the bushes . . .'

Regis, who was dealing with the burns on the girl's arm, interrupted their conversation.

'The dressing must be changed daily,' he said to the dwarf. 'I'll leave you the ointment and some gauze which won't stick to the burns.'

'Thank you, barber-surgeon.'

'Her arm will heal,' the vampire said softly, looking at the Witcher. 'With time the scar will even vanish from her young skin. What's happening in the poor girl's head is worse, though. My ointments can't cure that.'

Geralt said nothing. Regis wiped his hands on a rag.

'It's a curse,' he said in hushed tones, 'to be able to sense a sickness – the entire essence of it – in the blood, but not be able to treat it . . .'

'Indeed.' Zoltan sighed. 'Patching up the skin is one thing, but when the mind's addled, you're helpless. All you can do is give a damn and look after them. . . Thank you for your aid, barber-surgeon. I see you've also joined the Witcher's company.'

'It just seemed to happen.'

'Mmm,' Zoltan said and stroked his beard. 'And which way will you head in search of Ciri?'

'We're heading east, to Caed Dhu, to the druids' circle. We're counting on the druids' help . . .'

'No help,' said the girl with the bandaged arm in a ringing, metallic voice. 'No help. Only blood. And a baptism of fire. Fire purifies. But also kills.'

Zoltan was dumbfounded. Regis gripped his arm tightly and gestured him to remain silent. Geralt, who could recognise a hypnotic trance, said nothing and did not move.

'He who has spilt blood and he who has drunk blood,' the girl said, her head still lowered, 'shall pay in blood. Within three days one shall die in the other, and something shall die in each. They shall die inch by inch, piece by piece . . . And when finally the iron-shod clogs wear out and the tears dry, then the last shreds will pass. Even that which never dies shall die.'

'Speak on,' Regis said softly and gently. 'What can you see?'

'Fog. A tower in the fog. It is the Tower of Swallows . . . on a lake bound by ice.'

'What else do you see?'

'Fog.'

'What do you feel?'

'Pain . . .'

Regis had no time to ask another question. The girl jerked her head, screamed wildly, and whimpered. When she raised her eyes there really was nothing but fog in them.

Zoltan, Geralt recalled, still running his fingers over the rune-covered blade, *started to respect Regis more after that incident, altogether dropping the familiar tone he normally used in conversations with the barber-surgeon.*

Regis requested they did not say a single word to the others about the strange incident. The Witcher was not too concerned about it.

He had seen similar trances in the past and tended towards the view that the ravings of people under hypnosis were not prophecy but the regurgitation of thoughts they had intercepted and the suggestions of the hypnotist. Of course in this case it was not hypnosis but a vampire spell, and Geralt mused over what else the girl might have picked up from Regis's mind, had the trance lasted any longer.

They marched with the dwarves and their charges for half a day. Then Zoltan Chivay stopped the procession and took the Witcher aside.

'It is time to part company,' he declared briefly. 'We have made a decision, Geralt. Mahakam is looming up to the north, and this valley leads straight to the mountains. We've had enough adventures. We're going back home. To Mount Carbon.'

'I understand.'

'It's nice that you want to understand. I wish you and your company luck. It's a strange company, if you don't mind me saying so.'

'They want to help,' the Witcher said softly. 'That's something new for me. Which is why I've decided not to enquire into their motives.'

'That's wise,' Zoltan said, removing the dwarven sihil in its lacquered scabbard, wrapped in catskins, from his back. 'Here you go, take it. Before we go our separate ways.'

'Zoltan . . .'

'Don't say anything, just take it. We'll sit out the war in the mountains. We have no need of hardware. But it'll be pleasant to recall, from time to time, that this Mahakam-forged sihil is in safe hands and whistles in a just cause. That it won't bring shame on itself. And when you use the blade to slaughter your Ciri's persecutors, take one down for Caleb Stratton. And remember Zoltan Chivay and the dwarven forges.'

'You can be certain I will,' Geralt said, taking the sword and slinging it across his back. 'You can be certain I'll remember. In this rotten world, Zoltan Chivay, goodness, honesty and integrity become deeply engraved in the memory.'

'That is true,' the dwarf said, narrowing his eyes. 'Which is why I won't forget about you and the marauders in the forest clearing, nor about Regis and the horseshoe in the coals. While we're talking about reciprocity . . .'

He broke off, coughed, hawked and spat.

'Geralt, we robbed a merchant near Dillingen. A wealthy man, who'd got rich as a hawker. We waylaid him after he'd loaded his gold and jewels onto a wagon and fled the city. He defended his property like a lion and was yelling for help, so he took a few blows of an axe butt to the pate and became as quiet as a lamb. Do you remember the chest we lugged along, then carried on the wagon, and finally buried in the earth by the River O? Well, it contained his goods. Stolen loot, which we intend to build our future on.'

'Why are you telling me this, Zoltan?'

'Because I reckon you were still being misled by false appearances not so long ago. What you took for goodness and integrity was rottenness hidden under a pretty mask. You're easy to deceive, Witcher, because you don't look into motives. But I don't want to deceive you. So don't look at those women and children . . . don't take the dwarf who's standing in front of you as virtuous and noble. Before you stands a thief, a robber and possibly even a murderer. Because I can't be certain the hawker we roughed up didn't die in the ditch by the Dillingen highway.'

A lengthy silence followed, as they both looked northwards at the distant mountains enveloped in clouds.

'Farewell, Zoltan,' Geralt finally said. 'Perhaps the forces, the existence of which I'm slowly becoming convinced about, will permit us to meet again one day. I hope our paths cross again. I'd like to introduce Ciri to you, I'd like her to meet you. But even if it never happens, know that I won't forget you. Farewell, dwarf.'

'Will you shake my hand? Me, a thief and a thug?'

'Without hesitation. Because I'm not as easy to deceive as I once was. Although I don't enquire into people's motives, I'm slowly learning the art of looking beneath masks.'

Geralt swung the sihil and bisected a moth that was flying past.

After parting with Zoltan and his group, he recalled, *we happened upon a group of wandering peasants in the forest. Some of them took*

314

flight on seeing us, but Milva stopped a few by threatening them with her
bow. The peasants, it turned out, had been captives of the Nilfgaardians
not long before. They had been forced to fell cedar trees, but a few days
ago their guards had been attacked and overcome by a unit of soldiers
who freed them. Now they were going home. Dandelion insisted they
describe their liberators. He pushed them aggressively and asked sharp
questions.

'Those soldiers,' the peasant repeated, 'they serve the White Queen.
They're giving the Black infantry a proper hiding! They said they're
carrying out baboon attacks on the enemy's rear lines.'

'What?'

'I'm telling you, aren't I? Baboon attacks.'

'Bollocks to those baboons,' Dandelion said, grimacing and
waving a hand. 'Good people . . . I asked you what banners the army
were bearing.'

'Divers ones, sire. Mainly cavalry. And the infantry were wearing
something crimson.'

The peasant picked up a stick and described a rhombus in the
sand.

'A lozenge,' Dandelion, who was well versed in heraldry, said in
astonishment. 'Not the Temerian lily, but a lozenge. Rivia's coat of
arms. Interesting. It's two hundred miles from here to Rivia. Not
to mention the fact that the armies of Lyria and Rivia were utterly
annihilated during the fighting in Dol Angra and at Aldersberg, and
Nilfgaard has since occupied the country. I don't understand any of
this!'

'That's normal,' the Witcher interrupted. 'Enough talking. We
need to go.'

'Ha!' the poet cried. He had been pondering and analysing the information extracted from the peasants the whole time. 'I've got it! Not
baboons – guerrillas! Partisans! Do you see?'

'We see.' Cahir nodded. 'In other words, a Nordling partisan
troop is operating in the area. A few units, probably formed from
the remains of the Lyrian and Rivian armies, which were defeated

at Aldersberg in the middle of July. I heard about that battle while I was with the Squirrels.'

'I consider the news heartening,' Dandelion declared, proud he had been able to solve the mystery of the baboons. 'Even if the peasants had confused the heraldic emblems, we don't seem to be dealing with the Temerian Army. And I don't think news has reached the Rivian guerrillas about the two spies who recently cheated Marshal Vissegerd's gallows. Should we happen upon those partisans we have a chance to lie our way out of it.'

'Yes, we have a chance .. ..,' Geralt agreed, calming the frolicking Roach. 'But, to be honest, I'd prefer not to try our luck.'

'But they're your countrymen, Witcher,' Regis said. 'I mean, they call you Geralt of Rivia.'

'A slight correction,' he replied coldly. 'I call myself that to make my name sound fancier. It's an addition that inspires more trust in my clients.'

'I see,' the vampire said, smiling. 'And why exactly did you choose Rivia?'

'I drew sticks, marked with various grand-sounding names. My witcher preceptor suggested that method to me, although not initially. Only after I'd insisted on adopting the name Geralt Roger Eric du Haute-Bellegarde. Vesemir thought it was ridiculous; pretentious and idiotic. I dare say he was right.'

Dandelion snorted loudly, looking meaningfully at the vampire and the Nilfgaardian.

'My full name,' Regis said, a little piqued by the look, 'is authentic. And in keeping with vampire tradition.'

'Mine too,' Cahir hurried to explain. 'Mawr is my mother's given name, and Dyffryn my great-grandfather's. And there's nothing ridiculous about it, poet. And what's your name, by the way? Dandelion must be a pseudonym.'

'I can neither use nor betray my real name,' the bard replied mysteriously, proudly putting on airs. 'It's too celebrated.'

'It always sorely annoyed me,' added Milva, who after being silent and gloomy for a long while had suddenly joined in the conversation, 'when I was called pet names like Maya, Manya or Marilka.

When someone hears a name like that they always think they can pinch a girl's behind.'

It grew dark. The cranes flew off and their trumpeting faded into the distance. The breeze blowing from the hills subsided. The Witcher sheathed the sihil.

It was only this morning. This morning. And all hell broke loose in the afternoon.

We should have suspected earlier, he thought. *But which of us, apart from Regis, knew anything about this kind of thing? Naturally everyone noticed that Milva often vomited at dawn. But we all ate grub that turned our stomachs. Dandelion puked once or twice too, and on one occasion Cahir got the runs so badly he feared it was dysentery. And the fact that the girl kept dismounting and going into the bushes, well I took it as a bladder infection . . .*

I was an ass.

I think Regis realised the truth. But he kept quiet. He kept quiet until he couldn't keep quiet any longer. When we stopped to make camp in a deserted woodmen's shack, Milva led him into the forest, spoke to him at length and at times in quite a loud voice. The vampire returned from the forest alone. He brewed up and mixed some herbs, and then abruptly summoned us all to the shack. He began rather vaguely, in his annoying patronising manner.

'I'm addressing all of you,' Regis said. 'We are, after all, a fellowship and bear collective responsibility. The fact that the one who bears ultimate responsibility . . . direct responsibility, so to speak . . . is probably not with us doesn't change anything.'

'Spit it out,' Dandelion said, irritated. 'Fellowship, responsibility . . . What's the matter with Milva? What's she suffering from?'

'She's not suffering from anything,' Cahir said softly.

'At least not strictly speaking,' Regis added. 'Milva's pregnant.'

Cahir nodded to show it was as he suspected. Dandelion, however, was dumbstruck. Geralt bit his lip.

'How far gone is she?'

'She declined, quite rudely, to give any dates at all, including the date of her last period. But I'm something of an expert. The tenth week.'

'Then refrain from your pompous appeals to direct responsibility,' Geralt said sombrely. 'It's not one of us. If you had any doubts at all in this regard, I hereby dispel them. You were absolutely right, however, to talk about collective responsibility. She's with us now. We have suddenly been promoted to the role of husbands and fathers. So let's listen carefully to what the physician says.'

'Wholesome, regular meals,' Regis began to list. 'No stress. Sufficient sleep. And soon the end of horseback riding.'

They were all quiet for a long time.

'We hear you, Regis,' Dandelion finally said. 'My fellow husbands and fathers, we have a problem.'

'It's a bigger problem than you think,' the vampire said. 'Or a lesser one. It all depends on one's point of view.'

'I don't understand.'

'Well you ought to,' Cahir muttered.

'She demanded,' Regis began a short while later, 'that I prepare and give her a strong and powerful . . . medicament. She considers it a remedy for the problem. Her mind is made up.'

'And have you?'

Regis smiled.

'Without talking to the other fathers?'

'The medicine she's requesting,' Cahir said quietly, 'isn't a miraculous panacea. I have three sisters, so I know what I'm talking about. She thinks, it seems to me, that she'll drink the decoction in the evening, and the next morning she'll ride on with us. Not a bit of it. For about ten days there won't be a chance of her even sitting on a horse. Before you give her that medicine, Regis, you have to tell her that. And we can only give her the medicine after we've found a bed for her. A clean bed.'

'I see,' Regis said, nodding. 'One voice in favour. What about you, Geralt?'

'What about me?'

'Gentlemen.' The vampire swept across them with his dark eyes. 'Don't pretend you don't understand.'

'In Nilfgaard,' Cahir said, blushing and lowering his head, 'the woman decides. No one has the right to influence her decision. Regis said that Milva is certain she wants the . . . medicament. Only for that reason, absolutely only for that reason, have I begun – in spite of myself – to think of it as an established fact. And to think about the consequences. But I'm a foreigner, who doesn't know . . . I ought not to get involved. I apologise.'

'What for?' the troubadour asked, surprised. 'Do you think we're savages, Nilfgaardian? Primitive tribes, obeying some sort of shamanic taboo? It's obvious that only the woman can make a decision like that. It's her inalienable right. If Milva decides to—'

'Shut up, Dandelion,' the Witcher snapped. 'Please shut up.'

'You don't agree?' the poet said, losing his temper. 'Are you planning to forbid her or—'

'Shut your bloody mouth, or I won't be answerable for my actions! Regis, you seem to be conducting something like a poll among us. Why? You're the physician. The agent she's asking for . . . yes, the agent. The word medicament doesn't suit me somehow . . . Only you can prepare and give her this agent. And you'll do it should she ask you for it again. You won't refuse.'

'I've already prepared the agent,' Regis said, showing them all a little bottle made of dark glass. 'Should she ask again, I shall not refuse. Should she ask again,' he repeated with force.

'What's this all about then? Unanimity? Total agreement? Is that what you're expecting?'

'You know very well what it's about,' the vampire answered. 'You sense perfectly what ought to be done. But since you ask, I shall tell you. Yes, Geralt, that's precisely what it's about. Yes, that's precisely what ought to be done. And no, it's not me that's expecting it.'

'Could you be clearer?'

'No, Dandelion,' the vampire snapped. 'I can't be any clearer. Particularly since there's no need. Right, Geralt?'

'Right,' the Witcher said, resting his forehead on his clasped hands. 'Yes, too bloody right. But why are you looking at me? You want me to do it? I don't know how. I can't. I'm not suited for this role at all . . . Not at all, get it?'

'No,' Dandelion interjected. 'I don't get it at all. Cahir? Do you get it?'

The Nilfgaardian looked at Regis and then at Geralt.

'I think I do,' he said slowly. 'I think so.'

'Ah,' the troubadour said, nodding. 'Ah. Geralt understood right away and Cahir thinks he understands. I, naturally, demand to be enlightened, but first I'm told to be quiet, and then I hear there's no need for me to understand. Thank you. Twenty years in the service of poetry, long enough to know there are things you either understand at once, even without words; or you'll never understand them.'

The vampire smiled.

'I don't know anyone,' he said, 'who could have put it more elegantly.'

It was totally dark. The Witcher got to his feet.

It's now or never, he thought. *I can't run away from it. There's no point putting it off. It's got to be done. And that's an end to it.*

Milva sat alone by the tiny fire she had started in the forest, in a pit left by a fallen tree, away from the woodmen's shack where the rest of the company were sleeping. She didn't move when she heard his footsteps. It was as though she was expecting him. She just shifted along, making space for him on the fallen tree trunk.

'Well?' she said harshly, not waiting for him to say anything. 'We're in a fix, aren't we, eh?'

He didn't answer.

'You didn't expect this when we set off, did you? When you let me join the company? You thought: "So what if she's a peasant; a foolish, country wench?" You let me join. "I won't be able to talk to her about brainy things on the road," you thought, "but she might come in useful. She's a healthy, sturdy lass. She shoots a straight arrow, she won't get a sore arse from the saddle, and if it gets nasty she won't shit her britches. She'll come in useful." And it turns out she's no use, just a hindrance. A millstone. A typical bloody woman!'

'Why did you come after me?' he asked softly. 'Why didn't you stay in Brokilon? You must have known . . .'

'I did,' she interrupted. 'I mean, I was with the dryads, they always know what's wrong with a girl; you can't keep anything secret from them. They realised quicker than me . . . But I never thought I'd start feeling poorly so soon. I thought I'd drink some ergot or some other decoction, and you wouldn't even notice, wouldn't even guess . . .'

'It's not that simple.'

'I know. The vampire told me. I spent too long dragging my feet, meditating, hesitating. Now it won't be so easy . . .'

'That's not what I meant.'

'Bollocks,' she said a moment later. 'Imagine this. I had more than one string to my bow . . . I saw how Dandelion puts on a brave face; but thought him weak, soft, not used to hardship. I was just waiting for him to give up and then we'd have to offload him. I thought if it got hard I'd go back with Dandelion . . . Now just look: Dandelion's the hero, and I'm . . .'

Her voice suddenly cracked. Geralt embraced her. And he knew at once it was the gesture she had been waiting for, which she needed more than anything else. The roughness and hardness of the Brokilon archer disappeared just like that, and what remained was the trembling, gentle softness of a frightened girl. But it was she who interrupted the lengthening silence.

'And that's what you told me . . . in Brokilon. That I would need a . . . a shoulder to lean on. That I would call out, in the darkness . . . You're here, I can feel your arm next to mine . . . And I still want to scream . . . Oh dear, oh dear . . . Why are you trembling?'

'It's nothing. A memory.'

'What will become of me?'

He didn't answer. The question wasn't meant for him.

'Daddy once showed me . . . Where I come from there's a black wasp that lives by the river and lays its eggs in a live caterpillar. The young wasps hatch and eat the caterpillar alive . . . from the inside. . . Something like that's in me now. In me, inside me, in my own belly. It's growing, it keeps growing and it's going to eat me alive . . .'

'Milva—'

321

'Maria. I'm Maria, not Milva. What kind of Red Kite am I? A mother hen with an egg, not a Kite . . . Milva laughed with the dryads on the battleground, pulled arrows from bloodied corpses. Waste of a good arrow shaft or a good arrowhead! And if someone was still breathing, a knife across the throat! Milva was treacherous, she led those people to their fate and laughed . . . Now their blood calls. That blood, like a wasp's venom, is devouring Maria from the inside. Maria is paying for Milva.'

He remained silent. Mainly because he didn't know what to say. The girl snuggled up closer against his shoulder.

'I was guiding a commando to Brokilon,' she said softly. 'It was in Burnt Stump, in June, on the Sunday before summer solstice. We were chased, there was a fight, seven of us escaped on horseback. Five elves, one she-elf and me. About half a mile to the Ribbon, but the cavalry were behind us and in front of us, darkness all around, swamps, bogs . . . At night we hid in the willows, we had to let ourselves and the horses rest. Then the she-elf undressed without a word, lay down . . . and the first elf lay with her . . . It froze me, I didn't know what to do . . . Move away, or pretend I couldn't see? The blood was pounding in my temples, but I heard it when she said: "Who knows what tomorrow will bring? Who will cross the Ribbon and who will perish? *En'ca minne.*" *En'ca minne*, a little love. Only this way, she said, can death be overcome. Death or fear. They were afraid, she was afraid, I was afraid . . . So I undressed too and lay down nearby. I placed a blanket under my back . . . When the first one embraced me I clenched my teeth, for I wasn't ready, I was terrified and dry . . . But he was wise – an elf, after all – he only seemed young . . . wise . . . tender . . . He smelled of moss, grass and dew . . . I held my arms out towards the second one myself . . . desiring . . . a little love? The devil only knows how much love there was in it and how much fear, but I'm certain there was more fear . . . For the love was fake. Perhaps well faked, but fake even so, like a pantomime, where if the actors are skilled you soon forget what's playacting and what's the truth. But there was fear. There was real fear.'

Geralt remained silent.

'Nor did we manage to defeat death. They killed two of them at

322

dawn, before we reached the bank of the Ribbon. Of the three who survived I never saw any of them again. My mother always told me a wench knows whose fruit she's bearing . . . But I don't know. I didn't even know the names of those elves, so how could I tell? How?'

He said nothing. He let his arm speak for him.

'And anyway, why do I need to know? The vampire will soon have the draft ready . . . The time will come for me to be left in some village or other . . . No, don't say a word; be silent. I know what you're like. You won't even give up that skittish mare, you won't leave her, you won't exchange her for another, even though you keep threatening to. You aren't the kind that leaves others behind. But now you have no choice. After I drink it I won't be able to sit in the saddle. But know this; when I've recovered I'll set off after you. For I would like you to find your Ciri, Witcher. To find her and get her back, with my help.'

'So that's why you rode after me,' he said, wiping his forehead. 'That's why.'

She lowered her head.

'That's why you rode after me,' he repeated. 'You set off to help rescue someone else's child. You wanted to pay; to pay off a debt, that you intended to incur even when you set off . . . Someone else's child for your own, a life for a life. And I promised to help you should you be in need. But, Milva, I can't help you. Believe me, I cannot.'

This time she remained silent. But he could not. He felt compelled to speak.

'Back there, in Brokilon, I became indebted to you and swore I'd repay you. Unwisely. Stupidly. You offered me help in a moment when I needed help very much. There's no way of paying off a debt like that. It's impossible to repay something that has no price. Some say everything in the world – everything, with no exception – has a price. It's not true. There are things with no price, things that are priceless. But you realise it belatedly: when you lose them, you lose them forever and nothing can get them back for you. I have lost many such things. Which is why I can't help you today.'

'But you have helped me,' she replied, very calmly. 'You don't even know how you've helped me. Now go, please. Leave me alone. Go away, Witcher. Go, before you destroy my whole world.'

When they set off again at dawn, Milva rode at the head, calm and smiling. And when Dandelion, who was riding behind her, began to strum away on his lute, she whistled the melody.

Geralt and Regis brought up the rear. At a certain moment the vampire glanced at the Witcher, smiled, and nodded in acknowledgement and admiration. Without a word. Then he took a small bottle of dark glass out of his medical bag and showed it to Geralt. Regis smiled again and threw the bottle into the bushes.

The Witcher said nothing.

When they stopped to water the horses, Geralt led Regis away to a secluded place.

'A change of plans,' he informed briefly. 'We aren't going through Ysgith.'

The vampire remained silent for a moment, boring into him with his black eyes.

'Had I not known,' he finally said, 'that as a witcher you are only afraid of real hazards, I should have thought you were worried by the preposterous chatter of a deranged girl.'

'But you do know. And you're sure to be guided by logic.'

'Indeed. However, I should like to draw your attention to two matters. Firstly, Milva's condition, which is neither an illness nor a disability. The girl must, of course, take care of herself, but she is utterly healthy and physically fit. I would even say more than fit. The hormones—'

'Drop the patronising, superior tone,' Geralt interrupted, 'because it's getting on my nerves.'

'That was the first matter of the two I intended to bring up,' Regis continued. 'Here's the second: when Milva notices your overprotectiveness, when she realises you're making a fuss and mollycoddling her, she'll be furious. And then she'll feel stressed; which is absolutely inadvisable for her. Geralt, I don't want to be patronising. I want to be rational.'

Geralt did not answer.

'There's also a third matter,' Regis added, still watching the Witcher carefully. 'We aren't being compelled to go through Ysgith by enthusiasm or the lust for adventure, but by necessity. Soldiers are roaming the hills, and we have to make it to the druids in Caed Dhu. I understood it was urgent. That it was important for you to acquire the information and set off to rescue your Ciri as quickly as possible.'

'It is,' Geralt said, looking away. 'It's very important to me. I want to rescue Ciri and get her back. Until recently I thought I'd do it at any price. But no. I won't pay that price, I won't consent to taking that risk. We won't go through Ysgith.'

'The alternative?'

'The far bank of the Yaruga. We'll go upstream, far beyond the swamps. And we'll cross the Yaruga again near Caed Dhu. If it turns out to be difficult, only the two of us will meet the druids. I'll swim across and you'll fly over as a bat. Why are you staring at me like that? I mean, rivers being obstacles to vampires is another myth and superstition. Or perhaps I'm wrong.'

'No, you are not wrong. But I can only fly during a full moon, not at any other time.'

'That's only two weeks away. When we reach the right place it'll almost be full moon.'

'Geralt,' the vampire said, still not taking his eyes away from the Witcher. 'You're a strange man. To make myself clear, I wasn't being critical. Right, then. We give up on Ysgith, which is dangerous for a woman with child. We cross to the far bank of the Yaruga, which you consider safer.'

'I'm capable of assessing the level of risk.'

'I don't doubt it.'

'Not a word to Milva or the others. Should they ask, it's part of our plan.'

'Of course. Let us begin to look for a boat.'

They didn't have to look for long, and the result of their search surpassed their expectations. They didn't find just a boat, but a ferryboat. Hidden among the willows, craftily camouflaged with branches and bunches of bulrushes, it was betrayed by the painter connecting it to the left bank.

The ferryman was also found. While they were approaching he quickly hid in the bushes, but Milva spotted him and dragged him from the undergrowth by the collar. She also flushed out his helper, a powerfully built fellow with the shoulders of an ogre and the face of an utter simpleton. The ferryman shook with fear, and his eyes darted around like a couple of mice in an empty granary.

'To the far bank?' he whined, when he found out what they wanted. 'Not a chance! That's Nilfgaardian territory and there's a war on! They'll catch us and stick us on a spike! I'm not going! You can kill me, but I'm not going!'

'We can kill you,' Milva said, grinding her teeth. 'We can also beat you up first. Open your trap again and you'll see what we can do.'

'I'm sure the fact there's a war on,' the vampire said, boring his eyes into the ferryman, 'doesn't interfere with smuggling, does it, my good man? Which is what your ferry is for, after all, craftily positioned as it is far from the royal and Nilfgaardian toll collectors. Am I right? Go on, push it into the water.'

'That would be wise,' Cahir added, stroking his sword hilt. 'Should you hesitate, we shall cross the river ourselves, without you, and your ferry will remain on the far bank. To get it back you'll have to swim across doing the breaststroke. This way you ferry us across and return. An hour of fear and then you can forget all about it.'

'But if you resist, you halfwit,' Milva snapped, 'I'll give you such a beating you won't forget us till next winter!'

The ferryman yielded in the face of these hard, indisputable arguments, and soon the entire company was on the ferry. Some of the horses, particularly Roach, resisted and refused to go aboard, but the ferryman and his dopey helper used twitches made of sticks and rope. The skill with which they calmed the animals proved it was not the first time they had smuggled stolen mounts across the Yaruga. The giant simpleton got down to turning the wheel which drove the ferry, and the crossing began.

When they reached the peaceful waters and felt the gentle breeze, their moods improved. Crossing the Yaruga was something new, a clear milestone, marking progress in their trek. In front of them was the Nilfgaardian bank, the frontier, the border. They all suddenly cheered up. It even affected the ferryman's foolish helper, who began to whistle an inane tune. Even Geralt was strangely euphoric, as though Ciri would emerge at any moment from the alder grove on the far bank and shout out joyfully on seeing him.

Instead of that the ferryman began shouting. And not joyfully in the least.

'By the Gods! We're done for!'

Geralt looked towards where he was pointing and cursed. Suits of armour flashed and hooves thudded among the alders on the high bank. A moment later the jetty on the left bank was teeming with horsemen.

'Black Riders!' the ferryman screamed, paling and releasing the wheel. 'Nilfgaardians! Death! Gods, save us!'

'Hold the horses, Dandelion!' Milva yelled, trying to remove her bow from her saddle with one hand. 'Hold the horses!'

'They aren't imperial forces,' Cahir said. 'I don't think . . .'

His voice was drowned out by the shouts of the horsemen on the jetty and the ferryman's yelling. Urged on by the yelling, the daft helper seized a hatchet, swung it and brought the blade down powerfully on the rope. The ferryman came forward to help him with another hatchet. The horsemen on the jetty noticed it and also began to yell. Several of them rode into the water, to seize the rope. Others began swimming towards the ferry.

'Leave that rope alone!' Dandelion shouted. 'It's not Nilfgaard! Don't cut it—'

It was too late, however. The loose end of the rope sank heavily into the water, the ferry turned a little and began to float downstream. The horsemen on the bank started yelling.

'Dandelion's right,' Cahir said grimly. 'They aren't imperial forces . . . They're on the Nilfgaardian bank, but it isn't Nilfgaard.'

'Of course they aren't!' Dandelion called. 'I recognise their livery! Eagles and lozenges! It's Lyria's coat of arms! They're the Lyrian guerrillas! Hey, you men . . .'

'Get down, you idiot!'

The poet, as usual, rather than listen to the warning, wanted to know what it was all about. And right then arrows whistled through the air. Some of them thudded into the side of the ferry, some of them flew over the deck and splashed into the water. Two flew straight for Dandelion, but the Witcher already had his sword in his hand, leapt forward and deflected both of them with swift blows.

'By the Great Sun,' Cahir grunted. 'He deflected two arrows! Remarkable! I've never seen anything like it . . .'

'And you never will again! That's the first time I've ever managed two in a row! Now get down, will you!'

However, the soldiers by the jetty had stopped shooting, seeing the current pushing the drifting ferryboat straight towards their bank. Water foamed beside the horses which had been driven into the river. The ferry station was filling up with more horsemen. There were at least two hundred of them.

'Help!' the ferryman yelled. 'Seize the poles, m'lords! We're being carried to the bank!'

They understood at once, and fortunately there were plenty of poles. Regis and Dandelion held the horses, and Milva, Cahir and the Witcher aided the efforts of the ferryman and his duffer of an assistant. Pushed off by five poles, the ferryboat turned and began to move more quickly, clearly heading towards the midstream. The soldiers on the bank started yelling again, and took up their bows once again. Again, several arrows whistled past and one of their horses neighed wildly. The ferryboat, carried away by a more powerful current, was fortunately travelling quickly and began to move further from the bank, beyond the range of an effective arrow shot.

They were now floating in the middle of the river, on calm waters. The ferryboat was spinning like a turd in an ice hole and the horses stamped and whinnied, tugging at the reins, which were being held by Dandelion and the vampire. The horsemen on the bank yelled and shook their fists at them. Geralt suddenly noticed a rider on a white steed among them, who was waving a sword and issuing orders. A moment later the cavalcade withdrew into the forest and galloped along the edge of the high bank. Their armour flashed among the riverside undergrowth.

'They aren't letting us go,' the ferryman groaned. 'They know that the rapids round the corner will push us over towards the bank again . . . Keep those poles at the ready, m'lords! When it turns towards the right bank, we'll have to help the old tub get the better of the current and land . . . Else we're doomed . . .'

They floated, turning, drifting slightly towards the right bank; a steep, high bluff, bristling with crooked pine trees. The left bank, the one that was moving away from them, had become flat and jutted into the river in a semi-circular, sandy spit. Horsemen galloped onto the spit, their momentum taking them into the water. By the spit there was clearly a sand-bank channel, a shallow, and before the water had reached the height of the horses' bellies, the horsemen had ridden quite far into the river.

'We're in arrow range,' Milva judged grimly. 'Get down.'

Arrows began whistling again and some of them thumped into the planks. But the current, pushing them away from the channel, quickly carried the ferryboat towards a sharp bend on the right.

'To the poles!' the trembling ferryman ordered. 'With a will. Let's land before the rapids carry us away!'

It wasn't so easy. The current was swift, the water deep and the ferryboat large, heavy and cumbersome. At first it did not react to their efforts at all, but finally the poles found more purchase on the riverbed. It looked as though they might succeed, when Milva suddenly dropped her pole and pointed wordlessly at the right bank.

'This time . . .' Cahir said, wiping sweat from his brow. 'This time it's definitely Nilfgaard.'

Geralt saw it too. The horsemen who had suddenly appeared on the right bank were wearing black and green cloaks, and the horses had typical Nilfgaardian blinders. There were at least a hundred of them.

'Now we're done for . . .' the ferryman whimpered. 'Mother of mine, it's the Black Riders!'

'To the poles!' the Witcher roared. 'To the poles and into the current! Away from the bank!'

Once again it turned out to be a difficult task. The current by the right bank was powerful and pushed the ferryboat straight under the high bluff, from which the shouts of the Nilfgaardians could be heard. A moment later, when Geralt, who was leaning on his pole, looked upwards, he saw pine branches above his head. An arrow shot from the top of the bluff penetrated the ferryboat's deck almost vertically, two feet from him. He deflected another, which was heading for Cahir, with a blow of his sword.

Milva, Cahir, the ferryman and his assistant pushed away – not from the riverbed, but from the bank where the bluff was. Geralt dropped his sword, caught up a pole and helped them, and the ferryboat began to drift towards the calm waters again. But they were still dangerously close to the right bank and to their pursuers galloping along the edge of it. Before they could move away, the bluff ended and Nilfgaardians flooded onto the flat, reedy bank. Fletchings screamed through the air.

'Get down!'

The ferryman's helper suddenly coughed strangely, dropping his pole into the water. Geralt saw a bloodied arrowhead and four inches of shaft sticking out of his back. Cahir's chestnut reared, neighed in pain, jerking its penetrated neck, knocked Dandelion down and leaped overboard. The remaining horses also neighed and thrashed, and the ferryboat shook from the impact of their hooves.

'Hold the horses!' the vampire yelled. 'Three—'

He suddenly broke off, fell backwards against the planks, and sat down with his head lolling. A black-feathered arrow was sticking out of his chest.

Milva saw it too. She screamed with fury, picked up her bow, knelt and emptied the quiver of arrows right on the deck. Then she began to shoot. Quickly. Arrow after arrow. Not one missed its target.

There was confusion on the bank, the Nilfgaardians retreating into the forest, leaving their dead and wounded in the reeds. Hidden in the undergrowth they continued to shoot, but their arrows were barely reaching the ferryboat, which was being carried towards the midstream by the swift current. The distance was too great for the Nilfgaardian archers to shoot accurately. But not too great for Milva.

Among the Nilfgaardians suddenly appeared an officer in a black cape and a helmet with raven's wings flapping on it. He was yelling, brandishing a mace and pointing downstream. Milva stood, took a broader stance, pulled the bowstring to her ear and quickly took aim. The arrow hissed in the air, and the officer bent backwards in his saddle and sagged in the arms of the soldiers holding him up. Milva drew her bow again and released her fingers from the bowstring. One of the Nilfgaardians holding up the officer screamed piercingly and lurched back off his horse. The others disappeared into the forest.

'Masterful shots,' Regis said calmly from behind the Witcher's back. 'But it'd be better if you grabbed the poles. We're still too close to the bank and we're being carried into the shallows.'

The archer and Geralt turned around.

'Aren't you dead?' they asked in in chorus.

'Did you think,' the vampire said, showing them the black-fletched shaft, 'I could be harmed by any old bit of wood?'

There was no time to be surprised. The ferryboat was once again turning around in the current and moving along the calm waters. But on the bend in the river another beach appeared, a sandbank and shallow channel, and the bank teemed with black-clad Nilfgaardians again. Some of them were riding into the river and preparing to shoot. Everyone, including Dandelion, rushed for the poles, which soon could not reach the bottom as – owing to the combined effort – the current finally carried the ferryboat towards swifter water.

'Good,' Milva panted, dropping her pole. 'Now they won't be able to reach us . . .'

'One of them's made it to the sandbank!' Dandelion cried. 'He's going to shoot! Get out of sight!'

'He'll miss,' Milva said coldly.

The arrow splashed into the water two yards from the ferryboat's bow.

'He's doing it again!' the troubadour yelled, peeping out from above the saxboard. 'Look out!'

'He'll miss,' Milva repeated, straightening the bracer on her left forearm. 'He's got a good bow, but he's as much an archer as my

331

old grannie. He's overexcited. After he releases, he trembles and shakes like a woman with a slug wriggling up her arse. Hold onto the horses, so I don't get knocked over.'

This time the Nilfgaardian shot too high and the arrow whistled over the ferryboat. Milva raised her bow, her stance firm, quickly pulled the bowstring to her cheek and released it gently, not changing her position by even a fraction of an inch. The Nilfgaardian tumbled into the water as though struck by lightning and began to float with the current. His black cape billowed out like a balloon.

'That's how it's done,' Milva said and lowered her bow. 'But it's too late for him to learn.'

'The others are galloping after us,' Cahir said, pointing towards the right bank. 'And I vouch they won't stop chasing us. Not now that Milva's shot their officer. The river's meandering and the current will carry us towards their bank again on the next bend. They know it and they'll be waiting . . .'

'Right now we have another worry,' the ferryman moaned, getting up from his knees and throwing off his dead helper. 'We're being pushed straight for the left bank . . . By the Gods, we're caught between two fires . . . And all because of you, m'lords! The blood will fall on your heads . . .'

'Shut your trap and grab a pole!'

The flat, left bank, which was now nearer, was teeming with horsemen, identified by Dandelion as Lyrian partisans. They were yelling and waving their arms. Geralt noticed a rider on a white horse among them. He wasn't certain, but he thought the rider was a woman. A fair-haired woman in armour, but without a helmet.

'What are they yelling?' Dandelion said, straining to listen. 'Something about a queen, is it?'

The shouting on the left bank intensified. They could also hear the clanging of steel distinctly now.

'It's a battle,' Cahir said bluntly. 'Look. Those are imperial forces running out of the forest. The Nordlings were fleeing from them, and now they've been caught in a trap.'

'The way out of the trap,' Geralt said, spitting into the water, 'was the ferry. I think they wanted to save at least their queen and their officers by ferrying them onto the other bank. And we hijacked the ferry. Oh, they won't like us now, no, no . . .'

'But they ought to!' Dandelion said. 'The ferry wouldn't have saved anyone, just carried them straight into the clutches of the Nilfgaardians on the right bank. Let's avoid the right bank too. We can parley with the Lyrians, but the Blacks will beat us to death without a second thought . . .'

'It's carrying us quicker and quicker,' Milva said, spitting into the water too and watching her saliva drift away. 'And right down the centre of the run. They can kiss our arses, both armies. The bends are gentle, the banks are level and overgrown with willows. We're heading down the Yaruga and they won't catch up with us. They'll soon get bored.'

'Bullshit,' the ferryman groaned. 'The Red Port is ahead of us . . . There's a bridge there! And shallows! The ferry will get stuck . . . If they overtake us, they'll be waiting for us . . .'

'The Nordlings won't overtake us,' Regis said, pointing at the left bank from the stern. 'They have their own worries.'

Indeed, a fierce battle was raging on the right bank. Most of the fighting took place in the forest and only betrayed itself by battle cries, but here and there the black and colourfully uniformed horsemen were delivering blows to each other in the water near the bank. Bodies were splashing into the Yaruga. The tumult and clang of steel quietened, and the ferryboat majestically, but quite quickly, headed downstream.

Finally no soldiers could be seen on the overgrown banks, and no sounds of their pursuers could be heard. Only when Geralt was starting to hope everything would end well did they see a wooden bridge spanning the two banks. The river flowed beneath the bridge, past sandbars and islands, the largest of which supported the bridge's piers. On the right bank lay the timber port; they could see thousands of logs piled up there.

'It's shallow all around,' the ferryman panted. 'We can only get through the middle, to the right of the island. The current is carrying us there now, but grab the poles, they might help if we get stuck . . .'

'There are soldiers on the bridge,' Cahir said, shielding his eyes with his hand. 'On the bridge and in the port . . .'

They could all see the soldiers. And they all saw the band of horsemen in black and green cloaks flooding out of the forest behind the port. They were even close enough to hear the noise of battle.

'Nilfgaard,' Cahir confirmed drily. 'The men who were pursuing us. So the men in the port are Nordlings . . .'

'To the poles!' the ferryman yelled. 'Maybe we'll sneak through while they're fighting!'

They did not manage to. They were very close to the bridge when it suddenly began to shake from the boots of running soldiers. The footmen were wearing white tunics, decorated with red lozenges over their hauberks. Most of them had crossbows, which they rested on the railing and aimed at the ferryboat approaching the bridge.

'Don't shoot, boys!' Dandelion yelled at the top of his voice. 'Don't shoot! We're with you!'

The soldiers did not hear, or did not want to hear.

The salvo of quarrels turned out to have tragic results. The only human to be hit was the ferryman, who was still trying to steer with his pole. A bolt pierced him right through. Cahir, Milva and Regis ducked down behind the side in time. Geralt seized his sword and deflected one quarrel, but there were too many of them. By an inexplicable miracle Dandelion, who was still yelling and waving his arms, was not hit. However, the hail of missiles caused real carnage among the horses. The grey slumped to its knees, struck by three quarrels. Milva's black fell, kicking. Regis's bay too. Roach, shot in the withers, reared and leaped overboard.

'Don't shoot!' Dandelion bellowed. 'We're with you!'

This time it worked.

The ferryboat, carried by the current, ploughed into a sandbank with a grinding sound and came to rest. They all jumped onto the island or into the water, escaping the hooves of the agonised, thrashing horses. Milva was the last, for her movements had suddenly become horrifyingly slow. *She's been hit*, the Witcher thought, seeing the girl clambering clumsily over the side and dropping inertly on the sand. He leapt towards her, but the vampire was quicker.

'Something's broken off in me,' the girl said very slowly. And very unnaturally. And then she pressed her hands to her womb. Geralt saw the leg of her woollen trousers darkening with blood.

'Pour that over my hands,' Regis said, handing Geralt a small bottle he had removed from his bag. 'Pour that over my hands, quickly.'

'What is it?'

'She's miscarrying. Give me a knife. I have to cut open her clothes. And go away.'

'No,' Milva said. 'I want him to stay . . .'

A tear trickled down her cheek.

The bridge above them thundered with soldiers' boots.

'Geralt!' Dandelion yelled.

The Witcher, seeing what the vampire was doing to Milva, turned his head away in embarrassment. He noticed soldiers in white tunics rushing across the bridge at great speed. An uproar could still be heard from the right bank and the timber port.

'They're running away,' Dandelion panted, running to him and tugging his sleeve. 'The Nilfgaardians are already on the right bridgehead! The battle is still raging there, but most of the army are fleeing to the left bank! Do you hear? We have to flee too!'

'We can't,' he said through clenched teeth. 'Milva's miscarried. She can't walk.'

Dandelion swore.

'We'll have to carry her then,' he declared. 'It's our only chance . . .'

'Not our only one,' Cahir said. 'Geralt, onto the bridge.'

'What do you mean?'

'We'll hold back their flight. If those Nordlings can hold the right bridgehead long enough, perhaps we'll be able to escape by the left one.'

'How do you plan to do it?'

'I'm an officer, don't forget. Climb up that pier and onto the bridge!'

On the bridge, Cahir demonstrated that he was indeed experienced at bringing panicked soldiers under control.

'Where are you going, scum? Where are you going, bastards?' he yelled. Each roar was accompanied by a punch, as he knocked a flee-ing soldier down onto the bridge's boards. 'Stop! Stop, you fucking swine!'

Some – but far from all – of the fleeing soldiers stopped, terrified by the roaring and flashing of the sword Cahir was whirling dramat-ically. Others tried to sneak behind his back. But Geralt had already drawn his sword and joined the spectacle.

'Where are you going?' he shouted, catching one of the soldiers in his tracks in a powerful grip. 'Where? Stand fast! Get back there!'

'Nilfgaard, sire!' the soldier screamed. 'It's a bloodbath! Let me go!'

'Cowards!' Dandelion roared in a voice Geralt had never heard, as he clambered onto the bridge. 'Base cowards! Chickenhearts! Would you flee to save your skins? To live out your days in igno-miny, you varlets?'

'They are too many, Sir Knight! We stand no chance!'

'The centurion's fallen . . .' another of them moaned. 'The decu-rions have taken flight! Death is coming!'

'We must run!'

'Your comrades,' Cahir yelled, brandishing his sword, 'are still fighting on the bridgehead and at the port! They are still fighting! Dishonour will be his who does not go to their aid! Follow me!'

'Dandelion,' the Witcher hissed. 'Get down onto the island. You and Regis will have to get Milva onto the left bank somehow. Well, what are you waiting for?'

'Follow me, boys!' Cahir repeated, whirling his sword. 'Follow me if the Gods are dear to you! To the timber port! Death to the dogs!'

About a dozen soldiers shook their weapons and took up the cry, their voices expressing very varied degrees of conviction. About a dozen of the men who had already run away turned back in shame and joined the ragtag army on the bridge. An army which was sud-denly being led by the Witcher and the Nilfgaardian.

They might really have set off for the timber port, but the bridgehead was suddenly black with the cavalrymen's cloaks. The

Nilfgaardians broke through the defence and forced their way onto the bridge. Horseshoes thudded on the planking. Some of the soldiers who had been stopped darted away, others stood indecisively. Cahir cursed. In Nilfgaardian. But no one apart from the Witcher paid any attention to it.

'What has been started must be finished,' Geralt snapped, gripping his sword tightly. 'Let's get them! We have to spur our men into action.'

'Geralt,' Cahir said, stopping and looking at him uncertainly. 'Do you want me to . . . to kill my own? I can't . . .'

'I don't give a shit about this war,' the Witcher said, grinding his teeth. 'This is about Milva. You joined the company, so make a choice. Follow me or join the black cloaks. But do it quickly.'

'I'm coming with you.'

And so it was that a witcher and a Nilfgaardian roared savagely, whirled their swords and leapt forward together without a second thought – two brothers in arms, two allies and comrades – in an encounter with their common foe, in an uneven battle. And that was their baptism of fire. A baptism of shared fighting, fury, madness and death. They were going to their deaths, the two of them. Or so they thought. For they could not know that they would not die that day, on that bridge over the River Yaruga. They did not know that they were both destined for other deaths, in other places and times.

The Nilfgaardians had silver scorpions embroidered on their sleeves. Cahir slashed two of them with quick blows of his long sword, and Geralt cut up two more with blows of his sihil. Then he jumped onto the bridge's railing, running along it to attack the rest. He was a witcher and keeping his balance was a trifle to him, but his acrobatic feat astonished the attackers. And amazed they died, from blows of his dwarven blade, which cut through their hauberks as though they were made of wool, their blood splashing the bridge's polished timbers.

Seeing their commanders' valour the now larger army on the bridge raised a cheer, a roar which expressed returning morale and a growing fighting spirit. And so it was that the previously panicked fugitives attacked the Nilfgaardians like fierce wolves, slashing with swords and battle-axes, stabbing with spears and halberds and striking with clubs and maces. The railing broke and horses plunged into the river with their black-cloaked riders. The roaring army hurtled onto the bridgehead, pushing their chance commanders ahead of them, not letting Geralt and Cahir do what they wanted to do. For they wanted to withdraw quietly, return to help Milva and flee to the left bank.

A battle was still raging at the timber port. The Nilfgaardians had surrounded and cut off the soldiers – who had not yet fled – from the bridge. Those in turn were defending themselves ferociously behind barricades built from cedar and pine logs. At the sight of the reinforcements the handful of soldiers raised a joyful cry. A little too hastily, however. The tight wedge of reinforcements swept the Nilfgaardians off the bridge. But now a flanking cavalry counter-attack began on the bridgehead. Had it not been for the barricades and timber port's woodpiles, which inhibited both escape and the cavalry's momentum, the infantry would have been scattered in an instant. Pressed against the woodpiles, the soldiers took up a fierce fight.

For Geralt it was something he did not know, a completely new kind of fighting. Swordsmanship was out of the question, it was simply a chaotic melee; a ceaseless parrying of blows falling from every direction. However, he continued to take advantage of the rather undeserved privilege of being the commander; the soldiers crowded around him covering his flanks, protected his back and cleared the area in front of him, creating space for him to strike and mortally wound. But it was becoming more and more cramped. The Witcher and his army found themselves fighting shoulder to shoulder with the bloody and exhausted handful of soldiers – mainly dwarven mercenaries – defending the barricade. They fought, surrounded on all sides.

And then came fire.

One side of the barricade, located between the timber port and the bridge, had been a huge pile of pine branches, as spiky as a hedgehog, an unsurmountable obstacle to horses and infantry. Now that pile was on fire; someone had thrown a burning brand into it.

The defenders retreated, assaulted by flames and smoke. Crowded together, blinded, hampering each other, they began to die under the blows of the attacking Nilfgaardians.

Cahir saved the day. Making use of his military experience, he did not allow the soldiers gathering around him on the barricade to be surrounded. He had been cut off from Geralt's group, but was now returning. He had even managed to acquire a horse in a black caparison, and now, hacking in all directions with his sword, he charged at the flank. Behind him, yelling wildly, halberdiers and spearmen in red-lozenged tunics forced their way into the gap.

Geralt put his fingers together and struck the burning pile with the Aard Sign. He did not expect any great effect, since he had been forced to make do without his witcher elixirs for several weeks. But he succeeded nonetheless. The pile of branches exploded and fell apart, showering sparks around.

'Follow me!' he roared, slashing a Nilfgaardian's temple when the man was trying to push his way onto the barricade. 'Follow me! Through the fire!'

And so they set off, scattering the still-burning pyre with their spears, throwing the flaming brands they had picked up with their bare hands at the Nilfgaardian horses.

A baptism of fire, the Witcher thought, furiously striking and parrying blows. *I was meant to pass through fire for Ciri. And I'm passing through fire in a battle which is of no interest to me at all. Which I don't understand in any way. The fire that was meant to purify me is just scorching my hair and face.*

The blood he was splattered with hissed and steamed.

'Onward, comrades! Cahir! To me!'

'Geralt!' Cahir shouted, sweeping another Nilfgaardian from the saddle. 'To the bridge! Force your way through to the bridge! We'll close ranks . . .'

He did not finish, for a cavalryman in a black breastplate, without a helmet, with flowing, bloodied hair, galloped at him. Cahir parried a blow of the rider's long sword, but was thrown from his horse, which sat down on its haunches. The Nilfgaardian leant over to pin him to the ground with his sword. But he did not. He stayed his thrust. The silver scorpion on his breastplate flashed.

'Cahir!' he cried in astonishment. 'Cahir aep Ceallach!'

'Morteisen . . .' no less astonishment could be heard in the voice of Cahir, spread-eagled on the ground.

A dwarven mercenary running alongside Geralt in a blackened and charred tunic with a red lozenge didn't waste time being astonished by anything. He plunged his bear spear powerfully into the Nilfgaardian's belly, unseating the enemy with the impetus of the blow. Another leapt forward, stamping on the fallen cavalryman's black breastplate with a heavy boot, and thrust his spear's blade straight into his throat. The Nilfgaardian wheezed, puking blood and raking the sand with his spurs.

At the same moment the Witcher received a blow in the base of his spine with something very heavy and very hard. His knees buckled beneath him. Falling, he heard a great, triumphant roar. He saw the horsemen in black cloaks fleeing into the trees. He heard the bridge thundering beneath the hooves of the cavalry arriving from the left bank, carrying a banner with an eagle surrounded by red lozenges.

And thus, for Geralt, ended the great battle for the bridge on the Yaruga. A battle which later chroniclers did not, of course, even mention.

'Don't worry, my lord,' the field surgeon said, tapping and feeling the Witcher's back. 'The bridge is down. We aren't in danger of being attacked from the other bank. Your comrades and the woman are also safe. Is she your wife?'

'No.'

'Oh, and I thought . . . For it's always dreadful, sire, when pregnant women suffer in wars . . .'

'Be silent. Not a word about it. What are those banners?'

'Don't you know who you were fighting for? Who would have thought such a thing were possible . . . That's the Lyrian Army. See, the black Lyrian eagle and the red Rivian lozenges. Good, I'm done here. It was only a bump. Your back will hurt a little, but it's nothing. You'll recover.'

'Thanks.'

'I should be thanking you. Had you not held the bridge, Nilfgaard would have slaughtered us on the far bank, forcing us back into the water. We wouldn't have been able to flee from them . . . You saved the queen! Well, farewell, sire. I have to go, others need me to tend to their wounds.'

'Thanks.'

He sat on a log in the port, weary, sore and apathetic. Alone. Cahir had disappeared somewhere. The golden-green Yaruga flowed between the piers of the ruined bridge, sparkling in the light of the sun, which was setting in the west.

He raised his head, hearing steps, the clatter of horseshoes and the clanking of armour.

'This is he, Your Majesty. Let me help you dismount . . .'

'Thtay away.'

Geralt lifted up his eyes. Before him stood a woman in a suit of armour, a woman with very pale hair, almost as pale as his own. He saw that the hair was not fair, but grey, although the woman's face did not bear the marks of old age. A mature age, indeed. But not old age.

The woman pressed a batiste handkerchief with lace hems to her lips. The handkerchief was heavily blood-stained.

'Rise, sire,' one of the knights standing alongside whispered to Geralt. 'And pay homage. It is the Queen.'

The Witcher stood up. And bowed, overcoming the pain in his lower back.

'Did you thafeguard the bridge?'

'I beg your pardon?'

The woman took the handkerchief away from her mouth and spat blood. Several red drops fell on her ornamented breastplate.

'Her Royal Highness Meve, Queen of Lyria and Rivia,' said a knight in a purple cloak decorated with gold embroidery, standing beside the woman, 'is asking if you led the heroic defence of the bridge on the Yaruga?'

'It just seemed to happen.'

'Theemed to happen?' the queen said, trying to laugh, but not

341

having much success. She scowled, swore foully but indistinctly, and spat again. Before she had time to cover her mouth he saw a nasty wound, and noticed she lacked several teeth. She caught his eye.

'Yes,' she said behind her handkerchief, looking him in the eye. 'Thome thon-of-a-bitch thmacked me right in the fathe. A trifle.'

'Queen Meve,' the knight in the purple cloak announced, 'fought in the front line, like a man, like a knight, opposing the superior forces of Nilfgaard! The wound hurts, but does not shame her! And you saved her and our corps. After some traitors had captured and hijacked the ferryboat, that bridge became our only hope. And you defended it valiantly . . .'

'Thtop, Odo. What ith your name, hero?'

'Mine?'

'Certainly,' the knight in purple said, looking at him menacingly. 'What is the matter with you? Are you wounded? Injured? Were you struck in the head?'

'No.'

'Then answer the Queen! You see, do you not, that she is wounded in the mouth and has difficulty speaking!'

'Thtop that, Odo.'

The purple knight bowed and then glanced at Geralt.

'Your name?'

Very well, he thought. *I've had enough of this. I will not lie.*

'Geralt.'

'Geralt from where?'

'From nowhere.'

'Has no one bethtowed a knighthood on you?' Meve asked, once more decorating the sand beneath her feet with a red splash of saliva mixed with blood.

'I beg your pardon? No, no. Nobody has. Your Majesty.'

Meve drew her sword.

'Kneel.'

He obeyed, still unable to believe what was happening. He was still thinking of Milva and the route he had chosen for her, fearing the swamps of Ysgith.

The queen turned to the Purple Knight.

'You will thpeak the formula. I am toothleth.'

'For outstanding valour in the fight for a just cause,' the Purple Knight recited with emphasis. 'For showing proof of virtue, honour and loyalty to the Crown, I, Meve, by grace of the Gods the Queen of Lyria and Rivia, by my power, right and privilege dub you a knight. Serve us faithfully. Bear this blow, shirk not away from pain.'

Geralt felt the touch of the blade on his shoulder. He looked into the queen's pale green eyes. Meve spat thick red gore, pressed the handkerchief to her face, and winked at him over the lace.

The Purple Knight walked over to her and whispered something. The Witcher heard the words: 'predicate', 'Rivian lozenges', 'banner' and 'virtue'.

'That ith tho,' Meve said, nodding. She spoke more and more clearly, overcoming the pain and sticking her tongue in the gap left by missing teeth. 'You held the bridge with tholdierth of Rivia, valiant Geralt of nowhere. It jutht theemed to happen, ha, ha. Well, it hath come to me to give you a predicate for that deed: Geralt of Rivia. Ha, ha.'

'Bow, sir knight,' the Purple Knight hissed.

The freshly dubbed knight, Geralt of Rivia, bowed low, so that Queen Meve, his suzerain, would not see the smile – the bitter smile – that he was unable to resist.

extras

meet the author

ANDRZEJ SAPKOWSKI was born in 1948 in Poland. He studied economy and business, but the success of his fantasy cycle about the sorcerer Geralt of Rivia turned him into a bestselling writer. He is now one of Poland's most famous and successful authors.

introducing

If you enjoyed
BAPTISM OF FIRE,
look out for

RED COUNTRY

by Joe Abercrombie

They burned her home.
They stole her brother and sister.
But vengeance is following.

Shy South hoped to bury her bloody past and ride away
smiling, but she'll have to sharpen up some bad old ways to
get her family back, and she's not a woman to flinch from
what needs doing. She sets off in pursuit with only a pair of
oxen and her cowardly old stepfather Lamb for company.
But it turns out Lamb's buried a bloody past of his own. And
out in the lawless Far Country the past never stays buried.

Their journey will take them across the barren plains to
a frontier town gripped by gold fever, through feud, duel and
massacre, high into the unmapped mountains to a reckoning
with the Ghosts. Even worse, it will force them into an alliance

extras

with Nicomo Cosca, infamous soldier of fortune, and his feckless lawyer Temple, two men no one should ever have to trust...

Some Kind of Coward

"Gold." Wist made the word sound like a mystery there was no solving. "Makes men mad."

Shy nodded. "Those that ain't mad already."

They sat in front of Stupfer's Meat House, which might've sounded like a brothel but was actually the worst place to eat within fifty miles, and that with some fierce competition. Shy perched on the sacks in her wagon and Wist on the fence, where he always seemed to be, like he'd such a splinter in his arse he'd got stuck there. They watched the crowd.

"I came here to get away from people," said Wist.

Shy nodded. "Now look."

Last summer you could've spent all day in town and not seen two people you didn't know. You could've spent some days in town and not seen two people. A lot can change with a few months and a gold find. Now Squaredeal was bursting at its ragged seams with bold pioneers. One-way traffic, headed west towards imagined riches, some charging through fast as the clutter would allow, some stopping off to add their own share of commerce and chaos. Wagon-wheels clattered, mules nickered and horses neighed, livestock honked and oxen bellowed. Men, women and children of all races and stations did plenty of their own honking and bellowing too, in every language and temper. It might've been quite the colourful spectacle if everywhere the blown dust hadn't leached each tone to that same grey ubiquity of dirt.

Wist sucked a noisy mouthful from his bottle. "Quite the variety, ain't there?"

Shy nodded. "All set on getting something for nothing."

All struck with a madness of hope. Or of greed, depending on the observer's faith in humanity, which in Shy's case stood less than brim-full. All drunk on the chance of reaching into some freezing pool out there in the great empty and plucking up a new life with both hands. Leaving their humdrum selves behind on the bank like a shed skin and taking a short cut to happiness.

"Tempted to join 'em?" asked Wist.

Shy pressed her tongue against her front teeth and spat through the gap between. 'Not me." If they made it across the Far Country alive, the odds were stacked high they'd spend a winter up to their arses in ice water and dig up naught but dirt. And if lightning did strike the end of your spade, what then? Ain't like rich folk got no trouble.

There'd been a time Shy thought she'd get something for nothing. Shed her skin and step away smiling. Turned out sometimes the short cut don't lead quite where you hoped, and cuts through bloody country, too.

"Just the rumour o' gold turns 'em mad." Wist took another swallow, the knobble on his scrawny neck bobbing, and watched two would-be prospectors wrestle over the last pickaxe at a stall while the trader struggled vainly to calm them. "Imagine how these bastards'll act if they ever close hands around a nugget."

Shy didn't have to imagine. She'd seen it, and didn't prize the memories. "Men don't need much beckoning on to act like animals."

"Nor women neither," added Wist.

Shy narrowed her eyes at him. "Why look at me?"

"You're foremost in my mind."

"Not sure I like being that close to your face."

Wist showed her his tombstone teeth as he laughed, and handed her the bottle. "Why don't you got a man, Shy?"

"Don't like men much, I guess."

"You don't like anyone much."

"They started it."

"All of 'em?"

"Enough of 'em." She gave the mouth of the bottle a good wipe and made sure she took only a sip. She knew how easy she could turn a sip into a swallow, and the swallow into a bottle, and the bottle into waking up smelling of piss with one leg in the creek. There were folk counting on her, and she'd had her fill of being a disappointment.

The wrestlers had been dragged apart and were spitting insults each in their own tongue, neither quite catching the details but both getting the gist. Looked like the pick had vanished in the commotion, more'n likely spirited away by a cannier adventurer while eyes were elsewhere.

"Gold surely can turn men mad," muttered Wist, all wistful as his name implied. "Still, if the ground opened and offered me the good stuff I don't suppose I'd be turning down a nugget."

Shy thought of the farm, and all the tasks to do, and all the time she hadn't got for the doing of 'em, and rubbed her roughed-up thumbs against her chewed-up fingers. For the quickest moment a trek into the hills didn't sound such a mad notion after all. What if there really was gold up there? Scattered on some stream bed in priceless abundance, longing for the kiss of her itchy fingertips? Shy South, luckiest woman in the Near Country...

"Hah." She slapped the thought away like a bothersome fly. High hopes were luxuries she couldn't stretch to. "In my experience, the ground ain't giving aught away. No more'n the rest of us misers."

"Got a lot, do you?"

"Eh?"

"Experience."

She winked as she handed his bottle back. "More'n you can imagine, old man." A damn stretch more'n most of the pioneers, that was sure. Shy shook her head as she watched the latest crowd coming through—a set of Union worthies, by their looks, dressed for a picnic rather than a slog across a few hundred miles of lawless empty. Folk who should've been satisfied with the comfortable lives they had, suddenly deciding they'd take any chance at grabbing more. Shy wondered how long it'd be before they were limping back the other way, broken and broke. If they made it back.

"Where's Gully at?" asked Wist.

"Back on the farm, looking to my brother and sister."

"Haven't seen him in a while."

"He ain't been here in a while. Hurts him to ride, he says."

"Getting old. Happens to us all. When you see him, tell him I miss him."

"If he was here he'd have drunk your bottle dry in one swallow and you'd be cursing his name."

"I daresay." Wist sighed. "That's how it is with things missed."

By then, Lamb was fording the people-flooded street, shag of grey hair showing above the heads around him for all his stoop, an even sorrier set to his heavy shoulders than usual.

"What did you get?" she asked, hopping down from the wagon.

Lamb winced, like he knew what was coming. "Twenty-seven?" His rumble of a voice tweaked high at the end to make a question of it, but what he was really asking was, *How bad did I fuck up?*

Shy shook her head, tongue wedged in her cheek, letting him know he'd fucked up middling to bad. "You're some kind

355

of a bloody coward, Lamb." She thumped at the sacks and sent up a puff of grain dust. "I didn't spend two days dragging this up here to give it away."

He winced a bit more, grey-bearded face creasing around the old scars and laughter lines, all weather-worn and dirt-grained. "I'm no good with the bartering, Shy, you know that."

"Remind me what it is y'are good with?" she tossed over her shoulder as she strode for Clay's Exchange, letting a set of pie-bald goats bleat past then slipping through the traffic sideways-on. "Except hauling the sacks?"

"That's something, ain't it?" he muttered.

The store was busier even than the street, smelling of sawn wood and spices and hard-working bodies packed tight. She had to shove between a clerk and some blacker'n black Southerner trying to make himself understood in no language she'd ever heard before, then around a washboard hung from the low rafters and set swinging by a careless elbow, then past a frowning Ghost, his red hair all bound up with twigs, leaves still on and everything. All these folk scrambling west meant money to be made, and woe to the merchant tried to put himself between Shy and her share.

"Clay?" she bellowed, nothing to be gained by whispering. "Clay!"

The trader frowned up, caught in the midst of weighing flour out on his man-high scales. "Shy South in Squaredeal. Ain't this my lucky day."

"Looks that way. You got a whole town full o' saps to *swindle*!" She gave the last word a bit of air, made a few heads turn and Clay plant his big fists on his hips.

"No one's swindling no one," he said.

"Not while I've got an eye on business."

"Me and your father agreed on twenty-seven, Shy."

"You know he ain't my father. And you know you ain't agreed shit 'til I've agreed it."

Clay cocked an eyebrow at Lamb and the Northman looked straight to the ground, shifting sideways like he was trying and wholly failing to vanish. For all Lamb's bulk he'd a weak eye, slapped down by any glance that held it. He could be a loving man, and a hard worker, and he'd been a fair stand-in for a father to Ro and Pit and Shy too, far as she'd given him the chance. A good enough man, but by the dead he was some kind of coward.

Shy felt ashamed for him, and ashamed of him, and that nettled her. She stabbed her finger in Clay's face like it was a drawn dagger she'd no qualms about using. "Squaredeal's a strange sort o' name for a town where you'd claw out a business! You paid twenty-eight last season, and you didn't have a quarter of the customers. I'll take thirty-eight."

"What?" Clay's voice squeaking even higher than she'd predicted. "Golden grain, is it?"

"That's right. Top quality. Threshed with my own blistered bloody hands."

"And mine," muttered Lamb.

"Shush," said Shy. "I'll take thirty-eight and refuse to be moved."

"Don't do me no favours!" raged Clay, fat face filling with angry creases. "Because I loved your mother I'll offer twenty nine."

"You never loved a thing but your purse. Anything short of thirty-eight and I'd sooner set up next to your store and offer all this through-traffic just a little less than what you're offering."

He knew she'd do it, even if it cost her. Never make a threat you aren't at least halfway sure you'll carry through on. "Thirty-one," he grated out.

357

"Thirty-five."

"You're holding up all these good folk, you selfish bitch!" Or rather she was giving the good folk notice of the profits he was chiselling and sooner or later they'd catch on.

"They're scum to a man, and I'll hold 'em up 'til Juvens gets back from the land of the dead if it means thirty-five."

"Thirty-two."

"Thirty-five."

"Thirty-three and you might as well burn my store down on the way out!"

"Don't tempt me, fat man. Thirty-three and you can toss in a pair o' those new shovels and some feed for my oxen. They eat almost as much as you." She spat in her palm and held it out.

Clay bitterly worked his mouth, but he spat all the same, and they shook. "Your mother was no better."

"Couldn't stand the woman." Shy elbowed her way back towards the door, leaving Clay to vent his upset on his next customer. "Not that hard, is it?" she tossed over her shoulder at Lamb.

The big old Northman fussed with the notch out of his ear. "Think I'd rather have settled for the twenty-seven."

"That's 'cause you're some kind of a bloody coward. Better to do it than live with the fear of it. Ain't that what you always used to tell me?"

"Time's shown me the downside o' that advice," muttered Lamb, but Shy was too busy congratulating herself.

Thirty-three was a good price. She'd worked over the sums, and thirty-three would leave something towards Ro's books once they'd fixed the barn's leaking roof and got a breeding pair of pigs to replace the ones they'd butchered in winter. Maybe they could stretch to some seed too, try and nurse the cabbage patch back to health. She was grinning, thinking on what she could put right with that money, what she could build.

extras

You don't need a big dream, her mother used to tell her when she was in a rare good mood, *a little one will do it.*

"Let's get them sacks shifted," she said.

He might've been getting on in years, might've been slow as an old favourite cow, but Lamb was strong as ever. No weight would bend the man. All Shy had to do was stand on the wagon and heft the sacks one by one onto his shoulders while he stood, complaining less than the wagon had at the load. Then he'd stroll them across, four at a time, and stack them in Clay's yard easy as sacks of feathers. Shy might've been half his weight, but had the easier task and twenty-five years advantage and still, soon enough, she was leaking water faster than a fresh-dug well, vest plastered to her back and hair to her face, arms pink-chafed by canvas and white-powdered with grain dust, tongue wedged in the gap between her teeth while she cursed up a storm.

Lamb stood there, two sacks over one shoulder and one over the other, hardly even breathing hard, those deep laugh lines striking out from the corners of his eyes. 'Need a rest, Shy?"

She gave him a look. "A rest from your carping."

"I could shift some o' those sacks around and make a little cot for you. Might be there's a blanket in the back there. I could sing you to sleep like I did when you were young."

"I'm still young."

"Ish. Sometimes I think about that little girl smiling up at me." Lamb looked off into the distance, shaking his head. "And I wonder—where did me and your mother go wrong?"

"She died and you're useless?" Shy heaved the last sack up and dropped it on his shoulder from as great a height as she could manage.

Lamb only grinned as he slapped his hand down on top. "Maybe that's it." As he turned he nearly barged into another

Northman, big as he was and a lot meaner-looking. The man started growling some curse, then stopped in the midst. Lamb kept trudging, head down, how he always did from the least breath of trouble. The Northman frowned up at Shy.

"What?" she said, staring right back.

He frowned after Lamb, then walked off, scratching at his beard.

The shadows were getting long and the clouds pink in the west when Shy dumped the last sack under Clay's grinning face and he held out the money, leather bag dangling from one thick forefinger by the drawstrings. She stretched her back out, wiped her forehead on the back of one glove, then worked the bag open and peered inside.

"All here?"

"I'm not going to rob you."

"Damn right you're not." And she set to counting it. *You can always tell a thief,* her mother used to say, *on account of all the care they take with their own money.*

"Maybe I should go through every sack, make sure there's grain in 'em not shit?"

Shy snorted. "If it was shit would that stop you selling it?"

The merchant sighed. "Have it your way."

"I will."

"She does tend to," added Lamb.

A pause, with just the clicking of coins and the turning of numbers in her head. "Heard Glama Golden won another fight in the pit up near Greyer," said Clay. "They say he's the toughest bastard in the Near Country and there's some tough bastards about. Take a fool to bet against him now, whatever the odds. Take a fool to fight him."

"No doubt," muttered Lamb, always quiet when violence was the subject.

"Heard from a man watched it he beat old Stockling Bear so hard his guts came out of his arse."

"That's entertainment, is it?" asked Shy.

"Beats shitting your own guts."

"That ain't much of a review."

Clay shrugged. "I've heard worse ones. Did you hear about this battle, up near Rostod?"

"Something about it," she muttered, trying to keep her count straight.

"Rebels got beat again, I heard. Bad, this time. All on the run now. Those the Inquisition didn't get a hold on."

"Poor bastards," said Lamb.

Shy paused her count a moment, then carried on. There were a lot of poor bastards about but they couldn't all be her problem. She'd enough worries with her brother and sister, and Lamb, and Gully, and the farm without crying over others' self-made misfortunes.

"Might be they'll make a stand up at Mulkova, but they won't be standing long." Clay made the fence creak as he leaned his soft bulk back on it, hands tucked under his armpits with the thumbs sticking up. "War's all but over, if you can call it a war, and there's plenty of people shook off their land. Shook off or burned out or lost what they had. Passes are opened up, ships coming through. Lots of folk seeing their fortune out west all of a sudden." He nodded at the dusty chaos in the street, still boiling over even as the sun set. "This here's just the first trickle. There's a flood coming."

Lamb sniffed. "Like as not they'll find the mountains ain't one great piece of gold and soon come flooding back the other way."

"Some will. Some'll put down roots. The Union'll be coming along after. However much land the Union get, they always

361

want more, and what with that find out west they'll smell money. That vicious old bastard Sarmis is sitting on the border and rattling his sword for the Empire, but his sword's always rattling. Won't stop the tide, I reckon." Clay took a step closer to Shy and spoke soft, like he had secrets to share. "I heard tell there's already been Union agents in Hormring, talking annexation."

"They're buying folk out?"

"They'll have a coin in one hand, sure, but they'll have a blade in the other. They always do. We should be thinking about how we'll play it, if they come to Squaredeal. We should stand together, those of us been here a while."

"I ain't interested in politics." Shy wasn't interested in anything might bring trouble.

"Most of us aren't," said Clay, "but sometimes politics takes an interest in us all the same. The Union'll be coming, and they'll bring law with 'em."

"Law don't seem such a bad thing," Shy lied.

"Maybe not. But taxes follow law quick as the cart behind the donkey."

"Can't say I'm an enthusiast for taxes."

"Just a fancier way to rob a body, ain't it? I'd rather be thieved honest with mask and dagger than have some bloodless bastard come at me with pen and paper."

"Don't know about that," muttered Shy. None of those she'd robbed had looked too delighted with the experience, and some a lot less than others. She let the coins slide back into the bag and drew the string tight.

"How's the count?" asked Clay. "Anything missing?"

"Not this time. But I reckon I'll keep watching just the same."

The merchant grinned. "I'd expect no less."

She picked out a few things they needed—salt, vinegar, some sugar since it only came in time to time, a wedge of dried beef, half a bag of nails which brought the predictable joke from Clay that she was half a bag of nails herself, which brought the predictable joke from her that she'd nail his fruits to his leg, which brought the predictable joke from Lamb that Clay's fruits were so small she might not get a nail through. They had a bit of a chuckle over each other's quick wits.

She almost got carried away and bought a new shirt for Pit which was more'n they could afford, good price or other price, but Lamb patted her arm with his gloved hand, and she bought needles and thread instead so she could make him a shirt from one of Lamb's old ones. She probably could've made five shirts for Pit from one of Lamb's, the boy was that skinny. The needles were a new kind, Clay said were stamped out of a machine in Adua, hundreds at a press, and Shy smiled as she thought what Gully would say to that, shaking his white head at them and saying, needles from a machine, what'll be thought of next, while Ro turned them over and over in her quick fingers, frowning down as she worked out how it was done.

Shy paused in front of the spirits to lick her lips a moment, glass gleaming amber in the darkness, then forced herself on without, haggled harder than ever with Clay over his prices, and they were finished.

"Never come to this store again, you mad bitch!" The trader hurled at her as she climbed up onto the wagon's seat alongside Lamb. "You've damn near ruined me!"

"Next season?"

He waved a fat hand as he turned back to his customers. "Aye, see you then."

She reached to take the brake off and almost put her hand in the beard of the Northman Lamb knocked into earlier. He was standing right beside the wagon, brow all ploughed up like he was trying to bring some foggy memory to mind, thumbs tucked into a sword-belt—big, simple hilt close to hand. A rough style of character, a scar born near one eye and jagged through his scraggy beard. Shy kept a pleasant look on her face as she eased her knife out, spinning the blade about so it was hidden behind her arm. Better to have steel to hand and find no trouble than find yourself in trouble with no steel to hand.

The Northman said something in his own tongue. Lamb hunched a little lower in his seat, not even turning to look. The Northman spoke again. Lamb grunted something back, then snapped the reins and the wagon rolled off, Shy swaying with the jolting wheels. She snatched a glance over her shoulder when they'd gone a few strides down the rutted street. The Northman was still standing in their dust, frowning after them.

"What'd he want?"

"Nothing."

She slid her knife into its sheath, stuck one boot on the rail and sat back, settling her hat brim low so the setting sun wasn't in her eyes. "The world's brimming over with strange people, all right. You spend time worrying what they're thinking, you'll be worrying all your life."

Lamb was hunched lower than ever, like he was trying to vanish into his own chest.

Shy snorted. "You're such a bloody coward."

He gave her a sideways look, then away. "There's worse a man can be."

They were laughing when they clattered over the rise and the shallow little valley opened out in front of them. Something Lamb had said. He'd perked up when they left town, as usual. Never at his best in a crowd.

It gave Shy's spirits a lift besides, coming up that track that was hardly more than two faded lines through the long grass.

extras

She'd been through black times in her younger years, midnight black times, when she thought she'd be killed out under the sky and left to rot, or caught and hanged and tossed out unburied for the dogs to rip at. More than once, in the midst of nights sweated through with fear, she'd sworn to be grateful every moment of her life if fate gave her the chance to tread this unremarkable path again. Eternal gratitude hadn't quite come about, but that's promises for you. She still felt that bit lighter as the wagon rolled home.

Then they saw the farm, and the laughter choked in her throat and they sat silent while the wind fumbled through the grass around them. Shy couldn't breathe, couldn't speak, couldn't think, all her veins flushed with ice-water. Then she was down from the wagon and running.

"Shy!" Lamb roared at her back, but she hardly heard, head full of her own rattling breath, pounding down the slope, land and sky jolting around her. Through the stubble of the field they'd harvested not a week before. Over the trampled-down fence and the chicken feathers crushed into the mud.

She made it to the yard—what had been the yard—and stood helpless. The house was all dead charred timbers and rubbish and nothing left standing but the tottering chimney-stack. No smoke. The rain must've put out the fires a day or two before. But everything was burned out. She ran around the side of the blacked wreck of the barn, whimpering a little now with each breath.

Gully was hanged from the big tree out back. They'd hanged him over her mother's grave and kicked down the headstone. He was shot through with arrows. Might've been a dozen, might've been more.

Shy felt like she was kicked in the guts and she bent over, arms hugged around herself, and groaned, and the tree groaned

365

with her as the wind shook its leaves and set Gully's corpse gently swinging. Poor old harmless bastard. He'd called to her as they'd rattled off on the wagon. Said she didn't need to worry 'cause he'd look to the children, and she'd laughed at him and said she didn't need to worry 'cause the children would look to him, and she couldn't see nothing for the aching in her eyes and the wind stinging at them, and she clamped her arms tighter, feeling suddenly so cold nothing could warm her.

She heard Lamb's boots thumping up, then slowing, then coming steady until he stood beside her.

"Where are the children?"

They dug the house over, and the barn. Slow, and steady, and numb to begin with. Lamb dragged the scorched timbers clear while Shy scraped through the ashes, sure she'd scrape up Pit and Ro's bones. But they weren't in the house. Nor in the barn. Nor in the yard. Wilder now, trying to smother her fear, and more frantic, trying to smother her hope, casting through the grass, and clawing at the rubbish, but the closest Shy came to her brother and sister was a charred toy horse Lamb had whittled for Pit years past and the scorched pages of some of Ro's books she let blow through her fingers.

The children were vanished.

She stood there, staring into the wind, back of one raw hand against her mouth and her chest going hard. Only one thing she could think of.

"They're stolen," she croaked.

Lamb just nodded, his grey hair and his grey beard all streaked with soot.

"Why?"

"I don't know."

She wiped her blackened hands on the front of her shirt and made fists of them. "We've got to get after."

"Aye."

She squatted down over the chewed-up sod around the tree. Wiped her nose and her eyes. Followed the tracks bent over to another battered patch of ground. She found an empty bottle trampled into the mud, tossed it away. They'd made no effort at hiding their sign. Horse-prints all around, circling the shells of the buildings. "I'm guessing at about twenty. Might've been forty horses, though. They left the spare mounts over here."

"To carry the children, maybe?"

"Carry 'em where?"

Lamb just shook his head.

She went on, keen to say anything that might fill the space. Keen to set to work at something so she didn't have to think. "My way of looking at it, they came in from the west and left going south. Left in a hurry."

"I'll get the shovels. We'll bury Gully."

They did it quick. She shinned up the tree, knowing every foot- and handhold. She used to climb it long ago, before Lamb came, while her mother watched and Gully clapped, and now her mother was buried under it and Gully was hanged from it, and she knew somehow she'd made it happen. You can't bury a past like hers and think you'll walk away laughing.

She cut him down, and broke the arrows off, and smoothed his bloody hair while Lamb dug out a hole next to her mother. She closed his popping eyes and put her hand on his cheek and it was cold. He looked so small now, and so thin, she wanted to put a coat on him but there was none to hand. Lamb lowered him in a clumsy hug, and they filled the hole together, and they dragged her mother's stone up straight again and tramped the thrashing grass around it, ash blowing on the cold wind in specks of black and grey, whipping across the land and off to nowhere.

"Should we say something?" asked Shy.

"I've nothing to say." Lamb swung himself up onto the wagon's seat. Might still have been an hour of light left.

"We ain't taking that," said Shy. "I can run faster'n those bloody oxen."

"Not longer, though, and not with gear, and we'll do no good rushing at this. They've got what? Two, three days' start on us? And they'll be riding hard. Twenty men, you said? We have to be realistic, Shy."

"Realistic?" she whispered at him, hardly able to believe it.

"If we chase after on foot, and don't starve or get washed away in a storm, and if we catch 'em, what then? We're not armed, even. Not with more'n your knife. No. We'll follow on fast as Scale and Calder can take us." Nodding at the oxen, grazing a little while they had the chance. "See if we can pare a couple off the herd. Work out what they're about."

"Clear enough what they're about!" she said, pointing at Gully's grave. "And what happens to Ro and Pit while we're fucking *following on*?" She ended up screaming it at him, voice splitting the silence and a couple of hopeful crows taking flight from the tree's branches.

The corner of Lamb's mouth twitched but he didn't look at her. "We'll follow." Like it was a fact agreed on. "Might be we can talk this out. Buy 'em back."

"Buy 'em? They burn your farm, and they hang your friend, and they steal your children and you want to *pay 'em* for the privilege? You're such a fucking coward!"

Still he didn't look at her. "Sometimes a coward's what you need." His voice was rough. Clicking in his throat. "No shed blood's going to unburn this farm now, nor unhang Gully neither. That's done. Best we can do is get back the little ones, any way we can. Get 'em back safe." This time the twitch started at his mouth and scurried all the way up his scarred cheek to the corner of his eye. "Then we'll see."

Shy took a last look as they lurched away towards the setting sun. Her home. Her hopes. How a day can change things about. Naught left but a few scorched timbers poking at the pinking sky. You don't need a big dream. She felt about as low as she ever had in all her life, and she'd been in some bad, dark, low-down places. Hardly had the strength all of a sudden to hold her head up.

"Why'd they have to burn it all?" she whispered.

"Some men just like to burn," said Lamb.

Shy looked around at him, the outline of his battered frown showing below his battered hat, the dying sun glimmering in one eye, and thought how strange it was, that he could be so calm. A man who hadn't the guts to argue over prices, thinking death and kidnap through. Being realistic about the end of all they'd worked for.

"How can you sit so level?" she whispered at him. "Like... like you knew it was coming."

Still he didn't look at her. "It's always coming."

introducing

If you enjoyed
BAPTISM OF FIRE,
look out for

THE BLACK PRISM

Lightbringer: Book 1

by Brent Weeks

*Gavin Guile is the Prism, the most powerful man
in the world. He is high priest and emperor, a man
whose power, wit, and charm are all that preserves
a tenuous peace. But Prisms never last, and Guile
knows exactly how long he has left to live: five years to
achieve five impossible goals.*

*But when Guile discovers he has a son, born in a far
kingdom after the war that put him in power, he must
decide how much he's willing to pay to protect a secret
that could tear his world apart.*

CHAPTER ONE

Kip crawled toward the battlefield in the darkness, the mist pressing down, blotting out sound, scattering starlight. Though the adults shunned it and the children were forbidden to come here, he'd played on the open field a hundred times—during the day. Tonight, his purpose was grimmer.

Reaching the top of the hill, Kip stood and hiked up his pants. The river behind him was hissing, or maybe that was the warriors beneath its surface, dead these sixteen years. He squared his shoulders, ignoring his imagination. The mists made him seem suspended, outside of time. But even if there was no evidence of it, the sun was coming. By the time it did, he had to get to the far side of the battlefield. Farther than he'd ever gone searching.

Even Ramir wouldn't come out here at night. Everyone knew Sundered Rock was haunted. But Ram didn't have to feed his family; *his* mother didn't smoke her wages.

Gripping his little belt knife tightly, Kip started walking. It wasn't just the unquiet dead that might pull him down to the evernight. A pack of giant javelinas had been seen roaming the night, tusks cruel, hooves sharp. They were good eating if you had a matchlock, iron nerves, and good aim, but since the Prisms' War had wiped out all the town's men, there weren't many people who braved death for a little bacon. Rekton was already a shell of what it had once been. The *alcaldesa* wasn't eager for any of her townspeople to throw their lives away. Besides, Kip didn't have a matchlock.

Nor were javelinas the only creatures that roamed the night. A mountain lion or a golden bear would also probably enjoy a well-marbled Kip.

A low howl cut the mist and the darkness hundreds of paces deeper into the battlefield. Kip froze. Oh, there were wolves too. How'd he forget wolves?

Another wolf answered, farther out. A haunting sound, the very voice of the wilderness. You couldn't help but freeze when you heard it. It was the kind of beauty that made you shit your pants.

Wetting his lips, Kip got moving. He had the distinct sensation of being followed. Stalked. He looked over his shoulder. There was nothing there. Of course. His mother always said he had too much imagination. Just walk, Kip. Places to be. Animals are more scared of you and all that. Besides, that was one of the tricks about a howl, it always sounded much closer than it really was. Those wolves were probably leagues away.

Before the Prisms' War, this had been excellent farmland. Right next to the Umber River, suitable for figs, grapes, pears, dewberries, asparagus—*everything* grew here. And it had been sixteen years since the final battle—a year before Kip was even born. But the plain was still torn and scarred. A few burnt timbers of old homes and barns poked out of the dirt. Deep furrows and craters remained from cannon shells. Filled now with swirling mist, those craters looked like lakes, tunnels, traps. Bottomless. Unfathomable.

Most of the magic used in the battle had dissolved sooner or later in the years of sun exposure, but here and there broken green luxin spears still glittered. Shards of solid yellow underfoot would cut through the toughest shoe leather.

Scavengers had long since taken all the valuable arms, mail, and luxin from the battlefield, but as the seasons passed and rains fell, more mysteries surfaced each year. That was what Kip was hoping for—and what he was seeking was most visible in the first rays of dawn.

The wolves stopped howling. Nothing was worse than hearing that chilling sound, but at least with the sound he knew where they were. Now...Kip swallowed on the hard knot in his throat.

As he walked in the valley of the shadow of two great unnatural hills—the remnant of two of the great funeral pyres where tens of thousands had burned—Kip saw something in the mist. His heart leapt into his throat. The curve of a mail cowl. A glint of eyes searching the darkness.

Then it was swallowed up in the roiling mists.

A ghost. Dear Orholam. Some spirit keeping watch at its grave.

Look on the bright side. Maybe wolves are scared of ghosts.

Kip realized he'd stopped walking, peering into the darkness. Move, fathead.

He moved, keeping low. He might be big, but he prided himself on being light on his feet. He tore his eyes away from the hill—still no sign of the ghost or man or whatever it was. He had that feeling again that he was being stalked. He looked back. Nothing.

A quick click, like someone dropping a small stone. And something at the corner of his eye. Kip shot a look up the hill. A click, a spark, the striking of flint against steel.

The mists illuminated for that briefest moment, Kip saw few details. Not a ghost—a soldier striking a flint, trying to light a slow-match. It caught fire, casting a red glow on the soldier's face, making his eyes seem to glow. He affixed the slow-match to the match-holder of his matchlock and spun, looking for targets in the darkness.

His night vision must have been ruined by staring at the brief flame on his match, now a smoldering red ember, because his eyes passed right over Kip.

The soldier turned again, sharply, paranoid. "The hell am I supposed to see out here, anyway? Swivin' wolves."

Very, very carefully, Kip started walking away. He had to get deeper into the mist and darkness before the soldier's night vision recovered, but if he made noise, the man might fire blindly. Kip walked on his toes, silently, his back itching, sure that a lead ball was going to tear through him at any moment.

But he made it. A hundred paces, more, and no one yelled. No shot cracked the night. Farther. Two hundred paces more, and he saw light off to his left, a campfire. It had burned so low it was barely more than coals now. Kip tried not to look directly at it to save his vision. There was no tent, no bedrolls nearby, just the fire.

Kip tried Master Danavis's trick for seeing in darkness. He let his focus relax and tried to view things from the periphery of his vision. Nothing but an irregularity, perhaps. He moved closer.

Two men lay on the cold ground. One was a soldier. Kip had seen his mother unconscious plenty of times; he knew instantly this man wasn't passed out. He was sprawled unnaturally, there were no blankets, and his mouth hung open, slack-jawed, eyes staring unblinking at the night. Next to the dead soldier lay another man, bound in chains but alive. He lay on his side, hands manacled behind his back, a black bag over his head and cinched tight around his neck.

The prisoner was alive, trembling. No, weeping. Kip looked around; there was no one else in sight.

"Why don't you just finish it, damn you?" the prisoner said.

Kip froze. He thought he'd approached silently.

"Coward," the prisoner said. "Just following your orders, I suppose? Orholam will smite you for what you're about to do to that little town."

Kip had no idea what the man was talking about.

Apparently his silence spoke for him.

"You're not one of them." A note of hope entered the prisoner's voice. "Please, help me!"

Kip stepped forward. The man was suffering. Then he stopped. Looked at the dead soldier. The front of the soldier's shirt was soaked with blood. Had this prisoner killed him? How?

"Please, leave me chained if you must. But please, I don't want to die in darkness."

Kip stayed back, though it felt cruel. "You killed him?"

"I'm supposed to be executed at first light. I got away. He chased me down and got the bag over my head before he died. If dawn's close, his replacement is coming anytime now."

Kip still wasn't putting it together. No one in Rekton trusted the soldiers who came through, and the alcaldesa had told the town's young people to give any soldiers a wide berth for a while—apparently the new satrap Garadul had declared himself free of the Chromeria's control. Now he was King Garadul, he said, but he wanted the usual levies from the town's young people. The alcaldesa had told his representative that if he wasn't the satrap anymore, he didn't have the right to raise levies. King or satrap, Garadul couldn't be happy with that, but Rekton was too small to bother with. Still, it would be wise to avoid his soldiers until this all blew over.

On the other hand, just because Rekton wasn't getting along with the satrap right now didn't make this man Kip's friend.

"So you *are* a criminal?" Kip asked.

"Of six shades to Sun Day," the man said. The hope leaked out of his voice. "Look, boy—you are a child, aren't you? You sound like one. I'm going to die today. I can't get away. Truth to tell, I don't want to. I've run enough. This time, I fight."

"I don't understand."

"You will. Take off my hood."

Though some vague doubt nagged Kip, he untied the half-knot around the man's neck and pulled off the hood.

At first, Kip had no idea what the prisoner was talking about. The man sat up, arms still bound behind his back. He was perhaps thirty years old, Tyrean like Kip but with a lighter complexion, his hair wavy rather than kinky, his limbs thin and muscular. Then Kip saw his eyes.

Men and women who could harness light and make luxin—drafters—always had unusual eyes. A little residue of whatever color they drafted ended up in their eyes. Over the course of their life, it would stain the entire iris red, or blue, or whatever their color was. The prisoner was a green drafter—or had been. Instead of the green being bound in a halo within the iris, it was shattered like crockery smashed to the floor. Little green fragments glowed even in the whites of his eyes. Kip gasped and shrank back.

"Please!" the man said. "Please, the madness isn't on me. I won't hurt you."

"You're a color wight."

"And now you know why I ran away from the Chromeria," the man said.

Because the Chromeria put down color wights like a farmer put down a beloved, rabid dog.

Kip was on the verge of bolting, but the man wasn't making any threatening moves. And besides, it was still dark. Even color wights needed light to draft. The mist did seem lighter, though, gray beginning to touch the horizon. It was crazy to talk to a madman, but maybe it wasn't too crazy. At least until dawn.

The color wight was looking at Kip oddly. "Blue eyes." He laughed.

Kip scowled. He hated his blue eyes. It was one thing when a foreigner like Master Danavis had blue eyes. They looked fine on him. Kip looked freakish.

"What's your name?" the color wight asked.

Kip swallowed, thinking he should probably run away.

"Oh, for Orholam's sake, you think I'm going to hex you with your name? How ignorant is this backwater? That isn't how chromaturgy works—"

"Kip."

The color wight grinned. "Kip. Well, Kip, have you ever wondered why you were stuck in such a small life? Have you ever gotten the feeling, Kip, that you're special?"

Kip said nothing. Yes, and yes.

"Do you know *why* you feel destined for something greater?"

"Why?" Kip asked, quiet, hopeful.

"Because you're an arrogant little shit." The color wight laughed.

Kip shouldn't have been taken off guard. His mother had said worse. Still, it took him a moment. A small failure. "Burn in hell, coward," he said. "You're not even good at running away. Caught by ironfoot soldiers."

The color wight laughed louder. "Oh, they didn't *catch* me. They recruited me."

Who would recruit madmen to join them? "They didn't know you were a—"

"Oh, they knew."

Dread like a weight dropped into Kip's stomach. "You said something about my town. Before. What are they planning to do?"

"You know, Orholam's got a sense of humor. Never realized that till now. Orphan, aren't you?"

"No. I've got a mother," Kip said. He instantly regretted giving the color wight even that much.

"Would you believe me if I told you there's a prophecy about you?"

"It wasn't funny the first time," Kip said. "What's going to happen to my town?" Dawn was coming, and Kip wasn't going to stick around. Not only would the guard's replacement come then, but Kip had no idea what the wight would do once he had light.

"You know," the wight said, "you're the reason I'm here. Not here here. Not like 'Why do I exist?' Not in Tyrea. In chains, I mean."

"What?" Kip asked.

"There's power in madness, Kip. Of course…" He trailed off, laughed at a private thought. Recovered. "Look, that soldier has a key in his breast pocket. I couldn't get it out, not with—" He shook his hands, bound and manacled behind his back.

"And I would help you why?" Kip asked.

"For a few straight answers before dawn."

Crazy, and cunning. *Perfect.* "Give me one first," Kip said.

"Shoot."

"What's the plan for Rekton?"

"Fire."

"What?" Kip asked.

"Sorry, you said one answer."

"That was no answer!"

"They're going to wipe out your village. Make an example so no one else defies King Garadul. Other villages defied the king too, of course. His rebellion against the Chromeria isn't popular everywhere. For every town burning to take vengeance on the Prism, there's another that wants nothing to do with war. Your village was chosen specially. Anyway, I had a little spasm of conscience and objected. Words were exchanged. I punched my superior. Not totally my fault. They know us greens don't do rules and hierarchy. Especially not once we've broken the halo." The color wight shrugged. "There, straight. I think that deserves the key, don't you?"

It was too much information to soak up at once—broken the halo?—but it *was* a straight answer. Kip walked over to the dead man. His skin was pallid in the rising light. Pull it together, Kip. Ask whatever you need to ask.

Kip could tell that dawn was coming. Eerie shapes were emerging from the night. The great twin looming masses of Sundered Rock itself were visible mostly as a place where stars were blotted out of the sky.

What do I need to ask?

He was hesitating, not wanting to touch the dead man. He knelt. "Why my town?" He poked through the dead man's pocket, careful not to touch skin. It was there, two keys.

"They think you have something that belongs to the king. I don't know what. I only picked up that much by eavesdropping."

"What would Rekton have that the king wants?" Kip asked.

"Not Rekton you. You you."

It took Kip a second. He touched his own chest. "Me? Me personally? I don't even own anything!"

The color wight gave a crazy grin, but Kip thought it was a pretense. "Tragic mistake, then. Their mistake, your tragedy."

"What, you think I'm lying?!" Kip asked. "You think I'd be out here scavenging luxin if I had any other choice?"

"I don't really care one way or the other. You going to bring that key over here, or do I need to ask real nice?"

It was a mistake to bring the keys over. Kip knew it. The color wight wasn't stable. He was dangerous. He'd admitted as much. But he had kept his word. How could Kip do less?

Kip unlocked the man's manacles, and then the padlock on the chains. He backed away carefully, as one would from a wild animal. The color wight pretended not to notice, simply rubbing his arms and stretching back and forth. He moved over to the guard and poked through his pockets again. His hand emerged with a pair of green spectacles with one cracked lens.

"You could come with me," Kip said. "If what you said is true—"

"How close do you think I'd get to your town before someone came running with a musket? Besides, once the sun comes up... I'm ready for it to be done." The color wight took a deep breath, staring at the horizon. "Tell me, Kip, if you've done bad things your whole life, but you die doing something good, do you think that makes up for all the bad?"

"No," Kip said, honestly, before he could stop himself.

"Me neither."

"But it's better than nothing," Kip said. "Orholam is merciful."

"Wonder if you'll say that after they're done with your village."

There were other questions Kip wanted to ask, but everything had happened in such a rush that he couldn't put his thoughts together.

In the rising light Kip saw what had been hidden in the fog and the darkness. Hundreds of tents were laid out in military precision. Soldiers. Lots of soldiers. And even as Kip stood, not two hundred paces from the nearest tent, the plain began winking. Glimmers sparkled as broken luxin gleamed, like stars scattered on the ground, answering their brethren in the sky.

It was what Kip had come for. Usually when a drafter released luxin, it simply dissolved, no matter what color it was. But in battle, there had been so much chaos, so many drafters, some sealed magic had been buried and protected from the sunlight that would break it down. The recent rain had uncovered more.

But Kip's eyes were pulled from the winking luxin by four soldiers and a man with a stark red cloak and red spectacles walking toward them from the camp.

"My name is Gaspar, by the by. Gaspar Elos." The color wight didn't look at Kip.

"What?"

"I'm not just some drafter. My father loved me. I had plans. A girl. A life."

"I don't—"

"You will." The color wight put the green spectacles on; they fit perfectly, tight to his face, lenses sweeping to either side so that wherever he looked, he would be looking through a green filter. "Now get out of here."

As the sun touched the horizon, Gaspar sighed. It was as if Kip had ceased to exist. It was like watching his mother take that first deep breath of haze. Between the sparkling spars of darker green, the whites of Gaspar's eyes swirled like droplets of green blood hitting water, first dispersing, then staining the whole. The emerald green of luxin ballooned through his eyes, thickened until it was solid, and then spread. Through his cheeks, up to his hairline, then down his neck, standing out starkly when it finally filled his lighter fingernails as if they'd been painted in radiant jade.

Gaspar started laughing. It was a low, unreasoning cackle, unrelenting. Mad. Not a pretense this time.

Kip ran.

He reached the funerary hill where the sentry had been, taking care to stay on the far side from the army. He had to get to Master Danavis. Master Danavis always knew what to do.

There was no sentry on the hill now. Kip turned around in time to see Gaspar change, transform. Green luxin spilled out of his hands onto his body, covering every part of him like a shell, like an enormous suit of armor. Kip couldn't see the soldiers or the red drafter approaching Gaspar, but he did see a fireball the size of his head streak toward the color wight, hit his chest, and burst apart, throwing flames everywhere.

Gaspar rammed through it, flaming red luxin sticking to his green armor. He was magnificent, terrible, powerful. He ran toward the soldiers, screaming defiance, and disappeared from Kip's view.

Kip fled, the vermilion sun setting fire to the mists.

CHAPTER TWO

Gavin Guile sleepily eyed the papers that slid under his door and wondered what Karris was punishing him for this time. His rooms occupied half of the top floor of the Chromeria, but the panoramic windows were blackened so that if he slept at all, he could sleep in. The seal on the letter pulsed so gently that Gavin couldn't tell what color had been drafted into it. He propped himself up in bed so he could get a better look and dilated his pupils to gather as much light as possible.

Superviolet. Oh, sonuva—

On every side, the floor-to-ceiling blackened windows dropped into the floor, bathing the room in full-spectrum light as the morning sun was revealed, climbing the horizon over the dual islands. With his eyes dilated so far, magic flooded Gavin. It was too much to hold.

Light exploded from him in every direction, passing through him in successive waves from superviolet down. The sub-red was last, rushing through his skin like a wave of flame. He jumped out of bed, sweating instantly. But with all the windows open, cold summer morning winds blasted through his chambers, chilling him. He yelped, hopping back into bed.

His yelp must have been loud enough for Karris to hear it and know that her rude awakening had been successful, because he heard her unmistakable laugh. She wasn't a superviolet, so she must have had a friend help her with her little prank. A quick shot of superviolet luxin at the room's controls threw the windows closed and set the filters to half. Gavin extended a hand to blast his door open, then stopped. He wasn't going to give Karris the satisfaction. Her assignment to be the White's fetch-and-carry girl had ostensibly been intended to teach her humility and gravitas. So far that much had been a spectacular failure, though the White always played a deeper game. Still, Gavin couldn't help grinning as he rose and swept the folded papers Karris had tucked under the door into his hand.

He walked to his door. On a small service table just outside, he found his breakfast on a platter. It was the same every morning: two squat bricks of bread and a pale wine in a clear glass cup. The bread was made of wheat, barley, beans, lentils, millet, and spelt, unleavened. A man could live on that bread. In fact, a man *was* living on that bread. Just not Gavin. Indeed, the sight of it made his stomach turn. He could order a different breakfast, of course, but he never did.

He brought it inside, setting the papers on the table next to the bread. One was odd, a plain note that didn't look like the White's personal stationery, nor any official hard white stationery the Chromeria used. He turned it over. The Chromeria's message office had marked it as being received from "ST, Rekton": Satrapy of Tyrea, town of Rekton. It sounded familiar, maybe one of those towns near Sundered Rock? But then, there had once been so many towns there. Probably someone begging an audience, though those letters were supposed to be screened out and dealt with separately.

Still, first things first. He tore open each loaf, checking that nothing had been concealed inside it. Satisfied, he took out a bottle of the blue dye he kept in a drawer and dribbled a bit into the wine. He swirled the wine to mix it, and held the glass up against the granite blue sky of a painting he kept on the wall as his reference.

He'd done it perfectly, of course. He'd been doing this for

almost six thousand mornings now. Almost sixteen years. A long time for a man only thirty-three years old. He poured the wine over the broken halves of the bread, staining it blue—and harmless. Once a week, Gavin would prepare a blue cheese or blue fruit, but it took more time.

He picked up the note from Tyrea.

"I'm dying, Gavin. It's time you meet your son Kip. —Lina"

Son? I don't have a—

Suddenly his throat clamped down, and his chest felt like his heart was seizing up, no matter that the chirurgeons said it wasn't. Just relax, they said. Young and strong as a warhorse, they said. They didn't say, Grow a pair. You've got lots of friends, your enemies fear you, and you have no rivals. You're the Prism. What are you afraid of? No one had talked to him that way in years. Sometimes he wished they would.

Orholam, the note hadn't even been sealed.

Gavin walked out onto his glass balcony, subconsciously checking his drafting as he did every morning. He stared at his hand, splitting sunlight into its component colors as only he could do, filling each finger in turn with a color, from below the visible spectrum to above it: sub-red, red, orange, yellow, green, blue, superviolet. Had he felt a hitch there when he drafted blue? He double-checked it, glancing briefly toward the sun.

No, it was still easy to split light, still flawless. He released the luxin, each color sliding out and dissipating like smoke from beneath his fingernails, releasing the familiar bouquet of resinous scents.

He turned his face to the sun, its warmth like a mother's caress. Gavin opened his eyes and sucked in a warm, soothing red. In and out, in time with his labored breaths, willing them to slow. Then he let the red go and took in a deep icy blue. It felt like it was freezing his eyes. As ever, the blue brought clarity, peace, order. But not a plan, not with so little information. He let go of the colors. He was still fine. He still had at least five of his seven years left. Plenty of time. Five years, five great purposes.

Well, maybe not five *great* purposes.

Still, of his predecessors in the last four hundred years, aside from those who'd been assassinated or died of other causes, the rest had served for exactly seven, fourteen, or twenty-one years after becoming Prism. Gavin had made it past fourteen. So, plenty of time. No reason to think he'd be the exception. Not many, anyway.

He picked up the second note. Cracking the White's seal—the old crone sealed everything, though she shared the other half of this floor and Karris hand-delivered her messages. But everything had to be in its proper place, properly done. There was no mistaking that she'd risen from Blue.

The White's note read, "Unless you would prefer to greet the students arriving late this morning, my dear Lord Prism, please attend me on the roof."

Looking beyond the Chromeria's buildings and the city, Gavin studied the merchant ships in the bay cupped in the lee of Big Jasper Island. A ragged-looking Atashian sloop was maneuvering in to dock directly at a pier.

Greeting new students. Unbelievable. It wasn't that he was too good to greet new students—well, actually, it *was* that. He, the White, and the Spectrum were supposed to balance each other. But though the Spectrum feared him the most, the reality was that the crone got her way more often than Gavin and the seven Colors combined. This morning she had to be wanting to experiment on him again, and if he wanted to avoid something more onerous like teaching he'd better get to the top of the tower.

Gavin drafted his red hair into a tight ponytail and dressed in the clothes his room slave had laid out for him: an ivory shirt and a wellcut pair of black wool pants with an oversize gem-studded belt, boots with silverwork, and a black cloak with harsh old Ilytian runic designs embroidered in silver thread. The Prism belonged to all the satrapies, so Gavin did his best to honor the traditions of every land—even one that was mainly pirates and heretics.

He hesitated a moment, then pulled open a drawer and drew out his brace of Ilytian pistols. They were, typical for Ilytian work, the most advanced design Gavin had ever seen. The firing mechanism was far more reliable than a wheellock—they were calling it a flintlock. Each pistol had a long blade beneath the barrel, and even a beltflange so that when he tucked them into his belt behind his back they were held securely and at an angle so he didn't skewer himself when he sat. The Ilytians thought of everything.

And, of course, the pistols made the White's Blackguards nervous. Gavin grinned.

When he turned for the door and saw the painting again, his grin dropped.

He walked back to the table with the blue bread. Grabbing one use-smoothened edge of the painting, he pulled. It swung open silently, revealing a narrow chute.

Nothing menacing about the chute. Too small for a man to climb up, even if he overcame everything else. It might have been a laundry chute. Yet to Gavin it looked like the mouth of hell, the evernight itself opening wide for him. He tossed one of the bricks of bread into it, then waited. There was a thunk as the hard bread hit the first lock, a small hiss as it opened, then closed, then a smaller thunk as it hit the next lock, and a few moments later one last thunk. Each of the locks was still working. Everything was normal. Safe. There had been mistakes over the years, but no one had to die this time. No need for paranoia. He nearly snarled as he slammed the painting closed.